TO

Washington
banks and
the machines came up with a name:

James Barbour Matlock

the perfect man for the assignment.

An assignment that would mean horror and pain to Matlock, that would mean the savaging of the girl he loved—and almost surely his own death. But the soundless machines and the faceless men who monitored them didn't care as long as the conspiracy called Nimrod was destroyed along with him.

THE MATLOCK PAPER

"A scorching story!" —*Hartford Courant*

"Suspense, violence and total readability!"
—*Chicago Tribune*

"A winner!" —*King Features Syndicate*

"A compelling, zipping story that it is quite impossible not to finish!"
—*Library Journal*

Other Books by the Author:

THE SCARLATTI INHERITANCE
THE OSTERMAN WEEKEND
*THE RHINEMANN EXCHANGE
*THE GEMINI CONTENDERS
THE CHANCELLOR MANUSCRIPT
THE HOLCROFT COVENANT
THE MATARESE CIRCLE
THE BOURNE IDENTITY
THE PARSIFAL MOSAIC

*Available in Dell Editions.

THE MATLOCK PAPER

Robert Ludlum

A DELL BOOK

For Pat and Bill—
As the ancient Bagdhivi proverb says:
When giants cast shadows, hope for the shade.
The "Due Macellis" are giants!

Published by
DELL PUBLISHING CO., INC.
1 Dag Hammarskjold Plaza
New York, New York 10017

ISBN: 0-440-15538-X

Reprinted by arrangement with
The Dial Press
New York, New York 10017
Printed in the United States of America
First Dell printing—May 1974
Twenty-sixth Dell printing—May 1983

1

Loring walked out the side entrance of the Justice Department and looked for a taxi. It was nearly five thirty, a spring Friday, and the congestion in the Washington streets was awful. Loring stood by the curb and held up his left hand, hoping for the best. He was about to abandon the effort when a cab that had picked up a fare thirty feet down the block stopped in front of him.

"Going east, mister? It's O.K. This gentleman said he wouldn't mind."

Loring was always embarrassed when these incidents occurred. He unconsciously drew back his right forearm, allowing his sleeve to cover as much of his hand as possible—to conceal the thin black chain looped around his wrist, locked to the briefcase handle.

"Thanks, anyway. I'm heading south at the next corner."

He waited until the taxi reentered the flow of traffic and then resumed his futile signaling.

Usually, under such conditions, his mind was alert, his feelings competitive. He would normally dart his eyes in both directions, ferreting out cabs about to disgorge passengers, watching the corners for those dimly lit roof signs that meant this particular vehicle was for hire if you ran fast enough.

Today, however, Ralph Loring did not feel like running. On this particular Friday, his mind was obsessed with a terrible reality. He had just borne witness to a man's being sentenced to death. A man he'd never met but knew a great deal about. An unknowing man of thirty-three who lived and worked in a small New England town four hundred miles away and who had no idea of Loring's existence, much less of the Justice Department's interest in him.

Loring's memory kept returning to the large conference room with the huge rectangular table around which sat the men who'd pronounced the sentence.

He had objected strenuously. It was the least he could do for the man he'd never met, the man who was being maneuvered with such precision into such an untenable position.

"May I remind you, Mr. Loring," said an assistant attorney general who'd once been a judge advocate in the navy, "that in any combat situation basic risks are assumed. A percentage of casualties is anticipated."

"The circumstances are different. This man isn't trained. He won't know who or where the enemy is. How could he? We don't know ourselves."

"Just the point." The speaker then had been another assistant AG, this one a recruit from some corporation law office, fond of committee meetings, and, Loring suspected, incapable of decisions without them. "Our subject is highly mobile. Look at the psychological profile, 'flawed but mobile in the extreme.' That's exactly what it says. He's a logical choice."

" 'Flawed but mobile'! What in heaven's name does that mean? May *I* remind this committee that I've worked in the field for fifteen years. Psychological profiles are only screening guidelines, hit-and-miss judgments. I would no more send a man into an infiltration problem without knowing him thoroughly than I would assume the responsibility for NASA mathematics."

The chairman of the committee, a career professional, had answered Loring.

"I understand your reservations; normally, I'd agree. However, these aren't normal conditions. We have barely three weeks. The time factor overrides the usual precautions."

"It's the risk we have to assume," said the former judge advocate pontifically.

"*You're* not assuming it," Loring replied.

"Do you wish to be relieved of the contact?" The chairman made the offer in complete sincerity.

"No, sir. I'll make it. Reluctantly. I want that on the record."

"One thing before we adjourn." The corporation lawyer leaned forward on the table. "And this comes right from the top. We've all agreed that our subject is motivated. The profile makes that clear. What must also be made clear is that any assistance given this committee by the subject is given freely and on a voluntary basis. We're vulnerable here. We cannot, repeat *cannot*, be responsible. If it's possible, we'd like the record to indicate that the subject came to *us*."

Ralph Loring had turned away from the man in disgust.

If anything, the traffic was heavier now. Loring had about made up his mind to start walking the twenty-odd blocks to his apartment when a white Volvo pulled up in front of him.

"Get in! You look silly with your hand up like that."

"Oh, it's you. Thanks very much." Loring opened the door and slid into the small front seat, holding his briefcase on his lap. There was no need to hide the thin black chain around his wrist. Cranston was a field man, too; an overseas route specialist. Cranston had done most of the background work on the assignment which was now Loring's responsibility.

"That was a long meeting. Accomplish anything?"

"The green light."

"It's about time."

"Two assistant AGs and a concerned message from the White House were responsible."

"Good. Geo division got the latest reports from Force-Mediterranean this morning. It's a regular mass conversion of source routes. It's confirmed. The fields in Ankara and Konya in the north, the projects in Sidi Barrani and Rashid, even the Algerian contingents are systematically cutting production. It's going to make things very difficult."

"What the hell do you want? I thought the objective was to rip them out. You people are never satisfied."

"Neither would you be. We can exert controls over routes we know about; what in God's name do we know about places like . . . Porto Belócruz, Pilcomayo, a half dozen unpronounceable names in Paraguay, Brazil, Guiana? It's a whole goddamn new ballgame, Ralph."

"Bring in the SA specialists. CIA's crawling with them."

"No way. We're not even allowed to ask for maps."

"That's asinine."

"That's espionage. We stay clean. We're strictly according to Interpol-Hoyle; no funny business. I thought you knew that."

"I do," replied Loring wearily. "It's still asinine."

"You worry about New England, USA. We'll handle the pampas, or whatever they are—it is."

"New England, USA, is a goddamn microcosm. That's what's frightening. What happened to all those poetic descriptions of rustic fences and Yankee spirit and ivied brick walls?"

"New poetry. Get with it."

"Your sympathy is overwhelming. Thanks."

"You sound discouraged."

"There isn't enough time. . . ."

"There never is." Cranston steered the small car into a faster lane only to find it bottlenecked at Nebraska and Eighteenth. With a sigh, he shoved the gearshift into neutral and shrugged his shoulders. He looked at Loring, who was staring blankly at the windshield. "At least you got the green light. That's something."

"Sure. With the wrong personnel."

"Oh . . . I see. Is that him?" Cranston gestured his head toward Loring's briefcase.

"That's him. From the day he was born."

"What's his name?"

"Matlock. James B. Matlock II. The *B* is for Barbour, very old family—two very old families. James Matlock, B.A., M.A., Ph.D. A leading authority in the field of social and political influences on Elizabethan literature. How about that?"

"Jesus! Are those his qualifications? Where does he start asking questions? At faculty teas for retired professors?"

"No. That part of it's all right; he's young enough. His qualifications are included in what Security calls 'flawed but mobile in the extreme.' Isn't that a lovely phrase?"

"Inspiring. What does it mean?"

"It's supposed to describe a man who isn't very nice. Probably because of a loused-up army record, or a divorce—I'm sure it's the army thing—but in spite of that insurmountable handicap, is very well liked."

"I like him already."

"That's my problem. I do, too."

The two men fell into silence. It was clear that Cranston had been in the field long enough to realize when a fellow professional had to think by himself. Reach certain conclusions—or rationalizations—by himself. Most of the time, it was easy.

Ralph Loring thought about the man whose life was detailed so completely in his briefcase, culled from a score of data-bank sources. James Barbour Matlock was the name, but the person behind the name refused to come into focus. And that bothered Loring; Matlock's life had been shaped by disturbing, even violent, inconsistencies.

He was the surviving son of two elderly, immensely wealthy parents who lived in handsome retirement in Scarsdale, New York. His education had been properly Eastern Establishment: Andover and Amherst, with the proper expectations of a Manhattan-based profession—banking, brokerage, advertising. There was nothing in his precollege or undergraduate record to indicate a deviation from this pattern. Indeed, marriage to a socially prominent girl from Greenwich seemed to confirm it.

And then things happened to James Barbour Matlock, and Loring wished he understood. First came the army.

It was the early sixties, and by the simple expedient of agreeing to a six-month extension of service, Matlock could have sat comfortably behind a desk as a supply officer somewhere—most likely, with his family's connections, in Washington or New York. Instead, his service file read like a hoodlum's: a series of infractions and insubordinations that guaranteed him the least desirable of assignments—Vietnam and its escalating hostilities. While in the Mekong Delta, his military behavior also guaranteed him two summary courts-martial.

Yet there appeared to be no ideological motivation behind his actions, merely poor, if any, adjustment.

His return to civilian life was marked by continuing difficulties, first with his parents and then with his wife. Inexplicably, James Barbour Matlock, whose academic record had been gentlemanly but hardly superior, took a small apartment in Morningside Heights and attended Columbia University's graduate school.

The wife lasted three and a half months, opting for a quiet divorce and a rapid exit from Matlock's life.

The following several years were monotonous intelligence material. Matlock, the incorrigible, was in the process of becoming Matlock, the scholar. He worked around the calendar, receiving his master's degree in fourteen months, his doctorate two years later. There was a reconciliation of sorts with his parents, and a position with the English department at Carlyle University in Connecticut. Since then Matlock had published a number of books and articles and acquired an enviable reputation in the academic community. He was obviously popular—"mobile in the extreme" (silly goddamn expression); he was moderately well off and apparently possessed none of the antagonistic traits he'd displayed during the hostile years. Of course, there was damn little reason for him to be discontented, thought Loring. James Barbour Matlock II had his life nicely routined; he was covered on all flanks, thank you, including a girl. He was currently, with discretion, involved with a graduate student named Patricia Ballantyne. They kept separate residences, but according to the data, were lovers. As near as could be determined, however, there was no marriage in sight. The girl was completing her doctoral studies in archeology, and a dozen foundation grants awaited her. Grants that led to distant lands and unfamiliar facts. Patricia Ballantyne was not for marriage; not according to the data banks.

But what of Matlock? wondered Ralph Loring. What did the facts tell him? How could they possibly justify the choice?

They didn't. They couldn't. Only a trained professional could carry out the demands of the current situation. The problems were far too complex, too filled with traps for an amateur.

The terrible irony was that if this Matlock made errors, fell into traps, he might accomplish far more far quicker than any professional.

And lose his life doing so.

"What makes you all think he'll accept?" Cranston was nearing Loring's apartment and his curiosity was piqued.

"What? I'm sorry, what did you say?"

"What's the motive for the subject's acceptance? Why would he agree?"

"A younger brother. Ten years younger, as a matter of fact. The parents are quite old. Very rich, very detached. This Matlock holds himself responsible."

"For what?"

"The brother. He killed himself three years ago with an overdose of heroin."

Ralph Loring drove his rented car slowly down the wide, tree-lined street past the large old houses set back beyond manicured lawns. Some were fraternity houses, but there were far fewer than had existed a decade ago. The social exclusivity of the fifties and early sixties was being replaced. A few of the huge structures had other identifications now. *The House, Aquarius* (naturally), *Afro-Commons, Warwick, Lumumba Hall.*

Connecticut's Carlyle University was one of those medium-sized "prestige" campuses that dot the New England landscape. An administration, under the guidance of its brilliant president, Dr. Adrian Sealfont, was restructuring the college, trying to bring it into the second half of the twentieth century. There were inevitable protests, proliferation of beards, and African studies balanced against the quiet wealth, club blazers, and alumni-sponsored regattas. Hard rock and faculty tea dances were groping for ways to coexist.

Loring reflected, as he looked at the peaceful campus in the bright spring sunlight, that it seemed inconceivable that such a community harbored any real problems.

Certainly not the problem that had brought him there.

Yet it did.

Carlyle was a time bomb which, when detonated, would claim extraordinary victims in its fallout. That it *would* explode, Loring knew, was inevitable. What happened before then was unpredictable. It was up to him to engineer the best possible probabilities. The key was James Barbour Matlock, B.A., M.A., Ph.D.

Loring drove past the attractive two-story faculty residence that held four apartments, each with a separate entrance. It was considered one of the better faculty houses and was usually occupied by bright young families before they'd reached the tenure necessary for outlying homes of their own. Matlock's quarters were on the first floor, west section.

Loring drove around the block and parked diagonally across the street from Matlock's door. He couldn't stay long; he kept turning in the seat, scanning the cars and Sunday morning pedestrians, satisfied that he himself wasn't being observed. That was vital. On Sunday, according to Matlock's surveillance file, the young professor usually read the papers till around noon and then drove to the north end of Carlyle where Patricia Ballantyne lived in one of the efficiency apartments reserved for graduate students. That is, he drove over if she hadn't spent the night with him. Then the two generally went out into the country for lunch and returned to Matlock's apartment or went south into Hartford or New Haven. There were variations, of course. Often the Ballantyne girl and Matlock took weekends together, registering as man and wife. Not this weekend, however. Surveillance had confirmed that.

Loring looked at his watch. It was twelve forty, but Matlock was still in his apartment. Time was running short. In a few minutes, Loring was expected to be at Crescent Street. 217 Crescent. It was where he would make cover-contact for his second vehicle transfer.

He knew it wasn't necessary for him to physically watch Matlock. After all, he'd read the file thoroughly, looked at scores of photographs, and even talked briefly with Dr. Sealfont, Carlyle's president. Nevertheless, each agent had his own working methods, and his included watching subjects for a period of hours before making contact. Several colleagues at Justice claimed it gave him a sense of power. Loring knew only that it gave him a sense of confidence.

Matlock's front door opened and a tall man walked out into the sunlight. He was dressed in khaki trousers, loafers, and a tan turtleneck sweater. Loring saw that he was modestly good looking with sharp features and fairly long blond hair. He checked the lock on his door, put on a pair of sunglasses, and walked around the sidewalk to what Loring presumed was a small parking area. Several minutes later, James Matlock drove out of the driveway in a Triumph sportscar.

The government man reflected that his subject seemed to have the best of a pleasant life. Sufficient income, no responsibilities, work he enjoyed, even a convenient relationship with an attractive girl.

Loring wondered if it would all be the same for James Barbour Matlock three weeks from then. For Matlock's world was about to be plunged into an abyss.

2

Matlock pressed the Triumph's accelerator to the floor and the low-slung automobile vibrated as the speedometer reached sixty-two miles per hour. It wasn't that he was in a hurry—Pat Ballantyne wasn't going anywhere—just that he was angry. Well, not angry, really; just irritated. He was usually irritated after a phone call from home. Time would never eliminate that. Nor money, if ever he made any to speak of—amounts his father considered respectable. What caused his irritation was the infuriating condescension. It grew worse as his mother and father advanced in years. Instead of making peace with the situation, they dwelled on it. They insisted that he spend the spring midterm vacation in Scarsdale so that he and his father could make daily trips into the city. To the banks, to the attorneys. To make ready for the inevitable, when and if it ever happened.

". . . There's a lot you'll have to digest, son," his father had said sepulchrally. "You're not exactly prepared, you know. . . ."

". . . You're all that's left, darling," his mother had said with obvious pain.

Matlock knew they enjoyed their anticipated, martyred leave-taking of this world. They'd made their mark—or at least his father had. The amusing part was that his parents were as strong as pack mules, as healthy as wild horses. They'd no doubt outlast him by decades.

The truth was that they wanted him with them far more than he wished to be there. It had been that way for the past three years, since David's death at the Cape. Perhaps, thought Matlock, as he drew up in front of Pat's apartment, the roots of his irritation were in his own guilt. He'd never quite made peace with himself about David. He never would.

And he didn't want to be in Scarsdale during the midterm holidays. He didn't want the memories. He had someone now who was helping him forget the awful years—of death, no love, and indecision. He'd promised to take Pat to St. Thomas.

The name of the country inn was the Cheshire Cat, and, as its title implied, it was Englishy and pubbish. The food was decent, the drinks generous, and those factors made it a favorite spot of Connecticut's exurbia. They'd finished their second Bloody Mary and had ordered roast beef and Yorkshire pudding. There were perhaps a dozen couples and several families in the spacious dining area. In the corner sat a single man reading *The New York Times* with the pages folded vertically, commuter fashion.

"He's probably an irate father waiting for a son who's about to splash out. I know the type. They take the Scarsdale train every morning."

"He's too relaxed."

"They learn to hide tension. Only their druggists know. All that Gelusil."

"There are always signs, and he hasn't any. He looks positively self-satisfied. You're wrong."

"You just don't know Scarsdale. Self-satisfaction is a

registered trademark. You can't buy a house without it."

"Speaking of such things, what are you going to do? I really think we should cancel St. Thomas."

"I don't. It's been a rough winter; we deserve a little sun. Anyway, they're being unreasonable. There's nothing I want to learn about the Matlock manipulations; it's a waste of time. In the unlikely event that they ever *do* go, others'll be in charge."

"I thought we agreed that was only an excuse. They want you around for a while. I think it's touching they do it this way."

"It's not touching, it's my father's transparent attempt at bribery. . . . Look. Our commuter's given up." The single man with the newspaper finished his drink and was explaining to the waitress that he wasn't ordering lunch. "Five'll get you ten he pictured his son's hair and leather jacket—maybe bare feet—and just panicked."

"I think you're wishing it on the poor man."

"No, I'm not. I'm too sympathetic. I can't stand the aggravation that goes with rebellion. Makes me self-conscious."

"You're a very funny man, Private Matlock," said Pat, alluding to Matlock's inglorious army career. "When we finish, let's go down to Hartford. There's a good movie."

"Oh, I'm sorry, I forgot to tell you. We can't today. . . . Sealfont called me this morning for an early evening conference. Said it was important."

"About what?"

"I'm not sure. The African studies may be in trouble. That 'Tom' I recruited from Howard turned out to be a beaut. I think he's a little to the right of Louis XIV."

She smiled. "Really, you're terrible."

Matlock took her hand.

The residence of Dr. Adrian Sealfont was imposingly appropriate. It was a large white colonial mansion with wide marble steps leading up to thick double doors carved in relief. Along the front were Ionic pillars spanning the width of the building. Floodlights from the lawn were turned on at sundown.

Matlock walked up the stairs to the door and rang the bell. Thirty seconds later he was admitted by a maid, who ushered him through the hallway toward the rear of the house, into Dr. Sealfont's huge library.

Adrian Sealfont stood in the center of the room with two other men. Matlock, as always, was struck by the presence of the man. A shade over six feet, thin, with aquiline features, he radiated a warmth that touched all who were near him. There was about him a genuine humility which concealed his brilliance from those who did not know him. Matlock liked him immensely.

"Hello, James." Sealfont extended his hand to Matlock. "Mr. Loring, may I present Dr. Matlock?"

"How do you do? Hi, Sam." Matlock addressed this last to the third man, Samuel Kressel, dean of colleges at Carlyle.

"Hello, Jim."

"We've met before, haven't we?" asked Matlock, looking at Loring. "I'm trying to remember."

"I'm going to be very embarrassed if you do."

"I'll bet you will!" laughed Kressel with his sardonic, slightly offensive humor. Matlock also liked Sam Kressel, more because he knew the pain of Kressel's job—what he had to contend with—than for the man himself.

"What do you mean, Sam?"

"I'll answer you," interrupted Adrian Sealfont. "Mr. Loring is with the federal government, the Justice Department. I agreed to arrange a meeting between the three of you, but I did not agree to what Sam and Mr. Loring have just referred to. Apparently Mr. Loring has seen fit to have you—what is the term—under surveillance. I've registered my strong objections." Sealfont looked directly at Loring.

"You've had me *what?*" asked Matlock quietly.

"I apologize," said Loring persuasively. "It's a personal idiosyncrasy and has nothing to do with our business."

"You're the commuter in the Cheshire Cat."

"The what?" asked Sam Kressel.

"The man with the newspaper."

"That's right. I knew you'd noticed me this afternoon. I thought you'd recognize me the minute you saw me again. I didn't know I looked like a commuter."

"It was the newspaper. We called you an irate father."

"Sometimes I am. Not often, though. My daughter's only seven."

"I think we should begin," Sealfont said. "Incidentally, James, I'm relieved your reaction is so understanding."

"My only reaction is curiosity. And a healthy degree of fear. To tell you the truth, I'm scared to death." Matlock smiled haltingly. "What's it all about?"

"Let's have a drink while we talk." Adrian Sealfont smiled back and walked to his copper-topped dry bar in the corner of the room. "You're a bourbon and water man, aren't you, James? And Sam, a double Scotch over ice, correct? What's yours, Mr. Loring?"

"Scotch'll be fine. Just water."

"Here, James, give me a hand." Matlock crossed to Sealfont and helped him.

"You amaze me, Adrian," said Kressel, sitting down in a leather armchair. "What in heaven's name prompts you to remember your subordinates' choice of liquor?"

Sealfont laughed. "The most logical reason of all. And it certainly isn't confined to my . . . colleagues. I've raised more money for this institution with alcohol than with hundreds of reports prepared by the best analytic minds in fund-raising circles." Here Adrian Sealfont paused and chuckled—as much to himself as to those in the room. "I once gave a speech to the Organization of University Presidents. In the question and answer period, I was asked to what I attributed Carlyle's endowment. . . . I'm afraid I replied, 'To those ancient peoples who developed the art of fermenting the vineyards.' . . . My late wife roared but told me later I'd set the fund back a decade."

The three men laughed; Matlock distributed the drinks.

"Your health," said the president of Carlyle, raising his glass modestly. The toast, however, was brief. "This is a bit awkward, James . . . Sam. Several weeks ago I was contacted by Mr. Loring's superior. He asked me to come to Washington on a matter of utmost importance, relative to Carlyle. I did so and was briefed on a situation I still refuse to accept. Certain information which Mr. Loring will impart to you seems incontrovertible on the surface. But that is the surface: rumor; out-of-context statements, written and verbal; constructed evidence which may be meaningless. On the other hand, there might well be a degree of substance. It is on that possibility that I've agreed to this meeting. I must make it clear, however, that I cannot be a party to it. Carlyle *will not* be a party to it. Whatever may take place in this room has my unacknowledged approval but not my official sanction. You act as individuals, not as members of the faculty or staff of Carlyle. If, indeed, you decide to act at all. . . . Now, James, if that doesn't 'scare you,' I don't know what will." Sealfont smiled again, but his message was clear.

"It scares me," said Matlock without emphasis.

Kressel put down his glass and leaned forward on the chair. "Are we to assume from what you've said that you don't endorse Loring's presence here? Or whatever it is he wants?"

"It's a gray area. If there's substance to his charges, I certainly cannot turn my back. On the other hand, no university president these days will openly collaborate with a government agency on speculation. You'll forgive me, Mr. Loring, but too many people in Washington have taken advantage of the academic communities. I refer specifically to Michigan, Columbia, Berkeley . . . among others. Simple police matters are one thing, infiltration . . . well, that's something else again."

"Infiltration? That's a pretty strong word," said Matlock.

"Perhaps too strong. I'll leave the terms to Mr. Loring."

Kressel picked up his glass. "May I ask why we—Matlock and I—have been chosen?"

"That, again, will be covered in Mr. Loring's discussion. However, since I'm responsible for *your* being here, Sam, I'll tell you *my* reasons. As dean, you're more closely attuned to campus affairs than anyone else. . . . You will also be aware of it if Mr. Loring or his associates overstep their bounds. . . . I think that's all I have to say. I'm going over to the assembly. That filmmaker, Strauss, is speaking tonight and I've got to put in an appearance." Sealfont walked back to the bar and put his glass on the tray. The three other men rose.

"One thing before you go," said Kressel, his brow wrinkled. "Suppose one or both of us decide we want no part of Mr. Loring's . . . business?"

"Then refuse." Adrian Sealfont crossed to the library door. "You are under no obligation whatsoever; I want that perfectly clear. Mr. Loring understands. Good evening, gentlemen." Sealfont walked out into the hallway, closing the door behind him.

3

The three men remained silent, standing motionless. They could hear the front entrance open and close. Kressel turned and looked at Loring.

"It seems to me you've been put on the spot."

"I usually am in these situations. Let me clarify my position; it will partly explain this meeting. The first thing you should know is that I'm with the Justice Department, *Narcotics* Bureau."

Kressel sat down and sipped at his drink. "You haven't traveled up here to tell us forty percent of the student body is on pot and a few other items, have you? Because if so, it's nothing we don't know."

"No, I haven't. I assume you *do* know about such things. Everyone does. I'm not sure about the percentage, though. It could be a low estimate."

Matlock finished his bourbon and decided to have another. He spoke as he crossed to the copper bar table. "It may be low or high, but comparatively speaking—in relation to other campuses—we're not in a panic."

"There's no reason for you to be. Not about that."

"There's something else?"

"Very much so." Loring walked to Sealfont's desk and bent down to pick up his briefcase from the floor. It was apparent that the government man and Carlyle's president had talked before Matlock and Kressel arrived. Loring put the briefcase on the desk and opened it. Matlock walked back to his chair and sat down.

"I'd like to show you something." Loring reached into the briefcase and withdrew a thick page of silver-colored stationery, cut diagonally as if with pinking shears. The silver coating was now filthy with repeated handling and blotches of grease or dirt. He approached Matlock's chair and handed it to him. Kressel got up and came over.

"It's some kind of letter. Or announcement. With numbers," said Matlock. "It's in French; no, Italian, I think. I can't make it out."

"Very good, professor," said Loring. "A lot of both and not a predominance of either. Actually, it's a Corsican dialect, written out. It's called the Oltremontan strain, used in the southern hill country. Like Etruscan, it's not entirely translatable. But what codes are used are simple to the point of not being codes at all. I don't think they were meant to be; there aren't too many of these. So there's enough here to tell us what we need to know."

"Which is?" asked Kressel, taking the strange-looking paper from Matlock.

"First I'd like to explain how we got it. Without that explanation, the information is meaningless."

"Go ahead." Kressel handed the filthy silver paper back to the government agent, who carried it to the desk and carefully returned it to his briefcase.

"A narcotics courier—that is, a man who goes into a specific source territory carrying instructions, money, messages—left the country six weeks ago. He was more than a courier, actually; he was quite powerful in the distribution hierarchy; you might say he was on a busman's holiday, Mediterranean style. Or perhaps he was checking investments. . . . At any rate, he was killed by some mountain people in the Toros Daglari—that's Turkey, a growing district. The story is, he canceled operations there and the violence followed. We accept that; the Mediterranean fields are closing down right and left, moving into South America. . . . The paper was found on his body, in a skin belt. As you saw, it's been handed around a bit. It brought a succession of prices from Ankara to Marrakesh. An Interpol undercover man finally made the purchase and it was turned over to us."

"From Toros Dag-whatever-it-is to Washington. That paper's had quite a journey," said Matlock.

"And an expensive one," added Loring. "Only it's not in Washington now, it's here. From Toros Daglari to Carlyle, Connecticut."

"I assume that means something." Sam Kressel sat down, apprehensively watching the government man.

"It means the information in that paper concerns Carlyle." Loring leaned back against the desk and spoke calmly, with no sense of urgency at all. He could have been an instructor in front of a class explaining a dry but necessary mathematics theorem. "The paper says there'll be a conference on the tenth of May, three weeks from tomorrow. The numbers are the map coordinates of the Carlyle area—precision decimals of longitude and latitude in Greenwich units. The paper itself identifies the holder to be one of those summoned. Each paper has either a matching half or is cut from a pattern that can be matched—simple additional security. What's missing is the precise location."

"Wait a minute." Kressel's voice was controlled but sharp; he was upset. "Aren't you ahead of yourself,

Loring? You're giving us information—obviously restricted—before you state your request. This university administration isn't interested in being an investigative arm of the government. Before you go into facts, you'd better say what you want."

"I'm sorry, Mr. Kressel. You said I was on the spot and I am. I'm handling it badly."

"Like hell. You're an expert."

"Hold it, Sam." Matlock raised his hand off the arm of the chair. Kressel's sudden antagonism seemed uncalled for. "Sealfont said we had the option to refuse whatever he wants. If we exercise that option—and we probably will—I'd like to think we did so out of judgment, not blind reaction."

"Don't be naïve, Jim. You receive restricted or classified information and instantly, *post facto*, you're involved. You can't deny receiving it; you can't say it didn't happen."

Matlock looked up at Loring. "Is that true?"

"To a degree, yes. I won't lie about it."

"Then why should we listen to you?"

"Because Carlyle University *is* involved; has been for years. And the situation is critical. So critical that there are only three weeks left to act on the information we have."

Kressel got out of his chair, took a deep breath, and exhaled slowly. "Create the crisis—without proof—and force the involvement. The crisis fades but the records show the university was a silent participant in a federal investigation. That was the pattern at the University of Wisconsin." Kressel turned to Matlock. "Do you remember that one, Jim? Six days of riots on campus. Half a semester lost on teach-ins."

"That was Pentagon oriented," said Loring. "The circumstances were entirely different."

"You think the Justice Department makes it more palatable? Read a few campus newspapers."

"For Christ's sake, Sam, let the man talk. If you don't want to listen, go home. I want to hear what he has to say."

Kressel looked down at Matlock. "All right. I think I understand. Go ahead, Loring. Just remember, no obligations. And we're not bound to respect any conditions of confidence."

"I'll gamble on your common sense."

"That may be a mistake." Kressel walked to the bar and replenished his drink.

Loring sat on the edge of the desk. "I'll start by asking both of you if you've ever heard of the word *nimrod.*"

"Nimrod is a Hebrew name," Matlock answered. "Old Testament. A descendant of Noah, ruler of Babylon and Nineveh. Legendary prowess as a hunter, which obscures the more important fact that he founded, or built, the great cities in Assyria and Mesopotamia."

Loring smiled. "Very good again, professor. A *hunter* and a *builder*. I'm speaking in more contemporary terms, however."

"Then, no, I haven't. Have you, Sam?"

Kressel walked back to his chair, carrying his glass. "I didn't even know what you just said. I thought a nimrod was a casting fly. Very good for trout."

"Then I'll fill in some background. . . . I don't mean to bore you with narcotics statistics; I'm sure you're bombarded with them constantly."

"Constantly," said Kressel.

"But there's an isolated geographical statistic you may not be aware of. The concentration of drug traffic in the New England states is growing at a rate exceeding that of any other section of the country. It's a startling pattern. Since 1968, there's been a systematic erosion of enforcement procedures. . . . Let me put it into perspective, geographically. In California, Illinois, Louisiana, narcotics controls have improved to the point of at least curtailing the growth curves. It's really the best we can hope for until the international agreements have teeth. But not in the New England area. Throughout this section, the expansion has gone wild. It's hit the colleges hard."

"How do you know that?" asked Matlock.

"Dozens of ways and always too late to prevent distribution. Informers, marked inventories from Mediterranean, Asian, and Latin American sources, traceable Swiss deposits; that *is* restricted data." Loring looked at Kressel and smiled.

"Now I know you people are crazy." Kressel spoke disagreeably. "It seems to me that if you can substantiate those charges, you should do so publicly. And loud."

"We have our reasons."

"Also restricted, I assume," said Kressel with faint disgust.

"There's a side issue," continued the government man, disregarding him. "The eastern prestige campuses—large and small, Princeton, Amherst, Harvard, Vassar, Williams, Carlyle—a good percentage of their enrollments include VIP kids. Sons and daughters of very important people, especially in government and industry. There's a blackmail potential, and we think it's been used. Such people are painfully sensitive to drug scandals."

Kressel interrupted. "Granting what you say is true, and I don't, we've had less trouble here than most other colleges in the northeast area."

"We're aware of that. We even think we know why."

"That's esoteric, Mr. Loring. Say what you want to say." Matlock didn't like the games some people played.

"Any distribution network which is capable of systematically servicing, expanding, and controlling an entire section of the country has got to have a base of operations. A clearing house—you might say, a command post. Believe me when I tell you that this base of operations, the command post for the narcotics traffic throughout the New England states, is Carlyle University."

Samuel Kressel, dean of the colleges, dropped his glass on Adrian Sealfont's parquet floor.

Ralph Loring continued his incredible story. Matlock and Kressel remained in their chairs. Several times during his calm, methodical explanation, Kressel began to interrupt, to object, but Loring's persuasive narrative cut him short. There was nothing to argue.

The investigation of Carlyle University had begun eighteen months ago. It had been triggered by an accounts ledger uncovered by the French Sureté during one of its frequent narcotics investigations in the port of Marseilles. Once the ledger's American origins were established, it was sent to Washington under Interpol agreement. Throughout the ledger's entries were references to "C-22°-59°" consistently followed by the name *Nimrod.* The numbered degree marks were found to be map coordinates of northern Connecticut, but not decimally definitive. After tracing hundreds of possible trucking routes from Atlantic seaboard piers and airports relative to the Marseilles operation, the vicinity of Carlyle was placed under maximum surveillance.

As part of the surveillance, telephone taps were ordered on persons known to be involved with narcotics distribution from such points as New York, Hartford, Boston, and New Haven. Tapes were made of conversations of underworld figures. All calls regarding narcotics to and from the Carlyle area were placed to and from public telephone booths. It made the intercepts difficult, but not impossible. Again, restricted methods.

As the information files grew, a startling fact became apparent. The Carlyle group was independent. It had no formal ties with structured organized crime; it was beholden to no one. It *used* known criminal elements, was not used *by* them. It was a tightly knit unit, reaching into the majority of New England universities. And it did not—apparently—stop at drugs.

There was evidence of the Carlyle unit's infiltration into gambling, prostitution, even postgraduate employment placement. Too, there seemed to be a purpose, an objective beyond the inherent profits of the illegal activities. The Carlyle unit could have made far greater profit with less complications by dealing outright with known criminals, acknowledged suppliers in all areas. Instead, it spent its own money to set up its organization. It was its own master, controlling its own sources, its own distribution. But what its ultimate objectives were was unclear.

It had become so powerful that it threatened the leadership of organized crime in the Northeast. For this reason, leading figures of the underworld had demanded a conference with those in charge of the Carlyle operation. The key here was a group, or an individual, referred to as *Nimrod.*

The purpose of the conference, as far as could be determined, was for an accommodation to be reached between Nimrod and the overlords of crime who felt threatened by Nimrod's extraordinary growth. The conference would be attended by dozens of known and unknown criminals throughout the New England states.

"Mr. Kressel." Loring turned to Carlyle's dean and seemed to hesitate. "I suppose you have lists—students, faculty, staff—people you know or have reason to suspect are into the drug scene. I can't assume it because I don't know, but most colleges do have."

"I won't answer that question."

"Which, of course, gives me my answer," said Loring quietly, even sympathetically.

"Not for a minute! You people have a habit of assuming exactly what you want to assume."

"All right, I stand rebuked. But even if you'd said yes, it wasn't my purpose to ask for them. It was merely by way of telling you that we *do* have such a list. I wanted you to know that."

Sam Kressel realized he'd been trapped; Loring's ingenuousness only annoyed him further. "I'm sure you do."

"Needless to say, we'd have no objection to giving you a copy."

"That won't be necessary."

"You're pretty obstinate, Sam," said Matlock. "You burying your head?"

Before Kressel could reply, Loring spoke. "The dean knows he can change his mind. And we've agreed, there's no crisis here. You'd be surprised how many people wait for the roof to cave in before asking for help. Or accepting it."

"But there aren't many surprises in your organization's proclivity for turning difficult situations into disasters, are there?" countered Sam Kressel antagonistically.

"We've made mistakes."

"Since you have names," continued Sam, "why don't you go after them? Leave us out of it; do your own dirty work. Make arrests, press charges. Don't try to deputize *us*."

"We don't want to do that. . . . Besides, most of our evidence is inadmissible."

"That occurred to me," interjected Kressel.

"And what do we gain? What do *you* gain?" Loring leaned forward, returning Sam's stare. "We pick up a couple of hundred potheads, a few dozen speedfreaks; users and low-level pushers. Don't you understand, that doesn't *solve* anything."

"Which brings us to what you really want, doesn't it?" Matlock sank back into the chair; he watched the persuasive agent closely.

"Yes," answered Loring softly. "We want Nimrod. We want to know the location of that conference on May 10. It could be anywhere within a radius of fifty to a hundred miles. We want to be prepared for it. We want to break the back of the Nimrod operation, for reasons that go way beyond Carlyle University. As well as narcotics."

"How?" asked James Matlock.

"Dr. Sealfont said it. Infiltration. . . . Professor Matlock, you are what's known in intelligence circles as a highly mobile person within your environment. You're widely accepted by diverse, even conflicting factions —within both the faculty and the student body. We have the names, you have the mobility." Loring reached into his briefcase and withdrew the scissored page of filthy stationery. "Somewhere out there is the information we need. Somewhere there's someone who has a paper like this; someone who knows what we have to know."

James Barbour Matlock remained motionless in his chair, staring at the government man. Neither Loring nor Kressel could be sure what he was thinking but both had an idea. If thoughts were audible, there would have been full agreement in that room at that moment. James Matlock's mind had wandered back three, almost four years ago. He was remembering a blond-haired boy of nineteen. Immature for his age, perhaps, but good, kind. A boy with problems.

They'd found him as they'd found thousands like him in thousands of cities and towns across the country. Other times, other Nimrods.

James Matlock's brother, David, had inserted a needle in his right arm and had shot up thirty mg. of white fluid. He had performed the act in a catboat in the calm waters of a Cape Cod inlet. The small sailboat had drifted into the reeds near shore. When they found it, James Matlock's brother was dead.

Matlock made his decision.

"Can you get me the names?"

"I have them with me."

"Just hold it." Kressel stood up, and when he spoke, it wasn't in the tone of an angry man—it was with fear. "Do you realize what you're asking him to do? He has no experience in this kind of work. He's not trained. Use one of your *own* men."

"There isn't time. There's no time for one of our men. He'll be protected; you can help."

"I can *stop* you!"

"No, you can't, Sam," said Matlock from the chair.

"Jim, for Christ's sake, do you know what he's asking? If there's *any* truth to what he's said, he's placing you in the worst position a man can be in. An informer."

"You don't have to stay. My decision doesn't have to be your decision. Why don't you go home?" Matlock rose and walked slowly to the bar, carrying his glass.

"That's impossible now," said Kressel, turning toward the government agent. "And *he knows it.*"

Loring felt a touch of sadness. This Matlock was a good man; he was doing what he was doing because he felt he owed a debt. And it was coldly, professionally projected that by accepting the assignment, James Matlock was very possibly going to his death. It was a terrible price, that possibility. But the objective was worth it. The conference was worth it.

Nimrod was worth it.

That was Loring's conclusion.

It made his assignment bearable.

4

Nothing could be written down; the briefing was slow, repetition constant. But Loring was a professional and knew the value of taking breaks from the pressures of trying to absorb too much too rapidly. During these periods, he attempted to draw Matlock out, learn more about this man whose life was so easily expendable. It was nearly midnight; Sam Kressel had left before eight o'clock. It was neither necessary nor advisable that the dean be present during the detailing of the specifics. He was a liaison, not an activist. Kressel was not averse to the decision.

Ralph Loring learned quickly that Matlock was a private man. His answers to innocuously phrased questions were brief, thrown-away replies constituting no more than self-denigrating explanations. After a while, Loring gave up. Matlock had agreed to do a job, not make public his thoughts or his motives. It wasn't necessary; Loring understood the latter. That was all that mattered. He was just as happy not to know the man too well.

Matlock, in turn—while memorizing the complicated information—was, on another level, reflecting on his own life, wondering in his own way why he'd been selected. He was intrigued by an evaluation that could describe him as being *mobile;* what an awful word to have applied!

Yet he knew he was precisely what the term signified. He *was* mobile. The professional researchers, or psychologists, or whatever they were, were accurate. But he doubted they understood the reasons behind his . . . "mobility."

The academic world had been a refuge, a sanctuary. Not an objective of long-standing ambition. He had fled into it in order to buy time, to organize a life that was falling apart, to understand. To get his *head straight,* as the kids said these days.

He had tried to explain it to his wife, his lovely, quick, bright, ultimately hollow wife, who thought he'd lost his senses. What was there to understand but an *awfully* good job, an *awfully* nice house, an *awfully* pleasant club, and a *good* life within an *awfully* rewarding social and financial world? For her, there *was* nothing more to understand. And he understood that.

But for him that world had lost its meaning. He had begun to drift away from its core in his early twenties, during his last year at Amherst. The separation became complete with his army experience.

It was no one single thing that had triggered his rejection. And the rejection itself was not a violent act, although violence played its role in the early days of the Saigon mess. It had begun at home, where most life-styles are accepted or rejected, during a series of disagreeable confrontations with his father. The old gentleman—too old, too gentlemanly—felt justified in demanding a better performance from his first son. A direction, a sense of purpose not at all in evidence. The senior Matlock belonged to another era—if not another century—and believed the gap between father and son a desirable thing, the lower element being dismissible until it had proved itself in the marketplace. Dismissible but, of course, malleable. In ways, the father was like a benign ruler who, after generations of power, was loath to have the throne abandoned by his rightful issue. It was inconceivable to the elder Matlock that his son would not assume the leadership of the family business. Businesses.

But for the younger Matlock, it was all *too* conceivable. And preferable. He was not only uncomfortable thinking about a future in his father's *marketplace,* he was also afraid. For him there was no joy in the regimented pressures of the financial world; instead, there was an awesome fear of inadequacy, emphasized by his father's strong—overpowering—competence. The closer he came to entering that world, the more pronounced was his fear. And it occurred to him that along with the delights of extravagant shelter and unnecessary creature comforts had to come the justification for doing what was expected in order to possess these things. He could not find that justification. Better the shelter should be less extravagant, the creature comforts somewhat limited, than face the prospects of continuing fear and discomfort.

He had tried to explain *that* to his father. Whereas his wife had claimed he'd lost his senses, the old gentleman pronounced him a misfit.

Which didn't exactly refute the army's judgment of him.

The army.

A disaster. Made worse by the knowledge that it was of his own making. He found that blind physical discipline and unquestioned authority were abhorrent to him. And he was large enough and strong enough and had a sufficient vocabulary to make his unadjustable, immature objections known—to his own disadvantage.

Discreet manipulations by an uncle resulted in a discharge before his tour of service was officially completed; for that he *was* grateful to an influential family.

And at this juncture of his life, James Barbour Matlock II was a mess. Separated from the service less than gloriously, divorced by his wife, dispossessed—symbolically if not actually—by his family, he felt the panic of belonging nowhere, of being without motive or purpose.

So he'd fled into the secure confines of graduate school, hoping to find an answer. And as in a love affair begun on a sexual basis but growing into psychological dependence, he had married that world; he'd found what had eluded him for nearly five vital years. It was the first real commitment he'd ever experienced.

He was free.

Free to enjoy the excitement of a meaningful challenge; free to revel in the confidence that he was equal to it. He plunged into his new world with the enthusiasm of a convert but without the blindness. He chose a period of history and literature that teemed with energy and conflict and contradictory evaluations. The apprentice years passed swiftly; he was consumed and pleasantly surprised by his own talents. When he emerged on the professional plateau, he brought fresh air into the musty archives. He made startling innovations in long-unquestioned methods of research. His doctoral thesis on court interference with English Renaissance literature—news management—blew into the historical ashcan several holy theories about one benefactress named Elizabeth.

He was the new breed of scholar: restless, skeptical, unsatisfied, always searching while imparting what he'd learned to others. Two and a half years after receiving his doctorate, he was elevated to the tenured position of associate professor, the youngest instructor at Carlyle to be so contracted.

James Barbour Matlock II made up for the lost years, the awful years. Perhaps best of all was the knowledge that he could communicate his excitement to others. He was young enough to enjoy sharing his enthusiasm, old enough to direct the inquiries.

Yes, he was *mobile;* God, was he! He couldn't, *wouldn't* turn anyone off, shut anyone out because of disagreement—even dislike. The depth of his own gratitude, the profoundness of his relief was such that he unconsciously promised himself never to discount the concerns of another human being.

"Any surprises?" Loring had completed a section of the material that dealt with narcotics purchases as they'd been traced.

"More a clarification, I'd say," replied Matlock. "The old-line fraternities or clubs—mostly white, mostly rich—get their stuff from Hartford. The black units like Lumumba Hall go to New Haven. Different sources."

"Exactly; that's student orientation. The point being that none buy from the Carlyle suppliers. From Nimrod."

"You explained that. The Nimrod people don't want to be advertised."

"But they're here. They're used."

"By whom?"

"Faculty and staff," answered Loring calmly, flipping over a page. This *may* be a surprise. Mr. and Mrs. Archer Beeson . . ."

Matlock immediately pictured the young history instructor and his wife. They were Ivy League conformity itself—falsely arrogant, aesthetically precious. Archer Beeson was a young man in an academic hurry; his wife, the perfect faculty ingenue, carelessly sexy, always in awe.

"They're with LSD and the methedrines. Acid and speed."

"Good Lord! They fooled the hell out of me. How do you know?"

"It's too complicated to go into, also restricted. To oversimplify: they, he, used to purchase heavily from a distributor in Bridgeport. The contact was terminated and he didn't show up on any other lists. But he's not off. We think he made the Carlyle connection. No proof, though . . . Here's another."

It was the coach of varsity soccer, a jock who worked in physical education. His items were marijuana and amphetamines; his previous source, Hartford. He was considered a pusher on campus, not a user. Although the Hartford source was no longer employed, the man's varied and dummied bank accounts continued to grow. Assumption: Nimrod.

And another. This one frightening to Matlock. The assistant dean of admissions. An alumnus of Carlyle who returned to the campus after a brief career as a salesman. He was a flamboyant, open-handed man; a proselytizer for the cause of Carlyle. A popular enthusiast in these days of cynicism. He, too, was considered a distributor, not a user. He covered himself well through second- and third-level pushers.

"We think he came back here through the Nimrod organization. Good positioning on Nimrod's part."

"Goddamn scarey. That son of a bitch makes parents think he's a combination of astronaut and chaplain."

"Good positioning, as I said. Remember? I told you and Kressel: the Nimrod people have interests that go beyond drugs."

"But you don't know what they are."

"We'd better find out. . . . Here's the breakdown of the kids."

The names of the students seemed endless to Matlock. There were 563 out of a total enrollment of 1200 plus. The government man admitted that many were included not because of confirmation of individual use, but due to their campus affiliations. Clubs and fraternities were known to pool resources for the purchase of narcotics.

"We haven't the time to ascertain the validity of every name. We're looking for relationships; any, no matter how remote. You've got to have all kinds of avenues; we can't restrict them. . . . And there's one aspect to this list; I don't know whether you see it or not."

"I certainly do. At least, I think I do. Twenty or thirty names here ring loud bells in several high places. Some very influential parents. Industry, government. Here." Matlock pointed. "The president's cabinet, if I'm not mistaken. And I'm not."

"You see." Loring smiled.

"Has any of this had any effect?"

"We don't know. Could have, could be. The Nimrod tentacles are spreading out fast. That's why the alarms are sounding; louder than your bells. Speaking unofficially, there could be repercussions no one's dreamed of. . . . Defense overruns, union contracts, forced installations. You name it. It *could* be related."

"Jesus Christ," said Matlock softly.

"Exactly."

The two men heard the front door of Sealfont's mansion open and shut. As if by reflex, Loring calmly took the papers from Matlock's hand and quickly replaced them in his briefcase. He closed the case and then did an unexpected thing. He silently, almost unobtrusively, whipped back his jacket and curled his fingers around the handle of a revolver in a small holster strapped to his chest. The action startled Matlock. He stared at the hidden hand.

The library door opened and Adrian Sealfont walked in. Loring casually removed his hand from inside his coat. Sealfont spoke kindly.

"I *do try*. I honestly do. I understand the words and the pictures and take no offense whatsoever at the braided hair. What confuses me is the hostility. Anyone past thirty is the natural enemy of these fellows."

"That was Strauss, wasn't it?" asked Matlock.

"Yes. Someone inquired about the New Wave influence. He replied that the New Wave was ancient history. Prehistoric, was his word. . . . I won't interrupt you gentlemen. I would, however, like to know Kressel's status, Mr. Loring. Obviously, James has accepted."

"So has Mr. Kressel, sir. He'll act as liaison between us."

"I see." Sealfont looked at Matlock. There was a sense of relief in his eyes. "James, I can tell you now. I'm extremely grateful you've decided to help."

"I don't think there's an alternative."

"There isn't. What's frightening is the possibility of such total involvement. Mr. Loring, I'll want to be advised the minute you have anything concrete. At that point, I shall do whatever you wish, follow any instructions. All I ask is that you supply me with proof and you'll have my complete, my official cooperation."

"I understand, sir. You've been very helpful. More than we had a right to expect. We appreciate it."

"As James said, there is no alternative. But I must impose limits; my first obligation is to this institution. The campuses these days might appear dormant; I think that's a surface evaluation. . . . You have work to do and I have some reading to finish. Good night, Mr. Loring. James."

Matlock and the government man nodded their goodnights as Adrian Sealfont closed the library door.

By one o'clock, Matlock could absorb no more. The main elements—names, sources, conjectures—were locked in; he would never forget them. Not that he could recite everything by rote; that wasn't expected. But the sight of any particular individual on the lists would trigger a memory response. He knew Loring was right about that. It was why the agent insisted that he say the names out loud, repeating them several times each. It would be enough.

What he needed now was a night's sleep, if sleep would come. Let everything fall into some kind of perspective. Then in the morning he could begin to make initial decisions, determine which individuals should be approached, selecting those least likely to come in contact with one another. And this meant familiarizing himself with immediate friends, faculty or student body status—dozens of isolated fragments of information beyond the data supplied by Loring. Kressel's files—the ones he disclaimed having—would help.

Once in conversations he'd have to make his way carefully—thrusting, parrying, watching for signs, looks, betrayals.

Somewhere, with someone, it would happen.

"I'd like to go back to something," said Loring. "Background material."

"We've covered an awful lot. Maybe I should digest what I've got."

"This won't take a minute. It's important." The agent reached into his briefcase and withdrew the filthy, scissored paper. "Here, this is yours."

"Thanks for I-don't-know-what." Matlock took the once-shining silver paper and looked at the strange script.

"I told you it was written in Oltremontan-Corsican and, except for two words, that's correct. At the bottom, on a single line, you'll see the phrase *Venerare Omerta*. That's not Corsican, it's Sicilian. Or a Sicilian contraction, to be precise."

"I've seen it before."

"I'm sure you have. It's been given wide distribution in newspapers, movies, fiction. But that doesn't lessen its impact on those concerned by it. It's very real."

"What does it mean?"

"Roughly translated: Respect the law of Omerta. Omerta is an oath of allegiance *and* silence. To betray either is asking to be killed."

"Mafia?"

"It's involved. You might say it's the party of the second part. Bear in mind that this little announcement was issued jointly by two factions trying to reach an accommodation. 'Omerta' goes across the board; it's understood by both."

"I'll bear it in mind, but I don't know what I'm supposed to do with it."

"Just know about it."

"O.K."

"One last item. Everything we've covered here tonight is related to narcotics. But if our information is correct, the Nimrod people are involved in other fields. Sharking, prostitution, gambling . . . perhaps, and it's only perhaps, municipal controls, state legislatures, even the federal government. . . . Experience tells us that narcotics is the weakest action, the highest rate of collapse among these activities, and that's why we've centered on it. In other words, concentrate on the drug situation but be aware that other avenues exist."

"It's no secret."

"Maybe not to you. Let's call it a night."

"Shouldn't you give me a number where I can reach you?"

"Negative. Use Kressel. We'll check with him several times a day. Once you start asking questions, you may be put under a microscope. Don't call Washington. And *don't* lose our Corsican invitation. It's your ultimate clout. Just find another one."

"I'll try."

Matlock watched as Loring closed his briefcase, looped the thin black chain around his wrist, and snapped the built-in lock.

"Looks very cloak-and-daggerish, doesn't it?" Loring laughed.

"I'm impressed."

"Don't be. The custom began with diplomatic couriers who'd take their pouches to hell with them, but today it's simply a protection against purse-snatching. . . . So help me, that's what they think of us."

"I don't believe a word you say. That's one of those cases that make smoke screens, send out radio signals, and trigger bombs."

"You're right. It does all those things and more. It's got secret compartments for sandwiches, laundry, and God knows what else." Loring swung the briefcase off the desk. "I think it'd be a good idea if we left separately. Preferably one from the front, one from the rear. Ten minutes apart."

"You think that's necessary?"

"Frankly, no, but that's the way my superiors want it."

"O.K. I know the house. I'll leave ten minutes after you do, from the kitchen."

"Fine." Loring extended his right hand by steadying the bottom of his case with his left. "I don't have to tell you how much we appreciate what you're doing."

"I think you know why I'm doing it."

"Yes, we do. Frankly, we counted on it."

Loring let himself out of the library and Matlock waited until he heard the outer door open and close. He looked at his watch. He'd have one more drink before he left.

By one twenty Matlock was several blocks away from the house. He walked slowly west toward his apartment, debating whether to detour around the campus. It often helped him to walk out a problem; he knew sleep would come fitfully. He passed a number of students and several faculty members, exchanging low-keyed, end of the weekend greetings with those he recognized. He'd about made up his mind to turn north on High Street, away from the direction of his apartment, when he heard the footsteps behind him. First the footsteps, then the harshly whispered voice.

"Matlock! Don't turn around. It's Loring. Just keep walking and listen to me."

"What is it?"

"Someone knows I'm here. My car was searched. . . ."

"Christ! How do you know?"

"Field threads, preset markings. All over the car. Front, back, trunk. A very thorough, very professional job."

"You're sure?"

"So goddamn sure I'm not going to start that engine!"

"Jesus!" Matlock nearly stopped.

"Keep walking! If anyone was watching me—and you can be damned sure someone was—I made it clear I'd lost my ignition key. Asked several people who passed by where a pay phone was and waited till I saw you far enough away."

"What do you want me to do? There's a phone booth on the next corner. . . ."

"I know. I don't think you'll have to do anything, and for both our sakes, I hope I'm right. I'm going to jostle you as I pass—pretty hard. Lose your balance, I'll shout my apologies. Pretend you twisted an ankle, a wrist, anything you like; *but buy time!* Keep me in sight until a car comes for me and *I nod that it's o.k.* Do you have all that? I'll get to the booth in a hurry."

"Suppose you're still phoning when I get there?"

"Keep walking but *keep checking.* The car's cruising."

"What's the point?"

"This briefcase. That's the point. There's only one thing Nimrod—if it *is* Nimrod—would like more than this briefcase. And that's the paper in your coat pocket. So be careful!"

Without warning, he rushed up beside Matlock and pushed him off the sidewalk.

"Sorry, fella! I'm in an awful hurry!"

Matlock looked up from the ground, reflecting that he'd had no reason to *pretend* to fall. The force of Loring's push eliminated that necessity. He swore and rose awkwardly. Once on his feet, he limped slowly toward the phone booth several hundred yards away. He wasted nearly a minute lighting a cigarette. Loring was inside the booth now, sitting on the plastic seat, hunched over the phone.

Any second, Matlock expected Loring's car to drive up the street.

Yet none came.

Instead, there was the tiniest break in the spring noises. A rush of air through the new leaves. Or was it the crush of a stone beneath a foot, or a small twig unable to take the weight of the new growth in the trees? Or was it Matlock's imagination? He couldn't be sure.

He approached the booth and remembered Loring's orders. *Walk by and pay no attention.* Loring was still huddled over the phone, his briefcase resting on the floor, its chain visible. But Matlock could hear no conversation, could see no movement from the man within. Instead, again, there was a sound: now, the sound of a dial tone.

Despite his instructions, Matlock approached the booth and opened the door. There was nothing else he could do. The government man had not even *begun* his call.

And in an instant, he understood why.

Loring had fallen into the gleaming gray metal of the telephone. He was dead. His eyes wide, blood trickling out of his forehead. A small circular hole no larger than a shirt button, surrounded by a spray of cracked glass, was ample evidence of what had happened.

Matlock stared at the man who had briefed him for hours and left him minutes ago. The dead man who had thanked him, joked with him, then finally warned him. He was petrified, unsure of what he should do, *could* do.

He backed away from the booth toward the steps of the nearest house. Instinct told him to stay away but not to run away. Someone was out there in the street. Someone with a rifle.

When the words came, he realized they were his, but he didn't know when he'd decided to shout them. They just emerged involuntarily.

"Help . . . *Help!* There's a man out here! He's been *shot!*"

Matlock raced up the steps of the corner house and began pounding on the door with all his strength. Several lights went on in several different homes. Matlock continued shouting.

"For God's *sake*, someone call the *police! There's a dead man out here!*"

Suddenly, from the shadows underneath the full trees in the middle of the block, Matlock heard the roar of an automobile engine, then the sound of swerving tires as the vehicle pulled out into the middle of the street and started forward. He rushed to the edge of the porch. The long black automobile plunged out of the darkness and sped to the corner. Matlock tried to see the license plates and, realizing that was impossible, took a step down to identify the make of the car. Suddenly he was blinded. The beam of a searchlight pierced the dimly lit spring night and focused itself on him. He pulled his hands up to shield his eyes and then heard the quiet slap, the instant rush of air he had heard minutes ago.

A rifle was being fired at him. A rifle with a silencer.

He dove off the porch into the shrubbery. The black car sped away.

5

He waited alone. The room was small, the window glass meshed with wire. The Carlyle Police Station was filled with officers and plainclothesmen called back on duty; no one could be sure what the killing signified. And none discounted the possibility that others might follow.

Alert. It was the particular syndrome of midcentury America, thought Matlock.

The gun.

He'd had the presence of mind after reaching the police to call Sam Kressel. Kressel, in shock, told him he would somehow contact the appropriate men in Washington and then drive down to the station house.

Until further instructions, they both agreed Matlock would restrict himself to a simple statement on finding the body and seeing the automobile. He had been out for a late night walk, that was all.

Nothing more.

His statement was typed out; questions as to time, his reasons for being in the vicinity, descriptions of the "alleged perpetrator's vehicle," direction, estimated speed—all were asked routinely and accepted without comment.

Matlock was bothered by his unequivocal negative to one question.

"Did you ever see the deceased before?"

"No."

That hurt. Loring deserved more than a considered, deliberate lie. Matlock recalled that the agent said he had a seven-year-old daughter. A wife and a child; the husband and father killed and he could not admit he knew his name.

He wasn't sure why it bothered him, but it did. Perhaps, he thought, because he knew it was the beginning of a great many lies.

He signed the short deposition and was about to be released when he heard a telephone ring inside an office beyond the desk. Not *on* the desk, beyond it. Seconds later, a uniformed policeman emerged and said his name in a loud voice, as if to make sure he had not left the building.

"Yes, officer?"

"We'll have to ask you to wait. If you'll follow me, please."

Matlock had been in the small room for nearly an hour; it was 2:45 A.M. and he had run out of cigarettes. It was no time to run out of cigarettes.

The door opened and a tall, thin man with large, serious eyes walked in. He was carrying Loring's briefcase. "Sorry to detain you, Dr. Matlock. It is 'Doctor,' isn't it?"

" 'Mister' is fine."

"My identification. Name's Greenberg, Jason Greenberg. Federal Bureau of Investigation. I had to confirm your situation. . . . It's a hell of a note, isn't it?"

" 'A hell of a note'? Is that all you can say?"

The agent looked at Matlock quizzically. "It's all I care to share," he said quietly. "If Ralph Loring had completed his call, he would have reached me."

"I'm sorry."

"Forget it. I'm out-briefed—that is, I know something but not much about the Nimrod situation; I'll get filled in before morning. Incidentally, this fellow Kressel is on his way over. He knows I'm here."

"Does this change anything? . . . That sounds stupid, doesn't it? A man is killed and I ask you if it changes anything. I apologize again."

"No need to; you've had a terrible experience. . . . Any change is up to you. We accept the fact that Ralph's death could alter tonight's decision. We ask only that you keep your own counsel in what was revealed to you."

"You're offering me a chance to renege?"

"Of course. You're under no obligation to us."

Matlock walked to the small, rectangular window with the wire-enclosed glass. The police station was at the south end of the town of Carlyle, about a half a mile from the campus, the section of town considered industrialized. Still, there were trees along the streets. Carlyle was a very clean town, a neat town. The trees by the station house were pruned and shaped.

And Carlyle was also something else.

"Let me ask you a question," he said. "Does the fact that I found Loring's body associate me with him? I mean, would I be considered a part of whatever he was doing?"

"We don't think so. The way you behaved tends to remove you from any association."

"What do you mean?" Matlock turned to face the agent.

"Frankly, you panicked. You didn't run, you didn't take yourself out of the area; you flipped out and started shouting your head off. Someone who's programmed for an assignment wouldn't react like that."

"I wasn't programmed for *this.*"

"Same results. You just found him and lost your head. If this Nimrod even *suspects* we're involved . . ."

"Suspects!" interrupted Matlock. "They *killed* him!"

"*Someone* killed him. It's unlikely that it's any part of Nimrod. Other factions, maybe. No cover's absolutely foolproof, even Loring's. But his was the closest."

"I don't understand you."

Greenberg leaned against the wall and folded his arms, his large, sad eyes reflective. "Ralph's field cover was the best at Justice. For damn near fifteen years." The agent looked down at the floor. His voice was deep, with faint bitterness. "The kind of goddamn cover that works best when it doesn't matter to a man anymore. When it's finally used, it throws everyone off balance. And insults his family."

Greenberg looked up and tried to smile, but no smile would come.

"I still don't understand you."

"It's not necessary. The main point is that you simply stumbled on the scene, went into panic, and had the scare of your life. You're dismissible, Mr. Matlock. . . . So?"

Before Matlock could respond, the door swung open and Sam Kressel entered, his expression nervous and frightened.

"Oh, Christ! This is terrible! Simply terrible. You're Greenberg?"

"And you're Mr. Kressel."

"Yes. What's going to happen?" Kressel turned to Matlock, speaking in the same breath. "Are you all right, Jim?"

"Sure."

"Well, Greenberg, what's *happening!?* They told

me in Washington that you'd let us know."

"I've been talking to Mr. Matlock and . . ."

"Listen to me," interrupted Kressel suddenly. "I called Sealfont and we're of the same opinion. What happened was terrible . . . tragic. We express our sympathies to the man's family, but we're most anxious that any use of the Carlyle name be cleared with us. We assume this puts everything in a different light and, therefore, we insist we be kept out of it. I think that's understandable."

Greenberg's face betrayed his distaste. "You race in here, ask me what's happening, and before you give me a chance to answer, you tell me what *must* happen. Now, how do you want it? Do I call Washington and let them have *your* version or do you want to listen first? Doesn't make a particle of difference to me."

"There's no reason for antagonism. We never asked to be involved."

"Nobody does." Greenberg smiled. "Just please let me finish. I've offered Matlock his out. He hasn't given me his answer, so I can't give you mine. However, if he says what I think he's going to say, Loring's cover will be activated immediately. It'll be activated anyway, but if the professor's in, we'll blow it up a bit."

"What the hell are you talking about?" Kressel stared at the agent.

"For years Ralph was a partner in just about the most disreputable law firm in Washington. Its clients read like a cross section of a Mafia index. . . . Early this morning, there was the first of two vehicle transfers. It took place in a Hartford suburb, Elmwood. Loring's car with the D.C. plates was left near the home of a well-advertised capo. A rented automobile was waiting for him a couple of blocks away. He used that to drive to Carlyle and parked it in front of 217 Crescent Street, five blocks from Sealfont's place. 217 Crescent is the residence of a Dr. Ralston. . . ."

"I've met him," interjected Matlock. "I've heard he's . . ."

". . . an abortionist," completed Greenberg.

"He's in no way associated with this university!" said Kressel emphatically.

"You've had worse," countered Greenberg quietly. "And the doctor is still a Mafia referral. At any rate, Ralph positioned the car and walked into town for the second transfer. I covered him; this briefcase is prime material. He was picked up by a Bell Telephone truck which made routine stops—including one at a restaurant called the Cheshire Cat—and finally delivered him to Sealfont's. No one could have known he was there. If they had, they would have intercepted him outside; they were watching the car on Crescent."

"That's what he told me," said Matlock.

"He knew it was possible; the trace to Crescent was intentionally left open. When he confirmed it, to his satisfaction, he acted fast. I don't know what he did, but he probably used whatever stragglers he could find until he spotted you."

"That's what he did."

"He wasn't fast enough."

"What in God's name does this have to do with *us?* What *possible* bearing can it have?" Kressel was close to shouting.

"If Mr. Matlock wants to go on, Loring's death will be publicized as an underworld killing. Disreputable lawyer, maybe a bag man; undesirable clients. The capo and the doctor will be hauled in; they're expendable. The smoke screen's so thick everyone's off balance. Even the killers. Matlock's forgotten. It'll work; it's worked before."

Kressel seemed astonished at Greenberg's assured glibness, his confidence, his calm professionalism. "You talk awfully fast, don't you?"

"I'm very bright."

Matlock couldn't help but smile. He liked Greenberg; even in—perhaps because of—the sadly disagreeable circumstances. The agent used the language well; his mind was fast. He was, indeed, bright.

"And if Jim says he washes his hands of it?"

Greenberg shrugged. "I don't like to waste words. Let's hear him say it."

Both the men looked at Matlock.

"I'm afraid I'm not going to, Sam. I'm still in."

"You can't be serious! That man was killed!"

"I know. I found him."

Kressel put his hand on Matlock's arm. It was the gesture of a friend. "I'm not an hysterical shepherd watching over a flock. I'm concerned. I'm *frightened.* I see a man being manipulated into a situation he's not qualified to handle."

"That's subjective," broke in Greenberg quietly. "We're concerned, too. If we didn't think he was capable, we never would have approached him."

"I think you would," said Kressel. "I don't for a minute believe such a consideration would stop you. You use the word *expendable* too easily, Mr. Greenberg."

"I'm sorry you think so. Because I don't. We don't. . . . I haven't gotten the detailed briefing, Kressel, but aren't you supposed to act as liaison? Because if that's true, I suggest you remove yourself. We'll have someone else assigned to the job."

"And give you a clear field? Let you run roughshod over this campus? Not on your life."

"Then we work together. As disagreeable as that may be for both of us . . . You're hostile; perhaps that's good. You'll keep me on my toes. You protest too much."

Matlock was startled by Greenberg's statement. It was one thing to form an antagonistic coalition, quite another to make veiled accusations; insulting to use a literary cliché.

"That remark requires an explanation," said Kressel, his face flushed with anger.

When Greenberg replied, his voice was soft and reasonable, belying the words he spoke. "Pound sand, mister. I lost a very good friend tonight. Twenty minutes ago I spoke with his wife. I don't give explanations under those conditions. That's where my employers and me part company. Now, shut up and I'll write out the hours of contact and give you the emergency telephone numbers. If you don't want them, get the hell out of here."

Greenberg lifted the briefcase onto a small table and opened it. Sam Kressel, stunned, approached the agent silently.

Matlock stared at the worn leather briefcase, only hours ago chained to the wrist of a dead man. He knew the deadly pavanne had begun. The first steps of the dance had been taken violently.

There were decisions to make, people to confront.

6

The implausible name below the doorbell on the two-family faculty house read: Mr. and Mrs. Archer Beeson. Matlock had elicited the dinner invitation easily. History instructor Beeson had been flattered by his interest in coordinating a seminar between two of their courses. Beeson would have been flattered if a faculty member of Matlock's attainments had asked him how his wife was in bed (and most wondered). And since Matlock was very clearly male, Archer Beeson felt that "drinks and din" with his wife wriggling around in a short skirt might help cement a relationship with the highly regarded professor of English literature.

Matlock heard the breathless shout from the second-floor landing. "Just a sec!"

It was Beeson's wife, and her broad accent, overcultivated at Miss Porter's and Finch, sounded caricatured. Matlock pictured the girl racing around checking the plates of cheese and dip—very unusual cheese and dip, conversation pieces, really—while her husband put the final touches on the visual aspects of his bookcases—perhaps several obscure tomes carelessly, carefully, placed on tables, impossible for a visitor to miss.

Matlock wondered if these two were also secreting small tablets of lysergic acid or capsules of methedrine.

The door opened and Beeson's petite wife, dressed in the expected short skirt and translucent silk blouse that loosely covered her large breasts, smiled ingenuously.

"Hi! I'm Ginny Beeson. We met at several *mad* cocktail parties. I'm *so* glad you could come. Archie's just finishing a paper. Come on up." She preceded Matlock up the stairs, hardly giving him a chance to acknowledge. "These stairs are *horrendous!* Oh, well, the price of starting at the bottom."

"I'm sure it won't be for long," said Matlock.

"That's what Archie keeps saying. He'd better be right or I'll have muscles all over my legs!"

"I'm sure he is," said Matlock, looking at the soft, unmuscular, large expanse of legs in front of him.

Inside the Beeson apartment, the cheese and dip were prominently displayed on an odd-shaped coffee table, and the anticipated showcase volume was one of Matlock's own. It was titled *Interpolations in Richard II* and it resided on a table underneath a fringed lamp. Impossible for a visitor to miss.

The minute Ginny closed the door, Archie burst into the small living room from what Matlock presumed was Beeson's study—also small. He carried a sheaf of papers in his left hand; his right was extended.

"Good-oh! Glad you could make it, old man! . . . Sit, sit. Drinks are due and overdue! God! I'm flaked out for one! . . . Just spent three hours reading twenty versions of the Thirty Years' War!"

"It happens. Yesterday I got a theme on *Volpone* with the strangest ending I ever heard of. Turned out the kid never read it but saw the film in Hartford."

"With a new ending?"

"Totally."

"God! That's marvy!" injected Ginny semihysterically. "What's your drink preference, Jim? I may call you Jim, mayn't I, Doctor?"

"Bourbon and a touch of water, and you certainly better, Ginny. I've never gotten used to the 'doctor.' My father calls it fraud. Doctors carry stethoscopes, not books." Matlock sat in an easy chair covered with an Indian serape.

"Speaking of doctors, I'm working on my dissertation now. That and two more hectic summers'll do the trick." Beeson took the ice bucket from his wife and walked to a long table underneath a window where bottles and glasses were carelessly arranged.

"It's worth it," said Ginny Beeson emphatically. "Isn't it worth it, Jim?"

"Almost essential. It'll pay off."

"That and *publishing.*" Ginny Beeson picked up the cheese and crackers and carried them to Matlock. "This is an interesting little Irish *fromage.* Would you believe, it's called 'Blarney'? Found it in a little shop in New York two weeks ago."

"Looks great. Never heard of it."

"Speaking of publishing. I picked up your *Interpolations* book the other day. *Damned fascinating!* Really!"

"Lord, I've almost forgotten it. Wrote it four years ago."

"It should be a *required text!* That's what Archie said, isn't it, Archie?"

"Damned right! Here's the poison, old man," said Beeson, bringing Matlock his drink. "Do you work through an agent, Jim? Not that I'm nosy. I'm years from writing anything."

"That's not true, and you know it," Ginny pouted vocally.

"Yes, I do. Irving Block in Boston. If you're working on something, perhaps I could show it to him."

"Oh, no, I wouldn't . . . that'd be awfully presumptuous of me. . . ." Beeson retreated with feigned humility to the couch with his drink. He sat next to his wife and they—involuntarily, thought Matlock—exchanged satisfied looks.

"Come on, Archie. You're a bright fellow. A real comer on this campus. Why do you think I asked you about the seminar? *You* could be doing *me* the favor. I might be bringing Block a winner. That rubs off, you know."

Beeson's expression had the honesty of gratitude. It embarrassed Matlock to return the instructor's gaze until he saw something else in Beeson's eyes. He couldn't define it, but it was there. A slight wildness, a trace of panic.

The look of a man whose mind and body knew drugs.

"That's *damned* good-oh of you, Jim. I'm touched, *really*."

The cheese, drinks, and dinner somehow passed. There were moments when Matlock had the feeling he was outside himself, watching three characters in a scene from some old movie. Perhaps on board ship or in a sloppily elegant New York apartment with the three of them wearing tightly fitted formal clothes. He wondered why he visualized the scene in such fashion—and then he knew. The Beesons had a thirties quality about them. The thirties that he had observed on the late night television films. They were somehow an anachronism, of this time but not of the time. It was either more than camp or less than put-on; he couldn't be sure. They were not artificial in themselves, but there was a falseness in their emphatic small talk, their dated expressions. Yet the truth was that they were the *now* of the present generation.

Lysergic acid and methedrine.

Acid heads. Pill poppers.

The Beesons were somehow forcing themselves to show themselves as part of a past and carefree era. Perhaps to deny the times and conditions in which they found themselves.

Archie Beeson and his wife were frightening.

By eleven, after considerable wine with the "interesting-little-veal-dish-from-a-recipe-in-an-old-Italian cookbook," the three of them sat down in the living room. The last of the proposed seminar problems was ironed out. Matlock knew it was time to begin; the awful, awkward moment. He wasn't sure how; the best he could do was to trust his amateur instincts.

"Look, you two. . . . I hope to hell this won't come as too great a shock, but I've been a long time without a stick." He withdrew a thin cigarette case from his pocket and opened it. He felt foolish, uncomfortably clumsy. But he knew he could not show those feelings. "Before you make any judgments, I should tell you I don't go along with the pot laws and I never have."

Matlock selected a cigarette from the dozen in the case and left the case open on the table. Was that the proper thing to do? He wasn't sure; he didn't know. Archie and his wife looked at each other. Through the flame in front of his face, Matlock watched their reaction. It was cautious yet positive. Perhaps it was the alcohol in Ginny, but she smiled hesitantly, as if she was relieved to find a friend. Her husband wasn't quite so responsive.

"Go right ahead, old man," said the young instructor with a trace of condescension. "We're hardly on the attorney general's payroll."

"Hardly!" giggled the wife.

"The laws are archaic," continued Matlock, inhaling deeply. "In all areas. Control and an abiding sense of discretion—self-discretion—are all that matter. To deny experience is the real crime. To prohibit any intelligent individual's right to fulfillment is . . . goddamn it, it's repressive."

"Well, I think the key word is *intelligent*, Jim. *Indiscriminate* use among the *un*intelligent leads to chaos."

"Socratically, you're only half right. The other half is 'control.' Effective control among the 'iron' and 'bronze' then frees the 'gold'—to borrow from *The Republic*. If the intellectually superior were continually kept from thinking, experimenting, because their thought processes were beyond the comprehension of their fellow citizens, there'd be no great works—artistically, technically, politically. We'd still be in the Dark Ages."

Matlock inhaled his cigarette and closed his eyes. Had he been too strong, too positive? Had he sounded too much the false proselytizer? He waited, and the wait was not long. Archie spoke quietly, but urgently nevertheless.

"Progress is being made every day, old man. Believe that. It's the truth."

Matlock half opened his eyes in relief and looked at Beeson through the cigarette smoke. He held his gaze steady without blinking and then shifted his stare to Beeson's wife. He spoke only two words.

"You're children."

"That's a relative supposition under the circumstances," answered Beeson, still keeping his voice low, his speech precise.

"And that's talk."

"Oh, don't be so sure about that!" Ginny Beeson had had enough alcohol in her to be careless. Her husband reached for her arm and held it. It was a warning. He spoke again, taking his eyes off Matlock, looking at nothing.

"I'm not at all sure we're on the same wavelength . . ."

"No, probably not. Forget it. . . . I'll finish this and shove off. Be in touch with you about the seminar." Matlock made sure his reference to the seminar was offhanded, almost disinterested.

Archie Beeson, the young man in an academic hurry, could not stand that disinterest.

"Would you mind if I had one of those?"

"If it's your first, yes, I would. . . . Don't try to impress me. It doesn't really matter."

"My first? . . . Of what?" Beeson rose from the couch and walked to the table where the cigarette case lay open. He reached down, picked it up, and held it to his nostrils. "That's passable grass. I might add, just passable. I'll try one . . . for openers."

"For openers?"

"You seem to be very sincere but, if you'll forgive me, you're a bit out of touch."

"From what?"

"From where it's at." Beeson withdrew two cigarettes and lit them in *Now, Voyager* fashion. He inhaled deeply, nodding and shrugging a reserved approval, and handed one to his wife. "Let's call this an hors d'oeuvre. An appetizer."

He went into his study and returned with a Chinese lacquered box, then showed Matlock the tiny peg which, when pushed, enabled the holder to flip up a thin layer of wood on the floor of the box, revealing a false bottom. Beneath were two dozen or so white tablets wrapped in transparent plastic.

"This is the main course . . . the entrée, if you're up to it."

Matlock was grateful for what knowledge he possessed and the intensive homework he'd undertaken during the past forty-eight hours. He smiled but his tone of voice was firm.

"I only take white trips under two conditions. The first is at *my* home with very good, very old friends. The second is with very good, very old friends at *their* homes. I don't know you well enough, Archie. Self-discretion. . . . I'm not averse to a small red journey, however. Only I didn't come prepared."

"Say no more. I just may be." Beeson took the Chinese box back into his study and returned with a small leather pouch, the sort pipe smokers use for tobacco, and approached Matlock's chair. Ginny Beeson's eyes grew wide; she undid a button on her half-unbuttoned blouse and stretched her legs.

"Dunhill's best." Beeson opened the top flap and held the pouch down for Matlock to see inside. Again there was the clear plastic wrapped around tablets. However, these were deep red and slightly larger than the white pills in the Chinese box. There were at least fifty to sixty doses of Seconal.

Ginny jumped out of the chair and squealed. "I *love* it! It's the pinky-groovy!"

"Beats the hell out of brandy," added Matlock.

"We'll trip. Not too much, old man. Limit's five. That's the house rules for new old friends."

The next two hours were blurred for James Matlock, but not as blurred as they were for the Beesons. The history instructor and his wife quickly reached their "highs" with the five pills—as would have Matlock had he not been able to pocket the final three while pretending to have swallowed them. Once on the first plateau, it wasn't too hard for Matlock to imitate his companions and then convince Beeson to go for another dosage.

"Where's the almighty discretion, Doctor?" chuckled Beeson, sitting on the floor in front of the couch, reaching occasionally for one of his wife's legs.

"You're better friends than I thought you were."

"Just the *beginning* of a beautiful, *beautiful* friendship." The young wife slowly reclined on the couch and giggled. She seemed to writhe and put her right hand on her husband's head, pushing his hair forward.

Beeson laughed with less control than he had shown earlier and rose from the floor. "I'll get the magic then."

When Beeson walked into his study, Matlock watched his wife. There was no mistaking her action. She looked at Matlock, opened her mouth slowly, and pushed her tongue out at him. Matlock realized that one of Seconal's side effects was showing. As was most of Virginia Beeson.

The second dosage was agreed to be three, and Matlock was now easily able to fake it. Beeson turned on his stereo and played a recording of "Carmina Burana." In fifteen minutes Ginny Beeson was sitting on Matlock's lap, intermittently rubbing herself against his groin. Her husband was spread out in front of the stereo speakers, which were on either side of the turntable. Matlock spoke as though exhaling, just loud enough to be heard over the music.

"These are some of the best I've had, Archie. . . . Where? Where's the supply from?"

"Probably the same as yours, old man." Beeson turned over and looked at Matlock and his wife. He laughed. "Now, I don't know what you mean. The magic or the girl on your lap. Watch her, Doctor. She's a minx."

"No kidding. Your pills are a better grade than mine and my grass barely passed inspection. Where? Be a good friend."

"You're funny, man. You keep asking. Do I ask you? No. . . . It's not polite. . . . Play with Ginny. Let me listen." Beeson rolled back over face down on the floor.

The girl on Matlock's lap suddenly put her arms around his neck and pressed her breasts against his chest. She put her head to the side of his face and began kissing his ears. Matlock wondered what would happen if he lifted her out of the chair and carried her into the bedroom. He wondered, but he didn't want to find out. Not then. Ralph Loring had not been murdered to increase his, Matlock's, sex life.

"Let me try one of your joints. Let me see just how advanced your taste is. You may be a phony, Archie."

Suddenly Beeson sat up and stared at Matlock. He wasn't concerned with his wife. Something in Matlock's voice seemed to trigger an instinctive doubt. Or was it the words? Or was it the too normal pattern of speech Matlock used? The English professor thought of all these things as he returned Beeson's look over the girl's shoulder. Archie Beeson was suddenly a man warned, and Matlock wasn't sure why. Beeson spoke haltingly.

"Certainly, old man. . . . Ginny, don't annoy Jim." He began to rise.

"Pinky groovy . . ."

"I've got several in the kitchen. . . . I'm not sure where but I'll look. Ginny, I told you not to tease Jim. . . . Be nice to him, be good to him." Beeson kept staring at Matlock, his eyes wide from the Seconal, his lips parted, the muscles of his face beyond relaxation. He backed away toward the kitchen door, which was open. Once inside, Archie Beeson did a strange thing. Or so it appeared to James Matlock.

He slowly closed the swing-hinged door and held it shut.

Matlock quickly eased the drugged girl off his lap and she quietly stretched out on the floor. She smiled angelically and reached her arms up for him. He smiled down, stepping over her.

"Be right back," he whispered. "I want to ask Archie something." The girl rolled over on her stomach as Matlock walked cautiously toward the kitchen door. He ruffled his hair and purposely, silently, lurched, holding onto the dining room table as he neared the entrance. If Beeson suddenly came out, he wanted to appear irrational, drugged. The stereo was a little louder now, but through it Matlock could hear the sound of Archie's voice talking quietly, excitedly on the kitchen telephone.

He leaned against the wall next to the kitchen door and tried to analyze the disjointed moments that caused Archie Beeson to panic, to find it so imperative to reach someone on the telephone.

Why? What?

Had the grand impersonation been so obvious? Had he blown his first encounter?

If he had, the least he could do was try to find out who was on the other end of the line, who it was that Beeson ran to in his disjointed state of anxiety.

One fact seemed clear: whoever it was had to be more important than Archer Beeson. A man—even a drug addict—did not panic and contact a lesser figure on his own particular totem.

Perhaps the evening wasn't a failure; or his failure—conversely—a necessity. In Beeson's desperation, he might let slip information he never would have revealed if he *hadn't* been desperate. It wasn't preposterous to force it out of the frightened, drugged instructor. On the other hand, that was the least desirable method. If he failed in that, too, he was finished before he'd begun. Loring's meticulous briefing would have been for nothing; his death a rather macabre joke, his terrible cover—so painful to his family, so inhuman somehow—made fruitless by a bumbling amateur.

There was no other way, thought Matlock, but to try. Try to find out who Beeson had reached *and* try to put the pieces of the evening back where Beeson might accept him again. For some insane reason, he pictured Loring's briefcase and the thin black chain dangling from the handle. For an even crazier reason, it gave him confidence; not much, but some.

He assumed a stance as close to the appearance of collapse as he could imagine, then moved his head to the door frame and slowly, quarter inch by quarter inch, pushed it inward. He fully expected to be met by Beeson's staring eyes. Instead, the instructor's back was to him; he was hunched over like a small boy trying to control his bladder, the phone clutched to his thin scrunched neck, his head bent to the side. It was obvious that Beeson thought his voice was muffled, indistinguishable beneath the sporadic crescendos of the "Carmina Burana." But the Seconal had played one of its tricks. Beeson's ear and his speech were no longer synchronized. His words were not only clear. They were emphasized by being spaced out and repeated.

". . . You *do not* understand me. I want you to understand me. *Please,* understand. He keeps asking questions. He's not *with* it. He *is not with it.* I swear to Christ he's a plant. Get hold of Herron. Tell Herron to reach him for *God's* sake. Reach him, *please!* I could lose everything! . . . No. No, I can tell! I *see* what I *see, man!* When that bitch turns horny I have *problems.* I mean there are appearances, old man. . . . Get Lucas. . . . For Christ's sake *get* to him! I'm in *trouble* and I can't. . . ."

Matlock let the door swing slowly back into the frame. His shock was such that thought and feeling were suspended; he saw his hand still on the kitchen door, yet he felt no wood against his fingers. What he had just heard was no less horrible than the sight of Ralph Loring's lifeless body in the telephone booth.

Herron. *Lucas Herron!*

A seventy-year-old legend. A quiet scholar who was as much revered for his perceptions of the human condition as he was for his brilliance. A lovely man, an honored man. There had to be a mistake, an explanation.

There was no time to ponder the inexplicable.

Archer Beeson thought he was a "plant." And now, someone else thought so, too. He couldn't allow that. He had to think, force himself to *act.*

Suddenly he understood. Beeson himself had told him what to do.

No informer—no one not narcotized—would attempt it.

Matlock looked over at the girl lying face down on the living room floor. He crossed rapidly around the dining table and ran to her side, unbuckling his belt as he did so. In swift movements, he took off his trousers and reached down, rolling her over on her back. He lay down beside her and undid the remaining two buttons on her blouse, pulling her brassiere until the hasp broke. She moaned and giggled, and when he touched her exposed breasts, she moaned again and lifted one leg over Matlock's hip.

"Pinky groovy, pinky groovy . . ." She began breathing through her mouth, pushing her pelvis into Matlock's groin; her eyes half open, her hands reaching down, stroking his leg, her fingers clutching at his skin.

Matlock kept his eyes toward the kitchen door, praying it would open.

And then it did, and he shut his eyes.

Archie Beeson stood in the dining area looking down at his wife and guest. Matlock, at the sound of Beeson's footsteps, snapped his head back and feigned terrified confusion. He rose from the floor and immediately fell back down again. He grabbed his trousers and held them in front of his shorts, rising once more unsteadily and finally falling onto the couch.

"Oh, Jesus! Oh, sweet Jesus, Archie! Christ, young fella! I didn't think I was this freaked out! . . . I'm far out, Archie! What the hell, what do I *do?* I'm *gone,* man, I'm sorry! Christ, I'm sorry!"

Beeson approached the couch, his half-naked wife at his feet. From his expression it was impossible to tell what he was thinking. Or the extent of his anger.

Or was it anger?

His audible reaction was totally unexpected: he started to laugh. At first softly, and then with gathering momentum, until he became nearly hysterical.

"Oh, *God,* old man! I said it! I *said* she was a minx! . . . Don't worry. No tattle tales. No rapes, no dirty-old-man-on-the-faculty. But we'll have our *seminar.* Oh, Christ, yes! That'll be some *seminar!* And you'll tell them all you picked *me!* Won't you? Oh, yes! That's what you'll tell them, isn't it?"

Matlock looked into the wild eyes of the addict above him.

"Sure. Sure, Archie. Whatever you say."

"You better believe it, old man! And don't apologize. No apologies are necessary! The apologies are mine!" Archer Beeson collapsed on the floor in laughter. He reached over and cupped his wife's left breast; she moaned and giggled her maddening, high-pitched giggle.

And Matlock knew he had won.

7

He was exhausted, both by the hour and by the tensions of the night. It was ten minutes past three and the choral strains of the "Carmina Burana" were still hammering in his ears. The image of the bare-breasted wife and the jackal-sounding husband—both writhing on the floor in front of him—added revulsion to the sickening taste in his mouth.

But what bothered him most was the knowledge that Lucas Herron's name was used within the context of such an evening.

It was inconceivable.

Lucas Herron. The "grand old bird," as he was called. A reticent but obvious fixture of the Carlyle campus. The chairman of the Romance languages department and the embodiment of the quiet scholar with a deep and abiding compassion. There was always a glint in his eyes, a look of bemusement mixed with tolerance.

To associate him—regardless of how remotely—with the narcotics world was unbelievable. To have heard him sought after by an hysterical addict—for essentially, Archer Beeson *was* an addict, psychologically if not chemically—as though Lucas were some sort of power under the circumstances was beyond rational comprehension.

The explanation had to lie somewhere in Lucas Herron's immense capacity for sympathy. He was a friend to many, a dependable refuge for the troubled, often the deeply troubled. And beneath his placid, aged, unruffled surface, Herron was a strong man, a leader. A quarter of a century ago, he had spent countless months of hell in the Solomon Islands as a middle-aged infantry officer. A lifetime ago, Lucas Herron had been an authentic hero in a vicious moment of time during a savage war in the Pacific. Now over seventy, Herron was an institution.

Matlock rounded the corner and saw his apartment half a block away. The campus was dark; aside from the street lamps, the only light came from one of his rooms. Had he left one on? He couldn't remember.

He walked up the path to his door and inserted his key. Simultaneously with the click of the lock, there was a loud crash from within. Although it startled him, his first reaction was amusement. His clumsy, long-haired house cat had knocked over a stray glass or one of those pottery creations Patricia Ballantyne had inflicted on him. Then he realized such a thought was ridiculous, the product of an exhausted mind. The crash was too loud for pottery, the shattering of glass too violent.

He rushed into the small foyer, and what he saw pushed fatigue out of his brain. He stood immobile in disbelief.

The entire room was in shambles. Tables were overturned; books pulled from the shelves, their pages torn from the bindings, scattered over the floor; his stereo turntable and speakers smashed. Cushions from his couch and armchairs were slashed, the stuffing and foam rubber strewn everywhere; the rugs upended, lumped in folds; the curtains ripped from their rods, thrown over the upturned furniture.

He saw the reason for the crash. His large casement window, on the far right wall bordering the street, was a mass of twisted lead and broken glass. The window consisted of two panels; he remembered clearly that he had opened both before leaving for the Beesons. He liked the spring breezes, and it was too early in the season for screens. So there was no reason for the window to be smashed; the ground was perhaps four or five feet below the casement, sufficient to dissuade an intruder, low enough for a panicked burglar to negotiate easily.

The smashing of the window, therefore, was not for escape. It was intended.

He had been watched, and a signal had been given.

It was a warning.

And Matlock knew he could not acknowledge that warning. To do so was to acknowledge more than a robbery; he was not prepared to do that.

He crossed rapidly to his bedroom door and looked inside. If possible, his bedroom was in more of a mess than the living room. The mattress was thrown against the wall, ripped to shreds. Every drawer of his bureau was dislodged, lying on the floor, the contents scattered all around the room. His closet was like the rest —suits and jackets pulled from the clothes rod, shoes yanked from their recesses.

Even before he looked he knew his kitchen would be no better off than the rest of his apartment. The foodstuffs in cans and boxes had not been thrown on the floor, simply moved around, but the soft items had been torn to pieces. Matlock understood again. One or two crashes from the other rooms were tolerable noise levels; a continuation of the racket from his kitchen might arouse one of the other families in the building. As it was, he could hear the faint sounds of footsteps above him. The final crash of the window had gotten someone up.

The warning was explicit, but the act itself was a search.

He thought he knew the object of that search, and again he realized he could not acknowledge it. Conclusions were being made as they had been made at Beeson's; he had to ride them out with the most convincing denials he could manufacture. That much he knew instinctively.

But before he began that pretense, he had to find out if the search was successful.

He shook the stammering lethargy out of his mind and body. He looked once again at his living room; he studied it. All the windows were bare, and the light was sufficient for someone with a pair of powerful binoculars stationed in a nearby building or standing on the inclining lawn of the campus beyond the street to observe every move he made. If he turned off the lights, would such an unnatural action lend credence to the conclusions he wanted denied?

Without question. A man didn't walk into a house in shambles and proceed to turn off lights.

Yet he had to reach his bathroom, at that moment the most important room in the apartment. He had to spend less than thirty seconds inside to determine the success or failure of the ransacking, and do so in such a way as to seem innocent of any abnormal concerns. If anyone *was* watching.

It was a question of appearance, of gesture, he thought. He saw that the stereo turntable was the nearest object to the bathroom door, no more than five feet away. He walked over and bent down, picking up several pieces, including the metal arm. He looked at it, then suddenly dropped the arm and brought his finger to his mouth, feigning an imagined puncture on his skin. He walked into the bathroom rapidly.

Once inside, he quickly opened the medicine cabinet and grabbed a tin of Band-Aids from the glass shelf. He then swiftly reached down to the left of the toilet bowl where the cat's yellow plastic box was placed and picked up a corner of the newspaper underneath the granules of litter. Beneath the newspaper he felt the coarse grain of the two layers of canvas he had inserted and lifted up an edge.

The scissored page was still intact. The silver Corsican paper that ended in the deadly phrase *Venerare Omerta* had not been found.

He replaced the newspaper, scattered the litter, and stood up. He saw that the frosted glass of the small window above the toilet was partially opened, and he swore.

There was no time to think of that.

He walked back into the living room, ripping the plastic off a Band-Aid.

The search had failed. Now the warning had to be ignored, the conclusions denied. He crossed to the telephone and called the police.

"Can you give me a list of what's missing?" A uniformed patrolman stood in the middle of the debris. A second policeman wandered about the apartment making notes.

"I'm not sure yet. I haven't really checked."

"That's understandable. It's a mess. You'd better

look, though. The quicker we get a list, the better."

"I don't think anything *is* missing, officer. What I mean is, I don't have anything particularly valuable to anyone else. Except perhaps the stereo . . . and that's smashed. There's a television set in the bedroom, that's okay. Some of the books could bring a price, but look at them."

"No cash, jewelry, watches?"

"I keep money in the bank and cash in my wallet. I wear my watch and haven't any jewelry."

"How about exam papers? We've been getting a lot of that."

"In my office. In the English department."

The patrolman wrote in a small black notebook and called to his partner, who had gone into the bedroom. "Hey, Lou, did the station confirm the print man?"

"They're getting him up. He'll be over in a few minutes."

"Have you touched anything, Mr. Matlock?"

"I don't know. I may have. It was a shock."

"Particularly any of the broken items, like that record player? It'd be good if we could show the fingerprint man specific things you haven't touched."

"I picked up the arm, not the casing."

"Good. It's a place to start."

The police stayed for an hour and a half. The fingerprints specialist arrived, did his work, and departed. Matlock thought of phoning Sam Kressel, but reasoned that there wasn't anything Kressel could do at that hour. And in the event someone outside *was* watching the building, Kressel shouldn't be seen. Various people from the other apartments had wakened and had come down offering sympathy, help, and coffee.

As the police were leaving, a large patrolman turned in the doorway. "Sorry to take so much time, Mr. Matlock. We don't usually lift prints in a break and entry unless there's injury or loss of property, but there's been a lot of this sort of thing recently. Personally, I think it's those weirdos with the hair and the beads. Or the niggers. We never had trouble like this before the weirdos and the niggers got here."

Matlock looked at the uniformed officer, who was so confident of his analysis. There was no point in objecting; it would be useless, and Matlock was too tired. "Thanks for helping me straighten up."

"Sure thing." The patrolman started down the cement path, then turned again. "Oh, Mr. Matlock."

"Yes?" Matlock pulled the door back.

"It struck us that maybe someone was looking for something. What with all the slashing and books and everything . . . you know what I mean?"

"Yes."

"You'd tell us if that was the case, wouldn't you?"

"Of course."

"Yeah. It'd be stupid to withhold information like that."

"I'm not stupid."

"No offense. Just that sometimes you guys get all involved and forget things."

"I'm not absentminded. Very few of us are."

"Yeah." The patrolman laughed somewhat derisively. "I just wanted to bring it up. I mean, we can't do our jobs unless we got all the facts, you know?"

"I understand."

"Yeah. Good."

"Good night."

"Good night, Doctor."

He closed the door and walked into his living

room. He wondered if his insurance would cover the disputable value of his rarer books and prints. He sat down on the ruined couch and surveyed the room. It was still a mess; the carnage had been thorough. It would take more than picking up debris and righting furniture. The warning had been clear, violent.

The startling fact was that the warning existed at all.

Why? From whom?

Archer Beeson's hysterical telephone call? That was possible, even preferable, perhaps. It might encompass a motive unrelated to Nimrod. It could mean that Beeson's circle of users and pushers wanted to frighten him enough to leave Archie alone. Leave them all alone; and Loring had specifically said there was no proof that the Beesons were involved with the Nimrod unit.

There was no proof that they weren't, either.

Nevertheless, if it *was* Beeson, the alarm would be called off in the morning. There was no mistaking the conclusion of the night's engagement. The "near-rape" by a dirty, drugged "old man." He was Beeson's academic ladder.

On the other hand, and far less preferable, there was the possibility that the warning *and* the search were centered on the Corsican paper. What had Loring whispered behind him on the sidewalk?

". . . There's only one thing they want more than this briefcase; that's the paper in your pocket."

It was then reasonable to assume that he'd been linked to Ralph Loring.

Washington's assessment that his panic at finding Loring dissociated him from the agent was in error, Jason Greenberg's confidence misplaced.

Still again, as Greenberg had suggested, they might

test him. Press him before issuing a clean bill of health.

Might, could, possible, still again.

Conjectures.

He had to keep his head; he couldn't allow himself to overreact. If he was to be of *any* value, he had to play the innocent.

Might have, could have, it was possible.

His body ached. His eyes were swollen and his mouth still had the terrible aftertaste of the combined dosages of Seconal, wine, and marijuana. He was exhausted; the pressures of trying to reach unreachable conclusions were overtaking him. His memory wandered back to the early days in 'Nam and he recalled the best advice he'd ever been given in those weeks of unexpected combat. That was to rest whenever he could, to sleep if it was at all possible. The advice had come from a line sergeant who, it had been rumored, had survived more assaults than any man in the Mekong Delta. Who, it was also rumored, had slept through an ambush which had taken most of his company.

Matlock stretched out on the barely recognizable couch. There was no point in going into the bedroom —his mattress was destroyed. He unbuckled his belt and kicked off his shoes. He could sleep for a few hours; then he'd talk to Kressel. Ask Kressel and Greenberg to work out a story for him to use about the invasion of his apartment. A story approved by Washington and, perhaps, the Carlyle police.

The police.

Suddenly he sat up. It hadn't struck him at the time, but now he considered it. The crass but imperiously polite patrolman whose primitive detection powers had centered on the "weirdos and niggers" had addressed him as "Mister" throughout the nearly two hours of police investigation. Yet when he was leaving, when he insultingly referred to the possibility of Matlock's withholding information, he had called him "Doctor." The "mister" was normal. The "doctor" was most unusual. No one outside the campus community—and rarely there—ever called him "Doctor," ever called *any* Ph.D. "Doctor." It struck most holders of such degrees as fatuous, and only the fatuous expected it.

Why had the patrolman used it? He didn't know him, he had never seen him to his knowledge. How would the patrolman know he was even entitled to the name "doctor"?

As he sat there, Matlock wondered if the combined efforts and pressures of the last hours were taking their toll. Was he now finding unreasonable meanings where no meanings existed? Was it not entirely plausible that the Carlyle police had a list of the Carlyle faculty and that a desk sergeant, or whoever took emergency calls, had checked his name against the list and casually stated his title? Was he not, perhaps, consigning the patrolman to a plateau of ignorance because he disliked the officer's prejudices?

A lot of things were possible.

And disturbing.

Matlock fell back onto the couch and closed his eyes.

At first the noise reached him as a faint echo might from the far end of a long, narrow tunnel. Then the noise became identifiable as rapid, incessant tapping. Tapping which would not stop, tapping which became louder and louder.

Matlock opened his eyes and saw the blurred light

coming from two table lamps across from the couch. His feet were drawn up under him, his neck perspiring against the rough surface of the sofa's corduroy cover. Yet there was a cool breeze coming through the smashed, lead-framed window.

The tapping continued, the sound of flesh against wood. It came from the foyer, from his front door. He flung his legs over the side onto the floor and found that they both were filled with pins and needles. He struggled to stand.

The tapping and the knocking became louder. Then the voice. "Jamie! Jamie!"

He walked awkwardly toward the door.

"Coming!" He reached the door and opened it swiftly. Patricia Ballantyne, dressed in a raincoat, silk pajamas evident underneath, walked rapidly inside.

"Jamie, for God's sake, I've been trying to call you."

"I've been here. The phone didn't ring."

"I know it didn't. I finally got an operator and she said it was out of order. I borrowed a car and drove over as fast as I could and . . ."

"It's not out of order, Pat. The police—the police were here and a quick look around will explain why—they used it a dozen times."

"Oh, good Lord!" The girl walked past him into the still-disheveled room. Matlock crossed to the telephone and picked it up from the table. He quickly held it away from his ear as the piercing tone of a disengaged instrument whistled out of the receiver.

"The bedroom," he said, replacing the telephone and going to his bedroom door.

On his bed, on top of the slashed remains of his mattress, was his bedside phone. The receiver was off the hook, *underneath* the pillow, muffling the harsh sound of the broken connection so it would not be heard. Someone had not wanted it to ring.

Matlock tried to remember everyone who'd been there. All told, more than a dozen people. Five or six policemen—in and out of uniform; husbands and wives from other apartments; several late-night passersby who had seen the police cars and wandered up to the front door. It had been cumulatively blurred. He couldn't remember all the faces.

He put the telephone back on the bedside table and was aware that Pat stood in the doorway. He gambled that she hadn't seen him remove the pillow.

"Someone must have knocked it over straightening out things," he said, pretending irritation. "That's rotten; I mean your having to borrow a car. . . . Why did you? What's the matter?"

She didn't reply. Instead, she turned and looked back into the living room. "What happened?"

Matlock remembered the patrolman's language. "They call it 'break and entry.' A police phrase covering human tornadoes, as I understand it. . . . Robbery. I got myself robbed for the first time in my life. It's quite an experience. I think the poor bastards were angry because there wasn't anything of any value so they ripped the place apart. . . . Why'd you come over?"

She spoke softly, but the intensity of her voice made Matlock realize that she was close to panic. As always, she imposed a control on herself when she became emotional. It was an essential part of the girl.

"A couple of hours ago—at quarter to four to be exact—my phone rang. The man, it was a man, asked for you. I was asleep, and I suppose I didn't make much sense, but I pretended to be upset that anyone would think you were there. . . . I didn't know what to do. I was confused. . . ."

"Okay, I understand that. So?"

"He said he didn't believe me. I was a liar. I . . . I was so surprised that anyone would phone then—at quarter to four—and call me a liar . . . I was confused. . . ."

"What did you say?"

"It's not what *I* said. It's what *he* said. He told me to tell you to . . . not to stay 'behind the globe' or 'light the lower world.' He said it *twice!* He said it was an awful joke but you'd understand. It was frightening! . . . Do you? Do you understand?"

Matlock walked past her into the living room. He looked for his cigarettes and tried to remain calm. She followed him. "What did he mean?"

"I'm not sure."

"Has it anything to do with . . . this?" She gestured her hand over the apartment.

"I don't think so." He lit his cigarette and wondered what he should tell her. The Nimrod people hadn't wasted any time finding associations. If it *was* Nimrod.

"What did he mean by . . . 'standing behind the globe'? It sounds like a riddle."

"It's a quote, I think." But Matlock did not have to think. He knew. He recalled Shakespeare's words precisely: *Knowest thou not that when the searching eye of heaven is hid behind the globe and lights the lower world . . . then thieves and robbers range abroad unseen . . . in murders and in outrage bloody here.*

"What does it mean?"

"I don't *know!* I can't remember it. . . . Somebody's confusing me with someone else. That's the only thing

I can imagine. . . . What did he sound like?"

"Normal. He was angry but he didn't shout or anything."

"No one you recognized? Not specifically, but did you ever hear the voice before?"

"I'm not sure. I don't think so. No one I could pick out, but . . ."

"But what?"

"Well, it was a . . . cultivated voice. A little actorish, I think."

"A man used to lecturing." Matlock made a statement, he did not ask a question. His cigarette tasted sour so he crushed it out.

"Yes, I guess that would describe it."

"And probably not in a science lab. . . . That reduces the possibilities to roughly eighty people on campus."

"You're making assumptions I don't understand! That phone call *did* have something to do with what happened here."

He knew he was talking too much. He didn't want to involve Pat; he *couldn't* involve her. Yet someone else had—and that fact was a profound complication. "It might have. According to the best sources—naturally I refer to television detectives—thieves make sure people aren't home before they rob a place. They were probably checking me out."

The girl held his wavering eyes with her gaze. "Weren't you home then? At quarter to four? . . . The question is not inquisitorial, my darling, simply a point of information."

He swore at himself silently. It was the exhaustion, the Beeson episode, the shock of the apartment. Of course the question wasn't inquisitorial. He was a free agent. And, of course, he was home at quarter to four.

"I'm not sure. I wasn't that concerned with the time. It was one hell of a long evening." He laughed feebly. "I was at Archie Beeson's. Proposed seminars with young instructors promote a lot of booze."

She smiled. "I don't think you understand me. I really don't mind what Poppa Bear was doing. . . . Well, of course, I do, but right now I don't understand why you're lying to me. . . . You were *here* two hours ago, and that phone call wasn't any thief checking your whereabouts and you *know* it."

"Momma Bear's reaching. That doesn't go with the territory." Matlock was rude. It, too, like the lying, was obviously false. Whatever his past rebellions, whatever his toughness, he was a kind person and she knew that.

"All right. I apologize. I'll ask one more question and then I'll leave. . . . What does *Omerta* mean?"

Matlock froze. "What did you say?"

"The man on the phone. He used the word *Omerta*."

"How?"

"Very casually. Just a reminder, he said."

8

Field Agent Jason Greenberg walked through the borderless door of the squash court. "You're working up quite a sweat there, Dr. Matlock."

"I'd hate to have it analyzed. . . . Anyway, it was your idea. I would have been just as happy at Kressel's office or even downtown somewhere."

"This is better. . . . We've got to talk quickly, though. The gym registry has me listed as an insurance surveyor. I'm checking the extinguishers in the corridors."

"They probably need checking." Matlock walked to a corner where a gray sweatshirt was wrapped in a towel. He unwound it and slipped it over his head. "What have you come up with? Last night was a little hairy."

"If you discount confusion, we haven't come up with a thing. At least nothing specific. A couple of theories, that's all. . . . We think you handled yourself very well."

"Thanks. I was confused. What are the theories? You sound academic, and I'm not sure I like that."

Greenberg's head suddenly shifted. From the right wall there could be heard a dull thumping. "Is that another court?"

"Yes. There are six of them on this side. They're

practice courts, no balconies. But you know that."

Greenberg picked up the ball and threw it hard against the front wall. Matlock understood and caught it on the bounce. He threw it back; Greenberg returned it. They maintained a slow rhythm, neither man moving more than a foot or two, each taking his turn to throw. Greenberg spoke softly, in a monotone.

"We think you're being tested. That's the most logical explanation. You *did* find Ralph. You made a statement about seeing the car. Your reasons for being in the area were weak; so weak we thought they were plausible. They want to make sure, that's why they brought in the girl. They're being thorough."

"Okay. Theory number one. What's number two?"

"I said that was the most logical. . . . It's the only one, really."

"What about Beeson?"

"What about him? You were there."

Matlock held the squash ball in his hand for a few seconds before lobbing it against the side wall. The wall away from Greenberg's stare.

"Could Beeson have been smarter than I thought and sent out an alarm?"

"He could have. We think it's doubtful. . . . The way you described the evening."

But Matlock had *not* described the *entire* evening. He had not told Greenberg or anyone of Beeson's telephone call. His reasons weren't rational, they were emotional. Lucas Herron was an old man, a gentle man. His sympathy for troubled students was legendary; his concern for young, untried, often arrogant new instructors was a welcomed sedative in faculty crises. Matlock had convinced himself that the "grand old bird" had befriended a desperate young man, helping him in a desperate situation. He had no right to surface Herron's name on the basis of a phone call made by a panicked drug user. There were too many possible explanations. Somehow he'd speak with Herron, perhaps over coffee at the Commons, or in the bleachers at a baseball game—Herron loved baseball—talk to him, tell him he should back away from Archer Beeson.

"—about Beeson?"

"What?" Matlock had not heard Greenberg.

"I asked you if you had second thoughts about Beeson."

"No. No, I haven't. He's not important. As a matter of fact, he'll probably throw away the grass and the pills—except for *my* benefit—if he thinks he can use me."

"I won't try to follow that."

"Don't. I just had momentary doubts. . . . I can't believe you arrived at only one theory. Come on. What else?"

"All right. Two others and they're not even plausible—both from the same egg. The first is that there might be a leak in Washington. The second—a leak here at Carlyle."

"Why not plausible?"

"Washington first. There are fewer than a dozen men who know about this operation, and that includes Justice, Treasury, and the White House. They're the caliber of men who exchange secret messages with the Kremlin. Impossible."

"And Carlyle?"

"You, Adrian Sealfont, and the obnoxious Samuel Kressel. . . . I'd like nothing better than pointing at Kressel—he's a prick—but, again, impossible. I'd also take a certain ethnic delight in knocking a venerated

WASP like Sealfont off his pedestal, but there, too—no sense. That leaves you. Are you the one?"

"Your wit is staggering." Matlock had to run to catch the ball which Greenberg threw into a corner. He held it in his hand and looked at the agent. "Don't misunderstand me—I like Sam, or at least I think I do—but why is he 'impossible'?"

"Same as Sealfont. . . . In an operation like this we start at the beginning. And I *mean* the *beginning.* We don't give a goddamn about positions, status, or reputation—good or bad. We use every trick in the books to prove someone guilty, not innocent. We try to find even the flimsiest reason *not* to clear him. Kressel's as clean as John the Baptist. Still a prick, but clean. Sealfont's worse. He's everything they say. A goddamn saint—Church of England, of course. So, again, that leaves you."

Matlock whipped the ball up in a spinning reverse shot into the rear left ceiling. Greenberg stepped back and slashed the ball in midair into the right wall. It bulleted back between Matlock's legs.

"I gather you've played the game," said Matlock with an embarrassed grin.

"The bandit of Brandeis. What about the girl? Where is she?"

"In my apartment. I made her promise not to leave till I got back. Outside of safety, it's one way to get the place cleaned up."

"I'm assigning a man to her. I don't think it's necessary, but it'll make *you* feel better." Greenberg looked at his watch.

"It will and thanks."

"We'd better hurry. . . . Now, listen. We're letting everything take its normal course. Police blotter, newspapers, everything. No covers, no counter stories, nothing to obstruct normal curiosity or your perfectly normal reactions. Someone broke into your apartment and smashed up the place. That's all you know. . . . And there's something else. You may not like it, but we think it's best—and safest."

"What?"

"We think Miss Ballantyne should report the phone call she received to the police."

"Hey, come on! The caller expected to find me there at four o'clock in the morning. You don't spell that kind of thing out. Not if you're on a fellowship and expect to work for museum foundations. They still revere McKinley."

"The eye of the beholder, Dr. Matlock. . . . She just received a phone call; some man asked for you, quoted Shakespeare, and made an unintelligible reference to some foreign word or city. She was goddamn mad. It wouldn't rate five lines in a newspaper, but since your apartment was broken into, it's logical she report it."

Matlock was silent. He walked over to the corner of the squash court where the ball had settled and picked it up. "We're a couple of ciphers who got pushed around. We don't know what happened; just that we don't like it."

"That's the idea. Nothing is so convincing as someone who's a bewildered injured party and lets everybody know it. Make an insurance issue about those old books of yours. . . . I've got to go. There aren't that many extinguishers in the building. Anything else? What are you doing next?"

Matlock bounced the ball on the floor. "A fortuitous invitation. Fortuitously received over a number of beers at the Afro-Commons. I'm invited to a staged version of the original puberty rites of the Mau Mau tribes. Tonight at ten o'clock in the cellars of Lumumba Hall. . . . It used to be the Alpha Delt fraternity house. I can tell you there are a lot of white Episcopalians spinning in hell over that one."

"Again, I'm not following, Doctor."

"You don't do your homework, either. . . . Lumumba Hall is very large on your list."

"Sorry. You'll phone me in the morning?"

"In the morning."

"I'll call you Jim if you'll call me Jason."

"No kiss, but agreed."

"O.K. Practice some more in here. I'll take you when this is over."

"You're on."

Greenberg let himself out. He looked up and down the narrow corridor, satisfied that no one was there; no one had seen him enter or leave the court. Continuous thumping could be heard within the walls. All the courts were in use. Greenberg wondered, as he was about to turn the corner into the main hallway, why the Carlyle gymnasium was so heavily attended at eleven o'clock in the morning. It was never the case at Brandeis; not fifteen years ago. Eleven o'clock in the morning was a time for class.

He heard a strange noise that was not the sound of a hard ball against thick wood and turned quickly.

No one.

He entered the main hall and turned once again. No one. He left quickly.

The sound he heard was that of a stubborn latch. It came from the door next to Matlock's court. Out of that door a man emerged. He, too, as Greenberg had done less than a minute before, looked up and down the narrow corridor. But instead of being satisfied that no one was there, he was annoyed. The obstinate latch had caused him to miss seeing the man who'd met with James Matlock.

Now the door of court four opened and Matlock himself stepped into the corridor. The man ten feet away was startled, pulled his towel up to his face, and walked away, coughing.

But the man wasn't quick enough. Matlock knew that face.

It was the patrolman from his apartment at four o'clock in the morning.

The patrolman who had called him "Doctor." The man in uniform who knew beyond a doubt that the campus troubles were caused by the "weirdos and the niggers."

Matlock stared at the retreating figure.

9

Over the large cathedral doors one could see—if one looked closely, or the sun was shining at a certain angle—the faded imprint of the Greek letters ΑΔΦ. They had been there in bas-relief for decades, and no amount of sand blasting or student damage could eradicate them completely. The fraternity house of Alpha Delta Phi had gone the way of other such buildings at Carlyle. Its holy order of directors could not find it within themselves to accept the inevitable. The house had been sold—lock, stock, leaking roof, and bad mortgage—to the blacks.

The blacks had done well, even extremely well, with what they had to work with. The decrepit old house had been totally refurbished inside and out. All past associations with its former owners were obliterated wherever possible. The scores of faded photographs of venerated alumni were replaced with wildly theatrical portraits of the new revolutionaries—African, Latin American, Black Panther. Throughout the ancient halls were the new commands, screeched in posters and psychedelic art: *Death to the Pigs! Up Whitey! Malcolm Lives! Lumumba the Black Christ!*

Between these screams for recognition were replicas of primitive African artifacts—fertility masks, spears, shields, animal skins dipped in red paint, shrunken heads suspended by hair with complexions unmistakably white.

Lumumba Hall wasn't trying to fool anyone. It reflected anger. It reflected fury.

Matlock didn't have to use the brass knocker set beside the grotesque iron mask at the edge of the doorframe. The large door opened as he approached it, and a student greeted him with a bright smile.

"I was hoping you'd make it! It's gonna be a groove!"

"Thanks, Johnny. Wouldn't miss it." Matlock walked in, struck by the proliferation of lighted candles throughout the hallway and adjoining rooms. "Looks like a wake. Where's the casket?"

"That's later. Wait'll you see!"

A black Matlock recognized as one of the campus extremists walked up to them. Adam Williams' hair was long—African style and clipped in a perfect semicircle above his head. His features were sharp; Matlock had the feeling that if they met in the veldt, Williams would be assumed to be a tribal chief.

"Good evening," Williams said with an infectious grin. "Welcome to the seat of revolution."

"Thanks very much." They shook hands. "You don't look so revolutionary as you do funereal. I was asking Johnny where the casket was."

Williams laughed. His eyes were intelligent, his smile genuine, without guile or arrogance. In close quarters, the black radical had little of the firebrand quality he displayed on the podium in front of cheering supporters. Matlock wasn't surprised. Those of the faculty who had Williams in their courses often remarked on his subdued, good-humored approach. So different from the image he projected in campus—

rapidly becoming national—politics.

"Oh, Lord! We're lousing up the picture then! This is a happy occasion. A little gruesome, I suppose, but essentially joyful."

"I'm not sure I understand," Matlock smiled.

"A youngster from the tribe reaches the age of manhood, the brink of an active, responsible life. A jungle Bar Mitzvah. It's a time for rejoicing. No caskets, no weeping shrouds."

"That's right! That's right, Adam!" said the boy named Johnny enthusiastically.

"Why don't you get Mr. Matlock a drink, brother." And then he turned to Matlock. "It's all the same drink until after the ceremony—it's called Swahili punch. Is that O.K.?"

"Of course."

"Right." Johnny disappeared into the crowd toward the dining room and the punch bowl. Adam smiled as he spoke.

"It's a light rum drink with lemonade and cranberry juice. Not bad, really. . . . Thank you for coming. I mean that."

"I was surprised to be invited. I thought this was a very 'in' thing. Restricted to the tribe. . . . That didn't come out the way I meant it."

Williams laughed. "No offense. I used the word. It's good to think in terms of tribes. Good for the brothers."

"Yes, I imagine it is. . . ."

"The collective, protective social group. Possessing an identity of its own."

"If that's the purpose—the constructive purpose—I endorse it."

"Oh, it is. Tribes in the bush don't always make war on each other, you know. It's not all stealing, looting, carrying away women. That's a Robert Ruark hang-up. They trade, share hunting and farming lands together, coexist in the main probably better than nations or even political subdivisions."

It was Matlock's turn to laugh. "All right, professor. I'll make notes *after* the lecture."

"Sorry. Avocational hazard."

"Avocational or occupational?"

"Time will tell, won't it? . . . One thing I should make clear, however. We don't need your endorsement."

Johnny returned with Matlock's cup of Swahili punch. "Hey, you know what? Brother Davis, that's Bill Davis, says you told him you were going to flunk him, then at midterm you gave him a High Pass!"

"Brother Davis got off his fat ass and did a little work." Matlock looked at Adam Williams. "You don't object to that kind of endorsement, do you?"

Williams smiled broadly and placed his hand on Matlock's arm. "No, sir, bwana. . . . In that area you run King Solomon's Mines. Brother Davis is here to work as hard as he can and go as far as his potential will let him. No argument there. Bear down on the brother."

"You're positively frightening." Matlock spoke with a lightness he did not feel.

"Not at all. Just pragmatic. . . . I've got some last-minute preparations to look after. See you later." Williams hailed a passing student and walked through the crowd toward the staircase.

"Come on, Mr. Matlock. I'll show you the new alterations." Johnny led Matlock into what used to be Alpha Delt's common room.

In the sea of dark faces, Matlock saw a minimum of

guarded, hostile looks. There were, perhaps, less overt greetings than he might expect outside on the campus, but by and large, his presence was accepted. He thought for a moment that if the brothers knew why he had come, the inhabitants of Lumumba Hall might turn on him angrily. He was the only white person there.

The alterations in the common room were drastic. Gone were the wide moldings of dark wood, the thick oak window seats beneath the huge cathedral windows, the solid, heavy furniture with the dark red leather. Instead, the room was transformed into something else entirely. The arched windows were no longer. They were now squared at the top, bordered by jet-black dowels an inch or two in diameter, which looked like long, rectangular slits. Spreading out from the windows into the walls was a textured pattern of tiny wooden bamboo strips shellacked to a high polish. This same wall covering was duplicated on the ceiling, thousands of highly glossed reeds converging towards the center. In the middle of the ceiling was a large circle, perhaps three feet in width, in which there was placed a thick pane of rippled glass. Beyond the glass shone a bright yellowish white light, its flood diffused in ripples over the room. What furniture he could see through the mass of bodies was not really furniture at all. There were various low-cut slabs of thick wood in differing shapes on short legs—these Matlock assumed were tables. Instead of chairs, there were dozens of pillows in vibrant colors scattered about the edge of the walls.

It didn't take Matlock long to realize the effect.

Alpha Delta Phi's common room had been transformed brilliantly into the replica of a large thatched

African hut. Even to the point of the blazing equatorial sun streaming through the enclosure's vent to the skies.

"This is remarkable! Really remarkable. It must have taken months."

"Almost a year and a half," Johnny said. "It's very comfortable, very relaxing. Did you know that lots of top designers are going in for this sort of thing now? I mean the back-to-nature look. It's very functional and easy to maintain."

"That sounds dangerously like an apology. You don't have to apologize. It's terrific."

"Oh, I'm *not* apologizing." Johnny retreated from his explanation. "Adam says there's a certain majesty in the primitive. A very proud heritage."

"Adam's right. Only he's not the first person to make that observation."

"Please don't put us down, Mr. Matlock. . . ."

Matlock looked at Johnny over the rim of his cup of Swahili punch. Oh, Christ, he thought, the more things change, the more they remain the same.

The high-ceilinged chapter room of Alpha Delta Phi had been carved out of the cellars at the farthest end of the fraternity house. It had been built shortly after the turn of the century when impressive alumni had poured impressive sums into such hobbies as secret societies and debutante cotillions. Such activities promulgated and propagandized a way of life, yet assuredly kept it selective.

Thousands of starched young men had been initiated in this chapel-like enclosure, whispering the secret pledges, exchanging the unfamiliar handshakes explained to them by stern-faced older children, vowing till death to keep the selected faith. And afterward, getting drunk and vomiting in corners.

Matlock thought these thoughts as he watched the Mau Mau ritual unfold before him. It was no less childish, no less absurd than the preceding scenes in this room, he considered. Perhaps the physical aspects—the simulated physical aspects—were more brutal in what they conveyed, but then the roots of the ceremony were not based in the delicate steps of a cotillion's pavanne but, instead, in harsh, animal-like pleas to primitive gods. Pleas for strength and survival. Not supplications for continued exclusivity.

The tribal rite itself was a series of unintelligible chants, each one growing in intensity, over the body of a black student—obviously the youngest brother in Lumumba Hall—stretched out on the concrete floor, naked except for a red loincloth strapped around his waist and legs, covering his genitals. At the finish of each chant, signifying the end of one canto and the commencement of the succeeding song, the boy's body was raised above the crowd by four extremely tall students, themselves naked to the waist, wearing jet-black dance belts, their legs encased in spirals of rawhide strips. The room was lighted by dozens of thick candles mounted on stands, causing shadows to dance across the upper walls and the ceiling. Adding to this theatrical effect was the fact that the five active participants in the ritual had their skins covered with oil, their faces streaked in diabolical patterns. As the singing grew wilder, the young boy's rigid body was thrown higher and higher until it left the hands of its four supporters, returning split seconds later into the outstretched arms. Each time the black body with the red loincloth was flung into the air, the crowd responded with growing volumes of guttural shouts.

And then Matlock, who had been watching with a degree of detachment, suddenly found himself frightened. Frightened for the small Negro whose stiff, oiled body was being flung into air with such abandon. For two additional blacks, dressed like the others, had joined the four in the center of the floor. However, instead of helping toss the now soaring figure, the two blacks crouched between the rectangular foursome—beneath the body—and withdrew long-bladed knives, one in each hand. Once in their squatting positions, they stretched out their arms so that the blades were held upright, as rigid, as stiff as the body above them. Each time the small Negro descended, the four blades inched closer to the falling flesh. One slip, one oily miscalculation on the part of just one of the four blacks, and the ritual would end in death for the small student. In murder.

Matlock, feeling that the ritual had gone as far as he could allow, began scanning the crowd for Adam Williams. He saw him in front, on the edge of the circle, and started pushing his way toward him. He was stopped—quietly but firmly—by the blacks around him. He looked angrily at a Negro who held his arm. The black didn't acknowledge his stare; he was hypnotized by the action now taking place in the center of the room.

Matlock saw why instantly. For the body of the small boy was now being *spun*, alternately face up and face down with each elevation. The danger of error was increased tenfold. Matlock grabbed the hand on his arm, twisted it inward, and flung it off him. He looked once more in the direction of Adam Williams.

He wasn't there. He was nowhere in sight! Matlock stood still, undecided. If he raised his voice between the crowd's roaring crescendos, it was entirely possible that he might cause a break in the concentration of those handling the body. He couldn't risk that, and yet he couldn't allow the dangerous absurdity to continue.

Suddenly Matlock felt another hand, this one on his shoulder. He turned and saw the face of Adam Williams behind him. It startled him. Had some primitive tribal signal been transmitted to Williams? The black radical gestured with his head for Matlock to follow him through the shouting crowd to the outer edge of the circle. Williams spoke between the roars.

"You look worried. Don't be."

"Look! This crap's gone far enough! That kid could be killed!"

"No chance. The brothers have rehearsed for months. . . . It's really the most simplistic of the Mau Mau rites. The symbolism is fundamental. . . . See? The child's eyes remain open. First to the sky, then facing the blades. He is constantly aware—every second—that his life is in the hands of his brother warriors. He cannot, he *must* not show fear. To do so would betray his peers. Betray the confidence he must place in their hands—as they will someday place their lives in *his* hands."

"It's childish, *dangerous stupidity*, and you *know* it!" cut in Matlock. "Now, I'm telling you, Williams, you put a stop to it or *I* will!"

"Of course," continued the black radical, as if Matlock had not spoken, "there are anthropologists who insist that the ceremony is essentially one of fertility. The unsheathed knives representing erections, the four protectors guarding the child through its formative years. Frankly, I think that's reaching. Also, it strikes me as contradictory even for the primitive mind. . . ."

"Goddamn you!" Matlock grabbed Williams by the front of his shirt. Immediately other blacks closed in on him.

Suddenly there was total silence in the eerily lit room. The silence lasted only a moment. It was followed by a series of mind-shattering screams from the mouths of the four Negroes in the center of the crowd in whose hands the life of the young student depended. Matlock whipped around and saw the shining black body descending downward from an incredible height above the outstretched hands.

It couldn't be true! It wasn't happening! Yet it was!

The four blacks suddenly, in unison, crouched into kneeling positions *away* from the center, their arms slashed to their sides. The young student came crashing down, *face toward the blades.* Two further screams followed. In a fraction of a second, the students holding the huge knives swung their weapons across one another and in an unbelievable display of wrist strength, *caught* the body on the flat of the blades.

The crowd of blacks went wild.

The ceremony was over.

"Do you believe me now?" Williams asked, speaking in a corner with Matlock.

"Whether I do or not doesn't change what I said. You can't *do* this sort of thing! It's too goddamn dangerous!"

"You exaggerate. . . . Here, let me introduce another guest." Williams raised his hand and a tall thin black with close-cropped hair and glasses, dressed in an expensively cut tan suit, joined them. "This is Julian Dunois, Mr. Matlock. Brother Julian is our expert. Our choreographer, if you like."

"A pleasure." Dunois extended his hand, speaking with a slight accent.

"Brother Julian is from Haiti. . . . Harvard Law out of Haiti. A most unusual progression, I think you'll agree."

"It certainly is. . . ."

"Many Haitians, even the Ton Ton Macoute, still get upset when they hear his name."

"You exaggerate, Adam," said Julian Dunois with a smile.

"That's what I just said to Mr. Matlock. *He* exaggerates. About the danger of the ceremony."

"Oh, there's danger—as there's danger if one crosses the Boston Commons wearing a blindfold. The petcock of safety, Mr. Matlock, is that those holding the knives watch closely. In the training there is as much emphasis on being able to drop the knives instantly as there is in holding them up."

"That may be so," Matlock acknowledged. "But the margin for error terrifies me."

"It's not as narrow as you think." The lilt in the Haitian's voice was as reassuring as it was attractive. "Incidentally, I'm a fan of yours. I've enjoyed your works on the Elizabethans. May I add, you're not exactly what I expected. I mean, you're far, far younger."

"You flatter me. I didn't think I was known in law schools."

"My undergraduate major was English literature."

Adam interrupted politely. "You two enjoy yourselves. There'll be drinks upstairs in a few minutes; just follow the crowd. I've got things to do. . . . I'm glad you've met. You're both strangers, in a way. Strangers should meet in unfamiliar areas. It's comforting."

He gave Dunois an enigmatic look and walked rapidly away through the crowd.

"Why does Adam feel he has to talk in what I'm sure he considers are profound riddles?" Matlock asked.

"He's very young. He strives constantly to make emphasis. Very bright, but very young."

"You'll pardon me, but you're not exactly ancient. I doubt more than a year or two older than Adam."

The black in the expensively cut tan suit looked into Matlock's eyes and laughed gently.

"Now you flatter *me*," he said. "If the truth were known—and why shouldn't it be?—and if my tropic color did not disguise the years so well, you'd know that I was precisely one year, four months, and sixteen days *older* than *you*."

Matlock stared at the Negro, speechless. It took him nearly a full minute to assimilate the lawyer's words and the meaning behind those words. The black's eyes did not waver. He returned Matlock's stare in equal measure. Finally, Matlock found his voice.

"I'm not sure I like this game."

"Oh, come, we're both here for the same reason, are we not? You from your vantage point, I from mine . . . Let's go upstairs and have a drink. . . . Bourbon and soda, isn't it? Sour mash, if it's available, I understand."

Dunois preceded Matlock through the crowd, and Matlock had no other course but to follow.

Dunois leaned against the brick wall.

"All right," Matlock said, "the amenities are over.

Everyone's acknowledged your show downstairs, and there's no one left for me to impress my white skin on. I think it's time you started explaining."

They were alone now, outside on the porch. Both held drinks.

"My, aren't we professional? Would you care for a cigar? I can assure you it's Havana."

"No cigar. Just talk. I came here tonight because these are my friends. I felt privileged to be invited. . . . Now, you've attached something else and I don't like it."

"Bravo! Bravo!" said Dunois, raising his glass. "You do that very well. . . . Don't worry, they know nothing. Perhaps they suspect, but believe me, only in the vaguest terms."

"What the hell are you talking about?"

"Finish your drink and let's walk out on the lawn." Dunois drained his rum and, as if by reflex, Matlock drank the remainder of his bourbon. The two men walked down the steps of the Lumumba Hall, Matlock following the black to the base of a large elm tree. Dunois turned suddenly and grabbed Matlock by the shoulders.

"Take your goddamn hands off me!"

"Listen to me! I want that paper! I *must have* that paper! And you must tell me *where it is!*"

Matlock flung his hands up to break Dunois's grip. But his arms did not respond. They were suddenly heavy, terribly heavy. And there was a whistling. A growing, piercing whistling in his head.

"What? What? . . . What paper? I don't have any paper. . . ."

"Don't be difficult! We'll get it, you know! . . . Now, just tell me where it is!"

Matlock realized that he was being lowered to the

ground. The outline of the huge tree above him began to spin, and the whistling in his brain became louder and louder. It was unendurable. He fought to find his mind again.

"What are you doing? What are you doing to me!?"

"The paper, Matlock! Where is the Corsican *paper?*"

"Get *off* me!" Matlock tried to yell. But nothing came from his lips.

"The silver paper, goddamn you to hell!"

"No paper . . . no. Haven't paper! No!"

"Listen to me! You just had a drink, remember the drink? . . . You just finished that drink. Remember? . . . You can't be alone now! You don't *dare* be alone!"

"What? . . . What? Get off me! You're crushing me!"

"I'm not even *touching* you. The drink is! You just consumed three tabs of *lysergic acid!* You're in trouble, Doctor! . . . *Now! You tell me where that paper is!"*

From his inner recesses he found an instant of clarity. From the spinning, turning, whirling spirals of mind-blasting colors, he saw the form of the man above him and he lashed out. He grabbed at the white shirt between the dark borders of the jacket and pulled it down with all the strength he could summon. He brought his fist up and hit the descending face as hard as he could. Once the face was jarred, he began hammering at the throat beneath it mercilessly. He could feel the shattering of the glasses and he knew his fist had found the eyes and crushed the glass into the rolling head.

It was over in a period of time he could never ascertain. Dunois's body was beside him, unconscious.

And he knew he had to run. Run furiously away! What had Dunois said? . . . Don't dare be alone. Don't *dare!* He had to find Pat! Pat would know what to do. He had to find her! The chemical in his body was going to take full effect soon and he knew it! Run, for Christ's sake!

But where?! Which way?! He didn't know *the way!* The *goddamn fucking way!* The street was there, he raced along the street, but was it the *right way?!* Was it the *right street?!*

Then he heard a car. It *was* a car, and it was coming close to the curb and the driver was looking at him. Looking at him, so he ran faster, tripping once over the curb and falling into the pavement and rising again. Running, for Christ Almighty's sake, running till the breath in his lungs was gone and he could no longer control the movement of his feet. He felt himself swerve, unable to stop himself, toward the wide gulf of the street, which suddenly became a river, a black putrid river in which he would drown.

He vaguely heard the screech of the brakes. The lights blinded him, and the figure of a man reached down and poked at his eyes. He didn't care any longer. Instead, he laughed. Laughed through the blood which flowed into his mouth and over his face.

He laughed hysterically as Jason Greenberg carried him to the car.

And then the earth, the world, the planet, the galaxy, and the entire solar system went crazy.

10

The night was agony.

The morning brought a degree of reality, less so for Matlock than for the two people sitting beside him, one on either side of the bed. Jason Greenberg, his large, sad eyes drooping, his hands calmly crossed on his lap, leaned forward. Patricia Ballantyne, her arm stretched out, held a cool washcloth on Matlock's forehead.

"The schvugs gave you one hell of a party, friend."

"Shh!" whispered the girl. "Leave him alone."

Matlock's eyes wandered as best they could around the room. He was in Pat's apartment, in her bedroom, her bed.

"They gave me acid."

"You're telling *us* . . . We had a doctor—a real doctor—brought in from Litchfield. He's the nice fella you kept trying to take the eyeballs from. . . . Don't worry, he's federal. No names."

"Pat? How come . . ."

"You're a very sweet acid head, Jamie. You kept yelling my name."

"It also made the best sense," interrupted Greenberg. "No hospitals. No out-patient records. Nice and private; good thinking. Also, you're very persuasive when you're violent. You're a hell of a lot stronger than

I thought. Especially for such a lousy handball player."

"You shouldn't have brought me here. Goddamn it, Greenberg, you shouldn't have *brought* me here!"

"Forgetting for the moment that it was your idea . . ."

"I was drugged!"

"It was a *good* idea. What would you have preferred? The emergency clinic? . . . 'Who's that on the stretcher, Doctor? The one screaming.' . . . 'Oh, just Associate Professor Matlock, Nurse. He's on an acid trip.' "

"You know what I mean! You could have taken me home. Strapped me down."

"I'm relieved to see you don't know much about acid," said Greenberg.

"What he means, Jamie . . . ," Pat took his hand, ". . . if it's bad, you should be with someone you know awfully well. The reassurance is necessary."

Matlock looked at the girl. And then at Greenberg. "What have you told her?"

"That you volunteered to help us; that we're grateful. With your help we may be able to prevent a serious situation from getting worse." Greenberg spoke in a monotone; it was obvious that he didn't wish to expand.

"It was a very cryptic explanation," Pat said. "He wouldn't have given me that if I hadn't threatened him."

"She was going to call the police." Greenberg sighed, his sad eyes sadder. "She was going to have me locked up for dosing you. I had no choice."

Matlock smiled.

"Why are you doing this, Jamie?" Pat found nothing amusing.

"The man said it: the situation's serious."

"But why *you?*"

"Because I can."

"What? Turn in kids?"

"I told you," said Jason. "We're not interested in students. . . ."

"What's Lumumba Hall, then? A branch of General Motors?"

"It's one contact point; there are others. Frankly, we'd rather *not* have gotten involved with that crowd; it's ticklish. Unfortunately, we can't choose."

"That's offensive."

"I don't think there's much I could say that wouldn't be offensive to you, Miss Ballantyne."

"Perhaps not. Because I thought the FBI had more important work to do than harassing young blacks. Obviously, you don't."

"Hey, come on." Matlock squeezed the girl's hand. She took it from him.

"No, I mean that, Jamie! No games, no radical chic. There are drugs all over this place. Some of it's a bad scene, most of it's pretty standard. We *both* know that. Why all of a sudden are the kids at Lumumba singled out?"

"We wouldn't *touch* those kids. Except to help them." Greenberg was weary from the long night. His irritation showed.

"I don't like the way you people help people and I don't like what happened to Jamie! Why did you send him there?"

"He didn't *send* me. I maneuvered that myself."

"Why?"

"It's too complicated and I'm too washed out to explain it."

"Oh, Mr. Greenberg did that. He explained all right. They've given you a badge, haven't they? They can't do it themselves so they pick a nice, easygoing fellow to do it for them. You take all the risks; and when it's over, you'll never be trusted on this campus again. Jamie, for God's sake, this is your *home*, your *work!*"

Matlock held the girl's eyes with his own, doing his best to calm her. "I know that better than you do. My home needs to be helped—and that's no game either, Pat. I think the risks are worth it."

"I won't pretend to understand that."

"You can't understand it, Miss Ballantyne, because we can't tell you enough to make it reasonable. You'll have to accept that."

"Do I?"

"I'm asking you to," said Matlock. "He saved my life."

"I wouldn't go that far, Professor." Greenberg shrugged as he spoke.

Pat stood up. "I think he threw you overboard and tossed you a rope as an afterthought. . . . Are you all right?"

"Yes," answered Matlock.

"I have to go; I won't if you don't want me to."

"No, you go ahead. I'll call you later. Thanks for the ministrations."

The girl looked briefly at Greenberg—it was not a pleasant look—and crossed to her dresser. She picked up a brush and rapidly stroked her hair, slipping an orange headband into place. She watched Greenberg through the mirror. He returned the stare.

"The man who's been following me, Mr. Greenberg. Is he one of your men?"

"Yes."

"I don't like it."

"I'm sorry."

Pat turned. "Will you remove him, please?"

"I can't do that. I'll tell him to be less obvious."

"I see." She took her purse from the dresser top and reached down to the floor, picking up her accordion briefcase. Without speaking further, the girl walked out of the bedroom. Several seconds later, the two men could hear the apartment door open and shut firmly.

"That is one very strong-willed young lady," said Jason.

"There's a good reason."

"What do you mean?"

"I thought you fellows were so familiar with the people you had to deal with. . . ."

"I'm still getting briefed. I'm the back-up, remember?"

"Then I'll save you time. In the late fifties her father got McCarthyized out of the State Department. Of course, he was very dangerous. He was a language consultant. He was cleared for translating newspapers."

"Shit."

"That's the word, brother. He never made it back. She's had scholarships all her life; the cupboard's bare. She's a little sensitive to your type."

"Boy, do you pick 'em!"

"You picked *me*, remember?"

Matlock opened the door to his apartment and walked into the foyer. Pat had done a good job putting the rooms in order—as he knew she would. Even the curtains were rehung. It was a little after three—most of the day wasted. Greenberg had insisted that the two of them drive over to Litchfield for a reexamination by the doctor. Shaken but operable, was the verdict.

They stopped for lunch at the Cheshire Cat. During

the meal, Matlock kept looking over at the small table where four days ago Ralph Loring had sat with his folded newspaper. The lunch was quiet. Not strained —the two men were comfortable in each other's company—but quiet, as if each had too much to think about.

On the road back to Carlyle, Greenberg told him to stay in his apartment until he contacted him. Washington hadn't issued any new instructions. They were evaluating the new information, and until they confirmed any further involvement, Matlock was to remain "OOS"—a term the English professor found hard to equate with grownups: *out of strategy.*

It was just as well, he thought. He had his own strategy to think about—Lucas Herron. The "grand old bird," the campus elder statesman. It was time to reach him, to warn him. The old man was out of his element, and the quicker he retreated, the better for everyone—Carlyle included. Yet he didn't want to telephone him, he didn't want to arrange a formal meeting—he had to be subtler than that. He didn't want to alarm old Lucas, have him talking to the wrong people.

It occurred to Matlock that he was acting as some sort of protector for Herron. That presumed Lucas was innocent of any serious involvement. He wondered if he had the right to make that assumption. On the other hand, by civilized standards, he had no right to make any other.

The telephone rang. It couldn't be Greenberg, he thought. He'd just left him at the curb. He hoped it wasn't Pat; he wasn't ready to talk to her yet. Reluctantly he lifted the instrument to his ear. "Hello!"

"Jim! Where have you *been!?* I've been calling since eight this morning! I was so goddamn worried I went over there twice. Got your key from maintenance." It was Sam Kressel. He sounded as though Carlyle had lost its accreditation.

"It's too involved to go into now, Sam. Let's get together later. I'll come over to your place after dinner."

"I don't know if it can wait that long. Jesus! What the hell got *into* you?"

"I don't understand."

"At Lumumba last night!"

"What are you talking about? What have you heard?"

"That black bastard, Adam Williams, handed in a report to my office accusing you of just about everything short of advocating slavery! He claims the only reason he's not filing police charges is that you were blind drunk! Of course, the alcohol stripped you of your pretenses and showed clearly what a racist you are!"

"What?!"

"You broke up furniture, slapped around some kids, smashed windows. . . ."

"You know damned well that's bullshit!"

"I figured as much." Kressel lowered his voice. He was calming down. "But my knowing it doesn't help, can't you see that? This is the kind of thing we've got to *avoid*. Polarization! The government walks onto a campus, polarization follows."

"Listen to me. Williams' statement is a decoy—if that's the word. It's camouflage. They drugged me last night. If it hadn't been for Greenberg, I don't know where I'd be right now."

"Oh, God! . . . Lumumba's on your list, isn't it? That's all we *need!* The blacks'll scream persecution. Christ knows what'll happen."

Matlock tried to speak calmly. "I'll come over

around seven. Don't do anything, don't say anything. I've got to get off the phone. Greenberg's supposed to call."

"Wait a minute, Jim! One thing. This Greenberg . . . I don't trust him. I don't trust any of them. Just remember. Your loyalty's to Carlyle. . . ." Kressel stopped, but he had not finished. Matlock realized he was at a loss for words.

"That's a strange thing to say."

"I think you know what I mean."

"I'm not sure I do. I thought the idea was to work together. . . ."

"Not at the expense of ripping this campus apart!" The dean of colleges sounded nearly hysterical.

"Don't worry," Matlock said. "It won't tear. I'll see you later." Matlock hung up the phone before Kressel could speak again. His mind needed a short rest, and Kressel never let anyone rest where his domain was concerned. Sam Kressel, in his own way, was as militant as any extremist, and, perhaps, quicker to cry "foul."

These thoughts led Matlock to another consideration—two considerations. Four days ago, he had told Pat that he didn't want to change their plans for St. Thomas. Carlyle's midterm holiday, a short ten days at the end of April, would start after classes on Saturday, in three days. Under the circumstances, St. Thomas was out—unless Washington decided to retire him, and he doubted that. He'd use his parents as the excuse. Pat would understand, even be sympathetic. The other thought was his own classes. He had fallen behind. His desk was piled with papers—mostly themes and essay exams. He had also missed his two classes earlier in the day. He was not so much concerned for his students—his method was to accelerate in the fall and winter and relax in the spring—but he didn't want to add any fuel to such fires as Williams' false complaint. An absentee associate professor was a target for gossip. His class load for the next three days was medium—three, two, and two. He'd organize the work later. Between now and seven o'clock, however, he had to find Lucas Herron. If Greenberg called while he was out, he'd blame it on a forgotten graduate conference.

He decided to shower, shave, and change clothes. Once in the bathroom, he checked the litter box. The Corsican paper was there—he knew it would be.

The shave and shower completed, Matlock walked into his bedroom, selecting clothes and a course of action. He didn't know Herron's daily schedule, although it would be a simple matter to find out if Lucas had any late afternoon classes or seminars. If he didn't, Matlock knew Herron's house; it would take about fifteen minutes to get there by car. Herron lived eight miles from the campus, on a rarely traveled back road in a section once a part of the old Carlyle family estate. Herron's home had been a carriage house. It was out of the way, but as Lucas kept saying, "Once there, it's worth it."

The rapid tapping of the door knocker broke his concentration. It also frightened him—he felt himself gasping for breath; that was disturbing.

"Be right there," he yelled, slipping a white sport shirt over his head. He walked barefoot to the front door and opened it. It was impossible for him to conceal his shock. In the doorframe stood Adam Williams—alone.

"Afternoon."

"Jesus! . . . I don't know whether to hit you in the

mouth right now or first call the police! What the hell do you want? Kressel's already called me, if that's what you're checking on."

"Please let me talk to you. I'll be quick." The black spoke with urgency, trying, thought Matlock, to conceal his fear.

"Come on in. And *make* it quick." Matlock slammed the door as Williams passed by him into the foyer. The black turned and tried to smile, but there was no humor in his eyes.

"I'm sorry about that report. Truly sorry. It was an unpleasant necessity."

"I don't buy that and you can't sell it! What did you want Kressel to do? Bring me up before the board and burn me out of here? Did you think I'd just sit down and play doormat? You're a goddamn maniac!"

"We didn't think *anything* would happen. That's precisely why we did it. . . . We couldn't be sure where you went. You disappeared, you know. You might say we had to take the offensive and then later agree that it was all a disagreeable misunderstanding. . . . It's not a new tactic. I'll send Kressel another report, backing off—but not entirely. In a couple of weeks, it'll be forgotten."

Matlock raged, as much against Williams' attitude as his conscienceless pragmatism. But when he spoke he did not raise his voice. "Get out. You disgust me."

"Oh, come off it, man! Haven't we *always disgusted* you?!" Matlock had hit a nerve and Williams responded in kind. But just as suddenly, he took hold of himself. "Let's not argue theoretical practicalities. Let me get to the point and leave."

"By all means."

"All right. Listen to me. Whatever Dunois wanted

from you, *give* it to him! . . . That is, give it to me and I'll send it on. No forked tongue; it's last-extremity language!"

"Too pat a phrase. No sale. Why would I have anything Brother Julian wanted? Did he say so? Why doesn't he come over himself?"

"Brother Julian doesn't stay long in any one place. His talents are in great demand."

"Staging Mau Mau puberty rituals?"

"He really does that, you know. It's a hobby."

"Send him to me." Matlock crossed in front of Williams and went to the coffee table. He reached down and picked up a half-empty pack of cigarettes. "We'll compare notes on associative body movements. I've a hell of a collection of sixteenth-century folk dances."

"Talk seriously. There's no *time!*"

Matlock lit a cigarette. "I've got all the time in the world. I just want to see Brother Julian again; I want to put him in jail."

"No chance! No chance. I'm here for *your* benefit! If I leave without it, I can't *control* it!"

"Two pronouns signifying the same or different objects?"

"Oh, you're too much! You're really too much! Do you know who Julian Dunois *is?*"

"Part of the Borgia family? Ethiopian branch?"

"*Stop it, Matlock!* Do what he says! People could be hurt. Nobody wants that."

"I *don't* know who Dunois is and I don't much give a damn. I just know he drugged me and assaulted me and is exercising a dangerous influence on a bunch of children. Beyond this, I suspect he had my apartment broken into and many of my personal belongings destroyed. I want him put away. From you *and* from me."

"Be reasonable, *please!*"

Matlock walked swiftly to the curtains in front of his casement window and with a flourish, yanked them down, displaying the shattered glass and twisted lead.

"Is this one of Brother Julian's calling cards?"

Adam Williams stared, obviously shocked, at the mass of destruction. "No, man. Absolutely, no. That's not Julian's style. . . . That's not even my style. That's someone else."

11

The road to Lucas Herron's house was dotted with the potholes of winter. Matlock doubted that the town of Carlyle would fill them in; there were too many other commercially traveled streets still showing the effects of the New England freeze. As he approached the old carriage house, he slowed his Triumph to barely ten miles an hour. The bumps were jarring, and he wanted to reach Herron's house with little noise.

Thinking that Jason Greenberg might have had him followed, Matlock took the long route to Herron's, driving four miles north on a parallel road and then doubling back on Herron's street. There was no one behind him. The nearest houses to Herron's were a hundred yards away on either side, none in front. There'd been talk of turning the area into a housing development just as there'd been talk of enlarging Carlyle University, but nothing came of either project. Actually, the first depended upon the second, and there was strong alumni opposition to any substantial physical change at Carlyle. The alumni were Adrian Sealfont's personal cross.

Matlock was struck by the serenity of Herron's home. He'd never really looked at the house before. A dozen times, more or less, he'd driven Lucas home after faculty meetings, but he'd always been in a hurry. He'd never accepted Lucas's invitations for a drink and, as a result, he had never been inside the house.

He got out of the car and approached the old brick structure. It was tall and narrow; the faded stone covered with thousands of strands of ivy heightened the feeling of isolation. In front, on the large expanse of lawn, were two Japanese willow trees in full spring bloom, their purple flowers cascading toward the earth in large arcs. The grass was cut, the shrubbery pruned, and the white gravel on the various paths was gleaming. It was a house and grounds which were loved and cared for, yet one had the feeling that they were not shared. It was the work of and for one person, not two or a family. And then Matlock remembered that Lucas Herron had never married. There were the inevitable stories of a lost love, a tragic death, even a runaway bride-to-be, but whenever Lucas Herron heard about such youthful romanticizing he countered with a chuckle and a statement about being "too damned selfish."

Matlock walked up the short steps to the door and rang the bell. He tried practicing an opening smile, but it was false; he wouldn't be able to carry it off. He was afraid.

The door swung back and the tall, white-haired Lucas Herron, dressed in wrinkled trousers and a half-unbuttoned, oxford-blue shirt, stared at him.

It was less than a second before Herron spoke, but in that brief instant, Matlock knew that he'd been wrong. Lucas Herron knew why he had come.

"Well, Jim! Come in, come in, my boy. A pleasant surprise."

"Thank you, Lucas. I hope I'm not interrupting anything."

"Not a thing. You're just in time, as a matter of fact. I'm dabbling in alchemy. A fresh fruit gin Collins. Now I won't have to dabble alone."

"Sounds good to me."

The inside of Herron's house was precisely as Matlock thought it would be—as his own might be in thirty-odd years, if he lived that long alone. It was a mixed bag, an accumulated total of nearly half a century of unrelated gatherings from a hundred unrelated sources. The only common theme was comfort; there was no concern for style or period or coordination. Several walls were lined with books, and those which were not were filled with enlarged photographs of places visited abroad—one suspected during sabbaticals. The armchairs were thick and soft, the tables within arm's reach—the sign of practiced bachelorhood, thought Matlock.

"I don't think you've ever been here—inside, I mean."

"No, I haven't. It's very attractive. Very comfortable."

"Yes, it's that. It's comfortable. Here, sit down, I'll finish the formula and bring us a drink." Herron started across the living room toward what Matlock presumed was the door to the kitchen and then stopped and turned. "I know perfectly well that you haven't come all the way out here to liven up an old man's cocktail hour. However, I have a house rule: at least one drink—religion and strong principles permitting—before any serious discussion." He smiled and the myriad lines around his eyes and temples became more pronounced. He was an *old,* old man. "Besides, you look terribly serious. The Collins'll lessen the degree, I promise you."

Before Matlock could answer, Herron walked rapidly through the door. Instead of sitting, Matlock walked to the wall nearest him, against which was a small writing desk, above it a half-dozen photographs that hung in no discernible pattern. Several were of Stonehenge taken from the same position, the setting sun at dramatically different angles. Another was of a rock-bound coast, mountains in the distance, fishing boats moored offshore. It looked Mediterranean, possibly Greece or the Thracian Islands. Then there was a surprise. On the lower right side of the wall, only inches above the desk, was a small photograph of a tall, slender army officer standing by the trunk of a tree. Behind him the foliage was profuse, junglelike; to the sides were the shadows of other figures. The officer was helmetless, his shirt drenched with sweat, his large right hand holding the stock of a submachine gun. In his left hand the officer held a folded piece of paper—it looked like a map—and the man had obviously just made a decision. He was looking upward, as though toward some high terrain. The face was taut but not excited. It was a good face, a strong face. It was a dark-haired, middle-aged Lucas Herron.

"I keep that old photograph to remind me that time was not always so devastating."

Matlock snapped up, startled. Lucas had reentered and had taken him off guard. "It's a good picture. Now I know who really won that war."

"No doubt about it. Unfortunately, I never heard of that particular island either before or since. Someone said it was one of the Solomons. I think they blew it up in the fifties. Wouldn't take much. Couple of fire crackers'd do it. Here." Herron crossed to Matlock, handing him his drink.

"Thanks. You're too modest. I've heard the stories."

"So have I. Impressed the hell out of me. They grow better as I grow older. . . . What do you say we sit in the back yard. Too nice to stay indoors." Without waiting for a reply, Herron started out and Matlock followed.

Like the front of the house, the back was precisely manicured. On a flagstone patio, there were comfortable-looking, rubber-stranded beach chairs, each with a small table by its side. A large wrought-iron table with a sun umbrella was centered in the middle of the flagstones. Beyond, the lawn was close cropped and full. Dogwood trees were dotted about, each spaded around its trunk, and two lines of flowers—mostly roses—stretched lengthwise to the end of the lawn, about a hundred feet away. At the end of the lawn, however, the pastoral effect abruptly stopped. Suddenly there were huge trees, the underbrush thick, mangled, growing within itself. The side borders were the same. Around the perimeters of the sculptured back lawn was an undisciplined, overgrown forest.

Lucas Herron was surrounded by a forbidding green wall.

"It *is* a good drink, you'll admit." The two men were seated.

"It certainly is. You'll convert me to gin."

"Only in spring and summer. Gin's not for the rest of the year. . . . All right, young fellow, the house rule's been observed. What brings you to Herron's Nest?"

"I think you have an idea."

"Do I?"

"Archie Beeson." Matlock watched the old man, but Herron's concentration was on his glass. He showed no reaction.

"The young history man?"

"Yes."

"He'll make a fine teacher one day. Nice little filly of a wife, too."

"Nice . . . and promiscuous, I think."

"*Appearances,* Jim." Herron chuckled. "Never thought of you as Victorian. . . . One grows infinitely more tolerant of the appetites as one gets older. And the innocent whetting of them. You'll see."

"Is that the key? The tolerance of appetites?"

"Key to what?"

"Come on. He wanted to reach you the other night."

"Yes, he did. And you were there. . . . I understand your behavior left something to be desired."

"My behavior was calculated to leave that impression." For the first time Herron betrayed a trace of concern. It was a small reaction, the blinking of his eyes in rapid succession.

"That was reprehensible." Herron spoke softly and looked up at his imposing green wall. The sun was going below the line of tall trees; long shadows were cast across the lawn and patio.

"It was necessary." Matlock saw the old man's face wince in pain. And then he recalled his own reaction to Adam Williams' description of the "unpleasant necessity" of sending Sam Kressel the false report of his actions at Lumumba Hall. The parallel hurt.

"The boy's in trouble. He's sick. It's a disease and he's trying to cure himself. That takes courage. . . . This is no time for campus Gestapo tactics." Herron took a long drink from his glass while his free hand gripped the arm of the chair.

"How did you know about it?"

"That might be privileged information. Let's say I heard from a respected co-worker of ours—in the medical line—who ran across the symptoms and became concerned. What difference does it make? I tried to help the boy and I'd do it again."

"I'd like to believe that. It's what I wanted to believe."

"Why is that difficult for you?"

"I don't know. . . . Something at the front door a few minutes ago. Perhaps this house. I can't put my finger on it. . . . I'm being completely honest with you."

Herron laughed but still avoided Matlock's eyes. "You're too wound up in the Elizabethans. The plots and counterplots of *The Spanish Tragedy*. . . . You young faculty crusaders should stop trying to be an amateur Scotland Yard. Not too long ago it was fashionable around here to have Red Dogs for breakfast. You're just magnifying the situation out of proportion."

"That's not true. I'm not a faculty crusader. I'm no part of that crowd, and I think you know it."

"What was it then? Personal interest? In the boy. Or his wife? . . . I'm sorry, I shouldn't have said that."

"I'm glad you did. I have no interest in Virginia Beeson—sexual or otherwise. Although I can't imagine what else there would be."

"Then you put on quite an act."

"I certainly did. I took extreme measures to keep Beeson from knowing why I was there. It was that important."

"To whom?" Herron slowly put his glass down with his right hand, his left still gripped the arm of the chair.

"To people beyond this campus. Washington people. The federal authorities . . ."

Lucas Herron took a sudden, sustained intake of breath through his nostrils. In front of Matlock's eyes,

Herron's face began to drain itself of color. When he spoke, he did so barely above a whisper.

"What are you saying?"

"That I was approached by a man from the Justice Department. The information he showed me was frightening. Nothing was trumped up, nothing over-dramatized. It was straight data. I was given a free choice whether to cooperate or not."

"And you accepted?" Herron's words were uttered softly in disbelief.

"I didn't feel there was an alternative. My younger brother . . ."

"You didn't feel there was an *alternative?*" Herron rose from his chair, his hands began to shake, his voice grew in intensity. "You didn't *feel* there was an *alternative?*"

"No, I didn't," Matlock remained calm. "That's why I came out here. To warn you, old friend. It's much deeper—far more dangerous . . ."

"*You* came out here to warn *me?!* What have you *done?* What in the name of everything sacred *have you done?* . . . Now, you listen to me! You listen to what I say!" Herron backed off, bumping into the small side table. In one whip of his left arm, he sent it crashing onto the flagstones. "You let it *go,* do you hear me! You go back and tell them *nothing! Nothing exists!* It's all . . . all in their imaginations! *Don't touch it! Let it go!*"

"I can't do that," said Matlock gently, suddenly afraid for the old man. "Even Sealfont will have to agree. He can't fight it any longer. It's there, Lucas. . . ."

"Adrian! Adrian's been told? . . . Oh, my God, do you know what you're doing? *You'll destroy so much.*

So many, many . . . Get out of here! *Get out!* I don't know you! Oh, *Jesus! Jesus!*"

"Lucas, what is it?" Matlock got up and took several steps toward the old man. Herron continued backing away, an old man in panic.

"Don't come near me! Don't you *touch me!*"

Herron turned and started running as well as his ancient legs could carry him across the lawn. He stumbled, falling to the ground, and picked himself up. He didn't look back. Instead he ran with all his might toward the rear of the yard, toward the overgrown woods. And then he disappeared through his huge green wall.

"Lucas! For Christ's sake!" Matlock raced after the old man, reaching the edge of the woods only seconds behind him. Yet he was nowhere in sight. Matlock whipped at the overgrowth in front of him and stepped into the tangled mass of foliage. Branches slashed back at him, and the intricate webbings of giant weeds ensnared his feet as he kicked his way into the dense woods.

Herron was gone.

"Lucas! Where are you?!"

There was no answer, only the rustling of the disturbed growth behind him. Matlock went farther into the forest, ducking, crouching, sidling by the green barriers in front of him. There was no sign of Lucas Herron, no sound.

"Lucas! For God's sake, Lucas, answer me!"

Still no reply, no hint of presence.

Matlock tried to look around him, tried to spot a break in the patterns of foliage, a route to follow. He could see none. It was as if Lucas were matter one moment, vapor the next.

And then he heard it. Indistinct, from all sides of him, echoing softly from some unknown place. It was a deep-throated moan, a wail. Near, yet far in the dense distance. And then the wail diminished and became a plaintive sob. A single sob, punctuated by a single word—clear, and spoken in hatred.

The word was—

"Nimrod . . ."

12

"Goddamn it, Matlock! I told you to stay put until I contacted you!"

"Goddamn it, Greenberg! How did you get into my apartment?!"

"You didn't get your window fixed."

"You haven't offered to pay for it."

"We're even. Where have you been?"

Matlock threw his car keys on the coffee table and looked at his broken stereo set in the corner. "It's an involved story and I suspect . . . pathetic. I'll tell you all about it after I've had a drink. My last one was interrupted."

"Get me one, too. I've also got a story and mine's *definitely* pathetic."

"What do you drink?"

"Very little, so whatever you're having is fine."

Matlock looked out his front window. The curtains were strewn on the floor where he had torn them in front of Adam Williams. The sun was almost down now. The spring day was over. "I'm going to squeeze some lemons and have a fresh fruit Tom Collins."

"Your file says you drink bourbon. Sour mash."

Matlock looked at the federal agent. "Does it?"

Greenberg followed Matlock into the kitchen and watched in silence as he fixed their drinks. Matlock handed the federal man his glass.

"Looks fancy."

"It's not . . . Whose pathetic story gets first telling?"

"I'll want to hear yours, of course, but under the circumstances, mine has priority."

"You sound ominous."

"No. Just pathetic. . . . I'll start by asking you if you'd care to know where I've been since I dropped you off." Greenberg leaned against the counter.

"Not particularly, but you'll tell me anyway."

"Yes, I will. It's part of the pathos. I was out at your local airport—Bradley Field—waiting for a jet dispatched by Justice a few hours ago from Dulles. There was a man on the plane who brought me two sealed envelopes which I had to sign for. Here they are." Greenberg reached into his jacket pocket and took out two long business envelopes. He put one on the counter and began to open the second.

"They look very official," said Matlock, edging himself up so that he sat next to the sink, his long legs dangling over the side in front of the cabinets.

"They couldn't be more official. . . . This envelope contains the summary of our conclusions based on information you gave us—gave me. It ends with a specific recommendation. I'm allowed to convey this information in my own words as long as I cover all the facts. . . ."

"Jason Greenberg gets two points."

"However," continued the federal man without acknowledging Matlock's interruption, "the contents of the second envelope must be delivered verbatim. You are to read it thoroughly—*should it be necessary*—and if it's acceptable, you've got to acknowledge that by your signature."

"This gets better and better. Am I running for the Senate?"

"No, you're just running. . . . I'll start as instructed." Greenberg glanced at the unfolded paper and then looked across at Matlock. "The man at Lumumba Hall named Julian Dunois—alias Jacques Devereaux, Jésus Dambert, and probably several others we don't know about—is a legal strategist for the Black Left militants. The term *legal strategist* covers everything from court manipulations to agent provocateur. When involved with the former, he uses the name of Dunois, the latter—any number of aliases. He operates out of unusual places geographically. Algiers, Marseilles, the Caribbean—including Cuba—and, we suspect, Hanoi and probably Moscow. Perhaps even Peking. In the States he has a regular, bona fide law office in upper Harlem and a West Coast affiliate in San Francisco. . . . He's generally in the background, but wherever he's in evidence, bad news usually follows. Needless to say, he's on the attorney general's list of undesirables, and these days that's not respectable any longer. . . ."

"These days," broke in Matlock, "that includes almost everyone to the left of AT&T."

"No comment. To continue. The surfacing of Dunois in this operation adds a dimension not anticipated—a new aspect not considered before. It goes beyond domestic lawbreakers and enters the area of international crime and/*or* subversion. *Or* a combination of *both.* In light of the fact that drugs were used on you, your apartment broken into and ripped apart, your friend, Miss Ballantyne, indirectly threatened—and don't kid yourself, that's what it was—in light of all this, the recommendation is as follows. You withdraw from any further participation in this investigation. Your involvement is beyond the realm of reasonable risk." Greenberg dropped the paper on the counter and took several swallows of his drink. Matlock swung his legs slowly back and forth in front of the cabinet beneath him. "What say you, in the docket?" asked Greenberg.

"I'm not sure. It seems to me you're not finished."

"I'd like to be. Right here. The summary's accurate, and I think you should agree with the recommendation. Pull out, Jim."

"Finish first. What's the other letter? The one I'm supposed to read verbatim?"

"It's only necessary if you reject the recommendation. Don't reject it. I'm not instructed to lean that way, so that's off the record."

"You know damned well I'm going to reject it, so why waste time?"

"I *don't* know that. I don't want to *believe* that."

"There's no way out."

"There are counter explanations I can activate in an hour. Get you off the hook, out of the picture."

"Not any longer."

"What? Why?"

"That's *my* pathetic story. So you'd better continue."

Greenberg searched Matlock's eyes for an explanation, found none, and so picked up the second envelope and opened it.

"In the unlikely and ill-advised event that you reject our recommendation to cease and desist, you must understand that you do so against the express wishes of the Justice Department. Although we will offer whatever protection we can—as we would any citizen—you act under your own responsibility. We cannot be held liable for any injuries or inconveniences of any nature."

"Is that what it says?"

"No, that's *not* what it says, but that's what it means," said Greenberg, unfolding the paper. "It's much simpler and even more inclusive. Here." The federal agent handed Matlock the letter.

It was a statement signed by an assistant attorney general with a separate line on the left for Matlock's signature.

> An investigative office of the Department of Justice accepted the offer of James B. Matlock to make inquiries of a minor nature with regard to certain illegal acts alleged to have occurred within the vicinity of Carlyle University. However, the Department of Justice now considers the situation to be a professional matter, and any further participation on the part of Professor Matlock is deemed unwarranted and against the policies of the Department. Therefore, the Department of Justice hereby informs James B. Matlock that it appreciates his previous cooperation but requests him to remove himself from any further involvement in the interest of safety and investigatory progress. It is the opinion of the Department that further actions on the part of Professor Matlock might tend to interfere with the aims of the Investigation in the Carlyle area. Mr. Matlock has received the original of this letter and so signifies by his signature below.

"What the hell are you talking about? This says that I agree to pull out."

"You'd make a lousy lawyer. Don't buy a bicycle on time before talking to me."

"What?"

"Nowhere! No*where* does your signing this little stinkpot say you *agree* to retire from the scene. Only that Justice *requested* you to."

"Then why in hell should I sign it?"

"Excellent question. You may buy a bicycle. . . . You sign it if, as you say, you reject the recommendation to pull out."

"Oh, for Christ's sake!" Matlock slipped down from the edge of the sink and threw the paper across the counter next to Greenberg. "I may not know law but I know language. You're talking in contradictions!"

"Only on the surface. . . . Let me ask you a question. Say you continue playing undercover agent. Is it conceivable that you may want to ask for help? An emergency, perhaps?"

"Of course. Inevitable."

"You get no help whatsoever without that letter going back signed. . . . Don't look at *me!* I'll be replaced in a matter of days. I've been in the area too long already."

"Kind of hypocritical, isn't it? The only way I can count on any assistance—any protection—is to sign a statement that says I won't need it."

"It's enough to send me into private practice. . . . There's a new term for this sort of thing these days. It's called 'hazardless progress.' Use whatever—*who*ever—you can. But don't take the blame if a *game plan* gets fucked up. Don't be responsible."

"And I jump without a parachute if I don't sign."

"I told you. Take some free advice—I'm a good lawyer. Quit. Forget it. But *forget it.*"

"And I told *you*—I can't."

Greenberg reached for his drink and spoke softly. "No matter what you do, it's not going to bring your brother out of his grave."

"I know that." Matlock was touched, but he answered firmly.

"You might prevent other younger brothers but you probably won't. In either case, someone else can be recruited from professional ranks. I hate like hell to admit it, but Kressel was right. And if we don't get this conference—this convocation of peddlers in a couple of weeks—there'll be others."

"I agree with everything you say."

"Then why hesitate? Pull out."

"Why? . . . I haven't told you *my* pathetic little story, that's why. Remember? You had priority, but I've still got my turn."

"So tell."

And Matlock told him. Everything he knew about Lucas Herron—legend, giant, the "grand old bird" of Carlyle. The terror-stricken skeleton who had run into his personal forest. The wail of the single word: "Nimrod." Greenberg listened, and the longer Matlock talked, the sadder Jason Greenberg's eyes became. When Matlock finished, the federal agent drank the last of his drink and morosely nodded his head in slow motion.

"You spelled out everything for him, didn't you? You couldn't come to *me*, you had to go to *him*. Your campus saint with a bucket of blood in his hands. . . . Loring was right. We had to reach a conscience-stricken amateur. . . . Amateurs in front of us and amateurs behind us. At least I'll say this for you. You got a conscience. That's more than I can say for the rear flank."

"What should I do?"

"Sign the stinkpot." Greenberg picked up the Justice Department letter from the counter and handed it to Matlock. "You're going to need help."

Patricia Ballantyne preceded Matlock to the small side table at the far end of the Cheshire Cat. The drive out had been strained. The girl had hammered away—quietly, acidly—at Matlock's cooperating with the government, in particular and specifically the Federal Bureau of Investigation. She claimed not to be reacting to a programmed liberal response; there was simply too much overwhelming evidence that such organizations had brought the country ten steps from its own particular police state.

She knew firsthand. She'd witnessed the anguished aftermath of one FBI exercise and knew it wasn't isolated.

Matlock held her chair as she sat down, touching her shoulders as she did so. Touching, reaffirming, lessening the imagined hurt. The table was small, next to a window, several feet from a terrace that soon—in late May—would be in use for outside dining. He sat across from her and took her hand.

"I'm not going to apologize for what I'm doing. I think it has to be done. I'm not a hero and I'm not a fink. I'm not asked to be heroic, and the information they want ultimately will help a lot of people. People who need help—desperately."

"Will those people *get* help? Or will they simply be prosecuted? Instead of hospitals and clinics . . . will they find themselves in jail?"

"They're not interested in sick kids. They want the ones who make them sick. So do I."

"But in the process, the kids get hurt." A statement.

"Some may be. As few as possible."

"That's contemptible." The girl took her hand away from Matlock's. "It's so condescending. Who makes *those* decisions? You?"

"You're beginning to sound like a one-track tape."

"I've *been* there. It's not pleasant."

"This is entirely different. I've met just two men; one . . . left. The other's Greenberg. They're not your nightmares from the fifties. Take my word for that."

"I'd like to."

The manager of the Cheshire Cat approached the table. "There's a telephone call for you, Mr. Matlock."

Matlock felt a twinge of pain in his stomach. It was the nerves of fear. Only one person knew where he was—Jason Greenberg.

"Thanks, Harry."

"You can take it by the reservations desk. The phone's off the hook."

Matlock got out of his chair and looked briefly at Pat. In the months and months of their going out together, from restaurants to parties to dinners, he had never received a telephone call, had never been interrupted that way. He saw that realization in her eyes. He walked rapidly away from the table to the reservations desk.

"Hello?"

"Jim?" It *was* Greenberg, of course.

"Jason?"

"Sorry to bother you. I wouldn't if I didn't have to."

"What is it, for heaven's sake?"

"Lucas Herron's dead. He committed suicide about an hour ago."

The pain in Matlock's stomach suddenly returned. It wasn't a twinge this time, but instead a sharp blow that left him unable to breathe. All he could see in front of his eyes was the picture of the staggering, panicked old man running across the manicured lawn and disappearing into the dense foliage bordering his property. And then the wailing sound of a sob and the name of Nimrod whispered in hatred.

"Are you all right?"

"Yes. Yes, I'm all right." For reasons he could not fathom, Matlock's memory focused on a small, black-framed photograph. It was an enlarged snapshot of a dark-haired, middle-aged infantry officer with a weapon in one hand, a map in the other, the face lean and strong, looking up toward the high ground.

A quarter of a century ago.

"You'd better get back to your apartment. . . ." Greenberg was issuing an order, but he had the sense to be gentle about it.

"Who found him?"

"My man. No one else knows yet."

"Your man?"

"After our talk, I put Herron under surveillance. You get to spot the signs. He broke in and found him."

"How?"

"Cut his wrists in the shower."

"Oh, Christ! What have I done?"

"Cut that out! Get back here. We've got people to reach. . . . Come on, Jim."

"What can I tell Pat?" Matlock tried to find his mind but it kept wandering back to a helpless, frightened old man.

"As little as possible. But hurry."

Matlock replaced the receiver and took several deep breaths. He searched his pockets for cigarettes and remembered that he'd left them at the table.

The table. Pat. He had to go back to the table and think of something to say.

The truth. Goddamn it, the *truth.*

He made his way around two antique pillars toward the far end of the room and the small side table by the window. In spite of his panic, he felt a degree of relief and knew it was because he had decided to be honest with Pat. God knew he had to have someone other than Greenberg and Kressel to talk to.

Kressel! He was supposed to have gone to Kressel's house at seven. He'd forgotten all about it!

But in an instant Sam Kressel went out of his thoughts. He saw the small side table by the window and there was no one there.

Pat was gone.

13

"No one saw her leave?" Greenberg followed a frustrated Matlock into the living room from the foyer. Sam Kressel's voice could be heard from the bedroom, shouting excitedly into a telephone. Matlock took notice of it, his attention split in too many areas.

"That's Sam in there, isn't it?" he asked. "Does he know about Herron?"

"Yes. I called him after I talked to you. . . . What about the waitresses? Did you ask them?"

"Of course, I did. None of them were sure. It was busy. One said she thought she might have gone to the ladies' room. Another hinted, s'help me, hinted, that she might have been the girl who left with a couple from another table."

"Wouldn't they have had to pass you on the way out? Wouldn't you have seen her?"

"Not necessarily. We were in the back. There are two or three doors which lead to a terrace. In summer, especially when it's crowded, they put tables on the terrace."

"You drove out in your car?"

"Naturally."

"And you didn't see her outside, walking on the road, on the grounds?"

"No."

"Did you recognize any of the other people there?"

"I didn't really look. I was . . . preoccupied." Matlock lit a cigarette. His hand shook as he held the match.

"If you want my opinion, I think she spotted someone she knew and asked for a lift home. A girl like that doesn't go anywhere she doesn't want to go without a fight."

"I know. That's occurred to me."

"Have a fight?"

"You might say it was diminishing but not over. The phone call probably set her off again. Old English teachers rarely get calls while out at restaurants."

"I'm sorry."

"It's not your fault. I told you, she's uptight. She keeps thinking about her father. I'll try her apartment when Sam gets off the phone."

"*He's* a funny man. I tell him about Herron—naturally he goes off the deep end. He says he's got to talk privately with Sealfont so he goes into the bedroom and shouts so loud they can hear him in Poughkeepsie."

Matlock's thoughts shifted quickly to Herron. "His death—his *suicide*—is going to be the biggest shock this campus has had in twenty years. Men like Lucas simply don't die. They certainly don't die like *this*. . . . Does Sam know I saw him?"

"He does. I couldn't withhold that. I told him pretty much what you told me—shorter version, of course. He refuses to believe it. The implications, I mean."

"I don't blame him. They're not easy to believe. What do we do now?"

"We wait. I've made a report. Two lab men from

the Hartford Bureau are out there now. The local police have been called in."

At the mention of the police, Matlock suddenly remembered the patrolman out of uniform in the squash court corridor, who had walked rapidly away at the moment of recognition. He'd told Greenberg and Greenberg had never given him an explanation—if there was one. He asked again.

"What about the cop in the gym?"

"The story's reasonable. At least so far. The Carlyle police are assigned three mornings a week for limited use of the facilities. Town-gown relations. Coincidence."

"You're settling for that?"

"I said, 'so far.' We're running a check on the man. Nothing's turned up but an excellent record."

"He's a bigot, a nasty bastard."

"This may surprise you, but that's no crime. It's guaranteed in the Bill of Rights."

Sam Kressel walked through the bedroom door quickly, emphatically. Matlock saw that he was as close to pure fear as he'd ever seen a man. There was an uncomfortable similarity between Sam's face and the bloodless expression of Lucas Herron before the old man had raced into the woods.

"I heard you come in," Kressel said. "What are we going to *do*? What in hell are we *going to do*? . . . Adrian doesn't believe that absurd story any more than *I* do! *Lucas Herron! It's insane!*"

"Maybe. But it's true."

"Because *you* say so? How can you be sure? You're no professional in these matters. As I understand it, Lucas admitted he was helping a student through a drug problem."

"He . . . they aren't students."

"I see." Kressel stopped briefly and looked back and forth between Matlock and Greenberg. "Under the circumstances, I demand to know the identities."

"You'll get them," said Greenberg quietly. "Go on. I want to hear why Matlock's so wrong, the story so absurd."

"Because Lucas Herron isn't . . . wasn't the only member of the faculty concerned with these problems. There are dozens of us giving aid, helping wherever we can!"

"I don't follow you." Greenberg stared at Kressel. "So you help. You don't go and kill yourself when a fellow member of the faculty finds out about it."

Sam Kressel removed his glasses and looked momentarily reflective, sad. "There's something else neither of you know about. I've been aware of it for some time but not so knowledgeably as Sealfont. . . . Lucas Herron was a very sick man. One kidney was removed last summer. The other was also cancerous and he knew it. The pain must have been unbearable for him. He hadn't long."

Greenberg watched closely as Kressel returned his glasses to his face. Matlock bent down and crushed out his cigarette in an ashtray on the coffee table. Finally, Greenberg spoke.

"Are you suggesting that there's no relationship between Herron's suicide and Matlock's seeing him this afternoon?"

"I'm not suggesting any such thing. I'm sure there's a relationship. . . . But you didn't know Lucas. His whole life for nearly half a century, except for the war years, was Carlyle University. It's been his total, complete existence. He loved this place more than any man could love a woman, more than any parent a child. I'm sure Jim's told you. If he thought for a moment that his world here was going to be defaced, torn apart—that would be a greater pain than the physical torture his body gave him. What better time to take his own life?"

"*Goddamn you!*" roared Matlock. "You're saying ***I killed him!***"

"Perhaps I am," Kressel said quietly. "I hadn't thought of it in those terms. I'm sure Adrian didn't either."

"But that's what you're *saying!* You're saying I went off half-cocked and killed him as much as if I'd slashed his wrists! . . . Well, you weren't there. *I was!*"

Kressel spoke gently. "I didn't say you went off half-cocked. I said you were an amateur. A very well-intentioned amateur. I think Greenberg knows what I mean."

Jason Greenberg looked at Matlock. "There's an old Slovak proverb: 'When the old men kill themselves, the cities are dying.' "

The telephone bell suddenly pierced the air; its sound acted as a jolt to the three men. Matlock answered it, then turned to Greenberg. "It's for you."

"Thanks." The federal agent took the phone from Matlock. "Greenberg. . . . O.K. I understand. When will you know? . . . I'll probably be on the road by then. I'll call you back. Talk later." He replaced the telephone and stood by the desk, his back to Matlock and Kressel. The dean of colleges couldn't contain himself.

"What was it? What happened?"

Greenberg turned and faced them. Matlock thought his eyes seemed sadder than usual, which Matlock had learned was a sign of trouble in Greenberg.

"We're making a request of the police—the courts—for an autopsy."

"*Why?!*" Kressel shouted as he approached the agent. "For God's sake, *why?!* The man killed himself! He was in *pain!* . . . Jesus Christ, you can't *do* this! If news of it gets out . . ."

"We'll handle it quietly."

"That can't be done and you *know* it! It'll leak out and all hell'll break loose around here! I won't *permit* it!"

"You can't stop it. Even I couldn't stop it. There's sufficient evidence to indicate that Herron didn't take his own life. That he was killed." Greenberg smiled wryly at Matlock. "And not by words."

Kressel argued, threatened, made another call to Sealfont, and finally, when it was obvious that all were to no avail, he left Matlock's apartment in fury.

No sooner had Kressel slammed the door than the telephone rang again. Greenberg saw that the sound disturbed Matlock—not merely annoyed him, but disturbed him; perhaps frightened him.

"I'm sorry. . . . I'm afraid this place has to be a kind of patrol base for a while. Not long. . . . Maybe it's the girl."

Matlock picked up the phone, listened, but did not say anything into it. Instead, he turned to Greenberg. He said only one word.

"You."

Greenberg took the telephone, uttered his name softly, and then spent the next minute staring straight ahead. Matlock watched Greenberg for half the time and then wandered into his kitchen. He didn't wish to stand awkwardly to one side while the agent listened to a superior's instructions.

The voice at the other end of the line had initially identified itself by saying, "Washington calling."

On the counter lay the empty envelope in which the brutally hypocritical statement had come from the Department of Justice. It had been one more sign that his worst fantasies were gradually becoming real. From that infinitesimal portion of the mind which concerns itself with the unthinkable, Matlock had begun to perceive that the land he had grown up in was changing into something ugly and destructive. It was far more than a political manifestation, it was a slow, all-embracing sense of morality by strategy. A corruption of intentions. Strong feelings were being replaced with surface anger, convictions and compromise. The land was becoming something other than its promise, its commitment. The grails were empty vessels of flat wine, impressive solely because they were possessed.

"I'm off the phone now. Would you like to try reaching Miss Ballantyne?"

Matlock looked up at Greenberg, standing in the frame of the kitchen door. Greenberg, the walking contradiction, the proverb-quoting agent deeply suspicious of the system for which he worked.

"Yes. Yes, I'd like to." He started into the living room as Greenberg stepped aside to let him pass. Matlock reached the center of the room and stopped. "That's one hell of a quotation. What was it? 'When the old men kill themselves, the cities are dying.' " He turned and looked at the agent. "I think that's the saddest proverb I've ever heard."

"You're not Hassidic. Of course, neither am I, but the Hassidim wouldn't think it sad. . . . Come to think of it, no true philosopher would."

"Why not? It *is* sad."

"It's truth. Truth is neither joyful nor sad, neither good nor bad. It is simply truth."

"Someday let's debate that, Jason." Matlock picked up the telephone, dialed Pat's number, and let it ring a dozen times. There was no answer. Matlock thought of several of Pat's friends and wondered whether to call them or not. When angry or upset, Pat usually did one of two things. She either went off by herself for an hour or so, or, conversely, sought out one or two friends and drove off to a film in Hartford or an out-of-the-way bar. It was just over an hour. He'd give her another fifteen minutes before phoning around. It had, of course, occurred to him that she might have been taken involuntarily—that had been his first thought. But it wasn't logical. The Cheshire Cat had been filled with people, the tables close together. Greenberg was right. Wherever she went, she went because she wanted to go.

Greenberg stood by the kitchen door. He hadn't moved. He'd been watching Matlock.

"I'll try in a quarter of an hour. Then, if there's no answer, I'll call some friends of hers. As you said, she's one strong-willed young lady."

"I hope you're not from the same cloth."

"What does that mean?"

Greenberg took several steps into the living room. When he spoke, he looked directly into Matlock's eyes.

"You're out. Finished. Forget the letter, forget Loring, forget me. . . . That's the way it's got to be. We understand you have reservations for St. Thomas on Pan Am for Saturday. Enjoy it, because that's where you're going. Much better this way."

Matlock returned the government man's look. "Any decision like that will be made by me. I've got a gentle old man on my conscience; and you've got that stinkpot in your pocket. I signed it, remember?"

"The stinkpot doesn't count anymore. D.C. wants you out. You go."

"Why?"

"Because of the gentle old man. If he *was* killed, you could be, too. If that happened, certain records might be subpoenaed, certain men who had reservations about recruiting you might voice those reservations to the press. You were maneuvered. I don't have to tell you that."

"So?"

"The directors at Justice have no wish to be called executioners."

"I see." Matlock took his eyes off Greenberg and wandered toward the coffee table. "Suppose I refuse?"

"Then I remove you from the scene."

"How?"

"I have you arrested on suspicion of murder one."

"*What?*"

"You were the last person of record to see Lucas Herron alive. By your own admission, you went out to his house to threaten him."

"To *warn* him!"

"That's subject to interpretation, isn't it?"

When the thunderous crash came, it was so ear-shattering both men threw themselves to the floor. It was as if the whole side of the building had collapsed in rubble. Dust was everywhere, furniture toppled, glass shattered, splinters of wood and plaster flew through the air, and the terrible stench of burning sulfur settled over the room. Matlock knew the smell of that kind of bomb, and his reflexes knew how to operate. He clung to the base of his couch waiting, waiting for a second explosion—a delayed detonator which would kill any who rose in panic. Through the mist, he saw Greenberg start to get up, and he leaped forward, tackling the agent at his knees.

"Get down! Stay. . . ."

The second explosion came. Parts of the ceiling blackened. But Matlock knew it was not a killer explosive. It was something else, and he could not figure it out at the moment. It was an eyegrabber, a camouflage—not meant to kill, but to deflect all concentration. A huge firecracker.

Screams of panic could now be heard mounting from all parts of the building. The sounds of rushing feet pounded on the floor above his apartment.

And then a single screech of terror from outside Matlock's front door. It would not stop. The horror of it caused Matlock and Greenberg to struggle to their feet and race to the source. Matlock pulled the door open and looked down upon a sight no human being should ever see more than once in a lifetime, if his life must continue beyond that instant.

On his front step was Patricia Ballantyne wrapped in a bloodsoaked sheet. Holes were cut in the areas of her naked breasts, blood flowing from gashes beneath the nipples. The front of her head was shaved; blood poured out of lacerations where once had been the soft brown hair. Blood, too, came from the half-open mouth, her lips bruised and split. The eyes were blackened into deep crevasses of sore flesh—but they moved! The eyes moved!

Saliva began forming at the corners of her lips. The half-dead corpse was trying to speak.

"Jamie . . ." was the only word she managed and then her head slipped to one side.

Greenberg threw his whole weight against Matlock, sending him sprawling into the gathering crowd. He roared orders of "Police!" and "Ambulance!" until he saw enough people running to execute his commands. He put his mouth to the girl's mouth, to force air into the collapsing lungs, but he knew it wasn't really necessary. Patricia Ballantyne wasn't dead; she'd been tortured by experts, and the experts knew their business well. Every slash, every crack, every bruise meant utmost pain but did not mean death.

He started to pick the girl up but Matlock stopped him. The English professor's eyes were swollen with tears of hate. He gently removed Greenberg's hands and lifted Pat into his arms. He carried her inside and stretched her out on the half-destroyed sofa. Greenberg went into the bedroom and returned with a blanket. Then he brought a bowl of warm water from the kitchen and several towels. He lifted the blanket and held a towel beneath the bleeding breasts. Matlock, staring in horror at the brutally beaten face, then took the edge of another towel and began wiping away the blood around the shaven head and the mouth.

"She'll be all right, Jim. I've seen this before. She'll be all right."

And as Greenberg heard the sounds of the sirens in the near distance, he wondered, really, if this girl would ever be right again.

Matlock, helpless, continued to wipe the girl's face, his tears now streaming down his cheeks, his eyes unblinking. He spoke through his controlled sobs.

"You know what this means, don't you? No one

pulls me out now. They try, I'll kill them."

"I won't let them," said Greenberg simply.

The screeching of brakes could be heard outside and the flashing lights of the police cars and the ambulances whipped in circles through the windows.

Matlock's face fell into the cushion beside the unconscious girl and he wept.

14

Matlock awoke in the antiseptic whiteness of a hospital room. The shade was up, and the sun reflected harshly on the three walls he could see. At his feet a nurse was writing efficiently, emphatically, on top of a clipboard attached to the base of the bed by a thin keychain. He stretched his arms, then quickly brought his left back, aware of a sharp pain in his forearm.

"You feel those the next morning, Mr. Matlock," droned the nurse without looking up from the clipboard. "Heavy intravenous sedations are murder, I can tell you. Not that I've ever had one, but Lord knows, I've seen enough who have."

"Is Pat . . . Miss Ballantyne here?"

"Well, not in the same *room!* Lord, you campus types!"

"She's here?"

"Of course. Next room. Which I intend to keep *locked!* Lord, you people from the hill! . . . There! You're all accounted for." The nurse let the clipboard crash down and vibrate back and forth. "Now. *You've* got special privileges. *You're* allowed breakfast even though it's past breakfast time—*way* past! That's probably because they want you to pay your bill. . . . You can be discharged any time after twelve."

"What time is it? Someone took my watch."

"It's eight minutes to nine," said the nurse, glancing at her wrist. "And no one *took* your watch. It's with any other valuables you had when you were admitted."

"How *is* Miss Ballantyne?"

"We don't discuss other patients, Mr. Matlock."

"Where's her doctor?"

"He's the same as yours, I understand. Not one of *ours*." The nurse made sure the statement was hardly complimentary. "According to your chart, he'll be here at nine thirty unless we phone for an emergency."

"Call him. I want him here as soon as possible."

"Now, really. There's no emergency. . . ."

"Goddamn it, get him here!"

As Matlock raised his voice the door of his room opened. Jason Greenberg came in quickly. "I could hear you in the corridor. That's a good sign."

"How's Pat?!"

"Just a minute, sir. We have regulations. . . ."

Greenberg took out his identification and showed it to the nurse. "This man is in my custody, Miss. Check the front desk, if you like, but leave us alone."

The nurse, ever professional, scrutinized the identification and walked rapidly out the door.

"How's Pat?"

"A mess, but with it. She had a bad night; she's going to have a worse morning when she asks for a mirror."

"The hell with that! Is she *all right?*"

"Twenty-seven stitches—body, head, mouth, and, for variety, one on her left foot. But she's going to be fine. X-rays show only bone bruises. No fractures, no ruptures, no internal bleeding. The bastards did their usual professional job."

"Was she able to talk?"

"Not really. And the doctor didn't advise it. She needs sleep more than anything else. . . . You need a little rest, too. That's why we put you here last night."

"Anyone hurt at the apartment?"

"Nope. It was a crazy bombing. We don't think it was intended to kill anyone. The first was a short two-inch stick taped below the window exterior; the second—activated by the first—wasn't much more than a July Fourth rocket. You expected the second blast, didn't you?"

"Yes. I guess I did. . . . Terror tactics, wasn't it?"

"That's what we figure."

"Can I see Pat?"

"Rather you waited. The doctor thinks she'll sleep into the afternoon. There's a nurse in there with ice packs and stuff if localized pain bothers her. Let her rest."

Matlock cautiously sat up on the edge of the bed. He began flexing his legs, arms, neck, and hands, and found that he wasn't much below par. "I feel sort of like a hangover without the headache."

"The doctor gave you a heavy dose. You were . . . understandably . . . very emotional."

"I remember everything. I'm calmer, but I don't retract one goddamned word. . . . I have two classes today. One at ten and the other at two. I want to make them."

"You don't have to. Sealfont wants to see you."

"I'll talk to him after my last class. . . . Then I'll see Pat." Matlock stood on his feet and walked slowly to the large hospital window. It was a bright, sunlit morning; Connecticut had had a string of beautiful days. As he stared outside, Matlock remembered that he'd looked out another window five days ago when he'd first met Jason Greenberg. He'd made a decision then as he was making one now. "Last night you said you wouldn't let them pull me out. I hope you haven't changed your mind. I'm *not* going to be on that Pan Am flight tomorrow."

"You won't be arrested. I promised you that."

"Can you prevent it? You also said you were going to be replaced."

"I can prevent it. . . . I can morally object, an enigmatic phrase which is translated to mean I can embarrass people. However, I don't want to mislead you. If you create problems, you could be taken into protective custody."

"They can if they can find me."

"That's a condition I don't like."

"Forget you heard it. Where are my clothes?" Matlock walked to the single closet door and opened it. His slacks, jacket, and shirt were hung on hangers; his loafers were on the floor with his socks carefully inserted. The lone bureau held his undershorts and a hospital-furnished toothbrush. "Will you go down and see whoever you've got to see to get me out of here? Also, I'll need my wallet, cash, and watch. Will you do that, please?"

"What do you mean—if they could find you? What are you going to do?" Greenberg made no move to leave.

"Nothing earth-shattering. Merely continue making those inquiries . . . of a minor nature. That's the way the statement from your employers phrased it, wasn't it? Loring said it. Somewhere out there is the other half of that paper. I'm going to find it."

"You listen to me first! I don't deny you have a right . . ."

"You don't *deny!*" Matlock turned on the federal

agent. His voice was controlled but vicious. "That's not good enough. That's *negative* approval! I've got several *big* rights! They include a kid brother in a sailboat, a black son of a bitch named Dunois or whatever you call him, a man by the name of Lucas Herron, and that girl in there! I suspect you and the doctor know the rest of what happened to her last night, and I can *guess!* Don't talk to me about *a right!*"

"In principle, we agree. I just don't want your 'rights' to land you next to your brother. This is a job for professionals. Not an amateur! If you work at all, I want you to work with whoever takes my place. That's important. I want your word on it."

Matlock took off the top of his pajamas and gave Greenberg a short, embarrassed smile. "You have it. I don't really see myself as a one-man ranger team. Do you know who's taking your place?"

"Not yet. Probably someone from D.C. They won't take a chance on using a Hartford or a New Haven man. . . . The truth is . . . they don't know who's been bought. He'll be in touch. I'll have to brief him myself. No one else can. I'll instruct him to identify himself with . . . what would you like?"

"Tell him to use your proverb. 'When the old men kill themselves, the cities are dying.' "

"You like that, don't you?"

"I don't like it or dislike it. It's simply the truth. Isn't that the way it should be?"

"And very applicable. I see what you mean."

"Very."

"Jim, before I go this afternoon, I'm going to write out a telephone number for you. It's a Bronx number—my parents. They won't know where I am, but I'll check with them every day. Use it if you have to."

"Thanks, I will."

"I want your word on it."

"You have it." Matlock laughed a short laugh of gratitude.

"Of course, under the circumstances, I may just be on the other end of the line if you do call."

"Back in private practice?"

"The possibility is less remote than you think."

15

Between his two classes, Matlock drove to the small brokerage office in the town of Carlyle and emerged with a check for $7,312. It represented his total investment in the market, mostly from royalties. The broker had tried to dissuade him; it was no time to sell, especially at current prices. But Matlock had made up his mind. The cashier reluctantly issued the check.

From there Matlock went to his bank and transferred his entire savings into his checking account. He added the $7,312 to the slip and looked at the sum total of his immediate cash value.

It came to $11,501.72.

Matlock stared at the figure for several minutes. He had mixed feelings about it. On the one hand, it proved solvency; on the other, it was a little frightening to think that after thirty-three years of living he was able to pinpoint so accurately his net financial worth. There was no house, no land, no hidden investments anywhere. Only an automobile, a few possessions of minor value, and some published words of such a specialized nature that there would be no significant commercial rewards.

Yet by many standards, it was a great deal of money.

Only nowhere *near* enough. He knew that. It was why Scarsdale, New York, was on the day's schedule.

The meeting with Sealfont had been unnerving, and Matlock wasn't sure how much more his shattered nerves could take. The cold fury of Carlyle's president was matched only by the depth of his anguish.

The bewildering shadow world of violence and corruption was a world he could never come to grips with because it was not within the realm of his comprehension. Matlock had been startled to hear Sealfont say, as he sat in his chair staring out the bay window overlooking the most beautiful lawn on the Carlyle campus, that he might well resign.

"If this whole sordid, unbelievable business is true—and who can doubt it—I have no right to sit in this chair."

"That's not so," Matlock had answered. "If it's true, this place is going to need you more than ever before."

"A blind man? No one needs a blind man. Not in this office."

"Not blind. Unexposed."

And then Sealfont had swung around in his chair and pounded on the top of his desk in an enormous display of strength.

"Why *here?! Why here?!*"

As he sat in front of Sealfont's desk, Matlock looked at the pained face of Carlyle's president. And for a second he thought the man might weep.

The trip down the Merritt Parkway was made at high speed. He had to race; it was necessary for him. It helped take his mind off the sight of Pat Ballantyne as he had seen her a few minutes before leaving. He had gone from Sealfont's to the hospital; still he hadn't been able to talk with her. No one had yet.

She had awakened at noon, he'd been told. She'd gone into severe hysterics. The doctor from Litchfield had administered further sedatives. The doctor was worried, and Matlock knew it was Pat's mind he was worried about. The nightmare of terror inflicted upon her body had to touch her brain.

The first minutes with his parents at the huge Scarsdale house were awkward. His father, Jonathan Munro Matlock, had spent decades in the highest spheres of his marketplace and knew instinctively when a man came to him without strength.

Without strength but with need.

Matlock told his father as simply and unemotionally as he could that he wanted to borrow a large sum of money; he could not guarantee its repayment. It would be used to help—ultimately help—young people like his dead brother.

The dead son.

"How?" asked Jonathan Matlock softly.

"I can't tell you that." He looked into his father's eyes and the irrevocable truth of the son's statement was accepted by the father.

"Very well. Are you qualified for this undertaking?"

"Yes. I am."

"Are there others involved?"

"By necessity, yes."

"Do you trust them?"

"I do."

"Have they asked for this money?"

"No. They don't know about it."

"Will it be at their disposal?"

"No. Not that I can foresee. . . . I'll go further than that. It would be wrong for them to learn of it."

"I'm not restricting you, I'm asking."

"That's my answer."

"And you believe that what you're doing will help, in some way, boys like David? Practical help, not theoretical, not dream stuff, not charity."

"Yes. It has to."

"How much do you want?"

Matlock took a deep breath silently. "Fifteen thousand dollars."

"Wait here."

Several minutes later, the father came out of his study and gave the son an envelope.

The son knew better than to open it.

Ten minutes after the exchange—and Matlock knew it *was* an exchange—he left, feeling the eyes of his parents as they stood on the enormous porch and watched him drive out through the gates.

Matlock pulled into the apartment driveway, shut off the lights and the engine, and wearily climbed out. As he approached the old Tudor house, he saw that every light he owned was turned on. Jason Greenberg wasn't taking chances, and Matlock assumed that some part of Greenberg's silent, unseen army was watching his place from varying distances—none too far away.

He unlocked the door and pushed it open. There was no one there. At least, not in sight. Not even his cat.

"Hello? Jason? . . . Anybody here? It's Matlock."

There was no answer and Matlock was relieved. He wanted only to crawl into bed and sleep. He'd stopped at the hospital to see Pat, and the request had been denied. At least he'd learned that ". . . she is resting and her condition is deemed satisfactory." That was a step up. That afternoon she'd still been on the critical list. He would see her at nine in the morning.

Now was the time for him to sleep—peaceably if possible. Sleep at all costs. There was a great deal to do in the morning.

He went into his bedroom, passing the still unrepaired sections of wall and window as he did so. Carpenter's and plasterer's tools were neatly stacked in corners. He removed his jacket and his shirt and then thought, with a degree of self-ridicule, that he was becoming far too confident. He walked rapidly out of the bedroom and into his bathroom. Once the door was shut, he reached down to the litter box and lifted up the newspaper to the layer of canvas. The Corsican paper was there, the tarnished silver coating reflecting the light.

Back in the bedroom, Matlock removed his wallet, cash, and car keys, placing them on top of his bureau. As he did so, he remembered the envelope.

He hadn't been fooled. He knew his father, perhaps better than his father realized. He presumed there was a short note with the check stating clearly that the money was a gift, not a loan, and that no repayment was anticipated.

The note was there, folded inside the envelope, but the written words were not what Matlock expected.

I believe in you. I always have.
Love,
Dad

On top of the note, clipped to the paper on the reverse side, was the check. Matlock slipped it off and read the figure.

It was for fifty thousand dollars.

16

Much of the swelling on her face and around her eyes had subsided. He took her hand and held it tightly, putting his face once more next to hers.

"You're going to be fine," were the innocuous words he summoned. He had to hold himself in check to stop himself from screaming out his anger and his guilt. That this could be done to a human being by other human beings was beyond his endurance. And he was responsible.

When she spoke, her voice was hardly audible, like a small child's, the words only partially formed through the immobile lips.

"Jamie . . . Jamie?"

"Shh . . . Don't talk if it hurts."

"*Why?*"

"I don't know. But we'll find out."

"No! . . . No, don't! They're . . . they're . . ." The girl had to swallow; it was nearly impossible for her. She pointed to a glass of water on the bedside table. Matlock quickly reached for it and held it to her lips, supporting her by the shoulders.

"How did it happen? Can you tell me?"

"Told . . . Greenberg. Man and woman . . . came to the table. Said you were . . . waiting . . . outside."

"Never mind, I'll talk to Jason."

"I . . . feel better. I hurt but . . . feel better, I . . . really do. . . . Am I going to be all right?"

"Of course you are. I spoke with the doctor. You're bruised, but nothing broken, nothing serious. He says you'll be out of bed in a few days, that's all."

Patricia Ballantyne's eyes brightened, and Matlock saw the terrible attempt of a smile on her sutured lips. "I fought. . . . I fought and I fought . . . until I . . . couldn't remember any more."

It took all of Matlock's strength not to burst into tears. "I know you did. Now, no more talking. You rest, take it easy. I'll just sit here and we'll talk with our eyes. Remember? You said we always communicate around other people with our eyes. . . . I'll tell you a dirty joke."

When the smile came, it *was* from her eyes.

He stayed until a nurse forbade him to stay longer. Then he kissed her softly on the lips and left the room. He was a relieved man; he was an angry man.

"Mr. Matlock?" The young doctor with the freshly scrubbed face of an intern approached him by the elevator.

"Yes?"

"There's a telephone call for you. You can take it at the second floor reception, if you'll follow me."

The caller's voice was unknown. "Mr. Matlock, my name's Houston. I'm a friend of Jason Greenberg's. I'm to get in touch with you."

"Oh? How's Jason?"

"Fine. I'd like to get together with you as soon as possible."

Matlock was about to name a place, any place, after his first class. And then he stopped. "Did Jason leave any message . . . where he is now, or anything?"

"No sir. Just that I was to make contact pronto."

"I see." Why didn't the man say it? Why didn't Houston identify himself? "Greenberg definitely told me he'd leave word . . . a message . . . where he'd be. I'm sure he said that."

"Against department regulations, Mr. Matlock. He wouldn't be allowed to."

"Oh? . . . Then he didn't leave any message at all?"

The voice on the other end of the line hesitated slightly, perceptively. "He may have forgotten. . . . As a matter of fact, I didn't speak to him myself. I received my orders directly from Washington. Where shall we meet?"

Matlock heard the anxiety in the man's voice. When he referred to Washington, his tone had risen in a small burst of nervous energy. "Let me call you later. What's your number?"

"Now listen, Matlock. I'm in a telephone booth and we have to meet. I've got my orders!"

"Yes, I'll bet you do. . . ."

"What?"

"Never mind. Are you downtown? In Carlyle?"

The man hesitated again. "I'm in the area."

"Tell me, Mr. Houston. . . . Is the city dying?"

"What? What are you talking about?"

"I'm going to be late for my class. Try me again. I'm sure you'll be able to reach me." Matlock hung up the phone. His left hand shook and perspiration had formed on his brow.

Mr. Houston was the enemy.

The enemy was closing in.

His first Saturday class was at eleven, which gave him just about an hour to make what he felt were the most logical arrangements for the money. He didn't want to think that he had to physically be in the town of Carlyle—at the Carlyle Bank—on Monday morning. He wasn't sure it would be possible. He wasn't sure where he would be on Monday.

Since, on the surface, Carlyle was a typical New England college town, it had a particular way of life common to such places. One knew, generally on a first-name basis, all the people whose jobs made day-to-day living the effortless, unhurried existence that it was. The garage mechanic was "Joe" or "Mac," the manager at J. Press was "Al," the dentist "John" or "Warren," the girl at the dry cleaners "Edith." In Matlock's case, the banker was "Alex." Alex Anderson, a Carlyle graduate of forty, a local boy who'd made the jump from town to gown and then coordinated both. Matlock called him at home and explained his problem. He was carrying around a large check from his father. He was making some private family investments in his own name, and they were confidential. Since the robbery at his apartment, he wanted to divest himself of the check immediately. Could Alex suggest anything? Should he put it in the mail? How best to get it into his account, since he wasn't sure he would be in Carlyle on Monday, and he needed it cleared, the money available. Alex Anderson suggested the obvious. Matlock should endorse the check, put it in an envelope marked for Anderson's attention, and drop it in the night deposit box at the bank. Alex would take care of the rest first thing Monday morning.

And then Alex Anderson asked him the denomination and Matlock told him.

The account problem solved, Matlock concentrated on what he began to think of as his point of departure. There was no other phrase he could find, and he needed a phrase—he needed the discipline of a definition. He had to start precisely right, knowing that what might follow could be totally *undisciplined*—completely without plan or orthodoxy. For he had made up his mind.

He was going to enter the world of Nimrod. The builder of Babylon and Nineveh, the hunter of wild animals, the killer of children and old men, the beater of women.

He was going to find Nimrod.

As were most adults not wedded to the precept that all things enjoyable were immoral, Matlock was aware that the state of Connecticut, like its sister states to the north, the south, and the west, was inhabited by a network of men only too eager to supply those divertissements frowned upon by the pulpits and the courts. What Hartford insurance executive in the upper brackets never heard of that string of "Antique Shoppes" on New Britain Avenue where a lithe young girl's body could be had for a reasonable amount of petty cash? What commuter from Old Greenwich was oblivious to the large estates north of Green Farms where the gambling often rivaled the Vegas stakes? How many tired businessmen's wives from New Haven or Westport were really ignorant of the various "escort" services operating out of Hamden and Fairfield? And over in the "old country," the Norfolks? Where the rambling mansions were fading apotheoses to the *real* money, the blooded first families who migrated just a little west to avoid the new rich? The "old country" had the strangest diversions, it was rumored. Houses in shadows, lighted by candles, where the bored could become aroused by observation. Voyeurs of the sickest scenes. Female, male, animal—all types, all combinations.

Matlock knew that in this world Nimrod could be found. It had to be. For although narcotics were but one aspect of the services rendered within this network, they were available—as was everything else.

And of all these games of indulgence, none had the fire and ice, none had the magnetism, of the gambling houses. For those thousands who couldn't find time for the junkets to San Juan, London, or Paradise Island, there were the temporary excursions into the manic moments where daily boredom could be forgotten—a stone's throw from home. Reputations were made quickly over the green felt tables—with the roll of the dice or a turn of a card. It was here that Matlock would find his point of departure. It was in these places where a young man of thirty-three years was prepared to lose thousands—until someone asked who he was.

At twelve thirty Matlock walked across the quadrangle toward his apartment. The time had come to initiate his first move. The vague outline of a plan was coming into focus.

He should have heard the footsteps, but he didn't. He only heard the cough, a smoker's cough, the cough of a man who'd been running.

"Mr. Matlock?"

Matlock turned and saw a man in his middle thirties, like himself, perhaps a bit older and, indeed, out of breath.

"Yes?"

"Sorry, I keep missing you. I got to the hospital just as you'd left, then waited in the wrong damn building for you, after your class. There's a very confused biology teacher with a name similar to yours. Even looks a little like you. Same height, build, hair . . ."

"That's Murdock. Elliott Murdock. What's the matter?"

"He couldn't understand why I kept insisting that when 'old men kill themselves, the cities are dying'!"

"You're from Greenberg!"

"That's it. Morbid code, if you don't mind my saying so. Keep walking. We'll separate at the end of the path. Meet me in twenty minutes at Bill's Bar & Grill by the freight depot. It's six blocks south of the railroad station. O.K.?"

"Never heard of it."

"I was going to suggest you remove your necktie. I'll be in a leather jacket."

"You pick classy spots."

"Old habit. I cheat on the expense account."

"Greenberg said I was to work with you."

"You better believe it! He's up to his Kosher ass in boiling oil for you. I think they're shipping him out to a job in Cairo. . . . He's one hell of a guy. We field men like him. Don't louse him up."

"All I wanted to ask was your name. I didn't expect a sermon."

"It's Houston. Fred Houston. See you in twenty minutes. Get rid of the tie."

17

Bill's Bar & Grill was a part of Carlyle Matlock had never seen before. Railroad laborers and freight-yard drifters were its predominant clientele. He scanned the filthy room; Houston sat in a back booth.

"It's cocktail hour, Matlock. A little early by campus standards, but the effects aren't much different. Not even the clothes these days."

"It's quite a place."

"It serves the purpose. Go up to the bar and get yourself a drink. The bunnies don't come on till sundown."

Matlock did as Houston instructed and brought back the best bourbon he could find. It was a brand he had given up when he reached a living wage.

"I think I should tell you right away. Someone using your name telephoned me at the hospital."

It was as if Houston had been hit in the stomach. "My God," he said quietly. "What did he say? How did you handle it?"

"I waited for him to identify himself . . . with Greenberg's proverb. I gave him a couple of chances but he didn't. . . . So I told him to call me later and hung up."

"He used *my* name?! *Houston.* You're sure?"

"Absolutely."

"That doesn't make sense. He *couldn't!*"

"Believe me. He did."

"No one knew I was the replacement. . . . *I* didn't know it until three this morning."

"Someone found out."

Houston took several swallows of his beer. "If what you say is true, I'll be out of here within a couple of hours. Incidentally, that was good thinking. . . . Let me give you an extra hint, though. Never accept a contact made by telephone."

"Why not?"

"If that *had* been me calling—how would *I* know it was *you* I was talking to?"

"I see what you mean. . . ."

"Common sense. Most everything we do is common sense. . . . We'll keep the same code. The 'old men' and 'the cities.' Your next contact will be made tonight."

"You're sure you'll be leaving?"

"I've been *spotted.* I'm not *about* to stick around. Maybe you forgot Ralph Loring. . . . We gave big at the office."

"All right. Have you talked to Jason? Did he brief you?"

"For two hours. From four till six this morning. My wife said he drank thirteen cups of coffee."

"What can you tell me about Pat? Patricia Ballantyne. What happened?"

"You know the medical facts. . . ."

"Not all of them."

"I don't know *all* of them, either."

"You're lying."

Houston looked at Matlock without offense. When he replied, he did so compassionately. "All right.

There was evidence of rape. That's what you want to know, isn't it?"

Matlock gripped his glass. "Yes," he said softly.

"However, you should know this, too. The girl doesn't know it. Not at this stage of her recovery. I understand the mind plays tricks. It rejects things until it thinks—or something tells it—that the remembering can be handled."

"Thanks for the lesson in psychology. . . . Animals. Filthy animals . . ." Matlock pushed his glass away. The liquor was intolerable to him now. The thought of dulling his senses even slightly was abhorrent.

"I'm supposed to play this by ear, so if I read you wrong, all I can do is apologize. . . . Be around when the puzzle gets put together for her. She's going to need you."

Matlock looked up from the table, from the sight of his tensed hands. "It was that bad?" he asked almost inaudibly.

"Preliminary lab tests—fingernails, hair, what have you—indicate that the assault was carried out by more than one person."

Matlock's hatred could find only one expression. He closed his eyes and lashed out at the glass, sending it across the floor, where it smashed in front of the bar. The bartender dropped his soiled rag and started toward his latch, looking over at the man who threw the glass. Then he stopped. Houston held up a bill quickly, gesturing the man to stay away.

"Get hold of yourself!" Houston said. "You're not going to do anyone any good like that. You're just calling attention to us. . . . Now, listen. You're cleared to make further inquiries, but there are two stipulations. The first is to check with our man—it was supposed to be me—before approaching anyone. The second—keep your subjects to students and only students. No faculty, no staff, no one outside—just students. . . . Make your reports every night between ten and eleven. Your contact will reach you daily as to where. Have you got that?"

Matlock stared at the agent in disbelief. He understood what the man was saying—even why he said it—but he couldn't believe that anyone who'd been briefed by Jason Greenberg would think he could deliver such instructions. "Are you serious?"

"The orders are explicit. No deviations. That's holy writ."

It was there again for Matlock. Another sign, another compromise. Another plastic order from the unseen plastic leaders.

"I'm there but I'm *not* there, is that the idea? I'm consigned to the outer limits and that fulfills the bargain?"

"Frig that."

Matlock's eyes wandered upward, at nothing. He was trying to buy a few seconds of sweet reason. "Frigga is the Norse goddess of the sky. She shares the heavens with Odin. Don't insult the lady, Houston."

"You're a nut!" said the agent. "I'm not sorry I'm getting out of here. . . . Look, it's for the best, take my word for it. And one last thing. I've got to take back the paper Loring gave you. That's a *must do.*"

"Is it, really?" Matlock slid across the filthy leatherette seat and started to get up. "I don't see it that way. You go back to Washington and tell them I see it as a *must don't.* Take care of yourself, holy writ."

"You're playing around with preventive custody!"

"We'll see who's playing," said Matlock as he pushed himself away from the table, angling it to block the agent's exit, and started for the door. He could hear the screech of the table's legs as Houston moved it out of his way. He heard Houston call his name softly, intensely, as if he were confused, wanting to make Matlock come back, yet afraid of identifying him. Matlock reached the door, turned right on the sidewalk, and started running as fast as he could. He found a narrow alley and realized that it was, at least, in the right direction. He raced into it and stopped, pressing himself into a doorway. At the base of the alley, on the freight-yard thoroughfare, he saw Houston walking rapidly past the phlegmatic noonday laborers on their lunch breaks. Houston looked panicked; Matlock knew he couldn't return to his apartment.

It was a funny thing to do, he considered, as he sat in the booth of Bill's Bar & Grill. Returning to the place he couldn't wait to get out of twenty minutes ago. But it made vague sense to him—as much as anything made sense at the moment. He had to be by himself and think. He couldn't take the chance of wandering the streets where some part of the Greenberg-Houston unseen army might spot him. Ironically, the bar seemed safest.

He'd made his apologies to a wary bartender, offering to pay for the broken glass. He implied that the man he'd had words with before was a deadbeat—into him for a lot of money with no ability to pay. This explanation, given by the now-relaxed customer, was not only accepted by the bartender, it elevated him to a status not often seen in Bill's Bar & Grill.

He had to marshal his thoughts. There were checkpoints he'd mentally outlined which were to be passed before he began his journey to Nimrod. Now, there was another checkpoint. Houston had supplied it, although he'd never know. Pat had to be totally safe. He couldn't have that worry on his mind. All other items on his list were subservient to this. The clothes, the ready cash, the unfamiliar automobile, all would have to wait. He might have to alter his strategy now, Matlock thought. Nimrod's associates would be watched, his apartment would be watched, every name and location on the Justice list would be under surveillance.

But first, Pat. He'd have her guarded night and day, around the clock, every minute. Guarded openly, with no pretense of secrecy. Guarded in such a way as to be a signal to both the unseen armies, a warning that she was out of the game. Money was no problem now, none at all. And there were men in Hartford whose professions would fit his requirements. He knew that. The huge insurance companies used them incessantly. He remembered an ex-faculty member from the math department who'd left Carlyle for the lucrative field of insurance actuaries. He worked for Aetna. He looked for a telephone inside the dingy bar.

Eleven minutes later, Matlock returned to the booth. The business was concluded with Blackstone Security, Incorporated, Bond Street, Hartford. There would be three men daily on eight-hour shifts, three hundred dollars for each twenty-four-hour period the subject was covered by Blackstone, Inc. There would, of course, be the additional charges for any expenses incurred and a fee attached for the use of a "Tel-electronic" if it was required. The Tel-electronic was a small device which signaled the bearer with short beeps if the telephone number designated was called. Blackstone, of course, suggested a different telephone number from a resident phone—which, of course, they would have activated within twelve hours and for which, of course, there was an additional charge.

Matlock agreed to everything, was grateful *for* everything, and said he'd be in Hartford to sign the papers later in the afternoon. He wanted to meet Mr. Blackstone—for another reason now. Blackstone, however, made it clear that since the head of Aetna's actuarial department had personally contacted him regarding Mr. Matlock, the formalities were not pressing. He'd dispatch his team to the Carlyle Hospital within the hour. And by any chance, was Mr. Matlock related to Jonathan Munro Matlock . . . ? The head of Aetna's actuarial department had mentioned . . .

Matlock was relieved. Blackstone *could* be useful. The ex-faculty member at Aetna had assured him that there was none better than Blackstone. Expensive, but the best. Blackstone's personnel for the most part were former officers of the Special Forces and Marine Intelligence team. It was more than a business gimmick. They were smart, resourceful, and tough. They were also licensed and respected by the state and local police.

The next item on his list was clothes. He had planned to go to his apartment and pack a suit, several pairs of slacks, and a jacket or two. Now that was out. At least for the time being. He would buy clothes—what he needed—as he went along. The ready cash could prove more of a problem, considering the amount he wanted. It was Saturday—he wasn't going to waste a Saturday night. The banks were closed, the large money sources unavailable.

Alex Anderson would have to solve the problem. He'd lie to Alex Anderson, tell him Jonathan Munro Matlock would look kindly—financially kindly—on

Anderson if the banker would made available a large sum of cash on a Saturday afternoon. It would be confidential on both sides, of course. There would be a gratuity rendered for a coveted favor on a Saturday afternoon. Nothing which could be construed remotely indelicate. And, of course, again, confidential.

Matlock rose from the ripped, stained, dirty leatherette seat and returned to the telephone.

Anderson had only fleeting doubts about accommodating Jonathan Munro Matlock's son, and they concerned not the act but the confidence of the act. Once that concern was allayed, the fact that he was giving aid in the best traditions of banking became clear. It was important for any bank to accommodate the better client. If a particular client wished to show gratitude . . . well, that was up to the client.

Alex Anderson would secure James Matlock five thousand dollars in cash on a Saturday afternoon. He would deliver it to him at three outside the Plaza Movie Theatre, which was showing a revival of *A Knife in the Water*—with subtitles.

An automobile would be the least of his problems. There were two rent-a-car offices in the town, a Budget-National and a Luxor-Elite. The first for students, the second for affluent parents. He would rent a Luxor Cadillac or Lincoln and drive into Hartford to another Luxor lot and change cars. From Hartford he'd go to a Luxor branch in New Haven and do the same. With money, there would be the minimum of questions; with decent tips, there might even be cooperation.

He'd moved to his point of departure.

"Hey, mister. Your name Matlock?" The hairy bartender leaned over the table, the soiled bar rag squeezed in his right hand.

"Yes," answered the startled Matlock with a short, violent intake of breath.

"Guy just came up t' me. Said for me to tell you you forgot something outside. On the curb, he said. You should hurry, he said."

Matlock stared at the man. The pain in his stomach was the fear again, the panic. He reached into his pocket and pulled out several bills. Separating a five, he held it up to the bartender. "Come to the door with me. Just to the window. Tell me if he's outside."

"Sure. . . . To the window." The hairy bartender switched the soiled rag to his left hand and took the bill. Matlock got out of the booth and walked beside the man to the half-curtained, filthy glass looking out on the street. "No, he's not there. There's no one there. . . . Just a dead . . ."

"I see," said Matlock, cutting the man off. He didn't have to go outside, it wasn't necessary.

Lying on the edge of the curb, its body draping down into the gutter, was Matlock's cat.

Its head was severed, held to the rest of its body by a small piece of flesh. The blood poured out, staining the sidewalk.

18

The killing preyed on Matlock's mind as he approached the West Hartford town line. Was it another warning or had they found the paper? If they *had* found the paper, it didn't vitiate the warning, only reinforced it. He wondered whether to have a member of the Blackstone team check his apartment, check the litter box. He wasn't even sure why he hesitated. Why not have a Blackstone man find out? For three hundred dollars a day, plus charges, such an errand was hardly too much to ask. He was going to ask far more of Blackstone, Incorporated, but they didn't know it. Yet he kept balking. If the paper *was* secure, sending a man to check it might reveal its location.

He'd almost made up his mind to take the chance when he noticed the tan sedan in his rear-view mirror. It was there again. It had been there, off and on, since he'd entered Highway 72 a half hour ago. Whereas other cars turned off, passed him, or fell behind, this tan sedan was never really out of sight. Weaving in and around the traffic, it always managed to stay three or four cars behind him. There was one way to find out if it was coincidence. Off the next exit into West Hartford was a narrow street which wasn't a street at all but a cobblestone alley used almost exclusively for deliveries. He and Pat thought it was a shortcut one hectic afternoon and had been hemmed in for five minutes.

He swung off the exit and down the main street toward the alley. He made a sharp left and entered the narrow cobblestone lane. Since it was Saturday afternoon, there were no delivery trucks, and the alley was clear. He raced through, emerging in a crowded A & P parking lot, which in turn led to a parallel main road. Matlock drove to an empty parking space, shut off his motor, and lowered himself on the seat. He angled his side-view mirror so that it reflected the entrance of the alley. In roughly thirty seconds, the tan sedan came into view.

The driver was obviously confused. He slowed down, looking at the dozens of automobiles. Suddenly, behind the tan sedan, another car began blowing its horn. The driver was impatient; the tan sedan was blocking his progress. Reluctantly, the driver of the tan sedan started up; but before he did, he turned his face, craning his neck over his right shoulder in such a way that Matlock, now looking directly at the automobile, recognized him.

It was the patrolman. The police officer who'd been in his demolished apartment after the Beeson episode, the man who had covered his face with a towel and raced down the corridor of squash alley two days ago.

Greenberg's "coincidence."

Matlock was perplexed. He was also frightened.

The patrolman in mufti drove the tan sedan haltingly toward a parking lot exit, still obviously searching. Matlock saw the car turn into the flow of traffic and drive away.

The offices of Blackstone Security, Incorporated, Bond Street, Hartford, looked more like a wealthy, sedate insurance company than an investigatory agency. The furniture was heavy colonial, the wallpaper a subdued, masculine stripe. Expensive hunting prints above the glow of brass table lamps. The effect was immediately one of strength, virility, and financial solidity. Why not? thought Matlock, as he sat in the Early American two-seater in the outer office. At three hundred dollars a day, Blackstone Security, Incorporated, probably rivaled Prudential in ratio of investment to profits.

When he was at last ushered into the office, Michael Blackstone rose from his chair and walked around the cherrywood desk to greet him. Blackstone was a short, compact man, neatly dressed. He was in his early fifties, obviously a physical person, very active, probably very tough.

"Good afternoon," he said. "I hope you didn't drive down here just for the papers. They could have waited. Just because *we* work seven days a week, doesn't mean we expect the rest of the world to do so."

"I had to be in Hartford, anyway. No problem."

"Sit down, sit down. Can I offer you anything? A drink? Coffee?"

"No thanks." Matlock sat in a huge black leather chair, the kind of chair usually found in the oldest, most venerated men's clubs. Blackstone returned to his desk. "Actually, I'm in somewhat of a hurry. I'd like to sign our agreement, pay you, and leave."

"Certainly. The file's right here." Blackstone picked up a folder on his desk and smiled. "As I mentioned on the phone, there are questions we'd like answered, of course. Beyond what you've instructed us to do. It would help us carry out your orders. Take just a few minutes."

Matlock expected the request. It was part of his plan, why he wanted to see Blackstone. His assumption—once Blackstone entered the picture—was that Blackstone might be able to offer him shortcuts. Perhaps not willingly, but if it was a question of "an additional charge." . . . It was for this reason that he had to meet Blackstone face to face. If Blackstone could be bought, a great deal of time could be saved.

"I'll answer what I can. As I'm sure you've checked out, the girl was beaten severely."

"We know that. What puzzles us is the reluctance of anyone to say why. No one's given that sort of beating for kicks. Oh, it's possible, but that kind of case is generally handled quickly and efficiently by the police. There's no need for us. . . . Obviously you have information the police don't have."

"That's true. I do."

"May I ask why you haven't given it to them? Why you hired us? . . . The local police will gladly furnish protection if there's sufficient cause, and far less expensively."

"You sound like you're turning away business."

"We often do." Blackstone smiled. "It's never done happily, I can tell you that."

"Then why . . ."

"You're a highly recommended client," interrupted Blackstone, "the son of a very prominent man. We want you to know your alternatives. That's our reasoning. What's yours?"

"You're plainspoken. I appreciate it. I assume what you're saying is that you don't want your reputation tarnished."

"That's good enough."

"Good. That's my reasoning, too. Only it's not *my* reputation. It's the girl's. Miss Ballantyne's. . . . The simplest way to put it is that she showed bad judgment in her choice of friends. She's a brilliant girl with an exciting future, but unfortunately that intelligence didn't carry over into other areas." Matlock purposely stopped and took out a pack of cigarettes. Unhurriedly, he removed one and lit it. The pause had its effect. Blackstone spoke.

"Did she profit financially from these associations?"

"Not at all. As I see it, she was used. But I can understand why you asked. There's a lot of money to be made on campuses these days, isn't there?"

"I wouldn't know. Campuses aren't our field." Blackstone smiled again, and Matlock knew he was lying. Professionally, of course.

"I guess not."

"All right, Mr. Matlock. Why was she beaten? And what do you intend to do about it?"

"It's my opinion she was beaten to frighten her from revealing information *she doesn't have*. I intend to find the parties involved and tell them that. Tell them to leave her alone."

"And if you go to the police, her associations—past associations, I assume—become a matter of record and jeopardize this brilliant future of hers."

"Exactly."

"That's a tight story. . . . Who are these parties involved?"

"I don't know them by name. . . . However, I know their occupations. The main line of work seems to be gambling. I thought you might be able to help me here. Naturally, I would expect an additional charge for the service."

"I see." Blackstone got up and walked around his chair. For no particular reason, he fingered the dials on his inoperative air conditioner. "I think you presume too much."

"I wouldn't expect names. I'd like them, of course, and I'd pay well for them. . . . But I'd settle for locations. I can find them myself, and you know I can. You'd be saving me time, though."

"I gather you're interested in . . . private clubs. *Private* social organizations where members may meet to pursue activities of their choice."

"Outside the eye of the law. Where private citizens can follow their perfectly natural inclinations to place bets. That's where I'd like to start."

"Could I dissuade you? Is it possible I could convince you to go to the police, instead?"

"No."

Blackstone walked to a file cabinet on the left wall, took out a key, and opened it. "As I said, a tight story. Very plausible. And I don't believe a word of it. . . . However, you seem determined; that concerns me." He took a thin metal case from the file cabinet and carried it back to the desk. Selecting another key from his chain, he unlocked it and withdrew a single sheet of paper. "There's a Xerox machine over there," he said, pointing to a large gray copier in the corner. "To use it one places a page face down under the metal flap and dials the required duplicates. Records are kept of the numbers automatically. There's rarely a reason for more than one. . . . If you'll excuse me for approximately two minutes, Mr. Matlock, I must make a phone call in another office."

Blackstone held up the single sheet of paper, then placed it face down on top of Matlock's file folder. He stood erect, and, with the fingers of both hands, tugged at the base of his jacket in the manner of a man used to displaying expensive suits. He smiled and walked around his desk toward the office door. He opened it and turned back.

"It may be what you're looking for, and then again, it may not. I wouldn't know. I've simply left a confidential memorandum on my desk. The charge will be listed on your billing as . . . additional surveillance."

He went out the door, closing it firmly behind him. Matlock rose from the black leather chair and crossed behind the desk. He turned the paper over and read the typed heading.

FOR SURVEILLANCE: HARTFORD—NEW HAVEN AXIS
PRIVATE CLUBS: LOCATIONS AND CONTACTS (MANAGERS)
AS OF 3—15. NOT TO BE REMOVED FROM OFFICE

Beneath the short, capitalized paragraph were twenty-odd addresses and names.

Nimrod was closer now.

19

The Luxor-Elite Rental Agency on Asylum Street, Hartford, had been cooperative. Matlock now drove a Cadillac convertible. The manager had accepted the explanation that the Lincoln was too funereal, and since the registration papers were in order, the switch was perfectly acceptable.

So was the twenty-dollar tip.

Matlock had analyzed Blackstone's list carefully. He decided to concentrate on the clubs northwest of Hartford for the simple reason that they were nearer the Carlyle area. They weren't the nearest, however. Two locations were within five and seven miles of Carlyle respectively—in opposite directions—but Matlock decided to hold them off for a day or so. By the time he reached them—if he did so—he wanted the managements to know he was a heavy plunger. Not a mark, just heavy. The network gossip would take care of that—if he handled himself properly.

He checked off his first location. It was a private swimming club west of Avon. The contact was a man named Jacopo Bartolozzi.

At nine thirty Matlock drove up the winding driveway to a canopy extending from the entrance of the Avon Swim Club. A uniformed doorman signaled a parking attendant, who appeared out of nowhere and slid into the driver's seat the moment Matlock stepped onto the pavement. Obviously no parking ticket was to be given.

As he walked toward the entrance, he looked at the exterior of the club. The main building was a sprawling, one-story white brick structure with a tall stockade fence extending from both ends into the darkness. On the right, quite far behind the fence, was the iridescent glow of greenish blue light and the sound of water splashing. On the left was a huge tent-like canopy under which could be seen the shimmering light of dozens of patio torches. The former was obviously an enormous pool, the latter some kind of dining area. Soft music could be heard.

The Avon Swim Club appeared to be a very luxurious complex.

The interior did nothing to dispel this observation. The foyer was thickly carpeted and the various chairs and odd tables against the damask walls seemed genuine antiques. On the left was a large checkroom, and further down on the right was a white marble counter not unlike a hotel information desk. At the end of the narrow lobby was the only incongruous structure. It was a black, ornate wrought-iron gate, and it was closed, obviously locked. Beyond the grilled enclosure could be seen an open-air corridor, subtly lit, with an extended covering supported by a series of thin Ionic pillars. A large man in a tuxedo was standing at attention behind the iron gate.

Matlock approached him.

"Your membership card, sir?"

"I'm afraid I don't have one."

"Sorry, sir, this is a private swimming club. Members only."

"I was told to ask for Mr. Bartolozzi."

The man behind the grill stared at Matlock, frisking him with his eyes.

"You'd better check the front desk, sir. Right over there."

Matlock walked back to the counter, to be greeted by a middle-aged, slightly paunchy desk clerk who had not been there when he first came in.

"May I help you?"

"You may. I'm fairly new in the area. I'd like to become a member."

"We're sorry. Membership's full right now. However, if you'll fill out an application, we'll be glad to call you if there's an opening. . . . Would that be a family application or individual, sir?" The clerk, very professionally, reached below the counter and brought up two application forms.

"Individual. I'm not married. . . . I was told to ask for Mr. Bartolozzi. I was told specifically to ask for him. Jacopo Bartolozzi."

The clerk gave the name only the slightest indication of recognition. "Here, fill out an application and I'll put it on Mr. Bartolozzi's desk. He'll see it in the morning. Perhaps he'll call you, but I don't know what he can do. Membership's full and there's a waiting list."

"Isn't he here now? On such a busy night?" Matlock said the words with a degree of incredulity.

"I doubt it, sir."

"Why don't you find out? Tell him we have mutual friends in San Juan." Matlock withdrew his money clip and removed a fifty-dollar bill. He placed it in front of the clerk, who looked at him sharply and slowly picked up the money.

"San Juan?"

"San Juan."

Matlock leaned against the white marble counter and saw the man behind the wrought-iron gate watching him. If the San Juan story worked and he got through the gate, he realized that he would have to part with another large-sized bill. The San Juan story *should* work, thought Matlock. It was logical to the point of innocence. He had spent a winter vacation in Puerto Rico two years ago, and although no gambler, he'd traveled with a crowd—and a girl—who made the nightly rounds of the casinos. He'd met a number of people from the Hartford vicinity, although he couldn't for the life of him remember a single name.

A foursome emerged from inside the grilled entrance, the girls giggling, the men laughing resignedly. The women had probably won twenty or thirty dollars, thought Matlock, while the men had probably lost several hundred. Fair exchange for the evening. The gate closed behind them; Matlock could hear the electric click of the latch. It was a very well-locked iron gate.

"Excuse me, sir?" It was the paunchy desk clerk, and Matlock turned around.

"Yes?"

"If you'll step inside, Mr. Bartolozzi will see you."

"Where? How?" There was no door except the wrought-iron gate and the clerk had gestured with his left hand, away from the gate.

"Over here, sir."

Suddenly a knobless, frameless panel to the right of the counter swung open. The outline was barely discernible when the panel was flush against the damask wall; when shut, no border was in evidence. Matlock walked in and was taken by the clerk to the office of Jacopo Bartolozzi.

"We got mutual friends?" The obese Italian spoke hoarsely as he leaned back in his chair behind the desk. He made no attempt to rise, gave no gesture of welcome. Jacopo Bartolozzi was a short, squat caricature of himself. Matlock couldn't be sure, but he had the feeling that Bartolozzi's feet weren't touching the floor beneath his chair.

"It amounts to the same thing, Mr. Bartolozzi."

"What amounts? Who's in San Juan?"

"Several people. One fellow's a dentist in West Hartford. Another's got an accounting firm in Constitution Plaza."

"Yeah. . . . Yeah?" Bartolozzi was trying to associate people with the professions and locations Matlock described. "What's the names? They members here?"

"I guess they are. They gave me *your* name."

"This is a swim club. Private membership. . . . Who are they?"

"Look, Mr. Bartolozzi, it was a crazy night at the Condado casino. We all had a lot to drink and . . ."

"They don't drink in the Puerto Rican casinos. It's a law!" The Italian spoke sharply, proud of his incisive knowledge. He was pointing his fat finger at Matlock.

"More honored in the breach, believe me."

"What?"

"We drank. Take my word for it. I'm just telling you I don't remember their names. . . . Look, I can go downtown on Monday and stand all day outside the Plaza and I'll find the CPA. I could also go out to West Hartford and ring every dentist's doorbell. What difference does it make? I like to play and I've got the money."

Bartolozzi smiled. "This is a swim club. I don't know what the hell you're talking about."

"O.K.," said Matlock with a disgruntled edge to his voice. "This place happened to be convenient, but if you want to show three lemons, there are others. My San Juan friends also told me about Jimmy Lacata's down in Middletown, and Sammy Sharpe's in Windsor Shoals. . . . Keep your chips, fink." He turned to the door.

"Hold it! Wait a minute!"

Matlock watched the fat Italian get out of the chair and stand up. He'd been right. Bartolozzi's feet couldn't have been touching the floor.

"What for? Maybe your limit's too small here."

"You know Lacata? Sharpe?"

"Know *of* them, I told you. . . . Look, forget it. You've got to be careful. I'll find my CPA on Monday and we'll both come back some other time. . . . I just felt like playing tonight."

"O.K. O.K. Like you said, we gotta be careful." Bartolozzi opened his top drawer and pulled out some papers. "C'mere. Sign 'em. You got an itch. Maybe I'll take your money. Maybe you'll take mine."

Matlock approached the desk. "What am I signing?"

"Just a couple of forms. Initiation's five hundred. Cash. You got it? No checks, no credit."

"I've got it. What are the forms?"

"The first is a statement that you understand that this is a nonprofit corporation and that any games of chance are for charitable purposes. . . . What are you laughing at? I built the Church of the Blessed Virgin down in Hamden."

"What's this other? It's a long one."

"That's for our files. A certificate of general partnership. For the five hundred you get a classy title. You're a partner. Everybody's a partner. . . . Just in case."

"In case?"

"In case anything good happens to us, it happens just as good to you. Especially in the newspapers."

The Avon Swim Club was certainly a place for swimming, no doubt about it. The enormous pool curved back nearly two hundred feet, and scores of small, elegant cabanas bordered the far side. Beach chairs and tables were dotted about the grassy edges beyond the tiled deck of the pool, and the underwater floodlights made the setting inviting. All this was on the right of the open-air corridor. On the left, Matlock could see fully what was only hinted at from the outside. A huge green-and-white-striped tent rose above dozens of tables. Each table had a candled lantern in the center, and patio torches were safely placed about the whole enclosure. At the far end was a long table filled with roasts, salads, and buffet food. A bar was adjacent to the long table; scores of couples were milling about.

The Avon Swim Club was a lovely place to bring the family.

The corridor led to the rear of the complex, where there was another sprawling, white-bricked structure similar to the main building. Above the large, black-enameled double doors was a wooden sign, in old English scroll:

The Avon Spa

This part of the Avon Swim Club was not a lovely place to bring the family.

Matlock thought he was back in a San Juan casino—his only experience in gambling rooms. The wall-to-wall carpet was sufficiently thick to muffle sound almost completely. Only the click of the chips and the low-keyed but intense mutterings of the players and the board men were heard. The craps tables were lined along the walls, the blackjack counters in the center. In between, in staggered positions to allow for the flow of traffic, were the roulette wheels. In the middle of the large room, raised on a platform, was the cashier's nest. All of the Avon Spa's employees were in tuxedos, neatly groomed and subservient. The players were less formal.

The gate man, pleased with Matlock's crisp fifty-dollar bill, led him to the half-circle counter in front of the cashier's platform. He spoke to a man counting out slips of paper.

"This is Mr. Matlock. Treat him good, he's a personal friend."

"No other way," said the man with a smile.

"I'm sorry, Mr. Matlock," muttered the gate man quietly. "No markers the first time around."

"Naturally. . . . Look, I'm going to wander about. . . ."

"Sure. Get the feel of the action. . . . I tell you, it ain't Vegas. Between you and me, it's Mickey Mouse most of the time. I mean for a guy like you, you know what I mean?"

Matlock knew exactly what the gate man meant. A fifty-dollar bill was not the ordinary gratuity in Avon, Connecticut.

It took him three hours and twelve minutes to lose $4,175. The only time he felt panic was when he had a streak at the craps table and had built up his reserves to nearly $5,000. He had begun the evening properly—for his purposes. He went to the cashier often enough to realize that the average purchase of chips was $200 to $300. Hardly "Mickey Mouse" in his book. So his first purchase was $1,500. The second was $1,000; the third, $2,000.

By one in the morning, he was laughing with Jacopo Bartolozzi at the bar underneath the green-and-white-striped tent.

"You're a game one. Lots'a creeps would be screaming 'ice pick' if they went for a bundle like you did. Right now I'd be showing them a few papers in my office."

"Don't you worry, I'll get it back. I always do. . . . You said it before. My itch was too much. Maybe I'll come back tomorrow."

"Make it Monday. Tomorrow it's only swimming."

"How come?"

"Sunday. Holy day."

"Shit! I've got a friend coming in from London. He won't be here Monday. He's a big player."

"Tell you what. I'll call Sharpe over in Windsor Shoals. He's a Jew. Holy days don't mean a fucking thing to him."

"I'd appreciate that."

"I may even drop over myself. The wife's got a Mothers of Madonna meeting, anyway."

Matlock looked at his watch. The evening—his point of departure—had gone well. He wondered if he should press his luck. "Only real problem coming into a territory is the time it takes to find the sources."

"What's your problem?"

"I've got a girl over in the motel. She's sleeping, we

traveled most of the day. She ran out of grass—no hard stuff—just grass. I told her I'd pick some up for her."

"Can't help you, Matlock. I don't keep none here, what with the kids around during the day. It's not good for the image, see? A few pills, I got. No needle crap, though. You want some pills?"

"No, just grass. That's all I let her use."

"Very smart of you. . . . Which way you headed?"

"Back into Hartford."

Bartolozzi snapped his fingers. A large bartender sprang into position instantly. Matlock thought there was something grotesque about the squat little Italian commandeering in such fashion. Bartolozzi asked the man for paper and pencil.

"Here. Here's an address. I'll make a phone call. It's an afterhours place right off the main drag. Down the street from G. Fox. Second floor. Ask for Rocco. What you couldn't use, he's got."

"You're a prince." And as Matlock took the paper, he meant it.

"For four grand the first night, you got privileges. . . . Hey, y'know what? You never filled out an application! That's a gas, huh?"

"You don't need credit references. I play with cash."

"Where the hell do you keep it?"

"In thirty-seven banks from here to Los Angeles." Matlock put down his glass and held out his hand to Bartolozzi. "It's been fun. See you tomorrow?"

"Sure, sure. I'll walk you to the door. Don't forget now. Don't give Sammy all the action. Come on back here."

"My word on it."

The two men walked back to the open-air corridor,

the short Italian placing his fat hand in the middle of Matlock's back, the gesture of a new friend. What neither man realized as they stepped onto the narrow causeway was that one well-dressed gentleman at a nearby table who kept punching at a fluidless lighter was watching them. As the two men passed his table, he put his lighter back into his pocket while the woman across from him lit his cigarette with a match. The woman spoke quietly through a smile.

"Did you get them?"

The man laughed softly. "Karsh couldn't have done better. Even got close-ups."

20

If the Avon Swim Club was an advantageous point of departure, the Hartford Hunt Club—under the careful management of Rocco Aiello—was an enviable first lap. For Matlock now thought of his journey to Nimrod as a race, one which had to end within two weeks and one day. It would end with the convocation of the Nimrod forces and the Mafiosi somewhere in the Carlyle vicinity. It would be finished for him when someone, somewhere produced another silver Corsican paper.

Bartolozzi's telephone call was effective. Matlock entered the old red stone building—at first he thought he had the wrong address, for no light shone through the windows, and there was no sign of activity within—and found a freight elevator at the end of the hallway with a lone Negro operator sitting in a chair in front of the door. No sooner had he come in than the black rose to his feet and indicated the elevator to Matlock.

In an upstairs hallway a man greeted him. "Very nice to make your acquaintance. Name's Rocco. Rocco Aiello." The man held out his hand and Matlock took it.

"Thanks. . . . I was puzzled. I didn't hear anything. I thought maybe I was in the wrong place."

"If you had heard, the construction boys would have taken me. The walls are eighteen inches thick, sound-proofed both sides; the windows are blinds. Very secure."

"That's really something."

Rocco reached into his pocket and withdrew a small wooden cigarette case. "I got a box of joints for you. No charge. I'd like to show you around, but Jock-O said you might be in a hurry."

"Jock-O's wrong. I'd like to have a drink."

"Good! Come on in. . . . Only one thing, Mr. Matlock. I got a nice clientele, you know what I mean? Very rich, very cube. Some of them know about Jock-O's operation, most of them don't. You know what I mean?"

"I understand. I was never much for swimming anyway."

"Good, good. . . . Welcome to Hartford's finest." He opened the thick steel door. "I hear you went for a bundle tonight."

Matlock laughed as he walked into the complex of dimly lit rooms crowded with tables and customers. "Is that what it's called?"

"In Connecticut, that's what it's called. . . . See? I got two floors—a duplex, like. Each floor's got five big rooms, a bar in each room. Very private, no bad behavior. Nice place to bring the wife, or somebody else, you know what I mean?"

"I think I do. It's quite something."

"The waiters are mostly college boys. I like to help them make a few dollars for their education. I got niggers, spics, kikes—I got no discrimination. Just the hair, I don't go for the long hair, you know what I mean?"

"College kids! Isn't that dangerous? Kids talk."

"Hey, what d'you think?! This place was originally started by a Joe College. It's like a fraternity home. Everybody's a bona fide, dues-paying member of a private organization. They can't getcha for that."

"I see. What about the other part?"

"What other part?"

"What I came for."

"What? A little grass? Try the corner newsstand."

Matlock laughed. He didn't want to overdo it. "Two points, Rocco. . . . Still, if I knew you better, maybe I'd like to make a purchase. Bartolozzi said what I couldn't use, you've got. . . . Forget it, though. I'm bushed. I'll just get a drink and shove off. The girl's going to wonder where I've been."

"Sometimes Bartolozzi talks too much."

"I think you're right. By the way, he's joining me tomorrow night at Sharpe's over in Windsor Shoals. I've got a friend flying in from London. Care to join us?"

Aiello was obviously impressed. The players from London were beginning to take precedence over the Vegas and Caribbean boys. Sammy Sharpe's wasn't that well known, either.

"Maybe I'll do that. . . . Look, you need something, you feel free to ask, right?"

"I'll do that. Only I don't mind telling you, the kids make me nervous."

Aiello took Matlock's elbow with his left hand and walked him toward the bar. "You got it wrong. These kids—they're not kids, you know what I mean?"

"No, I don't. Kids are kids. I like my action a little more subdued. No sweat. I'm not curious." Matlock looked up at the bartender and withdrew what was left of his bankroll. He removed a twenty-dollar bill and placed it on the bar. "Old Fitz and water, please."

"Put your money away," Rocco said.

"Mr. Aiello?" A young man in a waiter's jacket approached them. He was perhaps twenty-two or twenty-three, Matlock thought.

"Yeah?"

"If you'll sign this tab. Table eleven. It's the Johnsons. From Canton. They're O.K."

Aiello took the waiter's pad and scribbled his initials. The young man walked back toward the tables.

"See that kid? That's what I mean. He's a Yalie. He got back from Nam six months ago."

"So?"

"He was a lieutenant. An officer. Now he's studying business administration. . . . He fills in here maybe twice a week. Mostly for contacts. By the time he gets out, he'll have a real nest egg. Start his own business."

"What?"

"He's a supplier. . . . These kids, that's what I mean. You should hear their stories. Saigon, Da Nang. Hong Kong, even. Real peddling. Hey, these kids today, they're great! They know what's up. Smart, too. No worries, believe me!"

"I believe you." Matlock took his drink and swallowed quickly. It wasn't that he was thirsty, he was trying to conceal his shock at Aiello's revelation. The graduates of Indochina were not the pink-cheeked, earnest, young-old veterans of Armentières, Anzio, or even Panmunjom. They were something else, something faster, sadder, infinitely more knowing. A hero in Indochina was the soldier who had contacts on the docks and in the warehouses. That man in Indochina was the giant among his peers. And such young-old men were almost all back.

Matlock drank the remainder of his bourbon and

let Rocco show him the other rooms on the third floor. He displayed the controlled appreciation Aiello expected and promised he'd return. He said no more about Sammy Sharpe's in Windsor Shoals. He knew it wasn't necessary. Aiello's appetite had been whetted.

As he drove away, two thoughts occupied his mind. Two objectives had to be accomplished before Sunday afternoon was over. The first was that he had to produce an Englishman; the second was that he had to produce another large sum of money. It was imperative that he have both. He had to be at Sharpe's in Windsor Shoals the next evening.

The Englishman he had in mind lived in Webster, an associate professor of mathematics at a small parochial campus, Madison University. He had been in the country less than two years; Matlock had met him—quite unprofessionally—at a boat show in Saybrook. The Britisher had lived on the Cornwall coast most of his life and was a sailing enthusiast. Matlock and Pat had liked him immediately. Now Matlock hoped to God that John Holden knew something about gambling.

The moncy was a more serious problem. Alex Anderson would have to be tapped again, and it was quite possible that he'd find enough excuses to put him off. Anderson was a cautious man, easily frightened. On the other hand, he had a nose for rewards. That instinct would have to be played upon.

Holden had seemed startled but not at all annoyed by Matlock's telephone call. If he was anything other than kind, it was curious. He repeated the directions to his apartment twice and Matlock thanked him, assuring him that he remembered the way.

"I'll be perfectly frank, Jim," said Holden, admitting Matlock into his neat three-room apartment. "I'm simply bursting. Is anything the matter? Is Patricia all right?"

"The answers are yes and no. I'll tell you everything I can, which won't be a hell of a lot. . . . I want to ask you a favor, though. Two favors, actually. The first, can I stay here tonight?"

"Of course—you needn't ask. You look peaked. Come, sit down. Can I get you a drink?"

"No, no thanks." Matlock sat on Holden's sofa. He remembered that it was one of those hide-a-beds and that it was comfortable. He and Pat had slept in it one happy, alcoholic night several months ago. It seemed ages ago.

"What's the second favor? The first is my pleasure. If it's cash, I've something over a thousand. You're entirely welcome to it."

"No, not money, thanks just the same. . . . I'd like you to impersonate an Englishman for me."

Holden laughed. He was a small-boned man of forty, but he laughed the way older, fatter men laughed.

"That shouldn't be too demanding, now should it? I suspect there's still a trace of Cornwall in my speech. Hardly noticeable, of course."

"Hardly. With a little practice you may even lose the Yankee twang. . . . There's something else, though, and it may not be so easy. Have you ever gambled?"

"Gambled? You mean horses, football matches?"

"Cards, dice, roulette?"

"Not substantially, no. Of course, as any reasonably imaginative mathematician, I went through a phase when I thought that by applying arithmetical principles—logarithmic averages—one could beat the gambling odds."

"Did they work?"

"I said I went through the phase, I didn't stay there. If there's a mathematical system, it eluded me. Still does."

"But you've played? You know the games."

"Rather well, when you come right down to it. Laboratory research, you might say. Why?"

Matlock repeated the story he had told Blackstone. However, he minimized Pat's injuries and lightened the motives of those who assaulted her. When he finished, the Englishman, who'd lit his pipe, knocked the ashes out of the bowl into a large glass ashtray.

"It's right out of the cinema, isn't it? . . . You say Patricia's not seriously hurt. Frightened but nothing much more than that?"

"Right. If I went to the police it might louse up her scholarship money."

"I see. . . . Well, I don't really, but we'll let it go. And you'd rather I lost tomorrow night."

"That doesn't matter. Just that you bet a great deal."

"But you're *prepared* for heavy losses."

"I am."

Holden stood up. "I'm perfectly willing to go through with this performance. It should prove rather a lark. However, there's a great deal you're not telling me and I wish you would. But I shan't insist upon it. I will tell you that your story is boggled with a large mathematical inconsistency."

"What's that?"

"As I understand it, the money you are prepared to lose tomorrow evening is far in excess of any amount Patricia might realize in scholarship aid. The logical assumption, therefore, is that you do not wish to go to the police. Or perhaps, you can't."

Matlock looked up at the Englishman and wondered at his own stupidity. He felt embarrassed and very inadequate. "I'm sorry. . . . I haven't consciously lied to you. You don't have to go through with it; maybe I shouldn't have asked."

"I never implied that you lied—not that it matters. Only that there was much you haven't told me. Of course, I'll do it. I just want you to know I'm a willing audience when and if you decide to tell me everything that's happened. . . . Now, it's late and you're tired. Why don't you take my room."

"No, thanks. I'll sack out here. It has pleasant memories. A blanket's all I need. Also I have to make a phone call."

"Anything you say. A blanket you'll get, and you know where the phone is."

When Holden left, Matlock went to the phone. The Tel-electronic device he'd agreed to lease would not be ready until Monday morning.

"Blackstone."

"This is James Matlock. I was told to call this number for any messages."

"Yes, Mr. Matlock. There is a message, if you'll hold on while I get the card. . . . Here it is. From the Carlyle team. Everything is secure. The subject is responding nicely to medical treatment. The subject had three visitors. A Mr. Samuel Kressel, a Mr. Adrian Sealfont, and a Miss Lois Meyers. The subject received two telephone calls, neither of which the physician allowed to be taken. They were from the same individual, a Mr. Jason Greenberg. The calls were from Wheeling, West Virginia. At no time was the subject separated from the Carlyle team. . . . You can relax."

"Thank you. I will. You're very thorough. Good night." Matlock breathed deeply in relief and exhaustion. Lois Meyers lived across the hall from Pat in the graduate apartment house. The fact that Greenberg had called was comforting. He missed Greenberg.

He reached up and turned off the table lamp by the sofa. The bright April moon shone through the windows. The man from Blackstone's service was right—he could relax.

What he couldn't allow to relax were his thoughts about tomorrow—and after tomorrow. Everything had to remain accelerated; one productive day had to lead into another. There could be no letup, no sense of momentary satisfaction which might slow his thrust.

And after tomorrow. After Sammy Sharpe's in Windsor Shoals. If all went according to his calculations, it would be the time to head into the Carlyle area. Matlock closed his eyes and saw Blackstone's printed page in front of his mind.

CARMOUNT COUNTRY CLUB—CONTACT: HOWARD STOCKTON

WEST CARLYLE SAIL AND SKI RESORT—CONTACT: ALAN CANTOR

Carmount was east of Carlyle near the border of Mount Holly. The Sail and Ski was west, on Lake Derron—a summer and winter resort area.

He'd find some reason to have Bartolozzi or Aiello, or, perhaps, Sammy Sharpe, make the proper introductions. And once in the Carlyle area, he would drop the hints. Perhaps more than hints—commands, requirements, necessities. This was the boldness he needed to use, this was the way of Nimrod.

His eyes remained closed, the muscles in his body sagged, and the pitch darkness of exhausted sleep came over him. But before sleeping he remembered the paper. The Corsican paper. He had to get the paper now. He would need the silver paper. He would need the invitation to Nimrod.

His invitation now. His paper.

The Matlock paper.

21

If the elders at the Windsor Shoals Congregational Church had ever realized that Samuel Sharpe, attorney at law, the very bright Jewish lawyer who handled the church's finances, was referred to as Sammy the Runner by most of North Hartford and South Springfield, Massachusetts, vespers would have been canceled for a month. Fortunately, such a revelation had never been made to them and the Congregational Church looked favorably on him. He had done remarkable things for the church's portfolio and gave handsomely himself during fund drives. The Congregational Church of Windsor Shoals, as indeed most of the town, was nicely disposed toward Samuel Sharpe.

Matlock learned all of this in Sharpe's office inside the Windsor Valley Inn. The framed citations on the wall told half the story, and Jacopo Bartolozzi good-naturedly supplied the rest. Jacopo was actually making sure that Matlock and his English friend were aware that Sharpe's operation, as well as Sharpe himself, lacked the fine traditions of the Avon Swim Club.

Holden surpassed Matlock's expectations. Several times he nearly laughed out loud as he watched Holden take hundred-dollar bills—rushed into Webster by a harassed, nervous Alex Anderson—and flick them nonchalantly at a croupier, never bothering to count the chips but somehow letting everyone at whatever table he was at realize that he knew—to the dollar—the amount given him. Holden played intelligently, cautiously, and at one point was ahead of the house by nine thousand dollars. By the end of the evening, he had cut his winnings to several hundred and the operators of the Windsor Valley breathed grateful sighs of relief.

James Matlock cursed his second night of terrible luck and took his twelve-hundred-dollar loss for what it meant to him—nothing.

At four in the morning Matlock and Holden, flanked by Aiello, Bartolozzi, Sharpe, and two of their cronies, sat at a large oak table in the colonial dining room. They were alone. A waiter and two busboys were cleaning up; the gambling rooms on the third floor of the inn had closed.

The husky Aiello and the short, fat Bartolozzi kept up a running commentary about their respective clientele, each trying to upstage the other with regard to their customers' status; each allowing that "it might be nice" for the other to become "acquainted" with a Mr. and Mrs. Johnson of Canton or a certain Dr. Wadsworth. Sharpe, on the other hand, seemed more interested in Holden and the action in England. He told several funny, self-effacing stories about his visits to London clubs and his insurmountable difficulty with British currency in the heat of betting.

Matlock thought, as he watched Sammy Sharpe, that he was a very charming man. It wasn't hard to believe that Sharpe was considered a respectable asset to Windsor Shoals, Connecticut. He couldn't help comparing Sharpe to Jason Greenberg. And in the comparison, he found an essential difference. It was told in the eyes. Greenberg's were soft and compassionate, even in anger. Sharpe's were cold, hard, incessantly darting—strangely in conflict with the rest of his relaxed face.

He heard Bartolozzi ask Holden where he was off to next. Holden's offhand reply gave him the opportunity he was looking for. He waited for the right moment.

"I'm afraid I'm not at liberty to discuss my itinerary."

"He means where he's going," injected Rocco Aiello.

Bartolozzi shot Aiello a withering glance. "I just thought you should drop over to Avon. I got a real nice place I think you'd enjoy."

"I'm sure I would. Perhaps another time."

"Johnny'll be in touch with me next week," Matlock said. "We'll get together." He reached for an ashtray and crushed out his cigarette. "I have to be in . . . Carlyle, that's the name of the place."

There was the slightest pause in the conversation. Sharpe, Aiello, and one of the other two men exchanged looks. Bartolozzi, however, seemed oblivious to any deep meaning.

"The college place?" asked the short Italian.

"That's right," answered Matlock. "I'll probably stay at Carmount or the Sail and Ski. I guess you fellows know where they are."

"I guess we do." Aiello laughed softly.

"What's your business in Carlyle?" The unidentified man—at least no one had bothered to introduce him by name—drew deeply on a cigar as he spoke.

"*My* business," said Matlock pleasantly.

"Just asking. No offense."

"No offense taken. . . . Hey, it's damned near four thirty! You fellows are too hospitable." Matlock pushed his chair back, prepared to stand.

The man with the cigar, however, had to ask another question.

"Is your friend going to Carlyle with you?"

Holden held up his hand playfully. "Sorry, no itineraries. I'm simply a visitor to your pleasant shores and filled with a tourist's plans. . . . We really must go."

Both men rose from the table. Sharpe stood, too. Before the others could move, Sharpe spoke.

"I'll see the boys to their car and show them the road out. You fellows wait here—we'll settle accounts. I owe you money, Rocco. Frank owes me. Maybe I'll come out even."

The man with the cigar, whose name was obviously Frank, laughed. Aiello looked momentarily perplexed but within seconds grasped the meaning of Sharpe's statement. The men at the table were to remain.

Matlock wasn't sure he'd handled the situation advantageously.

He had wanted to pursue the Carlyle discussion just enough to have someone offer to make the necessary calls to Carmount and the Sail and Ski. Holden's refusal to speak about his itinerary precluded it, and Matlock was afraid that it also implied that he and Holden were so important that further introductions were unnecessary. In addition, Matlock realized that as his journey progressed, he banked more and more on the dead Loring's guarantee that none of those invited to the Carlyle conference would discuss delegates among themselves. The meaning of "Omerta" was supposedly so powerful that silence was inviolate. Yet Sharpe had just commanded those at the table to remain.

He had the feeling that perhaps he had gone too far with too little experience. Perhaps it was time to reach Greenberg—although he'd wanted to wait until he had more concrete knowledge before doing so. If he made contact with Greenberg now, the agent might force him—what was the idiotic phrase?—out of strategy. He wasn't prepared to face that problem.

Sharpe escorted them to the near-deserted parking lot. The Windsor Vally Inn wasn't crowded with overnight guests.

"We don't encourage sleeping accommodations," Sharpe explained. "We're known primarily as a fine restaurant."

"I can understand that," said Matlock.

"Gentlemen," began Sharpe haltingly. "May I make a request that might be considered impolite?"

"Go right ahead."

"May I have a word with you, Mr. Matlock? Privately."

"Oh, don't concern yourself," said Holden, moving off. "I understand fully. I'll just walk around."

"He's a very nice fellow, your English friend," Sharpe said.

"The nicest. What is it, Sammy?"

"Several points of information, as we say in court."

"What are they?"

"I'm a cautious man, but I'm also very curious. I run a fine organization, as you can see."

"I can see."

"I'm growing nicely—cautiously, but nicely."

"I'll accept that."

"I don't make mistakes. I've a trained legal mind and I'm proud that I don't make mistakes."

"What are you driving at?"

"It strikes me—and I must be honest with you, it has also occurred to my partner Frank and to Rocco Aiello—that you may have been sent into the territory to make certain observations."

"Why do you think that?"

"Why? . . . From nowhere comes a player like you. You got powerful friends in San Juan. You know our places like the back of your hand. Then you have a very rich, very nice associate from the London scene. That all adds up. . . . But most important—and I think you know it—you mention this business in Carlyle. Let's be honest. That speaks a whole big book, doesn't it?"

"Does it?"

"I'm not foolhardy. I told you, I'm a cautious man. I understand the rules and I don't ask questions I'm not supposed to ask or talk about things I'm not privileged to know about. . . . Still, I want the generals to realize they have a few intelligent, even ambitious, lieutenants in the organization. Anyone can tell you. I don't skim, I don't hold back."

"Are you asking me to give you a good report?"

"That about sizes it up. I have value. I'm a respected attorney. My partner's a very successful insurance broker. We're naturals."

"What about Aiello? It seems to me you're friendly with him."

"Rocco's a good boy. Maybe not the quickest, but solid. He's a kind person, too. However, I don't believe he's in our league."

"And Bartolozzi?"

"I have nothing to say about Bartolozzi. You'll have to make up your own mind about him."

"By saying nothing, you're saying a lot, aren't you?"

"In my opinion, he talks too much. But that could be his personality. He rubs me the wrong way. Not Rocco, though."

Matlock watched the methodical Sharpe in the predawn light of the parking lot and began to understand what had happened. It was logical; he, himself, had planned it, but now that it was taking place, he felt curiously objective. Observing himself; watching reacting puppets.

He had entered Nimrod's world a stranger; possibly suspect, certainly devious.

Yet suddenly, that suspicion, that deviousness, was not to be scorned but *honored.*

The suspect honored for his deviousness—because it *had* to come from a higher source. He was an emissary from the upper echelons now. He was feared.

What had Greenberg called it? The shadow world. Unseen armies positioning their troops in darkness, constantly on the alert for stray patrols, unfriendly scouts.

The thin line he had to tread was precarious. But it was his now.

"You're a good man, Sharpe. Goddamn smart, too. . . . What do you know about Carlyle?"

"Nothing! Absolutely nothing."

"Now you're lying, and that's *not* smart."

"It's true. I don't *know anything*. Rumors I've heard. Knowledge and hearsay are two different kinds of testimony." Sharpe held up his right hand, his two forefingers separated.

"What rumors? Give it straight, for your own sake."

"Just rumors. A gathering of the clan, maybe. A meeting of very highly placed individuals. An agreement which has to be reached between certain people."

"Nimrod?"

Sammy Sharpe closed his eyes for precisely three seconds. During those moments he spoke.

"Now you talk language I don't want to hear."

"Then you didn't hear it, did you?"

"It's stricken from the record, I assure you."

"O.K. You're doing fine. And when you go back inside, I don't think it would be such a good idea to discuss the rumors you've heard. That would be acting like a stupid lieutenant, wouldn't it?"

"Not only stupid—insane."

"Why did you tell them to stay, then? It's late."

"For real. I wanted to know what everybody thought of you and your English friend. I'll tell you now, though—since you have mentioned a certain name, no such discussion will take place. As I said, I understand the rules."

"Good. I believe you. You've got possibilities. You'd better go back in. . . . Oh, one last thing. I want you . . . *we* want you to call Stockton at Carmount and Cantor at the Sail and Ski. Just say I'm a personal friend and I'll be showing up. Nothing else. We don't want any guards up. That's important, Sammy. Nothing else."

"It's my pleasure. And you won't forget to convey my regards to the others?"

"I won't forget. You're a good man."

"I do my best. It's all a person can do . . ."

Just then, the quiet of the predawn was shattered by five loud reports. Glass smashed. The sounds of people running and screaming and furniture crashing came from within the inn. Matlock threw himself to the ground.

"John! John!"

"Over here! By the car! Are you all right?!"

"Yes. Stay there!"

Sharpe had run into the darkness by the base of the building. He crouched into a corner, pressing himself against the brick. Matlock could barely see the outline of his form, but he could see enough to watch Sharpe withdraw a revolver from inside his jacket.

Again there was a volley of shots from the rear of the building, followed once more by screams of terror. A busboy crashed through the side door and crawled on his hands and knees toward the edge of the parking lot. He shouted hysterically in a language Matlock could not understand.

Several seconds later, another of the inn's employees in a white jacket ran through the door pulling a second man behind him, this one obviously wounded, blood pouring from his shoulder, his right arm dangling, immobile.

Another shot rang out of nowhere and the waiter who had been screaming fell over. The wounded man behind him went pummeling forward, crashing face down into the gravel. Within the building, men were shouting.

"Let's go! Get *out!* Get to the *car!*"

He fully expected to see men come scrambling out of the side door into the parking lot, but no one came. Instead, from another section of the property, he heard the gunning of an engine and, moments later, the screeching of tires as an automobile made a sharp turn. And then, to his left, about fifty yards away, a black sedan came racing out of the north driveway toward the main road. The car had to pass under a street light, and Matlock saw it clearly.

It was the same automobile that had plunged out of the darkness moments after Ralph Loring's murder.

Everything was still again. The grayish light of dawn was getting brighter.

"Jim! Jim, come here! I think they've gone!"

It was Holden. He had left the sanctuary of the automobile and was crouching over the man in the white jacket.

"Coming!" said Matlock, getting off the ground.

"This fellow's dead. He was shot between the shoulders. . . . This one's still breathing. Better get an ambulance." Holden had walked over to the unconscious busboy with the bloodied, immobile right arm.

"I don't hear anything. Where's Sharpe?"

"He just went inside. That door. He had a gun."

The two men walked carefully to the side entrance of the inn. Matlock slowly opened the door and preceded Holden into the foyer. Furniture was overturned, chairs and tables on their sides; blood was glistening on the wooden floor.

"Sharpe? Where are you?" Matlock raised his voice cautiously. It was several seconds before the reply came. When it did, Sharpe could hardly be heard.

"In here. In the dining room."

Matlock and Holden walked through the oak-framed arch. Nothing in either man's life had prepared him for what he saw.

The overpowering horror was the sight of the bodies literally covered with blood. What was left of Rocco Aiello was sprawled across the red-soaked tablecloth, most of his face blown off. Sharpe's partner, the unintroduced man named Frank, was on his knees, his torso twisted back over the seat of a chair, blood flowing out of his neck, his eyes wide open in death. Jacopo Bartolozzi was on the floor, his obese body arched around the leg of a table, the front of his shirt ripped up to the collar, revealing his bulging stomach, the flesh pierced with a score of bullet holes, blood still trickling out over the coarse black hair. Bartolozzi had tried to tear his shirt away from his battered chest, and a portion of cloth was clutched in his dead hand. The fourth man lay behind Bartolozzi, his head resting on Bartolozzi's right foot, his arms and legs extended in a spread-eagle pattern, his entire back covered with a thick layer of blood, portions of his intestines pushed through the skin.

"Oh, my God!" muttered Matlock, not fully believing what he saw. John Holden looked as though he might become sick. Sharpe spoke softly, rapidly, wearily.

"You'd better go. You and your English friend better leave quickly."

"You'll have to call the police," said Matlock, bewildered.

"There's a man outside, a boy. He's still alive." Holden stuttered as he spoke.

Sharpe looked over at the two men, the revolver at his side, his eyes betraying only the slightest degree of suspicion. "I have no doubt the lines have been cut. The nearest houses are farms at least half a mile from here. . . . I'll take care of everything. You'd better get out of here."

"Do you think we should?" asked Holden, looking at Matlock.

Sharpe replied. "Listen, Englishman, personally I couldn't care less what either of you do. I've got enough to think about, enough to figure out. . . . For your own good, get out of here. Less complications, less risk. Isn't that right?"

"Yes, you're right," Matlock said.

"In case you're picked up, you left here a half hour ago. You were friends of Bartolozzi, that's all I know."

"All right."

Sharpe had to turn away from the sight of the murdered men. Matlock thought for a moment that the Windsor Shoals attorney was going to weep. Instead, he took a deep breath and spoke again.

"A trained legal mind, Mr. Matlock. I'm valuable. You tell them that."

"I will."

"You also tell them I need protection, *deserve* protection. You tell them that, too."

"Of course."

"Now, get out." Suddenly Sharpe threw his revolver on the floor in disgust. And then he screamed, as the tears came to his eyes, "Get out for Christ's sake! *Get out!*"

22

Matlock and Holden agreed to separate immediately. The English professor dropped off the mathematician at his apartment and then headed south to Fairfield. He wanted to register at a highway motel far enough away from Windsor Shoals to feel less panicked, yet near enough to Hartford so he could get to Blackstone's by two in the afternoon.

He was too exhausted, too frightened to think. He found a third-rate motel just west of Stratford and surprised the early morning clerk by being alone.

During the registration, he mumbled unpleasant criticisms about a suspicious wife in Westport, and with a ten-dollar bill convinced the clerk to enter his arrival at 2:00 A.M., single. He fell into bed by seven and left a call for twelve thirty. If he slept for five hours, he thought, things had to become clearer.

Matlock slept for five hours and twenty minutes and nothing much had changed. Very little had cleared up for him. If anything, the massacre at Windsor Shoals now appeared more extraordinary than ever. Was it possible that he was meant to be a victim? Or were the killers waiting outside, waiting silently for him to leave before committing their executions?

Mistake or warning?

By one fifteen he was on the Merritt Parkway. By

one thirty he entered the Berlin Turnpike, taking the back roads into Hartford. By five minutes past two he walked into Blackstone's office.

"Look," said Michael Blackstone, leaning over his desk, staring at Matlock, "we ask a minimum of questions, but don't for one minute think that means we give our clients blank checks!"

"It seems to me you like that process reversed."

"Then take your money and go somewhere else. We'll survive!"

"Just hold it! You were hired to protect a girl, that's all! That's what I'm paying three hundred dollars a day for! Anything else is marginal, and I'm paying for that, too, I expect."

"There'll be no extra charges. I don't know what you're talking about." Suddenly Blackstone bent his elbows, crouching forward. He whispered hoarsely. "Christ, Matlock? Two *men!* Two men on that goddamn list were murdered last night! If you're a hopped-up maniac, I don't want anything to do with you! That's no part of any deal here! I don't care *who* your old man is or *how* much money you've got!"

"Now I don't know what *you're* talking about. Except what I read in the papers. I was at a motel in Fairfield last night. I was registered there at two this morning. According to the papers, those killings took place around five."

Blackstone pushed himself off the desk and stood up. He looked at Matlock suspiciously. "You can verify that?"

"Do you want the name and number of the motel? Give me a phone book, I'll get it for you."

"No! . . . No. I don't want to know a thing. You were in Fairfield?"

"Get the phone book."

"All right. All right, forget it. I think you're lying, but you've covered yourself. As you say, we're only hired to protect the girl."

"Any change from Sunday afternoon? Is everything all right?"

"Yes. . . . Yes." Blackstone seemed preoccupied. "I've got your Tel-electronic. It's operative. It's an additional twenty dollars a day."

"I see. Wholesale price."

"We never implied we were cheap."

"You couldn't."

"We don't." Blackstone remained standing, pushed a button on his office intercom, and spoke into it. "Bring in Mr. Matlock's Tel-electronic, please."

Seconds later an attractive girl came into the office carrying a metal device no larger than a pack of cigarettes. She put it on Blackstone's desk and placed an index card beside it. She left as rapidly as she had entered.

"Here you are," Blackstone said. "Your code is Charger Three-zero. Meaning—Carlyle area, three-man team. The telephone number you call is five, five, five, six, eight, six, eight. We keep a list of numbers on reserve which we feel are easy to commit. The Tel-electronic will signal you by short beeps. You can shut it off by pushing this button here. When the signal is emitted, you are to call the number. A recording machine on that telephone will give you the message from the team. Often it will be to phone another number to make direct contact. Do you understand everything? It's really very simple."

"I understand," said Matlock, taking the small metal box. "What confuses me is why you don't just have the men call this office and then you contact me.

Outside of whatever profit there is, wouldn't it be easier?"

"No. Too much room for error. We handle a great many clients. We want our clients to be in direct contact with the men they're paying for."

"I see."

"Also, we respect the privacy of our clients. We don't think it's such a good idea for information to be transmitted through third and fourth parties. Incidentally, you can reach the team by the same procedures. Each one has a machine. Just phone the number and record the message for them."

"Commendable."

"Professional." And then Blackstone, for the first time since Matlock had entered the office, sat in his chair and leaned back. "Now I'm going to tell you something, and if you want to take it as a threat, you'd be justified. Also, if you want to cancel our services on the strength of what I say, that's O.K., too. . . . We know that you're being actively sought by agents of the Justice Department. However, there are no charges leveled against you, no warrants for your arrest. You have certain rights which the federal men often overlook in their zealousness—it's one of the reasons we're in business. However, *again,* we want you to know that should your status change, should there *be* charges or a warrant for your arrest, our services are terminated immediately, and we won't hesitate to cooperate with the authorities regarding your whereabouts. Whatever information we possess will be held for your attorneys—it's privileged—but not your whereabouts. *Capiche?*"

"I do. That's fair."

"We're more than fair. That's why I'm going to demand ten days' advance payment from you—unused portion returnable. . . . In the event the situation changes and the federal men get a court order for you, you will receive—*only once*—the following message on the telephone recorder. Just *these words.*"

Blackstone paused for emphasis.

"What are they?"

"'*Charger Three-zero is canceled.*'"

Out on Bond Street Matlock felt a sensation he knew wouldn't leave him until his journey, his race was over. He thought people were staring at him. He began to think strangers were watching him. He found himself involuntarily turning around, trying to find the unseen, observing eyes. Yet there were none.

None that he could distinguish.

The Corsican paper now had to be gotten out of his apartment. And considering Blackstone's statements, there was no point in his attempting to get it himself. His apartment would be under surveillance—from both camps, the seekers and the quarry.

He would use the Blackstone team, one of them, putting to the test the sartorial Blackstone's guarantee of privileged information. He would reach them—him—as soon as he placed one prior telephone call. A call that would make it clear whether the silver Corsican invitation was really necessary or not. A call to Samuel Sharpe, attorney at law, Windsor Shoals, Connecticut.

Matlock decided to show Sharpe a temporary, more compassionate side of his acquired personality. Sharpe himself had displayed a momentary lapse of control. Matlock thought it was the moment to indicate that even such men as himself—men who had influential friends in San Juan and London—had feelings beyond personal survival.

He walked into the lobby of the Americana Hotel and called him. Sharpe's secretary answered.

"Are you in an office where Mr. Sharpe can return your call momentarily?"

"No, I'm in a telephone booth. I'm also in a hurry."

There was silence, preceded by the click of a hold button. The wait was less than ten seconds.

"May I have the number you're calling from, Mr. Matlock? Mr. Sharpe will get back to you within five minutes."

Matlock gave the girl the number and hung up.

As he sat in the plastic seat, his memory wandered back to another telephone booth and another plastic seat. And a black sedan which raced past the dead man slouched in that booth, on that seat, with a bullet hole in his forehead.

The bell sounded; Matlock lifted the receiver.

"Matlock?"

"Sharpe?"

"You shouldn't call me at the office. You should know better. I had to go down to the lobby here, to a pay phone."

"I didn't think a respected attorney's telephone would be any risk. I'm sorry."

There was a pause at the other end of the line. Sharpe obviously never expected an apology. "I'm a cautious man, I told you. What is it?"

"I just wanted to know how you were. How everything went. It was a terrible thing, last night."

"I haven't had time for a reaction. There's so much to do. Police, funeral arrangements, reporters."

"What are you saying? How are you handling it?"

"There won't be any major mistakes. In a nutshell—if it comes to that—I'm an innocent victim. Frank's a victim, too, only he's dead. . . . I'm going to miss

Frank. He was a very good fellow. I'll close down the upstairs, of course. The state police have been paid. By you people, I assume. It'll be what the papers say it was. A bunch of Italian hoodlums shot up in a nice country restaurant."

"You're a cool operator."

"I told you," replied Sharpe sadly, "I'm a cautious man. I'm prepared for contingencies."

"Who did it?"

Sharpe did not answer the question. He did not speak at all.

"I asked you, who do you think did it?"

"I expect you people will find out before I do. . . . Bartolozzi had enemies; he was an unpleasant person. Rocco, too, I suppose. . . . But why Frank? You tell me."

"I don't know. I haven't been in touch with anyone."

"Find out for me. Please. It wasn't right."

"I'll try. That's a promise. . . . And, Sammy, make those calls to Stockton and Cantor, don't forget."

"I won't. I've got them listed on my afternoon calendar. I told you. I'm a methodical man."

"Thanks. My sympathies about Frank. He seemed like a nice guy."

"He was a prince."

"I'm sure he was. . . . I'll be in touch, Sammy. I haven't forgotten what I said I'd do for you. You've really impressed me. I'll . . ."

The sound of coins dropping into the telephone receptacle at Windsor Shoals interrupted Matlock. The time limit was up, and there was no point in prolonging the conversation. He had found out what he needed to know. He had to have the Corsican paper now. The horror of the dawn massacre had not caused the methodical Sharpe to forget the telephone calls he'd promised to make. Why it hadn't was a miracle to Matlock, but there it was. The cautious man had not panicked. He was ice.

The telephone booth was stuffy, close, uncomfortable, filled with smoke. He opened the door and walked rapidly across the hotel lobby to the front exit.

He rounded the corner of Asylum Street looking for an appropriate restaurant. One in which he could have lunch while awaiting the return call from Charger Three-zero. Blackstone had said that he should leave a number; what better than a restaurant?

He saw the sign: The Lobster House. The kind of place frequented by business executives.

He was given a booth to himself, not a table. It was nearly three; the luncheon crowd had thinned. He sat down and ordered a bourbon on the rocks, asking the waitress the whereabouts of the nearest telephone. He was about to get out of the booth to make his call to 555-6868 when he heard the muted, sharp, terrifying sound of the Tel-electronic from within his jacket. At first it paralyzed him. It was as if some part of his person, an hysterical organ perhaps, had gone mad and was trying to signal its distress. His hand shook as he reached inside his coat and withdrew the small metal device. He found the shut-off button and pressed it as hard as he could. He looked around, wondering if the sound had attracted attention.

It had not. No one returned his looks. No one had heard a thing.

He got out of his seat and walked quickly toward the telephone. His only thought was Pat—something had happened, something serious enough for Charger Three-zero to activate the terrible, insidious machine which had panicked him.

Matlock pulled the door shut and dialed 555-6868.

"Charger Three-zero reporting." The voice had the once-removed quality of a taped recording. "Please telephone five, five, five; one, nine, five, one. There is no need for alarm, sir. There's no emergency. We'll be at this number for the next hour. The number again is five, five, five; one, nine, five, one. Out."

Matlock realized that Charger Three-zero took pains to allay his fears immediately, perhaps because it was his first experience with the Tel-electronic. He had the feeling that even if the town of Carlyle had gone up in thermonuclear smoke, Charger Three-zero's words would have a palliative quality about them. The other reasoning, perhaps, was that a man thought more clearly when unafraid. Whatever, Matlock knew that the method worked. He was calmer now. He reached into his pocket and took out some change, making a mental note as he did so to convert some dollar bills into coins for future use. The pay telephone had become an important part of his life.

"Is this five, five, five; nineteen fifty-one?"

"Yes," said the same voice he had heard on the recording. "Mr. Matlock?"

"Yes. Is Miss Ballantyne all right?"

"Doing very well, sir. That's a good doctor you've got. She sat up this morning. A lot of the swelling's gone down. The doctor's quite pleased. . . . She's asked for you a number of times."

"What are you telling her?"

"The truth. That we've been hired by you to make sure she's not bothered."

"I mean about where I am."

"We've simply said you had to be away for several days. It might be a good idea to telephone her. She can take calls starting this afternoon. We'll screen them, of course."

"Of course. Is that why you contacted me?"

"In part. The other reason is Greenberg. Jason Greenberg. He keeps calling for you. He insists that you get in touch with him."

"What did he say? Who talked to him?"

"I did. Incidentally, my name's Cliff."

"O.K., Cliff, what did he say?"

"That I should tell you to call him the minute I reached you. It was imperative, critical. I've got a number. It's in Wheeling, West Virginia."

"Give it to me." Matlock withdrew his ballpoint pen and wrote the number on the wooden shelf under the telephone.

"Mr. Matlock?"

"What?"

"Greenberg also said to tell you . . . that 'the cities weren't dying, they were dead.' Those were his words. 'The cities were dead.' "

23

Cliff agreed without comment to retrieve the Corsican paper from Matlock's apartment. A rendezvous would be arranged later by telephone. In the event the paper was missing, Charger Three-zero would alert him immediately.

Matlock restricted himself to one drink. He picked at his lunch and left the Lobster House by three thirty. It was time to regroup his forces, resupply his ammunition. He had parked the Cadillac in a lot several blocks south of Blackstone's office on Bond Street. It was one of those municipal parking areas, each slot with its own meter. It occurred to Matlock as he approached it that he hadn't returned to insert additional coins since going to Blackstone's. The meters were only good for an hour; he'd been there for nearly two. He wondered what rental-car businesses did with the slew of traffic violations which had to mount up with transients. He entered the lot and momentarily wondered if he was in the right aisle. Then he realized he was not. The Cadillac was two lanes over, in the fourth aisle. He started to sidle past the closely parked vehicles toward his own and then he stopped.

In between the automobiles, he saw the blue and white stripes of a Hartford patrol car. It was parked directly behind his Cadillac. One police officer was trying the Cadillac's door handle, a second patrolman was leaning against the police vehicle talking into a radio phone.

They'd found the car. It frightened him, but somehow it didn't surprise him.

He backed away cautiously, prepared to run if he was spotted. His thoughts raced ahead to the problems to which this newest complication gave rise. First and most immediate was an automobile. Second was the fact that they knew he was in the Hartford vicinity. That ruled out other means of transportation. The railroad stations, the bus terminals, even the hack bureaus would be alerted. It came back to finding another car.

And yet he wondered. Blackstone made it clear there were no charges against him, no warrants. If there were, he would have received the message from 555-6868. He would have heard the words: "Charger Three-zero is canceled."

He hadn't. There'd been no hint of it. For a moment he considered going back to the patrol car, accepting a ticket for overtime.

He dismissed the thought. These police were not meter maids. There had been a previous parking lot beyond an alley, at the rear of an A&P. And another policeman—in civilian clothes—following him. A pattern was there, though it eluded definition.

Matlock walked swiftly up Bond Street away from the municipal lot. He turned into the first side street and found himself beginning to break into a run. Instantly he slowed down. There is nothing in a crowded street more noticeable than a man running—unless it is a woman. He resumed a pace equal to the afternoon shoppers, doing his best to melt into the flow of human traffic. He even paused now and then to stare blankly into store-front windows, not really seeing the displays of merchandise. And then he began to reflect on what was happening to him. The primitive instincts of the hunted were suddenly working inside his brain. The protective antennae of the would-be trapped animal were thrusting, parrying with their surroundings and, chameleonlike, the body did its best to conform to the environment.

Yet he wasn't the hunted! He was the hunter! Goddamn it, he was the *hunter!*

"Hello, Jim! How the hell are you? What are you doing in the big city?"

The shock of the greeting caused Matlock to lose his balance. To actually *lose his balance* and trip. He fell to the sidewalk and the man who had spoken to him reached down and helped him up.

"Oh! Oh, hello, Jeff! Christ, you startled me. Thanks." Matlock got up and brushed himself off. He looked around wondering who else besides Jeff Kramer was watching him.

"A long lunch, buddy?" Kramer laughed. He was a Carlyle alumnus with a graduate degree in psychology that had been impressive enough for an expensive public relations firm.

"Lord, no! Just have something on my mind. My bumbling old professor bag." And then Matlock looked at Jeff Kramer. Jeff Kramer was not only with an expensive firm, but he also had an expensive wife and two very expensive kids in extremely expensive prep schools. Matlock felt he should reemphasize his previous point. "For a fact, I had one unfinished bourbon."

"Why don't we rectify that," said Kramer, pointing

at the Hogshead Tavern across the street. "I haven't seen you in months. I read in *The Courant* you got yourself robbed."

"Goddamn, *did* I! The robbery I could take, but what they did to the apartment! And the *car!*" Matlock headed toward the Hogshead Tavern with Jeff Kramer. "That's why I'm in town. Got the Triumph in a garage here. That's my problem, as a matter of fact."

The hunted not only had antennae which served to warn the host of its enemies, but also the uncanny —if temporary—ability to turn disadvantage into advantage. Conceivable liabilities into positive assets.

Matlock sipped his bourbon and water while Kramer went through half his Scotch in several swallows. "The idea of a bus down to Scarsdale, with changes at New Haven and Bridgeport, defeats me."

"*Rent* a car, for Christ's sake."

"Just tried two places. The first can't let me have one until tonight, the second not until tomorrow. Some kind of convention, I guess."

"So wait until tonight."

"Can't do it. Family business. My father called his council of economic advisers. For dinner—and if you think I'm going to Scarsdale without my own wheels, you're out of it!" Matlock laughed and ordered another round of drinks. He reached into his pocket and put a fifty-dollar bill on the bar. The bill had to attract the attention of Jeff Kramer, who had such an expensive wife.

"Never thought you could balance a checkbook, say nothing of being an economic adviser."

"Ah, but I'm the prince royal. Can't forget that, can we?"

"Lucky bastard, that's what I can't forget. Lucky bastard."

"Hey! I've got one hell of an idea. Your car in town?"

"Hey, wait a minute, good buddy. . . ."

"No, listen." Matlock took out his bills. "The old man'll pay for it. . . . Rent me *your* car. Four or five days. . . . Here. I'll give you two, three hundred."

"You're nuts!"

"No, I'm not He wants me down. He'll pay!"

Matlock could sense Kramer's mind working. He was estimating the cost of a low-priced rent-a-car for a week. Seventy-nine fifty and ten cents a mile with an average daily mileage of, perhaps, fifteen or twenty. Tops, $105, and maybe $110, for the week.

Kramer had that expensive wife and those two very expensive kids in extremely expensive prep schools.

"I wouldn't want to take you like that."

"Not *me!* Christ, no. *Him!*"

"Well . . ."

"Here, let me write out a bill. I'll give it to him the minute I get there." Matlock grabbed a cocktail napkin and turned it over to the unprinted side. He took out his ballpoint pen and began writing. "Simple contract. . . . 'I, James B. Matlock, agree to pay Jeffrey Kramer three hundred' . . . what the hell, it's his money . . . 'four hundred dollars for the rental of his . . .' —what's the make?"

"Ford wagon. A white Squire. Last year's." Kramer's eyes alternately looked at the napkin and the roll of bills Matlock carelessly left next to Kramer's elbow on the bar.

" 'Ford Wagon, for a period of' . . . let's say one week, O.K.?"

"Fine." Kramer drank the remainder of his second Scotch.

" 'One week. . . . Signed, James B. Matlock!' There you are, friend. Countersign. And here's four hundred. Courtesy of Jonathan Munro. Where's the car?"

The hunted's instincts were infallible, thought Matlock, as Kramer pocketed the bills and wiped his chin, which had begun to perspire. Kramer removed the two car keys and the parking lot ticket from his pocket. True to Matlock's anticipation. Jeff Kramer wanted to part company. With his four hundred dollars.

Matlock said he would phone Kramer in less than a week and return the automobile. Kramer insisted on paying for the drinks and rapidly left the Hogshead Tavern. Matlock, alone, finished his drink and thought out his next move.

The hunted and the hunter were now one.

24

He sped out Route 72 toward Mount Holly in Kramer's white station wagon. He knew that within the hour he would find another pay telephone and insert another coin and make another call. This time to one Howard Stockton, owner of the Carmount Country Club. He looked at his watch; it was nearly eight thirty. Samuel Sharpe, attorney at law, should have reached Stockton several hours ago.

He wondered how Stockton had reacted. He wondered about Howard Stockton.

The station wagon's headlights caught the reflection of the road sign.

MOUNT HOLLY. INCORPORATED 1896

And just beyond it, a second reflection.

MOUNT HOLLY ROTARY
HARPER'S REST
TUESDAY NOON
ONE MILE

Why not? thought Matlock. There was nothing to lose. And possibly something to gain, even learn.

The hunter.

The white stucco front and the red Narragansett neons in the windows said all there was to say about Harper's cuisine. Matlock parked next to a pickup truck, got out, and locked the car. His newly acquired suitcase with the newly acquired clothes lay on the back seat. He had spent several hundred dollars in Hartford; he wasn't about to take a chance.

He walked across the cheap, large gravel and entered the bar area of Harper's Restaurant.

"I'm on my way to Carmount," said Matlock, paying for his drink with a twenty-dollar bill. "Would you mind telling me where the hell it is?"

"About two and a half miles west. Take the right fork down the road. You got anything smaller than a twenty? I only got two fives and singles. I need my singles."

"Give me the fives and we'll flip for the rest. Heads you keep it, tails I have one more and you still keep it." Matlock took a coin from his pocket and threw it on the formica bar, covering it with his hand. He lifted his palm and picked up the coin without showing it to the bartender. "It's your unlucky night. You owe me a drink—the ten's yours."

His conversation did not go unheeded by the other customers—three men drinking draft beer. That was fine, thought Matlock, as he looked around for a telephone.

"Men's room's in the rear around the corner," said a rustic-looking drinker in a chino jacket, wearing a baseball cap.

"Thanks. Telephone around?"

"Next to the men's room."

"Thanks again." Matlock took out a piece of paper

on which he had written: Howard Stockton, Carmount C.C., #203-421-1100. He gestured for the bartender, who came toward him like a shot. "I'm supposed to phone this guy," said Matlock quietly. "I think I got the name wrong. I'm not sure whether it's Stackton or Stockton. Do you know him?"

The bartender looked at the paper and Matlock saw the instant reflex of recognition. "Sure. You got it right. It's Stockton. Mr. Stockton. He's vice-president of the Rotary. Last term he was president. Right, boys?" The bartender addressed this last to his other customers.

"Sure."

"That's it. Stockton."

"Nice fella."

The man in the chino jacket and baseball cap felt the necessity of elaborating. "He runs the country club. That's a real nice place. Real nice."

"Country club?" Matlock implied the question with a trace of humor.

"That's right. Swimming pool, golf course, dancing on the weekends. Very nice." It was the bartender who elaborated now.

"I'll say this, he's highly recommended. This Stockton, I mean." Matlock drained his glass and looked toward the rear of the bar. "Telephone back there, you say?"

"That's right, Mister. Around the corner."

Matlock reached into his pocket for some change and walked to the narrow corridor where the rest rooms and telephone were located. The instant he rounded the corner, he stopped and pressed himself against the wall. He listened for the conversation he knew would be forthcoming.

"Big spender, huh?" The bartender spoke.

"They all are. Did I tell you? My kid caddied there a couple of weeks ago—some guy got a birdie and give the kid a fifty-dollar bill. Che-ryst! Fifty dollars!"

"My old woman says all them fancy dames there are *whoores.* Real whoores. She works a few parties there, my old woman does. Real whoores. . . ."

"I'd like to get my hands on some of them. Jee-*sus!* I swear to Christ most of 'em got no brazzieres!"

"Real whoores. . . ."

"Who gives a shit? That Stockton's O.K. He's O.K. in my book. Know what he did? The Kings. You know, Artie King who had a heart attack—dropped dead doin' the lawns up there. Old Stockton not only give the family a lotta dough—he set up a regular charge account for 'em at the A&P. No shit. He's O.K."

"Real whoores. They lay for money. . . ."

"Stockton put most of the cash up for the grammar school extension, don't forget that. You're fuckin' right, he's O.K. I got two kids in that school!"

"Not only—y'know what? He give a pocketful to the Memorial Day picnic."

"Real, honest-to-Christ whoores. . . ."

Matlock silently sidestepped his way against the wall to the telephone booth. He closed the door slowly with a minimum of noise. The men at the bar were getting louder in their appreciation of Howard Stockton, proprietor of the Carmount Country Club. He was not concerned that they might hear his delayed entrance into the booth.

What concerned him in an odd way was himself. If the *hunted* had instincts—protective in nature—the *hunter* had them also—aggressive by involvement. He understood now the necessity of tracking the scent, following the spoor, building a fabric of comprehensive habit. It meant that the hunter had abstract tools to complement his weapons. Tools which could build a base of entrapment, a pit in which the hunted might fall.

He ticked them off in his mind.

Howard Stockton: former president, current vice-president of the Mount Holly Rotary; a charitable man, a compassionate man. A man who took care of the family of a deceased employee named Artie King; who financed the extension of a grammar school. The proprietor of a luxurious country club in which men gave fifty-dollar tips to caddies and girls were available for members in good standing. Also a good American who made it possible for the town of Mount Holly to have a fine Memorial Day picnic.

It was enough to start with. Enough to shake up Howard Stockton if—as Sammy Sharpe had put it—"it came to that." Howard Stockton was not the formless man he was fifteen minutes ago. Matlock still didn't know the man's features, but other aspects, other factors were defined for him. Howard Stockton had become a *thing* in Mount Holly, Connecticut.

Matlock inserted the dime and dialed the number of the Carmount Country Club.

"It *suh*tainly is a pleasure, Mr. Matlock!" exclaimed Howard Stockton, greeting Matlock on the marble steps of the Carmount Country Club. "The boy'll take your car. Heah! Boy! Don't wrap it up, now!"

A Negro parking attendant laughed at his southern gentleman's command. Stockton flipped a half-dollar in the air and the black caught it with a grin.

"Thank you, suh!"

"Treat 'em good, they'll treat you good. That right, boy? Do I treat you good?!"

"*Real* good, Mister Howard!"

Matlock thought for a moment that he was part of an odious television commercial until he saw that Howard Stockton was the real item. Right up to his grayish blond hair, which topped a sun-tanned face, which, in turn, set off his white moustache and deep blue eyes surrounded by crow's nests of wrinkles belonging to a man who lived well.

"Welcome to Carmount, Mr. Matlock. It's not Richmond, but on the other hand, it ain't the Okefenokee."

"Thank you. And the name is Jim."

"Jim? Like that name. It's got a good, honest ring to it! My friends call me Howard. You call me Howard."

The Carmount Country Club, what he could see of it, reminded Matlock of all those pictures of antebellum architecture. And why not, considering the owner? It was rife with potted palms and delicate chandeliers and light blue toile wallpaper depicting rococo scenes in which cavorted prettified figures in powdered wigs. Howard Stockton was a proselytizer of a way of life which had collapsed in 1865, but he wasn't going to admit it. Even the servants, mostly black, were in liveries—honest-to-god liveries, knickers and all. Soft, live music came from a large dining room, at the end of which was a string orchestra of perhaps eight instruments gracefully playing in a fashion long since abandoned. There was a slowly winding staircase in the center of the main hall which would have done honor to Jefferson Davis—or David O. Selznick. Attractive women were wandering around, linked with not-so-attractive men.

The effect was incredible, thought Matlock, as he walked by his host's side toward what his host modestly claimed was his private library.

The southerner closed the thick paneled door and strode to a well-stocked mahogany bar. He poured without asking a preference.

"Sam Sharpe says you drink sour mash. You're a man of taste, I tell you that. That's *my* drink." He carried two glasses to Matlock. "Take your pick. A Virginian has to disarm a northerner with his complete lack of bias these days."

"Thank you," said Matlock, taking a glass and sitting in the armchair indicated by Stockton.

"This Virginian," continued Howard Stockton, sitting opposite Matlock, "also has an unsouthern habit of getting to the point. . . . I don't even know if it's wise for you to be in my place. I'll be honest. That's why I ushered you right in here."

"I don't understand. You could have told me on the phone not to come. Why the game?"

"Maybe you can answer that better than I can. Sammy says you're a real big man. You're what they call . . . *international.* That's just dandy by me. I like a bright young fella who goes up the ladder of success. Very commendable, that's a fact. . . . But I pay my bills. I pay every month on the line. I got the best combined operation north of Atlanta. I don't want trouble."

"You won't get it from *me.* I'm a tired businessman making the rounds, that's all I am."

"What happened at Sharpe's? The papers are full of it! I don't want *nothin'* like that!"

Matlock watched the southerner. The capillaries in the suntanned face were bloodred, which was probably why the man courted a year-round sunburn. It covered a multitude of blemishes.

"I don't think you understand." Matlock measured his words as he lifted the glass to his lips. "I've come a long way because I *have* to be here. I don't *want* to be here. Personal reasons got me into the area early, so I'm doing some sightseeing. But it's only that. I'm just looking around. . . . Until my appointment."

"What appointment?"

"An appointment in Carlyle, Connecticut."

Stockton squinted his eyes and pulled at his perfectly groomed white moustache. "You've got to be in Carlyle?"

"Yes. It's confidential, but I don't have to tell you that, do I?"

"You haven't told me anything." Stockton kept watching Matlock's face, and Matlock knew the southerner was looking for a false note, a wrong word, a hesitant glance which might contradict his information.

"Good. . . . By any chance, do you have an appointment in Carlyle, too? In about a week and a half?"

Stockton sipped his drink, smacking his lips and putting the glass on a side table as though it were some precious *objet d'art*. "I'm just a southern cracker tryin' to make a dollar. Livin' the good life and makin' a dollar. That's all. I don't know about any appointments in Carlyle."

"Sorry I brought it up. It's a . . . major mistake on my part. For both our sakes, I hope you won't mention it. Or *me*."

"That's the *last* thing I'd do. Far as I'm concerned, you're a friend of Sammy's lookin' for a little action . . . and a little hospitality." Suddenly Stockton leaned forward in his chair, his elbows on his knees, his hands folded. He looked like an earnest minister questioning a parishioner's sins. "What in tarnation happened at Windsor Shoals? What in hell was it?"

"As far as I can see, it was a local vendetta. Bartolozzi had enemies. Some said he talked too goddamn much. Aiello, too, I suppose. They were show-offs. . . . Frank was just there, I think."

"Goddamn *Eye*talians! Mess up everything! *That* level, of course, you know what I mean?"

There it was again. The dangling interrogative—but in this southerner's version, it wasn't really a question. It was a statement.

"I know what you mean," said Matlock wearily.

"I'm afraid I got a little bad news for you, Jim. I closed the tables for a few days. Just plum scared as a jackrabbit after what happened at the Shoals."

"That's not bad news for me. Not the way my streak's been going."

"I heard. Sammy told me. But we got a couple of other diversions. You won't find Carmount lacking in hospitality, I promise you that."

The two men finished their drinks, and Stockton, relieved, escorted his guest into the crowded, elegant Carmount dining room. The food was extraordinary, served in a manner befitting the finest and wealthiest plantation of the antebellum South.

Although pleasant—even relaxing, in a way—the dinner was pointless to Matlock. Howard Stockton would not discuss his "operation" except in the vaguest terms and with the constant reminder that he catered to the "best class of Yankee." His speech was peppered with descriptive anachronisms, he was a walking contradiction in time. Halfway through the meal, Stockton excused himself to say good-bye to an important member.

It was the first opportunity Matlock had to look at Stockton's "best class of Yankee" clientele.

The term applied, thought Matlock, if the word *class* was interchangeable with *money*, which he wasn't willing to concede. Money screamed from every table. The first sign was the proliferation of suntans in the beginning of a Connecticut May. These were people who jetted to the sun-drenched islands at will. Another was the easy, deep-throated laughter echoing throughout the room; also the glittering reflection of jewelry. And the clothes—softly elegant suits, raw silk jackets, Dior ties. And the bottles of sparkling vintage wines, standing majestically in sterling silver stands upheld by cherrywood tripods.

But something was wrong, thought Matlock. Something was missing or out of place, and for several minutes he couldn't put his finger on what it was. And then he did.

The suntans, the laughter, the wrist jewelry, the jackets, the Dior ties—the money, the elegance, the aura was predominantly *male*.

The contradiction was the women—the girls. Not that there weren't some who matched their partners, but in the main, they didn't. They were younger. Much, much younger. And different.

He wasn't sure what the difference was at first. Then, abstractly, it came to him. For the most part, the girls—and they *were* girls—had a look about them he knew very well. He'd referred to it often in the past. It was the campus look—as differentiated from the office look, the secretary look. A slightly more careless attitude in conversation. The look of girls not settling into routines, not welded to file cabinets or typewriters. It was definable because it was real. Matlock had been exposed to that look for over a decade—it was unmistakable.

Then he realized that within this contradiction there was another—minor—discrepancy. The clothes the girls wore. They weren't the clothes he expected to find on girls with the campus look. They were too precisely cut, too designed, if that was the word. In this day of unisex, simply too feminine.

They wore costumes!

Suddenly, in a single, hysterically spoken sentence from several tables away, he knew he was right.

"Honest, I mean it—it's too groovy!"

That voice! *Christ, he knew that voice!*

He wondered if he was meant to hear it.

He had his hand up to his face and slowly turned toward the direction of the giggling speaker. The girl was laughing and drinking champagne, while her escort—a much older man—stared with satisfaction at her enormous breasts.

The girl was Virginia Beeson. The "pinky groovy" perennial undergraduate wife of Archer Beeson, Carlyle University's history instructor.

The man in an academic hurry.

Matlock tipped the black who carried his suitcase up the winding staircase to the large, ornate room Stockton had offered him. The floor was covered with a thick wine-colored carpet, the bed canopied, the walls white with fluted moldings. He saw that on the bureau was an ice bucket, two bottles of Jack Daniels, and several glasses. He opened the suitcase, picked out his toilet articles, and put them on the bedside table. He then removed a suit, a lightweight jacket, and two pairs of slacks, and carried them to the closet. He returned to the suitcase, lifted it from the bed, and laid it across the two wooden arms of a chair.

There was a soft tapping on his door. His first thought was that the caller was Howard Stockton, but he was wrong.

A girl, dressed in a provocative deep-red sheath, stood in the frame and smiled. She was in her late teens or very early twenties and terribly attractive.

And her smile was false.

"Yes?"

"Compliments of Mr. Stockton." She spoke the words and walked into the room past Matlock.

Matlock closed the door and stared at the girl, not so much bewildered as surprised.

"That's very thoughtful of Mr. Stockton, isn't it?"

"I'm glad you approve. There's whisky, ice, and glasses on your bureau. I'd like a short drink. Unless you're in a hurry."

Matlock walked slowly to the bureau. "I'm in no hurry. What would you like?"

"It doesn't matter. Whatever's there. Just ice, please."

"I see." Matlock poured the girl a drink and carried it over to her. "Won't you sit down?"

"On the bed?"

The only other chair, besides the one on which the suitcase was placed, was across the room by a French window.

"I'm sorry." He removed the suitcase and the girl sat down. Howard Stockton, he thought, had good taste. The girl was adorable. "What's your name?"

"Jeannie." She drank a great deal of her drink in several swallows. The girl may not have perfected a selection in liquor, but she knew how to drink. And then, as the girl took the glass from her mouth, Matlock noticed the ring on her third right finger.

He knew that ring very well. It was sold in a campus bookstore several blocks from John Holden's apartment in Webster, Connecticut. It was the ring of Madison University.

"What would you say if I told you I wasn't interested?" asked Matlock, leaning against the thick pole of the bed's anachronistic canopy.

"I'd be surprised. You don't look like a fairy."

"I'm not."

The girl looked up at Matlock. Her pale blue eyes were warm—but professionally warm—meaning, yet not meaning at all. Her lips were young. And full; and taut.

"Maybe you just need a little encouragement."

"You can provide that?"

"I'm good." She made the statement with quiet arrogance.

She was so young, thought Matlock, yet there was age in her. And hate. The hate was camouflaged, but the cosmetic was inadequate. She was performing—the costume, the eyes, the lips. She may have detested the role, but she accepted it.

Professionally.

"Suppose I just want to talk?"

"Conversation's something else. There are no rules about that. I've equal rights in that department. Quid pro, Mister No-name."

"You're facile with words. Should that tell me something?"

"I don't know why."

"'Quid pro quo' isn't the language of your eight to three hooker."

"This place—in case you missed it—isn't the Avenida de las Putas, either."

"Tennessee Williams?"

"Who knows?"

"I think you do."

"Fine. All right. We can discuss Proust in bed. I mean, that *is* where you want me, isn't it?"

"Perhaps I'd settle for the conversation."

The girl suddenly, in alarm, whispered hoarsely, "Are you a cop?"

"I'm the furthest thing from a cop," laughed Matlock. "You might say that some of the most important policemen in the area would like to find me. Although I'm no criminal. . . . Or a nut, by the way."

"Now *I'm* not interested. May I have another drink?"

"Surely." Matlock got it for her. Neither spoke until he returned with her glass.

"Do you mind if I stay here awhile? Just long enough for you to have balled me."

"You mean you don't want to lose the fee?"

"It's fifty dollars."

"You'll probably have to use part of it to bribe the dormitory head. Madison University's a little old-fashioned. Some coed houses still have weekday check-ins. You'll be late."

The shock on the girl's face was complete. "You *are* a cop! You're a lousy *cop!*" She started to get out of the chair, but Matlock quickly stood in front of her, holding her shoulders. He eased her back into the chair.

"I'm not a cop, I told you that. And you're not interested, remember? But *I'm* interested. I'm *very* interested, and you're going to tell me what I want to know."

The girl started to get up and Matlock grabbed her arms. She struggled; he pushed her back violently. "Do you always get 'balled' with your ring on? Is that to show whoever gets laid there's a little class to it?!"

"Oh, my God! Oh, Jesus!" She grabbed her ring and twisted her finger as if the pressure might make it disappear.

"Now, listen to me! You answer my questions or I'll be down in Webster tomorrow morning and I'll start asking them down there! Would you like that better?"

"Please! *Please!*" Tears came to the girl's eyes. Her hands shook and she gasped for breath.

"How did you get here?!"

"No! No . . ."

"*How?*"

"I was recruited. . . ."

"By whom?"

"Other . . . Others. We recruit each other."

"How many are there?"

"Not many. Not very many. . . . It's quiet. We have to keep it quiet. . . . Let me go, *please*. I want to *go*."

"Oh, no. Not yet. I want to know how many and *why!*"

"I told you! Only a few, maybe seven or eight girls."

"There must be thirty downstairs!"

"I don't *know* them. They're from other places. We don't ask each other's *names!*"

"But you know where they're from, don't you!"

"Some. . . . Yes."

"Other schools?"

"Yes. . . ."

"*Why*, Jeannie? For Christ's sake, *why?*"

"Why do you *think? Money!*"

The girl's dress had long sleeves. He grabbed her

right arm and ripped the fabric up past the elbow. She fought him back but he overpowered her.

There were no marks. No signs.

She kicked at him and he slapped her face, hard enough to shock her into momentary immobility. He took her left arm and tore the sleeve.

There they were. Faded. Not recent. But there.

The small purple dots of a needle.

"I'm not on it now! I haven't been in *months!*"

"But you need the money! You need fifty or a hundred dollars every time you come over here! . . . What is it *now?* Yellows? Reds? *Acid? Speed?* What the hell is it *now?* Grass isn't that expensive!"

The girl sobbed. Tears fell down her cheeks. She covered her face and spoke—moaned—through her sobs.

"There's so much trouble! So much . . . *trouble!* Let me *go, please!*"

Matlock knelt down and cradled the girl's head in his arms, against his chest.

"What trouble? tell me, please. What trouble?"

"They *make* you do it. . . . You *have* to. . . . So many need help. They won't help *anyone* if you don't do it. Please, whatever your name is, let me alone. Let me go. Don't say anything. Let me *go! . . . Please!*"

"I will, but you've got to clear something up for me. Then you can go and I won't say anything. . . . Are you down here because they threatened you? Threatened the other kids?"

The girl nodded her head, gasping quietly, breathing heavily. Matlock continued. "Threatened you with what? Turning you in? . . . Exposing a habit? That's not worth it. Not today. . . ."

"Oh, you're outta sight!" The girl spoke through her

tears. "They can ruin you. For life. Ruin your family, your school, maybe later. Maybe. . . . Some rotten prison. Somewhere! Habit, pushing, supplying . . . a boy you know's in trouble and *they* can get him off. . . . Some girl's in her third month, she needs a doctor . . . *they* can get one. No noise."

"You don't need *them!* Where've you *been?!* There are agencies, counseling!"

"Oh, Jesus Christ, mister! Where have *you* been?! . . . The drug courts, the doctors, the judges! They run them *all!* . . . There's nothing *you* can do about it. Nothing *I* can do about it. So leave me alone, leave *us* alone! Too many people'll get hurt!"

"And you're just going to keep doing what they say! Frightened, spoiled little bastards who keep on whining! Afraid to wash your hands, or your *mouths,* or your *arms!*" He pulled at her left elbow and yanked it viciously.

The girl looked up at him, half in fear, half in contempt.

"That's right," she said in a strangely calm voice. "I don't think you'd understand. You don't know what it's all about. . . . We're different from you. My friends are all I've got. All any of us have got. We help each other. . . . I'm not interested in being a hero. I'm only interested in my friends. I don't have a flag decal in my car window and I don't like John Wayne. I think he's a shit. I think you all are. All shits."

Matlock released the girl's arm. "Just how long do you think you can keep it up?"

"Oh, I'm one of the lucky ones. In a month I'll have that scroll my parents paid for and I'm out of it. They hardly ever try to make contact with you later. They say they will, but they rarely do. . . . You're just supposed to live with the possibility."

He understood the implications of her muted testimony and turned away. "I'm sorry. I'm very, very sorry."

"Don't be. I'm one of the lucky ones. Two weeks after I pick up that piece of engraved crap my parents want so badly, I'll be on a plane. I'm leaving this goddamn country. And I'll never come back!"

25

He had not been able to sleep, nor had he expected to. He had sent the girl away with money, for he had nothing else he could give her, neither hope nor courage. What he advocated was rejected, for it involved the risk of danger and pain to untold children committed to the well-being of each other. He could not demand; there was no trust, no threat equal to the burdens they carried. Ultimately, it was the children's own struggle. They wanted no help.

He remembered the Bagdhivi admonition: *Look ye to the children; look and behold. They grow tall and strong and hunt the tiger with greater cunning and stronger sinews than you. They shall save the flocks better than you. Ye are old and infirm. Look to the children. Beware of the children.*

Were the children hunting the tiger better? And even if they were, whose flocks would they save? And who was the tiger?

Was it the "goddamn country"?

Had it come to that?

The questions burned into his mind. How many Jeannies were there? How extensive was Nimrod's recruiting?

He had to find out.

The girl admitted that Carmount was only one port

of call; there were others, but she didn't know where. Friends of hers had been sent to New Haven, others to Boston, some north to the outskirts of Hanover.

Yale. Harvard. Dartmouth.

The most frightening aspect was Nimrod's threat of a thousand futures. What had she said?

"They hardly ever make contact. . . . They say they will. . . . You live with the possibility."

If such was the case, Bagdhivi was wrong. The children had far less cunning, possessed weaker sinews; there was no reason to beware. Only to pity.

Unless the children were subdivided, led by other, stronger children.

Matlock made up his mind to go down to New Haven. Maybe there were answers there. He had scores of friends at Yale University. It would be a side trip, an unconsidered excursion, but intrinsic to the journey itself. Part of the Nimrod odyssey.

Short, high-pitched sounds interrupted Matlock's concentration. He froze, his eyes swollen in shock, his body tense on top of the bed. It took him several seconds to focus his attention on the source of the frightening sound. It was the Tel-electronic, still in his jacket pocket. But where had he put his jacket? It wasn't near his bed.

He turned on the bedside lamp and looked around, the unrelenting, unceasing sounds causing his pulse to hammer, his forehead to perspire. Then he saw his coat. He had put it on top of the chair in front of the French window, halfway across the room. He looked at his watch: 4:35 A.M. He ran to the jacket, pulled out the terrible instrument, and shut it off.

The panic of the hunted returned. He picked up the telephone on the bedside table. It was a direct line, no switchboard.

The dial tone was like any other dial tone outside the major utility areas. A little fuzzy, but steady. And if there was a tap, he wouldn't be able to recognize it anyway. He dialed 555-6868 and waited for the call to be completed.

"Charger Three-zero reporting," said the mechanized voice. "Sorry to disturb you. There is no change with the subject, everything is satisfactory. However, your friend from Wheeling, West Virginia, is very insistent. He telephoned at four fifteen and said it was imperative you call him at once. We're concerned. Out."

Matlock hung up the telephone and forced his mind to go blank until he found a cigarette and lit it. He needed the precious moments to stop the hammering pulse.

He hated that goddamn machine! He hated what its terrifying little beeps did to him.

He drew heavily on the smoke and knew there was no alternative. He had to get out of the Carmount Country Club and reach a telephone booth. Greenberg wouldn't have phoned at four in the morning unless it was an emergency. He couldn't take the chance of calling Greenberg on the Carmount line.

He threw his clothes into the suitcase and dressed quickly.

He assumed there'd be a night watchman, or a parking attendant asleep in a booth, and he'd retrieve his, Kramer's, automobile. If not, he'd wake up someone, even if it was Stockton himself. Stockton was still frightened of trouble, Windsor Shoals trouble—he wouldn't try to detain him. Any story would do for the purveyor of young, adorable flesh. The sunburned southern flower of the Connecticut Valley. The stench of Nimrod.

Matlock closed the door quietly and walked down the silent corridor to the enormous staircase. Wall sconces were lighted, dimmed by rheostats to give a candlelight effect. Even in the dead of night, Howard Stockton couldn't forget his heritage. The interior of the Carmount Country Club looked more than ever like a sleeping great hall of a plantation house.

He started for the front entrance, and by the time he reached the storm carpet, he knew it was as far as he would go. At least for the moment.

Howard Stockton, clad in a flowing velour, nineteenth-century dressing gown, emerged from a glass door next to the entrance. He was accompanied by a large, Italian-looking man whose jet black eyes silently spoke generations of the Black Hand. Stockton's companion was a killer.

"Why, Mr. Matlock! Are you leavin' us?"

He decided to be aggressive.

"Since you tapped my goddamn phone, I assume you gather I've got problems! They're *my business, not yours!* If you want to know, I resent your intrusion!"

The ploy worked. Stockton was startled by Matlock's hostility.

"There's no reason to be angry. . . . I'm a businessman, like you. Any invasion of your privacy is for your protection. Goddamn! That's *true, boy!*"

"I'll accept the lousy explanation. Are my keys in the car?"

"Well, not in your *car*. My friend Mario here's got 'em. He's a real high-class Eyetalian, let me tell you."

"I can see the family crest on his pocket. May I have my keys?"

Mario looked at Stockton, obviously confused.

"Now, just a minute," Stockton said. "Wait a bit,

Mario. Let's not be impulsive. . . . I'm a reasonable man. A very reasonable, rational person. I'm merely a Virginia . . ."

"*Cracker*, trying to make a dollar!" interrupted Matlock. "I'll buy that! Now get the hell out of my way and give me the keys!"

"Good Lord, *you all* are downright *mean!* I mean, *mean!* Put yourself in my place! . . . Some crazy code like 'Chargin' Three-zero' and an urgent call from Wheelin', West *Virginia!* And instead of usin' my perfectly good telephone, you gotta make space and get *outta* here! C'mon, Jim. What would *you* do?!"

Matlock kept his voice chillingly precise. "I'd try to understand *who* I was dealing with. . . . We've made a number of inquiries, Howard. My superiors are concerned about you."

"What-do-you-mean?" Stockton's question was asked so swiftly the words had no separation.

"They think . . . we think you've called too much attention to yourself. President and vice-president of a *Rotary Club!* Jesus! A one-man fund-raiser for new school buildings; the big provider for widows and orphans—charge accounts included; Memorial Day picnics! Then hiring locals to spread rumors about the girls! Half the time the kids walk around half naked. You think the local citizens don't talk? *Christ*, Howard!"

"Who the hell are you?"

"Just a tired businessman who gets annoyed when he sees another businessman make an ass of himself. What the hell do you think you're running for? Santa Claus? Have you any idea how prominent that costume is?"

"Goddamn it, you got it in for me! I've got the finest combined operation north of Atlanta! I don't know who you people been talkin' to, but I tell you—this l'il old Mount Holly'd go to hell in a basket for me! Those things you people dug up—they're *good* things! *Real* good! . . . You twist 'em, make 'em sound bad! That ain't *right!*"

Stockton took out a handkerchief and patted his flushed, perspiring face. The southerner was so upset his sentences spilled over into one another, his voice strident. Matlock tried to think swiftly, cautiously. Perhaps the time was now—with Stockton. It had to be sometime. He had to send out his own particular invitation. He had to start the last lap of his journey to Nimrod.

"Calm down, Stockton. Relax. You may be right. . . . I haven't time to think about it now. We've got a crisis. All of us. That phone call was serious." Matlock paused, looking hard at the nervous Stockton, and then put his suitcase on the marble floor. "Howard," he said slowly, choosing his words carefully, "I'm going to trust you with something and I hope to hell you're up to it. If you pull it off, no one'll bother your operation—ever."

"What's that?"

"Tell *him* to take a walk. Just down the hall, if you like."

"You heard the man. Go smoke a cigar."

Mario looked both hostile and confused as he trudged slowly toward the staircase. Stockton spoke.

"What do you want me to do? I told you, I don't want trouble."

"We're *all* going to have trouble unless I reach a few delegates. That's what Wheeling was telling me."

"What do you mean . . . delegates?"

"The meeting over at Carlyle. The conference with our people and the Nimrod organization."

"That's not my affair!" Stockton spat out the words. "I don't know a thing about that!"

"I'm sure you don't; you weren't meant to. But now it concerns all of us. . . . Sometimes rules have to be broken; this is one of those times. Nimrod's gone too far, that's all I can tell you."

"You tell *me*? I live with those *preachers!* I *parlay* with them, and when I complain, you know what our own people say? They say, 'That's the way it is, old Howie, we all do business'! What kind of talk is that? Why do *I* have to do business with them?"

"Perhaps you won't much longer. That's why I have to reach some of the others. The delegates."

"They don't include me in those meetings. I don't know anyone."

"Of course you don't. Again, you weren't meant to. The conference is heavy; very heavy and very quiet. So quiet we may have screwed ourselves: we don't know who's in the area. From what organization; from what family? But I have my orders. We've got to get through to one or two."

"I can't help you."

Matlock looked harshly at the southerner. "I think you can. Listen to me. In the morning, get on the phone and pass the word. *Carefully!* We don't want panic. Don't talk to anyone you don't know and don't use my name! Just say you've met someone who has the Corsican paper, the silver Corsican paper. He's *got* to meet quietly with someone else who has it, too. We'll start with one person if we have to. Have you got that?"

"I got it but I don't like it! It's none of *my business!*"

"Would you rather close down? Would you rather lose this magnificent relic of yours and stare out of a cell window for ten or twenty years? I understand prison funerals are very touching."

"All right! . . . All right. I'll call my bag boy. I'll say I don't know nothin'! I'm just passin' along a message."

"Good enough. If you make a contact, tell whoever it is that I'll be at the Sail and Ski tonight or tomorrow. Tell him to bring the paper. I won't talk to anyone without the paper!"

"Without the paper. . . ."

"Now let me have my keys."

Stockton called Mario back. Matlock got his keys.

He swung south on Route 72 out of Mount Holly. He didn't remember precisely where, but he knew he'd passed several highway telephone booths on his way up from Hartford. It was funny how he was beginning to notice public telephones, his only connecting link with solidity. Everything else was transient, hit or miss, unfamiliar and frightening. He'd phone Greenberg as Charger Three-zero requested, but before he did, he was going to reach one of Blackstone's men.

A rendezvous would have to be arranged immediately. He now had to have the Corsican paper. He'd put out the word; he'd have to keep his end of the bargain or he would learn nothing. *If* Stockton's message got through and *if* someone *did* make contact, that someone would kill or be killed before breaking the oath of "Omerta" unless Matlock produced the paper.

Or was it all for nothing? Was he the amateur Kressel and Greenberg said he was? He didn't know. He tried so hard to think things through, look at all sides of every action, use the tools of his trained, academic imagination. But was it enough? Or was it possible that his sense of commitment, his violent feelings of vengeance and disgust were only turning him into a Quixote?

If that were so, he'd live with it. He'd do his goddamnedest and live with it. He had good reasons—a brother named David; a girl named Pat; a gentle old man named Lucas; a nice fellow named Loring; a confused, terrified student from Madison named Jeannie. The sickening whole *scene!*

Matlock found a booth on a deserted stretch of Route 72 and called the inanimate receiver at the other end of 555-6868. He gave the number of the telephone booth and waited for Charger Three-zero to answer his call.

A milk truck lumbered by. The driver was singing and waved to Matlock. Several minutes later a huge Allied Van Lines sped past, and shortly after a produce truck. It was nearing five thirty, and the day was brightening. Brightening to a dull gray, for there were rain clouds in the sky.

The telephone rang.

"Hello!"

"What's the problem, sir? Did you reach your friend in West Virginia? He said he's not kidding anymore."

"I'll call him in a few minutes. Are you the fellow named Cliff?" Matlock knew it was not; the voice was different.

"No, sir. I'm Jim. Same name as yours."

"All right, Jim. Tell me, did the other fellow do what I asked him to? Did he get the paper for me?"

"Yes, sir. If it's the one on silver paper, written in Italian. I think it's Italian."

"That's the one. . . ."

Matlock arranged for the pickup in two hours. It

was agreed that the Blackstone man named Cliff meet him at an all-night diner on Scofield Avenue near the West Hartford town line. Charger Three-zero insisted that the delivery be made rapidly, in the parking lot. Matlock described the car he was driving and hung up the phone.

The next call would have to be Jason Greenberg in Wheeling. And Greenberg was furious.

"Schmuck! It isn't bad enough you break your word, you've got to hire your own army! What the hell do you think those clowns can do that the United States Government can't?"

"Those clowns are costing me three hundred dollars a day, Jason. They'd better be good."

"You ran out! Why did you do that? You gave me your word you wouldn't. You said you'd work with our man!"

"Your man gave me an ultimatum I couldn't live with! And if it was your idea, I'll tell you the same thing I told Houston."

"What does that mean? What ultimatum?"

"You know goddamn well! Don't play that game. And you listen to me. . . ." Matlock took a break before plunging into the lie, giving it all the authority he could summon. "There's a lwayer in Hartford who has a very precise letter signed by me. Along the same lines as the letter I signed for you. Only the information's a bit different: it's straight. It describes in detail the story of my recruitment; how you bastards sucked me in and then how you let me hang. How you forced me to sign a lie. . . . You try anything, he'll release it and there'll be a lot of embarrassed manipulators at the Justice Department. . . . You gave me the idea, Jason. It was a damn good idea. It might even make a few militants decide to tear up the Carlyle campus. Maybe launch a string of riots, with luck, right across the country. The academic scene's ready to be primed out of its dormancy; isn't that what Sealfont said? Only this time it won't be the war or the draft or drugs. They'll find a better label: government infiltration, police state . . . *Gestapo* tactics. Are you prepared for that?"

"For Christ's sake, cut it out! It won't do you any good. You're not that important. . . . Now, what the hell are you talking about? *I briefed him!* There weren't any conditions except that you keep him informed of what you were doing."

"Bullshit! I wasn't to leave the campus; I wasn't to talk to anyone on the faculty or the staff. I was restricted to student inquiries, and I gathered those were to be cleared *first!* Outside of those minor restrictions, I was free as a bird! Come on! You *saw* Pat! You saw what they did to her. You know what else they did—the word is *rape,* Greenberg! Did you people expect me to *thank* Houston for being so *understanding?*"

"Believe me," said Greenberg softly, in anger. "Those conditions were added after the briefing. They should have told me, that's true. But they were added for your own protection. You can see that, can't you?"

"They weren't part of our bargain!"

"No, they weren't. And they should have told me. . . ."

"Also, I wonder whose protection they were concerned with. Mine or theirs."

"A good question. They should have told me. They can't delegate responsibility and always take away the authority. It's not logical."

"It's not *moral.* Let me tell you something. This little odyssey of mine is bringing me closer and closer to the sublime question of morality."

"I'm glad for you, but I'm afraid your odyssey's coming to an end."

"Try it!"

"They're going to. Statements in lawyers' offices won't mean a damn. I told them I'd try first. . . . If you don't turn yourself over to protective custody within forty-eight hours, they'll issue a warrant."

"On what grounds?!"

"You're a menace. You're mentally unbalanced. You're a nut. They'll cite your army record—two courts-martial, brig time, continuous instability under combat conditions. Your use of drugs. And alcohol—they've got witnesses. You're also a racist—they've got that Lumumba affidavit from Kressel. And now I understand, although I haven't the facts, you're consorting with known criminals. They have photographs—from a place in Avon. . . . Turn yourself in, Jim. They'll ruin your life."

26

Forty-eight hours! Why forty-eight hours? Why not twenty-four or twelve or immediately? It didn't make sense! Then he understood and, alone in the booth, he started to laugh. He laughed out loud in a telephone booth at five thirty in the morning on a deserted stretch of highway in Mount Holly, Connecticut.

The practical men were giving him just enough time to accomplish something—if he *could* accomplish something. If he couldn't, and anything happened, they were clean. It was on record that they considered him a mentally unbalanced addict with racist tendencies who consorted with known criminals, and they had given him warning. In deference to the delicate balance of dealing with such madmen, they allocated *time* in the hopes of reducing the danger. Oh, Christ! The manipulators!

He reached the West Hartford diner at six forty-five and ate a large breakfast, somehow believing that the food would take the place of sleep and give him the energy he needed. He kept glancing at his watch, knowing that he'd have to be in the parking lot by seven thirty.

He wondered what his contact at Charger Three-zero would look like.

The man was enormous, and Matlock had never considered himself small. Cliff of Charger Three-zero reminded Matlock of those old pictures of Primo Carnera. Except the face. The face was lean and intelligent and smiled broadly.

"Don't get out, Mr. Matlock." He reached in and shook Matlock's hand. "Here's the paper; I put it in an envelope. By the way, we had Miss Ballantyne laughing last night. She's feeling better. Encephalograph's steady, metabolism's coming back up to par, pupil dilation's receding. Thought you'd like to know."

"I imagine that's good."

"It is. We've made friends with the doctor. He levels."

"How's the hospital taking your guard duty?"

"Mr. Blackstone solves those problems in advance. We have rooms on either side of the subject."

"For which, I'm sure, I'll be charged."

"You know Mr. Blackstone."

"I'm getting to. He goes first class."

"So do his clients. I'd better get back. Nice to meet you." The Blackstone man walked rapidly away and got into a nondescript automobile several years old.

It was time for Matlock to drive to New Haven.

He had no set plan, no specific individuals in mind; he wasn't leading, he was being led. His information was, at best, nebulous, sketchy, far too incomplete to deal in absolutes. Yet perhaps there was enough for someone to make a connection. But whoever made it, or was capable of making it, had to be someone with an overall view of the university. Someone who dealt, as did Sam Kressel, with the general tensions of the campus.

However, Yale was five times the size of Carlyle; it was infinitely more diffuse, a section of the New Haven city, not really isolated from its surroundings as was Carlyle. There *was* a focal point, the Office of Student Affairs; but he didn't know anyone there. And to arrive off the street with an improbable story of college girls forming—or being formed into—a prostitution ring reaching, as so far determined, the states of Connecticut, Massachusetts, and New Hampshire, would create havoc if he was taken seriously. And he wasn't sure he *would* be taken seriously, in which case he'd learn nothing.

There was one possibility; a poor substitute for Student Affairs, but with its own general view of the campus: the Department of Admissions. He knew a man, Peter Daniels, who worked in Yale's admissions office. He and Daniels had shared a number of lecterns during prep school recruitment programs. He knew Daniels well enough to spell out the facts as he understood them; Daniels wasn't the sort to doubt him or to panic. He'd restrict his story to the girl, however.

He parked on Chappel Street near the intersection of York. On one side of the thoroughfare was an arch leading to the quadrangle of Silliman College, on the other a large expanse of lawn threaded with cement paths to the Administration Building. Daniels's office was on the second floor. Matlock got out of the car, locked it, and walked toward the old brick structure with the American flag masted next to the Yale banner.

"That's preposterous! This is the age of Aquarius and then some. You don't pay for sex; it's exchanged freely."

"I know what I saw. I know what the girl told me; she wasn't lying."

"I repeat. You can't be sure."

"It's tied in with too many other things. I've seen them, too."

"May I ask the obvious question? Why don't you go to the police?"

"Obvious answer. Colleges have been in enough trouble. What facts I have are isolated. I need more information. I don't want to be responsible for indiscriminate name-calling, any widespread panic. There's been enough of that."

"All right, I'll buy it. But I can't help you."

"Give me several names. Students *or* faculty. People you know . . . you're certain are messed up, seriously messed up. Near the center. You've got those kinds of names, I know you do; we do. . . . I swear, they'll never know who gave them to me."

Daniels got out of his chair, lighting his pipe. "You're being awfully general. Messed up how? Academically, politically . . . narcotics, alcohol? You're covering a wide territory."

"Wait a minute." Daniels's words evoked a memory. Matlock recalled a dimly lit, smoke-filled room inside a seemingly deserted building in Hartford. Rocco Aiello's Hunt Club. And a tall young man in a waiter's jacket who had brought over a tab for Aiello to sign. The veteran of Nam and Da Nang. The Yalie who was *making contacts, building up his nest egg* . . . the *business administration* major. "I know who I want to see."

"What's his name?"

"I don't know. . . . But he's a veteran—Indochina, about twenty-two or three; he's pretty tall, light brown hair . . . majoring in business administration."

"A description which might fit five hundred students. Except for premed, law, and engineering, it's all lumped under liberal arts. We'd have to go through every file."

"Application photographs?"

"Not allowed anymore, you know that."

Matlock stared out the window, his eyebrows wrinkled in thought. He looked back at Daniels. "Pete, it's May. . . ."

"So? It could be November; that wouldn't change the Fair Practices law."

"Graduation's in a month. . . . Senior class photographs. Yearbook portraits."

Daniels understood instantly. He took his pipe from his mouth and started for the door.

"Come with me."

His name was Alan Pace. He was a senior and his curriculum was not centered on business administration; he was a government major. He lived off campus on Church Street near the Hamden town line. According to his records, Alan Pace was an excellent student, consistent honors in all subjects, a fellowship in the offing at the Maxwell School of Political Science at Syracuse. He had spent twenty-eight months in the army, four more than was required of him. As with most veterans, his university extracurricular activities were minimal.

While Pace was in service, he was an officer attached to inventory and supply. He had volunteered for a four-month extended tour of duty in the Saigon

Corps—a fact noted with emphasis on his reapplication form. Alan Pace had given four months of his life more than necessary to his country. Alan Pace was obviously an honorable man in these days of cynicism.

He was a winner, thought Matlock.

The drive out Church Street toward Hamden gave Matlock the chance to clear his mind. He had to take one thing at a time; one item crossed off—on to the next. He couldn't allow his imagination to interpret isolated facts beyond their meaning. He couldn't lump everything together and total a sum larger than the parts.

It was entirely possible that this Alan Pace played a solo game. Unattached, unencumbered.

But it wasn't logical.

Pace's apartment house was an undistinguished brown brick building, so common on the outskirts of cities. Once—forty or fifty years ago—it had been the proud symbol of a rising middle class extending themselves out beyond the cement confines toward the country, but not so courageous as to leave the city completely. It wasn't so much run down as it was . . . not spruced up. The most glaring aspect of the apartment house to Matlock, however, was that it seemed to be a most unlikely place for a student to reside.

But he was there now; Peter Daniels had ascertained that.

Pace had not wanted to unlatch the door. It was only Matlock's strong emphasis on two points that made the student relent. The first point was that he wasn't from the police; the second, the name of Rocco Aiello.

"What do you want? I've got a lot of work to do;

I don't have time to talk. I've got comprehensives tomorrow."

"May I sit down?"

"What for? I told you, I'm busy." The tall, brown-haired student crossed back to his desk, piled with books and papers. The apartment was neat—except for the desk—and quite large. There were doors and short corridors leading to other doors. It was the sort of apartment that usually was shared by four or five students. But Alan Pace had no roommates.

"I'll sit down anyway. You owe that much to Rocco."

"What does that mean?"

"Just that Rocco was my friend. I was the one with him the other night when you brought him a tab to sign. Remember? And he was good to you. . . . He's dead."

"I know. I read about it. I'm sorry. But I didn't owe him anything."

"But you bought from him."

"I don't know what you're talking about."

"Come on, Pace. You don't have the time and neither do I. You're not connected to Aiello's death, I know that. But I've got to have information, and you're going to supply it."

"You're talking to the wrong person. I don't know you. I don't know *anything.*"

"I know *you.* I've got a complete rundown on you. Aiello and I were considering going into business together. Now, that's none of your concern, I realize that, but we exchanged . . . personnel information. I'm coming to you because, frankly, Rocco's gone and there are areas that need filling. I'm really asking a favor, and I'll pay for it."

"I told you, I'm not your man. I hardly knew Aiello. I picked up a few dollars waiting tables. Sure, I heard rumors, but that's *all.* I don't know what you want, but you'd better go to someone else."

Pace was sharp, thought Matlock. He was disengaging himself but not foolishly claiming complete innocence. On the other hand, perhaps he was telling the truth. There was only one way to find out.

"I'll try again. . . . Fifteen months in Vietnam. Saigon, Da Nang; excursions to Hong Kong, Japan. I&S officer; the dullest, most exasperating kind of work for a young man with the potential that earns him honors at a very tough university."

"I&S was good duty; no combat, no sweat. Everybody made the tourist hops. Check the R&R route sheets."

"Then," continued Matlock without acknowledging Pace's interruption, "the dedicated officer returns to civilian life. After a four-month voluntary extension in Saigon—I'm surprised you weren't caught up on *that* one—he comes back with enough money to make the proper investments, and certainly not from his army pay. He's one of the biggest suppliers in New Haven. Do you want me to go on?"

Pace stood by the desk and seemed to stop breathing. He stared at Matlock, his face white. When he spoke, it was the voice of a frightened young man.

"You can't prove anything. I haven't done anything. My army record, my record here—they're both good. They're very good."

"The best. Unblemished. They're records to be proud of; I mean that sincerely. And I wouldn't want to do anything to spoil them; I mean that, too."

"You couldn't. I'm clean!"

"No, you're not. You're up to your fellowship neck. Aiello made that *clear*. On *paper*."

"You're lying!"

"You're stupid. You think Aiello would do business with *anyone* he didn't run a check on? Do you think he'd be *allowed* to? He kept very extensive books, Pace, and I've *got* them. I told you; we were going into business together. You don't form a partnership without audit disclosures, you should know that."

Pace spoke barely above a whisper. "There are no books like that. There never are. Cities, towns, codes. No names. Never any names."

"Then why am I here?"

"You saw me in Hartford; you're reaching for a connection."

"You know better than that. Don't be foolish."

Matlock's quickly put implications were too much for the tall, shocked young man. "Why did you come to me? I'm not that important. You say you know about me; then you know I'm not important."

"I told you. I need information. I'm reluctant to go to the high priests, anyone with real authority. I don't want to be at a disadvantage. That's why I'm willing to pay; why I'm prepared to tear up everything I've got on you."

The prospect of being cut free of the stranger's grip was obviously all that was on Pace's mind. He replied quickly.

"Suppose I can't answer your questions? You'll think I'm lying."

"You can't be worse off. All you can do is try me."

"Go ahead."

"I met a girl . . . from a nearby college. I met her under circumstances that can only be described as professional prostitution. Professional in every sense of the word. Appointments, set fees, no prior knowledge of clients, the works. . . . What do you know about it?"

Pace took several steps toward Matlock. "What do you mean, what do I know? I know it's there. What else is there to know?"

"How extensive?"

"All over. It's not news."

"It is to me."

"You don't know the scene. Take a walk around a few college towns."

Matlock swallowed. Was he really that far out of touch? "Suppose I were to tell you I'm familiar with a lot of . . . college towns?"

"I'd say your circles were cubed. Also, I'm no part of that action. What else?"

"Let's stick to this for a minute. . . . Why?"

"Why what?"

"Why do the girls do it?"

"Bread, man. Why does anyone do anything?"

"You're too intelligent to believe that. . . . Is it organized?"

"I guess so. I told you, I'm no part of it."

"Watch it! I've got a lot of paper on you. . . ."

"All right. Yes, it's organized. Everything's organized. If it's going to work."

"Where *specifically* are the operations?"

"I *told* you! All *over*."

"Inside the colleges?"

"No, not inside. On the outskirts. A couple of miles usually, if the campuses are rural. Old houses, away from the suburbs. If they're in cities—downtown hotels, private clubs, apartment houses. But not *here*."

"Are we talking about . . . Columbia, Harvard, Radcliffe, Smith, Holyoke? And points south?"

"Everyone always forgets Princeton," replied Pace with a wry smile. "A lot of nice old estates in those back roads. . . . Yes, we're talking about those places."

"I never would have believed it. . . ." Matlock spoke as much to himself as to Pace. "But, *why?* Don't give me the 'bread' routine. . . ."

"Bread is *freedom*, man! For these kids it's freedom. They're not psyched-up freaks; they're not running around in black berets and field jackets. Very few of us are. We've *learned.* Get the money, fella, and the nice people will like you. . . . Also, whether you've noticed it or not, the straight money's not as easy to come by as it once was. Most of these kids need it."

"The girl I mentioned before; I gathered she was forced into it."

"Oh, Jesus, nobody's *forced!* That's crap."

"She was. She mentioned a few things. . . . Controls is as good a word as any. Courts, doctors, even jobs. . . ."

"I wouldn't know anything about that."

"And afterward. Making contact later—perhaps a few years later. Plain old-fashioned blackmail. Just as I'm blackmailing you now."

"Then she was in trouble before; this girl, I mean. If it's a bummer, she doesn't have to make the trip. Unless she's into somebody and owes what she can't pay for."

"Who is Nimrod?" Matlock asked the question softly, without emphasis. But the question caused the young man to turn and walk away.

"I don't know that. I don't have that information."

Matlock got out of the chair and stood motionless. "I'll ask you just once more, and if I don't get an answer, I'll walk out the door and you'll be finished.

A very promising life will be altered drastically—if you have a life. . . . Who is Nimrod?"

The boy whipped around and Matlock saw the fear again. The fear he had seen on Lucas Herron's face, in Lucas Herron's eyes.

"So help me Christ, I can't answer that!"

"Can't or won't?"

"Can't. I *don't know!*"

"I think you do. But I said I'd only ask you once. That's it." Matlock started for the apartment door without looking at the student.

"No! . . . Goddamn it, I *don't know!* . . . How *could* I know? You can't!" Pace ran to Matlock's side.

"Can't what?"

"Whatever you said you'd do. . . . Listen to me! I don't know who they are! I don't have . . ."

"They?"

Pace looked puzzled. "Yeah. . . . I guess 'they.' I don't know. I don't have any contact. Others do; I don't. They haven't bothered me."

"But you're aware of them." A statement.

"Aware. . . . Yes, I'm aware. But *who,* honest to God, *no!*"

Matlock turned and faced the student. "We'll compromise. For now. Tell me what you *do* know."

And the frightened young man did. And as the words came forth, the fear infected James Matlock.

Nimrod was an unseen master puppeteer. Faceless, formless, but with frightening, viable authority. It wasn't a *he* or a *they*— it was a *force,* according to Alan Pace. A complex abstraction that had its elusive tentacles in every major university in the Northeast, every municipality that served the academic landscape, all the financial pyramids that funded the complicated structures of New England's higher education. "And points south," if the rumors had foundation.

Narcotics was only one aspect, the craw in the throats of the criminal legions—the immediate reason for the May conference, the Corsican letter.

Beyond drugs and their profits, the Nimrod imprimatur was stamped on scores of college administrations. Pace was convinced that curriculums were being shaped, university personnel hired and fired, degree and scholarship policies, all were expedited on the Nimrod organization's instructions. Matlock's memory flashed back to Carlyle. To Carlyle's assistant dean of admissions—a Nimrod appointee, according to the dead Loring. To Archer Beeson, rapidly rising in the history department; to a coach of varsity soccer; to a dozen other faculty and staff names on Loring's list.

How many more were there? How deep was the infiltration?

Why?

The prostitution rings were subsidiary accommodations. Recruitments were made by the child-whores among themselves; addresses were provided, fees established. Young flesh with ability and attractiveness could find its way to Nimrod and make the pact. And there was "freedom," there was "bread" in the pact with Nimrod.

And "no one was hurt"; it was a victimless crime.

"No crime at all, just freedom, man. No pressures over the head. No screaming zonkers over scholarship points."

Alan Pace saw a great deal of good in the elusive, practical Nimrod. More than good.

"You think it's all so different from the outside—straight? You're wrong, mister. It's mini-America: organized, computerized, and very heavy with the corporate structure. Hell, it's patterned on the American syndrome; it's company *policy*, man! It's GM, ITT, and Ma Bell—only someone was smart enough to organize the groovy groves of academe. And it's growing fast. Don't fight it. Join it."

"Is that what you're going to do?" asked Matlock.

"It's the way, man. It's the faith. For all I know *you're* with it now. Could be, you're a recruiter. You guys are everywhere; I've been expecting you."

"Suppose I'm not?"

"Then you're out of your head. And over it, too."

27

If one watched the white station wagon and its driver heading back toward the center of New Haven, one would have thought—if he thought at all—that it was a rich car, suitable to a wealthy suburb, the man at the wheel appropriately featured for the vehicle.

Such an observer would not know that the driver was barely cognizant of the traffic, numbed by the revelations he'd learned within the hour; an exhausted man who hadn't slept in forty-eight hours, who had the feeling that he was holding onto a thin rope above an infinite chasm, expecting any instant that his lifeline would be severed, plunging him into the infinite mist.

Matlock tried his best to suspend whatever thought processes he was capable of. The years, the specific months during which he'd run his academic race against self-imposed schedules had taught him that the mind—at least his mind—could not function properly when the forces of exhaustion and overexposure converged.

Above all, he had to function.

He was in uncharted waters. Seas where tiny islands were peopled by grotesque inhabitants. Julian Dunoises, Lucas Herrons; the Bartolozzis, the Aiellos, the Sharpes, the Stocktons, and the Paces. The poisoned and the poisoners.

Nimrod.

Uncharted waters?

No, they weren't uncharted, thought Matlock.

They were well traveled. And the travelers were the cynics of the planet.

He drove to the Sheraton Hotel and took a room.

He sat on the edge of the bed and placed a telephone call to Howard Stockton at Carmount. Stockton was out.

In brusque, officious tones, he told the Carmount switchboard that Stockton was to return his call—he looked at his watch; it was ten of two—in four hours. At six o'clock. He gave the Sheraton number and hung up.

He needed at least four hours' sleep. He wasn't sure when he would sleep again.

He picked up the telephone once more and requested a wake-up call at five forty-five.

As his head sank to the pillow, he brought his arm up to his eyes. Through the cloth of his shirt he felt the stubble of his beard. He'd have to go to a barbershop; he'd left his suitcase in the white station wagon. He'd been too tired, too involved to remember to bring it to his room.

The short, sharp three rings of the telephone signified the Sheraton's adherence to his instructions. It was exactly quarter to six. Fifteen minutes later there was another ring, this one longer, more normal. It was precisely six, and the caller was Howard Stockton.

"I'll make this short, Matlock. You got a contact.

Only he doesn't want to meet *inside* the Sail and Ski. You go to the East Gorge slope—they use it in spring and summer for tourists to look at the scenery—and take the lift up to the top. You be there at eight thirty this evenin'. He'll have a man at the top. That's all I've got to say. It's none of *mah business!*"

Stockton slammed down the telephone and the echo rang in Matlock's ear.

But he'd made it! *He'd made it!* He had made the contact with Nimrod! With the conference.

He walked up the dark trail toward the ski lift. Ten dollars made the attendant at the Sail and Ski parking lot understand his problem: the nice-looking fellow in the station wagon had an assignation. The husband wasn't expected till later—and, what the hell, that's life. The parking lot attendant was very cooperative.

When he reached the East Gorge slope, the rain, which had threatened all day, began to come down. In Connecticut, April showers were somehow always May thunderstorms, and Matlock was annoyed that he hadn't thought to buy a raincoat.

He looked around at the deserted lift, its high double lines silhouetted against the increasing rain, shining like thick strands of ship hemp in a fogged harbor. There was a tiny, almost invisible light in the shack which housed the complicated, hulking machines that made the lines ascend. Matlock approached the door and knocked. A small, wiry-looking man opened the door and peered at him.

"You the fella goin' up?"

"I guess I am."

"What's your name?"

"Matlock."

"Guess you are. Know how to catch a crossbar?"

"I've skied. Arm looped, tail on the slat, feet on the pipe."

"Don't need no help from me. I'll start it, you get it."

"Fine."

"You're gonna get wet."

"I know."

Matlock positioned himself to the right of the entrance pit as the lumbering machinery started up. The lines creaked slowly and then began their halting countermoves, and a crossbar approached. He slid himself onto the lift, pressed his feet against the footrail, and locked the bar in front of his waist. He felt the swinging motion of the lines lifting him off the ground.

He was on his way to the top of the East Gorge, on his way to his contact with Nimrod. As he swung upward, ten feet above the ground, the rain became, instead of annoying, exhilarating. He was coming to the end of his journey, his race. Whoever met him at the top would be utterly confused. He counted on that, he'd planned it that way. If everything the murdered Loring and the very-much-alive Greenberg had told him was true, it couldn't be any other way. The total secrecy of the conference; the delegates, unknown to each other; the oath of "Omerta," the subculture's violent insistence on codes and countercodes to protect its inhabitants—it *was* all true. He'd seen it all in operation. And such complicated logistics—when sharply interrupted—inevitably led to suspicion and fear and ultimately confusion. It was the confusion Matlock counted on.

Lucas Herron had accused him of being influenced by plots and counterplots. Well, he wasn't *influenced* by them—he merely *understood* them. That was different. It was this understanding which had led him one step away from Nimrod.

The rain came harder now, whipped by the wind which was stronger off the ground than on it. Matlock's crossbar swayed and dipped, more so each time he reached a rung up the slope. The tiny light in the machine shack was now barely visible in the darkness and the rain. He judged that he was nearly halfway to the top.

There was a jolt; the machinery stopped. Matlock gripped the waist guard and peered above him through the rain trying to see what obstruction had hit the wheel or the rung. There was none.

He turned awkwardly in the narrow perch and squinted his eyes down the slope toward the shack. There was no light now, not even the slightest illumination. He held his hand up in front of his forehead, keeping the rain away as best he could. He had to be mistaken, the downpour was blurring his vision, perhaps the pole was in his line of sight. He leaned first to the right, then to the left. But still there was no light from the bottom of the hill.

Perhaps the fuses had blown. If so, they would have taken the bulb in the shack with them. Or a short. It was raining, and ski lifts did not ordinarily operate in the rain.

He looked beneath him. The ground was perhaps fifteen feet away. If he suspended himself from the footrail, the drop would only be eight or nine feet. He could handle that. He would walk the rest of the way up the slope. He had to do it quickly, however. It might take as long as twenty minutes to climb to the top, there was no way of telling. He couldn't take the chance of his contact's panicking, deciding to leave before he got to him.

"Stay right where you are! Don't unlatch that harness!"

The voice shot out of the darkness, cutting through the rain and wind. Its harsh command paralyzed Matlock as much from the shock of surprise as from fear. The man stood beneath him, to the right of the lines. He was dressed in a raincoat and some kind of cap. It was impossible to see his face or even determine his size.

"Who are you?! What do you want?!"

"I'm the man you came to meet. I want to see that paper in your pocket. Throw it down."

"I'll show you the paper when I see *your* copy. That's the deal! That's the deal I made."

"You don't understand, Matlock. Just throw the paper down. That's all."

"What the hell are you talking about?!"

The glare of a powerful flashlight blinded him. He reached for the guard rail latch.

"Don't touch that! Keep your hands straight out or you're dead!"

The core of the high-intensity light shifted from his face to his chest, and for several seconds all Matlock saw were a thousand flashing spots inside his eyes. As his sight returned, he could see that the man below him was moving closer to the lines, swinging the flashlight toward the ground for a path. In the glow of the beam, he also saw that the man held a large, ugly automatic in his right hand. The blinding light returned to his face, now shining directly beneath him.

"Don't threaten me, punk!" yelled Matlock, remembering the effect his anger had on Stockton at four that morning. "Put that goddamn gun away and help me down! We haven't much time and I don't like games!"

The effect now was not the same. Instead, the man beneath him began to laugh, and the laugh was sickening. It was, more than anything else, utterly genuine. The man on the ground was enjoying himself.

"You're very funny. You look funny sitting there on your ass in midair. You know what you look like? You look like one of those bobbing monkey targets in a shooting gallery! *You know what I mean?* Now, cut the bullshit and throw down the paper!"

He laughed again, and at the sound everything was suddenly clear to Matlock.

He hadn't made a contact. He hadn't cornered anyone. All his careful planning, all his thought-out actions. All for nothing. He was no nearer Nimrod now than he was before he knew Nimrod existed.

He'd been trapped.

Still, he had to try. It was all that was left him now.

"You're making the mistake of your life!"

"Oh, for Christ's sake, knock it off! Give me the paper! We've been looking for that fucking thing for a week! My orders are to get it *now!*"

"I can't give it to you."

"I'll blow your head off!"

"I said I *can't!* I didn't say I *wouldn't!*"

"Don't shit me. You've got it on you! You wouldn't have come here without it!"

"It's in a packet strapped to the small of my back."

"Get it out!"

"I told you, I can't! I'm sitting on a four-inch slat of wood with a footrail and I'm damn near twenty feet in the air!"

His words were half lost in the whipping rain. The man below was frustrated, impatient.

"I said get it out!"

"I'll have to drop down. I can't reach the straps!" Matlock yelled to be heard. "I can't *do* anything! I haven't got a gun!"

The man with the large, ugly automatic moved back several feet from the lines. He pointed both the powerful beam and his weapon at Matlock.

"O.K., come on down! You cough wrong and your head's blown off!"

Matlock undid the latch, feeling like a small boy on top of a ferris wheel wondering what could happen if the wheel stopped permanently and the safety bar fell off.

He held onto the footrail and let the rest of him swing beneath it. He dangled in the air, the rain soaking him, the beam of light blinding him. He had to think now, he had to create an instant strategy. His life was worth far less than the lives at Windsor Shoals to such men as the man on the ground.

"Shine the light down! I can't see!"

"Fuck that! Just drop!"

He dropped.

And the second he hit the earth, he let out a loud, painful scream and reached for his leg.

"Aaaahhh! My ankle, my foot! I broke my goddamn ankle!" He twisted and turned on the wet overgrowth, writhing in pain.

"Shut up! Get me that paper! *Now!*"

"*Jesus Christ!* What do you *want* from me? My ankle's turned *around!* It's *broken!*"

"Tough! Give me the paper!"

Matlock lay prostrate on the ground, his head moving back and forth, his neck straining to stand the pain. He spoke between short gasps.

"Strap's here. Undo the strap." He tore at his shirt displaying part of the canvas belt.

"Undo it yourself. Hurry up!"

But the man came closer. He wasn't sure. And closer. The beam of light was just above Matlock now. Then it moved to his midsection and Matlock could see the large barrel of the ugly black automatic.

It was the second, the instant he'd waited for.

He whipped his right hand up toward the weapon, simultaneously springing his whole body against the legs of the man in the raincoat. He held the automatic's barrel, forcing it with all his strength toward the ground. The gun fired twice, the impact of the explosions nearly shattering Matlock's hand, the sounds partially muted by wet earth and the slashing rain.

The man was beneath him now, twisting on his side, thrashing with his legs and free arm against the heavier Matlock. Matlock flung himself on the pinned arm and sank his teeth into the wrist above the hand holding the weapon. He bit into the flesh until he could feel the blood spurting out, mingled with the cold rain.

The man released the automatic, screaming in anguish. Matlock grabbed for the gun, wrested it free, and smashed it repeatedly into the man's face. The powerful flashlight was in the tall grass, its beam directed at nothing but drenched foliage.

Matlock crouched over the half-conscious, bloody face of his former captor. He was out of breath, and the sickening taste of the man's blood was still in his mouth. He spat a half dozen times trying to cleanse his teeth, his throat.

"O.K.!" He grabbed the man's collar and yanked his head up. "Now you tell me what happened! This was a trap, wasn't it?"

"The paper! I gotta get the paper." The man was hardly audible.

"I was *trapped, wasn't I!* The whole last week was a trap!"

"Yeah. . . . Yeah. The paper."

"That paper's pretty important, isn't it?"

"They'll kill you . . . they'll kill you to get it! You stand no chance, mister. . . . No chance . . ."

"Who's *they?!*"

"I don't know . . . don't know!"

"*Who's Nimrod?*"

"I don't know . . . 'Omerta'! . . . 'Omerta'!"

The man opened his eyes wide, and in the dim spill of the fallen flashlight, Matlock saw that something had happened to his victim. Some thought, some concept overpowered his tortured imagination. It was painful to watch. It was too close to the sight of the panicked Lucas Herron, the terrified Alan Pace.

"Come on, I'll get you down the slope. . . ."

It was as far as he got. From the depths of his lost control, the man with the blood-soaked face lunged forward, making a last desperate attempt to reach the gun in Matlock's right hand. Matlock yanked back; instinctively he fired the weapon. Blood and pieces of flesh flew everywhere. Half the man's neck was blown off.

Matlock stood up slowly. The smoke of the automatic lingered above the dead man, the rain forcing it downward toward the earth.

He reached into the grass for the flashlight, and as he bent over he began to vomit.

28

Ten minutes later he watched the parking lot below him from the trunk of a huge maple tree fifty yards up the trail. The new leaves partially protected him from the pouring rain, but his clothes were filthy, covered with wet dirt and blood. He saw the white station wagon near the front of the area, next to the stone gate entrance of the Sail and Ski. There wasn't much activity now; no automobiles entered, and those drivers inside would wait until the deluge stopped before venturing out on the roads. The parking lot attendant he'd given the ten dollars to was talking with a uniformed doorman under the carport roof of the restaurant entrance. Matlock wanted to race to the station wagon and drive away as fast as he could, but he knew the sight of his clothes would alarm the two men, make them wonder what had happened on the East Gorge slope. There was nothing to do but wait, wait until someone came out and distracted them, or both went inside.

He hated the waiting. More than hating it, he was frightened by it. There'd been no one he could see or hear near the wheel shack, but that didn't mean no one was there. Nimrod's dead contact probably had a partner somewhere, waiting as Matlock was waiting now. If the dead man was found, they'd stop him, kill him—if not for revenge, for the Corsican paper.

He had no choice now. He'd gone beyond his depth, his abilities. He'd been manipulated by Nimrod as he'd been maneuvered by the men of the Justice Department. He would telephone Jason Greenberg and do whatever Greenberg told him to do.

In a way, he was glad his part of it was over, or soon would be. He still felt the impulse of commitment, but there was nothing more he could do. He had failed.

Down below, the restaurant entrance opened and a waitress signaled the uniformed doorman. He and the attendant walked up the steps to speak with the girl.

Matlock ran down to the gravel and darted in front of the grills of the cars parked on the edge of the lot. Between automobiles he kept looking toward the restaurant door. The waitress had given the doorman a container of coffee. All three were smoking cigarettes, all three were laughing.

He rounded the circle and crouched in front of the station wagon. He crept to the door window and saw to his relief that the keys were in the ignition. He took a deep breath, opened the door as quietly as possible, and leaped inside. Instead of slamming it, he pulled the door shut quickly, silently, so as to extinguish the interior light without calling attention to the sound. The two men and the waitress were still talking, still laughing, oblivious.

He settled himself in the seat, switched on the ignition, threw the gears into reverse, and roared backward in front of the gate. He raced out between the stone posts and started down the long road to the highway.

Back under the roof, on the steps by the front door,

the three employees were momentarily startled. Then, from being startled they became quickly bewildered—and even a little curious. For, from the rear of the parking lot, they could hear the deep-throated roar of a second, more powerful engine. Bright headlights flicked on, distorted by the downpour of rain, and a long black limousine rushed forward.

The wheels screeched as the ominous-looking automobile swerved toward the stone posts. The huge car went to full throttle and raced after the station wagon.

There wasn't much traffic on the highway, but he still felt he'd make better time taking the back roads into Carlyle. He decided to go straight to Kressel's house, despite Sam's proclivity toward hysteria. Together they could both call Greenberg. He had just brutally, horribly killed another human being, and whether it was justified or not, the shock was still with him. He suspected it would be with him for the remainder of his life. He wasn't sure Kressel was the man to see.

But there was no one else. Unless he returned to his apartment and stayed there until a federal agent picked him up. And then again, instead of an agent, there might well be an emissary from Nimrod.

There was a winding S-curve in the road. He remembered that it came before a long stretch through farmland where he could make up time. The highway was straighter, but the back roads were shorter as long as there was no traffic to speak of. As he rounded the final half-circle, he realized that he was gripping the wheel so hard his forearms ached. It was the muscular defenses of his body taking over, controlling his shaking limbs, steadying the car with sheer unfeeling strength.

The flat stretch appeared; the rain had let up. He pushed the accelerator to the floor and felt the station wagon surge forward in overdrive.

He looked twice, then three times, up at his rear-view mirror, wary of patrol cars. He saw headlights behind him coming closer. He looked down at his speedometer. It read eighty-seven miles per hour and still the lights in the mirror gained on him.

The instincts of the hunted came swiftly to the surface; he knew the automobile behind him was no police car. There was no siren penetrating the wet stillness, no flashing light heralding authority.

He pushed his right leg forward, pressing the accelerator beyond the point of achieving anything further from the engine. His speedometer reached ninety-four miles per hour—the wagon was not capable of greater speed.

The headlights were directly behind him now. The unknown pursuer was feet, inches from his rear bumper. Suddenly the headlights veered to the left, and the car came alongside the white station wagon.

It was the same black limousine he had seen after Loring's murder! The same huge automobile that had raced out of the darkened driveway minutes after the massacre at Windsor Shoals! Matlock tried to keep part of his mind on the road ahead, part on the single driver of the car, which was crowding him to the far right of the road. The station wagon vibrated under the impact of the enormous speed; he found it more and more difficult to hold the wheel.

And then he saw the barrel of the pistol pointed at him through the window of the adjacent automobile. He saw the look of desperation in the darting eyes behind the outstretched arm, trying to steady itself for a clean line of fire.

He heard the shots and felt the glass shattering into his face and over the front seat. He slammed his foot into the brake and spun the steering wheel to the right, jumping the shoulder of the road, careening violently into and through a barbed-wire fence and onto a rock-strewn field. The wagon lunged into the grass, perhaps fifty or sixty feet, and then slammed into a cluster of rocks, a property demarcation. The headlights smashed and went out, the grill buckled. He was thrown into the dashboard, only his upheld arms keeping his head from crashing into the windshield.

But he was conscious, and the instincts of the hunted would not leave him.

He heard a car door open and close, and he knew the killer was coming into the field after his quarry. After the Corsican paper. He felt a trickle of blood rolling down his forehead—whether it was the graze of a bullet or a laceration from the flying glass, he couldn't be sure—but he was grateful it was there. He'd need it now, he needed the sight of blood on his forehead. He remained slumped over the wheel, immobile, silent.

And under his jacket he held the ugly automatic he had taken from the dead man in the raincoat on the slope of East Gorge. It was pointed under his left arm at the door.

He could hear the mushed crunch of footsteps on the soft earth outside the station wagon. He could literally feel—as a blind man feels—the face peering through the shattered glass looking at him. He heard the click of the door button as it was pushed in and the creaking of the hinges as the heavy panel was pulled open.

A hand grabbed his shoulder. Matlock fired his weapon.

The roar was deafening; the scream of the wounded man pierced the drenched darkness. Matlock leaped out of the seat and slammed the full weight of his body against the killer, who had grabbed his left arm in pain. Wildly, inaccurately, Matlock pistol-whipped the man about his face and neck until he fell to the ground. The man's gun was nowhere to be seen, his hands were empty. Matlock put his foot on the man's throat and pressed.

"I'll stop when you signal you're going to talk to me, you son of a bitch! Otherwise I *don't* stop!"

The man sputtered, his eyes bulged. He raised his right hand in supplication.

Matlock took his foot away and knelt on the ground over the man. He was heavy set, black-haired, with the blunt features of a brute killer.

"Who sent you after me? How did you know this car?"

The man raised his head slightly as though to answer. Instead, the killer whipped his right hand into his waist, pulled out a knife, and rolled sharply to his left, yanking his gorilla-like knee up into Matlock's groin. The knife slashed into Matlock's shirt, and he knew as he felt the steel point crease his flesh that he'd come as close as he would ever come to being killed.

He crashed the barrel of the heavy automatic into the man's temple. It was enough. The killer's head snapped back; blood matted itself around the hairline. Matlock stood up and placed his foot on the hand with the knife.

Soon the killer's eyes opened.

And during the next five minutes, Matlock did what he never thought he would be capable of doing—he tortured another man. He tortured the killer with the killer's own knife, penetrating the skin around and below the eyes, puncturing the lips with the same steel point that had scraped his own flesh. And when the man screamed, Matlock smashed his mouth with the barrel of the automatic and broke pieces of ivory off the killer's teeth.

It was not long.

"The paper!"

"What else?"

The writhing killer moaned and spat blood, but would not speak. Matlock did; quietly, in total conviction, in complete sincerity.

"You'll answer me or I'll push this blade down through your eyes. I don't care anymore. Believe me."

"The old man!" The guttural words came from deep inside the man's throat. "He said he wrote it down. . . . No one knows. . . . You talked to him. . . ."

"What old . . ." Matlock stopped as a terrifying thought came into his mind. *"Lucas Herron?! Is that who you mean?!"*

"He said he wrote it down. They think you know. Maybe he lied. . . . For Christ's sake, he could have lied. . . ."

The killer fell into unconsciousness.

Matlock stood up slowly, his hands shaking, his whole body shivering. He looked up at the road, at the huge black limousine standing silently in the diminishing rain. It would be his last gamble, his ultimate effort.

But something was stirring in his brain, something

elusive but palpable. He had to trust that feeling, as he had come to trust the instincts of the hunter and the hunted.

The old man!

The answer lay somewhere in Lucas Herron's house.

29

He parked the limousine a quarter of a mile from Herron's Nest and walked toward the house on the side of the road, prepared to jump into the bordering woods should any cars approach.

None did.

He came upon one house, then another, and in each case he raced past, watching the lighted windows to see if anyone was looking out.

No one was.

He reached the edge of Herron's property and crouched to the ground. Slowly, cautiously, silently he made his way to the driveway. The house was dark; there were no cars, no people, no signs of life. Only death.

He walked up the flagstone path and his eye caught sight of an official-looking document, barely visible in the darkness, tacked onto the front door. He approached it and lit a match. It was a sheriff's seal of closure.

One more crime, thought Matlock.

He went around to the back of the house, and as he stood in front of the patio door, he remembered vividly the sight of Herron racing across his manicured lawn into the forbidding green wall which he parted so deftly and into which he disappeared so completely.

There was another sheriff's seal on the back door. This one was glued to a pane of glass.

Matlock removed the automatic from his belt and as quietly as possible broke the small-paned window to the left of the seal. He opened the door and walked in.

The first thing that struck him was the darkness. Light and dark were relative, as he'd come to understand during the past week. The night had light which the eyes could adjust to; the daylight was often deceptive, filled with shadows and misty blind spots. But inside Herron's house the darkness was complete. He lit a match and understood why.

The windows in the small kitchen were covered with shades. Only they weren't ordinary window shades, they were custom built. The cloth was heavy and attached to the frames with vertical runners, latched at the sills by large aluminum hasps. He approached the window over the sink and lit another match. Not only was the shade thicker than ordinary, but the runners and the stretch lock at the bottom insured that the shade would remain absolutely flat against the whole frame. It was doubtful that any light could go out or come in through the window.

Herron's desire—or need—for privacy had been extraordinary. And if all the windows in all the rooms were sealed, it would make his task easier.

Striking a third match, he walked into Herron's living room. What he saw in the flickering light caused him to stop in his tracks, his breath cut short.

The entire room was a shambles. Books were strewn on the floor, furniture overturned and ripped apart, rugs upended, even sections of the wall smashed. He could have been walking into his own apartment the night of the Beeson dinner. Herron's living room had been thoroughly, desperately searched.

He went back to the kitchen to see if his preoccupation with the window shades and the darkness had played tricks on his eyes. They had. Every drawer was pulled open, every cabinet ransacked. And then he saw on the floor of a broom closet two flashlights. One was a casement, the other a long-stemmed Sportsman. The first wouldn't light, the second did.

He walked rapidly back into the living room and tried to orient himself, checking the windows with the beam of the flashlight. Every window was covered, every shade latched at the sill.

Across the narrow hallway in front of the narrower stairs was an open door. It led to Herron's study, which was, if possible, more of a mess than his living room. Two file cabinets were lying on their sides, the backs torn off; the large leather-topped desk was pulled from the wall, splintered, smashed on every flat surface. Parts of the wall, as the living room, were broken into. Matlock assumed these were sections which had sounded hollow when tapped.

Upstairs, the two small bedrooms and the bath were equally dismantled, equally dissected.

He walked back down the stairs, even the steps had been pried loose from their treads.

Lucas Herron's home had been searched by professionals. What could he find that they hadn't? He wandered back into the living room and sat down on what was left of an armchair. He had the sinking feeling that his last effort would end in failure also. He lit a cigarette and tried to organize his thoughts.

Whoever had searched the house had not found

what they were looking for. Or had they? There was no way to tell, really. Except that the brute killer in the field had screamed that the old man "had written it down." As if the fact was almost as important as the desperately coveted Corsican document. Yet he had added: ". . . maybe he lied, he could have lied." *Lied?* Why would a man in the last extremity of terror add that qualification to something so vital?

The assumption had to be that in the intricate delicacy of a mind foundering on the brink of madness, the worst evil was rejected. Had to be rejected so as to hold onto what was left of sanity.

No. . . . No, they had not found whatever it was they *had to find.* And since they hadn't found it after such exhaustive, extraordinary labors—it didn't *exist.*

But he knew it did.

Herron may have been involved with Nimrod's world, but he was not born of it. His was not a comfortable relationship—it was a tortured one. Somewhere, someplace he had left an indictment. He was too good a man not to. There had been a great decency in Lucas Herron. Somewhere . . . someplace.

But where?

He got out of the chair and paced in the darkness of the room, flicking the flashlight on and off, more as a nervous gesture than for illumination.

He reexamined minutely every word, every expression used by Lucas that early evening four days ago. He was the hunter again, tracking the spoor, testing the wind for the scent. And he was close; goddamn it, he was close! . . . Herron had *known* from the second he'd opened his front door what Matlock was after. That instantaneous, fleeting moment of recognition had been in his eyes. It had been unmistakable to Matlock. He'd even said as much to the old man, and the old man had laughed and accused him of being influenced by plots and counterplots.

But there'd been something else. Before the plots and counterplots. . . . Something *inside*. In this room. Before Herron suggested sitting *outside*. . . . Only he hadn't *suggested*, he'd made a statement, given a command.

And just before he'd given the command to rear-march toward the backyard patio, he'd walked in silently, *walked in silently*, and startled Matlock. He had opened the swinging door, *carrying* two filled glasses, and Matlock *hadn't heard* him. Matlock pushed the button on the flashlight and shot the beam to the base of the kitchen door. There was no rug, nothing to muffle footsteps—it was a hardwood floor. He crossed to the open swing-hinged door, walked through the frame, and shut it. Then he pushed it swiftly open in the same direction Lucas Herron had pushed it carrying the two drinks. The hinges clicked as such hinges do if they are old and the door is pushed quickly—*normally*. He let the door swing shut and then he pressed against it slowly, inch by inch.

It was silent.

Lucas Herron had made the drinks and then *silently* had eased himself back into the living room so he wouldn't be heard. So he could observe Matlock without Matlock's knowing it. And then he'd given his firm command for the two of them to go outside.

Matlock forced his memory to recall *precisely* what Lucas Herron said and did at that *precise* moment.

". . . we'll go out on the patio. It's too nice a day to stay inside. Let's go."

Then, *without waiting for an answer*, even a mildly enthusiastic agreement, Herron had walked *rapidly* back through the kitchen door. No surface politeness, none of the courtly manners one expected from Lucas.

He had given an order, the firm command of an officer and a gentleman.

By Act of Congress.

That was *it!* Matlock swung the beam of light over the writing desk.

The photograph! The photograph of the marine officer holding the map and the Thompson automatic in some tiny section of jungle on an insignificant island in the South Pacific.

"I keep that old photograph to remind myself that time wasn't always so devastating."

At the precise moment Herron walked through the door, Matlock had been looking closely at the photograph! The fact that he was doing so disturbed the old man, disturbed him enough for him to insist that they go outside instantly. In a curt, abrupt manner so unlike him.

Matlock walked rapidly to the desk. The small cellophane-topped photograph was still where it had been—on the lower right wall above the desk. Several larger glass-framed pictures had been smashed; this one was intact. It was small, not at all imposing.

He grabbed the cardboard frame and pulled the photo off the single thumbtack which held it to the wall. He looked at it carefully, turning it over, inspecting the thin edges.

The close, harsh glare of the flashlight revealed scratches at the upper corner of the cardboard. Fingernail scratches? Perhaps. He pointed the light down on the desk top. There were unsharpened pencils, scraps of note paper, and a pair of scissors. He took the scissors and inserted the point of one blade between the thin layers of cardboard until he could rip the photograph out of the frame.

And in that way he found it.

On the back of the small photograph was a diagram drawn with a broad-tipped fountain pen. It was in the shape of a rectangle, the bottom and top lines filled in with dots. On the top were two small lines with arrows, one straight, the other pointing to the right. Above each arrowhead was the numeral 30. Two 30s.

Thirty.

On the sides, bordering the lines, were childishly drawn trees.

On the top, above the numbers, was another simplified sketch. Billowy half-circles connected to one another with a wavy line beneath. A cloud. Underneath, more trees.

It was a map, and what it represented was all too apparent. It was Herron's back yard; the lines on three sides represented Herron's forbidding green wall.

The numerals, the 30s, were measurements—but they were also something else. They were contemporary symbols.

For Lucas Herron, chairman for decades of Romance Languages, had an insatiable love for words and their odd usages. What was more appropriate than the symbol "30" to indicate finality?

As any first year journalism student would confirm, the number 30 at the bottom of any news copy meant the story was finished. It was over.

There was no more to be said.

Matlock held the photograph upside down in his left hand, his right gripping the flashlight. He entered the woods at midsection—slightly to the left—as indicated on the diagram. The figure 30 could be feet, yards, meters, paces—certainly not inches.

He marked off thirty twelve-inch spaces. Thirty feet straight, thirty feet to the right.

Nothing.

Nothing but the drenched, full overgrowth and underbrush which clawed at his feet.

He returned to the green wall's entrance and decided to combine yards and paces, realizing that paces in such a dense, jungle-like environment might vary considerably.

He marked off the spot thirty paces directly ahead and continued until he estimated the point of yardage. Then he returned to the bent branches where he had figured thirty paces to be and began the lateral trek.

Again nothing. An old rotted maple stood near one spot Matlock estimated was thirty steps. There was nothing else unusual. He went back to the bent branches and proceeded to his second mark.

Thirty yards straight out. Ninety feet, give or take a foot or two. Then the slow process of thirty yards through the soaking wet foliage to his next mark. Another ninety feet. Altogether, one hundred and eighty feet. Nearly two-thirds of a football field.

The going was slower now, the foliage thicker, or so it seemed. Matlock wished he had a machete or at least some kind of implement to force the wet branches out of his way. Once he lost count and had to keep in mind the variation as he proceeded—was it twenty-one or twenty-three large steps? Did it matter? Would the difference of three to six feet really matter?

He reached the spot. It was either twenty-eight or thirty. Close enough if there was anything to be seen. He pointed the flashlight to the ground and began slowly moving it back and forth laterally.

Nothing. Only the sight of a thousand glistening weeds and the deep-brown color of soaked earth. He kept swinging the beam of light, inching forward as he did so, straining his eyes, wondering every other second if he had just covered that particular section or not—everything looked so alike.

The chances of failure grew. He could go back and begin again, he thought. Perhaps the 30s connoted some other form of measurement. Meters, perhaps, or multiples of another number buried somewhere in the diagram. The dots? Should he count the dots on the bottom and top of the rectangle? Why were the dots there?

He had covered the six-foot variation and several feet beyond.

Nothing.

His mind returned to the dots, and he withdrew the photograph from his inside pocket. As he positioned himself to stand up straight, to stretch the muscles at the base of his spine—pained by crouching—his foot touched a hard, unyielding surface. At first he thought it was a fallen limb, or perhaps a rock.

And then he knew it was neither.

He couldn't see it—whatever it was, was underneath a clump of overgrown weeds. But he could feel the outline of the object with his foot. It was straight, precisely tooled. It was no part of a forest.

He held the light over the cluster of weeds and saw that they weren't weeds. They were some kind of small-budded flower in partial bloom. A flower which did not need sunlight or space.

A jungle flower. Out of place, purchased, replanted.

He pushed them out of the way and bent down. Underneath was a thick, heavily varnished slab of wood about two feet wide and perhaps a foot and a half long. It had sunk an inch or two into the ground; the surface had been sanded and varnished so often that the layers of protective coating reached a high gloss, reflecting the beam of the flashlight as though it were glass.

Matlock dug his fingers into the earth and lifted up the slab. Beneath it was a weathered metal plaque, bronze perhaps.

For Major Lucas N. Herron, USMCR
In Gratitude from the Officers and Men of
Bravo Company, Fourteenth Raider Battalion,
First Marine Division
Solomon Islands—South Pacific
May 1943

Seeing it set in the ground under the glare of light, Matlock had the feeling he was looking at a grave.

He pushed away the surrounding mud and dug a tiny trench around the metal. On his hands and knees, he slowly, awkwardly lifted the plaque up and carefully placed it to one side.

He had found it.

Buried in earth was a metal container—the type used in library archives for valuable manuscripts. Airtight, weatherproofed, vacuumed, a receptacle for the ages.

A coffin, Matlock thought.

He picked it up and inserted his cold, wet fingers under the lever of the coiled hasp. It took considerable strength to pull it up, but finally it was released.

There was the rush of air one hears upon opening a tin of coffee. The rubber edges parted. Inside Matlock could see an oilcloth packet in the shape of a notebook.

He knew he'd found the indictment.

30

The notebook was thick, over three hundred pages, and every word was handwritten in ink. It was in the form of a diary, but the lengthy entries varied enormously. There was no consistency regarding dates. Often days followed one another; at other times entries were separated by weeks, even months. The writing also varied. There were stretches of lucid narrative followed by incoherent, disjointed rambling. In the latter sections the hand had shaken, the words were often illegible.

Lucas Herron's diary was a cry of anguish, an outpouring of pain. A confessional of a man beyond hope.

As he sat on the cold wet ground, mesmerized by Herron's words, Matlock understood the motives behind Herron's Nest, the forbidding green wall, the window shades, the total isolation.

Lucas Herron had been a drug addict for a quarter of a century. Without the drugs, his pain was unendurable. And there was absolutely nothing anyone could do for him except confine him to a ward in a Veterans' Hospital for the remainder of his unnatural life.

It was the rejection of this living death that had plunged Lucas Herron into another.

Major Lucas Nathaniel Herron, USMCR, attached to Amphibious Assault Troops, Raider Battalions, Fleet Marine Force, Pacific, had led numerous companies of the Fourteenth Battalion, First Marine Division, in ranger assaults on various islands throughout the Japanese-held Solomons and Carolinas.

And Major Lucas Herron had been carried off the tiny island of Peleliu in the Carolinas on a stretcher, having brought two companies back to the beach through jungle fire. None thought he could survive.

Major Lucas Herron had a Japanese bullet imbedded at the base of his neck, lodged in a section of his nervous system. He was not expected to live. The doctors, first in Brisbane, then San Diego, and finally at Bethesda, considered further operations unfeasible. The patient could not survive them; he would be reduced to a vegetable should even the slightest complication set in. No one wished to be responsible for that.

They put the patient under heavy medication to relieve the discomfort of his wounds. And he lay there in the Maryland hospital for over two years.

The stages of healing—partial recovery—were slow and painful. First, there were the neck braces and the pills; then the braces and the metal frames for walking, and still the pills. At last the crutches, along with the braces and always the pills. Lucas Herron came back to the land of the living—but not without the pills. And in moments of torment—the needle of morphine at night.

There were hundreds, perhaps thousands, like Lucas Herron, but few had his extraordinary qualifications—for those who sought him out. An authentic hero of the Pacific war, a brilliant scholar, a man above reproach.

He was perfect. He could be used perfectly.

On the one hand, he could not live, could not endure, without the relief afforded him by the narcotics—the pills and the increasingly frequent needles. On the other hand, if the degree of his dependence was known medically, he would be returned to a hospital ward.

These alternatives were gradually, subtly made clear to him. Gradually in the sense that his sources of supply needed favors now and then—a contact to be made in Boston, men to be paid in New York. Subtly, in that when Herron questioned the involvement, he was told it was really quite harmless. Harmless but *necessary*.

As the years went by, he became enormously valuable to the men he needed so badly. The contact in Boston, the men to be paid in New York, became more and more frequent, more and more *necessary*. Then Lucas was sent farther and farther afield. Winter vacations, spring midterms, summers: Canada, Mexico, France . . . the Mediterranean.

He became a courier.

And always the thought of the hospital ward on his tortured body and brain.

They had manipulated him brilliantly. He was never exposed to the results of his work, never specifically aware of the growing network of destruction he was helping to build. And when finally he learned of it all, it was too late. The network had been built.

Nimrod had his power.

April 22, 1951. At midterm they're sending me back to Mexico. I'll stop at the U. of M.—as usual—and on the way back at Baylor. A touch of irony: the bursar here called me in, saying Carlyle would be pleased to help defray my "research" expenses. I declined, and told him the *disability allowance* was sufficient. Perhaps I should have accepted. . . .

June 13, 1956. To Lisbon for three weeks. A routing map, I'm told, for a small ship. Touching the Azores, through Cuba (a mess!), finally into Panama. Stops—for me—at the Sorbonne, U. of Toledo, U. of Madrid. I'm becoming an academic gadfly! I'm not happy about methods—who could be?—but neither am I responsible for the archaic laws. So many, many can be helped. They need help! I've been in touch with scores on the telephone—they put me in touch—men like myself who couldn't face another day without help. . . . Still, I worry. . . . Still, what can I do? Others would do it, if not me . . .

February 24, 1957. I'm alarmed but calm and reasonable (I hope!) about my concerns. I'm told now that when they send me to make contacts I am the *messenger* from *"Nimrod"!* The name is a code—a meaningless artifice, they say—and will be honored. It's all so foolish—like the intelligence information we'd receive from MacArthur's HQ in So-Pac. *They* had *all* the codes and *none* of the *facts*. . . . The pain is worse, the medics said it would get worse. But . . . "Nimrod's" considerate. . . . As I am. . . .

March 10, 1957. They were angry with me! They withheld my dosage for two days—I thought I would kill myself! I started out in my car for the VA hospital in Hartford, but they stopped me on the highway. They were in a Carlyle *patrol car*—I should have known they had the police here! . . . It was either *compromise* or the *ward!* . . . They were right! . . . I'm off to Canada and the job is to bring in a man from North Africa. . . . I *must* do it! The calls to me are constant. This evening a man—Army, 27th—Naha casualty—from East Orange, N.J., said that he and six others *depended* on me! There are so many like ourselves! Why? Why, for God's sake, are we *despised?* We need *help* and all that's offered to us are the *wards!* . . .

August 19, 1960. I've made my position clear! They go too far . . . "Nimrod" is not just a code name for a location, it's also a *man!* The geography doesn't change but the man does. They're not helping men like me any longer—well, maybe they are—but it's more than *us!* They're reaching out—they're *attracting* people—for a great deal of money! . . .

August 20, 1960. Now they're threatening me. They say I'll have no more once my cabinet's empty. . . . I don't care! I've enough for a week—with luck—a week and a half. . . . I wish I liked alcohol more, or that it didn't make me sick. . . .

August 28, 1960. I shook to my ankles but I went to the Carlyle Police Station. I wasn't thinking. I asked to speak with the highest man in authority and they said it was after five o'clock—he had gone home. So I said I had information about narcotics and within ten minutes the chief of police showed up. . . . By now I was obvious—I couldn't control myself—I urinated through my trousers. The chief of police took me into a small room and opened his kit and administered a needle. He was from Nimrod! . . .

October 7, 1965. This Nimrod is displeased

with me. I've always gotten along with the Nimrods—the two I've met, but this one is sterner, more concerned with my accomplishments. I refuse to touch *students,* he accepts that, but he says I am getting silly in my classroom lectures, I'm not bearing down. He doesn't care that I don't *solicit*—he doesn't want me to—but he tells me that I should be—well, be more conservative in my outlook. . . . It's strange. His name is Matthew Orton and he's an insignificant aide to the lieutenant governor in Hartford. But he's Nimrod. And I'll obey. . . .

November 14, 1967. The back is intolerable now—the doctors said it would *disintegrate*—that was *their* word—but not like *this!* I can get through forty minutes of a lecture and then I *must* excuse myself! . . . I ask always—is it worth it? . . . It must be or I wouldn't go on. . . . Or am I simply too great an egoist—or too much a coward—to take my life? . . . Nimrod sees me tonight. In a week it's *Thanksgiving*—I wonder where I will go. . . .

January 27, 1970. It *has* to be the end now. In C. Fry's beautiful words, the "seraphic strawberry, beaming in its bed" must turn and show its nettles. There's nothing more for me and Nimrod has infected too many, too completely. I will take my life—as painlessly as possible—there's been so much pain. . . .

January 28, 1970. I've tried to kill myself! I can't *do* it! I bring the gun, then the knife to the point, but it *will not happen!* Am I *really* so infused, so infected that I cannot accomplish that which is most to be desired? . . . Nimrod will kill me. I know that and he knows it better.

January 29, 1970. Nimrod—he's now *Arthur Latona!* Unbelievable! The same *Arthur Latona* who built the middle-income housing projects in Mount Holly!—At any rate, he's given me an unacceptable order. I've *told* him it's *unacceptable.* I'm far too valuable to be discarded and I've told him that, *too.* . . . He wants me to carry a great deal of money to Toros Daglari in Turkey! . . . Why, oh why, can't my life be *ended?* . . .

April 18, 1971. It's a wondrously strange world. To survive, to exist and breathe the air, one does so much one comes to loathe. The total is frightening . . . the excuses and the rationalizations are worse. . . . Then something happens which suspends—or at least postpones—all necessity of judgment. . . . The pains shifted from the neck and spine to the lower sides. I knew it had to be something else. Something *more.* . . . I went to Nimrod's doctor—as I must—always. My weight has dropped, my reflexes are pathetic. He's worried and tomorrow I enter the private hospital in Southbury. He says for an exploratory. . . . I know they'll do their best for me. They have other trips—very important trips, Nimrod says. I'll be traveling throughout most of the summer, he tells me. . . . If it wasn't me, it would be someone else. The pains are terrible.

May 22, 1971. The old, tired soldier is home. Herron's Nest is my salvation! I'm minus a kidney. No telling yet about the other, the doctor says. But I know better. I'm dying. . . . Oh, God, I welcome it! There'll be no more trips, no more threats. Nimrod can do no more. . . . They'll keep me alive, too. As long as they can. *They have to now!* . . . I hinted to the doctor that I've kept a record over the years. He just stared at me speechless. I've never seen a man so frightened. . . .

May 23, 1971. Latona—Nimrod—dropped by this morning. Before he could discuss anything, I told him I knew I was dying. That nothing mattered to me now—the decision to end my life was made, not by me. I even told him that I was prepared—relieved; that I had tried to end it myself but couldn't. He asked about *"what you told the doctor."* He wasn't able to say the *words!* His *fear* blanketed the living room like a heavy mist. . . . I answered calmly, with great authority, I think. I told him that whatever records there were would be given to him—*if my last days or months were made easier for me.* He was furious but he knew there wasn't anything he could do. What can a person do with an old man in pain who knows he's going to die? What arguments are left?

August 14, 1971. Nimrod is dead! Latona died of a coronary! Before *me,* and there's irony in that! . . . Still the business continues without change. Still I'm brought my supplies every week and every week the frightened messengers ask the questions—where are they? Where are the records?—they come close to threatening me but I remind them that Nimrod had the word of a dying old man. Why would I change that? . . . They retreat into their fear. . . . A new Nimrod will be chosen soon. . . . I've said I didn't want to know—and I don't!

September 20, 1971. A new year begins for Carlyle. My last year, I know that—what responsibilities I can assume, that is. . . . Nimrod's death has given me courage. Or is it the knowledge of my own? God knows I can't undo much but I can try! . . . I'm reaching out, I'm finding a few who've been hurt badly, and if nothing else I offer help. It may only be words, or advice, but just the knowledge that *I've been there* seems to be comforting. It's always such a shock to those I speak with! Imagine! The "grand old bird"! The pains and the numbness are nearly intolerable. I may not be able to wait. . . .

December 23, 1971. Two days before my last Christmas. I've said to so many who've asked me to their homes that I was going into New York. Of course, it's not so. I'll spend the days here at the Nest. . . . A disturbing note. The messengers tell me that the new Nimrod is the sternest, strongest one of all. They say he's ruthless. He orders executions as easily as his predecessors issued simple requests. Or are they telling me these things to frighten me? That can't frighten me!

February 18, 1972. The doctor told me that he'd prescribe heavier "medication" but warned me not to overdose. He, too, spoke of the new Nimrod. Even he's worried—he implied that the man was mad. I told him I didn't want to know anything. I was out of it.

February 26, 1972. I can't believe it! Nimrod *is* a *monster!* He's *got* to be *insane!* He's demanded that all those who've been working here over three years be cut off—sent out of the country—and if they refuse—be killed! The doctor's leaving next week. Wife, family, practice. . . . Latona's widow was murdered in an "automobile accident"! One of the messengers—Pollizzi —was shot to death in New Haven. Another—Capalbo—OD'd and the rumor is that the dose was administered!

April 5, 1972. From Nimrod to me—deliver to the messengers any and all records or he'll shut off my supplies. My house will be watched around the clock. I'll be followed wherever I go. I'll not be allowed to get any medical attention whatsoever. The combined effects of the cancer and the withdrawal will be beyond anything I can imagine. What Nimrod doesn't know is that before he left the doctor gave me enough for several months. He frankly didn't believe I'd last that long. . . . For the first time in this terrible, horrible life, I'm dealing from a position of strength. My life is firmer than ever because of death.

April 10, 1972. Nimrod is near the point of hysterics with me. He's threatened to expose me—which is meaningless. I've let him know that through the messengers. He's said that he'll destroy the whole Carlyle campus, but if he does that he'll destroy himself as well. The rumor is that he's calling together a conference. An important meeting of powerful men. . . . My house is now watched—as Nimrod said it would be—around the clock. By the Carlyle police, of course. Nimrod's private army!

April 22, 1972. Nimrod has won! It's horrifying, but he's won! He sent me two newspaper clippings. In each a student was killed by an overdose. The first a girl in Cambridge, the second a boy from Trinity. He says that he'll keep adding to the list for every week I withhold the records. . . . Hostages are executed!—He's got to be *stopped!* But how? What can I *do?* . . . I've got a plan but I don't know if I can do it—I'm going to try to *manufacture* records. Leave them intact. It will be difficult—my hands shake so sometimes! Can I possibly get through it?—I have to. I said I'd deliver a *few* at a time. For my *own* protection. I wonder if he'll agree to that?

April 24, 1972. Nimrod's unbelievably evil, but he's a realist. He knows he can do nothing else! We both are racing against the time of my death. Stalemate! I'm alternating between a typewriter and different fountain pens and various types of paper. The killings are suspended but I'm told they will resume if I miss *one* delivery! Nimrod's hostages are in my hands! Their executions can be prevented only by me!

April 27, 1972. Something strange is happening! The Beeson boy phoned our contact at Admissions. Jim Matlock was there and Beeson suspects him. He asked questions, made an ass of himself with Beeson's wife. . . . Matlock isn't on any list! He's no part of Nimrod—on either side. He's never purchased a thing, never sold. . . . The Carlyle patrol cars are always outside now. Nimrod's army is alerted. What is it?

April 27, 1972—P.M. The messengers came—two of them—and what they led me to believe is so incredible I cannot write it here. . . . I've never asked the identity of Nimrod, I never wanted to know. But panic's rampant now, something is happening beyond even Nimrod's control. And

> the messengers told me who Nimrod is. . . . They *lie! I cannot, will not believe it!* If it is true we are all in hell!

Matlock stared at the last entry helplessly. The handwriting was hardly readable; most of the words were connected with one another as if the writer could not stop the pencil from racing ahead.

> *April 28.* Matlock was here. He knows! Others know! He says the government men are involved now. . . . It's over! But what they can't understand is what will happen—a bloodbath, killings—executions! Nimrod can do *no less!* There will be so much *pain.* There will be mass killing and it will be provoked by an insignificant teacher of the Elizabethans. . . . A messenger called. Nimrod *himself* is coming out. It is a confrontation. Now I'll know the truth—who he really is. . . . If he's who I've been led to believe—somehow I'll get this record out—somehow. It's all that's left. It's my turn to threaten. . . . It's over now. The pain will soon be over, too. . . . There's been so much pain . . . I'll make one final entry when I'm sure. . . .

Matlock closed the notebook. What had the girl named Jeannie said? *They* have the *courts,* the *police,* the *doctors.* And Alan Pace. He'd added the major university administrations—all over the Northeast. Whole academic policies; employments, deployments, curriculums—sources of enormous financing. *They* have it *all.*

But Matlock had the indictment.

It was enough. Enough to stop Nimrod—whoever he was. Enough to stop the bloodbath, the executions.

Now he *had* to reach Jason Greenberg.

Alone.

31

Carrying the oilcloth packet, he began walking toward the town of Carlyle, traveling the back roads on which there was rarely any night traffic. He knew it would be too dangerous to drive. The man in the field had probably recovered sufficiently to reach someone—reach Nimrod. An alarm would be sent out for him. The unseen armies would be after him now. His only chance was to reach Greenberg. Jason Greenberg would tell him what to do.

There was blood on his shirt, mud caked on his trousers and jacket. His appearance brought to mind the outcasts of Bill's Bar & Grill by the railroad freight yards. It was nearly two thirty in the morning, but such places stayed open most of the night. The blue laws were only conveniences for them, not edicts. He reached College Parkway and descended the hill to the yards.

He brushed his damp clothes as best he could and covered the bloodstained shirt with his jacket. He walked into the filthy bar; the layers of cheap smoke were suspended above the disheveled customers. A jukebox was playing some Slovak music, men were yelling, a stand-up shuffleboard was being abused. Matlock knew he melted into the atmosphere. He would find a few precious moments of relief.

He sat down at a back booth.

"What the hell happened to *you?*"

It was the bartender, the same suspicious bartender whom he'd finally befriended several days ago. Years . . . ages ago.

"Caught in the rainstorm. Fell a couple of times. Lousy whisky. . . . Have you got anything to eat?"

"Cheese sandwiches. The meat I wouldn't give you. Bread's not too fresh either."

"I don't care. Bring me a couple of sandwiches. And a glass of beer. Would you do that?"

"Sure. Sure, mister. . . . You sure you want to eat here? I mean, I can tell, this ain't your kind of place, you know what I mean?"

There it was again. The incessant, irrelevant question; the dangling interrogative. *You know what I mean . . . ?* Not a question at all. Even in his few moments of relief he had to hear it once more.

"I know what you mean . . . but I'm sure."

"It's your stomach." The bartender trudged back to his station.

Matlock found Greenberg's number and went to the foul-smelling pay phone on the wall. He inserted a coin and dialed.

"I'm sorry, sir," the operator said, "the telephone is disconnected. Do you have another number where the party can be reached?"

"Try it again! I'm sure you're wrong."

She did and she wasn't. The supervisor in Wheeling, West Virginia, finally informed the operator in Carlyle, Connecticut, that any calls to a Mr. Greenberg were to be routed to Washington, D.C. It was assumed that whoever was calling would know where in Washington.

"But Mr. Greenberg isn't expected at the Washington number until early A.M.," she said. "Please inform the party on the line."

He tried to think. Could he trust calling Washington, the Department of Justice, Narcotics Division? Under the circumstances, might not Washington—for the sake of speed—alert someone in the Hartford vicinity to get to him? And Greenberg had made it clear—he didn't trust the Hartford office, the Hartford agents.

He understood Greenberg's concern far better now. He had only to think of the Carlyle police—Nimrod's private army.

No, he wouldn't call Washington. He'd call Sealfont. His last hope was the university president. He dialed Sealfont's number.

"James! Good Lord, James! Are you all right?! Where in heaven's name have you *been*?!"

"To places I never knew were there. Never knew existed."

"But you're all right? That's all that matters! Are you all right?!"

"Yes, sir. And I've got everything. I've got it all. Herron wrote everything down. It's a record of twenty-three years."

"Then he *was* part of it?"

"Very much so."

"Poor, *sick* man. . . . I don't understand. However, that's not important now. That's for the authorities. Where are you? I'll send a car. . . . No, I'll come myself. We've all been so worried. I've been in constant touch with the men at the Justice Department."

"Stay where you are," Matlock said quickly. "I'll get to you myself—everyone knows your car. It'll be less dangerous this way. I know they're looking for me. I'll have a man here call me a taxi. I just wanted to make sure you were home."

"Whatever you say. I must tell you I'm relieved. I'll call Kressel. Whatever you have to say, he should know about it. That's the way it's to be."

"I agree, sir. See you shortly."

He went back to the booth and began to eat the unappetizing sandwiches. He had swallowed half the beer when from inside his damp jacket, the short, hysterical beeps of Blackstone's Tel-electronic seared into his ears. He pulled out the machine and pressed the button. Without thinking of anything but the number 555-6868 he jumped up from the seat and walked rapidly back to the telephone. His hand trembling, he awkwardly manipulated the coin and dialed.

The recorded words were like the lash of a whip across his face.

"Charger Three-zero is canceled."

Then there was silence. As Blackstone had promised, there was nothing else but the single sentence—stated but once. There was no one to speak to, no appeal. Nothing.

But there had to be! He would not, *could not*, be cut off like this! If Blackstone was canceling him, he had a right to know *why!* He had a right to know that Pat was *safe!*

It took several minutes and a number of threats before he reached Blackstone himself.

"I don't have to talk to you!" The sleepy voice was belligerent. "I made that clear! . . . But I don't mind because if I can put a trace on this call I'll tell them where to find you the second you hang up!"

"Don't threaten me! You've got too much of my

money to threaten me. . . . Why am I canceled? I've got a right to know that."

"Because you stink! You stink like garbage!"

"That's not good enough! That doesn't *mean* anything!"

"I'll give you the rundown then. A warrant is out for you. Signed by the court and . . ."

"For *what,* goddamn it? Protective custody?! *Preventive detention?!*"

"For *murder,* Matlock! For conspiracy to distribute *narcotics!* For aiding and abetting known narcotics *distributors!* . . . You sold *out!* Like I said, you *smell!* And I hate the business you're in!"

Matlock was stunned. Murder? Conspiracy! What was Blackstone talking about?

"I don't know what you've been told, but it's not true. None of it's *true!* I risked my life, my *life,* do you *hear* me! To bring what I've got . . ."

"You're a good talker," interrupted Blackstone, "but you're careless! You're also a ghoulish bastard! There's a guy in a field outside of Carlyle with his throat slit. It didn't take the government boys ten minutes to trace that Ford wagon to its owner!"

"I didn't *kill* that man! I swear to Christ I *didn't kill him!*"

"No, of course not! And you didn't even *see* the fellow whose head you shot off at East Gorge, did you? Except that there's a parking lot attendant and a couple of others who've got you on the scene! . . . I forgot. You're also stupid. You left the parking ticket under your windshield wiper!"

"Now, wait a minute! *Wait a minute!* This is all *crazy!* The man at East Gorge asked to meet me there! He tried to *murder me!*"

"Tell that to your lawyer. We got the whole thing

—straight—from the Justice boys! I demanded that. I've got a damned good reputation. . . . I'll say this. When you sell out, you sell *high!* Over sixty thousand dollars in a *checking* account. Like I said, you *smell,* Matlock!"

He was so shocked he could not raise his voice. When he spoke, he was out of breath, hardly audible. "Listen to me. You've *got* to listen to me. Everything you say . . . there are explanations. Except the man in the field. I don't understand that. But I don't care if you believe me or not. It doesn't matter. I'm holding in my hand all the vindication I'll ever need. . . . What *does* matter is that you watch *that girl!* Don't cancel me out! *Watch her!*"

"Apparently you don't understand English very well. You *are* canceled! Charger Three-zero is *canceled!*"

"What about the girl?"

"We're not irresponsible," said Blackstone bitterly. "She's perfectly safe. She's under the protection of the Carlyle police."

There was a general commotion at the bar. The bartender was closing up and his customers resented it. Obscenities were shouted back and forth over the beer-soaked, filthy mahogany, while cooler or more drunken heads slowly weaved their way toward the front door.

Paralyzed, Matlock stood by the foul-smelling telephone. The roaring at the bar reached a crescendo but he heard nothing; the figures in front of his eyes were only blurs. He felt sick to his stomach, and so he held the front of his trousers, the oilcloth packet with Lucas Herron's notebook between his hands and his belt. He thought he was going to be sick as he had been sick beside the corpse on the East Gorge slope.

But—there was no time. Pat was held by Nimrod's private army. He had to act *now.* And when he acted, the spring would be sprung. There would be no rewinding.

The horrible truth was that he didn't know where to begin.

"What's the matter, mister? The sandwiches?"

"What?"

"Ya look like you're gonna throw up."

"Oh? . . . No." Matlock saw for the first time that almost everyone had left the place.

The notebook! The notebook would be the ransom! There would be no tortured decision—not for the plastic men! Not for the *manipulators!* Nimrod could have the notebook! The indictment!

But then what? Would Nimrod let her live? Let him live? . . . What had Lucas Herron written: "The new Nimrod is a monster . . . ruthless. He orders executions. . . ."

Nimrod had murdered with far less motive than someone's knowledge of Lucas Herron's diaries.

"Look, mister. I'm sorry, but I gotta close up."

"Will you call a taxi for me, please?"

"A taxi? It's after three o'clock. Even if there was one, he wouldn't come down *here* at three o'clock in the morning."

"Have you got a car?"

"Now wait a minute, mister. I gotta clean up and ring out. I had some action tonight. The register'll take me twenty minutes."

Matlock withdrew his bills. The smallest denomination was a hundred. "I've got to have a car—right away. How much do you want? I'll bring it back in an hour—maybe less."

The bartender looked at Matlock's money. It wasn't a normal sight. "It's a pretty old heap. You might have trouble driving it."

"I can drive *anything!* Here! Here's a hundred! If I wreck it you can have the whole roll. Here! Take it, for Christ's sake!"

"Sure. Sure, mister." The bartender reached under his apron and took out his car keys. "The square one's the ignition. It's parked in the rear. Sixty-two Chevy. Go out the back door."

"Thanks." Matlock started for the door indicated by the bartender.

"Hey, mister!"

"What?"

"What's your name again? . . . Something 'rock'? I forgot. I mean, for Christ's sake, I give you the car, I don't even know your name!"

Matlock thought for a second. "Rod. Nimrod. The name's Nimrod."

"That's no name, mister." The burly man started toward Matlock. "That's a spin fly for catchin' trout. Now, what's your name? You got my car, I gotta know your name."

Matlock still held the money in his hand. He peeled off three additional hundreds and threw them on the floor. It seemed right. He had given Kramer four hundred dollars for his station wagon. There should be symmetry somewhere. Or, at least, meaningless logic.

"That's four hundred dollars. You couldn't get four hundred dollars for a '62 Chevy. I'll bring it back!" He ran for the door. The last words he heard were those of the grateful but confused manager of Bill's Bar & Grill.

"Nimrod. Fuckin' joker!"

The car was a heap, as its owner had said. But it moved, and that was all that mattered. Sealfont would help him analyze the facts, the alternatives. Two opinions were better than one; he was afraid of assuming the total responsibility—he wasn't capable of it. And Sealfont would have people in high places he could contact. Sam Kressel, the liaison, would listen and object and be terrified for his domain. No matter; he'd be dismissed. Pat's safety was uppermost. Sealfont would see that.

Perhaps it was time to threaten—as Herron ultimately had threatened. Nimrod had Pat; he had Herron's indictment. The life of one human being for the protection of hundreds, perhaps thousands. Even Nimrod had to see their bargaining position. It was irrefutable, the odds were on their side.

He realized as he neared the railroad depot that this kind of thinking, by itself, made him a manipulator, too. Pat had been reduced to *quantity X*, Herron's diaries, *quantity Y*. The equation would then be postulated and the mathematical observers would make their decisions based on the data presented. It was the ice-cold logic of survival; emotional factors were disregarded, consciously despised.

Frightening!

He turned right at the station and started to drive up College Parkway. Sealfont's mansion stood at the end. He went as fast as the '62 Chevy would go, which wasn't much above thirty miles an hour on the hill. The streets were deserted, washed clean by the storm. The store fronts, the houses, and finally the campus were dark and silent.

He remembered that Kressel's house was just a half block off College Parkway on High Street. The detour would take him no more than thirty seconds. It was worth it, he thought. If Kressel hadn't left for Sealfont's, he would pick him up and they could talk on the way over. Matlock *had* to talk, *had* to begin. He couldn't stand the isolation any longer.

He swung the car to the left at the corner of High Street. Kressel's house was a large gray colonial set back from the street by a wide front lawn bordered by rhododendrons. There were lights on downstairs. With luck, Kressel was still home. There were two cars, one in the driveway; Matlock slowed down.

His eyes were drawn to a dull reflection at the rear of the driveway. Kressel's kitchen light was on; the spill from the window illuminated the hood of a third car, and the Kressels were a two-car family.

He looked again at the car in front of the house. It was a Carlyle patrol car. The Carlyle police were in Kressel's house!

Nimrod's private army was with *Kressel!*

Or was Nimrod's private army with *Nimrod?*

He swerved to the left, narrowly missing the patrol car, and sped down the street to the next corner. He turned right and pressed the accelerator to the floor. He was confused, frightened, bewildered. If Sealfont had called Kressel—which he had obviously done—and Kressel worked with Nimrod, or *was* Nimrod, there'd be other patrol cars, other soldiers of the private army waiting for him.

His mind went back to the Carlyle Police Station—a century ago, capsuled in little over a week—the night of Loring's murder. Kressel had disturbed him then. And even before that—with Loring and Greenberg—Kressel's hostility to the federal agents had been outside the bounds of reason.

Oh, Christ! It was so clear now! His instincts had been right. The instincts which had served him as the *hunted* as well as the *hunter* had been true! He'd been watched *too* thoroughly, his every action anticipated. Kressel, the *liaison,* was, in fact, Kressel the tracker, the seeker, the supreme killer.

Nothing was ever as it appeared to be—only what one sensed behind the appearance. Trust the senses.

Somehow he had to get to Sealfont. Warn Sealfont that the Judas was Kressel. Now they *both* had to protect themselves, establish some base from which they could strike back.

Otherwise the girl he loved was lost.

There couldn't be a second wasted. Sealfont had certainly told Kressel that he, Matlock, had Lucas Herron's diaries, and that was all Kressel would need to know. All Nimrod needed to know.

Nimrod had to get possession of both the Corsican paper *and* the diaries; now he knew where they were. His private army would be told that this was its moment of triumph or disaster. They would be waiting for him at Sealfont's; Sealfont's mansion was the trap they expected him to enter.

Matlock swung west at the next corner. In his trouser pocket were his keys, and among them was the key to Pat's apartment. To the best of his knowledge, no one knew he had such a key, certainly no one would expect him to go there. He had to chance it; he couldn't risk going to a public telephone, risk being seen under a street lamp. The patrol cars would be searching everywhere.

He heard the roar of an engine behind him and felt the sharp pain in his stomach. A car was following him—closing in on him. And the '62 Chevrolet was no match for it.

His right leg throbbed from the pressure he exerted on the pedal. His hands gripped the steering wheel as he turned wildly into a side street, the muscles in his arms tensed and aching. Another turn. He spun the wheel to the left, careening off the edge of the curb back into the middle of the road. The car behind him maintained a steady pace, never more than ten feet away, the headlights blinding in the rear-view mirror.

His pursuer was *not* going to close the gap between them! Not then. Not at that moment. He could have done so a hundred, two hundred yards ago. He was waiting. Waiting for something. But what?

There was so *much* he couldn't understand! So much he'd miscalculated, misread. He'd been outmaneuvered at every important juncture. He was what they said—an amateur! He'd been beyond his depth from the beginning. And now, at the last, his final assault was ending in ambush. They would kill him, take the Corsican paper, the diaries of indictment. They would kill the girl he loved, the innocent child whose life he'd thrown away so brutally. Sealfont would be finished—he knew too much now! God knew how many others would be destroyed.

So be it.

If it had to be this way, if hope really had been taken from him, he'd end it all with a gesture, at least. He reached into his belt for the automatic.

The streets they now traveled—the pursuer and the pursued—ran through the outskirts of the campus, consisting mainly of the science buildings and a number of large parking lots. There were no houses to speak of.

He swerved the Chevrolet as far to the right as possible, thrusting his right arm across his chest, the barrel of the pistol outside the car window, pointed at the pursuing automobile.

He fired twice. The car behind him accelerated; he

felt the repeated jarring of contact, the metal against metal as the car behind hammered into the Chevrolet's left rear chassis. He pulled again at the trigger of the automatic. Instead of a loud report, he heard and felt only the single click of the firing pin against an unloaded chamber.

Even his last gesture was futile.

His pursuer crashed into him once more. He lost control; the wheel spun, tearing his arm, and the Chevrolet reeled off the road. Frantic, he reached for the door handle, desperately trying to steady the car, prepared to jump if need be.

He stopped all thought; all instincts of survival were arrested. Within those split seconds, time ceased. For the car behind him had drawn parallel and he saw the face of his pursuer.

There were bandages and gauze around the eyes, beneath the glasses, but they could not hide the face of the black revolutionary. Julian Dunois.

It was the last thing he remembered before the Chevrolet swerved to the right and skidded violently off the road's incline.

Blackness.

32

Pain roused him. It seemed to be all through his left side. He rolled his head, feeling the pillow beneath him.

The room was dimly lit; what light there was came from a table lamp on the other side. He shifted his head and tried to raise himself on his right shoulder. He pushed his elbow into the mattress, his immobile left arm following the turn of his body like a dead weight.

He stopped abruptly.

Across the room, directly in line with the foot of the bed, sat a man in a chair. At first Matlock couldn't distinguish the features. The light was poor and his eyes were blurred with pain and exhaustion.

Then the man came into focus. He was black and his dark eyes stared at Matlock beneath the perfectly cut semicircle of an Afro haircut. It was Adam Williams, Carlyle University's firebrand of the Black Left.

When Williams spoke, he spoke softly and, unless Matlock misunderstood—once again—there was compassion in the black's voice.

"I'll tell Brother Julian you're awake. He'll come in to see you." Williams got out of the chair and went to the door. "You've banged up your left shoulder. Don't try to get out of bed. There are no windows in here. The hallway is guarded. Relax. You need rest."

"I don't have *time* to rest, you *goddamn fool!*" Matlock tried to raise himself further but the pain was too great. He hadn't adjusted to it.

"You don't have a choice." Williams opened the door and walked rapidly out, closing it firmly behind him.

Matlock fell back on the pillow. . . . Brother Julian. . . . He remembered now. The sight of Julian Dunois's bandaged face watching him through the speeding car window, seemingly inches away from him. And his ears had picked up Dunois's words, his commands to his driver. They had been shouted in his Caribbean dialect.

"Hit him, mon! Hit him again! Drive him *off*, mon!"

And then everything had become dark and the darkness had been filled with violent noise, crashing metal, and he had felt his body twisting, turning, spiraling into the black void.

Oh, God! How long ago was it? He tried to lift up his left hand to look at his watch, but the arm barely moved; the pain was sharp and lingering. He reached over with his right hand to pull the stretch band off his wrist, but it wasn't there. His watch was gone.

He struggled to get up and finally managed to perch on the edge of the bed, his legs touching the floor. He pressed his feet against the wood, thankful that he could sit up. . . . He had to put the pieces together, to reconstruct what had happened, where he was going.

He'd been on his way to Pat's. To find a secluded telephone on which to reach Adrian Sealfont. To warn him that Kressel was the enemy, Kressel was Nimrod. And he'd made up his mind that Herron's diaries would be Pat's ransom. Then the chase had begun, only it wasn't a chase. The car behind him, commanded by Julian Dunois, had played a furious game of terror. It had toyed with him as a lethal mountain cat might play with a wounded goat. Finally it had attacked—steel against steel—and driven him to darkness.

Matlock knew he had to escape. But *from where* and *to whom*?

The door of the windowless room opened. Dunois entered, followed by Williams.

"Good morning," said the attorney. "I see you've managed to sit up. That's good. It augurs well for your very abused body."

"What time is it? Where am I?"

"It's nearly four thirty. You are in a room at Lumumba Hall. You see? I withhold nothing from you. . . . Now, you must reciprocate. You must withhold nothing from me."

"Listen to me!" Matlock kept his voice steady. "I have no fight with you, with *any* of you! I've got . . ."

"Oh, I disagree," Dunois smiled. "Look at my *face*. It's only through enormous good fortune that I wasn't blinded by you. You tried to crush the lenses of my glasses into my eyes. Can you imagine how my work would suffer if I were blind?"

"Goddamn it! You filled me with acid!"

"And you provoked it! You were actively engaged in pursuits inimicable to our brothers! Pursuits you had no *right* to engage in . . . But this is concentric debate. It will get us nowhere. . . . We *do* appreciate what you've brought us. Beyond our most optimistic ambitions."

"You've got the notebook. . . ."

"*And* the Corsican document. The Italian invitation

we knew existed. The notebook was only a rumor. A rumor which was fast being ascribed to fiction until tonight—this morning. You should feel proud. You've accomplished what scores of your more experienced betters failed to accomplish. You found the treasure. The *real* treasure."

"I've got to have it back!"

"Fat chance!" said Williams, leaning against the wall, watching.

"If I don't get it back, a girl will *die!* Do whatever you goddamn well please with me, but let me *use* it to get her back. Christ! Please, *please!*"

"You feel deeply, don't you? I see tears in your eyes. . . ."

"Oh, *Jesus!* You're an *educated man!* You can't *do* this! . . . *Listen!* Take whatever information you want out of it! Then give it to me and let me go! . . . I swear to you I'll come back. Give her a chance. Just give her a *chance!*"

Dunois walked slowly to the chair by the wall, the chair in which Adam Williams sat when Matlock awoke. He pulled it forward, closer to the bed, and sat down, crossing his knees gracefully. "You feel helpless, don't you? Perhaps . . . even without hope."

"I've been through a great deal!"

"I'm sure you have. And you appeal to my reason . . . as an *educated man.* You realize that it is within my scope to help you and therefore I am superior to you. You would not make such an appeal if it were not so."

"Oh, Christ! Cut that out!"

"Now you know what it's like. You are helpless. Without hope. You wonder if your appeal will be lost on a deaf ear. . . . Do you really, for one second, think that I care for the life of Miss Ballantyne? Do you honestly believe she has any priority for me? Any *more* than the lives of *our* children, *our* loved ones mean anything to you!"

Matlock knew he had to answer Dunois. The black would offer nothing if he evaded him. It was another game—and he had to play, if only briefly.

"I don't deserve this and you know it. I loathe the people who won't do anything for them. You know me—you've made that clear. So you must know that."

"Ahh, but I *don't* know it! You're the one who made the choice, the decision to work for the superior mon! The *Washington* mon! For decades, two *centuries, my* people have appealed to the *superior Washington mon!* 'Help us,' they cry. 'Don't leave us without hope!' they scream. But nobody listens. Now, you expect me to listen to you?"

"Yes, I *do!* Because I'm not your enemy. I may not be everything you want me to be, but I'm not your enemy. If you turn me—and men like me—into objects of hatred, you're *finished.* You're outnumbered, don't forget that, Dunois. We won't storm the barricades every time you yell 'foul,' but we hear you. We're willing to help; we want to help."

Dunois looked coldly at Matlock. "Prove it."

Matlock returned the black's stare. "Use me as your bait, your hostage. Kill me if you have to. But get the girl out."

"We can do that—the hostaging, the killing—without your consent. Brave but hardly proof."

Matlock refused to allow Dunois to disengage the stare between them. He spoke softly. "I'll give you a statement. Written, verbal—on tape; freely, without force or coercion. I'll spell it all out. How I was used, what I did. Everything. You'll have your Washington men as well as Nimrod."

Dunois folded his arms and matched Matlock's quiet voice. "You realize you would put an end to your professional life; this life you love so much. No university administration worthy of its name would consider you for a position. You'd never be trusted again. By any factions. You'd become a pariah."

"You asked for proof. It's all I can offer you."

Dunois sat immobile in the chair. Williams had straightened up from his slouching position against the wall. No one spoke for several moments. Finally Dunois smiled gently. His eyes, surrounded by the gauze, were compassionate.

"You're a good man. Inept, perhaps, but persevering. You shall have the help you need. We won't leave you without hope. Do you agree, Adam?"

"Agreed."

Dunois got out of the chair and approached Matlock.

"You've heard the old cliché, that politics make strange bedfellows. Conversely, practical objectives often make for strange political alliances. History bears this out. . . . We want this Nimrod as much as you do. As well as the Mafiosi he tries to make peace with. It is they and their kind who prey upon the children. An example must be made. An example which will instill terror in other Nimrods, other Mafiosi. . . . You shall have help, but this is the condition we demand."

"What do you mean?"

"The disposition of Nimrod and the others will be left to us. We don't trust your judges and your juries. Your courts are corrupt, your legalistics no more than financial manipulations. . . . The barrio addict is thrown into jail. The rich gangsters appeal. . . . No, the disposition must be left to us."

"I don't care about that. You can do whatever you like."

"Your not caring is insufficient. We demand more than that. We must have our guarantee."

"How can I give a guarantee?"

"By your silence. By not acknowledging our presence. We will take the Corsican paper and somehow we will find the conference and be admitted. We will extract what we want from the diaries—that's being done now, incidentally. . . . But your *silence* is the paramount issue. We will help you now—on a best-efforts basis, of course—but you must never mention our involvement. Irrespective of what may happen, you must not, directly or indirectly, allude to our participation. Should you do so, we will take your life and the life of the girl. Is this understood?"

"It is."

"Then we are in agreement?"

"We are."

"Thank you," said Dunois, smiling.

33

As Julian Dunois outlined their alternatives and began to formulate strategy, it became clearer to Matlock why the blacks had sought him out with such concentration—and why Dunois was willing to offer help. He, Matlock, had the basic information they needed. Who were his contacts? Both inside and without the university? Who and where were the government men? How were communications expedited?

In other words—whom should Julian Dunois *avoid* in his march to Nimrod?

"I must say, you were extraordinarily unprepared for contingencies," Dunois said. "Very slipshod."

"That occurred to me, too. But I think I was only partially to blame."

"I dare say you were!" Dunois laughed, joined by Williams. The three men remained in the windowless room. A card table had been brought in along with several yellow pads. Dunois had begun writing down every bit of information Matlock supplied. He double-checked the spelling of names, the accuracy of addresses—a professional at work; Matlock once again experienced the feeling of inadequacy he had felt when talking with Greenberg.

Dunois stapled a number of pages together and

started on a fresh pad. "What are you doing?" asked Matlock.

"These will be duplicated by a copier downstairs. The information will be sent to my office in New York. . . . As will a photostat of every page in Professor Herron's notebook."

"You don't fool around, do you?"

"In a word—no."

"It's all I've got to give you. Now, what do we do? What do *I* do? I'm frightened, I don't have to tell you that. I can't even let myself think what might happen to her."

"*Nothing* will happen. Believe me when I tell you that. At the moment, your Miss Ballantyne is as safe as if she were in her mother's arms. Or yours. She's the bait, not you. The bait will be kept fresh and unspoiled. For you have what they want. They can't survive without it."

"Then let's make the offer. The sooner the better."

"Don't worry. It will be made. But we must decide carefully—aware of the nuances—how we do it. So far, we have two alternatives, we agreed upon that. The first is Kressel, himself. The direct confrontation. The second, to use the police department, to let your message to Nimrod be delivered through it."

"Why do that? Use the police?"

"I'm only listing alternatives. . . . Why the police? I'm not sure. Except that the Herron diaries state clearly that Nimrod was replaced in the past. This current Nimrod is the third since the position's inception, is that not correct?"

"Yes. The first was a man named Orton in the lieutenant governor's office. The second, Angelo Latona, a builder. The third, obviously, Kressel. What's your point?"

"I'm speculating. Whoever assumes the position of Nimrod has authoritarian powers. Therefore, it is the position, not the man. The man can make whatever he can of the office."

"But the office," interrupted Williams, "is given and taken away. Nimrod isn't the last voice."

"Exactly. Therefore, it might be to Matlock's advantage to let the word leak out very specifically that it is *he* who possesses the weapon. That Kressel—Nimrod—must exercise great caution. For everyone's sake."

"Wouldn't that mean that more people would be after me?"

"Possibly. Conversely, it could mean that there'd be a legion of anxious criminals protecting you. Until the threat you impose is eliminated. No one will act rashly until that threat is taken away. No one will want Nimrod to act rashly."

Matlock lit a cigarette, listening intently. "What you're trying to do then is to partially separate Nimrod from his own organization."

Dunois snapped the fingers of both hands, the sound of castanets, applause. He smiled as he spoke.

"You're a quick student. It's the first lesson of insurgency. One of the prime objectives of infiltration. Divide. Divide!"

The door opened; an excited black entered. Without saying a word, he handed Dunois a note. Dunois read it and closed his eyes for several moments. It was his way of showing dismay. He thanked the black messenger calmly and dismissed him politely. He looked at Matlock but handed the note to Williams.

"Our stratagems may have historic precedence, but I'm afraid for us they're empty words. Kressel and his wife are dead. Dr. Sealfont has been taken forcibly from his house under guard. He was driven away in a Carlyle patrol car."

"What? Kressel! I don't believe it! It's not true!"

"I'm afraid it is. Our men report that the two bodies were carried out not more than fifteen minutes ago. The word is murder and suicide. Naturally. It would fit perfectly."

"Oh, Christ! Oh, Jesus Christ! It's my fault! I made them do it! I *forced* them! Sealfont! Where did they take him?"

"We don't know. The brothers on watch didn't dare follow the patrol car."

He had no words. The paralysis, the fear, was there again. He reeled blindly into the bed and sank down on it, sitting, staring at nothing. The sense of futility, of inadequacy, of defeat was now overwhelming. He had caused so much pain, so much death.

"It's a severe complication," said Dunois, his elbows on the card table. "Nimrod has removed your only contacts. In so doing, he's answered a vital question, prevented us from making an enormous error—I refer to Kressel, of course. Nevertheless, to look at it from another direction, Nimrod has reduced our alternatives. You have no choice now. You must deal through his private army, the Carlyle police."

Matlock looked numbly across at Julian Dunois. "Is that all you can *do*? Sit there and coolly decide a next move? . . . Kressel's *dead*. His *wife* is *dead*. Adrian Sealfont's probably killed by now. These were my *friends!*"

"And you have my sympathies, but let me be honest: I don't regret the loss of the three individuals. Frankly, Adrian Sealfont is the only *real* casualty—we might have worked with him, he was brilliant—but this loss does not break my heart. We lose thousands in the barrios every month. I weep for them more readily. . . . However, to the issue at hand. You really don't have a choice. You must make your contact through the police."

"But that's where you're wrong." Matlock felt suddenly stronger. "I *do* have a choice. . . . Greenberg left West Virginia early this morning. He'll be in Washington by now. I have a number in New York that can put me in touch with him. I'm getting hold of Greenberg." He'd done enough, caused enough anguish. He couldn't take the chance with Pat's life. Not any longer. He wasn't capable.

Dunois leaned back in his chair, removing his arms from the card table. He stared at Matlock. "I said a little while ago that you were an apt student. I amend that observation. You are quick but obviously superficial. . . . You will *not* reach Greenberg. He was not part of our agreement and you *will not* violate that agreement. You will carry through on the basis we agree upon or you will be subject to the penalties I outlined."

"Goddamn it, don't threaten me! I'm sick of threats!" Matlock stood up. Dunois reached under his jacket and took out a gun. Matlock saw that it was the black automatic he had taken from the dead man on the East Gorge slope. Dunois, too, rose to his feet.

"The medical report will no doubt estimate your death to be at dawn."

"For God's sake! The girl is being held by killers!"

"So are you," Dunois said quietly. "Can't you *see* that? Our motives are different, but make no mistake about it. We are *killers*. We *have* to be."

"You wouldn't go that far!"

"Oh, but we would. We have. And much, much further. We would drop your insignificant corpse in front of the police station with a note pinned to your bloodstained shirt. We would *demand* the death of the girl prior to any negotiations. They would readily agree, for neither of us can take the chance of her living. Once she, too, is dead, the giants are left to do battle by themselves."

"You're a monster."

"I am what I have to be."

No one spoke for several moments. Matlock shut his eyes, his voice a whisper. "What do I do?"

"That's much better." Dunois sat down, looking up at the nervous Adam Williams. Briefly, Matlock felt a kinship with the campus radical. He, too, was frightened, unsure. As Matlock, he was ill-equipped to deal with the world of Julian Dunois or Nimrod. The Haitian seemed to read Matlock's thoughts.

"You must have confidence in yourself. Remember, you've accomplished far more than anyone else. With far less resources. And you have extraordinary courage."

"I don't feel very courageous."

"A brave man rarely does. Isn't that remarkable? Come, sit down." Matlock obeyed. "You know, you and I are not so different. In another time, we might even be allies. Except, as many of my brothers have noted, I look for saints."

"There aren't any," Matlock said.

"Perhaps not. And then again, perhaps . . . we'll debate it some other time. Right now, we must plan. Nimrod will be expecting you. We can't disappoint him. Yet we must be sure to guard ourselves on all flanks." He pulled closer to the table, a half-smile on his lips, his eyes shining.

The black revolutionary's strategy, if nothing else, was a complex series of moves designed to protect Matlock and the girl. Matlock grudgingly had to acknowledge it.

"I have a double motive," Dunois explained. "The second is, frankly, more important to me. Nimrod will not appear himself unless he has no other choice, and I want Nimrod. I will not settle for a substitute, a camouflage."

The essence of the plan was Herron's notebook itself, the last entries in the diary.

The identity of Nimrod.

"Herron states explicitly that he *would* not write the name intimated by the messengers. Not that he couldn't. His feeling obviously was that he could not implicate that man if the information was incorrect. Guilt by innuendo would be abhorrent to him. Like yourself, Matlock; you refused to offer up Herron on the basis of an hysterical phone call. He knew that he might die at any given moment; his body had taken about as much abuse as it could endure. . . . He had to be positive." Dunois, by now, was drawing meaningless geometric shapes on a blank page of yellow paper.

"And then he was murdered," said Matlock. "Made to look like suicide."

"Yes. If nothing else, the diaries confirm that. Once Herron had proved to himself who Nimrod was, he would have moved heaven and earth to include it in the notebook. Our enemy cannot know that he did not. That is our Damocletian sword."

Matlock's first line of protection was to let the chief

of the Carlyle police understand that he, Matlock, knew the identity of Nimrod. He would reach an accommodation solely with Nimrod. This accommodation was the lesser of two evils. He was a hunted man. There was a warrant out for his arrest of which the Carlyle police surely were aware. He might conceivably be exonerated from the lesser indictments, but he would not escape the charge of murder. Possibly, two murders. For he had killed, the evidence was overwhelming, and he had no tangible alibis. He did not know the men he had killed. There were no witnesses to corroborate self-defense; the manner of each killing was grotesque to the point of removing the killer from society. The best he could hope for was a number of years in prison.

And then he would spell out his terms for an accommodation with Nimrod. Lucas Herron's diaries for his life—and the life of the girl. Certainly the diaries were worth a sum of money sufficient for both of them to start again somewhere.

Nimrod could do this. Nimrod *had* to do it.

"The key to this . . . let's call it phase one . . . is the amount of conviction you display." Dunois spoke carefully. "Remember, you are in panic. You have taken lives, killed other human beings. You are not a violent man but you've been forced, coerced into frightening crimes."

"It's the truth. More than you know."

"Good. Convey that feeling. All a panicked man wants is to get away from the scene of his panic. Nimrod must believe this. It guarantees your immediate safety."

A second telephone call would then be made by Matlock—to confirm Nimrod's acceptance of a meeting. The location, at this point, could be chosen by

Nimrod. Matlock would call again to learn where. But the meeting must take place before ten o'clock in the morning."

"By now, you, the fugitive, seeing freedom in sight, suddenly possess doubts," said Dunois. "In your gathering hysteria, you need a guarantee factor."

"Which is?"

"A third party; a mythical third party. . . ."

Matlock was to inform the contact at the Carlyle Police Headquarters that he had written up a complete statement about the Nimrod operation. Herron's diaries, identities, everything. This statement had been sealed in an envelope and given to a friend. It would be mailed to the Justice Department at ten in the morning unless Matlock instructed otherwise.

"Here, phase two depends again on conviction, but of another sort. Watch a caged animal whose captors suddenly open the gate. He's wary, suspicious; he approaches his escape with caution. So, too, must our fugitive. It will be expected. You have been most resourceful during the past week. By logic you should have been dead by now, but you survived. You must continue that cunning."

"I understand."

The last phase was created by Julian Dunois to guarantee—as much as was possible in a "best-efforts situation"—the reclaiming of the girl and the safety of Matlock. It would be engineered by a third and final telephone call to Nimrod's contact. The object of the call was to ascertain the specific location of the meeting and the precise time.

When informed of both, Matlock was to accept without hesitation.

At first.

Then moments later—seemingly with no other reason than the last extremity of panic and suspicion—he was to reject Nimrod's choice.

Not the time—the location.

He was to hesitate, to stutter, to behave as close to irrationality as he could muster. And then, suddenly, he was to blurt out a second location of his *own* choice. As if it had just come to mind with no thoughts of it before that moment. He was then to restate the existence of the nonexistent statement which a mythical friend would mail to Washington at ten in the morning. He was then to hang up without listening further.

"The most important factor in phase three is the recognizable consistency of your panic. Nimrod must see that your reactions are now primitive. The act itself is about to happen. You lash out, recoil, set up barriers to avoid his net, should that net exist. In your hysteria, you are as dangerous to him as a wounded cobra is deadly to the tiger. For rationality doesn't exist, only survival. He now must meet you himself, he now must bring the girl. He will, of course, arrive with his palace guard. His intentions won't change. He'll take the diaries, perhaps discuss elaborate plans for your accommodation, and when he learns that there is no written statement, no friend about to mail it, he'll expect to kill you both. . . . However, none of his intentions will be carried out. For we'll be waiting for him."

"How? How will you be waiting for him?"

"With my own palace guard. . . . We shall now, you and I, decide on that hysterically arrived at second location. It should be in an area you know well, perhaps frequent often. Not too far away, for it is presumed you have no automobile. Secluded, because you are hunted by the law. Yet accessible, for you must travel fast, most likely on back roads."

"You're describing Herron's Nest. Herron's house."

"I may be, but we can't use it. It's psychologically inconsistent. It would be a break in our fugitive's pattern of behavior. Herron's Nest is the root of his fear. He wouldn't go back there. . . . Someplace else."

Williams started to speak. He was still unsure, still wary of joining Dunois's world. "I think, perhaps . . ."

"What, Brother Williams? What do you think?"

"Professor Matlock often dines at a restaurant called the Cheshire Cat."

Matlock snapped his head up at the black radical. "You too? You've had me followed."

"Quite often. We don't enter such places. We'd be conspicuous."

"Go on, brother," broke in Dunois.

"The Cheshire Cat is about four miles outside Carlyle. It's set back from the highway, which is the normal way to get there, about half a mile, but it also can be reached by taking several back roads. Behind and to the sides of the restaurant are patios and gardens used in the summer for dining. Beyond these are woods."

"Anyone on the premises?"

"A single night watchman, I believe. It doesn't open until one. I don't imagine cleanup crews or kitchen help get there before nine thirty or ten."

"Excellent." Dunois looked at his wristwatch. "It's now ten past five. Say we allow fifteen minutes between phases one, two, and three and an additional twenty minutes for traveling between stations, that would make it approximately six fifteen. Say six thirty for contingencies. We'll set the rendezvous for seven. Behind the Cheshire Cat. Get the notebook, brother. I'll alert the men."

Williams rose from his chair and walked to the door. He turned and addressed Dunois. "You won't change your mind? You won't let me come with the rest of you?"

Dunois didn't bother to look up. He answered curtly. "Don't annoy me. I've a great deal to think about."

Williams left the room quickly.

Matlock watched Dunois. He was still sketching his meaningless figures on the yellow pad, only now he bore down on the pencil, causing deep ridges on the paper. Matlock saw the diagram emerging. It was a series of jagged lines, all converging.

They were bolts of lightning.

"Listen to me," he said. "It's not too late. Call in the authorities. Please, for Christ's sake, you can't risk the lives of these kids."

From behind his glasses, surrounded by the gauze bandages, Dunois's eyes bore into Matlock. He spoke with contempt. "Do you for one minute think I would allow these children to tread in waters I don't even know *I* can survive? We're not your Joint Chiefs of Staff, Matlock. We have greater respect, greater love for our young."

Matlock recalled Adam Williams' protestations at the door. "That's what Williams meant then? About coming with you."

"Come with me."

Dunois led Matlock out of the small, windowless room and down the corridor to a staircase. There were a few students milling about, but only a few. The rest of Lumumba Hall was asleep. They proceeded down two flights to a door Matlock remembered as leading to the cellars, to the old, high-ceilinged chapter room in which he'd witnessed the frightening performance of the African tribal rite. They descended the stairs and, as Matlock suspected, went to the rear of the cellars, to the thick oak door of the chapter room. Dunois had not spoken a word since he'd bade Matlock follow him.

Inside the chapter room were eight blacks, each well over six feet tall. They were dressed alike: dark, tight-fitting khakis with open shirts and black, soft leather ankle boots with thick rubber soles. Several were sitting, playing cards; others were reading, some talking quietly among themselves. Matlock noticed that a few had their shirt sleeves rolled up. The arms displayed were tautly muscular, veins close to the skin. They all nodded informally to Dunois and his guest. Two or three smiled intelligently at Matlock, as if to put him at ease. Dunois spoke softly.

"The palace guard."

"My God!"

"The elite corps. Each man is trained over a period of three years. There is not a weapon he cannot fire or fix, a vehicle he cannot repair . . . or a philosophy he cannot debate. Each is familiar with the most brutal forms of combat, traditional as well as guerrilla. Each is committed until death."

"The terror brigade, is that it? It's not new, you know."

"Not with that description, no, it wouldn't be. Don't forget, I grew up with such dogs at my heels. Duvalier's Ton Ton Macoute were a pack of hyenas; I witnessed their work. These men are no such animals."

"I wasn't thinking of Duvalier."

"On the other hand, I acknowledge the debt to Papa Doc. The Ton Ton's concept was exciting to me. Only I realized it had to be restructured. Such units are springing up all over the country."

"They sprung up once before," Matlock said. "They

were called 'elite' then, too. They were also called 'units'—SS units."

Dunois looked at Matlock and Matlock saw the hurt in his eyes. "To reach for such parallels is painful. Nor is it justified. We do what we have to do. What is right for us to do."

"Ein Volk, Ein Reich, Ein Fuehrer," said Matlock softly.

34

Everything happened so fast. Two of Dunois's elite guard were assigned to him, the rest left for the rendezvous with Nimrod, to prepare themselves to meet another elite guard—the selected few of Nimrod's private army who undoubtedly would accompany him. Matlock was ushered across the campus by the two huge blacks after the word came back from scouts that the path was clear. He was taken to a telephone booth in the basement of a freshman dormitory, where he made his first call.

He found that his fear, his profound fear, aided the impression Dunois wanted to convey. It wasn't difficult for him to pour out his panicked emotions, pleading for sanctuary, for, in truth, he *felt* panicked. As he spoke hysterically into the phone, he wasn't sure which was the reality and which the fantasy. He wanted to be free. He wanted Pat to live and be free with him. If Nimrod could bring it all about, why not deal with Nimrod in good faith?

It was a nightmare for him. He was afraid for a moment that he might yell out the truth and throw himself on the mercy of Nimrod.

The sight of Dunois's own Ton Ton Macoute kept bringing him back to his failing senses, and he ended the first telephone call without breaking. The Carlyle police "superintendent" would forward the information, receive an answer, and await Matlock's next call.

The blacks received word from their scouts that the second public telephone wasn't clear. It was on a street corner, and a patrol car had been spotted in the area. Dunois knew that even public phones could be traced, although it took longer, and so he had alternate sites for each of the calls, the last one to be made on the highway. Matlock was rushed to the first alternate telephone booth. It was on the back steps of the Student Union.

The second call went more easily, although whether that was an advantage was not clear. Matlock was emphatic in his reference to the mythical statement that was to be mailed at ten in the morning. His strength had its effect, and he was grateful for it. The "superintendent" was frightened now, and he didn't bother to conceal it. Was Nimrod's private army beginning to have its doubts? The troops were, perhaps, picturing their own stomachs blown out by the enemy's shells. Therefore, the generals had to be more alert, more aware of the danger.

He was raced to a waiting automobile. It was an old Buick, tarnished, dented, inconspicuous. The exterior, however, belied the inside. The interior was as precisely tooled as a tank. Under the dashboard was a powerful radio; the windows were at least a half-inch thick, paned, Matlock realized, with bulletproof glass. Clipped to the sides were high-powered, short-barreled rifles, and dotted about the body were rubber-flapped holes into which these barrels were to be inserted. The sound of the engine impressed Matlock instantly. It was as powerful a motor as he'd ever heard.

They followed an automobile in front of them at

moderate speed; Matlock realized that another car had taken up the rear position. Dunois had meant it when he said they were to cover themselves on all flanks. Dunois was, indeed, a professional.

And it disturbed James Matlock when he thought about the profession.

It was black. It was also *Ein Volk, Ein Reich, Ein Fuehrer.*

As was Nimrod and all he stood for.

The words came back to him.

"*. . . I'm getting out of this goddamn country, mister. . . .*"

Had it come to that?

And: "*. . . You think it's all so different? . . . It's mini-America! . . . It's company policy, man!*"

The land was sick. Where was the cure?

"Here we are. Phase three." The black revolutionary in command tapped him lightly on the arm, smiling reassuringly as he did so. Matlock got out of the car. They were on the highway south of Carlyle. The car in front had pulled up perhaps a hundred yards ahead of them and parked off the road, its lights extinguished. The automobile behind had done the same.

In front of him stood two aluminum-framed telephone booths, placed on a concrete platform. The second black walked to the right booth, pushed the door open—which turned on the dull overhead light—and quickly slid back the pane of glass under the light, exposing the bulb. This he rapidly unscrewed so that the booth returned to darkness. It struck Matlock—impressed him, really—that the Negro giant had eliminated the light this way. It would have been easier, quicker, simply to have smashed the glass.

The objective of the third and final call, as Dunois

had instructed, was to reject Nimrod's meeting place. Reject it in a manner that left Nimrod no alternative but to accept Matlock's panicked substitute: the Cheshire Cat.

The voice over the telephone from the Carlyle police was wary, precise.

"Our mutual friend understands your concerns, Matlock. He'd feel the same way you do. He'll meet you with the girl at the south entrance of the athletic field, to the left of the rear bleachers. It's a small stadium, not far from the gym and the dormitories. Night watchmen are on; no harm could come to you. . . ."

"All right. All right, that's O.K." Matlock did his best to sound quietly frantic, laying the groundwork for his ultimate refusal. "There are people around; if any of you tried anything, I could scream my head off. And I *will!*"

"Of course. But you won't have to. Nobody wants anyone hurt. It's a simple transaction; that's what our friend told me to tell you. He admires you. . . ."

"How can I be sure he'll bring Pat? I have to be sure!"

"The *transaction*, Matlock." The voice was oily, there was a hint of desperation. Dunois's "cobra" was unpredictable. "That's what it's all about. Our friend wants what you found, remember?"

"I remember. . . ." Matlock's mind raced. He realized he had to maintain his hysteria, his unpredictability. But he had to switch the location. Change it without being suspect. If Nimrod became suspicious, Dunois had sentenced Pat to death. "And you tell our *friend* to remember that there's a statement in an envelope addressed to men in Washington!"

"He knows that, for Christ's sake, I mean . . . he's

concerned, you know what I mean? Now, we'll see you at the field, O.K.? In an hour, O.K.?"

This was the moment. There might not come another.

"No! Wait a minute. . . . I'm not going on that campus! The Washington people, they've got the whole place watched! They're all around! They'll put me away!"

"No, they won't. . . ."

"How the hell do you know?"

"There's nobody. So help me, it's *O.K.* Calm down, please."

"That's easy for you, not me! No, I'll tell you where. . . ."

He spoke rapidly, disjointedly, as if thinking desperately while talking. First he mentioned Herron's house, and before the voice could either agree or disagree, he rejected it himself. He then pinpointed the freight yards, and immediately found irrational reasons why he could not go there.

"Now, don't get so excited," said the voice. "It's a simple transaction. . . ."

"That restaurant! Outside of town. The Cheshire Cat! Behind the restaurant, there's a garden. . . ."

The voice was confused trying to keep up with him, and Matlock knew he was carrying off the ploy. He made last references to the diaries and the incriminating affidavit and slammed the telephone receiver into its cradle.

He stood in the booth, exhausted. Perspiration was dripping down his face, yet the early morning air was cool.

"That was handled very nicely," said the black man in command. "Your adversary chose a place within the college, I gather. An intelligent move on his part. Very nicely done, sir."

Matlock looked at the uniformed Negro, grateful for his praise and not a little astonished at his own resourcefulness. "I don't know if I could do it again."

"Of course you could," answered the black, leading Matlock toward the car. "Extreme stress activates a memory bank, not unlike a computer. Probing, rejecting, accepting—all instantaneously. Until panic, of course. There are interesting studies being made regarding the varying thresholds."

"Really?" said Matlock as they reached the car door. The Negro motioned him inside. The car lurched forward and they sped off down the highway flanked by the two other automobiles.

"We'll take a diagonal route to the restaurant using the roads set back in the farm country," said the black behind the wheel. "We'll approach it from the southwest and let you off about a hundred yards from a path used by employees to reach the rear of the building. We'll point it out to you. Walk directly to the section of the gardens where there's a large white arbor and a circle of flagstones surrounding a goldfish pond. Do you know it?"

"Yes, I do. I'm wondering how *you* do, though."

The driver smiled. "I'm not clairvoyant. While you were in the telephone booth, I was in touch with our men by radio. Everything's ready now. We're prepared. Remember, the white arbor and the goldfish pond. . . . And here. Here's the notebook and the envelope." The driver reached down to a flap pocket on the side of his door and pulled out the oilcloth package. The envelope was attached to it by a thick elastic band.

"We'll be there in less than ten minutes," said the man in command, shifting his weight to get comfortable. Matlock looked at him. Strapped to his leg—sewn into the tight-fitting khaki, actually—was a leather scabbard. He hadn't noticed it before and knew why. The bone-handled knife it contained had only recently been inserted. The scabbard housed a blade at least ten inches long.

Dunois's elite corps was now, indeed, prepared.

35

He stood at the side of the tall white arbor. The sun had risen over the eastern curve, the woods behind him still heavy with mist, dully reflecting the light of the early morning. In front of him the newly filled trees formed corridors for the old brick paths that converged into this restful flagstone haven. There were a number of marble benches placed around the circle, all glistening with morning moisture. From the center of the large patio, the bubbling sounds of the man-made goldfish pond continued incessantly with no break in the sound pattern. Birds could be heard activating their myriad signals, greeting the sun, starting the day's foraging.

Matlock's memory wandered back to Herron's Nest, to the forbidding green wall which isolated the old man from the outside world. There were similarities, he thought. Perhaps it was fitting that it should all end in such a place.

He lit a cigarette, extinguishing it after two intakes of smoke. He clutched the notebook, holding it in front of his chest as though it were some impenetrable shield, his head snapping in the direction of every sound, a portion of his life suspended with each movement.

He wondered where Dunois's men were. Where had

the elite guard hidden itself? Were they watching him, laughing quietly among themselves at his nervous gestures—his so obvious fear? Or were they spread out, guerrilla fashion? Crouched next to the earth or in the low limbs of the trees, ready to spring, prepared to kill?

And who would they kill? In what numbers and how armed would be Nimrod's forces? Would Nimrod come? Would Nimrod bring the girl he loved safely back to him? And if Nimrod did, if he finally saw Pat again, would the two of them be caught in the massacre which surely had to follow?

Who *was* Nimrod?

His breathing stopped. The muscles in his arms and legs contorted spastically, stiffened with fear. He closed his eyes tightly—to listen or to pray, he'd never really know, except that his beliefs excluded the existence of God. And so he listened with his eyes shut tight until he was sure.

First one, then two automobiles had turned off the highway and had entered the side road leading to the entrance of the Cheshire Cat. Both vehicles were traveling at enormous speeds, their tires screeching as they rounded the front circle leading into the restaurant parking area.

And then everything was still again. Even the birds were silent; no sound came from anywhere.

Matlock stepped back under the arbor, pressing himself against its lattice frame. He strained to hear—anything.

Silence. Yet not silence! Yet, again, a sound so blended with stillness as to be dismissed as a rustling leaf is dismissed.

It was a scraping. A hesitant, halting scraping from one of the paths in front of him, one of the paths hidden amongst the trees, one of the old brick lanes leading to the flagstone retreat.

At first it was barely audible. Dismissible. Then it became slightly clearer, less hesitant, less unsure.

Then he heard the quiet, tortured moan. It pierced into his brain.

"Jamie . . . Jamie? Please, Jamie. . . ."

The single plea, his name, broke off into a sob. He felt a rage he had never felt before in his life. He threw down the oilcloth packet, his eyes blinded by tears and fury. He lunged out of the protective frame of the white arbor and yelled, roared so that his voice startled the birds, who screeched out of the trees, out of their silent sanctuary.

"Pat! Pat! Where are you? Pat, my God, where? *Where!*"

The sobbing—half relief, half pain—became louder.

"Here. . . . Here, Jamie! Can't see."

He traced the sound and raced up the middle brick path. Halfway to the building, against the trunk of a tree, sunk to the ground, he saw her. She was on her knees, her bandaged head against the earth. She had fallen. Rivulets of blood were on the back of her neck; the sutures in her head had broken.

He rushed to her and gently lifted up her head.

Under the bandages on her forehead were layers of three-inch adhesive tape, pushed brutally against the lids of her eyes, stretched tight to her temples—as secure and unmovable as a steel plate covering her face. To try and remove them would be a torture devised in hell.

He held her close and kept repeating her name over and over again.

"Everything will be all right now. . . . Everything will be all right. . . ."

He lifted her gently off the ground, pressing her face against his own. He kept repeating those words of comfort which came to him in the midst of his rage.

Suddenly, without warning, without any warning at all, the blinded girl screamed, stretching her bruised body, her lacerated head.

"Let them have it, for God's sake! Whatever it is, *give it to them!*"

He stumbled down the brick path back to the flagstone circle.

"I will, I will, my darling. . . ."

"Please, Jamie! Don't let them touch me again! *Ever again!*"

"No, my darling. Not ever, not ever. . . ."

He slowly lowered the girl onto the ground, onto the soft earth beyond the flagstones.

"Take the tape off! Please take the tape off."

"I can't now, darling. It would hurt too much. In a little . . ."

"I don't *care!* I can't stand it any longer!"

What could he do? What was he supposed to *do?* Oh, God! Oh, God, you son-of-a-bitching God! *Tell me! Tell me!*

He looked over at the arbor. The oilcloth packet lay on the ground where he had thrown it.

He had no choice now. He did not care now.

"Nimrod! . . . Nimrod! Come to me now, Nimrod! Bring your goddamn army! Come on and get it, Nimrod! I've got it here!"

Through the following silence, he heard the footsteps.

Precise, surefooted, emphatic.

On the middle path, Nimrod came into view.

Adrian Sealfont stood on the edge of the flagstone circle.

"I'm sorry, James."

Matlock lowered the girl's head to the ground. His mind was incapable of functioning. His shock was so total that no words came, he couldn't assimilate the terrible, unbelievable fact in front of him. He rose slowly to his feet.

"Give it to me, James. You have your agreement. We'll take care of you."

"No. . . . No. No, I don't, I *won't believe* you! This isn't so. This isn't the way it can be. . . ."

"I'm afraid it is." Sealfont snapped the fingers of his right hand. It was a signal.

"No. . . . No! No! No!" Matlock found that he was screaming. The girl, too, cried out. He turned to Sealfont. "They said you were taken away! I thought you were dead! I blamed myself for your death!"

"I wasn't taken, I was escorted. Give me the diaries." Sealfont, annoyed, snapped his fingers again. "And the Corsican paper. I trust you have both with you."

There was the slightest sound of a muffled cough, a rasp, an interrupted exclamation. Sealfont looked quickly behind him and spoke sharply to his unseen forces.

"Get out here!"

"Why?"

"Because we *had* to. *I* had to. There was no alternative."

"No alternative?" Matlock couldn't believe he had heard the words. "No alternative to *what?*"

"Collapse! We were financially exhausted! Our last reserves were committed; there was no one left to appeal to. The moral corruption was complete: the pleas of higher education became an unprofitable, national bore. There was no other answer but to assert our own leadership . . . over the corruptors. We did so, and we survived!"

In the agonizing bewilderment of the moment, the pieces of the puzzle fell into place for Matlock. The unknown tumblers of the unfamiliar vault locked into gear and the heavy steel door was opened. . . . Carlyle's extraordinary endowment. . . . But it was more than Carlyle; Sealfont had just said it. The *pleas* had become a *bore!* It was subtle, but it was there!

Everywhere!

The raising of funds throughout all the campuses continued but there were no cries of panic these days; no threats of financial collapse that had been the themes of a hundred past campaigns in scores of colleges and universities.

The general assumption to be made—if one bothered to make it—was that the crises had been averted. Normality had returned.

But it *hadn't*. The norm had become a monster.

"Oh, my God," said Matlock softly, in terrified consternation.

"He was no help, I can assure you," replied Sealfont. "Our accomplishments are extremely human. Look at us now. *Independent!* Our strength growing systematically. Within five years every major university in the Northeast will be part of a self-sustaining federation!"

"You're diseased. . . . You're a *cancer!*"

"We *survive!* The choice was never really that difficult. No one was going to stop the way things were. Least of all ourselves. . . . We simply made the decision ten years ago to alter the principal players."

"But *you* of all people . . ."

"Yes. I was a good choice, wasn't I?" Sealfont turned once again in the direction of the restaurant, toward the sleeping hill with the old brick paths. He shouted. "I told you to come out here! There's nothing to worry about. Our friend doesn't care who you are. He'll soon be on his way. . . . Won't you, James?"

"You're *insane*. You're . . ."

"Not for a *minute!* There's no one saner. Or more practical. . . . History repeats, you should know that. The fabric is torn, society divided into viciously opposing camps. Don't be fooled by the dormancy; scratch the surface—it bleeds profusely."

"You're *making* it bleed!" Matlock screamed. There was nothing left; the spring had sprung.

"On the contrary! You pompous, self-righteous *ass!*" Sealfont's eyes stared at him in cold fury, his voice scathing. "Who gave you the right to make pronouncements? Where were you when men like myself—in *every institution*—faced the very real prospects of closing our doors! You were safe; we *sheltered* you. . . . And our appeals went unanswered. There wasn't room for our needs . . ."

"You didn't try! Not hard enough . . ."

"Liar! *Fool!*" Sealfont roared now. He was a man possessed, thought Matlock. Or a man tormented. "What was *left?* Endowments? Dwindling! There are other, more *viable tax incentives!* . . . Foundations? Small-minded tyrants—smaller allocations! . . . The Government? *Blind! Obscene!* Its priorities are bought! Or returned in kind at the ballot box! We had no funds; we bought no votes! For us, the system had collapsed! It was finished! . . . And no one knew it better than I did. For years . . . begging, pleading; palms outstretched to the ignorant men and their pompous *committees*. . . . It was hopeless; we were killing ourselves. Still no one listened. And always . . . *always*—behind the excuses and the delays—there was the snickering, the veiled reference to our common God-given frailty. After all . . . we were *teachers*. Not *doers*. . . ."

Sealfont's voice was suddenly low. And hard. And utterly convincing as he finished. "Well, young man, we're *doers now*. The system's damned and rightly so. The leaders never learn. Look to the children. They saw. They understood. . . . And we've enrolled them. Our alliance is no coincidence."

Matlock could do no more than stare at Sealfont. Sealfont had said it: *Look to the children. . . . Look, and behold. Look and beware.* The leaders never learn. . . . Oh, God! Was it so? Was it really the way things were? The Nimrods and the Dunoises. The "federations," the "elite guards." Was it happening all over again?

"Now James. Where is the letter you spoke of? Who has it?"

"Letter? What?"

"The letter that is to be mailed this morning. We'll stop it now, won't we?"

"I don't understand." Matlock was trying, trying *desperately* to make contact with his senses.

"Who has the letter!"

"The letter?" Matlock knew as he spoke that he was saying the wrong words, but he couldn't help himself. He couldn't stop to think, for he was incapable of thought.

"The letter! . . . There *is* no *letter, is there?!* There's . . . no 'incriminating statement' typed and ready to be mailed at ten o'clock in the morning! You were lying!"

"I was lying. . . . Lying." His reserves had been used up. There was nothing now but what was so.

Sealfont laughed softly. It wasn't the laugh Matlock was used to hearing from him. There was a cruelty he'd not heard before.

"Weren't you clever? But you're ultimately weak. I knew that from the beginning. You were the government's perfect choice, for you have no really firm commitments. They called it mobility. I knew it to be unconcerned flexibility. You talk but that's all you do. It's meaningless. . . . You're very representative, you know." Sealfont spoke over his shoulder toward the paths. "All right, *all* of you! Dr. Matlock won't be in a position to reveal any names, any identities. Come out of your hutches, you rabbits!"

"Augh . . ."

The guttural cry was short, punctuating the stillness. Sealfont whipped around.

Then there was another gasp, this the unmistakable sound of a human windpipe expunging its last draft of air.

And another, this coupled with the beginnings of a scream.

"Who is it? Who's up there?" Sealfont rushed to the path from which the last cry came.

He was stopped by the sound of a terrifying shout—cut short—from another part of the sanctuary. He raced back; the beginnings of panic were jarring his control.

"Who's up there?! Where are all of you? *Come down here!*"

The silence returned. Sealfont stared at Matlock.

"What have you done? What have you done, you

unimportant little man? Whom have you brought with you? *Who is up there? Answer me!*"

Even if he'd been capable, there was no need for Matlock to reply. From a path at the far end of the garden, Julian Dunois walked into view.

"Good morning, Nimrod."

Sealfont's eyes bulged. "Who *are* you? Where are my men?!"

"The name is Jacques Devereaux, Heysoú Daumier, Julian Dunois—take your choice. You were no match for us. You had a complement of ten, I had eight. No match. Your men are dead and how their bodies are disposed of is no concern of yours."

"Who *are you?*"

"Your enemy."

Sealfont ripped open his coat with his left hand, plunging his right inside. Dunois shouted a warning. Matlock found himself lurching forward toward the man he'd revered for a decade. Lunging at him with only one thought, one final objective, if it had to be the end of his own life.

To kill.

The face was next to his. The Lincoln-like face now contorted with fear and panic. He brought his right hand down on it like the claw of a terrified animal. He ripped into the flesh and felt the blood spew out of the distorted mouth.

He heard the shattering explosion and felt a sharp, electric pain in his left shoulder. But still he couldn't stop.

"Get off, Matlock! For God's sake, get off!"

He was being pulled away. Pulled away by huge black muscular arms. He was thrown to the ground, the heavy arms holding him down. And through it all he heard the cries, the terrible cries of pain and his name being repeated over and over again.

"Jamie . . . Jamie . . . Jamie . . ."

He lurched upward, using every ounce of strength his violence could summon. The muscular black arms were taken by surprise; he brought his legs up in crushing blows against the ribs and spines above him.

For a few brief seconds, he was free.

He threw himself forward on the hard surface, pounding his arms and knees against the stone. Whatever had happened to him, whatever was meant by the stinging pain, now spreading throughout the whole left side of his body, he had to reach the girl on the ground. The girl who had been through such terror for him.

"Pat!"

The pain was more than he could bear. He fell once more, but he had reached her hand. They held each other's hands, each trying desperately to give comfort to the other, fully aware that both might die at that moment.

Suddenly Matlock's hand went limp.

All was darkness for him.

He opened his eyes and saw the large black kneeling in front of him. He had been propped up into a sitting position at the side of a marble bench. His shirt had been removed; his left shoulder throbbed.

"The pain, I'm sure, is far more serious than the wound," said the black. "The upper left section of your body was badly bruised in the automobile, and the bullet penetrated below your left shoulder cartilage. Compounded that way, the pain would be severe."

"We gave you a local anesthetic. It should help." The speaker was Julian Dunois, standing to his right.

"Miss Ballantyne has been taken to a doctor. He'll remove the tapes. He's black and sympathetic, but not so much so to treat a man with a bullet wound. We've radioed our own doctor in Torrington. He should be here in twenty minutes."

"Why didn't you wait for him to help Pat?"

"Frankly, we have to talk. Briefly, but in confidence. Secondly, for her own sake, those tapes had to be removed as quickly as possible."

"Where's Sealfont?"

"He's disappeared. That's all you know, all you'll ever know. It's important that you understand that. Because, you see, if we must, we will carry out our threat against you and Miss Ballantyne. We don't wish to do that. . . . You and I, we are not enemies."

"You're wrong. We are."

"Ultimately, perhaps. That would seem inevitable. Right now, however, we've served each other in a moment of great need. We acknowledge it. We trust you do also."

"I do."

"Perhaps we've even learned from each other."

Matlock looked into the eyes of the black revolutionary. "I understand things better. I don't know what you could have learned from me."

The revolutionary laughed gently. "That an individual, by his actions—his courage, if you like—rises above the stigma of labels."

"I don't understand you."

"Ponder it. It'll come to you."

"What happens now? To Pat? To me? I'll be arrested the minute I'm seen."

"I doubt that sincerely. Within the hour, Greenberg will be reading a document prepared by my organization. By me, to be precise. I suspect the contents will become part of a file buried in the archives. It's most embarrassing. Morally, legally, and certainly politically. Too many profound errors were made. . . . We'll act this morning as your intermediary. Perhaps it would be a good time for you to use some of your well-advertised money and go with Miss Ballantyne on a long, recuperative journey. . . . I believe that will be agreed upon with alacrity. I'm sure it will."

"And Sealfont? What happens to him. Are you going to kill him?"

"Does Nimrod deserve to die? Don't bother to answer; we'll not discuss the subject. Suffice it to say he'll remain alive until certain questions are answered."

"Have you any idea what's going to happen when he's found to be missing?"

"There will be explosions, ugly rumors. About a great many things. When icons are shattered, the believers panic. So be it. Carlyle will have to live with it. . . . Rest, now. The doctor will be here soon." Dunois turned his attention to a uniformed Negro who had come up to him and spoken softly. The kneeling black who had bandaged his wound stood up. Matlock watched the tall, slender figure of Julian Dunois, quietly, confidently issuing his instructions, and felt the pain of gratitude. It was made worse because Dunois suddenly took on another image.

It was the figure of death.

"Dunois?"

"Yes?"

"Be careful."

EPILOGUE

The blue-green waters of the Caribbean mirrored the hot afternoon sun in countless thousands of swelling, blinding reflections. The sand was warm to the touch, soft under the feet. This isolated stretch of the island was at peace with itself and with a world beyond that it did not really acknowledge.

Matlock walked down to the edge of the water and let the miniature waves wash over his ankles. Like the sand on the beach, the water was warm.

He carried a newspaper sent to him by Greenberg. Part of a newspaper, actually.

KILLINGS IN CARLYLE, CONN.

23 SLAIN, BLACKS AND WHITES, TOWN STUNNED, FOLLOWS DISAPPEARANCE OF UNIVERSITY PRESIDENT

CARLYLE, MAY 10—On the outskirts of this small university town, in a section housing large, old estates, a bizarre mass killing took place yesterday. Twenty-three men were slain; the federal authorities have speculated the killings were the result of an ambush that claimed many lives of both the attackers and the attacked. . . .

There followed a cold recitation of identities, short summaries of police file associations.

Julian Dunois was among them.

The specter of death had not been false; Dunois hadn't escaped. The violence he engendered had to be the violence that would take his life.

The remainder of the article contained complicated speculations on the meaning and the motives of the massacre's strange cast of characters. And the possible connection to the disappearance of Adrian Sealfont.

Speculations only. No mention of Nimrod, nothing of himself; no word of any long-standing federal investigation. Not the truth; nothing of the truth.

Matlock heard his cottage door open, and he turned around. Pat was standing on the small veranda fifty yards away over the dune. She waved and started down the steps toward him.

She was dressed in shorts and a light silk blouse; she was barefoot and smiling. The bandages had been removed from her legs and arms, and the Caribbean sun had tanned her skin to a lovely bronze. She had devised a wide orange headband to cover the wounds above her forehead.

She would not marry him. She said there would be no marriage out of pity, out of debt—real or imagined. But Matlock knew there would be a marriage. Or there would be no marriages for either of them. Julian Dunois had made it so.

"Did you bring cigarettes?" he asked.

"No. No cigarettes," she replied. "I brought matches."

"That's cryptic."

"I used that word—cryptic—with Jason. Do you remember?"

"I do. You were mad as hell."

"You were spaced out . . . In hell. Let's walk down to the jetty."

"Why did you bring matches?" He took her hand, putting the newspaper under his arm.

"A funeral pyre. Archeologists place great significance in funeral pyres."

"What?"

"You've been carrying around that damned paper all day. I want to burn it." She smiled at him, gently.

"Burning it won't change what's in it."

Pat ignored his observation. "Why do you think Jason sent it to you? I thought the whole idea was several weeks of nothing. No newspapers, no radios, no contact with anything but warm water and white sand. He made the rules and he broke them."

"He *recommended* the rules and knew they were difficult to live by."

"He should have let someone else break them. He's not as good a friend as I thought he was."

"Maybe he's a better one."

"That's sophistry." She squeezed his hand. A single, overextended wave lapped across their bare feet. A silent gull swooped down from the sky into the water offshore; its wings flapped against the surface, its neck shook violently. The bird ascended screeching, no quarry in its beak.

"Greenberg knows I've got a very unpleasant decision to make."

"You've made it. He knows that, too."

Matlock looked at her. Of course Greenberg knew; she knew, too, he thought. "There'll be a lot more pain; perhaps more than justified."

"That's what they'll tell you. They'll tell you to let them do it their way. Quietly, efficiently, with as little embarrassment as possible. For everyone."

"Maybe it's best; maybe they're right."

"You don't believe that for a second."

"No, I don't."

They walked in silence for a while. The jetty was in front of them, its rocks placed decades, perhaps centuries ago, to restrain a long-forgotten current. It was a natural fixture now.

As Nimrod had become a natural fixture, a logical extension of the anticipated; undesirable but nevertheless expected. To be fought in deep cover.

Mini-America . . . just below the surface.

Company policy, man.

Everywhere.

The hunters, builders. The killers and their quarry were making alliances.

Look to the children. They understand . . . We've enrolled them.

The leaders never learn.

A microcosm of the inevitable? Made unavoidable because the needs were real? Had been real for years?

And still the leaders would not learn.

"Jason said once that truth is neither good nor bad. Simply truth. That's why he sent me this." Matlock sat down on a large flat rock; Pat stood beside him. The tide was coming in and the sprays of the small waves splashed upward. Pat reached over and took the two pages of the newspaper.

"This is the truth then." A statement.

"Their truth. Their judgment. Assign obvious labels and continue the game. The good guys and the bad guys and the posse will reach the pass on time. Just in time. This time."

"What's your truth?"

"Go back and tell the story. All of it."

"They'll disagree. They'll give you reasons why you shouldn't. Hundreds of them."

"They won't convince me."

"Then they'll be against you. They've threatened; they won't accept interference. That's what Jason wants you to know."

"That's what he wants me to think about."

Pat held the pages of the newspaper in front of her and struck a wooden island match on the dry surface of a rock.

The paper burned haltingly, retarded by the Caribbean spray.

But it burned.

"That's not a very impressive funeral pyre," said Matlock.

"It'll do until we get back."

THE GEMINI CONTENDERS IS:

"THE READ OF THE YEAR! Ludlum grabs you by the throat . . . intense suspense."

—*Boston Herald Advertiser*

"HIS MOST AMBITIOUS NOVEL . . . ALSO HIS BEST . . . its twists and turns carry the reader on a fast bobsled run . . . a marvelously unflagging imagination."

—*New York Times*

"PACKED FULL OF EXCITEMENT . . . if you like a good thriller you had better read the book and not wait for the movie."

—*Denver Post*

"A MASTERFUL JOB . . . his most complex, thought-provoking, and intricately plotted novel to date."

—*San Diego Union*

Other Books by the Author:

THE SCARLATTI INHERITANCE
THE OSTERMAN WEEKEND
*THE RHINEMANN EXCHANGE
*THE GEMINI CONTENDERS
THE CHANCELLOR MANUSCRIPT
THE HOLCROFT COVENANT
THE MATARESE CIRCLE
THE BOURNE IDENTITY
THE PARSIFAL MOSAIC

*Available in Dell Editions.

THE GEMINI CONTENDERS

ROBERT LUDLUM

A DELL BOOK

Published by
DELL PUBLISHING CO., INC.
1 Dag Hammarskjold Plaza
New York, N.Y. 10017

ISBN: 0-440-12859-5

Reprinted by arrangement with
The Dial Press

Printed in the United States of America

First Dell printing—April 1977
Twenty-seventh Dell printing—May 1983

For Richard Marek, Editor.

Brilliance cloaked in great humor. Perception beyond any writer's imagination. Simply, the best there is.

And for lovely Margot, who makes it all perfect.

BOOK ONE

PROLOGUE

DECEMBER 9, 1939
SALONIKA, GREECE

One by one the trucks struggled up the steep road in the predawn light of Salonika. Each went a bit faster at the top; the drivers were anxious to return to the darkness of the descending country road cut out of the surrounding forests.

Yet each of the five drivers in the five trucks had to control his anxiety. None could allow his foot to slip from a brake or press an accelerator beyond a certain point; eyes had to be squinted, sharpening the focus, alert for a sudden stop or an unexpected curve in the darkness.

For it was darkness. No headlights were turned on; the column traveled with only the gray light of the Grecian night, low-flying clouds filtering the spill of the Grecian moon.

The journey was an exercise in discipline. And discipline was not foreign to these drivers, or to the riders beside the drivers.

Each was a priest. A monk. From the Order of Xenope, the harshest monastic brotherhood under the control of the Patriarchate of Constantine. Blind obedience coexisted with self-reliance; they were disciplined to the instant of death.

In the lead truck, the young bearded priest removed his cassock, under which were the clothes of a laborer, a heavy shirt and trousers of thick fabric. He rolled up the cassock and placed it in the well behind the high-backed seat, shoving it down between odd items of canvas and cloth. He spoke to the robed driver beside him.

"It's no more than a half mile now. The stretch of track parallels the road for about three hundred feet. In the open; it will be sufficient."

"The train will be there?" asked the middle-aged, powerfully built monk, narrowing his eyes in the darkness.

"Yes. Four freight cars, a single engineer. No stokers. No other men."

"You'll be using a shovel, then," said the older priest, smiling but with no humor in his eyes.

"I'll be using the shovel," replied the younger man simply. "Where's the weapon?"

"In the glove compartment."

The priest in the laborer's clothes reached forward and released the catch on the compartment panel. It fell open. He put his hand inside the recess and withdrew a heavy, large-calibered pistol. Deftly, the priest sprung the magazine out of the handle, checked the ammunition, and cracked the thick steel back into the chamber. The metallic sound had a finality to it.

"A powerful instrument. Italian, isn't it?"

"Yes," answered the older priest without comment, only the sadness in his voice.

"That's appropriate. And, I suppose, a blessing." The younger man shoved the weapon into his belt. "You'll call his family?"

"I've been so ordered——" It was obvious that the driver wanted to say something more, but he controlled himself. Silently he gripped the wheel more firmly than necessary.

For a moment the moonlight broke through the night clouds, illuminating the road cut out of the forest.

"I used to play here as a child," said the younger man. "I would run through the woods and get wet in the streams . . . then I would dry off in the mountain caves and pretend I had visions. I was happy in these hills. The Lord God wanted me to see them again. He is merciful. And kind."

The moon disappeared. There was darkness once more.

The trucks entered a sweeping curve to the west; the woods thinned out and in the distance, barely visible, were the outlines of telegraph poles, black shafts silhouetted against gray night. The road straightened and widened and became one with a clearing that stretched perhaps a hundred yards from forest to forest. A flat, barren area imposed on the myriad hills and woodlands. In the center of the clearing, its hulk obscured by the darkness beyond, was a train.

Immobile but not without movement. From the engine came curls of smoke spiraling up into the night.

"In the old days," said the young priest, "the farmers would herd their sheep and cart their produce here. There was always a great deal of confusion, my father told me. Fights broke out constantly over what belonged to whom. They were amusing stories. . . . There he is!"

The beam of a flashlight shot out from the black. It circled twice and then remained stationary, the white shaft directed now at the last freight car. The priest in laborer's clothes unclipped a pencil light from his shirt pocket, held it forward and pressed the button for precisely two seconds. The reflection off the truck's windshield briefly illuminated the small enclosure. The younger man's eyes were drawn swiftly to the face of his brother monk. He saw that his companion had bitten his lip; a rivulet of blood trickled down his chin, matting itself in the close-cropped gray beard.

There was no reason to comment on it.

"Pull up to the third car. The others will turn around and start unloading."

"I know," said the driver simply. He swung the wheel gently to the right and headed toward the third freight car.

The engineer, in overalls and a goatskin cap, approached the truck as the young priest opened the door and jumped to the ground. The two men looked at each other and then embraced.

"You look different without your cassock, Petride. I'd forgotten how you looked——"

"Oh, come now. Four years out of twenty-seven is hardly the better part."

"We don't see you often enough. Everyone in the family remarks about it." The engineer removed his large, calloused hands from the priest's shoulders. The moon broke through the clouds again; the spill lighted the trainman's face. It was a strong face, nearer fifty than forty, filled with the lines of a man constantly exposing his skin to the wind and the sun.

"How's mother, Annaxas?"

"Well. A little weaker with each month of age, but alert."

"And your wife?"

"Pregnant again and not laughing this time. She scolds me."

"She should. You're a lustful old dog, my brother. But better to serve the church, I rejoice to say." The priest laughed.

"I'll tell her you said that," said the engineer, smiling.

There was a moment of silence before the young man replied. "Yes. You tell her." He turned to the activity taking place at the freight cars. The loading doors had been opened and lanterns hung inside, shedding their muted light sufficiently for packing, but not bright enough to be obvious outside. The figures of robed priests began walking swiftly back and forth between the trucks and the doors, carrying crates, boxes of heavy cardboard framed with wood. Prominently displayed on each crate was the crucifix and thorns of the Order of Xenope.

"The food?" inquired the engineer.

"Yes," answered his brother. "Fruits, vegetables, dried meats, grain. The border patrols will be satisfied."

"Then where?" It was not necessary to be clearer.

"This vehicle. In the middle section of the carriage, beneath tobacco nets. You have the lookouts posted?"

"On the tracks and the road; both directions for over a mile. Don't worry. Before daybreak on a Sunday morning, only you priests and novices have work to do and places to go."

The young priest glanced over at the fourth freight car. The work was progressing rapidly; the crates were being stacked inside. All those hours of practice were showing their value. The monk who was his driver stopped briefly by the muted light of the loading door, a carton in his hands. He exchanged looks with the younger man, then forced his attention away, back to the carton which he swung up into the well of the freight car.

Father Petride turned to his brother. "When you picked up the train, did you speak with anyone?"

"Only the dispatcher. Naturally. We had black tea together."

"What did he say?"

"Words I wouldn't offend you with, for the most part. His papers said the cars were to be loaded by the fathers of Xenope in the outlying yards. He didn't ask any questions."

Father Petride looked over at the second freight car, on his right. In minutes all would be completed; they would be ready for the third car. "Who prepared the engine?"

"Fuel crews and mechanics. Yesterday afternoon. The orders said it was a standby; that's normal. Equipment breaks down all the time. We are laughed at in Italy. . . . Naturally, I checked everything myself several hours ago."

"Would the dispatcher have any reason to telephone the freight yards? Where supposedly we are loading the cars?"

"He was asleep, or practically so, before I left his tower. The morning schedule won't start——" the engineer looked up at the gray black sky "——for at least another hour. He'd have no reason to call anyone, unless the wireless reported an accident."

"The wires were shorted out; water in a terminal box," said the priest quickly, as if talking to himself.

"Why?"

"In case you did have problems. You spoke to *no one* else?"

"Not even a drifter. I checked the cars to make sure none were inside."

"You've studied our schedule by now. What do you think?"

The trainman whistled softly, shaking his head. "I think I'm astounded, my brother. Can so much be . . . so arranged?"

"The arrangements are taken care of. What about the time? That's the important factor."

"If there are no track failures the speed can be maintained. The Slav border police at Bitola are hungry for bribes; and a Greek freight at Banja Luka is fair game. We'll have no trouble at Sarajevo or Zagreb; they look for larger fish than food for the religious."

"The time, not the bribes."

"They *are* time. One haggles."

"Only if *not* haggling would seem suspicious. Can we reach Monfalcone in three nights?"

"If your arrangements are successful, yes. If we lose time we could make it up during the daylight hours."

"Only as a last resort. We travel at night."

"You're obstinate."

"We're cautious." Again the priest looked away. Freight cars one and two were secure, the fourth would be loaded and packed before the minute was up. He turned back to his brother. "Does the family think you're taking a freight to Corinth?"

"Yes. To Navpaktos. To the shipyards on the straits of Patrai. They don't expect me back for the better part of a week."

"There are strikes at Patrai. The unions are angry. If you were a few days longer, they'd understand."

Annaxas looked closely at his brother. He seemed startled at the young priest's worldly knowledge. There was a hesitancy in his reply. "They'd understand. Your sister-in-law would understand."

"Good." The monks had gathered by Petride's truck, watching him, waiting for instructions. "I'll join you at the engine shortly."

"All right," said the trainman as he walked away, glancing at the priests.

Father Petride removed the pencil light from his shirt pocket and in the darkness approached the other monks at the truck. He searched out the powerfully built man who was his driver. The monk understood and stepped away from the others, joining Petride at the side of the vehicle.

"This is the last time we speak," said the young priest. "May the blessings of God——"

"Please," interrupted Petride. "There's no time. Just commit to memory each move we make here tonight. *Everything.* It must be duplicated exactly."

"It will be. The same roads, the same orders or trucks, the same drivers, identical papers across the borders to Monfalcone. Nothing will change, except one of us will be missing."

"That's the will of God. For the glory of God. It's a privilege beyond my worth."

There were two master padlocks on the truck's panel. Petride had one key; his driver held the other. Together they approached the locks and inserted the keys. The irons sprung; the locks were lifted out of the steel hasps, the hasps slapped up, and the doors opened. A lantern was hung high on the edge of the panel.

Inside were the crates with the symbols of the crucifix and thorns stenciled on the sides between the strips of wood. The monks began to remove them, maneuvering like dancers—robes flowing in the eerie light. They carried the cartons to the loading door of the third freight car. Two men leaped up into the heavy-beamed deck of the car and started stacking the boxes at the south end.

Several minutes later half the truck was empty. In the center of the van, separated from the surrounding cartons, was a single crate draped in black cloth. It was somewhat larger than the cases of produce and not rectangular in shape. Instead, it was a perfect cube: three feet in height, three in width, and three in depth.

The priests gathered in a semicircle in front of the open panels of the truck. Shafts of filtered white moonlight mingled with the yellow spill of the lantern. The combined effect of the strange admixture of light, the cavernous truck, and the robed figures made Father Petride think of a catacomb, deep in the earth, housing the true relics of the cross.

The reality was not much different. Except that what lay sealed inside the iron vault—for that was what it was—was infinitely more meaningful than the petrified wood of the crucifixion.

Several of the monks had closed their eyes in prayer; others were staring, transfixed by the presence of the holy thing, their thoughts suspended, their faith drawing sustenance from what they believed was within the tomblike chest—itself a catafalque.

Petride watched them, feeling apart from them, and that was how it should be. His mind wandered back to what seemed only hours ago, but was in reality six weeks. He had been ordered out of the fields and taken to the white concrete rooms of the Elder of Xenope. He was ushered into the presence of that most holy father; there was one other priest with the old prelate, no one else.

"Petride Dakakos," the holy man had begun, sitting behind his thick wooden table, "you have been chosen above all others here at Xenope for the most demanding task of your existence. For the glory of God and the preservation of Christian sanity."

The second priest had been introduced. He was an ascetic-looking man with wide, penetrating eyes. He spoke slowly, precisely. "We are the custodians of a vault, a sarcophagus, if you will, that has remained sealed in a tomb deep in the earth for over fifteen hundred years. Within that vault are documents that would rend the Christian world apart, so devastating are their writings. They are the ultimate proof of our most sacred beliefs, yet their exposure would set religion against religion, sect against sect, entire peoples against one another. In a holy war. . . . The German conflict is spreading. The vault must be taken out of Greece, for its existence has been rumored for decades. The search for it would be as thorough as a hunt for microbes. Arrangements have been made to remove it where none will find it. I should say, most of the arrangements. You are the final component."

The journey had been explained. The *arrangements*. In all their glory. And fear.

"You will be in contact with only one man. Savarone Fontini-Cristi, a great *padrone* of northern Italy, who lives in the vast estates of Campo di Fiori. I, myself, have traveled there and spoken with him. He's an extraordinary man, of unparalleled integrity and utter commitment to free men."

"He is of the Roman church?" Petride had asked incredulously.

"He is of no church, yet *all* churches. He is a powerful force for men who care to think for themselves. He is the friend of the Order of Xenope. It is he who will conceal the vault. . . . You and he alone. And then you . . . but we will get to that; you are the most privileged of men."

"I thank my God."

"As well you should, my son," said the holy father of Xenope, staring at him.

"We understand you have a brother. An engineer for the railroads."

"I do."

"Do you trust him?"

"With my life. He's the finest man I know."

"You shall look into the eyes of the Lord," said the holy father, "and you will not waver. In His eyes you will find perfect grace."

"I thank my God," said Petride once again.

He shook his head and blinked his eyes, forcing the reflections out of his mind. The priests by the truck were still standing immobile; the hum of whispered chants came from rapidly moving lips in the darkness.

There was no time for meditation or prayer. There was no time for anything but swift movement—to carry out the commands of the Order of Xenope. Petride gently parted the priests in front of him and jumped up into the truck. He knew why he had been chosen. He was capable of such harshness; the holy father of Xenope had made that clear to him.

There was a time for such men as himself.

God forgive him.

"Come," he said quietly to those on the ground. "I'll need help."

The monks nearest the truck looked uncertainly at one another. Then, one by one, five men climbed into the van.

Petride removed the black drape that covered the vault. Underneath, the holy receptacle was encased in the heavy cardboard, wood framing, and the stenciled symbols of Xenope; identical except for size and shape to all the other crates. But the casing was the only similarity. It required six strong backs, pushing and pulling, to nudge it to the edge of the van and onto the freight car.

The moment it was in place, the dancelike activity resumed. Petride remained in the freight car, arranging the crates so that they concealed the holy thing, obscuring it as one among so many. Nothing unusual, nothing to catch the eye.

The freight car was filled. Petride pulled the doors shut and inserted the iron padlock. He looked at the radium dial of his wristwatch; it had all taken eight minutes and thirty seconds.

It had to be, he supposed, yet still it annoyed him: His fellow priests knelt on the ground. A young man—younger than he, a powerful Serbo-Croat barely out of his novitiate—could not help himself. As the tears rolled down his cheek, the young priest began the chant of Nicaea. The others picked it up and Petride knelt also, in his laborer's clothes, and listened to the holy words.

But not speaking them. There was no *time! Couldn't they understand?*

What was happening to him? In order to take his mind off the holy whispers, he put his hand inside his shirt and checked the leather pouch that was strapped to his chest. Inside that flat, uncomfortable dispatch case were the orders that would lead him across hundreds of miles of uncertainty. Twenty-seven separate pages of paper. The pouch was secure; the straps cut into his skin.

The prayer over, the priests of Xenope rose silently. Petride stood in front of them and each in turn approached him and embraced him and held him in love. The last was his driver, his dearest friend in the order. The tears that filled the rims of his eyes and rolled down his strong face said everything there was to say.

The monks raced back to the trucks; Petride ran to the front of the train and climbed up into the pilot's cabin. He nodded to his brother who began to pull levers and turn wheels. Grinding shrieks of metal against metal filled the night.

In minutes the freight was traveling at high speed. The journey had begun. The journey for the glory of one Almighty God.

Petride held on to an iron bar that protruded from the iron wall. He closed his eyes and let the hammering vibrations and rushing wind numb his thoughts. His fears.

And then he opened his eyes—briefly—and saw his brother leaning out the window, his massive right hand on the throttle, his stare directed to the tracks ahead.

Annaxas the Strong, everyone called him. But Annaxas was more than strong; he was good. When their father had died, it was Annaxas who had gone out to the yards—a huge boy of thirteen—and worked the long, hard hours that exhausted grown men. The money Annaxas brought home kept them all together, made it possible for his brothers and sisters to get what schooling they could. And one brother got more. Not for the family, but for the glory of God.

The Lord God tested men. As He was testing now.

Petride bowed his head and the words seared through his brain and out of his mouth in a whisper that could not be heard.

I believe in one God, the Father Almighty, maker of all things both visible and invisible, and in one Lord, Jesus Christ, Teacher, Son of God, Only begotten of the Father. God of God, Light of Light, Very God of Very God, begotten not made. . . .

They reached the sidings at Edhessa; a switch was thrown by unseen, unauthorized hands, and the freight from Salonika plunged into the northern darkness. The Yugoslav border police at Bitola were as anxious for Greek news as they were for Greek bribes. The northern conflict was spreading rapidly, the armies of Hitler were maniacs; the Balkans were next to fall, everyone said so. And the unstable Italians were filling the piazzas, listening to the screams of war mouthed by the insane Mussolini and his strutting *fascisti*. The talk everywhere was of invasion.

The Slavs accepted several crates of fruit—Xenope fruit was the best in Greece—and wished Annaxas better fortune than they believed he would have, especially since he traveled north.

They sped through the second night north into Mitrovica. The Order of Xenope had done its work; a track was cleared on which no train was scheduled and the freight from Salonika proceeded east to Sarajevo, where a man came out of the shadows and spoke to Petride.

"In twelve minutes the track will be shifted. You will head north to Banja Luka. During the day you'll stay in the yards. They're very crowded. You'll be contacted at nightfall."

In the crowded freight yards at Banja Luka, at precisely quarter past six in the evening, a man came to them dressed in overalls. "You've done well," he said to Petride. "According to the dispatcher's flagging schedules, you don't exist."

At six thirty-five a signal was given; another switch was thrown, and the train from Salonika entered the tracks for Zagreb.

At midnight, in the quiet yards of Zagreb, another man, emerging from other shadows, gave Petride a long manila envelope. "These are papers signed by *Il Duce*'s *Ministro di Viaggio*. They say your freight is part of the Venice *Ferrovia*. It is Mussolini's pride; no one stops it for anything. You will hold at the Sezana depot and pick up the *Ferrovia* out of Trieste. You'll have no trouble with the Monfalcone border patrols."

Three hours later they waited on the Sezana track, the huge locomotive idling. Sitting on the steps, Petride watched Annaxas manipulate the valves and levers.

"You're remarkable," he said, meaning the compliment sincerely.

"It's a small talent," replied Annaxas. "It takes no schooling, just doing it over and over."

"I think it's a remarkable talent. I could never do it."

His brother looked down at him; the glow of the coals washed over his large face, with the wide-set eyes, so firm and strong and gentle. He was a bull of a man, this brother. A decent man. "You could do anything," said Annaxas awkwardly. "You have the head for thoughts and words far beyond mine."

"That's nonsense," laughed Petride. "There was a time when you'd slap my backside and tell me to tend to my chores with more brains."

"You were young; that was many years ago. You tended to your books, you did that. You were better than the freight yards; you got out of them."

"Only because of you, my brother."

"Rest, Petride. We must both rest."

They had nothing in common any longer, and the reason they had nothing was because of Annaxas's goodness and generosity. The older brother had provided the means for the younger to escape, to grow beyond he who provided . . . until there was nothing in common. What made the reality unbearable was that Annaxas the Strong understood the chasm between them now. In Bitola and Banja Luka he had also insisted they rest, not talk. They would get little sleep once they crossed the borders at Monfalcone. In Italy there would be no sleep at all.

The Lord God tested.

In the silence between them, in the open cabin, the black sky above, the dark ground below, the incessant straining of the engine's fires filling the night outside, Petride felt an odd suspension of thought and feeling. Thinking and feeling once-removed, as though he were examining another's experiences from some isolated perch, looking down through a glass. And he began to consider the man he would meet in the Italian Alps. The man who had provided the Order of Xenope with the complicated schedules of transportation through northern Italy. The expanding circles within circles that led inexorably across the Swiss borders in a way that was untraceable.

Savarone Fontini-Cristi was his name. His estate was called Campo di Fiori. The Elders of Xenope said the Fontini-Cristis were the most powerful family in Italy north of Venice. Quite possibly the richest north of Rome. The power and the wealth certainly were borne out by the twenty-seven separate papers in the leather pouch strapped so securely around his chest. Who but an extraordinarily influential man could provide them? And how did the Elders reach him? Through what means? And why would a man named Fontini-Cristi, whose origins had to be of the Roman Church, deliver such assistance to the Order of Xenope?

The answers to these questions were not within his province, but nevertheless the questions burned. He knew what lay sealed in the vault of iron in the third freight car. It was more than what his brother priests believed.

Far more.

The Elders had told him so he would understand. *It* was the holiest of compelling motives that would allow him to look into the eyes of God without doubt or hesitation. And he needed that assurance.

Unconsciously, he put his hand under the coarse shirt and felt the pouch. A rash had formed around the straps; he could feel the swelling and the rough, abrasive surface of his skin. It would be infected soon. But not before the twenty-seven papers did their work. Then it did not matter.

Suddenly, a half mile away on the northern track, the Venice *Ferrovia* could be seen speeding out of Trieste. The Sezana contact raced out of the control tower and ordered them to proceed without delay.

Annaxas fired up and throttled the idling locomotive as rapidly as possible and they plunged north behind the *Ferrovia* toward Monfalcone.

The guards at the border accepted the manila envelope and gave it to their superior officer. The officer shouted at the top of his lungs for the silent Annaxas to fire up quickly. *Proceed!* The freight was part of the *Ferrovia!* The engineer was not to delay!

The madness began at Legnago, when Petride gave the dispatcher the first of Fontini-Cristi's papers. The man blanched and became the most obsequious of public servants. The young priest could see the dispatcher searching his eyes, trying to unearth the level of authority Petride represented.

For the strategy devised by Fontini-Cristi was brilliant. Its strength was in its simplicity, its power over men based in fear—the threat of instant retaliation from the state.

The Greek freight was not a Greek freight at all. It was one of the highly secretive investigating trains sent out by

Rome's Ministry of Transportation, the inspectors general of the Italian rail system. Such trains roamed the tracks throughout the country, manned by officials ordered to examine and evaluate all rail operations and submit reports that some said were read by Mussolini himself.

The world made jokes about *Il Duce*'s railroads, but behind the humor was respect. The Italian rail system was the finest in Europe. It maintained its excellence by the time-honored method of the fascist state: secret efficiency ratings compiled by unknown investigators. A man's livelihood—or absence of it—depended on the judgments of the *esaminatori*. Retentions, advancements, and dismissals were often the results of a few brief moments of observation. It stood to reason that when an *esaminatore* revealed himself, absolute cooperation and confidentiality were given.

The freight from Salonika was now an Italian train with the covert imprimatur of Rome as its shield. Its movements were subject only to the authorizations contained in the papers supplied the dispatchers. And the orders within those authorizations were bizarre enough to have come from the convoluted machinations of *Il Duce* himself.

The circuitous route began. The towns and villages fled by—San Giorgio, Latisana, Motta di Levenza—as the freight from Salonika entered tracks behind Italian boxcars and passenger trains. Treviso, Montebelluna, and Valdagno, west to Malcesine on the Lago di Garda; across the large expanse of water on the sluggish freight boat and immediately north to Breno and Passo della Presolana.

There was only frightened cooperation. Everywhere.

When they reached Como the circling stopped and the dash began. They sped north on the land route and swung south to Lugano, following the tracks on the Swiss borders south and west again to Santa Maria Maggiore, crossing into Switzerland at Saas Fee, where the freight from Salonika resumed its identity, with one minor alteration.

This was determined by the twenty-second authorization in Petride's pouch. Fontini-Cristi had once again provided the simple explanation: The Swiss International Aid Commission at Geneva had granted permission for the Eastern church to cross borders and supply its retreat on the outskirts of Val de Gressoney. What was implied was that the borders would soon be closed to such supply trains. The war was gaining a terrible momentum; soon there would be no trains whatever from the Balkans or Greece.

From Saas Fee the freight rolled south into the yards at Zermatt. It was night; they would wait for the yards to close operations and a man who would come to them and confirm that another switch had been thrown. They would make the incursion south into the Italian Alps of Champoluc.

At ten minutes to nine a trainman appeared in the distance, coming out of the shadows across the Zermatt freight yard. He ran the last several hundred feet and raised his voice.

"Hurry! The rails are clear for Champoluc. There's no time to waste! The switch is tied to a master line; it could be spotted. Get *out* of here!"

Once more Annaxas went about the business of releasing the enormous pressures built up in the fires of the iron fuselage, and once again the train plunged into the darkness.

The signal would come in the mountains, high near an Alpine pass. No one knew just where.

Only Savarone Fontini-Cristi.

A light snow was falling, adding its thin layer to the alabaster cover on the moonlit ground. They passed through tunnels carved out of rock, swinging westward around the ledges of the mountains, the steep gorges menacingly beneath them on their right. It was so much colder. Petride had not expected that; he had not thought about temperatures. The snow and the ice; there was ice on the tracks.

Every mile they traveled seemed like ten, every minute that passed could have been an hour. The young priest peered through the windshield, seeing the beam of the train's searchlight reflecting off the falling snow. He leaned out; he could see only the giant trees that rose up in the darkness.

Where *was* he? Where was the Italian *padrone,* Fontini-Cristi? Perhaps he had changed his mind. O merciful God, that could not be! He could not allow himself to think such thoughts. What they carried in that holy vault would plunge the world into chaos. The Italian knew that; the Patriarchate had total confidence in the *padrone.* . . .

Petride's head was aching, his temples pounded. He sat on the steps of the tender; he had to control himself. He looked at the radium dial of his watch. *Merciful God!*

They'd traveled too far! In a half hour they'd be out of the mountains!

"There is your signal!" shouted Annaxas.

Petride leaped to his feet and leaned over the side, his pulse wild, his hands trembling as he gripped the roof ladder. Down the track no more than a quarter of a mile, a lantern was being raised and lowered, its light flickering through the thin sheets of snow.

Annaxas braked the locomotive. The belching engine drew out its roars like the subsiding giant furnace it was. In the snow-lit, moonlit distance, aided by the beam of the locomotive's single headlight, Petride saw a man standing next to an odd-shaped vehicle in a small clearing at the side of the rails. The man was dressed in heavy clothing, collar and cap of fur. The vehicle was both a truck and not a truck. Its rear wheels were much larger than those in front, as though belonging to a tractor. Yet the hood beyond the windshield was not a truck's hood, or a tractor's, thought the priest. It resembled something else.

What was it?

Then he knew and he could not help but smile. He had seen hundreds of such pieces of equipment during the past four days. In front of the strange vehicle's hood was a vertically controlled cargo platform.

Fontini-Cristi was as resourceful as the monks in the Order of Xenope. But then the pouch strapped to his chest had told him that.

"You are the priest of Xenope?" Savarone Fontini-Cristi's voice was deep, aristocratic, and very used to authority. He was a tall man and slender beneath the Alpine clothing, with large, penetrating eyes recessed in the aquiline features of his face. And he was a much older man than Petride thought he would be.

"I am, *signore*," said Petride, climbing down into the snow.

"You're very young. The holy men have given you an awesome responsibility."

"I speak the language. I know that what I do is right."

The *padrone* stared at him. "I'm sure you do. What else is left for you?"

"Don't you believe it?"

The *padrone* replied simply. "I believe in only one thing, my young father. There is but a single war that must be fought. There can be no divisions among those who battle the fascist. *That* is the extent of what I believe." Fontini-Cristi looked up abruptly at the train. "Come. There's no time to waste. We must return before daybreak. There are clothes for you in the tractor. Get them. I'll instruct the engineer."

"He doesn't speak Italian."

"I speak Greek. Hurry!"

The freight car was lined up with the tractor. Laterally operated chains were placed around the holy vault, and the heavy iron receptacle encased in strips of wood was pulled, groaning under the tension, out onto the platform. It was secured by the chains in front; taut straps buckled over the top.

Savarone Fontini-Cristi tested the harnessing on all sides. He was satisfied; he stood back, the beam of his flashlight illuminating the monastic symbols stenciled on the encasement.

"So after fifteen hundred years it comes out of the earth. Only to be returned to the earth," said Fontini-Cristi quietly. "Earth and fire and sea. I should have chosen the last two, my young priest. Fire or the sea."

"That is not the will of God."

"I'm glad your communication is so direct. You holy men never cease to amaze me with your sense of the absolute." Fontini-Cristi turned to Annaxas and spoke fluently now in Greek. "Pull up so that I may clear the tracks. There's a narrow trail on the other side of the woods. We'll be back before dawn."

Annaxas nodded. He was uncomfortable in the presence of such a man as Fontini-Cristi. "Yes, Your Excellency."

"I'm no such thing. And you're a fine engineer."

"Thank you." Annaxas, embarrassed, walked toward the engine.

"That man is your brother?" asked Fontini-Cristi softly of Petride.

"Yes."

"He doesn't know?"

The young priest shook his head.

"You'll need your God then." The Italian turned swiftly and started for the driver's side of the enclosed tractor. "Come, Father. We have work to do. This machine was built for the avalanche. It will take our cargo where no human being could carry it."

Petride climbed into the seat. Fontini-Cristi started the powerful engine and expertly shifted gears. The platform in front of the hood was lowered, permitting visibility, and the vehicle lunged forward, vibrating across the tracks into the Alpine forest.

The priest of Xenope sat back and closed his eyes in prayer. Fontini-Cristi maneuvered the powerful machine through the rising woods toward the upper trails of the Champoluc mountains.

"I have two sons older than you," said Fontini-Cristi after a while. And then he added, "I'm taking you to the grave of a Jew. I think it's appropriate."

They returned to the Alpine clearing as the black sky was turning gray. Fontini-Cristi stared at Petride as the young priest climbed out of the strange machine. "You know where I live. My house is your house."

"We all reside in the house of the Lord, *signore*."

"So be it. Good-bye, my young friend."

"Good-bye. May God go with you."

"If He chooses."

The Italian pushed the gearshift into place and drove quickly down the barely visible road below the tracks. Petride understood. Fontini-Cristi could not lose a minute now. Every hour he was away from his estate would add to the questions that might be asked. There were many in Italy who considered the Fontini-Cristis to be enemies of the state.

They were watched. All of them.

The young priest ran through the snow toward the engine. And his brother.

Dawn came over the waters of Lago Maggiore. They were on the Stresa freight barge; the twenty-sixth authorization in the pouch was their passport. Petride wondered what would greet them in Milan, although he realized that it did not really matter.

Nothing mattered now. The journey was coming to an end.

The holy thing was in its resting place. Not to be unearthed for years; perhaps to be buried for a millennium. There was no way to tell.

They sped southeast on the main track through Varese into Castiglione. They did not wait for nightfall . . . nothing mattered now. On the outskirts of Varese, Petride saw a roadsign in the bright Italian sunlight.

CAMPO DI FIORI. 20 KIL.

God had chosen a man from Campo di Fiori. The holy secret now belonged to Fontini-Cristi.

The countryside rushed by; the air was clear and cold and exhilarating. The skyline of Milan came into view. The haze of factory smoke intruded on God's sky and lay suspended like a flat, gray tarpaulin above the horizon. The freight slowed and entered the tracks of the depot sidings. They held at a stop until a disinterested *spedizioniere* in the uniform of the state railroads pointed to a curve in the rails where a green disc snapped up in front of a red one. It was the signal to enter the Milan yards.

"We're here!" shouted Annaxas. "A day's rest, then home! I must say you people are remarkable!"

"Yes," said Petride simply. "We're remarkable."

The priest looked at his brother. The sounds of the freight yard were music to Annaxas; he sang a Greek song, his whole upper body swaying rhythmically to the sharp, fast beats of the melody.

It was strange, the song Annaxas sang. It was not a song of the railroads; it belonged to the sea. A chanty that was a favorite of the fishermen of Thermaïkós. There was something appropriate, thought Petride, about such a song at such a moment.

The sea was God's source of life. It was from the sea that He created earth.

I believe in one God . . . maker of all things. . . .

The priest of Xenope removed the large Italian pistol from under his shirt. He took two steps forward, toward his beloved brother, and raised the barrel of the weapon. It was inches from the base of Annaxas's skull.

. . . both visible and invisible . . . and in one Lord, Jesus Christ . . . only begotten of the Father. . . .

He pulled the trigger.

The explosion filled the cabin. Blood and flesh and things most terrible flew through the air and matted onto glass and metal.

. . . substance of the Father . . . God of God . . . light of light . . . very God of very God. . . .

The priest of Xenope closed his eyes and shouted in exaltation as he held the weapon against his own temple.

"*. . . begotten, not made! I will look into the eyes of the Lord and I shall not waver!*"

He fired.

PART ONE

1

DECEMBER 29, 1939
MILAN, ITALY

Savarone walked past his son's secretary into his son's office and across the heavily carpeted floor to the window overlooking the vast factory complex that was the Fontini-Cristi Industries. His son, of course, was nowhere to be seen. His son, his *eldest* son, was rarely in his office; he was rarely in Milan, for that matter. The first son, the heir-apparent to all of Fontini-Cristi, was incorrigible. And arrogant, and far too concerned with his own creature comforts.

Vittorio was also brilliant. A far more brilliant man than the father who had trained him. And that fact only served to further infuriate Savarone; a man possessing such gifts had greater responsibilities than other men. *He* did not settle for the daily accomplishments that came naturally. He did not carouse and whore and gamble at roulette and baccarat. Or waste sleepless nights with the naked children of the Mediterranean. Neither did he turn his back on the events that were crippling his country, veering it into chaos.

Savarone heard a slight cough behind him and turned. Vittorio's secretary had come into the office.

"I've left word for your son at the Borsa Valori. I believe he was to see his broker this afternoon."

"You may believe it, but I doubt you'll find it on his calendar." Savarone saw the girl flush. "I apologize. You're not accountable for my son. Although you've probably done so, I suggest you try whatever private numbers he's given you. This is a familiar office to me. I'll wait." He removed his overcoat of light camel's hair and his hat, a

Tyrolean of green felt. He threw them on the armchair at the side of the desk.

"Yes, sir." The girl left quickly, closing the door behind her.

It *was* a familiar office, thought Fontini-Cristi, although it had been necessary to call it to the girl's attention. Until two years ago, it had been his. Very little remained of his presence, now; only the dark wood paneling. All the furniture had been changed. Vittorio had accepted the four walls. Nothing else.

Savarone sat in the large swivel chair behind the desk. He did not like such chairs; he was too old to let his body be suddenly turned and sprung back by unseen springs and hidden ball bearings. He reached into his pocket and took out the telegram that had brought him to Milan from Campo di Fiori, the telegram from Rome that said the Fontini-Cristis were marked.

But marked for what? By whom? On whose orders?

Questions that could not be asked on the telephone, for the telephone was an instrument of the state. The state. Always the state. Seen and unseen. Observing, following, listening, prying. No telephone could be used and no answer given by the informer in Rome who employed the simple codes.

We have received no reply from Milan, therefore we take the liberty of wiring you personally. Five shipments of aircraft piston hammers defective. Rome insists on immediate replacement. Repeat: immediate. Please confirm by telephone before the end of the day.

The number "five" referred to the Fontini-Cristis, because there were five men in the family—a father and four sons. Anything to do with the word "hammer" meant sudden, extreme danger. The repetition of the word "immediate" was self-explanatory: not a moment could be lost, confirmation of receipt was to be made by telephone to Rome within minutes of the telegram's arrival in Milan. Other men would then be contacted, strategies analyzed, plans made. It was too late now.

The wire had been sent to Savarone that afternoon. Vittorio must have received his cable by eleven. And yet his son had neither replied to Rome nor alerted him in Campo di Fiori. The end of the day was at hand. Too late.

It was unforgivable. Men daily risked their lives and the lives of their families in the fight against Mussolini.

It had not always been so, thought Savarone, as he stared at the office door, hoping that any second the secretary would reappear with news of Vittorio's whereabouts. It had all been very different once. In the beginning, the Fontini-Cristis had endorsed *Il Duce*. The weak, indecisive Emmanuel was letting Italy die. Benito Mussolini had offered an alternative; he had come himself to Campo di Fiori to meet with the patriarch of the Fontini-Cristis, seeking alliance—as Machiavelli once so sought the backing of the princes—and he had been alive, and committed, and filled with promise for all Italy.

That was sixteen years ago; since that time Mussolini had fed upon his own rhetoric. He had robbed the nation of its right to think, the people of their freedom to choose; he had deceived the aristocrats—used them and denied their common objectives. He had plunged the country into an utterly useless African war. All for the personal glory of this Caesar Maximus. He had plundered the soul of Italy, and Savarone had vowed to stop him. Fontini-Cristi had gathered the northern "princes" together, and quietly the revolt was taking place.

Mussolini could not risk an open break with the Fontini-Cristis. Unless the charge of treason could be sustained with such clarity that even the family's most avid supporters would have to conclude they had been—if nothing else—stupid. Italy was gearing for its own entry into the German war. Mussolini had to be careful. That war was not popular, the Germans less so.

Campo di Fiori had become the meeting place of the disaffected. The sprawling acres of lawns and forests and hills and streams were suited to the clandestine nature of the conferences which generally took place at night. But not always; there were other gatherings that required the daylight hours, where younger men were trained by other experienced younger men in the arts of a new, strange warfare. The knife, the rope, the chain, and the hook. They had even coined a name for themselves: *partigiani.*

The partisans. A name that was spreading from nation to nation.

These were the games of Italy, thought Savarone. "The games of Italy" was what his son called them, a term used in derision by an arrogant, self-centered *aristocratico* who took seriously only his own pleasures. . . . No, that was not entirely true. Vittorio also took seriously the running of Fontini-Cristi, as long as pressures of the marketplace conformed to his own schedules. And he made them conform. He used his financial power ruthlessly, his expertise—the expertise he had learned at his father's side—arrogantly.

The telephone rang; Savarone was tempted to pick it up, but he did not. It was his son's office, his son's telephone. Instead, he got out of the terrible chair and walked across the room to the door. He opened it. The secretary was repeating a name.

". . . Signore Tesca?"

Savarone interrupted harshly. "Is that Alfredo Tesca?"

The girl nodded.

"Tell him to stay on the telephone. I'll speak with him."

Savarone walked rapidly back to his son's desk and the telephone. Alfredo Tesca was a foreman in one of the factories; he was also a *partigiano*.

"Fontini-Cristi," Savarone said.

"*Padrone?* I'm glad it's you. This line is clear; we check it every day."

"Nothing changes. It only accelerates."

"Yes, *padrone*. There's an emergency. A man has flown up from Rome. He must meet with a member of your family."

"Where?"

"The Olona house."

"When?"

"As soon as possible."

Savarone looked at the overcoat and the green felt hat he had thrown over the chair. "Tesca? Do you remember two years ago? The meeting at the apartment on the Duomo?"

"Yes, *padrone*. It will be six o'clock soon. I'll be waiting for you."

Fontini-Cristi hung up the telephone and reached for his overcoat and his hat. He put them on and checked his watch. It was five forty-five; he had to wait a few minutes. The walk across the concrete lot to the factory was short. He had to time it so that he entered the building at the height of the crowds; when the day shift was leaving and the night shift came to work.

His son had taken full advantage of *Il Duce*'s war machine. The Fontini-Cristi Industries operated around the clock. When the father had reproached the son, the son had replied, "We don't make munitions. We're not geared for that. The conversion would be too expensive. We make only profits, father."

His son. The most capable of them all had a hollowness in him.

Savarone's eyes fell on the photograph in the silver frame on Vittorio's desk. Its very existence was a cruel, self-inflicted joke. The face in the picture was that of a young woman, pretty in the accepted sense, with the pert, set features of a spoiled child growing into spoiled maturity. She had been Vittorio's wife. Ten years ago.

It had not been a good marriage. It had been more an industrial alliance between two immensely wealthy families. And the bride brought little to the union; she was a pouting, self-indulgent woman whose outlook was guided by possessions.

She died in an automobile crash in Monte Carlo, early in the morning after the casinos had closed. Vittorio never talked about that early morning; he had not been with his wife. Another had.

His son had spent four years in turbulent discomfort with a wife he could not stand, and yet the photograph was on his desk. Ten years later. Savarone once asked him why.

"Being a widower lends a certain respectability to my life-style."

It was seven minutes to six. Time to begin. Savarone walked out of his son's office and spoke to the secretary. "Please call downstairs and have my car brought around to the west gate. Tell my chauffeur I have a meeting at the Duomo."

"Yes, sir. . . . Do you wish to leave a number where your son can reach you?"

"Campo di Fiori. But by the time he calls, I'll no doubt be asleep."

Savarone took the private elevator to the ground floor and went out the executive entrance onto the concrete. Thirty yards away his chauffeur was walking toward the limousine with the crest of Fontini-Cristi on the door panels. The two men exchanged looks. The chauffeur nodded slightly; he knew what to do. He was a *partigiano*.

Savarone crossed the yard, aware that people were

watching him. That was good; that was the way it had been two years ago when *Il Duce*'s secret police were tracking his every move, trying to unearth the whereabouts of an antifascist cell. The factory whistles blew; the day shift was released and within minutes the yard and the corridors would be crowded. The incoming workers—due at their stations at six fifteen—were flooding through the west gate.

He climbed the steps to the employees' entrance and entered the crowded, noisy corridor, removing his coat and hat in the confusion. Tesca stood by the wall, halfway toward the doors that led to the workers' lockers. He was tall and slender, very much like Savarone, and he took Savarone's coat and hat and helped Fontini-Cristi into his own worn, three-quarter-length raincoat with a newspaper in the pocket. Then he handed Savarone a large cloth visor cap. The exchange was completed without words in the jostling crowds. Tesca accepted Savarone's assistance in putting on the camel's hair coat; the employer saw that the employee had taken the trouble—as he had done two years ago—to change into pressed trousers, shined shoes, and a white whirt and tie.

The *partigiano* entered the flow of human traffic to the exit doors. Savarone followed ten yards behind, then stood immobile on the crowded platform outside the constantly opening doors, pretending to read the newspaper.

He saw what he wanted to see. The camel's hair coat and the green Tyrolean hat stood out among the worn leather jackets and frayed workers' clothing. Two men beyond the throngs signaled each other and began the chase, making their way through the crowd as best they could in an effort to catch up. Savarone squeezed himself into the stream of workers and arrived at the gate in time to see the door of the Fontini-Cristi limousine close and the huge automobile roll into the traffic of the Via di Sempione. The two pursuers were at the curb; a gray Fiat pulled up and they climbed in.

The Fiat took up the chase. Savarone turned north and walked swiftly to the corner bus stop.

The house on the riverfront was a relic that once, perhaps a decade ago, had been painted white. From the outside it looked dilapidated, but inside the rooms were small, neat, and organized; they were places of work, an antifascist headquarters.

Savarone entered the room with the windows overlooking the murky waters of the Olona River, made black by the darkness of night. Three men rose from straight-backed chairs around a table and greeted him with feeling and respect. Two were known to him; the third, he presumed, was from Rome.

"The hammer code was sent this morning," said Savarone. "What does it mean?"

"You *received* the wire?" asked the man from Rome incredulously. "All telegrams to Fontini-Cristi in Milan were intercepted. It's why I'm here. All communications to your factories were stopped."

"I received mine at Campo di Fiori. Through the telegraph office in Varese, I imagine, not Milan." Savarone felt a minor relief in knowing his son had not disobeyed. "Have you the information?"

"Not all, *padrone*," replied the man. "But enough to know it's extremely serious. And imminent. The military is suddenly very concerned with the northern movement. The generals want it crippled; they intend to see your family exposed."

"As what?"

"As enemies of the new Italy."

"On what grounds?"

"For holding meetings of a treasonable nature at Campo di Fiori. Spreading antistate lies; of attempting to undermine Rome's objectives and corrupt the industrial arm of the country."

"Words."

"Nevertheless, an example is to be made. They demand it, they say."

"Nonsense. Rome wouldn't dare move against us on such tenuous grounds."

"That is the problem, *signore*," said the man hesitantly. "It's not Rome. It's Berlin."

"What?"

"The Germans are everywhere, giving orders to everyone. The word is that Berlin wants the Fontini-Cristis stripped of influence."

"They look to the future, don't they," stated one of the

other two men, an older *partigiano* who had walked to the window.

"How do they propose to accomplish this?" asked Savarone.

"By smashing a meeting at Campo di Fiori. Forcing those there to bear witness to the treasons of the Fontini-Cristis. That would be less difficult than you think, I believe."

"Agreed. It's the reason we've been careful. . . . When will this happen? Do you have any idea?"

"I left Rome at noon. I can only assume the code word 'hammer' was used correctly."

"There's a meeting tonight."

"Then 'hammer' was called for. Cancel it, *padrone*. Obviously, word got out."

"I'll need your help. I'll give you names . . . our telephones are unsafe." Fontini-Cristi began writing in a notebook on the table with a pencil supplied by the third *partigiano*.

"When's the meeting scheduled?"

"Ten thirty. There's enough time," replied Savarone.

"I hope so. Berlin is thorough."

Fontini-Cristi stopped writing and looked over at the man. "That's a strange thing to say. The Germans may bark orders in the Campidoglio; they're not in Milan."

The three partisans exchanged glances. Savarone knew there was further news he had not received. The man from Rome finally spoke.

"As I said, our information is not complete. But we know certain things. The degree of Berlin's interest, for example. The German high command wants Italy to openly declare itself. Mussolini wavers; for many reasons, not the least of which is the opposition of such powerful men as yourself——" The man stopped; he was unsure. Not, apparently, of his information, but how to say it.

"What are you driving at?"

"They say that Berlin's interest in the Fontini-Cristis is Gestapo inspired. It's the Nazis who demand the example; who intend to crush Mussolini's opposition."

"I gathered that. So?"

"They have little confidence in Rome, none in the provinces. The raiding party will be led by Germans."

"A German raiding party out of *Milan?*"

The man nodded.

Savarone put down the pencil and stared at the man from Rome. But his thoughts were not on the man; they were on a Greek freight from Salonika he had met high in the mountains of Champoluc. On the cargo that train carried. A vault from the Patriarchate of Constantine, now buried in the frozen earth of the upper regions.

It seemed incredible, but the incredible was commonplace in these times of madness. Had Berlin found out about the train from Salonika? Did the Germans know about the vault? *Mother of Christ,* it had to be kept from them! And all—*all—like* them!

"You're sure of your information?"

"We are."

Rome could be managed, thought Savarone. Italy needed the Fontini-Cristi Industries. But if the German intrusion was linked to the vault from Constantine, Berlin would not consider Rome's needs in the slightest. The possession of the vault was *everything.*

And, therefore, the protection of it essential beyond all life. Above all things its secret could not fall into the wrong hands. Not now. Perhaps not ever, but certainly not now.

The key was Vittorio. It was always Vittorio, the most capable of them all. For whatever else he was, Vittorio was a Fontini-Cristi. He would honor the family's commitment; he was a match for Berlin. The time had come to tell him about the train from Salonika. Detail the family's arrangements with the monastic Order of Xenope. The timing was right, the strategy complete.

A date marked in stone, etched for a millennium, was only a hint, a clue in case of a sudden failing of the heart, death from abrupt natural or unnatural causes. It was not enough.

Vittorio had to be told, charged with a responsibility beyond anything in his imagination. The documents from Constantine made everything else pale into insignificance.

Savarone looked up at the three men. "The meeting will be canceled tonight. The raiding party will find only a large family gathering. A holiday dinner party. All my children and their children. However, for it to be complete, my oldest son must be at Campo di Fiori. I've tried calling him all afternoon. Now you must find him. Use your telephones.

Call everyone in Milan if you have to, but *find him!* If it gets late, tell him to use the stable road. It wouldn't do for him to enter with the raiding party."

2

DECEMBER 29, 1939
LAKE COMO, ITALY

The white, twelve-cylinder Hispano-Suiza, its off-white leather top rolled halfway back, uncovering the front, red leather seat, took the long curve at high speed. Below on the left were the winter-blue waters of Lake Como, to the right the mountains of Lombardy.

"Vittorio!" shrieked the girl beside the driver, holding her wind-shocked blonde hair with one hand, her collar of Russian pony with the other. "I'll be undone, my lamb!"

The driver smiled, his squinting gray eyes steady on the onrushing road in the sunlight, his hands expertly, almost delicately, feeling the play in the ivory steering wheel. "The Suiza is a far better car than the Alfa-Romeo. The British Rolls is no comparison."

"You don't have to prove it to *me*, darling. My God, I refuse to look at the speedometer! And I'll be an absolute mess!"

"Good. If your husband's in Bellagio, he won't recognize you. I'll introduce you as a terribly sweet cousin from Verona."

The girl laughed. "If my husband's in Bellagio, he'll have a terribly sweet cousin to introduce to *us*."

They both laughed. The curve came to an end, the road straightened, and the girl slid over next to the driver. She slipped her hand under the arm of his tan suede jacket, enlarged by the heavy wool of the white turtleneck sweater beneath; briefly she placed her face against his shoulder.

"It was sweet of you to call. I really had to get away."

"I knew that. It was in your eyes last night. You were bored to death."

"Well, God, weren't *you?* Such a dreary dinner party! Talk, talk, talk! War this, war that. Rome yes, Rome no, Benito always. I'm positively sick of it! Gstaad closed! St. Moritz filled with Jews throwing money at everyone! Monte Carlo an absolute fiasco! The casinos are closing, you know. Everybody says so. It's all such a *bore!*"

The driver let his right hand drop from the steering wheel and reached for the fold of the girl's overcoat. He separated the fur and caressed her inner thigh as expertly as he fingered the ivory steering wheel. She moaned pleasantly and craned her neck, putting her lips to his ear, her tongue darting.

"You continue that, we'll end up in the water. I suspect it's damned cold."

"You started it, my lovely Vittorio."

"I'll stop it," he said smiling, returning his hand to the wheel. "I won't be able to buy another car like this for a long time. Today everything is the tank. Far less profit in the tank."

"Please! No war talk."

"You'll get none from me," said Fontini-Cristi, laughing again. "Unless you want to negotiate a purchase for Rome. I'll sell you anything from conveyor belts to motorcycles to uniforms, if you like."

"You don't make uniforms."

"We own a company that does."

"I forgot. Fontini-Cristi owns everything north of Parma and west of Padua. At least, that's what my husband says. Quite enviously, of course."

"Your husband, the sleepy count, is a dreadful businessman."

"He doesn't mean to be."

Vittorio Fontini-Cristi smiled as he braked the long white automobile for a descending curve in the road toward the lakeshore. Halfway down, on the promontory that was Bellagio, stood the elegant Villa Lario, named for the ancient poet of Como. It was a resort lodge known for its extraordinary beauty, as well as its marked exclusivity.

When the elite moved north, they played at Villa Lario. Money and family were their methods of entry. The *commessi* were diffident, soft-spoken, aware of their clientele's every proclivity, and most alert as to the scheduling of reservations. It was uncommon for a husband or a wife, a lover or a mistress, to receive a quiet, cautioning phone call suggesting another date for arrival. Or rapid departure.

The Hispano-Suiza swerved into the parking lot of blue brick; two uniformed attendants raced from the heated booth to both sides of the automobile, opening the doors and bowing.

The attendant at Vittorio's side spoke. "Welcome to Villa Lario, *signore*."

It was never nice-to-see-you-again-*signore*.

Never.

"Thank you. We have no luggage. We're here only for the day. See to the oil and petrol. Is the mechanic around?"

"Yes, sir."

"Have him check the alignment. There's too much play."

"Of course, *signore*."

Fontini-Cristi got out of the car. He was a tall man, over six feet in height. His straight, dark-brown hair fell over his forehead; his features were sharp—as aquiline as his father's—and his eyes, still squinting in the bright sunlight, were at once passive and alert. He walked in front of the white hood, absently feeling the radiator cap, and smiled at his companion, the Contessa d'Avenzo. Together they crossed to the stone steps leading up to the entrance of Villa Lario.

"Where did you tell the servants you were off to?" asked Fontini-Cristi.

"Treviglio. You are a horse trainer who wants to sell me an Arabian."

"Remind me to buy you one."

"And you? What did you say at your office?"

"Nothing, really. Only my brothers might ask for me; everyone else waits patiently."

"But not your brothers." The Contessa d'Avenzo smiled. "I like that. The important Vittorio is hounded in business by his brothers."

"Hardly! My sweet younger brothers have between them three wives and eleven children. Their problems are continuously and forever domestic. I think sometimes I'm a referee. Which is fine; they keep occupied and *away* from business."

They stood on the terrace outside the glass doors that led

to the lobby of Villa Lario and looked down at the enormous lake and across to the mountains beyond.

"It's beautiful," said the contessa. "You've arranged for a room?"

"A suite. The penthouse. The view's magnificent."

"I've heard of it. I've never been up there."

"Few people have."

"I imagine you lease it by the month."

"That's not really necessary," said Fontini-Cristi, turning toward the huge glass doors. "You see, as it happens I own Villa Lario."

The Contessa d'Avenzo laughed. She preceded Vittorio into the lobby. "You are an *impossible, a*moral man. You get richer from your own kind. My God, you could blackmail half of Italy!"

"Only *our* Italy, my dear."

"That's enough!"

"Hardly. But I've never had to, if it relieves your mind. I'm merely a guest. Wait here, please."

Vittorio walked over to the front desk. The tuxedoed clerk behind the marble counter greeted him. "How good of you to come to see us, Signore Fontini-Cristi."

"Are things going well?"

"Extremely so. Would you care to——?"

"No, I should not," interrupted Vittorio. "I assume my rooms are ready."

"Of course, *signore.* As you requested, an early supper is being prepared. Caviar Iranian, cold pressed duck, Veuve Cliquot twenty-eight."

"And?"

"There are flowers, naturally. The masseur is prepared to cancel his other appointments."

"And . . ?"

"There are no complications for the Contessa d'Avenzo," answered the clerk quickly, rapidly. "None of her circle is here."

"Thank you." Fontini-Cristi turned, only to be stopped by the sound of the clerk's voice.

"Signore?"

"Yes?"

"I realize you do not care to be disturbed except in emergencies, but your office called."

"Did my office say it was an emergency?"

"They said your father was trying to locate you."
"That's not an emergency. It's a whim."

"I think you may be that Arabian, after all, lamb," mused the contessa out loud, lying beside Vittorio in the feather bed. The eiderdown quilt was pulled down to her naked waist. "You're marvelous. And so patient."

"But not patient enough, I think," replied Fontini-Cristi. He sat up against the pillow, looking down at the girl; he was smoking a cigarette.

"Not patient enough," agreed the Contessa d'Avenzo, turning her face and smiling up at him. "Why don't you put out the cigarette?"

"In a little while. Be assured of it. Some wine?" He gestured at the silver ice bucket within arm's reach. It stood on a tripod; an open bottle draped with a linen towel was pushed into the melting crushed ice.

The contessa stared at him, her breath coming shorter. "You pour the wine. I'll drink my own."

In swift, gentle movements, the girl turned and reached under the soft quilt with both hands to Vittorio's groin. She raised the cover and placed her face underneath, over Vittorio. The quilt fell back, covering her head as her throaty moans grew louder and her body writhed.

The waiters cleared away the dishes and rolled out the table, a *commesso* lighted a fire in the fireplace and poured brandy.

"It's been a lovely day," said the Contessa d'Avenzo. "May we do it often?"

"I think we should set up a schedule. By your calendar, of course."

"Of course." The girl laughed throatily. "You're a very practical man."

"Why not? It's easier."

The telephone rang. Vittorio looked over at it, annoyed. He rose from the chair in front of the fireplace and crossed angrily to the bedside table. He picked up the instrument and spoke harshly. "Yes?"

The voice at the other end was vaguely familiar. "This is Tesca. Alfredo Tesca."

"Who?"

"One of the foremen in the Milan factories."

"You're *what?* How *dare* you call here! How did you get this number?"

Tesca was silent for a moment. "I threatened the life of your secretary, young *padrone.* And I would have killed her had she not given it to me. You may fire me tomorrow. I am your foreman, but I am a *partigiano* first."

"You *are* fired. *Now.* As of this moment!"

"So be it, *signore.*"

"I want no part——."

"Basta!" shouted Tesca. "There's no time! Everyone's looking for you. The *padrone*'s in danger. Your whole *family*'s in danger! Go to Campo di Fiori! At once! Your father says to use the stable road!"

The telephone went dead.

Savarone walked through the great hall into the enormous dining room of Campo di Fiori. Everything was as it should be. The room was filled with sons and daughters, husbands and wives, and a thoroughly boisterous crowd of grandchildren. The servants had placed silver trays of antipasto on the tops of marble tables. A tall pine that reached the high beamed ceiling was a magnificent Christmas tree, its myriad lights and glittering ornament filling the room with reflections of color that bounced off the tapestries and the ornate furniture.

Outside in the circular drive in front of the marble steps of the entrance were four automobiles illuminated by the floodlights that beamed down from the eaves. They could easily be mistaken for anyone's automobiles, which was what Savarone intended. For when the raiding party arrived, all it would find was an innocent, festive family gathering. A holiday dinner. Nothing else.

Except an imperiously aggravated patriarch of one of Italy's most powerful clans. The *padrone* of the Fontini-Cristis, who would demand to know who was responsible for such a barbarous intrusion.

Only Vittorio was missing; and his presence was vital. Questions might be raised that could lead to other questions. The unwilling Vittorio, who scoffed at their work, could become an unjustified target of suspicion. What was a holiday family dinner without the eldest son, the primary heir? Further, if Vittorio appeared *during* the intrusion, arrogantly reluctant—as his custom—to give an account of himself to anyone, there could be trouble. His son refused to acknowledge the extent, but Rome *was* under Berlin's thumb.

Savarone beckoned his next eldest, the serious Antonio, who stood with his wife as she admonished one of their children.

"Yes, father?"

"Go to the stables. See Barzini. Tell him that if Vittorio arrives during the fascists' visit, he's to say he was detained at one of the plants."

"I can call him on the stable phone."

"No. Barzini's getting on. He pretends it's not so, but he's growing deaf. Make sure he understands."

The second son nodded dutifully. "Yes, of course, father. Anything you say."

What in God's name had his father *done*? What *could* he do that would give Rome the confidence, the *excuse,* to move openly against the house of Fontini-Cristi?

Your whole family is in danger.

Preposterous!

Mussolini courted the northern industrialists; he needed them. He knew that most were old men, set in their ways, and knew he could achieve more with honey than vinegar. What did it matter if a few Savarones played their silly games? Their time was past.

But then there was only one Savarone. Separate and apart from all other men. He had become, perhaps, that terrible thing, a symbol. With his silly, goddamned *partigiani.* Ragtail lunatics who raced around the fields and the woods of Campo di Fiori pretending they were some kind of primitive tribesmen hunting tigers and killer lions.

Jesus! *Children!*

Well, it would all come to a stop. *Padrone* or no *padrone,* if his father had gone too far and embarrassed them, there would be a confrontation. He had made it clear to Savarone two years ago that when he assumed the reins of Fontini-Cristi, it meant that all the leather was in his hands.

Suddenly Vittorio remembered. Two weeks ago, Savarone had gone to Zürich for a few days. At least, he *said* he was going to Zürich. It wasn't really clear; he, Vittorio, had not been listening closely. But during those few days, it was unexpectedly necessary to get his father's signature on several contracts. So necessary that he had telephoned every hotel in Zürich, trying to locate Savarone. He was nowhere to be found. No one had seen him, and his father was not easily overlooked.

And when he returned to Campo di Fiori, he would not say where he had been. He was maddeningly enigmatic, telling his son that he would explain everything in a few days. An incident would take place in Monfalcone and when it occurred, Vittorio would be told. Vittorio *had* to be told.

What in hell was his father talking about? *What* incident at Monfalcone? Why would *anything* taking place at Monfalcone concern them?

Preposterous!

But Zürich wasn't preposterous at all. Banks were in Zürich. Had Savarone manipulated money in Zürich? Had he transferred extraordinary sums out of Italy into Switzerland? There was specific laws against that these days. Mussolini needed every *lira* he could keep. And God knew the family had sufficient reserves in Berne and Geneva; there was no lack of Fonti-Cristi capital in Switzerland.

Whatever Savarone had done, it would be his last gesture. If his father was so politically involved, let him go somewhere else and proselytize. America, perhaps.

Vittorio shook his head slowly in defeat, as he steered the Hispano-Suiza onto the road out of Varese. What was he thinking of? Savarone was—Savarone. The head of the house of Fontini-Cristi. No matter the son's talents or expertise, the son was not the *padrone.*

Use the stable road.

What was the point of that? The stable road started at the north end of the property, three miles from the east gates. Nevertheless, he would use it; his father must have had a reason for giving the order. No doubt as implausible as the foolish games he indulged in, but a surface filial obedience was called for; the son was going to be very firm with the father.

What had happened in Zürich?

He passed the main gates on the road out of Varese and proceeded to the intersecting west road three miles beyond. He turned left and drove nearly two miles to the north gate, turning left again into Campo di Fiori. The stables were three-quarters of a mile from the entrance; the road was dirt. It was easier on the horses, for this was the road used by riders heading for the fields and trails north and west of the forest at the center of Campo di Fiori. The forest behind the great house that was bisected by the wide stream that flowed from the northern mountains.

In the headlights he saw the figure of old Guido Barzini waving his arms, signaling him to stop. The gnarled Barzini was something: a fixture at Campo di Fiori who had spent his life in the service of the house.

"Quickly, Signore Vittorio!" said Barzini through the open window. "Leave your car here. There's no more time."

"Time for what?"

"The *padrone* spoke to me not five minutes ago. He said if you drove in now, you were to call him on the stable telephone before you went to the house. It's nearly half past the hour."

Vittorio looked at the dashboard clock. It was twenty-eight minutes past ten. "What's going on?"

"Hurry, *signore*! *Please!* The *fascisti!*"

"What *fascisti*?"

"The *padrone*. He'll tell you."

Fontini-Cristi got out of the car and followed Barzini down the stone path into the entrance of the stables. It was a tack room; bits and braces and halters and leather were hung neatly on the walls, surrounding countless plaques and ribbons, proof of the superiority of the Fontini-Cristi colors. Also on the wall was the telephone that connected the stables to the great house.

"What's going on, father? Have you any idea who called me in Bellagio?"

"Basta!" roared Savarone over the telephone. "They'll be here any moment. A German raiding party."

"Germans?"

"Yes. Rome expects to find a *partigiano* meeting taking place. They won't, of course. They'll intrude on a family dinner. *Remember!* A family dinner party was on your calendar. You were detained in Milan."

"What have Germans got to do with Rome?"

"I'll explain later. Just remember——"

Suddenly, over the telephone, Vittorio heard the sounds of screeching tires and powerful motors. A column of automobiles was speeding toward the great house from the east gates.

"Father!" yelled Vittorio. "Has this anything to do with your trip to Zürich?"

There was silence over the phone. Finally Savarone spoke. "It may have. You must stay where you are——"

"What happened? What happened in Zürich?"

"Not Zürich. Champoluc."

"What?"

"Later! I have to get back to the others. Stay where you are! Out of sight! We'll talk when they leave."

Vittorio heard the click. He turned to Barzini. The old stable master was riffling through a low chest of drawers filled with odd bits and braces; he found what he was looking for: a pistol and a pair of binoculars. He pulled them out and handed both to Vittorio.

"Come!" he said, his old eyes angry. "We'll watch. The *padrone* will teach them a lesson."

They ran down the dirt road toward the house and the gardens above and behind it. When the dirt became pavement they cut to their left and climbed the embankment overlooking the circular drive. They were in darkness; the whole area below bathed in floodlights.

Three automobiles sped up the east-gate road; long, black, powerful vehicles, their headlights emerging out of the darkness, swallowed by the floodlamps that washed the area in white light. The cars entered the circular drive, careening to the left of the other automobiles, stopping suddenly, equidistant from each other in front of the stone steps that led to the thick oak doors of the entrance.

Men leaped out of the cars. Men dressed alike in black suits and black overcoats; men carrying weapons.

Carrying *weapons!*

Vittorio stared as the men—seven, eight, nine—raced up the steps to the door. A tall man in front assumed command; he held his hand up to those behind, ordering them to flank the doors, four on each side. He pulled the bell chain with his left hand, his right holding a pistol at his side.

Vittorio put the binoculars to his eyes. The man's face was turned away toward the door, but the weapon in his hand came into focus. It was a German Luger. Vittorio swung the binoculars to those on both sides of the doors.

The weapons were all German. Four Lugers, four Bergmann MP38 submachine guns.

Vittorio's stomach suddenly convulsed; his mind caught fire as he watched in disbelief. What had Rome *permitted?* It was incredible!

He focused the binoculars on the three automobiles. In each was a man; all were in shadows, only the backs of their heads seen through the rear windows. Vittorio concentrated on the nearest car, on the man inside that car.

The man shifted his position in the seat and looked back to his right; the light from the floodlamps caught his hair. It was close-cropped, grayish hair, but with a white streak shooting up from his forehead. There was something familiar about the man—the shape of the head, the streak of white in the hair—but Vittorio could not place him.

The door of the house opened; a maid stood in the frame, startled by the sight of the tall man with a gun. Vittorio stared in fury at the scene below. Rome would pay for the insult. The tall man pushed the maid aside and burst through the door, followed by the squad of eight men, their weapons held in front of them. The maid disappeared in the phalanx of bodies.

Rome would pay dearly!

There were shouts from inside. Vittorio could hear his father's roar and the subsequent shouted objections of his brothers.

There was a loud crash, a combination of glass and wood. Vittorio reached for the pistol in his pocket. He felt a powerful hand grip his wrist.

It was Barzini. The old stable master held Vittorio's hand, but he was looking over his shoulder, staring below.

"There are too many guns. You'll solve nothing," he said simply.

A third crash came from below, the sound nearer now. The left panel of the huge oak double door had been thrown open and figures emerged. The children, first, bewildered, some crying in fear. Then the women, his sisters and his brothers' wives. Then his mother, her head defiant, the youngest child in her arms. His father and his brothers followed, prodded violently by the weapons in the hands of the black-suited men.

They were herded onto the pavement of the circular

drive. His father's voice roared above the others, demanding to know who was responsible for the outrage.

But the outrage had not begun.

When it did, the mind of Vittorio Fontini-Cristi snapped. Cracks of thunder deafened him, streaks of lightning blinded him. He lunged forward, every ounce of his strength trying to wrench his hand free of Barzini's grip, twisting, turning, trying desperately to free his neck and his jaw from Barzini's stranglehold.

For the black-suited men below had opened fire. Women threw themselves over the children, his brothers lurched at the weapons that shattered the night with fire and death. The screams of terror and pain and outrage swelled in the blinding light of the execution grounds. Smoke billowed; bodies froze in midair—suspended in blood-soaked garments. Children were cut in half, the bullets ripping out mouths and eyes. Pieces of flesh and skull and intestine shot through the swirling mists. A child's body exploded in its mother's arms. And still Vittorio Fontini-Cristi could not free himself, could not go to his own.

He felt dead weight pressing him downward, then a clawing, choking, pulling at his lower jaw that blocked all sound from his lips.

And then the words pierced through the cacophony of gunshot and human screams below. The voice was tremendous, its thunder chopped by the firepower of submachine guns, but not stopped.

It was his father. Calling to him over the chasms of death.

"*Champoluc* . . . Zürich is *Champoluc*. . . . Zürich is the *river* . . . *Champoluuuc*. . . ."

Vittorio gnashed his teeth down on the fingers inside his mouth, pulling his jaw out of its socket. He wrenched his hand free for an instant—the hand with the weapon—and tried to raise the pistol and fire below.

But suddenly he could not. The sea of heaviness was over him again, his wrist twisted beyond endurance; the pistol was shaken loose. The enormous hand that had gripped his jaw was pushing his face into the cold earth. He could feel the blood in his mouth, over his lips, mingled with dirt.

And the horrible scream from the abyss of death came once more.

"Champoluc!"

And then was stilled.

3

DECEMBER 30, 1939

"Champoluc . . . Zürich is Champoluc . . . Zürich is the river. . . ."

The words were screams and they were blurred in agony. His mind's eye was filled with white light and explosions of smoke and deep red streaks of blood; his ears heard the screams of jolting shock, and terror, and the outrage of infinite pain and terrible murder.

It had happened. He had borne witness to the tableau of execution: strong men, trembling childen, wives and mothers. His own.

Oh, my God!

Vittorio twisted his head and buried his face into the coarse cloth of the primitive bed, the tears flowing down his cheeks. It was cloth, not cold rough dirt; he had been moved. The last thing he remembered was his face being pressed with enormous strength into the hard ground of the embankment. Pressed down and held furiously immobile, his eyes blinded, his lips filled with warm blood and cold earth.

Only his ears bearing witness to the agony.

"Champoluc!"

Mother of God, it had happened!

The Fontini-Cristis were massacred in the white lights of Campo di Fiori. All the Fontini-Cristis but one. And that one would make Rome pay. The last Fontini-Cristi would cut the flesh, layer by layer, from *Il Duce*'s face; the eyes would be last, the blade would enter slowly.

"Vittorio. Vittorio."

He heard his name and yet he did not hear it. It was a whisper, an urgent whisper, and whispers were dreams of agony.

"Vittorio." The weight was on his arms again; the whisper came from above, in the darkness. The face of Guido Barzini was inches from his, the sad strong eyes of the stablemaster were reflected in a shaft of dim light.

"Barzini?" It was all he could manage to say.

"Forgive me. There was no choice, no other way. You would have been killed with the rest."

"Yes, I know. Executed. But *why?* In the name of God, *why?*"

"The Germans. That's all we know at the moment. The Germans wanted the Fontini-Cristis dead. They want you dead. The ports, the airfields, the roads, all of northern Italy is sealed off."

"Rome allowed it." Vittorio could still taste the blood in his mouth, still feel the pain in his jaw.

"Rome hides," said Barzini softly. "Only a few speak."

"What do they say?"

"What the Germans want them to say. That the Fontini-Cristis were traitors, killed by their own people. That the family was aiding the French, sending arms and monies across the borders."

"Preposterous."

"Rome is preposterous. And filled with cowards. The informer was found. He hangs naked from his feet in the Piazza del Duomo, his body riddled, his tongue nailed to his head. A *partigiano* placed a sign below; it says, 'This pig betrayed Italy, his blood flows from the stigmata of the Fontini-Cristis.' "

Vittorio turned away. The images burned; the white smoke in the white light, the bodies suspended, abruptly immobile in death, a thousand sudden blots of thick red; the execution of children.

"Champoluc," whispered Vittorio Fontini-Cristi.

"I beg your pardon?"

"My father. As he was dying, as the gunfire ravaged him, he shouted the name, Champoluc. Something happened in Champoluc."

"What does it mean?"

"I don't know. Champoluc is in the Alps, deep in the

mountains. 'Zürich is Champoluc. Zürich is the river.' He said that. He shouted it as he died. Yet there's no river in the Champoluc."

"I cannot help you," said Barzini, sitting up, the anxiety in his questioning eyes and in the awkward rubbing together of his large hands. "There's not a great deal of time to dwell on it, or to think. Not now."

Vittorio looked up at the huge, embarrassed farmhand sitting on the side of the primitive bed. They were in a room built of heavy wood. There was a door, only partially open, ten or fifteen feet away, on his left, but no windows. There were several other beds; he could not tell how many. It was a barracks for laborers.

"Where are we?"

"Across the Maggiore, south of Baveno. On a goat farm."

"How did we get here?"

"A wild trip. The men at the riverfront drove us out. They met us with a fast car on the road west of Campo di Fiori. The *partigiano* from Rome knows the drugs; he gave you a hypodermic needle."

"You carried me from the embankment to the west road?"

"Yes."

"It's more than a mile."

"Perhaps. You're large, but not so heavy." Barzini stood up.

"You saved my life." Vittorio pressed his hands on the coarse blanket and raised himself to a sitting position, his back against the wall.

"Revenge is not found in one's own death."

"I understand."

"We must both travel. You out of Italy, me to Campo di Fiori."

"You're going back?"

"It's where I can do the most good. The most damage."

Fontini-Cristi stared for a moment at Barzini. How quickly the unimaginable became the practical reality. How rapidly did men react savagely to the savage; and how necessary was that reaction. But there was no time. Barzini was right; the thinking would come later.

"Is there a way for me to get out of the country? You said all of northern Italy was sealed off."

"All the usual routes. It is a manhunt mounted by Rome, directed by the Germans. There are other ways. The British will help, I am told."

"The British?"

"That is the word. They have been on *partigiano* radios all through the night."

"The British? I don't understand."

The vehicle was an old farm truck with poor brakes and a sliding clutch, but it was strudy enough for the badly paved back roads. It was no match for motorcycles or official automobiles, but excellent for traveling from one point to another in the farm country—one more truck carrying a few livestock that lurched unsteadily in the open, slatted van.

Vittorio was dressed, as was his driver, in the filthy, dung-encrusted, sweat-stained clothes of a farm laborer. He was provided with a dirty, mutilated identification card that gave his name as Aldo Ravena, former *soldato semplice* in the Italian army. It could be assumed his schooling was minimal; any conversation he might have with the police would be simple, blunt, and perhaps a touch hostile.

They had been driving since dawn, southwest into Torino, where they swung southeast toward Alba. With no serious interruptions they would reach Alba by nightfall.

At an *espresso* bar in Alba's main piazza, San Giorno, they would make contact with the British; two operatives sent in by MI6. It would be their job to get Fontini-Cristi down to the coast and through the patrols that guarded every mile of waterfront from Genoa to San Remo. Italian personnel, German efficiency, Vittorio was told.

This area of the coast in the Gulf of Genoa was considered the most conducive to infiltration. For years it had been a primary source route for Corsican smugglers. Indeed the *Unio Corso* claimed the beaches and rocky ocean cliffs as their own. They called this coast the soft belly of Europe; they knew every inch.

Which was fine as far as the British were concerned. They employed the Corsicans, whose services went to the highest bidders. The *Unio Corso* would aid London in getting Fontini-Cristi through the patrols and out on the water where, in a prearranged rendezvous north of Rogliano on the Corsican coast, a submarine from the Royal Navy would surface and pick him up.

This was the information Vittorio was given—by the ragtail lunatics he had scorned as children playing primitive games. The unkempt, wild-eyed fools who had formed an untenable alliance with such men as his father had saved his life. *Were* saving his life. Skinny peasant thugs who had direct communication with the far-off British . . . far off and not so distant. No farther than Alba.

How? Why? What in the name of God were the English doing? Why were they doing it? What were men he had barely acknowledged, hardly spoken to in his life before—except to order and ignore—what were *they* doing. And *why?* He was no friend; no enemy, perhaps, but certainly no friend.

These were the questions that frightened Vittorio Fontini-Cristi. A nightmare had exploded in white light and death, and he was not capable of fathoming—even wanting—his own survival.

They were eight miles from Alba on a curving dirt road that paralleled the main highway from Torino. The *partigiano* driver was weary, his eyes bloodshot from the long day of bright sunlight. The shadows of early evening were now playing tricks on his eyes; his back obviously ached from the constant strain. Except for infrequent fuel stops he had not left his seat. Time was vital.

"Let me drive for a while."

"We're nearly there, *signore.* You don't know this road; I do. We'll enter Alba from the east, on the Canelli highway. There may be soldiers at the municipal limits. Remember what you're to say."

"As little as possible, I think."

The truck entered the light traffic on the Via Canelli and maintained a steady speed with the other vehicles. As the driver had predicted, there were two soldiers at the municipal line.

For any of a dozen reasons, the truck was signaled to stop. They pulled off the road onto the shoulder of sand and waited. A sergeant approached the driver's window, a private stood laconically outside Fontini-Cristi's.

"Where are are you from?" asked the sergeant.

"A farm south of Baveno," the *partigiano* said.

"You've come a long way for such a small delivery. I count five goats."

"Breeding stock. They're better animals than they look. Ten thousand *lire* for the males; eight for the females."

The sergeant raised his eyebrows. He did not smile as he spoke. "You don't look like *you're* worth that, *paisan.* Your identification."

The partisan reached into his rear pocket and pulled out a worn billfold. He withdrew the state card and handed it to the soldier.

"This says you're from Varallo."

"I come from Varallo. I work in Baveno."

"*South* of Baveno," corrected the soldier coldly. *"You,"* said the sergeant, addressing Vittorio. "Your identification."

Fontini-Cristi put his hand into his jacket, bypassing the handle of his pistol, and removed the card. He handed it to the driver, who gave it to the soldier.

"You were in Africa?"

"Yes, sergeant," replied Vittorio bluntly.

"What corps?"

Fontini-Cristi was silent. He had no answer. His mind raced, trying to recall from the news a number, or a name. "The Seventh," he said.

"I see." The sergeant returned the card; Vittorio exhaled. But the relief was short-lived. The soldier reached for the handle of the door, yanked it downward and pulled the door open swiftly. "Get out! Both of you!"

"What? Why?" objected the partisan in a loud whine. "We have to make our delivery by nightfall! There's barely time!"

"Get *out.*" The sergeant had removed his army revolver from the black leather holster and was pointing it at both men. He barked his orders across the hood to the private. "Pull him out! Cover him!"

Vittorio looked at the driver. The partisan's eyes told him to do as he was told. But to stay alert, be ready to move; the man's eyes told him that also.

Out of the truck on the shoulder of sand, the sergeant commanded both men to walk toward the guardhouse that stood next to a telephone pole. A telephone wire sagged down from a junction box and was attached to the roof of the small enclosure; the door was narrow, and open.

On the Via Canelli the twilight traffic was heavier now; or it seemed heavier to Fontini-Cristi. There were mostly cars, with a scattering of trucks, not unlike the farm trucks they were driving. A number of drivers slowed perceptibly at the sight of the two soldiers, their weapons drawn, marching the two civilians to the guardhouse. Then the drivers speeded up, anxious to be away.

"You have no right to stop us!" cried the partisan. "We've done nothing illegal. It's no crime to earn a living!"

"It's a crime to give false information, *paisan*."

"We gave no false information! We are workers from Baveno, and, by the Mother of God, that's the truth!"

"Be careful," said the soldier sarcastically. "We'll add sacrilege to the charges. Get inside!"

The roadside guardhouse seemed even smaller than it appeared from the Via Canelli. The depth was no more than five feet, the length perhaps six. There was barely enough room for the four of them. And the look in the partisan's eyes told Vittorio that the close quarters was an advantage.

"Search them," ordered the sergeant.

The private placed his rifle on the floor, barrel up. The partisan driver then did a strange thing. He pulled his arms across his chest, protectively over his coat, as though it were a conscious act of defiance. Yet the man was not armed; he had made that clear to Fontini-Cristi.

"You'll steal!" he said, louder than was necessary, his words vibrating in the wooden shack. "Soldiers steal!"

"We're not concerned with your *lire, paisan*. There are more impressive vehicles on the highway. Take your hands from your coat."

"Even in Rome reasons are given! *Il Duce,* himself, says the workers are not to be treated so! I march with the fascist guards; my rider served in Africa!"

What was the man doing? thought Vittorio. *Why was he behaving so? It would only anger the soldiers.* "You try my patience, pig! We look for a man from Maggiore. Every road post looks for this man. You were stopped because the license on your truck is from the Maggiore district . . . Hold out your arms!"

"*Baveno!* Not Maggiore! We are from *Baveno!* Where are the lies?"

The sergeant looked at Vittorio. "No soldier in Africa says he was with the Seventh Corps. It was disgraced."

The army guard had barely finished when the partisan screamed his command.

"*Now, signore!* Take the other!" The driver's hand swept down, lashing at the revolver in the sergeant's grip, only inches from his stomach. The suddenness of the action and the shattering roar of the partisan's voice in the small enclosure had the effect of an unexpected collision. Vittorio had no time to watch; he could only hope his companion knew what he was doing. The private had lurched for his rifle, his left hand on the barrel, his right surging down to the stock. Fontini-Cristi threw his weight against the man, slamming him into the wall, both hands on the side of the soldier's head, crashing the head into the hard, wooden surface. The private's barracks cap fell off; blood matted instantly throughout the hairline and streaked down over the man's head. He slumped to the floor.

Vittorio turned. The sergeant was wedged into the corner of the tiny guardhouse, the partisan over him, pistol-whipping him with his own weapon. The soldier's face was a mass of torn flesh, the blood and ripped skin sickening.

"*Quickly!*" cried the partisan as the sergeant fell. "Bring the truck to the front! Directly to the front; squeeze it between the road and the guardhouse. Keep the motor running."

"Very well," said Fontini-Cristi, confused by the brutality as well as the swift decisiveness of the last thirty seconds.

"And, *signore!*" shouted the partisan, as Vittorio had one foot out the door.

"Yes?"

"Your gun, please. Let me use it. These army issues are like thunder."

Fontini-Cristi hesitated, then withdrew the weapon and handed it to the man. The partisan reached over to the crank-telephone on the wall and ripped it out.

Vittorio steered the truck to the front of the guardhouse, the left wheels by necessity on the hard surface of the highway; there was not sufficient room on the shoulder to pull completely off the road. He hoped the rear lights were sufficiently bright for the onrushing traffic—far heavier now—to see the obstruction and skirt it.

The partisan came out of the guardhouse and spoke through the window. "Race the motor, *signore.* As loud and as fast as you can."

Fontini-Cristi did so. The partisan ran back to the guard house. Gripped in his right hand was Vittorio's pistol.

The two shots were deep and sharp; muffled combustions that were sudden, terrible outbursts within the sounds of the rushing traffic and racing motor. Vittorio stared, his emotions a mixture of awe and fear and, inexplicably, sorrow. He had entered a world of violence he did not understand.

The partisan emerged from the guardhouse, pulling the narrow door shut behind him. He jumped into the truck, slammed the door panel, and nodded to Vittorio. Fontini-Cristi waited several moments for a break in the traffic, then let out the clutch. The old truck lurched forward.

"There is a garage on the Via Monte that will hide the truck, paint it, and alter the license plates. It's less than a mile from the Piazza San Giorno. We'll walk there from the garage. I'll tell you where to turn."

The partisan held out the pistol for Vittorio. "Thank you," said Fontini-Cristi awkwardly, as he shoved the weapon into his jacket pocket. "You killed them?"

"Of course," was the simple reply.

"I suppose you had to."

"Naturally. You'll be in England, *signore.* I, in Italy. I could be identified."

"I see," answered Vittorio, the hesitancy in his voice.

"I don't mean disrespect, Signor Fontini-Cristi, but I don't think you *do* see. You people at Campo di Fiori, it's all new to you. It's not new to us. We've been at war for twenty years; I, myself, for ten."

"War?"

"Yes. Who do you think trains your *partigiani?*"

"What do you mean?"

"I am a Communist, *signore.* The powerful, capitalist Fontini-Cristis are shown how to fight by Communists."

The truck was rushing forward; Vittorio held the wheel firmly, astonished but strangely unmoved by his companion's words.

"I didn't know that," he replied.

"It's peculiar, isn't it?" said the partisan. "No one ever asked."

4

DECEMBER 30, 1939
ALBA, ITALY

The *espresso* bar was crowded, the tables full, the voices loud. Vittorio followed the partisan through the mass of gesturing hands and reluctantly parted bodies to the counter; they ordered coffee with Strega.

"Over there," said the partisan, indicating a table in the corner with three laborers seated around it, their soiled clothes and stubbled faces testifying to their status. There was one empty chair.

"How do you know? I thought we were to meet two men, not three. And British. Besides, there's not enough room; there's only one chair."

"Look at the heavyset man on the right. The identification is on the shoes. There are splotches of orange paint, not much but visible. *He's* the Corsican. The other two are English. Go over and say 'Our trip was uneventful'; that's all. The man with the shoes will get up; take his seat."

"What about you?"

"I'll join you in a minute. I must talk with the *Corso*."

Vittorio did as he was told. The heavyset man with the drippings of paint on his shoes got up, heaving a sigh of discomfort; Fontini-Cristi sat down. The British across from him spoke. His Italian was grammatically proper but hesitant; he had learned the language but not the idiom.

"Our sincerest regrets. Absolutely dreadful. We'll get you out."

"Thank you. Would you prefer speaking English? I'm fluent."

"Good," said the second man. "We weren't sure. We've had precious little time to read up on you. We were flown out of Lakenheath this morning. The *Corsos* picked us up in Pietra Ligure."

"Everything's happened so fast," said Vittorio. "The shock hasn't worn off."

"Don't see how it could," said the first man. "But we're not clear yet. You'll have to keep your wits about you. Our orders are to make bloody sure we get you to London: not to come back without you, and that's a fact."

Vittorio looked alternately at both men. "May I ask you why? Please understand, I'm grateful, but your concern seems to me extraordinary. I'm not humble, but neither am I a fool. Why am I so important to the British?"

"Damned if we know," replied the second agent. "But I can tell you, all hell broke loose last night. *All* night. We spent from midnight till four in the morning at the Air Ministry. All the radio dials in every operations room were beaming like mad. We're working with the Corsicans, you know."

"Yes, I was told."

The partisan walked through the crowds to the table. He pulled out the empty chair and sat down, a glass of Strega in his hand. The conversation was continued in Italian.

"We had trouble on the Canelli road. A checkpoint. Two guards had to be taken out."

"What's the A-span?" asked the agent on Fontini-Cristi's right. He was a slender man, somewhat more intense than his partner. He saw the puzzled expression on Vittorio's face and clarified. "How long does he think we have before the alarm goes out?"

"Midnight. When the twelve o'clock shift arrives. No one bothers with unanswered telephones. The equipment breaks down all the time."

"Well done," said the agent across the table. He was rounder in the face than his fellow Englishman; he spoke more slowly, as if constantly choosing his words. "You're a Bolshevik, I imagine."

"I am," replied the partisan, his hostility near the surface.

"No, no, please," added the agent. "I like working with you chaps. You're very thorough."

"M.I.-*Sei* is polite."

"By the way," said the Britisher on Vittorio's right, "I'm Apple; he's Pear."

"We know who you are," said Pear to Fontini-Cristi.

"And my name's not important," said the partisan with a slight laugh. "I'll not be going with you."

"Let's run through that, shall we?" Apple was anxious, but controlled to the point of being reserved. "The going. Also, London wants to set up firmer communications."

"We knew London would."

The three men fell into a professional conversation that Vittorio found extraordinary. They spoke of routes and codes and radio frequencies as though they were discussing prices on the stock exchange. They touched on the necessity of *taking-out, eliminating* various people in specific positions—not men, not human beings, but *factors* that had to be killed.

What kind of men were these three? "Apple," "Pear," a Bolshevik with no name, only a false identification card. Men who killed without anger, without remorse.

He thought of Campo di Fiori. Of blinding white floodlights, and gunfire and death. *He* could kill now. Viciously, savagely—but he could not speak of death as these men spoke of it.

". . . get us to a trawler known to the coastal patrols. Do you understand?" Apple was speaking to him, but he had not been listening.

"I'm sorry," said Vittorio. "My mind was elsewhere."

"We've a long way to go," said Pear. "Over fifty miles to the coast, then a minimum of three hours on the water. A lot can happen."

"I'll try to be more attentive."

"Do better than try," replied Apple, his tone one of controlled irritation. "I don't know what you've done to the Foreign Office, but you happen to be a high-priority subject. It's our asses if we don't bring you out. So *listen!* The Corsicans will take us to the coast. There will be four changes of vehicles——"

"Wait!" The partisan reached over the table and gripped Apple's arm. "The man who was seated with you, the paint-spattered shoes. Where did you pick him up? *Quickly.*"

"Here in Alba. About twenty minutes ago."

"Who made contact first?"

Both Englishmen looked at each other. Briefly, with instant concern. "He did," said Apple.

"Get out of here! Now! Use the kitchen!"

"What?" Pear was looking over at the *espresso* counter.

"He's leaving," said the partisan. "He was to wait for me."

The heavyset man was making his way through the crowds toward the door. He was doing so as unobtrusively as possible; a drinker going to the men's room, perhaps.

"What do you think?" asked Apple.

"I think that there are a great many men throughout Alba with paint on their shoes. They wait for strangers whose eyes stray to the floor." The Communist rose from the table. "The contact code was broken. It happens. The Corsicans will have to change it. Now, *go!*"

The two Englishmen got out of their chairs, but not with any overt sense of urgency. Vittorio took his cue and stood up. He reached out and touched the partisan's sleeve. The Communist was startled; his eyes were on the heavyset man; he was about to plunge into the crowds.

"I want to thank you."

The partisan stared for an instant. "You're wasting time," he said.

The two Britishers knew exactly where the kitchen was, and therefore the exit *from* that kitchen. The alley outside was filthy; garbage cans were lined against the dirty stucco walls, refuse overflowing. The alley was a link between the Piazza San Giorno and the street behind, but so dimly lit and strewn with trash it was not a popular shortcut.

"This way," said Apple, turning left, away from the piazza. "Quickly now."

The three men ran out of the alley. The street was sufficiently filled with pedestrians and shopkeepers to provide them with cover. Apple and Pear fell into a casual walk; Vittorio followed suit. He realized that the two agents had maneuvered him between them.

"I'm not sure the Bolshie was right," said Pear. "Our *Corso* might simply have spotted a friend. He was damned convincing."

"The Corsicans have their own language," interjected Vittorio, excusing himself as he nearly collided with an oncoming stroller.

"Couldn't he tell by talking to him?"

"Don't do that," said Apple incisively.

"What?"

"Don't be so damned polite. It hardly goes with the clothes. To answer your question, the Corsicans employ regional contacts everywhere. We all do. They're minor level, just messengers."

"I see." Fontini-Cristi looked at the man who called himself Apple. He was walking casually, but his eyes kept shifting about in the night-cloaked street. Vittorio turned his head and looked at Pear. He was doing precisely what his countryman was doing: observing the faces in the crowds, the vehicles, the recesses in the buildings on both sides of the street.

"Where are we going?" asked Fontini-Cristi.

"To within a block of where our Corsican told us to be," replied Apple.

"But I thought you suspected him."

Pear spoke. "They won't see us because they don't know what to look for. The Bolshevik will catch the *Corso* in the piazza. If everything's on the up-and-up, they'll arrive together. If not, and if your friend is competent, he'll be the only one."

The shopping area curved to the left, into the south entrance of the Piazza San Giorno. The entrance was marked by a fountain, the circular pool at its base littered with discarded papers and bottles. Men and women sat on the ledge dipping their hands in the dirty water; children shouted and ran on the cobblestones under their parents' watchful eyes.

"The road beyond," said Apple, lighting a cigarette, gesturing toward the wide pavement seen through the spray of the fountain, "is the Via Ligata. It leads to the coastal highway. Two hundred yards down is a side street where the *Corso* said a taxi would be waiting."

"Would the side street, by any chance, be a dead end?" Pear asked the question with a degree of disdain. He did not really expect an answer.

"Isn't that a coincidence? I was wondering the same thing. Do let's find out. You," said Apple to Vittorio, "stay with my partner and do *exactly* as he says." The agent threw the match to the ground, inhaled deeply on his cigarette, and walked rapidly over the cobblestones toward the fountain. When he was within several feet of the pool, he slowed down, and then, to Vittorio's astonishment, he disappeared, lost entirely in the crowds.

"He does that rather in top form, doesn't he?" said Pear.

"I can't make him out. I don't see him."

"Not supposed to. A good race-and-melt, done in the proper light, can be very effective." He shrugged. "Come along. Keep abreast and chatter a bit. And gesture. You people wave your hands like mad."

Vittorio smiled at the Englishman's bromide. But as they walked into the crowds, he was conscious of moving hands and flailing arms and sudden exclamations. The Britisher knew his Italians. He kept pace with the agent, fascinated by the man's decisiveness. Suddenly, Pear grabbed Vittorio's sleeve and yanked him to the left, propelling them both toward a newly vacated space on the fountain's ledge. Fontini-Cristi was startled; he thought their objective was to reach the Via Ligata as rapidly and as unobtrusively as possible.

Then he understood. The Britisher's experienced, professional eyes had seen what the amateur's had not seen: the signal.

Vittorio sat on the agent's right, his head down. The first objects that came into focus were a pair of worn shoes with the splotches of orange paint on the scuffed leather. A single pair of immobile shoes in the moving shadows of moving bodies. Then Vittorio raised his head and froze. The partisan driver was cradling the heavyset body of the Corsican contact, as though succoring a friend who had drunk too much. But the contact was not drunk. His head was slumped, his eyes open, staring downward into the moving darkness. He was dead.

Vittorio leaned back on the ledge, mesmerized by the sight below. A steady, narrow stream of blood was soaking the back of the Corsican's shirt, rolling down the stone of the fountain's inner wall, mingling with the filthy water, forming circles and swirling half circles in the intermittent light of the piazza's street lamps.

The partisan's hand gripped the cloth, bunching the shirt around the blood-soaked area, knuckles and wrist drenched. And in his grip was the handle of a knife.

Fontini-Cristi tried to control his shock.

"I was hoping you'd stop," said the Communist to the Englishman.

"Nearly didn't," replied Pear in his overly grammatical Italian. "Until I noticed the couple leap up here." The agent indicated the ledge on which he and Vittorio sat. "They're yours, I presume."

"No. When you were closest, I told them my friend was about to vomit. It's a trap, of course. Fishnet variety; they don't know what they'll catch. They broke the code—last night. There are a dozen or so *provocatori* in the area, flushing out what targets they can. A roundup."

"We'll tell the Corsicans."

"It won't do much good. The code changes tomorrow."

"The taxi's the snare, then?"

"No. The second bait. They're not taking chances. The taxi drives the targets into the net. Only the driver knows where; he's upper level."

"There must be others nearby." Pear brought his hand to his mouth; it was a gesture of thought.

"Certainly."

"But which ones?"

'There's a way to find out. Where's Apple?"

"In the Via Ligata by now. We wanted to separate in case you had trouble."

"Join him; the trouble wasn't mine."

"Yes. I can see that——"

"Mother of God!" exclaimed Vittorio under his breath, incapable of silence. "You're holding a dead man in the middle of the piazza and you chatter like women!"

"We have things to say, *signore.* Be quiet and listen." The partisan returned his eyes to the Englishman, who had barely taken notice of Fontini-Cristi's outburst. "I'll give you two minutes to reach Apple. Then I'll let our *Corso* friend here slide into the pool, back up, knife visible. There'll be chaos. I'll start the shouting myself. It will carry. It'll be enough."

"And we keep our eyes on the taxi," interrupted Pear.

"Yes. As the shouting grows, see who speaks together. See who leaves to investigate."

"Then take the bloody taxi and be off," added the agent with finality. "Good show! I look forward to working with you again." The Britisher rose; Vittorio did the same, feeling Pear's hand on his arm.

"You," said the partisan, looking up at Vittorio while cradling the limp, heavyset body in the noisy, jostling, shadow-filled darkness. "Something to remember. A conversation in the midst of many people is often the safest.

And a blade in a crowd is the hardest to trace. Remember these things."

Vittorio looked down at the man, not sure whether the Communist meant his words to be insulting or not.

"I'll remember," said Vittorio.

They walked swiftly into the Via Ligata. Apple was on the other side, slowly making his way toward the side street where the Corsican contact said the taxi would be waiting. The street lamps were dimmer than in the piazza.

"Hurry, now. There he is," said Pear in English. "Take longer steps, but don't run."

"Shouldn't we go over and meet him?" asked Vittorio.

"No. One person crossing the street is less obvious than two. . . . All right. Stop now."

Pear removed a box of matches from his pocket; he struck one. The instant it flared, he waved it out, throwing it to the pavement—as if the flame had seared his finger—and immediately struck a second, holding it to the cigarette he had placed in his lips.

Less than a minute passed before Apple joined them by the wall of a building. Pear told him the partisan's strategy. The three walked in silence, between the strollers, down the pavement to the end of the block opposite the side street. Across, in the dim white wash of the streetlights, was the taxi, thirty feet from the corner.

"Isn't that a coincidence," said Apple, lifting his foot to a low ledge on the building, pulling up his sock. "It's a dead end."

"The troops can't be far away. Is your pillow attached? Mine isn't."

"Yes. Fix yours."

Pear turned into the building and removed an automatic form inside his jacket. With his other hand he reached into his pocket and withdrew a cylinder about four inches long, with perforations on the iron surface, and twisted it into the barrel of his weapon. He replaced the gun inside his jacket just as the cries from the piazza began.

There were only a few at first, almost indistinguishable. And then a crescendo of sound erupted.

"Polizia!" "A quale punto polizia!" "Assassinio!" "Omicidio!" Women and children ran out of the square; men followed, shouting orders and information at no one and everyone. Among the screams came the words: *"Uomo*

con arancia scarpe," a man with orange shoes. The partisan had done his job well.

And then the partisan himself was among the crowds running down the pavement. He stopped ten feet from Fontini-Cristi and the two Englishmen and roared in a loud voice to any who would listen.

"I *saw* him! I saw *them!* I was right *next* to him! This man—his shoes were *painted*—they put a knife into his back!"

From the dark recess of a building a figure came dashing across the street, heading for the partisan. "You! Come here!"

"What?"

"I'm with the police. What did you see?"

"The police. Thank God! Come with me! There were two men! In sweaters——"

Before the official could adjust, the partisan started to race back toward the entrance of the piazza through the crowds. The policeman hesitated, then looked across the dimly lit street. Three men were talking together several yards in front of the taxi. The policeman gestured; two of the men broke away and started after the officer, who was now racing toward San Giorno and the disappearing partisan.

"The man left at the car. He's the driver," said Apple. "Here we go."

The next moments were a blur. Vittorio followed the two agents across the Via Ligata into the side street. The man at the taxi had climbed into the driver's seat. Apple approached the car, opened the door, and without saying a word raised his gun. A muted explosion burst from the mouth of his revolver. The man slumped forward; Apple rolled him over the seat toward the opposite door. Pear spoke to Fontini-Cristi.

"Into the back. Quickly, now!"

Apple turned the ignition; the taxi was old, the engine new and powerful. The automobile's make was the usual Fiat, Vittorio thought, but the motor was a Lamborgini.

The car lurched forward, turned right at the corner and gathered speed on the Via Ligata. Apple spoke over his shoulder, addressing Pear. "Check the glove compartment, will you? This bloody wreck belongs to some very *important people.* I daresay it would do well at Le Mans."

Pear lunged from the seat in the speeding car, over the felt back, and across the corpse of the Italian. He pulled open the glove compartment panel, grabbed the papers, bunching them together in his hand. As he pushed himself off the dashboard, the car swerved; Apple had swung the wheel to pass two automobiles. The body of the dead Italian fell across Pear's arm. He gripped the lifeless neck and threw the corpse violently back into the corner.

Vittorio stared at the scene, sick and uncomprehending. Behind them a heavyset man floated in death in a piazza fountain, the handle of a knife protruding from his blood-soaked shirt. Here, in an unmarked, speeding police car disguised as a taxi, a man slumped in the front seat, a bullet in his lifeless body. Miles away in a small guardhouse on the Via Canelli, two other men lay dead, killed by the Communist who had saved his life. The continuing nightmare was destroying his mind. He held his breath, desperately trying to find an instant of sanity.

"Here we are!" shouted Pear, holding up a rectangular sheet of heavy paper he had been studying in the inadequate light. "By God, it's a clean wicket!"

"An inland passport, I expect," said Apple, slowing down for a curve in the road.

"Indeed it is! The bloody *veicolo* is assigned to the *ufficiale segreto!* That bunch has access to Mussolini himself."

"It had to be something like that," agreed Apple, nodding his head. "The motor in this tacky box is a bloody marvel."

"It is a Lamborgini," said Vittorio quietly.

"What?" Apple raised his voice to be heard over the roar of the engine on the now straightaway road. They were approaching the outskirts of Alba.

"I said it's a Lamborgini."

"Yes," replied Apple, obviously unfamiliar with the engine. "Well, you keep coming up with things like that. Things Italian, that is. We're going to need your words before we reach the coast."

Pear turned to Fontini-Cristi. The Englishman's pleasant face was barely discernible in the darkness. He spoke gently, but there was no mistaking the quiet urgency in his voice.

"I'm sure this is all very strange to you, and damned

uncomfortable, I should think. But that Bolshevik had a point. Remember what you can. The most difficult part of this work isn't the *doing;* it's getting *used* to the doing, if you see what I mean. Just accepting the fact that it's real, that's the leg up a fellow needs. We've all been through it, go through it constantly, as a matter of fact. It's all so bloody outrageous, in a way. But someone's got to do it; that's what they tell us. And I'll say this: You're getting some very practical on-the-job training. Wouldn't you agree?"

"Yes," said Vittorio softly, turning front, his eyes mesmerized by the onrushing road outlined by the beams of the headlights, and his mind frozen by the sudden question he could not avoid.

Training for what?

5

DECEMBER 31, 1939
CELLE LIGURE, ITALY

It was two hours of madness. They turned off the coastal highway and carried the body of the dead driver into a field, stripping it naked, removing all identification.

They returned to the highway and sped south toward Savona. The road checks were similar to those on the Via Canelli: single guardhouses next to telephone booths, two soldiers in attendance at each. There were four checkpoints; three were passed easily. The thick, official document that proclaimed the vehicle assigned to the *ufficiale segreto* was read with respect and not a little fear. Fontini-Cristi did the talking at all three posts.

"You're damned quick," said Apple from the front, shaking his head in agreeable surprise. "And you were right about staying back there. You roll down that window like a Punjab prince."

The road sign was caught in the headlights.

ENTRARE MONTENOTTE SUD

Vittorio recognized the name; it was one of those medium-sized towns surrounding the Gulf of Genoa. He recognized it from a decade ago, when he and his wife had driven down the coast road on their last trip to Monte Carlo. A journey that had ended a week later in death. In a speeding car at night.

"The coast's about fifteen miles from here, I think," said Apple hesitantly, interrupting Fontini-Cristi's thoughts.

"Nearer eight," corrected Vittorio.

"You know this area?" asked Pear.

"I've driven to Cap Ferrat and Villefranche a number of times." *Why didn't he say Monte Carlo; was the name too much of a symbol?* "Usually on the Torino road, but several times on the shore route from Genoa. Montenotte Sud is known for its inns."

"Then would you know a dirt road that cuts north of Savona—through some hills, I gather—into Celle Ligure?"

"No. There are hills everywhere. . . . But I know Celle Ligure. It's on the waterfront just beyond Albisolla. Is that where we're going?"

"Yes," said Apple. "It's our backup rendezvous with the Corsicans. In case anything happened, we were to make our way to Celle Ligure, to a fishing pier south of the marina. It'll be marked with a green wind sock."

"Well, *something* happened, as they say," interjected Pear. "I'm sure there's a *Corso* wandering around Alba wondering where we are."

Several hundred yards ahead in the glare of the headlights, two soldiers stood in the center of the road. One held a rifle at port arms; the other had his hand raised, signaling them to stop. Apple slowed the Fiat, the transposed motor emitting the low sounds of its decelerating power. "Do your bitchy act," he said to Vittorio. "Be arrogant as hell." The Britisher kept the car in the center of the road, a sign that the inhabitants expected no interruption; pulling off to the side was unnecessary.

One of the soldiers was a lieutenant, his companion a

corporal. The officer approached Apple's open window and saluted the unkempt civilian smartly.

Too smartly, thought Vittorio.

"Your identification, *signore,*" said the soldier courteously.

Too courteously.

Apple held up the thick official paper and gestured toward the back seat. It was Vittorio's cue.

"We are the *ufficiale segreto,* Genoa garrison, and in a great hurry. We have business in Savona. You've done your job; pass us through immediately."

"My apologies, *signore.*" The officer took the heavy paper in Apple's hand and scrutinized it. He creased the folds as his eyes scanned downward in the very dim light. He continued politely. "I must see your identifications. There is so little traffic on the road at this hour. All vehicles must be checked."

Fontini-Cristi slammed his hand down on the top of the front seat in sudden irritation. "You're out of order! Don't let our appearances fool you. We're on official business and we're late for Savona!"

"Yes. Well, I must read this——"

But he was *not* reading it, thought Vittorio. A man in inadequate light did not fold a page of paper *toward* him; if he folded it at all, it would be *away*—to catch more light. The soldier was stalling. And the corporal had moved to the right front of the Fiat, his rifle still held across his chest; but the left hand was now lower on the barrel grip. Any hunter knew the stance; it was ready-at-fire.

Fontini-Cristi sat back in the seat, swearing furiously as he did so. "I demand your name and the name of your commanding officer!"

In the front, Apple had edged his shoulders to the right, trying to see into the rearview mirror, unable to do so without being obvious. But in his pretended anger, Fontini-Cristi had no such difficulty. He whipped his hand up behind Pear's shoulders, as if his irritation had reached the breaking point.

"Perhaps you did not hear me, soldier! Your name and that of your commanding officer!"

Through the rearview mirror he saw it. Quite far in the distance, beyond the clear range of the mirror, not easily seen through the window itself. A car had pulled off the road . . . so far off, it was half into the field bordering the highway. Two men were getting out of the front seat, the figures barely visible, moving slowly.

". . . Marchetti, *signore*. My commanding officer is Colonel Balbo. Genoa garrison, *signore*."

Vittorio caught Apple's eye in the rearview mirror, nodded slightly, and moved his head in a slow arc toward the back window. At the same time, he tapped his fingers rapidly on Pear's neck in the darkness. The agent understood.

Without warning, Vittorio opened his door. The rifle-bearing corporal jerked his weapon forward. "Put that *down, caporale*. Since your superior sees fit to take up my time, I will put it to use. I am Major Aldo Ravena, *ufficiale segreto*, from Rome. I will inspect your quarters. I will also relieve myself."

"*Signore!*" shouted the officer from across the Fiat's hood.

"Are you addressing me?" asked Fontini-Cristi arrogantly.

"My apologies, major." The officer could not help himself; he stole a quick glance to his right, to the road behind. "There are no facilities inside the guardhouse."

"Surely you are not immaculate in your bowels, man. The fields must be inconvenient. Perhaps Rome will install such facilities. I'll see."

Vittorio walked swiftly toward the door of the small structure; it was open. As he expected, the corporal went with him. He walked rapidly through the door. The instant the corporal entered behind him, Fontini-Cristi turned and jammed the pistol up under the man's chin. He pushed the weapon into the flesh of the corporal's throat and with his left hand grabbed the barrel of the rifle.

"If you so much as cough, I'll have to kill you!" whispered Vittorio. "I don't wish to do that."

The corporal's eyes widened in shock; he had no stomach for heroics. Fontini-Cristi held the rifle and gave his order quietly, precisely.

"Call the officer. Say I'm using your telephone and you don't know what to do. Tell him I'm calling the Genoa garrison. For that Colonel Balbo. *Now!*"

The corporal shouted the words, conveying both his confusion and his fear. Vittorio pressed his back against the wall by the door. The reply from the lieutenant betrayed the officer's own fear; perhaps he had made a dreadful mistake.

"I am only following orders! I received orders from Alba!"

"Tell him Colonel Balbo is coming to the telephone," whispered Fontini-Cristi. *"Now!"*

The corporal did so. Vittorio heard the footsteps of the officer running from the Fiat to the guardhouse.

"If you wish to live, Lieutenant, remove your pistol belt—just unbuckle both straps—and join the corporal at the wall."

The lieutenant was stunned. His jaw dropped, his lips parted in fright. Fontini-Cristi prodded him with the rifle, lancing the barrel into his stomach. The bewildered officer winced and gasped and did as he was told. Vittorio called outside, in English.

"I've disarmed them. Now I'm not sure what to do."

Pear's half-whispered shout came back. "What to *do?* My God, you're a bloody marvel! Send the officer back outside. Make sure he knows we have our weapons on him. Tell him to return to Apple's window right off. We'll take it from there."

Fontini-Cristi translated the instructions. The officer, prodded by the barrel of Vittorio's pistol, lurched out the doors and crossed swiftly in front of the car's headlights to the driver's window.

Ten seconds later the officer's shouts were heard on the road outside.

"You men from Alba! This is not the vehicle! A mistake has been made!"

A moment passed before other voices replied. Two voices, loud and angry.

"What happened? Who are they?"

Vittorio could see the figures of two men come out of the darkness of the field. They were soldiers and held guns at their sides. The officer answered.

"These are *segreti* from Genoa. They, too, look for the vehicle from Alba."

"Mother of Christ! How many *are* there?"

Suddenly, the officer pushed himself away from the window, screaming as he dove for the front of the automobile.

"Shoot! Open fire! They are——"

The muffled explosions of the British pistols erupted.

Pear leaped out of the right rear door, covered by the automobile, and fired at the approaching soldiers. A rifle answered; it was a wild shot that thumped into the tarred surface of the road, triggered by a dying man. The checkpoint lieutenant sprang to his feet and started to race toward the opposite field into the darkness. Apple fired; three muted reports accompanied the sharp, abrupt flashes of his weapon. The officer screamed and arched his back. He fell into the dirt off the road.

"Fontini!" yelled Apple. "Kill your man and get out here!"

The corporal's lips trembled, his eyes watered. He had heard the muted explosions, the screams, and he understood the command.

"No," said Fontini-Cristi.

"Goddamn you!" roared Apple. "You do as I *say!* You're under *my* orders! We've no time to waste *or* chances to take!"

"You're wrong. We would waste more time and take greater risks if we could not find the road into Celle Ligure. This soldier will surely know it."

He did. Vittorio drove, the soldier beside him in the front seat. Fontini-Cristi knew the area; if they ran into trouble, he could handle it. He had proved that.

"Relax," said Vittorio in Italian to the frightened corporal. "Continue to be helpful; you'll be all right."

"What will happen to me? They'll say I deserted my post."

"Nonsense. You were ambushed, forced at the point of a gun to accompany us, to act as a shield. You had no choice."

They drove into Celle Ligure at ten forty; the streets of the fishing village were nearly deserted. The majority of its inhabitants began their days at four in the morning; ten at night was late. Fontini-Cristi drove into the sandy parking area behind an open fish market that fronted the wide ocean street. Across was the main section of the marina.

"Where are the sentries?" asked Apple. "Where do they meet?"

At first the corporal seemed confused. Vittorio explained. "When you are on duty here, where do you turn around?"

"I see." The corporal was relieved; he was obviously trying to help. "Not here, not at this section. Up farther; I mean, down farther."

"*Damn* you!" Apple was forward in the back seat. He grabbed the Italian by the hair.

"You'll get nowhere like that," said Vittorio in English. "The man's frightened."

"So am I!" countered the agent. "There's a dock across there with a green wind sock on it, and a boat in that dock we have to find! We don't know what's happened behind us; there are soldiers on the piers with weapons—one shot would alert the whole area. And we have no idea what orders have been radioed the water patrols. *I'm damned* frightened!"

"I remember!" cried the corporal. "On the left. Up the street on the left! The trucks stopped and we would walk through to the piers and wait for the man on duty. He would give us the patrol sheet and be relieved."

"Where? *Exactly* where, Corporal?" Pear spoke urgently.

"The next street. I'm sure of it."

"That's roughly one hundred yards, wouldn't you say?" asked Pear, looking at Fontini-Cristi. "And the street below this another one hundred, give or take some."

"What's your idea?" Apple had released the corporal, but kept his hands menacingly on the top of the seat.

"Same as yours," replied Pear. "Take the sentry at mid-point; less chance of his being seen there. Once he's out we walk south to the wind sock, where, I trust, a Corsican or two will show themselves."

They crossed the ocean road into an alley that led to the dock complex. The smell of fish and the sounds of half a hundred boats creaking in rhythmic rest in their slips filled the darkness. Nets were hung everywhere; the wash of the sea could be heard beyond the planked walkway that fronted the piers. A few lanterns were swaying on ropes over decks; a concertina played a simple tune in the distance.

Vittorio and Pear walked casually out of the alley, their footsteps muted by moist planks. Apple and the corporal remained in the shadows. The walkway was bordered by a railing of metal tubing above the lapping water.

"Do you see the sentry?" asked Fontini-Cristi softly.

"No. But I hear him," answered the agent. "He's rapping the pipe as he walks. Listen."

It took Vittorio several seconds before he could distinguish the faint metal sounds among the rhythmic creakings of wood on water. But they were there. The unconscious, irregular tattoo of a bored man performing a dull task.

Several hundred feet south on the walkway, the figure of the soldier came under the spill of a pier light, his rifle angled down to the deck through his left arm. He was beside the railing, his right hand aimlessly tapping out his steps.

"When he gets here, ask him for a cigarette," said Pear calmly. "Pretend you're drunk. I will, too."

The sentry approached. The instant he saw them he snapped up his rifle and cracked the bolt, holding his position fifteen feet away.

"Halt! Who's *there?"*

"Two fishermen without cigarettes," replied Fontini-Cristi, slurring his words. "Be a nice fellow and give us a couple. Even one; we'll share it."

"You're drunk," said the soldier. "There's a curfew tonight on the piers. How come you're here? It was on the loudspeakers all day."

"We've been with two whores in Albisolla," answered Vittorio, lurching, steadying himself on the railing. "Only things we heard were music on a phonograph and creaking beds."

"Very nice," mumbled Pear.

The sentry shook his head in disapproval. He lowered his rifle and approached, reaching into the pocket of his tunic for cigarettes. "You *Ligurini* are worse than the *Napoletani.* I've done duty there."

Behind the soldier, Vittorio could see Apple coming out of the shadows. He had forced the corporal to lie down on his back in the corner of the alley; the corporal would not move. In Apple's hands were two spools.

Before Vittorio could realize what was happening, Apple sprang out of the passageway, his arms stretched, angled upward. In two swift moves, the agent's hands whipped over the sentry's head, and with his knee jammed into the small of the soldier's back, he yanked violently, causing the guard to arch spastically and then collapse.

The only noise was an abrupt, horrible expunging of air,

and the quiet fall of the man's body into the soft, moist wood.

Pear rushed to the corporal; he held his pistol against the soldier's temple. "Not a sound. Understood?" It was a command that left no room for debate. The corporal rose silently.

Fontini-Cristi looked down in the dim light at the guard on the walkway. What he could see he wished he had not seen. The man's neck was severed half off his body, the blood was pouring out in a dark-red stream from what had been the man's throat. Apple rolled the body through a wide space in the railing. It hit the water with a muffled splash. Pear picked up his rifle and spoke in English.

"Off we go. Down this way."

"Come on," said Fontini-Cristi, his hand on the trembling corporal's arm. "You have no choice."

The green wind sock was limp, no breeze billowing its cloth. The pier was only half filled with boats; it seemed to extend farther out into the water than the others. The four of them walked down the steps, Apple and Pear in front, their hands in their pockets. The two Englishmen were obviously hesitant. It was apparent to Vittorio that they were concerned.

Without warning or sound, men suddenly appeared on both sides of them, their weapons drawn. They were on the decks of the boats; five, no, six men dressed as fishermen.

"Be you George the Fifth?" said the gruff voice of the man nearest the agents, standing on the deck of a small trawler.

"Thank *God!*" said Pear in relief. "We've had a nasty time of it."

At the spoken English, weapons were replaced in belts and pockets. The men converged, a number talking at once.

The language was Corsican.

One man, obviously the leader, turned to Apple. "Go to the end of the pier. We've got one of the fastest trawlers in Bastia. We'll take care of the Italian. They won't find him for a month!"

"No!" Fontini-Cristi stepped between the two men. He looked at Pear. "We gave our word. If he cooperated, he lived."

Apple replied, instead, his whispered voice drawn out in

irritation. "Now, you see here. You've been a help, I'll not deny it, but you're not running this show. Get out to the bloody boat."

"Not until this man is back on the walkway. We gave our word!" He spoke to the corporal. "Go back. You won't be harmed. Strike a match when you reach a passageway to the ocean road."

"And if I say *no?*" Apple continued to grip the soldier's tunic.

"Then I'll remain here."

"Damn!" Apple released the soldier.

"Walk with him part way," said Fontini-Cristi to the Corsican. "Make sure your men let him pass."

The Corsican spat on the pier.

The corporal ran as fast as he could toward the base of the dock. Fontini-Cristi looked at the two Englishmen.

"I am sorry," he said simply. "There's been enough killing."

"You're a damn fool," replied Apple.

"Hurry," said the Corsican leader. "I want to get started. The water's rough beyond the rocks. And you people are crazy!"

They walked out to the end of the long pier, one by one jumping over the gunwale onto the deck of the huge trawler. Two Corsicans remained on the dock by the pilings; they unwound the thick greasy ropes while the gruff captain started the engines.

It happened without warning.

A fusillade of gunfire from the walkway. Then the blinding shaft of a searchlight shot out of the darkness, accompanied by the shouts of soldiers at the base of the pier. The voice of the corporal could be heard.

"Out *there!* At the end of the dock! The *fishing trawler!* Send out the alarms!"

One of the Corsicans was hit; he plunged to the ground, at the last second freeing the rope from the piling.

"The *light!* Shoot out the light!" screamed the Corsican from the open wheelhouse, revving the engines, heading for open water.

Apple and Pear unscrewed their silencers for greater accuracy. Apple was the first to raise himself over the protection of the gunwale; he squeezed his trigger repeatedly, steadying his hand on the wooden rail. In the distance the searchlight exploded. Simultaneously, fragments of wood burst around Apple; the agent reeled back, screaming in pain.

His hand was shattered.

But the Corsican had steered the fast-moving trawler out into the protective darkness of the sea. They were free of Celle Ligure.

"Our price goes up, English!" shouted the man at the wheel. "You whoreson bastards! You'll pay for this craziness!" He looked at Fontini-Cristi crouched beneath the starboard gunwale. Their eyes met; the Corsican spat furiously.

Apple sat back sweating against a pile of ropes. In the night light reflecting the ocean's spray, Vittorio saw that the Englishman was staring at the bloody mass of flesh that was his hand, holding it by the wrist.

Fontini-Cristi got up and crossed to the agent, tearing off part of his shirt as he did so. "Let me wrap that for you. Stop the bleeding——"

Apple jerked his head up and spoke in quiet anger. "Stay the hell away from me. Your goddamned principles cost too much."

The seas were heavy, the winds strong, the rolls violent and abrupt. They had plowed through the drenching waves of the open water for thirty-eight minutes. Arrangements had been made, the blockade run; the trawler's engines were now idling.

Beyond the swells, Vittorio could see a small flashing blue disc: on for a beat, off for a beat. The signal from a submarine. The Corsican on the bow with the lantern began his own signal. He lowered and raised the lamp, using the gunwale as a shutter, imitating the timing of the blue disc half a mile away over the waters.

"Can't you radio him?" Pear shouted his question.

"Frequencies are monitored," replied the Corsican. "The patrol boats would circle in; we can't bribe them all."

The two vessels began their cautious pavane over the rough seas, the trawler making most of the moves until the huge undersea marauder was directly off the starboard rail. Fontini-Cristi was hypnotized by its size and black majesty.

The two ships drifted within fifty feet of each other, the submarine considerably higher on the mountainous waves.

Four men could be seen on the deck; they were hanging on to a metal railing, the two in the center trying to manipulate some kind of machine.

A heavy rope shot through the air and crashed against the midships of the trawler. Two Corsicans leaped at it, holding on desperately, as if the line had a hostile will of its own. They lashed the rope to an iron winch in the center of the deck and signaled the men on the submarine.

The action was repeated. But the second rope was not the only item that had been shot from the submarine. There was a canvas pouch with metal rings on the edges, and from one of these rings was a thick coil of wire that extended back to the crew on the sub's deck.

The Corsicans ripped open the canvas pack and pulled out a shoulder harness. Fontini-Cristi recognized it immediately; it was a rig used to cross crevasses in the mountains.

Pear, bracing himself as he lurched forward on the rolling deck, approached Vittorio.

"It's a bit skin-crawling, but it's safe!" he yelled.

Vittorio shouted back "Send your man Apple first. His hand should be looked after."

"You're the priority. And frankly, if the damn thing doesn't hold, I'd rather we find out with you!"

Fontini-Cristi sat on the iron bunk inside the small metal room and drank from the thick china mug of coffee. He pulled the Royal Navy blanket around his shoulders, feeling the wet clothes beneath. The discomfort did not bother him; he was grateful to be alone.

The door of the small metal room opened. It was Pear. He carried an armful of clothing which he dropped on the bunk.

"Here's a dry change for you. It wouldn't do for you to croak off with pneumonia now. That'd be a clanker in the balls, wouldn't it?"

"Thank you," said Vittorio, getting up. "How's your friend?"

"The ship's doctor is afraid he'll lose the use of his hand. The doctor hasn't told him, but he knows."

"I'm sorry. I was naïve."

"Yes," agreed the Britisher simply. "You were naïve." He left, leaving the door open.

From the narrow metal corridors outside the tiny metal room, there was a sudden eruption of noise. Men raced by the door, all running in the same direction, fore or aft, Fontini-Cristi could not tell. Over the ship's intercom a piercing, deafening whistle shrieked without letup; metal doors slammed, the shouting increased.

Vittorio lunged at the open door; his breathing stopped. The panic of helplessness under the sea gripped him.

He collided with a British sailor. But the sailor's face was not contorted in panic. Or fear. Or anything but carefree laughter.

"Happy New Year, mate!" cried the sailor. "Midnight, chum! We're in 1940. A bloody new decade!"

The sailor raced on to the next hatchway, which he opened with a crash. Beyond, Fontini-Cristi could see the mess quarters. Men were gathered around holding out mugs into which two officers were pouring whiskey. The shouts merged into laughter. "Auld Lang Syne" began to fill the metal chambers.

The new decade.

The old one had ended in death. Death everywhere, most horribly in the blinding white light of Campo di Fiori. Father, mother, brothers, sisters . . . the children. *Gone.* Gone in a minute of shattering violence that was burned into his mind. A memory he would live with for the rest of his life.

Why? *Why?* Nothing made sense!

And then he remembered. Savarone had said he had gone to Zürich. But he had not gone to Zürich; he had gone somewhere else.

In that somewhere else lay the answer. But what?

Vittorio walked into the small metal room of the submarine and sat down on the iron ridge of the bed.

The new decade had begun.

PART TWO

6

JANUARY 2, 1940
LONDON, ENGLAND

Sandbags.

London was a city of sandbags. Everywhere. In doorways, windows, storefronts; piled in mounds on street corners. The sandbag was the symbol. Across the Channel, Adolf Hitler vowed the destruction of all England; quietly the English believed his threat, and quietly, firmly, they steeled themselves in anticipation.

Vittorio had reached the Lakenheath military airfield late on the previous night, the first day of the new decade. He had been taken off an unmarked plane flown out of Majorca and whisked into operations, the purpose of which was to confirm his identity for the Naval Ministry. And now that he was safely in the country, the voices suddenly became calm and solicitous: Would he care to rest up after his grueling journey? Perhaps the Savoy? It was understood that the Fontini-Cristis stayed at the Savoy when in London. Would a conference tomorrow afternoon at fourteen hundred hours be convenient? At the Admiralty, Intelligence Sector Five. Alien operations.

Of course. For God's sake, *yes!* Why have you English done what you've done? I must know, but I will be silent until you tell me.

The Savoy desk provided him with toilet articles and nightclothes, including a Savoy robe. He had drawn a very hot bath in the enormous hotel tub and immersed himself for such a length of time the skin on his fingertips wrinkled. He then proceeded to drink too many glasses of brandy and fell into bed.

He had left a wake-up call for ten but, of course, it was unnecessary. He was fully alert by eight thirty; showered and shaved by nine. He ordered an English breakfast from the floor steward and while waiting, telephoned Norcross, Limited, on Savile Row. He needed clothes immediately. He could not walk around London in a borrowed raincoat, a sweater, and the ill-fitting trousers provided by an agent named Pear on a submarine in the Mediterranean.

As he hung up the phone, it struck Vittorio that he had no money other than ten pounds courtesy of Lakenheath dispersals. He assumed his credit was good; he would have funds transferred from Switzerland. He had not had time to concentrate on the logistics of living; he had been too preoccupied with staying alive.

It occurred to Fontini-Cristi that he had many things to do. And if only to control the terrible memory—the infinite pain—of Campo di Fiori, he had to keep active. Force his mind to concentrate first on the simple things, everyday things. For when the great things came into focus he could go mad pondering them.

Please, dear God, the *little* things! Spare me the time to find my sanity.

He saw her first across the Savoy lobby while waiting for the day manager to arrange for immediate monies. She was sitting in an armchair, reading the *Times*, dressed in the stern uniform of a branch of the women's service, what branch he had no idea. Beneath the officer's visor cap her dark brunette hair fell in waves to her shoulders, outlining her face. It was a face he had seen before; it was a face one remembered. But it was a younger version of that face that stuck in his mind. The woman was, perhaps, in her middle thirties; the face he recalled had been no more than twenty-two or twenty-three. The cheekbones were high, the nose more Celtic than English—sharp, slightly upturned, and delicate above the full lips. He could not see the eyes clearly, but he knew what they looked like: a very intense blue, as blue as he had ever seen a woman's eyes.

That's what he remembered. Angry blue eyes staring up at him. Angry and filled with disdain. He had not encountered that reaction often in his life; it had irritated him.

Why did he remember? When was it?

"Signor Fontini-Cristi." The Savoy manager walked briskly out of the cashier's arch, an envelope in his hand. "As you requested, a thousand pounds."

Vittorio took the envelope and shoved it in the raincoat pocket. "Thank you."

"We've arranged for your limousine, sir. It should be here shortly. If you'd care to return to your suite, we'll ring you the moment it arrives."

"I'll wait here. If you can put up with these clothes, I can."

"Please, *signore*. It is always a great pleasure to welcome a member of the Fontini-Cristis. Will your father be joining you this trip? We trust he's well."

England marched to the sudden drums of war and the Savoy inquired about families.

"He'll not be joining me." Vittorio saw no point in further explanations. The news had not reached England, or if it had, the war dispatches made it insignificant. "By the way, do you know that lady over there? The one seated. In the uniform."

The manager unobtrusively glanced across the sparsely crowded lobby. "Yes, sir. She's Mrs. Spane. I should say *was* Mrs. Spane; they're divorced. I believe she's remarried now. Mr. Spane is. We don't see her often."

"Spane?"

"Yes, sir. I see she's with Air Defense. They're a no-nonsense group, they are."

"Thank you," said Vittorio, dismissing the manager courteously. "I shall wait for my car."

"Yes, of course. If there's anything we can do to make your stay more pleasant, don't hesitate to call upon us."

The manager nodded and walked away. Fontini-Cristi looked again at the woman. She glanced at her watch, and then returned to her reading.

He remembered the name Spane because of its spelling, and because of the spelling, he remembered the man. It had been eleven, no, twelve years ago; he had accompanied Savarone to London to observe his father in negotiations with British Haviland—the observation a part of his training. Spane had been introduced to him one night at Les Ambassadeurs, a youngish man two or three years older than he was. He found the Englishman mildly amusing but basically tiring. Spane was a Mayfair product quite content to enjoy the fruits of ancestral labors without contributing much of anything himself, other than his expertise at the races. His father had disapproved of Spane and said as much to his eldest son, which, quite naturally, goaded the son into a brief acquaintanceship.

But it had been brief, and Vittorio suddenly remembered why. That it had not first come to mind was merely further proof that he had blocked her existence from much of his memory: not the woman across the lobby, but his wife.

His wife had come to England with them twelve years ago, the *padrone* feeling that her presence would have a restraining influence on a headstrong, wandering son. But Savarone did not know his daughter-in-law that well; he did later, but not at the time. The heady atmosphere of Mayfair at the height of the season was a tonic to her.

His wife was attracted to Spane; one or the other seduced one or the other. He had not paid much attention; he had been occupied himself.

And somewhere along the way there'd been a disagreeable confrontation. Recriminations had been hurled, and the angry blue eyes had stared up at him.

Vittorio walked across the lobby toward the armchair. The Spane woman glanced up as he approached. There was a moment of hesitancy in her eyes, as if she were unsure. And then she *was* sure and there was no hesitance at all; the disdain he recalled so vividly replaced the hesitation. Their eyes locked for a second—no more—and she returned to the newspaper.

"Mrs. Spane?"

She looked up. "The name is Holcroft."

"We've met."

"We have. It's Fontini——" She paused.

"Fontini-Cristi. Vittorio Fontini-Cristi."

"Yes. A long time ago. You'll forgive me, but I've a full day. I'm waiting for someone and I shan't have the chance to get through the paper again." She went back to her reading.

Vittorio smiled. "You dismiss me efficiently."

"I find it quite easy to do so," she replied without looking at him.

"Mrs. Holcroft, it *was* a long time ago. The English poet says that nothing so becomes change as the years."

"The English poet also maintains that leopards do not change their spots. I'm really quite occupied. Good day."

Vittorio started to nod his departure when he saw that her hands trembled ever so slightly. Mrs. Holcroft was somewhat less confident than her demeanor implied. He was not sure why he stayed; it was a time to be alone. The terrible memories of white light and death burned; he did not care to share them. On the other hand, he wanted to talk. To someone. About anything.

"Is an apology offered for childish behavior twelve years ago a decade too late?"

The lieutenant glanced up. "How *is* your wife?"

"She died in an automobile crash ten years ago."

The look in her eyes was steady; the hostility lessened. She blinked in discomfort, mildly embarrassed. "I'm sorry."

"It is my place to apologize. Twelve years ago you were seeking an explanation. Or comfort. And I had neither to give."

The woman allowed herself the trace of a smile. Her blue eyes had an element—if only an element—of warmth in them. "You were a very arrogant young man. And I'm afraid I had very little grace under pressure. I came to have more, of course."

"You were better than the games we played. I should have understood."

"That's a very disarming thing to say. . . . And I think we've said enough about the subject."

"Will you and your husband have dinner with me tonight, Mrs. Holcroft?" He heard the words he had spoken, not sure he had said them. It was the impulse of the moment.

She stared at him briefly before answering. "You mean that, don't you?"

"Certainly. I left Italy in somewhat of a rush, courtesy of your government, as these clothes are the courtesy of your countrymen. I haven't been to London in several years. I have very few acquaintances here."

"Now that's a provocative thing to say."

"I beg your pardon?"

"That you left Italy in a rush and you're wearing someone else's clothes. It raises questions."

Vittorio hesitated, then spoke quietly. "I would appreciate your having the understanding I lacked ten years ago. I would prefer those questions not be raised. But I'd like to have dinner with you. And your husband, of course."

She held his gaze, looking up at him curiously. Her lips curved into a gentle smile; she had made her decision. "My husband's name was Spane. Holcroft's my own. Jane Holcroft. And I'll have dinner with you."

The Savoy doorman interrupted. "Signor Fontini-Cristi, your car has arrived, sir."

"Thank you," he replied, his eyes on Jane Holcroft. "I'll be right there."

"Yes, sir." The doorman nodded and walked away.

"May I pick you up this evening? Or send my car for you?"

"Petrol's getting scarce. I'll meet you here. Eight o'clock?"

"Eight o'clock. *Arrivederci.*"

"Until then."

He walked down the long corridor at the Admiralty, escorted by a Commander Neyland who had met him at the entrance desk. Neyland was middle-aged, properly military, and quite impressed with himself. Or perhaps he was not at all impressed with Italians. In spite of Vittorio's fluency in English, Neyland insisted on using the simplest terms, and raising his voice as though addressing a retarded child. Fontini-Cristi was convinced that Neyland had not listened to his replies; a man did not hear of pursuit, death, and escape, and respond with such banalities as "You don't say." . . . "Odd, isn't it?" . . . "The Genoa gulf can be choppy in December, can't it?"

As they walked, Vittorio balanced his negative reaction to the commander with his gratitude for old Norcross on Savile Row.

Where the commander floundered, Norcross performed. The old tailor had clothed him in a matter of hours.

The little things; concentrate on the every*day* things.

Above all, maintain a control that bordered on ice during the conference with whatever, or whoever, comprised Intelligence Sector Five. There was so much to learn, to understand. So much that was beyond his comprehension. In the cold recital of the events that were the horror of Campo di Fiori, he could not let the agony cloud his perceptions; the recital, therefore, *would* be cold and understated.

"Through here, old man," said Neyland, indicating a cathedral-arched doorway that was more reminiscent of some venerable men's club than a military building. The commander opened the heavy door, gleaming with brass hardware, and Vittorio walked in.

There was nothing about the large room that belied the concept of a subdued but richly appointed club. Two huge windows overlooked a courtyard; everything was heavy and ornate: the drapes, the furniture, the lamps, and to some degree the three men who sat at the thick mahogany table in the center. Two were in uniform—the insignia and breast decorations duly proclaiming advanced ranks unknown to Fontini-Cristi. The man in civilian clothes had an archly diplomatic look about him, complete with a waxed moustache. Such men had come and gone in Campo di Fiori. They spoke in soft voices, their words ambiguous; they were seekers of elastic. The civilian was at the head of the table, the officers seated at the sides. There was one empty chair, obviously for him.

"Gentlemen," said Commander Neyland, as if he were announcing a petitioner at the Court of St. James, "Signor Savarone Fontini-Cristi of Milan."

Vittorio stared at the fatuous Englishman; the man had not heard a word he said.

The three men at the table rose as one. The civilian spoke. "May I introduce myself, sir. I am Anthony Brevourt. For a number of years I was the crown's ambassador of the Greek court of George the Second in Athens. On my left, Vice Admiral Hackett, Royal Navy; on my right, Brigadier Teague, Military Intelligence."

At first there were formal nods of acknowledgment, then Teague broke the formality by coming around his chair, his hand held out for Vittorio.

"I'm glad you're here, Fontini-Cristi. I received the preliminary reports. You've had a hell of a time of it."

"Thank you," said Vittorio, shaking the general's hand.

"Do sit down," said Brevourt, indicating the expected chair to Vittorio and returning to his own. The two officers took their seats—Hackett rather formally, even pompously; Teague quite casually. The general withdrew a cigarette case from his pocket and offered it to Fontini-Cristi.

"No, thank you," said Vittorio. To smoke with these men would imply a casualness he neither felt nor wanted them to think he felt. A lesson from Savarone.

Brevourt quickly continued. "I think we'd better get on

with it. I'm sure you know the subject of our anxieties. The Greek consignment."

Vittorio looked at the ambassador. And then at the two officers. They were staring at him, apparently in anticipation. "The Greek? I know nothing of a 'Greek consignment.' However, I know the gratitude I feel. There are no words to express it in either language. You saved my life; men were killed doing so. What more can I say?"

"I think," said Brevourt slowly, "that we should like to hear you say something about an extraordinary delivery made to the family Fontini-Cristi by the Eastern Brotherhood of Xenope."

"I beg your pardon?" Vittorio was stunned. The words had no meaning for him. Some extraordinary error had been made.

"I told you. I was the crown's ambassador to Athens. During the tenure of my office, diplomatic liaisons were formed throughout the country, including, of course, the religious. For, in spite of the turmoil Greece is experiencing, the church hierarchy remains a powerful force."

"I'm sure it does," agreed Vittorio. "But I have no idea why it concerns me."

Teague leaned forward, the smoke curling in front of his face, his eyes riveted on Fontini-Cristi. "Please. We've done our share, you know. As you've said—I think quite properly—we saved your life. We sent in our best men, paid thousands to the *Corsos,* took considerable gambles in dangerous waters with a submarine—of which we have precious few—and activated a barely developed aircraft escape route. All these just to get you out." Teague paused, put down his cigarette and smiled ever so slightly. "All human life is sacred, perhaps, but there are limits to the expenditures one makes to prolong it."

"Speaking for the navy," said Hackett with controlled irritation, "we followed blindly, given only the barest facts, urged by the most commanding figures in the government. We jeopardized a vital area of operations; a decision that could cost a great many lives in the near future. Our expense was considerable. And the full tally's not in yet."

"These gentlemen—the government itself—acted on my most urgent entreaties," said Ambassador Anthony Brevourt with measured precision. "I was convinced beyond any doubt that *whatever* the cost, it was imperative to get you out of Italy. Quite simply put, Signor Fontini-Cristi, it was not your life. It was the information you possess relative to the Patriarchate of Constantine. That is my conduit. Now, if you please, the location of the delivery. Where is the vault?"

Vittorio returned Brevourt's stare until he could feel the sting in his eyes. No one spoke; the silence was strained. Things were being alluded to that moved the highest echelons of government and Fontini-Cristi knew he was the focus. But that was all he knew.

"I cannot tell you what I know nothing about."

"The freight from Salonika." Brevourt's voice was cutting. The flat of his hand descended delicately on the table, the soft slap of flesh against the wood as startling as it was abrupt. "Two dead men in the railroad yards of Milan. One a priest. Somewhere beyond Banja Luka, north of Trieste, past Monfalcone, somewhere in Italy, or Switzerland you met that train. Now *where?*"

"I met no train, *signore*. I know nothing of Banja Luka, or Trieste. Monfalcone, yes, but it was only a phrase, and meaningless to me. An 'incident' would 'take place at Monfalcone.' That was all. My father did not elaborate. His position was that I would be given the information *after* the incident at Monfalcone. Not before."

"What of the two dead men in Milan? In the railroad yards." Brevourt would not let up; his intensity was electric.

"I read of the two men you speak of—shot in the Milan freight yards. It was a newspaper story. It did not seem terribly important to me."

"They were *Greeks*."

"I understand that."

"You *saw* them. They made the *delivery* to you."

"I saw no Greeks. No delivery was made to me."

"Oh, my God!" Brevourt drew out the words in a pained whisper. It was obvious to all at the table that the diplomat was suddenly gripped in his own particular fear; he was not feigning for negotiable effect.

"Easy," said Vice Admiral Hackett vacuously. The diplomat started to speak again, slowly, carefully, as though marshaling his thoughts.

"An agreement was made between the Elders of Xenope and the Italian Fontini-Cristis. It was a matter of incalculable priority. Sometime between December ninth and sixteenth—the dates the train left Salonika and arrived in Milan—it was met and a crate removed from the third freight car. Of such value was this cargo that the train's itinerary was prepared in isolated stages. There was only a single master plan, itself a sequence of documents, held by one man, a priest of Xenope. These, too, were destroyed before the priest took his own life and that of the engineer. Only he knew where the transfer was to be made, where the crate was to be removed. He and those responsible for removing it. The Fontini-Cristis." Brevourt paused, his deepset eyes riveted on Vittorio. "These are facts, sir; given to me by a courier from the Patriarchate. Coupled with the measures my government has taken, I presume they are sufficient to convince you to give us the information."

Fontini-Cristi shifted his position in the chair and looked away from the quietly intense face of the ambassador. He was sure the three men thought he was dissembling; he would have to dissuade them of that. But first he had to think. So this was the reason. An unknown train from Salonika had caused the British government to take extraordinary measures to—what had Teague said?—prolong his life. Yet it was not his life that was important, as Brevourt had made clear. It was the information they assumed he possessed.

Which, of course, he did not.

December 9 through 16. His father had left for Zürich on the twelfth. But Savarone had not been in Zürich. And he would not tell his son where he had been. . . . Brevourt might well have cause for his anxieties. Still, there were other questions; the pattern was unclear. Vittorio turned back to the diplomat.

"Bear with me. You say Fontini-Cristis. You use the plural. A father and four sons. The father's name was Savarone. Your Commander Neyland inaccurately introduced me by that name."

"Yes." Brevourt was barely audible, as if he were being forced to confront a conclusion he refused to accept. "I was aware of that."

"So Savarone is the name you received from the Greeks. Is that correct?"

"He could not have done it alone." Again Brevourt spoke hardly above a whisper. "You're the eldest son; you run the companies. He would have advised you. He needed your help. There were over twenty separate documents to be prepared, we know that. He *needed* you!"

"It is what you apparently—perhaps desperately—wish to believe. And because you believed it, you took extraordinary measures to save my life, to get me out of Italy. You obviously know what happened at Campo di Fiori."

Brigadier Teague spoke. "We picked it up first through the partisans. The Greeks weren't far behind. The Greek embassy in Rome was keeping close tabs on the Fontini-Cristis; it wasn't told why, apparently. The Athens conduit reached the ambassador and he, in turn, got in touch with us."

"And now you are implying," said Brevourt icily, "that it was all for nothing."

"I'm not implying it. I'm stating it. During the period you spoke of, my father said he was traveling to Zürich. I'm afraid I wasn't paying much attention at the time, but several days later I had an urgent reason to ask him to return to Milan. I tried contacting him; I called every hotel in Zürich; he was nowhere to be found. He never told me where he was, where he had been. That's the truth, gentlemen."

The two officers looked at the diplomat. Brevourt leaned slowly back in his chair—it was a gesture of futility and exhaustion; he stared at the table top. Finally, he spoke.

"You have your life, Signor Fontini-Cristi. For all our sakes, I hope the cost was not too great."

"I can't answer that, of course. Why was this agreement made with my father?"

"*I* can't answer *that*," replied Brevourt, his eyes still on the table. "Apparently someone, somewhere, believed he was resourceful enough, or powerful enough, to carry it off. Either or both of which have been borne out. Perhaps we'll never know. . . ."

"What was on the train from Salonika? What was in the vault that caused you to do what you did?"

Anthony Brevourt raised his eyes and looked at Vittorio and lied. "I don't know."

"That's preposterous."

"I'm sure it must appear that way. I know only the . . . implications of its significance. There is no price on such things. It's an abstract value."

"And on that judgment you made these decisions, convinced your highest authorities to make them? Moved your government?"

"I did, sir. I would do it again. And that's all I'll say on the subject." Brevourt rose from the table. "It's pointless to go on. Others may be in touch with you. Good day, Signor Fontini-Cristi."

The ambassador's action startled the two officers, but they said nothing. Vittorio got out of his chair, nodded, and walked silently to the door. He turned and looked at Brevourt; the man's eyes were noncommittal.

Outside, Fontini-Cristi was surprised to see Commander Neyland standing at attention between two enlisted men. Intelligence Sector Five, Alien Operations, was taking no chances. The door of the conference room was being guarded.

Neyland turned, astonishment in his face. He obviously expected the meeting to last far longer.

"You've been released, I see."

"I didn't think I was being held," answered Vittorio.

"Figure of speech."

"I never realized how unattractive it was. Are you to escort me past the desk?"

"Yes, I'll sign you out."

They approached the Admiralty's huge entrance desk. Neyland checked his watch, gave Vittorio's last name to the guard. Fontini-Cristi was asked to initial the departure time; he did so, and as he stood up from the desk he was greeted by the commander's very formal salute. He nodded—formally—turned and walked across the marble floor to the huge double doors to the street.

He was on the fourth step when the words came to him. They shot through the swirling mists of white light and the shattering staccato of gunfire.

"Champoluc . . . Zürich is Champoluc . . . Zürich is the river!"

And then no more. Only the screams, and the white light, and the bodies suspended in death.

He stopped on the marble step, seeing nothing but the terrible visions of his mind.

"Zürich is the river! Champoluc. . . ."

Vittorio controlled himself. He stood motionless and breathed deeply, vaguely aware that people on the pavement and the steps were staring at him. He wondered if he should walk back through the doors of the Admiralty and down a long corridor to the cathedral arch that was the conference room of Intelligence Sector Five.

Calmly he made his decision. *Others may contact you.* Let the others come. He would not share with Brevourt, the seeker of elastic who lied to him.

"If I may, Sir Anthony," said Vice Admiral Hackett, "I believe there was a great deal more ground we might have covered——"

"I agree," interrupted Brigadier Teague, his irritation showing. "The admiral and I have our differences, but not in *this,* sir. We barely scratched the surface. We made an extraordinary investment and got nothing for it; there was more to be had."

"It was useless," said Brevourt wearily, walking slowly to the draped window overlooking the courtyard. "It was in his eyes. Fontini-Cristi told the truth. He was stunned by the information. He knows nothing."

Hackett cleared his throat, a prelude to judgment. "He didn't strike me as foaming at the mouth. He seemed to take it rather in stride, I'd say."

The diplomat stared absently out the window as he replied quietly. "If he had foamed at the mouth, I would have kept him in that chair for a week. He behaved precisely the way such a man reacts to deeply disturbing news. The shock was too profound for theatrics."

"Granting your premise," said Teague coldly, "it does not eliminate mine. He may not *realize* what he knows. Secondary information often leads to a primary source. In our business it nearly always does. I must object, Sir Anthony."

"Your objection is noted. You're perfectly free to make further contact; I made that clear. But you'll learn no more than we did this afternoon."

"How can you be so *sure?*" asked the Intelligence man quickly, his irritation rapidly turning into anger.

Brevourt turned from the window, his expression pained, his eyes in reflection. "Because I knew Savarone Fontini-Cristi. Eight years ago in Athens. He was a neutral emissary, I think is the term, from Rome. The only man Athens would trust. The circumstances are not relevant here; the methods of Fontini-Cristi are. He was a man possessed with a sense of discretion. He could move economic mountains, negotiate the most difficult international agreements, because all parties knew his word was better than any written contract. In a strange way, it was why he was feared; beware the man of total integrity. Our only hope was if he had called in his son. If he had needed him."

Teague absorbed the diplomat's words, then leaned forward, his arms on the table. "What was on the train from Salonika? In that damned vault?"

Brevourt paused before answering. The two officers understood that whatever the ambassador was about to say, it was *all* he would say.

"Documents hidden from the world for fourteen centuries. They could tear the Christian world apart, setting church against church . . . nation against nation, perhaps; forcing millions to choose sides in a war as profound as Hitler's."

"And by so doing," interrupted Teague in the form of a question, "dividing those who fight Germany."

"Yes. Inevitably."

"Then we'd better pray they're not found," concluded Teague.

"Pray strenuously, general. It's strange. Over the centuries men have willingly given their lives to protect the sanctity of those documents. Now they've disappeared. And all who knew where are dead."

PART THREE

7

JANUARY 1940 TO SEPTEMBER 1945
EUROPE

The telephone rang on the antique desk in the Savoy suite. Vittorio was at the casement window overlooking the Thames, watching the barges make their way slowly up and down the river in the afternoon rain. He checked his watch; it was exactly four thirty. The caller had to be MI6's Alec Teague.

Fontini-Cristi had learned many things about Teague over the past three weeks; one was that the man was punctual to a fault. If he said he would telephone *around* four thirty, then he would do so *at* four thirty. Alec Teague ran his life by a clock; it made for abrupt conversations.

Vittorio picked up the telephone. "Yes?"

"Fontini?" The Intelligence man was also given to brevity when it came to names. Apparently he saw no reason to add the Cristi when the Fontini was sufficient.

"Hello, Alec, I've been expecting you."

"I've got the papers," said Teague rapidly. "And your orders. The Foreign Office was reluctant. It's an equal wager whether they were concerned for your well-being, or whether they thought you'd present the crown with a bill."

"The latter, I can assure you. My father drove 'hard bargains,' I think is the term. Frankly, I've never understood the phrase; can bargains be soft?"

"Damned if I know." Teague was not really listening. "I think we should meet right off. How's your evening?"

"I'm having dinner with Miss Holcroft. Under the circumstances I can cancel, of course."

"Holcroft? Oh, the Spane woman."

"I think she prefers Holcroft."

"Yes, can't blame her. He's a bloody fool. Still, you can't deny the ceremony."

"She's doing her best to, I believe."

Teague laughed. "Damned gutsy girl. I think I'd like her."

"Which means you don't know her, and you want *me* to know you've had me followed. I never mentioned her married name to you."

Teague laughed again. "For your own benefit, not ours."

"Shall I cancel?"

"Don't bother. When will you be finished?"

"Finished?"

"Dinner. Damn, I forgot; you're Italian."

Vittorio smiled. Alec's recollection was made in complete sincerity. "I can see the lady home by ten thirty . . . ten o'clock. I gather you wish to meet tonight."

"I'm afraid we have to. Your orders call for you to leave tomorrow. For Scotland. In the morning."

The restaurant in Holborn was named Fawn's. Black curtains were drawn tautly across the windows, stretched and tacked, inhibiting any light from spilling a single shaft into the street. He was in the bar, seated at a corner stool with a clear view of the lounge and the shrouded entrance. She would arrive any minute now and he smiled at himself, realizing that he wanted to see her very much.

He knew when it had begun with Jane—their swiftly developing relationship that would shortly lead to the splendid comfort of the bed. It was not their meeting in the Savoy lobby; nor was it their first evening together. Those were pleasant distractions; he had sought no more, wanted no more.

The beginning was five days later when he had been sitting alone in his rooms. There'd been a knock on the foyer door. He had opened it; Jane was standing in the hallway. In her hand was a slightly worn copy of the *Times*. He had not seen it.

"For God's sake, what happened?" she asked.

He had shown her in without answering, unsure of her meaning. She'd handed him the newspaper. In the lower left corner of the front page was a brief article circled in red pencil.

MILAN, Jan. 2 (Reuters)—A news blackout has been lowered on the Fontini-Cristi Industries here as government officials moved in assuming managerial control. No member of the Fontini-Cristi family has been seen, and the police have sealed off the family estate at Campo di Fiori. Rumors abound as to the fate of this powerful dynasty headed by the financier Savarone Fontini-Cristi and his eldest son, Vittorio. Reliable sources indicate they may have been killed by patriots, infuriated by recent company decisions many felt were inimicable to Italy's interests. It was reported that the mutilated body of an "informer" (unseen by this journalist) was found hanging in the Piazza del Duomo, with a sign that would seem to confirm the rumors of execution. Rome has issued only the statement that the Fontini-Cristis were enemies of the state.

Vittorio had put down the paper and walked across the room, away from the girl. He knew she meant well; he did not fault her concern. Yet he was profoundly annoyed. The anguish was his alone and he did not care to share it. She had intruded.

"I'm sorry," she'd said quietly. "I presumed. I had no right to do that."

"When did you first read this?"

"Less than a half hour ago. It was left on my desk. I've mentioned you to friends. I saw no reason not to."

"And you came right over?"

"Yes."

"Why?"

"I cared," had been her simple answer. The honesty of it had touched him. "I'll go now."

"Please——"

"Do you want me to stay?"

"Yes. I think I do."

And so he had told her. In measured tones at first, his sentences gathering momentum as he approached the hideous night of white light and death that was Campo di Fiori. His throat was dry. He did not wish to go on.

And Jane did a strange thing. Separated by the short distance between their opposing chairs, making no move to diminish that separation, she forced him to continue.

"For God's sake, *say* it. *All* of it."

She whispered, but the whisper was a command and in his confusion and anguish he accepted it.

When he was done, relief swept over him. For the first time in days an unbearable weight had been lifted. Not permanently, it would return; but for the moment he had found his sanity; really found it, not an imposed pretense that left his breath always a little short.

Jane had known what he had not understood. She had said it.

"Did you think you could go on keeping it inside? Not saying the words; not hearing them. What kind of man do you think you *are?*"

What kind of man? He did not really know. He had not actually thought about the kind of man he was; it was not a question that had concerned him beyond certain limits. He was Vittorio Fontini-Cristi, first son of Savarone. Now he would find out what else he was. He wondered whether Jane could be a part of his new world. Or whether the hate and the war would be all-consuming. He knew only the war—and the hate—were his springboards back to life.

Which was why he had encouraged Alec Teague when the MI6 man contacted him after the disastrous conference with Brevourt at Intelligence Sector Five. Teague wanted background material—seemingly unimportant conversations, offhand remarks, oddly repeated words—anything that might have a bearing on the train from Salonika. But Vittorio wanted something, too. From Teague. So he spaced out the isolated scraps of information: a river that might or might not have anything to do with Zürich, a district in the Italian Alps that bore the name Champoluc, but possessed no river. Whatever the puzzle was, its pieces remained separate. Still Teague probed.

And while he probed, Vittorio drew out the conceivable options MI6 might have for him. He was fluent in English and Italian, more than proficient in French and German; he had an intimate working knowledge of a score of major European industries, had negotiated with the leading financial figures throughout Europe. Certainly there was *something.*

Teague said he would look. Yesterday Teague said he would call him today at four thirty; there might be something. This afternoon at precisely four thirty Teague had called; he had Vittorio's "orders." There *had* been something. Fontini-Cristi wondered what it was, and even more, why the abruptness of his departure for Scotland.

"Have you been waiting long?" asked Jane Holcroft, suddenly standing beside him in the dimly lit bar.

"I'm *sorry*." Vittorio was; he had not seen her in the lounge. Yet he had been staring at the door. "No, not at all."

"You were miles away. You looked right at me and when I smiled, you scowled. I trust it's not indicative."

"Good heavens, no. You were right; I was miles away. In Scotland."

"I beg your pardon?"

"I'll tell you about it at the table. What I know, which is very little."

They were led to their table and ordered drinks. "I've told you about Teague," he said, lighting her cigarette, holding the flame of the match for his own.

"Yes. The man from Intelligence. You didn't say a great deal about him. Only that he seemed to be a good chap who asked a lot of questions."

"He had to. My family required it." Fontini-Cristi had not told Jane about the freight from Salonika; there was no point. "I've been pestering him for several weeks to find me a job."

"In the service?"

"In any service. He was a logical man to approach; he knows people everywhere. We both agreed I have qualifications that might be useful to someone."

"What will you be doing?"

"I don't know, but whatever it is, it begins in Scotland."

The waiter arrived with their drinks. Vittorio nodded his thanks, aware that Jane kept her eyes on his face.

"There are training camps in Scotland," she said quietly. "Several are listed as highly classified. They're quite secret and heavily guarded."

Vittorio smiled. "They can't be *too* secret."

The girl returned his smile, the full explanation in her eyes, only half of it in her words. "There's an elaborate system of air defense warning-relays throughout the areas. Overlapping sectors; extremely difficult for aircraft to penetrate. Especially single-engine light aircraft."

"I forgot. The Savoy manager said you were no-nonsense people."

"We're also given extensive training in all existing systems. As well as those in development stages. Systems vary considerably from sector to sector. When are you leaving?"

"Tomorrow."

"I see. For how long?"

"I don't know."

"Of course. You said that."

"I'm to meet with Teague tonight. After dinner, but there's no need to rush. I'm not seeing him until ten thirty. I presume I'll know more then."

Jane was silent for several moments. She locked her eyes with his and then spoke simply. "When your meeting with Teague is over, will you come to me? To my flat? Tell me what you can."

"Yes. I will."

"I don't care what time it is." She placed her hand over his. "I want us to be together."

"So do I."

Brigadier Alec Teague removed his creased officer's cap and army overcoat and threw them on the Savoy chair. He unbuttoned his tunic and his collar and loosened his tie. He lowered his large, powerful frame into the soft couch and exhaled a sigh of relaxation. He grinned at Fontini-Cristi, who stood in front of an opposing armchair and held his palms up in supplication.

"Since I've been at it since seven this morning, I do think you should offer me a drink. Whiskey neat would be splendid."

"Of course." Vittorio crossed to the small bar against the wall, poured two short glasses, and returned with the drinks.

"Mrs. Spane's a most attractive woman," Teague said. "And you're quite right, you know, she does prefer her maiden name. At the Air Ministry the 'Spane' is in brackets. She's called Flying Officer Holcroft."

"Flying Officer?" Vittorio did not know why but the title seemed faintly amusing to him. "I hadn't thought of her in such military terms."

"Yes, I see what you mean." Teague finished his drink quickly and placed his glass on the coffee table. Vittorio gestured for a refill. "No more, thank you. It's time for serious talk." The Intelligence man looked at his wristwatch; Fontini-Cristi wondered if Teague really scheduled himself to the precise half-minute for social conversation.

"What's in Scotland?"

"Your place of residence for the next month or so. Should you accept the terms of employment. The pay's not exactly what you're accustomed to, I'm afraid." Teague grinned again. "As a matter of fact, we rather arbitrarily placed it at a captain's rate. I don't have the figures in my head."

"The figures aren't my concern. You say I have a choice, but before you said that my orders had arrived. I don't understand."

"We have no hold over you. You can reject the employment and I'll cancel the orders. It's as simple as that. However, in the interests of time, I made the purchase first. Frankly, to be sure it *could* be made."

"All right. What is it?"

"That's rather difficult to answer quickly. If at all, really. You see, it's pretty much up to you."

"To *me?*"

"Yes. The circumstances surrounding your getting out of Italy were unique, we all understand that. But you're not the only continental who's fled Europe. We've got dozens and dozens. And I'm not talking about the Jews and the Bolsheviks; they're in the thousands. I'm referring to scores of men like yourself. Businessmen, professionals, scientists, engineers, university people who, for one reason or another—we'd like to think it was moral repugnance—couldn't function where they lived. That's about where we are."

"I don't understand. Where are you?"

"In Scotland. With forty or fifty ragtail continentals—all quite successful in their previous livelihoods—in search of a leader."

"And you think I am *he?*"

"The more I think about it, the more convinced I become. Rather natural qualifications, I'd say. You've moved in the monied circles, you speak the languages. Above all, you're a businessman, you've developed markets all over Europe. Good heavens, man, the Fontini-Cristi Industries are *enormous;* you were its chief executive. Adapt to the conditions. Do what you've done splendidly for the past half-dozen years or so. Only do it from the *opposite point of view. Mis*management."

"What *are* you talking about?"

The brigadier continued, speaking rapidly. "We have men in Scotland who've worked in scores of occupations and professions in all the major cities in Europe. One step always leads to another, doesn't it?"

"That's what you're counting on, isn't it? We both ask questions."

Teague leaned forward, suddenly reflective. "These are hectic and complicated times. There are more questions than there are answers. But one answer was right in front of our eyes only we didn't see it. We were training these men for the wrong things! That is, we weren't sure *what* we were training them for; vaguely for underground contacts, routine information runs, it was amorphous. There's something better; damned ingenious, if I say so myself. The strategy, the concept is to send them back to *disrupt* the marketplace, create havoc—not so much physical sabotage, we've enough people doing that, but bureaucratic chaos. Let them operate in their former bailiwicks. Accounting offices consistently out of balance, bills of lading constantly inaccurate, delivery schedules at sixes and sevens, mass confusion in the factories: exemplary *mis*management at all *costs!*"

Teague was excited, his enthusiasm infectious. It was difficult for Vittorio to keep his concentration on the essence of his original question. "But why do I have to leave in the morning?"

"To put it bluntly, I said I might lose you if there were any further delays."

"Further? How can you say that? I've been here less than——"

"Because," broke in Teague, "no more than five people in England know why we *really* got you out of Italy. Your complete lack of information about the train from Salonika has them stunned. They took an extraordinary gamble and lost. What you've told me leads nowhere; our agents in Zürich, Berne, Trieste, Monfalcone . . . they can trace nothing. So I stepped in with a different version of why we got you out and saved a few heads in the bargain. I said this new operation was *your* idea. They leaped at it! After all, you are a Fontini-Cristi. Will you accept?"

Vittorio smiled. " 'Mismanagement at all costs.' That is a credo I doubt has a precedent. Yes, I do see the possibilities. Whether they are enormous—or theoretical—remains to be seen. I accept."

Teague smiled slyly. "There's one thing more. About your name——"

"Victor Fontine?" Jane laughed beside him on the couch in the Kensington flat, warmed by the glow of the burning logs in the fireplace. "That's British cheek if I ever heard it. They've *colonized* you."

"And made me an officer in the process," chuckled Captain Victor Fontine, holding up the envelope and dropping it on the coffee table. "Teague was amusing. He approached the subject rather the way one expects from the cinema. 'We must find you a *name*. Something immediately recognizable, easy to use in cables.' I was intrigued. I was to be given a code name, something quite dramatic, I imagined. A precious stone, perhaps, with a number. Or an animal's name. Instead, he merely Anglicized my own and lopped it off." Victor laughed. "I'll get used to it. It's not for a lifetime."

"I don't know if I can, but I'll try. It's rather a letdown, frankly."

"We must all sacrifice. Am I correct in assuming a *capitano* is a higher rank than a flying officer?"

"The 'flying officer' has no intention of giving orders. I don't think either of us is very military. Nor is Kensington. What about Scotland?"

He told her sketchily, keeping what facts he knew unspecific. As he spoke, he saw and could feel her unusually light-blue eyes probing his, looking beyond the offhand phrases, knowing surely there was more, or would be. She was dressed in a comfortable lounging robe of pale yellow that accentuated her very dark brown hair and emphasized the blue of her eyes. Underneath the robe, between the wide lapels, he could see the soft white of her nightgown and he knew she meant him to see it, and to want to touch her.

It was so comfortable, thought Fontine. There was no sense of urgency or maneuver. At one point during his monologue he touched her shoulder; she slowly, gently reached up and held his hand, her fingers caressing his. She led his hand down to her lap and cupped it with her other hand as he finished.

"So there we have it. 'Mismanagement at all costs' wherever it can be inflicted."

She was quiet for a moment, her eyes still probing, and then she smiled. "It's a marvelous idea. Teague's right, the possibilities are enormous. How long will you be in Scotland? Did he say?"

"Not specifically. A 'number of weeks.'" He withdrew his hand from hers and casually, naturally reached around her shoulders and drew her to him. Her head rested on his upper chest; he kissed her soft hair. She pulled back and looked up at him—her eyes still searching. She parted her lips as she moved toward him, taking his hand and casually, perfectly naturally, leading it between the lapels of her robe, inside over her breast. When ther lips met, Jane moaned and widened her mouth, accepting the full moisture of his own.

"It's been a long time," she whispered finally.

"You're lovely," he replied, stroking her soft hair with his hand, kissing her eyes.

"I wish you didn't have to go away. I don't want you to go."

They stood up in front of the small couch. She helped him take off his jacket, pausing to press her face against his chest. They kissed again, holding each other at first gently, and then with gathering strength. For the briefest time, Victor placed his hands on her shoulders and moved her back; her lovely face was below him and he spoke into her blue eyes. "I'll miss you terribly. You've given me so much."

"And you've given me what I was afraid to find," she answered, her lips forming a gentle, quiet smile. "Afraid to look for, actually. Good heavens, I was petrified!"

She took his hand and they walked across the room to a doorway. Inside was the bedroom; a single ivory lamp shone on a night table, its yellowish white glow throwing light up on the walls of soft blue and across the ivory-colored, simple furniture. The silk spread over the bed was, again, blue and white and filled with the intricate circles of a floral design. It was all so peaceful, so away, so lovely, as Jane was lovely.

"This is a room of great privacy. And warmth," said

Fontine, struck by simple beauty. "It's an extraordinary room, because it's your room and you care for it. Do I sound foolish?"

"You sound Italian," she answered softly, smiling, her blue eyes filled with love and urgency. "The privacy and the warmth are for you to share. I want you to share them."

She walked to one side of the bed, he to the other. Together they folded back the silk spread; their hands touched and they looked at each other. Jane walked around the bed to him. As she did so, she reached up and unbuttoned the top of her negligee, and then untied the ribbon of her gown. The fabric fell away, her round, full breasts emerged from the folds of silk, the nipples pink, taut.

He took her into his arms, his lips seeking hers in moist, soft excitement. She pressed her body against his. He could never remember being so completely, so totally aroused. Her long legs trembled and once again she pressed against him. She opened her mouth, her lips covered his, low moans of sweet pleasure coming from her throat.

"Oh, God, *take* me, Vittorio. Quickly, *quickly*, my love!"

The telephone rang on Alec Teague's desk. He looked at the office clock on the wall, then at his wristwatch. It was ten minutes to one in the morning. He picked up the receiver.

"Teague here."

"Reynolds in surveillance. We have the report. He's still in Kensington at the Holcroft flat. We think he'll stay the night."

"Good! We're on schedule. Everything according to plan."

"I wish we knew what was said. We could have set it up, sir."

"Quite unnecessary, Reynolds. Deposit a file-insertion for the morning: Parkhurst at the Air Ministry is to be contacted. Flying Officer Holcroft is to be given flexible consideration, including a tour of the Loch Torridon warning relays in Scotland, if it can be arranged quietly. Now, I'm off for some sleep. Good night."

8

Loch Torridon was west of the northwest highlands on the edge of the water, the source of the loch in the sea leading to the Hebrides. Inland there were scores of deep ravines, with streams rolling down from the upper regions, water that was icy and clear and formed pockets of marsh. The compound was between the coast and the hills. It was rough country. Isolated, invulnerable, patrolled by guards armed with weapons and dogs. Six miles northeast was a small village with a single main street that wound between a few shops and became a dirt road on the outskirts.

The hills themselves were steep, the abrupt inclines profuse with tall trees and thick foliage. It was in the hills that the continentals were put through the rigors of physical training. But the training was slow and laborious. The recruits were not soldiers but businessmen, teachers, and professionals, incapable of sustaining harsh physical exertion.

The common denominator was a hatred of the Germans. Twenty-two had their roots in Germany and Austria; in addition, there were eight Poles, nine Dutch, seven Belgians, four Italians, and three Greeks. Fifty-three once-respectable citizens who had made their own calculations months earlier.

They understood that one day they would be sent back to their homelands. But as Teague had noted, it was a formless sort of objective. And this undefined, seemingly low-level, participation was unacceptable to the continentals; undercurrents of discontent were heard in the four barracks in the middle of the camp. As the news of German victories came with alarming rapidity over the radio, the frustrations grew.

For God's sake! When? Where? How? *We are wasted!*

The camp commander greeted Victor Fontine with not a

little wariness. He was a blunt officer of the Regulars and a graduate of MI6's various schools of covert operations.

"I won't pretend to understand much," he said at first meeting. "My instructions are muddy, which is what they're supposed to be, I imagine. You'll spend three weeks, more or less—until Brigadier Teague gives us the order—training with our group as one of the men. You'll do everything they do, nothing out of the ordinary."

"Yes, of course."

With these words Victor entered the world of Loch Torridon. A strange, convoluted world that had little in common with anything he had experienced in his life before. And he understood, although he was not sure why, that the lessons of Loch Torridon would merge with the teachings of Savarone and shape the remaining years of his life.

He was issued regulation combat fatigues and equipment, including a rifle and a pistol (without ammunition), a carbine bayonet that doubled as a knife, a field pack with mess utensils, and a blanket roll. He moved into the barracks, where he was greeted casually, with as few words as possible and no curiosity. He learned quickly that there was not much camaraderie in Loch Torridon. These men lived in and with their immediate pasts; they did not seek friendship.

The daylight hours were long and exhausting; the nights spent memorizing codes and maps and the deep sleep necessary to ease aching bodies. In some ways Victor began to think of Loch Torridon as an extension of other, remembered games. He might have been back at the university, in competition with his classmates on the field, on the courts, on the mats, or up on the slopes racing downhill against a stopwatch. Except that the classmates at Loch Torridon were different; most were older than he was and none had known even vaguely what it was like to have been a Fontini-Cristi. He gathered that much from brief conversations; it was easy to keep to himself, and therefore to compete against himself. It was the cruelest competition.

"Hello? My name is Mikhailovic." The man grinning and speaking to Victor sank to the ground, breathing heavily. He released the straps of his field pack and let the bulky canvas slip from his shoulders. It was midpoint in a ten-minute break between a forced march and a tactical maneuver exercise.

"Mine's Fontine," replied Victor. The man was one of the two new recruits who had arrived in Loch Torridon less than a week ago. He was in his mid-twenties, the youngest trainee in the compound.

"You're Italian, aren't you? In Barracks Three?"

"Yes."

"I'm Serbo-Croat, Barracks One."

"Your English is very good."

"My father is an exporter—was, I should say. The money's in the English-speaking countries." Mikhailovic pulled out a pack of cigarettes from his fatigues pocket and offered it to Fontine.

"No, thanks. I just finished one."

"I ache all over," said the Slav, grinning, lighting a cigarette. "I don't know how the old men do it."

"We've been here longer."

"I don't mean you. I mean the others."

"Thank you." Victor wondered why Mikhailovic complained. He was a stocky, powerfully built man, with a bull neck and large shoulders. Too, something about him was odd: there was no perspiration whatsoever on Mikhailovic's forehead, while Fontine's own was matted with sweat.

"You got out of Italy before Mussolini made you a lackey to the German, eh?"

"Something like that."

"Machek's taking the same road. He'll run all of Yugoslavia soon, mark my word."

"I didn't know that."

"Not many people do. My father did." Mikhailovic drew on his cigarette, his eyes across the field. He added quietly, "They executed him."

Fontine looked compassionately at the younger man. "I'm sorry. It's painful, I know."

"Do you?" The Slav turned; there was bewilderment in his eyes.

"Yes. We'll talk later. We must concentrate on the maneuver. The object is to reach the top of the next hill through the woods without being tagged." Victor stood and held out his hand. "My first name's Vittor—Victor. What's yours?"

The Serbo-Croat accepted the handshake firmly. "Petride. It's Greek. My grandmother was Greek."

"Welcome to Loch Torridon, Petride Mikhailovic."

As the days went by, Victor and Petride worked well together. So well, in fact, the compound sergeants paired them off against superior numbers in the infiltration exercises. Petride was allowed to move into Victor's barracks.

For Victor, it was like having one of his younger brothers suddenly return to life; curious, often bewildered, but strong and obedient. In some ways Petride filled a void, lessened the pain of his memories. If there was a liability in the relationship it was merely one of excess on the Serbo-Croat's part. Petride was an excessive talker, forever questioning, always volunteering information about his personal life, expecting Victor to reciprocate.

Beyond a point, Fontine could not. He simply was not so inclined. He had shared the anguish of Campo di Fiori with Jane; there would be no one else. Occasionally he found it necessary to reprimand Petride Mikhailovic.

"You're my friend. Not my priest."

"Did you have a priest?"

"Actually, no. It was a figure of speech."

"Your family was religious. It must have been."

"Why?"

"Your real name. 'Fontini-Cristi.' It means fountains of Christ, doesn't it?"

"In a language several centuries old. We're not religious in the accepted sense; not for a long time."

"I'm very, *very* religious."

"It's your right."

The fifth week came and went and still there was no word from Teague. Fontine wondered if he'd been forgotten; whether MI6 had developed second thoughts over the concept of "mismanagement at all costs." Regardless, life at Loch Torridon had taken his mind off his self-destructive memories; he actually felt quite strong and capable again.

The compound's lieutenants had devised what they called a "long-pursuit" exercise for the day. The four barracks operated separately, each taking forty-five degrees of the compass within a ten-mile radius of Loch Torridon. Two men from each barracks were given a fifteen-minute head start before the remaining recruits took chase; the object being for the hunted to elude the hunters for as long as possible.

It was natural for the sergeants to choose the best two

from each barracks to begin the exercise. Victor and Petride were the first eluders in Barracks Three.

They raced down the rocky slope toward the Loch Torridon woods.

"Quickly now!" ordered Fontine as they entered the thick foliage of the forest. "We'll go left. The *mud;* step into the mud! Break as many branches as you can."

They ran no more than fifty yards, snapping limbs, stamping their feet into the moist corridor of soft earth that angled through the woods. Victor issued his second command.

"Stop! This is far enough. Now, carefully. We'll make footprints up onto the dry ground. . . . That's enough. All right, step backward, directly on the prints. *Across* the mud. . . . Good. Now, we'll head back."

"Head back?" asked the bewildered Petride. "Head back where?"

"To the edge of the woods. Where we entered. We've still got eight minutes. That's enough time."

"For what?" The Serbo-Croat looked at his older friend as if Fontine was amusingly mad.

"To climb a tree. Out of sight."

Victor selected a tall Scotch pine in the center of a cluster of lower trees and started up, shinnying to the first level of branches. Petride followed, his boyish face elated. Both men reached the three-quarter height of the pine, bracing themselves on opposite sides of the trunk. They were obscured by the surrounding branches; the ground beneath, however, was visible to them.

"We've nearly two minutes to spare," whispered Victor, looking at his watch. "Kick any loose limbs away. Rest your weight solidly."

Two minutes and thirty second later, their pursuers passed far below them. Fontine leaned forward toward the young Serbo-Croat.

"We'll give them thirty seconds and then climb down. We'll head for the other side of the hill. A section of it fronts a ravine. It's a good hiding place."

"A stone's throw from the starting line!" Petride grinned. "How did you think of it?"

"You never had brothers to play games with. Race-and-hide was a favorite."

Mikhailovic's smile disappeared. "I have many brothers," he said enigmatically, and looked away.

There was no time to pursue Petride's statement. Nor did Victor care to. During the past eight days or so, the young Serbo-Croat had behaved quite strangely. Morose one minute, antic the next; and incessantly asking questions that were beyond the bounds of a six-week friendship. Fontine looked at his watch. "I'll start down first. If there's no one in sight, I'll yank the branches. That's your signal to follow."

On the ground, Victor and Petride crouched and ran east at the edge of the woods, the base of the starting hill. Three hundred yards, around the circle of the hill was a slope of jagged rock that overlooked a deep ravine. It was carved out of the hill by a crack of a glacier eons ago, a natural sanctuary. They made their way literally across the gorge. Breathing hard, Fontine lowered himself into a sitting position, his back against the stone cliff. He opened the pocket of his field jacket and took out a pack of cigarettes. Petride sat in front of him, his legs over the side of the ledge. Their isolated perch was no more than seven feet across, perhaps five in depth. Again, Victor looked at his watch. There was no need to whisper now.

"In half an hour, we'll climb over the crest and surprise the lieutenants. Cigarette?"

"No, thank you," replied Mikhailovic harshly, his back to Fontine.

The note of anger could not be overlooked. "What's the matter? Did you hurt yourself?"

Petride turned. His eyes bore into Victor. "In a manner of speaking, yes."

"I won't try to follow that. You either hurt yourself or you didn't. I'm not interested in manners of speech." Fontine decided that if this was to be one of Mikhailovic's periods of depression, they could do without conversation. He was beginning to think that beneath his wide-eyed innocence, Petride Mikhailovic was a disturbed young man.

"You *choose* what interests you, don't you, Victor? You turn the world off at will. With a switch in your head, all is void. Nothing." The Serbo-Croat stared at Fontine as he spoke.

"Be quiet. Look at the scenery, smoke a cigarette, leave me alone. You're becoming a bore."

Mikhailovic slowly pulled his legs over the ledge, his eyes still riveted on Victor. "You must not dismiss me. You cannot. I've shared my secrets with you. Openly, willingly. Now you must do the same."

Fontine watched the Serbo-Croat, suddenly apprehensive. "I think you mistake our relationship. Or, perhaps, I've mistaken your preferences."

"Don't insult me."

"Merely clarification——"

"My time has *run out!*" Petride raised his voice; his words formed a cry as his eyes remained wide, unblinking. "You're not blind! You're not deaf! Yet you pretend these things!"

"Get out of here," ordered Victor quietly. "Go back to the starting line. To the sergeants. The exercise is over."

"My name," Mikhailovic whispered, one leg pulled up beneath his powerful, crouching body. "From the beginning you refused to acknowledge it! *Petride!*"

"It is your name. I acknowledge it."

"You've never heard it before? Is that what you're saying?"

"If I have, it made no impression."

"That's a lie! It's the name of a priest. And you *knew that priest!*" Again the words floated upward, a cry shouted in desperation.

"I've known a number of priests. None with that name——"

"A priest on a *train!* A man devoted to the glory of God! Who walked in the grace of His holy work! You cannot, *must* not deny him!"

"*Mother of Christ!*" Fontine spoke inaudibly; the shock was overpowering. "Salonika. The freight from Salonika."

"Yes! That most holy train; documents that are the blood, the *soul* of the *one incorruptible, immaculate* church! You've taken them from us!"

"You're a priest of Xenope," said Victor, incredulous at the realization. "My God, you're a monk from Xenope!"

"With all my heart! With all my *mind* and *soul* and *body!*"

"How did you get here? How did you penetrate Loch Torridon?"

Mikhailovic pulled his other leg up; he was fully crouched now, a mad animal prepared to spring. "It's irrelevant. I must know where that vault was taken, where it was hidden. You'll tell me, *Vittorio Fontini-Cristi!* You've no choice!"

"I'll tell you what I told the British. I know *nothing!* The English saved my life; why would I lie?"

"Because you gave your word. To another."

"Who?"

"Your father."

"No! He was killed before he could say the words! If you know anything, you know that!"

The priest of Xenope's eyes became suddenly fixed. His stare was clouded, his lids wide, almost thyroid. He reached under his field jacket and withdrew a small, snub-nosed automatic. With his thumb he snapped up the safety. "You're insignificant. We're both insignificant," he whispered. "We're nothing."

Victor held his breath. He pulled his knees up; the split second approached when he would have the one opportunity to save his life, when he would lash his feet out at the maniacal priest. One boot at the weapon, the other at Mikhailovic's weighted leg, sending him over the precipice. It was all there was left—if he could do it.

Abruptly, the vocal intrusion startling, the priest spoke, his tone chantlike, transfixed. "You're telling me the truth," he said, closing his eyes. "You have told me the truth," he repeated hypnotically.

"Yes." Fontine took a deep, deep breath. As he exhaled, he knew he would plunge both legs out; the moment had come.

Petride stood up, his powerful chest expanding beneath the soldier's clothes. But the weapon was no longer aimed at Victor. Instead, both Mikhailovic's arms were extended in an attitude of crucifixion. The priest raised his head to the skies and shouted.

"I believe in one God, the Father Almighty! I will look into the eyes of the Lord and I shall not waver!"

The priest of Xenope bent his right arm and put the barrel of the automatic to his temple.

He fired.

"You got your first kill," said Teague casually, sitting in a chair in front of Fontine's desk in the small, enclosed cubicle.

"I did not kill him!"

"It doesn't matter how it happens, or who pulls the bloody trigger. The result's the same."

"For the wrong reason! That *train,* that damned, *unholy train!* When will it stop? When will it *go away?"*

"He was your enemy. That's all I'm saying."

"If he was, you should have known it, spotted it! You're a fool, Alec."

Teague shifted his legs in irritation. "That's rather harsh language for a captain to employ with a brigadier."

"Then I'd be delighted to purchase your command and set it right," said Victor, returning to the papers in manila folders on his desk.

"One doesn't do that in the military."

"It's the only reason for your continuity. You wouldn't last a week as one of my executives."

"I don't believe this." Teague spoke in astonishment. "I'm sitting here being cashiered by a ragtail guinea."

Fontine laughed. "Don't exaggerate. I'm only doing what you asked me to do." He gestured at the manila folders on the desk. "Refine Loch Torridon. In that process, I've tried to learn how this priest of Xenope, this Mikhailovic, got in."

"Have you?"

"I think so. It's a basic weakness with every one of these dossiers. There are no clear financial appraisals; there are endless words, histories, judgments—but very few figures. It should be corrected wherever possible before we make our final personnel decisions."

"What on earth are you talking about?"

"Money. Men are proud of it; it's the symbol of their productivity. It can be traced, confirmed in a dozen different ways. Records abound. Where possible, I want financial statements on every recruit in Loch Torridon. There was none on Petride Mikhailovic."

"Financial——"

"A financial statement," completed Fontine, "is a most penetrating look into a man's character. These are businessmen and professionals, by and large. They'll be anxious to oblige. Those that are not we'll question at length."

Teague uncrossed his legs, his voice respectful. "We'll get at it, there are forms for that sort of thing."

"If not," said Victor glancing up, "any bank or brokerage house can supply them. The more complex, the better."

"Yes, of course. And beyond this, how are things going?"

Fontine shrugged, waving his hand again over the pile of the folders on the desk. "Slowly. I've read all the dossiers several times, making notes, cataloging by professions and related professions. I've detailed geographical patterns, linguistic compatibilities. But where it's all led me, I'm not sure. It'll take time."

"And a lot of work," interrupted Teague. "Remember, I told you that."

"Yes. You also said it would be worthwhile. I hope you're right."

Teague leaned forward. "I have one of the finest men in the service to work with you. He'll be your communications man for the whole show. He's a crackerjack; knows more codes and ciphers than any ten of our best cryptographers. He's damned decisive, a shark at quick decisions. Which is what you'll want, of course."

"Not for a long time."

"Before you know it."

"When do I meet him? What's his name?"

"Geoffrey Stone. I brought him up with me."

"He's in Loch Torridon?"

"Yes. No doubt checking the cryp's quarters. I want him in at the beginning."

Victor was not sure why but Teague's information disturbed him. He wanted to work alone, without distraction. "All right. I imagine we'll see him at the dinner mess."

Teague smiled again and looked at his watch.

"Well, I'm not sure you'll want to dine at the Torridon mess."

"One never *dines* at the mess, Alec. He eats."

"Yes, well, the cuisine notwithstanding. I've a bit of news for you. A friend of yours is in the sector."

"Sector? Is Loch Torridon a sector?"

"For air warning-relays."

"Good Lord! *Jane* is here?"

"I found out the night before last. She's on tour for the Air Ministry. Of course, she had no idea you were in this area, until I reached her yesterday. She was in Moray Firth, on the coast."

"You're a terrible manipulator!" Fontine laughed. "And so obvious. Where the devil *is* she?"

"I swear to you," said Teague with convincing innocence, "I knew nothing. Ask her yourself. There's an inn on the outskirts of town. She'll be there at five thirty."

My God, I've missed her! I've really missed her. It was rather extraordinary; he had not realized how deeply he felt. Her face with its sharp yet delicate features, her dark, soft hair that fell so beautifully around her shoulders; her eyes, so intensely blue; all were etched in his mind. "I assume you'll give me a pass to leave the compound."

Teague nodded. "And arrange a vehicle for you. But you've a while before you should drive off. Let's spend it on specifics. I realize you've only begun, but you must have reached a conclusion or two."

"I have. There are fifty-three men here. I doubt twenty-five will survive Loch Torridon, as I believe it should be run——"

They talked for nearly an hour. The more Fontine expanded his views, the more completely, he realized, did Teague accept them. Good, thought Victor. He was going to make many requests, including a continuing hunt for Loch Torridon talent. But now his thoughts turned to Jane.

"I'll walk you to your barracks," Teague said, sensing his impatience. "We might drop in at the officers' club for a minute—I promise no longer. Captain Stone will be there by now; you should meet him."

But it was not necessary to stop off at the officers' bar to find Captain Geoffrey Stone. As they walked down the steps of the field complex, Victor saw the figure of a tall man in an army overcoat. He stood about thirty feet away in the compound, his back to them, talking to a sergeant major. There was something familiar about the officer's build, a kind of unmilitary slouch in the shoulders. Most striking was the man's right hand. It was encased in a black glove obviously several sizes too large to be normal. It was a medical glove; the hand was bandaged beneath the black leather.

The man turned; Fontine halted in his tracks, his breath suspended.

Captain Geoffrey Stone was the agent named Apple, who was shot on the pier in Celle Ligure.

* * *

They held each other. Neither spoke, for words were extraneous. It had been ten weeks since they'd been together. Ten weeks since the splendid, exciting moments of lovemaking.

At the inn, the old woman who sat in a rocking chair behind the front desk had greeted him.

"Flying Officer Holcroft arrived a half hour ago. 'A trust you're the captain, though the clothes dinna' say it. She said you're t' go up, if you're a mind to. She's a direct lass. Dinna' care for sly words, that one. Top of the stairs, turn left, room four."

He had knocked softly at the door, the pounding in his chest ridiculously adolescent. He wondered if she was possessed by the same tension.

She stood inside, her hand on the doorknob, her inquisitive blue eyes bluer and more searching than he could remember ever having seen them. The tension was there, yet there was confidence, too.

He stepped in and took her hand. He shut the door; they closed the distance between them and slowly reached for each other. When their lips touched, all the questions were put to rest, the answers obvious in silence.

"I was frightened, do you know that?" whispered Jane, holding his face in her hands, kissing his lips tenderly, repeatedly.

"Yes. Because I was frightened, too."

"I wasn't sure what I was going to say."

"Neither was I. So here we are talking about our uncertainties. It's healthy, I suppose."

"It's probably childish," she said, tracing his forehead and his cheek with her fingers.

"I think not. To want . . . to *need* . . . with such feeling is a thing apart. One is afraid it may not be returned." He took her hand from his face and kissed it, then kissed her lips and then her soft dark hair that fell, framing the soft smooth skin of her lovely face. He reached around her and pulled her to him, holding her close, and whispered "I *do* need you. I've missed you."

"You're a love to say it, my darling, but you don't have to. I don't require it, I won't ask for it."

Victor pulled away gently and cupped her face, staring into her eyes, so close to his. "Isn't it the same with you?"

"Very much the same." She leaned into him, her lips against his cheeks. "I think of you far too often. And I'm a very busy girl."

He knew she wanted him as fully and completely as he wanted her. The tension each had felt was transferred to their bodies, release to be found only in the act of love. Yet the swelling, aching urgency in them did not demand swiftness. Instead, they held each other in the warm excitement of the bed, explored each other in tenderness and growing insistence. And they talked softly in whispers as their excitement grew.

Oh, God, he loved her so.

They lay naked under the covers, spent. She rose on her elbow and reached across him, touching his shoulder, tracing the skin with her fingers down to his thighs. Her dark hair fell over his chest; behind it, below her delicate face and penetrating blue eyes, her breasts were suspended over his flesh. He moved his right hand and reached for her, a signal that the act of love would begin again. And it suddenly occurred to Vittorio Fontini-Cristi, as they lay naked together, that he never wanted to lose this woman.

"How long can you stay in Loch Torridon?" he asked, pulling her face down to his.

"You're a horrid manipulating spoiler of not-so-young girls," she whispered, laughing softly in his ear. "I am currently in a state of erotic anxiety, with the memory of thunderbolts and erogenous pleasure still rippling up my most private—and you ask me how long I can stay! Forever and ever, of course. Until I return to London in three days."

"Three days! It's better than two days. Or twenty-four hours."

"For what? To reduce us both to babbling idiots?"

"We'll be married."

Jane raised her head and looked at him. She looked at him for a long time before she spoke, her eyes locked with his. "You've been through a great deal of sorrow. And terrible confusion."

"You don't want to marry me?"

"More than my *life*, my darling. God, more than all the world. . . ."

"But you don't say yes."

"I'm yours. You don't have to marry me."

"I *want* to marry you. Is it wrong?"

"It's the rightest thing I can imagine. But you have to be sure."

"Are *you* sure?"

She lowered her cheek on his. "Yes. It's you. *You* must be sure."

With his hand he swept her soft dark hair away from her face and answered her with his eyes.

Ambassador Anthony Brevourt sat behind the enormous desk in his Victorian study. It was nearly midnight, the household retired, the city of London dark. Everywhere men and women were on rooftops and on the river and in the parks talking quietly into wireless sets, watching the skies. Waiting for the siege they knew would come, but had not yet begun.

It was a matter of weeks; Brevourt knew it, the records projected it. But he could not keep his attention on the horrors that would reshape history as inevitably as the events moved forward. He was consumed by another catastrophe. Less immediately dramatic, but in many ways no less profound. It was contained in the file folder in front of him. He stared at the handwritten code name he had created for himself. And a few—very few—others.

SALONIKA

So simple in the reading, yet so complex in meaning.

How in God's name could it have happened? What were they thinking of? How could the movements of a single freight crossing half a dozen national borders be untraceable? The key had to be with the subject.

From below, in a locked drawer of his desk, a telephone rang. Brevourt unlocked the drawer and pulled it open. He lifted the receiver.

"Yes?"

"Loch Torridon," was the flat reply.

"Yes, Loch Torridon? I'm alone."

"The subject was married yesterday. To the candidate."

Brevourt momentarily stopped breathing. Then inhaled deeply. The voice on the other end of the line spoke again. "Are you there, London? Do you hear me?"

"Yes, Torridon. I heard you. It's more than we might have hoped for, isn't it? Is Teague pleased?"

"Not actually. I think he would have preferred a convenient relationship. Not the marriage. I don't think he was prepared for that."

"Probably not. The candidate might be considered an obstruction. Teague will have to adjust. Salonika has far greater priority."

"Don't you ever tell M.I.-Six that, London."

"At this juncture," said Brevourt coldly, "I trust all files relative to Salonika have been *removed* from M.I.-Six. That was our understanding, Loch Torridon."

"It is correct. Nothing remains."

"Good. I'll be traveling with Churchill to Paris. You may reach me through the official Foreign Office channel, Code Maginot. Stay in contact; Churchill wants to be kept informed."

9

LONDON

Fontine entered the stream of pedestrians moving toward Paddington Station. There was a numbness in the streets, a sense of disbelief that resulted in pockets of silence. Eyes searched other eyes, strangers took notice of the other strangers.

France had fallen.

Victor turned into Marylebone; he saw people buying newspapers in silence. It had happened; it had *really happened*. Across the Channel was the enemy—victorious, invincible.

The Dover boats from Calais held no crowds of laughing tourists on holiday any longer. Now there were different journeys; everyone had heard of them. The Calais boats sailed under cover of night, as men and women, some bloodied, some whole, all desperate, crouched below decks, hidden by nets and canvas, bringing out the stories of agony and defeat that were Normandy, Rouen, Strasbourg, and Paris.

Fontine remembered Alec Teague's words: *The concept, the strategy is to send them back to disrupt the marketplace . . . create havoc! Mismanagement at all costs!*

The marketplace was now all of Western Europe. And Captain Victor Fontine was ready to send out his Loch Torridon mismanagers of that marketplace.

Of the original fifty-three continentals, twenty-four remained; others would be added—slowly, selectively—as losses demanded. These twenty-four were as diverse as they were accomplished, as inventive as they were devious. They were German, Austrian, Belgian, Polish, Dutch, and Greek, but their nationalities were secondary. Labor forces were shipped across borders daily. For in Berlin, the *Reichsministerium* of Industry was pressing into service people from all occupied terrotories—it was a sweeping policy that would accelerate as new lands were brought under control. It was not unusual for a Hollander to be working in a Stuttgart factory. Already—only days after Paris fell—Belgians were being shipped to captured plants in Lyon.

Acting on this knowledge, the underground leaders were scouring the labor-transfer lists. Objectives: Find specialized temporary "employment" for twenty-four skilled professionals.

In the confusion that resulted from the German obsession for maximum productivity, positions were unearthed everywhere. Krupp and I.G. Farben were exporting so many experts to get factories and laboratories rolling in conquered countries that German industrialists complained bitterly to Berlin. It led to haphazard organization, slipshod management; it reduced the effectiveness of German plants and offices.

It was into this morass that the French, Dutch, Belgian, Polish, and German undergrounds infiltrated. Job recruitment directives were sent by espionage couriers to London, for the scrutiny of Captain Victor Fontine.

Item: Frankfurt, Germany. Messerschmidt subsupplier. Three plant foremen sought.

Item: Kraków, Poland. Axle division, automobile plant. Draftsmen needed.

Item: Antwerp, Belgium. Railroad yards. Freight and scheduling divisions. Management scarce.

Item: Mannheim, Germany. Government printing offices. Bilingual technical translators needed imperatively.

Item: Turin, Italy. Turin Aircraft. Source partigiano. *Mechanical engineers in short supply.*

Item: Linz, Austria. Berlin claims consistent overpayment fabrics company. Cost accountants needed.

Item: Dijon, France. Wehrmacht legal department. Lawyers demanded by occupation forces. . . . (So like the French, Victor had thought. In the midst of defeat, the Gallic mind sought debate in practical legalities.)

And so they went. Scores of "requirements," dozens of possibilities that would grow in numbers as the German demands for productivity grew.

There was work to be had, to be done, by the small brigade of Loch Torridon continentals. It was now merely a question of proper allocations and Fontine would personally oversee the specifics. He carried in his briefcase a very small strip of reusable tape that could be attached to any part of the body. The adhesive had the tensile strength of steel, but could be removed by a simple solution of water, sugar, and citrus juice.

Within that tape were twenty-four dots, each containing a microfilm. On each microfilm was a microscopically reduced photograph and a brief résumé of talents. They would be used in concert with the underground leaders. Twenty-four positions of employment would be found . . . temporary, to be sure, for such skilled personnel would be desirable in many locations during the coming months.

But first things first, and the first item on Fontine's agenda was a business trip of undetermined length. He would be parachuted into France, in the province of Lorraine near the Franco-Swiss border. His first conference would take place in the small town of Montbéliard, where he would stay for several days. It was a strategic geographical point, affording maximum accessibility for the underground from northern and central France and southern Germany.

From Montbéliard he would head north on the Rhine as far as Wiesbaden, where contingents of anti-Reichists from Bremen, Hamburg, Berlin, and points north and west would gather for meetings. From Wiesbaden he would take the underground's routes east to Prague, then northwest into Poland and Warsaw. Schedules would be created, codes refined, official work papers provided for eventual duplication in London.

From Warsaw he would return to Lorraine. The decision would then be made whether to head south into his beloved Italy. Captain Geoffrey Stone was against it in principle. The agent Fontine had known as Apple made that clear. All things Italian filled Stone with loathing, his revulsion traced to a pier in Celle Ligure and a hand shattered because of Italian naïveté and betrayal. Stone saw no reason to waste their resources on Italy; there were too many other pressure points. The nation of incompetents was its own worst enemy.

Fontine reached Paddington and waited for the Kensington bus. He had discovered buses in London; he had never taken public conveyances in his life before. The discovery was partly defensive. Whenever official cars were used, they were shared, calling for conversation between the passengers. None was called for on a bus.

There were times, of course, when he carried highly sensitive material home to read, when Alec Teague simply refused to allow him his newfound indulgence. It was too dangerous. Tonight had been a case in point, but Victor had fought his superior; the official car had two other riders and he wanted to think. It was his last night in England. Jane had to be told.

"For heaven's sake, Alec! I'll be traveling several thousand miles in hostile territory. If I lose a briefcase that's chained to my wrist with a combination lock on a London bus, I think we're all in for immense trouble!"

Teague had capitulated, checking the chain and the lock himself.

The bus pulled up and he climbed in, threading his way down the crowded corridor to a seat in the front. It was by a window; he looked out and let his thoughts dwell first on Loch Torridon.

They *were* ready. The concept *was* valid. They *could* place their personnel in succeeding managerial positions. All that remained was the implementation of the strategy. He would accomplish a great deal of that on his trip. He would find the right positions for the right personnel . . . the chaos and the havoc would shortly follow.

He was primed for the moment of departure. Yet he was not really prepared for the one thing that faced him now: telling Jane the moment had finally come.

He had moved into her Kensington flat when he returned from Scotland. She'd rejected his offer of considerably grander quarters. And these past weeks were the happiest in his life.

And now the moment had come and fear would replace the comfort of daily existence together. It made no difference that thousands upon thousands were going through the same experience; there was no comfort in mathematics.

His stop was next. The June twilight washed the trees and scrubbed the houses. Kensington was peaceful, the war remote. He got off the bus and started down the quiet street when suddenly his attention was drawn away from the entrance gate. He had learned over the past months not to betray his concern, so he pretended to wave to an unseen neighbor in a window across the way. By doing so, while squinting his eyes against the setting sun, he was able to see more clearly the small Austin sedan parked on the opposite side of the street fifty yards diagonally in front of him. It was gray. He had seen that gray Austin before. Exactly five days ago. He remembered vividly. He and Stone had been driving up to Chelmsford to interview a Jewess who had worked for the Kraków civil service until just before the invasion. They had stopped at a service station outside of Brentwood.

The gray Austin sedan had driven in behind them to the pump beside theirs. Victor had noticed it only because an attendant who sold the driver petrol was caustic when the pump registered less than two gallons . . . and the Austin's tank was full.

"That's bein' a mite greedy," the attendant had said.

The driver had looked embarrassed, turned the ignition, and sped out on the highway.

Fontine had noticed because the driver was a priest. The driver of the gray Austin across from him now was a priest. The white collar could be seen clearly.

And the man, he knew, was staring at him.

Fontine walked casually to the gate of the house. He lifted the latch, entered, turned, and closed the gate; the priest in the gray Austin sat motionless, his eyes—behind what appeared to be thick glasses—still directed at him. Victor approached the door and let himself inside. The moment he was in the hallway he shut the door and moved quickly to the narrow column of windows that flanked the doorframe. A blackout curtain was draped over the glass; he parted the edge and looked out.

The priest had inched his way over to the right window of his car and was looking out and up at the front of the building. The man was grotesque, thought Fontine. He was extremely pale and thin, and the lenses of his glasses were thick.

Victor let the curtain fall back and walked rapidly to the staircase, climbing the steps two at a time to the third floor, their floor. He could hear music within; the radio was on; Jane was home. As he closed the door behind him, he heard her humming in the bedroom. There was no time to shout greetings; he wanted to get to the window. And he did not wish to alarm her if he could avoid it.

His binoculars were in the bookshelf on the fireplace wall. He pulled the case from its recess between a section of books and took out the binoculars, went to the window and focused the glass below.

The priest was talking to someone in the back seat of the small automobile. Fontine had not seen anyone else in the car. The rear seat was in shadow and he had been concentrating on the driver. He edged the binoculars behind the priest and refined the focus.

Victor froze. The blood rushed to his head.

It was a nightmare! A nightmare that repeated itself! *Fed* upon itself!

The streak of white in the close-cropped hair! He had seen that shock of white from an embankment . . . inside an automobile . . . under the glaring lights . . . soon to erupt in smoke and death!

Campo di Fiori!

The man in the back seat of the gray Austin below had been in another back seat! Fontine had looked down at him from the darkness as he was now looking down at him thousands of miles away in a Kensington street! One of the German commanders! One of the German executioners!

"Good heavens! You startled me," said Jane, walking into the room. "What are you——?"

"Get Teague on the telephone! Now!" shouted Victor, dropping the binoculars, struggling with the combination lock on his briefcase.

"What *is* it, darling?"

"Do as I say!" He fought to keep control. The numbers came; the lock sprang open.

Jane stared at her husband; she dialed rapidly, asking no further questions.

Fontine raced into the bedroom. He pulled his service revolver from between a pile of shirts and tore it from its holster, running back into the living room toward the door.

"*Victor! Stop!* For God's sake!"

"Tell Teague to get over here! Tell him a German from Campo di Fiori is below!"

He ran out into the corridor and raced down the narrow staircase, manipulating his thumb beneath the barrel of the weapon, unlatching the safety. As he reached the top of the first flight, he heard the gunning of an engine. He yelled and plunged down to the hallway, to the front door, yanking furiously at the knob, pulling the door open with such force that it crashed against the wall. He ran outside to the gate.

The gray Austin was speeding down the street; pedestrians were on the sidewalks. Fontine chased it, dodging two oncoming cars, their tires screeching as they braked. Men and women shouted at him; Victor understood. A man racing in the middle of the street at seven in the evening with a gun in his hand was a cause for violent alarms. But he could not dwell on such thoughts; there was only the gray Austin and a man in the back seat with a shock of white in his hair.

The *executioner.*

The Austin turned right at the corner! Oh, God! The traffic on the throughfare was light, only a few taxis and private cars! The Austin accelerated, speeding, weaving between the vehicles. It jumped a traffic light, narrowly missing a delivery truck which jolted to a stop, blocking all vision beyond.

He had lost it. He stopped, his heart pounding, sweat pouring down his face, his weapon at his side. But he had not lost everything. There were six numbers on the gray Austin's license plate. He'd managed to distinguish four of them.

* * *

"The automobile in question is registered to the Greek embassy. The attaché assigned to it claims it must have been removed from the embassy grounds late this afternoon." Teague spoke rapidly, annoyed not only with his conceivably false information but with the entire incident itself. It was an obstruction, a serious obstruction. The Loch Torridon operation could not tolerate barriers at this moment.

"Why the German? Who is he? I know *what* he is." Victor spoke quietly, with enormous feeling.

"We're putting on every trace we can come up with. A dozen experienced field men are pulling the files. They're going back years, getting everything we have. The description you gave the artist was good; his sketch quite accurate, you said. If he's there, we'll find him."

Fontine got out of the chair, started for the window and saw that heavy black drapes had been drawn, shutting in all light. He turned and looked absently at a large map of Europe on Teague's wall. There were dozens of red mark-pins protruding from the thick paper.

"It's the train from Salonika, isn't it?" He asked the question softly, not needing an answer.

"That wouldn't explain the German. If he is a German."

"I *told* you," interrupted Victor, turning to face the brigadier. "He was there. In Campo di Fiori. I remembered then that I'd thought I'd seen him before."

"And you've never been able to recall where?"

"No. There are times when it drives me mad. I don't *know!*"

"Can you associate? Go back. Think in terms of cities, or hotels; start with business dealings, contracts. Fontini-Cristi had investments in Germany."

"I've tried all that. There's nothing. Only the face, and that not terribly clear. But the white streak in the hair, that's what stays in my mind." Wearily, Victor returned to the chair and sat down again. He leaned back, both hands over his closed eyes. "Oh, God, Alec, I'm frightened to death."

"You've no reason to be."

"You weren't in Campo di Fiori that night."

"There'll be no repetition in London. Or anywhere else, for that matter. Tomorrow morning your wife will be escorted to the Air Ministry, where she will turn over her workload—files, letters, maps, everything—to another officer. The ministry has assured me the transition can be concluded by early afternoon. Thereupon, she'll be driven to very comfortable quarters in the countryside. Isolated and totally secure. She'll stay there until you return, or until we find your man. And break him."

Fontine lowered his hands from his eyes. He looked questioningly at Teague. "When did you do this? There's been no time."

Teague smiled, but it was not the unsettling smile Victor was used to. It was, if anything, gentle. "It's been a contingency plan since the day you were married. Within hours, as a matter of fact."

"She'll be safe?"

"No one in England more so. Frankly, I've a twofold motive. Your wife's safety is directly related to your state of mind. You've a job to do, so I'll do mine."

Teague looked at the wall clock, then at his wristwatch. The clock had lost nearly a minute since he'd last adjusted it. When *was* that? It must have been eight, ten days ago; he would have to bring it back to the watchsmith's in Leicester Square.

It was a foolish preoccupation, he supposed, this obsession with time. He'd heard the names: "Stopwatch Alec," "Timer Teague." His colleagues often chided him; he wouldn't be so damned concerned with time if he had a wife and small ones clattering about. But he had made that decision years ago; in his profession he was better off without such attachments. He was no monk. There had, of course, been women. But no marriage. It was out of the question; it was a hindrance, an obstacle.

These passive thoughts gave rise to an active consideration: Fontine and *his* marriage. The Italian was the perfect coordinator for the Loch Torridon operation, yet now there was an obstacle—his wife.

Goddamn it! He had cooperated with Brevourt because he really *did* want to use Fontini-Cristi. If a convenient relationship with an English girl served both objectives, he was willing to go along. But not *this* far!

And now, where the hell was Brevourt? He had given up. He had faded away after having made extraordinary demands of Whitehall in the name of an unknown freight from Salonika.

Or had he merely pretended to fade away?

It seemed that Brevourt knew when to cut his losses, when to back away from an embarrassing failure. There'd been no further instructions regarding Fontine; he was now the property of MI6. Just like that. It was as though Brevourt wanted to put as much distance as possible between himself and the Italian *and* the goddamned train. When the report of the infiltrating priest of Xenope was given to Brevourt, he feigned only a mild interest, ascribing the episode to a lone fanatic.

For a man who had moved his government to do what it did, that wasn't natural. Because the priest of Xenope had not acted alone. Teague knew it; Brevourt knew it, too. The ambassador was reacting too simply, his sudden disinterest too obvious.

And that girl, Fontine's wife. When she appeared, Brevourt had snapped up her existence like a true MI-Sixer himself. She was a short-range anchor. She could be appealed to, used. If Fontine's behavior became suddenly strange, if he entered into or sought abnormal contacts that could be traced to the train from Salonika, she was to be called in and given her instructions: *report everything*. She was an English patriot; she would comply.

But no one had even considered a marriage. That *was* mismanagement-at-all-costs! Instructions could be given to a convenient mistress; they were not given to a wife.

Brevourt had taken this news with an equanimity that was again unnatural.

Something was happening that Teague did not understand. He had the uncomfortable feeling that Whitehall was using MI6 and that meant using him, tolerating Loch Torridon because it might lead Brevourt to a greater objective than the scattered disruption of enemy industry.

Back to the train from Salonika.

So two parallel strategies were being played out: Loch Torridon, and the search for the documents of Constantine. They allowed him the former; he was dismissed from the latter.

Dismissed and left with a married Intelligence officer—the most vulnerable kind.

It was ten minutes to three in the morning. In six hours he would be driving down to Lakenheath with Fontine to see him off.

A man with a streak of white in his hair. A sketch that eluded thousands of photographs and file descriptions, a hunt that led nowhere. A dozen MI6 staffers were down in the archives continuing the search. The field agent who broke the identity would not be overlooked when choice assignments were passed around.

His telephone rang, startling him.

"Yes?"

"It's Stone, sir. I think I have something."

"I'll be right down."

"If it's all the same to you, I'd prefer coming up. It's a bit mad. I'd rather see you alone."

"Very well."

What had Stone found? What could be so odd that it required in-house security?

"Here is the sketch Fontine approved, general," said Captain Geoffrey Stone, standing in front of Teague's desk, placing the charcoal portrait on the blotter. An envelope was clamped awkwardly between his arm and his chest, above the immobile, gloved right hand. "It matched nothing in the Himmler files, or any other German—or German-related—sources, including collaborationist circles in Poland, Czechoslovakia, France, the Balkans, and Greece."

"And Italy? What of the Italians?"

"That was our first consideration. Regardless of what Fontine claims to have seen that night in Campo di Fiori, he *is* Italian. The Fontini-Cristis made enemies among the fascists. But we found nothing, no one faintly resembling the subject in question. Then quite frankly, sir, I began thinking about the man. His marriage. We didn't expect that, did we, sir?"

"No, captain. We did not expect that."

"A small vicarage in Scotland. A church of England ceremony. Not exactly what one would have thought."

"Why not?"

"I've worked the Italian sectors, general. The Catholic influence is most pervasive."

"Fontine's not a religious man. What in hell are you driving at?"

"Just that. Everything's a question of degree, isn't it? One never is just this or just that. Especially a man who has wielded such power. I went back to *his* file; we've photostats of every damned thing we could lay our hands on. Including his marriage application and certificate. Under the heading of 'denomination' he inserted one word: 'Christian.' "

"Get to the point."

"I'm doing so. One thing always leads to another. An immensely wealthy, powerful family in a Catholic country, and the surviving son purposely denies any association with its church."

Teague narrowed his eyes. "Go on, captain."

"He *was denying*. Perhaps unconsciously, we don't know. 'Christian' is not a denomination. We were looking for the wrong Italians, pulling out the wrong files." Stone raised the envelope with his left hand, unwound the small string and opened the flap. He took out a newspaper clipping, a cropped photograph of a bareheaded man with a shock of white in his dark hair. The bareheaded man wore the black robes of the church; the picture was taken at the altar of St. Peter's. The man was kneeling, facing the cross. Above him was a pair of outstretched hands. They were holding the three-cornered hat of a cardinal.

"My God!" Teague looked up at Stone.

"The Vatican files. We keep records of all ecclesiastical elevations."

"But *this*——"

"Yes, sir. The subject's name is Guillamo Donatti. He's one of the most powerful cardinals in the Curia."

10

MONTBÉLIARD

The aircraft began its ninety-degree turn. They were at 3,-000 feet, the night clear, the wind stream rushing past the open hatch with such force Fontine thought he would be sucked out before the red light above him was extinguished, replaced by the sudden glare of the white bulb that was his signal to leap. He gripped the handles at the sides of the hatch, bracing himself; his thick boots were pressed against the steel deck of the Haviland bomber; he waited to jump.

He thought of Jane. At first, she'd objected strenuously to her confinement. She had earned her position at the Air Ministry, weeks and months of "just plain damned hard work," were now taken away in a matter of hours. And then she abruptly stopped, seeing, he was sure, the pain in his eyes. She wanted him back. If isolation in the countryside would help his return, she would go.

He thought, too, of Teague; partially of what he said, mostly of what he did not say. MI6 had a line on the German executioner, the man-monster with the streak of white in his hair who had coldly observed the horror of Campo di Fiori. The service assumed him to be a ranking member of the *Geheimdienst Korps,* Himmler's secret police, a man who stayed far in the background, never expecting to be identified. Someone who had been stationed at the German consulate in Athens, perhaps.

"Assumed." "Perhaps." Words of equivocation. Teague was concealing information. For all his experience, the Intelligence man could not hide his omissions. Nor was he entirely convincing when he subtly introduced a subject that had little to do with anything:

"——it's standard procedure, Fontine. When a man

goes on assignment we list his religious affiliation. Just like a birth certificate or a passport——"

No, he had no formal affiliation. No, he was not Catholic, nor was that extraordinary; there *were* non-Catholics in Italy. Yes, Fontini-Cristi was a derivative combination that was translated as the "fountains of Christ"; yes, the family for centuries had been allied with the church, but a number of decades ago had broken with the Vatican. But, no, he did not place undue emphasis on the break; he rarely thought about it.

What was Teague after?

The red light went off. Victor bent his knees as he had learned to do, and held his breath.

The white bulb flashed. The tap came—sharp, assured, solid. Fontine whipped his hands into reverse grips on the latch handles, leaned back, and propelled himself through the open hatch into the furious slipstream of the aircraft. He was buffeted away from the huge fuselage, the force of the wind crashing into his body with the sudden velocity and weight of a giant wave.

He was in free fall. He forced his legs into a V, feeling the harness of his chute cutting into his thighs. He thrust his arms forward and diagonally out at his side. The spread-eagle configuration did what it was supposed to do: It stabilized his fall through the sky, just enough for Victor to concentrate on the dark earth below.

He saw them! Two tiny flares to his left.

He pulled his right hand in against the rushing air and tugged at a small ring beside the parachute release. There was a momentary flash above him, like an instantly fading spit of a Roman candle. It would be enough for those on the ground to get a sighting. The moment fell back into darkness; he yanked the rubber handle of the parachute release. The billowing folds of cloth shot out of the pack; the massive jolt came, causing him to expunge his breath, his every muscle taut in counterthrust.

He floated, swinging in quarter circles in the night sky, toward the earth.

The conferences in Montbéliard went well. It was strange, thought Victor, but in spite of the crude, even primitive surroundings—an abandoned warehouse, a barn, a rock-strewn pasture—the conferences were not unlike smoothly run management meetings, with himself acting as a visiting consultant from the home office. The objective of each conference with the teams of underground leaders who made their covert treks into Lorraine was the same: projected recruitment for the pool of skilled personnel now in exile in England.

Management personnel were in demand everywhere, for everywhere within the Third Reich's expanding sphere production facilities were instantly appropriated and geared for maximum output. But there was a major flaw in the German obsession for immediate efficiency: Control remained in Berlin. Requests were processed by the *Reichsministerium* of Industry and Armaments; orders were cleared and issued hundreds of miles away from the place of origin.

Orders could be intercepted enroute; requests could be altered at the source, within the ministries; infiltrated at the clerical level.

Positions could be created; personnel could be replaced. In the chaos that was the Berlin fever for instant, total efficiency, fear was inherent. Orders were rarely questioned.

Everywhere the bureaucratic environment was ripe for Loch Torridon.

"You will be taken to the Rhine and put aboard a river barge at Neuf-Brisach," said the Frenchman, going to the small window in the rooming house overlooking Montbéliard's rue de Bac. "Your escort will bring the papers. I understand they describe you as river garbage, strong back and small head. A loading stevedore who spends most of his waking hours drunk with very cheap wine."

"That should be interesting."

THE RHINE

It wasn't. It was grueling, physically exhausting, and made almost intolerable by the stench below decks. German patrols prowled the river, stopping vessels continuously, subjecting crews to brutal interrogations. The Rhine was an underground courier route; it took no great perception to know that. And because the river "garbage" deserved no better, the patrols took delight in wielding clubs and rifle stocks when bones and flesh were the objects of impact. Fontine's cover was successful, if revolting. He drank enough rancid wine and induced sufficient vomit to give his breath the putrid foulness of a confirmed, unkempt alcoholic.

What kept him from losing his sensibilities altogether was his escort. The man's name was Lübok, and Victor knew that whatever risks he was taking, Lübok's were far greater.

Lübok was a Jew and a homosexual. He was a blond-haired, blue-eyed, middle-aged ballet master whose Czechoslovakian parents had emigrated to Berlin thirty years ago. Fluent in the Slovak languages, as well as German, he held papers identifying him as a translator for the Wehrmacht. Along with the papers were several letters on High Command stationery that proclaimed Lübok's loyalty to the Reich.

The papers and the letterheads were genuine, the loyalty false. Lübok operated as an underground courier across the Czechoslovakian and Polish borders. At such times he wore his homosexual inclinations outrageously on his sleeve; it was common knowledge that such circles existed in the Officer *Korps*. Checkpoints never knew who was favored by powerful men who preferred to bed with other men. And the middle-aged ballet master was an encyclopedia of truths, half-truths and gossip as they pertained to the sexual practices and aberrations practiced by the German High Command in any given sector or zone he entered. It was his inventory; it was his weapon.

Lübok had volunteered for the Loch Torridon assignment, to be the MI6 escort out of Montbéliard, through Wiesbaden, east to Prague and north to Warsaw. And as the journey progressed and the days and the miles went by, Fontine was grateful. Lübok was the best. Beneath the well-tailored suits was a powerful man whose acid tongue and withering stare guaranteed a hot but intelligent temper.

WARSAW, POLAND

Lübok drove the motorcycle with Victor in the sidecar, dressed in the uniform of a Wehrmacht *Oberst* attached to Occupation Transport. They sped out of Lódz on the road to Warsaw, reaching the final checkpoint a little before midnight.

Lübok performed outrageously before the patrols, dropping the names of *Kommandanten* and *Oberführerin* in acid rapidity, implying all manner of recriminations if their vehicle was detained. The embarrassed guards were not anxious to test him. The bike was waved through; they entered the city.

It was chaos. Although it was dark, rubble could be discerned everywhere. Street after street was deserted. Candles shone in windows—most electricity was out. Wires sagged, automobiles and trucks were immobilized—scores overturned, lying like giant steel insects waiting to be impaled on a laboratory table.

Warsaw was dead. Its armed killers walked in groups, themselves afraid of the corpse.

"We head for the Casimir," said Lübok softly. "The underground's waiting for you. It's no more than ten streets from here."

"What's the Casimir?"

"An old palace on the Kraków Boulevard. In the middle of the city. For years it was the university; now the Germans use it for barracks and offices."

"We go in *there?*"

Lübok smiled in the darkness. "You can put Nazis in universities, but it guarantees no instruction. The maintenance crews for all the buildings and the grounds are *podziemna.* Underground, to you. At least the beginnings of one."

Lübok squeezed the motorcycle between two staff cars on the Kraków Boulevard, halfway down the block, across from the main gate to the Casimir. Except for the guards at the gatehouse, the street was deserted. Only two streetlamps were working, but within the Casimir's grounds floodlights shot up from the grass, lighting the ornate facades of the buildings.

Out of the shadows walked a German soldier, an enlisted man. He approached Lübok and spoke quietly in Polish. Lübok nodded; the German continued diagonally across the wide boulevard up toward the Casimir gate.

"He's with the *podziemna,*" said Lübok. "He used the correct codes. He said you should go in first. Ask for Captain Hans Neumann, Block Seven."

"Captain Hans Neumann," repeated Victor. "Block Seven. What then?"

"He's tonight's contact in the Casimir. He'll take you to the others."

"What about you?"

"I'm to wait ten minutes and follow. I'm to ask for an Oberst Schneider, Block Five."

Lübok seemed concerned. Victor understood. Never before had they been separated at their point of contact with the underground leaders. "This is an unusual procedure, isn't it? You look troubled."

"They must have their reasons."

"But you don't know what they are. And that fellow didn't tell you."

"He wouldn't know. He's a messenger."

"Do you sense a trap?"

Lübok leveled his gaze at Fontine. He was thinking as he spoke. "No, that's not really possible. The commandant of this sector has been compromised. On film. I won't bore you with details, but his proclivity for children has been duly recorded. He's been shown the results and told negatives exist. He lives in fear, and we live with *him*. . . . He's a Berlin favorite, a close friend of Göring's. No, it's not a trap."

"But you're worried."

"Needlessly. He *had* the codes; they're complicated and very precise. I'll see you later."

Victor got out of the cramped sidecar and started across the boulevard toward the gates of the Casimir. He stood erect, the picture of arrogance, prepared to arrogantly display false papers that would gain him admittance.

As he walked across the Casimir's floodlit grounds, he could see German soldiers strolling in pairs and threes down the paths. A year ago these men might have been students and professors, recapping the events of the academic day. Now they were conquerors, peacefully removed from the devastation that was everywhere outside the walls of the Casimir. Death, hunger, and mutilation were within the sound of their commands, yet they talked quietly on clean paths, oblivious to the consequences of their acts.

Campo di Fiori. There were floodlights at Campo di Fiori. And death with mutilation.

He forced the images out of his mind; he could not allow his concentration to be weakened. The entranceway with the filigreed arch framing the thick double doors below the number seven was directly ahead. A Wehrmacht guard stood at attention on the single marble step.

Fontine recognized him: the soldier who had whispered in Polish to Lübok on the Kraków Boulevard.

"You're efficient," said Victor softly in German.

The guard nodded, reached for the door and opened it. "Be quickly now. Do use the staircase to the left. You will be met on the first landing."

Fontine walked rapidly through the door into the huge marble hall, crossed to the stairs, and started up. Halfway to the landing he slowed his pace. A silent alarm went off in his brain.

The guard's voice, his use of German. The words were odd, strangely awkward. *Be quickly. . . . Do use the staircase. . . .*

Watch for the lack of idiom, the excessively grammatical, or conversely, unmatching end syllables. Loch Torridon.

The guard was not German. Yet why should he be? He was from the *podziemna.* Yet, again, the *podziemna* would not take chances. . . .

Two German officers appeared on the landing, their pistols drawn and leveled down at him. The man on the right spoke.

"Welcome to the Casimir, Signor Fontini-Cristi."

"Please don't stop, *padrone.* We must hurry," said the second man.

The language they spoke was Italian, but their speech was not native. Victor recognized the source. The officers above him were no more German than the guard was German. They were *Greek.* The train from Salonika had reappeared!

There was the crack of a pistol bolt behind him, followed by rapid footsteps. Within seconds, the barrel was jammed into the small of his back, propelling him farther up the staircase.

There was no way he could move, no diversion he could employ, to distract his confronters. Weapons covered him, eyes watched his hands, bullets were locked in chambers.

Above, somewhere in an unfamiliar corridor, he heard laughter. Perhaps if he shouted, raising alarms of an enemy within the enemy camp; the concentric circle of thought was numbing.

"Who are you?" *Words*. Begin with words. If he could raise his voice in sequence, natural sequence that would minimize the chance of triggers pulled. "You're not German!"

Louder. *Now* louder.

"What are you *doing* here?"

The barrel of the pistol slid up his back and was jabbed into the base of his skull. The jolt caused him to stop. A closed fist punched him in the left kidney; he lurched forward, caught by the silent, staring Greeks in front of him.

He started to shout; there was no other way. The laughter above was growing louder, nearer. Other men were descending the staircase.

"I warn you——"

Suddenly, both his hands were yanked back, his arms bent and locked, the wrists turned inward. A large, coarse cloth was shoved into his face, saturated with acrid, foul-smelling liquid.

He was blinded; a breathless vacuum was being imposed on him, without light, without air. His tunic was ripped away, the cross strap pulled up from his chest. He tried to lash out his arms.

As he did so, he could feel the long needle entering his flesh; he was not sure where. Instinctively, he raised his hands in protest. They were *free*; and they were useless as his resistance was useless.

He heard the laughter again; it was deafening. He was aware of being propelled forward, and downward.

But that was all.

"You betray those who saved your life."

He opened his eyes; images came into focus slowly. There was a burning sensation in his left arm, or shoulder. He reached for it; the touch was painful.

"You feel the antidote," said the voice of the blurred figure somewhere in front of him. "It raises a welt, but it isn't harmful."

Fontine's eyes began to clear. He was sitting on a cement floor, his back against a wall of stone. Across from him, perhaps twenty feet away, a man stood in front of an opposite wall. They were on some kind of raised platform in a large tunnel. The tunnel appeared to be deep underground, carved out of rock, both ends disappearing into darkness.

On the floor of the tunnel were old, narrow tracks; they were cracked, rusted. Light came from several thick candles inserted in ancient brackets on the walls.

His focus refined, Fontine concentrated on the man across from him. He wore a black suit; around his neck was a white collar. The man was a priest.

He was bald, but not from age. The head was shaved; the man was no more than forty-five or fifty, the face ascetic, the body slender.

Beside the priest was the guard in the Wehrmacht uniform. The two Greeks impersonating German officers stood by an iron door in the left wall facing the tunnel. The priest spoke.

"We've followed you since Montbéliard. You're a thousand miles from London. The English can't protect you. We have routes south they know nothing about."

"The English?" Fontine stared at the priest trying to understand. "You're from the Order of Xenope."

"We are."

"Why do you fight the English?"

"Because Brevourt's a liar. He breaks his word."

"Brevourt?" Victor was stunned; nothing made sense. "You're out of your mind! Everything, *everything* he's done in *your name!* For *you.*"

"Not for us! For England. He wants the vault of Constantine for *England!* Churchill demands it! It's a more powerful weapon than a hundred armies, and they all know it! We would never see it again!" The priest's eyes were wide, furious.

"You believe that?"

"Don't be an ass!" spat the monk from Xenope. "As Brevourt breaks his word, we broke Code *Maginot.* Messages were intercepted; communications between . . . shall we say, interested parties."

"You're *crazy!*" Fontine tried to think. Anthony Brevourt had faded away; there'd been no word from him—or about him—in months. "You say you've followed me since Montbéliard. *Why?* I don't have what you want! I never did have it! I know nothing about that goddamned train!"

"Mikhailovic believed you," said the priest softly. "I don't."

"Petride——" The sight of the child monk taking his

own life on the rocky ledge in Loch Torridon came back to Victor.

"Petride was not his name——"

"You killed him!" said Fontine. "You killed him as surely as if you'd pulled the trigger yourself. You're insane! All of you."

"He failed. He knew what was expected. It was understood."

"You're *sick!* You infect everyone you touch! You can believe me or not, but I'm telling you for the last time! I don't have the information you want!"

"Liar!"

"You're mad!"

"Then why do you travel with Lübok? Tell me that, Signor Fontini-Cristi! Why Lübok?"

Victor recoiled; the shock of Lübok's name caused him to arch his back against the stone. "Lübok?" he whispered incredulously. "If you know his work, you know the answer to that."

"Loch Torridon?" asked the priest sarcastically.

"I never heard of Lübok before in my life. I only know he does his job. He's a Jew, a . . . he takes great risks."

"He works *for Rome!*" roared the priest of Xenope. "He conveys offers to Rome! *Your* offers!"

Victor was silent; his astonishment was so complete he had no words. The monk of Xenope continued, his voice low, penetrating. "Strange, isn't it? Of all the escorts in the occupied territories, Lübok is chosen. He just shows up in Montbéliard. Do you expect us to believe that?"

"Believe what you will. This is madness."

"It is *betrayal!*" the priest shouted again, taking several steps away from the wall. "A degenerate who can pick up a telephone and blackmail half of Berlin! And most outrageous—for you—a dog who works for the monster of——"

"*Fontine! Dive!*" The piercing command came from the black hole of the tunnel. It was screamed in Lübok's high-pitched voice, the sound bouncing off the receding walls of rock, overriding the shouts of the priest.

Victor reeled and sprang forward, rolling down the stone wall, crashing from the platform to the hard ground by the old rusted track. Above him he heard the spits of bullets shattering the air, followed by two thunderous explosions of unsilenced Lugers.

In the flickering light he could see the figures of Lübok and several others lurch out of the darkness, angling their weapons, taking rapid, accurate aim; firing and spinning back into the protection of the rock.

It was over in seconds. The priest of Xenope had fallen; he was hit in the neck, his left ear blown off his head. He had crawled to the ledge of the platform, dying, staring down at Fontine. In imminent death his whispered voice was a rasp.

"We . . . are not your enemies. For the mercy of God, bring the documents to us——"

A final, muted spit was heard; the priest's forehead exploded above his staring eyes.

Victor felt a grip on his left arm; it caused shooting pains throughout his shoulder and chest. He was being yanked to his feet.

"Get up!" was Lübok's command. "The shots may have been heard. Run!"

They raced into the tunnel. The beam of a flashlight pierced the black, held by one of Lübok's men up ahead. The man whispered his instructions in Polish. Lübok translated for Fontine, who ran beside him.

"About two hundred yards down there's a monks' cave. We'll be safe."

"A *what?*"

"Monks' cave," answered Lübok, breathing heavily. "The history of the Casimir goes back centuries. Escapes were needed."

They crawled on their hands and knees through a narrow, dark passageway cut out of rock. It led to the depths of a cave. The air was instantly different; there was an opening somewhere beyond in the darkness.

"I have to talk to you," said Victor quickly.

"To answer your questions, Captain Hans Neumann is a devoted officer of the Reich with a cousin in the Gestapo. Oberst Schneider wasn't on the roster; that was sticky. We knew it was a trap. . . . In all honesty we didn't expect to find you in the tunnel. That was a stroke of luck. We were on our way to Block Seven." Lübok turned to his comrades. He spoke first in Polish, then translated for Fontine. "We'll stay here for a quarter of an hour. That should be time enough. Then we'll proceed to the rendezvous in Seven. You'll conduct your business on schedule."

Fontine grabbed Lübok's arm and led him away from the *podziemna* men. Two of the men had turned on their flashlights. There was enough light to see the middle-aged courier's face, and Victor was grateful for that.

"It wasn't a German trap! Those men back there were Greek! One was a priest!" Fontine whispered, but there was no mistaking his intensity.

"You're mad," said Lübok casually, his eyes a perfect blank.

"They were from *Xenope.*"

"From what?"

"You heard me."

"I heard you, but I haven't the faintest idea what you're talking about."

"Goddamn you, Lübok! Who are you?"

"Many things to many people, thank heavens."

Victor grabbed the blond-haired Czech by the lapels of his jacket. Lübok's eyes became suddenly distant, filled with cold anger. "They said you worked for Rome. That you would convey offers to Rome! *What* offers? What does it mean?"

"I don't know," replied the Czech slowly.

"Who do you work for?"

"I work for many people. *Against* the Nazis. That's all you have to know. I keep you alive and see that you complete your negotiations. How I do it is none of your business."

"You know *nothing* about Salonika?"

"It is a city in Greece, on the Aegean Sea . . . . Now, take your hands off me."

Fontine relayed his grip but still held on. "Just in case—in *case*—the many people you speak of include men interested in that train from Salonika. I know *nothing*. I never did."

"If the subject ever comes up, and I can't imagine why, I'll convey the information. Now may we concentrate on your negotiations in Warsaw? We must complete them tonight. In the morning arrangements have been made for two couriers to fly out on the Berlin military shuttle. I'll check the airfield myself before daybreak. We'll get off at Müllheim. It's near the Franco-Swiss border, a night's trip to Montbéliard. Your business in Europe is finished."

"*Fly* out?" Victor removed his hands. "On a German plane?"

"Courtesy of a very distraught Warsaw commandant. He's seen too many motion pictures in which he was a prominent player. Sheer pornography."

11

AIR CORRIDOR, MUNICH WEST

The trimotored Fokker was stationary as maintenance crews checked the engines and a fuel truck filled the tanks. They were in Munich; they had left Warsaw early in the morning with a stop at Prague. Most of the passengers had gotten off at Munich.

Müllheim was next, the last leg of their journey. Victor sat uncomfortably beside a seemingly relazed Lübok in the quiet cabin of the aircraft. There was one other passenger: an aging corporal on leave to Stuttgart.

"I'd like it better if there were a few more hitchhikers," whispered Lübok. "With so small a number, the pilot may insist everyone stay on board at Müllheim. He could gas up quickly and be on his way. He takes on most of his passengers in Stuttgart."

He was interrupted by the sound of clattering footsteps on the metal stairs outside the aircraft. Raucous, uninhibited laughter accompanied the unsteady clattering and grew louder as the new passengers approached the cabin door. Lübok looked at Fontine and smiled in relief. He returned to the newspaper provided by the attendant and sank back in the seat. Victor turned; the Munich contingent came into view.

There were three Wehrmacht officers and a woman. They were drunk. The girl was in a light-covered cloth coat; she was pushed through the narrow door by two of the Wehrmacht and shoved into a seat by the third. She did not object; instead she laughed and made funny faces. A willing, participating toy.

She was in her late twenties, pleasant-looking but not attractive. There was a frantic quality in her face, an intensity that made her appear somehow frayed. Her light-brown, windswept hair was a little too thick; it had not fallen free in the wind. The mascara about her eyes was too pronounced, the lipstick too red, the rouge too obvious.

"What are *you* looking at?" The question was shouted above the roar of the revving motors. The speaker was the third Wehrmacht officer, a broad-chested, muscular man in his thirties. He had walked past his two comrades and addressed Victor.

"I'm sorry," said Fontine, smiling weakly. "I didn't mean to be rude."

The officer squinted his eyes; he was a brawler, it was unmistakable. "We've got a *fancy* one. Listen to the lace-pants!"

"I meant no offense."

The officer turned to his comrades; one had pulled the not-unwilling girl over on his lap, the other was in the aisle. "The lace-pants meant no offense! Isn't that nice?"

The two fellow officers groaned derisively. The girl laughed; a little too hysterically, thought Victor. He turned front, hoping the Wehrmacht boor would go away.

Instead, a huge hand reached over the seat and grabbed him by the shoulder blade. "That's not good enough." The officer looked at Lübok. "You two move up front."

Lübok's eyes sought Victor's. The message was clear: Do as the man ordered.

"Certainly." Fontine and Lübok rose and walked swiftly up the aisle. Neither spoke. Fontine could hear the uncorking of bottles. The Wehrmacht party had begun.

The Fokker sped down the runway and left the ground. Lübok had taken the aisle seat, leaving him the window. He riveted his eyes on the sky, withdrawing into the cocoon of himself, hoping to produce a blankness that would make the journey to Müllheim pass more swiftly. It could not pass swiftly enough.

The blankness would not come. Instead, involuntarily, he thought of the Xenope priest in the underground tunnel of the Casimir.

You travel with Lübok. Lübok works for Rome.

Lübok.

We are not your enemies. For the mercy of God, bring the documents to us.

Salonika. It was never far away. The vault from Constantine was capable of violently dividing men who fought a common enemy.

He heard laughter from the rear of the cabin, then a whispered voice behind him.

"*No!* Don't turn around. *Please!*" It was the flight attendant, barely audible through the narrow space between the seats. "Don't get up. They're *Kommandos.* They just let off steam, so don't concern yourselves. Pretend there is nothing!"

"*Kommandos?*" whispered Lübok. "In Munich? They're stationed north, in the Baltic zones."

"Not these. These operate across the mountains in the Italian sectors. Execution teams. There are many——"

The words struck with the impact of silent thunderbolts. Victor inhaled; the muscles of his stomach hardened into a wall of stone.

. . . *execution teams.* . . .

He gripped the armrests of his seat and arched his back. Then, pressing his back into the seat, he stretched his neck and turned his eyes toward the rear of the cabin, over the metal rim of the headrest. He could not believe what he saw.

The wild-eyed girl was on the floor, her coat open; she was naked except for torn undergarments, her legs spread, her buttocks moving. A Wehrmacht officer, his trousers and shorts pulled down to his knees, lowered himself on her, his penis stabbing. Kneeling above the girl's head was a second Wehrmacht, his trousers removed, an erection protruding from the opening in his shorts. He held the girl by the hair and lanced his erection around the flesh of her face; she opened her mouth and accepted it, moaning and coughing. The third Wehrmacht was sitting, bent over on the armrest above the rape. He was breathing in gasps through parted lips, his left hand extended, rubbing the girl's naked breasts in a rhythm that matched the masturbating motions of his right hand.

"*Animali!*" Fontine lunged from the seat, ripping Lübok's fingers from his wrist, hurling himself forward. The Wehrmacht were stunned beyond movement, their shock total. The officer on the armrest gaped. Victor's open hand gripped his hair and crashed the man's head into the steel rim of the seat. The skull cracked; an eruption of blood sprayed the face of the Wehrmacht lying between the spread legs of the girl. The officer caught his knees in his trousers; he fell forward on top of the girl, his hands lashing out to grab support. He rolled on his back, crushing the girl in the narrow aisle. Fontine raised the heel of his right boot and propelled it into the soft throat of the Wehrmacht. The blow was pulverizing; the veins in the German's neck swelled into huge tubes of bluish-black under the skin. His eyes rolled up into his sockets, the eyeballs white gelatine, blank and horrible.

The screams of the girl beneath were now mingled with the cries of agony from the third officer, who had sprung forward, propelling himself off the Fokker's deck toward the rear bulkhead. The man's underwear was matted with blood.

Fontine lunged; the German rolled hysterically away. His bloody, trembling hand reached under his tunic; Victor knew what he was after: the four-inch *Kommando* knife, strapped next to his flesh beneath his armpit. The Wehrmacht whipped out the blade—short, razor sharp—and slashed it diagonally in front of him. Fontine rose from his crouch, prepared to leap.

Suddenly an arm was lashed around Victor's neck. He struck back with his elbows, but the grip was unbreakable.

His neck was yanked back and a long knife sped through the air and imbedded itself deep in the German's chest. The man was dead before his body slumped to the floor of the cabin.

Abruptly Fontine's neck was released. Lübok slapped him across the face, the blow powerful, stinging his flesh.

"*Enough!* Stop it! I won't die for *you!*"

Dazed, Victor looked around. The throats of the other two Wehrmacht had been cut. The girl had crawled away, vomiting and weeping between two seats. The flight attendant lay sprawled in the aisle—dead or unconscious, there was no way to tell.

And the old corporal who had stared at nothing—in fear—only minutes ago, stood by the pilot's cabin door, a pistol in his hand.

Suddenly the girl started screaming as she got to her feet. "They'll *kill* us! Oh, God! Why did you do it?"

Stunned, Fontine stared at the girl and spoke quietly with what breath he had left. "*You?* You can ask that?"

"Yes! Oh, my God!" She pulled her filthy coat around her as best she could. "They'll kill me. I don't want to die!"

"You don't want to live like *that*."

She returned his stare maniacally, her head trembling. "They took me from the camps," she whispered. "I understood. They gave me drugs when I needed them, wanted them." She pulled at her loose right sleeve; there were scores of needle marks from her wrist to her upper arm. "But I understood. And I lived!"

"Basta!" roared Victor stepping toward the girl, raising his hand. "Whether you live or die is immaterial to me. I didn't act for you!"

"Whatever you did is done, Captain," said Lübok quickly, touching his arm. "Snap out of it! You've had your confrontation, there can be no more. Understand?"

Fontine saw the strength in Lübok's eyes. Breathing heavily, Victor pointed in astonishment at the fortyish corporal who stood silently by the cabin door, his weapon drawn. "He's one of you, isn't he?"

"No," said Lübok. "He's a German with a conscience. He doesn't know who or what we are. At Müllheim he'll be unconscious, an innocent bystander who can tell them whatever he likes. I suspect it will be nothing. Stay with the girl."

Lübok took charge. He went back to the bodies of the Wehrmacht and removed identification papers and weapons. In the tunic of one, he found a hypodermic kit and six vials of narcotics. He gave them to the girl, who sat by the window next to Fontine. She accepted them gratefully and without so much as looking at Victor, she proceeded to break a capsule, fill the hypodermic, and insert the needle into her left arm.

She carefully repacked the kit and shoved it into the pocket of her bloodstained coat. She leaned back and breathed deeply.

"Feel better?" asked Fontine.

She turned and looked at him. Her eyes were calmer now, only contempt showing in them. "You understand,

Captain. I don't *feel*. There are no feelings. One just goes on living."

"What will you do?"

She took her eyes away from him and returned to the window. She answered him quietly, dreamily—out of contact. "Live, if I can. It's not up to me. It's up to you."

In the aisle the flight attendant stirred. He shook his head and got to his knees. Before he could focus, Lübok was in front of him, his gun at the attendant's head.

"If you want to stay alive, you'll do exactly as I say at Müllheim."

Obedience was in the soldier's eyes.

Fontine got up. "What about the girl?" he whispered.

"What about her?" countered Lübok.

"I'd like to bring her out with us."

The Czech ran an exasperated hand through his hair. "Oh, Christ! Well, it's that or killing her. She'd identify me for a drop of morphine." He looked down at the girl. "Get her to clean up. There's a raincoat in the back. She can put it on."

"Thanks," said Victor.

"Don't," replied Lübok. "I'd kill her in a second if I thought it was a better solution. But she could be valuable; she's been with a *Kommando* unit where we didn't know one existed."

The Resistance fighters met the automobile on a back road of Lörrach, near the Franco-Swiss border. Victor was given clean but ragged clothes to replace the German uniform. They crossed the Rhine at nightfall. The girl was taken west to a Resistance camp in the hills; she was too drugged, too erratic to make the trip south to Montbéliard.

The flight attendant was simply taken away. Fontine kept his own counsel. There'd been another corporal from another army on a pier in Celle Ligure.

"I leave you now," said Lübok, crossing to him on the riverbank. The Czech's hand was extended.

Fontine was surprised. The plan had been for Lübok to go with him to Montbéliard; London might have new instructions for him. He took Lübok's hand, protesting.

"Why? I thought——"

"I know. But things change. There are problems in Wiesbaden."

Victor held the Czech's right hand with his own, covering it with his left. "It's difficult to know what to say. I owe you my life."

"Whatever I did, you would have done the same. I never doubted that."

"You're generous as well as brave."

"That Greek priest said I was a degenerate who could blackmail half of Berlin."

"Could you?"

"Probably," answered Lübok quickly, looking over at a Frenchman who was beckoning him to the boat. He acknowledged with a nod of his head. He turned back to Victor. "Listen to me," he said softly, removing his hand. "That priest told you something else. That I worked for Rome. You said you didn't know what that meant."

"I don't, specifically. But I'm not blind; it has to do with the train from Salonika."

"It has *everything* to do with it."

"You do work for Rome, then? For the church?"

"The church is not your enemy. Believe that."

"The Order of Xenope claims *it* is not my enemy. Yet certainly I have one. But you don't answer my question. Do you work for Rome?"

"Yes. But not in the way you think."

"Lübok!" Fontine grabbed the middle-aged Czech by the shoulders. "I *have* no thoughts! I don't *know!* Can't you understand that?"

Lübok stared at Victor; in the dim night light his eyes were searching. "I believe you. I gave you a dozen opportunities; you seized none of them."

"Opportunities? *What* opportunities?"

The Frenchman by the boat called again, this time harshly. "You! Peacock! Let's get out of here."

"Right away," replied Lübok, his eyes still on Fontine. "For the last time. There are men—on both sides—who think this war is insignificant compared to the information they believe you have. In some ways I agree with them. But you don't have it, you never did. And this war must be fought. And won. In fact, your father was wiser than all of them."

"Savarone? What do you——?"

"I go now." Lübok raised his hands, with strength but no hostility, and removed Victor's arms. "For these reasons, I did what I did. You'll know soon enough. That priest in the Casimir was right: there are monsters. He was one of them. There are others. But don't blame churches; they are innocent. They harbor the fanatics, but they're innocent."

"Peacock! No more delay!"

"Coming!" said Lübok in a shouted whisper. "Good-bye, Fontine. If for one minute I thought you were not what you say you are, I would have wracked you myself for the information. Or killed you. But you are what you are, caught in the middle. They'll leave you alone now. For a while."

The Czech touched Victor's face briefly, gently, and ran down to the boat.

The blue lights flashed above the Montbéliard field at precisely five minutes past midnight. Instantly two rows of small flares were ignited; the runway was marked, the plane circled and made its approach.

Fontine ran across the field carrying his briefcase. By the time he reached the side of the rolling plane, the hatch was open; two men were standing in the frame, gripping the sides, their arms extended. Victor heaved the briefcase inside and reached up, making contact with the arm on his right. He ran faster, jumped, and was pulled in through the opening; he lay face down on the deck. The hatch was slammed shut, a command shouted out to the pilot, and the engines roared. The plane sprang forward, the tail of the fuselage rising in seconds, and seconds later they were airborne.

Fontine raised his head and crawled to the ribbed wall outside the hatch. He pulled the briefcase to his side and breathed deeply, letting his head fall back against the metal.

"Oh, my God!" came the words spoken in shock out of the darkness. "It's *you!*"

Victor snapped his head to the left, in the direction of the indistinguishable figure who spoke with such alarm in his voice. The first shafts of moonlight came from the windows of the open pilot area. Fontine's eyes were drawn to the right hand of the speaker. It was encased in a black glove.

"Stone? What are you doing here?"

But Geoffrey Stone was incapable of answering. The

moonlight grew brighter, illuminating the hollow shell that was the aircraft's fuselage. Stone's eyes were wide, his lips parted, immobile.

"Stone? It *is* you?"

"Oh, Jesus! We've been tricked. They've done it!"

"What are you talking about?"

The English continued in a monotone. "You were reported killed. Captured and executed in the Casimir. We were told that only one man escaped. With your papers——"

"Who?"

"The courier, Lübok."

Victor got to his feet unsteadily, holding on to a metal brace that protruded from the wall of the vibrating aircraft. The geometric pieces were coming together. "Where did you get this information?"

"It was relayed to us this morning."

"By whom? Who picked it up? Who relayed it?"

"The Greek embassy," replied Stone barely above a whisper.

Fontine sank back down to the deck of the plane. Lübok had said the words.

I gave you a dozen opportunities; you seized none. There are men who think this war is insignificant. . . . For these reasons I did what I did. You'll know soon enough. . . . They'll leave you alone now. For a while.

Lübok had made his move. He had checked an airfield in Warsaw before daybreak and sent a false message to London.

It did not take a great deal of imagination to know what that message accomplished.

"We're immobilized. We've exposed ourselves and been taken out. We all watch each other now, but no one can make a move, or admit what we're looking for. No one can afford that." Brevourt spoke as he stood by the leaded window overlooking the courtyard in Alien Operations. "Checkmate."

Across the room, standing by the long conference table, was a furious Alec Teague. They were alone.

"I don't give a *damn*. What concerns me is your blatant manipulation of Military Intelligence! You've placed an entire network in jeopardy. Loch Torridon may well have been crippled!"

"Create another strategy," said Brevourt absently, looking out the window. "It's your job, isn't it?"

"Damn you!"

"For God's sake, Teague, *stop* it!" Brevourt reeled from the window. "Do you for one minute think I was the final authority?"

"I think you compromised that authority! I should have been consulted!"

Brevourt started to reply, then stopped. He nodded his head as he walked slowly across the room to the table opposite Teague. "You may be right, general. Tell me, you're the expert. What was our mistake?"

"Lübok," said the brigadier coldly. "He faded you. He took your money and turned to Rome, then made up his own mind. He was the wrong man."

"He was your man. From your files."

"Not for that job. You interfered."

"He can go anywhere in Europe," continued Brevourt almost plaintively, as if Teague had not interrupted. "He's untouchable. If Fontini-Cristi broke away, Lübok could have followed him anywhere. Even into Switzerland."

"You expected that, didn't you?"

"Frankly, yes. You're too good a salesman, general. I believed you. I thought Loch Torridon *was* Fontini-Cristi's brainchild. How logical it all seemed. The Italian goes back under perfect cover to make his own arrangements." Brevourt sat down wearily, clasping his hands in front of him on the table.

"Didn't it occur to you that if such was the case, he would have come to us? To you?"

"No. We couldn't return his lands or his factories."

"You don't know him," concluded Teague with finality. "You never took the trouble. That was your first mistake."

"Yes, I expect it was. I've lived most of my life with liars. The corridors of mendacity. The simple truth is elusive." Brevourt suddenly looked up at the Intelligence man. His face was pathetic, his pallid skin taut, the hollows of his eyes proof of exhaustion. "You didn't believe it, did you? You didn't believe he was dead."

"No."

"I couldn't take the chance, you see. I accepted what you said, that the Germans wouldn't execute him, that they'd put a trace on him, find out who he was, use him.

But the report said otherwise. So, if he *was* dead, it meant the fanatics in Rome or Xenope had killed him. They wouldn't do that unless—*unless*—they'd learned his secret."

"And if they had, the vault would be theirs. Not yours. Not England's. It was never yours to begin with."

The ambassador looked away from Teague and sank back in the chair, closing his eyes. "Nor could it be allowed to fall into the hands of maniacs. Not now. We know who the maniac is in Rome. The Vatican will watch Donatti now. The Patriarchate will suspend activities; we've been given assurance."

"Which was Lübok's objective, of course."

Brevourt opened his eyes. "Was it really?"

"In my judgment, yes. Lübok's a Jew."

Brevourt turned his head and stared at Teague. "There'll be no more interference, general. Get on with your war. Mine is at a standoff."

Anton Lübok crossed Prague's Wenceslaus Square and walked up the steps of the bombed-out cathedral. Inside, the late afternoon sun streaked through the huge gaps of stone where *Luftwaffe* bombs had exploded. Whole sections of the left wall were destroyed; primitive scaffolds had been erected everywhere for support.

He stood in the far right aisle and checked his watch. It was time.

An old priest came out of the curtained apse and crossed in front of the confessional booths. He paused briefly at the fourth. It was Lübok's signal.

He walked down the aisle cautiously, his attention on the dozen or so worshipers in the church. None was watching him. He parted the curtains and walked inside the confessional. He knelt before the tiny Bohemian crucifix, the flickering light of the prayer candle throwing shadows on the draped walls.

"Forgive me, Father, for I have sinned," Lübok began softly. "I have sinned in excess. I have debased the body and blood of Christ."

"One cannot debase the Son of God," came the proper reply from behind the drapes. "One can only debase oneself."

"But we are in the image of God. As was Himself."

"A poor and imperfect image," was the correct response.

Lübok exhaled slowly, the exercise was completed. "You are Rome?"

"I am the conduit," said the voice in quiet arrogance.

"I didn't think you were the city, you damn fool."

"This is the house of God. Watch your tongue."

"And you revile this house," whispered Lübok. "All who work for Donatti revile it!"

"*Silence*. We are the way of Christ!"

"You're *dirt!* Your Christ would spit on you."

The breathing beyond the drapes was filled with controlled loathing. "I shall pray for your soul," came the forced words. "What of Fontini-Cristi?"

"He had no other purpose but Loch Torridon. Your projections were wrong."

"That won't do!" The priest's whisper was strident. "He had to have other objectives! We're positive!"

"He never left my side from the moment we met in Montbéliard. There were no additional contacts other than those we knew about."

"*No!* We don't believe that!"

"In a matter of days it won't make any difference what you believe. You're finished. All of you. Good men will see to it."

"What have you done, *Jew?*" The voice behind the drapes was low now, the loathing absolute.

"What had to be done, priest." Lübok rose to his feet and put his left hand into his pocket. With his right he suddenly ripped the drapes in front of him.

The priest was revealed. He was huge, the black robes giving him the appearance of immensity. His face was the face of a man who hated deeply; the eyes were the eyes of a predator.

Lübok withdrew an envelope from his pocket and dropped it on the prayer stall in front of the stunned priest. "Here's your money. Give it back to Donatti. I wanted to see what you looked like."

The priest answered quietly. "You'd better know the rest. My name is Gaetamo. Enrici Gaetamo. And I'll come back for you."

"I doubt it," replied Lübok.

"Don't," said Enrici Gaetamo.

Lübok stood for a moment looking down at the priest. When their eyes were locked, the blond-haired Czech wet the fingers of his right hand and reached for the prayer candle, extinguishing its flame. All was darkness. He parted the drapes and walked out of the confessional.

PART FOUR

12

The cottage was on the grounds of a large estate west of Aylesbury in Oxfordshire. Tall metal poles strung with electrified barbed wire surrounded the area. Killer dogs guarded the enormous compound.

There was only one entrance, a gate at the base of a long, straight driveway flanked by open lawns. At the main house, a quarter of a mile from the gate, the drive split off right and left, then split again with several smaller roads leading to the various cottages.

There were fourteen cottages in all, houses built in and around the woods of the estate. The residents were men and women who needed the security: defectors and their families, double agents, couriers who'd been exposed—targets who'd been marked for an assassin's bullet.

Jane's cottage became their home and Victor was grateful for its remoteness. For nightly the *Luftwaffe* streaked through the skies, the fires of London grew, the battle for Britain had begun.

And so had Loch Torridon.

For weeks at a time, Victor was away from their miniature house in Oxfordshire, away from Jane, his mind at rest because she was safe. Teague moved the Loch Torridon headquarters into the cellars of MI6. Day and night had no essential meaning. Men worked around the clock with files and shortwave radios, and with complicated equipment that reproduced perfectly the documents required in the occupied lands: work papers, travel permits, clearances from the *Reichsministerium* of Armaments and Industry. Other men were called into the cellars and given their instructions by Captains Fontine and Stone. And they were sent to Lakenheath and beyond.

As was Victor on a growing number of occasions. At such times, he knew Alec Teague was right: *Your wife's safety is directly related to your state of mind. You have a job to do; I'll do mine.*

Jane could not be touched by the maniacs of Rome or Xenope. It was all that mattered. The freight from Salonika became a strange, painful memory. And the war went on.

AUGUST 24, 1940
ANTWERP, BELGIUM

(Intercepted dispatch—duplicate—Commandant: Occupation Forces, Antwerp, to Reichsminister Speer, Armaments.)

The railroad yards at Antwerp are chaos! Supply trains crossing Schelde River are overloaded through carelessness in shipping orders, causing cracks throughout bridge structure. Schedules and signaling codes altered without proper notice. From offices managed by *German personnel!* Reprisals ludicrous. No alien responsibility. Trains meet one another from opposing directions on the same tracks! Freights pull up for loading at sidings and depots where there are no trucks! No shipments! The situation is intolerable and I must insist that the *Reichsministerium* coordinate more thoroughly. . . .

SEPTEMBER 19, 1940
VERDUN-SUR-MEUSE, FRANCE

(Excerpts from letter received by the second command legal office of *Gesetzbuch Besitzergreifung*—from a Colonel Grepschedit, Verdun-Meuse.)

. . . It was agreed that we prepare specific rules of occupation to adjudicate disputes between ourselves and the conquered who laid down their arms. The regulations were circulated. We now find additional regulations—circulated by *your* offices—that contradict whole sections of the previous codes. We are in constant debate with even those who *welcome* us! Entire days are taken up with occupation hearings. Our own officers are faced with conflicting orders from your couriers—all under proper signatures and validated by your seals. We are at a boiling point over inconsequentials. We are going out of our minds. . . .

MARCH 20, 1941
BERLIN, GERMANY

(Extracted minutes of the meeting between accounts stabilizers of the *Finanzministerium* and the officials of *Reichsordnung.* File removed—duplicate.)

. . . The substance of Ordnance's unending difficulties are to be found with the *Finanzministerium*'s consistent errors in funds allocations. Accounts go unsettled for months, payrolls are miscalculated, monies are transferred to wrong dispersal depots—often to wrong geographical sectors! Whole battalions have gone without pay because the funds were somewhere in Yugoslavia when they should have been in Amsterdam! . . .

JUNE 23, 1941
BREST-LITOVSK, RUSSIAN FRONT

(Courier dispatch from General Guderian to his commander, General Bock, Hdqtrs: Pripet, Poland. Intercept: Bialystok. Not delivered.)

. . . In two days of the offensive we are within forty-eight hours of Minsk. The Dnieper will be crossed in a matter of weeks, the Don and Moscow not far beyond! The speed of our assault requires instant communications—in the main—radio communications, but there are increasing difficulties with our radio equipment. Specifically in what the engineers tell me is frequency calibration. More than half our divisional equipment is set in differing graduations. Unless extreme caution is taken, communications are sent out on unintended frequencies, often *enemy* frequencies. It is a factory problem. Our concern is that it is impossible to determine which equipment has malfunctioning calibrations. I, myself, initiated a communication to Kleist on Rundstedt's south flank and reached our forces in eastern Lithuania. . . .

FEBRUARY 2, 1942
BERLIN, GERMANY

(Removed from correspondence file of Manfried Probst, Official, *Reichsindustrie* from Hiru Kayanaka, attaché, Japanese Embassy, Berlin.)

Dear Reichsoffiziell Probst:

Since we are now comrades in battle as well as spirit we must attempt to strive further for the perfection expected of us by our leaders.

To the subject at hand, my dear *Reichsoffiziell.* As you know, our respective governments have entered into joint radar development experiments.

We flew—at great risk—our foremost electronic scientists to Berlin to enter conferences with your people. That was six weeks ago and to date there have been no conferences whatsoever. I am now informed that our foremost scientists were flown to Greifswald on the Baltic Sea by error. They are not concerned with the rocket experiments, but with radar, my dear *Reichsoffiziell.* Unfortunately, none speak your language and the interpreters you assigned are less than fluent in ours.

Word reached my desk an hour ago that our foremost scientists are now on their way to Würzburg, where there are radio transmitters. My dear *Reichsoffiziell,* we do not know where Würzburg is. And our foremost scientists are not concerned with radio transmitters, but with *radar!*

Can you please locate our foremost scientists? When are the radar conferences? Our foremost scientists are traveling all over Germany for what purpose? . . .

MAY 25, 1942
ST. VALÉRY-EN-CAUX, FRANCE

(Report filed by Captain Victor Fontine, who was dropped behind lines in the Héricourt district. Returned by trawler, Isle of Wight.)

. . . The armaments shipments along the coastal regions are primarily offensive in nature, with little thought at this point given to defensive weapons. The shipments are routed from Essen, through Düsseldorf, across the border to Roubaix and then to the French coast. The key is fuel. We have placed our people in the petrol depots. They are receiving continuous "instructions" from the *Reichsministerium* of Industry to divert shipments of fuel immediately out of Brussels to Rotterdam, where rails will begin the journey to the Russian front. At last report, there were fourteen miles of standard armaments vehicles choking the roads between Louvain and Brussels, their tanks empty. And, of course, no reprisals. We estimate that the ploy will be operable for another four days, at which point Berlin will be forced to move in and our people will move out. Coordinate air strikes at this time. . . .

(Note: Loch Torridon Command. For record. Cleared, Brigadier General Teague. Captain Victor Fontine granted leave upon return from Wight. Recommendation for majority approved——)

Fontine sped out of London on the Hempstead road toward Oxfordshire. He thought the debriefing session with Teague and Stone would never end! *God!* The repetitions! His coadministrator, Stone, was always furious when he returned from one of his trips behind the German lines. It was work Stone had been trained to do, but now was impossible for him. His shattered hand ruled out such incursions and he spent his rage on Victor. He would subject Fontine to rapid, harsh, repetitive interrogation, looking for errors in every phase of a mission. What charity Victor once felt for the cryptographer had disappeared over the months. Months? Mother of Christ, it was nearly two and a half years!

But tonight Stone's delaying tactics were unforgivable. The *Luftwaffe* strikes over England had lessened, but they had not disappeared. Should the air raid sirens begin, it might be impossible for him to drive out of London.

And Jane was nearly due. The doctors had said it was a matter of a fortnight. That was a week ago, when he had flown out of Lakenheath to France and dropped into the grazing fields of Héricourt.

He reached the outskirts of Aylesbury and looked at his watch, holding it under the dim light of the dashboard. It was twenty minutes past two in the morning. They would both laugh at that; he was always coming back to her at ridiculous hours.

But he was coming back. He'd be at the compound in ten minutes.

Behind him, in the distance, he could hear the wail of the sirens rising and falling in plaintive fugues. There was not the jolting, breath-catching anxiety that used to accompany the terrible sound. The sound itself had taken on a weariness; repetition had dulled its terror.

He swung the wheel of the automobile to the right; he was now on the back road that led to the Oxfordshire estate. Another two or three miles and he'd be with his wife. His foot pressed down on the accelerator. There were no cars on the road; he could speed.

Instinctively, his ears listened for the distant rumbling of the bombing. But there was no faraway thunder, only the incessant whines of the sirens. Suddenly, there were sounds intruding where no sounds should be; he caught his breath, realizing instantly the return of forgotten anxiety. He wondered for a moment whether his exhaustion was causing tricks to be played. . . .

It was no trick! No trick at all! The sounds were overhead and unmistakable. He'd heard them too often, both over London and across the Channel in scores of different, covert locations.

Heinkel aircraft. Twin-engine, German, long-range bombers. They'd passed London. And if London was bypassed, it was a good bet that Heinkels would take a northwest heading toward the Birmingham district and the munitions factories.

My God! The aircraft were *losing altitude*. They were pitching down in rapid descent.

Directly *above* him!

In *front* of him!

A bombing run! An airstrike in the countryside of *Oxfordshire!* What in God's name? . . .

Jesus! Oh, Jesus Christ!

The compound!

The one place in England without parallel in security. From the ground, but *not* from the skies!

A low-altitude air strike had been called against the compound!

Fortine held the accelerator to the floor, his body trembling, his breath coming in short, spurting expulsions, his eyes riveted to the onrushing road.

The skies exploded. The screams of diving aircraft mingled with the manmade thunder: detonation after detonation. Immense flashes of white and yellow—jagged, shapeless, horrible—filled the open spaces above and between the woods of Oxfordshire.

He reached the compound's gate, tires screeching as he braked the car into a turn. The iron gates were open.

Evacuation.

He stabbed the pedal to the floor and sped into the long straight drive. Beyond, fires were everywhere, explosions everywhere, people running in panic—everywhere.

The main house had taken a direct hit. The entire left front wall was blown out; the roof was collapsing in weirdly shapeless splendor, bricks and stone cascading to the ground. Smoke spread in vertical swirls of black and gray—fires beyond, spurting upward, jagged, yellow, terrifying.

A deafening crash; the car lurched, the ground swelled, the windows shattered, hurling fragments of glass—everywhere. Fontine felt blood streaking down his face, but he could see and that was all that mattered.

The bomb had struck less than fifty yards to his right. In the light of the fires he could see the ripped-out earth of the lawn. He swung the car to the right, skirting the crater, cutting across the grass toward the dirt road that led to their cottage. Bombs did not strike twice in the same zero target, he thought.

The road was blocked; trees had fallen, fires consuming them—everywhere.

He lurched out of the car and raced between the flaming barriers. He saw their cottage. A huge oak had been blown out of the ground, its massive trunk crashed into the pipe-tiled roof.

"Jane! Jane!

God of hatred, do not do this to me! Do not do this to me again!

He smashed through the door, sending it hurtling off its hinges. Inside was total wreckage; tables, lamps, chairs were scattered, overturned, broken into a thousand fragments. Fires were burning—on the couch, in the open roof where the oak had crashed.

"Jane!"

"Here. . . ."

Her voice came from the kitchen. He raced through the narrow doorway and felt for an instant that he should fall to his knees in supplication. Jane stood gripping the edge of the counter, her back to him, her body shaking, her head nodding up and down. He rushed to her and held her shoulders, his face against her cheek, the spastic rhythm of her movements uninterrupted.

"My darling."

"Vittorio. . . ." Suddenly Jane contracted violently, gasping as she did so. "Sheets. . . . Sheets, my love. And blankets, I think I'm not sure, really——"

"Don't talk." He picked her up and saw the pain in her face in the darkness. "I'll take you to the clinic. There's a clinic, a doctor, nurses——"

"We can't get there!" she screamed. "Do as I say." She coughed in a spasm of pain. "I'll show you. Carry me."

In her hand she gripped a knife. Hot water had been running over the blade; she had been prepared to give birth alone.

Through the incessant detonations, Victor could hear the aircraft ascending, scrambling to higher altitudes. The strike was coming to an end; the distant, furious whines of Spitfires converging into the sector was a signal no *Luftwaffe* pilot overlooked.

He did as his wife told him to do, holding her in his arms, awkwardly gathering up whatever she ordered.

He kicked his way through the wreckage and the spreading flames and carried his wife out the door. Like an animal seeking sanctuary, he hurried into the woods and found a lair that was their own.

They were together. The frenzy of death that was several hundred yards away could not deter life. He delivered his wife of two male infants.

The sons of Fontini-Cristi were born.

Smoke spiraled up lazily, vertical coils of dignified, dead vapor interrupting the shafts of early morning sunlight. Stretchers were everywhere. Blankets covered the faces of the dead; the living and partly living were staring upward, mouths open, the shock imbedded. Ambulances were everywhere. And fire engines and police vehicles.

Jane was in an ambulance, a mobile medical unit, they called it. His sons were with their mother.

The doctor came out of the lean-to canvas extension of the strange vehicle and walked across the short stretch of lawn toward Victor. The doctor's face was haggard; he had escaped death but he lived with the dying.

"She's had a hard time of it, Fontine. I told her she would under normal circumstances——"

"Will she be all right?" interrupted Victor.

"Yes, she'll be all right. However, she'll need a long, *long* rest. I told her several months ago I suspected a multiple birth. She was not—shall I say—designed for such a delivery. In some ways it's rather amazing that she made it."

Fontine stared at the man. "She never mentioned that to me."

"Didn't think she would. You're in a precarious business. Can't have too much on your mind."

"May I see her?"

"Not for a while. She's solidly corked off; the infants are quiet. Let her be."

The doctor's hand was gently on his arm, leading him away from the ambulance toward what remained of the main house. An officer approached them and took Victor aside.

"We found what we were looking for. We knew it was here, or something like it. The strike was far too accurate. Even German instruments couldn't do it, and night pilotage was out; we checked. There were no markings, no flares."

"Where are we going? What are you talking about?" Victor had heard the officer speak, but the words were elliptical.

". . . high-arc transmitter."

The words still did not penetrate. "I'm sorry. What did you say?"

"I said the room's still standing. It's at the rear of the right wing. The bastard was operating a simple high-arc transmitter."

"A transmitter?"

"Yes. That's how the Huns came in on pinpoint. They were guided by a radio beam. The chaps at M.I.-Five and

-Six had no objection to my showing you. As a matter of fact, I think they were pleased. They're afraid with all the confusion here someone'll disturb things. You can confirm that we haven't."

They threaded their way through the rubble and the intermittent piles of smoking debris to the right side of the large house. The major opened the door and they turned right down a corridor that seemed to be newly partitioned, as if for offices.

"A radio beam could bring a squadron into the area," said Fontine, walking beside the officer. "But only the area, not the target. These were bombers. I was on the road; they dove to the lowest levels. They would need more sophisticated equipment than a simple high-arc——."

"When I said there were no markings, no flares," interrupted the major, "I meant in a pattern; points A to B to C. Once they were over the target area, the bastard simply opened his window and shot up fireworks. He *did* use flares then. A fucking box full, from what we've found on the ground."

At the end of the corridor a door was flanked by two uniformed guards. The officer opened it and stepped inside; Victor followed.

The room was immaculate, miraculously no part of the surrounding carnage. On a table against the wall was an open briefcase, a circular aerial protruding out of it, attached to radio equipment beneath, secured in the case.

The officer gestured to his left, to the bed, not at first visible from the doorway.

Fontine froze. His eyes locked on the sight now in front of him.

On the bed was the body of a man, the back of his head blown off, a pistol beside his right hand. In his left hand was gripped a large crucifix.

The man was in the black robes of a priest.

"Damned strange," said the major. "His papers said he was a member of some Greek monastic brotherhood. The Order of Xenope."

13

He vowed it! There would be no more.

Jane and their two infant sons were taken secretly to Scotland. North of Glasgow, to an isolated house in the countryside of Dunblane. Victor would not rely on compounds *without-parallel-in-security,* nor on any guarantees from MI6 or the British government. Instead, he used his own funds, employed former soldiers, exhaustively screened by himself, and turned the house and grounds into a small but impenetrable fortress. He would not tolerate Teague's suggestions *or* objections *or* excuses. He was being pursued by forces he could not understand, an enemy beyond control, removed from the war and yet part of it.

He wondered if it would be so for the rest of his life. Mother of Christ, why didn't they believe him? How could he reach the fanatics and the killers and roar his denials? He knew nothing! *Nothing!* A train had left Salonika three years ago, at dawn on the ninth of December 1939, and he knew *nothing!* Only of its existence. Nothing more!

"Do you intend to remain here for the rest of the war?" Teague had come up to Dunblane for the day; they walked in the gardens behind the house, in sight of the high brick wall and the guards. It had been five months since they'd seen each other, although Victor permitted calls over redirected scrambler-telephones. He was too much a part of Loch Torridon; his knowledge was vital.

"You have no hold over me, Alec. I'm not British. I've sworn no allegiance to you."

"I never thought that was necessary. I did make you a major, however." Teague smiled.

Victor laughed. "Without ever having been formally inducted into the service? You're a disgrace to military tradition."

"Absolutely. I get things done." The brigadier stopped.

He bent over to pick up a long blade of grass and rose, looking at Fontine. "Stone can't do it alone."

"Why not? You and I talk several times a week. I tell you what I can. Stone expedites the decisions. It's a sound arrangement."

"It's not the same and you know it."

"It will have to do. I can't fight two wars." Fontine paused, remembering. "Savarone was right."

"Who?"

"My father. He must have known that whatever was on that train could make men enemies even when they fought for a common survival."

They reached the edge of the path. A guard was thirty yards away across the lawn by the wall; he smiled and stroked the fur of a leashed Great Dane that snarled at the sight and scent of the stranger.

"One day it will have to be resolved," said Teague. "You, Jane, the children: You can't live with it for the rest of your lives."

"I've said that to myself more times than I can count. But I'm not sure how it can be."

"Perhaps I do. At least, I'm willing to try. And I have at my disposal the finest Intelligence service in existence."

Victor glanced at him, interested. "Where would you start?"

"The question is not where, but when."

"Then, *when?*"

"When this war is over."

"Please, Alec. No more words, no strategies. Or tricks."

"No tricks. A simple, uncomplicated agreement. I need you. The war has turned; Loch Torridon enters its most important phase. I intend to see that it does its job."

"You're obsessed."

"So are you. Quite rightfully. But you'll learn nothing of 'Salonika'—that's Brevourt's code name, incidentally—until this war is won, take my word for it. And the war *will* be won."

Fontine held Teague's eyes with his own. "I want facts, not rhetoric."

"Very well. We have identities you don't have, nor, for your own safety and the safety of your family, will I reveal them to you."

"The man in the car? In Kensington, Campo di Fiori. The streak of white? The *executioner?*"

"Yes."

Victor held his breath, controlling a nearly overpowering urge to grab the Englishman and force the words from him. "You've taught me to kill; I could kill you for that."

"To what end? I'd protect you with my life, and you know it. The point is, he's immobilized. Under control. If, indeed, he *was* the executioner."

Victor let his breath out slowly. The muscles in his jaw pained from the tension. "What other identities?"

"Two elders of the Patriarchate. Through Brevourt. They command the Order of Xenope."

"Then they're responsible for *Oxfordshire.* My *God,* how can you——?"

"They're *not,*" interrupted Teague quickly. "They were, if possible, more shocked than we were. As was pointed out, the last thing they wanted was your death."

"The man who guided those planes was a priest! From Xenope!"

"Or someone made to appear so."

"He killed himself," said Fontine softly, "in the prescribed manner."

"No one has a quota on fanatics."

"Go on." Victor began walking back on the path, away from the guard and the dog.

"These people are the worst kind of extremists. They're mystics; they believe they're involved in a holy war. Their war permits only confrontation by violence, not negotiation. But we know the pressure points, those whose word cannot be disobeyed. We can bring about a confrontation through Whitehall pressure, if need be, and demand a resolution. At least one that removes you from their concerns—once and for all. You can't do this by yourself. We can. Will you come back?"

"If I do, all this will be set in motion? I, myself, a part of the planning?"

"We'll mount it with the precision we mounted Loch Torridon."

"Has my cover in London been kept absolute?"

"Not a dent. You're somewhere in Wales. All our telephone calls are placed to the Swansea area and tripped north. Mail is regularly sent to a post office box in the village of Gwynliffen, where it's quietly put in other envelopes and returned only to me. Right now, if I'm needed, Stone places a call to a Swansea number."

"No one knows where we are? *No one?*"

"Not even Churchill."

"I'll talk with Jane."

"One thing," said Teague, his hand on Fontine's arm. "I've given my word to Brevourt. There'll be no more trips across the Channel for you."

"She'll like that."

Loch Torridon flourished. The principle of mismanagement-at-all-costs became a thorn in the German craw.

In the Mannheim printing plants, 130,000 *Commandmant Manuals for Occupation* came off the presses with all negatives dropped in vital restrictions. Shipments to the Messerschmidt factories in Frankfurt were routed to the Stuka assembly lines in Leipzig. In Kalach on the Russian front, it was found that three quarters of the radio equipment now operated on varying frequency calibrations. In the Krupp plants at Essen, engineering miscalculations resulted in malfunctions in the firing mechanisms of all cannon with the bore number 712. In Kraków, Poland, in the uniform factories, fabric bypassed a chemical saturation process and 200,000 units were sent out, subject to instant flammability. In Turin, Italy, where the Germans ran the aircraft plants, designs were implemented that caused metal fatigue after twenty hours of flight; entire sections of squadrons structurally collapsed in midair.

In late April of 1944, Loch Torridon concentrated on the offshore patrols throughout the coastal zones of Normandy. A strategy was conceived that would alter the patrol schedules as they were issued to the German naval personnel from the base at Pointe de Barfleur. Brigadier Teague brought the explosive report to Supreme Headquarters, Allied Command, and handed it personally to Dwight Eisenhower.

> The German coastal predawn patrols will be removed from Normandy zones during the first eleven days in June. That is the calendar target. Repeat: 1 June through 11 June.

The supreme commander responded appropriately. "I'll be goddamned. . . ."

Overlord was executed and the invading armies progressed. Under Badoglio and Grandi, the outlines of the Italian collaboration were negotiated in Lisbon.

It was a trip Alec Teague permitted Major Fontine. He was entitled to it.

And in a small room in Lisbon, a weary Badoglio faced Victor. "So the son of Fontini-Cristi brings us our ultimatum. There must be a certain gratification in that for you."

"No," replied Victor simply. "Merely contempt."

JULY 26, 1944
WOLFSSCHANZE, EAST PRUSSIA

(Excerpts from the Gestapo investigation of the assassination attempt on Adolf Hitler at the Wolfsschanze High Command Headquarters. File removed and destroyed.)

. . . The aides of the traitor, Gen. Claus von Stauffenberg, have broken. They described a widespread conspiracy implicating such generals as Olbricht, von Falkenhausen, Hoepner, and possibly Kluge and Rommel. This conspiracy could not have been coordinated without enemy assistance. All normal channels of communication were avoided. A network of unknown couriers was employed, and a code name surfaced, unheard of previously. It is of Scottish origin, the name of a district or a village: Loch Torridon. . . . We have captured . . .

Alec Teague stood in front of the map on his office wall. Fontine sat dejectedly in the chair by Teague's desk, his eyes on the brigadier across the room.

"It was a gamble," said Teague. "We lost. Can't expect to win every time. You've had too few losses, that's your trouble, you're not used to them." He removed three pins from the map and walked back to his desk. He sat down slowly and rubbed his eyes. "Loch Torridon has been an extremely effective operation. We have every reason to be proud."

Fontine was startled. "Past tense?"

"Yes. The Allied ground offensive toward the Rhine will

commence maximum effort by October first. The Supreme Command wants no complications; they anticipate widespread defections. We're a complication, possibly a detriment. Loch Torridon will be phased out over the next two months. Terminated by the end of September."

Victor watched Teague as the brigadier made the pronouncement. A part of the old soldier died with the words. It was painful to watch Alec. Loch Torridon was his moment in the military sun; he would get no nearer, and jealousies were not out of the question regarding its termination. But decisions had been made. They were irrevocable, and to fight them *was* out of the question. Teague was a soldier.

Fontine examined his own thoughts. At first he experienced neither elation nor depression; more a suspension, as if time were abruptly arrested. Then slowly, painfully, there was the momentary feeling of what now? Where is my purpose? What do I do?

And then suddenly these vague concerns were swiftly replaced. The obsession that was never far from his mind came sharply into focus. He got out of the chair and stood in front of Alec's desk. "Then I call in your debt," he said quietly to Teague. "There's another operation that must be mounted 'with all the precision of Loch Torridon.' That's the way you phrased it."

"It will be. I gave you my word. The Germans can't last a year; surrender feelers already come from the generals. Six, eight months, and the war will be over. 'Salonika' will be mounted then. With all the precision of Loch Torridon."

14

It took twelve weeks to close the books and bring the men back to England. Loch Torridon was finished; twenty-two cabinets of accomplishments were all that remained. They were put under lock and seal and stored in the vaults of Military Intelligence.

Fontine returned to the isolated compound in Scotland. To Jane and the twins, Andrew and Adrian, named for the British saint and any of several acceptable Romans. But they were neither saintly nor imperial; they were two and a half years old, with all the energy that age implied.

Victor had been surrounded by the children of his brothers all his adult life, but these were *his*. In themselves they were different. They alone would carry on the Fontini-Cristis. Jane could have no more children; the doctors had agreed. The injuries at Oxfordshire were too extensive.

It was strange. After four years of furious activity and strain he was suddenly, abruptly, totally passive. The five months in '42 when he remained in Dunblane could not be considered a period of tranquility. Jane's recovery had been slow and dangerous; the fortifying of the compound had obsessed him. There'd been no letup of pressure then.

There was now. And the transition was unbearable. As unbearable as the wait for "Salonika" to begin. It was the inactivity that gnawed at him; he was not a man for idleness. In spite of Jane and the children, Dunblane became his prison. There were men outside, across the Channel, deep within Europe and the Mediterranean, who sought him as intensely as he sought them. There was nothing until that movement could begin.

Teague would not go back on his word, Victor understood that. But neither would he deviate from it. The end of the war would mark the commencement of the strategy that would lead to the men of Salonika. Not before. With each new victory, each new penetration within Germany, Fontine's mind raced. The war *was* won; it was not over, but it was won. Lives all over the world had to be picked up, the pieces put back together and decisions made, for years of living had to be faced. For him, for Jane, everything depended on the forces that sought a vault that came out of Greece five years ago—at dawn on the ninth of December.

The inactivity was his own particular hell.

During the waiting he had reached one decision: he would not return to Campo di Fiori after the war. When he thought of his house and looked at his wife, he saw other wives slain in the white mists of light. When he saw his sons, he saw other sons, helpless, terrified, riddled by gunfire. The tortures of the mind were too vivid still. He could not go back to the killing ground, or to anything or anyone associated with it. They would build a new life somewhere else. The Fontini-Cristi Industries would be returned to him, the Court of Reparations in Rome had sent word to London.

And he had sent word back through MI6. The factories, the plants, all lands and properties—except Campo di Fiori—would go to the highest bidder. He would make separate arrangements for Campo di Fiori.

It was the night of March 10. The children were asleep across the hall; the last of the winter winds blew in gusts outside the windows of their bedroom. Victor and Jane lay under the covers, the coals in the fireplace throwing an orange glow on the ceiling. And they talked quietly, as they always talked in the final hours of the day.

"Barclay's will handle everything," said Victor. "It's a simple auction, really. I've put a cellar on the total; however they want to divide the entire purchase is up to them."

"Are there buyers?" asked Jane, lying on her elbow, looking at him.

Fontine laughed softly. "Packs of them. Mostly in Switzerland, mostly American. There are fortunes to be made in the reconstruction. Those who have manufacturing bases will have the advantage."

"You sound like an economist."

"I sincerely hope so. My father would be terribly disappointed if I didn't." He fell silent. Jane touched his forehead, brushing aside his hair.

"What's the matter?"

"Just thinking. It'll be over with soon. First the war, then 'Salonika'; that will be finished, too. I trust Alec. He'll bring it off if he has to blackmail all the diplomats in the Foreign Office. The fanatics will be forced to accept the fact that I don't know a damn thing about their ungodly train."

"I thought it was supposed to be awfully godly." She smiled.

"Inconceivable." He shook his head. "What kind of god would allow it?"

"Checkmate, my darling."

Victor raised himself on the pillow. He looked over at

the windows; a March snow was silently careening off the dark panes of glass, carried by the winds. He turned to his wife. "I can't go back to Italy."

"I know. You've told me. I understand."

"But I don't want to stay here. In England. Here I will always be Fontini-Cristi. Son of the massacred family of *padrones*. Equal parts reality, legend, and myth."

"You *are* Fontini-Cristi."

Victor looked down at Jane in the dim light of the fire. "No. For five years now I've been Fontine. I've gotten rather used to it. What do you think?"

"It doesn't lose too much in the translation," said Jane, smiling again. "Except, perhaps, a flavor of landed gentry."

"That's part of what I mean," he replied quickly. "Andrew and Adrian shouldn't be burdened with such nonsense. Times are not what they were; those days will never return."

"Probably not. It's a little sad to see them go, but it's for the best, I suppose." His wife suddenly blinked her eyes and looked questioningly up to him. "If not Italy, *or* England, then where?"

"America. Would you live in America?"

Jane stared at him, her eyes still searching. "Of course. I think that's very exciting. . . Yes, it's right. For all of us."

"And the name? You don't mind really, do you?"

She laughed, reaching up to touch his face. "It doesn't matter. I married a man, not a name."

"You matter," he said, pulling her to him.

Harold Latham walked out of the old, brass-grilled elevator and looked at the arrows and the numbers on the wall. He had been transferred to the Burma theater three years ago; it had been that long since he'd been in the corridors of M16-London.

He tugged at the jacket of his new suit. He was a civilian now; he had to keep reminding himself of that. Soon there would be thousands upon thousands of civilians—*new* civilians. Germany had collapsed. He'd wagered five pounds that the formal announcement of surrender would come before the first of May. There were three days to go, and he didn't give a damn about the five quid. It was over; that was all that mattered.

He started walking down the hallway toward Stone's office. Good old, poor old, angry Geoff Stone. The *Apple* to his *Pear*. Rotten fucking luck it was, old Apple's hand shot to bits because of a high-handed guinea; and so early on, too.

Still, it bloody well might have saved his life. An awful lot of two-handed operatives never came back. In some ways Stone was damned fortunate. As he had been fortunate. He had a few pieces of metal in his back and stomach, but if he was careful they said he'd do fine. Practically normal, they said. Discharged him early, too.

Apple and Pear had survived. They'd made it! *Goddamn,* that called for a month of whiskies!

He had tried to call Stone but hadn't been able to reach him. He telephoned for two days straight, both the flat and the office, but there was never an answer. There was no point in leaving messages; his own plans were so ragtail he wasn't sure how long he could stay in London.

It was better this way. Just barge in and demand to know why old Apple had taken so long to win the war.

The door was locked. He knocked; there was no answer. *Damn!* The front desk had Stone checked in; that was to say he hadn't checked *out* last night, or the night before, which was not unusual these days. Office couches were beds these days. All the Intelligence services were working around the clock, going through files, destroying records that could be embarrassing, and probably saving a few thousand lives in the process. When the dust of victory and defeat settled, informers were the least popular survivors.

He knocked louder. Nothing.

Yet there was light shining through the thin, lateral crack at the base of the door. Perhaps Stone had stepped out for a minute. To the W.C. or the cafeteria.

And then Latham's eyes strayed to the round lock cylinder. There was something odd, something wrong. A speck of dull gray seemed to cling to the brass, a tiny scratch above it, to the right of the keyhole. Latham looked closer; he drew a match and struck it, almost afraid to do what he was about to do.

He held the flame directly below the speck of gray matter. It melted instantly and fell away; solder.

It was also an obscure but time-tested device that Apple favored. He had used it on numerous occasions when they worked together. Come to think of it, Latham couldn't remember anyone else ever using it.

Melt the end of a small solder wire and shove the soft liquid into the lock with its key. It jammed the tumblers but did not prevent the key from going in.

It merely prevented any key from opening the lock. In quiet situations that called for a little time while a man raced out of a trap, it provided that time without raising any sudden alarms. A perfectly normal-looking lock malfunctioned; most locks were old. One did not break down a door; one called a locksmith.

Had Apple needed time? Was there a trap?

Something *was* wrong.

"Good Christ! Don't touch anything! Get a *doctor!"* shouted Teague, lunging into the office beyond the unhinged door. "And keep this tight!"

"He's dead," said Latham quietly at the brigadier's side.

"I know that," answered Teague curtly. "I want to know how *long* he's been dead."

"Who is he?" asked Latham, looking down at the dead man. The body had been stripped; only the undershorts and shoes remained. There was a single, clean gunshot wound in the upper center of the naked chest; the rivulet of blood had dried.

"Colonel Aubrey Birch. Officer of the vaults." Teague turned and spoke to the two guards holding the door. A third soldier had gone for the MI6 house surgeon on the second floor. "Put that door back. Admit no one. Say nothing. Come with me, Latham."

They rode the elevator to the cellars. Latham saw that Teague was not only in a state of shock, he was frightened.

"What do you think happened, sir?"

"I gave him his separation papers two nights ago. He hated me for it."

Latham was silent for a moment. Then he spoke without looking at Teague, his eyes straight ahead. "I'm a civilian, so I'll say it. That was a rotten, goddamned thing to do. Stone was once the best man you had."

"Your objection is noted," said the brigadier coldly. "You were the one they called Pear, weren't you?"

"Yes."

Teague glanced at the discharged Intelligence agent; the panel light indicated that the cellars had been reached. "Well, the apple soured, Mr. Pear. It became rancid. What concerns me now is how far the rot penetrated."

The door opened. They walked out of the elevator and turned right toward a wall of steel that closed off the corridor. In the center of the wall was a thick steel door, its frame was barely discernible. There was a plate of bulletproof glass in the upper section, a black button to the left, a thin rubber slot below, a metal sign above.

SECURITY AREA

No Admittance Without Proper Authorisation
Ring Bell—Place Authorisation In Vacuum Slot

Teague approached the glass, pushed the button and spoke firmly. "Code Hyacinth. No delays, please; make visual confirmation. This is Brigadier Teague. I'm accompanied by one Mr. Harold Latham, cleared by me."

There was a whirring sound. The steel door receded, then was slid manually to the side. An officer on the other side saluted.

"Good afternoon, general. There's been no Hyacinth report down here."

Teague acknowledged the salute with a nod of his head. "I'm delivering it myself, major. Nothing is to be removed until further orders. What does the duty ledger read on Colonel Birch?"

The officer turned to a metal desk that was attached to the metal wall. "Here it is, sir," he said, holding open a black leather notebook. "Colonel Birch signed out the night before last at nineteen hundred hours. He's due back in the morning. Oh seven hundred, sir."

"I see. Was anyone with him?"

The major looked again at the large notebook. "Yes, sir. Captain Stone, sir. His checkout time is the same."

"Thank you. Mr. Latham and I will be in Vault Seven. May I have the keys, please? And the combination figures."

"Of course."

Inside the metal room were twenty-two file cabinets. Teague stopped at the fourth cabinet against the far wall opposite the door. He looked at the page of figures in his hand and began manipulating the combination lock in the upper right corner of the cabinet. As he did so, he held out the page of figures for Latham.

"Save time," he said brusquely, his voice hoarse. "Locate the cabinet with the Brevourt file. B-r-e-v-o-u-r-t. Extract it."

Latham took the paper, returned to the left wall and found the cabinet.

The lock sprung. Teague reached over and pulled out the second cabinet drawer. Rapidly his fingers separated the files.

Then he separated them again. Slowly, allowing for no oversight.

It wasn't there. The file on Victor Fontine was gone.

Teague closed the cabinet drawer and stood erect. He looked over at Latham, who knelt by the bottom drawer of his cabinet, an open folder in his hand. He was staring at it, his expression one of stunned bewilderment.

"I asked you to find it, not to read it," said the brigadier icily.

"There's nothing to read," replied Latham quietly, removing a single page of paper from the folder. "Except this. . . . What the hell have you bastards *done?*"

The paper was a photostat. It had a black border, with room at the bottom for two seals of approval. Both men knew exactly what it was.

An order for execution. An official license to kill.

"Who's the target?" asked Teague in a monotone, remaining by the cabinet.

"Vittorio Fontini-Cristi."

"Who approved of it?"

"Foreign Office seal, Brevourt's signature."

"Who *else?* There must be *two!*"

"The prime minister."

"And Captain Stone is the assignee——"

Latham nodded, although Teague had not asked a question. "Yes."

Teague breathed deeply, closing his eyes for a moment. He opened them and spoke. "How well did you know Stone? His methods?"

"We worked together for eighteen months. We were like brothers."

"Brothers? Then I remind you, Mr. Latham, that in spite of your separation from the service, the Official Secrets Act still binds you."

15

Teague spoke into the telephone, his phrases precise, his voice cutting. "From the beginning he was your man. From the day we placed him in Loch Torridon. His interrogations, the endless questions, Lübok's name in our files, the traps. Fontine's every move was reported to you."

"I make no apologies," said Anthony Brevourt on the other end of the line. "For reasons you well know. 'Salonika' was, and still remains, a highest priority of the Foreign Office."

"I want an explanation for that order of execution! It was never cleared, never reported——"

"Nor was it *meant* to be," interrupted Brevourt. "That order was our backup. You may subscribe to your own immortality, brigadier, but we don't. Air raids aside, you're a strategist for covert operations; a potential mark for assassination. If you were killed, that order permitted Stone immediate access to Fontini-Cristi's whereabouts."

"Stone convinced you of that?"

There was a pause before the ambassador replied. "Yes. Several years ago."

"Did Stone also tell you he hated Fontine?"

"He didn't approve of him; he wasn't alone."

"I said *hated!* Bordering on the pathological."

"If you knew that, why didn't you replace him?"

"Because, damn it, he controlled it! As long as he had a reason to. He has *none* now."

"I don't see——"

"You're a goddamn fool, Brevourt! Stone left us a photostat; he kept the original. You're helpless and he wants you to know it."

"What are you talking about?"

"He's walking around with an official document that gives him a warrant to kill Fontine. Countermanding it now is meaningless. It would have been meaningless two *years* ago! He has the paper; he's a professional. He intends to carry out the assignment and place that document where you can't get it. Can the British government—can *you,* or the foreign secretary, or Churchill, himself, justify that execution? Would any of you care to even *comment* on it?"

Brevourt replied swiftly, urgently. "It was a contingency. That was *all* it was."

"It was the best," agreed Teague harshly. "Startling enough to cut through red tape. Sufficiently dramatic to break down bureaucratic walls. I can hear Stone mounting his argument."

"Stone must be found. He must be stopped." Brevourt's breathing could be heard over the line.

"We've reached one area of agreement," said the brigadier wearily.

"What are you going to do?"

"To begin with, tell Fontine everything."

"Is that wise?"

"It's fair."

"We expect to be kept informed. If need be, hourly."

Teague looked absently across the office at his wall clock. It was nine forty-five; moonlight streamed through the windows, no curtains blocked it now. "I'm not sure that's possible."

"What?"

"You're concerned with a vault taken out of Greece five years ago. I'm concerned with the lives of Victor Fontine and his family."

"Has it occurred to you," said Brevourt, drawing out his words, "that the two are inseparable?"

"Your conjecture is noted." Teague hung up and leaned back in his chair. He would have to call Fontine now. Warn him.

There was a knock on his door.

"Come in."

Harold Latham walked in first, followed by one of the best investigating officers in MI6. A middle-aged, former

Scotland Yard forensic specialist. He carried a manila file folder in his hand.

A few weeks ago, Pear would not have walked into Teague's office smoking a cigarette. He did so now; it was important to him. Yet, thought Teague, Latham's hostility had lessened. Pear was first and foremost a professional. Civilian status would not change that.

"Did you find anything?" asked Teague.

"Scratchings," said Latham. "They may mean something, they may not. Your man here is sharp. He can lift a book off a pinhead."

"He knew where to point me," added the analyst. "He was familiar with the subject's habits."

"What have we got?"

"Nothing on the premises; his office was clean. Nothing but case work, dossiers marked for the ovens, all quite legitimate. His flat was something else. He was a thorough chap. But the arrangements of the hangers in the closets, the clothes in his bureau, the toilet supplies . . . they all indicate that Stone had been planning his departure for some time."

"I see. And these scratchings?"

Pear answered. The professional in him needed recognition. "Stone had a disagreeable habit. He would lie in bed making notes. Words, brackets, figures, arrows, names—doodling, I call it. But before he turned in he'd tear off the pages and burn them. We found a writing pad on the shelf of the bedside table. There was nothing on it, of course, but the Yarder here knew what to do."

"There were depressions, sir. It wasn't difficult; we lifted them under spectrograph." The officer handed Teague the folder across the desk. "Here are the results."

Teague opened the folder and stared at the spectrogram. As Pear had described, there were numbers, brackets, arrows, words. It was a disjointed puzzle, a wild diagram of incoherent meanderings.

And then the name leaped up from the mass of incoherence.

Donatti.

The man with the streak of white in his hair. The executioner of Campo di Fiori. One of the most powerful cardinals in the Curia.

"Salonika" had begun.

". . . Guillamo Donatti."

Fontine heard the name and it triggered the memory locked in his mind. The name was the key, the lock was sprung, and the memory revealed.

He was a child, no more than nine or ten years old. It was evening and his brothers were upstairs preparing for bed. He had come down in his pajamas to find a book, when he'd heard the shouting from his father's study.

The door was open, no more than a foot, and the curious child had approached it. What he saw inside so shocked his sensibilities that he stood there hypnotized. A priest was in front of his father's desk, roaring at Savarone, pounding the top of the desk with his fist, his face pinched in anger, his eyes wide in fury.

That anyone could behave this way in his father's presence, even—perhaps especially—a priest, so startled the child that he involuntarily, audibly gasped.

When he did the priest whipped around, the burning eyes looking at the child, and it was then that Victor had seen the streak of white in the black hair. He had run away from the living room and up the staircase.

The next morning Savarone had taken his son aside and explained; his father never left explanations suspended. What the violent argument referred to was obscured with time, but Fontine recalled that his father had identified the priest as Guillamo Donatti, a man who was a disgrace to the Vatican . . . someone who issued edicts to the uninformed and enforced them by fear. They were words a child remembered.

Guillamo Donatti, firebrand of the Curia.

"Stone's after his own, now," said Teague over the line from London, bringing Victor's focus back to the present. "He wants you, and whatever price you'll bring. We were looking in the wrong areas; we've traced him now. He used Birch's papers and got a military flight out of Lakenheath. To Rome."

"To the cardinal," corrected Fontine. "He's not taking chances with long-distance negotiations."

"Precisely. He'll come back for you. We'll be waiting."

"No," said Victor into the telephone. "That's not the way. We won't wait, we'll go after them."

"Oh?" The doubt was in Teague's voice.

"We know Stone's in Rome. He'll stay out of sight, probably with informer cells; they're used to hiding men."

"Or with Donatti."

"That's doubtful. He'll insist on neutral territory. Donatti's dangerous, unpredictable. Stone realizes that."

"I don't care what you're thinking, but I can't——"

"Can you circulate a rumor from reliable sources?" interrupted Fontine.

"What kind of rumor?"

"That I'm about to do what everyone expects me to do: return to Campo di Fiori. For unknown reasons of my own."

"Absolutely not! It's out of the question!"

"For God's *sake*," shouted Victor. "I can't hide out for the rest of my life! I can't live in fear that each time my wife or my children leave the house there is a Stone or a Donatti or an execution team waiting for them! You promised me a confrontation. I want it *now*."

There was silence on the line from London. Finally Teague spoke. "There's still the Order of Xenope."

"One step leads to another. Hasn't that been your premise all along? Xenope will be forced to acknowledge what *is*, not what it thinks *should* be. Donatti and Stone will be proof. There can be no other conclusion."

"We have men in Rome, not many——"

"We don't *want* many. Very few. My being in Italy must not be linked with M.I.-Six. The cover will be the Court of Reparations. The government wants to control our factories, the properties. The court bids higher every week; they don't want the Americans."

"Court of Reparations," said Teague, obviously writing a note.

"There is an old man named Barzini," continued Fontine. "Guido Barzini. He used to be at Campo di Fiori, he tended the stables. He could give us background. Put a trace on him in the Milan district. If he's alive, he'll be found through the *partigiani*."

"Barzini, Guido," repeated Teague. "I'll want safety factors."

"So do I, but very low profile, Alec. We want to force them out in the open, not further underground."

"Assuming the bait's taken, what will you do?"

"Make them listen. It's as simple as that."

"I don't think it is," said Teague.

"Then I'll kill them," said Victor.

The word went out. The *padrone* was alive; he had returned. In a small hotel several blocks from the Duomo, he was *seen*. Fontini-Cristi was in Milan. The news was known even in Rome.

There was a knock on the hotel door. Barzini. It was a moment Victor both looked forward to and dreaded. The memories of white light and death inadvertently came into focus. He suppressed them as he walked across the room to the door.

The old farmhand stood in the hallway, his once muscular body now bent and thin, lost within the coarse fabric of his cheap black coat. His face was wrinkled; the eyes were rheumy. The hands that had held Victor's writhing, lashing body to the earth, the fingers that had clawed at his face and saved his life, were withered, gnarled. And they shook.

To Fontine's sorrow and embarrassment, Barzini fell to his knees, his thin arms outstretched, grasping Victor's legs.

"It's true. You're alive!"

Fontine pulled him to his feet and embraced him. In silence he led the old man into the room, to the couch. Beyond his age, it was obvious that Barzini was ill. Victor offered food; Barzini asked for tea and brandy. Both were brought quickly by the hotel waiters, and when both were finished, Fontine learned the salient facts of Campo di Fiori since the night of the massacre.

For months after the German killings, the fascist troops kept the estate under guard. The servants were allowed to take their possessions and leave; the maid who had witnessed the shooting was murdered that night. No one was permitted to live in Campo di Fiori except Barzini, who was obviously mentally deficient.

"It was not difficult. The *fascisti* always thought everyone else was crazy but themselves. It was the only way they could think, and face themselves in the morning."

In his position of stablehand and groundkeeper, Guido was able to watch the activity at Campo di Fiori. Most startling were the priests. Groups of priests were permitted in; never more than three or four at a time, but there were many such groups. At first Guido believed they had been sent by the holy father to pray for the souls of the house of

Fontini-Cristi. But priests on sacred missions did not behave as these priests behaved. They went through the main house, then the cottages and, finally, the stables, searching with precision. They tagged everything; furniture was pried apart; walls tapped for hollow sections and panels removed; floors ripped up—not in anger but as experienced carpenters might do; lifted and replaced. And the grounds were combed as though they were fields of gold.

"I asked several of the young fathers what they were looking for. I don't think they really knew. They always replied, 'thick boxes, old man. Cartons of steel and iron.' And then I realized that there was one priest, an older priest, who came every day. He was forever checking the work of the others."

"A man in his sixties," said Victor softly, "with a streak of white in his hair."

"Yes! That was he! How did you know?"

"He was expected. How long did the searching go on?"

"For nearly two years. It was an unbelievable thing. And then it stopped."

All activity stopped, according to Barzini, except German activity. The Wehrmacht Officer Corps appropriated Campo di Fiori, turning it into an elaborate retreat for the higher echelon commanders.

"Did you do as the Englishman from Rome told you, old friend?" Fontine poured Barzini more brandy; the trembling had partially subsided.

"Yes, *padrone*. For the past two days I have gone to the markets in Laveno, in Varese, and Legnano. I say the same to a few chosen loudmouths: 'Tonight I see the *padrone!* He returns! I go to Milan to meet him, but no one is to know!' They will know, son of Fontini-Cristi." Barzini smiled.

"Did anyone ask you *why* I insisted you come to Milan?"

"Most did. I say only that you wish to talk with me privately. I tell them I am honored. And I am."

"It should be enough." Victor picked up the phone and gave a number to the hotel switchboard. While he waited for the call to be placed, he turned to Barzini. "When this is over, I want you to come back with me. To England, then America. I'm married, old friend. You'll like the *signora*. I have sons, two sons. Twins."

Barzini's eyes shone. "You have sons? I give thanks to God——"

There was no answer on the line. Fontine was concerned. It was *imperative* that the MI6 man be at that telephone! He was stationed halfway between Varese and Campo di Fiori. He was the contact for the others, spread out on the roads leading from Stresa, Lugano, and Morcote; he was the focal point of communications. Where the hell *was* he?

Victor hung up the phone and took his wallet out of his pocket. In a concealed recess was another telephone number. In Rome.

He gave it to the operator.

"What do you mean there's no answer?" asked the precise English voice that answered.

"Is there a clearer way to say it?" responded Fontine. "There *is* no *answer*. When did you last hear from him?"

"About four hours ago. Everything was on schedule. He was in radio contact with all vehicles. You got the message, of course."

"What message?"

There was a momentary silence. "I don't like this, Fontine."

"What *message?*"

"He said he might have been zeroed, but we weren't to worry. He'd reach you at the hotel when you arrived. He spotted up the car himself. It was on the road that passes the main gates at Campo di Fiori. He didn't reach you?"

Victor suppressed a desire to shout. "He didn't reach me. There were no messages for me. What car?"

"A green Fiat. The license was from Savona, that's on the Genoa gulf. One of the descriptions matched a Corsican in the police files. A contrabandist London believes worked for us. The others are also Corsos, we think. And *him.*"

"I presume you mean——"

"Yes. Stone's the fourth man."

Stone had taken the bait. Apple had gone back to Celle Ligure, back to the Corsicans to find his recruits. And Apple, the professional, had removed the contact in Varese.

Eliminate the couriers. Immoblize communications. Loch Torridon.

"Thank you," said Victor to the man in Rome.

"See *here,* Fontine!" came the harried voice over the telephone. "You're to do *nothing!* Stay where you are!"

Without answering, Victor replaced the phone and walked back to Barzini. "I need some men. Men we can trust, who are willing to take risks."

Barzini look away; the old man was embarrassed. "Things are not what they were, *padrone.*"

"Partigiani?" said Fontine.

"Mostly Communists. They're concerned with themselves now. With ther pamphlets, their meetings. They——" Barzini stopped. "Wait. There are two men who don't forget. They hid in the mountains; I brought them food, news of their families. We can trust them."

"They'll have to do," said Victor, starting for the bedroom door. "I'm going to change clothes. Can you reach them?"

"There's a telephone number," answered Barzini, getting up from the couch.

"Call them. Tell them to meet me at Campo di Fiori. I assume there are guards."

"Only a nightwatchman now. From Laveno. And myself."

Fontine stopped and turned to Barzini. "Would these men know the back road north of the stables?"

"They can find it."

"Good. Tell them to start out now and wait for me on the bridle path at the rear of the stables. It's still there, isn't it?"

"It is still there. What are you going to do, *padrone?*"

Victor realized as he spoke that he was repeating the words he had used over the phone to Teague five days ago. "What everyone expects me to do." He turned and continued toward the bedroom.

16

The lessons of Loch Torridon were always present, thought Victor, as he stood in front of the hotel desk, his arms on the marble counter, watching the night clerk carry out his request. He had demanded a car for hire in a voice loud enough to draw attention. It was a difficult order considering the hour; vehicles were hard enough to come by during the day, much less in the middle of the night. But they could be had if the money was sufficient. Then, too, the argument at the front desk was sufficiently disagreeable to alert any observer. Also, there were the clothes he wore: dark gray trousers, boots, and a dark hunting jacket. It was not the hunting season.

There were only a few stragglers in the lobby; several businessmen making unsteady treks to their rooms after long, liquid conferences; a couple arguing over one or the other's behavior; a nervous, rich youth signing in with a whore who waited discreetly in a chair. And a dark, swarthy man with the hard leather face of the sea, who was across the lobby in an armchair reading a magazine, seemingly oblivious to the hotel's night scene. A Corsican, thought Victor.

It was this man who could carry the message to other Corsicans. To the Englishman named Stone.

It was simply a matter of coordinating the upcoming sequence. To make sure there was a green Fiat on the street, probably in shadows, ready to take up a discreet position when the rented car drove away. If there was no such automobile, Victor could find reasons to delay until it arrived.

No delay was necessary. The Fiat could be seen in the middle of the next block. Captain Geoffrey Stone was sure of himself. The auto was positioned in front of Fontine's car, heading west, toward the road to Varese. To Campo di Fiori.

Barzini sat in the front with Victor. The brandy had done its work. The old man's head kept falling to his chest.

"Sleep," said Victor. "It's a long drive and I'll want you rested when we get there."

They drove through the open gates and into the long winding entrance of Campo di Fiori. Although he was braced for it, the sight of the house filled his chest with pain; hammering seared through his temples. He approached the execution grounds. The sights and sounds of that agony returned, but he knew he could not permit them to overwhelm him. The lessons of Loch Torridon: *Divided concentrations were dangerous.*

He contracted the muscles of his stomach taut and stopped the car.

Barzini was awake, staring at him. The nightwatchman emerged from the thick oak doors beyond the marble steps, the beam of his flashlight examining the car and those inside. Barzini stepped out and spoke.

"I bring the son of Fontini-Cristi. He's the *padrone* of this house."

The watchman threw the beam over at Victor, who had gotten out of the car and stood by the hood. His voice was respectful. And not a little frightened.

"I am honored, *padrone.*"

"You may go home to Laveno," Fontine told him. "If you don't mind, use the north road. You probably do anyway. It's the shortest way."

"Much the shortest, *signore.* Thank you, *signore.*"

"There may be two friends waiting for me at the stables. Don't be alarmed, I asked them to drive through the north gate. If you see them, please tell them I'll be there shortly."

"Of course, *padrone.*" The nightwatchman nodded and walked rapidly down the marble steps into the drive. There was a bicycle in the shadows by the shrubbery. He mounted and pedaled off into the darkness toward the stables.

"Quickly," said Victor, turning to Barzini. "Tell me. Are the telephones as they were? Is there still a line connecting the house with the stables?"

"Yes. In your father's study and in the hall."

"Good. Go in and turn on all the lights in the hall and in the dining room. Then go back to the study, keeping those lights out. Stay by a window. When I reach your friends, I'll call you from the stables and tell you what to do. Soon the Corsicans will appear. On foot, I'm sure. Watch for small flashlights. Tell me what you see."

"Very well. *Padrone?*"

"Yes?"

"I have no gun. Weapons are outlawed."

"Take mine." Victor reached into his belt and removed his Smith & Wesson. "I don't think you'll need it. Don't fire unless your life depends on it."

Thirty seconds later the lights in the great hall shone through the stained-glass windows above the huge entrance doors. Victor hurried along the side of the house and waited by the edge of the building. The chandeliers in the dining room were switched on. The whole north section of the house was a blaze of light, the south section in darkness.

There were still no signs of life on the road; no beams of flashlights or flares or matches. It was as it should be. Stone was a professional. When he moved it would be with extreme caution.

So be it. *His* moves would be cautious also.

Victor ran into the north road toward the stables. He kept low to the ground and alert, listening for the unusual. Stone might have opted for the north gates as his means of entry, but it was unlikely. Stone was anxious; he would move in swiftly, close behind his quarry, and seal off the exits.

"*Partigiani.* It's Fontini-Cristi." Victor walked down the bridle path at the rear of the stables. The few horses left inside were old and weary, the whinnies intermittent.

"*Signore.*" The whisper came from the woods to the right of the path; Fontine approached. Suddenly a flashlight beam shot out from the opposite side. From the left. And another voice spoke.

"Stay where you are! Don't turn!"

He felt the hand of the man behind him on the small of his back, holding him steady. The flashlight moved forward over his shoulder, shining in his face, blinding him.

"It's him," said the voice in the darkness.

The flashlight was removed. Fontine blinked and rubbed his eyes, trying to erase the residual image of the blinking light. The *partigiano* came out of the darkness. He was a tall man, nearly as tall as Victor, dressed in a worn American field jacket. The second man came from behind; he was much shorter than his comrade and barrel-chested.

"Why are we here?" asked the tall man. "Barzini's old and doesn't think clearly. We agreed to watch you, warn you . . . nothing else. We do this because we owe Barzini much. And for old time's sake; the Fontini-Cristis fought against the fascists."

"Thank you."

"What do the Corsicans want? And this Englishman?" The second man moved to his friend's side.

"Something they believe I have, which I don't have." Victor stopped. From the stables there was a soft, tired snort followed by a series of hoof thumps. The partisans heard it, too; the flashlight was extinguished.

A crack of a limb. A pebble dislodged under a footstep. Someone approached, following the same path Fontine had taken. The partisans separated; the stocky man moved forward and disappeared into the foliage. His brother did the same in the opposite direction. Victor stepped to his right and crouched off the path.

Silence. The footsteps scratching over the dry earth became clearer. Suddenly the figure was there, only inches in front of Fontine, outlined in the forest night.

And then it happened. A powerful beam of light burst out of the darkness, piercing the opposite woods; at the same instant there was the sudden, muted spit of a pistol, its noise contained by a silencer.

Victor sprang up, lashing his left arm around the throat of the man, his right surging beyond for the weapon, forcing it downward. As the man's back arched, Victor crashed his knee into the base of the spine. The man's breath was expunged; Fontine yanked with all his strength at the taut neck in his hammerlock. There was a snap, sickening and final. The light rolled on the path.

The tall *partigiano* raced out of the woods, crushing the light underfoot, his pistol in his hand. He and Victor plunged into the foliage, both silently acknowledging the fear that their ally was dead.

He was not. The bullet had only creased his arm. He lay wild-eyed in shock, his mouth open, his breathing loud. Fontine knelt beside him, tearing off the partisan's shirt to check the wound. The man's friend remained standing, his gun on the stable path.

"Mother of Christ! You damn fool! Why didn't you *shoot* him?" The wounded *partigiano* winced in pain. "Another second and he would have killed me!"

"I had no weapon," replied Victor quietly, wiping the blood from the man's flesh.

"Not even a knife?"

"No." Fontine bound the wound and knotted the cloth. The *partigiano* stared at him.

"You've got balls," he said. "You could have waited out of sight. My comrade has a gun."

"Come on, stand up. There are two other *Corsi* somewhere. I want them. But without gunfire." Victor bent down and picked up the dead man's pistol. There were four bullets in the chamber; the silencer was one of the best. He beckoned the tall partisan off the path and spoke to both. "I'm going to ask a favor of you. You can refuse me and I'll understand."

"What is it?" asked the larger man.

"The other two Corsicans are back there. One's probably watching the main road, the other may be behind the house, in the gardens, there's no way to tell. The Englishman will stay out of sight, near the house. I'm sure the *Corsi* won't kill me. They'll watch every move I make, but they will not open fire."

"That one," said the wounded partisan, pointing to the dead man, "did not hesitate to pull his trigger."

"These *Corsi* know me by sight. He could see you weren't me."

The strategy was clean. Victor was the bait; he would walk openly down to the circular drive and turn into the gardens at the rear of the house. The partisans were to follow him, staying out of sight in the trees. If Fontine was right, a Corsican would be seen. And taken. Or killed silently. It did not matter; these *Corsi* murdered Italians.

The strategy would then be repeated on the main entrance road, the partisans crossing diagonally far behind the embankment, meeting him at a juncture a quarter of a mile away. Somewhere between the circular drive and the gates, the third and last Corsican would be stationed.

The positions were logical, and Stone was nothing if not a logical man. And thorough. He *would* seal off the exits.

"You don't have to do this for me," said Victor. "I'll pay generously, but I understand——."

"Keep your money," interrupted the wounded man, looking first at his comrade. "You didn't have to do what you did for me."

"There's a telephone in the stables. I must talk with Barzini. Then start down the road."

The surmise was confirmed. Stone had covered both roads and the gardens. And the remaining Corsicans were taken, their lives ended with partisan knives.

They met at the stables. Fontine was sure that Stone had been watching him from the embankment. The quarry was walking the killing ground; the return was painful. Loch Torridon had taught them both to anticipate reactions. It was a weapon.

"Where's your car?" Victor asked the *partigiani*.

"Outside the north gate," replied the tall one.

"You have my thanks. Get your friend to a doctor. Barzini will know where I can send a more concrete form of gratitude."

"You want the Englishman for yourself?"

"There'll be no trouble. He's a man with one hand, without his *Corsi*. Barzini and I know what to do. Get to a doctor."

"Good-bye, *signore*," said the tall man. "Our debts are canceled. To old Barzini. To you, perhaps. The Fontini-Cristis were good to this land once."

"Many thanks."

The partisans nodded a last time and made their way swiftly up the road into the darkness toward the north gate. Fontine went down the path and let himself into the stables through a side door. He walked by the stalls, past the horses and Barzini's small bedroom, into the tack room. He found a wooden box and began filling it with braces and bits and musty, framed citations from the walls. He crossed to the telephone by the door and pushed a button beneath it.

"All is well, old friend."

"Thank God."

"What about the Englishman?"

"He's waiting across the drive, in the high grass. On the embankment. The same——" Barzini stopped.

"I understand. I'm starting out now. You know what to

do. Remember, at the door speak slowly, clearly. The Englishman hasn't spoken Italian in recent years."

"Old men talk louder than they must," said Barzini, humor in his voice. "Because we hear poorly, so must everyone else."

Fontine replaced the phone and checked the pistol the partisans had left him; it had been taken from a dead Corsican. He unscrewed the silencer and put the weapon in his pocket. He picked up the box and went out the tack room door.

He walked slowly down the road to the circular drive opposite the embankment. In front of the steps, in the spill of light from the windows, he paused, giving his arms a moment of rest, conveying the fact that the box was heavier than its size might indicate.

He continued up the steps to the large oak doors. He then did the most natural thing that came to him: he kicked at the right door.

In seconds the door was opened by Barzini. Their exchange was simple, without strain. The old man spoke clearly.

"You're sure I can't bring you something, *padrone?* A pot of tea, coffee?"

"No, thank you, old friend. Get some sleep. We have a lot to do in the morning."

"Very well. The horses will eat early today." Barzini walked past Victor to the steps and down into the circular drive. He turned left toward the stables.

Victor stood in the great hall; everything was as it had been. The Germans knew when not to mar a thing of beauty. He turned into the darkened south section, into the enormous drawing room toward the doors of his father's study. As he walked through the familiar space, he felt pains of anguish in his chest and the catching of breath in his throat.

He went into his father's study, Savarone's *sanctum sanctorum*. Instinctively, he turned right in the darkness; the huge desk was where it had always been. He put the box down and turned on the green-shaded lamp he remembered; it was the same lamp. Nothing had changed.

He sat down in his father's chair and removed the pistol from his pocket. He placed it on the desk, behind the wooden box, concealing it from the front.

The waiting had begun. And for the second time his life was in Barzini's hands. He could not imagine a firmer grip. For Barzini would not reach the stables. He would walk up the stable road and enter the woods, doubling back into the gardens, to the rear of the house. He would let himself in through one of the patio doors, and wait for the Englishman to come.

Stone was trapped.

The minutes dragged on. Absently, Fontine opened the drawers of his father's desk. He found sheets of Wehrmacht stationery, and methodically he placed them sheet by sheet in separate piles, a game of solitaire with huge blank playing cards.

He waited.

At first, he did not hear any sound. Instead, he felt the presence. It was unmistakable, filling the air between himself and the intruder. Then the creak of a floorboard pierced the silence, followed by two distant footsteps, bold, unconcealed; Fontine's hand moved toward the gun.

Suddenly, out of the dark space, a light-colored object came flying through the shadows toward him, *at* him! Victor recoiled as the object came into focus, trailing rivulets of blood in the air. There was a harsh slap—flesh against wood—and the horrible thing made contact with the top of the desk and rolled obscenely under the spill of the lamp.

Fontine expelled his breath in an instant of total revulsion.

The object was a hand. A severed right hand cut crudely above the wrist. The fingers were old and withered and clawlike in spastic contraction, the tendons iced at the instant of primitive surgery.

It was the hand of Guido Barzini. Thrown by a maniac who had lost his own on a pier in Celle Ligure.

Victor shot up from the chair, suppressing the revulsion that welled up beside him, stabbing for the gun.

"Don't touch that! You do, you're dead!" Stone's words were spat out in English. He crouched in the shadows across the room, behind a high-backed armchair.

Victor withdrew his hand. He had to force himself to think. To survive. "You killed him."

"They'll find him in the woods. It's odd *I* found him there, isn't it?"

Fontine stood motionless, accepting the awful news, suspending emotion. "Odder still," said Victor quietly, "that your Corsican didn't."

Stone's eyes reacted; only a flicker of recognition, but the reaction was there. "The walk you took. I wondered." The Englishman nodded his head. "Yes, you could have done that. You could have taken them out."

"I didn't. Others did."

"Sorry, Fontini. That doesn't wash."

"How can you be sure?"

"Because if there were others, you wouldn't use an old man for the last job; that's stupid. You're an arrogant son of a bitch, but you're not stupid. We're alone, all right. Just you and me and that box. *Christ!* It must have been in one hell of a hole. Enough people looked for it."

"Then you made your deal with Donatti?"

"He thinks so. Strange, isn't it? You took everything from me. I crawled out of Liverpool and made my way up, and you took it all away on a fucking guinea pier five years ago. Now I've got it all back and then some. I may hold the biggest auction anyone's ever heard of."

"For what? Old hunt prizes? Faded citations?"

Stone snapped the hammer of his weapon into firing position. His black glove slapped the back of the chair, his eyes bore through the shadows. "Don't make jokes!"

"No jokes. I'm not stupid, remember? And you're not in any position to pull that trigger. You've only got one chance to deliver the contents of that vault. If you don't, another order of execution can easily be issued. Those powerful men who hired you five years ago don't like embarrassing speculations."

"Shut up! *Stop it!*" Furiously, Stone raised the clawlike glove above the chair and smashed it down. "Those tactics won't work on me, you guinea bastard! I used them before you ever heard of Loch Torridon."

"Loch Torridon was based on *error*. Miscalculation! *Mismanagement!* That was its *premise*. Remember?" Fontine took a step backward, pushing the chair with his legs, extending his hands out in a gesture of helplessness. "Come on. Look for yourself. You wouldn't kill me before you saw what the bullet cost you."

"Move back! *Farther!*" Stone came around the chair, his immobile right hand stretched out directly in front of him like a protruding lance. His left hand held the weapon with the cocked hammer; the slightest squeeze of the trigger and the pin would spring forward, exploding the shell.

Victor did as he was commanded, his eyes riveted on the pistol. His moment would come; it had to come or there was nothing.

The Englishman approached the desk, each step the movement of a man filled with loathing and wariness, prepared to destroy at the split second of imbalance. He took his eyes from Fontine and stared at the top of the desk. At the severed, mutilated hand of Guido Barzini. At the box. At the pile of debris inside the box.

"No," he whispered. *"No!"*

The moment came: the shock of revelation was in Stone's eyes. It would not come again.

Victor sprang forward over the desk, his long arms plunging for the weapon; it had wavered with only a heartbeat, but that was all he could hope for.

The explosion was deafening, but Fontine's grip had deflected the shot. Only inches, but it was enough. The bullet shattered the top of the desk, hurling splinters of wood everywhere. Victor held Stone's wrist, wrenching with all the power he possessed, feeling and not feeling the blows delivered to his face and neck by the hard gloved hand. Stone brought his right knee up, pummeling Fontine's groin and stomach; the pistol would not be dislodged. The Englishman screamed and went into a paroxysm of frenzy. He would not, *could* not be bested by strength alone.

Victor did the only thing left for him. For an instant he stopped all movement, then yanked Stone's wrist forward as if jamming the pistol into his own stomach. As the gun was about to touch the cloth of his jacket, he suddenly twisted his body and Stone's wrist, inverting the weapon, and shoved it with his full weight upward.

The explosion came. For a second Fontine was blinded, his flesh ice cold with fireburn, and for that instant he believed he had been killed.

Until he felt the body of Geoffrey Stone collapse, pulling him downward to the floor.

He opened his eyes. The bullet had entered the flesh beneath Stone's jaw, its trajectory upward, through the skull, ripping open the top of Stone's head.

And next to the mass of blood and tissue was the severed hand of Guido Barzini.

He carried Barzini's body out of the woods and to the stables. He placed the mutilated corpse on the bed and covered it with a sheet. He stood over the body, for how long he would never remember, trying to understand pain and terror and love.

Campo di Fiori was still. For him its secret was buried, never to be known. The mystery of Salonika was a confidence Savarone had not shared. And the son of Savarone would no longer dwell on it. Let others do so, if they cared to. Let Teague take care of the rest. He was finished.

He walked down the north road from the stables to the drive in front of the house and climbed into the rented car. It was dawn. The orange summer sun broke over the Italian countryside. He took one last look at the home of his childhood and started the ignition.

The trees rushed by, the foliage became a blur of green and orange and yellow and white. He looked at the speedometer. Over eighty. Eighty-four kilometers an hour on the twisting entrance road cut out of the forest. He should brake the speed, he knew that. It was foolhardy, if not dangerous. Yet his foot would not obey his mind.

Oh, God! He had to get away!

There was a long hairpin curve that preceded the gate. In the old days—years ago—it was the custom to blow one's horn when one approached the curve. There was no cause to do so now; and he was relieved to find his foot relaxing its pressure on the pedal. Instinct was intact. Still, he took the curve at fifty, the tires screeching as he came out of the turn and headed for the gates. Automatically, on the straightaway, he accelerated. He would whip past the gateposts and swing out the road for Varese. Then Milan. Then London!

He was not sure when he saw it. *Them*. His mind had wandered, his eyes on the immediate ground in front of the hood. He only knew that he slammed the brakes with such force he was thrown against the steering wheel, his head inches from the windshield. The car swerved, the the tires screamed, dust billowed up from the wheels, and the automobile skidded diagonally through the gates, stopping only feet from the two black limousines that had converged out of nowhere, blocking the road beyond the stone posts.

His body was jolted back against the seat; the whole car shook in its sudden, violent arrest. Stunned, it took Fontine several seconds to shake off the effects of the near collision. He blinked his eyes, quickly regaining focus. His fury was suspended in astonishment at what he saw.

Standing in front of the two limousines were five men in black suits and white clerical collars. They stared impassively at him. Then the rear door of the limousine on the right opened and a sixth man got out. He was a man of about sixty, in the black robes of the church.

With a shock of white in his hair.

17

The cardinal had the eyes of a fanatic and the strained, clipped voice of a man possessed. He moved in slow, fluid motions, never permitting his audience's attention to waver. He was at once theatrical and ominous. It was a cultivated appearance, refined over the years in the corridors of the Vatican. Donatti was an eagle who fed on sparrows. He was beyond righteousness; he *was* righteousness.

At the sight of the man Victor lost control of himself. That this killer of the church could approach Campo di Fiori was an obscenity he could not stand. He lunged at the vile, cassocked figure, all sense of reason and survival and sanity itself destroyed in the instant of memory.

The priests were ready for him. They converged, as the limousines had converged, blocking his path of assault. They held him, twisting his arms high up behind his back; a hand with powerful fingers gripped his throat, forcing his head into an agonizing arch, choking off all speech, but not sight or hearing.

"The car," said Donatti quietly.

The two priests who were not restraining Fontine raced to the rented car and began the search. Victor could hear the doors and the trunk and the hood being opened. Then the ripping of upholstery and the crashing of metal as the car was torn apart. For nearly a quarter of an hour the ransacking continued. Throughout, Fontine's eyes were locked with the cardinal's. Only at the end of the search did the priest of the Curia look over at the automobile, when the two men approached and spoke simultaneously.

"There is nothing, Your Grace."

Donatti gestured to the priest whose powerful hand held Victor's throat. The grip was eased; Fontine swallowed repeatedly. His arms were still stretched taut behind his back. The cardinal spoke.

"The heretics of Constantine chose well: the apostates of Campo di Fiori. The enemies of Christ."

"Animal! Butcher!" Victor could barely whisper; the muscles of his neck and windpipe had been damaged severely. "You *murdered* us! I *saw* you!"

"Yes. I thought you might have." The cardinal spoke with quiet venom. "I would have fired the weapons myself, had it been required. And thinking thus, you are quite correct. Theologically, I was the executioner." Donatti's eyes grew wide. "Where is the crate from Salonika?"

"I don't know."

"You'll tell me, heretic. Believe the word of a true priest. You haven't got a choice."

"You hold me against my will! In the name of *God,* I presume!" said Fontine coldly.

"In the name of preserving the *mother church!* No laws take precedence over that. *Where is the shipment from Salonika?"*

The eyes, the high-pitched voice triggered the memory of years ago—a small child outside a study door. "If that knowledge was so important to you, why did you execute my father? He was the only one who knew. . . ."

"A *lie!* That is a *lie!"* Donatti caught himself, his lips trembling.

Fontine understood. A raw nerve had been exposed. An error of extraordinary magnitude had been made, and the cardinal could not bear to face it. "You know it's the truth," said Victor quietly. "*Now* you know it's the truth and you can't stand it. *Why?* Why was he *killed?"*

The priest lowered his voice. "The enemies of Christ deceived us. The heretics of Xenope fed lies to us." And once more Donatti roared abruptly. "*Savarone Fontini-Cristi* was the *communicator of those lies!"*

"What lies could *he* tell *you?* You never believed him when he told you the truth."

Again the cardinal trembled. He could barely be heard. "There were two freights out of Salonika. Three days apart. The first we knew nothing about; the second we picked up at Monfalcone, making sure that Fontini-Cristi would not meet it. We did not know then that he had already made contact with the first train. And now you will tell us what we wish to know. What we *must* know."

"I can't give you what I don't have."

Donatti looked at the priests and said one word. "Now."

Victor could never remember the length of time, for there was not time, only pain. Excruciating, harrowing, stinging, convulsive pain. He was dragged within the gates of Campo di Fiori and taken into the forest. There the holy apostolic priests began the torture. They started with his bare feet; every toe was broken, the ankles twisted until they cracked. The legs and knees were next: crushed, inverted, racked. And then the groin and stomach——*O God! He wished to die!*——And always, above him, blurred in the vision of tears of pain, was the priest of the Curia with the shock of white in his hair.

"*Tell us! Tell us! Enemy of Christ!*"

His arms were sprung from their sockets. His wrists were turned inward until the capillaries burst, spreading purple fluid throughout the skin. There were moments of blessed void, ended suddenly by hands slapping him back to consciousness.

"*Tell us! Tell us!*" The words became a hundred thousand hammers, echoes within echoes. "*Tell us! Enemy of Christ!*"

And all was void again. And through the dark tunnels of feeling, he sensed the rhythm of waves and air and suspension. A floating that deep within his brain told him he was near death.

There was a final, convulsive crash, yet he could not feel it. He was beyond feeling.

Yet he heard the words from far, far away in the distance, spoken in a chant.

"*In nomine Patris, et Filii et Spiritus sancti. Amen. Dominus vobiscum. . . .*"

Last rites.

He had been left to die.

There was the floating again. The waves and the air. And voices, indistinct, too far away to be really heard. And touch. He felt touching, each contact sending shafts of pain throughout his body. Yet these were not the touches of torture; the voices in the distance were not the voices of tormentors.

The blurred images at last came into focus. He was in a white room. In the distance were shining bottles with tubes cascading in the air.

And above him was a face. The face he knew he would never see again. What was left of his mind was playing horrible tricks on him.

The face was crying; tears rolled down the cheeks.

His wife Jane whispered. "My love. My dearest love. Oh, *God*, what have they done to you?"

Her beautiful face was next to his. Touching his.

And there was no pain.

He had been found by worried men of MI6. The priests had carried him to a car, driven him to the circular drive, and left him to die in Campo di Fiori. That he did not die was not to be explained by the doctors. He *should* have died. His recovery would take months, perhaps years. And, in truth, he would never completely recover. But with care he would regain the use of his arms and legs; he would be ambulatory, and that in itself was a miracle.

By the eighth week he was able to sit up. He concluded his business with Rome's Court of Reparations. The lands, the factories, the properties were sold for seventy-five million pounds sterling. As he had promised himself, the transaction did not include Campo di Fiori.

For Campo di Fiori he made separate arrangements, through a trusted lawyer in Milan. It, too, was to be sold but he never wanted to know the name of the buyer. There were two inviolate restrictions: The purchaser was to have nowhere in his history any connection with the fascists. Nor was he to have any association whatsoever, regardless of denomination, with any religious body.

On the ninth week an Englishman was flown over from London on instructions of his government.

Sir Anthony Brevourt stood at the foot of Fontine's bed, his jaw firm, his eyes compassionate and yet not without hardness. "Donatti's dead, you know. He threw himself off the balustrade of St. Peter's. Nobody mourns him, least of all the Curia."

"Yes, I knew that. At the end an act of insanity."

"The five priests who were with him have been punished. Three were excommunicated, prosecuted, and in prison for several decades. The other two are under life penance in the Transvaal. What was done in the church's name horrifies its leaders."

"It seems to me that too many churches permit the fanatics, then look back in astonishment, amazed at what was done in 'their names.' It's not restricted to Rome. Trappings often obscure purposes, don't they? That goes for governments, too. I want *questions answered!*"

Brevourt blinked several times at Fontine's outburst and replied rapidly, mechanically. "I'm prepared to offer them where I can. I've been instructed to withhold nothing."

"First, Stone. The order of execution has been explained; I have no comment. I want to know the rest. All of it."

"Precisely what you've been told. I didn't trust you. I was convinced when you first arrived in London that you'd made up your mind to reveal nothing about the train from Salonika. I expected you to make your own arrangements, on your own terms. We couldn't let that happen."

"Stone reported my movements then?"

"Every one. You made eleven trips across the Channel, and one to Lisbon. With Stone's help we had you covered each time. In the event of capture, we were prepared to negotiate an exchange with the enemy."

"Suppose I'd been killed?"

"In the beginning it was a risk we calculated, overshadowed by the fact that you might have bolted, made contact with regard to 'Salonika.' And in June of forty-two, after Oxfordshire, Teague agreed not to send you across any longer."

"What happened at Oxfordshire? The priest—if he *was* a priest—who led those planes in was Greek. From the Order of Xenope. Your first constituency, I believe."

Brevourt pursed his lips and breathed deeply. Admissions were being made that both pained and embarrassed him. "Stone, again. The Germans had tried for two years to locate the compound at Oxfordshire. He leaked the precise bearings to Berlin, and at the same time made his own arrangements with the Greeks. He convinced them there was a way to break you. It was worth trying; a broken man talks. He didn't give a damn himself about 'Salonika,' but the raid served his primary aim. He put a fanatic priest in the compound and coordinated the strike."

"For God's sake, *why?*"

"To kill your wife. If she'd been killed, even severely wounded, he assumed you'd turn on all things British, get out of M.I.-Six. He was right. You nearly did, you know. He hated you; blamed you for ruining a brilliant career. As I understand it, he tried to keep you in London that night."

Victor remembered the horrible night. Stone, the methodical psychopath, had counted the minutes, projected the speed of a car. Fontine reached for his cigarettes on the bedside table. "The last question. And don't lie to me. What was on the train from Salonika?"

Brevourt walked away from the bed. He crossed to the hospital window and was silent for a moment.

"Parchments, writings from the past which, if made public, could bring chaos to the religious world. Specifically, they would tear the Christian world apart. Accusations and denials would be hurled back and forth, governments might have to choose sides. Above everything, the documents in enemy hands would have been an ideological weapon beyond anything imaginable."

"Documents can do this?" asked Fontine.

"These documents can," replied Brevourt, turning away from the window. "Have you ever heard of the Filioque Clause?"

Victor inhaled. His mind went back over the years to the impartial lessons of his childhood. "It's part of the Creed of Nicaea."

"More properly, the Nicene Creed of the year 381; there were many councils, subtle alterations of the creed. The Filioque was a later addition that once and for all established the Christ figure as one substance with God. It's rejected by the Eastern church as misleading. For the Eastern church, especially the sects that followed the scholar-priest Arius, Christ as the son of God was the teacher; his divinity was not equal to God's. No such equality could exist for them in those times. When the Filioque was first proposed, the Patriarchate of Constantine recognized it for what it was: a doctrinal division that favored Rome. A theological symbol that was the excuse to divide and conquer new territories. And quite right they were. The Holy Roman Empire became a global force—as the globe was known. Its influence spread throughout the world on that single premise, this specialized divinity of Christ: *Conquer* in the name of *Christ*." Brevourt stopped, as if searching for words. He walked slowly back toward the foot of the bed.

"Then the documents in that vault," said Victor, "refute the Filioque? If so, they challenge the foundation of the Roman church and all the Christian divisions that followed."

"Yes, they do that," replied Brevourt quietly. "Collectively they're called the denials . . . the Filioque denials. They include agreements between crowns and caesars from as far away as Spain, in the sixth century, where the Filioque originated, for what many believe were purely political reasons. Others trace what they term the 'theological corruption.' . . . But if that was *all* they did, the world could live with them. Son of God, teacher, one substance. These are theological differences, subjects for biblical scholars to debate. They do more, I'm afraid. In the Patriarchate's fervor to deny the Filioque, it sent out priests to search the holy lands, meet with the Aramaic scholars, unearth everything that ever existed relative to Jesus. They unearthed more than they were looking for. There were rumors of scrolls written during the years just preceding and after the mark of the first century. They traced them, discovered several, and brought them back to Constantine. It is said that one Aramaic scroll raises profound and very specific doubts as to the man known as Jesus. He may never have existed at all."

The ocean liner headed toward the open waters of the Channel. Fontine stood at the railing and watched the skyline of Southampton. Jane was at his side, one hand gently around his waist, the other crossed in front of her, over his hand on the railing. The crutches with the large metal clasps that held his forearms were to his left, the shiny half circles of stainless steel glistening in the sunlight. He had designed them himself. If it was going to be necessary, as the doctors said, for him to use crutches for a year or more he could damn well improve on the existing product.

Their two sons, Andrew and Adrian, were with their nurse from Dunblane—one of those who had elected to sail to America with the Fontines.

Italy, Campo di Fiori, the train for Salonika were in the past. The cataclysmic parchments that had been taken from the archives of Xenope were somewhere in the vast range of the Italian Alps. Buried for a millennium; perhaps never to be found.

It was better that way. The world had passed through an era of devastation and doubt. Reason demanded that a calm be restored, at least for a while, if only on the surface. It was no time for the vault from Salonika.

The future began with the rays of the afternoon sun on the waters of the English Channel. Victor leaned toward his wife and put his face next to hers. Neither spoke; she held his hand in silence.

There was a commotion on the deck. Thirty yards aft the twins has gotten into a quarrcl. Andrew was angry with his brother Adrian. Childish blows were exchanged. Fontine smiled.

Children.

PART ONE
BOOK TWO

18

JUNE 1973

Men.

They were men, thought Victor Fontine as he watched his sons thread separately through the guests in the bright sunlight. And twins, second. It was an important distinction, he felt, although it wasn't necessary to dwell on it. It seemed years since anyone had referred to them as the twins. Except Jane and himself, of course. Brothers, yes; but not twins. It was strange how that word had fallen into disuse.

Perhaps the party would revive it for a while. Jane would like that. They were always the twins to Jane. Her Geminis.

The afternoon party at the North Shore house on Long Island was *for* Andrew and Adrian; it was their birthday. The lawns and gardens behind the house, above the boathouse and the water, had been turned into an enormous outdoor *fête champêtre,* as Jane called it. "A ruddy, grownup picnic! No one has them anymore. We will."

A small orchestra played at the south edge of the terrace, its music serving as an undercurrent to a hundred conversations. Long tables heaped with food were organized on the large expanse of manicured lawn; two bars did brisk business at either end of the rectangular buffet. *Fête champêtre*. Victor had never heard the term before. In thirty-four years of marriage, he had never heard it.

How the years had flown! It was as though three decades had been compressed into a time capsule and shot through the skies at incredible speed, only to land and be opened and scanned by participants who had merely grown older.

Andrew and Adrian were near each other now. Andy chatted with the Kempsons by the canapé table. Adrian was at the bar, talking to several young people whose clothes were the only vague evidence of their gender. It was right, somehow, that Andrew should be with the Kempsons. Paul Kempson was president of Centaur Electronics; he was well thought of by the Pentagon. As, of course, was Andrew. Adrian, no doubt, had been cornered by several university students who wanted to question the singularly outspoken attorney who was Victor's son.

Victor noted with a certain satisfaction that both twins were taller than those around them. It was to be expected; neither he nor Jane were short. And they looked somewhat alike, but not identical. Andrew's hair was very light, nearly blond; Adrian's was dark, auburn. Their features were sharp, a combination of his and Jane's, but each with his own identity. The only physical thing they shared in common was their eyes: they were Jane's. Light blue and penetrating.

At times, in very bright sunlight or in dim shadows, they could be mistaken for each other. But only at such times, under such conditions. And they did not seek them. Each was very much his own man.

The light-haired Andrew was in the army, a dedicated professional. Victor's influence had secured a congressional appointment to West Point, where Andrew had excelled. He'd made two tours of duty in Vietnam, although he despised the way the war was fought. "Win or get out" was his credo, but none listened, and he wasn't sure it made any difference. There was no way to win for losing. Saigon corruption was like no other corruption on the face of the earth.

Yet Andrew was not a spoiler within the ranks, either. Victor understood that. His son was a *believer*. Deep, concerned, unwavering: The military was America's strength. When all the words were said and done, there remained only the power at hand. To be used wisely, but to be *used*.

For the dark-haired Adrian, however, there was *no* limit to be placed on the use of words, and no excuse for armed confrontation. Adrian, the lawyer, was as dedicated in his fashion as his brother, although his demeanor might seem to deny it. Adrian slouched; he gave the appearance of nonchalance where none existed. Legal adversaries had learned never to be lulled by his humor or his seeming lack of concern. Adrian *was* concerned. He was a shark in the courtroom. At least he *had* been for the prosecutor's office in Boston. He was in Washington now.

Adrian had gone from prep school to Princeton to Harvard Law, with a year taken off to wander and grow a beard and play a guitar and sleep with available girls from San Francisco to Bleecker Street. It had been a year when Victor and Jane had held their collective breath, though not always their tempers.

But the life of the open road, the provincial confines of a half-dozen communes palled on Adrian. He could no more accept the aimlessness of unprovoked experience than Victor had nearly thirty years ago at the end of the European war.

Fontine's thoughts were interrupted. The Kempsons were heading over to his chair, excusing their way through the crowd. They would not expect him to get up—no one ever did—but it annoyed Victor that he could not. Without help.

"Damn fine boy," said Paul Kempson. "He's got his head on straight, that Andrew does. I told him if he ever wants to chuck the uniform, Centaur has a place for him."

"I told him he should *wear* his uniform," added Kempson's wife brightly. "He's such a handsome man."

"I'm sure he thinks it would be disconcerting," said Fontine, not at all sure. "No one wants to be reminded of the war at a birthday party."

"How long's he home for, Victor?" asked Kempson.

"Home? Here? Only for a few days. He's stationed in Virginia now. At the Pentagon."

"Your other boy's in Washington, too, isn't he? Seems I read something about him in the papers."

"Yes, I'm sure you did." Fontine smiled.

"Oh, then they're together. That's nice," said Alice Kempson.

The orchestra finished one number and began another. The younger couples flocked to the terrace; the party was accelerating. The Kempsons floated away with nods and smiles. Briefly, Victor thought about Alice Kempson's remark.

. . . *they're together. That's nice.* But Andrew and Adrian were not together. They worked within twenty minutes of each other but lived separate lives. At times, Fontine thought, *too* separate. They did not laugh together as they once did as children. As men, something had happened between them. Fontine wondered what it was.

Jane acknowledged for roughly the hundredth time that the party *was* a success, wasn't it. A statement. Thank heavens the weather held. The caterers had sworn they could erect the tents in less than an hour, if it was necessary, but by noon the sun was bright, the promise of a beautiful day confirmed.

Not, however, a beautiful evening. Far in the distance, over the water near Connecticut, the sky was gray. Weather reports predicted scattered-nocturnal-thundershowers-with-increasingly-steady-precipitation, whatever all *that* meant. Why didn't they simply say it would rain later on?

Two o'clock to six o'clock. Good hours for a Sunday *fête champêtre*. She had laughed at Victor's ignorance of the term. It was so pretentiously Victorian; the fun was in using it. It looked ridiculous on the invitations. Jane smiled, then stifled a laugh. She really *should* control her foolishness, she supposed. She was much too old for that sort of thing.

Across the lawn between the crowds, Adrian was smiling at her. Had he read her thoughts? Adrian, her dark-haired Gemini, had inherited her slightly mad English humor.

He was thirty-one years old. *They* were thirty-one years old. Where had those years gone? It seemed like only months ago they'd all arrived in New York on the ship. Followed by months of activity that had Victor flying all over the States and back to Europe, furiously building.

And Victor had done it. Fontine, Ltd. became one of the most sought-after consulting firms in America, Victor's expertise primarily aimed at European reconstruction. The name Fontine on a corporation's presentation was an industrial plus. Knowledge of a given marketplace was assured.

Victor had involved himself totally, not merely for the sake of pride, or instinctive productivity, but for something else. Jane knew it, and at the same time knew she could do nothing to help him. It took his mind off the pain. Her husband was rarely without pain; the operations prolonged his life, but did little to lessen the pain.

She looked at Victor across the lawn, sitting in his hard

wooden chair with the straight back, the shiny metal cane at his side. He had been so proud when the two crutches were replaced by the single cane that made it possible for him to walk without being so obvious a cripple.

"Hi, Mrs. Fontine," said the young man with the very long hair. "It's one terrific party! Thanks for letting me bring my friends. They really wanted to meet Adrian."

The speaker was Michael Reilly. The Reillys were their nearest neighbors on the shore, about a half a mile down the beach. Michael was in law school at Columbia. "That's very flattering!"

"Hey, *he's great!* He wrapped up that Tesco antitrust in Boston when even the federal courts thought it was too loose. Everyone knew it was a Centaur company, but it took Adrian to nail it."

"Don't discuss it with Mr. Kempson."

"Don't worry. I saw him at the club and he told me to get a haircut. What the hell, so did my father."

"You won, I see."

Michael grinned. "He's mad as a bull but he can't say anything. I'm on the honors list. We made a deal."

"Good for you. Make him live up to it."

The Reilly boy laughed and leaned over, kissing her cheek. "You're outta sight!" He grinned again and left, beckoned by a girl at the edge of the patio.

Young people liked her, thought Jane. It was a comforting realization these days when the young found so little to like, or to approve. They liked her in spite of the fact that she refused to make concessions to youth. Or to age. Her hair was streaked—God, more than streaked—with gray; her face was lined—as it should be lined—and there were no discussions of a skin nip here, or a tuck there, as so many of her friends had done. She thanked her stars she'd kept her figure. All things considered, not bad for sixty . . . *plus,* damn it.

"Excuse me, Mrs. Fontine?" It was the maid; she'd come out of the turmoil that was the kitchen.

"Yes, Grace? Problems?"

"No, ma'am. There's a gentleman at the door. He asked for you or Mr. Fontine."

"Tell him to come out."

"He said he'd rather not. He's a foreign gentleman. A priest. I thought with so many people, Mr. Fontine——"

"Yes, you were right," interrupted Jane, understanding the maid's concerns. Victor did not relish walking among his guests as he was forced to walk. "I'll go see him."

The priest stood in the hallway, his black suit ill-fitting and old, his face thin and tired. He appeared awed, frightened.

Jane spoke coldly. She could not help herself. "I'm Mrs. Fontine."

"Yes, you are the *signora,*" replied the priest awkwardly, a large, stained envelope in his hand. "I have seen the pictures. I did not mean to intrude. So many automobiles."

"What is it?"

"I have come from Rome, *signora.* I bring a letter for the *padrone.* You will see that he gets it, please?" The priest held out the envelope.

Andrew watched his brother at the bar with the long-haired students, dressed in their uniforms of denim and suede, medallions around their necks. Adrian would never learn; his audience was useless. They were fakes. It was not simply the profusion of unkempt hair and the offbeat clothes that bothered the soldier; those were only symptoms. It was the pretense that went with these shallow expressions of nonconformity. By and large they were insufferable; antagonistic people with unkempt minds.

They spoke so intensely, so knowingly, of "movements" and "countermovements" as though they were participants, shifters of political thought. *This* world . . . the *third* world. And that was the biggest joke of all, because not one in ten thousand would know how to act as a revolutionary. They had neither the commitment nor the guts nor the savvy.

They were misfits who threw plastic bags of shit when no one paid attention to their ravings. They were . . . freaks, and, Christ, he couldn't stand the freaks. But Adrian did not understand; his brother looked for values where there weren't any. Adrian was a fool; but then he learned that seven years ago. Seven years ago he had discovered just how big a fool his brother was. Adrian was a misfit in the worst sense: He had every reason not to be.

Adrian glanced up at him from the bar; he turned away. His brother was a bore, and the sight of him proselytizing to that particular audience was distasteful.

The soldier hadn't always felt this way. Ten years ago when he'd gotten out of The Point he hadn't *hated* with the vehemence he felt now. He didn't think much of Adrian and his collection of misfits, but there was no hatred. The way the Johnson crowd began handling Southeast Asia, there was something to be said for the dissenters' attitude. *Get out.*

Translated: *Obliterate Hanoi. Or get out.*

He had explained his position time and again. To the freaks. To Adrian. But no one wanted to hear it from a soldier. "Soldierboy," that's what they called him. And "shell-head," and "missile-fingers," and "blast-ass."

But it wasn't the names. Anyone who'd gone through West Point and Saigon could handle that. Ultimately, it was their stupidity. They didn't simply turn off the people who mattered, they antagonized them, infuriated them, and finally *embarrassed* them. And *that* was the final stupidity. They drove even those who agreed with them into opposing positions.

Seven years ago in San Francisco, Andrew tried to make his brother see that, tried to make him understand that what he was doing was wrong and stupid—and very dangerous to the brother who was a soldier.

He'd gotten back from two and a half years in the Mekong Delta with one of the finest record sheets in the army. His company had the highest body count in the battalion; he'd been decorated twice, his first lieutenancy lasting a month before he was given his captain's bars. He was that rare commodity in armed forces: a young, brilliant military strategist from an immensely wealthy, influential family. He was on his way up to the top—where he belonged. He was being flown back for reassignment, which was another way of the Pentagon's saying: *That's our man. Keep your eye on him. Rich, solid, future Joint Chiefs material. A few more combat tours—in selected areas, a few short years—and it's the War College.*

It never hurt the Pentagon to favor a man like him, especially when it was justified. The army needed men from powerful families, they had precious few.

But regardless of what the Pentagon favored or the army needed, G2 agents had shown up when he got off that plane in California seven years ago. They'd taken him to an office and given him a two-month-old newspaper. On the second page was a story about an insurrection at the Army's Presidio in San Francisco. Accompanying the article were photographs of the riot, one showing a group of civilians marching in support of the mutineering enlisted men. A face had been circled in a red pencil.

It was Adrian. It seemed impossible, but there he was! He wasn't supposed to be there; he was in his last year at law school. In Boston. But he was not in Boston, he was in San Francisco harboring three convicted deserters who had escaped; that's what the G2 men said. His twin brother was working for the *enemy!* Goddamn it, that's what they *were* and that's what he was *doing!* The Pentagon wouldn't look upon *that* with a whole lot of laughs. Jesus! His brother! His *twin!*

So G2 flew him up north and, out of uniform, he had wandered the streets of Haight-Ashbury until he'd found Adrian.

"These aren't men, they're confused kids," his brother said in a quiet bar. "They were never even told what their legal alternatives were; they've been railroaded."

"They took oaths like everybody else. You can't make exceptions," Andrew had replied.

"Oh, come on. Two of them didn't know what that oath meant, and the other one genuinely changed his mind. But nobody wants to listen. The judge advocates want examples, and the defense attorneys don't want to make waves."

"Sometimes examples *have* to be made," the soldier had insisted.

"And the law says they're entitled to competent counsel. Not barracks drinking buddies who want to look good——"

"Get with it, Adrian!" he interrupted. "There's a war out there! The firepower's real! Bastards like these cost *lives.*"

"Not if they're over here."

"Yes, they do! Because others will begin to wonder why they're over *there.*"

"Maybe they should."

"For Christ's sake, you're talking about *rights,* aren't you?" asked the soldier.

"You better believe it."

"Well, doesn't the poor son of a bitch on patrol in a rice paddy have any? Maybe *he* didn't know what he was getting into; he just went along because the law said he had to. Maybe *he* changed his mind. But he doesn't have time to think about it; he's trying to stay alive. He gets confused, he gets sloppy, he gets *killed!*"

"We can't reach everybody; it's one of the law's oversights, an abuse built into the system. But we do what we can."

Adrian would not give him any information seven years ago. He refused to tell him where the deserters were hidden. So the soldier said good-bye in the quiet bar and waited in a San Francisco alley until his brother came out. He followed Adrian for three hours through the acid streets. The soldier was an expert in tracking stray patrols in jungles; San Francisco was just another jungle.

His brother made contact with one of the deserters five blocks from the waterfront. The boy was a Black, with a growth of beard on his face. He was tall and thin and matched the photograph in Andrew's pocket. His twin gave the deserter money; it was a simple matter to follow the Black down to the waterfront, to a filthy tenement that was as good a hiding place as any in the area.

The phone call was made to the military police. Ten minutes later three convicted deserters were dragged out of the filthy tenement, to spend eight years in the stockades.

The misfit network went to work; the crowds gathered screeching their epithets, swaying to their adolescent, useless chants. And throwing their plastic bags of feces.

His brother came up to him in the crowds that night and for several moments just stared at him. Finally he said, "You've driven me back. Thanks."

Then Adrian had walked swiftly away to the barricades of would-be revolutionaries.

Andrew's reflections were interrupted by Al Winston, nee Weinstein, an engineer with an aerospace company. Winston had called out his name and was making his way over. Al Winston was heavy into air force contracts, and lived in the Hamptons. Andrew didn't like Winston-Weinstein. Whenver he ran into him he thought of another Jew—and compared them. The Jew he thought of was stationed at the Pentagon after four years under heavy fire in the worst sections of the Delta. Captain Martin Greene was a tough son of a bitch, a great soldier—not a flabby Winston-Weinstein from the Hamptons. And Greene didn't gouge profits from cost overruns; instead he watched them, catalogued them. Marty Greene was one of *them.* One of Eye Corps.

"Many happy returns, major," said Winston, raising his glass.

"Thanks, Al. How are you?"

"Be a lot better if I could sell you boys something. I get no support from the ground troops." Winston grinned.

"You do pretty well *off* the ground. I read where you're in on the Grumman contract."

"Nickels and dimes. I've got a laser honing device that can be adapted to heavy artillery. But I can't get to first base."

Andrew toyed with the idea of sending Winston-Weinstein to Martin Greene. By the time Greene got finished with him, Al Winston would wish he'd never heard of the Pentagon. "I'll see what I can do. I'm not in procurement——"

"They *listen* to you, Andy."

"You never stop working, Al."

"Big house, big bills, rotten kids." Winston grinned again, then stopped smiling long enough to get across his point. "Put in a word for me. I'll make it worth your while."

"With what?" asked Andrew, his eyes straying toward the boathouse and the Chris-Craft and the sailboats moored in the water. "Money?"

Winston's grin returned, now nervous, awkward. "No offense," said the engineer softly.

Andrew looked at the Jew, thinking again of Captain Martin Greene and the difference between the two men. "No offense," he said, walking away.

Christ! Next to the freaks, he despised the *corrupters.* No, that wasn't true. Next to the corrupters, he despised those who allowed themselves to *be* corrupted. They were everywhere. Sitting in boardrooms, playing the golf courses in Georgia and Palm Springs, lapping up the sauce in the country clubs of Evanston and Grosse Pointe. They'd sold their ranks!

Colonels, generals, commanders, admirals. The whole goddamned military establishment was riddled with a new brand of thieves. Men who winked and smiled and put their signatures on committee recommendations, on procurements approvals, on contracts, on overruns. Because there were understandings made. Today's brigadier was tomorrow's "consultant" or "Washington representative."

Christ, it was easy to hate! The misfits, the corrupters, the corrupted. . . .

It was why Eye Corps was formed. A very small, select group of officers who were sick to death of the apathy and corruption and venality that pervaded every branch of the armed forces. Eye Corps was the answer, the medicine that would cure the sickness. For Eye Corps was compiling records from Saigon to Washington. The men of Eye Corps were putting it all together: names, dates, connections, illegal profits.

To hell with the so-called proper channels: up the chain of command. To the inspector general. To the secretary of the army. Who vouched for command? Who for the IG? Who in his right *mind* would vouch for the civilians?

No one they trusted. So they would do it themselves. Every general—every brigadier and admiral—*anyone* who tolerated any form of deviation would be smoked out and confronted with his crimes.

Eye Corps. That's what it was all about. A handful of the best young officers in the field. And one day they'd walk into the Pentagon and take over. None would dare stand in their way. The Eye Corps indictments would hang like grenades over the heads of the high brass. The grenades would explode if the brass didn't move out, leaving their chairs for men of the Eye Corps. The Pentagon belonged to them. They would give it meaning again. Strength. *Their* strength.

Adrian Fontine leaned on the bar and listened to the intense young students arguing, aware that his brother was staring at them. He looked up at Andrew; the soldier's cold eyes held their usual veiled contempt and then glanced away as Al Winston approached, raising his glass to the major.

Andrew was beginning to wear his contempt too openly, thought Adrian. His brother had lost some of his well-known cool; things aggravated the soldier too quickly these days.

God, how they'd veered from each other! They'd been so close once. The Geminis . . . brothers, twins, friends. The Geminis were the *best!* And somewhere along the line—in their teens, in prep school—it all started to change. Andrew began to think he was better than best, and Adrian became less than convinced he was adequate. Andrew never questioned his abilities; Adrian wasn't sure he had very many.

He was sure now. The terrible years of indecision were over; he'd passed through uncertainty and found his own way. Thanks in large measure to his very positive brother, the soldier.

And today, on their birthday, he had to confront his brother and ask some very disturbing questions. Questions that went to the core of Andrew's strength.

Core? It was appropriate; the sound was right, the spelling wrong.

Eye Corps was the name they'd uncovered. His brother was on the list. Eight self-deluded elitists who concealed evidence for their own purposes. A small band of officers who had convinced themselves they should run the Pentagon through what amounted to sheer blackmail. The situation might have been comic except that the evidence was there, and Eye Corps had it. The Pentagon was not above being manipulated by fear. Eye Corps was dangerous; it had to be ripped out.

They'd settle for that. They'd hand over a blanket subpoena to the army lawyers and let them handle it quietly. As long as the army lawyers did handle it and did not cover up. Perhaps it wasn't the time for demoralizing trials and long prison sentences. The guilt was so widespread and the motives so complex. But there was one irreducible condition. *Get the elitists out of uniform; clean your military house.*

Jesus, the irony of it! In San Francisco, Andrew had blown a crude whistle in the name of military law. Now, seven years later, he, Adrian, was blowing the whistle. Less crudely, he hoped, but the law was no less specific. The charge was obstruction of justice.

So much had changed. Nine months ago he was an assistant prosecutor in Boston, happy doing what he was doing, building a reputation that could lead to just about anywhere. Building it *himself*. Not having it *given* to him because he was Adrian Fontine, son of Victor Fontine, Limited; brother of West Point's celebrated Major Andrew Fontine, immaculate warrior.

Then a man had called him in early October, asking him to have drinks at the Copely bar late in the afternoon. The man's name was James Nevins and he was Black; he was also an attorney, and he worked for the Justice Department in Washington.

Nevins was the spokesman for a small contingent of harassed, disaffected government lawyers who burned under the tactics of the most politicized Justice Department in memory. The phrase "White House calling" simply meant another manipulation was taking place. The lawyers were worried, genuinely worried. Those manipulations were taking the country too close to the specter of a police state.

The lawyers needed help. From the outside. Someone to whom they could funnel their information. Someone who could organize and evaluate, who could set up and pay for a command center where they could meet privately and discuss their progress.

Someone, frankly, who could not be harassed. For reasons more obvious than not, one Adrian Fontine fit the bill. Would he accept?

Adrian hadn't wanted to leave Boston. He had his work; he had his girl. A slightly mad, brilliant girl he adored. Barbara Pierson, B.A., M.A., Ph.D. Associate Professor, Anthropology Laboratories, Harvard University. She of the quick deep laugh, the light-brown hair and the dark-brown eyes. They'd been living together for a year and a half; it wasn't easy to leave. But Barbara had packed for him and sent him on his way because she knew he had to go.

Just as he had to go seven, eight years ago. He had to leave Boston then, too. A depression had swept over him. He was the wealthy son of a powerful father; the twin brother of a man the army paraded in dispatches as one of the brightest young lights in the military.

What was left? For him? Who *was* he?

So he fled the trappings of a lifetime to see what he could find for himself. That was *his*. It was his own personal crisis; he couldn't explain it to anyone. And he ended up in San Francisco where there was a fight, a struggle he could understand. Where he could help. Until the immaculate warrior came along and ripped the scene apart.

Adrian smiled, remembering the morning after the terrible night in San Francisco. He'd gotten roaring drunk and woke up in the house of a legal aid lawyer in Cape Mendocino sick and vomiting.

"If you're who you say you are, you can do more than any of us," said the lawyer in Cape Mendocino that morning. "Hell, my old man was a janitor at the May Company."

In the seven intervening years Adrian had tried. But he knew he had only just begun.

"It's a constitutional ambiguity! Isn't that right, Adrian?"

"What? Sorry, I didn't hear what you said." The students at the bar had been arguing among themselves; now all eyes were on him.

"Free press versus pretrial bias," said an intense young girl, stumbling over the words.

"It's a gray area, I think," replied Adrian. "Each case is judged by itself."

The youngsters wanted more than he gave them, so they went back to yelling at each other.

Gray area. Saigon's Eye Corps had been a gray area only weeks ago. Rumors had filtered back to Washington that a small cadre of young senior officers were regularly harassing enlisted personnel on the docks and in the warehouses, insisting on copies of shipment manifests and destinations schedules. Shortly after, in one of the numerous, halfheartedly pursued antitrust cases at Justice, there was a plaintiff's allegation that records had been stolen from the corporation's Saigon offices, thus constituting illegally obtained evidence. The case would be dropped.

The lawyers at Justice wondered whether there was a connection between the strange group of officers who scoured the shipment manifests and corporations under contract to the Pentagon. Had the military gone that far? The conjecture was enough to send Jim Nevins to Saigon.

The Black attorney found what he was looking for. In a warehouse in the Tan Son Nhut cargo area. An officer was in the process of illegally transcribing security-related information on armaments supplies. Threatened with charges, the officer broke, and Eye Corps was revealed for everything it was. There were eight officers; the man caught knew the names of seven. The eighth was in Washington, that's all he knew.

Andrew Fontine headed the list of those identified.

Eye Corps. Nice fellows, thought Adrian. Just what the country needed; storm troopers out to save the nation.

Seven years ago in San Francisco his brother had not given him any warning before the action started, and the sirens came screaming into Haight-Ashbury. Adrian would be more considerate. He was going to give Andrew five days. There'd be no sirens, no riots . . . no eight-year sentences in the stockades. But the celebrated Major Andrew Fontine would be out of the army.

And although the work in Washington was nowhere near completed, Adrian would go back to Boston for a while. Back to Barbara.

He was tired. And sick with what faced him in an hour or so. The pain was real. Whatever else, Andrew was his brother.

The final guests had left. The orchestra was packing its instruments, and the caterers were cleaning up the lawn. The sky was growing darker, as much because of the threatening clouds over the water as by the approach of nightfall.

Adrian walked across the lawn to the flagstone steps and down to the boathouse. Andrew was waiting for him; he had told the soldier to be there.

"Happy birthday, counselor," said Andrew as Adrian came through the boathouse door. The soldier leaned against the wall beyond the boat slip, his arms folded, smoking a cigarette.

"Same to you," answered Adrian, stopping at the edge of the slip. "You staying tonight?"

"Are you?" asked Andrew.

"I thought I might. The old man looks pretty bad."

"Then I won't," said the soldier politely.

Adrian paused; he knew he was expected to speak. He wasn't quite sure how to begin, so instead he looked around the boathouse. "We had some good laughs down here."

"Did you want to reminisce? Is that why you asked me to come down here?"

"No. . . . I wish it were that simple."

The soldier flipped the cigarette into the water. "I hear you left Boston. You're in Washington."

"Yes. For a while. I keep thinking we'll run into each other."

"I doubt it," said the major, smiling. "We don't travel in the same circles. You working for a D.C. firm?"

"No. I guess you might say I'm a consultant."

"That's the best job in Washington." Andrew's voice was laced with quiet contempt. "Who are you counseling?"

"Some people who are very upset——"

"Oh, a consumer group; isn't that nice." It was an insulting statement. "Good for you!"

Adrian stared at his brother; the soldier returned the look. "Don't dismiss me, Andy. You're in no position to do that. You're in trouble. I'm not here to help you, I can't do that. I'm here to warn you."

"What the hell are you talking about?" asked the major softly.

"A deposition was taken from an officer in Saigon by one of our people. We have a complete statement about the activities of a group of eight men who call themselves Eye Corps."

Andrew bolted upright against the wall, his face pinched, his fingers stretched, curved, immobile. He seemed to freeze; he spoke barely above a whisper, spacing his words out. "Who is 'we'?"

"You'll know the origin soon enough. It's on the subpoena."

"Sub-poena?"

"Yes. The Justice Department, a specialist division. . . . I won't tell you the individual attorneys, but I will tell you that your name heads the Eye Corps list. We know there are eight of you; seven have been identified, the eighth is at the Pentagon. In procurement. We'll find him."

Andrew held his position against the wall; everything about him remained immobile, except the muscles of his jaw, which moved slowly, steadily. Once again his voice was low, measured. "What have you done? What have you bastards *done?*"

"Stopped you," answered Adrian simply.

"What do you know? What have you been told?"

"The truth. We've no reason to doubt it."

"You need proof for a subpoena!"

"You need probable cause. We have that."

"One deposition! *Nothing!*"

"Others'll follow. What difference does it make? You're finished."

Andrew's voice calmed. He spoke matter-of-factly. "Officers complain. Up and down the zones, officers complain every day——"

"Not this way. There's no fine line between complaints and blackmail. It's very defined, very distinct. You crossed over it."

"*Who have we blackmailed?*" asked Andrew swiftly. "No one!"

"Records were kept, evidence suppressed; the intent was clear. That's in the deposition."

"There *are* no records!"

"Oh, come on, they're *somewhere*," said Adrian wearily. "But I repeat, who gives a goddamn? You're finished."

The soldier moved. He breathed deeply and stood erect against the wall. "Listen to me," he said quietly, his voice strained. "You don't know what you're doing. You say you're a consultant to men who are upset. We both know what that means; we're the Fontines. Who needs resources when they have us?"

"I don't see it that way," broke in Adrian.

"It's *true!*" shouted the soldier. And then he lowered his voice. "You don't have to spell out what you're doing, the Boston newspapers did that. You nail the big fellows, the vested interests, you call them. You're good. Well, what the hell do you think *I'm* doing? We're nailing them, too! You stop Eye Corps, you're destroying the finest young senior officers in the field, men who want to rip out the garbage! Don't *do* that, Adree! *Join* us! I mean that."

"Join——" Adrian repeated the word in disbelief. Then he added quietly. "You're out of your mind. What makes you think that's remotely possible?"

Andrew took a step away from the wall; his eyes were steady on his brother. "Because we want the same thing."

"No, we don't."

"*Think,* for God's sake! 'Vested interests.' You use that a lot, 'vested interests.' I read your summation in the Tesco case; you repeated it continuously."

"It applied. One company owning many, setting a single policy when there should have been competition. What's your point?"

"You use the term negatively because that's the way you

find it. Okay, I'll buy that. But I submit there's another way to look at it. There can be *good* vested interests. Like us. Our interests isn't ourselves; we don't *need* anything. Our interests is the country and our resources are considerable. We're in positions to *do* something. I'm doing it. For Christ's sake, don't *stop* me!"

Adrian turned away from his brother and walked aimlessly along the moist planks of the boathouse toward the huge opening that led to the open water. The waves slapped against the pilings. "You're very glib, Andy. You were always very glib and sure and truly confident. But it's not going to work." He turned again and faced the soldier diagonally across the slip. "You say we don't need anything. I think we do; we both need—want—something. And what you want frightens me because I've got an idea what your concept of finest is. Frankly, it scares the hell out of me. The thought of your 'finest senior officers' controlling the country's hardware is enough to send me running to the library to reread the Constitution."

"That's arrogant horseshit! You don't know them!"

"I know the way they operate, the way you operate. If it'll make you feel better, you made some sense in San Francisco. I didn't like it, but I recognized it." Adrian walked back along the slip. "You're not making sense now, which is why I'm warning you. Save what you can of your neck, I owe you that much. Get out as gracefully as you can."

"You can't force me," said Andrew scathingly. "My record's one of the best. Who the hell are *you?* One lousy statement from a disgruntled officer in a combat zone. Bullshit!"

"I'll spell it out!" Adrian stopped by the boathouse doorway, raising his voice. "In five days—next Friday, to be precise—a blanket subpoena will be served on the adjutant general of the Courts of Military Justice. He'll have the weekend to negotiate his arrangements. Arrangements *can* be negotiated, but there's one irrevocable condition. You're *out*. All of you."

The soldier started forward, then stopped, his foot on the edge of the slip, as if he were about to spring across, lunging at his enemy. He held himself in check; waves of nausea and fury seemed to pass over him and through him. "I could . . . kill you," he whispered. "You're everything I despise."

"I guess I am," said Adrian, closing his eyes briefly, rubbing them in weariness. "You'd better get to the airport," he continued, now looking at his brother. "You've got a lot to do. I suggest you start with this so-called evidence you've been sitting on. We understand you've been collecting it for damn near three years. Get it to the proper authorities."

In angry silence the soldier lurched in rapid strides around the slip, past Adrian, and out to the boathouse steps. He began climbing, taking the flatstone stairs two at a time.

Adrian moved swiftly to the door and called out, halting his brother on the border of the lawn.

"Andy!"

The soldier stood motionless. But he did not turn around, or speak. So the lawyer continued.

"I admire your strength, I always have. Just as I admire father's. You're part of him, but you're not all of him. You missed something, so let's understand each other. You're everything I consider dangerous. I guess that means you're everything *I* despise."

"We understand each other," said Andrew, repeating the words in a monotone. He started up across the lawn toward the house.

19

The orchestra and the caterers left. Andrew was driven to LaGuardia Airport. There was a nine o'clock plane to Washington.

Adrian remained on the beach by himself for nearly thirty minutes after his brother left. Finally he wandered up to the house to talk to his parents. He told them he had intended to stay the night but now thought he should leave. He had to get back to Washington.

"You should have gone with your brother," said Jane at the front door.

"Yes, I should have," said Adrian softly. "I didn't think." He said his good-byes.

When he left, Jane walked out to the terrace, carrying the letter brought by the priest. She held it out for her husband, unable to conceal her fear. "A man brought this. About three hours ago. He was a priest. He said he was from Rome."

Victor looked up at his wife. There was no comment in his eyes, and by the lack of it, there was. "Why did you wait?"

"Because it was your sons' birthday."

"They're strangers to each other," said Fontine, taking the envelope. "They're both our children, but they're very far apart."

"It won't last. It's the war."

"I hope you're right," said Victor, opening the envelope and taking out the letter. It ran several pages, the handwriting small but precise. "Do we know a man named Aldobrini?"

"Who?"

"Guido Aldobrini. That's the signature." Fontine held up the last page.

"I don't think so," answered Jane, sitting down in the nearest chair, her eyes on the threatening sky. "Can you see in this light? It's getting darker."

"It is sufficient." Victor put the pages in sequence and began to read.

Signor Fontini-Cristi:

You do not know me although we met many years ago. That meeting cost me the better part of my life. I have spent over a quarter of a century in the Transvaal in holy penance for an act of shame. I did not touch you myself, but I observed and did not raise my voice for mercy, which was an indecent and unholy thing.

Yes, Signore, I was one of the priests with the Cardinal Donatti that dawn at Campo di Fiori. For what we believed was the preservation of Christ's Mother

Church on earth, the Cardinal convinced us that there were no laws of God or man or mercy standing between our actions and the preservation of God's Church. All our scholastic training and vows of obedience—not only to our superiors, but to the highest authority of conscience—were twisted by the power of Donatti's influence. I have spent twenty-five years trying to understand, but that is another story not pertinent here. One would have had to know the Cardinal to understand.

I am retired from my cloth. The illnesses of the African forests have taken their toll, and thanks be to Christ I do not fear death. For I have given of myself as fully as I knew how. I am cleansed and await the judgment of God.

Before I face our merciful Lord, however, there is information I must impart to you, for to withhold it now would be no less a sin than that for which I have paid holy penance.

The work of Donatti continues. A man, one of the three defrocked priests who were imprisoned by the civil court for their assault on you, has been released. As you perhaps know, one took his own life, the other died of natural causes while in prison. This third man survives and for motives beyond my comprehension, has rededicated himself to the pursuit of the Salonika documents. I say beyond my comprehension, for Cardinal Donatti was discredited in the highest circles of the Vatican. The Grecian documents cannot affect the Holy Mother Church. Divine revelation cannot be contravened by the hand of mortal man.

This defrocked priest goes by the name of Enrici Gaetamo, and he is taken to wearing the collar denied him by apostolic decree. It is my understanding that his years spent in the criminal institution have done nothing to enlighten his soul or show him the ways of a merciful Christ. On the contrary, I am told he is Donatti incarnate. A man to be feared.

He currently, painstakingly, researches every detail he can unearth relative to the train from Salonika thirty-three years ago. His travels have carried him from the yards of Edhessa, through the Balkans, over the rail routes beyond Monfalcone into the northern

Alpine regions. He seeks out all he can find who knew the son of Fontini-Cristi. He is a man possessed. He subscribes to the code of Donatti. There is no law of God or man that will interfere with his "journey for Christ," as he phrases it. Nor will he reveal to anyone the objective of his journey. But I know, and now you do. And soon I shall depart this life.

Gaetamo resides in a small hunting lodge in the hills of Varese. I'm sure the proximity to Campo di Fiori does not escape you.

This is all I can tell you; it is all I know. That he will attempt to reach you, I am certain. That you be warned and remain safe in God's hands, is my prayer.

In sorrow and personal anguish for my past, I remain,

Guido Aldobrini

There was the sound of thunder over the water; Fontine wished the symbolism were not so crudely simple. The clouds were above them now; the sun was gone and the rains began. He was grateful for the diversion. He looked at Jane. She was staring at him; somehow he had communicated to her his profound uneasiness.

"Go in," he said softly. "I'll follow in a minute or two."

"The letter——?"

"Of course," he answered her unspoken question as he replaced the pages in the envelope and handed it to her. "Read it."

"You'll be drenched. The rain will get stronger."

"It's refreshing; you know I like the rain." He smiled up at her. "Then perhaps you'll help me change the brace while we talk."

She stood above him for a moment, and he could feel her eyes on him. But as always, she would leave him alone when he wished it.

He was chilled by his thoughts, not the rain. The letter from Aldobrini was not the first time Salonika had reappeared. He had said nothing to Jane for there was nothing concrete, only a series of obscurely disturbing—seemingly minor—occurrences.

Three months ago he had gone to Harkness for yet another week of corrective surgery. Several days after the operation he'd had a visitor whose appearance startled him; a monsignor from the Archdiocese of New York. His name was Land, he said. He had returned to the United States after many years in Rome, and wanted to meet Victor because of information he had come across in the Vatican archives.

The priest was solicitous; what struck Fontine was that the cleric knew a great deal about his physical condition, far more than a casual visitor would know.

It was a very odd half hour. The priest was a student of history, he said. He had come across archive documents that raised profoundly disturbing questions between the house of Fontini-Cristi and the Vatican. Historical questions that led to the break between the *padroni* of the north and the Holy See. When Victor was well again, perhaps they could discuss the past. The *historical* past. He had ended his good-byes with a direct reference to the assault at Campo di Fiori. The pain and anguish inflicted by one maniacal prelate could not be laid at the soul of the church, he said.

About five weeks later there'd been a second incident. Victor had been in his Washington office, preparing to testify before a congressional committee looking into the tax concessions enjoyed by American shippers sailing under the Paraguayan flag, when his intercom buzzed.

"Mr. Fontine, Mr. Theodore Dakakos is here. He says he wants to pay his respects."

Dakakos was one of the young Greek shipping giants, an impertinent rival of Onassis and Niarchos, and far better liked. Fontine told his secretary to send him in.

Dakakos was a large man with a blunt, open expression on his face that might become an American football player more than a shipping tycoon. He was around forty years of age; his English was precise, the language of a student.

He had flown to Washington to observe the hearings, perhaps to learn something, he said smiling. Victor laughed; the Greek's reputation for integrity was matched only by the legend of his acute business sense. Fontine told him so.

"I was most fortunate. At a very young age I was given the advantages of an education by a sympathetic but remote religious brotherhood."

"You were, indeed, fortunate."

"My family was not wealthy, but they served their church, I'm told. In ways that today I do not understand."

The young Greek magnate was saying something beyond his words, but Victor could not determine what it was. "Gratitude as well as God, then, moves in strange ways," said Victor smiling. "Your reputation is a fine one. You do credit to those who aided you."

"Theodore is my first name, Mr. Fontine. My full name is Theodore Annaxas Dakakos. Throughout my schooling I was known as Annaxas the Younger. Does that mean anything to you?"

"In what way?"

"The name Annaxas."

"I've dealt with literally hundreds of your countrymen over the years. I don't think I've ever run across the name Annaxas."

The Greek had remained silent for several moments. Then he spoke quietly. "I believe you."

Dakakos left soon after.

The third occurrence was the strangest of all; it triggered a memory of violence so sharply into focus that Fontine lost his breath. It had happened only ten days ago in Los Angeles. He was at the Beverly Hills Hotel for conferences between two widely divergent companies trying to merge their interests. He had been called in to salvage what he could; the task was impossible.

Which was why he was taking the sun in the early afternoon, instead of sitting inside the hotel listening to lawyers trying to justify their retainers. He was drinking a Campari at a table in the outside pool area, astonished at the number of good-looking people who apparently did not have to work for a living.

"*Guten Tag, mein Herr.*"

The speaker was a woman in her late forties or early fifties, that age so well cosmeticized by the well-to-do. She was of medium height, quite well proportioned, with streaked blond hair. She wore white slacks and a blue blouse. Covering her eyes was a pair of large silver-rimmed sunglasses. Her German was natural, not studied. He replied in his own, academic, less natural, as he rose awkwardly.

"Good afternoon. Have we met? I'm sorry, but I don't seem to remember."

"Please, sit down. It's difficult for you. I know that."

"You do? Then we *have* met."

The woman sat down opposite him. She continued in English. "Yes. But you had no such difficulties then. You were a soldier then."

"During the war?"

"There was a flight from Munich to Müllheim. And a whore from the camps escorted on that flight by three Wehrmacht pigs. More pigs than she, I try to tell myself."

"My God!" Fontine caught his breath. "You were a *child*. What happened to you?"

She told him briefly. She had been taken by the French Resistance fighters to a transit camp southwest of Montbéliard. There for several months she endured agonies best left undescribed, as she experienced the process of narcotics withdrawal. She had tried to commit suicide numerous times, but the Resistance people had other ideas. They banked on the fact that once the drugs were expunged, her memories would be motive enough to turn her into an effective underground agent. She was already tough; that much they could see.

"They were right, of course," the woman said, ten days ago at the table on the patio of the Beverly Hills Hotel. "They kept watch over me night and day, men and women. The men had more fun; the French never waste anything, do they?"

"You survived the war," Fontine replied, not caring to probe.

"With a bucket full of medals. *Croix de guerre, Légion d'honneur, Légion de résistance.*"

"And so you became a great motion picture star and I was too stupid to recognize you." Victor smiled gently.

"Hardly. Although I've had occasions to be associated, as it were, with many prominent people of the motion picture industry."

"I'm afraid I don't understand."

"I became—and at the risk of sounding immodest, still am—the most successful madame in the south of France. The Cannes Film Festival alone provides sufficient income for a perfectly adequate subsistence." It was the woman's turn to smile. It was a good smile, thought Fontine. Genuine, alive.

"Then I'm very happy for you. I'm Italian enough to find a certain honorableness in your profession."

"I knew you were. And would. I'm here on a talent hunt. It would be my pleasure to grant any request you might have. There are a number of my girls out there in the pool."

"No, thank you. You're most kind, but, as you said, I am not the man I was."

"I think you're magnificent," she said simply. "I always have." She smiled at him. "I must go. I recognized you and wanted to speak to you, that's all." She rose from the table and extended her hand. "Don't get up."

The handshake was firm. "It's been a pleasure—and a relief—to see you again," he said.

She held his eyes and spoke quietly. "I was in Zürich a few months ago. They traced me through a man named Lübok. To you. He was a Czech. A queen, I'm told. He was the man on the plane with us, wasn't he?"

"Yes. A very brave man, I must add. A king, in my judgment." Victor was so startled he replied instinctively, without comprehending. He had not thought of Lübok in years.

"Yes, I remember. He saved all of us. They broke him." The woman released his hand.

"Broke him? About *what?* My God, the man, if he's alive, is my age or more. Seventy or better. Who would be interested in such old men? What are you talking about?"

"About a man named Vittorio Fontini-Cristi, son of Savarone."

"You're talking nonsense. Nonsense I understand, but I don't see how it might concern you. *Or* Lübok."

"I don't know any more. Nor do I care to. A man in Zürich came to my hotel room and asked questions about you. Naturally, I couldn't answer them. You were merely an Allied Intelligence officer who saved a whore's life. But he knew about Anton Lübok."

"Who was this man?"

"A priest. That is all I know. Good-bye, *Kapitän.*" She turned and walked away, waving and smiling at various girls who were splashing about in the pool and laughing too obviously.

A priest. In Zürich.

. . . He seeks out all he can find who knew the son of Fontini-Cristi. . . .

Now he understood the enigmatic meeting at the poolside in Los Angeles. A defrocked priest had been released after nearly thirty years in prison and revived the hunt for the documents of Constantine.

The work of Donatti continues, the letter said. *He currently, painstakingly, researches every detail he can unearth . . . his travels have carried him from the yards at Edhessa, through the Balkans . . . beyond Monfalcone into the northern Alpine regions.*

He seeks out all he can find who knew the son of Fontini-Cristi.

And thousands of miles away in New York City, another priest—very much *of* the cloth—comes into a hospital room and speaks of an act of barbarism that could not be separated from those documents. Lost three decades ago and hunted still.

And in Washington, a young industrial giant walks into an office and for no apparent reasons says his family served the church in ways he did not understand.

". . . I was given . . . advantages . . . by a sympathetic but remote religious brotherhood. . . ."

The *Order of Xenope*. It was suddenly so very clear.

Nothing was coincidence.

It had come back. The train from Salonika had plunged through thirty years of sleep and reawakened. It had to be controlled before the hatreds collided, before the fanatics turned the search into a holy war, as they had done three decades ago. Victor knew he owed that much to his father, his mother, to the loved ones slain in the white lights of Campo di Fiori; to those who had died at Oxfordshire. To a misguided young monk named Petride who took his own life on a rocky slope in Loch Torridon, to a man named Teague, to an undergrounder named Lübok, to an old man named Guido Barzini who had saved him from himself.

The violence could not be allowed to return.

The rain came faster now, harder, in diagonal sheets blown by the wind. Fontine reached for the wrought iron chair beside him and struggled to his feet, his arm clamped within the steel band of his cane.

He stood on the terrace looking out over the water. The

wind and the rain cleared his mind. He knew what he had to do, where he had to go.

To the hills of Varese.

To Campo di Fiori.

20

The heavy car approached the gates of Campo di Fiori. Victor stared out the window, aware of the spasm in his back; the eye was recording, the mind remembering.

His life had been altered, in pain, on the stretch of ground beyond the gates. He tried to control the memory; he could not suppress it. The images he observed were forced out of his mind's eye, replaced by black suits and white collars.

The car went through the gates; Victor held his breath. He had flown into Milan from Paris as unobtrusively as possible. In Milan he had taken a single room at the Albergo Milano, registering simply as: V. Fontine, New York City.

The years had done their work. There were no raised eyebrows, no curious glances; the name triggered no surprises. Thirty years ago a Fontine or a Fontini in Milan would be reason enough for comment. Not now.

Before he left New York he had made one inquiry—any more might have raised an alarm. He had learned the identity of the owners of Campo di Fiori. The purchase had been made twenty-seven years ago; there had been no change of ownership since that time. Yet the name had no impact in Milan. None had heard of it.

Baricours, Père et Fils. A Franco-Swiss company out of Grenoble, that's what the transfer papers said. Yet there was no Baricours, Père et Fils, in Grenoble. No details could be learned from the lawyer who had negotiated the sale. He had died in 1951.

The automobile rolled past the embankment into the circular drive in front of the main house. The spasm in Victor's back was compounded by a sharp stinging sensation behind his eyes; his head throbbed as he reentered the execution grounds.

He gripped his wrist and dug his fingers into his own flesh. The pain helped; he was able to look out the window and see what was there now, not thirty-three years ago.

What he saw was a mausoleum. Dead but cared for. Everything was as it had been, but not for the living. Even the orange rays of the setting sun had a dead quality to them: majestically ornamental, but not alive.

"Aren't there groundkeepers or men at the gates?" he asked.

The driver turned in the seat. "Not this afternoon, *padrone*," he replied. "There are no guards. And no priests of the Curia."

Fontine lurched forward in the seat; his metal cane slipped. He stared at the driver.

"I've been tricked."

"Watched. Expected. Not tricked, really. Inside, a man is waiting for you."

"One man?"

"Yes."

"Would his name be Enrici Gaetamo?"

"I told you. There are no priests of the Curia here. Please, go inside. Do you need help?"

"No, I can manage." Victor got out of the car slowly, each movement a struggle, the pain in his eyes receding, the spasm in his back subsiding. He understood. His mind was refocusing itself. He had come to Campo di Fiori for answers. For a confrontation. But he had not expected it to be this way.

He walked up the wide marble steps to the oak door of his childhood. He paused and waited for what he thought was inevitable: a sense of overwhelming sorrow. But it did not come, because there was no life here.

He heard the gunning of the engine behind him and turned. The driver had swung the car out into the curve, and driven past the embankment into the road toward the main gate. Whoever he was, he wanted to be away as rapidly as possible.

As he watched, Victor heard the metallic sound of a latch. He turned again to the huge oak door; it had opened.

The shock was impossible to conceal. Nor did he bother to hide it. The rage inside him welled; his whole body trembled in anger.

The man at the door was a *priest!* Dressed in the black cassock of the church. He was an old man and frail. Had he been otherwise, Fontine might have struck out at him.

Instead he stared at the old man and spoke quietly. "That a priest would be in this house is most painful to me."

"I'm sorry you feel that way," replied the priest in a foreigner's Italian, his voice thin but firm. "We revered the *padrone* of the Fontini-Cristis. We placed our most precious treasures in his hands."

Their eyes were locked; neither wavered, but the anger within Victor was slowly replaced with incredulity. "You're Greek," he said, barely audible.

"I am, but that's not relevant. I'm a monk from Constantine. Please. Come in." The old priest stepped back to allow Victor to pass. He added softly, "Take your time. Let your eyes roam. Little has changed; photographs and inventories were taken of each room. We have maintained everything as it was."

A mausoleum.

"So did the Germans." Fontine walked into the enormous hall. "It's strange that those who went to such lengths to own Campo di Fiori don't want to change it."

"One doesn't cut a great jewel or deface a worthy painting. There's nothing strange in that."

Victor did not reply. Instead, he gripped his cane and walked with difficulty toward the staircase. He stopped in front of the arch that led to the huge drawing room on the left. Everything *was* as it had been. The paintings, the half-tables against the massive walls, the glazed antique mirrors above the tables, the oriental rugs covering the polished floor, the wide staircase, its balustrade glistening.

He looked over through the north arch into the dining room. Twilight shadows fell across the enormous table, now bare, polished, empty, where once the family had sat. He pictured them now; he could hear the chatter and the laughter. Arguments and anecdotes, never-ending talk; dinners were important events at Campo di Fiori.

The figures froze, the voices disappeared. It was time to look away.

Victor turned. The monk gestured at the south arch. "Shall we go into your father's study?"

He preceded the old man into the drawing room. Involuntarily—for he did not care to activate memories—his eyes fell on the furnishings, suddenly so familiar. Every chair, every lamp, every tapestry and sconce and table was precisely as he remembered it.

Fontine breathed deeply and closed his eyes for a moment. It was macabre. He was passing through a museum that had once been a living part of his existence. In some ways it was the cruelest form of anguish.

He continued on through the door into Savarone's study; it had never been his, although his life nearly ended in that room. He passed by the doorframe through which a severed, bloody hand had been thrown in the shadows.

If there was anything that startled him it was the desk lamp; and the light that spilled downward over the floor from the green shade. It was *precisely* as it was nearly three decades ago. His memory of it was vivid, for it was the light from the lamp that had washed over the shattered skull of Geoffrey Stone.

"Would you care to sit down?" asked the priest.

"In a minute."

"May I?"

"I beg your pardon?"

"May I sit at your father's desk?" said the monk. "I've watched your eyes."

"It's your house, your desk. I'm a visitor."

"But not a stranger."

"Obviously. Am I speaking with a representative of Baricours, Père et Fils?"

The old priest nodded silently. He walked slowly around the desk, pulled out the chair, and lowered his frail body into it. "Don't blame the lawyer in Milan; he couldn't have known. Baricours met your conditions, we made sure of it. Baricours is the Order of Xenope."

"And my enemy," said Victor quietly. "In 1942 there was an M.I.-Six compound in Oxfordshire. You tried to kill my wife. Many innocent people lost their lives."

"Decisions were made beyond the control of the Elders. The extremists had their way; we couldn't stop them. I don't expect you to accept that."

"I don't. How did you know I was in Italy?"

"We are not what we once were, but we still have resources. One in particular keeps his eye on you. Don't ask me who it is; I won't tell you. Why did you come back? After thirty years, why did you return to Campo di Fiori?"

"To find a man named Gaetamo," answered Fontine. "Enrici Gaetamo."

"Gaetamo lives in the hills of Varese," said the monk.

"He's still looking for the train from Salonika. He's traveled from Edhessa, through the Balkans, across Italy, into the northern mountains. Why have you stayed here all these years?"

"Because the *key* is here," replied the monk. "A pact was made. In October of 1939, I traveled to Campo di Fiori. It was I who negotiated Savarone Fontini-Cristi's participation, I who sent a dedicated priest on that train with his brother, an engineer. And demanded their deaths in the name of God."

Victor stared at the monk. The spill of the lamp illuminated the pale, taut flesh and the sad, dead eyes. Fontine recalled the visitor in his Washington office. "A Greek came to me saying his family served their church once in ways he didn't understand. Was this priest's brother the engineer, named Annaxas?"

The old cleric's head snapped up; the eyes became briefly alive. "Where did you hear that name?"

Fontine looked away, his eyes falling on a painting beneath a Madonna on the wall. A hunting scene, birds being flushed from a thicket by men with guns. Other birds flew above. "We'll trade information," he said quietly. "Why did my father agree to work with Xenope?"

"You know the answer. He had only one concern: not to divide the Christian world. The defeat of the fascists was all he cared about."

"Why was the vault taken from Greece in the first place?"

"The Germans were scavengers and Constantine was marked. That was the information we received from Poland and Czechoslovakia. The Nazi commanders stole from museums, tore apart retreats and monasteries. We couldn't take the chance of leaving it there. Your father engineered the removal. Brilliantly. Donatti was tricked."

"By the use of a second train," added Victor. "Mounted and routed identically. Sent three days later."

"Yes. Word of this second train was leaked to Donatti through the Germans, who had no concept of the significance of the vault from Constantine. They looked for treasures—paintings, sculpture, art objects—not obscure writings they were told were valuable only to scholars. But Donatti, the fanatic, could not resist; the Filioque denials had been rumored for decades. He had to possess them." The priest of Xenope paused, the memory painful. "The cardinal's and the German interests coincided. Berlin wanted Savarone Fontini-Cristi's influence destroyed; Donatti wanted to keep him from that train. At all costs."

"Why was Donatti involved at all?"

"Again, your father. He knew the Nazis had a powerful friend in the Vatican. He wanted Donatti exposed for what he was. The cardinal could not know about that second train unless the Germans told him. Your father intended to make use of this fact. It was the only price Fontini-Cristi asked of us. As it turned out, that price brought about the executions of Campo di Fiori."

Victor could hear his father's voice piercing through the decades. . . . *He issues edicts to the uninformed and enforces them by fear. . . . A disgrace to the Vatican.* Savarone knew the enemy, but not the extremes of his monstrousness.

The brace across Fontine's back was cutting into his flesh. He had been standing too long. He gripped his cane and walked toward the chair in front of the desk. He sat down.

"Do you know what was on that train?" asked the old monk gently.

"Yes. Brevourt told me."

"Brevourt never knew. He was told part of the truth. Not all of it. What did he tell you?"

Victor was suddenly alarmed. He locked eyes once again with the priest.

"He spoke of the Filioque denials, studies that refuted the divinity of Christ. The most damaging of which was an Aramaic scroll that raised questions as to whether Jesus ever existed at all. The conclusion would appear that he did not."

"It was never the denials. Never the scroll. It was—*is*—a confession written in its entirety that predates all the other documents." The priest of Xenope looked away. He raised his hands; his bony fingers touched the pale skin of his cheek. "The Filioque denials are artifacts for scholars to ponder. As one of them, the Aramaic scroll, was ambiguous, as the scrolls of the Dead Sea were ambiguous when studied fifteen hundred years later. However, thirty years ago at the height of a moral war—if that's not a contradiction in terms—that scroll's exposure might have been catastrophic. It was enough for Brevourt."

Fontine was mesmerized. "What is this confession? I've never heard it mentioned."

The monk returned his eyes to Victor. During the brief silence before he spoke, the old priest conveyed the pain of his immediate decision. "It is everything. It was written on a parchment brought out of a Roman prison in the year sixty-seven. We know the date because the document speaks of the death of Jesus in terms of the Hebrew calendar that places the figure at thirty-four years. It coincides with anthropological scholarship. The parchment was written by a man who wandered blindly; he speaks of Gethsemane and Capernaum, Gennesaret and Corinth, Pontus, Galatia and Cappadocia. The writer can be no one else but Simon of Bethsaida, given the name of Peter by the man he called Christ. What is contained in that parchment is beyond anything in your imagination. It must be found."

The priest stopped and stared across at Victor.

"And destroyed?" asked Fontine softly.

"Destroyed," replied the monk. "But not for any reason you might think of. For *nothing* is changed, yet *all* is changed. My vows forbid me to tell you more. We're old men; we haven't much time. If you can help, you must. That parchment can alter history. It should have been destroyed centuries ago, but arrogance prevailed. It could plunge a great part of the world into a terrible agony. No one can justify the pain."

"But you say nothing is changed," replied Victor, repeating the monk's words, "yet *all* is changed. One cancels the other; it doesn't make sense."

"The confession on that parchment makes sense. In all its anguish. I can tell you no more."

Fontine held the priest's eyes. "Did my father know about the parchment? Or was he told only what Brevourt was told?"

"He knew," said the monk of Xenope. "The Filioque denials were like your American articles of impeachment, charges for canonical debate. Even the most damaging—as you called it—the Aramaic scroll, was subject to the linguistic interpretations of antiquity. Fontini-Cristi would have perceived these issues; Brevourt did not. But the confession on that parchment is not debatable. It was the single, awesome thing that demanded Fontini-Cristi's commitment. He understood and accepted it."

"A confession on a parchment taken out of a Roman prison." Fontine spoke quietly; the issue was clear. "That's what the vault of Constantine is all about."

"Yes."

Victor let the moment pass. He leaned forward in the chair, his hand on his metal cane. "You said the key is here. But why? Donatti searched—every wall, every floor, every inch of ground. You've remained here for twenty-seven years, and still there's nothing. What's left for you?"

"Your father's words, said in this room."

"What were they?"

"That the markings would be here in Campo di Fiori. Etched for a millennium. That was the phrase he used: 'etched for a millennium.' And his son would understand. It was part of his childhood. But his son was told nothing. We came to know that."

Fontine refused a bed in the great house. He would rest in the stables, in the bed on which he had placed the dead Barzini a lifetime ago.

He wanted to be alone, isolated, and above all, out of the house, away from the dead relics. He had to think, to go back over the horror again and again until he found the missing connection. For it was there now; the pattern existed. What remained missing was the line that completed the design.

Part of his childhood. No, not there, not yet. Don't start there; it would come later. Begin with what one knew, one saw, one heard for himself.

He reached the stables and walked through the empty rooms and past the empty stalls. There was no electricity now; the old monk had given him a flashlight. Barzini's room was as he remembered it. Bare, without ornament; the narrow bed, the worn-out armchair, the simple trunk for his few possessions.

The tack room, too, was as he had seen it last. Bridles and leather straps on the walls. He sat down on a small wooden stirrup bench, exhaling in pain as he did so. He put out the flashlight. The moon shone through the windows. He inhaled deeply and forced his mind back to the horrible night.

The shattering of machine gun fire filled his ears, evoking the memory he abhorred. The swirling clouds of smoke were there, the arched bodies of loved ones in succeeding instants of death, seen in the blinding light of the floodlamps.

Champoluc is the river! Zürich is the river!

The words were screamed, then repeated, twice, three times! Roared up at him but aimed higher than where he was, above him, as the bullets pierced his father's chest and stomach.

Champoluc is the river!

The head raised? Was that it? The head, the *eyes.* It's always in *the eyes!* A split fraction of time before the words poured out, his father's eyes had *not* been on the embankment, *not* on *him.*

They had been leveled to his right, on a diagonal. Savarone had been staring at the automobiles, into the *third automobile.*

Savarone had seen Guillamo Donatti! He had recognized him in the shadows of the back seat of the car. At the instant of death, he knew the identity of his executioner.

And the roars of fury had poured forth, up at his son, but beyond his son. Up and beyond and . . . what *was* it? What *was* it his father had done at that last instant of life? It was the missing connection, the line that completed the pattern!

Oh, Christ! Some part of his body. His head, his shoulders, his hands. What *was* it?

The *whole* body! My God, it was the gesture in *death* of the *whole body!* Head, arms, hands. Savarone's body had been stretched in one final gesture! *To his left!* But not the house, not the lighted rooms so viciously invaded, but beyond the house. *Beyond the house!*

Champoluc is the river. . . .

Beyond the house!

The *woods* of Campo di Fiori!

The *river!* The wide mountain stream in the forest! Their own personal *"river"!*

It was part of his childhood. The river of his childhood was a quarter of a mile beyond the gardens of Campo di Fiori!

Sweat fell from Victor's face; his breath was erratic, his hands trembled. He gripped the edge of the stirrup bench in the darkness. He was spent, but certain; it was all suddenly, totally clear.

The *river* was not in the Champoluc, nor in Zürich. It was minutes away from *here.* A brief walk down a forest path made by generations of children.

Etched for a millennium.

Part of his *childhood.*

He pictured the woods, the flowing stream, the rocks . . . the rocks . . . the *rocks.* The *boulders* that bordered the stream in the deepest section of the water! There was one *large* boulder used for diving and jumping and lying in the sun, and *scratching initials,* and childish *messages,* and secret *codes* between very young brothers!

Etched for a millennium. His *childhood!*

Had Savarone chosen *this rock* on which to etch his message?

It was suddenly so clear. So *consistent.*

Of course he had.

21

The night sky turned gradually to gray, but no rays of the Italian sun broke through the overcast. Instead, there would be rain soon, and a cold summer wind whipping down from the northern mountains.

Victor walked down the stable road into the gardens. It was too dark to make out the colors. Then, too, there were not the rows of flowers bordering the paths as there had been; he could see that much.

He found the path with difficulty, only after examining the uncut grass, angling the beam of his flashlight into the ground, looking for signs of the past. As he penetrated the woods beyond the garden familiar things came back to him: a gnarled olive tree with thick limbs; a cluster of white birches, now concealed by beechwood vine and dying spruce.

The stream was no more than a hundred yards away, diagonally to his right, if memory served. There were birches and tall pines; giant weeds formed a wall of tentacles, soft but uncomfortable to the touch.

He stopped. There was a rustle of bird wings, the snap of a twig. He turned and peered into the black shapes of the overgrowth.

Silence.

Then the sound of a small animal intruded on the quiet. He had probably disturbed a hare. Strange, he should assume so naturally that it was a hare. The surroundings jogged memories long forgotten; as a boy he had trapped hares in these woods.

He could smell the water now. He had always been able to smell the moistness when he approached the stream, smell it before he heard the sound of the flow. The foliage nearest the water was thick, almost impenetrable. Seepage from the stream had fed a hundred thousand roots, allowing rampant, uncontrolled growth. He had to force back limbs and spread thickets to approach the stream.

His left foot was ensnared in a tangle of ground vine. He stepped back on his right and, with his cane, worked it free, losing his balance as he did so. The cane whipped out of his hand, spiraling into the darkness. He grabbed for a branch to break his fall; the small limb cracked, stripping itself from its source. On one knee, he used the thick stick to push himself off the ground; his cane was gone; he could not see it. He held onto the stick and threaded his way through the mass of foliage to the water's edge.

The stream seemed narrower than he remembered. Then he realized it was the gray darkness and the overgrown forest that made it appear so. Three decades of inattention had allowed the woods to impinge upon the water.

The massive boulder was on his right, upstream, no

more than twenty feet away, but the wall of overgrowth was such that it might have been half a mile. He began edging his way toward it, crouching, rising, separating, each movement a struggle. Twice he butted against hard obstacles in the earth, too high, too thin and narrow, for rocks. He swung the beam of the flashlight down; the obstacles were iron stakes, rusted and pitted as though relics from a sunken galleon.

He reached the base of the huge rock; its body extended over the water. He looked below, the flashlight illuminating the separation of earth and flowing stream, and realized the years had made him cautious. The distance to the water was only a few feet, but it appeared a gulf to him now. He sidestepped his way down into the stream, the thick stick in his left hand prodding the depth.

The water was cold—as he remembered, it was always cold—and came up to his thighs, lapped over his waist below the brace, sending chills throughout his body. He shivered and swore at the years.

But he was *here*. It was all that mattered.

He focused the flashlight on the rock. He was several feet from the edge of the bank; he would have to organize his search. Too many minutes could be wasted going over areas twice or three times because he could not remember examining them. He was honest with himself: He was not sure how long he could take the cold.

He reached up, pressing the end of the stick into the surface of the rock. The moss that covered it peeled easily. The details of the boulder's surface, made vivid by the harsh, white beam of the flashlight, looked like thousands of tiny craters and ravines.

His pulse accelerated at the first signs of human intrusion. They were faint, barely visible, but they were there. And they were his marks, from more than half a century ago. Descending lines scratched deeply into the rock as part of a long forgotten boyhood game.

The **V** was the clearest letter; he had made sure his mark was vivid, properly recorded. Then there was **b**, followed by what might have been numbers. And a **t**, again followed by what were probably numbers. He had no idea what they meant.

He peeled the moss above and below the scratchings. There were other faint markings; some seemed meaningful.

Initials, mainly; here and there, rough drawings of trees and arrows and quarter circles drawn by children.

His eyes strained under the glare of the flashlight; his fingers peeled and rubbed and caressed a larger and larger area. He made two vertical lines with the stick to show where he had searched and moved farther into the cold water; but soon the cold grew too much and he climbed onto the bank, seeking warmth. His hands and arms and legs were trembling with cold and age. He knelt in the damp overgrowth and watched the vapor of his breath diffuse itself in the air.

He went back into the water, to the point where he had left off. The moss was thicker; underneath he found several more markings similar to the first set nearer the embankment. **V**'s and **b**'s and **t**'s and very faint numbers.

Then it came back to him through the years—faintly, as faintly as the letters and the numbers. And he *knew* he was right to be in that stream, at that boulder.

Burrone! Traccia! He had forgotten but now recalled. "Ravine," "trail." He had always scratched—recorded—their journeys into the mountains!

Part of his childhood.

My God, what a part! Every summer Savarone gathered his sons together and took them north for several days of climbing. Not dangerous climbing, more hiking and camping. For them all, a high point of the summers. And he gave them maps so they knew where they had been; and Vittorio, the eldest, would indelibly, soberly record the journeys on the boulder down at the stream, their "river."

They had christened the rock The Argonaut. And the scratchings of The Argonaut served as a permanent record of their mountain odysseys. Into the mountains of their boyhood.

Into the mountains.

The train from Salonika had gone into the mountains! The vault of Constantine was somewhere in the mountains!

He balanced himself with the stick and continued. He was near the face of the rock; the water came up to his chest, chilling the steel brace beneath his clothes. The farther out he went the more convinced he became; he was *right* to be there! The faint scratching—the faded scars of half lines and zigzags—were more and more numerous.

The Argonaut's hull was covered with graffiti related to journeys long forgotten.

The cold water sent a spasm through the base of his spine; the stick fell from his hands. He slapped at the water, grabbing the stick, shifting his fee in the effort. He fell—glided, actually—into the rock and righted himself by pressing the stick into the mud below for balance.

He stared at the sight inches from his eyes in the water. There was a short, straight, horizontal line deeply defined in the rock. It was *chiseled.*

He braced himself as best he could, transferred the stick to his right hand, manipulating it between his thumb and the flashlight, and pressed his fingers into the surface of the boulder.

He traced the line. It angled sharply downward into the water; across and down and then it abruptly stopped.

7. It was a 7.

Unlike any other faded hieroglyphics on the rock; not scratches made by awkward, youthful hands, but a work of precision. The figure was no more than two inches high—but the impression itself was a good half inch deep.

He'd *found* it! *Etched for a millennium!* A message carved in rock, *chiseled in stone!*

He brought the flashlight closer and carefully moved his trembling fingers about the area. My God, was this *it?* Was this the *moment?* In spite of the cold and the wet, the blood raced to his head, his heart accelerated. He felt like shouting; but he had to be *sure!*

At midpoint of the vertical line of the 7, about an inch to its right, was a dash. Then another single vertical line . . . a 1, followed by yet another vertical that was shorter, angling to the right . . . and intersected by a line straight up and down. . . . A 4. It was a 4.

Seven—dash—one—four. More below the surface of the water than above it.

Beyond the 4 was another short, horizontal line. A dash. It was followed by a . . . Z, but not a Z. The angles were not abrupt, they were rounded.

2.

Seven—dash—one—four—dash—two. . . .

There was a final impression but it was not a figure. It was a series of four short, straight lines joined together. A box . . . a square. A perfect geometric square.

Of course, it *was* a figure! A *zero!*

0.

Seven—dash—one—four—dash—two—zero.

What did it *mean?* Had Savarone's age caused him to leave a message that meant nothing to anyone but *him?* Had everything been so brilliantly logical but the message itself? It meant *nothing.*

7—14—20. . . . A date? Was it a *date?*

My God! thought Victor. 7–14. July 14! His birthday! Bastille Day. Throughout his life that had been a minor source of amusement. A Fontini-Cristi born on the celebrated day of the French Revolution.

July 14 . . . two-zero . . . 20. 1920.

That was Savarone's key. Something had happened on July 14, 1920. What was it? What incident had occurred that his father considered so meaningful to his first son? Something that had a significance beyond other times, other birthdays.

A shaft of pain—the second of what he knew would be many—shot through his body, originating, once again, at the base of his spine. The brace was like ice; the cold of the water had chilled his skin and penetrated the tendons and muscle tissue.

With the sensitivity of a surgeon, he pressed his fingers around the area of the chiseled numbers. There was only the date; all else was flat and unspoiled. He took the stick in his left hand and thrust it below the water into the mud. Painfully, he sidestepped his way back toward the embankment, until the level of the water had receded to his thighs. Then he paused for breath. The flashes of pain accelerated; he had done more damage to himself than he had realized. A full convulsion was developing; he tensed the muscles of his jaw and throat. He had to get out of the water and lie down. Lurching for the overhanging vines on the embankment, he fell to his knees in the water. The flashlight spun out of his hand and rolled over some matted fern, its beam shooting out into the dense woods. He grabbed a cluster of thick, exposed roots and pulled himself up toward the ground, pushing the stick behind him into the mud for propulsion.

All movement was arrested in a paralyzing instant of shock.

Above him, in the darkness on the embankment, stood

the figure of a man. A huge man dressed in black, and motionless, staring down at him. Around his throat—in jarring counterpoint to the pitch-black clothing—was a rim of white. A priest's collar. The face—what he could see of it in the dim forest light—was impassive. But the eyes that bore down at him had fire in them, and hatred.

The man spoke. His speech was deliberate, slow, born of loathing.

"The enemy of Christ returns."

"You are Gaetamo," said Fontine.

"A man came in an automobile to watch my cabin in the hills. I knew that automobile, that man. He serves the heretic of Xenope. The monk who lives his life in Campo di Fiori. He was there to keep me away."

"But he couldn't."

"No." The defrocked priest elaborated no further. "So this is where it was. All those years and the answer was here." His deep voice seemed to float, beginning anywhere, ending abruptly in midstatement. "What did he leave? A name? Of what? A bank? A building in the Milan factories? We thought of those; we took them apart."

"Whatever it was, it has no meaning for you. Nor for me."

"Liar," replied Gaetamo quietly, in his chilling monotone. He turned his head right, then left; he was remembering. "We staked out every inch of these woods. We ran yellow strings from stake to stake and marked each area as we studied it. We considered burning, cutting . . . but were afraid of what we might destroy. We damned the stream and probed the mud. The Germans gave us instruments . . . but always nothing. The large rocks were filled with meaningless markings, including the birthdate of an arrogant seventeen-year-old who had to leave his conceit in stone. And always nothing."

Victor tensed. *Gaetamo had said it.* In one brief phrase the defrocked priest had unlocked the door! *An arrogant seventeen-year-old,* leaving his mark in stone. But *he* had not left it! Donatti had found the key but had not recognized it! The reasoning was so simple, so uncomplicated: a seventeen-year-old carving a memorable day on a familiar rock. It was so logical, so essentially unremarkable. And so *clear.*

As the memory was now clear. Most of it.

7–14–20. His seventeenth birthday. It came back to him because there had been none like it in his life. My God, thought Victor, Savarone was incredible! *Part of his childhood.* It was on his seventeenth birthday that his father had given him the present he had wanted so badly he had dreamed of it, pleaded for it: The chance to go up into the mountains without his younger brothers. To really do some climbing . . . *above* the usual and—for him—dreary campsites in the foothills.

On his seventeenth birthday, Savarone had presented him with an authentic Alpine pack, the sort used by experienced climbers. Not that his father was about to take him up the Jungfrau; they never really scaled anything extraordinary. But that first trip—*alone with his father*—was a landmark in his early manhood. That pack and that journey were symbols of something very important to him: proof that he was growing up in his father's eyes.

He had forgotten; he was not sure of it even now, for there had been other trips, other years. Had it—that first trip—been in the Champoluc? It must have been, but *where*? That *was* beyond memory.

". . . end your life in this water."

Gaetamo had spoken, but Fontine had not heard him: only the threat had penetrated. Of all men—all priests—this madman could be told nothing. "I found only meaningless scribblings. Childish markings, as you said."

"You found what rightfully belongs to *Christ!*" Gaetamo's words sliced through the forest. He lowered himself to one knee, his immense chest and head inches from Victor, his eyes wide and burning. "You found the *sword of the archangel of hell!* No more lies. Tell me what you've found!"

"Nothing."

"Liar! Why are you *here?* An old man in water and mud! What was in this stream? On this *rock!*"

Victor stared at the grotesque eyes. "Why am I here?" he repeated, stretching his neck, arching his tortured back, his features pinched. "I'm old. With memories. I convinced myself that the answer *might* be here. When we were children we left messages for one another here. You saw for yourself. Childish markings, scribblings, stone scratched against stone. I thought perhaps—— But I found nothing. If there was anything, it's gone now."

"You examined the rock, and then you stopped! You were prepared to leave."

"*Look* at me! How long do you think I can stay in this water?"

Gaetamo shook his head slowly. "I watched you. You were a man who found what he had come to find."

"You saw what you wanted to see. Not what was there."

Victor's foot slipped; the stick that braced him in the water slid in the mud, sinking deeper. The priest thrust out a hand and grabbed Fontine's hair. He yanked viciously, pulling Victor into the embankment, forcing his head and neck to one side. The sudden contortion was unbearable; wrenching pain spread throughout Fontine's body. The wide maniacal eyes above him in the dim light were not those of an aging man in the clothes of a priest but, instead, the eyes of a young fanatic thirty years ago.

Gaetamo saw. And understood. "We thought you were dead then. There was no way you could have survived. The fact that you did convinced our holy man that you were from *hell!* . . . You remember. For now I'll continue what was begun thirty years ago! And with each crack of your bones you'll have the chance—as you did then—to tell me what you've found. But don't lie. The pain will only stop when you tell me the truth."

Gaetamo bent forward. He began to twist Victor's head, pressing the face downward into the rocky embankment, cutting the flesh, forcing the air out of Fontine's throat.

Victor tried to pull back; the priest slammed his forehead into a gnarled root. Blood spurted from the gash, flowing into Victor's eyes, blinding him, infuriating him. He raised his right hand, grappling for Gaetamo's wrist; the defrocked prest clasped the hand and wrenched it inward, snapping the fingers. He pulled Fontine higher on the ground, twisting, always twisting his head and neck, causing the brace to cut into his back.

"It won't end until you tell me the truth!"

"*Pig! Pig from Donatti!*" Victor lurched to the side. Gaetamo countered by crashing his fist into Fontine's rib cage. The impact was paralyzing, the pain excruciating.

The stick. The *stick!* Fontine rolled to his left, his left hand below, still gripped around the broken limb, gripped as one holds an object in a moment of agony. Gaetamo had felt the brace; he pulled on it, wrenching it back and forth until the steel lacerated the surrounding flesh.

Victor inched the long stick up by pressing it into the embankment. It touched his chest; he felt it. The end was jagged. If he could only find the smallest opening between himself and the monster above, space enough to thrust it upward, toward the face, the neck.

It came. Gaetamo raised one knee. It was *enough.*

Fontine shoved the stick up, driving it with every ounce of strength he could summon, impaling it into the stunned body above. He heard a cry of shock, a scream that filled the forest.

And then an explosion filled the gray darkness. A powerful gun had been fired. The screeches of birds and animals swelled in the woods—and the body of Gaetamo fell forward on top of him. It rolled to the side.

The stick was lodged in his throat. Below his neck a huge gaping mass of torn flesh saturated with blood was in his upper chest; he had been blown apart by the gun that had been fired out of the darkness.

"May God forgive me," said the monk of Xenope from the shadows.

A black void came over Victor; he felt himself slipping into the water as trembling hands grabbed him. His last thoughts—strangely peaceful—were of his sons. The Geminis. The hands might have been the hands of his sons, trying to save him. But his sons' hands did not tremble.

PART TWO

22

Major Andrew Fontine sat rigidly at his desk, listening to the sounds of morning. It was five minutes to eight; the offices were beginning to fill up. Voices rose and fell in the corridors as the Pentagon started the day.

He had five days to think. No, not to think, to *move.* There wasn't that much to think about; it was only necessary to move out and cut *down.* Stop whatever Adrian and his "concerned citizens" had started.

Eye Corps was the most legitimate clandestine unit in the army. It was doing exactly what the dissenters *thought they* were doing, but without tearing down the system, without revealing weakness. Maintain strength and the illusion of strength. It was all important. They'd tried it the other way. Eye Corps wasn't born in Georgetown, over brandy and cigars and pictures of the Pentagon on the walls. *Bullshit!* It was born in a hut in the Mekong Delta. After he had come back from Saigon and told his three subordinate officers what had happened at command headquarters.

He had gone to Saigon with legitimate field complaints, proof of corruption in the supply lines. Hundred of thousands of dollars' worth of equipment was being drained off all over the Mekong every week, abandoned by ARVN troops at the first sign of hostilities, routed back into the black market. Payrolls were banked by ARVN commanders, drugs bought and distributed by Vietnamese networks out of Hue and Da-nang. Millions were piped out of the Southeast Asia operation, and no one seemed to know what to do about it.

So he brought his proof to Saigon, right up to the command brass. And what did the brass do? They thanked him and said they would investigate. What was there to investigate? He'd brought enough proof to institute a dozen charges.

A brigadier had taken him out for a drink.

"Listen, Fontine. Better a little corruption than blow the whole ammo dump. These people are thieves by nature, we're not going to change that."

"We could make a few examples, sir. Openly."

"For Christ's sake! We've got enough Stateside problems! That kind of publicity would play right into the antimilitary hands. Now, you've got a fine record; don't louse it up."

That's when it started, when Eye Corps was born. The name itself said it: a unit of men who watched and recorded. And as the months went on, the four of them expanded to five, then seven. Recently, they'd added the eighth man: Captain Martin Greene, in the Pentagon. They were born of disgust. The army was led by weak-kneed whores—*women—afraid* to *offend.* What kind of stature was that for the military leaders of the strongest nation on earth?

Something else happened, too, along the way. As the records grew and the enemies within tagged for what they were, the obvious stared the men of Eye Corps in the face: *they* were the inheritors! They were the incorruptible; they were the elite.

Since regular channels didn't work, they would do it their way. Build up the records, get files on every misfit, every deviate, ever corrupter, large and small. Strength lay with those who could confront the misfits and make them crawl. Make them do exactly what strong, incorruptible men wanted them to do.

Eye Corps was nearly there. Almost three years' worth of recorded garbage. Christ! Southeast Asia was the place to find it. They'd take over soon; go right into the Pentagon and take over! It was men like themselves who had the skill and training and the commitment to oversee the vast complexities that were the armed might of the country. It was not a delusion; they *were* the elite.

It was so logical for him, too. His father would understand that, if he could ever talk to him about it. And one day he might. Since his earliest memories, he felt the presence of influence, of pride, of consequence. And power . . . yes, power. It wasn't a dirty word! It belonged to those who knew how to handle it; it was his birthright.

And Adrian wanted to tear it down! Well, the spoiler was not going to tear it down. He was not going to rip Eye Corps apart.

. . . *arrangements can be made.* That's what Adrian had said in the boathouse.

How right he was! Arrangements could be made; but not any arrangements considered by Adrian and his concerned citizens. A lot would happen before then.

Five days. Adrian wasn't trained to consider the options. Practical, physical alternatives, not words and abstractions and "positions." The army would have a hell of a time trying to reach him five days from now if he was 10,000 miles away in a combat zone, involved in operations covered by an umbrella of security. He had enough clout to do that; to get over there and build that umbrella.

There was a weakling in Saigon who had betrayed them. Betrayed the rest of Eye Corps. To learn who he was—and he was one of six—was the first reason to get over there. Find him . . . then make a decision.

Once he was found—and the decision made—the rest was easy. He'd brief the remaining men of Eye Corps. The stories would be integrated, synchronized.

Even the army needed proof. And there was no way it could get that proof.

Here in Washington, Eye Corps' eighth member could take care of himself. Captain Martin Greene was steel and leather. And smart. He could hold his own against any flak leveled at him. His people had come from the Irgun, the toughest fighters in Jew history. If the D.C. brass gave him any static, he'd cut out for Israel in a second, and the Jew army would be better for it.

Andrew looked at his watch. It was a little past eight, time to reach Greene. He couldn't take the chance last night. Adrian and his civilians were trying to find an unknown officer who worked at the Pentagon. Outside telephones could not be trusted. He and Marty would have to talk; they couldn't wait for their next scheduled meeting. He would be on a plane for Saigon before the day was over.

They had agreed never to be seen together. If they met by chance at a conference or a cocktail party, both pretended they were meeting for the first time. It was vital that no connection between them be apparent. When they did meet, it was in out-of-the-way places and always by prearranged schedule. During the meetings they would combine whatever damaging information they'd culled from Pentagon files during the week, seal the pages in an envelope, and mail it to a post office box in Baltimore. The enemies of Eye Corps were being catalogued everywhere.

In times of emergencies, or when one needed the other's immediate advice, they sent word to each other by placing a "mistaken" call through the Pentagon switchboard. It was the signal to invent some excuse, get out of the office, and head for a bar in downtown Washington. Andrew had made the "mistaken" call two hours ago.

The bar was dark and cheap and gaudy, with booths in the back that afforded a clear view of the entrance. Andrew sat in a booth by the back wall, toying with his bourbon, not interested in it. He kept looking up at the entrance fifty feet away. Whenever the door opened, the morning sun burst through briefly, a harsh intruder on the interior darkness. Greene was late; it wasn't like him to be late.

The door opened again and the silhouette of a stocky, muscular man with broad, thick shoulders was arrested in the glare. It was Marty; he was out of uniform, dressed in an open white shirt and what appeared to be plaid trousers. He nodded to the bartender and started toward the rear of the bar. Everything about Greene was powerful, thought Andrew. From his thick legs to the shock of bright-red hair, shaped in a bristling crew cut.

"Sorry it took me so long," said Greene, sliding into the booth opposite Andrew. "I stopped off at the apartment to change. Then I went out the back way."

"Any particular reason?"

"Maybe, maybe not. Last night I took the car out of the garage and thought I picked up surveillance—a dark-green Electra. I reversed directions; it was still there. I went home."

"What time was it?"

"Around eight thirty, quarter to nine."

"It figures. It's why I called you. They expect me to contact someone in your section; set up a meeting right away. They probably had half a dozen others followed."

"Who?"

"One of them's my brother."

"Your *brother?*"

"He's a lawyer. He's working with——"

"I know *exactly* who he is," interrupted Greene, "*and* who he's working with. They're about as subtle as jackals."

"You never mentioned him to me. How come?"

"There was no reason to. They're a bunch of hotheads over at Justice. They were organized by a Black named Nevins. We keep close tabs on them; they mess around with hardware contracts more than we'd like. But they haven't got anything to do with *us*."

"They do now. It's why I called you. One of the six in Nam broke. They've got a deposition. A list. Eight officers, seven identified."

Greene's cold eyes narrowed. He spoke slowly, quietly. "What the hell are you saying?"

Andrew told him. When he finished, Greene spoke without moving an inch of his powerful body.

"That Black son of a bitch, Nevins, flew to Saigon two weeks ago. The matter wasn't related."

"It is now," said the major.

"Who has the deposition? Are there copies?"

"I don't know."

"Why is the subpoena being delayed?"

"Again, I don't know," said Andrew.

"There must be a reason! For Christ's sake, why didn't you ask?"

"Hold it, Marty. Everything came as a shock——"

"We're trained for shock," interrupted Greene icily. "Can you find out?"

Andrew swallowed part of his bourbon. He had not seen the captain like this before. "I can't call my brother. He wouldn't tell me if I did."

"Nice family. May the brothers live and be well. Maybe I can do better. We've got people at Justice; procurement covers itself. I'll do what I can. Where are our files in Saigon? They're the bottom line."

"They're not in Saigon. They're in Phan-thiet on the coast. In a fenced-off area of a warehouse, I'm the only one who knows the location. A couple of cabinets among a thousand G-Two crates."

"Very smart." Greene nodded his head in approval.

"I'll check them the first thing. I'm flying out this afternoon. A sudden inspection trip."

"Very nice." Greene nodded again. "You'll find the man?"

"Yes."

"Check Barstow. He's a smartass. Too many decorations."

"You don't know him."

"I know the way he operates," said Greene.

Andrew was stung by the similarity of words. His brother had applied them to Eye Corps. "He's a good man in the field——"

"Bravery," interrupted the captain, "hasn't got a goddamn thing to do with it. Check Barstow first."

"I will." Andrew smarted under Greene's pronouncements. He had to get some of his own back. "What about Baltimore? I'm worried about that."

The envelopes in Baltimore were picked up by Greene's twenty-year-old nephew.

"He's perfect. He'd kill himself first. I was up there last weekend. I would have known."

"Are you sure?"

"It's not worth discussing. I want to know more about that goddamned deposition. When you crack Barstow make sure you get every word he put down. They probably gave him a copy; see if he's got a military lawyer."

The major drank again, averting Greene's narrow eyes. Andrew did not like the captain's tone of voice. He was actually giving orders; he was out of line. But on the bottom line Greene was a good man to have around in a crisis. "What can you find out over at Justice?"

"More than that Black bastard would ever guess. We've got funds set up for the mavericks who interfere with armaments contracts. We don't care who makes a few extra dollars, we want the hardware. You'd be surprised how the lowly paid government lawyers take to Caribbean vacations." Greene smiled and sat back in the booth. "I think we can handle this. The subpoena won't mean a damn thing without our records. Line officers bitch all the time, what else is new?"

"That's what I told my brother," said Andrew.

"Him I can't figure," said Greene. And then the captain leaned forward. "Whatever you do in Nam, think it out. If you use prejudice, get your facts and do it by remote."

"I think I've had more experience in those areas than you." Andrew lighted a cigarette; his hand was steady in spite of his increased irritation. He was pleased with that.

"You probably do," said Greene casually. "Now, I've got something for you. I figured it could wait till our next meeting, but there's no point in holding it."

"What is it?"

"A congressional tracer came in last Friday. From a pol named Sandor; he's on the Armed Services Committee. It concerned you, so I pulled it."

"What did they want?"

"Limited. Your rotation schedule. How permanent you were in Washington. I inserted a routine response. You were high-echelon material, War College candidate. Very permanent."

"I wonder what—"

"I haven't finished," interrupted Greene. "I called this Sandor's aide and asked why the congressman was interested in you. He checked his papers and said the request came from a friend of Sandor's, a man named Dakakos. Theodore Dakakos."

"Who is he?"

"A Greek shipper. In your family's class. He's got millions."

"Dakakos? Never heard of him."

"These Greeks are pistols. Maybe he wants to give you a present. Like a small yacht or your own battalion."

Fontine shrugged. "Dakakos? I can buy a yacht. I'll take the battalion."

"You can buy that, too," said Greene, sliding across the seat out of the booth. "Have a prosperous trip. Call me when you get back."

"What are you going to do?"

"Find out everything there is to know about a Black son of a bitch named Nevins."

Greene walked rapidly past the booths toward the entrance. Andrew would wait five minutes before leaving. He had to get to his apartment and back. His plane left at one thirty.

Dakakos? Theodore Dakakos.

Who was he?

Adrian got out of the bed slowly, one foot after the other, as quietly as possible so he would not wake her. Barbara was asleep, but her sleep was fitful.

It was barely nine thirty in the evening. He had picked her up at the airport shortly after five. She'd canceled her Thursday and Friday seminars, too excited to lecture detached summer students.

She had been awarded a grant to assist the anthropologist Sorkis Khertepian at the University of Chicago. Khertepian was in the process of analyzing artifacts taken from the site of the Aswan Dam. Barbara was exhilarated; she had to fly down and tell Adrian all about it. She was intensely alive when things went right in her world, a scholar who would never lose her sense of wonder.

It was strange. Both he and Barbara had entered their professions in a sense of outrage. His was traced to the acid streets of San Francisco, hers to a brilliant mother denied her rightful place in a midwest college because she *was* a mother. A woman who had no place in the higher offices of a university. Yet each had found values that far outweighed the anger.

It was part of the bond between them.

He walked quietly across the room and sat down in an armchair. His eyes fell on his briefcase on the bedroom desk. He never left it in the sitting room at night; Jim Nevins had cautioned him about being careless. Nevins was at times a little paranoid about such matters.

Nevins, too, had come to his profession in outrage. It was the outrage that often sustained him. Not merely the frustrations of a Black man climbing over the barriers erected by a skeptical white establishment, but the anger of a lawyer who saw so much illegality in the city where laws were made.

But nothing outraged Nevins more than the discovery of Eye Corps. The idea of military elitists suppressing evidence of massive corruption for their own ends was more dangerous than anything the Black lawyer could think of.

When Major Andrew Fontine's name appeared on the list, Nevins had asked Adrian to remove himself. Adrian had become one of his closest friends, but nothing could stand in the way of prosecuting Eye Corps.

Brothers were brothers. Even white brothers.

"You look so serious. And so naked." Barbara swept her

light-brown hair away from her face, and rolled on her side, hugging the pillow.

"I'm sorry. Did I wake you?"

"Heavens, no. I was only dozing."

"Correction. Your snoring could be heard on Capitol Hill."

"You lie through your legal teeth. . . . What time is it?"

"Twenty of ten," he answered, looking at his watch.

She sat up and stretched. The sheet fell away to her waist; her lovely, full breasts separated, their slow expansion, the movement of the nipples holding his eyes, arousing him. She saw him watching her and smiled, pulling the sheet over her as she leaned against the headrest.

"We talk," she said firmly. "We have three days to wear ourselves to a frazzle. While you're out during the day slaying bears, I'll preen myself like a concubine. Satisfaction guaranteed."

"You should do all those things nonacademic ladies do. Spend hours at Elizabeth Arden's, wallow in milk baths, eat bonbons with your gin. You're a tired girl."

"Let's put me aside," said Barbara smiling. "I've been talking about me all night—almost. How's everything down here? Or shouldn't you say? I'm sure Jim Nevins thinks the suite is bugged."

Adrian laughed, crossing his legs. He reached for a pack of cigarettes next to a lighter on the armchair table. "Jim's conspiracy complex remains undaunted. He refuses to leave case files at the office anymore. He keeps all his important papers in his briefcase, which is the biggest damn thing you ever saw." Adrian chuckled.

"Why does he do that?"

"He doesn't want copies made. He knows the crowd upstairs would take him off half the cases if they knew how much progress he was making."

"That's astonishing."

"It's chilling," he said.

The telephone rang. Adrian got out of the chair quickly and crossed to the bedside table.

It was his mother. She could not hide the anxiety in her voice. "I've heard from your father."

"What do you mean, you've *heard* from him?"

"He flew to Paris last Monday. Then he went on to Milan——"

"*Milan*? What for?"

"He'll tell you himself. He wants you and Andrew here on Sunday."

"Wait a minute." Adrian's mind raced. "I don't think I can do that."

"You *must*."

"You don't understand, and I can't explain right now. But Andy's not going to want to see me. I'm not sure I want to see him. I'm not even sure it's advisable under the circumstances."

"What are you talking about?" His mother's voice was suddenly cold. "What have you done?"

Adrian paused before answering. "We're on the opposite sides of a . . . dispute."

"Whatever it is, it doesn't matter! Your father *needs* you." She was losing control. "Something happened to him. Something *happened* to him! He could barely talk!"

There were several clicks on the line, followed by the urgent voice of a hotel operator. "Mr. Fontine, I'm sorry to break in, but there's an emergency call for you."

"Oh, God." His mother whispered over the line from New York. "Victor——"

"I'll call you back if it's got anything to do with him. I promise you that," said Adrian swiftly. "All right, operator. I'll take——"

It was as far as he got. The voice now on the line was hysterical. It was a woman, crying and screaming and barely coherent.

"*Adrian!* My *God, Adrian!* He's *dead!* He was *killed!* They *killed him!* Adri*annnnnnnn!*"

The screams filled the room. And the terror of the screams filled Adrian with a shock he had never felt before. . . . Death. Death that touched *him*.

The woman on the telephone was Carol Nevins. Jim's wife.

"I'll be right there!"

"Call my mother," he told Barbara, as he dressed as fast as he could. "The North Shore number. Tell her it's not dad."

"Who is it?"

"Nevins."

"Oh, my God!"

He raced into the corridor and down to the elevators. He kept his finger on the button; the elevators were slow—*too* slow! He ran to the exit doors, crashed them open and leaped down the angling staircase to the lobby. He sped to the glass doors of the entrance.

"Excuse me! Pardon me! Let me through, *please!*"

Out on the curb he ran to his right, to the lighted sign of an empty taxi. He gave the address of Nevins's apartment.

What had happened? What in God's name *had happened?!* What did Carol mean? *They killed him! Who* killed him. Jesus! Was he *dead?!*

Jim Nevins dead? Corruption, yes. Greed, of course. Mendacity, normal. But not *murder!*

There was a traffic light at New Hampshire, and he thought he would go mad. Two more blocks!

The cab plunged forward the instant the light flickered. The driver accelerated, then halfway down the block came to a sudden stop. The street was jammed with traffic. There were circling lights up ahead; nothing was moving.

Adrian jumped out on the street and began threading his way as fast as possible between the cars. Across Florida Avenue police cars blocked the entrance. Patrolmen were blowing whistles, signaling with iridescent orange gloves, funneling the traffic west.

He ran into the blockade; two police officers several yards away at either side yelled at him.

"No one goes past here, mister!"

"Get back, buddy! You don't want to go in there!"

But he did want to go; he had to go! He ducked between two patrol cars and raced toward the swirling lights near a mass of twisted metal and shattered glass that Adrian instantly recognized. It was Jim Nevins's car. What was left of it.

An ambulance's rear doors were open; a stretcher on which a body lay strapped, covered completely with a white hospital blanket, was being carried from the wreckage by two attendants. A third man, holding a black medical bag, walked alongside.

Adrian approached, pushing away a policeman who held out a prohibiting arm. "Get out of the way," he said firmly, but with his voice trembling.

"Sorry, mister. I can't let——"

"I'm an attorney! And that man, I *think*, is my friend."

The doctor heard the desperation in his words and waved the officer away. Adrian reached down for the blanket; the doctor's hand shot out and held his wrist.

"Is your friend Black?"

"Yes."

"With identification that says his name is Nevins?"

"Yes."

"He's dead, take my word for it. You don't want to look."

"You don't understand. I *have* to look."

Adrian pulled back the blanket. Nausea swept over him; he was at once hypnotized and terrified at what he saw. Nevins's face was half ripped off, blood and bone more apparent than flesh. The area of the throat was worse; half his neck was gone.

"Oh, Jesus. My *God!*"

The doctor replaced the blanket and ordered the attendants to continue on. He was a young man with long blond hair and the face of a boy. "You better sit down," he said to Adrian. "I tried to tell you. Come on, let me take you to a car."

"No. No, thanks." Adrian suppressed the sickness and tried to breathe. There wasn't enough air! "What happened?"

"We don't know all the details yet. Are you really a lawyer?"

"Yes. And he was my friend. What happened?"

"Seems he made a left turn to go into the apartment driveway and halfway across, some outsized rig rammed him at full speed."

"Rig?"

"A trailer truck, the kind with steel gridwork. It barrel-assed down like it was on a freeway."

"Where is it?"

"We don't know. It stopped for a couple of moments, its horn blasting like hell, then pulled out. A witness said it was a rental; it had one of those rent-a-truck signs on the side. You can bet the cops have APB's out all over the place."

Suddenly, Adrian remembered, amazed that he was able to do so. He grabbed the doctor's sleeve. "Can you get me through the police to his car? It's important."

"I'm a doctor, not a cop."

"Please. Will you try?"

The young doctor sucked air through his teeth, then nodded his head. "Okay. I'll take you over. Don't pull any shit, though."

"I just want to see something. You said a witness saw the truck stop."

"I *know* it stopped," replied the blond-haired doctor enigmatically. "Come on!"

They walked over to the wreck. Nevins's car was caved in on the left side, metal stripped everywhere, windows shattered. Foam had been sprayed around the gas tank; white globules had drifted through the smashed windows.

"Hey, Doc! What are *you* doing?" The policeman's voice was tired and angry.

"Come on, kid, get back. You, too!" A second patrolman yelled.

The young doctor raised his black bag. "Forensic washout, fellas. Don't argue with me, call the station!"

"What?"

"What forensic?"

"Pathology, for Christ's sake!" He propelled Adrian forward. "Come on, lab man, take the samples and let's get out of here. I'm beat." Adrian looked into the car. "See anything?" asked the doctor pointedly.

Adrian did. Nevins's briefcase was missing.

They walked back through the cordon of police to the ambulance.

"Did you really find anything?" asked the young doctor.

"Yes," answered Adrian, numbed, not sure he was thinking clearly. "Something that should have been there, but wasn't."

"Okay. Good. Now I'll tell you why I took you over."

"What?"

"You saw your friend; I wouldn't let his wife see him. His face and neck were blown apart with broken glass and metal fragments."

"Yes . . . I know. I saw." Adrian felt the wave of nausea spreading over him again.

"But it's a pretty warm night. I think the window on the driver's side was rolled down. I couldn't swear to it—that car's totaled—but your friend could have taken a short blast from a shotgun."

Adrian raised his eyes. Something inside his head snapped; the words his brother said seven years ago in San Francisco seared into his brain.

"*. . . There's a war out there . . . the firepower's real!*"

Among the papers in Nevins's briefcase was the deposition taken from an officer in Saigon. The indictment of Eye Corps.

And he had given his brother five days' warning.

Oh, God! What had he done?

He took a cab to the precinct police station. His credentials as an attorney gained him a brief conversation with a sergeant.

"If there's foul play involved, we'll find it," said the man, looking at Adrian with the distaste the police reserved for lawyers who followed up accidents.

"He was a friend of mine and I have reason to believe there was. Did you find the truck?"

"Nope. We know it's not on any of the highways. The state troopers are watching for it."

"It was a rental."

"We know that, too. The rental agencies are being checked. Why don't you go home, mister?"

Adrian bent over the sergeant's desk, his hands on the edge. "I don't think you're taking me very seriously."

"Fatality sheets come into this station a dozen an hour. Now, what the hell do you want me to do? Suspend everything else and put a whole goddamned platoon on one hit-and-run?"

"I'll tell you what I want, sergeant. I want a pathology report on all cranial injuries sustained by the deceased. Is that clear?"

"What are you talking about?" replied the police officer disdainfully. "Cranial——"

"I want to know what blew that man apart."

23

The train from Salonika had claimed its last sacrifice, thought Victor, as he lay in his bed, the morning sun streaming through the oceanside windows of the North Shore house. There was no reason on earth why any further life should be lost in its name. Enrici Gaetamo was the last victim, and there was no sorrow in that death.

He himself had very little time remaining. He could see it in Jane's eyes, in the eyes of the doctors. It was to be expected; he had been granted too many reprieves.

He had dictated everything he could remember about that day in July a lifetime ago. He had probed forgotten recesses in his mind, refused the narcotics that would numb the pain because they would equally numb the memories. The vault from Constantine had to be found, its contents evaluated by responsible men. What had to be prevented—however remote it might be—was a chance discovery, exposure without thought. He would charge his sons. Salonika was now theirs. The Geminis. They would do what he could not do: find the vault of Constantine.

But there was a piece of the puzzle that was missing. He had to find it before he spoke with his sons. What did Rome know? How much had the Vatican learned about Salonika? Which was why he had asked a man to visit him this morning. A priest named Land, the monsignor from New York's archdiocese who had come to his hospital room months ago.

Fontine heard the footsteps outside the bedroom, and the quiet voices of Jane and the visitor. The priest had arrived.

The heavy door opened silently. Jane ushered in the monsignor, then went back into the hallway, closing the door behind her. The priest stood across the room, a leather book in his hand.

"Thank you for coming," Victor said.

The priest smiled. He touched the leather cover of the book. "*Conquest with Mercy. In the Name of God.* The history of the Fontini-Cristis. I thought you might like this, Mr. Fontine. I found it in a bookshop in Rome years ago."

The monsignor placed the book on the bedside table. They shook hands; each, Victor realized, was appraising the other.

Land was no more than fifty. He was of medium height, broad in the chest and shoulders. His features were sharp, Anglican; his eyes hazel beneath generous eyebrows that were darker than his short, graying hair. It was a pleasant face with intelligent eyes.

"A vanity publication, I'm afraid. A custom of dubious value at the turn of the century. It's long been out of print. The language is Italian——"

"An obsolete northern idiom," completed Land. "Court Victorian would be the English equivalent, I think. Somewhere between 'you' and 'thee.' "

"You have the advantage over me. My knowledge of languages is not nearly so erudite."

"It was sufficient for Loch Torridon," said the priest.

"Yes, it was. Please sit down, Monsignor Land." Victor gestured to the chair by the bed. The priest sat. The two men looked at each other. Fontine spoke.

"Several months ago you came to my hospital room. Why?"

"I wanted to meet the man whose life I had studied so thoroughly. Shall I speak frankly?"

"You wouldn't have come here this morning if you meant to do otherwise."

"I was told you might die. I was presumptuous enough to hope you'd allow me to administer last rites."

"That *is* frank. And *was* presumptuous."

"I realized that. It's why I never returned. You're a courteous man, Mr. Fontine, but you couldn't conceal your feelings."

Victor examined the priest's face. There was the same sorrow he had remembered in the hospital. "Why did you study my life? Does the Vatican still investigate? Wasn't Donatti's cause rejected?"

"The Vatican is always engaged in study. In examination. It doesn't stop. And Donatti was more than rejected.

He was excommunicated, his remains refused the sanctity of Catholic burial."

"You answer my last two questions. Not the first. Why you?"

The monsignor crossed his legs, clasping his hands in front of him on his knees, his fingers entwined. "I'm a political and social historian. Which is another way of saying that I look for incompatible relationships between the church and its environs at given periods of time." Land smiled, his eyes reflective. "The original reason for such work was to prove the virtue of the church and the error of any who opposed her. But virtue wasn't always found. And it certainly wasn't found in the countless lapses of judgment, or morality, as they were exposed." Land's smile had gone; his admission was clear.

"The execution of the Fontini-Cristis was a lapse? Of *judgment? Morality?*"

"Please." The priest spoke swiftly, his voice soft but emphatic. "You and I both know what it was. An act of murder. Impossible to sanction and unforgivable."

Victor saw once again the sorrow in the man's eyes. "I accept what you say. I don't understand it, but I accept it. So I became an object of your social and political examinations?"

"Among many other questions of the time. I'm sure you're aware of them. Although there was a great deal of good during those years, there was *much* that was unforgivable. You and your family were obviously in this category."

"You became interested in me?"

"You became my obsession." Land smiled again, awkwardly. "Remember, I'm American. I was studying in Rome, and the name Victor Fontine was well known to me. I had read of your work in postwar Europe; the newspapers were filled with it. I was aware of your influence in both the public and the private sectors. You can imagine my astonishment when, in studying the period, I found that Vittorio Fontini-Cristi and Victor Fontine were the same person."

"Was there a great deal of information in your Vatican files?"

"About the Fontini-Cristis, yes." Land gestured his head toward the leather-bound volume he had placed on the bedside table. "As that book, somewhat biased, I'm afraid.

Hardly as flattering, naturally. But of you, there was substantively nothing. Your existence was acknowledged: the first male child of Savarone, now an American citizen known as Victor Fontine. Nothing more. The files ended abruptly with the information that the remaining Fontini-Cristis had been executed by the Germans. It was an incomplete ending. Even the date was missing."

"The less written down, the better."

"Yes. So I studied the records of the court of Reparations. They were far more complete. What began as curiosity turned into shock. You made accusations to the tribunal of judges. Accusations I found unbelievable, intolerable, for you included the church. And you named a man of the Curia, Guillamo Donatti. That was the link that was missing. It was all I needed."

"Are you telling me Donatti's name was nowhere in the files of the Fontini-Cristis?"

"It is now. It wasn't then. It was as if the archivists couldn't bring themselves to acknowledge the connection. Donatti's papers had been sealed, as usual with excommunicants. After his death, they had been found in possession of an aide——"

"Father Enrici Gaetamo. Defrocked," interrupted Fontine softly.

Land paused. "Yes. Gaetamo. I received permission to break the seals. I read the paranoid ramblings of a madman, a self-canonized fanatic." Again the monsignor stopped briefly, his eyes wandering. "What I found there took me to England. To a man named Teague. I met with him only once, at his country house. It was raining and he repeatedly got up to stoke the fire. I never saw a man finger a watch so. Yet he was retired and had no place to go."

Victor smiled. "It was an annoying habit, that watch. I told him so many times."

"Yes, you were good friends, I learned that quickly. He was in awe of you, you know."

"In awe of me? Alec? I can't believe that. He was far too direct."

"He said he never admitted it to you, but he was. He said he felt inadequate around you."

"He didn't convey it."

"He said a great deal more, too. Everything. The execution at Campo di Fiori, the escape through Celle Ligure,

Loch Torridon, Oxfordshire, your wife, your sons. And Donatti; how he kept the name from you."

"He had no choice. The knowledge would have interfered with Loch Torridon."

Land unclasped his hands and uncrossed his legs. He seemed to have difficulty finding the words. "It was the first time I had heard of the train from Salonika."

Victor raised his eyes abruptly; they had been focused on the priest's hands. "That's not logical. You read Donatti's papers."

"And suddenly they were clear. The insane ramblings, the disjointed phrases, the seemingly deranged references to out-of-the-way places and times . . . suddenly made sense. Even in his most private papers, Donatti wouldn't spell it out; his fear was too great. . . . Everything was reduced to that train. And whatever was on it."

"You don't know?"

"I came to. I would have learned more quickly, but Brevourt refused to see me. He died several months after I tried to reach him.

"I went to the prison where Gaetamo was held. He spat at me through the wire mesh, clawing his hands over it until they were bleeding. Still, I had the source. Constantine. The Patriarchate. I gained an audience with a priest of the Elders. He was a very old man and he told me. The train from Salonika carried the Filioque denials."

"That was all?"

Monsignor Land smiled. "Theologically speaking, it was enough. To that old man and his counterparts in Rome, the Filioque documents represented triumph and cataclysm."

"They don't represent the same to you?" Victor watched the priest closely, concentrating on the steady hazel eyes.

"No. The church isn't the church of past centuries, even past generations. Simply put, it couldn't survive if it were. There are the old men who cling to what they believe is incontrovertible . . . in most cases it's all they have left; there's no need to strip them of their convictions. Time mandates change gracefully; nothing is as it was. With each year—as the old guard leaves us—the church moves more swiftly into the realm of social responsibility. It has the power to effect extraordinary good, the wherewithal—spiritually and pragmatically—to alleviate enormous suffering. I speak with a certain expertise, for I am part of this movement. We're in every diocese over the globe. It's our future. We are *with* the world now."

Fontine looked away. The priest had finished; he had described a force for good in a sadly lacking world. Victor turned back to Land.

"You don't know precisely, then, what is in those documents from Salonika."

"What does it matter? At the worst, theological debate. Doctrinal equivocation. A man *existed* and his name was Jesus of Nazareth . . . or the Essenian Archangel of Light . . . and he spoke from the heart. His words have come down to us, historically authenticated by the Aramaics and Biblical scholars, Christian and non-Christian alike. What difference does it really make whether he is called carpenter, or prophet, or son of God? What matters is that he spoke the truth as he saw it, as it was *revealed* to him. His sincerity, if you will, is the only issue, and on that there is no debate."

Fontine caught his breath. His mind raced back to Campo di Fiori, to an old monk of Xenope who spoke of a parchment taken out of a Roman prison.

. . . what is contained in that parchment is beyond anything in your imagination . . . it must be found . . . destroyed . . . for nothing has changed yet all is changed. . . .

Destroyed.

. . . what matters is that he spoke the truth as he saw it, as it was revealed to him. . . . His sincerity is the only issue, and on that there is no debate. . . .

Or was there?

Was this scholar-priest, this good man beside him, prepared to face what had to be faced? Was it remotely fair to ask him to do so?

For nothing has changed, yet all is changed.

Whatever those contradictory words meant, it would take exceptional men to know what to do. He would prepare a list for his sons.

The priest named Land was a candidate.

The four massive overhead blades slowed to a stop, sending metallic thuds throughout the aircraft. An airman opened the hatch and sprang the lever that swung the short flight of steps out from the undercarriage. Maj. Andrew

Fontine emerged into the morning sunlight and climbed down the metal stairs onto the helicopter pad at Air Force Base Cobra in Phan-thiet.

His paper authorized priority transportation and access to the restricted warehouses down at the waterfront. He would commandeer a jeep from the officers' pool and head directly to the piers. And to a file cabinet in Warehouse Four. The Eye Corps records were there; and they would stay there, the safest place in Southeast Asia, once he saw for himself that nothing was disturbed. He had two more stops to make after the warehouse: north to Da-nang, then south again, past Saigon into the Delta. To Can-tho.

Captain Jerome Barstow was in Can-tho. Marty Greene was right; it was Barstow who had betrayed Eye Corps. The others agreed; his behavior was that of a man who had broken. He had been seen in Saigon with a legal officer named Tarkington. It wasn't difficult to understand what had happened: Barstow was preparing a defense, and if that was so, a defense meant he would testify. Barstow did not know where the Eye Corps records were, but he had seen them. Seen them, *hell!* He'd prepared twenty or thirty himself. Barstow's testimony could finish Eye Corps. They could not allow that.

The legal officer named Tarkington was in Da-nang. He didn't know it but he was going to meet another man from Eye Corps. It would be the last person he met. In an alley, with a knife in his stomach, and whiskey on his shirt and in his mouth.

And then Andrew would fly to the Delta. To the betrayer named Barstow. Barstow would be shot by a whore; they were easy to buy.

He walked across the hot concrete toward the transit building. A lieutenant colonel was waiting for him. At first Andrew was alarmed; had something gone wrong? The five days weren't up! Then he saw that the colonel was smiling, somewhat patronizingly, but nevertheless in friendship.

"Major Fontine?" The greeting was accompanied by an extension of the hand; no salute was expected.

"Yes, sir?" The handshake was brief.

"Washington cable, straight from the secretary of the army. You have to get home, major. As soon as possible. I'm sorry to be the one to tell you, but it concerns your father."

"My *father?* Is he dead?"

"It's only a matter of time. You have priority clearance for any aircraft leaving Tan Son Nhut." The colonel handed him a red-bordered envelope with the imprimatur of General Headquarters, Saigon, across the top. It was the sort of envelope reserved for White House liaisons and couriers from the Joint Chiefs.

"My father's been a sick man for many years," said Fontine slowly. "This isn't unexpected. I have another day's work here. I'll be at Tan San Nhut tomorrow night."

"Whatever you say. The main thing is we found you. You've got the message."

"I've got the message," said Andrew.

In the phone booth, Adrian listened to the weary voice of the police sergeant. The sergeant was lying; more credible still, someone had lied to him. The pathology report on Nevins, James, Black male, victim of hit-and-run, showed no apparent evidence of cranial, neck, or upper thorax injuries unrelated to the impact of collision.

"Send the report and the X-rays to me," said Adrian curtly. "You've got my address."

"There were no X-rays accompanying the pathology report," replied the police officer mechanically.

"Get them," said Adrian, hanging up the phone.

Lies. Everywhere lies and evasions.

His was the biggest lie of all; he lied to himself, and accepted that lie and used it to convince others. He had stood up in front of a group of very frightened young lawyers from the Justice Department and told them that under the circumstances, the subpoena on Eye Corps should be delayed. They needed to regroup their evidence, obtain a second deposition; to go to the adjutant general with only a list of names was meaningless.

It *wasn't* meaningless! The moment was right to confront the military and demand an immediate investigation. A man was murdered; the evidence he carried with him removed from the scene of his death. That evidence was the indictment of Eye Corps! Here are the names! This is the gist of the deposition!

Now, *move* on it!

But he could not do that. His brother's name was at the top of that list. To serve the subpoena was to charge his brother with murder. There was no other conclusion. Andrew was his brother, his twin, and he was not prepared to call him killer.

Adrian walked out of the phone booth and down the block toward his hotel. Andrew was on his way back from Saigon. He had left the country last Monday; it didn't take a great deal of imagination to know why. His brother wasn't stupid; Andrew was building his defense at the source of his crimes; crimes that included conspiracy, suppression of evidence, and obstruction of justice. Motives: complex and not without fundamental substance, but still crimes.

But no murder at night in a Washington street.

Oh, Christ! Even now he lied to himself! Or to be charitable, he refused to face the possible. Come on! *Say it, think it!*

The probable.

There was an eighth member of Eye Corps in Washington. Whoever that man was, he was Nevins's killer. And Nevins's killer could not have acted without the knowledge given by brother to brother in a boathouse on Long Island's North Shore.

When Andrew's plane landed, he would learn that the subpoena had not been served. Eye Corps was intact for a while longer, free to maneuver and manipulate.

There was one thing that would stop it, though. Stop it instantly and recharge a group of frightened lawyers who wondered if what happened to Nevins could happen to them; they were attorneys, not commandos.

Adrian would look into his brother's eyes, and if he saw Jim Nevins's death in them, he would avenge it. If the soldier had given the order of execution, then the soldier would be destroyed.

Or was he lying to himself again? Could he call his brother killer? Could he *really?*

What the hell did his father want? What difference did it make?

24

The two chairs were placed on opposite sides of the bed. It was proper this way. It could divide his attention between his sons; they were different people, their reactions would be different. Jane preferred to stand. He had asked a terrible thing of her: to tell his sons the story of Salonika. Everything, leaving out nothing. They had to be made to understand that powerful men, institutions, even governments could be moved by the vault from Constantine. As they had been moved three decades before.

He could not tell the story himself. He was dying; his mind was clear enough to know that. He had to have the simple energy to answer their questions; he had to have the strength to give his charge to his sons. For theirs was now the responsibility of the Fontini-Cristis.

They walked into the room with their mother. So tall, so alike, yet so different. One in uniform, the other in a nondescript tweed jacket and flannel trousers. Blond-haired Andrew was angry. It was in his face, the continuous tensing of his jaw muscles, the firm set of his mouth, the neutral, clouded gaze of his eyes.

Adrian, on the other hand, seemed unsure of himself. His blue eyes were questioning, his mouth slack, the lips parted. He drew his hand through his dark hair as he stared down, his expression equal parts of compassion and astonishment.

Victor indicated the chairs. The brothers looked at each other briefly; it was impossible to define the communication. Whatever had happened to alienate them had to be erased. Their responsibility demanded it. They sat down, the Xeroxed pages of his recollections of July 14, 1920, in their hands. He had instructed Jane to give them each a copy; they were to read them through before seeing him.

No moments were to be lost on explanations that could be covered beforehand. He hadn't the strength.

"We won't waste words on sentiment. You've heard your mother; you've read what I've written. You'll have questions."

Andrew spoke. "Assuming this vault can be found—and we'll get to that—what then?"

"I'll prepare a list of names. Five or six men, no more; they are not easily arrived at. You'll bring the vault to them."

"What'll they do?" pressed Andrew.

"That will depend on what the vault contains, *specifically*. Release it, destroy it, rebury it."

Adrian interrupted quietly. The lawyer was suddenly disturbed. "Is there a choice? I don't think so. It doesn't belong to us; it should be public knowledge."

"With public chaos? The consequences have to be weighed."

"Does anyone else have the key?" asked the soldier. "The location of this trip on July 14, 1920?"

"No. It would be meaningless. There are only a few left who knew of the train, knew what was *really* on it. Old men from the Patriarchate; one remains in Campo di Fiori and cannot have much time."

"And we're to say nothing to anyone," continued the major. "No one but ourselves is to know."

"No one. There are those who would trade off half the arsenals in this world for the information."

"I wouldn't go that far."

"Then you wouldn't be thinking. I'm sure your mother explained. Besides the Filioque denials, including the Aramaic scroll, in that vault there is a parchment on which is written a confession that could alter religious history. If you think governments, whole nations, are disinterested bystanders, you are grossly mistaken."

Andrew fell silent. Adrian looked at him and then at Victor.

"How long do you figure it'll take? To find this . . . this vault?" he asked.

"I'd estimate a month. You'll need equipment, Alpine guides, a week of instruction—no more, I should think."

Adrian raised the Xeroxed pages several inches. "Can you estimate how large an area there is to cover?"

"It's difficult to day; much will depend on what you find, what has changed. But if my memory serves, no more than five to eight square miles."

"Five to eight! That's out of the question," said Andrew emphatically, but without raising his voice. "I'm sorry, but it's crazy. It could take years. You're talking about the Alps. One hole in the ground, a box no larger than a coffin, anywhere in a dozen mountains."

"The most logical recesses are limited; they are reduced to one of perhaps three or four passes, high above, I suspect, where we were never allowed to climb."

"I've mapped terrain in half a hundred field situations," said the soldier slowly, so courteously his words bordered on condescension. "You're minimizing an unbelievably difficult problem."

"I don't think so. I meant what I just said to Adrian. Much will depend on what you find. Your grandfather was nothing if not meticulous. He considered all aspects of a situation, and most eventualities." Victor stopped and shifted his position on the pillows. "Savarone was an old man; there was a war going on and no one knew it better than he did. He would leave nothing that was recognizable to anyone in Camp di Fiori, but I can't believe he would not leave *something* within the area itself. A sign, a message—something. He was like that."

"Where would we look?" asked Adrian, his eyes straying for an instant to his brother in the leather chair opposite him. The major was staring at the pages in his hand.

"I've written down the possibilities," said Victor. "There was a family of guides in the village of Champoluc. The Goldonis. They were used by my father, his father before him. And there was an inn north of the village. Run for generations by a family named Capomonti. We never traveled to the Champoluc without staying there. These were the people closest to Savarone. If he spoke with anyone, it would be to them."

"That's over fifty years ago," protested Adrian softly.

"Families in the mountains are closely knit. Two generations isn't a particularly wide gap. If Savarone left word it would be passed on from father to eldest child. Remember that: *child*. Son *or* daughter." He smiled weakly at them. "What else occurs to you? Questions may trigger further memories."

The questions began but they triggered nothing. Victor had traced and retraced all he could. Whatever else remained was beyond memory.

Until Jane caught something. And as he listened to her words, Victor smiled. His blue-eyed, English Jane was remarkable for details.

"You wrote that the tracks of the railroad wound through the mountains south of Zermatt and descended into Champoluc, past flagging stops. Clearings between stations for the convenience of climbers and skiers."

"Yes. Before the war. Nowadays, vehicles are more flexible in the snow."

"It seems logical that a train carrying a vault, described to you as heavy and awkward, would find it necessary to stop at one of those clearings. For it to be transferred to another vehicle."

"Agreed. What's your point?"

"Well, there are, or *were,* only so many stops between Zermatt and Champoluc. How many would you say?"

"Quite a few. At least nine or ten."

"That's not much help. I'm sorry."

"North of Champoluc, the first clearing was called Eagle's Peak, I believe. Then Crow's Lookout, and Condor's——" Victor stopped. *Birds.* The *names* of *birds.* A memory had been triggered, but it was not a memory that reached back three decades. It was barely days ago. In Campo di Fiori. "The painting," he said softly.

"What painting?" asked Adrian.

"Beneath the Madonna. In my father's study. A hunting scene, with *birds.*"

"And each clearing on the tracks," said Andrew swiftly, sitting forward in the chair, "is—or was—described in part with the name of a bird. What were the birds in the painting?"

"I don't remember. The light was dim and I was trying to find a few moments to think. I didn't concentrate on that painting."

"Was it your father's?" asked Adrian.

"I'm not sure."

"Can you call?" said the major, his question less a request than an order.

"No. Campo di Fiori is a tomb without lines of communication. Only a postal box in Milan, and that under the name of Baricours, Père et Fils."

"Mother told us an old priest lives there. How does he exist?" The soldier was not satisfied.

"I never thought to ask," replied the father. "There was a man, a driver who picked me up in Milan. I assumed he was the monk's contact with the outside. The old priest and I talked most of the night, but my concerns were limited. He was still my enemy. He understood that."

Andrew looked over at his brother. "We stop at Campo di Fiori," said the soldier curtly.

Adrian nodded and turned back to Victor. "There's no way I can convince you to turn this over to the others? To responsible scholars?"

"No," answered Victor simply. "The scholars will come later. Before then, nothing. Bear in mind what you're dealing with. The contents of that vault are as staggering to the civilized world as anything in history. The confession on that parchment is a devastating weapon, make no mistake about it. No *committee* can be asked to assume the responsibility at this stage. The dangers are too great."

"I see," said Adrian, sitting back in his chair, looking at the pages. "You mention the name Annaxas, but you're not clear about it. You say the 'father of Annaxas was the engineer on the train,' killed by the priest of Xenope? Who is Annaxas?"

"In the event those papers fell into hands other than yours, I wanted no connections made. Annaxas is Theodore Dakakos."

There was a snap. The soldier was holding a wooden pencil in his hand. He had broken it in half. Father and brother looked at him. Andrew said one word.

"Sorry."

"I've heard the name," continued Adrian. "I'm not sure where."

"He's Greek. A very successful shipper. The priest on that train was his father's brother, his uncle. Brother killed brother. It was ordered by Xenope, the location of the vault buried with them."

"Dakakos knows this?" asked the soldier quietly.

"Yes. Where he precisely fits in, I don't know. I know only that he's looking for answers. And for the vault."

"Can you trust him?" asked the lawyer.

"No. I trust no one where Salonika is concerned." Victor inhaled deeply. It was difficult to talk now; his breath was shorter, his strength going.

"Are you all right?" Jane crossed quickly in front of Adrian to her husband. She leaned over and placed her hand on his cheek.

"Yes," he answered, smiling up at her. And then he looked at Andrew and Adrian, holding each with his eyes.

"I don't ask what I ask of you lightly. You have your own lives, your interests are your own. You have money." Victor raised a hand quickly. "I hasten to add that this, too, was your right. I was given no less, nor should you be. In this respect we are a privileged family. But this privilege extracts responsibilities from those who enjoy it. There must inevitably come periods when you're asked to suspend your own pursuits for an unexpected urgency. I submit to you that such an urgency now exists.

"You've separated. Opponents, I suspect, philosophically and politically. There's nothing wrong with that, but these differences are insignificant compared to what faces you now. You're brothers, the grandsons of Savarone Fontini-Cristi, and you must now do what *his* son can't do. There's no appeal from privilege. Don't look for it."

He was finished. It was all he could say; each breath was painful.

"All these years, you never said——" Adrian's eyes were questioning once again; there was awe and sadness in them. "My God, how you must have felt."

"I had two choices," replied Victor, barely audible. "To be productive or die a neuter. It was not a difficult choice."

"You should have killed them," said the soldier quietly.

They stood outside in the drive in front of the North Shore house. Andrew leaned against the hood of his rented Lincoln Continental, his arms folded across his pressed uniform, the afternoon sun bouncing off the brass buttons and the insignia.

"He's going," he said.

"I know," answered Adrian. "He knows it, too."

"And here we are."

"Here we are," agreed the lawyer.

"What he wants is easier for me than it is for you." Andrew looked up at the windows of the front bedroom on the second floor.

"What does that mean?"

"I'm practical. You're not. We'll do better working together than apart."

"I'm surprised you concede I might help. It must hurt your vanity."

"There's no ego in field decisions. It's the objective that counts." Andrew spoke casually. "We can cut the time in half if we divide the possibilities. His recollections are disjointed, he wanders all over the place. His terrain-recall is confused; I've had some experience in that." Andrew straightened up, away from the car. "I think we'll have to go back, Adrian. Seven years ago. Before San Francisco. Can you do that?"

Adrian stared at his brother. "You're the only one who can answer that. And please don't lie; you were never any good at lying. Not with me."

"Nor you with me."

Their eyes locked; neither wavered.

"A man was killed Wednesday night. In Washington."

"I was in Saigon. You know that. Who was he?"

"A Black lawyer from Justice. A man named——"

"Nevins," completed Andrew, interrupting his brother.

"My God! You *knew!*"

"*About* him, yes. About his being *killed*, no. Why would I?"

"Eye Corps! He took a deposition on Eye Corps! It was with him! It was taken from his car!"

"Are you out of your goddamned mind?" The soldier spoke slowly, without urgency. "You may not like us, but we're not stupid. A target like that man, even remotely linked to us, would bring on the I.G. investigators by the hundreds. There are better ways. Killing's an instrument; you don't use it against yourself."

Adrian continued to look at his brother, searching his eyes. Finally, he spoke. Softly, barely above a whisper. "I think that's the most cold-blooded thing I've ever heard."

"What is?"

" 'Killing's an instrument.' You mean it, don't you?"

"Of course I do. It's the truth. Have I answered your question?"

"Yes," said Adrian quietly. "We'll go back . . . before

San Francisco. For a while; you have to know that. Only until this is over."

"Good. . . . You've got things to straighten up before we leave, and so do I. Let's say a week from tomorrow."

"All right. A week from tomorrow."

"I'm catching the six o'clock plane to Washington. Want to come along?"

"No, I'm meeting someone in town. I'll use one of the cars here."

"It's funny," said Andrew, shaking his head slowly, as if what he was about to say wasn't funny at all. "I've never asked for your telephone number, or where you lived."

"It's the District Towers. On Nebraska."

"The District Towers. All right. A week from tomorrow. I'll make the plane reservations. Straight through to Milan. Is your passport current?"

"I think so. It's at the hotel. I'll check."

"Good. I'll call you. A week from tomorrow." Andrew reached for the door handle. "Incidentally, what happened to that subpoena?"

"You know what happened. It wasn't served."

The soldier smiled as he climbed into the car. "It wouldn't have worked anyway."

They sat at a corner table in the St. Moritz sidewalk café on Central Park South. They were partial to such places; they would select pedestrians and invent instant biographies.

They invented none now. Instead, Adrian decided that his father's instructions to tell no one about the train from Salonika would not include Barbara. His decision was based on his belief that were their roles reversed, she would tell him. He wasn't going to leave the country for five to ten weeks without saying why. She deserved better than that.

"So there it is. Religious documents that go back fifteen hundred years, an Aramaic scroll that made the British government go half out of its collective mind in the middle of the war, and a confession written on a parchment two *thousand* years ago that contains God only knows what. That vault's caused more violence than I want to think about. If what my father says is true, those documents, that scroll—the parchment, most of all—could alter a large part of history."

Barbara leaned back in the chair, her brown eyes leveled at him. She watched him without replying for several moments. "That seems highly unlikely. Documents are unearthed every day. History doesn't change," she said simply.

"Have you ever heard of something called the Filioque Clause?"

"Certainly. It was incorporated in the Nicene Creed. It was the first issue that separated the Western and Eastern church. The debate went on for hundreds of years, and led to the Photian schism in . . . the ninth century. I think. Which in turn brought about the schism of 1054. The issue ultimately became papal infallibility."

"How the hell do you know that?"

Barbara laughed. "It's my field. Remember? At least the behavioral aspects."

"You said the ninth century. My father said fifteen hundred years——"

"Early Christian history is confusing, date-happy. From the first to the seventh centuries there were so many councils, so much seesawing back and forth, so much debate over *this* doctrine and *that* law, it's nearly impossible to sort out. Do these documents concern the Filioque? Are they supposed to be the denials?"

Adrian's glass was suspended on the way to his lips. "Yes. That's what my father said; he used the term. The Filioque denials."

"They don't exist."

"What?"

"They were destroyed—ceremonially, I believe—in Istanbul, in the Mosque of Saint Sophia early in the Second World War. There's documentation . . . witnesses, if I remember correctly. Even charred fragments confirmed by spectrochemical analyses."

Adrian stared at her. Something was terribly wrong. It was all too simple. Too negatively simple. "Where did you get that information?"

"Where? You mean *specifically* where?"

"Yes."

Barbara leaned forward, moving her glass absently in thought. Her forehead was creased. "It's not my area, but I can find out, of course. It goes back several years. I *do* remember that it was quite a shock to a lot of people."

"Do me a favor," he said rapidly. "When you get back, find out everything you can about that fire. It doesn't make sense! My father would know about it."

"I don't know why. It's awfully academic stuff."

"It still doesn't make sense——"

"Speaking of Boston," she interrupted. "My answering service had two calls from someone trying to locate you. A man named Dakakos."

"Dakakos?"

"Yes. A Theodore Dakakos. He said it was urgent."

"What did you say?"

"That I'd give you the message. I wrote down the number. I didn't *want* to give it to you. You don't need hysterical phone calls from Washington. You've had a horrid few days."

"He's not from Washington."

"The phone calls were."

Adrian looked up from the table, past the miniature hedges in the boxes bordering the café. He saw what he was looking for: a telephone booth.

"I'll be right back."

He walked to the phone and called the District Towers in Washington.

"Front desk, please."

"Yes, Mr. Fontine. We've had several calls from a Mr. Dakakos. There's an aide to Mr. Dakakos in the lobby now waiting for you."

Adrian thought quickly. His father's words came back to him; he had asked his father if he could trust Dakakos. *Where Salonika is concerned, I trust no one. . . .*

"Listen to me. Tell the man in the lobby you just heard from me. I won't be back for several days. I don't want to see this Dakakos."

"Of course, Mr. Fontine."

Adrian hung up. His passport was in Washington. In the room. He'd go by way of the garage. But not tonight; that was too soon. He'd wait until tomorrow. He'd stay in New York tonight. . . . His father. His father should be told about Dakakos. He called the North Shore house.

Jane's voice was strained. "The doctor's with him now. Thank God he allowed them to give him something. I don't think he could have stood it much longer. He's had spasms——"

"I'll phone you tonight."

Adrian walked out of the booth and threaded his way between the strollers back into the café, to the table.

"What *is* it?" Barbara was alarmed.

"Get in touch with your service in Boston. Tell them to call Dakakos and say we missed each other. I had to fly to—hell, Chicago. On business. That was the message for you at the hotel here."

"You really don't want to see him, do you?"

"I've got to avoid him. I want to throw him off the track. He's probably tried to reach my brother."

The path in Rock Creek Park. It was Martin Greene's idea, his selection. Greene had sounded strange on the telephone, somehow defiant. As though he didn't care about anything anymore.

Whatever was gnawing at Greene would vanish in the time it took to tell him the story. My God, would it! In one afternoon, Eye Corps had taken a giant step! Beyond anything they could have imagined. If the things his father said about that vault—the lengths powerful men, entire *governments* went to possess it—if it was all only half true, Eye Corps was in the catbird seat! Unreachable!

His father said he was going to prepare a list. Well, his father didn't have to; there *was* a list. The seven men of Eye Corps would control that vault. And he would control the seven men of Eye Corps.

Christ, it was incredible! But events did not lie; his father did not lie. Whoever possessed those documents, that parchment from a forgotten Roman prison, had the leverage to make extraordinary demands. Everywhere! An omission of recorded history, kept from the world out of unbelievable fear. Its revelation could not be tolerated. Well, fear, too, was an instrument. As great a one as death. Often greater.

Bear in mind that the contents of that vault are as staggering to the civilized world as anything in history. . . .

The decisions of extraordinary men—in peace and in war—supported his father's judgment. And now other extraordinary men, led by one extraordinary man, would find that vault and help shape the last quarter of the twentieth century. One had to begin to think like that, think in large blocks, concepts beyond ordinary men. His training, his heritage: All was coming into focus, and he was ready for the weight of enormous responsibility. He was primed for it; it was his with a vault buried in the Italian Alps.

Adrian would have to be immobilized. Not seriously; his brother was weak, indecisive, no contender at all. It would be enough to slow him down. He would visit his brother's rooms and do just that.

Andrew started down the Rock Creek path. There were very few strollers; the park was not a place for walking at night. Where *was* Greene? He should have been there; his apartment was a lot closer than the airport. And Greene had told him to hurry.

Andrew walked out on the grass and lighted a cigarette. There was no point standing under the spill of the park lamps. He'd see Greene when he came down the path.

"Fontine!"

The soldier turned around, startled. Twenty yards away at the side of a tree trunk stood Martin Greene. He was in civilian clothes; there was a large briefcase in his left hand.

"Marty? What the hell——"

"Get over here," ordered the captain tersely.

Andrew walked rapidly into the cluster of trees. "What's going on?"

"It's gone, Fontine. The whole goddamned thing. I've been calling you since yesterday morning."

"I was in New York. What are you talking about?"

"Five men are in a maximum security jail in Saigon. Want to take a guess who?"

"*What?* The subpoena wasn't served! You confirmed it, *I* confirmed it!"

"Nobody needed a subpoena. The I.G. crawled out of the rocks. They hit us on all points. My guess is that I've got about twelve hours before they figure I'm the one in procurement. You, you're marked."

"Wait a minute. Just wait a minute! This is crazy! The subpoena was canceled!"

"I'm the only one who benefits from that. You never mentioned my name in Saigon, did you?"

"Of course not. Just that we've got a man here."

"That's all they'll need; they'll put it together."

"How?"

"A dozen different ways. Locking in and comparing my checkout times with yours is the first that comes to mind. Something happened over there; something blew everything apart." Greene's eyes strayed.

Andrew breathed steadily, staring down at the captain. "No, it didn't," he said softly. "It happened over here. Last Wednesday night."

Greene's head snapped up. "What *about* Wednesday night?"

"That Black lawyer. Nevins. You had him killed, you stupid son of a bitch. My brother accused me! Accused *us!* He believed me because I believed it myself! It was too stupid!" The soldier's voice was a strained whisper. It was all he could do to keep from lashing out at the man staring up at him.

Greene replied calmly, with assurance. "You're getting the right total but the wrong numbers. I had it done, that's true, and I've got that bastard's briefcase, including the deposition against us. But the contract was so remote the people who did it don't know I exist. To bring you up to date, they were caught this morning. In West Virginia. They've got laundered money that can be traced to a company up for fraud. And we're not it. . . . No, Fontine, it wasn't me. Whatever it was, happened over there. I think you blew it."

Andrew shook his head. "Impossible. I handled——"

"Please. No burdens. I don't want to know, because I don't give a damn anymore. I've got a suitcase at Dulles and a one-way ticket to Tel Aviv. But I'm going to do you one last favor. When everything hit, I called a few friends at I.G., they owed me. That deposition from Barstow we worried so much about wasn't even in the prize money."

"What do you mean?"

"Remember the routine congressional inquiry? The Greek you never heard of——?"

"Dakakos?"

"That's right. Theodore Dakakos. Over at I.G. they call it the Dakakos probe. It was him. Nobody knows how, but that Greek was the one who got everything there was to get on Eye Corps. He funneled it piece by piece into the I.G. files."

Theodore Dakakos, thought Andrew. Theodore Annaxas Dakakos, son of a Greek trainman slain thirty years ago in the Milan freight yards by a priest who was his brother. Extraordinary men went to extraordinary lengths to control the vault of Constantine. A calm swept over the soldier.

"Thanks for telling me," he said. Greene held up the briefcase. "By the way, I made a trip to Baltimore."

"The Baltimore records are among the best," said Fontine.

"Where I'm going, we may need some quick firepower in the Negev. These could get it."

"Very possibly."

Greene hesitated, and then asked quietly, "You want to come along? We can hide you. You could do worse."

"I can do better."

"Stop kidding yourself, Fontine! Use some of your well-advertised money and get out of here as fast as you can. Buy sanctuary. You're *finished*."

"You're wrong. I've just begun."

25

Washington's noonday traffic was slowed further by the June thunderstorm. It was one of the deluges without spells of relief that allowed pedestrians to dash from doorway to awning to doorway. Windshield wipers did little but intrude on the sheets of water that blanketed the glass, distorting all vision.

Adrian sat in the back seat of a taxi, his thoughts divided equally in three parts, on three people. Barbara, Dakakos, and his brother.

Barbara was in Boston, probably in the library archives by now, researching the information—the extraordinary information—about the destructions of the Filioque denials. If those ancient documents had been in the vault from Constantine, and proof of their destruction established beyond doubt . . . had the vault been found? A equals B equals C. Therefore A equals C. Or did it?

Theodore Dakakos, the indefatigable Annaxas, would be scouring the Chicago hotels and law firms looking for him. There was no reason for the Greek not to; a business trip to Chicago was perfectly normal. The distraction was all Adrian needed. He would go up to his rooms, grab his passport, and call Andrew. They could both get out of Washington, avoiding Dakakos. The assumption had to be that Dakakos was trying to stop them. Which meant that somehow Dakakos-Annaxas knew what their father had planned. It was easy enough. An old man returns from Italy, his life expectancy short. And he summons his two sons.

One of those sons was Adrian's third concern. Where was his brother? He had telephoned Andrew's apartment in Virginia repeatedly throughout the night. What bothered Adrian, and the admission wasn't easy for him, was that his brother was more equipped to deal with someone like Dakakos than he. Move and countermove was part of his life, not thesis and antithesis.

"Garage entrance," said the cab driver. "Here it is."

Adrian dashed through the rain into the District Towers's garage. He had to orient himself before walking toward the elevator. As he did so, he reached into his pocket for the key with the plastic tag; he never left it at the front desk.

"Hi, Mr. Fontine. How are ya?"

It was the garage attendant; Adrian vaguely remembered the face. A sallow, twenty-year-old hustler with the eyes of a ferret.

"Hello," replied Adrian, pushing the elevator button.

"Hey, thanks again. I appreciated it, ya know what I mean? I mean it was real nice of you."

"Sure," Adrian said blankly, wishing the elevator would arrive.

"Hey." The attendant winked at him. "You look a lot better'n you did last night. A real broiler, huh?"

"What?"

The attendant smiled. No, it wasn't a smile, it was a leer. "I tied one on, too. Real good. Just like you said."

"What did you say? You saw me last night?"

"Hey, come on. Ya don't remember even? I gotta admit, you was fried, man."

Andrew! Andrew could do it when he wanted to!

Slouch, wear a hat, draw out his words. He'd pulled that caricature dozens of times.

"Tell me, I'm a little hazy. What time did I get in?"

"Jee-*sus!* You was flat out. Around eight o'clock, don't you remember? You gimme——" The attendant stopped; the hustler in him prevented full disclosure.

The elevator doors opened. Adrian walked inside. So Andrew had come to see him while he was trying to call *him* in Virginia. Had Andy found out about Dakakos? Had he already left town? Maybe Andy was upstairs now. Again the realization was disquieting, but Adrian felt a certain relief at the prospect. His brother would know what to do.

Adrian walked down the corridor to the door of his suite and let himself in. As he did so, he heard the footsteps behind him. He whipped around and saw an army officer standing in the bedroom door; not Andrew, a colonel.

"Who the hell are you?"

The officer did not immediately reply. Instead, he stood immobile, his eyes angry. When he did speak there was a slight drawl in his cold voice.

"Yeah, you do look like him. Put on a uniform and straighten you up and you could *be* him. Now, all you have to do is tell me where he is."

"How did you get in here? Who the hell let you in?"

"No question for a question. Mine comes first."

"What comes first is that you're trespassing." Adrian walked rapidly to the telephone, crossing in front of the officer. "Unless you've got a warrant from a civilian court, you're going to march into a civilian police station."

The colonel undid one button on his tunic, reached inside, and took out a pistol. He snapped the safety catch and leveled the weapon.

Adrian held the telephone in his left hand, his right poised above the dial. Stunned, he stopped all movement; the expression on the officer's face had not changed.

"You listen to me," said the colonel softly. "I could shoot both your kneecaps off just for looking like him. Can you understand that? I'm a civilized man, a lawyer like you; but where Eye Corps' Major Fontine is concerned, all the rules go out the window. I'll do anything to get that son of a bitch. Do you read me?"

Adrian slowly put down the telephone. "You're a maniac."

"Minor compared to him. Now, you tell me where he is."

"I don't know."

"I don't believe you."

"Wait a minute!" In his shock, Adrian had not been sure of what he'd heard. Now he was. "What do you know about *Eye Corps?"*

"A lot more than you paranoid bastards want me to know. Did you two really think you could pull it off?"

"You're way off base! You'd know that if you knew anything about me! About Eye Corps we're on the same side! Now, for God's sake, what have you got on him?"

The officer replied slowly. "He killed two men. A captain named Barstow, and a legal officer named Tarkington. Both killings were made to look *kai-sai*—whore-and-booze oriented. They weren't. In Tarkington's case it was inconsistent. He didn't drink."

"Oh, Christ!"

"And a file was taken from Tarkington's Saigon office. Which *was* consistent. What they didn't know was that we had a complete copy."

"Who's 'we'?"

"The Inspector General's Office." The colonel did not lower his pistol; his answers were delivered in a flat Southwestern drawl. "Now, I just gave you the benefit of a doubt. You know why I want him, so tell me where he is. My name's Tarkington, too. I drink and I'm not mild-mannered and I want the son of a bitch who killed my brother."

Adrian felt the breath leave his lungs. "I'm sorry——"

"Now you know why this gun is out and why I'll use it. Where did he go? How did he go?"

It took Adrian a moment to focus. "Where? How? I didn't know he *was* gone. Why are you sure he is?"

"Because he knows we're after him. We know he got the word; we made the connection this morning. A captain named Greene in the Pentagon. In procurement. Needless to say, he's gone, too. Probably halfway across the world by now."

. . . *halfway across the world* . . . the words penetrated, the realization began to surface. *Halfway across the world. To Italy. Campo di Fiori. A painting on the wall and the memories of a half a century ago. The vault from Constantine!*

"Did you check the airports?"

"He has a standard military passport. All military. . . ."

"Oh, Jesus!" Adrian started for the bedroom.

"Hold it!" The colonel grabbed his arm.

"Let me go!" Fontine shook off the officer's hand and raced into the bedroom. To the bureau.

He pulled open the right-hand top drawer. From behind the colonel's hand shot out and slammed it, trapping his wrist.

"You pull out anything I don't like, you're dead." The colonel released the drawer.

Fontine could feel the pain and see the swelling on his wrist. He could not think about either. He opened a large leather case. His passport was gone. So, too, his international driver's license and his Banque Genève checkbook with the coded numbers and photograph on the flap.

Adrian turned and walked across the room in silence. He dropped the leather pouch on the bed and continued to the window. The rain outside came down in torrents against the glass.

His brother had stalled him. Andrew had gone after the vault, leaving him behind, wanting no assistance at all, never having wanted it. The vault from Constantine was Andrew's final weapon. In his hands a deadly thing.

The irony was, reflected Adrian, that the army officer behind him in that room could *help*. He could break down bureaucratic barriers, provide instant transportation;—but the army officer could be told nothing about the train from Salonika.

There are those who would trade off half the arsenals in this world for the information. His father's words.

He spoke quietly. "There's your proof, colonel."

"I guess so."

Adrian turned and faced the officer. "Tell me, as one brother to another—how did you lock in on Eye Corps?"

The colonel put away the gun. "A man named Dakakos."

"Dakakos?"

"Yes, he's Greek. You know him?"

"No, I don't."

"The data came in slowly at first. Right into my department, marked for me by name. When Barstow broke and gave his deposition in Saigon, there was Dakakos again. He sent word to my brother to get to Barstow. Eye Corps was covered both over here and over there——"

"By two brothers who could pick up a phone and keep it all together," said Adrian, interrupting. "Without bureaucratic interference."

"We figured that. We don't know why, but this Dakakos was after Eye Corps."

"He certainly was," agreed Adrian, marveling at Dakakos's clarity of method.

"Yesterday, *everything* came in. Dakakos had Fontine followed to Phan-thiet. To a warehouse. We've got Eye Corps' records now, we've got the proof——"

The telephone rang, interrupting the army man. Adrian barely heard it, so total was his concentration on the colonel's words.

It rang again.

"May I?" asked Adrian.

"You'd better." Tarkington's eyes became cold again. "I'll be right next to you."

It was Barbara, calling from Boston. "I'm in the archives. I've got the information on that church fire in forty-one that destroyed the Filioque——"

"Just a minute." Adrian turned his head toward the officer, the phone between them. He wondered if he could sound natural. "You can get on a line in the other room, if you like. It's just some research I asked for."

The ruse worked. Tarkington shrugged and walked to the window.

"Go ahead," he said into the phone.

Barbara spoke as an expert does, scanning a report whose form is familiar; her voice rose and fell as salient points were enumerated. "There was a gathering of elders on January 9, 1941, at eleven o'clock in the evening at the Mosque of Saint Sophia, Istanbul, a ceremony of deliverance. According to the witnesses a consigning of holy property to the heavens . . . sloppy work here; it's all narrative. There should be direct quotes and literal translations. Anyway, it goes on to verify the act and list the laboratories in Istanbul and Athens where fragments of the ash were confirmed for age and materials. There you are, my doubting Thomas."

"What about those witnesses? The narrative?"

"I'm being overly critical. I could be more so; the report should include authorizing credentials and graphic plate numbers, but that's all academic lacework. The main thing is, it's got the archival seal; you don't buy that. You can't play games with it. It means someone beyond reproach was at the scene and confirmed the burning. The Annaxas grant got what it paid for. The seal says it."

"What grant?" he asked quietly.

"Annaxas. It's the company that put up the money for the research."

"Thanks. I'll talk to you later." He hung up. Tarkington was standing by the window, looking out at the rain. This was the man he had to get away from; he had to get to the vault!

Barbara was right in one respect. Dakakos-Annaxas got *exactly* what he paid for: a false report in the archives.

He knew where he had to go.

Campo di Fiori.

Dakakos.

Dakakos, Dakakos, *Dakakos!*

The name burned into Andrew's brain as he watched the coast of Italy go by 30,000 feet below. Theodore Annaxas Dakakos had destroyed Eye Corps for the sole purpose of destroying *him,* eliminating *him* from the search for a vault buried in the mountains. What triggered his decision? How did he do it? It was vital to learn all he could about the man himself. The better one knew his enemy, the better he could fight. As things stood, Dakakos was the only barrier, the only contender.

There was a man in Rome who could help. He was a banker who showed up with increasing frequency in Saigon, a large-scale buyer who bought whole piers, shipped the contents back to Naples and sold the stolen goods throughout Italy. Eye Corps had nailed him and used him; he had provided names that went right back to Washington.

Such a man would know about Dakakos.

The announcement came over the Air Canada loudspeaker. They would begin their descent into Rome's Leonardo da Vinci Airport in fifteen minutes.

Fontine took out his passport. He had bought it in Quebec. Adrian's passport had gotten him through Canadian customs, but he knew it would be worthless after that. Washington would flash the name Fontine to every airport in the hemisphere.

Ironically, he made a connection with several army deserters at two in the morning in Montreal. The exiled moralists needed money; morality could not be proselytized without hard cash. A stringy-haired intellectual in a GI field jacket took him to an apartment that reeked of hash, and for $10,000 he got a passport within an hour.

Adrian was so far behind he'd never catch up.

. . . He could dismiss Adrian. If Dakakos wanted to stop one of them, he obviously wanted to stop both. The Greek was no match for the soldier; he was more than a match for the lawyer. And if Dakakos didn't stop Adrian, the lack of a passport would slow him down more than enough. His brother was out of the picture, no contender at all.

The plane touched ground. Andrew unbuckled his seat belt; he would be among the first out of the aircraft. He was in a hurry to get to a telephone.

The evening crowds on the Via Veneto were heavy, the sidewalk tables under the awnings of the Café de Paris nearly filled. The banker had secured one near the service door, where the traffic was concentrated. He was a gaunt, middle-aged, impeccably dressed man, and he was cautious. No listener could overhear anything said at that table.

Their greeting was perfunctory, the banker obviously anxious to have the meeting over with as quickly as possible.

"I won't ask why you're in Rome. No address, out of your celebrated uniform." The Italian spoke rapidly in a monotone that gave no emphasis to any word and thus emphasis to all. "I honored your demand to make no inquiries. It wasn't necessary. You're a hunted man."

"How do you know that?"

The slender Italian paused, his thin lips stretched into a slight smile. "You just told me."

"I warn you——"

"Oh, stop it. A man flies in unannounced, says he'll meet only in crowds. It's enough to send me to Malta so I won't run into you. Besides, it's all over your face. You're uncomfortable."

The banker was essentially right. He *was* uncomfortable. He would have to adjust better, be more relaxed. "You're clever, but then we knew that in Saigon."

"I never saw you before in my life," replied the Italian, signaling a waiter. "*Due* Campari, *per favore.*"

"I don't drink Campari. . . ."

"Then don't. Two Italians who order Campari on the Via Veneto are not conspicuous. Which is precisely what I intend to be. What did you wish to discuss?"

"A man named Dakakos. A Greek."

The banker raised his eyebrows. "If by Dakakos you mean Theo Dakakos, he is indeed Greek."

"You know him?"

"Who in the world of finance doesn't? You have business with Dakakos?"

"Maybe. He's a shipper, isn't he?"

"Among many other interests. He's also quite young and very powerful. Even the colonels in Athens think twice before issuing edicts unfavorable to him. His older competitors are wary of him. What he lacks in experience he makes up for in energy. He's a bull."

"What are his politics?"

The Italian's eyebrows once more rose. "Himself."

"What are his interests in Southeast Asia? Whom does he work for out of Saigon?"

"He doesn't work *for* anyone." The waiter returned with the drinks. "He ships middle-manned supplies to the A.I.D. in Vientiane. Into northern Laos and Cambodia. As you know, it's all intelligence-operated. He pulled out, I understand."

That was it, thought Fontine, pushing away the glass of Campari. Eye Corps had tagged the corruption in AID, and Dakakos had tagged *them*. "He went to a lot of trouble to interfere."

"Did he succeed in interfering? . . . I see he did. Annaxas the Younger usually does succeed; he's perverse and predictable in that department." The Italian raised his glass delicately.

"What was that name?"

"Annaxas. Annaxas the Younger, son of Annaxas the Strong. Sounds Theban, does it not? The Greek bloodlines, however insignificant, are always on the tips of their tongues. Pretentious, I think."

"Does he use it a lot?"

"Not often for himself. His yacht is named *Annaxas,* several planes are *Annaxas—One, Two, Three.* He works the name into a few corporate titles. It's an obsession with him. Theodore Annaxas Dakakos. The first son of a poor family raised by some religious order in the north. The circumstances are cloudy; he doesn't encourage curiosity." The Italian drained his glass.

"That's interesting."

"Have I told you something you didn't know?"

"Maybe," said Fontine casually. "It's not important."

"By which you mean it is." The Italian smiled his thin, bloodless smile. "Dakakos is in Italy, you know."

Fontine concealed his surprise. "Is he really?"

"So you *do* have business with him. Is there anything else?"

"No."

The banker rose and walked rapidly into the crowds of the Via Veneto.

Andrew remained at the table. So Dakakos was in Italy. Andrew wondered where they would meet. He wanted that meeting very much; almost as much as he wanted to find the vault from Salonika.

He wanted to kill Theodore Annaxas Dakakos. The man who had destroyed Eye Corps did not deserve to live.

Andrew got up from the table. He could feel the bulge of papers in his jacket pocket. His father's recollections of half a century ago.

26

Adrian shifted the soft leather suitcase into his left hand and fell behind the surge of passengers in the wide corridor of London's Heathrow Airport. He did not wish to be among the first in the passport line. He wanted to be in the middle group, even the last section; he would have more time to look around, be less conspicuous doing so. He wondered who among the scores of people in the terminal had him in their sights.

Colonel Tarkington was no fool; he'd know within minutes of the application that one Adrian Fontine was at the emigration offices in Rockefeller Center waiting for the issuance of a substitute passport. It was entirely possible that an IG agent had picked him up before he'd left the building. If no one had, he knew it was only a question of time. And because of that certainty, Adrian had flown to London, not Rome.

Tomorrow he would begin the chase, an amateur against professionals. His first step was to disappear, but he wasn't sure how. On the one hand it seemed simple: a single human being among millions; how difficult could it be? Then came second thoughts: one had to travel across national borders—that meant clearly one had to have identification; one had to sleep and eat—that meant shelter and purchases, places that could be watched, alerted.

It wasn't simple at all; not if the single human being in question had no experience. He had no contacts in the underworld; he wouldn't know how to behave if he met them. He doubted that he could approach someone and say the words *"I'll pay for a false passport,"* . . . or *"Get me to Italy illegally,"* . . . or even *"I won't tell you my name but I'll give money for certain services."* Such boldness belonged in fiction. Normal men and women did not do such things; their awkwardness would be laughed at. But professionals—the sort he was up against—were not normal. They did such things quite easily.

He saw the passport lines. There were six in all; he chose the longest. Yet as he walked over to it, he realized that the decision was amateurish. True, he had more time to look around, but conversely, so did others.

"Occupation, sir?" asked the immigration officer.

"I'm a lawyer."

"Here on business?"

"In a manner of speaking. Also pleasure."

"Anticipated length of stay?"

"I'm not sure. No more than a week."

"Do you have hotel accommodations?"

"I didn't make reservations. Probably the Savoy."

The official glanced up; it was difficult to tell whether he was impressed or whether he resented Adrian's tone. Or whether the name Fontine, A. was on a concealed list somewhere in the drawer of his lectern, and he wanted to look at the face.

Regardless, he smiled mechanically, stamped the pages of the newly issued passport, and handed it to Adrian. "Have a pleasant stay in Great Britain, Mr. Fontine."

"Thank you."

The Savoy found him a room above the court, offering to switch him to a suite on the Thames side as soon as one became available. He accepted the offer, saying he expected to remain in England for the better part of the month. He would be traveling around—away from London for much of the time—but would like a suite available during the period of his stay.

What astonished him was the ease with which he lied. It all flowed casually, with a certain businesslike assurance. It wasn't an important maneuver, but the fact that he was able to do it so well gave him a sense of confidence. He had seized an advantage when it was presented; that was the important thing. He had spotted an opportunity and acted on it.

He sat on the bed, airline schedules scattered over the spread. He found what he wanted. An SAS flight from Paris to Stockholm at 10:30 A.M. And an Air Afrique from Paris to Rome. Time: 10:15 A.M. The SAS left from the de Gaulle field, the Air Afrique from Orly.

Fifteen minutes between flights, departure before arrival, from adjacent airfields. He wondered—almost academically now—if he was capable of conceiving a deception, organizing the facts and executing the manipulation from beginning to end.

Odd things would have to be considered. Items that were part of the . . . "dressing," that was the word. Part of the ruse that would draw the proper attention in a crowded, bustling airport. He picked up a Savoy note pad and wrote:

Three suitcases—unusual.
Overcoat—conspicuous.
Glasses.

Hat—wide-brimmed.
Small paste-on beard.

The last item—the beard—caused him to smile uncomfortably, embarrassed at his own imagination. Was he crazy? Who did he think he was? What did he think he was doing? He moved the pencil instinctively to the left of the line, prepared to cross it out. Then he stopped. He wasn't crazy. It was part of the boldness he had to absorb, the unnatural with which he had to be comfortable. He took the pencil away and without thinking wrote the name: "Andrew."

Where was he now? Had his brother reached Italy? Had he traveled halfway around the world without being found? Would he be waiting for him at Campo di Fiori?

And if he *was* waiting, what would they say to each other? He hadn't thought about that; he hadn't wanted to think about it. Like a difficult summation in front of a hostile jury, he could not rehearse the words. He could only marshal the facts in his head and trust his thought processes when the moment came. But what did one say to a twin who was the killer of Eye Corps? What was there *to* say?

. . . *Bear in mind, the contents of that vault are as staggering to the civilized world as anything in history.* . . .

His brother had to be stopped. It was as simple as that.

He looked at his watch. It was one in the morning. He was thankful that he had gotten little sleep during the past several days. It would make sleeping possible now. He had to rest; he had a great deal to do tomorrow. Paris.

He walked up to the desk clerk in the Hôtel Pont Royale and handed him the room key. He hadn't been to the Louvre in five years; it would be a cultural sin to avoid it since it was so close by. The clerk agreed politely, but Adrian saw the shaded curiosity in the man's eyes. It was further confirmation of what Adrian suspected: he was being followed; questions were being asked.

He walked into the bright sunlight on the rue de Bac. He nodded, smiling, at the doorman and shook his head in response to the offer of a taxi.

"I'm going to the Louvre. I'll walk, thanks."

At the curb he lit a cigarette, turning slightly as if to

avoid a breeze, and let his eyes wander over to the large windows of the hotel. Inside, through the glass, obscured by the sun's reflection, he could see the clerk talking to a man in a light-brown topcoat. Adrian was not certain, but he was fairly sure he had seen that gabardine coat at the airport two hours ago.

He started east down the rue de Bac, toward the Seine and the Pont Royale bridge.

The Louvre was crowded. Tourists mingled with busloads of students. Adrian climbed the steps past Winged Victory and continued up the staircase to the right, to the second landing, and into the hall of nineteenth-century masters. He fell in with a group of German tourists.

The Germans moved in unison down to the next painting, a Delacroix. Adrian was now in the center of the group. Keeping his head below the level of the tallest German, he turned and looked between the sagging bodies, beyond the impassive faces. He saw what he was both afraid and wanted to see.

The light-brown topcoat.

The man was fifty feet away, pretending to read from a museum pamphlet, relating it to an Ingres in front of him. But he was neither reading nor relating; his eyes kept straying up from the paper to the crowd of Germans.

The group turned the corner into the intersecting corridor. Adrian was against the wall. He parted the bodies in front of him, excusing himself, until he was past the guide and free of the group. He walked swiftly down the right side of the enormous hall and turned left into a dimly lit room. Tiny spotlights shone down from the dark ceiling on a dozen marble statues.

It suddenly occurred to him that if the man in the light-brown gabardine topcoat came into that room, there was no way out.

On the other hand, if the man entered there was no way out for him, either. Adrian wondered which of them had more to lose. He had no answer and so he stood in the shadows at the farthest end of the room, beyond the shafts of light, and waited.

He could see the group of Germans go past the doorway. Seconds later there was the blur of the light-brown topcoat; the man was running, actually running.

Adrian went to the door, paused long enough to see the

Germans swing left into yet another intersecting corridor, turned right and walked rapidly toward the hall to the stairs.

The crowds on the staircase were denser than before. There was a contingent of uniformed schoolgirls entering the steps. Behind the girls was the man in the light-brown gabardine topcoat, frustrated in his attempt to pass and reach the steps.

It was suddenly clear to Adrian. The man had lost him and would wait at the exit.

There remained the obvious: reach the main doors first.

Adrian hurried down the steps, doing his best to look unhurried; a man late for a lunch date.

Out on the steps in front of the entrance a taxi was disgorging four Japanese. An elderly couple, obviously British, was walking across the pavement toward the cab. He ran, overtaking the couple, and reached the taxi first.

"Dépêchez-vous s'il vous plaît. Très important."

The driver grinned and started up the car. Adrian turned in the seat and looked out the rear window. On the steps the man in the light-brown topcoat stood looking up and down, confused and angry.

"Orly Airport," ordered Adrian. "Air Afrique."

There were more crowds and more lines but the line he was in was short. And nowhere in sight was the light-brown topcoat. No one seemed interested in him at all.

The Black girl in the Air Afrique uniform smiled at him.

"I'd like a ticket to Rome on your ten fifteen flight tomorrow morning. The name's Llewellyn. That's two *l*'s in front, two in back, with a *y*. First class, please, and if it's possible, I'd like seat location now. I'll be very rushed in the morning, but hold the reservation. I'll pay in cash."

He walked out the automatic doors of the Orly terminal and hailed another taxi.

"De Gaulle field, please. SAS."

The line was longer, the service slower, there was a man staring at him beyond a row of plastic chairs. There'd been no one looking at him like that in Orly terminal. He wondered; he hoped.

"Round trip to Stockholm," he said arrogantly to the SAS attendant behind the counter. "You have a flight tomorrow at ten thirty. That's the one I want."

The attendant looked up from his papers. "I'll see what

we have, sir," he replied in muted irritation, his accent heavily Scandinavian. "What would be the return date?"

"I'm not sure, so leave it open. I'm not interested in bargains. The name's Fontine."

Five minutes later the tickets were processed, the payment made.

"Please be here an hour prior to departure, sir," said the clerk, smarting under Adrian's impatience.

"Of course. Now, there's a small problem. I have some valuable, very fragile objects in my luggage. I'd like——"

"We cannot take responsibility for such things," interrupted the attendant.

"Don't be a damn fool. I know you can't. I just want to make sure you have 'Fragile' stickers in Swedish or Norwegian or whatever the hell it is. My bags are easily recognized——"

He left the de Gaulle terminal convinced he'd alienated a very nice fellow who would complain to his colleagues about him, and got into a taxi.

"The Hôtel Pont Royale, please. Rue de Bac."

Adrian saw him at a table in a small sidewalk café on the rue Dumont. He was an American, drinking white wine, and looked like a student who would nurse a drink because of the price. His age was no problem; he seemed tall enough. Adrian walked up to him.

"Hello!"

"Hi," replied the young man.

"May I sit down? Buy you a drink?"

"Hell, why not?"

Adrian sat. "You go to the Sorbonne?"

"Nope. L'École des Beaux Arts. I'm a bona-fide, real-life painter. I'll sketch you for thirty *francs*. How about it?"

"No, thanks. But I'll give you a lot more than that if you'll do something else for me."

The student eyed him suspiciously, distastefully. "I don't smuggle anything for anybody. You'd better beat it. I'm a very legal type."

"I'm more than that. I'm a lawyer. A prosecuting attorney, as a matter of fact. With a card to prove it."

"You don't sound it."

"Just hear me out. What can it cost? Five minutes and some decent wine?"

At nine fifteen in the morning, Adrian emerged from the limousine in front of the glass doors of SAS at de Gaulle terminal. He was dressed in a long, flared Edwardian overcoat of white fabric; he looked like an ass, but he couldn't be missed. On his head he wore a matching white, wide-brimmed fedora, the cloth pulled down over his face in Barrymore style, his features in shadow. Beneath the hat were huge dark glasses that covered far more than his eyes, and below his chin was a blue silk scarf, billowing above and out of the white coat.

The uniformed chauffeur scrambled around to the trunk of the limousine, opened it, and called for skycaps to serve his very important passenger. Three large, white leather suitcases were stacked on a hand rack, to Adrian's complaints that they were being scuffed.

He strode through the electronically parted doors and up to the SAS counter.

"I feel like hell!" he said scathingly, conveying the effects of a hangover, "and I would appreciate as little difficulty as possible. I want my luggage to be loaded last; please keep it behind the counter until the final baggage call. It's done for me all the time. The gentleman yesterday assured me there'd be no trouble."

The clerk behind the counter looked bewildered. Adrian slapped his ticket envelope down.

"Gate forty-two, sir," the clerk said, handing back the envelope. "Boarding time is at ten o'clock."

"I'll wait over there," replied Adrian, indicating the line of plastic chairs inside the SAS area. "I meant what I said about the luggage. Where's the men's room?"

At twenty minutes to ten, a tall, slender man in khaki trousers, cowboy boots, and an American army field jacket came through the doors of the terminal. On his face there was a pronounced chin beard; on his head a wide Australian bush hat. He entered the men's room.

At eighteen minutes to ten, Adrian got out of the plastic chair and walked across the crowded terminal. He pushed the door marked "Hommes" and entered.

Inside a toilet stall they awkwardly manipulated the exchange of clothes.

"This is weird, man. You swear there's nothing in that crazy coat?"

"It's not even old enough to have lint. . . . Here are the tickets, go to gate forty-two. You can throw away the baggage stubs, I don't care. Unless you want the suitcases; they're damned expensive. And clean."

"In Stockholm no one busts me. You guarantee."

"As long as you use your *own* passport and don't say you're me. I gave you my tickets, that's all. You've got my note to prove it. Take my word for it, nobody'll press you. You don't know where I am and there's no warrant. There's nothing."

"You're a nut. But you've paid my tuition for a couple of years, plus some nice living expenses. You're a good nut."

"Let's hope I'm good enough. Hold the mirror for me." Adrian pressed the beard on his chin; it adhered quickly. He studied the results and, satisfied, put on the bush hat, pulling it down on the side of his head. "Okay, let's go. You look fine."

At eleven minutes to ten, a man in a long white coat, matching white hat, blue scarf, and dark glasses strode past the SAS desk toward gate forty-two.

Thirty seconds later a bearded young man—obviously American—in a soiled field jacket, khaki trousers, cowboy boots, and bush hat slipped out the door of the men's room, turned sharply left into the crowds, and headed for the exit door. Out on the pavement he rushed to a waiting taxi, got in and removed the beard.

"The name's Llewellyn!" he shouted to the Air Afrique attendant at the lectern by the departure gate. "I'm sorry I'm late; did I make it?"

The pleasant-faced Black smiled and replied in a French accent. "Just barely, *monsieur.* We've given the last call. Do you have any hand luggage?"

"Not a thing."

At twenty-three minutes past ten, the ten fifteen Air Afrique flight to Rome taxied out toward runway seven. By ten twenty-eight it was airborne. It was only thirteen minutes late.

The man who called himself Llewellyn sat by the window, the bush hat on his left in the adjacent, empty first-class seat. He felt the hardening globules of facial cement on his chin, and he rubbed them in a kind of wonder.

He had done it. Disappeared.

The man in the light-brown topcoat boarded the SAS flight to Stockholm at ten twenty-nine. Departure was delayed. As he walked toward the economy section, he passed the fashionably dressed passenger in the long white overcoat and matching white hat. He thought to himself that the man he followed was a fucking idiot. Who did he think he was, wearing that outfit?

By ten fifty the flight to Stockholm was airborne. It was twenty minutes late, not unusual. The man in the economy section had removed his topcoat and was seated in the forward area of the cabin, diagonally behind the target of his surveillance. When the curtains were parted—as they were now—he could see the subject clearly.

Twelve minutes into the flight the pilot turned off the seat-belt sign. The fashionably dressed subject in the first-class section rose from his aisle seat and removed the long white overcoat and matching white hat.

The man diagonally behind in the economy section bolted forward in his seat, stunned.

"Oh, shit," he muttered.

27

Andrew peered through the windshield at the sign caught in the dull wash of the headlights. It was dawn but pockets of fog were everywhere.

MILANO 5 KM.

He had driven through the night, renting the fastest car he could find in Rome. The journey at night minimized the risk of being followed. Headlights were giveaways on long stretches of dark roads.

But he had not expected to be followed. In Rock Creek Park, Greene said he was marked. What the Jew did not know was that if IG wanted him that quickly, they could have picked him up at the airport. The Pentagon knew exactly where he was; a cable from the secretary of the army had brought him back from Saigon.

So the word to take him had not been given. That it would within days, perhaps hours, was not the issue; of course it would. But he was the son of Victor Fontine. The Pentagon would not be hasty issuing any formal orders for arrest. The army did not bring charges against a Rockefeller or a Kennedy or a Fontine lightly. The Pentagon would insist on flying back the Eye Corps officers for corroborating testimony. The Pentagon would leave nothing to chance or error.

Which meant he had the time to get out. For by the time the army was prepared to move, he would be in the mountains tracing a vault that would change the ground rules as they had never been changed before.

Andrew stepped on the accelerator. He needed sleep. A professional knew when the body hungered for rest in spite of the high-pitched moment, and the eyes became aware of their sockets. He would find a small boardinghouse or country inn and sleep for most of the day. Late in the afternoon he would drive north to Campo di Fiori and find a picture on the wall. The first clue in the search for a vault buried in the mountains.

He drove by the crumbling stone gates of the entrance without slowing down, and continued for several miles. He allowed two cars to pass him, observing the drivers; they were not interested in him. He turned around and went past the gates a second time. There was no way to tell what was inside; whether there were any security measures—trip alarms or dogs. All he could see was a winding paved road that disappeared into the woods.

The sound of an automobile on that road would be its own alarm. He could not chance that; he had no intention of announcing his arrival at Campo di Fiori. He slowed the car down, and turned into the bordering woods, driving as far off the road as possible.

Five minutes later he approached the gates. By habit he checked for wires and photoelectric cells; there were none, and he passed through the gates and walked down the road cut out of the woods.

He stayed at the edge, concealed by the trees and the

overgrowth until he was in sight of the main house. It was as his father had described: more dead than alive.

The windows were dark, no lamps were on inside. There should have been. The house was in shadows. An old man living alone needed light; old men did not trust their eyes. Had the priest died?

Suddenly, out of nowhere, there came the sound of a voice, high-pitched and plaintive. Then footsteps. They came from the road beyond the north bend of the drive; the road he remembered his father describing as leading to the stables. Fontine dropped to the ground, below the level of the grass, and remained motionless. He raised his head by inches; he waited and watched.

The old priest came into view. He was wearing a long black cassock and carried a wicker basket. He spoke out loud, but Andrew could not see who he was talking to. Nor could he understand the words. Then the monk stopped and turned and spoke again.

There was a reply. It was rapid, authoritative, in a language Fontine did not immediately recognize. Then he saw the monk's companion and instantly appraised him as one might an adversary. The man was large, the shoulders wide and heavy, encased in a camel's hair jacket above well-tailored slacks. The last rays of the sun illuminated both men; not well—the light was at their backs—but enough to distinguish the faces.

Andrew concentrated on the younger, powerfully built man walking behind the priest. His face was large, the eyes wide apart, beneath light brows and a tanned forehead that set off short, sun-bleached hair. He was in his middle forties, certainly no more. And the walk: It was that of a deliberate man, capable of moving swiftly, but not anxious for observers to know it. Fontine had commanded such men.

The old monk proceeded toward the marble steps, shifting the small basket to his left arm, his right hand lifting the folds of his habit. He stopped on the top step and turned again to the younger man. His voice was calmer, resigned to the layman's presence or instructions or both. He spoke slowly and Fontine had no trouble now recognizing the language. It was Greek.

As he listened to the priest he reached another, equally

obvious conclusion. The powerfully built man was Theodore Annaxas Dakakos. *He is a bull.*

The priest continued across the wide marble porch to the doors; Dakakos climbed the steps and followed. Both men went inside.

Fontine lay in the grass on the border of the drive for several minutes. He had to think. What brought Dakakos to Campo di Fiori? What was here for him?

And as the questions formed, the single answer was apparent. Dakakos, the loner, was the unseen power here. The conversation that had just taken place in the circular drive was not a conversation between strangers.

What had to be established was whether Dakakos had come alone to Campo di Fiori. Or had he brought his own protection, his own firepower? There was no one in the house, no lights in the windows, no sounds from inside. That left the stables.

Andrew scrambled backward in the wet grass until all sightlines from the windows were blocked by the overgrowth. He rose behind a clump of bushes and removed a small Beretta revolver from his pocket. He climbed the embankment above the drive and estimated the angle of the stable road across the knoll. If Dakakos's men were in the stables, it would be a simple matter to eliminate them. Without gunfire; that was essential. The weapon was merely a device; men collapsed under its threat.

Fontine crouched and weaved his way across the knoll toward the stable road. The early evening breezes bent the upper grass and the branches of trees; the professional soldier fell instinctively into the rhythm of their movement. The roofs of the stables came into view and he stepped silently down the incline toward the road.

In front of the stable door was a long steel-gray Maserati, its tires caked with mud. There were no voices, no signs of life; there was only the quiet hum of the surrounding woods. Andrew lowered himself to his knees, picked up a handful of dirt, and threw it twenty yards in the air across the road, hitting the stable windows.

No one emerged. Fontine repeated the action, using more dirt mixed with small pieces of rock. The splattering was louder; there was no way it could go unobserved.

Nothing. No one.

Cautiously, Andrew walked out on the road toward the

car. He stopped before he reached it. The surface of the road was hard, but still partially wet from the earlier rain. The Maserati was headed north; there were no footsteps on the passenger side of the car in front of him. He walked around the automobile; there were distinct imprints on the driver's side: the shoe marks of a man. Dakakos had come alone.

There was no time to waste now. There was a picture on a wall to be taken, and a journey to Champoluc that had to begin. Too, there was a fine irony in finding Dakakos at Campo di Fiori. The informer's life would end where his obsession had begun. Eye Corps was owed that much.

He could see lights inside the house now, but only in the windows to the left of the main entrance. Andrew kept to the wall, ducking under the ledges, until he was at the side of the window where the light was brightest. He inched his face to the frame and looked inside.

The room was huge. There were couches and chairs and a fireplace. Two lamps were lit; one by the far couch, the second nearer, to the right of an armchair. Dakakos was standing by the mantel, gesturing in slow, deliberate movements with his hands. The priest was in the chair, his back to Fontine, and barely visible. Their conversation was muted, indistinguishable. It was impossible to determine whether the Greek had a weapon; the assumption had to be that he did.

Andrew pried a brick loose from the border of the drive and returned to the window. He rose, the Beretta in his right hand, the brick gripped in his left. Dakakos approached the priest in the chair; the Greek was pleading, or explaining, his concentration absolute.

The moment was now.

Shielding his eyes with the gun, Fontine extended his left arm behind him, then arced it forward, hurling the brick into the center of the window, shattering glass and wood strips everywhere. On impact he smashed the remaining, obstructing glass with the Beretta, thrusting the weapon through the space, and screamed at the top of his voice.

"You move one inch, you're dead!"

Dakakos froze. "*You?*" he whispered. "You were *taken!*"

The Greek's head slumped forward, the gashes from the pistol barrel on his face deep, ugly, and bleeding profusely.

There was nothing that so became this man as a painful death, thought Fontine.

"In the name of God have *mercy!*" screamed the priest from the opposite chair, where he sat bound and helpless.

"Shut up!" roared the soldier, his eyes on Dakakos. "Why did you do it? Why are you here?"

The Greek stared, his breathing erratic, his eyes swollen. "They said you were taken. They had everything they needed." He could barely be heard, speaking as much to himself as to the man above him.

"They made a mistake," said Andrew. "Their signals got crossed. You didn't expect them to wire you their apologies, did you? What did they tell you? That they were picking me up?"

Dakakos remained silent, blinking from the rivulets of blood that rolled down his forehead into his eyes. Fontine could hear the Pentagon commanders. *Never admit. Never explain. Take the objective, the rest is no strain.*

"Forget it," he said quietly, icily to Dakakos. "Just tell me why you're here."

The Greek's eyes swam in his head; his lips moved. "You are *filth.* And we'll *stop you!*"

"Who's we?"

Dakakos arched his neck, thrusting it forward, and spat into the soldier's face. Fontine swung the barrel of the pistol up into the Greek's jaw. The head slumped forward.

"Stop!" cried the monk. "I'll tell you. There's a priest named Land. Dakakos and Land work together."

"Who?" Fontine turned abruptly to the monk.

"It's all I know. The name! They've been in contact for years."

"Who is he? *What* is he?"

"I don't know. Dakakos doesn't say."

"Is he waiting for him? Is this priest coming here?"

The monk's expression suddenly changed. His eyelids quivered, his lips trembled.

Andrew understood. Dakakos was waiting for someone, but not a priest named Land. Fontine raised the barrel of the pistol and shoved it into the mouth of the semiconscious Greek. "All right, Father, you've two seconds to tell me who it is. Who's this son of a bitch waiting for?"

"The other one. . . ."

"The other *what?*"

The old monk stared at him. Fontine felt a hard emptiness in his stomach. He removed the pistol.

Adrian.

Adrian was on his way to Campo di Fiori! His brother had broken away and sold out to Dakakos!

The *picture!* He had to make sure the picture was there! He turned, looking for the door of the. . . .

When the blow came it was paralyzing. Dakakos had snapped the lamp cord binding his wrists and lunged forward, his first pummeling into Andrew's kidney, his other hand wrapped around the Beretta's barrel, twisting Fontine's forearm until he thought his elbow would crack.

Andrew countered by falling sideways, rolling with the force of Dakakos's lunge. The Greek sprang on top of him, crushing him like some elephantine hammer. He smashed Fontine's knuckles against the floor until the gun exploded, the bullet embedding itself in the wooden arch of the doorway. Andrew brought his knee up, pounding the base of Dakakos's groin, crushing the Greek's testicles until he arched his back, grimacing in torment.

Fontine rolled again, freeing his left hand, clawing the bleeding face above, tearing at the hanging flesh. Still, Dakakos would not retreat, would not let up; he slammed his forearms into Andrew's throat.

It was the instant! Andrew arched forward, sinking his teeth into the flesh of Dakakos's arm, biting deeply, as a mad dog would bite, feeling the warm blood glowing into his throat. The Greek pulled his arm up—his hand away—and it was the space Fontine needed. He crashed his knee up once again in Dakakos's groin, and slid his whole body under the giant; as he did so he shot his left hand into the well of Dakakos's armpit, and pressed the nerve with all the force he could summon.

The Greek raised his right side in agony. Andrew rolled to his left, kicking the heavy body away, pulling his arm free.

With the speed born of a hundred fire fights, Fontine was on his haunches, the Beretta leveled, spitting bullets into the exposed chest of the informer who had come to close to killing him.

Dakakos was dead. Annaxas was no more.

Andrew rose unsteadily; he was covered with blood, his whole body wracked. He looked at the priest of Xenope in the chair. The old man's eyes were closed, his lips moving in silent prayer.

There was one shell left in the Beretta. Andrew raised the gun and fired.

28

Stunned, Adrian took the cablegram held out for him by the desk clerk. He walked toward the front entrance of the hotel, stopped, and opened it.

> Mr. Adrian Fontine
> Excelsior Hotel
> Rome, Italy
> My dear Fontine:
> It is urgent we confer, for you must not act alone. You must trust me. You have nothing to fear from me. I understand your anxieties, consequently there will be no intermediaries, none of my people will intercept you. I will wait for you alone and alone we can make our decisions. Check your source.
> Theo Dakakos

Dakakos had traced him! The Greek expected to *meet.* But where? How?

Adrian knew that once he passed through customs in Rome, there was no way he could stop those looking for him from knowing he'd come to Italy; it was the reason for the next step in his strategy. But that Dakakos would openly contact him seemed extraordinary. It was as though Dakakos assumed they were working *together*. Yet it was Dakakos who had gone after Andrew; gone after his brother relentlessly, ingeniously, wrapping up Eye Corps in a seditious ribbon that had eluded the combined efforts of the inspector general and the Justice Department.

The sons of Victor Fontine—the grandsons of Savarone

Fontini-Cristi—were after the vault. Why would Dakakos stop one and not the other?

The answer had to be that he was trying to do just that. Carrots held out in front of the donkey's nose; offers of safety and trust that were translated to mean *control, confinement.*

. . . I will wait for you alone and alone we can make our decisions. Check your source. . . .

Was Dakakos on his way to Campo di Fiori? How was that possible? And what was the *source?* An IG colonel named Tarkington with whom Dakakos had set up lines of communication to trap Eye Corps? What other source did he and Dakakos have in common?

"Signor Fontine?" It was the Excelsior manager; the door to his office was open behind him. He had come out quickly.

"Yes?"

"I tried your room, of course. You were not there." The man smiled nervously.

"Right," said Adrian. "I'm here. What is it?"

"Our guests are always our first consideration." The Italian smiled again. It was maddening.

"Please. I'm in a hurry."

"A few moments ago we had a call from the American embassy. They say they are calling all the hotels in Rome. They are looking for you."

"What did you say?"

"Our guests are always——"

"What did you *say?*"

"That you had checked out. You *have* checked out, *signore.* However, if you wish to use my telephone. . . ."

"No, thank you," said Adrian, starting toward the entrance. Then stopped and turned to the manager. "Call the embassy back. Tell them where I've gone. The front desk knows."

It was the second part of his strategy in Rome, and when he conceived it, he realized it was merely an extension of what he had done in Paris. Before the day was over the professionals who followed him would know exactly where he was. Computers and passport entries and international cooperation made for swift relays of information. He had to make them all think he was going somewhere that he wasn't.

Rome was the best place to start. Had he flown to

Milan, the IG men would dig into their files; Campo di Fiori would appear. He could not allow that.

He had asked the front desk of the Excelsior to draw up a route for a drive south. To Naples, Salerno, and Policastro, along roads that would take him east through Calabria to the Adriatic. He had rented a car at the airport.

Now Theodore Dakakos had joined the hunt. Dakakos, whose relays of information were faster than those of United States Army Intelligence, and far more dangerous. Adrian knew what the United States Army wanted: the killer for Eye Corps. But Dakakos wanted the vault from Constantine. It was a greater prize.

Adrian drove through Rome's melodramatic traffic back to Leonardo da Vinci Airport. He returned the rented car and bought a ticket on Itavia Airlines for Milan. He stood in line at the departure gate, his head down, his body slouched, seeking the protective cover of the crowd. As he was jostled forward—and for reasons he didn't know—the words of an extraordinary lawyer came back to him.

You can run with the pack, in the middle of the pack, but if you want to do something, get to the edges and peel away. Darrow.

In Milan he would call his father. He'd lie about Andrew; he'd invent *something*, he couldn't think about that now. But he had to know more about Theodore Dakakos.

Dakakos was closing in.

He sat on his bed in Milan's Hotel di Piemonte as he'd sat on the bed at the Savoy in London, staring at papers in front of him. But these were not airline schedules, they were the Xeroxed pages of his father's recollection of fifty years ago. He was rereading them—not for any new information; he knew the contents—but because the reading postponed the moment when he would pick up the phone. He wondered how thoroughly his brother had studied these pages, with their rambling descriptions and hesitant, often obsure reflections. Andrew would probably pore over them with the scrutiny of a soldier in combat. There were names. Goldoni, Capomonti, Lefrac. Men who had to be reached.

Adrian knew he could not procrastinate any longer. He folded the pages, put them in his jacket pocket, and reached for the telephone.

Ten minutes later the switchboard called him back; the

phone 5,000 miles away in the North Shore house was ringing. His mother answered and when she said the words, she did so simply, without the trappings of grief, for they were extraneous, the grief private.

"Your father died last night."

Neither spoke for several moments. The silence conveyed a sense of love. As though they were touching.

"I'll come home right away," he said.

"No, don't do that. He wouldn't want you to. You know what you have to do."

Again there was silence. "Yes," he said finally.

"Adrian?"

"Yes?"

"I have two things to tell you, but I don't want to discuss them. Can you understand that?"

Adrian paused. "I think so."

"An army officer came to see us. A Colonel Tarkington. He was kind enough to speak only with me. I know about Andrew."

"I'm sorry."

"Bring him back. He needs help. All the help we can give him."

"I'll try."

"It's so easy to look back and say 'Yes, I see now. I realize.' He always saw the results of strength; he never understood its complications, its essential compassion, I think."

"Let's not discuss it," reminded the son.

"Yes. I don't want to discuss——. Oh, God, I'm so *frightened!*"

"*Please,* mother."

Jane breathed deeply, the sound carried over the wire. "There's something else. Dakakos was here. He spoke to your father. To both of us together. You must trust him. Your father wished it; he was convinced of it. So am I."

. . . *check your source.* . . .

"He sent me a cable. He said he'd be waiting for me."

"At Campo di Fiori," completed Jane.

"What did he say about Andrew?"

"That he thought your brother might be delayed. He didn't elaborate; he talked only about you. He used your name repeatedly."

"You're sure you don't want me to come home?"

"No. There's nothing you can do here. He wouldn't want it." She paused for a moment. "Adrian, tell your brother his father never knew. He died thinking both his Geminis were the men he believed them to be."

"I'll tell him. I'll call again soon."

They said quiet good-byes.

His father was dead. The source was gone, and the void was terrible. He sat by the telephone, aware that perspiration had formed on his forehead, though the room was cool. He got up from the bed; there were things to do and he had to move quickly. Dakakos was on his way to Campo di Fiori. So was the killer of Eye Corps, and Dakakos did not know that.

So he sat down at the desk and began writing. He might have been back in his Boston apartment, jotting down items in preparation for the next day's cross-examination.

But in this case it was not the next day. It was tonight. And very few items came to mind.

He stopped the car at the fork in the road, picked up the map, and held it under the dashboard light. The fork was detailed on the map. There were no other roads until the town of Laveno. His father had said there were large stone gateposts on the left; they were the entrance to Campo di Fiori.

He started the car up, straining his eyes in the darkness, waiting to catch a glimpse of erected stone in the wall of forest on his left. Four miles up the road he found them. He stopped the car opposite the huge, crumbling stone pillars and aimed his flashlight out the window. There was the winding road beyond as his father had described it, angling sharply, disappearing into the woods.

He swung the automobile to the left and drove through the gates. His mouth was suddenly dry, his heart accelerated, its beat echoing in his throat. It was the fear of the immediate unknown that gripped him. He wanted to face it quickly, before the fear controlled him. He drove faster.

There were no lights anywhere.

The enormous white house stood in eerie stillness, a deathlike splendor in the darkness. Adrian parked the car on the left side of the circle, opposite the marble steps, shut off the motor and, reluctantly, the headlights. He got out, took the flashlight from his raincoat pocket, and started across the rutted pavement toward the stairs.

Dull moonlight briefly illuminated the macabre setting and then disappeared. The sky was overcast but no rain would come; the clouds were everywhere above, but thin and traveling too fast. The air was dry; everything was still.

Adrian reached the bottom step and switched on his flashlight to look at his watch. It was eleven thirty. Dakakos was not there. Nor his brother. Either or both would have heard the car; neither nor both would be asleep at this hour. That left the old priest. An old man in the country would have gone to bed by now. He called out.

"Hello in there! My name is Adrian Fontine and I'd like to talk to you!"

Nothing.

And not nothing! There was movement. A pattering, a series of scratches accompanied by tiny, indistinguishable screeches. He swung the flashlight to the source. In its beam was caught the blurred, rushing figures of rats—three, four, five—scampering over the ledge of an open window.

He held the flashlight steady. The windows was smashed; he could see jagged edges of glass. He approached it slowly, suddenly afraid.

His feet sank into the earth; his shoes crunched broken glass. He stood in front of the window and raised the flashlight.

He lost his breath in an involuntary gasp as two pairs of animal's eyes were suddenly caught in the blinding shaft. They darted up, startled yet furious, and a terrible muted screeching was heard as the creatures fled into the darkness of another part of the house. There was a crash. A crazed, frightened animal had collided with an unstable object of china or glass.

Adrian breathed again, then shuddered. His nostrils were filled with an overpowering stench, a putrid, rotting aroma that caused his eyes to water and his throat to swell and choke. He held his breath and he climbed over the window ledge. He pressed his open left hand against his mouth and his nose, filtering the foul stench; he cast the beam of the flashlight over the enormous room.

The shock of it staggered him. The figures of two dead

men, one in torn robes strapped to a chair, the other half-naked on the floor, were hideous. The clothes were torn by animal teeth, flesh ripped out by animal jaws, dried blood made moist by animal urine and saliva.

Adrian reeled. Vomit spewed out of his mouth. He lurched to his left; the light caught a doorway and he lunged into it gasping for breath, for air that could be swallowed.

He was in the study of Savarone Fontini-Cristi, a man he never knew, but now hated with all the hatred of which he was capable. The grandfather who had triggered a chain of killing and suspicion that in itself brought more death and greater hatred.

Over *what? For* what?

"*Goddamnnn youuu! . . .*"

He screamed uncontrollably; he gripped the high back of an old chair and threw it crashing to the floor.

Suddenly, in silence and in full knowledge of what he had to do, Adrian stood immobile and aimed the flashlight on the wall behind the desk. To the right, he remembered, beneath a painting of the Madonna.

The frame was there, the glass shattered.

And the painting was gone.

He sank to his knees, trembling. Tears welled his eyes and he sobbed uncontrollably.

"Oh, *God,*" he whispered, the pain unbearable. "Oh, my brother!"

PART THREE

29

Andrew pulled the Land Rover off to the side of the Alpine road and poured steaming hot coffee into the lid of the thermos. He had made good time; according to the Michelin map he was ten miles from the village of Champoluc. It was morning; the rays of the early sun shot up from behind the surrounding mountains. In a little while he would drive into Champoluc and buy the equipment he needed.

Adrian was far behind. Andrew knew he could slow down for a while, think things out. Besides, his brother was walking into a situation that would paralyze him. Adrian would find the bodies at Campo di Fiori and panic; his thoughts would be confused, indecisive. He wouldn't know what to do next. His brother wasn't trained to confront death from violence; it was too far removed from him. It was different for soldiers: It was different for him. The physical confrontation—even the bloodshed—primed his senses, infused him with an intense feeling of exhilaration. His energies were peaked, he was confident, sure of his movements.

The vault was as good as his. Now was the time to concentrate. Study each word, each clue. His took his father's Xeroxed pages and held them up, catching the morning light through the windshield.

. . . *In the village of Champoluc was the family Goldoni. According to current Zermatt records, they exist still and are scattered throughout the area. The present head of the family is one Alfredo Goldoni. He resides in the house of his father—and father before him—on several acres of land at the base of the mountains in the west outskirts. For generations, the Goldonis have been the most experienced guides in the Italian Alps. Savarone employed them frequently, and beyond this, they were "northern friends"—a phrase my father used to distinguish men of the land from those in the marketplace. His trust was placed in the former far more quickly than in the latter. It is possible that he left information with Alfredo Goldoni's father. With his death, arrangements would be made to pass this information on to the surviving eldest child—whether man or woman—as is the Italian-Swiss custom. Therefore, should Alfredo not be the eldest, look for an older sister.*

North, into the mountains—between the railroad clearings Krahen Aüsblick and Greier Gipfel, I believe—is a small inn run by the family Capomonti. Again, according to Zermatt (I made no inquiries in the Champoluc district to avoid raising suspicion) the inn, too, still exists. I gather it has been somewhat expanded. It is currently under the management of Naton Lefrac, a descendent by marriage of the Capomontis. I remember this man. He was not a man then, of course, for he was one or two years younger than I, the son of a merchant who dealt with the Capomontis. We became quite good friends. I recall clearly that he was much beloved of the Capomontis and the hope was that he would marry a daughter of the house. Obviously he did so.

As children—and young men—we never went into the Champoluc without staying at Locanda Capomonti. I have recollections of warm welcomes and laughter and roaring fireplaces and much comfort. The family was simple—in the uncomplicated sense—and extremely outgoing and sincere. Savarone was particularly taken with them. If there were secrets to leave in the Champoluc, old Capomonti would have been a rock of silence and trust. . . .

Andrew put down the pages and picked up the Michelin road map. Once again he traced the minute markings of the Zermatt railroad, his concern returning. Of the many clearings his father recalled, only four remained. And none bore the name of *hawk.*

For the hunting picture in the study at Campo di Fiori was not as his father remembered; it did not show birds being flushed from bushes. Instead, there were hunters in overgrown fields, their eyes and weapons leveled forward as hawks flew lazily above in the distant sky; an artist's comment on the futility of the hunt.

His father said that the clearings were called Eagle's Peak, Condor's Lookout, and Crow's Summit. There had to be a clearing with the name hawk in it. But if there had been, it no longer existed. And a half century had gone by; obscure railroad clearings below Alpine passes scores of miles apart were not landmarks. Who recalled the precise location of a trolley stop thirty years after the tracks were covered with asphalt? He put down the map and picked up the Xeroxed pages again. The initial key was somewhere in these words.

We stopped in the center of the village for a late lunch, or afternoon tea, I cannot remember which—and Savarone left the restaurant to check the telegraph office for messages—I do remember that. When he returned he was very upset, and I feared our trip to the mountains would be canceled before it began. However, during the meal another message was delivered and Savarone was both placated and relieved. There was no more talk of returning to Campo di Fiori. The dreadful moment had passed for an anxious seventeen-year-old.

From the restaurant we dropped by the shop of a merchant whose name was German in sound and spelling, not Italian or French. My father was prone to order supplies and equipment from this man because he felt sorry for him. He was a Jew and for Savarone, who fought bitterly against the czarist pogroms and dealt on a handshake with the Rothschilds, such thinking was indefensible. There is a blurred memory of an unpleasant incident at the store that evening. What the unpleasant incident specifically entailed, I have no recall, but it was most serious and provoked my father to quiet but definite anger. A sad anger if, again, memory serves. I seem to have the vague impression that details were withheld from me, but now, so many years later, it is only an impression and could well be false.

We left the merchant's shop and proceeded by horsecart to the Goldoni farm. I remember showing off my Alpine pack with its straps and hammer and cleats and forged double-clamps for the ropes. I was terribly proud of it, believing it signified manhood. Again there is a dim impression that while at the Goldonis' an undercurrent of distress was prevalent, but not obvious. I cannot tell you why this feeling remains after so many years, but I relate it to the fact that I had difficulty holding the attention of the male Goldonis while exhibiting my new pack. The father, an uncle or two, and certainly the older sons seemed distracted. Arrangements were made with one of the Goldoni sons to meet us the next day and take us into the mountains. We stayed at the Goldonis for several hours before leaving to resume our journey by cart to the Locando Capomonti. I do recall it was dark when we left, and, as it was summer, the hour had to be past 7:30 or 8:00.

What were the facts, thought Andrew. Man and boy arrived at the village, had something to eat, bought supplies from a disliked Jew, went to the house of the guides they were hiring, and a spoiled child was insulted because not enough attention was paid to his mountain-climbing equipment. The relevant information was reduced to the name Goldoni.

Andrew finished the coffee and screwed the lid back on the thermos. The sun was higher now; it was time to move. Exhilaration filled him. All the years of training and experience and decisions in the field had prepared him for the next few days. There was a vault in the mountains and he would find it!

Eye Corps would be paid in full.

The soldier turned the ignition and gunned the motor. He had clothing and equipment and weapons to buy. And a man named Goldoni to see. Perhaps a woman named Goldoni; he'd know shortly.

Adrian sat in the darkness behind the wheel of the stationary car and wiped his mouth with his handkerchief. He could not erase the taste of sickness in his throat any more than he could erase the sight of the ravaged bodies inside the house from his mind's eye. Or the stench of death from his nostrils.

Sweat rolled down his face, produced by tension he had never known, a fear he had never experienced.

He felt the need to vomit returning; he suppressed it by inhaling rapidly. He had to find some semblance of sanity, he had to function. He could not remain in darkness, in an immobile car for the rest of the night. He had to pass through the shock and find his mind again. It was all he had left: the ability to think.

Instinctively, he pulled the pages of his father's memories from his pocket and switched on the flashlight. Words had come to be his refuge; he was an analyst of words—their shadings, their subtle interpretations, their simplicity and complexity. He was an expert with words, as much an expert as his brother was with death.

Adrian separated the pages, reading slowly, meticulously. Child and man had come to the village of Champoluc; there were immediate impressions of discord, perhaps more than discord. *When he returned he was very upset . . . I feared for our trip.* There was the shop of a Jew, and anger. *What the unpleasant incident specifically entailed, I have no recall . . . it was most serious and provoked my father.* And sadness. *A sad anger if, again, memory serves.* Then the anger and the sadness faded away, replaced by vague feelings of distress and embarrassment; the child was not heeded by those whose attentions he sought. *The father, an uncle or two, and certainly the older sons were distracted.* Their attentions were elsewhere—on the anger, the discord? The sadness? And these obscure recollections were in turn displaced by memories of warmth, and an inn north of the village, *a warm welcome, which was like a dozen other similar welcomes.* This peaceful interlude was followed a short while later once again by vague feelings of distress and concern.

At the Capomonti inn there is little I can recall specifically except a warm welcome, which was like a dozen other similar welcomes. One thing I do remember was that for the first time in the mountains I had my own room, no younger brothers sharing it with me. It was a significant departure and I felt quite grown up. There was another meal, and my father and old Capomonti drank a good deal of whiskey afterward. I recall this because I went to bed, thinking of the next day's climbing, and later heard loud, belligerent voices below, and wondered if the noise might wake the other guests. It was a small inn then and there were perhaps three or four others registered. This concern was unusual for I had never seen my father drunk. I do not know to this day if he was, but the noise was considerable. To a young man on his seventeenth birthday, about to be given the present of his life—a real climb in the Champoluc—the thoughts of a weakened, angry father in the morning were disturbing.

It was not the case, however. The Goldoni guide arrived with our supplies, shared breakfast with us, and we departed.

A Capomonti son—or it might have been young Lefrac—drove the three of us several miles north in the horse-cart. We bade him good-bye and it was agreed he would meet us at the same place late in the afternoon on the following day. Two days in the mountains and an overnight camp with adults! I was overjoyed for I knew we would make camp at a higher altitude than was ever possible with younger brothers in tow.

Adrian put down the pages on the seat of the car. The remaining paragraphs described sketchily remembered hills and trails and views that seemed to overlap. The journey into the mountains had begun.

Specific information might well lie in these rambling descriptions. Isolated landmarks might be revealed, and a pattern emerge; but which landmarks, which patterns?

Oh, God! The painting on the wall. Andrew had the painting!

Adrian suppressed his sudden alarm. The painting from Savarone's study might narrow down the location of a clearing, but what then? Fifty years had passed. A half century of ice and water and summer thaws and natural growth and erosion.

The painting on the wall might well be one clue, perhaps the most important. But Adrian had the feeling that there were others as vital as that painting. They were contained in the words of his father's testament. Memories that survived fifty years of extraordinary living.

Something had happened fifty years ago that had nothing to do with a father and son going into the mountains.

He had found part of his mind again. He was exercising his ability to think. The shock and the horror were still there, but he was passing through to the beginnings of sanity.

. . . *Bear in mind, the contents of that vault are as staggering to the civilized world as anything in history*. . . .

He had to reach it, find it. He had to stop the killer from Eye Corps.

30

Andrew parked the Land Rover by a fence bordering a field. The Goldoni farmhouse was two hundred yards down the road, on the left; the field was part of the Goldoni property. There was a man driving the tractor along rows of upturned earth, his living body turned in the seat, watching the progress behind him. There were no other houses in the area, no other people in sight. Andrew decided to stop and speak to the man.

It was shortly past five in the afternoon. He had spent the day wandering about Champoluc, buying clothes, supplies, and climbing equipment, including the finest Alpine pack available, filled with those items recommended for the mountains, and one that was not. A Magnum .357-caliber pistol. He had made these purchases at the much-expanded shop referred to in his father's recollections. The name was Leinkraus; it had a mezuzah on the doorframe of the front entrance. The clerk behind the counter allowed that Leinkraus had been selling the finest equipment in the Italian Alps since 1913. There were now branches in Gstaad and Lake Lucerne.

Andrew got out of the Land Rover and walked to the fence, waving his hand back and forth to get the attention of the man on the tractor. He was a short, stocky Italian-Swiss, ruffled brown hair above the dark eyebrows, and the rugged, sharp features of a northern Mediterranean. He was at least ten years older than Fontine; his expression was cautious, as if he were not used to unfamiliar faces.

"Do you speak English?" Andrew asked.

"Passably, *signore,*" said the man.

"I'm looking for Alfredo Goldoni. I was directed out here."

"You were directed correctly," replied the Italian-Swiss in more than passable English. "Goldoni is my uncle. I tend his land for him. He can't work for himself." The man stopped, offering no further clarification.

"Where can I find him?"

"Where he always is. In the back room of his house. My aunt will show you to him. He likes visitors."

"Thank you." Andrew turned toward the Land Rover.

"You're American?" asked the man.

"No. Canadian," he replied, extending his cover for any of a dozen immediate possibilities. He climbed into the vehicle and looked at the man through the open window. "We sound the same."

"You look the same, dress the same," countered the farmhand quietly, eyeing the fur-lined Alpine jacket. "The clothes are new," he added.

"Your English isn't," said Fontine. He turned the ignition.

Goldoni's wife was gaunt and ascetic-looking. Her straight gray hair was pulled back, the taut bun a crown of self-denial. She ushered the visitor through the several neat, sparsely furnished rooms to a doorway at the rear of the house. There was no door attached; where once there'd been a sill in the frame, it had been removed, the floor leveled. Fontine walked through; he entered the bedroom. Alfredo Goldoni sat in a wheelchair by a window overlooking the fields at the base of the mountains.

He had no legs. The stubs of his once-massive limbs were encased in the folds of his trousers, the cloth held together by safety pins. The rest of his body, like his face, was large and awkward. Age and mutilation had extracted their price.

Old Goldoni greeted him with false energy. A tired cripple afraid of offending a newcomer, grateful for the all-too-infrequent interruption.

The introductions over, the directions and the journey from town described, and wine brought by a sullen wife, Fontine sat down in a chair opposite the legless man. The stumps were within an arm's reach; the word *grotesque* came repeatedly to his mind. Andrew did not like ugliness; he did not care to put up with it.

"You don't recognize the name Fontine?"

"I do not, sir. It's French, I think. But you're American."

"Do you recognize the name Fontini-Cristi?"

Goldoni's eyes changed. A long-forgotten alarm was triggered. "Yes, of course, I recognize it," replied the amputee, his voice also changing, his words measured. "Fontine; Fontini-Cristi. So the Italian becomes French and the possessor American. It's been many years. You're a Fontini-Cristi?"

"Yes. Savarone was my grandfather."

"A great *padrone* from the northern provinces. I remember him. Not well, of course. He stopped coming to Champoluc in the late twenties, I believe."

"The Goldonis were his guides. Father and sons."

"We were everyone's guides."

"Were you ever a guide for my grandfather?"

"It's possible. I worked the mountains as a very young man."

"Can't you remember?"

"In my time I have taken thousands into the Alps——"

"You just said you remembered him."

"Not well. And more by the name than by the person. What is it you want?"

"Information. About a trip to the mountains taken by my father and grandfather fifty years ago."

"Are you joking?"

"Hardly. My father, Victor—Vittorio Fontini-Cristi—sent me from America to get that information. At great inconvenience to me. I haven't much time, so I need your help."

"It's freely given, but I wouldn't know where to begin. A single climb fifty years ago! Who would remember?"

"The man who led them. The guide. According to my father he was a son of Goldoni. The date is July fourteenth, 1920."

Fontine could not be sure—perhaps the grotesque cripple merely suppressed a sharp pain from his massive stumps, or shifted his legless clump of a body in reflection—but Goldoni *did react*. It was the *date*. He reacted to the date. And immediately covered that reaction by talking.

"July of 1920. It's two generations ago. It's impossible. You must have something more, how do you say, specific than that?"

"The *guide*. He was a Goldoni."

"Not I. I was no more than fifteen years old. I went into

the mountains young, but not that young. Not as a *prima guida*."

Andrew held the cripple's eyes with his own. Goldoni was uncomfortable; he did not like the exchange of stares and looked away. Fontine leaned forward. "But you remember something, don't you?" he asked quietly, unable to keep the coldness out of his voice.

"No, Signor Fontini-Cristi. There's nothing."

"Just a few seconds ago, I gave you the date: July fourteenth, 1920. You knew that date."

"I knew only that it was too long ago for me to think about."

"I should tell you, I'm a soldier. I've interrogated hundreds of men; very few ever fooled me."

"It wouldn't be my intention, *signore*. For what purpose? I should like to be helpful to you."

Andrew continued to stare. "Years ago there were clearings on the railroad tracks south of Zermatt."

"A few are left," added Goldoni. "Not many, of course. They're not necessary these days."

"Tell me. Each was given the name of a bird——"

"Some," interrupted the Alpiner. "Not all."

"Was there a *hawk?* A hawk's . . . *something?*"

"A hawk? Why do you ask that?" The outsized amputee looked up, his gaze now steady, unwavering.

"Just tell me. Was there a clearing with 'hawk' as part of its name?"

Goldoni remained silent for several moments. "No," he said finally.

Andrew sat back in the chair. "Are you the eldest son of the Goldoni family?"

"No. It was obviously one of my brothers who was hired for that climb fifty years ago."

Fontine was beginning to understand. Alfredo Goldoni was given the house because he had lost his legs. "Where are your brothers? I'll talk with them."

"Again, I must ask if you joke, *signore*. My brothers are dead, everyone knows that. My brothers, an uncle, two cousins. All dead. There are no Goldoni guides left in Champoluc."

Andrew's breathing stopped. He absorbed the information and inhaled deeply. His shortcut had been eliminated with a single sentence.

"I find that hard to believe," he said coldly. "*All* those men dead? What killed them?"

"Avalanche, *signore*. A whole village was buried in sixty-eight. Near Valtournanche. Rescue teams were sent from as far north as Zermatt, south from Châtillon. The Goldonis led them. Three nations awarded us their highest honors. They were of little good to the rest. For me, they provide a small pension. I lost my legs through exposure." He tapped the stumps of his once muscular legs.

"And you have no information about that trip on July fourteenth, 1920?"

"Without particular details, how can I?"

"I have descriptions. Written down by my father." Fontine withdrew the Xeroxed pages from his jacket.

"Good! You should have said so before! Read them to me."

Andrew did so. The descriptions were disjointed, the pictures evoked contradictory. Time sequences jumped back and forth, and landmarks seemed to be confused with each other.

Goldoni listened; every now and then he closed his puffed, creased eyes and turned his neck to one side, as though conjuring up his own visual recollections. When Fontine finished he shook his head slowly. "I'm sorry, *signore*. What you have read could be any of twenty, thirty different trails. Much that's there doesn't even exist in our district. Forgive me, but I think that your father has confused trails farther west in Valais. It's easy to do."

"There's nothing that sounds familiar?"

"On the contrary. Everything. *And* nothing. Fragments of many locations for hundreds of square miles. I'm sorry. It's impossible."

Andrew was confused. He still had the gut feeling that the Alpiner was lying. There was another option to pursue before he forced the issue. If it, too, led nowhere, he would come back and face the cripple with different tactics.

. . . *Should Alfredo not be the eldest, look for a sister*. . . .

"Are you the oldest surviving member of the family?"

"No. Two sisters were born before me. One lives."

"Where?"

"In Champoluc. On the Via Sestina. Her son works my land."

"What's the name? Her married name."

"Capomonti."

"Capomonti? That's the name of the people who run the inn."

"Yes, *signore*. She married into the family."

Fontine got out of the chair, putting the Xeroxed pages into his pocket. He reached the door and turned. "It's possible I'll be back."

"It will be a pleasure to welcome you."

Fontine got into the Land Rover and started the engine. Across the fence in the field, the nephew-farmhand sat motionless on the tractor and watched him, his vehicle idling. The gut feeling returned; the look on the farmhand's face seemed to be saying, *Get out of here. I must run to the house and hear what you said.*

Andrew released the brake and pressed the accelerator. The Land Rover shot forward on the road; he made a rapid U-turn and started back toward the village.

Suddenly his eyes riveted on the most obvious, unstartling sight in the world. He swore. It was so obvious he had not taken notice.

The road was lined with telephone poles.

There was no point in looking for an old woman on the Via Sestina; she would not be there. Another strategy came to the soldier's mind. The odds favored it.

"Woman!" shouted Goldoni.

"Quickly! Help me! The telephone!"

Goldoni's wife walked swiftly into the room and gripped the handles of the chair. "Should I make the calls?" she asked, wheeling him to the telephone.

"No. I'll do it." He dialed. "Lefrac? Can you hear me? . . . He's come. After all these years. Fontini-Cristi. But he does not bring the words. He seeks a clearing named for *hawks*. He tells me nothing else, and that's nothing. I don't trust him. I must reach my sister. Gather the others. We'll meet in an hour. . . . . Not *here!* At the inn."

Andrew lay prone in the field across from the farmhouse. He focused the binoculars alternately on the door and on the windows. The sun was going down behind the western Alps; it would be dark soon. Lights had been put on in the farmhouse; the shadows moved back and forth. There was activity.

A car was being backed out of a dirt drive to the right of the house; it stopped and the farmhand-nephew got out. He raced to the front door; it opened.

Goldoni was in his wheelchair, his wife behind him. The nephew replaced her and started wheeling his legless uncle across the lawn toward the automobile, whose motor was idling.

Goldoni was clutching something in his arms. Andrew focused the binoculars on the object.

It was a large book; but it was more than a book. It was some kind of heavy, wide volume. A ledger.

At the car Goldoni's wife held the door while the nephew grabbed the grotesque amputee under the arms and swung the carcass across into the seat. Goldoni twitched and squirmed; his wife drew a strap across him and buckled it.

Through the frame of the open door's window, Andrew had a clear view of the legless, former Alpine guide. The center of focus once again was the huge ledger in Goldoni's arms, held almost desperately, though it were a thing of extraordinary value he dared not let go. Then Andrew realized there was something else in Goldoni's arms, something infinitely more familiar to the soldier. A shaft of glistening metal was wedged between the large volume and the Alpiner's thick chest. It was the barrel of a small, powerful shotgun; a model particularly identified with warring Italian families in the south. In Sicily. It was called the *lupo,* the "wolf." It was without much accuracy beyond twenty yards, but at short range could blow a man ten feet off the ground.

Goldoni was guarding the volume in his arms with a weapon more powerful than the .357 Magnum in the soldier's Alpine pack. Briefly, Andrew focused on Goldoni's nephew; the man had a new addition to his garb. Jammed into his belt was a pistol, the large handle indicative of its heavy caliber.

Both Alpiners were guarding that ledger. No one could get near it. What was——

Christ! Suddenly, Fontine understood. *Records!* Records of *journeys into the mountains!* It couldn't be anything else! It never occurred to him—*or* to Victor—to ask if such records were kept. Especially in light of the years; it was simply not a consideration. My God, a half century had passed!

But according to his father, and *his* father, the Goldonis were the finest guides in the Alps. Such professionals with such a collective reputation to uphold *would* keep records; it was the most natural thing to do. Records of past trips into the mountains, going back decades!

Goldoni had lied. The information his visitor wanted was in that house. But Goldoni did not want the visitor to have it.

Andrew watched. The nephew collapsed the wheelchair, opened the trunk of the car, threw it in, and ran to the driver's side. He climbed behind the wheel as Goldoni's wife closed her husband's door.

The car lurched out of the drive and headed north toward Champoluc. Goldoni's wife returned to the house.

The soldier lay prone in the grass and slowly replaced the binoculars in the case as he considered his options. He could race to the hidden Land Rover and go after Goldoni, but to what purpose, and how great a risk? The Alpiner was only half a man, but the *lupo* in his hands more than made up for his missing legs. Too, the surly nephew wouldn't hesitate to use the pistol in his belt.

If the ledger carried by Goldoni was what he suspected, it was being rushed away to be hidden. Not to be destroyed; one did not destroy a record of such incalculable value.

If. He had to be sure, certain of his judgment. Then he could move.

It was funny. He had not expected Goldoni to leave; he had expected others to come to him. That Goldoni did leave meant that panic had set in. A legless man who never went anywhere did not race away into the indignity and discomfort of the outside world unless the motive was extraordinary.

The soldier made up his mind. The circumstances were optimum; Goldini's wife was alone. First, he would find out if that ledger was what he thought it was; then he would find out where Goldoni had gone.

Once he learned these things, the decision would be made: whether to follow or to wait.

Andrew rose from the grass; there was no point wasting time. He started for the house.

"There is no one here, *signore,*" said the stunned, gaunt woman, her eyes frightened. "My husband has gone with his nephew. They play cards in the village."

Andrew pushed the woman aside without replying. He walked directly through the house to Goldoni's room. There was nothing but old magazines and out-of-date Italian newspapers. He looked in a closet; it was at once ugly and pathetic. Trousers hung, the cloth folded, the folds held in place by safety pins. There were no books, no ledgers like the one the Alpiner had clutched in his arms.

He returned to the front room. The sullen, frightened wife was at the telephone, depressing the bar in short, panicked jabs with her bony fingers.

"The wire's cut," he said simply, approaching her.

"No," the woman whispered. "What do you want? I have nothing! *We* have nothing!"

"I think you do," answered Fontine, backing the woman against the wall, his face inches above hers. "Your husband lied to me. He said he couldn't tell me anything, but he left in a hurry carrying a very large book. It was a journal, wasn't it! An old journal that described a climb in the mountains fifty years ago. The journals! Show me the journals!"

"I do not know what you talk about, *signore!* We have nothing! We live on a *pensionare!*"

"Shut up! Give me those records!"

"Per favore. . . ."

"Goddamn you!" Fontine grabbed the woman's straight gray hair and yanked it forward, then suddenly, brutally backward, crashing her head into the wall. "I haven't got time. Your husband lied to me. Show me where those books are! *Now!"* He wrenched the hair again, and again slammed her skull into the wall. Blood appeared on her wrinkled neck, tears welled in her unfocused eyes.

The soldier realized he had gone too far. The combat option was now defined; it wouldn't be the first time. There'd been no lack of uncooperative peasants in Nam. He pulled the woman away from the wall.

"Do you understand me?" he said in a monotone. "I'll light a match in front of your eyes. Do you know what happens then? I'm asking you for the last time. Where are those records?"

Goldoni's wife collapsed, sobbing. Fontine held her by the cloth of her dress. With a trembling arm and frenzied, shaking fingers, she pointed to a door in the right wall of the room.

Andrew dragged her across the floor. He withdrew his Beretta and smashed the door with his boot. It crashed open. There were no one inside.

"The light switch. Where is it?"

She raised her head, her mouth open, the breath coming shorter, and moved her eyes to the left. *"Lampada, lampada,"* she whispered.

He pulled her inside the small room, releasing the cloth of her dress, and found the lamp. She lay trembling, curled up on the floor. The light reflected off the glass-enclosed bookcase on the opposite wall. There were five shelves, and on each a row of books. He rushed to the case, grabbed a knob in the middle and tried to raise the pane of glass. It was locked; he tried the others. All locked.

With his Beretta he smashed the glass of two panels. The light from the lamp was dim but sufficient. The faded, handwritten letters and numbers on the brown binding were clear enough.

Each year was divided into two six-month periods, the volumes differing in thickness. The books were handmade. He looked at the upper left panel; he had not broken the glass and the reflection of light obscured the lettering. He smashed it, clearing the fragments of glass away with repeated thrusts of the steel barrel.

The first volume read 1907. There was no month noted underneath; that was a system which had evolved.

He raced the barrel over the volumes to the year 1920. January to June was there.

July to December was missing. In its place, filling the space, was a hastily inserted volume dated *1967*.

Alfredo Goldoni, the legless cripple, had outrun him. He had removed the key from the locked door that held the secret of a journey into the mountains fifty years ago, and raced away. Fontine turned to Goldoni's wife. She was on her knees, her gaunt arms supporting her shaking, gaunt body.

It would not be difficult to do what he had to do, learn what had to be learned.

"Get up," he said.

He carried the lifeless body across the field and into the woods. There was still no moon; instead the air smelled of impending rain, the sky pitch black with clouds, no stars in evidence. The beam of the flashlight wavered up and down with his footsteps.

Time. Time was the only thing that counted now.

And shock. He would need shock.

Alfredo Goldoni had gone to the inn of the Capomontis, according to the dead woman. They had all gone there, she said. The *consigliatori of Fontini-Cristi* had gathered together. A stranger had come among them bringing the wrong words.

31

Adrian drove back to Milan but he did not go to the hotel, he followed the highway signs to the airport, not entirely sure of *how* he was going to do what he had to do, but certain that he would do it.

He had to get to Champoluc. A killer was loose and that killer was his brother.

Somewhere in the vast complex of the Milan airport was a pilot and a plane. Or someone who knew where both could be found, for whatever price was necessary.

He drove as fast as he could, all the windows open, the wind whipping through the car. It helped him control himself; it helped him not to think, for thought was too painful.

"There's a small, private field on the outskirts of Champoluc, used by the rich in the mountains," said the unshaven pilot who had been awakened and summoned to the airport by a well-tipped clerk on the night shift for Alitalia. "But it's not operational at these hours."

"Can you fly in?"

"It's not so far away, but the terrain's bad."

"Can you *do* it?"

"I'll have enough petrol to return if I cannot. That will will be my decision, not yours. But not one *lira* will be given back; is that understood?"

"I don't care."

The pilot turned to the Alitalia clerk, speaking authoritatively, obviously for the benefit of the man who would pay such money for such a flight. "Get me the weather. Zermatt, stations south, heading two-eighty degrees sweep to two-ninety-five out of Milan. I want radar fronts."

The Alitalia clerk shrugged and sighed.

"You'll be paid," said Adrian curtly.

The clerk picked up a red telephone. "*Operazioni,*" he said officiously.

The landing at Champoluc was not as hazardous as the pilot wanted Adrian to believe. The field, it was true, was not operational—there was no radio contact, no tower to guide a plane in—but the single strip was outlined, the east and west perimeters marked by red lights.

Adrian walked across the field toward the only structure with lights on inside. It was a semicircular metal shell, perhaps fifty feet long, twenty-five feet high at its midpoint. It was a hangar for small private aircraft. The door opened, brighter light spilled out on the ground, and a man in overalls was silhouetted in the doorway. He hunched his shoulders, peering out into the darkness; then he stretched, stifling a yawn.

"Can you speak English?" asked Fontine.

The man did—reluctantly and poorly, but clearly enough to be understood. And the information Adrian was given was pretty much what he expected. It was four in the morning and there was no place open at all. What pilot was crazy enough to fly into Champoluc at such an hour? Perhaps the *polizia* should be called.

Fontine withdrew several large bills from his pocket and held them in the light of the doorway. The watchman's eyes riveted on the money. Adrian suspected it was over a month's pay for the angry man.

"I came a long way to find someone. I've done nothing wrong except hire a plane to fly me here from Milan. The police are not interested in me, but *I must* find the person I'm looking for. I need a car and directions."

"You're no criminal? Flying up at such an hour——"

"No criminal," interrupted Adrian, suppressing his impatience, speaking as calmly as he could. "I'm a lawyer. An . . . *avvocato,*" he added.

"*Avvocato?*" The man's voice conveyed his respect.

"I must find the house of Alfredo Goldoni. That's the name I've been given."

"The legless one?"

"I didn't know that."

The automobile was an old Fiat with torn upholstery and cracked side windows. The Goldoni farmhouse was eight to ten miles out of town, according to the watchman, on the west road. The man drew a simple diagram; it was easy to follow.

A post-and-rail fence could be seen in the glare of the headlights, the outlines of a house farther in the distance. And there was a dim wash of light coming from the house, shining through windows, dimly illuminating cascading branches of pine trees that fronted the old building near the road. Adrian removed his foot from the Fiat's accelerator, wondering whether he should stop and walk the rest of the way on foot. Lights on in a farmhouse at a quarter to five in the morning was not what he expected.

He saw the telephone poles. Had the night watchman at the airport called Goldoni and told him to expect a visitor? Or did farmers in Champoluc normally rise at such an early hour?

He decided against approaching on foot. If the watchman had telephoned, or the Goldonis were starting their day, an automobile was not the alarming intruder a man alone, walking quietly in the night, would be.

Adrian turned into a wide dirt path between the tall pines; there was no other entrance for a car. He pulled up parallel to the house; the dirt drive extended far back into the property, ending at a barn. Farm equipment could be seen through the open barn doors in the wash of the headlights. He got out of the car, passed the lighted front windows covered by curtains, and walked to the front door. It was a farmhouse door—wide and thick, the upper section a panel by itself, separated from the lower to let in the summer breezes and keep the animals out. There was a heavy, pitted brass knocker in the center. He used it.

He waited. There was no response, no sounds of movement within.

He rapped again, louder, with longer spaces between the sharp metallic reports.

There was a sound from behind the door. Indistinct, brief. A rustle of cloth or paper; a hand scratching on fabric? What?

"Please," he called out courteously. "My name's Fontine. You knew my father, and his father. From Milan. From Campo di Fiori. Please let me speak to you! I mean no harm."

Only silence now. Nothing.

He stepped back onto the grass and walked to the lighted windows. He put his face against the glass and tried to see through the white sheer curtains beyond. They were in opaque folds. The blurred images inside were further distorted by the thick glass of the Alpine window.

Then he saw it, and for a moment—as his eyes adjusted to the blurred distortion—he thought he had lost his mind for the second time that night.

At the far left side of the room was the figure of a legless man writhing in short, spastic twitches across the floor. The deformed body was large from the waist up, dressed in some kind of shirt that ended at the huge stumps, what remained of the legs hidden in the cloth of white undershorts.

The legless one.

Alfredo Goldoni. Adrian watched now as Goldoni maneuvered himself into a dark corner at the far wall. He carried something in his arms, clutching it as though it were a lifeline in a heavy sea. It was a rifle, a large-barreled rifle. Why?

"*Goldoni! Please!*" Fontine cried out at the window. "I just want to *talk* to you. If the watchman called you, he must have told you that."

The report was thunderous; glass shattered in all directions, fragments penetrating Adrian's raincoat and jacket. At the last instant he had seen the black barrel raised and had lurched to the side, covering his face. Thick, jagged points of glass were like a hundred pieces of ice across his arm. But for the heavy sweater he had bought in Milan, he would have been a mass of blood. As it was, his arms and neck were bleeding slightly.

Above, through the billows of smoke and the shattered glass of the window, he could hear the metallic snap of the rifle; Goldoni had reloaded. He sat up, his back against the stone foundation of the house. He felt along his left arm and removed as much of the glass as he could. He could feel the rivulets of blood on his neck.

He sat there, breathing heavily, ministering to himself, then called out again. Goldoni could not possibly negotiate the space between the dark corner and the window. They were two prisoners, one intent on killing the other, held at bay by an invisible, unclimbable wall.

"Listen to me! I don't know what you've been told, but it's not true! I'm not your enemy!"

"*Animale!*" roared Goldoni from within. "I'll see you dead!"

"For God's sake, why? I don't want to harm you!"

"You are Fontini-Cristi! You are a killer of women! An abductor of children! *Maligno! Animale!*"

He was too late. Oh, Jesus! He was *too late!* The killer had reached Champoluc before him.

But the killer was still loose. There was a chance.

"One last time, Goldoni," he said, without shouting now. "I'm a Fontini-Cristi, but I'm not the man you want dead. I'm not a killer of women and I've abducted no children. I know the man you're talking about and he's not me. That's as clear and as simple as I can put it. Now, I'm going to stand up in front of this window. I haven't got any gun—I've never owned one. If you don't believe me, I guess you'll have to shoot. I haven't got time to argue any longer. And I don't think you do, either. Any of you."

Adrian pressed his bleeding hand on the ground and rose unsteadily. He walked slowly in front of the shattered glass of the window.

Alfredo Goldoni called out quietly, "Walk in with your arms in front of you. There's no way you'll live if you hesitate or break your step."

Fontine came out of the shadows of the darkened back room. The legless man had directed him to a window through which he could enter; the cripple would not risk the manipulations required of him to open the front door. As Adrian emerged from the darkness, Goldoni cocked the hammer of the rifle, prepared to fire. He spoke in a whisper.

"You're the man and, yet, you are not the man."

"He's my brother," said Adrian softly. "And I have to stop him."

Goldoni stared at him in silence. Finally, his eyes still concentrated on Fontine's face, he uncocked the rifle and lowered it beside him in the corner.

"Help me into my chair," he said.

Adrian sat in front of the legless man, bare to the waist, his back within the reach of Goldoni's hands. The Italian-Swiss had removed the fragments of glass, applying an alcohol solution that stung but did its work; the bleeding stopped.

"In the mountains blood is precious. Our countrymen in the north call this fluid *leimen*. It's better than the powder. I doubt the medical doctors approve, but it does the trick. Put on your shirt."

"Thank you." Fontine rose and did as he was told. They had spoken only briefly of things that had to be said. With an Alpiner's practicality, Goldoni had ordered Adrian to remove his clothes where the glass had penetrated. A wounded man, uncared for, was of little good to anyone. His role of rural physician, however, did not lessen his anger or his agony.

"He's a man from hell," said the cripple as Fontine buttoned his shirt.

"He's sick, though I realize that's no help for you. He's looking for something. A vault, hidden somewhere in the mountains. It was carried there years ago, before the war, by my grandfather."

"We know. We've known someone would come someday. But that's all we know. We don't know where in the mountains."

Adrian didn't believe the legless man and yet he could not be sure. "You said killer of women. Who?"

"My wife. She's gone."

"Gone? How do you know she's dead?"

"He lied. He said she ran away down the road. That he took chase and caught her and keeps her hidden in the village."

"It's possible."

"It is not. I can't walk, *signore*. My wife can't run. She has the swollen veins in her legs. She wears thick shoes to get around this house. Those shoes are in front of your eyes."

Adrian looked down where Goldoni gestured. A pair of heavy, ugly shoes were placed neatly at the side of a chair.

"People do things they don't think they can do——"

"There's blood on the floor," interrupted Goldoni, his voice trembling, pointing to an open doorway. "There were no wounds on the man who calls himself a soldier. Go! Look for yourself."

Fontine walked to the open door and went inside the small room. A glass bookcase was smashed, sharp fragments everywhere. He reached inside and removed a volume behind one of the shattered panels. He opened it. In clear handscript were pages detailing successive climbs into the mountains. The dates extended back beyond 1920. And there was blood on the floor by the door.

He was too late.

He walked swiftly back into the front room.

"Tell me everything. As quickly as you can. *Everything.*"

The soldier had been thorough. He had immobilized his enemy, rendered them helpless through fear and panic. The major from Eye Corps had mounted his own invasion of the Capomonti inn. He had done so swiftly, without a wasted move, finding Lefrac and the members of the Capomonti and Goldoni families in an upstairs room where they were holding their hastily summoned conference.

The door of the room had crashed open, a terrified desk clerk propelled through it so harshly he fell to the floor. The soldier entered quickly, closing the door before any in the room knew what was happening, and held them all rigid at the point of a gun.

The soldier then issued his demands. First, the old ledger describing a journey into the mountains over fifty years ago. And maps. Minutely detailed maps used by climbers in the Champoluc district. Second, the services of either Lefrac's son or eighteen-year-old grandson to lead him into the hills. Third, the granddaughter as a second hostage. The child's father had lost his head and lunged at the man with the gun; but the soldier was expert and the father subdued without a shot.

Old Lefrac was ordered to open the door and call for a housemaid. Proper clothing was brought to the room and the children dressed under gunpoint. It was then that the man-from-hell told Goldoni his wife was a prisoner. He was to return to his house and remain there alone, sending his driver—his nephew—away. If he stopped to reach the police, he would never see his wife again.

"Why?" asked Adrian quickly. "Why did he do that? Why did he want you back here alone?"

"He separates us. My sister returns with my nephew to her house on the Via Sestina; Lefrac and his son remain at the inn. Together we might make each other bold. Apart we're frightened, helpless. A gun against a child's head is not easily forgotten. He knows that alone we'll do nothing but wait."

Adrian closed his eyes. "God," he said.

"The soldier's an expert, that one." Goldoni's voice was low, the hatred seething.

Fontine glanced at him. *I have run with the pack—in the middle of the pack—but now I have reached the edges and I will peel away.*

"Why did you shoot at me? If you thought it was him, how could you take the chance? Not knowing what he did."

"I saw your face against the glass. I wanted to blind you, not to kill you. A dead man can't tell me where he's taken my wife. Or the body of my wife. Or the children. I'm a good shot; I fired inches above your head."

Fontine crossed to the chair where he had thrown his jacket and took out the Xeroxed pages of his father's recollections of fifty years ago. "You must have read that journal. Can you remember what was written?"

"You can't go after him. He'll kill."

"Can you *remember?*"

"It was a two-day climb with many crossing trails! He could be anywhere. He narrows down the place he seeks. He travels blindly. If he saw you, he'd kill the children."

"He won't see me. Not if I get there first! Not if I *wait* for him!" Adrian unfolded the Xeroxed pages.

"They've been read to me. There's nothing that can help you."

"There has to be! It's *here!*"

"You're wrong," said Goldoni, and Adrian knew he was not lying. "I tried to tell *him* that, but he wouldn't listen. Your grandfather made his arrangements, but the *padrone* did not consider unexpected death, or human failing."

Fontine looked up from the pages. Helplessness was in the old man's eyes. A killer was in the mountains and he was helpless. Death would surely follow death, for surely his wife was gone.

"What were these arrangements?" asked Adrian softly.

"I'll tell you. You're not your brother. We've kept the secret for thirty-five years, Lefrac, the Capomontis, and ourselves. And one other—not one of us—whose death came suddenly, before he made his own arrangements."

"Who was that?"

"A merchant named Leinkraus. We didn't know him well."

"Tell me."

"We've waited all these years for a Fontini-Cristi to come." So the legless man began:——

The man they—the Goldonis, Lefrac, and the Capomontis—expected would come quietly, in peace, seeking the iron crate buried high in the mountains. This man would speak of the journey taken so many years ago by father and son, and he would know that journey was recorded in the Goldoni ledgers—as all who employed the Goldoni guides would know. And because that climb lasted for two days over considerable terrain, the man would specify an abandoned railroad clearing known as *Sciocchezza di Cacciatori*—Hunter's Folly. The clearing had been left to nature over forty years ago, long before the iron crate had been buried, but it had existed when father and son journeyed to Champoluc in the summer of 1920.

"I thought those clearings were given——"

"The names of birds?"

"Yes."

"Most were, not all. The soldier asked if there was a clearing known by the name of the hawk. There are no hawks in the mountains of Champoluc."

"The painting on the wall," said Adrian, more to himself than for the benefit of the Alpiner.

"What?"

"My father remembered a painting on a wall in Campo

di Fiori, a painting of a hunt. He thought it might be significant."

"The soldier did not speak of it. Nor did he speak of why he sought the information; only that he had to have it. He wouldn't mention the *search* to me. *Or* the ledgers. Or the reason why the railroad clearing was important. He was *secretive*. And, clearly, he did not come in peace. A soldier who threatens a legless man is a hollow commander. I didn't trust him."

Everything his brother had done was contrary to the memory of the Fontini-Cristis as these people remembered them. It might have been so simple had he been open with them, had he *come in peace*; but the soldier couldn't do that. He was always at war.

"Then the area around this abandoned clearing—Hunter's Folly—is where the vault is buried?"

"Presumably. There are several old trails to the east that lead away from the tracks, up to the higher ridges. But which trail, which ridge? We do not know."

"The records would describe it."

"If one knew where to look. The soldier doesn't."

Adrian thought. His brother had traveled across the world, eluding the Intelligence network of the most powerful nation on earth. "You may be underestimating him."

"He's not one of us. He's not a man of the mountains."

"No," mused Fontine quietly. "He's something else. What would he *look* for? That's what we have to think about."

"An inaccessible place. Away from the trails. Ground that would not be traveled easily for any of several reasons. There are many such areas. The mountains are filled with them."

"But you said it a few minutes ago. He'd narrow down his . . . options."

"*Signore?*"

"Nothing. I was thinking of—never mind. You see, he knows what *not* to look for. He knows that the vault was heavy; it had to be transported—mechanically. He starts with something *besides* the record book."

"We weren't aware of that."

"He is."

"It will do him little good in the darkness."

"Look at the window," said Adrian. Outside, the first

morning light could be seen. "Tell me about this other man. The merchant."

"Leinkraus?"

"Yes. How was he involved?"

"That answer went with his death. Even Francesca doesn't know."

"Francesca?"

"My sister. When my brothers died, she was the eldest. The envelope was given to her. . . ."

"*Envelope?* What envelope?"

"Your grandfather's instructions."

. . . Therefore, should Alfredo not be the eldest, look for a sister, as is the Italian-Swiss custom. . . .

Adrian unfolded the pages of his father's testament. If such fragments of truth came through the distance of years with such accuracy, more attention had to be paid to his father's disjointed remembrances.

"My sister has lived in Champoluc since her marriage to Capomonti. She knew the Leinkraus family better than any of us. Old Leinkraus died in his store. There was a fire; many thought it wasn't accidental."

"I don't understand."

"The family Leinkraus are Jews."

"I see. Go on." Adrian shifted the pages.

. . . The merchant was not popular. He was a Jew and for one who fought bitterly . . . Such thinking was indefensible.

Goldoni continued. The man who came to Champoluc and spoke of the iron crate and the long-forgotten journey and the old railroad clearing was to be given the envelope left with the eldest Goldoni.

"You must understand, *signore.*" The legless man interrupted himself. "We are *all* family now. The Capomontis and the Goldonis. After so many years and no one came, we discussed it between ourselves."

"You're ahead of me."

"The envelope directed the man who had come to Champoluc to old Capomonti. . . ."

Adrian turned back the pages. *If there were secrets to leave in the Champoluc, old Capomonti would have been a rock of silence and trust.*

"When Capomonti died, he gave *his* instructions to his son-in-law, Lefrac."

"Then Lefrac *knows.*"

"Only one word. The name Leinkraus."

Fontine bolted forward in his seat. He remained on the edge, bewildered. Yet something was triggered in his mind. As in long, complex cross-examination, isolated phrases and solitary words were suddenly brought into focus, given meaning where no meaning had existed previously.

The *words.* Look to the words, as his brother looked to violence.

He scanned the pages in his hands, turning them rapidly until he found what he was looking for.

. . . There is a blurred memory of an unpleasant incident . . . what the unpleasant incident specifically entailed, I have no recall . . . serious and provoked my father . . . a sad anger . . . impression that details were withheld from me. . . .

Withheld. Anger. Sadness.

. . . provoked my father. . . .

"Goldoni, listen to me. You've got to think back. Way back. Something happened. Something unpleasant, sad, angry. And it concerned the Leinkraus family."

"No."

Adrian stopped. The legless Goldoni had not let him finish. "What do you mean 'no'?" he asked quietly.

"I told you. I didn't know them well. We barely spoke."

"Because they were Jews? Is that the way it came down from the north in those days?"

"I don't understand you."

"I think you do." Adrian stared at him; the Alpiner avoided his eyes. Fontine continued softly. "You didn't have to know them—at all, perhaps. But for the first time, you're lying to me. Why?"

"I'm not lying. They weren't friends of the Goldonis."

"Or the Capomontis?"

"*Or* the Capomontis!"

"You didn't like them?"

"We didn't *know* them! They kept to themselves. Other Jews came and they lived among their own. It's that simple."

"It's *not.*" Adrian knew the answer was within reach. Hidden, perhaps, from Goldoni himself. "Something happened in July of 1920. What was it?"

Goldoni sighed. "I can't remember."

"July fourteenth, 1920! What *happened?*"

Goldoni's breath was shorter, his large jaws taut. The massive stumps that once were legs twitched in his wheelchair. "It doesn't mean anything," he whispered.

"Let me be the judge of that," said Adrian.

"Times have changed. So much has changed in a lifetime," said the Alpiner, his voice faltering. "The same was felt by everyone."

"July *fourteenth, 1920!*" Adrian zeroed in on his witness.

"I tell you! It is meaningless!"

"*Goddamn you!*" Adrian leaped from the chair. Striking the helpless old man was not out of the question. Then the words came.

"A Jew was beaten. A young Jew who entered the church school . . . was beaten. He died three days later."

The Alpiner had said it. But only part of it. Fontine backed away from the wheelchair. "Leinkraus's son?" he asked.

"Yes."

"The church school?"

"He couldn't enter the state school. It was a place to learn. The priests accepted him."

Fontine sat down slowly, keeping his eyes on Goldoni. "There's more, isn't there? Who gave the beating?"

"Four boys from the village. They didn't know what they were doing. Everyone said so."

"I'm sure everyone did. It's easier that way. Ignorant children who had to be protected. And what was the life of one Jew?"

Tears came to the eyes of Alfredo Goldoni. "Yes."

"You were one of those boys, weren't you?"

Goldoni nodded his head in silence.

"I think I can tell you what happened," continued Adrian. "Leinkraus was threatened. His wife, his other children. Nothing was said, nothing reported. A young Jew had died, that was all."

"So many years ago," Goldoni whispered as the tears fell down his face. "No one thinks like that anymore. And we have lived with what we did. At the end of my life, it grows even more difficult. The grave is close at hand now."

Adrian stopped breathing, stunned by Goldoni's words. The *grave* is close. . . . The *grave.* My God! Was that *it?* He wanted to jump out of the chair and roar his questions until the legless Alpiner remembered! *Exactly*. But he could not do that. He kept his voice low, incisive.

"What happened then? What did Leinkraus do?"

"Do?" Goldoni shrugged slowly, sadness in the gesture. "What could he do? He kept silent."

"Was there a funeral? A burial?"

"If there was, we knew nothing of it."

"Leinkraus's son had to be buried. No Christian cemetery would accept a Jew. Was there a burial place for Jews?"

"No, not then. There is now."

"Then! What about then? Where was he *buried?* Where was the *murdered son* of Leinkraus *buried?*"

Goldoni reacted as though struck in the face. "It was said the father and the brothers—the men of the family—took the dead son into the mountains. Where the boy's body would not be further abused."

Adrian got out of the chair. There was his answer.

The grave of the Jew. The vault from Salonika.

Savarone Fontini-Cristi had found an eternal truth in a village tragedy. He had used it. In the end, not letting the holy men forget.

Paul Leinkraus was in his late forties, the grandson of the merchant and a merchant himself, but of a different time. There was little he could relate of a grandfather he barely knew, or of an era of obsequiousness and fear he had never known. But he was a man of acumen, bespeaking the expansion for which he was responsible. As such, he had recognized the urgency and the legitimacy of Adrian's sudden call.

Leinkraus had taken Fontine into the library, away from his wife and child, and removed the family Torah from the shelf. The diagram filled the entire back panel of the binding. It was a precisely drawn map that showed the way to the grave of Reuven Leinkraus's first son, buried in the mountains on July 17, 1920.

Adrian had traced every line, then matched his drawing with the original. It was precise; he had his last passport. To where, he was certain. To what, he could not know.

He had made a final request of Leinkraus. An overseas telephone call to London for which, of course, he would pay.

"Your grandfather made all the payments this house can accept. Make your call."

"Please stay. I want you to hear."

He had placed a call to the Savoy in London. His request was uncomplicated. When the American embassy opened, would the Savoy please leave a message for Colonel Tarkington of the inspector general's office. If he was not in London, the embassy would know where to reach him.

Colonel Tarkington was to be directed to a man named Paul Leinkraus in the town of Champoluc in the Italian Alps. The message was to be signed Adrian Fontine.

He was going into the mountains on the hunt, but he had no illusions. He was not ultimately a match for the soldier. His gesture might be only that: a gesture ending in futility. And very possibly his own death; he understood that, too.

The world could survive very well without his presence. He wasn't particularly remarkable, although he liked to think he had certain talents. But he wasn't at all sure how the world would fare if Andrew walked out of the Champoluc with the contents of an iron crate that had been carried on a train from Salonika over thirty years ago.

If only one brother came out of the mountains and that man was the killer of Eye Corps, he had to be taken.

The call finished, Adrian had looked up at Paul Leinkraus. "When Colonel Tarkington makes contact with you, tell him exactly what happened here this morning."

Fontine nodded to Leinkraus in the doorway. He opened the door of the Fiat and climbed in, noticing that he had been so agitated upon his arrival that he'd left the keys in the car. It was the kind of carelessness no soldier would be guilty of.

The realization caused him to reach over and pull down the panel of the glove compartment. He put his hand inside and took out a heavy, black, magazine-clip pistol; the loading mechanism had been explained to him by Alfredo Goldoni.

He started the ignition and rolled down the window, suddenly needing the air. His breath came rapidly; his heartbeat vibrated in his throat. And he remembered.

He had fired a pistol only once in his life. Years ago at a boys' camp in New Hampshire when the counselors had taken them to a local police range. His brother had been beside him, and they had laughed together, excited children.

Where had the laughter gone?

Where had his brother gone?

Adrian drove down the tree-lined street and turned left into the road that would take him north to the mountains. Above, the early morning sun was hidden behind a blanket of gathering clouds.

The sky was angry.

32

The girl shrieked and slipped on the rock; her brother whipped around and grabbed her hand, preventing the fall. The plunge was no more than twenty feet, and the soldier wondered whether it might be better to break the grip between them and let her fall. If the girl snapped an ankle or a leg, she wouldn't go anywhere; she certainly could not make it down through the trails to the flat ground and the road below. It was twelve miles behind them now. They had covered the initial terrain during the night.

He could bypass the initial trails of that journey into the mountains fifty years ago. If others began the search, they wouldn't know that; he did. He could read maps the way most men read simple books. From symbols, colors, and numbers, he could visualize terrain with the accuracy of a camera. There was no one better in the army. He was a master of everything *real,* from men to machines to maps.

The detailed map used by climbers in the Champoluc district showed the railroad from Zermatt angling west around the curve of the mountains. It straightened out for approximately five miles before the station at Champoluc The areas directly east of the final flat stretches of track were heavily traversed throughout the year. These were the first trails described in Goldoni's journal. No one concealing anything of value would consider them.

Yet farther north, at the start of the railroad's western curve, were the old clearings that led to the numerous trails specifically listed in the pages he had ripped out of the Goldoni ledger for July 14 and 15 of 1920. Any of these might be the one. Once he saw them in daylight, and studied the possibilities, he could determine which of the trails he would trace.

Those selections would be based on fact. Fact one: The size and weight of the vault mandated vehicle or animal transportation. Fact two: The train from Salonika made its journey in the month of December—a time of year when the weather was bitter cold and the mountain passes clogged with snow. Fact three: The spring and summer thaws, with their rushing waters and erosion of earth, would call for a recess in the high ground to hide the vault, enveloped by rock for protection. Fact four: That recess would be away from frequently traveled areas, high above an established route, but with an offshoot trail that could be negotiated by an animal or a vehicle. Fact five: That trail had to emanate from a section of the track where a train could pull to a stop, the ground level on both sides flat and straight. Fact six: The specific clearing, in current use or abandoned, would lead into the crisscrossing trails recorded in the Goldoni ledger. By retracing each one to the tracks and picturing the feasibility of traveling over it—in the cold and snow, by animal or vehicle—the number of trails would be further reduced until there was one that led to the hiding place.

He had time. Days, if he needed them. He had supplies for a week strapped to his back. The stump, Goldoni, the woman, Capomonti, and Lefrac and his family were too frightened to make a move. He had covered himself brilliantly. The unseen was always more effective than the observable in combat. He had told the terrified Swiss that he had associates in Champoluc. They would be watching; they would get word to him in the mountains should a Goldoni or a Capomonti or a Lefrac reach the police. Communications were no problem for soldiers. And the result of their reaching him would be the execution of his hostages.

He had fantasized the presence of Eye Corps. Eye Corps the way it had been—efficient, strong, quick to maneuver.

He would build a new Corps one day, stronger and more efficient, without weakness. He would find the vault from Salonika, carry the documents out of the mountains, summon the holy men and watch their faces as he described the imminent, global collapse of their institutions.

. . . *The contents of that vault are as staggering to the civilized world as any in history.* . . .

That was comforting. It could not be in better hands.

They were on a flat stretch now, the first elevation to the west no more than a mile away. The girl fell to her knees, sobbing. Her brother looked at him, his eyes conveying hatred, fear, supplication. Andrew would kill them both, but not for a while. One disposed of hostages when they no longer served a purpose.

Only fools killed indiscriminately. Death was an instrument, a means to be used in reaching an objective or completing an assignment, and that was all it was.

Adrian drove the Fiat off the road into the fields. The rocks ripped the undercarriage. He could drive no farther; he had reached the first of several step hills that led to the first plateau described on the Leinkraus diagram. He was eight and a half miles north of Champoluc. The grave was precisely five miles beyond the first of the plateaus that were the landmarks of the journey to the burial ground.

He got out of the car and walked across the field of tall grass. He looked up. The hill in front of him sprang suddenly out of the ground, an impromptu bulge of nature, more rock than greenery, with no discernible path on which to scale it. He knelt down and retied the laces on his rubber-soled shoes as tightly as he could. The weight of the pistol was heavy in his raincoat pocket.

For a moment he closed his eyes. *He could not think. O God! Keep me from thinking!*

He was a mover now. He got to his feet and started to climb.

The first two railroad clearings proved negative. There was no way animal or vehicle could traverse the routes from the Zermatt railway to the eastern slopes. Two more clearings remained. The names on the old Champoluc map were Hunter's Folly and Sparrow's Rook; no mention of hawk. Still, it had to be one of them!

Andrew looked at his hostages. Brother and sister sat together on the ground, talking in quiet, frightened whispers, their eyes darting up at him. The hatred was gone now, only fear and supplication remained. There was something ugly about them, thought the soldier. And then he realized what it was. Across the world in the jungles of Southeast Asia, people their age fought battles, weapons strapped to their backs over uniforms that looked like pajamas. They were his enemy over there, but he respected that enemy.

He had no respect for these children. There was no strength in their faces. Only fear, and fear was repulsive to the major from Eye Corps.

"Get up!" He could not help himself; he shouted angrily at the sight of these pampered, weak brats with no dignity in their faces.

Christ, he despised the spineless!

They would not be missed.

Adrian looked back across the ridge to the plateau in the distance, thankful that old Goldoni had given him gloves. Even without the cold, his bare hands and fingers would have been a bleeding mass of flesh. It wasn't that the climb was difficult; a man used to minimum exercise in the mountains would find it simple. But he had never been in the mountains except on skis, where tows and trams did the uphill work. He was using muscles rarely employed and had little confidence in his sense of balance.

The last several hundred yards had been the most difficult. The trail in the Leinkraus diagram was landmarked: a cluster of gray rock at the base of a crystalline schistose embankment that all climbers knew should be avoided, for it cracked easily. The crystalline rock evolved into a cliff that rose about a hundred feet from the schist, its edge sharply defined. To the left of the crystalline sheet were abrupt, dense Alpine woods that grew vertically out of the slope, a sudden, thick forest surrounded by rock. The Leinkraus trail was marked off at ten paces from the embankment. It led to the top of the wooded slope whose ridge was the second plateau: the end of the second leg of the journey.

The trail was nowhere to be found. It had disappeared; years of disuse and overgrowth had concealed it. Yet the ridge could be seen clearly above the trees. That he could see it was an indication of the angle of ascent.

He had walked into the dense Alpine underbrush and made his way, yard by yard, up the steep incline, through nettled bush and the skin-piercing needles of the pines.

He sat on the ridge, breathing heavily, his shoulders aching from the constant tension. He estimated the distance from the first plateau to be at least three miles. It had taken nearly three hours. A mile an hour, over rocks and down miniature valleys, and across cold streams, and up endless hills. Just three miles. If that were so, he had two miles to go, perhaps less. He looked up. The overcast had lasted the entire morning. It would continue on throughout the day. The sky above was like the North Shore sky before a heavy squall.

They used to sail in squalls together. Laughing as they bested the weather, sure of their abilities in the water, pitting themselves against the rain and the wind of the Sound.

No, he would not think of that. He got to his feet and looked at his tracing of the Leinkraus diagram, copied from the inside binding of a family Torah.

The diagram was clear but the rising terrain beyond him wasn't. He saw the objective—due northeast, the third plateau, isolated above a sea of Alpine spruce. But the ridge he was on swept to the right, due *east*, leading into the base of yet another mountain of boulders, away from any direct line to the pleateau in the distance. He walked around the ledge past the border of the dark, sloping woods he had climbed through. The drop below was sheer and the rocks beneath rose like a bubbling river of stone. The trail as marked in the diagram went from forest to ledge to forest; there was no mention of intersecting rock.

Geological changes had taken place in the intervening years since any member of the Leinkraus family had journeyed to the burial ground. A sudden shift of nature—a quake or an avalanche—had eliminated the trail.

Still, he could see the plateau. What separated him from it seemed impenetrable, but once through it—and over it—he could make out a winding trail on the higher ground that led to the plateau. It was doubtful that that had been altered. He slid down the embankment onto the river of stone, and awkwardly, trying to keep his feet from slipping into a hundred miniature crevices, climbed toward the forest of spruce.

The third clearing was it! *Sciocchezza di Cacciatori!* Hunter's Folly! Long abandoned but once perfect for removing the vault. The trail from the mountains to the Zermatt railway was passable, and the area around the tracks was flat and accessible. At first Andrew had not been sure; in spite of the level ground on either side of the tracks, the stretch was short, blocked by a curve. Then he remembered: his father had said that the train from Salonika had been a short freight. Four cars and an engine.

Five railway units could easily pull beyond the curve and come to a stop in a straight line. Whatever car the vault had been in could have been unloaded without difficulty.

But what now convinced him he was near his goal was an unexpected discovery. West of the tracks were the unmistakable signs of an abandoned road. The cut through the woods was defined, the trees in the cut shorter than those surrounding them, the brush closer to the ground. It was no longer a road—not even a path—but its former existence was undeniable.

"Lefrac!" he yelled at the eighteen-year-old. "What's down there?" He pointed northwest, where the cut in the forest sloped.

"A village. About five, six miles away."

"It's not on the railroad line?"

"No, *signore*. It's in farm country, below the mountains."

"What roads lead into it?"

"The main road from Zürich and——"

"All right." He stopped the boy for two reasons. He had heard what he wanted to hear, and twenty feet away the girl had gotten to her feet and was edging toward the woods on the eastern side of the tracks.

Fontine took out his pistol and fired two shots. The explosions thundered throughout the woods; the bullets detonated the ground on either side of the child. She screamed, terrified. Her brother lunged at him in a frenzy of tears; he sidestepped and smashed the barrel of his pistol on the side of the boy's head.

Lefrac's son fell to the ground, sobs of frustration and

anger filling the silence of the abandoned railroad clearing.

"You're better than I thought you were," said the soldier coldly, raising his eyes, turning to the girl. "Help him. He's not hurt. We're heading back."

Give the captured hope, reflected the soldier. The younger and more inexperienced they were, the more hope they should be given. It reduced the fear which was, in itself, detrimental to rapid travel. Fear was an instrument, too. Like death. It was to be used methodically.

He retraced the trail from the Zermatt tracks for a second time. He was certain now. There was nothing that would prevent an animal or a vehicle from negotiating it. The ground was clear and mostly hard. And more important, the terrain rose directly toward the eastern slopes, into the specific trails recorded in the faded pages of the ledger. Light snow and layers of frost covered the earth. With every yard the soldier in him told him he was nearing the enemy zone. For that was what it was.

They reached the first intersecting trail described by the Goldoni guide on the morning of July 14, 1920. To the right, the trail angled downward into some kind of forest, a thick wall of dark green, laced with a roof of white. It seemed impenetrable.

It was a possible hiding place. That mountain forest would not be tempting to the casual climber, and without interest for the experienced. On the other hand, it *was* forest—wood and earth, not rock—and because it was not rock he could not accept it. The vault would be protected by rock.

To the left, the trail continued up, veering obliquely into the side of a small mountain above them. The trail itself was wide, on solid rock, and bordered by foliage. Boulders rose sharply to the right, forming an abrupt sheer of heavy stone. An animal or a vehicle still had space to walk or roll; the direct line from the Zermatt tracks was unbroken.

"Move it!" he shouted, gesturing to the left. The Lefrac children looked at each other. To the right was the way to Champoluc—the way back. The girl grabbed her brother; Fontine stepped forward, broke the grip, and propelled the girl forward.

"*Signore!*" The boy shouted and stepped between them, his arms raised in front of him, his young palms flat—a very penetrable shield. "Don't do that," he stammered, his voice low, cracking with young fear, his own anger challenging himself.

"Let's go," said the soldier. He had no time to waste on children.

"You hear me, *signore!*"

"I heard you. Now, move."

At the western flank of the small mountain the width of the rising trail abruptly narrowed. It entered an enormous, natural archway cut out of the boulders and led to the face of a hill of sheer rock. The geologically formed archway was not only the logical extension of the trail, but the mountain of rock beyond must have been irresistible to novice climbers. It could be scaled without great effort, but was sufficiently awesome by its breadth and height to be a good start for the higher regions. Perfect for an enthusiastic seventeen year old, under the watchful eye of a guide and a father.

But the width under the arch *was* narrow, the rock floor too smooth, especially when heavier snows fell. An animal—a mule or a horse—might cross under but there was considerable danger that hooves would slip.

No vehicle could possibly get through.

Andrew turned and studied the approach they had just made. There were no other trails, but about thirty yards back on the left the ground was flat and filled with Alpine brush. It extended to a short wall of rock that rose up to the ridge of the mountain. That wall, that short cliff, was no more than twenty feet high, almost hidden by shrubs and small, gnarled trees growing out of the rock. But the ground beneath that cliff, beneath that ridge, was flat. Natural obstructions were everywhere else, but not there, not in that particular spot.

"Walk over there," he ordered the young Lefracs, both to keep them in sight and to provide perspective. "Go into that flat area between the rocks! Spread the bushes and walk in! As far as you can!"

He stepped back off the trail and studied the ridge above. It, too, was flat, or at least appeared so. And it was something else, something that might not be noticed except, perhaps, from where he stood. It was . . . defined. The edge, though jagged, formed a nearly perfect semicircle. If that circle continued, the ridge itself was like a small, out-of-the-way platform on a small, unimportant mountain, but still high above the lower Alpine hills.

He judged the height of Lefrac's son as five-ten or -eleven. "Raise your hands!" he shouted.

Arms extended, the boy's hands were just below the midpoint of the short cliff.

Suppose the method of transport was not an animal but a vehicle. A heavy-wheeled piece of machinery, the carriage a plow, or a tractor. It was consistent; there was no part of the route from the Zermatt tracks or up the Goldoni trail that such a piece of equipment could not traverse. And plows and tractors had winch machinery. . . .

"*Signore! Signore!*" It was the girl; her shouts conveyed a strange exaltation, a cross between hope and desperation. "If this is what you *look* for, let us *go!*"

Andrew raced back into the trail and toward the Lefracs. He sped into the tangled shrubbery to the face of the rock.

"Down there!" The girl shouted again.

On the ground in the light snow, barely seen through the underbrush, was an old ladder. The wood was rotted, the steps swollen out of their sockets in half a dozen places. But otherwise it was intact. It was not now usable, but neither had it been abused by man. It had lain in that shrubbery for years, perhaps decades, untouched except by nature and time.

Fontine knelt down and touched it, pried it off the ground, watched it crumble as he lifted it. He had found a human tool where none should be; he knew that not fifteen feet above him . . .

Above him! He whipped his head up and saw the blurred object crashing down. The impact came; his head exploded in a flashing of pain, followed by an instant of numbness, a hundred hammers pounding. He fell forward, struggling to shake the effects of the blow and find light again.

He heard the shouts.

"*Fuggi! Presto! In la traccia!*" The boy.

"*Non senza voi! Tu fuggi anche!*" The girl.

Lefrac's son had found a large rock on the ground. And in his hatred he had lost his fear; holding the primitive weapon in his hand, he had crashed it down on the soldier's head.

The light was returning. Fontine started to get up and,

again, he saw the unfocused hand descending, the rock slashing diagonally down.

"*You little fuck! You fuck!*"

Lefrac's son released the rock, hurling it into the soldier's body—anywhere, a final assault—and ran out of the snow-covered shrubbery onto the trail after his sister.

Andrew recognized the pitch of his own fury. He had felt it perhaps a dozen times in his life, and it had always been in the molten heat of combat when an enemy held an advantage he could not control.

He crawled out of the brush to the edge of the trail and looked below. Beneath him on the winding path were brother and sister, running as best they could over the slippery trail.

He reached under his jacket to the holster strapped to his chest. The Beretta was in his pocket. But a Beretta would be inadequate; it was not that accurate. He pulled out the .357-caliber Magnum he had bought at the Leinkraus store in Champoluc. His hostages were about forty yards away. The boy took the girl's hand; they were close together, the figures overlapping.

Andrew squeezed the trigger eight times in succession. Both bodies fell, writhing on the rocks. He could hear the screams. In seconds the screaming subsided into moans, the writhing became twists and lurches at nothing. They would die, but not for a while. They would go no farther.

The soldier crawled back through the shrubs into the flat *cul de sac* and removed the pack from his back, slipping the straps off slowly, moving his bleeding head as little as possible. He opened the pack and slipped out the canvas first-aid kit. He had to patch the broken skin and stop the bleeding as best he could. And move. For Christ's sake, *move!*

He had no hostages now. He could tell himself it made no difference, but he knew better. Hostages were a way out. If he came out of the mountains alone, they'd be watching. *Jesus,* they'd be watching for him—he was a dead man. They'd take the vault and kill him.

There was another way. The Lefrac boy had said it!

The abandoned road west of the abandoned clearing called Hunter's Folly! Past the tracks, down to a village whose main road led to Zürich.

But he was not going to that village, to that road that led

to Zürich, until the contents of the vault were his. And every instinct he possessed told him he'd found it.

Fifteen feet above.

He unwound the ropes clamped to the outside of the pack and spread the grappling hook from its axis; the prongs locked into position. He stood up. His temple throbbed and the wounds stung where he'd applied the antiseptic, but the bleeding had stopped. He was focusing clearly again.

He stepped back and lobbed the grappling hook up to the ledge. It caught. He yanked on the rope.

The rock splintered; fragments plummeted down, followed by larger sections of limestone. He sprang to the side to avoid the falling hook; it embedded itself through the thin layers of snow into the ground.

He swore and once more heaved the hook skyward, arcing it over the ledge, far into the flat surface above. He tugged in swift, short movements; the hook caught. He pulled harder; it held.

The line was ready; he could climb. He reached down, grabbed the straps of his pack and slipped his arms through, not bothering to secure the front clamps. He yanked on the rope a last time; he was satisfied. He jumped as high as he could, thrusting his legs out against the stone, allowing himself to swing back into the rock as he manipulated his hands—one over the other—in rapid ascent. He swung his left leg over the jagged ledge, and pushed his right hand against the stone beneath, forcing his body into a lateral roll that propelled him onto the surface. He started to get up, his eyes traveling to the source of the grappling hook's anchor.

But he remained kneeling in shock as he stared at the strange sight ten feet away, in the center of the plateau. Embedded in the stone was an old, rusted metal star: a Star of David.

The grappling hook enveloped it, the prongs moored around the iron.

He was looking at a grave.

He heard the echoes throughout the mountains like repeated, sharp cracks of thunder, one right after another. As if bolts of lightning had sliced through the roof of the forest, splitting the wood of a hundred trees around him. But they signified neither lightning nor thunder; they were gunshots.

In spite of the cold, perspiration stream down Adrian's face, and despite the darkness of the forest, his eyes were filled with unwanted images. His brother had killed again. The major from Eye Corps was efficiently going about his business of death. The screams that followed the shots were faint, muted by the forest barrier, but unmistakable.

Why? For God's sake, *why?!*

He could not think. Not about things like that. Not now. He had to think only on one level—the level of motion. He had made a half-dozen attempts to climb out of the dark labyrinth, each time allowing himself ten minutes to see the light of the forest's edge. Twice he had allowed himself extra time because his eyes played tricks, and in each case there was only further darkness, no end in sight.

He was rapidly going out of his mind. He was caught in a maze; thick shafts of bark and unending, prickling branches and cracked limbs creased his face and his legs. How many times had he gone in circles? He could not tell. Everything began to look like everything else. He'd *seen* that tree! That particular cluster of branches had been his wall five minutes ago! His flashlight was no help. Its illuminations imitated themselves; he could not tell one from another. He was lost in the middle of an impenetrable slope of Alpine woods. Nature had altered the trail in the decades since the Leinkraus mourners made their final pilgrimage. The seepage of melting summer snows had spread, inundating the once-negotiable forest, providing a bed of moist earth receptive to unlimited growth.

But knowing this was as useless as his flashlight's distortions. The initial reports of gunfire exploded from over *there*. In *that* direction. He had very little to lose except his breath and what remained of his sanity. He began to run, his head filled with the echoes of the gunfire he had heard seconds ago.

The faster he ran the straighter seemed his course. He slashed a path with his arms, bending, breaking, cracking everything that got in his way.

And he saw the light. He fell to his knees, out of breath, no more than thirty feet from the forest's edge. Gray stone, covered with patches of snow, rose beyond the dense trees and surged out of sight above the highest limbs. He had reached the base of the third plateau.

And so had his brother. The killer from Eye Corps had done what Goldoni believed he could not do: He had taken long-forgotten descriptions written down a half century ago and refined them, made them applicable to the present search. There was a time when brother would have taken pride in brother; that time had passed. There remained only the necessity of stopping him.

Adrian had tried not to think about it, wondering if he'd be capable of accepting it when the moment came. The moment of anguish unlike anything in his imagination. He was accepting it now. Calmly, strangely unmoved, though filled with a cold sadness. For it was the only eminently logical, undeniable response to the horror and the chaos.

He would kill his brother. Or his brother would kill him.

He got to his feet, walked slowly out of the forest and found the path of rock diagramed on the Leinkraus map. It wound up the mountain, a series of wide curves to lessen the angle of ascent, veering always clockwise until it reached the top. Or almost the top, for at the base of the plateau was a sheet of rock that Paul Leinkraus recalled was quite high. He had made the journey only twice—in the first and second years of the war—and was very young. The sheet of rock might not be as high as he remembered it to be, for the memory was in the context of a boy's perspective. But they had used a ladder, he recalled that clearly.

A solemn service for the dead and a young boy's sense of life were incompatible, Leinkraus had admitted. There was another way to the plateau, hardly practical for old men, but explored by a youngster lacking the proper respect for religious observance. It was at the very end of the seemingly vanished path, well past an enormous natural arch that was the continuation of the mountain trail. It consisted of a series of jagged rocks that followed the line of the narrowing summit, and necessitated sure feet and a willingness to take chances. His father and older brother had scolded him severely for using it. The drop was dangerous; probably not fatal, but sufficiently deep to break an arm or a leg.

If an arm or a leg were broken now, thought Adrian, the danger *was* fatal. An immobilized man was an easy target.

He started up the winding path, between the intermittent rocks, crouching to conceal his body below their height.

The plateau was three hundred to four hundred feet above the path, the distance of a football field. A light snow began to fall, settling itself delicately on the thin layer of white that already covered much of the rock. His feet slipped continuously; he balanced himself by grabbing shrubs and projections of jagged rock.

He reached the midpoint of the climb and pressed his back into a concave flute of stone to catch his breath unseen. He could hear sounds above him, metal against metal, or rock against rock. He lunged out of the recess and ran as fast as he could, up and around the next four bends of the trail, falling once to let untrapped, unswallowed air fill his lungs, to give his aching legs a chance to rest.

He pulled the Leinkraus diagram from his pocket and checked off the curves on the map; he had covered eight, he thought. Whatever, it wasn't any farther than a hundred feet to the arch, symbolized by an inverted U on the diagram. He raised his head, his face bitter cold from the temporary pillow of frost and snow. There was a straight stretch of trail, bordered on both sides by gray, gnarled shrubbery. According to the map, there were two more hairpin curves above that stretch and then the arch of rock. He jammed the diagram into his pocket, feeling the steel of his gun as he did so. He pulled his legs up under him into a crouch and raced on.

He saw the girl first. She was lying off the trail in the shrubs, her eyes wide, staring at the overcast sky, her legs stretched rigidly in front of her. There were two bullet holes above each knee, the blood matted about the cloth. A third puncture could be seen above her right breast, below her collar bone; blood had formed a solid stream down her white Alpine jacket.

She was alive, but in such a degree of shock that she did not blink her eyes against the particles of falling snow. Her lips were moving, trembling, melted snow forming rivulets of water at the edges. Adrian bent over her.

At the sight of his face, her eyes blinked into focus. She raised her head in convulsion, coughing the start of a scream. Gently, he pressed his gloved hand over the mouth, supporting her neck with his other hand.

"I'm not him," he whispered.

The brush above them moved. Adrian whipped up, releasing the girl as carefully as he could, and sprang back. A hand edged its way over the snow—what was left of a hand. It was bloodstained flesh, the glove blown off, the fingers shattered. Fontine crept over the girl and up into the tangled, gnarled shrubbery, ripping the intertwined branches apart. The boy lay on his stomach in a bed of wild mountain grass. A straight line of four bullet wounds angled diagonally along his back, across his spine.

Adrian rolled the youth carefully over on his side, cradling his head. Once again he gently pressed a hand over a mouth in shock. The boy's eyes locked with his and within seconds Adrian's meaning was clear: He was not the killer. That the boy could speak at all was extraordinary. His whisper was nearly covered by the growing wind, but Fontine heard him.

"*Mia sorella.*"

"I don't understand."

"*Sister?*"

"She's hurt. So are you. I'll do everything I can."

"*Pacco.* The pack. He wears a pack. *Medicina.*"

"Don't talk. Save your strength. A pack?"

"*Si!*"

. . . *An Alpine pack is not a mere collection of straps and leather casing. It is a work of master craftsmanship.* . . . His father had said that.

The boy would not stop. He knew he was dying. "A way out. The Zermatt railroad. A village. Not far, *signore.* North, not far. We were going to run."

"Shhh. Don't say any more. I'm going to put you next to your sister. Keep as warm as you can."

He half carried, half dragged the boy over the grass to the girl. They were children; his brother murdered children. He removed his raincoat and jacket, tearing the lining of the jacket in order to tie the strips around the girl's wounds. There wasn't much he could do about the boy's, so he avoided his eyes. He covered them both; they held each other.

He put the heavy pistol in his belt beneath the heavy black sweater and crawled out of the sanctuary of the bushes. He raced up the path to the arch, his eyes stinging but his breath steady, the pain in his legs gone.

It was one against one now. The way it had to be.

33

The sound of cracking came louder, hammerlike and furious. It was directly above him, above the sheer sheet of rock that sprang up, facing the small, defined plateau on the north side. The ground at his feet was disturbed; snow and earth were intermingled, footprints and broken shrubbery formed a semicircle beneath the overhang. Fragments of rock signified the method of ascent: A rope had been thrown above, with a hook attached, and the first throw or throws had not been successful.

A rotted ladder lay in the snow-laced, gray bushes, a number of its steps torn from the frame. It was the ladder Paul Leinkraus remembered. It was at least twenty feet long, on end, slightly higher than the sheet of rock in front of which Adrian crouched.

The burial ground is really a surface of shale. It cracks easily under the force of a pick to the earth beneath. The child's coffin was placed in the ground and a thin layer of concrete spread over it. The words of Paul Leinkraus.

Above him, his brother had broken through the layer of concrete described by Leinkraus. The hammering stopped; a metal instrument was thrown aside on the hard surface. Large particles of cement plummeted down, kicked by impatient feet, joining the fragments of rock on the ground and the bushes. Adrian got to his feet quickly and pressed himself into the miniature cliff. If he was seen, he was dead.

The spray of cement stopped. Adrian shivered; he knew he had to move. The cold was penetrating the black sweater, his breath formed billows of vapor in front of his face. The brief, light snowfall was letting up; a shaft of sunlight broke through the clouds, but brought no warmth.

He edged his way around the sheet of rock until he could go no farther, blocked by a projecting boulder bulging out of the mountaintop. He stepped forward onto the shrub-covered, snow-layered ground.

Suddenly, the earth gave way. Adrian leaped back and stood motionless, petrified, at the side of the boulder. The sounds of falling rock carried on the wind. He heard the foorsteps above—heavy, abrupt—and held his breath so no steam would emerge from his mouth or nostrils. The sound of footsteps stopped—except for the wind, only silence remained. Then the footsteps started again—less heavy, slower. The soldier's alarm had subsided.

Adrian looked down in front of him. He had come to the end of Paul Leinkraus's path; there was only mountain now. Below, beyond the edge of broken earth and wild grass, was a drop, a wide, sweeping crevasse whose empty space separated the ground of the summit from the shallow ledge of earth across from it that led to higher regions. The crevasse was far deeper than Leinkraus remembered; it was well over thirty feet to a floor of jagged rock. The boy had been reprimanded by his elders, but not so truthfully as to frighten him, or instill a fear of the mountains.

Adrian swung his body around and, clinging to the uneven surface, inch by inch, testing each, he moved out, pressing his chest and legs into the boulder, holding whatever sharp point he could grasp. On the other side was a narrow mass of indiscriminately formed rock that angled sharply up to the flat surface of the peak.

He was not sure he could reach it. A small boy could walk on the ledge away from the immediate base of the projecting boulder; it would not give way under his weight. A grown man was something else. It had not taken Adrian's weight; it would not take it.

The distance from the central point of the boulder—where he was—to the first promontory of rock was about five feet. He was over six. If he could angle his fall, with his arms outstretched, there was a good change his hands would reach. More of a chance if he could narrow the distance.

The muscles of his feet were in agony. He could feel cramps forming in both insteps: the strain on his calves swelled his skin, the tendons beneath arching nearly beyond endurance. He forced all thoughts of pain and risk out of his mind and concentrated only on the inches he could cover around the massive boulder.

He had gone no more than a foot when he felt the ground sinking beneath him—slowly, in minute, hypnotizing stages. Then he could hear—actually *hear*—the cracking of stone and frozen earth. He thrust out his arms at the last half second. The ledge fell away and for a moment he was in the void, suspended. His hands clutched out crazily; the wind whipped against his face in midair.

His right arm crashed over the jagged rock somewhere above him. His shoulder and head slammed into the rough, shagged surface. He clamped his hand around the sharp stone, arching his back instinctively to absorb the shock of the impact.

He swung like a puppet on the string of his own appendage, his feet dangling. He had to drag himself up. *Now!* There were no seconds to waste! No time to adjust to his own disbelief!

Move!

He clawed the uneven cliff with his free left hand; his feet pumped insanely until his right shoe caught a tiny ridge that supported his weight. It was enough. Like a panicked spider he scaled the wall of jagged rock, throwing his legs one after another over the diagonal incline, slamming his body into the base of the inner surface.

He was out of sight from above, not out of hearing. The sounds of the falling ledge brought Andrew to the edge of the plateau. The sun was behind him on his right, casting his shadow across the crevasse, over the rock and snow. Again, Adrian held his breath. He had a window on his own lantern show, played out in the now-blinding Alpine sun. The soldier's movements were not only clear, they were magnified. Andrew held an object in his left hand: a climber's folding shovel.

The soldier's right arm was angled at the elbow; the shadow of his forearm joined the shadow of his upper body. It took little imagination to visualize what the right hand held: a gun. Adrian moved his own right hand to his belt. The pistol was still there; he was grateful for its touch.

The shadow moved about the ledge above, three steps to the left, four to the right. It bent down and then stood up again, another object now in its right hand. The object was thrown off; a large fragment of cement plummeted down no more than two feet from Adrian's face and crashed on the floor of jagged rock below. The soldier stood motionless during the object's fall, as if counting off seconds, timing the descent. The last rolling spatters finished, the soldier walked away. His shadow disappeared, replaced by the harsh reflections of the sun.

Adrian lay in his recess, unaware of his discomfort, his face drenched with sweat. The curve of uneven rocks above his head swept sharply up, like a primitive spiral staircase in an ancient lighthouse. The sweep was about twenty-five feet in length; it was difficult to estimate for there was nothing beyond but sky and blazing sun. He could not move until he heard sounds from above. Sounds that meant the soldier was occupied, digging again.

They came. A loud crushing of stone, the scraping of metal against metal.

Andrew had found the vault!

Adrian crawled out of his shelter and, hand over hand, silent foot after silent foot, made his way up the jagged rock staircase. The ledge of the plateau was directly above; below was no longer the crevasse but a sheer drop of several hundred feet to the winding mountain pass. There were, perhaps, eight inches between him and the open space. The wind was steady. Its sound was a low whistle.

He reached for the pistol in his belt, removed it and—as Goldoni had instructed—checked the safety. It was in upright position, locked.

He snapped it level with the trigger and raised his head over the ledge.

The flat surface of the plateau was an oval, extending thirty-five feet or more in length, twenty or so in width. The soldier crouched in the center, next to a mound of earth covered with fragments of cracked cement. Beyond the dirt, partially concealed by the soldier's broad back, was a plain wooden casket with metal borders; it was remarkably preserved.

There was no vault. There was nothing but earth, the fragments of cement, and the coffin. But no vault!

Oh, my God, thought Adrian. We were *wrong! Both wrong!*

It wasn't possible. It was not possible. For if there were no vault, the killer from Eye Corps would be in a rage. He knew Andrew well enough to know that. But his brother was not angry. He was crouched in thought, his head angled down; he was staring at the grave. And Adrian understood: The vault was below, still in the earth. It had been buried beneath the coffin, that casket its final protection.

The soldier got to his feet and crossed to the Alpine pack which lay upright against the coffin. He bent over, unsnapped a strap, and pulled out a short, pointed iron bar. He returned to the grave, abruptly knelt by the edge, and reached down with the bar. Seconds later he yanked the bar up, letting it fall on the ground, and removed a gun from his jacket. Swiftly, but carefully, he angled the weapon down into the grave.

Three explosions followed. Adrian ducked his head below the edge of the plateau. He could smell the acrid odor of the gunfire, see the billows of smoke carried above him on the wind.

And then the words came and his whole body was locked in a fear he never believed he could experience. It was the shock of the knowledge of his own immediate execution.

"Put your head up, Lefrac," was the soft-spoken command, delivered in a monotone of ice. "It'll be quicker that way. You won't feel a thing. You won't even hear any noise."

Adrian rose from his narrow perch, his mind blank, beyond fear now. He was going to die; it was as simple as that.

But he was not what the soldier above him expected. Not *whom* the soldier expected. The killer from Eye Corps was suddenly, completely gripped in shock of his own. It was so total that his eyes widened in disbelief, his hand trembled and the weapon in its grasp wavered. He took an involuntary step backward, his mouth gaping, the skin on his face bloodless.

"*You!*"

Wildly, blindly, without thought or feeling, Adrian whipped up the heavy Italian pistol from the ledge of rock and fired at the stunned figure. He squeezed the trigger twice, three times. The gun jammed. The spits and smoke from the barrel-housing singed his flesh, stung his eyes. But he had hit the soldier! The killer from Eye Corps reeled backward, holding his stomach, his left leg buckling beneath him.

But Andrew still had the pistol in his hand. The explosion came; a crack of air detonated above Adrian's head.

He lunged at the fallen man, crashing the jammed pistol down in the area of the face. His right hand shot out, grabbing the hot steel of Andrew's gun, slamming it against the hard surface of the plateau. His own pistol found its mark; the bridge between the soldier's eyes erupted; blood flowed into the corners of his sockets, bluring his vision. Andrew's pistol flew out of his hand. Adrian sprang back.

He aimed his gun and squeezed the trigger with all his strength. It would not operate, it would not *fire*. The soldier got to his knees, rubbing his eyes, his mouth emitting grunts of fury. Adrian lashed out his foot, catching the killer from Eye Corps at the temple; the soldier's neck arched back, but his legs shot forward, twisting, kicking, slamming into Adrian's kneecaps, causing him to lurch to the side, his knees suddenly in agony.

Adrian could not stay on his feet. He rolled to his right as the major leaped up, still wiping his eyes. Andrew sprang off the ground, hands now outstretched like rigid hooks, directly at his intruder's neck. Adrian recoiled farther, crashing into the casket at the side of the grave. The soldier's lunge was uncontrolled; the screaming pitch of his anger caused him to lose his balance, and he fell, one arm plunged into the mound of earth and fragments of concrete. The earth flew; an eruption of dirt and snow and rock.

Adrian dove over the open space of the grave; on the opposite side was the iron bar. The soldier followed; he lunged up, screaming at Adrian, his hands locked above his head into a hammer—a monstrous bird screeching in for the kill. Adrian's fingers were on the bar, and he lashed it up at the plummeting figure.

The point plunged into the soldier's cheek, stunning him. Blood burst again from Andrew's flesh.

Adrian lurched away as fast as his exhausted, aching legs could propel him, dropping the bar. He saw the soldier's pistol lying across the flat stone surface; he lunged for it. His fingers wound around the handle; he raised it.

The iron bar came slicing through the air, creasing the skin of his left shoulder, tearing the sleeve half off his sweater. The shock sent him reeling back to the edge of the sheet of rock. He had brought the hand with the gun across his chest in panic; he knew the instant he did so it was the fraction of a second the soldier desperately needed. A wall of earth and stone came at him, the space between himself and the killer from Eye Corps was filled with debris. It smashed into him; sharp pieces of rock pummeled his face, his eyes. He could not see.

He fired. His hand recoiled violently from the explosion of the weapon; his fingers arched from the vibration.

He tried to get to his feet; a boot hammered into his neck. He caught the leg as he fell back, his shoulders over the edge of the sheet of rock. He rolled to his left, holding the leg until he felt the barrel of the gun against the flesh.

He pulled the trigger.

Flesh and bone and blood filled his universe. The soldier was blown off the ground, his right leg a mass of red-soaked cloth. Adrian started to crawl but he could not; there was no strength left, no air in his lungs. He raised himself on one hand and looked over at Andrew.

The major writhed back and forth, moans coming from his throat, his mouth filled with blood and saliva. He pushed himself off the ground, halfway to his knees, his eyes staring insanely at what was left of his leg. He looked over to his executioner. And then he screamed.

"*Help me!* You can't let me *die!* You *don't have the right!* Get me the *pack!*" He coughed, holding his shattered leg with one hand, his other trembling, gesturing at the Alpine pack against the coffin. The blood flowed everywhere, saturating his clothes. The poisons were spreading rapidly; he was dying.

"I don't have the right to let you live," said Adrian weakly, gasping for air. "Do you know what you've done? The people you killed?"

"Killing's an *instrument!*" screamed the soldier. "That's all it is!"

"Who decides when the instrument's used? *You?*"

"*Yes!* And men *like* me! We know who we are, what we can do. People like you, you're *not*——. For Christ's sake, *help me!*"

"You make the rules. Everybody else follows."

"Yes! Because we're willing to! People everywhere, they're not willing. They want the rules made for them! You can't deny that!"

"I do deny it," said Adrian quietly.

"Then you're lying. Or stupid! Oh, *Christ* . . ." The soldier's voice broke, interrupted by a spasm of coughing. He clutched his stomach and stared at his leg again, and then at the mound of dirt. He pulled his eyes away and looked at Adrian. "Here. Over *here*."

The major crawled toward the grave. Adrian rose slowly to his feet and watched, mesmerized by the horrible sight. What was left of his compassion told him to fire the weapon in his hand, end the life that was nearly finished. He could see the vault from Salonika in the ground; slats of rotted wood had been pulled away, revealing the iron beneath. Strips of metal had been shattered by gunfire, a coil of rope lay on top. There were torn pieces of heavy cardboard with faint markings that looked like circles of thorns around crucifixes.

They had found it.

"Don't you understand?" The soldier could barely be heard. "It's there. The answer. The *answer!*"

"What answer?"

"*Everything.* . . ." For several seconds his brother's eyes lost muscular control; they rolled in their sockets, and for an instant the pupils disappeared. Andrew's speech had the inflections of an angry child; his right hand extended into the grave. "I have it now. You can't interfere! Anymore! You can help me now. I'll let you help me. I used to let you help me, remember? You remember how I *always used to let you help me?*" The soldier screamed the question.

"It was always your decision, Andy. To let me help you, I mean," said Adrian softly, trying to understand the childlike rambling, hypnotized by the words.

"Of course my decision. It had to be *my decision.* Victor's and mine."

Adrian suddenly recalled their mother's words . . . *he saw the results of strength; he never understood its complications, its compassion.* . . . The lawyer in Adrian had to know. "What should we do with the vault? Now that we've got it, what should we do with——"

"*Use it!*" The soldier screamed again, pounding the loose rock at the edge of the grave. "*Use* it, use it! Make things *right!* We'll tell them we can ruin *everything!*"

"Suppose we can't? Suppose it doesn't matter? Maybe there's nothing there."

"We tell them *there is!* You don't know how to do it. We

tell them anything we *want* to tell them! They'll *crawl,* they'll *whine. . . .*"

"You want them to do that? To crawl and whine?"

"Yes! They're weak!"

"But you're not."

"No! I've *proved* it! Over and over and *over again!*" The soldier's neck arched and then snapped forward convulsively. "You think you see things *I* don't see. You're *wrong!* I see them but they don't make *any difference,* they don't *count!* What you think's so goddamned *important . . . doesn't . . . matter!*" Andrew spaced out the words; it was a child's cry of defiance.

"What's that, Andy? What is it I think is so important?"

"*People! What they think!* It doesn't *count,* doesn't *matter.* Victor knows that."

"You're wrong; you're *so* wrong," interrupted Adrian quietly. "He's dead, Andy. He died a couple of days ago."

The soldier's eyes regained part of their focus. There was elation in them. "Now everything's *mine!* I'll do it!" The coughing returned; the eyes wandered again. "Make them understand. They're not important. Never were. . . ."

"Only you."

"Yes! I don't hesitate. *You do!* You can't make up your mind!"

"You're decisive, Andy."

"Yes, *decisive.* That's important."

"And people don't count, so naturally they can't be trusted."

"What the hell are you trying to say?" The soldier's chest expanded in pain; his neck arched back, then shot forward, mucus and blood coughed through his lips.

"That you're *afraid!*" shouted Adrian. "You've always been afraid! You live scared to death that someone'll find that out! There's a big crack in your armor . . . you *freak!*"

A terrible, muted cry came from the soldier's throat; it was at once guttural and clear, a cross between a roar of final anger and a wail. "That's a *lie!* You and your goddamned words. . . ."

Suddenly there were no more words. The unbelievable was happening in the blinding Alpine sunlight, and Adrian knew only that he would move or die. The soldier's hand was in the grave. He whipped it out. In his grip was a rope;

he lurched off the ground, swinging the rope violently. Tied to the end was a grappling hook, its three prongs slashing through the air.

Adrian sprang to his left, firing the enormous weapon at the crazed killer from Eye Corps.

The soldier's chest exploded. The rope, held in a grip of steel, swung in a circle—the grappling hook spinning like an insanely off-course gyroscope—around the soldier's head. The body shot forward, over the sheet of rock, and plummeted down, its scream echoing, filling the mountains with its pitch of horror.

With a sudden, sickening vibration the rope sprang taut, quivering in the thin layer of disturbed snow.

There was the sound of cracking metal from the grave. Adrian whipped his eyes over to its source. The rope had been lashed to a steel band around the vault. The band snapped. The vault could be opened.

But Adrian did not go to it. He limped to the edge of the plateau and looked over the sheet of rock.

Suspended below was the soldier's body, the grappling hook imbedded in his neck. A prong had plunged up through Andrew's throat, its point protruding from the gaping mouth.

He filled the large Alpine pack with the three steel, airtight containers from the vault. He could not read the ancient writing etched in the metal. He did not have to; he knew what each container held. None were large. One was flat, thicker than the other two: within it were the documents compiled by the scholars of Constantine 1,500 years ago, studies that traced what they believed was a theological inconsistency—raising a holy man to one substance with God. Questions for new scholars to ponder. The second container was short, tubular; it held the Aramaic scroll that had so frightened powerful men thirty years ago that strategies of global war were secondary to its possession. But it was the third container, thin, no more than eight inches wide, ten high, that held the most extraordinary document of all: a confession written on a parchment, taken out of a Roman prison nearly 2,000 years ago. It was this receptacle—black, pitted, a relic of antiquity—that was the essence of the vault from Salonika.

All were the denials; only the confession on the Roman

parchment could produce an agony beyond men's minds. But that was not for him to judge. Or was it?

He put the plastic bottles of medicine into his pockets, threw the pack down on the ground, lowered himself over the edge of the sheet of rock—next to the soldier's body—and dropped to the earth beneath. He strapped the heavy pack on his back and started down the trail.

The boy was dead. The girl would live. Together they would somehow walk out of the mountains, of that Adrian was convinced.

They traveled slowly—a few steps at a time—down the trail toward the Zermatt tracks. He held the girl so that as little weight as possible was forced on her wounded legs.

He looked back up the mountain trail. In the distance the soldier's body hung suspended against the white sheet of rock. It could not be seen clearly—only if you knew where to look—but it was there.

Was Andrew the final death demanded by the train from Salonika? Were the documents in that vault worth so much life? So much violence for so many years? He had no answers.

He only knew insanity was given unearned stature in the name of holy things. Holy wars were primeval; they always would be. And he had killed a brother for their part of an unholy war.

He felt the terrible weight on his back. He was tempted to remove the steel containers and heave them into the deepest gorge in the mountains. Broken, left to wither into nothing with the first touch of air. Swept away by the Alpine winds into oblivion.

But he would not do that. The price had been too steep.

"Let's go," he said to the girl, gently placing her left arm around his neck. He smiled at the child's frightened face. "We're going to make it."

PART FOUR

34

Adrian stood by the window overlooking the dark expanse of Central Park. He was in the small staff lounge at the Metropolitan Museum. He held the telephone to his ear and listened to Colonel Tarkington in Washington. Across the room sat a priest from the Archdiocese of New York, the monsignor named Land. It was shortly past midnight; the army officer in Washington had been given the private number of the museum. He was told that Mr. Fontine expected his call, regardless of the hour.

Official documentation of events surrounding Eye Corps would be issued by the Pentagon in due time, the officer told Adrian. The administration wanted to avoid the scandal that would result from charges of corruption and insurrection within the armed forces. Especially as a prominent name was involved. It did not serve the interests of national security.

"Stage one," said Adrian. "Cover-up."

"Perhaps."

"You're going to settle for that?" asked Fontine quietly.

"It's your family," replied the colonel. "Your brother."

"And yours. I can live with it. Can't you? Can't Washington?"

There was silence on the other end of the line. Finally the officer spoke. "I got what I wanted. And maybe Washington can't. Not now."

"It's never 'now.' "

"Don't preach to me. Nobody's stopping you from holding a press conference."

It was now Adrian who was momentarily silent. "If I do, can I demand official documentation? Or would a dossier suddenly appear, describing——"

"Describing in psychiatric detail," interrupted the colonel, "a very disturbed young man who ran around the country living in hippie communes; who aided and abetted three convicted army deserters in San Francisco. Don't kid yourself, Fontine. It's on my desk."

"I thought it might be. I'm learning. You're thorough, aren't you? Which brother's the lunatic?"

"It goes much further. Family influence used to avoid military service; past membership in radical organizations—they're using dynamite these days. Your odd behavior recently in Washington, including a relationship with a Black attorney who was killed under strange circumstances, said Black lawyer suspected of criminal activities. Lots more. And that's only you."

"What?"

"Old truths—documented truths—are dragged up. A father who made a fortune operating all over the world with governments many believe are inimicable to our interests. A man who worked closely with the Communists, whose first wife was killed years ago under very odd circumstances in Monte Carlo. That's a disturbing pattern. Questions are raised. Can the Fontines live with *that?*"

"You make me sick."

"I make myself sick."

"Then why?"

"Because a decision had to be made that goes beyond you and me and our personal revulsions!" The colonel raised his voice in anger, then controlled himself. "I don't like a lot of bullshit players upstairs. I only know—or think I know—that maybe it isn't the time to talk about Eye Corps."

"So it goes on and on. You don't sound like the man I talked to in a hotel room."

"Maybe I'm not. I only hope for the sake of your righteous indignation you're never put in a position like this."

Adrian looked at the priest across the room. Land was staring at the dimly lit white wall, at nothing. Yet it was in his eyes, *it's always in the eyes.* A desperation that consumed him. The monsignor was a very strong man, but he was frightened now. "I hope I never am," he said to the colonel.

"Fontine?"

"Yes?"

"Let's have a drink sometime."

"Sure. We'll do that." Adrian hung up.

Was it up to him now? wondered Adrian. Everything? Was the time ever right to tell the truth?

There'd be one answer soon. He'd gotten the documents from the vault out of Italy with the colonel's help; the colonel owed him that much, and the colonel did not ask questions. The colonel's payment was a body suspended in front of a sheet of rock in the mountains of Champoluc. Brother for brother. Debt paid.

Barbara Pierson had known what to do with the documents. She contacted a friend who was a curator of relics and artifacts at the Metropolitan. A scholar who had devoted his life to study of the past. He had seen too much of antiquity to make judgments.

Barbara had flown down from Boston; she was in the laboratory with the scholar now. They'd been there since five-thirty. Seven hours. With the documents from Constantine.

But there was only one document that mattered now. It was the parchment taken out of a Roman prison 2,000 years ago. The parchment was everything. *Everything.* The scholar understood that.

Adrian left the window and walked across the room to the priest. Two weeks ago, when his father was close to death, Victor drew up his list of men to whom the vault of Constantine was to be delivered. Land's name was on that list. When Adrian contacted him, Land began saying things to him he had never said to Victor Fontine.

"Tell me about Annaxas," said Adrian, sitting down opposite the priest.

The monsignor looked away from the wall, startled. Not by the name, thought Fontine, but by the intrusion. His large, penetrating gray eyes under the dark brows were momentarily unfocused. He blinked, as if remembering where he was.

"Theodore Dakakos? What can I tell you? We first met in Istanbul. I was tracing what I knew was false evidence. The so-called destruction by fire of the Filioque documents. He found out I was there and flew up from Athens to meet the interfering priest from the Vatican archives. We talked; we were both curious. I, why such a prominent man of commerce was so interested in obscure theological artifacts. He, why a Roman scholar was pursuing—*allowed* to pursue, perhaps—a thesis hardly in the Vatican's interests. He was very knowledgeable. Each of us manuevered throughout the night, both of us finally exhausted. I think it was the exhaustion that caused it. And the fact that we thought we knew one another, perhaps even liked one another."

"Caused what?"

"The train from Salonika to be mentioned. Strange, I don't remember which of us said it first."

"He *knew* about it?"

"As much, or more, than I. The trainman was his father, the single passenger; the priest of Xenope, his father's brother. Neither man ever returned. In his search he found part of the answer. The police records in Milan contained an old entry from December 1939. Two dead men on a Greek train in the freight yards. Murder and suicide. No identification. Annaxas had to know why."

"What led him to Milan?"

"Over twenty years of asking questions. He had reason enough. He watched his mother go insane. She went mad because the church would give her no answers."

"Her church?"

"An arm of the church, if you will. The Order of Xenope."

"Then she knew about the train."

"She was never supposed to have known. It was believed she didn't. But men tell things to their wives they tell no one else. Before the elder Annaxas left early that morning in December of 1939, he said to his wife that he was not going to Corinth, as everyone believed. Instead, God would look favorably on them for he was joining his brother Petride. They were going on a journey very far away. They were doing God's work."

The priest fingered the gold cross hanging from a cord on the cloth beneath his collar. His touch was not gentle; there was anger in it.

"From which he never came back," said Adrian quietly. "And there was no brother in the church to reach because he was dead."

"Yes. I think we can both imagine how the woman—a good woman, simple, loving, left with six children—would react."

"She'd go out of her mind."

Land let the cross drop, his eyes straying back to the wall. "As an act of charity, the priests of Xenope took the mad woman in. Another decision was made. She died within a month."

Fontine slowly sat forward. "They killed her." It was not a question.

Land's gaze returned. There was a degree of supplication in his eyes now. "They weighed the consequences of her life. Not against the Filioque, but in relation to a parchment none of us in Rome ever knew existed. I'd never heard of it until this evening. It makes so many things so much clearer."

Adrian got out of the chair and walked back to the window. He was not ready to discuss the parchment. The holy men no longer had the right to direct inquiries. The attorney in Adrian disapproved of the priests. Laws were for all.

Down in Central Park, along a dimly lit path, a man was walking two huge Labrador retrievers, the animals straining at their leashes. He was straining on a leash of his own, but he could not let Land know it. He turned from the window. "Dakakos put it all together, didn't he?"

"Yes," replied Land, accepting Adrian's refusal to be led. "It was his legacy. He vowed to learn everything. We agreed to exchange information, but I was more forthright than he. The name Fontini-Cristi surfaced, but the parchment was never mentioned. The rest, I assume, you know."

Adrian was startled by the priest's words. "Don't assume anything. Tell me."

Land flinched. The rebuke was unexpected. "I'm sorry. I thought you knew. Dakakos took over the responsibility of Campo di Fiori. For years he paid the taxes—which were considerable—fended off buyers, real-estate developers, provided security, and upkeep——"

"What about Xenope?"

"The Order of Xenope is all but extinct. A small monastery north of Salonika. A few old priests on diminished farmland, with no money. For Dakakos, only one link remained: a dying monk at Campo di Fiori. He couldn't let it go. He extracted everything the old man knew. Ultimately, he was right. Gaetamo was released from prison; the banished priest, Aldobrini, came back from Africa dying of assorted fevers and, finally, your father returned to Campo di Fiori. The scene of his family's execution. The terrible search began all over again."

Adrian thought. "Dakakos stopped my brother. He went

to extraordinary lengths to trap him, expose Eye Corps."

"To keep him from the vault at all costs. The old monk must have told Dakakos that Victor Fontine knew about the parchment. He understood that your father would act outside the authorities, use his sons to find the vault. He had to. Weighing the consequences, there was no other course. Dakakos studied both of you. Actually he had you watched for several years. What he found in one son shocked him. Your brother could not be permitted to go further. He had to be destroyed. You, on the other hand, were someone he felt he could work with, if it came to that."

The priest had stopped. He inhaled deeply, his fingers once again around the gold cross on his chest. Thought had returned to him and it was obviously painful. Adrian understood; he had experienced the same feeling in the mountains of Champoluc.

"What would Dakakos have done if he'd found the vault?"

Land's penetrating gaze settled on Adrian. "I don't know. He was a compassionate man. He knew the anguish of seeking painful answers to very painful questions; his sympathy might have guided his judgment. Still, he was a man of truth. I think he would have weighed the consequences. Beyond this I can't help you."

"You use that phrase a lot, don't you? 'Weighing the consequences.' "

"I apologize if it offends you."

"It does."

"Then forgive me, but I must offend you further. I asked your permission to come here, but I've changed my mind. I'm going to leave." The priest got out of the chair. "I can't stay. I'll try to put it simply——"

"Simply *put,*" interrupted Adrian harshly, "I'm not interested."

"You have the advantage," replied Land quickly. "You see, I'm interested in *you,* in what you perceive." The priest would not be stopped; he took a step forward. "Do you think doubts are erased because vows are taken? You think seven thousand years of human communication is somehow voided for us? Any of us, whatever the vestments we wear? How many gods and prophets and holy men have been conjured over the centuries? Does the number lessen the devotion? I think not. For each accepts what he can accept, raising his own beliefs above all others. My doubts tell me that thousands of years from now scholars may study the remnants of what we were and conclude that our beliefs—our devotions—were singularly odd, consigning to myth what we think most holy. As we have consigned to myth the remnants of others. My intellect, you see, can conceive of this. But now, here, in my time—for me—the commitment is made. It's better to have it than not to have it. I do believe. I am convinced."

Adrian remembered the words. " 'Divine revelation cannot be contravened by mortal man'?"

"That's good enough. I'll accept that," said Land simply. "Ultimately, the lessons of Aquinas prevail. They're not the exclusive property of anyone, I might add. When reason is exhausted, at its last barrier, faith becomes the reason. I have that faith. But being mortal, I'm weak. I haven't the endurance to test myself further. I must retreat to the comfort of my commitment, knowing I'm better with it than without it." The priest held out his hand. "Good-bye, Adrian."

Fontine looked at the outstretched hand and accepted it. "You understand that it's the arrogance of your 'commitment,' your beliefs, that disturbs me. I don't know any other way to put it."

"I understand; your objection is noted. That arrogance is the first of the sins that lead to spiritual death. And the one most often overlooked: pride. It may kill us all one day. Then, my young friend, there'll be nothing."

Land turned and walked to the door of the small lounge. He opened it with his right hand, his left still holding the gold cross, enveloping it. The gesture was unmistakable. It was an act of protection. He looked once more at Adrian, then walked out of the room, closing the door behind him.

Fontine lighted a cigarette, then crushed it out. His mouth was sour from too many cigarettes and too little sleep. Instead, he went to a coffee maker and poured himself a cup.

An hour ago Land, testing the metal rim of the hot plate, had burned his fingers. It occurred to Adrian that the monsignor was the sort of man who tested most things in life. And yet he could not accept the final test. He merely walked away; there was a kind of honesty in that.

Far more than he had shown his mother, reflected Adrian. He had not lied to Jane; it would have been useless, the lie known for what it was. But neither had he told her the truth. He had done a far crueler thing: he had avoided her. He was not yet ready for confrontation.

He heard footsteps in the corridor outside the lounge. He put his coffee down and walked to the center of the room. The door opened and Barbara entered, the door held for her by the scholar, still in his laboratory smock, his horn-rimmed glasses somehow magnifying his face. Barbara's brown eyes, usually so filled with warmth and laughter, were sharp with professional involvement.

"Doctor Shire's finished," she said. "May we have coffee?"

"Sure." Adrian went back to the table and poured two cups. The scholar sat down in the chair from which Land had risen just minutes ago.

"Black, if you please," said Shire, placing a single page of paper in his lap. "Your friend has left?"

"Yes, he left."

"Did he know?" asked the old man, accepting the coffee.

"He knew because I told him. He made his decision. He left."

"I can understand," said Shire, blinking his old eyes beyond the glasses in the steam of his coffee. "Sit down, both of you."

Barbara took the coffee but did not sit. She and the scholar exchanged looks; she walked to the window as Adrian sat across from Shire.

"Is it authentic?" asked Fontine. "I imagine that's the first question."

"Authentic? As to time and materials and script and language . . . yes, I would say it will survive those examinations. I'm going under the assumption that it will. Chemical and prismatic analyses take a long time, but I've seen hundreds of documents from the period; it's authentic on these points. As to the authenticity of the contents. It was written by a half-crazed man facing death. A very cruel and painful form of death. That judgment will have to be made by others, if it's to be made at all." Shire glanced at Adrian as he placed the coffee cup on the table beside the chair and picked up the paper on his lap. Fontine remained silent. The scholar continued.

"According to the words on that parchment, the prisoner who was to lose his life in the arena on the following afternoon renounced the name of Peter, given him by the revolutionary named Jesus. He said he was not worthy of it. He wanted his death to be recorded as one Simon of Bethsaida, his name at birth. He was consumed with guilt, claiming he had betrayed his savior. . . . For the man who was crucified on Calvary was *not* Jesus of Nazareth."

The old scholar stopped, his words floating, suspended, as if broken off in midsentence.

"Oh, my God!" Adrian got out of the chair. He looked at Barbara by the window. She returned his gaze without comment. He turned back to Shire. "It's that specific?"

"Yes. The man was in torment. He writes that three of Christ's disciples acted on their own, *against* the carpenter's wishes. With the help of Pilate's guards, whom they bribed, they took an unconscious Jesus out of the dungeons and substituted a condemned criminal of the same size and general appearance, dressing him in the carpenter's clothes. In the hysterical crowds the next day, the shroud and the blood from the thorns were sufficient to obscure the features of the man under and on the cross. It was *not* the will of the man they called a messiah——"

" 'Nothing is changed,' " interrupted Adrian softly, remembering the words. " 'Yet all is changed.' "

"He was involuntarily removed. It was his intention to die, not to live. The parchment is clear on that."

"But he didn't die. He *did* live."

"Yes."

"He was *not* crucified."

"No. If one accepts the word of the man who wrote the document—under the conditions he wrote it. Barely on the brink of sanity, I should think. I wouldn't accept it merely because of its antiquity."

"Now you're making a judgment."

"An observation of probability," corrected Shire. "The writer of the parchment lapsed into wild prayer and lamentations. His thoughts were lucid one moment, unclear the next. Madman or self-flagellating ascetic? Pretender or penitent? Which one? Unfortunately, the physical fact that it's a document from two thousand years ago lends a credibility that would certainly be withheld under less striking circumstances. Remember, it was the time of Nero's persecutions, a period of social, political, and theological madness. People survived more often than not on sheer ingenuity. Who was it, *really?*"

"The document spells it out. Simon of Bethsaida."

"We have only the writer's word for it. There is no record of Simon Peter's having gone to his death with the early Christian martyrs. Certainly it would be part of the legend, yet there's no mention of it in biblical studies. If it were so, and overlooked, it's an awesome omission, isn't it?"

The scholar removed his glasses and wiped the thick lens with a corner of his smock. "What are you trying to say?" Adrian asked.

The old man put the glasses back on his face, magnifying his thoughtful, sad eyes. "Suppose a citizen of Rome, scheduled for a most horrible form of execution, invents a story that impugns the hated mark of an upstart, dangerous religion, and does so in a believable manner. Such a man might find favor with the praetors, the consuls, with a caesar himself. A great many tried it, you know. In one form or another. There are remnants of scores of such 'confessions.' And now one of them in its complete form comes down to us. Is there any reason to accept it more than the others? Merely because it *is* complete? Ingenuity and survival are commonplace in history."

Adrian watched the scholar closely as he spoke. There was a strange anxiety in the words. "What do *you* think, doctor?"

"It's not important what I think," said Shire, momentarily avoiding Adrian's eyes.

There was silence; it was profoundly moving. "You believe it, don't you?"

Shire paused. "It's an extraordinary document."

"Does it say what happened to the carpenter?"

"Yes," replied Shire, staring at Adrian. "He took his own life three days later."

"Took his *own life?* That's contrary to everything——"

"Yes, it is," interrupted the scholar softly. "The consistency is found in the time factor: three days. Consistency and inconsistency, where's the balance? The confession goes on to say that the carpenter reviled those who interfered, yet still at the end called upon his God to forgive them."

"That's consistent."

"Would you expect otherwise? Ingenuity and survival, Mr. Fontine."

Nothing is changed, yet all is changed.

"What's the condition of the parchment?"

"It's remarkably well preserved. A solution of animal oil, I think, pressed into a vacuum, covered by heavy rock glass."

"And the other documents?"

"I haven't examined them, other than to distinguish them from the parchment. The papers that I presume trace the Filioque agreements as seen by its opponents are barely intact. The Aramaic scroll is, of course, metallic and will take a great deal of time and care to unravel."

Adrian sat down. "Is that the literal translation of the confession?" he asked, pointed to the page of writing in the scholar's hand.

"Sufficiently so. It's unrefined. I wouldn't present it academically."

"May I have it?"

"You may have everything." Shire leaned forward. Adrian reached out and took the paper. "The parchment, the documents; they're yours."

"They don't belong to me."

"I know that."

"Then why? I'd think you'd be pleading with me to let you keep them. Examine them. Startle the world with them."

The scholar removed his thick glasses, his tired eyes creased with exhaustion, his voice quiet. "You've brought me a very strange discovery. And quite frightening. I'm too old to cope with it."

"I don't understand."

"Then I ask you to consider. A death was denied, not a *life*. But in that death was the symbol. If you raise that symbol into question, you risk casting doubt on everything that symbol has come to mean. I'm not sure that's justified."

Adrian was silent for a moment. "The price of truth is too steep. Is that what you're saying?"

"If it's true. But again, there's the terrible absolute of antiquity. Things are accepted because they exist. Homer creates fiction, and centuries later men trace sea routes in search of caves inhabited by one-eyed giants. Froisart chronicles history that never was and is hailed a true historian. I ask you to weigh the consequences."

Adrian got out of the chair and walked aimlessly to the wall. The same area of the wall that Land kept looking at: flat, dimly lit white paint. Nothing. "Can you keep everything here for a while?"

"It can be stored in a laboratory vault. I can send you a receipt of acknowledgment."

Fontine turned. "A vault?"

"Yes. A vault."

"It could have stayed in another."

"Perhaps it should have. For how long, Mr. Fontine?"

"How long?"

"How long will it remain here?"

"A week, a month, a century. I don't know."

He stood by the hotel window overlooking the Manhattan skyline. New York pretended to sleep, but the myriad lights below on the streets denied the pretense.

They had talked for several hours, how many he didn't really know. *He* had talked; Barbara had listened, gently forcing him to say it all.

There was so much to do, to go through, before he found his head again.

Suddenly—the sound somehow terrifying—the telephone rang. He wheeled around, too aware of the panic he felt, knowing it was in his eyes.

Barbara got out of her chair and walked calmly over to him. She reached up and held his face with her hands. The panic subsided.

"I don't want to talk to anyone. Not now."

"Then don't. Tell whoever it is to call in the morning."

It was so simple. The truth.

The telephone rang again. He crossed to the bedside table and picked it up, sure of his intention, confident of his strength.

"Adrian? For God's *sake!* We've been tracing you all over New York! A colonel at I.G. named Tarkington gave us the hotel."

The caller was one of the Justice lawyers recruited by Nevins.

"What is it?"

"It's happened! Everything we've worked for is falling into place. This town is blown apart. The White House is in panic. We're in touch with the Senate judiciary; we're after a special prosecutor. There's no other way it can be handled."

"You've got concrete evidence?"

"More than that. Witnesses, confessions. The thieves are running for cover. We're back in business, Fontine. Are you with us? We can *move* now!"

Adrian thought only briefly before he answered. "Yes, I'm with you."

It was important to keep moving. Certain struggles continued. Others had to be brought to a close. The wisdom was in deciding which.

A PAIR OF LOVERS IN A WHIRLPOOL OF DANGER AND DECEPTION

David Spaulding was a top secret American agent on a mission that he himself did not fully understand. Jean Cameron was a beautiful young widow who had been betrayed once by the havoc of war and was determined never to let herself be hurt that way again.

They came together in Buenos Aires, a wartime city of violence and intrigue where representatives of America and Nazi Germany played a deadly game with the fate of the world in perilous balance.

And even as David Spaulding and Jean Cameron began to realize they were in love, they discovered the monstrous nature of their roles in the strangest and most sinister deal that two nations at war ever made with each other . . .

THE RHINEMANN EXCHANGE

"A heady brew of fear, romance, racy dialogue, high readability and an intricate plot that builds to a bloody crescendo!"—*John Barkham Reviews*

"BREATHLESS!"
—*Cleveland Plain Dealer*

Other Books by the Author:

THE SCARLATTI INHERITANCE
THE MATLOCK PAPER
THE OSTERMAN WEEKEND
THE GEMINI CONTENDERS
THE CHANCELLOR MANUSCRIPT
THE HOLCROFT CONVENANT
THE MATARESE CIRCLE
THE BOURNE IDENTITY
THE PARSIFAL MOSAIC

THE RHINEMANN EXCHANGE

ROBERT LUDLUM

A Dell Book

For Norma and
Ed Marcum—For
So Many Things,
My Thanks

Published by
DELL PUBLISHING CO., INC.
1 Dag Hammarskjold Plaza
New York, N.Y. 10017

ISBN: 0-440-15079-5

Reprinted by arrangement with
The Dial Press
Printed in the United States of America
Previous Dell Edition #5079
New Dell Edition
First printing—March 1977
Twenty-third printing—May 1983

PREFACE

MARCH 20, 1944, WASHINGTON, D.C.

"David?"

The girl came into the room and stood silently for a moment, watching the tall army officer as he stared out the hotel window. The March rain fell through a March chill, creating pockets of wind and mist over the Washington skyline.

Spaulding turned, aware of her presence, not of her voice. "I'm sorry. Did you say something?" He saw that she held his raincoat. He saw, too, the concern in her eyes—and the fear she tried to conceal.

"It's over," she said softly.

"It's over," he replied. "Or will be in an hour from now."

"Will they all be there?" she asked as she approached him, holding the coat in front of her as though it were a shield.

"Yes. They have no choice. . . . I have no choice." Spaulding's left shoulder was encased in bandages under his tunic, the arm in a wide, black sling. "Help me on with that, will you? The rain's not going to let up."

Jean Cameron unfolded the coat reluctantly and opened it.

She stopped, her eyes fixed on the collar of his army shirt. Then on the lapels of his uniform.

All the insignia had been removed.

There were only slight discolorations in the cloth where the emblems had been.

There was no rank, no identifying brass or silver. Not even the gold initials of the country he served.

Had served.

He saw that she had seen.

"It's the way I began," he said quietly. "No name, no rank, no history. Only a number. Followed by a letter. I want them to remember that."

The girl stood motionless, gripping the coat. "They'll kill you, David." Her words were barely audible.

"That's the one thing they won't do," he said calmly. "There'll be no assassins, no accidents, no sudden orders flying me out to Burma or Dar es Salaam. That's finished. . . . They can't know what I've done."

He smiled gently and touched her face. Her lovely face. She breathed deeply and imposed a control on herself he knew she did not feel. She slipped the raincoat carefully over his left shoulder as he reached around for the right sleeve. She pressed her face briefly against his back; he could feel the slight trembling as she spoke.

"I won't be afraid. I promised you that."

He walked out the glass entrance of the Shoreham Hotel and shook his head at the doorman under the canopy. He did not want a taxi; he wanted to walk. To let the dying fires of rage finally subside and burn themselves out. A long walk.

It would be the last hour of his life that he would wear the uniform.

The uniform now with no insignia, no identification.

He would walk through the second set of doors at the War Department and give his name to the military police.

David Spaulding.

That's all he would say. It would be enough; no one would stop him, none would interfere.

Orders would be left by unnamed commanders—divisional recognition only—that would allow him to proceed down the grey corridors to an unmarked room.

Those orders would be at that security desk because another order had been given. An order no one could trace. No one comprehended. . . .

They claimed. In outrage.

But none with an outrage matching his.

They knew that, too, the unknown commanders.

Names meaning nothing to him only months ago would

be in the unmarked room. Names that now were symbols of an abyss of deceit that so revolted him, he honestly believed he had lost his mind.

Howard Oliver.

Jonathan Craft.

Walter Kendall.

The names were innocuous sounding in themselves. They could belong to untold hundreds of thousands. There was something so . . . American about them.

Yet these names, these men, had brought him to the brink of insanity.

They would be there in the unmarked room, and he would remind them of those who were absent.

Erich Rhinemann. Buenos Aires.

Alan Swanson. Washington.

Franz Altmüller. Berlin.

Other symbols. Other threads. . . .

The abyss of deceit into which he had been plunged by . . . enemies.

How in God's name had it *happened?*

How *could* it have happened?

But it did happen. And he had written down the facts as he knew them.

Written them down and placed . . . the document in an archive case inside a deposit box within a bank vault in Colorado.

Untraceable. Locked in the earth for a millennium . . . for it was better that way.

Unless the men in the unmarked room forced him to do otherwise.

If they did . . . if they forced him . . . the sanities of millions would be tested. The revulsion would not acknowledge national boundaries or the cause of any global tribe.

The leaders would become pariahs.

As he was a pariah now.

A number followed by a letter.

He reached the steps of the War Department; the tan stone pillars did not signify strength to him now. Only the appearance of light brown paste.

No longer substance.

He walked through the sets of double doors up to the

security desk, manned by a middle-aged lieutenant colonel flanked by two sergeants.

"Spaulding, David," he said quietly.

"Your I.D. . . ." the lieutenant colonel looked at the shoulders of the raincoat, then at the collar, "Spaulding. . . ."

"My name is David Spaulding. My source is Fairfax," repeated David softly. "Check your papers, soldier."

The lieutenant colonel's head snapped up in anger, gradually replaced by bewilderment as he looked at Spaulding. For David had not spoken harshly, or even impolitely. Just factually.

The sergeant to the left of the lieutenant colonel shoved a page of paper in front of the officer without interrupting. The lieutenant colonel looked at it.

He glanced back up at David—briefly—and waved him through.

As he walked down the grey corridor, his raincoat over his arm, Spaulding could feel the eyes on him, scanning the uniform devoid of rank or identification. Several salutes were rendered hesitantly.

None was acknowledged.

Men turned; others stared from doorways.

This was the . . . officer, their looks were telling him. They'd heard the rumors, spoken in whispers, in hushed voices in out-of-the-way corners. This was the man.

An order had been given. . . .

The *man.*

PROLOGUE

ONE

SEPTEMBER 8, 1939, NEW YORK CITY

The two army officers, their uniforms creased into steel, their hats removed, watched the group of informally dressed men and women through the glass partition. The room in which the officers sat was dark.

A red light flashed; the sounds of an organ thundered out of the two webbed boxes at each corner of the glass-fronted, lightless cubicle. There followed the distant howling of dogs—large, rapacious dogs—and then a voice—deep, clear, forbidding—spoke over the interweaving sounds of the organ and the animals.

> Wherever madness exists, wherever the cries of the helpless can be heard, there you will find the tall figure of Jonathan Tyne—waiting, watching in shadows, prepared to do battle with the forces of hell. The seen and the unseen. . . .

Suddenly there was a piercing, mind-splitting scream. "Eeaagh!" Inside the lighted, inner room an obese woman winked at the short man in thick glasses who had been reading from a typed script and walked away from the microphone, chewing her gum rapidly.

The deep voice continued.

> Tonight we find Jonathan Tyne coming to the aid of the terror-stricken Lady Ashcroft, whose husband disappeared into the misty Scottish moors at precisely midnight three weeks ago. And each night at precisely midnight, the howls of unknown dogs bay across the

darkened fields. They seem to be challenging the very man who now walks stealthily into the enveloping mist. Jonathan Tyne. The seeker of evil; the nemesis of Lucifer. The champion of the helpless victims of darkness. . . .

The organ music swelled once more to a crescendo; the sound of the baying dogs grew more vicious.

The older officer, a colonel, glanced at his companion, a first lieutenant. The younger man, his eyes betraying his concern, was staring at the group of nonchalant actors inside the lighted studio.

The colonel winced.

"Interesting, isn't it?" he said.

"What? . . . Oh, yes, sir. Yes, sir; very interesting. Which one is he?"

"The tall fellow over in the corner. The one reading a newspaper."

"Does he play Tyne?"

"Who? Oh, no, lieutenant. He has a small role, I think. In a Spanish dialect."

"A small role . . . in a Spanish dialect." The lieutenant repeated the colonel's words, his voice hesitant, his look bewildered. "Forgive me, sir, I'm confused. I'm not sure what we're *doing* here; what *he's* doing here. I thought he was a construction engineer."

"He is."

The organ music subsided to a pianissimo; the sound of the howling dogs faded away. Now another voice—this one lighter, friendlier, with no undercurrent of impending drama—came out of the two webbed boxes.

Pilgrim. The soap with the scent of flowers in May; the Mayflower soap. Pilgrim brings you once again . . . "The Adventures of Jonathan Tyne."

The thick corked door of the dark cubicle opened and a balding man, erect, dressed in a conservative business suit, entered. He carried a manila envelope in his left hand; he reached over and extended his right hand to the colonel. He spoke quietly, but not in a whisper. "Hello, Ed. Nice to see you again. I don't have to tell you your call was a surprise."

"I guess it was. How are you, Jack? . . . Lieutenant, meet Mr. John Ryan; formerly Major John N. M. I. Ryan of Six Corps."

The officer rose to his feet.

"Sit down, lieutenant," said Ryan, shaking the young man's hand.

"Nice to meet you, sir. Thank you, sir."

Ryan edged his way around the rows of black leather armchairs and sat down next to the colonel in front of the glass partition. The organ music once more swelled, matching the reintroduced sounds of the howling dogs. Several actors and actresses crowded around two microphones, all watching a man behind a panel in another glass booth—this one lighted—on the other side of the studio.

"How's Jane?" asked Ryan. "And the children?"

"She hates Washington; so does the boy. They'd rather be back in Oahu. Cynthia loves it, though. She's eighteen, now; all those D.C. dances."

A hand signal was given by the man in the lighted booth across the way. The actors began their dialogue.

Ryan continued. "How about you? 'Washington' looks good on the roster sheet."

"I suppose it does, but nobody knows I'm there. That won't help me."

"Oh?"

"G-2."

"You look as though you are thriving, Jack."

"Yes, I gathered that."

Ryan smiled a little awkwardly. "No sweat. Ten other guys in the agency could do what I'm doing . . . better. But they don't have the Point on their résumés. I'm an agency symbol, strong-integrity version. The clients sort of fall in for muster."

The colonel laughed. "Horseshit. You were always good with the beady-bags. Even the high brass used to turn the congressmen over to you."

"You flatter me. At least I *think* you're flattering me."

"Eeaagh!" The obese actress, still chewing her gum, had screeched into the second microphone. She backed away, goosing a thin, effeminate-looking actor who was about to speak.

"There's a lot of screaming, isn't there." The colonel wasn't really asking a question.

"And dogs barking and off-key organ music and a hell of a lot of groaning and heavy breathing. 'Tyne's' the most popular program we have."

"I admit I've listened to it. The whole family has; since we've been back."

"You wouldn't believe it if I told you who writes most of the scripts."

"What do you mean?"

"A Pulitzer poet. Under another name, of course."

"That seems strange."

"Not at all. Survival. We pay. Poetry doesn't."

"Is that why *he's* on?" The colonel gestured with a nod of his head toward the tall, dark-haired man who had put down the newspaper but still remained in the corner of the studio, away from the other actors, leaning against the white corked wall.

"Beats the hell out of me. I mean, I didn't know who he was—that is, I knew who he *was,* but I didn't know anything about him—until you called." Ryan handed the colonel the manila envelope. "Here's a list of the shows and the agencies he's worked for. I called around; implied that we were considering him for a running lead. The Hammerts use him a lot. . . ."

"The who?"

"They're packagers. They've got about fifteen programs; daytime serials and evening shows. They say he's reliable; no sauce problems. He's used exclusively for dialects, it seems. And language fluency when it's called for."

"German and Spanish." It was a statement.

"That's right. . . ."

"Only it's not Spanish, it's Portuguese."

"Who can tell the difference? You know who his parents are." Another statement, only agreement anticipated.

"Richard and Margo Spaulding. Concert pianists, very big in England and the Continent. Current status: semi-retirement in Costa del Santiago, Portugal."

"They're American, though, aren't they?"

"Very. Made sure their son was born here. Sent him to American settlement schools wherever they lived. Shipped him back here for his final two years in prep school and college."

"How come Portugal, then?"

"Who knows? They had their first successes in Europe

and decided to stay there. A fact I *think* we're going to be grateful for. They only return here for tours; which aren't very frequent anymore. . . . Did you know that he's a construction engineer?"

"No, I didn't. That's interesting."

"Interesting? Just 'interesting'?"

Ryan smiled; there was a trace of sadness in his eyes. "Well, during the last six years or so there hasn't been a lot of building, has there? I mean, there's no great call for engineers . . . outside of the CCC and the NRA." He lifted his right hand and waved it laterally in front of him, encompassing the group of men and women inside the studio. "Do you know what's in there? A trial lawyer whose clients—when he can get a few—can't pay him; a Rolls-Royce executive who's been laid off since thirty-eight; and a former state senator whose campaign a few years ago not only cost him his job but also a lot of potential employers. They think he's a Red. Don't fool yourself, Ed. You've got it good. The Depression isn't over by a long shot. These people are the lucky ones. They found avocations they've turned into careers. . . . As long as they last."

"If I do *my* job, *his* career won't last any longer than a month from now."

"I figured it was something like that. The storm's building, isn't it? We'll be in it pretty soon. And I'll be back, too. . . . Where do you want to use him?"

"Lisbon."

David Spaulding pushed himself away from the white studio wall. He held up the pages of his script as he approached the microphone, preparing for his cue.

Pace watched him through the glass partition, wondering how Spaulding's voice would sound. He noticed that as Spaulding came closer to the group of actors clustered around the microphone, there was a conscious—or it seemed conscious—parting of bodies, as if the new participant was in some way a stranger. Perhaps it was only normal courtesy, allowing the new performer a chance to position himself, but the colonel didn't think so. There were no smiles, no looks, no indications of familiarity as there seemed to be among the others.

No one winked. Even the obese woman who screamed

and chewed gum and goosed her fellow actors just stood and watched Spaulding, her gum immobile in her mouth.

And then it happened; a curious moment.

Spaulding grinned, and the others, even the thin, effeminate man who was in the middle of a monologue, responded with bright smiles and nods. The obese woman winked.

A curious moment, thought Colonel Pace.

Spaulding's voice—mid-deep, incisive, heavily accented—came through the webbed boxes. His role was that of a mad doctor and bordered on the comic. It *would* have been comic, thought Pace, except for the authority Spaulding gave the writer's words. Pace didn't know anything about acting, but he knew when a man was being convincing. Spaulding was convincing.

That would be necessary in Lisbon.

In a few minutes Spaulding's role was obviously over. The obese woman screamed again; Spaulding retreated to the corner and quietly, making sure the pages did not rustle, picked up his folded newspaper. He leaned against the wall and withdrew a pencil from his pocket. He appeared to be doing *The New York Times* crossword puzzle.

Pace couldn't take his eyes off Spaulding. It was important for him to observe closely any subject with whom he had to make contact whenever possible. Observe the small things: the way a man walked; the way he held his head; the steadiness or lack of it in his eyes. The clothes, the watch, the cuff links; whether the shoes were shined, if the heels were worn down; the quality—or lack of quality—in a man's posture.

Pace tried to match the human being leaning against the wall, writing on the newspaper, with the dossier in his Washington office.

His name first surfaced from the files of the Army Corps of Engineers. David Spaulding had inquired about the possibilities of a commission—not volunteered: what would his opportunities be? were there any challenging construction projects? what about the length-of-service commitment? The sort of questions thousands of men—skilled men—were asking, knowing that the Selective Service Act would become law within a week or two. If enlistment meant a shorter commitment and/or the continued practice of their professional skills, then better an enlistment than be drafted with the mobs.

Spaulding had filled out all the appropriate forms and had been told the army would contact him. That had been six weeks ago and no one had done so. Not that the Corps wasn't interested; it was. The word from the Roosevelt men was that the draft law would be passed by Congress any day now, and the projected expansion of the army camps was so enormous, so incredibly massive that an engineer—especially a *construction* engineer of Spaulding's qualifications—was target material.

But those high up in the Corps of Engineers were aware of the search being conducted by the Intelligence Division of the Joint Chiefs of Staff and the War Department.

Quietly, slowly. No mistakes could be made.

So they passed along David Spaulding's forms to G-2 and were told in turn to stay away from him.

The man ID was seeking had to have three basic qualifications. Once these were established, the rest of the portrait could be microscopically scrutinized to see if the whole being possessed the other desirable requirements. The three basics were difficult enough in themselves: the first was fluency in the Portuguese language; the second, an equal mastery of German; the third, sufficient professional experience in structural engineering to enable swift and accurate understanding of blueprints, photographs—even verbal descriptions—of the widest variety of industrial designs. From bridges and factories to warehousing and railroad complexes.

The man in Lisbon would need each of these basic requirements. He would employ them throughout the war that was to be; the war that the United States inevitably would have to fight.

The man in Lisbon would be responsible for developing an Intelligence network primarily concerned with the destruction of the enemy's installations deep within its own territories.

Certain men—and women—traveled back and forth through hostile territories, basing their undefined activities in neutral countries. These were the people the man in Lisbon would use . . . before others used them.

These plus those he would train for infiltration. Espionage units. Teams of bi- and trilingual agents he would send up through France into the borders of Germany. To bring back their observations; eventually to inflict destruction themselves.

The English agreed that such an American was needed in Lisbon. British Intelligence admitted its Portuguese weakness; they had simply been around too long, too obviously. And there were current, very serious lapses of security in London. MI-5 had been infiltrated.

Lisbon would become an American project.

If such an American could be found.

David Spaulding's preapplication forms listed the primary requisites. He spoke three languages, had spoken them since he was a child. His parents, the renowned Richard and Margo Spaulding, maintained three residences: a small, elegant Belgravia flat in London; a winter retreat in Germany's Baden-Baden; and a sprawling oceanside house in the artists' colony of Costa del Santiago in Portugal. Spaulding had grown up in these environs. When he was sixteen, his father—over the objections of his mother—insisted that he complete his secondary education in the United States and enter an American university.

Andover in Massachusetts; Dartmouth in New Hampshire; finally Carnegie Institute in Pennsylvania.

Of course, the Intelligence Division hadn't discovered *all* of the above information from Spaulding's application forms. These supplementary facts—and a great deal more—were revealed by a man named Aaron Mandel in New York.

Pace, his eyes still riveted on the tall, lean man who had put down his newspaper and was now watching the actors around the microphones with detached amusement, recalled his single meeting with Mandel. Again, he matched Mandel's information with the man he saw before him.

Mandel had been listed on the application under "References." *Power-of-attorney, parents' concert manager.* An address was given: a suite of rooms in the Chrysler Building. Mandel was a very successful artists' representative, a Russian Jew who rivaled Sol Hurok for clients, though not as prone to attract attention, or as desirous of it.

"David has been as a son to me," Mandel told Pace. "But I must presume you know that."

"Why must you? I know only what I've read on his application forms. And some scattered information; academic records, employment references."

"Let's say I've been expecting you. Or someone like you."

"I beg your pardon?"

"Oh, come. David spent a great many years in Germany; you might say he almost grew up there."

"His application . . . as a matter of fact his passport information, also includes family residences in London and a place called Costa del Santiago in Portugal."

"I said almost. He converses easily in the German language."

"Also Portuguese, I understand."

"Equally so. And its sister tongue, Spanish. . . . I wasn't aware that a man's enlistment in the army engineers called for a full colonel's interest. And passport research." Mandel, the flesh creased around his eyes, smiled.

"I wasn't prepared for you." The colonel's reply had been stated simply. "Most people take this sort of thing as routine. Or they convince themselves it's routine . . . with a little help."

"Most people did not live as Jews in tsarist Kiev. . . . What do you want from me?"

"To begin with, did you tell Spaulding you expected us? Or someone. . . ."

"Of course not," Mandel interrupted gently. "I told you, he is as a son to me. I wouldn't care to give him such ideas."

"I'm relieved. Nothing may come of it anyway."

"However, you hope it will."

"Frankly, yes. But there are questions we need answered. His background isn't just unusual, it seems filled with contradictions. To begin with, you don't expect the son of well-known musicians . . . I mean . . ."

"Concert artists." Mandel had supplied the term Pace sought.

"Yes, concert artists. You don't expect the children of such people to become engineers. Or accountants, if you know what I mean. And then—and I'm sure you'll understand this—it seems highly illogical that once that fact is accepted, the son *is* an engineer, we find that the major portion of his income is currently earned as a . . . as a radio performer. The pattern indicates a degree of instability. Perhaps more than a degree."

"You suffer from the American mania for consistency. I don't say this unkindly. I would be less than adequate as a neurosurgeon; you may play the piano quite well, but I doubt that I'd represent you at Covent Garden. . . . The questions you raise are easily answered. And, perhaps, the word *stability* can be found at the core. . . . Have you any idea, any *conception*, of what the world of the concert stage is like? *Madness*. . . . David lived in this world for nearly twenty years; I suspect . . . no, I don't suspect, I know . . . he found it quite distasteful. . . . And so often people overlook certain fundamental characteristics of musicianship. Characteristics easily inherited. A great musician is often, in his own way, an exceptional mathematician. Take Bach. A genius at mathematics. . . ."

According to Aaron Mandel, David Spaulding found his future profession while in his second year in college. The solidity, the permanence of structural creation combined with the precision of engineering detail were at once his answer to and escape from the mercurial world of the "concert stage." But there were other inherited characteristics equally at work inside him. Spaulding had an ego, a sense of independence. He needed approval, wanted recognition. And such rewards were not easily come by for a junior engineer, just out of graduate school, in a large New York firm during the late thirties. There simply wasn't that much to do; or the capital to do it with.

"He left the New York firm," Mandel continued, "to accept a number of individual construction projects where he believed the money would grow faster, the jobs be his own. He had no ties; he could travel. Several in the Midwest, one . . . no, two, in Central America; four in Canada, I think. He got the first few right out of the newspapers; they led to the others. He returned to New York about eighteen months ago. The money didn't really grow, as I told him it wouldn't. The projects were not his own; provincial . . . local interference."

"And somehow this led to the radio work?"

Mandel had laughed and leaned back in his chair. "As you may know, Colonel Pace, I've diversified. The concert stage and a European war—soon to reach these shores, as we all realize—do not go well together. These last few years my clients have gone into other performing areas, including the highly paid radio field. David quickly saw opportunities for himself and I agreed. He's done extremely well, you know."

"But he's not a trained professional."

"No, he's not. He has something else, however. . . . Think. Most children of well-known performers, or leading politicians, or the immensely rich, for that matter, have it. It's a public confidence, an assurance, if you will; no matter their private insecurities. After all, they've generally been on display since the time they could walk and talk. David certainly has it. And he has a good ear; as do both of his parents, obviously. An aural memory for musical or linguistic rhythms. . . . He doesn't act, he *reads.* Almost exclusively in the dialects or the foreign languages he knows fluently. . . ."

David Spaulding's excursion into the "highly paid radio field" was solely motivated by money; he was used to living well. At a time when owners of engineering companies found it difficult to guarantee themselves a hundred dollars a week, Spaulding was earning three or four hundred from his "radio work" alone.

"As you may have surmised," said Mandel, "David's immediate objective is to bank sufficient monies to start his own company. Immediate, that is, unless otherwise shaped by world or national conditions. He's not blind; anyone who can read a newspaper sees that we are being drawn into the war."

"Do you think we should be?"

"I'm a Jew. As far as I'm concerned, we're late."

"This Spaulding. You've described what seems to me a very resourceful man."

"I've described only what you could have found out from any number of sources. And *you* have described the conclusion you have drawn from that surface information. It's not the whole picture." At this point, Pace recalled, Mandel had gotten out of his chair, avoiding any eye contact, and walked about his office. He was searching for negatives; he was trying to find the words that would disqualify "his son" from the government's interests. And Pace had been aware of it. "What certainly must have struck you—from what I've told you—is David's preoccupation with himself, with his comforts, if you wish. Now, in a business sense this might be applauded; therefore, I disabused you of your concerns for stability. However, I would not be candid if I didn't tell you that David is abnormally headstrong. He operates —I think—quite poorly under authority. In a word, he's a selfish man, not given to discipline. It pains me to say this; I love him dearly. . . ."

And the more Mandel had talked, the more indelibly did Pace imprint the word *affirmative* on Spaulding's file. Not that he believed for a minute the extremes of behavior Mandel suddenly ascribed to David Spaulding—no man could function as "stably" as Spaulding had if it were true. But if it were only half true, it was no detriment; it was an asset.

The last of the requirements.

For if there were any soldier in the United States Army —in or out of uniform—who would be called upon to operate solely on his own, without the comfort of the chain of command, without the knowledge that difficult decisions could be made by his superiors, it was the Intelligence officer in Portugal.

The man in Lisbon.

OCTOBER 8, 1939, FAIRFAX, VIRGINIA

There were no names.

Only numbers and letters.

Numbers followed by letters.

Two-Six-B. Three-Five-Y. Five-One-C.

There were no personal histories, no individual backgrounds . . . no references to wives, children, fathers, mothers . . . no countries, cities, hometowns, schools, universities; there were only bodies and minds and separate, specific, reacting intelligences.

The location was deep in the Virginia hunt country, 220 acres of fields and hills and mountain streams. There were sections of dense forest bordering stretches of flat grasslands. Swamps—dangerous with body-sucking earth and hostile inhabitants, reptile and insect—were but feet from sudden masses of Virginia boulders fronting abrupt inclines.

The area had been selected with care, with precision.

It was bordered by a fifteen-foot-high hurricane fence through which a paralyzing—not lethal—electrical current flowed continuously; and every twelve feet there was a forbidding sign that warned observers that this particular section of the land . . . forest, swamp, grassland and hill . . . was the exclusive property of the United States government. Trespassers were duly informed that entry was not only prohibited, it was exceedingly dangerous. Titles and sections of the specific laws pertaining to the exclusivity were spelled out along with the voltage in the fence.

The terrain was as diverse as could be found within a reasonable distance from Washington. In one way or another—one place or another—it conformed remarkably to the topography of the locations projected for those training inside the enormous compound.

The numbers followed by the letters.

No names.

There was a single gate at the center of the north perimeter, reached by a back country road. Over the gate, between the opposing guard houses, was a metal sign. In block letters it read:

FIELD DIVISON HEADQUARTERS—FAIRFAX.

No other description was given, no purpose identified.

On the front of each guard house were identical signs, duplicates of the warnings placed every twelve feet in the fence, proclaiming the exclusivity, the laws and the voltage.

No room for error.

David Spaulding was assigned an identity—his Fairfax identity. He was Two-Five-L.

No name. Only a number followed by a letter.

Two—Five—L.

Translation: his training was to be completed by the fifth day of the second month. His destination: Lisbon.

It was incredible. In the space of four months a new way of life—of *living*—was to be absorbed with such totality that it strained acceptance.

"You probably won't make it," said Colonel Edmund Pace.

"I'm not sure I want to," had been Spaulding's reply.

But part of the training was motivation. Deep, solid, ingrained beyond doubt . . . but not beyond the psychological reality as perceived by the candidate.

With Two-Five-L, the United States government did not wave flags and roar espousals of patriotic causes. Such methods would not be meaningful; the candidate had spent his formative years outside the country in a sophisticated, international environment. He spoke the language of the enemy-to-be; he knew them as people—taxi drivers, grocers, bankers, lawyers—and the vast majority of those he knew were not the Germans fictionalized by the propaganda machines. Instead—and this was Fairfax's legitimate hook—they were goddamned fools being led by psychopathic criminals. The leaders were, indeed, fanatics, and the overwhelming evidence clearly established their crimes beyond doubt. Those crimes included wanton, indiscriminate murder, torture and genocide.

Beyond doubt.

Criminals.

Psychopaths.

Too, there was Adolf Hitler.

Adolf Hitler killed Jews. By the thousands—soon to be millions if his *final solutions* were read accurately.

Aaron Mandel was a Jew. His other "father" was a Jew; the "father" he loved more than the parent. And the goddamned fools tolerated an exclamation point after the word *Juden!*

David Spaulding could bring himself to hate the goddamned fools—the taxi drivers, the grocers, the bankers, the lawyers—without much compunction under the circumstances.

Beyond this very rational approach, Fairfax utilized a secondary psychological "weapon" that was standard in the compound; for some more than others, but it was never absent.

The trainees at Fairfax had a common gift—or flaw—depending on one's approach. None was accepted without it.

A highly developed sense of competition; a thrust to win.

There was no question about it; arrogance was not a despised commodity at Fairfax.

With David Spaulding's psychological profile—a dossier increasingly accepted by the Intelligence Division—the Fairfax commanders recognized that the candidate-in-training for Lisbon had a soft core which the field might harden—undoubtedly *would* harden if he lived that long—but whatever advances could be made in the compound, so much the better. Especially for the subject.

Spaulding was confident, independent, extremely versatile in his surroundings . . . all to the very good; but Two-Five-L had a weakness. There was within his psyche a slowness to take immediate advantage, a hesitancy to spring to the kill when the odds were his. Both verbally and physically.

Colonel Edmund Pace saw this inadequacy by the third week of training. Two-Five-L's abstract code of fairness would never do in Lisbon. And Colonel Pace knew the answer.

The mental adjustment would be made through the physical processes.

"Seizures, Holds and Releases" was the insipid title of the course. It disguised the most arduous physical training at Fairfax: hand-to-hand combat. Knife, chain, wire, needle, rope, fingers, knees, elbows . . . never a gun.

Reaction, reaction, reaction.

Except when one initiated the assault.

Two-Five-L had progressed nicely. He was a large man but possessed the quick coordination usually associated with a more compact person. Therefore his progress had to be stymied; the man himself humiliated. He would learn the practical advantages of the odds.

From smaller, more arrogant men.

Colonel Edmund Pace "borrowed" from the British commando units the best they had in uniform. They were flown over by the Bomber Ferry Command; three bewildered "specialists" who were subtly introduced to the Fairfax compound and given their instructions.

"Kick the shit out of Two-Five-L."

They did. For many weeks of sessions.

And then they could not do so with impunity any longer.

David Spaulding would not accept the humiliation; he was becoming as good as the "specialists."

The man for Lisbon was progressing.

Colonel Edmund Pace received the reports in his War Department office.

Everything was on schedule.

The weeks became months. Every known portable offensive and defensive weapon, every sabotage device, every conceivable method of ingress and egress—apparent and covert—was exhaustively studied by the Fairfax trainees. Codes and variations became fluent languages; instant fabrications second nature. And Two-Five-L continued to advance. Whenever there appeared a slackening, harsher instructions were given to the "specialists" in "Seizures, Holds and Releases." The psychological key was in the observable, physical humiliation.

Until it was no longer viable. The commandos were bested.

Everything on schedule.

"You may make it after all," said the colonel.

"I'm not sure what I've made," replied David in his first lieutenant's uniform, over a drink in the Mayflower Cocktail Lounge. And then he laughed quietly. "I suppose if they gave degrees in Advanced Criminal Activities, I'd probably qualify."

Two-Five-L's training would be completed in ten days. His twenty-four-hour pass was an irregularity, but Pace had demanded it. He had to talk with Spaulding.

"Does it bother you?" asked Pace.

Spaulding looked across the small table at the colonel. "If I had time to think about it, I'm sure it would. Doesn't it bother you?"

"No. . . . Because I understand the reasons."

"O.K. Then so do I."

"They'll become clearer in the field."

"Sure," agreed David tersely.

Pace watched Spaulding closely. As was to be expected, the young man had changed. Gone was the slightly soft, slightly pampered grace of inflection and gesture. These had been replaced by a tautness, a conciseness of movement and speech. The transformation was not complete, but it was well in progress.

The patina of the professional was beginning to show through. Lisbon would harden it further.

"Are you impressed by the fact that Fairfax skips you a rank? It took me eighteen months to get that silver bar."

"Again, time. I haven't had time to react. I haven't worn a uniform before today; I think it's uncomfortable." Spaulding flicked his hand over his tunic.

"Good. Don't get used to it."

"That's a strange thing to say. . . ."

"How do you feel?" said Pace, interrupting.

David looked at the colonel. For a moment or two, the grace, the softness—even the wry humor—returned. "I'm not sure. . . . As though I'd been manufactured on a very fast assembly line. A sort of high-speed treadmill, if you know what I mean."

"In some ways that's an accurate description. Except that you brought a lot to the factory."

Spaulding revolved his glass slowly. He stared at the floating cubes, then up at Pace. "I wish I could accept that as a compliment," he said softly. "I don't think I can. I know the people I've been training with. They're quite a collection."

"They're highly motivated."

"The Europeans are as crazy as those they want to fight. They've got their reasons; I can't question them. . . ."

"Well," interrupted the colonel, "we don't have that many Americans. Not yet."

"Those you do are two steps from a penitentiary."

"They're not army."

"I didn't know that," said Spaulding quickly, adding the obvious with a smile. "Naturally."

Pace was annoyed with himself. The indiscretion was minor but still an indiscretion. "It's not important. In ten days you'll be finished in Virginia. The uniform comes off then. To tell you the truth, it was a mistake to issue you one in the first place. We're still new at this kind of thing; rules of requisition and supply are hard to change." Pace drank and avoided Spaulding's eyes.

"I thought I was supposed to be a military attaché at the embassy. One of several."

"For the record, yes. They'll build a file on you. But there's a difference; it's part of the cover. You're not partial to uniforms. We don't think you should wear one. Ever." Pace put down his glass and looked at David. "You hustled yourself a very safe, very comfortable job because of the languages, your residences and your family connections. In a nutshell, you ran as fast as you could when you thought there was a chance your pretty neck might be in the real army."

Spaulding thought for a moment. "That sounds logical. Why does it bother you?"

"Because only one man at the embassy will know the truth. He'll identify himself. . . . After a while others may suspect—after a long while. But they won't know. Not the ambassador, not the staff. . . . What I'm trying to tell you is, you won't be very popular."

David laughed quietly. "I trust you'll rotate me before I'm lynched."

Pace's reply was swift and quiet, almost curt. "Others will be rotated. Not you."

Spaulding was silent as he responded to the colonel's look. "I don't understand."

"I'm not sure I can be clear about it." Pace put down his drink on the small cocktail table. "You'll have to start slowly, with extreme caution. British MI-5 has given us a few names—not many but something to start with. You'll have to build up your own network, however. People who will maintain contact only with you, no one else. This will entail a great deal of traveling. We think you'll gravitate to the north country, across the borders into Spain. Basque country . . . by and large anti-Falangist. We think those areas south of the Pyrenees will become the data and escape routes. . . . We're not kidding ourselves: the Maginot won't hold. France will fall. . . ."

"Jesus," interrupted David softly. "You've done a lot of projecting."

"That's almost *all* we do. It's the reason for Fairfax."

Spaulding leaned back in the chair, once more revolving his glass. "I understand about the network; in one form or another it's what the compound's training all of us for. This is the first I've heard about the north of Spain, the Basque areas. I know that country."

"We could be wrong. It's only a theory. You might find the water routes . . . Mediterranean, Málaga, or Biscay, or the Portuguese coast . . . more feasible. That's for you to decide. And develop."

"All right. I understand. . . . What's that got to do with rotation?"

Pace smiled. "You haven't reached your post. Are you angling for a leave already?"

"You brought it up. Sort of abruptly, I think."

"Yes, I did." The colonel shifted his position in the small chair. Spaulding was very quick; he locked in on words and used brief time spans to maximize their effectiveness. He would be good in interrogations. Quick, harsh inquiries. In the field. "We've decided that you're to remain in Portugal for the duration. Whatever normal and 'abnormal' leaves you take should be spent in the south. There's a string of colonies along the coast. . . ."

"Costa del Santiago among them," interjected Spaulding under his breath. "Retreats for the international rich."

"That's right. Develop covers down there. Be seen with your parents. Become a fixture." Pace smiled again; the smile was hesitant. "I could think of worse duty."

"You don't know those colonies. . . . If I read you—as we say in Fairfax—Candidate Two-Five-L had better take a good, hard look at the streets of Washington and New York because he's not going to see them again for a very long time."

"We can't risk bringing you back once you've developed a network, assuming you *do* develop one. If, for whatever reason, you flew out of Lisbon to Allied territory, there'd be an enemy scramble to microscopically trace every movement you made for months. It would jeopardize everything. *You're* safest—*our interests* are safest—if you remain permanent. The British taught us this. Some of their operatives have been local fixtures for years."

"That's not very comforting."

"You're not in MI-5. Your tour is for the duration. The war won't last forever."

It was Spaulding's turn to smile; the smile of a man caught in a matrix he had not defined. "There's something insane about that statement. . . . 'The war won't last forever.' . . ."

"Why?"

"We're not in it yet."

"You are," Pace said.

TWO

SEPTEMBER 8, 1943, PEENEMÜNDE, GERMANY

The man in the pinstriped suit, styled by tailors in Alte Strasse, stared in disbelief at the three men across the table. He would have objected strenuously had the three laboratory experts not worn the square red metal insignias on the lapels of their starched white laboratory jackets, badges that said these three scientists were permitted to walk through passageways forbidden to all but the elite of Peenemünde. He, too, had such a badge attached to his pinstriped lapel; it was a temporary clearance he was not sure he wanted.

Certainly he did not want it now.

"I can't accept your evaluation," he said quietly. "It's preposterous."

"Come with us," replied the scientist in the center, nodding to his companion on the right.

"There's no point procrastinating," added the third man.

The four men got out of their chairs and approached the steel door that was the single entrance to the room. Each man in succession unclipped his red badge and pressed it against a grey plate in the wall. At the instant of contact, a small white bulb was lighted, remained so for two seconds and then went off; a photograph had been taken. The last man—one of the Peenemünde personnel—then opened the door and each went into the hallway.

Had only three men gone out, or five, or any number not corresponding to the photographs, alarms would have been triggered.

They walked in silence down the long, starched-white corridor, the Berliner in front with the scientist who sat between the other two at the table, and was obviously the spokesman; his companions were behind.

They reached a bank of elevators and once more went through the ritual of the red tags, the grey plate and the tiny white light that went on for precisely two seconds. Below the plate a number was also lighted.

Six.

From elevator number six there was the sound of a single muted bell as the thick steel panel slid open. One by one each man walked inside.

The elevator descended eight stories, four below the surface of the earth, to the deepest levels of Peenemünde. As the four men emerged into yet another white corridor, they were met by a tall man in tight-fitting green coveralls, an outsized holster in his wide brown belt. The holster held a Lüger Sternlicht, a specially designed arm pistol with a telescopic sight. As the man's visor cap indicated, such weapons were made for the Gestapo.

The Gestapo officer obviously recognized the three scientists. He smiled perfunctorily and turned his attention to the man in the pinstriped suit. He held out his hand, motioning the Berliner to remove the red badge.

The Berliner did so. The Gestapo man took it, walked over to a telephone on the corridor wall and pushed a combination of buttons. He spoke the Berliner's name and waited, perhaps ten seconds.

He replaced the phone and crossed back to the man in the pinstriped suit. Gone was the arrogance he had displayed moments ago.

"I apologize for the delay, Herr Strasser. I should have realized. . . ." He gave the Berliner his badge.

"No need for apologies, Herr Oberleutnant. They would be necessary only if you overlooked your duties."

"Danke," said the Gestapo man, gesturing the four men beyond his point of security.

They proceeded toward a set of double doors; clicks could be heard as locks were released. Small white bulbs were lighted above the moldings; again photographs were taken of those going through the double doors.

They turned right into a bisecting corridor—this one not white, but instead, brownish black; so dark that Strasser's eyes took several seconds to adjust from the pristine brightness of the main halls to the sudden night quality of the passageway. Tiny ceiling lights gave what illumination there was.

"You've not been here before," said the scientist-spokesman to the Berliner. "This hallway was designed by an optics engineer. It supposedly prepares the eyes for the high-intensity microscope lights. Most of us think it was a waste."

There was a steel door at the end of the long, dark tunnel. Strasser reached for his red metal insignia automatically; the scientist shook his head and spoke with a slight wave of his hand.

"Insufficient light for photographs. The guard inside has been alerted."

The door opened and the four men entered a large laboratory. Along the right wall was a row of stools, each in front of a powerful microscope, all the microscopes equidistant from one another on top of a built-in workbench. Behind each microscope was a high-intensity light, projected and shaded on a goose-necked stem coming out of the immaculate white surface. The left wall was a variation of the right. There were no stools, however, and fewer microscopes. The work shelf was higher; it was obviously used for conferences, where many pairs of eyes peered through the same sets of lenses; stools would only interfere, men stood as they conferred over magnified particles.

At the far end of the room was another door; not an entrance. A vault. A seven-foot-high, four-foot-wide, heavy steel vault. It was black; the two levers and the combination wheel were in glistening silver.

The spokesman-scientist approached it.

"We have fifteen minutes before the timer seals the panel and the drawers. I've requested closure for a week. I'll need your counterauthorization, of course."

"And you're sure I'll give it, aren't you?"

"I am." The scientist spun the wheel right and left for the desired locations. "The numbers change automatically every twenty-four hours," he said as he held the wheel steady at its final mark and reached for the silver levers. He pulled the top one down to the accompaniment of a barely audible whirring sound, and seconds later, pulled the lower one up.

The whirring stopped, metallic clicks could be heard and the scientist pulled open the thick steel door. He turned to Strasser. "These are the tools for Peenemünde. See for yourself."

Strasser approached the vault. Inside were five rows of removable glass trays, top to bottom; each row had a total of one hundred trays, five hundred in all.

The trays that were empty were marked with a white

strip across the facing glass, the word *Auffüllen* printed clearly.

The trays that were full were so designated by strips of black across their fronts.

There were four and a half rows of white trays. Empty.

Strasser looked closely, pulled open several trays, shut them and stared at the Peenemünde scientist.

"This is the sole repository?" he asked quietly.

"It is. We have six thousand casings completed; God knows how many will go in experimentation. Estimate for yourself how much further we can proceed."

Strasser held the scientist's eyes with his own. "Do you realize what you're saying?"

"I do. We'll deliver only a fraction of the required schedules. Nowhere near enough. Peenemünde is a disaster."

SEPTEMBER 9, 1943, THE NORTH SEA

The fleet of B-17 bombers had aborted the primary target of Essen due to cloud cover. The squadron commander, over the objections of his fellow pilots, ordered the secondary mission into operation: the shipyards north of Bremerhaven. No one liked the Bremerhaven run; Messerschmitt and Stuka interceptor wings were devastating. They were called the Luftwaffe suicide squads, maniacal young Nazis who might as easily collide with enemy aircraft as fire at them. Not necessarily due to outrageous bravery; often it was merely inexperience or worse: poor training.

Bremerhaven-north was a terrible secondary. When it was a primary objective, the Eighth Air Force fighter escorts took the sting out of the run; they were not there when Bremerhaven was a secondary.

The squadron commander, however, was a hardnose. Worse, he was West Point; the secondary would not only be hit, it would be hit at an altitude that guaranteed maximum accuracy. He did not tolerate the very vocal criticism of his second-in-command aboard the flanking aircraft, who made it clear that such an altitude was barely logical *with* fighter escorts; *without* them, considering the heavy ack-ack fire, it was ridiculous. The squadron commander had replied with a terse recital of the new navigational headings and termination of radio contact.

Once they were into the Bremerhaven corridors, the German interceptors came from all points; the antiaircraft guns were murderous. And the squadron commander took his lead plane directly down into maximum-accuracy altitude and was blown out of the sky.

The second-in-command valued life and the price of aircraft more than his West Point superior. He ordered the squadron to scramble altitudes, telling his bombardiers to unload on anything below but for-God's-sake-release-the-goddamn-weight so all planes could reach their maximum heights and reduce antiaircraft and interceptor fire.

In several instances it was too late. One bomber caught fire and went into a spin; only three chutes emerged from it. Two aircraft were riddled so badly both planes began immediate descents. Pilots and crew bailed out. Most of them.

The remainder kept climbing; the Messerschmitts climbed with them. They went higher and still higher, past the safe altitude range. Oxygen masks were ordered; not all functioned.

But in four minutes, what was left of the squadron was in the middle of the clear midnight sky, made stunningly clearer by the substratosphere absence of air particles. The stars were extraordinary in their flickering brightness, the moon more a bombers' moon than ever before.

Escape was in these regions.

"Chart man!" said the exhausted, relieved second-in-command into his radio, "give us headings! Back to Lakenheath, if you'd be so kind."

The reply on the radio soured the moment of relief. It came from an aerial gunner aft of navigation. "He's dead, colonel. Nelson's dead."

There was no time in the air for comment. "Take it, aircraft three. It's your chart," said the colonel in aircraft two.

The headings were given. The formation grouped and, as it descended into safe altitude with cloud cover above, sped toward the North Sea.

The minutes reached five, then seven, then twelve. Finally twenty. There was relatively little cloud cover below; the coast of England should have come into sighting range at least two minutes ago. A number of pilots were concerned. Several said so.

"Did you give accurate headings, aircraft three?" asked the now squadron commander.

"Affirmative, colonel," was the radioed answer.

"Any of you chart men disagree?"

A variety of negatives was heard from the remaining aircraft.

"No sweat on the headings, colonel," came the voice of the captain of aircraft five. "I fault your execution, though."

"What the hell are you talking about?"

"You pointed two-three-niner by my reading. I figured my equipment was shot up. . . ."

Suddenly there were interruptions from every pilot in the decimated squadron.

"I read one-seven. . . ."

"My heading was a goddamned two-niner-two. We took a direct hit on . . ."

"*Jesus!* I had sixer-four. . . ."

"Most of our middle took a load. I discounted my readings totally!"

And then there was silence. All understood.

Or understood what they could not comprehend.

"Stay off all frequencies," said the squadron commander. "I'll try to reach base."

The cloud cover above broke; not for long, but long enough. The voice over the radio was the captain of aircraft three.

"A quick judgment, colonel, says we're heading due northwest."

Silence again.

After a few moments, the commander spoke. "I'll reach somebody. Do all your gauges read as mine? Fuel for roughly ten to fifteen minutes?"

"It's been a long haul, colonel," said aircraft seven. "No more than that, it's for sure."

"I figured we'd be circling, if we had to, five minutes ago," said aircraft eight.

"We're not," said aircraft four.

The colonel in aircraft two raised Lakenheath on an emergency frequency.

"As near as we can determine," came the strained, agitated, yet controlled English voice, "and by that I mean open lines throughout the coastal defense areas—water and land—you're approaching the Dunbar sector. That's the Scottish border, colonel. What in blazes are you doing there?"

"For Christ's sake, I don't *know!* Are there any fields?"

"Not for *your* aircraft. Certainly not a formation; perhaps one or two. . . ."

"I don't want to hear that, you son of a bitch! Give me emergency instructions!"

"We're really quite unprepared. . . ."

"Do you *read me?!* I have what's left of a very chopped-up squadron! We have less than six minutes' fuel! Now you *give!*"

The silence lasted precisely four seconds. Lakenheath conferred swiftly. With finality.

"We believe you'll sight the coast, probably Scotland. Put your aircraft down at sea. . . . We'll do our best, lads."

"We're eleven *bombers,* Lakenheath! We're not a bunch of ducks!"

"There isn't time, squadron leader. . . . The logistics are insurmountable. After all, we didn't guide you there. Put down at sea. We'll do our best. . . . Godspeed."

PART 1

1

SEPTEMBER 10, 1943, BERLIN, GERMANY

Reichsminister of Armaments Albert Speer raced up the steps of the Air Ministry on the Tiergarten. He did not feel the harsh, diagonal sheets of rain that plummeted down from the grey sky; he did not notice that his raincoat —unbuttoned—had fallen away, exposing his tunic and shirt to the inundation of the September storm. The pitch of his fury swept everything but the immediate crisis out of his mind.

Insanity! Sheer, unmitigated, unforgivable insanity!

The industrial reserves of all Germany were about exhausted; but he could handle that immense problem. Handle it by properly utilizing the manufacturing potential of the occupied countries; reverse the unmanageable practices of importing the labor forces. Labor forces? Slaves!

Productivity disastrous; sabotage continuous, unending.

What did they expect?

It was a time for sacrifice! Hitler could not continue to be all things to all people! He could not provide outsized Mercedeses and grand operas and populated restaurants; he had to provide, instead, tanks, munitions, ships, aircraft! *These* were the priorities!

But the Führer could never erase the memory of the 1918 revolution.

How totally inconsistent! The sole man whose will was shaping history, who was close to the preposterous dream of a thousand-year Reich, was petrified of a long-ago memory of unruly mobs, of unsatisfied masses.

Speer wondered if future historians would record the

fact. If they would comprehend just how weak Hitler really was when it came to his own countrymen. How he buckled in fear when consumer production fell below anticipated schedules.

Insanity!

But still *he*, the Reichsminister of Armaments, could control this calamitous inconsistency as long as he was convinced it was just a question of time. A few months; perhaps six at the outside.

For there was Peenemünde.

The rockets.

Everything reduced itself to Peenemünde!

Peenemünde was irresistible. Peenemünde would cause the collapse of London and Washington. Both governments would see the futility of continuing the exercise of wholesale annihilation.

Reasonable men could then sit down and create reasonable treaties.

Even if it meant the silencing of *un*reasonable men. Silencing Hitler.

Speer knew there were others who thought that way, too. The Führer was manifestly beginning to show unhealthy signs of pressure—fatigue. He now surrounded himself with mediocrity—an ill-disguised desire to remain in the comfortable company of his intellectual equals. But it went too far when the Reich itself was affected. A wine merchant, the foreign minister! A third-rate party propagandizer, the minister of eastern affairs! An erstwhile fighter pilot, the overseer of the *entire economy!*

Even himself. Even the quiet, shy architect; now the minister of armaments.

All that would change with Peenemünde.

Even himself. Thank *God!*

But first there *had* to be Peenemünde. There could be no *question* of its operational success. For without Peenemünde, the war was lost.

And now they were telling him there *was* a question. A flaw that might well be the precursor of Germany's defeat.

A vacuous-looking corporal opened the door of the cabinet room. Speer walked in and saw that the long conference table was about two-thirds filled, the chairs in cliquish separation, as if the groups were suspect of one another. As, indeed, they were in these times of progressively sharpened rivalries within the Reich.

He walked to the head of the table, where—to his right—sat the only man in the room he could trust. Franz Altmüller.

Altmüller was a forty-two-year-old cynic. Tall, blond, aristocratic; the vision of the Third Reich Aryan who did not, for a minute, subscribe to the racial nonsense proclaimed by the Third Reich. He did, however, subscribe to the theory of acquiring whatever benefits came his way by pretending to agree with anyone who might do him some good.

In public.

In private, among his *very* close associates, he told the truth.

When that truth might also benefit him.

Speer was not only Altmüller's associate, he was his friend. Their families had been more than neighbors; the two fathers had often gone into joint merchandising ventures; the mothers had been school chums.

Altmüller had taken after his father. He was an extremely capable businessman; his expertise was in production administration.

"Good morning," said Altmüller, flicking an imaginary thread off his tunic lapel. He wore his party uniform far more often than was necessary, preferring to err on the side of the archangel.

"That seems unlikely," replied Speer, sitting down rapidly. The groups—and they were groups—around the table kept talking among themselves but the voices were perceptibly quieter. Eyes kept darting over in Speer's direction, then swiftly away; everyone was prepared for immediate silence yet none wished to appear apprehensive, guilty.

Silence would come when either Altmüller or Speer himself rose from his chair to address the gathering. That would be the signal. Not before. To render attention before that movement might give the appearance of fear. Fear was equivalent to an admission of error. No one at the conference table could afford that.

Altmüller opened a brown manila folder and placed it in front of Speer. It was a list of those summoned to the meeting. There were essentially three distinct factions with subdivisions within each, and each with its spokesman. Speer read the names and unobtrusively—he thought—looked up to ascertain the presence and location of the three leaders.

At the far end of the table, resplendent in his general's uniform, his tunic a field of decorations going back thirty years, sat Ernst Leeb, Chief of the Army Ordnance Office. He was of medium height but excessively muscular, a condition he maintained well into his sixties. He smoked his cigarette through an ivory holder which he used to cut off his various subordinates' conversations at will. In some ways Leeb was a caricature, yet still a powerful one. Hitler liked him, as much for his imperious military bearing as for his abilities.

At the midpoint of the table, on the left, sat Albert Vögler, the sharp, aggressive general manager of Reich's Industry. Vögler was a stout man, the image of a burgomaster; the soft flesh of his face constantly creased into a questioning scowl. He laughed a great deal, but his laughter was hard; a device, not an enjoyment. He was well suited to his position. Vögler liked nothing better than hammering out negotiations between industrial adversaries. He was a superb mediator because all parties were usually frightened of him.

Across from Vögler and slightly to the right, toward Altmüller and Speer, was Wilhelm Zangen, the Reich official of the German Industrial Association. Zangen was thin-lipped, painfully slender, humorless; a fleshed-out skeleton happiest over his charts and graphs. A precise man who was given to perspiring at the edge of his receding hairline and below the nostrils and on his chin when nervous. He was perspiring now, and continuously brought his handkerchief up to blot the embarrassing moisture. Somewhat in contradiction to his appearance, however, Zangen was a persuasive debater. For he never argued without the facts.

They were all persuasive, thought Speer. And if it were not for his anger, he knew such men could—probably would—intimidate him. Albert Speer was honest in self-assessment; he realized that he had no substantial sense of authority. He found it difficult to express his thoughts forthrightly among such potentially hostile men. But now the potentially hostile men were in a defensive position. He could not allow his anger to cause them to panic, to seek only absolution for themselves.

They needed a remedy. Germany needed a remedy.

Peenemünde had to be saved.

"How would you suggest we begin?" Speer asked Altmüller, shading his voice so no one else at the table could hear him.

"I don't think it makes a particle of difference. It will take an hour of very loud, very boring, very obtuse explanations before we reach anything concrete."

"I'm not interested in explanations. . . ."

"Excuses, then."

"Least of all, excuses. I want a solution."

"If it's to be found at this table—which, frankly, I doubt—you'll have to sit through the excess verbiage. Perhaps something will come of it. Again, I doubt it."

"Would you care to explain that?"

Altmüller looked directly into Speer's eyes. "Ultimately, I'm not sure there is a solution. But if there is, I don't think it's at this table. . . . Perhaps I'm wrong. Why don't we listen first?"

"All right. Would you please open with the summary you prepared? I'm afraid I'd lose my temper midway through."

"May I suggest," Altmüller whispered, "that it will be necessary for you to lose your temper at some point during this meeting. I don't see how you can avoid it."

"I understand."

Altmüller pushed back his chair and stood up. Grouping by grouping the voices trailed off around the table.

"Gentlemen. This emergency session was called for reasons of which we assume you are aware. At least you should be aware of them. Apparently it is only the Reichsminister of Armaments and his staff who were not informed; a fact which the Reichsminister and his staff find appalling. . . . In short words, the Peenemünde operation faces a crisis of unparalleled severity. In spite of the millions poured into this most vital weaponry development, in spite of the assurances consistently offered by your respective departments, we now learn that production may be brought to a complete halt within a matter of weeks. Several months prior to the *agreed-upon* date for the first operational rockets. That date has never been questioned.

It has been the keystone for whole military strategies; entire armies have been maneuvered to coordinate with it. Germany's victory is predicated on it. . . . But now Peenemünde is threatened; Germany is threatened. . . . If the projections the Reichsminister's staff have compiled—*unearthed* and compiled—are valid, the Peenemünde complex will exhaust its supply of industrial diamonds in less than ninety days. Without industrial diamonds the precision tooling in Peenemünde cannot continue."

The babble of voices—excited, guttural, vying for attention—erupted the second Altmüller sat down. General Leeb's cigarette holder slashed the air in front of him as though it were a saber; Albert Vögler scowled and wrinkled his flesh-puffed eyes, placed his bulky hands on the table and spoke harshly in a loud monotone; Wilhelm Zangen's handkerchief was working furiously around his face and his neck, his high-pitched voice in conflict with the more masculine tones around him.

Franz Altmüller leaned toward Speer. "You've seen cages of angry ocelots in the zoo? The zookeeper can't let them hurl themselves into the bars. I suggest you lose your benign temper far earlier than we discussed. Perhaps now."

"That is not the way."

"Don't let them think you are cowed. . . ."

"Nor that I am cowering." Speer interrupted his friend, the slightest trace of a smile on his lips. He stood up. "Gentlemen."

The voices trailed off.

"Herr Altmüller speaks harshly; he does so, I'm sure, because I spoke harshly with him. That was this morning, very early this morning. There is greater perspective now; it is no time for recriminations. This is not to lessen the critical aspects of the situation, for they are great. But anger will solve nothing. And we need solutions. . . . Therefore, I propose to seek your assistance—the assistance of the finest industrial and military minds in the Reich. First, of course, we need to know the specifics. I shall start with Herr Vögler. As manager of Reich's Industry, would you give us your estimate?"

Vögler was upset; he didn't wish to be the first called. "I'm not sure I can be of much enlightenment, Herr

Reichsminister. I, too, am subject to the reports given me. They have been optimistic; until the other week there was no suggestion of difficulty."

"How do you mean, optimistic?" asked Speer.

"The quantities of bortz and carbonado diamonds were said to be sufficient. Beyond this there are the continuing experiments with lithicum, carbon and paraffin. Our intelligence tells us that the Englishman Storey at the British Museum reverified the Hannay-Moissan theories. Diamonds *were* produced in this fashion."

"Who verified the Englishman?" Franz Altmüller did not speak kindly. "Had it occurred to you that such data was meant to be passed?"

"Such verification is a matter for Intelligence. I am not with Intelligence, Herr Altmüller."

"Go on," said Speer quickly. "What else?"

"There is an Anglo-American experiment under the supervision of the Bridgemann team. They are subjecting graphite to pressures in excess of six million pounds per square inch. So far there is no word of success."

"Is there word of failure?" Altmüller raised his aristocratic eyebrows, his tone polite.

"I remind you again, I am not with Intelligence. I have received no word whatsoever."

"Food for thought, isn't it," said Altmüller, without asking a question.

"Nevertheless," interrupted Speer before Vögler could respond, "you had reason to assume that the quantities of bortz and carbonado were sufficient. Is that not so?"

"Sufficient. Or at least obtainable, Herr Reichsminister."

"How so obtainable?"

"I believe General Leeb might be more knowledgeable on that subject."

Leeb nearly dropped his ivory cigarette holder. Altmüller noted his surprise and cut in swiftly. "Why would the army ordnance officer have that information, Herr Vögler? I ask merely for my own curiosity."

"The reports, once more. It is my understanding that the Ordnance Office is responsible for evaluating the industrial, agricultural and mineral potentials of occupied territories. Or those territories so projected."

Ernst Leeb was not entirely unprepared. He *was* unprepared for Vögler's insinuations, not for the subject. He turned to an aide, who shuffled papers top to bottom as Speer inquired.

"The Ordnance Office is under enormous pressure these days; as is your department, of course, Herr Vögler. I wonder if General Leeb has had the time . . ."

"We *made* the time," said Leeb, his sharp military bearing pitted in counterpoint to Vögler's burgomaster gruffness. "When we received word—from Herr Vögler's subordinates—that a crisis was imminent—not upon us, but imminent—we immediately researched the possibilities for extrication."

Franz Altmüller brought his hand to his mouth to cover an involuntary smile. He looked at Speer, who was too annoyed to find any humor in the situation.

"I'm relieved the Ordnance Office is so confident, general," said Speer. The Reichsminister of Armaments had *little* confidence in the military and had difficulty disguising it. "Please, your extrication?"

"I said *possibilities,* Herr Speer. To arrive at practical solutions *will* take more time than we've been given."

"Very well. Your possibilities?"

"There is an immediate remedy with historical precedent." Leeb paused to remove his cigarette, crushing it out, aware that everyone around the table watched him intently. "I have taken the liberty of recommending preliminary studies to the General Staff. It involves an expeditionary force of less than four battalions. . . . Africa. The diamond mines east of Tanganyika."

"What?" Altmüller leaned forward; he obviously could not help himself. "You're not serious."

"Please!" Speer would not allow his friend to interrupt. If Leeb had even conceived of such drastic action, it might have merit. No military man, knowing the thin line of combat strength—chewed up on the Eastern Front, under murderous assault by the Allies in Italy—could suggest such an absurdity unless he had a realistic hope of success. "Go ahead, general."

"The Williamson Mines at Mwadui. Between the districts of Tanganyika and Zanzibar in the central sector. The mines at Mwadui produce over a million carats of the carbonado diamond annually. Intelligence—the intelligence that is forwarded regularly to me at my insistence—

informs us that there are supplies going back several months. Our agents in Dar es Salaam are convinced such an incursion would be successful."

Franz Altmüller passed a sheet of paper to Speer. On it he had scribbled: "He's lost his senses!"

"What is the historical precedent to which you refer?" asked Speer, holding his hand over Altmüller's paper.

"All of the districts east of Dar es Salaam rightfully belong to the Third Reich, German West Africa. They were taken from the fatherland after the Great War. The Führer himself made that clear four years ago."

There was silence around the table. An embarrassed silence. The eyes of even his aides avoided the old soldier. Finally Speer spoke quietly.

"That is justification, not precedent, general. The world cares little for our justifications, and although I question the logistics of moving battalions halfway around the globe, you may have raised a valid point. Where else nearer . . . in *East* Africa, perhaps, can the bortz or the carbonado be found?"

Leeb looked to his aides; Wilhelm Zangen lifted his handkerchief to his nostrils and bowed his thin head in the direction of the general. He spoke as if exhaling, his high voice irritating.

"I'll answer you, Herr Reichsminister. And then, I believe, you will see how fruitless this discussion is. . . . Sixty per cent of the world's crushing-bortz diamonds are in the Belgian Congo. The two principal deposits are in the Kasai and Bakwanga fields, between the Kanshi and the Bushimaie rivers. The district's governor-general is Pierre Ryckmans; he is devoted to the Belgian government in exile in London. I can assure Leeb that the Congo's allegiances to Belgium are far greater than ours ever were in Dar es Salaam."

Leeb lit a cigarette angrily. Speer leaned back in his chair and addressed Zangen.

"All right. Sixty per cent crushing-bortz; what of carbonado and the rest?"

"French Equatorial: totally allied to de Gaulle's Free French. Ghana and Sierra Leone: the tightest of British controls. Angola: Portuguese domination and their neutrality's inviolate; we know that beyond doubt. French West Africa: not only under Free French mandate but with Allied forces manning the outposts. . . . Here, there was only one possibility and we lost it a year and a half ago. Vichy abandoned the Ivory Coast. . . . There is no access in Africa, Reichsminister. None of a military nature."

"I see." Speer doodled on top of the paper Altmüller had passed to him. "You are recommending a nonmilitary solution?"

"There is no other. The question is what."

Speer turned to Franz Altmüller. His tall, blond associate was staring at them all. Their faces were blank. Baffled.

2

SEPTEMBER 11, 1943, WASHINGTON, D.C.

Brigadier General Alan Swanson got out of the taxi and looked up at the huge oak door of the Georgetown residence. The ride over the cobblestone streets had seemed like a continuous roll of hammering drums.

Prelude to execution.

Up those steps, inside that door, somewhere within that five-story brownstone and brick aristocratic home, was a large room. And inside that room thousands of executions would be pronounced, unrelated to any around the table within that room.

Prelude to annihilation.

If the schedules were kept. And it was inconceivable that they would be altered.

Wholesale murder.

In line with his orders he glanced up and down the street to make sure he hadn't been followed. Asinine! CIC had all of them under constant surveillance. Which of the pedestrians or slowly moving automobiles had him in their sights? It didn't matter; the choice of the meeting place was asinine, too. Did they really believe they could keep the crisis a secret? Did they think that holding conferences in secluded Georgetown houses would help?

Asses!

He was oblivious to the rain; it came down steadily, in straight lines. An autumn rainstorm in Washington. His raincoat was open, the jacket of his uniform damp and wrinkled. He didn't give a damn about such things; he couldn't think about them.

The only thing he could think about was packaged in a metal casing no more than seven inches wide, five high, and perhaps a foot long. It was designed for those dimensions; it had the appearance of sophisticated technology; it was tooled to operate on the fundamental properties of inertia and precision.

And it wasn't functional; it didn't work.

It failed test after test.

Ten thousand high-altitude B-17 bomber aircraft were emerging from production lines across the country. Without high-altitude, radio-beam gyroscopes to guide them, they might as well stay on the ground!

And without those aircraft, Operation Overlord was in serious jeopardy. The invasion of Europe would extract a price so great as to be obscene.

Yet to send the aircraft up on massive, round-the-clock, night and day bombing strikes throughout Germany without the cover of higher altitudes was to consign the majority to destruction, their crews to death. Examples were constant reminders . . . whenever the big planes soared too high. The labels of pilot error, enemy fire and instrument fatigue were not so. It was the higher altitudes. . . . Only twenty-four hours ago a squadron of bombers on the Bremerhaven run had scrambled out of the strike, exacting the maximum from their aircraft, and regrouped far above oxygen levels. From what could be determined, the guidance systems went crazy; the squadron ended up in the Dunbar sector near the Scottish border. All but one plane crashed into the sea. Three survivors were picked up by coastal patrols. Three out of God knows how many that had made it out of Bremerhaven. The one aircraft that attempted a ground landing had blown up on the outskirts of a town. . . . No survivors.

Germany was in the curve of inevitable defeat, but it would not die easily. It was ready for counterstrike. The Russian lesson had been learned; Hitler's generals were prepared. They realized that ultimately their only hope for any surrender other than *unconditional* lay in their ability to make the cost of an Allied victory so high it would stagger imagination and sicken the conscience of humanity.

Accommodation would then be reached.

And *that* was unacceptable to the Allies. *Unconditional surrender* was now a tripartite policy; the absolute had been so inculcated that it dared not be tampered with. The fever of total victory had swept the lands; the leaders had shaped that, too. And at this pitch of frenzy, the leaders stared into blank walls seeing nothing others could see and said heroically that losses would be tolerated.

Swanson walked up the steps of the Georgetown house. As if on cue, the door opened, a major saluted and Swanson was admitted quickly. Inside the hallway were four noncommissioned officers in paratroop leggings standing at ready-at-ease; Swanson recognized the shoulder patches of the Ranger battalions. The War Department had set the scene effectively.

A sergeant ushered Swanson into a small, brass-grilled elevator. Two stories up the elevator stopped and Swanson stepped out into the corridor. He recognized the face of the colonel who stood by a closed door at the end of the short hallway. He could not recall his name, however. The man worked in Clandestine Operations and was never much in evidence. The colonel stepped forward, saluting.

"General Swanson? Colonel Pace."

Swanson nodded his salute, offering his hand instead. "Oh, yes. Ed Pace, right?"

"Yes, sir."

"So they pulled you out of the cellars. I didn't know this was your territory."

"It's not, sir. Just that I've had occasion to meet the men you're seeing. Security clearances."

"And with you here they know we're serious." Swanson smiled.

"I'm sure we are, but I don't know what we're serious about."

"You're lucky. Who's inside?"

"Howard Oliver from Meridian. Jonathan Craft from Packard. And the lab man, Spinelli, from ATCO."

"They'll make my day; I can't wait. Who's presiding? Christ, there should be *one* person on our side."

"Vandamm."

Swanson's lips formed a quiet whistle; the colonel nodded in agreement. Frederic Vandamm was Undersecretary of State and rumored to be Cordell Hull's closest associate. If one wanted to reach Roosevelt, the best way was through Hull; if that avenue was closed, one pursued Vandamm.

"That's impressive artillery," Swanson said.

"When they saw him, I think he scared the hell out of Craft and Oliver. Spinelli's in a perpetual daze. He'd figure Patton for a doorman."

"I don't know Spinelli, except by rep. He's supposed to be the best gyro man in the labs. . . . Oliver and Craft I know *too* well. I wish to hell you boys had never cleared them for road maps."

"Not much you can do when they own the roads, sir." The colonel shrugged. It was obvious he agreed with Swanson's estimate.

"I'll give you a clue, Pace. Craft's a social-register flunky. Oliver's the bad meat."

"He's got a lot of it on him," replied the colonel, laughing softly.

Swanson took off his raincoat. "If you hear gunfire, colonel, it's only me fooling around. Walk the other way."

"I accept that as an order, general. I'm deaf," answered Pace as he reached for the handle and opened the door swiftly for his superior.

Swanson walked rapidly into the room. It was a library with the furniture pushed back against the walls and a conference table placed in the center. At the head of the table sat the white-haired, aristocratic Frederic Vandamm. On his left was the obese, balding Howard Oliver, a sheaf of notes in front of him. Opposite Oliver were Craft and a short, dark, bespectacled man Swanson assumed was Gian Spinelli.

The empty chair at the end of the table, facing Vandamm, was obviously for him. It was good positioning on Vandamm's part.

"I'm sorry to be late, Mr. Undersecretary. A staff car would have prevented it. A taxi wasn't the easiest thing to find. . . . Gentlemen?"

The trio of corporate men nodded; Craft and Oliver each uttered a muted "General." Spinelli just stared from behind the thick lenses of his glasses.

"I apologize, General Swanson," said Vandamm in the precise, Anglicized speech that bespoke a background of wealth. "For obvious reasons we did not want this conference to take place in a government office, nor, if known, did we wish any significance attached to the meeting itself. These gentlemen represent War Department gossip, I don't have to tell you that. The absence of urgency was desirable. Staff cars speeding through Washington—don't ask me why, but they never seem to slow down—have a tendency to arouse concern. Do you see?"

Swanson returned the old gentleman's veiled look. Vandamm was a smart one, he thought. It was an impetuous gamble referring to the taxi, but Vandamm had understood. He'd picked it up and used it well, even impartially.

The three corporate men were on notice. At this conference, they were the enemy.

"I've been discreet, Mr. Undersecretary."

"I'm sure you have. Shall we get down to points? Mr. Oliver has asked that he be permitted to open with a general statement of Meridian Aircraft's position."

Swanson watched the heavy-jowled Oliver sort out his notes. He disliked Oliver intensely; there was a fundamental gluttony about him. He was a manipulator; there were so many of them these days. They were everywhere in Washington, piling up huge sums of money from the war; proclaiming the power of the deal, the price of the deal, the price of the power—which they held.

Oliver's rough voice shot out from his thick lips. "Thank you. It's our feeling at Meridian that the . . . *assumed* gravity of the present situation has obscured the real advancements that *have* been made. The aircraft in question has proved beyond doubt its superior capabilities. The new, improved Fortress is ready for operational combat; it's merely a question of desired altitudes."

Oliver abruptly stopped and put his obese hands in front of him, over his papers. He had finished his statement; Craft nodded in agreement. Both men looked noncommittally at Vandamm. Gian Spinelli simply stared at Oliver, his brown eyes magnified by his glasses.

Alan Swanson was astounded. Not necessarily by the brevity of the statement but by the ingenuousness of the lie.

"If that's a position statement, I find it wholly unacceptable. The aircraft in question has *not* proved its capabilities until it's operational at the altitudes specified in the government contracts."

"It's operational," replied Oliver curtly.

"Operational. Not functional, Mr. Oliver. It is not functional until it can be guided from point A to point B at the altitudes called for in the specifications."

"*Specified* as 'intended maximum,' General Swanson," shot back Oliver, smiling an obsequious smile that conveyed anything but courtesy.

"What the hell does that mean?" Swanson looked at Undersecretary Vandamm.

"Mr. Oliver is concerned with a contractual interpretation."

"I'm *not*."

"I *have* to be," replied Oliver. "The War Department has refused payment to Meridian Aircraft Corporation. We have a contract. . . ."

"Take the goddamned contract up with someone else!"

"Anger won't solve anything." Vandamm spoke harshly.

"I'm sorry, Mr. Undersecretary, but I'm not here to discuss *contractual interpretations*."

"I'm afraid you'll have to, General Swanson." Vandamm now spoke calmly. "The Disbursement Office has withheld payment to Meridian on *your* negative authorization. You haven't cleared it."

"Why should I? The aircraft can't do the job we expected."

"It *can* do the job you contracted for," said Oliver, moving his thick neck from Vandamm to the brigadier general. "Rest assured, general, our best efforts are being poured into the *intended* maximum guidance system. We're expending all our resources. We'll reach a breakthrough, we're convinced of that. But until we do, we expect the contracts to be honored. We've met the guarantees."

"Are you suggesting that we take the aircraft *as is?*"

"It's the finest bomber in the air." Jonathan Craft spoke. His soft, high voice was a weak exclamation that floated to a stop. He pressed his delicate fingers together in what he believed was emphasis.

Swanson disregarded Craft and stared at the small face and magnified eyes of the ATCO scientist, Gian Spinelli. "What about the *gyros?* Can you give me an answer, Mr. Spinelli?"

Howard Oliver intruded bluntly. "Use the existing systems. Get the aircraft into combat."

"*No!*" Swanson could not help himself. His was the roar of disgust, let Undersecretary Vandamm say what he liked. "Our strategies call for round-the-clock strikes into the deepest regions of Germany. From all points—known and unknown. Fields in England, Italy, Greece . . . yes, even unlisted bases in Turkey and Yugoslavia; carriers in the Mediterranean and, goddamn it, the Black Sea! Thousands and thousands of planes crowding the air corridors for space. We need the extra altitude! We need the guidance systems to operate at those altitudes! Anything less is unthinkable! . . . I'm sorry, Mr. Vandamm. I believe I'm justifiably upset."

"I understand," said the white-haired Undersecretary of State. "That's why we're here this afternoon. To look for solutions . . . as well as money." The old gentleman shifted his gaze to Craft. "Can you add to Mr. Oliver's remarks, from Packard's vantage point?"

Craft disengaged his lean, manicured fingers and took a deep breath through his nostrils as if he were about to deliver essential wisdom. The executive font of knowledge, thought Alan Swanson, jockeying for a chairman's approval.

"Of course, Mr. Undersecretary. As the major subcontractor for Meridian, we've been as disturbed as the general over the lack of guidance results. We've spared nothing to accommodate. Mr. Spinelli's presence is proof of that. After all, we're the ones who brought in ATCO. . . ." Here Craft smiled heroically, a touch sadly. "As we all know, ATCO is the finest—and most costly. We've spared *nothing*."

"You brought in ATCO," said Swanson wearily, "because your own laboratories couldn't do the job. You submitted cost overruns to Meridian which were passed on to us. I don't see that you spared a hell of a lot."

"Good Lord, general!" exclaimed Craft with very little conviction. "The *time*, the *negotiations* . . . time is money, sir; make no mistake about *that*. I could show you. . . ."

"The general asked *me* a question. I should like to answer him."

The words, spoken with a trace of dialect, came from the tiny scientist, who was either dismissing Craft's nonsense, or oblivious to it, or, somehow, both.

"I'd be grateful, Mr. Spinelli."

"Our progress has been consistent, steady if you like. Not rapid. The problems are great. We believe the distortion of the radio beams beyond certain altitudes varies with temperatures and land-mass curvatures. The solutions lie in alternating compensations. Our experiments continuously narrow that field. . . . Our rate of progress would be more rapid were it not for constant interferences."

Gian Spinelli stopped and shifted his grotesquely magnified eyes to Howard Oliver, whose thick neck and jowled face were suddenly flushed with anger.

"You've had no interference from *us!*"

"And certainly not from Packard!" chimed in Craft. "We've stayed in almost daily contact. Our concerns have never flagged!"

Spinelli turned to Craft. "Your concerns . . . as those of Meridian . . . have been exclusively budgetary, as far as I can see."

"That's preposterous! Whatever financial inquiries were made, were made at the request of the . . . contractor's audit division. . . ."

"And totally necessary!" Oliver could not conceal his fury at the small Italian. "You *laboratory* . . . people don't reconcile! You're *children!*"

For the next thirty seconds the three agitated men babbled excitedly in counterpoint. Swanson looked over at Vandamm. Their eyes met in understanding.

Oliver was the first to recognize the trap. He held up his hand . . . a corporate command, thought Swanson.

"Mr. Undersecretary." Oliver spoke, stifling the pitch of his anger. "Don't let our squabbling convey the wrong impression. We turn out the products."

"You're not turning out this one," said Swanson. "I recall vividly the projections in your bids for the contract. You had everything *turned out then.*"

When Oliver looked at him, Alan Swanson instinctively felt he should reach for a weapon to protect himself. The Meridian executive was close to exploding.

"We relied on subordinates' evaluations," said Oliver slowly, with hostility. "I think the military has had its share of staff errors."

"Subordinates don't plan major strategies."

Vandamm raised his voice. "Mr. Oliver. Suppose General Swanson were convinced it served no purpose withholding funds. What kind of time limits could you *now* guarantee?"

Oliver looked at Spinelli. "What would you estimate?" he asked coldly.

Spinelli's large eyes swept the ceiling. "In candor, I cannot give you an answer. We *could* solve it next week. Or next year."

Swanson quickly reached into his tunic pocket and withdrew a folded page of paper. He spread it out in front of him and spoke swiftly. "According to this memorandum . . . our last communication from ATCO . . . once the guidance system *is* perfected, you state you need six weeks of inflight experimentation. The Montana Proving Grounds."

"That's correct, general. I dictated that myself," said Spinelli.

"Six weeks from next week. Or next year. And assuming the Montana experiments are positive, another month to equip the fleets."

"Yes."

Swanson looked over at Vandamm. "In light of this, Mr. Undersecretary, there's no other course but to alter immediate priorities. Or at least the projections. We can't meet the logistics."

"Unacceptable, General Swanson. We have to meet them."

Swanson stared at the old man. Each knew precisely what the other referred to.

Overlord. The invasion of Europe.

"We must postpone, sir."

"Impossible. That's the word, general."

Swanson looked at the three men around the table. The enemy.

"We'll be in touch, gentlemen," he said.

3

SEPTEMBER 12, 1943, THE BASQUE HILLS, SPAIN

David Spaulding waited in the shadows of the thick, gnarled tree on the rocky slope above the ravine. It was Basque country and the air was damp and cold. The late afternoon sun washed over the hills; his back was to it. He had years ago—it seemed a millennium but it wasn't—learned the advantage of catching the reflections of the sun off the steel of small weapons. His own rifle was dulled with burnt, crushed cork.

Four.

Strange, but the number *four* kept coming to mind as he scanned the distance.

Four.

Four years and four days ago exactly. And this afternoon's contract was scheduled for precisely four o'clock in the afternoon.

Four years and four days ago he had first seen the creased brown uniforms behind the thick glass partition in the radio studio in New York. Four years and four days ago since he had walked toward that glass wall to pick up his raincoat off the back of a chair and realized that the eyes of the older officer were looking at him. Steadily. Coldly. The younger man avoided him, as if guilty of intrusion, but not his superior, not the lieutenant colonel.

The lieutenant colonel had been studying him.

That was the beginning.

He wondered now—as he watched the ravine for signs of movement—when it would end. Would he be alive to see it end?

He intended to be.

He had called it a treadmill once. Over a drink at the Mayflower in Washington. Fairfax had *been* a treadmill; still, he had not known at the time how completely accurate that word would continue to be: a racing treadmill that never stopped.

It slowed down occasionally. The physical and mental pressures demanded deceleration at certain recognizable times—recognizable to him. Times when he realized he was getting careless . . . or too sure of himself. Or too absolute with regard to decisions that took human life.

Or might take his.

They were often too easily arrived at. And sometimes that frightened him. Profoundly.

During such times he would take himself away. He would travel south along the Portuguese coast where the enclaves of the temporarily inconvenienced rich denied the existence of war. Or he would stay in Costa del Santiago—with his perplexed parents. Or he would remain within the confines of the embassy in Lisbon and engross himself in the meaningless chores of neutral diplomacy. A minor military attaché who did not wear a uniform. It was not expected in the streets; it was inside the "territory." He did not wear one, however; no one cared. He was not liked very much. He socialized too frequently, had too many prewar friends. By and large, he was ignored . . . with a certain disdain.

At such times he rested. Forced his mind to go blank; to recharge itself.

Four years and four days ago such thoughts would have been inconceivable.

Now they consumed him. When he had the time for such thoughts.

Which he did not have now.

There was still no movement in the ravine. Something was wrong. He checked his watch; the team from San Sebastián was too far behind schedule. It was an abnormal delay. Only six hours ago the French underground had radioed that everything was secure; there were no complications, the team had started out.

The runners from San Sebastián were bringing out photographs of the German airfield installations north of Mont-de-Marsan. The strategists in London had been screaming for them for months. Those photographs had cost the lives of four . . . again, that goddamned number . . . four underground agents.

If anything, the team should have been early; the runners should have been waiting for the man from Lisbon.

Then he saw it in the distance; perhaps a half a mile away, it was difficult to tell. Over the ravine, beyond the opposite slope, from one of the miniature hills. A flashing.

An intermittent but rhythmic flashing. The measured spacing was a mark of intent, not accident.

They were being signaled. *He* was being signaled by someone who knew his methods of operation well; perhaps someone he had trained. It was a warning.

Spaulding slung the rifle over his shoulder and pulled the strap taut, then tighter still so that it became a fixed but flexible appendage to his upper body. He felt the hasp of his belt holster; it was in place, the weapon secure. He pushed himself away from the trunk of the old tree and, in a crouching position, scrambled up the remainder of the rock-hewn slope.

On the ridge he ran to his left, into the tall grass toward the remains of a dying pear orchard. Two men in mud-caked clothes, rifles at their sides, were sitting on the ground playing trick knife, passing the time in silence. They snapped their heads up, their hands reaching for their guns.

Spaulding gestured to them to remain on the ground. He approached and spoke quietly in Spanish.

"Do either of you know who's on the team coming in?"

"Bergeron, I think," said the man on the right. "And probably Chivier. That old man has a way with patrols; forty years he's peddled across the border."

"Then it's Bergeron," said Spaulding.

"What is?" asked the second man.

"We're being signaled. They're late and someone is using what's left of the sun to get our attention."

"Perhaps to tell you they're on their way." The first man put the knife back in his scabbard as he spoke.

"Possible but not likely. We wouldn't go anywhere. Not for a couple of hours yet." Spaulding raised himself partially off the ground and looked eastward. "Come on! We'll head down past the rim of the orchard. We can get a cross view there."

The three men in single file, separated but within hearing of each other, raced across the field below the high ground for nearly four hundred yards. Spaulding positioned himself behind a low rock that jutted over the edge of the ravine. He waited for the other two. The waters below were about a hundred feet straight down, he judged. The team from San Sebastián would cross them approximately two hundred yards west, through the shallow, narrow passage they always used.

The two other men arrived within seconds of each other.

"The old tree where you stood was the mark, wasn't it?" asked the first man.

"Yes," answered Spaulding, removing his binoculars from a case opposite his belt holster. They were powerful, with Zeiss Ikon lenses, the best Germany produced. Taken from a dead German at the Tejo River.

"Then why come down here? If there's a problem, your line of vision was best where you were. It's more direct."

"If there's a problem, they'll know that. They'll flank to their left. East. To the west the ravine heads *away* from the mark. Maybe it's nothing. Perhaps you were right; they just want us to know they're coming."

A little more than two hundred yards away, just west of the shallow passage, two men came into view. The Spaniard who knelt on Spaulding's left touched the American's shoulder.

"It's Bergeron and Chivier," he said quietly.

Spaulding held up his hand for silence and scanned the area with the binoculars. Abruptly he fixed them in one position. With his left hand he directed the attention of his subordinates to the spot.

Below them, perhaps fifty yards, four soldiers in Wehrmacht uniforms were struggling with the foliage, approaching the waters of the ravine.

Spaulding moved his binoculars back to the two Frenchmen, now crossing the water. He held the glasses steady against the rock until he could see in the woods behind the two men what he knew was there.

A fifth German, an officer, was half concealed in the tangled mass of weeds and low branches. He held a rifle on the two Frenchmen crossing the ravine.

Spaulding passed the binoculars quickly to the first Spaniard. He whispered, "Behind Chivier."

The man looked, then gave the glasses to his countryman.

Each knew what had to be done; even the methods were clear. It was merely a question of timing, precision. From a scabbard behind his right hip, Spaulding withdrew a short carbine bayonet, shortened further by grinding. His two associates did the same. Each peered over the rock at the Wehrmacht men below.

The four Germans, faced with waters waist high and a current—though not excessively strong, nevertheless considerable—strapped their rifles across their shoulders laterally and separated in a downstream column. The lead man started across, testing the depths as he did so.

Spaulding and the two Spaniards came from behind the rock swiftly and slid down the incline, concealed by the foliage, their sounds muffled by the rushing water. In less than half a minute they were within thirty feet of the Wehrmacht men, hidden by fallen tree limbs and overgrowth. David entered the water, hugging the embankment. He was relieved to see that the fourth man—now only fifteen feet in front of him—was having the most difficulty keeping his balance on the slippery rocks. The other three, spaced about ten yards apart, were concentrating on the Frenchmen upstream. Concentrating intently.

The Nazi saw him; the fear, the bewilderment was in the German's eyes. The split second he took to assimilate the shock was the time David needed. Covered by the sounds of the water, Spaulding leaped on the man, his knife penetrating the Wehrmacht throat, the head pushed violently under the surface, the blood mingling with the rushing stream.

There was no time, no second to waste. David released the lifeless form and saw that the two Spaniards were parallel with him on the embankment. The first man, crouched and hidden, gestured toward the lead soldier; the second nodded his head toward the next man. And David knew that the third Wehrmacht soldier was his.

It took no more than the time necessary for Bergeron and Chivier to reach the south bank. The three soldiers were dispatched, their blood-soaked bodies floating downstream, careening off rocks, filling the waters with streaks of magenta.

Spaulding signaled the Spaniards to cross the water to the north embankment. The first man pulled himself up beside David, his right hand bloodied from a deep cut across his palm.

"Are you all right?" whispered Spaulding.

"The blade slipped. I lost my knife." The man swore.

"Get out of the area," said David. "Get the wound dressed at the Valdero farm."

"I can put on a tight bandage. I'll be fine."

The second Spaniard joined them. He winced at the sight of his countryman's hand, an action Spaulding thought inconsistent for a guerrilla who had just minutes ago plunged a blade into the neck of a man, slicing most of his head off.

"That looks bad," he said.

"You can't function," added Spaulding, "and we don't have time to argue."

"I can. . . ."

"You *can't.*" David spoke peremptorily. "Go back to Valdero's. I'll see you in a week or two. Get going and stay out of sight!"

"Very well." The Spaniard was upset but it was apparent that he would not, could not, disobey the American's commands. He started to crawl into the woods to the east.

Spaulding called quietly, just above the rush of the water. "Thank you. Fine work today."

The Spaniard grinned and raced into the forest, holding his wrist.

Just as swiftly, David touched the arm of the second man, beckoning him to follow. They sidestepped their way along the bank upstream. Spaulding stopped by a fallen tree whose trunk dipped down into the ravine waters. He turned and crouched, ordering the Spaniard to do the same. He spoke quietly.

"I want him alive. I want to question him."

"I'll get him."

"No, I will. I just don't want you to fire. There could be a backup patrol." Spaulding realized as he whispered that the man couldn't help but smile. He knew why: his Spanish had the soft lilt of Castilian, a foreigner's Castilian at that. It was out of place in Basque country.

As he was out of place, really.

"As you wish, good friend," said the man. "Shall I cross farther back and reach Bergeron? He's probably sick to his stomach by now."

"No, not yet. Wait'll we're secure over here. He and the old man will just keep walking." David raised his head over the fallen tree trunk and estimated distances. The German officer was about sixty yards away, hidden in the woods. "I'll head in there, get behind him. I'll see if I can spot any signs of another patrol. If I do, I'll come back and we'll get out. If not, I'll try to grab him. . . . If anything goes wrong, if he hears me, he'll probably head for the water. Take him."

The Spaniard nodded. Spaulding checked the tautness of his rifle strap, giving it a last-second hitch. He gave his subordinate a tentative smile and saw that the man's hands—huge, calloused—were spread on the ground like claws. If the Wehrmacht officer headed this way, he'd never get by those hands, thought David.

He crept swiftly, silently into the woods, his arms and feet working like a primitive hunter's, warding off branches, sidestepping rocks and tangled foliage.

In less than three minutes he had gone thirty yards behind the German on the Nazi's left flank. He stood immobile and withdrew his binoculars. He scanned the forest and the trail. There were no other patrols. He doubled back cautiously, blending every movement of his body with his surroundings.

When he was within ten feet of the German, who was kneeling on the ground, David silently unlatched his holster and withdrew his pistol. He spoke sharply, though not impolitely, in German.

"Stay where you are or I'll blow your head off."

The Nazi whipped around and awkwardly fumbled for his weapon. Spaulding took several rapid steps and kicked it out of his hands. The man started to rise, and David brought his heavy leather boot up into the side of the German's head. The officer's visor hat fell to the ground; blood poured out of the man's temple, spreading throughout the hairline, streaking down across his face. He was unconscious.

Spaulding reached down and tore at the Nazi's tunic. Strapped across the Oberleutnant's chest was a traveling pouch. David pulled the steel zipper laterally over the waterproofed canvas and found what he was sure he would find.

The photographs of the hidden Luftwaffe installations north of Mont-de-Marsan. Along with the photographs were amateurish drawings that were, in essence, basic blueprints. At least, schematics. Taken from Bergeron, who had then led the German into the trap.

If he could make sense out of them—along with the photographs—he would alert London that sabotage units could inflict the necessary destruction, immobilizing the Luftwaffe complex. He would send in the units himself.

The Allied air strategists were manic when it came to bombing runs. The planes dove from the skies, reducing to rubble and crater everything that was—and was not—a target, taking as much innocent life as enemy. If Spaulding could prevent air strikes north of Mont-de-Marsan, it might somehow . . . abstractly . . . make up for the decision he now had to face.

There were no prisoners of war in the Galician hills, no internment centers in the Basque country.

The Wehrmacht lieutenant, who was so ineffectual in his role of the hunter . . . who might have had a life in some peaceful German town in a peaceful world . . . had to die. And he, the man from Lisbon, would be the executioner. He would revive the young officer, interrogate him at the point of a knife to learn how deeply the Nazis had penetrated the underground in San Sebastián. Then kill him.

For the Wehrmacht officer had seen the man from Lisbon; he could identify that man as David Spaulding.

The fact that the execution would be mercifully quick —unlike a death in partisan hands—was of small comfort to David. He knew that at the instant he pulled the trigger, the world would spin insanely for a moment or two. He would be sick to his stomach and want to vomit, his whole being in a state of revulsion.

But he would not show these things. He would say nothing, indicate nothing . . . silence. And so the legend would continue to grow. For that was part of the treadmill.

The man in Lisbon was a killer.

4

SEPTEMBER 20, 1943, MANNHEIM, GERMANY

Wilhelm Zangen brought the handkerchief to his chin, and then to the skin beneath his nostrils, and finally to the border of his receding hairline. The sweat was profuse; a rash had formed in the cleft below his lips, aggravated by the daily necessity to shave and the continuous pressure.

His whole face was stinging, his embarrassment compounded by Franz Altmüller's final words:

"Really, Wilhelm, you should see a doctor. It's most unattractive."

With that objective solicitousness, Altmüller had gotten up from the table and walked out the door. Slowly, deliberately, his briefcase—the briefcase containing the reports—held down at arm's length as though it had been some diseased appendage.

They had been alone. Altmüller had dismissed the group of scientists without acknowledging any progress whatsoever. He had not even allowed him, the Reich official of German Industry, to thank them for their contributions. Altmüller knew that these were the finest scientific minds in Germany, but he had no understanding of how to handle them. They were sensitive, they were volatile in their own quiet way; they needed praise constantly. He had no patience for tact.

And there *had* been progress.

The Krupp laboratories were convinced that the answer lay in the graphite experiments. Essen had worked around the clock for nearly a month, its managers undergoing one sleepless night after another. They had actually *produced carbon particles* in sealed iron tubes and were convinced these carbons held all the properties required for precision tooling. It was merely a question of time; time to create larger particles, sufficient for tolerance placement within existing machinery.

Franz Altmüller had listened to the Krupp team without the slightest indication of enthusiasm, although enthusiasm certainly had been called for under the circumstances. Instead, when the Krupp spokesman had finished his summary, Altmüller had asked one question. Asked it with the most bored expression imaginable!

"Have these . . . particles been subjected to the pressure of operational tooling?"

Of course they hadn't! How could they have been? They *had* been subjected to artificial, substitute pressures; it was all that was possible at the moment.

That answer had been unacceptable; Altmüller dismissed the most scientifically creative minds in the Reich without a single sentence of appreciation, only ill-disguised hostility.

"Gentlemen, you've brought me words. We don't need words, we need diamonds. We need them, we *must have* them within weeks. Two months at the outside. I suggest you return to your laboratories and consider our problem once again. Good day, gentlemen."

Altmüller was impossible!

After the scientists had left, Altmüller had become even more abrasive.

"Wilhelm," he had said with a voice bordering on contempt, "was *this* the nonmilitary solution of which you spoke to the minister of armaments?"

Why hadn't he used Speer's name? Was it necessary to threaten with the use of titles?

"Of course. Certainly more realistic than that insane march into the Congo. The mines at the Bushimaie River! Madness!"

"The comparison is odious. I overestimated you; I gave you more credit than you deserve. You understand, of course, that you failed." It was not a question.

"I disagree. The results aren't in yet. You can't make such a judgment."

"I can and I have!" Altmüller had slammed the flat of his hand against the tabletop; a crack of soft flesh against hard wood. An intolerable insult. "We have no time! We can't waste weeks while your laboratory misfits play with their bunsen burners, creating little stones that could fall apart at the first contact with steel! We need the *product!*"

"You'll have it!" The surface of Zangen's chin became an oily mixture of sweat and stubble. "The finest minds in all Germany are . . ."

"Are *experimenting.*" Altmüller had interrupted quietly, with scornful emphasis. "Get us the *product*. That's my order to you. Our powerful companies have long histories that go back many years. Certainly one of them can find an old friend."

Wilhelm Zangen had blotted his chin; the rash was agonizing. "We've covered those areas. Impossible."

"Cover them again." Altmüller had pointed an elegant finger at Zangen's handkerchief. "Really, Wilhelm, you should see a doctor. It's most unattractive."

SEPTEMBER 24, 1943, NEW YORK CITY

Jonathan Craft walked up Park Avenue and checked his wristwatch under the spill of a streetlamp. His long, thin fingers trembled; the last vestige of too many martinis, which he had stopped drinking twenty-four hours ago in Ann Arbor. Unfortunately, he had been drunk for the previous three days. He had not been to the office. The office reminded him of General Alan Swanson; he could not bear that memory. Now he had to.

It was a quarter to nine; another fifteen minutes and he would walk into 800 Park Avenue, smile at the doorman and go to the elevator. He did not want to be early, dared not be late. He had been inside the apartment house exactly seven times, and each occasion had been traumatic for him. Always for the same reason: he was the bearer of bad news.

But they needed him. He was the impeccable man. His family was old, fine money; he had been to the right schools, the best cotillions. He had access into areas—social and institutional—the *merchants* would never possess. No matter he was stuck in Ann Arbor; it was a temporary situation, a wartime inconvenience. A sacrifice.

He would be back in New York on the Exchange as soon as the damn thing was over.

He had to keep these thoughts in mind tonight because in a few minutes he would have to repeat the words Swanson had screamed at him in his Packard office. He had written a confidential report of the conversation . . . the *unbelievable* conversation . . . and sent it to Howard Oliver at Meridian.

If you've done what I think you've done, it falls under the heading of treasonable acts! And we're at war!

Swanson.

Madness.

He wondered how many would be there, in the apartment. It was always better if there were quite a few, say a dozen. Then they argued among themselves; he was almost forgotten. Except for his information.

He walked around the block, breathing deeply, calming himself . . . killing ten minutes.

Treasonable acts!

And we're at war!

His watch read five minutes to nine. He entered the building, smiled at the doorman, gave the floor to the elevator operator and, when the brass grill opened, he walked into the private foyer of the penthouse.

A butler took his overcoat and ushered him across the hall, through the door and down three steps into the huge sunken living room.

There were only two men in the room. Craft felt an immediate sharp pain in his stomach. It was an instinctive reaction partly brought on by the fact that there were only two other people for this extremely vital conference, but mainly caused by the sight of Walter Kendall.

Kendall was a man in shadows, a manipulator of figures who was kept out of sight. He was fiftyish, medium-sized, with thinning, unwashed hair, a rasping voice and an undistinguished—shoddy—appearance. His eyes darted continuously, almost never returning another man's look. It was said his mind concentrated incessantly on schemes and counterschemes; his whole purpose in life was apparently to outmaneuver other human beings—friend or enemy, it made no difference to Kendall, for he did not categorize people with such labels.

All were vague opponents.

But Walter Kendall was brilliant at what he did. As long as he could be kept in the background, his manipulations served his clients. And made him a great deal of money—which he hoarded, attested to by ill-fitting suits that bagged at the knees and sagged below the buttocks. But he was always kept out of sight; his presence signified crisis.

Jonathan Craft despised Kendall because he was frightened by him.

The second man was to be expected under the circumstances. He was Howard Oliver, Meridian Aircraft's obese debater of War Department contracts.

"You're on time," said Walter Kendall curtly, sitting down in an armchair, reaching for papers in an open, filthy briefcase at his feet.

"Hello, Jon." Oliver approached and offered a short, neutral handshake.

"Where are the others?" asked Craft.

"No one wanted to be here," answered Kendall with a furtive glance at Oliver. "Howard has to be, and I'm paid to be. You had one hell of a meeting with this Swanson."

"You've read my report?"

"He's read it," said Oliver, crossing to a copper-topped wheel-cart in the corner on which there were bottles and glasses. "He's got questions."

"I made everything perfectly clear. . . ."

"Those aren't the questions," interrupted Kendall while squeezing the tip of a cigarette before inserting it into his mouth. As he struck a match, Craft walked to a large velvet chair across from the accountant and sat down. Oliver had poured himself a whisky and remained standing.

"If you want a drink, Jon, it's over here," said Oliver.

At the mention of alcohol, Kendall glanced up at him from his papers with ferret-like eyes. "No, thank you," Craft replied. "I'd like to get this over with as soon as possible."

"Suit yourself." Oliver looked at the accountant. "Ask your questions."

Kendall, sucking on his cigarette, spoke as the smoke curled around his nostrils. "This Spinelli over at ATCO. Have you talked to him since you saw Swanson?"

"No. There was nothing to say; nothing *I* could say . . . without instructions. As you know, I spoke with Howard on the phone. He told me to wait; write a report and do nothing."

"Craft's the funnel to ATCO," said Oliver. "I didn't want him running scared, trying to smooth things over. It'd look like we were hiding something."

"We are." Kendall removed his cigarette, the ash falling on his trousers. He continued while slowly shuffling the papers on his lap. "Let's go over Spinelli's complaints. As Swanson brought them up."

The accountant touched briefly, concisely on each point raised. They covered Spinelli's statements regarding delayed deliveries, personnel transfers, blueprint holdups, a dozen other minor grievances. Craft replied with equal brevity, answering when he could, stating ignorance when he could not. There was no reason to hide anything.

He had been carrying out instructions, not issuing them.

"Can Spinelli substantiate these charges? And don't kid yourselves, these are charges, not complaints."

"What *charges?*" Oliver spat out the words. "That guinea bastard's fucked up everything! Who's he to make charges?"

"Get off it," said Kendall in his rasping voice. "Don't play games. Save them for a congressional committee, unless I can figure something."

At Kendall's words the sharp pain returned to Craft's stomach. The prospects of disgrace—even remotely associated—could ruin his life. The life he expected to lead back in New York. The financial boors, the *merchants*, could never understand. "That's going a little far. . . ."

Kendall looked over at Craft. "Maybe you didn't *hear* Swanson. It's not going far enough. You got the Fortress contracts because your *projections* said you could do the job."

"Just a minute!" yelled Oliver. "We . . ."

"*Screw* the legal crap!" countered Kendall, shouting over Oliver's interruption. "My firm . . . *me, I* . . . squared those projections. I know what they say, what they implied. You left the other companies at the gate. They wouldn't *say* what you said. Not Douglas, not Boeing, not Lockheed. You were hungry and you got the meat and now you're not delivering. . . . So what else is new? Let's go back: can Spinelli substantiate?"

"*Shit,*" exploded Oliver, heading for the bar.

"How do you mean . . . substantiate?" asked Jonathan Craft, his stomach in agony.

"Are there any memorandums floating around," Kendall tapped the pages in his hand, "that bear on any of this?"

"Well . . ." Craft hesitated; he couldn't stand the pain in his stomach. "When personnel transfers were expedited, they were put into interoffice. . . ."

"The answer's yes," interrupted Oliver in disgust, pouring himself a drink.

"What about financial cutbacks?"

Oliver once again replied. "We obscured those. Spinelli's requisitions just got lost in the paper shuffle."

"Didn't he scream? Didn't *he* shoot off memos?"

"That's Craft's department," answered Oliver, drinking most of his whisky in one swallow. "Spinelli was his little guinea boy."

"Well?" Kendall looked at Craft.

"Well . . . he sent numerous communications." Craft leaned forward in the chair, as much to relieve the pain as to appear confidential. "I removed everything from the files," he said softly.

"*Christ*," exploded Kendall quietly. "I don't give a *shit* what *you* removed. He's got copies. Dates."

"Well, I couldn't say. . . ."

"He didn't type the goddamned things *himself*, did he? You didn't take away the fucking secretaries, *too*, did you?"

"There's no call to be offensive. . . ."

"*Offensive!* You're a funny man! Maybe they've got fancy stripes for you in Leavenworth." The accountant snorted and turned his attention to Howard Oliver. "Swanson's got a case; he'll hang you. Nobody has to be a lawyer to see that. You held back. *You figured to use the existing guidance systems*."

"Only because the new gyroscopes couldn't be developed! Because that guinea bastard fell so far behind he couldn't catch up!"

"Also it saved you a couple of hundred million. . . . You should have primed the pumps, not cut off the water. You're big ducks in a short gallery; a blind man could knock you off."

Oliver put his glass down and spoke slowly. "We don't pay you for that kind of judgment, Walter. You'd better have something else."

Kendall crushed out his mutilated cigarette, his dirty fingernails covered with ash. "I do," he said. "You need company; you're in the middle of a very emotional issue. It'll cost you but you don't have a choice. You've got to make deals; ring in everybody. Get hold of Sperry Rand, GM, Chrysler, Lockheed, Douglas, Rolls-Royce, if you have to . . . every son of a bitch with an engineering laboratory. A patriotic crash program. Cross-reference your data, open up everything you've got."

"They'll steal us blind!" roared Oliver. "Millions!"

"Cost you more if you don't. . . . I'll prepare supplementary financial stats. I'll pack the sheets with so much ice, it'll take ten years to thaw. That'll cost you, too." Kendall smirked, baring soiled teeth.

Howard Oliver stared at the unkempt accountant. "It's crazy," he said quietly. "We'll be giving away fortunes for something that can't be bought because it doesn't exist."

"But you said it *did* exist. You told Swanson it existed —at least a hell of a lot more confidently than anybody else. You sold your great industrial know-how, and when you couldn't deliver, you covered up. Swanson's right. You're a menace to the war effort. Maybe you *should* be shot."

Jonathan Craft watched the filthy, grinning bookkeeper with bad teeth and wanted to vomit. But he was their only hope.

5

SEPTEMBER 25, 1943, STUTTGART, GERMANY

Wilhelm Zangen stood by the window overlooking Stuttgart's Reichssieg Platz, holding a handkerchief against his inflamed, perspiring chin. This outlying section of the city had been spared the bombing; it was residential, even peaceful. The Neckar River could be seen in the distance, its waters rolling calmly, oblivious to the destruction that had been wrought on the other side of the city.

Zangen realized he was expected to speak, to answer von Schnitzler, who spoke for all of I. G. Farben. The two other men were as anxious to hear his words as was von Schnitzler. There was no point in procrastinating. He had to carry out Altmüller's orders.

"The Krupp laboratories have failed. No matter what Essen says, there is no time for experimentation. The Ministry of Armaments has made that clear; Altmüller is resolute. He speaks for Speer." Zangen turned and looked at the three men. "He holds you responsible."

"How can that be?" asked von Schnitzler, his guttural lisp pronounced, his voice angry. "How can we be responsible for something we know nothing about? It's illogical. Ridiculous!"

"Would you wish me to convey that judgment to the ministry?"

"I'll convey it myself, thank you," replied von Schnitzler. "Farben is not involved."

"We are all involved," said Zangen quietly.

"How can *our* company be?" asked Heinrich Krepps, Direktor of Schreibwaren, the largest printing complex in

Germany. "Our work with Peenemünde has been practically nothing; and what there was, obscured to the point of foolishness. Secrecy is one thing; lying to ourselves, something else again. Do not include us, Herr Zangen."

"You *are* included."

"I reject your conclusion. I've studied our communications with Peenemünde."

"Perhaps you were not cleared for all the facts."

"Asinine!"

"Quite possibly. Nevertheless . . ."

"Such a condition would hardly apply to *me*, Herr Reich official," said Johann Dietricht, the middle-aged, effeminate son of the Dietricht Fabriken empire. Dietricht's family had contributed heavily to Hitler's National Socialist coffers; when the father and uncle had died, Johann Dietricht was allowed to continue the management—more in name than in fact. "Nothing occurs at Dietricht of which I am unaware. We've had nothing to do with Peenemünde!"

Johann Dietricht smiled, his fat lips curling, his blinking eyes betraying an excess of alcohol, his partially plucked eyebrows his sexual proclivity—excess, again. Zangen couldn't stand Dietricht; the man—although no man—was a disgrace, his life-style an insult to German industry. Again, felt Zangen, there was no point in procrastinating. The information would come as no surprise to von Schnitzler and Krepps.

"There are many aspects of the Dietricht Fabriken of which you know *nothing*. Your own laboratories have worked consistently with Peenemünde in the field of chemical detonation."

Dietricht blanched; Krepps interrupted.

"What is your purpose, Herr Reich official? You call us here only to insult us? You tell us, directors, that we are not the masters of our own companies? I don't know Herr Dietricht so well, but I can assure you that von Schnitzler and myself are not puppets."

Von Schnitzler had been watching Zangen closely, observing the Reich official's use of his handkerchief. Zangen kept blotting his chin nervously. "I presume you have specific information—such as you've just delivered to Herr Dietricht—that will confirm your statements."

"I have."

"Then you're saying that isolated operations—within our own factories—were withheld from us."

"I am."

"Then how can we be held responsible? These are insane accusations."

"They are made for practical reasons."

"Now you're talking in circles!" shouted Dietricht, barely recovered from Zangen's insult.

"I must agree," said Krepps, as if agreement with the obvious homosexual was distasteful, yet mandatory.

"Come, gentlemen. Must I draw pictures? These are *your companies*. Farben has supplied eighty-three per cent of all chemicals for the rockets; Schreibwaren has processed every blueprint; Dietricht, the majority of detonating compounds for the casing explosives. We're in a crisis. If we don't overcome that crisis, no protestations of ignorance will serve you. I might go so far as to say that there are those in the ministry and elsewhere who will deny that anything was withheld. You simply buried your collective heads. I'm not even sure myself that such a judgment is in error."

"Lies!" screamed Dietricht.

"Absurd!" added Krepps.

"But obscenely practical," concluded von Schnitzler slowly, staring at Zangen. "So this is what you're telling us, isn't it? What Altmüller tells us. We either employ our resources to find a solution—to come to the aid of our industrial *Schwachling*—or we face equilateral disposition in the eyes of the ministry."

"And in the eyes of the Führer; the judgment of the Reich itself."

"But *how?*" asked the frightened Johann Dietricht.

Zangen remembered Altmüller's words precisely. "Your companies have long histories that go back many years. Corporate and individual. From the Baltic to the Mediterranean, from New York to Rio de Janeiro, from Saudi Arabia to Johannesburg."

"And from Shanghai down through Malaysia to the ports in Australia and the Tasman Sea," said von Schnitzler quietly.

"They don't concern us."

"I thought not."

"Are you suggesting, Herr Reich official, that the solution for Peenemünde lies in our past associations?" Von Schnitzler leaned forward in his chair, his hands and eyes on the table.

"It's a crisis. No avenues can be overlooked. Communications can be expedited."

"No doubt. What makes you think they'd be exchanged?" continued the head of I. G. Farben.

"Profits," replied Zangen.

"Difficult to spend facing a firing squad." Von Schnitzler shifted his large bulk and looked up at the window, his expression pensive.

"You assume the commission of specific transactions. I refer more to acts of *omission.*"

"Clarify that, please," Krepps's eyes remained on the tabletop.

"There are perhaps twenty-five acceptable sources for the bortz and carbonado diamonds—acceptable in the sense that sufficient quantities can be obtained in a single purchase. Africa and South America; one or two locations in Central America. These mines are run by companies under fiat security conditions: British, American, Free French, Belgian . . . you know them. Shipments are controlled, destinations cleared. . . . We are suggesting that shipments can be sidetracked, destinations altered in neutral territories. By the expedient of omitting normal security precautions. Acts of incompetence, if you will; human error, not betrayal."

"Extraordinarily profitable mistakes," summed up von Schnitzler.

"Precisely," said Wilhelm Zangen.

"Where do you find such men?" asked Johann Dietricht in his high-pitched voice.

"Everywhere," replied Heinrich Krepps.

Zangen blotted his chin with his handkerchief.

6

NOVEMBER 29, 1943, BASQUE COUNTRY, SPAIN

Spaulding raced across the foot of the hill until he saw the converging limbs of the two trees. They were the mark. He turned right and started up the steep incline, counting off an approximate 125 yards; the second mark. He turned left and walked slowly around to the west slope, his body low, his eyes darting constantly in all directions; he gripped his pistol firmly.

On the west slope he looked for a single rock—one among so many on the rock-strewn Galician hill—that had been chipped on its downward side. Chipped carefully with three indentations. It was the third and final mark.

He found it, spotting first the bent reeds of the stiff hill grass. He knelt down and looked at his watch: two forty-five.

He was fifteen minutes early, as he had planned to be. In fifteen minutes he would walk down the west slope, directly in front of the chipped rock. There he would find a pile of branches. Underneath the branches would be a short-walled cave; in that cave—if all went as planned—would be three men. One was a member of an infiltration team. The other two were *Wissenschaftler*—German scientists who had been attached to the Kindorf laboratories in the Ruhr Valley. Their defections—escape—had been an objective of long planning.

The obstacles were always the same.

Gestapo.

The Gestapo had broken an underground agent and

was on to the *Wissenschaftler*. But, typical of the SS elite, it kept its knowledge to itself, looking for bigger game than two disaffected laboratory men. Gestapo *Agenten* had given the scientists wide latitude; surveillance dismissed, laboratory patrols relaxed to the point of inefficiency, routine interrogation disregarded.

Contradictions.

The Gestapo was neither inefficient nor careless. The SS was setting a trap.

Spaulding's instructions to the underground had been terse, simple: let the trap be sprung. With no quarry in its net.

Word was leaked that the scientists, granted a weekend leave to Stuttgart, were in reality heading due north through underground routing to Bremerhaven. There contact was being made with a high-ranking defecting German naval officer who had commandeered a small craft and would make a dramatic run to the Allies. It was common knowledge that the German navy was rife with unrest. It was a recruiting ground for the anti-Hitler factions springing up throughout the Reich.

The *word* would give everyone something to think about, reasoned Spaulding. And the Gestapo would be following two men it assumed were the *Wissenschaftler* from Kindorf, when actually they were two middle-aged Wehrmacht security patrols sent on a false surveillance.

Games and countergames.

So much, so alien. The expanded interests of the man in Lisbon.

This afternoon was a concession. Demanded by the German underground. He was to make the final contact alone. The underground claimed the man in Lisbon had created too many complications; there was too much room for error and counterinfiltration. There wasn't, thought David, but if a solo run would calm the nervous stomachs of the anti-Reichists, it was little enough to grant them.

He had his own Valdero team a half mile away in the upper hills. Two shots and they would come to his help on the fastest horses Castilian money could buy.

It was time. He could start toward the cave for the final contact.

He slid down the hard surface, his heels digging into the

earth and rocks of the steep incline until he was above the pile of branches and limbs that signified the hideout's opening. He picked up a handful of loose dirt and threw it down into the broken foliage.

The response was as instructed: a momentary thrashing of a stick against the piled branches. The fluttering of bird's wings, driven from the bush.

Spaulding quickly sidestepped his way to the base of the enclosure and stood by the camouflage.

"Alles in Ordnung. Kommen Sie," he said quietly but firmly. "There isn't much traveling time left."

"Halt!" was the unexpected shout from the cave.

David spun around, pressed his back into the hill and raised his Colt. The voice from inside spoke again. In English.

"Are you . . . Lisbon?"

"For God's sake, yes! Don't *do* that! You'll get your head shot off!" *Christ*, thought Spaulding, the infiltration team must have used a child, or an imbecile, or both as its runner. "Come on out."

"I am with apologies, Lisbon," said the voice, as the branches were separated and the pile dislodged. "We've had a bad time of it."

The runner emerged. He was obviously not anyone David had trained. He was short, very muscular, no more than twenty-five or twenty-six; nervous fear was in his eyes.

"In the future," said Spaulding, "don't acknowledge signals, then question the signaler at the last moment. Unless you intend to kill him. *Es ist Schwarztuch-chiffre.*"

"*Was ist das?* Black . . ."

"Black Drape, friend. Before our time. It means . . . confirm and terminate. Never mind, just don't do it again. Where are the others?"

"Inside. They are all right; very tired and very afraid, but not injured." The runner turned and pulled off more branches. "Come out. It's the man from Lisbon."

The two frightened, middle-aged scientists crawled out of the cave cautiously, blinking at the hot, harsh sun. They looked gratefully at David; the taller one spoke in halting English.

"This is a . . . minute we have waited for. Our very much thanks."

Spaulding smiled. "Well, we're not out of the woods, yet. *Frei*. Both terms apply. You're brave men. We'll do all we can for you."

"There was . . . *nichts* . . . remaining," said the shorter laboratory man. "My friend's socialist . . . *Politik* . . . was unpopular. My late wife was . . . *eine Jüdin*."

"No children?"

"*Nein*," answered the man. "*Gott seli dank*."

"I have one son," said the taller scientist coldly. "*Er ist . . . Gestapo*."

There was no more to be said, thought Spaulding. He turned to the runner, who was scanning the hill and the forests below. "I'll take over now. Get back to Base Four as soon as you can. We've got a large contingent coming in from Koblenz in a few days. We'll need everyone. Get some rest."

The runner hesitated; David had seen his expression before . . . so often. The man was now going to travel alone. No company, pleasant or unpleasant. Just alone.

"That is not my understanding, Lisbon. I am to stay with you. . . ."

"Why?" interrupted Spaulding.

"My instructions. . . ."

"From whom?"

"From those in San Sebastián. Herr Bergeron and his men. Weren't you informed?"

David looked at the runner. The man's fear was making him a poor liar, thought Spaulding. Or he was something else. Something completely unexpected because it was not logical; it was not, at this point, even remotely to be considered. Unless . . .

David gave the runner's frayed young nerves the benefit of the doubt. A benefit, not an exoneration. That would come later.

"No, I wasn't told," he said. "Come on. We'll head to Beta camp. We'll stay there until morning." Spaulding gestured and they started across the foot of the slope.

"I haven't worked this far south," said the runner, positioning himself behind David. "Don't you travel at night, Lisbon?"

"Sometimes," answered Spaulding, looking back at the scientists, who were walking side by side. "Not if we can help it. The Basques shoot indiscriminately at night. They have too many dogs off their leashes at night."

"I see."

"Let's walk single file. Flank our guests," said David to the runner.

The four traveled several miles east. Spaulding kept up a rapid pace; the middle-aged scientists did not complain but they obviously found the going difficult. A number of times David told the others to remain where they were while he entered the woods at various sections of the forest and returned minutes later. Each time he did so, the older men rested, grateful for the pauses. The runner did not. He appeared frightened—as if the American might not come back. Spaulding did not encourage conversation, but after one such disappearance, the young German could not restrain himself.

"What are you *doing?*" he asked.

David looked at the *Widerstandskämpfer* and smiled. "Picking up messages."

"Messages?"

"These are drops. Along our route. We establish marks for leaving off information we don't want sent by radio. Too dangerous if intercepted."

They continued along a narrow path at the edge of the woods until there was a break in the Basque forest. It was a grazing field, a lower plateau centered beneath the surrounding hills. The *Wissenschaftler* were perspiring heavily, their breaths short, their legs aching.

"We'll rest here for a while," said Spaulding, to the obvious relief of the older men. "It's time I made contact anyway."

"*Was ist los?*" asked the young runner. "Contact?"

"Zeroing our position," replied David, taking out a small metal mirror from his field jacket. "The scouts can relax if they know where we are. . . . If you're going to work the north country—what you call south—you'd better remember all this."

"I shall, I shall."

David caught the reflection of the sun on the mirror and beamed it up to a northern hill. He made a series of motions with his wrist, and the metal plate moved back and forth in rhythmic precision.

Seconds later there was a reply from halfway up the

highest hill in the north. Flashes of light shafted out of an infinitesimal spot in the brackish green distance. Spaulding turned to the others.

"We're not going to Beta," he said. "Falangist patrols are in the area. We'll stay here until we're given clearance. You can relax."

The heavyset Basque put down the knapsack mirror. His companion still focused his binoculars on the field several miles below, where the American and his three charges were now seated on the ground.

"He says they are being followed. We are to take up counterpositions and stay out of sight," said the man with the metal mirror. "We go down for the scientists tomorrow night. He will signal us."

"What's *he* going to do?"

"I don't know. He says to get word to Lisbon. He's going to stay in the hills."

"He's a cold one," the Basque said.

DECEMBER 2, 1943, WASHINGTON, D.C.

Alan Swanson sat in the back of the army car trying his best to remain calm. He looked out the window; the late morning traffic was slight. The immense Washington labor force was at its appointed destinations; machines were humming, telephones ringing, men were shouting and whispering and, in too many places, having the first drink of the day. The exhilaration that was apparent during the first hours of the working day faded as noon approached. By eleven thirty a great many people thought the war was dull and were bored by their mechanical chores, the unending duplicates, triplicates and quadruplicates. They could not understand the necessity of painstaking logistics, of disseminating information to innumerable chains of command.

They could not understand because they could not be given whole pictures, only fragments, repetitious statistics. Of course they were bored.

They were weary. As he had been weary fourteen hours ago in Pasadena, California.

Everything had failed.

Meridian Aircraft had initiated—was *forced* to initiate

—a crash program, but the finest scientific minds in the country could not eliminate the errors inside the small box that was the guidance system. The tiny, whirling spheroid discs would not spin true at maximum altitudes. They were erratic; absolute one second, deviant the next.

The most infinitesimal deviation could result in the midair collision of giant aircraft. And with the numbers projected for the saturation bombing prior to Overlord—scheduled to commence in less than four months—collisons *would* occur.

But this morning everything was different.

Could be different, if there was substance to what he had been told. He hadn't been able to sleep on the plane, hardly been able to eat. Upon landing at Andrews, he had hurried to his Washington apartment, showered, shaved, changed uniforms and called his wife in Scarsdale, where she was staying with a sister. He didn't remember the conversation between them; the usual endearments were absent, the questions perfunctory. He had no time for her.

The army car entered the Virginia highway and accelerated. They were going to Fairfax; they'd be there in twenty minutes or so. In less than a half hour he would find out if the impossible was, conversely, entirely possible. The news had come as a last-minute stay of execution; the cavalry in the distant hills—the sounds of muted bugles signaling reprieve.

Muted, indeed, thought Swanson as the army car veered off the highway onto a back Virginia road. In Fairfax, covering some two hundred acres in the middle of the hunt country, was a fenced-off area housing Quonset huts beside huge radar screens and radio signal towers that sprang from the ground like giant steel malformities. It was the Field Division Headquarters of Clandestine Operations; next to the underground rooms at the White House, the most sensitive processing location of the Allied Intelligence services.

Late yesterday afternoon, FDHQ-Fairfax had received confirmation of an Intelligence probe long since abandoned as negative. It came out of Johannesburg, South Africa. It had not been proved out, but there was sufficient evidence to believe that it could be.

High-altitude directional gyroscopes had been perfected. Their designs could be had.

DECEMBER 2, 1943, BERLIN, GERMANY

Altmüller sped out of Berlin on the Spandau highway toward Falkensee in the open Duesenberg. It was early in the morning and the air was cold and that was good.

He was so exhilarated that he forgave the theatrically secretive ploys of the Nachrichtendienst, code name for a select unit of the espionage service known to only a few of the upper-echelon ministers, not to many of the High Command itself. A Gehlen specialty.

For this reason it never held conferences within Berlin proper; always outside the city, always in some remote, secluded area or town and even then in private surroundings, away from the potentially curious.

The location this morning was Falkensee, twenty-odd miles northwest of Berlin. The meeting was to take place in a guest house on the estate belonging to Gregor Strasser.

Altmüller would have flown to Stalingrad itself if what he'd been led to believe was true.

The Nachrichtendienst had found the solution for Peenemünde!

The solution *was true*; it was up to others to expedite it.

The solution that had eluded teams of "negotiators" sent to all parts of the world to explore—unearth—prewar "relationships." Capetown, Dar es Salaam, Johannesburg, Buenos Aires. . . .

Failure.

No company, no individual would touch German negotiations. Germany was in the beginning of a death struggle. It would go down to defeat.

That was the opinion in Zürich. And what Zürich held to be true, international business did not debate.

But the Nachrichtendienst had found another truth.

So he was told.

The Duesenberg's powerful engine hummed; the car reached high speed; the passing autumn foliage blurred.

The stone gates of Strasser's estate came into view on the left, Wehrmacht eagles in bronze above each post. He swung into the long, winding drive and stopped at the gate guarded by two soldiers and snarling shepherd dogs. Altmüller thrust his papers at the first guard, who obviously expected him.

"Good morning, Herr Unterstaatssekretär. Please follow the drive to the right beyond the main house."

"Have the others arrived?"

"They are waiting, sir."

Altmüller maneuvered the car past the main house, reached the sloping drive and slowed down. Beyond the wooded bend was the guest cottage; it looked more like a hunting lodge than a residence. Heavy dark-brown beams everywhere; a part of the forest.

In the graveled area were four limousines. He parked and got out, pulling his tunic down, checking his lapels for lint. He stood erect and started toward the path to the door.

No names were ever used during a Nachrichtendienst conference; if identities were known—and certainly they had to be—they were never referred to in a meeting. One simply addressed his peer by looking at him, the group by gesture.

There was no long conference table as Altmüller had expected; no formal seating arrangement by some hidden protocol. Instead, a half dozen informally dressed men in their fifties and sixties were standing around the small room with the high Bavarian ceiling, chatting calmly, drinking coffee. Altmüller was welcomed as "Herr Unterstaatssekretär" and told that the morning's conference would be short. It would begin with the arrival of the final expected member.

Altmüller accepted a cup of coffee and tried to fall into the casual atmosphere. He was unable to do so; he wanted to roar his disapproval and demand immediate and serious talk. Couldn't they *understand?*

But this was the Nachrichtendienst. One didn't yell; one didn't demand.

Finally, after what seemed an eternity to his churning stomach, Altmüller heard an automobile outside the lodge. A few moments later the door opened; he nearly dropped his cup of coffee. The man who entered was known to him from the few times he had accompanied Speer to Berchtesgaden. He was the Führer's valet, but he had no subservient look of a valet now.

Without announcement, the men fell silent. Several sat in armchairs, others leaned against walls or stayed by the coffee table. An elderly man in a heavy tweed jacket stood in front of the fireplace and spoke. He looked at Franz, who remained by himself behind a leather couch.

"There is no reason for lengthy discussions. We believe we have the information you seek. I say 'believe,' for we gather information, we do not act upon it. The ministry may not care to act."

"That would seem inconceivable to me," said Altmüller.

"Very well. Several questions then. So there is no conflict, no misrepresentation." The old man paused and lit a thick meerschaum pipe. "You have exhausted all normal Intelligence channels? Through Zürich and Lisbon?"

"We have. And in numerous other locations—occupied, enemy and neutral."

"I was referring to the acknowledged conduits, Swiss, Scandinavian and Portuguese, primarily."

"We made no concentrated efforts in the Scandinavian countries. Herr Zangen did not think . . ."

"No names, please. Except in the area of Intelligence confrontation or public knowledge. Use governmental descriptions, if you like. Not individuals."

"The Reichsamt of Industry—which has continuous dealings in the Baltic areas—was convinced there was nothing to be gained there. I assume the reasons were geographical. There are no diamonds in the Baltic."

"Or they've been burnt too often," said a nondescript middle-aged man below Altmüller on the leather sofa. "If you want London and Washington to know what you're doing before you do it, deal with the Scandinavians."

"An accurate analysis," concurred another member of the Nachrichtendienst, this one standing by the coffee table, cup in hand. "I returned from Stockholm last week. We can't trust even those who publicly endorse us."

"Those least of all," said the old man in front of the fireplace, smiling and returning his eyes to Franz. "We gather you've made substantial offers? In Swiss currency, of course."

"Substantial is a modest term for the figures we've spoken of," replied Altmüller. "I'll be frank. No one will touch us. Those who could, subscribe to Zürich's judgment that we shall be defeated. They fear retribution; they even speak of postwar bank deposit reclamations."

"If such whispers reach the High Command there'll be a panic." The statement was made humorously by the Führer's valet, sitting in an armchair. The spokesman by the fireplace continued.

"So you must eliminate money as an incentive . . . even extraordinary sums of money."

"The negotiating teams were not successful. You know that." Altmüller had to suppress his irritation. Why didn't they get to the *point?*

"And there are no ideologically motivated defectors on the horizon. Certainly none who have access to industrial diamonds."

"Obviously, *mein Herr*."

"So you must look for another motive. Another incentive."

"I fail to see the point of this. I was told . . ."

"You will," interrupted the old man, tapping his pipe on the mantel. "You see, we've uncovered a panic as great as yours. . . . The enemy's panic. We've found the most logical motive for all concerned. Each side possesses the other's solution."

Franz Altmüller was suddenly afraid. He could not be sure he fully understood the spokesman's implications. "What are you saying?"

"Peenemünde has perfected a high-altitude directional guidance system, is this correct?"

"Certainly. Indigenous to the basic operation of the rockets."

"But there'll be no rockets—or at best, a pitiful few—without shipments of industrial diamonds."

"Obviously."

"There are business interests in the United States who face insurmountable . . .," the old man paused for precisely one second and continued, "*insurmountable* problems that can only be resolved by the acquisition of functional high-altitude gyroscopes."

"Are you suggesting . . ."

"The Nachrichtendienst does not suggest, Herr Unterstaatssekretär. We say what is." The spokesman removed the meerschaum from his lips. "When the occasion warrants, we transmit concrete information to diverse recipients. Again, only what is. We did so in Johannesburg. When the man I. G. Farben sent in to purchase diamonds from the Koening mines met with failure, we stepped in and confirmed a long-standing Intelligence probe we knew would be carried back to Washington. Our agents in California had apprised us of the crisis in the aircraft industry. We believe the timing was propitious."

"I'm not sure I understand. . . ."

"Unless we're mistaken, an attempt will be made to reestablish contact with one of the Farben men. We assume contingencies were made for such possibilities."

"Of course. Geneva. The acknowledged conduits."

"Then our business with you is concluded, sir. May we wish you a pleasant drive back to Berlin."

DECEMBER 2, 1943, FAIRFAX, VIRGINIA

The interior of the Quonset belied its stark outside. To begin with, it was five times larger than the usual Quonset structure, and its metal casing was insulated with a sound-absorbing material that swept seamless down from the high ceiling. The appearance was not so much that of an airplane hangar—as it should have been—as of a huge, windowless shell with substantial walls. All around the immense room were banks of complicated high-frequency radio panels; opposite each panel were glass-enclosed casings with dozens of detailed maps, changeable by the push of a button. Suspended above the maps were delicate, thin steel arms—markers, not unlike polygraph needles—that were manipulated by the radio operators, observed by men holding clipboards. The entire staff was military, army, none below the rank of first lieutenant.

Three-quarters into the building was a floor-to-ceiling wall that obviously was not the end of the structure. There was a single door, centered and closed. The door was made of heavy steel.

Swanson had never been inside this particular building. He had driven down to Field Division, Fairfax, many times—to get briefed on highly classified Intelligence findings, to observe the training of particular insurgence or espionage teams—but for all his brigadier's rank and regardless of the secrets he carried around in his head, he had not been cleared for this particular building. Those who were, remained within the two-hundred-acre compound for weeks, months at a time; leaves were rare and taken only in emergency and with escort.

It was fascinating, thought Swanson, who honestly believed he had lost all sense of awe. No elevators, no back staircases, no windows; he could see a washroom door in the left wall and without going inside, knew it was machine-ventilated. And there was only a single entrance. Once inside there was no place for a person to conceal himself for any length of time, or to exit without being checked out and scrutinized. Personal items were left at the entrance; no briefcases, envelopes, papers or materials were removed from the building without signed authorization by Colonel Edmund Pace and with the colonel personally at the side of the individual in question.

If there was ever total security, it was here.

Swanson approached the steel door; his lieutenant escort pushed a button. A small red light flashed above a wall intercom, and the lieutenant spoke.

"General Swanson, colonel."

"Thank you, lieutenant," were the words that came from the webbed circle below the light. There was a click in the door's lock and the lieutenant reached for the knob.

Inside, Pace's office looked like any other Intelligence headquarters—huge maps on the walls, sharp lighting on the maps, lights and maps changeable by pushbuttons on the desk. Teletype machines were equidistant from one another below printed signs designating theaters of operation—all the usual furnishings. Except the furniture itself. It was simple to the point of primitiveness. No easy chairs, no sofas, nothing comfortable. Just plain metal straight-backed chairs, a desk that was more a table than a desk, and a rugless hardwood floor. It was a room for concentrated activity; a man did not relax in such a room.

Edmund Pace, Commander of Field Division, Fairfax, got up from his chair, came around his table and saluted Alan Swanson.

There was one other man in the room, a civilian. Frederic Vandamm, Undersecretary of State.

"General. Good to see you again. The last time was at Mr. Vandamm's house, if I remember."

"Yes, it was. How are things here?"

"A little isolated."

"I'm sure." Swanson turned to Vandamm. "Mr. Undersecretary? I got back here as soon as I could. I don't have to tell you how anxious I am. It's been a difficult month."

"I'm aware of that," said the aristocratic Vandamm, smiling a cautious smile, shaking Swanson's hand perfunctorily. "We'll get right to it. Colonel Pace, will you brief the general as we discussed?"

"Yes, sir. And then I'll leave." Pace spoke noncommittally; it was the military's way of telegraphing a message to a fellow officer: *be careful.*

Pace crossed to a wall map, presented with markings. It was an enlarged, detailed section of Johannesburg, South Africa. Frederic Vandamm sat in a chair in front of the desk; Swanson followed Pace and stood beside him.

"You never know when a probe will get picked up. Or where." Pace took a wooden pointer from a table and indicated a blue marker on the map. "Or even if the location is important. In this case it *may* be. A week ago a member of the Johannesburg legislature, an attorney and a former director of Koening Mines, Ltd., was contacted by what he believed were two men from the Zürich Staats-Bank. They wanted him to middle-man a negotiation with Koening: simple transaction of Swiss francs for diamonds—on a large scale, with the anticipation that the diamond standard would remain more constant than the gold fluctuations." Pace turned to Swanson. "So far, so good. With lend-lease, and monetary systems going up in smoke everywhere, there's a lot of speculation in the diamond market. Postwar killings could be made. When he accepted the contact, you can imagine his shock when he arrived for the meeting and found that one of the 'Swiss' was an old friend—a very old and good friend—from the prewar days. A German he'd gone to school with—the Afrikaner's mother was Austrian; father a Boer. The two men had kept in close touch until thirty-nine. The German worked for I. G. Farben."

"What was the point of the meeting?" Swanson was impatient.

"I'll get to that. This background's important."

"O.K. Go on."

"There was no diamond market speculation involved, no transaction with any Zürich bank. It was a simple purchase. The Farben man wanted to buy large shipments of bortz and carbonado. . . ."

"Industrial diamonds?" interrupted Swanson.

Pace nodded. "He offered a fortune to his old friend if he could pull it off. The Afrikaner refused; but his long-standing friendship with the German kept him from reporting the incident. Until three days ago." Pace put down the pointer and started for his desk. Swanson understood that the colonel had additional information, written information, that he had to refer to; the general crossed to the chair beside Vandamm and sat down.

"Three days ago," continued Pace, standing behind the desk, "the Afrikaner was contacted again. This time there was no attempt to conceal identities. The caller said he was German and had information the Allies wanted; had wanted for a long time."

"The probe?" asked Swanson, whose impatience was carried by his tone of voice.

"Not exactly the probe we expected. . . . The German said he would come to the Afrikaner's office, but he protected himself. He told the lawyer that if any attempt was made to hold him, his old friend at I. G. Farben would be executed back in Germany." Pace picked up a sheet of paper from his desk. He spoke as he leaned across and handed it to Swanson. "This is the information, the report flown in by courier."

Swanson read the typewritten words below the Military Intelligence letterhead; above the large, stamped *Top Secret. Eyes Only. Fairfax 4–0.*

> Nov. 28, 1943. Johannesburg: Confirmed by Nachrichtendienst. Substratospheric directional gyroscopes perfected. All tests positive. Peenemünde. Subsequent contact: Geneva. Johannesburg contingent.

Swanson let the information sink in; he read the statement over several times. He asked a question of Edmund Pace with a single word: "Geneva?"

"The conduit. Neutral channel. Unofficial, of course."

"What is this . . . Nachrichtendienst?"

"Intelligence unit. Small, specialized; so rarefied it's above even the most classified crowds. Sometimes we wonder if it takes sides. It often appears more interested in observing than participating; more concerned with after the war than now. We suspect that it's a Gehlen operation. But it's never been wrong. Never misleading."

"I see." Swanson held out the paper for Pace.

The colonel did not take it. Instead, he walked around the desk toward the steel door. "I'll leave you gentlemen. When you're finished, please signify by pushing the white button on my desk." He opened the door and left quickly. The heavy steel frame closed into an airtight position; a subsequent click could be heard in the lock housing.

Frederic Vandamm looked at Swanson. "There is your solution, general. Your gyroscope. In Peenemünde. All you have to do is send a man to Geneva. Someone wants to sell it."

Alan Swanson stared at the paper in his hand.

7

DECEMBER 4, 1943, BERLIN, GERMANY

Altmüller stared at the paper in his hand. It was after midnight, the city in darkness. Berlin had withstood another night of murderous bombardment; it was over now. There would be no further raids until late morning, that was the usual pattern. Still, the black curtains were pulled tight against the windows. As they were everywhere in the ministry.

Speed was everything now. Yet in the swiftness of the planning, mandatory precautions could not be overlooked. The meeting in Geneva with the conduit was only the first step, the prelude, but it had to be handled delicately. Not so much *what* was said but *who* said it. The *what* could be transmitted by anyone with the proper credentials or acknowledged authority. But in the event of Germany's collapse, that *someone* could not represent the Third Reich. Speer had been adamant.

And Altmüller understood: if the war was lost, the label of traitor could not be traced to the Reichsministry. Or to those leaders Germany would need in defeat. In 1918 after Versailles, there had been mass internal recriminations. Polarization ran deep, unchecked, and the nation's paranoia over betrayal from within laid the groundwork for the fanaticism of the twenties. Germany had not been able to accept defeat, could not tolerate the destruction of its identity by traitors.

Excuses, of course.

But the prospects of repetition, no matter how remote, were to be avoided at all costs. Speer was himself fanatic on the subject. The Geneva representative was to be a figure isolated from the High Command. Someone from the ranks of German industry, in no way associated with the rulers of the Third Reich. Someone expendable.

Altmüller tried to point out the inconsistency of Speer's manipulation: high-altitude gyroscopic designs would hardly be given to an expendable mediocrity from German business. Peenemünde was buried—literally buried in the earth; its military security measures absolute.

But Speer would not listen, and Altmüller suddenly grasped the Reichsminister's logic. He was shifting the problem precisely where it belonged: to those whose lies and concealments had brought Peenemünde to the brink of disaster. And as with so much in the wartime Reich—the labor forces, the death camps, the massacres—Albert Speer conveniently looked away. He wanted positive results, but he would not dirty his tunic.

In this particular case, mused Altmüller, Speer was right. If there were to be risks of great disgrace, let German industry take them. Let the German businessman assume complete responsibility.

Geneva was vital only in the sense that it served as an introduction. Cautious words would be spoken that could —or could not—lead to the second stage of the incredible negotiation.

Stage two was geographical: the location of the exchange, should it actually take place.

For the past week, day and night, Altmüller had done little else but concentrate on this. He approached the problem from the enemy's viewpoint as well as his own. His worktable was covered with maps, his desk filled with scores of reports detailing the current political climates of every neutral territory on earth.

For the location had to be neutral; there had to be sufficient safeguards each side could investigate and respect. And perhaps most important of all, it had to be thousands of miles away . . . from either enemy's corridors of power.

Distance.

Remote.

Yet possessing means of instant communication.

South America.

Buenos Aires.

An inspired choice, thought Franz Altmüller. The Americans might actually consider it advantageous to them. It was unlikely that they would reject it. Buenos Aires had much each enemy considered its own; both had enormous influence, yet neither controlled with any real authority.

The third stage, as he conceived of it, was concerned with the human factor, defined by the word *Schiedsrichter*.

Referee.

A man who was capable of overseeing the exchange, powerful enough within the neutral territory to engineer the logistics. Someone who had the appearance of impartiality . . . above all, acceptable to the Americans.

Buenos Aires had such a man.

One of Hitler's gargantuan errors.

His name was Erich Rhinemann. A Jew, forced into exile, disgraced by Goebbels's insane propaganda machine, his lands and companies expropriated by the Reich.

Those lands and companies he had not converted before the misplaced thunderbolts struck. A minor percentage of his holdings, sufficient for the manic screams of the anti-Semitic press, but hardly a dent in his immense wealth.

Erich Rhinemann lived in exiled splendor in Buenos Aires, his fortunes secure in Swiss banks, his interests expanding throughout South America. And what few people knew was that Erich Rhinemann was a more dedicated fascist than Hitler's core. He was a supremacist in all things financial and military, an elitist with regard to the human condition. He was an empire builder who remained strangely—stoically—silent.

He had reason to be.

He would be returned to Germany regardless of the outcome of the war. He knew it.

If the Third Reich was victorious, Hitler's asinine edict would be revoked—as, indeed, might be the Führer's powers should he continue to disintegrate. If Germany went down to defeat—as Zürich projected—Rhinemann's expertise and Swiss accounts would be needed to rebuild the nation.

But these things were in the future. It was the present that mattered, and presently Erich Rhinemann was a Jew, forced into exile by his own countrymen, Washington's enemy.

He would be acceptable to the Americans.

And he would look after the Reich's interests in Buenos Aires.

Stages two and three, then, felt Altmüller, had the ring of clarity. But they were meaningless without an accord in Geneva. The prelude had to be successfully played by the minor instruments.

What was needed was a man for Geneva. An individual no one could link to the leaders of the Reich, but still one who had a certain recognition in the market place.

Altmüller continued to stare at the pages under the desk lamp. His eyes were weary, as he was weary, but he knew he could not leave his office or sleep until he had made the decision.

His decision; it was his alone. To be approved by Speer in the morning with only a glance. A name. Not discussed; someone instantly acceptable.

He would never know whether it was the letters in Johannesburg or the subconscious process of elimination, but his eyes riveted on one name, and he circled it. He recognized immediately that it was, again, an inspired choice.

Johann Dietricht, the bilious heir of Dietricht Fabriken; the unattractive homosexual given to alcoholic excess and sudden panic. A completely expendable member of the industrial community; even the most cynical would be reluctant to consider him a liaison to the High Command.

An expendable mediocrity.

A messenger.

DECEMBER 5, 1943, WASHINGTON, D.C.

The bass-toned chimes of the clock on the mantel marked the hour somberly. It was six in the morning and Alan Swanson stared out the window at the dark buildings that were Washington. His apartment was on the twelfth floor, affording a pretty fair view of the capital's skyline, especially from the living room, where he now stood in his bathrobe, no slippers on his feet.

He had been looking at Washington's skyline most of the night . . . most of the hours of the night for the past three days. God knew what sleep he managed was fitful, subject to sudden torments and awakenings; and always there was the damp pillow that absorbed the constant perspiration that seeped from the pores in the back of his neck.

If his wife were with him, she would insist that he turn himself in to Walter Reed for a checkup. She would force the issue with constant repetition until he was nagged into submission. But she was *not* with him; he had been adamant. She was to remain with her sister in Scarsdale. The nature of his current activities was such that his hours were indeterminate. Translation: the army man had no time for his army wife. The army wife understood: there was a severe crisis and her husband could not cope with even her minor demands and the crisis, too. He did not like her to observe him in these situations; he knew she knew that. She would stay in Scarsdale.

Oh, Christ! It was beyond belief!

None said the words; perhaps no one allowed himself to think them.

That was it, of course. The few—and there were *very* few—who had access to the data turned their eyes and their minds away from the ultimate judgment. They cut off the transaction at midpoint, refusing to acknowledge the final half of the bargain. That half was for others to contend with. Not them.

As the wily old aristocrat Frederic Vandamm had done.

There's your solution, general. Your guidance system. In Peenemünde. . . . Someone wants to sell it.

That's all.

Buy it.

None wanted to know the price. The price was insignificant . . . let others concern themselves with details. Under no circumstances—*no circumstances*—were insignificant details to be brought up for discussion! They were merely to be expedited.

Translation: the chain of command depended upon the execution of general orders. It did not—repeat, *not*—require undue elaboration, clarification or justification. Specifics were an anathema; they consumed time. And by all that was military holy writ, the highest echelons *had* no time. Goddamn it, man, there was a *war on!* We must tend to the great military issues of state!

The garbage will be sorted out by lesser men . . . whose

hands may on occasion reek with the stench of their lesser duties, but that's what the chain of command is all about.

Buy it!

We have no time. Our eyes are turned. Our minds are occupied elsewhere.

Carry out the order on your own initiative as a good soldier should who understands the chain of command. No one will be inquisitive; it is the result that matters. We all know that; the chain of command, old boy.

Insanity.

By the *strangest coincidence* an Intelligence probe is returned by a man in Johannesburg through which the purchase of industrial diamonds was sought. A purchase for which a fortune in Swiss currency was tendered by Germany's I. G. Farben, the armaments giant of the Third Reich.

Peenemünde had the guidance system; it could be had. For a price.

It did not take a major intellect to arrive at that price.

Industrial diamonds.

Insanity.

For reasons beyond inquiry, Germany desperately needed the diamonds. For reasons all too clear, the Allies desperately needed the high-altitude guidance system.

An exchange between enemies at the height of the bitterest war in the history of mankind.

Insanity. Beyond comprehension.

And so General Alan Swanson removed it from his immediate . . . totality.

The single deep chime of the clock intruded, signifying the quarter hour. Here and there throughout the maze of dark concrete outside, lights were being turned on in a scattering of tiny windows. A greyish purple slowly began to impose itself on the black sky; vague outlines of cloud wisps could be discerned above.

In the higher altitudes.

Swanson walked away from the window to the couch facing the fireplace and sat down. It had been twelve hours ago . . . eleven hours and forty-five minutes, to be precise . . . when he had taken the first step of *removal.*

He had placed . . . delegated the insanity where it belonged. To the men who had created the crisis; whose lies and manipulations had brought Overlord to the precipice of obscenity.

He had ordered Howard Oliver and Jonathan Craft to be in his apartment at six o'clock. Twelve hours and fifteen minutes ago. He had telephoned them on the previous day, making it clear that he would tolerate no excuses. If transportation were a problem, he would resolve it, but they were to be in Washington, in his apartment, by six o'clock.

Exposure was a viable alternative.

They had arrived at precisely six, as the somber chimes of the mantel clock were ringing. At that moment Swanson knew he was dealing from absolute strength. Men like Oliver and Craft—especially Oliver—did not adhere to such punctuality unless they were afraid. It certainly was not courtesy.

The transference had been made with utter simplicity.

There was a telephone number in Geneva, Switzerland. There was a man at that number who would respond to a given code phrase and bring together two disparate parties, act as an interpreter, if necessary. It was understood that the second party—for purposes of definition—had access to a perfected high-altitude guidance system. The first party, in turn, should have knowledge of . . . perhaps access to . . . shipments of industrial diamonds. The Koening mines of Johannesburg might be a place to start.

That was all the information they had.

It was recommended that Mr. Oliver and Mr. Craft act on this information immediately.

If they failed to do so, extremely serious charges involving individual and corporate deceit relative to armaments contracts would be leveled by the War Department.

There had been a long period of silence. The implications of his statement—with all its ramifications—were accepted gradually by both men.

Alan Swanson then added the subtle confirmation of their worst projections: whoever was chosen to go to Geneva, it could *not* be anyone known to him. Or to any War Department liaison with *any* of their companies. That was paramount.

The Geneva meeting was exploratory. Whoever went to Switzerland should be knowledgeable and, if possible, capable of spotting deception. Obviously a man who practiced deception.

That shouldn't be difficult for them; not in the circles they traveled. Surely they knew such a man.

They did. An accountant named Walter Kendall.

Swanson looked up at the clock on the mantel. It was twenty minutes past six.

Why did the time go so slowly? On the other hand, why didn't it stop? Why didn't everything stop but the sunlight? Why did there have to be the nights to go through?

In another hour he would go to his office and quietly make arrangements for one Walter Kendall to be flown on neutral routes to Geneva, Switzerland. He would bury the orders in a blue pouch along with scores of other transport directives and clearances. There would be no signature on the orders, only the official stamp of Field Division, Fairfax; standard procedure with conduits.

Oh, Christ! thought Swanson. If there could be control *. . . without participation.*

But he knew that was not possible. Sooner or later he would have to face the reality of what he had done.

8

DECEMBER 6, 1943, BASQUE COUNTRY, SPAIN

He had been in the north country for eight days. He had not expected it to be this long, but Spaulding knew it was necessary . . . an unexpected dividend. What had begun as a routine escape involving two defecting scientists from the Ruhr Valley had turned into something else.

The scientists were throwaway bait. Gestapo bait. The runner who had made their escape possible out of the Ruhr was not a member of the German underground. He was Gestapo.

It had taken Spaulding three days to be absolutely sure. The Gestapo man was one of the best he had ever encountered, but his mistakes fell into a pattern: he was *not* an experienced runner. When David *was* sure, he knew exactly what had to be done.

For five days he led his "underground" companion through the hills and mountain passes to the east as far as Sierra de Guara, nearly a hundred miles from the clandestine escape routes. He entered remote villages and held "conferences" with men he knew were Falangists—but who did *not* know him—and then told the Gestapo man they were partisans. He traveled over primitive roads and down the Guayardo River and explained that these routes were the avenues of escape. . . . Contrary to what the Germans believed, the routes were to the *east*, into the *Mediterranean, not* the Atlantic. This confusion was the prime reason for the success of the Pyrenees network. On two occasions he sent the Nazi into towns for supplies—both times he followed and observed the Gestapo man entering buildings that had thick telephone wires sagging into the roofs.

The information was being transmitted back to Germany. That was reason enough for the investment of five additional days. The German interceptors would be tied up for months concentrating on the eastern "routes"; the network to the west would be relatively unencumbered.

But now the game was coming to an end. It was just as well, thought David; he had work to do in Ortegal, on the Biscay coast.

The small campfire was reduced to embers, the night air cold. Spaulding looked at his watch. It was two in the morning. He had ordered the "runner" to stay on guard quite far from the campsite . . . out of the glow of the fire. In darkness. He had given the Gestapo man enough time and isolation to make his move, but the German had *not* made his move; he had remained at his post.

So be it, thought David. Perhaps the man wasn't as expert as he thought he was. Or perhaps the information his own men in the hills had given him was not accurate. There was no squad of German soldiers—suspected Alpine troops—heading down from the mountain borders to take out the Gestapo agent.

And him.

He approached the rock on which the German sat. "Get some rest. I'll take over."

"*Danke*," said the man, getting to his feet. "First, nature calls; I must relieve my bowels. I'll take a spade into the field."

"Use the woods. Animals graze here. The winds carry."

"Of course. You're thorough."

"I try to be," said David.

The German crossed back toward the fire, to his pack. He removed a camp shovel and started for the woods bordering the field. Spaulding watched him, now aware that his first impression was the correct one. The Gestapo agent *was* expert. The Nazi had not forgotten that six days ago the two Ruhr scientists had disappeared during the night—at a moment of the night when he had dozed. David had seen the fury in the German's eyes and knew the Nazi was now remembering the incident.

If Spaulding assessed the current situation accurately, the Gestapo man would wait at least an hour into his watch, to be sure he, David, was not making contact with unseen partisans in the darkness. Only then would the German give the signal that would bring the Alpine troops out of the forest. With rifles leveled.

But the Gestapo man had made a mistake. He had accepted too readily—without comment—Spaulding's statement about the field and the wind and the suggestion that he relieve himself in the woods.

They had reached the field during late daylight; it was barren, the grass was sour, the slope rocky. Nothing would graze here, not even goats.

And there was no wind at all. The night air was cold, but dead.

An experienced runner would have objected, no doubt humorously, and say he'd be damned if he'd take a crap in the pitch-black woods. But the Gestapo agent could not resist the gratuitous opportunity to make his own contact.

If there *was* such a contact to be made, thought Spaulding. He would know in a few minutes.

David waited thirty seconds after the man had disappeared into the forest. Then he swiftly, silently threw himself to the ground and began rolling his body over and over again, away from the rock, at a sharp angle from the point where the runner had entered the forest.

When he had progressed thirty-five to forty feet into the grass, he stood up, crouching, and raced to the border of the woods, judging himself to be about sixty yards away from the German.

He entered the dense foliage and noiselessly closed the distance between them. He could not see the man but he knew he would soon find him.

Then he saw it. The German's signal. A match was struck, cupped, and extinguished swiftly.

Another. This one allowed to burn for several seconds, then snuffed out with a short spit of breath.

From deep in the woods came two separate, brief replies. Two matches struck. In opposite directions.

David estimated the distance to be, perhaps, a hundred feet. The German, unfamiliar with the Basque forest, stayed close to the edge of the field. The men he had signaled were approaching. Spaulding—making no sound that disturbed the hum of the woods—crawled closer.

He heard the voices whispering. Only isolated words were distinguishable. But they were enough.

He made his way rapidly back through the overgrowth to his original point of entry. He raced to his sentry post, the rock. He removed a small flashlight from his field jacket, clamped separated fingers over the glass and aimed it southwest. He pressed the switch five times in rapid succession. He then replaced the instrument in his pocket and waited.

It wouldn't be long now.

It wasn't.

The German came out of the woods carrying the shovel, smoking a cigarette. The night was black, the moon breaking only intermittently through the thick cover of clouds; the darkness was nearly total. David got up from the rock and signaled the German with a short whistle. He approached him.

"What is it, Lisbon?"

Spaulding spoke quietly. Two words.

"Heil Hitler."

And plunged his short bayonet into the Nazi's stomach, ripping it downward, killing the man instantly.

The body fell to the ground, the face contorted; the only sound was a swallow of air, the start of a scream, blocked by rigid fingers thrust into the dead man's mouth, yanked downward, as the knife had been, shorting out the passage of breath.

David raced across the grass to the edge of the woods, to the left of his previous entry. Nearer, but not much, to the point where the Nazi had spoken in whispers to his two confederates. He dove into a cluster of winter fern as the moon suddenly broke through the clouds. He remained immobile for several seconds, listening for sounds of alarm.

There were none. The moon was hidden again, the darkness returned. The corpse in the field had not been spotted in the brief illumination. And that fact revealed to David a very important bit of knowledge.

Whatever Alpine troops were in the woods, they were not on the *edge* of the woods. Or if they were, they were not concentrating on the field.

They were waiting. Concentrating in other directions.

Or just waiting.

He rose to his knees and scrambled rapidly west through the dense underbrush, flexing his body and limbs to every bend in the foliage, making sounds compatible to the forest's tones. He reached the point where the three men had conferred but minutes ago, feeling no presence, seeing nothing.

He took out a box of waterproof matches from his pocket and removed two. He struck the first one, and the instant it flared, he blew it out. He then struck the second match and allowed it to burn for a moment or two before he extinguished it.

About forty feet in the woods there was a responding flash of a match. Directly north.

Almost simultaneously came a second response. This one to the west, perhaps fifty or sixty feet away.

No more.

But enough.

Spaulding quickly crawled into the forest at an angle. Northeast. He went no more than fifteen feet and crouched against the truck of an ant-ridden ceiba tree.

He waited. And while he waited, he removed a thin, short, flexible coil of wire from his field jacket pocket. At each end of the wire was a wooden handle, notched for the human hand.

The German soldier made too much noise for an Alpiner, thought David. He was actually hurrying, anxious to accommodate the unexpected command for rendezvous. That told Spaulding something else; the Gestapo agent he had killed was a demanding man. That meant the remaining troops would stay in position, awaiting orders. There would be a minimum of individual initiative.

There was no time to think of them now. The German soldier was passing the ceiba tree.

David sprang up silently, the coil held high with both hands. The loop fell over the soldier's helmet, the reverse pull so swift and brutally sudden that the wire sliced into the flesh of the neck with complete finality.

There was no sound but the expunging of air again.

David Spaulding had heard that sound so often it no longer mesmerized him. As it once had done.

Silence.

And then the unmistakable breaking of branches; footsteps crushing the ground cover of an unfamiliar path. Rushing, impatient; as the dead man at his foot had been impatient.

Spaulding put the bloody coil of wire back into his pocket and removed the shortened carbine bayonet from the scabbard on his belt. He knew there was no reason to hurry; the third man would be waiting. Confused, frightened perhaps . . . but probably not, if he was an Alpiner. The Alpine troops were rougher than the Gestapo. The rumors were that the Alpiners were chosen primarily for streaks of sadism. Robots who could live in mountain passes and nurture their hostilities in freezing isolation until the orders for attack were given.

There was no question about it, thought David. There was a certain pleasure in killing Alpiners.

The treadmill.

He edged his way forward, his knife leveled.

"*Wer? . . . Wer ist dort?*" The figure in darkness whispered in agitation.

"*Hier, mein Soldat,*" replied David. His carbine bayonet slashed into the German's chest.

The partisans came down from the hills. There were five men, four Basque and one Catalonian. The leader was a Basque, heavyset and blunt.

"You gave us a wild trip, Lisbon. There were times we thought you were *loco*. Mother of God! We've traveled a hundred miles."

"The Germans will travel many times that, I assure you. What's north?"

"A string of Alpiners. Perhaps twenty. Every six kilometers, right to the border. Shall we let them sit in their wastes?"

"No," said Spaulding thoughtfully. "Kill them. . . . All but the last three; harass them back. They'll confirm what we want the Gestapo to believe."

"I don't understand."

"You don't have to." David walked to the dying fire and kicked at the coals. He had to get to Ortegal. It was all he could think about.

Suddenly he realized that the heavyset Basque had followed him. The man stood across the diminished campfire; he wanted to say something. He looked hard at David and spoke over the glow.

"We thought you should know now. We learned how the pigs made the contact. Eight days ago."

"What are you talking about?" Spaulding was irritated. Chains of command in the north country were at best a calculated risk. He would get the written reports; he did not want conversation. He wanted to sleep, wake up, and get to Ortegal. But the Basque seemed hurt; there was no point in that. "Go on, *amigo*."

"We did not tell you before. We thought your anger would cause you to act rashly."

"How so? Why?"

"It was Bergeron."

"I don't believe that. . . ."

"It is so. They took him in San Sebastián. He did not break easily, but they broke him. Ten days of torture . . . wires in the genitals, among other devices, including hypodermics of the drug. We are told he died spitting at them."

David looked at the man. He found himself accepting the information without feeling. *Without feeling*. And that lack of feeling warned him . . . to be on guard. He had trained the man named Bergeron, lived in the hills with him, talked for hours on end about things only isolation produces between men. Bergeron had fought with him, sacrificed for him. Bergeron was the closest friend he had in the north country.

Two years ago such news would have sent him into furious anger. He would have pounded the earth and called for a strike somewhere across the borders, demanding that retribution be made.

A year ago he would have walked away from the bearer of such news and demanded a few minutes to be by himself. A brief silence to consider . . . by himself . . . the whole of the man who had given his life, and the memories that man conjured up.

Yet now he felt nothing.

Nothing at all.

And it was a terrible feeling to feel nothing at all.

"Don't make that mistake again," he said to the Basque. "Tell me next time. I don't act rashly."

9

DECEMBER 13, 1943, BERLIN, GERMANY

Johann Dietricht shifted his immense soft bulk in the leather chair in front of Altmüller's desk. It was ten thirty at night and he had not had dinner; there had been no time. The Messerschmitt flight from Geneva had been cramped, petrifying; and all things considered, Dietricht was in a state of aggravated exhaustion. A fact he conveyed a number of times to the Unterstaatssekretär.

"We appreciate everything you've been through, Herr Dietricht. And the extraordinary service you've rendered to your country." Altmüller spoke solicitously. "This will take only a few minutes longer, and then I'll have you driven anywhere you like."

"A decent restaurant, if you can find one open at this hour," said Dietricht petulantly.

"We apologize for rushing you away. Perhaps a pleasant evening; a really good meal. Schnapps, good company. Heaven knows you deserve it. . . . There's an inn several miles outside the city. Its patronage is restricted; mostly young flight lieutenants, graduates in training. The kitchen is really excellent."

There was no need for Johann Dietricht to return Altmüller's smiling look; he accepted certain things as indigenous to his life-style. He had been catered to for years. He was a very important man, and other men were invariably trying to please him. As Herr Altmüller was trying to please him now.

"That might be most relaxing. It's been a dreadful day. Days, really."

"Of course, if you've some other . . ."

"No, no. I'll accept your recommendation. . . . Let's get on with it, shall we?"

"Very well. Going back over several points so there's no room for error. . . . The American was not upset with regard to Buenos Aires?"

"He jumped at it. Revolting man; couldn't look you in the eye, but he meant what he said. Simply revolting, though. His clothes, even his fingernails. Dirty fellow!"

"Yes, of course. But you couldn't have misinterpreted?"

"My English is fluent. I understand even the nuances. He was very pleased. I gathered that it served a dual purpose: far removed—thousands of miles away—and in a city nominally controlled by American interests."

"Yes, we anticipated that reaction. Did he have the authority to confirm it?"

"Indeed, yes. There was no question. For all his uncouth manner, he's obviously highly placed, very decisive. Unquestionably devious, but most anxious to make the exchange."

"Did you discuss—even peripherally—either's motives?"

"My word, it was unavoidable! This Kendall was most direct. It was a financial matter, pure and simple. There were no other considerations. And I believe him totally; he talks only figures. He reduces everything to numbers. I doubt he has capacities for anything else. I'm extremely perceptive."

"We counted on that. And Rhinemann? He, too, was acceptable?"

"Immaterial. I pointed out the calculated risk we were taking in an effort to allay suspicions; that Rhinemann was in forced exile. This Kendall was impressed only by Rhinemann's wealth."

"And the time element; we must be thoroughly accurate. Let's go over the projected dates. It would be disastrous if I made any mistake. As I understand you, the American had graduated estimates of carbonado and bortz shipping requirements. . . ."

"Yes, yes," broke in Dietricht, as if enlightening a child. "After all, he had no idea of our needs. I settled on the maximum, of course; there was not that much difference in terms of time. They must divert shipments from points of origin; too great a risk in commandeering existing supplies."

"I'm not sure I understand that. It could be a ploy."

"They're trapped in their own security measures. As of a month ago, every repository of industrial diamonds has excessive controls, dozens of signatures for every kiloweight. To extract our requirements would be massive, lead to exposure."

"The inconvenience of the democratic operation. The underlings are given responsibility. And once given, difficult to divest. Incredible."

"As this Kendall phrased it, there would be too many questions, far too many people would be involved. It would be very sensitive. Their security is filled with Turks."

"We have to accept the condition," said Altmüller with resignation—his own, not for the benefit of Dietricht. "And the anticipated time for these shipment diversions is four to six weeks. It can't be done in less?"

"Certainly. If we are willing to process the ore ourselves."

"Impossible. We could end up with tons of worthless dirt. We must have the finished products, of course."

"Naturally. I made that clear."

"It strikes me as an unnecessary delay. I have to look for inconsistencies, Herr Dietricht. And you said this Kendall was devious."

"But anxious. I said he was anxious, too. He drew an analogy that lends weight to his statements. He said that their problem was no less than that of a man entering the national vaults in the state of Kentucky and walking out with crates of gold bullion. . . . Are we concluded?"

"Just about. The conduit in Geneva will be given the name of the man in Buenos Aires? The man with whom we make contact?"

"Yes. In three or four days. Kendall believed it might be a scientist named Spinelli. An expert in gyroscopics."

"That title could be questioned, I should think. He's Italian?"

"A citizen, however."

"I see. That's to be expected. The designs will be subject to scrutiny, of course. What remains now are the checks and counterchecks each of us employ up to the moment of the exchange. A ritual dance."

"*Ach!* That's for your people. I'm out of it. I have made the initial and, I believe, the most important contribution."

"There's no question about it. And, I assume, you have abided by the Führer's trust in you, conveyed through this office. You have spoken to no one of the Geneva trip?"

"No one. The Führer's trust is not misplaced. He knows that. As my father and his brother, my uncle, the Dietricht loyalty and obedience are unswerving."

"He's mentioned that often. We are finished, *mein Herr.*"

"Good! It's been absolutely nerve-wracking! . . . I'll accept your recommendation of the restaurant. If you'll make arrangements, I'll telephone for my car."

"As you wish, but I can easily have my personal driver take you there. As I said, it's somewhat restricted; my chauffeur is a young man who knows his way around." Altmüller glanced at Dietricht. Their eyes met for the briefest instant. "The Führer would be upset if he thought I inconvenienced you."

"Oh, very well. I suppose it *would* be easier. And we don't want the Führer upset." Dietricht struggled out of the chair as Altmüller rose and walked around the desk.

"Thank you, Herr Dietricht," said the Unterstaatssekretär, extending his hand. "When the time comes we will make known your extraordinary contribution. You are a hero of the Reich, *mein Herr*. It is a privilege to know you. The adjutant outside will take you down to the car. The chauffeur is waiting."

"Such a relief! Good evening, Herr Altmüller." Johann Dietricht waddled toward the door as Franz reached over and pushed a button on his desk.

In the morning Dietricht would be dead, the circumstances so embarrassing no one would care to elaborate on them except in whispers.

Dietricht, the misfit, would be eliminated.

And all traces of the Geneva manipulation to the leaders of the Reich canceled with him. Buenos Aires was now in the hands of Erich Rhinemann and his former brothers in German industry.

Except for him—for Franz Altmüller.

The true manipulator.

DECEMBER 15, 1943, WASHINGTON, D.C.

Swanson disliked the methods he was forced to employ. They were the beginnings, he felt, of an unending string of deceits. And he was not a deceitful man. Perhaps better than most at spotting deceitful men, but that was due to continuous exposure, not intrinsic characteristics.

The methods were distasteful: observing men who did not know they were being watched and listened to; who spoke without the inhibitions they certainly would have experienced had they any idea there were eyes and ears and wire recorders eavesdropping. It all belonged to that other world, Edmund Pace's world.

It had been easy enough to manipulate. Army Intelligence had interrogation rooms all over Washington. In the most unlikely places. Pace had given him a list of locations; he'd chosen one at the Sheraton Hotel. Fourth floor, Suite 4-M; two rooms in evidence and a third room that was not. This unseen room was behind the wall with openings of unidirectional glass in the two rooms of the suite. These observation holes were fronted by impressionist paintings hung permanently in the bedroom and the sitting room. Wire recorders with plug-in jacks were on shelves beneath the openings within the unseen room. Speakers amplified the conversation with minor distortion. The only visual obstructions were the light pastel colors of the paintings.

Not obstructions at all, really.

Neither had it been difficult to maneuver the three men to this room at the Sheraton. Swanson had telephoned Packard's Jonathan Craft and informed him that Walter Kendall was due in on an early afternoon flight from Geneva. The authoritative general also told the frightened civilian that it was possible the military might want to be in telephone communication. Therefore he suggested that Craft reserve a room at a busy, commercial hotel in the center of town. He recommended the Sheraton.

Craft was solicitous; he was running for his life. If the War Department suggested the Sheraton, then the Sheraton it would be. He had booked it without bothering to tell Meridian Aircraft's Howard Oliver.

The front desk took care of the rest.

When Walter Kendall had arrived an hour ago, Swanson was struck by the accountant's disheveled appearance. It was innate untidiness, not the result of traveling. A slovenliness that extended to his gestures, to his constantly darting eyes. He was an outsized rodent in the body of a medium-sized man. It seemed incongruous that men like Oliver and Craft—especially Craft—would associate with a Walter Kendall. Which only pointed up Kendall's value, he supposed. Kendall owned a New York auditing firm. He was a financial analyst, hired by companies to manipulate projections and statistics.

The accountant had not shaken hands with either man. He had gone straight to an easy chair opposite the sofa, sat down, and opened his briefcase. He had begun his report succinctly.

"The son of a bitch was a homo, I swear to Christ!"

As the hour wore on, Kendall described in minute detail everything that had taken place in Geneva. The quantities of bortz and carbonado agreed upon; the quality certifications; Buenos Aires; Gian Spinelli, the gyroscopic designs —*their* certifications and delivery; and the liaison, Erich Rhinemann, exiled Jew. Kendall was an authoritative rodent who was not awkward in the tunnels of negotiated filth. He was, in fact, very much at home.

"How can we be sure they'll bargain in good faith?" asked Craft.

"Good *faith?*" Kendall smirked and winced and grinned at the Packard executive. "You're too goddamned much. Good *faith!*"

"They might not give us the proper designs," continued Craft. "They could pass off substitutes, worthless substitutes!"

"He's got a point," said the jowled Oliver, his lips taut.

"And we could package crates of cut glass. You think that hasn't crossed their minds? . . . But they won't and we won't. For the same shit-eating reason. Our respective necks are on chopping blocks. We've got a common enemy and it's not each other."

Oliver, sitting across from Kendall, stared at the accountant. "Hitler's generals there; the War Department here."

"That's right. We're both lines of supply. For God, country and a dollar or two. And we're both in a lousy position. We don't tell the goddamned generals how to fight a war, and they don't tell us how to keep up production. If they screw up strategy or lose a battle, no screams come from us. But if we're caught short, if we don't deliver, those fuckers go after our necks. It's goddamned unfair. This homo Dietricht, he sees it like I do. We have to protect ourselves."

Craft rose from the couch; it was a nervous action, a gesture of doubt. He spoke softly, hesitantly. "This isn't exactly protecting ourselves in any normal fashion. We're dealing with the enemy."

"Which enemy?" Kendall shuffled papers on his lap; he did not look up at Craft. "But right, again. It's better than 'normal.' No matter who wins, we've each got a little something going when it's over. We agreed on that, too."

There was silence for several moments. Oliver leaned forward in his chair, his eyes still riveted on Kendall. "That's a dividend, Walter. There could be a lot of common sense in that."

"A lot," replied the accountant, allowing a short glance at Oliver. "We're kicking the crap out of their cities, bombing factories right off the map; railroads, highways—they're going up in smoke. It'll get worse. There's going to be a lot of money made putting it all back together. Reconstruction money."

"Suppose Germany wins?" asked Craft, by the window.

"Goddamned unlikely," answered Kendall. "It's just a question of how much damage is done to both sides, and we've got the hardware. The more damage, the more it'll cost to repair. That includes England. If you boys are smart, you'll be prepared to convert and pick up some of the postwar change."

"The diamonds. . . ." Craft turned from the window. "What are they for?"

"What difference does it make?" Kendall separated a page on his lap and wrote on it. "They ran out; their asses are in a sling. Same as yours with the guidance system. . . . By the way, Howard, did you have a preliminary talk with the mines?"

Oliver was deep in thought. He blinked and raised his eyes. "Yes. Koening. New York offices."

"How did you put it?"

"That it was top secret, War Department approval. The authorization would come from Swanson's office but even *he* wasn't cleared."

"They bought that?" The accountant was still writing.

"I said the money would be up front. They stand to make a few million. We met at the Bankers' Club."

"They bought it." A statement.

"Walter . . .," continued Oliver, "you said Spinelli before. I don't like it. He's a bad choice."

Kendall stopped writing and looked up at the Meridian man. "I didn't figure to tell him anything. Just that we were buying; he was to clear everything before we paid, make sure the designs were authentic."

"No good. He wouldn't be taken off the project. Not now; too many questions. Find somebody else."

"I see what you mean." Kendall put down the pencil. He picked his nose; it was a gesture of thought. "Wait a minute. . . . There *is* someone. Right in Pasadena. He's a weird son of a bitch, but he could be perfect." Kendall laughed while breathing through his mouth. "He doesn't even talk; I mean he *can't* talk."

"Is he any good?" asked Oliver.

"He's got problems but he may be better than Spinelli," replied Kendall, writing on a separate piece of paper. "I'll take care of it. . . . It'll cost you."

Oliver shrugged. "Include it in the overruns, you prick. What's next?"

"A contact in Buenos Aires. Someone who can deal with Rhinemann, work out the details of the transfer."

"Who?" asked Craft apprehensively, both hands clasped in front of him.

The accountant grinned, baring his discolored teeth. "You volunteering? You look like a priest."

"Good Lord, no! I was simply . . ."

"How much, Kendall?" interrupted Oliver.

"More than you want to pay but I don't think you've got a choice. I'll pass on what I can to Uncle Sam; I'll save you what I can."

"You do that."

"There's a lot of military down in Buenos Aires. Swanson will have to run some interference."

"He won't touch it," said Oliver quickly. "He was specific. He doesn't want to hear or see your name again."

"I don't give a shit if he does. But this Rhinemann's going to want certain guarantees. I can tell you that right now."

"Swanson will be upset." Craft's voice was high and intense. "We don't *want* him upset."

"Upset, shit! He wants to keep that pretty uniform nice and clean. . . . Tell you what, don't push him now. Give me some time; I've got a lot of things to figure out. Maybe I'll come up with a way to keep his uniform clean after all. Maybe I'll send him a bill."

He wants to keep that pretty uniform nice and clean. . . .

So devoutly to be wished, Mr. Kendall, thought Swanson as he approached the bank of elevators.

But not possible now. The uniform had to get dirty. The emergence of a man named Erich Rhinemann made that necessary.

Rhinemann was one of Hitler's fiascos. Berlin knew it; London and Washington knew it. Rhinemann was a man totally committed to power: financial, political, military. For him all authority must emanate from a single source and he would ultimately settle for nothing less than being at the core of that source.

The fact that he was a Jew was incidental. An inconvenience to end with the end of the war.

When the war was over, Erich Rhinemann would be called back. What might be left of German industry would demand it; the world's financial leaders would demand it.

Rhinemann would reenter the international market place with more power than ever before.

Without the Buenos Aires manipulation.

With it his leverage would be extraordinary.

His knowledge, his participation in the exchange would provide him with an unparalleled weapon to be used against all sides, all governments.

Especially Washington.

Erich Rhinemann would have to be eliminated.

After the exchange.

And if only for this reason, Washington had to have another man in Buenos Aires.

10

DECEMBER 16, 1943, WASHINGTON, D.C.

It was unusual for the ranking officer of Fairfax to leave the compound for any reason, but Colonel Edmund Pace was so ordered.

Pace stood in front of General Swanson's desk and began to understand. Swanson's instructions were brief, but covered more territory than their brevity implied. Intelligence files would have to be culled from dozens of double-locked cabinets, a number examined minutely.

Swanson knew that at first Pace disapproved. The Fairfax commander could not conceal his astonishment—at first. The agent in question had to be fluent in both German and Spanish. He had to have a working knowledge—not expert but certainly more than conversational—of aircraft engineering, including metallurgical dynamics and navigational systems. He had to be a man capable of sustaining a cover perhaps on the embassy level. That meant an individual possessing the necessary graces to function easily in monied circles, in the diplomatic arena.

At this juncture Pace had balked. His knowledge of the Johannesburg probe and the Geneva conduit caused him to object. He interrupted Swanson, only to be told to hold his remarks until his superior had finished.

The last qualification of the man for Buenos Aires—and the general conceded its inconsistency when included with the previous technical qualifications—was that the agent be experienced in "swift dispatch."

The man was to be no stranger to killing. Not combat fire with its adversaries separated, pitched into frenzy by the sights and sounds of battle. But a man who could kill in silence, facing his target. Alone.

This last qualification mollified Pace. His expression conveyed the fact that whatever his superiors were involved in, it was not wholly what he suspected it to be—might be. The War Department did not request such a man if it intended to keep surface agreements.

The ranking officer of Fairfax made no comment. It was understood that he, alone, would make the file search. He asked for a code, a name to which he could refer in any communications.

Swanson had leaned forward in his chair and stared at the map on his desk. The map that had been there for over three hours.

"Call it 'Tortugas,' " he said.

DECEMBER 18, 1943, BERLIN, GERMANY

Altmüller stared at the unbroken seal on the wide, brown manila envelope. He moved it under his desk lamp and took a magnifying glass from his top drawer. He examined the seal under the magnification; he was satisfied. It had not been tampered with.

The embassy courier had flown in from Buenos Aires—by way of Senegal and Lisbon—and delivered the envelope in person, as instructed. Since the courier was based permanently in Argentina, Altmüller did not want him carrying back gossip, so he indulged the man in innocuous conversation, referring to the communication several times in an offhand, derogatory manner. He implied it was a nuisance—a memorandum concerned with embassy finances and really belonged at the Finanzministerium, but what could he do? The ambassador was reputed to be an old friend of Speer's.

Now that the courier was gone and the door shut, Altmüller riveted his attention on the envelope. It was from Erich Rhinemann.

He sliced open the top edge. The letter was written by hand, in Rhinemann's barely decipherable script.

My Dear Altmüller:

To serve the Reich is a privilege I undertake with enthusiasm. I am, of course, grateful for your assurances that my efforts will be made known to my many old friends. I assumed you would do no less under the circumstances.

You will be pleased to know that in the coastal waters from Punta Delgada north to the Caribbean, my ships are honored under the neutrality of the Paraguayan flag. This convenience may be of service to you. Further, I have a number of vessels, notably small and medium-sized craft converted with high-performance engines. They are capable of traveling swiftly through the coastal waters, and there are refueling depots, thus enabling considerable distances to be traversed rapidly. Certainly no comparison to the airplane, but then the trips are made in utter secrecy, away from the prying eyes that surround all airfields these days. Even we neutrals must constantly outflank the blockades.

This information should answer the curiously obscure questions you raised.

I beg you to be more precise in future communications. Regardless, you may be assured of my commitment to the Reich.

Along these lines, associates in Berne inform me that your Führer is showing marked signs of fatigue. It was to be expected, was it not?

Remember, my dear Franz, the concept is always a greater monument than the man. In the current situation, the concept came *before* the man. *It* is the monument.

I await word from you.

Erich Rhinemann

How delicately unsubtle was Rhinemann! . . . *commitment to the Reich . . . associates in Berne . . . marked signs of fatigue . . . to be expected. . . .*

. . . a greater monument than the man. . . .

Rhinemann spelled out his abilities, his financial power, his "legitimate" concerns and his unequivocal commitment to Germany. By including, *juxtaposing* these factors, he elevated himself above even the Führer. And by so doing, condemned Hitler—for the greater glory of the Reich. No doubt Rhinemann had photostats made of his letter; Rhinemann would start a very complete file of the Buenos Aires operation. And one day he would use it to maneuver himself to the top of postwar Germany. Perhaps of all Europe. For he would have the weapon to guarantee his acceptance.

In victory *or* defeat. Unswerving devotion or, conversely, blackmail of such proportions the Allies would tremble at the thought of it.

So be it, thought Altmüller. He had no brief with Rhinemann. Rhinemann was an expert at whatever he entered into. He was methodical to the point of excess; conservative in progress—only in the sense of mastering all details before going forward. Above everything, he was boldly imaginative.

Altmüller's eyes fell on Rhinemann's words:

I beg you to be more precise in future communications.

Franz smiled. Rhinemann was right. He *had* been obscure. But for a sound reason: he wasn't sure where he was going; where he was being led, perhaps. He only knew that the crates of carbonado diamonds had to be thoroughly examined, and that would take time. More time than Rhinemann realized if the information he had received from Peenemünde was accurate. According to Peenemünde, it would be a simple matter for the Americans to pack thousands of low-quality bortz that, to the inexperienced eye, would be undetectable. Stones that would crack at the first touch to steel.

If the operation was in the hands of the British, that would be the expected maneuver.

And even the Americans had decent Intelligence manipulators. *If* the Intelligence services were intrinsic to the exchange. Yet Altmüller doubted their active involvement. The Americans were governmentally hypocritical. They would make demands of their industrialists and expect those demands to be met. However, they would close their eyes to the methods; the unsophisticated Puritan streak was given extraordinary lip service in Washington.

Such children. Yet angry, frustrated children were dangerous.

The crates would have to be examined minutely.

In Buenos Aires.

And once accepted, no risks could be taken that the crates would be blown out of the sky or the water. So it seemed logical to ask Rhinemann what avenues of escape were available. For somewhere, somehow, the crates would have to make rendezvous with the most logical method of transportation back to Germany.

Submarine.

Rhinemann would understand; he might even applaud the precision of future communications.

Altmüller got up from his desk and stretched. He walked absently around his office, trying to rid his back of the cramps resulting from sitting too long. He approached the leather armchair in which Johann Dietricht had sat several days ago.

Dietricht was dead. The expendable, misfit messenger had been found in a bloodsoaked bed, the stories of the evening's debauchery so demeaning that it was decided to bury them and the body without delay.

Altmüller wondered if the Americans had the stomach for such decisions.

He doubted it.

DECEMBER 19, 1943, FAIRFAX, VIRGINIA

Swanson stood silently in front of the heavy steel door inside the Quonset structure. The security lieutenant was on the wall intercom for only the length of time it took for him to give the general's name. The lieutenant nodded, replaced the phone, saluted the general for a second time. The heavy steel door clicked and Swanson knew he could enter.

The Fairfax commander was alone, as Swanson had ordered. He was standing to the right of his table-desk, a file folder in his hand. He saluted his superior.

"Good morning, general."

"Morning. You worked fast; I appreciate it."

"It may not be everything you want but it's the best we can come up with. . . . Sit down, sir. I'll describe the qualifications. If they meet with your approval, the file's yours. If not, it'll go back into the vaults."

Swanson walked to one of the straight-backed chairs in

front of the colonel's desk and sat down. He did so with a touch of annoyance. Ed Pace, as so many of his subordinates in Clandestine Operations, functioned as though he were responsible to no one but God; and even He had to be cleared by Fairfax. It struck Swanson that it would be much simpler if Pace simply gave him the file and let him read it for himself.

On the other hand, Fairfax's indoctrination had at its core the possibility—however remote—that any pair of eyes might be captured by the enemy. A man could be in Washington one week, Anzio or the Solomons the next. There was logic in Pace's methods; a geographical network of underground agents could be exposed with a single break in the security chain.

Still, it was annoying as hell. Pace seemed to enjoy his role; he was humorless, thought Swanson.

"The subject under consideration is a proven field man. He's acted as independently as anyone in one of our touchiest locations. Languages: acceptable fluency. Deportment and cover: extremely flexible. He moves about the civilian spectrum facilely, from embassy teacups to bricklayers' saloons—he's very mobile and convincing."

"You're coming up with a positive print, colonel."

"If I am, I'm sorry. He's valuable where he is. But you haven't heard the rest. You may change your mind."

"Go on."

"On the negative side, he's not army. I don't mean he's a civilian—he holds the rank of captain, as a matter of fact, but I don't think he's ever used it. What I'm saying is that he's never operated within a chain of command. He set up the network; he *is* the command. He has been for nearly four years now."

"Why is that negative?"

"There's no way to tell how he reacts to discipline. Taking orders."

"There won't be much latitude for deviation. It's cut and dried."

"Very well. . . . A second negative; he's not aeronautical. . . ."

"That *is* important!" Swanson spoke harshly; Pace was wasting his time. The man in Buenos Aires had to understand what the hell was going on; perhaps more than understand.

"He's in a related field, sir. One that our people say primes him for crash instructions."

"What is it?"

"He's a construction engineer. With considerable experience in mechanical, electrical and metal design. His background includes full responsibility for whole structures—from foundations through the finished productions. He's a blueprint expert."

Swanson paused, then nodded noncommittally. "All right. Go on."

"The most difficult part of your request was to find someone—someone with these technical qualifications—who had practical experience in 'dispatch.' You even conceded that."

"I know." Swanson felt it was the time to show a little more humanity. Pace looked exhausted; the search had not been easy. "I handed you a tough one. Does your nonmilitary, mobile engineer have any 'dispatches' of record?"

"We try to avoid records, because . . ."

"You know what I mean."

"Yes. He's stationed where it's unavoidable, I'm sorry to say. Except for the men in Burma and India, he's had more occasions to use last-extremity solutions than anyone in the field. To our knowledge, he's never hesitated to implement them."

Swanson started to speak, then hesitated. He creased his brow above his questioning eyes. "You can't help but wonder about such men, can you?"

"They're trained. Like anyone else they do a job . . . for a purpose. He's not a killer by nature. Very few of our really good men are."

"I've never understood your work, Ed. Isn't that strange?"

"Not at all. I couldn't possibly function in your end of the War Department. Those charts and graphs and civilian double-talkers confuse me. . . . How does the subject sound to you?"

"You have no alternates?"

"Several. But with each there's the same negative. Those that have the languages *and* the aeronautical training have no experience in 'dispatch.' No records of . . . extreme prejudice. I worked on the assumption that it was as important as the other factors."

"Your assumption was correct. . . . Tell me, do you know him?"

"Very well. I recruited him, I observed every phase of his training. I've seen him in the field. He's a pro."

"I want one."

"Then maybe he's your man. But before I say it, I'd like to ask you a question. I have to ask it, actually; I'll be asked the same question myself."

"I hope I can give you an answer."

"It's within bounds. It's not specific."

"What is it?"

Pace came to the edge of the desk toward Swanson. He leaned his back against it and folded his arms. It was another army signal: *I'm your subordinate but this puts us on equal footing right now—at this moment.*

"I said the subject was valuable where he is. That's not strong enough. He's *in*valuable, essential. By removing him from his station we jeopardize a very sensitive operation. We can handle it, but the risks are considerable. What I have to know is, does the assignment justify his transfer?"

"Let me put it this way, colonel," said Swanson, the tone of his voice gentle but strong. "The assignment has no priority equal, with the possible exception of the Manhattan Project. You've heard of the Manhattan Project, I assume."

"I have." Pace got off his desk. "And the War Department—through your office—will confirm this priority?"

"It will."

"Then here he is, general." Pace handed Swanson the file folder. "He's one of the best we've got. He's our man in Lisbon. . . . Spaulding. Captain David Spaulding."

11

DECEMBER 26, 1943, RIBADAVIA, SPAIN

David sped south on the motorcycle along the dirt road paralleling the Minho River. It was the fastest route to the border, just below Ribadavia. Once across he would swing west to an airfield outside Valença. The flight to Lisbon would take another two hours, if the weather held and if an aircraft was available. Valença didn't expect him for another two days; its planes might all be in use.

His anxiety matched the intensity of the spinning, careening wheels beneath him. It was all so extraordinary; it made no *sense* to him. There was *no one* in *Lisbon* who could issue such orders as he had received from Ortegal!

What had *happened?*

He felt suddenly as though a vitally important part of his existence was being threatened. And then he wondered at his own reaction. He had no love for his temporary world; he took no pleasure in the countless manipulations and countermanipulations. In fact, he despised most of his day-to-day activities, was sick of the constant fear, the unending high-risk factors to be evaluated with every decision.

Yet he recognized what bothered him so: he had grown in his work. He had arrived in Lisbon centuries ago, beginning a new life, and he had mastered it. Somehow it signified all the buildings he wanted to build, all the blueprints he wanted to turn into mortar and steel. There was precision and finality in his work; the results were there every day. Often many times every day. Like the hundreds of details in construction specifications, the information came to him and he put it all together and emerged with reality.

And it was this reality that others depended upon.

Now someone wanted him out of Lisbon! Out of Portugal and Spain! Was it as simple as that? Had his reports angered one general too many? Had a strategy session been nullified because he sent back the truth of a supposedly successful operation? Were the London and Washington brass finally annoyed to the point of removing a critical thorn? It was possible; he had been told often enough that the men in the underground rooms in London's Tower Road had exploded more than once over his assessments. He knew that Washington's Office of Strategic Services felt he was encroaching on their territory; even G-2, ostensibly his own agency, criticized his involvement with the escape teams.

But beyond the complaints there was one evaluation that overrode them all: he was good. He had welded together the best network in Europe.

Which was why David was confused. And not a little disturbed, for a reason he tried not to admit: he needed praise.

There were no buildings of consequence, no extraordinary blueprints turned into more extraordinary edifices. Perhaps there never would be. He would be a middle-aged engineer when it was over. A middle-aged engineer who had not practiced his profession in years, not even in the vast army of the United States, whose Corps of Engineers was the largest construction crew in history.

He tried not to think about it.

He crossed the border at Mendoso, where the guards knew him as a rich, irresponsible expatriate avoiding the risks of war. They accepted his gratuities and waved him over.

The flight from Valença to the tiny airfield outside Lisbon was hampered by heavy rains. It was necessary to put down twice—at Águeda and Pombal—before the final leg. He was met by an embassy vehicle; the driver, a cryptographer named Marshall, was the only man in the embassy who knew his real function.

"Rotten weather, isn't it?" said the code man, settling behind the wheel as David threw his pack in the back seat. "I don't envy you up in a crate like that. Not in this rain."

"Those grass pilots fly so low you could jump down. I worry more about the trees."

"I'd just worry." Marshall started up and drove toward the broken-down pasture gate that served as the field's entrance. On the road he switched on his high beams; it was not yet six o'clock, but the sky was dark, headlights necessary. "I thought you might flatter me and ask why an expert of my standing was acting as chauffeur. I've been here since four. Go on, ask me. It was a hell of a long wait."

Spaulding grinned. "Jesus, Marsh, I just figured you were trying to get in my good graces. So I'd take you north on the next trip. Or have I been made a brigadier?"

"You've been made something, David." Marshall spoke seriously. "I took the D.C. message myself. It was that high up in the codes: eyes-only, senior cryp."

"I'm flattered," said Spaulding softly, relieved that he could talk to someone about the preposterous news of his transfer. "What the hell is it all about?"

"I have no idea what they want you for, of course, but I can spell out one conclusion: they want you yesterday. They've covered all avenues of delay. The orders were to compile a list of your contacts with complete histories of each: motives, dates, repeats, currency, routings, codes . . . everything. Nothing left out. Subsequent order: alert the whole network that you're out of strategy."

"*Out of . . .*" David trailed off the words in disbelief. *Out of strategy* was a phrase used as often for defectors as it was for transfers. Its connotation was final, complete breakoff. "That's insane! This is *my network!*"

"Not anymore. They flew a man in from London this morning. I think he's Cuban; rich, too. Studied architecture in Berlin before the war. He's been holed up in an office studying your files. He's your replacement. . . . I wanted you to know."

David stared at the windshield, streaked with the harsh Lisbon rain. They were on the hard-surface road that led through the Alfama district, with its winding, hilly streets below the cathedral towers of the Moorish St. George and the Gothic Sé. The American embassy was in the Baixa, past the Terreiro do Paço. Another twenty minutes.

So it was really over, thought Spaulding. They were sending him out. A Cuban architect was now the man in

Lisbon. The feeling of being dispossessed took hold of him again. So much was being taken away and under such extraordinary conditions. *Out of strategy . . .*

"Who signed the orders?"

"That's part of the craziness. The use of high codes presumes supreme authority; no one else has access. But no one signed them, either. No name other than yours was in the cable."

"What am I supposed to do?"

"You get on a plane tomorrow. The flight time will be posted by tonight. The bird makes one stop. At Lajes Field on Terceira, the Azores. You pick up your orders there."

12

DECEMBER 26, 1943, WASHINGTON, D.C.

Swanson reached for the tiny lever on his desk intercom and spoke: "Send Mr. Kendall in." He stood up, remaining where he was, waiting for the door to open. He would not walk around his desk to greet the man; he would not offer his hand in even a symbol of welcome. He recalled that Walter Kendall had avoided shaking hands with Craft and Oliver at the Sheraton. The handshake would not be missed; his avoidance of it, however, might be noted.

Kendall entered; the door closed. Swanson saw that the accountant's appearance had changed little since the afternoon conference he had observed from the unseen room eleven days ago. Kendall wore the same suit, conceivably the same soiled shirt. God knew about his underwear; it wasn't a pleasant thought to dwell on. There was the slightest curl on Kendall's upper lip. It did not convey anger or even disdain. It was merely the way the man breathed: mouth and nostrils simultaneously. As an animal might breathe.

"Come in, Mr. Kendall. Sit down."

Kendall did so without comment. His eyes locked briefly with Swanson's but only briefly.

"You're listed on my appointment calendar as being called in to clarify a specific overrun on a Meridian contract," said the general, sitting down promptly. "Not to justify, simply enumerate. As the . . . outside auditing firm you can do that."

"But that's not why I'm here, is it?" Kendall reached into his pocket for a crumpled pack of cigarettes. He squeezed the end before lighting one. Swanson noted that the accountant's fingernails were unkempt, ragged, soiled at the tips. The brigadier began to see—but would not ponder it—that there was a sickness about Walter Kendall, the surface appearance merely one manifestation.

"No, that's not why you're here," he answered curtly. "I want to set up ground rules so neither of us misunderstands. . . . So *you* don't misunderstand, primarily."

"Ground rules mean a game. What's the game we're playing, general?"

"Perhaps . . . 'Clean Uniforms' might be a good name for it. Or how to run some 'Interference in Buenos Aires.' That might strike you as more inclusive."

Kendall, who had been gazing at his cigarette, abruptly shifted his eyes to the general. "So Oliver and Craft couldn't wait. They had to bring their teacher his big fat apple. I didn't think you wanted it."

"Neither Craft nor Howard Oliver has been in touch with this office—or with me—in over a week. Since you left for Geneva."

Kendall paused before speaking. "Then your uniform's pretty goddamned dirty now. . . . The Sheraton. I thought that was a little unritzy for Craft; he's the Waldorf type. . . . So you had the place *wired*. You trapped those fuckers." Kendall's voice was hoarse, not angry, not loud. "Well, you just remember how I got to where I was going. How I got to Geneva. You got that on the wire, too."

"We accommodated a request of the War Production Board; relative to a business negotiation with a firm in Geneva. It's done frequently. However, we often follow up if there's reason to think *anything prejudicial. . . .*"

"Horseshit!"

Swanson exhaled an audible breath. "That reaction is pointless. I don't want to argue with you. The *point* has been *made*. I have an . . . edited spool of wire that could send you straight to the hangman or the electric chair. Oliver, too. . . . Craft might get off with a life sentence. You ridiculed his doubts; you didn't let him talk. . . . The point, however, *has been made*."

Kendall leaned forward and crushed out his cigarette in an ashtray on Swanson's desk. His sudden fear made him look at the general; he was searching. "But you're more interested in Buenos Aires than the electric chair. That's right, isn't it?"

"I'm forced to be. As distasteful as it may be to me. As loathsome. . . ."

"Cut out the horseshit," Kendall interrupted sharply; he was no amateur in such discussions. He knew when to assert himself and his contributions. "As you said, the point's been made. I think you're in the barnyard with the rest of us pigs. . . . So don't play Jesus. Your halo smells."

"Fair enough. But don't you forget, I've got a dozen different pigsties to run to. A great big War Department that could get me to Burma or Sicily in forty-eight hours. You don't. You're right out there . . . in the barnyard. For everyone to see. And I've got a spool of wire that would make you *special. That's* the understanding I want you to have clear in your mind. I hope it is."

Kendall squeezed the tip of a second cigarette and lit the opposite end. The smoke drifted over his nostrils; he was about to speak, then stopped, staring at the general, his look a mixture of fear and hostility.

Swanson found himself consciously avoiding Kendall's eyes. To acknowledge the man at that moment was to acknowledge the pact. And then he realized what would make the pact bearable. It was the answer, *his* answer; at least a surface one. He was amazed it had not occurred to him before this moment.

Walter Kendall would have to be eliminated.

As Erich Rhinemann would be eliminated.

When Buenos Aires was in reach of completion, Kendall's death was mandatory.

And then all specific traces to the government of the United States would be covered.

He wondered briefly if the men in Berlin had the foresight for such abrupt decisions. He doubted it.

He looked up at the filthy—sick—accountant and returned his stare in full measure. General Alan Swanson was no longer afraid. Or consumed with guilt.

He was a soldier.

"Shall we continue, Mr. Kendall?"

The accountant's projections for Buenos Aires were well thought out. Swanson found himself fascinated by Walter Kendall's sense of maneuver and countermeasure. The man thought like a sewer rat: instinctively, probing sources of smell and light; his strength in his suspicions, in his constantly varying estimates of his adversaries. He was indeed an animal: predator and evader.

The Germans' prime concerns could be reduced to three: the quality of the bortz and carbonado diamonds; the quantity of the shipment; and finally the methods of safe transport to Germany. Unless these factors could be guaranteed, there would be no delivery of the gyroscopic designs—the guidance system.

Kendall assumed that the shipment of diamonds would be inspected by a team of experts—not one man or even two.

A team, then, three to five men, would be employed; the length of time required might extend to the better part of a week, depending upon the sophistication of the instruments used. This information he had learned from Koening in New York. During this period simultaneous arrangements would be agreed to that allowed an aerophysicist to evaluate the gyroscopic designs brought from Peenemünde. If the Nazis were as cautious as Kendall assumed they would be, the designs would be delivered in stages, timed to the schedule the inspection team considered adequate for its examination of the diamonds. The gyroscope scientist would no doubt be fed step-blueprints in isolation, with no chance of photostat or duplication until the diamond team had completed its work.

Once both sides were satisfied with the deliveries, Kendall anticipated that an ultimate threat would be imposed that guaranteed safe transport to the respective destinations. And it was logical that this "weapon" be identical for each party: threat of exposure. Betrayal of cause and country.

Penalties: death.

The same "weapon" the general held on him, on Walter Kendall.

What else was new?

Did Kendall think it was possible to get the designs and subsequently sabotage or reclaim the diamond shipment?

No. Not as long as it remained a civilian exchange. The threat of exposure was too complete; there was too much proof of contact. Neither crisis could be denied and names were known. The taint of collaboration could ruin men and corporations. "Authenticated" rumors could be circulated easily.

And if the military moved in, the civilians would move

out instantly—the responsibility of delivery no longer theirs.

Swanson should know this; it was precisely the situation he had engineered.

Swanson knew it.

Where would the diamonds be inspected? Where was the most advantageous location?

Kendall's reply was succinct: any location that seemed advantageous to one side would be rejected by the other. He thought the Germans foresaw this accurately and for that reason suggested Buenos Aires. It was on the spool of wire. Didn't Swanson listen?

Powerful men in Argentina were unquestionably, if quietly, pro-Axis, but the government's dependency on Allied economics took precedence. The neutrality essentially was controlled by the economic factors. Each side, therefore, had something: the Germans would find a sympathetic environment, but the Americans were capable of exerting a strong enough influence to counteract that sympathy—without eliminating it.

Kendall respected the men in Berlin who centered in on Buenos Aires. They understood the necessity of balancing the psychological elements, the need to give up, yet still retain spheres of influence. They were good.

Each side would be extremely cautious; the environment demanded it. Timing would be everything.

Swanson knew how the designs would be gotten out: a string of pursuit aircraft flying up the coastal bases under diplomatic cover. This cover would extend to the military. Only *he* would be aware of the operation; no one else in the services or, for that matter, in the government would be apprised. He would make the arrangements and give them to Kendall at the proper time.

What transport would the Germans arrive at? asked the general.

"They've got a bigger problem. They recognize it so they'll probably make some kind of airtight demands. They could ask for a hostage, but I don't think so."

"Why not?"

"Who've we got—that's involved—that's not expendable? Christ! If it was me, you'd be the first to say, 'Shoot the son of a bitch!' " Kendall again locked his eyes briefly with Swanson's. "Of course, you wouldn't know what particular safeguards *I* took; a lot of uniforms would be dirty as hell."

Swanson recognized Kendall's threat for what it was. He also knew he could handle it. It would take some thought, but such considerations could come later. It would be no insurmountable hurdle to prepare for Kendall's dispatch. The isolation would come first; then an elaborate dossier. . . .

"Let's concentrate on how they expect to ship out the bortz and carbonado. There's no point in going after each other," said Swanson.

"We're beyond that, then?"

"I think we are."

"Good. Just don't forget it," said Kendall.

"The diamonds will be brought to Buenos Aires. Have those arrangements been made?"

"They're being made. Delivery date in three, three-and-a-half weeks. Unless there's a fuck-up in the South Atlantic. We don't expect any."

"The inspection team does its work in Buenos Aires. We send the physicist . . . who will it be? Spinelli?"

"No. For both our sakes we ruled him out. But you know that. . . ."

"Yes. Who, then?"

"Man named Lyons. Eugene Lyons. I'll get you a file on him. You'll sweat bullets when you read it, but if there's anyone better than Spinelli, it's him. We wouldn't take any chances. He's in New York now."

Swanson made a note. "What about the German transport? Any ideas?"

"A couple. Neutral cargo plane north to Recife in Brazil, across east to Palmas or someplace in Guinea on the African coast. Then straight up to Lisbon and out. That's the fastest routing. But they may not want to chance the air corridors."

"You sound military."

"When I do a job, it's thorough."

"What else?"

"I think they'll probably settle for a submarine. Maybe two, for diversion purposes. It's slower but the safest."

"Subs can't enter Argentine ports. Our southern patrols would blow them out of the water. If they put in, they're impounded. We're not going to change those rules."

"You may have to."

"Impossible. There has to be another way."

"You may have to find it. Don't forget those clean uniforms."

Swanson looked away. "What about Rhinemann?"

"What about him? He's on his way back. With his kind of money, even Hitler can't freeze him out."

"I don't trust him."

"You'd be a goddamned fool if you did. But the worst he can do is hold out for market concessions—or money—from both sides. So what? He'll deliver. Why wouldn't he?"

"I'm sure he'll deliver; that's the one thing I'm positive about. . . . Which brings me to the main point of this meeting. I want a man in Buenos Aires. At the embassy."

Kendall absorbed Swanson's statement before replying. He reached for the ashtray and put it on the arm of his chair. "One of your men or one of ours? We need someone; we figured you'd have us supply him."

"You figured wrong. I've picked him."

"That could be dangerous. I tell you this with no charge . . . since I already said it."

"If we move in, the civilian contingent moves out?" A question.

"It makes sense. . . ."

"Only if the man I send *knows* about the diamonds. You're to make sure he doesn't." A statement. "Make *very* sure, Kendall. Your life depends on it."

The accountant watched Swanson closely. "What's the point?"

"There are six thousand miles between Buenos Aires and the Meridian Aircraft plants. I want that trip made without any mishaps. I want those designs brought back by a professional."

"You're taking a chance on dirtying up the uniforms, aren't you, general?"

"No. The man will be told that Rhinemann made a deal for the designs out of Peenemünde. We'll say Rhinemann brought in the German underground. For escape routings."

"Full of holes! Since when does the underground work for a price? Why would they go three thousand miles out of their way? Or work with Rhinemann?"

"Because they need him and he needs them. Rhinemann

was exiled as a Jew; it was a mistake. He rivaled Krupp. There are many in German industry still loyal to him; and he maintains offices in Berne. . . . Our crisis in gyroscopics is no secret, we know that. Rhinemann would use that knowledge; make deals in Berne."

"Why even bring in the underground?"

"I have my own reasons. They're not your concern." Swanson spoke curtly, clipping his words. It crossed his mind—fleetingly—that he was getting overtired again. He had to watch that; his strength was hollow when he was tired. And now he had to be convincing. He had to make Kendall obey without question. The important thing was to get Spaulding within reach of Erich Rhinemann. Rhinemann was the target.

The brigadier watched the filthy man in front of him. It sickened him to think that such a human slug was so necessary to the moment. Or was it, he wondered, that he was reduced to using such a man? Using him and then ordering his execution. It made their worlds closer.

"All right, Mr. Kendall, I'll spell it out. . . . The man I've picked for Buenos Aires is one of the best Intelligence agents we've got. He'll bring those designs back. But I don't want to take the slightest chance that he could learn of the diamond transfer. Rhinemann operating alone is suspect; the inclusion of the German underground puts it above suspicion."

Swanson had done his homework; everyone spoke of the French and Balkan undergrounds, but the *German* underground had worked harder and more effectively, with greater sacrifice, than all the others combined. The former man in Lisbon would know that. It would make the Buenos Aires assignment palatable and legitimate.

"Wait a minute. . . . Jesus Christ! *Wait* a minute." Kendall's disagreeable expression abruptly changed. It was as if suddenly—with reluctant enthusiasm—he had found merit in something Swanson said. "That could be a good device."

"What do you mean, *device?*"

"Just that. You say you're going to use it for this agent. The underground's above suspicion and all that shit. . . . O.K., let's go further. You just spelled out the guarantee we have to give."

"What guarantee?"

"That the shipment of Koening diamonds can get *out* of Buenos Aires. It's going to be *the* ball-breaker. . . . Let me ask you a couple of questions. And give me straight answers."

The *sewer rat*, thought Swanson, looking at the excited, disheveled figure-man. "Go ahead."

"This underground. They've gotten a lot of people out of Germany, very important people. I mean everybody knows that."

"They've—it's—been very effective."

"Does it have any hooks into the German *navy?*"

"I imagine so. Allied Central Intelligence would know specifically. . . ."

"But you don't want to go to them. Or do you?"

"Out of the question."

"But it is possible?"

"What?"

"The German *navy*, goddamn it! The submarine fleet!" Kendall was leaning forward, his eyes now boring into Swanson's.

"I would think so. I'm not . . . not primarily an Intelligence man. The German underground has an extensive network. I assume it has contacts in the naval command."

"Then it *is* possible."

"Yes, *anything's* possible." Swanson lowered his voice, turning away from his own words. "This is possible."

Kendall leaned back in the chair and crushed out his cigarette. He grinned his unattractive grin and wagged his forefinger at Swanson. "Then there's your story. Clean as a goddamned whistle and way above any goddamned suspicion. . . . While we're buying those designs, it just so happens that a German submarine is floating around, ready to surface and bring out one—even two, if you like —very important defectors. Courtesy of the underground. What better reason for a submarine to surface in hostile waters? Protected from patrols. . . . Only nobody gets off. Instead, some fresh cargo gets put on board."

Swanson tried to assimilate Kendall's rapidly delivered maneuvers. "There'd be complications. . . ."

"Wrong! It's *isolated*. *One* has nothing to do with the *other!* It's just talk anyway."

Brigadier General Alan Swanson knew when he had met

a man more capable in the field than himself. "It's possible. Radio blackout; Allied Central instructions."

Kendall rose from his chair; he spoke softly. "Details. I'll work them out. . . . And you'll pay me. Christ, will you pay."

13

DECEMBER 27, 1943, THE AZORES

The island of Terceira in the Azores, 837 miles due west of Lisbon, was a familiar stop to the trans-Atlantic pilots flying the southern route to the United States mainland. As they descended there was always the comfortable feeling that they would encounter minor traffic to be serviced by efficient ground crews who allowed them to be rapidly airborne again. Lajes Field was good duty; those assigned there recognized that and performed well.

Which was why the major in command of the B-17 cargo and personnel carrier which had a Captain David Spaulding as its single passenger couldn't understand the delay. It had begun at descent altitude, fourteen thousand feet. The Lajes tower had interrupted its approach instructions and ordered the pilot to enter a holding pattern. The major had objected; there was no necessity from his point of view. The field was clear. The Lajes tower radioman agreed with the major but said he was only repeating telephone instructions from American headquarters in Ponta Delgada on the adjacent island of São Miguel. Az-Am-HQ gave the orders; apparently it was expecting someone to meet the plane and that someone hadn't arrived. The tower would keep the major posted and, incidentally, was the major carrying some kind of priority cargo? Just curiosity.

Certainly not. There was *no* cargo; only a military attaché named Spaulding from the Lisbon embassy. One of those goddamned diplomatic teaparty boys. The trip was a routine return flight to Norfolk, and why the hell couldn't he land?

The tower would keep the major posted.

The B-17 landed at 1300 hours precisely, its holding pattern lasting twenty-seven minutes.

David got up from the removable seat, held to the deck by clamps, and stretched. The pilot, an aggressive major who looked roughly thirteen years old to Spaulding, emerged from the enclosed cockpit and told him a jeep was outside—or would be outside shortly—to drive the captain off the base.

"I'd like to maintain a decent schedule," said the young pilot, addressing his outranked elder humorlessly. "I realize you diplomatic people have a lot of friends in these social posts, but we've got a long lap to fly. Bear it in mind, please."

"I'll try to keep the polo match down to three chukkers," replied David wearily.

"Yeah, you do that." The major turned and walked to the rear of the cabin, where an air force sergeant had sprung open the cargo hatch used for the aircraft's exit. Spaulding followed, wondering who would meet him outside.

"My name's Ballantyne, captain," said the middle-aged civilian behind the wheel of the jeep, extending his hand to Spaulding. "I'm with Azores-American. Hop in; we'll only be a few minutes. We're driving to the provost's house, a few hundred yards beyond the fence."

David noticed that the guards at the gate did not bother to stop Ballantyne, they just waved him through. The civilian turned right on the road paralleling the field and accelerated. In less time than it took to adequately light a cigarette, the jeep entered the driveway of a one-story Spanish hacienda and proceeded past the house to what could only be described as an out-of-place gazebo.

"Here we are. Come on, captain," said Ballantyne, getting out, indicating the screen door of the screened enclosure. "My associate, Paul Hollander, is waiting for us."

Hollander was another middle-aged civilian. He was nearly bald and wore steel-rimmed spectacles that gave him an appearance beyond his years. As with Ballantyne, there was a look of intelligence about him. Both small and capital *I*. Hollander smiled genuinely.

"This is a distinct pleasure, Spaulding. As so many others, I've admired the work of the man in Lisbon."

Capital *I*, thought David.

"Thank you. I'd like to know why I'm not him any longer."

"I can't answer that. Neither can Ballantyne, I'm afraid."

"Perhaps they thought you deserved a rest," offered Ballantyne. "Good Lord, you've been there—how long is it now? Three years with no break."

"Nearer four," answered David. "And there were plenty of 'breaks.' The Costa Brava beats the hell out of Palm Beach. I was told that you—I assume it's you—have my orders. . . . I don't mean to seem impatient but there's a nasty teenager with a major's rank flying the plane. *He's* impatient."

"Tell him to go to blazes," laughed the man named Hollander. "We *do* have your orders and also a little surprise for you: you're a lieutenant colonel. Tell the major to get his uniform pressed."

"Seems I jumped one."

"Not really. You got your majority last year. Apparently you don't have much use for titles in Lisbon."

"Or military associations," interjected Ballantyne.

"Neither, actually," said David. "At least I wasn't broken. I had premonitions of walking guard duty around latrines."

"Hardly." Hollander sat down in one of the four deck chairs, gesturing David to do the same. It was his way of indicating that their meeting might not be as short as Spaulding had thought. "If it was a time for parades or revelations, I'm sure you'd be honored in the front ranks."

"Thanks," said David, sitting down. "That removes a very real concern. What's this all about?"

"Again, we don't have answers, only ex cathedra instructions. We're to ask you several questions—only one of which could preclude our delivering your orders. Let's get that over with first; I'm sure you'd like to know at least where you're going." Hollander smiled his genuine smile again.

"I would. Go on."

"Since you were relieved of your duties in Lisbon, have you made contact—intentional or otherwise—with *anyone* outside the embassy? I mean by this, even the most innocuous good-bye? Or a settling of a bill—a restaurant, a store; or a chance run-in with an acquaintance at the airport, or on the way to the airport?"

"No. And I had my luggage sent in diplomatic cartons; no suitcases, no traveling gear."

"You're thorough," said Ballantyne, still standing.

"I've had reason to be. Naturally, I had engagements for the week after I returned from the north country. . . ."

"From *where?*" asked Hollander.

"Basque and Navarre. Contact points below the border. I always scheduled engagements right after; it kept a continuity. Not many, just enough to keep in sight. Part of the cover. I had two this week: lunch and cocktails."

"What about them?" Ballantyne sat down next to David.

"I instructed Marshall—he's the cryp who took my orders—to call each just before I was supposed to show up. Say I'd be delayed. That was all."

"Not that you wouldn't *be* there?" Hollander seemed fascinated.

"No. Just delayed. It fit the cover."

"I'll take your word for it," laughed Hollander. "You answered affirmatively and then some. How does New York strike you?"

"As it always has: pleasantly for limited periods."

"I don't know for how long but that's your assignment. And out of uniform, colonel."

"I lived in New York. I know a lot of people there."

"Your new cover is simplicity itself. You've been discharged most honorably after service in Italy. Medical reasons, minor wounds." Hollander took out an envelope from the inside pocket of his jacket and handed it across to David. "It's all here. Terribly simple, papers . . . everything."

"O.K.," said David, accepting the envelope. "I'm a ruptured duck in New York. So far, very nice. You couldn't make it the real thing, could you?"

"The papers are simple, I didn't say authentic. Sorry."

"So am I. What happens then?"

"Someone's very solicitous of you. You have an excellent job; good pay, too. With Meridian Aircraft."

"Meridian?"

"Blueprint Division."

"I thought Meridian was in the Midwest. Illinois or Michigan."

"It has a New York office. Or it does now."

"Aircraft blueprints, I assume."

"I should think so."

"Is it counterespionage?"

"We don't know," answered Ballantyne. "We weren't given any data except the names of the two men you'll report to."

"They're in the envelope?"

"No," said Hollander. "They're verbal and to be committed. Nothing written until you're on the premises."

"Oh, Christ, this all sounds like Ed Pace. He loves this kind of nonsense."

"Sorry, again. It's above Pace."

"What? . . . I didn't think anything was, except maybe Holy Communion. . . . Then how do *you* report? And to whom?"

"Priority courier straight through to an address in Washington. No department listing, but transmission *and* priority cleared through Field Division, Fairfax."

Spaulding emitted a soft, nearly inaudible whistle. "What are the two names?"

"The first is Lyons. Eugene Lyons. He's an aerophysicist. We're to tell you that he's a bit strange, but a goddamned genius."

"In other words, reject the man; accept the genius."

"Something like that. I suppose you're used to it," said Ballantyne.

"Yes," answered Spaulding. "And the other?"

"A man named Kendall." Hollander crossed his legs. "Nothing on him; he's just a name. Walter Kendall. Have no idea what he does."

David pulled the strap across his waist in the removable seat. The B-17's engines were revving at high speed, sending vibrations through the huge fuselage. He looked about in a way he hadn't looked at an airplane before, trying to reduce the spans and the plating to some kind of imaginary blueprint. If Hollander's description of his assignment was accurate—and why shouldn't it be?—he'd be studying aircraft blueprints within a few days.

What struck him as strange were the methods of precaution. In a word, they were unreasonable; they went beyond even abnormal concerns for security. It would have been a simple matter for him to report to Washington, be reassigned, and be given an in-depth briefing. Instead, apparently there would be *no* briefing.

Why not?

Was he to accept open-ended orders from two men he'd never met before? Without the sanction of recognition—even introduction—from any military authority? What the hell was Ed Pace doing?

Sorry. . . . It's above Pace.

Those were the words Hollander had used.

. . . cleared through Field Division, Fairfax.

Hollander again.

Except for the White House itself, David realized that Fairfax was about as high up as one could go. But Fairfax was still *military*. And he wasn't being instructed by Fairfax, simply "cleared."

Hollander's remaining "questions" had not been questions at all, really. They had been introduced with interrogatory words: *do you, have you, can you*. But not questions; merely further instructions.

"Do you have friends in any of the aircraft companies? On the exective level?"

He didn't know, for God's sake. He'd been out of the country so damned long he wasn't sure he had any friends, period.

Regardless, Hollander had said, he was to avoid any such "friends"—should they exist. Report their names to Walter Kendall, if he ran across them.

"Have you any women in New York who are in the public eye?"

What kind of question was *that?* Silliest goddamned thing he'd ever heard of! What the hell did Hollander mean?

The balding, bespectacled Az-Am agent had clarified succinctly. It was listed in David's file that he had supplemented his civilian income as a radio performer. That meant he knew actresses.

And actors, Spaulding suggested. And so what?

Friendships with well-known actresses could lead to newspaper photographs, Hollander rejoined. Or speculations in columns; his name in print. That, too, was to be avoided.

David recalled that he did know—knew—several girls

who'd done well in pictures since he'd left. He'd had a short-lived affair with an actress who was currently a major star for Warner Brothers. Reluctantly he agreed with Hollander; the agent was right. Such contacts would be avoided.

"Can you absorb quickly, commit to memory, blueprint specifications unrelated to industrial design?"

Given a breakdown key of correlative symbols and material factors, the answer was probably yes.

Then he was to prepare himself—however it was done—for aircraft design.

That, thought Spaulding, was obvious.

That, Hollander had said, was all he could tell him.

The B-17 taxied to the west extreme of the Lajes runway and turned for takeoff. The disagreeable major had made it a point to be standing by the cargo hatch looking at his wristwatch when Spaulding returned. David had climbed out of the jeep, shaken hands with Ballantyne and held up three fingers to the major.

"The timer lost count during the last chukker," he said to the pilot. "You know how it is with these striped-pants boys."

The major had not been amused.

The aircraft gathered speed, the ground beneath hammered against the landing gear with increasing ferocity. In seconds the plane would be airborne. David bent over to pick up an Azores newspaper that Hollander had given him and which he'd placed at his feet when strapping himself in.

Suddenly it happened. An explosion of such force that the removable seat flew out of its clamps and jettisoned into the right wall of the plane, carrying David, bent over, with it. And he'd never know but often speculate on whether that Azores newspaper had saved his life.

Smoke was everywhere; the aircraft careened off the ground and spun laterally. The sound of twisting metal filled the cabin with a continuous, unending scream; steel ribs whipped downward from the top and sides of the fuselage—snapping, contorted, sprung from their mountings.

A second explosion blew out the front cabin; sprays of blood and pieces of flesh spat against the crumbling, spinning walls. A section of human scalp with traces of burnt hairline under the bright, viscous red fluid slapped into Spaulding's forearm. Through the smoke David could see the bright sunlight streaming through the front section of the careening plane.

The aircraft had been severed!

David knew instantly that he had only one chance of survival. The fuel tanks were filled to capacity for the long Atlantic flight; they'd go up in seconds. He reached for the buckle at his waist and ripped at it with all his strength. It was locked; the hurling fall had caused the strap to bunch and crowd the housing with cloth. He tugged and twisted, the snap sprung and he was free.

The plane—what was left of it—began a series of thundering convulsions signifying the final struggle to come to a halt on the rushing, hilly ground beyond the runway. David crashed backward, crawling as best he could toward the rear. Once he was forced to stop and hug the deck, his face covered by his arms, a jagged piece of metal piercing the back of his right shoulder.

The cargo hatch was blown open; the air force sergeant lay half out of the steel frame, dead, his chest ripped open from throat to rib cage.

David judged the distance to the ground as best his panic would allow and hurled himself out of the plane, coiling as he did so for the impact of the fall and the necessary roll away from the onrushing tail assembly.

The earth was hard and filled with rocks, but he was *free*. He kept rolling, rolling, crawling, digging, gripping his bloodied hands into the dry, hard soil until the breath in his lungs was exhausted.

He lay on the ground and heard the screaming sirens far in the distance.

And then the explosion that filled the air and shook the earth.

Priority high-frequency radio messages were sent back and forth between the operations room of Lajes Airfield and Field Division, Fairfax.

David Spaulding was to be airlifted out of Terceira on the next flight to Newfoundland, leaving in less than an hour. At Newfoundland he would be met by a pursuit fighter plane at the air force base and flown directly to Mitchell Field, New York. In light of the fact that Lieutenant Colonel Spaulding had suffered no major physical disability, there would be no change in the orders delivered to him.

The cause of the B-17 explosions and resultant killings was, without question, sabotage. Timed out of Lisbon or set during the refueling process at Lajes. An intensive investigation was implemented immediately.

Hollander and Ballantyne had been with David when he was examined and treated by the British army doctor. Bandages around the sutures in his right shoulder, the cuts on his hands and forearms cleaned, Spaulding pronounced himself shaken but operable. The doctor left after administering an intravenous sedative that would make it possible for David to rest thoroughly on the final legs of his trip to New York.

"I'm sure it will be quite acceptable for you to take a leave for a week or so," said Hollander. "My God, you're lucky to be among us!"

"*Alive* is the word," added Ballantyne.

"Am I a mark?" asked Spaulding. "Was it connected with me?"

"Fairfax doesn't think so," answered the balding Hollander. "They think it's coincidental sabotage."

Spaulding watched the Az-Am agent as he spoke. It seemed to David that Hollander hesitated, as if concealing something.

"Narrow coincidence, isn't it? I *was* the only passenger."

"If the enemy can eliminate a large aircraft and a pilot in the bargain, well, I imagine he considers that progress. And Lisbon security *is* rotten."

"Not where I've been. Not generally."

"Well, perhaps here at Terceira, then. . . . I'm only telling you what Fairfax thinks."

There was a knock on the dispensary door and Ballantyne opened it. A first lieutenant stood erect and spoke gently, addressing David, obviously aware that Spaulding had come very close to death.

"It's preparation time, sir. We should be airborne in twenty minutes. Can I help you with anything?"

"I haven't *got* anything, lieutenant. Whatever I had is in that mass of burnt rubble in the south forty."

"Yes, of course. I'm sorry."

"Don't be. Better it than me. . . . I'll be right with you."

David turned to Ballantyne and Hollander, shaking their hands.

As he said his last good-bye to Hollander, he saw it in the agent's eyes.

Hollander *was* hiding something.

The British naval commander opened the screen door of the gazebo and walked in. Paul Hollander rose from the deck chair.

"Did you bring it?" he asked the officer.

"Yes." The commander placed his attaché case on the single wrought iron table and snapped up the hasps. He took out an envelope and handed it to the American. "The photo lab did a rather fine job. Well lighted, front and rear views. Almost as good as having the real item."

Hollander unwound the string on the envelope's flap and removed a photograph. It was an enlargement of a small medallion, a star with six points.

It was the Star of David.

In the center of the face was the scrolled flow of a Hebrew inscription. On the back was the bas-relief of a knife with a streak of lightning intersecting the blade.

"The Hebrew spells out the name of a prophet named Haggai; he's the symbol of an organization of Jewish fanatics operating out of Palestine. They call themselves the Haganah. Their business, they claim, is vengeance—two thousand years' worth. We anticipate quite a bit of trouble from them in the years to come; they've made that clear, I'm afraid."

"But you say it was welded to the bottom main strut of the rear cabin."

"In such a way as to escape damage from all but a direct explosion. Your aircraft was blown up by the Haganah."

Hollander sat down, staring at the photograph. He looked up at the British commander. "Why? For God's sake, *why?*"

"I can't answer that."

"Neither can Fairfax. I don't think they even want to acknowledge it. They want it buried."

14

DECEMBER 27, 1943, WASHINGTON, D.C.

When the words came over his intercom in the soft, compensating voice of the WAC lieutenant who was his secretary, Swanson knew it was no routine communication.

"Fairfax on line one, sir. It's Colonel Pace. He says to interrupt you."

Since delivering David Spaulding's file, the Fairfax commander had been reluctant to call personally. He hadn't spoken of his reluctance, he simply relegated messages to subordinates. And since they all concerned the progress of getting Spaulding out of Portugal, Pace's point was clear: he would expedite but not personally acknowledge his participation.

Edmund Pace was still not satisfied with the murky "highest priority" explanations regarding his man in Lisbon. He would follow orders once-removed.

"General, there's a radio emergency from Lajes Field in Terceira," said Pace urgently.

"What the hell does that mean? *Where?*"

"Azores. The B-17 carrier with Spaulding on it was sabotaged. Blown up on takeoff."

"Jesus!"

"May I suggest you come out here, sir?"

"Is Spaulding dead?"

"Preliminary reports indicate negative, but I don't want to guarantee anything. Everything's unclear. I wanted to wait till I had further confirmations but I can't now. An unexpected development. Please, come out, general."

"On my way. Get the information on Spaulding!"

Swanson gathered the papers on his desk—the information from Kendall—that had to be clipped together, sealed in a thin metal box and locked in a file cabinet with two combinations and a key.

If there was ever a reason for total security, it was symbolized by those papers.

He spun the two combination wheels, turned the key and then thought for a second that he might reverse the process and take the papers with him. . . . No, that was unsound. They were safer in the cabinet. A file cabinet riveted to the floor was better than a cloth pocket on a man who walked in the street and drove in automobiles. A file cabinet could not have accidents; was not subject to the frailties of a tired, fifty-three-year-old brigadier.

He saluted the guard on duty at the entrance and walked rapidly down the steps to the curb. His driver was waiting, alerted by the WAC secretary, whose efficiency overcame her continuous attempts to be more than an efficient secretary to him. He knew that one day when the pressures became too much, he'd ask her in, lock the door and hump the ass off her on the brown leather couch.

Why was he thinking about his secretary? He didn't give a goddamn about the WAC lieutenant who sat so protectively outside his office door.

He sat back in the seat and removed his hat. He knew why he thought about his secretary: it gave him momentary relief. It postponed thoughts about the complications that may or may not have exploded on a runway in the Azores.

Oh *Christ!* The thought of rebuilding what he'd managed to put together was abhorrent to him. To go back, to reconstruct, to research for the right man was impossible. It was difficult enough for him to go over the details as they now stood.

The details supplied by the sewer rat.

Kendall.

An enigma. An unattractive puzzle even G-2 couldn't piece together. Swanson had run a routine check on him, based on the fact that the accountant was privy to Meridian's aircraft contracts; the Intelligence boys and Hoover's tight-lipped maniacs had returned virtually nothing but names and dates. They'd been instructed *not* to interview Meridian personnel or anyone connected with ATCO or

Packard; orders that apparently made their task close to impossible.

Kendall was forty-six, severely asthmatic and a CPA. He was unmarried, had few if any friends and lived two blocks from his firm, which he solely owned, in mid-Manhattan.

The personal evaluations were fairly uniform: Kendall was a disagreeable, antisocial individualist who happened to be a brilliant statistician.

The dossier might have told a desolate story—paternal abandonment, lack of privilege, the usual—but it didn't. There was no indication of poverty, no record of deprivation or hardship anywhere near that suffered by millions, especially during the Depression years.

No records of depth on anything, for that matter.

An enigma.

But there was nothing enigmatic about Walter Kendall's "details" for Buenos Aires. They were clarity itself. Kendall's sense of manipulation had been triggered; the challenge stimulated his already primed instincts for maneuvering. It was as if he had found the ultimate "deal"—and indeed, thought Swanson, he had.

The operation was divided into three isolated exercises: the arrival and inspection of the diamond shipment; the simultaneous analysis of the gyroscopic blueprints, as they, too, arrived; and the submarine transfer. The crates of bortz and carbonado from the Koening mines would be secretly cordoned off in a warehouse in the Dársena Norte district of the Puerto Nuevo. The Germans assigned to the warehouse would report only to Erich Rhinemann.

The aerophysicist, Eugene Lyons, would be billeted in a guarded apartment in the San Telmo district, an area roughly equivalent to New York's Gramercy Park—rich, secluded, ideal for surveillance. As the step-blueprints were delivered, he would report to Spaulding.

Spaulding would precede Lyons to Buenos Aires and be attached to the embassy on whatever pretext Swanson thought feasible. His assignment—as *Spaulding* thought it to be—was to coordinate the purchase of the gyroscopic designs, and if their authenticity was confirmed, authorize payment. This authorization would be made by a code radioed to Washington that supposedly cleared a transfer of funds to Rhinemann in Switzerland.

Spaulding would then stand by at a mutually agreed-upon airfield, prepared to be flown out of Argentina. He would be given airborne clearance when Rhinemann received word that "payment" had been made.

In reality, the code sent by Spaulding was to be a signal for the German submarine to surface at a prearranged destination at sea and make rendezvous with a small craft carrying the shipment of diamonds. Ocean and air patrols would be kept out of the area; if the order was questioned —and it was unlikely—the cover story of the underground defectors would be employed.

When the transfer at sea was made, the submarine would radio confirmation—Rhinemann's "payment." It would dive and start its journey back to Germany. Spaulding would then be cleared for takeoff to the United States.

These safeguards were the best either side could expect. Kendall was convinced he could sell the operation to Erich Rhinemann. He and Rhinemann possessed a certain objectivity lacking in the others.

Swanson did not dispute the similarity; it was another viable reason for Kendall's death.

The accountant would fly to Buenos Aires in a week and make the final arrangements with the German expatriate. Rhinemann would be made to understand that Spaulding was acting as an experienced courier, a custodian for the eccentric Eugene Lyons—a position Kendall admitted was desirable. But Spaulding was nothing else. He was not part of the diamond transfer; he knew nothing of the submarine. He would provide the codes necessary for the transfer, but he'd never know it. There was no way he could learn of it.

Airtight, ironclad: acceptable.

Swanson had read and reread Kendall's "details"; he could not fault them. The ferret-like accountant had reduced an enormously complicated negotiation to a series of simple procedures and separate motives. In a way Kendall had created an extraordinary deception. Each step had a checkpoint, each move a countermove.

And Swanson would add the last deceit: David Spaulding would kill Erich Rhinemann.

Origin of command: instructions from Allied Central Intelligence. By the nature of Rhinemann's involvement, he was too great a liability to the German underground. The former man in Lisbon could employ whatever methods he thought best. Hire the killers, do it himself; whatever the situation called for. Just make sure it was done.

Spaulding would understand. The shadow world of agents and double agents had been his life for the past several years. David Spaulding—if his dossier was to be believed—would accept the order for what it was: a reasonable, professional solution.

If Spaulding was alive.

Oh, Christ! What had *happened?* Where was it? Lapess, Lajes. Some goddamned airfield in the Azores! Sabotage. Blown up on takeoff!

What the hell did it *mean?*

The driver swung off the highway onto the back Virginia road. They were fifteen minutes from the Fairfax compound; Swanson found himself sucking his lower lip between his teeth. He had actually bitten into the soft tissue; he could taste a trickle of blood.

"We have further information," said Colonel Edmund Pace, standing in front of a photograph map frame. The map was the island of Terceira in the Azores. "Spaulding's all right. Shaken up, of course. Minor sutures, bruises; nothing broken, though. I tell you he pulled off a miracle. Pilot, copilot, a crewman: all dead. Only survivors were Spaulding and a rear aerial gunner who probably won't make it."

"Is he mobile? Spaulding?"

"Yes. Hollander and Ballantyne are with him now. I assumed you wanted him out. . . ."

"Jesus, *yes,*" interrupted Swanson.

"I got him on a Newfoundland transfer. Unless you want to switch orders, a coastal patrol flight will pick him up there and bring him south. Mitchell Field."

"When will he get in?"

"Late tonight, weather permitting. Otherwise, early morning. Shall I have him flown down here?"

Swanson hesitated. "No. . . . Have a doctor at Mitchell give him a thorough going-over. But keep him in New York. If he needs a few days' rest, put him up at a hotel. Otherwise, everything remains."

"Well . . ." Pace seemed slightly annoyed with his superior. "Someone's going to have to see him."

"Why?"

"His papers. Everything we prepared went up with the plane. They're a packet of ashes."

"Oh. Yes, of course. I didn't think about that." Swanson walked away from Pace to the chair in front of the stark, plain desk. He sat down.

The colonel watched the brigadier. He was obviously concerned with Swanson's lack of focus, his inadequate concentration. "We can prepare new ones easily enough, that's no problem."

"Good. Do that, will you? Then have someone meet him at Mitchell and give them to him."

"O.K. . . . But it's possible you may want to change your mind." Pace crossed to his desk chair but remained standing.

"Why? About what?"

"Whatever it is. . . . The plane was sabotaged, I told you that. If you recall, I asked you to come out here because of an unexpected development."

Swanson stared up at his subordinate. "I've had a difficult week. And I've told *you* the gravity of this project. Now, don't play Fairfax games with me. I make no claims of expertise in your field. I asked only for assistance; ordered it, if you like. Say what you mean without the preamble, please."

"I've tried to give you that assistance." Pace's tone was rigidly polite. "It's not easy, sir. And I've just bought you twelve hours to consider alternatives. That plane was blown up by the Haganah."

"The *what?*"

Pace explained the Jewish organization operating out of Palestine. He watched Swanson closely as he did so.

"That's insane! It doesn't make sense! How do you know?"

"The first thing an inspection team does at the site of sabotage is to water down, pick over debris, look for evidence that might melt from the heat, or burn, if explosives are used. It's a preliminary check and it's done fast. . . . A Haganah medallion was found riveted to the tail assembly. They wanted full credit."

"Good God! What did you say to the Azores people?"

"I bought you a day, general. I instructed Hollander to minimize any connection, keep it away from Spaulding. Frankly, to imply coincidence if the subject got out of hand. The Haganah is independent, fanatic. Most Zionist organizations won't touch it. They call it a group of savages."

"How could it get out of hand?" Swanson was disturbed on another level.

"I'm sure you're aware that the Azores are under British control. An old Portuguese treaty gives them the right to military installations."

"I know that," said Swanson testily.

"The British found the medallion."

"What will they do?"

"Think about it. Eventually make a report to Allied Central."

"But you know about it *now*."

"Hollander's a good man. He does favors; gets favors in return."

Swanson got out of the chair and walked aimlessly around it. "What do you think, Ed? Was it meant for Spaulding?" He looked at the colonel.

The expression on Pace's face let Swanson know that Pace was beginning to understand his anxiety. Not so much about the project—that was out of bounds and he accepted it—but that a fellow officer was forced to deal in an area he was out-of-sync with; territory he was not trained to cross. At such times a decent army man had sympathy.

"All I can give you are conjectures, very loose, not even good guesses. . . . It could be Spaulding. And even if it was, it doesn't necessarily mean it's connected with *your* project."

"What?"

"I don't know what Spaulding's field activities have been. Not specifically. And the Haganah is filled with psychopaths—deadly variety. They're about as rational as Julius Streicher's units. Spaulding may have had to kill a Portuguese or Spanish Jew. Or use one in a 'cover trap.' In a Catholic country that's all a Haganah cell would need. . . . Or it could be someone else on the plane. An officer or crewman with an anti-Zionist relative, especially a *Jewish* anti-Zionist relative. I'd have to run a check. . . . Unless you'd read the book, you couldn't possibly understand those kikes."

Swanson remained silent for several moments. When he

spoke he did so acknowledging Pace's attitude. "Thank you. . . . But it probably isn't any of those things, is it? I mean, Spanish Jews or 'cover traps' or some pilot's uncle . . . it's Spaulding."

"You don't *know* that. Speculate, sure; don't assume."

"I can't understand *how*." Swanson sat down again, thinking aloud, really. "All things considered . . ." His thought drifted off into silence.

"May I make a suggestion?" Pace went to his chair. It was no time to talk down to a bewildered superior.

"By all means," said Swanson, looking over at the colonel, his eyes conveying gratitude to this hard-nosed, confident Intelligence man.

"I'm not cleared for your project and, let's face it, I don't want to be. It's a DW exercise, and that's where it belongs. I said a few minutes ago that you should consider alternatives . . . maybe you should. But *only* if you see a direct connection. I watched you and you didn't."

"Because there isn't any."

"You're not involved—and even I don't see how, considering what I *do* know from the probe and Johannesburg—with the concentration camps? Auschwitz? Belsen?"

"Not even remotely."

Pace leaned forward, his elbows on the desk. "Those are Haganah concerns. Along with the 'Spanish Jews' and 'cover traps.' . . . Don't make any new decisions now, general. You'd be making them too fast, without supportive cause."

"Sup*port*. . . ." Swanson looked incredulous. "A plane was blown up. Men were killed!"

"And a medallion could be planted on a tail assembly by anyone. It's quite possible you're being tested."

"By *whom?*"

"I couldn't answer that. Warn Spaulding; it'll strike him as funny, he was *on* that aircraft. But let my man at Mitchell Field tell him there could be a recurrence; to be careful. . . . He's been there, general. He'll handle himself properly. . . . And in the meantime, may I also suggest you look for a replacement."

"A replacement?"

"For Spaulding. If there *is* a recurrence, it could be successful. He'd be taken out."

"You mean he'd be killed."

"Yes."

"What kind of world do you people live in?" asked Swanson softly.

"It's complicated," said Pace.

15

DECEMBER 29, 1943, NEW YORK CITY

Spaulding watched the traffic below from the hotel window overlooking Fifth Avenue and Central Park. The Montgomery was one of those small, elegant hotels his parents had used while in New York, and there was a pleasant sense of nostalgia in his being there again. The old desk clerk had actually wept discreet tears while registering him. Spaulding had forgotten—fortunately he remembered before his signature was dry—that the old man years ago had taken him for walks in the park. Over a quarter of a century ago!

Walks in the park. Governesses. Chauffeurs standing in foyers, prepared to whisk his parents away to a train, a concert, a rehearsal. Music critics. Record company executives. Endless dinner parties where he'd make his usual "appearance" before bedtime and be prompted by his father to tell some guest at what age Mozart composed the Fortieth; dates and facts he was forced to memorize and which he gave not one goddamn about. Arguments. Hysterics over an inadequate conductor or a bad performance or a worse review.

Madness.

And always the figure of Aaron Mandel, soothing, placating—so often fatherly to his overbearing father while his mother faded, waiting in a secondary status that belied her natural strength.

And the quiet times. The Sundays—except for concert Sundays—when his parents would suddenly remember his existence and try to make up in one day the attention they thought they had allocated improperly to governesses, chauffeurs and nice, polite hotel managements. At these times, the quiet times, he had felt his father's honest yet artificial attempts; had wanted to tell him it was all right, he wasn't deprived. They didn't have to spend autumn days wandering around zoos and museums; the zoos and museums were much better in Europe, anyway. It wasn't necessary that he be taken to Coney Island or the beaches of New Jersey in summer. What were they, compared to the Lido or Costa del Santiago? But whenever they were in America, there was this parental compulsion to fit into a mold labeled "An American Father and Mother."

Sad, funny, inconsistent; impossible, really.

And for some buried reason, he had never come back to this small, elegant hotel during the later years. There was rarely a need, of course, but he could have made the effort; the management was genuinely fond of the Spaulding family. Now it seemed right, somehow. After the years away he wanted a secure base in a strange land, secure at least in memories.

Spaulding walked away from the window to the bed where the bellboy had placed his new suitcase with the new civilian clothes he had purchased at Rogers Peet. Everything, including the suitcase. Pace had had the foresight to send money with the major who had brought him duplicates of the papers destroyed in Terceira. He had to sing for the money, not for the papers; that amused him.

The major who met him at Mitchell Field—on the field—had escorted him to the base infirmary, where a bored army doctor pronounced him fit but "run down"; had professionally criticized the sutures implanted by the British doctor in the Azores but saw no reason to change them; and suggested that David take two APCs every four hours and rest.

Caveat patient.

The courier-major had played a tune on the Fairfax piano and told him Field Division was still analyzing the Lajes sabotage; it could have been aimed at him for misdeeds out of Lisbon. He should be careful and report any unusual incidents directly to Colonel Pace at Fairfax. Further, Spaulding was to commit the name of Brigadier General Alan Swanson, DW. Swanson was his source control and would make contact in a matter of days, ten at the outside.

Why call Pace, then? Regarding any "incidents." Why

not get in touch directly with this Swanson? Since he was the SC.

Pace's instructions, replied the major—until the brigadier took over; just simpler that way.

Or further concealment, thought David, remembering the clouded eyes of Paul Hollander, the Az-Am agent in Terceira.

Something was happening. The source control transfer was being handled in a very unorthodox manner. From the unsigned, high-priority codes received in Lisbon to the extraordinary command: out of strategy. From the mid-ocean delivery of papers from Az-Am agents who said they had to question him first, to the strange orders that had him reporting to two civilians in New York without prior briefing.

It was all like a hesitation waltz. It was either very professional or terribly amateur; really, he suspected, a combination of both. It would be interesting to meet this General Swanson. He had never heard of him.

He lay down on the hotel bed. He would rest for an hour and then shower and shave and see New York at night for the first time in over three years. See what the war had done to a Manhattan evening; it had done little or nothing to the daylight hours, from what he'd seen—only the posters. It would be good to have a woman tonight. But if it happened, he'd want it to be comfortable, without struggle or urgency. A happy coincidence would be just right; a likable, really likable interlude. On the other hand, he wasn't about to browse through a telephone directory to create one. Three years and nine months had passed since he last picked up a telephone in New York City. During that time he had learned to be wary of the changes taking place over a matter of days, to say nothing of three years and nine months.

And he recalled pleasantly how the Stateside transfers to the embassy in Lisbon often spoke of the easy accessibility of the women back home. Especially in Washington and New York, where the numbers and the absence of permanency worked in favor of one-night stands. Then he remembered, with a touch of amused resignation, that these same reports usually spoke of the irresistible magnetism of an officer's uniform, especially captain and over.

He had worn a uniform exactly three times in the past

four years: at the Mayflower Hotel lounge with Ed Pace, the day he arrived in Portugal and the day he left Portugal. He didn't even own one now.

His telephone rang and it startled him. Only Fairfax and, he assumed, this brigadier, Swanson, knew where he was. He had called the Montgomery from the Mitchell Field infirmary and secured the reservation; the major had said to take seventy-two hours. He needed the rest; no one would bother him. Now someone was bothering him.

"Hello?"

"*David!*" It was a girl's voice; low, cultivated at the Plaza. "David *Spaulding!*"

"Who is this?" He wondered for a second if his just-released fantasies were playing tricks on reality.

"*Leslie*, darling! Leslie *Jenner!* My God, it must be nearly *five years!*"

Spaulding's mind raced. Leslie Jenner was part of the New York scene but not the radio world; she was the up-from-college crowd. Meeting under the clock at the Biltmore; late nights at LaRue; the cotillions—which he'd been invited to, not so much from social bloodlines as for the fact that he was the son of the concert Spauldings. Leslie was Miss Porter's, Finch and the Junior League.

Only her name had been changed to something else. She had married a boy from Yale. He didn't remember the name.

"Leslie, this is . . . well, Jesus, a surprise. How did you know I was here?" Spaulding wasn't engaging in idle small talk.

"*Nothing* happens in New York that I don't know about! I have eyes and ears everywhere, darling! A veritable spy network!"

David Spaulding could feel the blood draining from his face; he didn't like the girl's joke. "I'm serious, Leslie. . . . Only because I haven't called anyone. Not even Aaron. How did you find out?"

"If you must know, Cindy Bonner—she was Cindy Tottle, married Paul Bonner—Cindy was exchanging some dreary Christmas gifts for Paul at Rogers Peet and she *swore* she saw you trying on a suit. Well, you know Cindy! Just too shy for *words* . . ."

David *didn't* know Cindy. He couldn't even recall the

name, much less a face. Leslie Jenner went on as he thought about that.

". . . and so she ran to the nearest phone and called me. After all, darling, we *were* a major item!"

If a "major item" described a couple of summer months of weekending at East Hampton and bedding the daughter of the house, then David had to agree. But he didn't subscribe to the definition; it had been damned transient, discreet and before the girl's very social marriage.

"I'd just as soon you kept that information from your husband. . . ."

"Oh, *God*, you poor lamb! It's *Jenner*, darling, not Hawkwood! Didn't even keep the *name*. Damned if I would."

That was it, thought David. She'd married a man named Hawkwood: Roger or Ralph; something like that. A football player, or was it tennis?

"I'm sorry. I didn't know. . . ."

"Richard and I called it quits simply *centuries* ago. It was a *disaster*. The son of a bitch couldn't even keep his hands off my best friends! He's in London now; air corps, but very hush-hush, I think. I'm sure the English girls are getting their fill of him . . . and I do mean fill! I *know!*"

There was a slight stirring in David's groin. Leslie Jenner was proffering an invitation.

"Well, they're allies," said Spaulding humorously. "But you didn't tell me, how did you find me here?"

"It took exactly four telephone calls, my lamb. I tried the usual: Commodore, Biltmore and the Waldorf; and then I remembered that your dad and mum always stopped off at the Montgomery. Very Old World, darling. . . . I thought, with reservations simply *hell*, you might have thought of it."

"You'd make a good detective, Leslie."

"Only when the object of my detecting is worthwhile, lamb. . . . We *did* have fun."

"Yes, we did," said Spaulding, his thoughts on an entirely different subject. "And we can't let your memory prowess go to waste. Dinner?"

"If you hadn't asked, I would have *screamed*."

"Shall I pick you up at your apartment? What's the address?"

Leslie hesitated a fraction of a moment. "Let's meet at a restaurant. We'd never get out of here."

An invitation, indeed.

David named a small Fifty-first Street cafe he remembered. It was on Park. "At seven thirty? Eight?"

"Seven thirty's lovely, but not *there*, darling. It closed simply years ago. Why not the Gallery? It's on Forty-sixth. I'll make reservations; they know me."

"Fine."

"You poor lamb, you've been away so *long*. You don't know *anything*. I'll take you in tow."

"I'd like that. Seven thirty, then."

"Can't wait. And I promise not to cry."

Spaulding replaced the telephone; he was bewildered—on several levels. To begin with, a girl didn't call a former lover after nearly four war years without asking—especially in these times—where he'd been, how he was; at least the length of his stay in town. It wasn't natural, it denied curiosity in these curiosity-prone days.

Another reason was profoundly disturbing.

The last time his parents had been at the Montgomery was in 1934. And he had not returned since then. He'd met the girl in 1936; in October of 1936 in New Haven at the Yale Bowl. He remembered distinctly.

Leslie Jenner couldn't possibly know about the Montgomery Hotel. Not as it was related to his parents.

She was lying.

16

DECEMBER 29, 1943, NEW YORK CITY

The Gallery was exactly as David thought it would be: a lot of deep-red velvet with a generous sprinkling of palms in varying shapes and sizes, reflecting the soft-yellow pools of light from dozens of wall sconces far enough above the tables to make the menus unreadable. The clientele was equally predictable: young, rich, deliberately casual; a profusion of wrinkled eyebrows and crooked smiles and very bright teeth. The voices rose and subsided, words running together, the diction glossy.

Leslie Jenner was there when he arrived. She ran into his arms in front of the cloak room; she held him fiercely, in silence, for several minutes—or it seemed like minutes to Spaulding; at any rate, too long a time. When she tilted her head back, the tears had formed rivulets on her cheeks. The tears were genuine, but there was something—was it the tautness of her full mouth? the eyes themselves?—something artificial about the girl. Or was it him? The years away from places like the Gallery and girls like Leslie Jenner.

In all other respects she was as he remembered her. Perhaps older, certainly more sensual—the unmistakable look of experience. Her dark blonde hair was more a light brown now, her wide brown eyes had added subtlety to her innate provocativeness, her face was a touch lined but still sculptured, aristocratic. And he could feel her body against his; the memories were sharpened by it. Lithe, strong, full breasted; a body that centered on sex. Shaped by it and for it.

"God, God, God! Oh, *David!*" She pressed her lips against his ear.

They went to their table; she held his hand firmly, releasing it only to light a cigarette, taking it back again. They talked rapidly. He wasn't sure she listened, but she nodded incessantly and wouldn't take her eyes off him. He repeated the simple outlines of his cover: Italy, minor wounds; they were letting him out to go back into an essential industry where he'd do more good than carrying a rifle. He wasn't sure how long he'd be in New York. (He was honest about that, he thought to himself. He had no idea how long he'd be in town; he wished he did know.) He was glad to see her again.

The dinner was a prelude to bed. They both knew it; neither bothered to conceal the excitement of reviving the most pleasant of experiences: young sex that was taken in shadows, beyond the reprimands of elders. Enjoyed more because it was prohibited, dangerous.

"Your apartment?" he asked.

"No, lamb. I share it with my aunt, mum's younger sister. It's very chic these days to share an apartment; very patriotic."

The reasoning escaped David. "Then my place," he said firmly.

"David?" Leslie squeezed his hand and paused before speaking. "Those old family retainers who run the Montgomery, they know so many in our crowd. For instance, the Allcotts have a suite there, so do the Dewhursts. . . . I have a key to Peggy Webster's place in the Village. Remember Peggy? You were at their wedding. Jack Webster? You know Jack. He's in the navy; she went out to see him in San Diego. Let's go to Peggy's place."

Spaulding watched the girl closely. He hadn't forgotten her odd behavior on the telephone, her lie about the old hotel and his parents. Yet it was possible that his imagination was overworking—the years in Lisbon made one cautious. There could be explanations, memory lapses on his part; but now he was as curious as he was stimulated.

He was very curious. Very stimulated.

"Peggy's place," he said.

If there was anything beyond the sexual objective, it escaped him.

Their coats off, Leslie made drinks in the kitchen while David bunched newspapers beneath the fireplace grill and watched the kindling catch.

Leslie stood in the kitchen doorway looking down at him separating the logs, creating an airflow. She held their drinks and smiled. "In two days it's New Year's Eve. We'll jump and call this ours. Our New Year's. The start of many, I hope."

"Of many," he replied, standing up and going to her. He took both glasses, not the one extended. "I'll put them over here." He carried them to the coffee table in front of the small couch that faced the fireplace. He turned rapidly, politely to watch her eyes. She wasn't looking at the glasses. Or his placement of them.

Instead, she approached the fire and removed her blouse. She dropped it on the floor and turned around, her large breasts accentuated by a tight, transparent brassiere that had webbed stitching at the tips.

"Take off your shirt, David."

He did so and came to her. She winced at his bandages and gently touched them with her fingers. She pressed herself against him, her pelvis firm against his thighs, moving laterally, expertly. He reached around her back and undid the hasps of the brassiere; she hunched slightly as he pulled it away; then she turned, arching her breasts upward into his flesh. He cupped her left breast with his right hand; she reached down, stepping partially away, and undid his trousers.

"The drinks can wait, David. It's New Year's Eve. Ours, anyway."

Still holding her breast, he put his lips to her eyes, her ears. She felt him and moaned.

"Here, David," she said. "Right here on the floor." She sank to her knees, her skirt pulled up to her thighs, the tops of her stockings visible.

He lay down beside her and they kissed.

"I remember," he whispered with a gentle laugh. "The first time; the cottage by the boathouse. The floor. I remember."

"I wondered if you would. I've never forgotten."

It was only one forty-five in the morning when he took her home. They had made love twice, drunk a great deal of

Jack and Peggy Webster's good whisky and spoken of the "old days" mostly. Leslie had no inhibitions regarding her marriage. Richard Hawkwood, ex-husband, was simply not a man who could sustain a permanent relationship. He was a sexual glutton as long as the sex was spread around; not much otherwise. He was also a failure—as much as his family would allow—in the business world. Hawkwood was a man brought up to enjoy fifty thousand a year with the ability to make, perhaps, six.

The war was created, she felt, for men like Richard. They would excel in it, as her ex-husband had done. He should "go down in flames" somewhere, exiting brilliantly rather than return to the frustrations of civilian inadequacy. Spaulding thought that was harsh; she claimed she was being considerate. And they laughed and made love.

Throughout the evening David kept alert, waiting for her to say something, reveal something, ask something unusual. Anything to clarify—if nothing else—the reasons behind her earlier lies about finding him. There was nothing.

He asked her again, claiming incredulity that she would remember his parents and the Montgomery. She stuck to her infallible memory, adding only that "love makes any search more thorough."

She was lying again; he knew that. What they had was not love.

She left him in the taxi; she didn't want him to come up. Her aunt would be asleep; it was better this way.

They'd meet again tomorrow. At the Websters'. Ten o'clock in the evening; she had a dinner date she'd get rid of early. And she'd break her engagement for the real New Year's Eve. They'd have the whole day to themselves.

As the doorman let her in and the taxi started up toward Fifth Avenue, he thought for the first time that Fairfax had him beginning his assignment at Meridian Aircraft the day after tomorrow. New Year's Eve. He expected it would be a half-day.

It was strange. New Year's Eve. Christmas.

He hadn't even thought about Christmas. He'd remembered to send his parents' gifts to Santiago, but he'd done that before his trip to the north country. To the Basque Provinces and Navarre.

Christmas had no meaning. The Santa Clauses ringing their clinking bells on the New York streets, the decorations in the store windows—none had meaning for him.

He was sad about that. He had always enjoyed the holidays.

David paid the driver, said hello to the Montgomery night clerk and took the elevator to his floor. He got off and approached his door. Automatically, because his eyes were tired, he flipped his finger above the Do Not Disturb sign beneath the lock.

Then he felt the wood and looked down, punching his cigarette lighter for better vision.

The field thread was gone.

Second nature and the instructions from Fairfax to stay alert had caused him to "thread" his hotel room. Strands of invisible tan and black silk placed in a half-dozen locations, that if missing or broken meant a trespasser.

He carried no weapon and he could not know if anyone was still inside.

He returned to the elevator and pushed the button. He asked the operator if he had a passkey; his door wouldn't open. The man did not; he was taken to the lobby.

The night clerk obliged, ordering the elevator operator to remain at the desk while he went to the aid of Mr. Spaulding and his difficult lock.

As the two men walked out of the elevator and down the corridor, Spaulding heard the distinct sound of a latch being turned, snapped shut quietly but unmistakably. He rapidly turned his head in both directions, up and down the corridor, trying to locate the origin of the sound.

Nothing but closed hotel doors.

The desk clerk had no trouble opening the door. He had more difficulty understanding Mr. Spaulding's arm around his shoulder, ushering him into the single room with him.

David looked around quickly. The bathroom and closet doors were open as he had left them. There were no other places of concealment. He released the desk clerk and tipped him with a five-dollar bill.

"Thank you very much. I'm embarrassed; I'm afraid I had too much to drink."

"Not at all, sir. *Thank* you, sir." The man left, pulling the door shut behind him.

David rapidly began his thread check. In the closet: his jacket breast pocket, leafed out, centered.

No thread.

The bureau: the first and third drawers, inserted.

Both threads out of place. The first inside on top of a handkerchief; the second, wedged between shirts.

The bed: laterally placed along the spread in line with the pattern.

Nowhere. Nothing.

He went to his suitcase, which lay on a luggage rack by the window. He knelt down and inspected the right lock; the thread had been clamped inside the metal hasp up under the tiny hinge. If the suitcase was opened, it had to break.

It was broken, only one half remaining.

The inside of the suitcase housed a single strand at the rear, crossing the elastic flap three fingers from the left side.

It was gone.

David stood up. He crossed to the bedside table and reached underneath for the telephone directory. There was no point in delay; what advantage he had was in surprise. His room had been searched professionally; he was not expected to know.

He would get Leslie Jenner's number, return to her apartment house and find a telephone booth near the entrance—with luck, in sight of it. He would then call her, tell her some wildly incredible story about anything and ask to see her. No mention of the search, nothing of his borne-out suspicions. Throw her off completely and listen acutely to her reaction. If she agreed to see him, all well and good. If she didn't, he'd keep her apartment under surveillance throughout the night, if necessary.

Leslie Jenner had a story to tell and he'd find out what it was. The man in Lisbon had not spent three years in the north provinces without gaining expertise.

There was no Jenner at the address of the apartment building.

There were six Jenners listed in Manhattan.

One by one he gave the hotel switchboard the numbers, and one by one—in varying stages of sleep and anger—the replies were the same.

No Leslie Jenner. None known.

Spaulding hung up. He'd been sitting on the bed; he got up and walked around the room.

He would go to the apartment building and ask the doorman. It was possible the apartment was in the aunt's name but it wasn't plausible. Leslie Jenner would put her name and number in the Yellow Pages, if she could; for her the telephone was an instrument of existence, not convenience. And if he went to the apartment and started asking questions, he would be announcing unreasonable concern. He wasn't prepared to do that.

Who was the girl at Rogers Peet? The one exchanging Christmas gifts. Cynthia? Cindy? . . . Cindy. Cindy Tuttle . . . Tottle. But not Tottle. . . . Bonner. Married to Paul Bonner, exchanging "dreary gifts for Paul."

He crossed to the bed and picked up the telephone directory.

Paul Bonner was listed: 480 Park Avenue. The address was appropriate. He gave the number to the switchboard.

The voice of a girl more asleep than awake answered.

"Yes? . . . Hello?"

"Mrs. Bonner?"

"Yes. What is it? This is Mrs. Bonner."

"I'm David Spaulding. You saw me this afternoon at Rogers Peet; you were exchanging gifts for your husband and I was buying a suit. . . . Forgive me for disturbing you but it's important. I had dinner with Leslie . . . Leslie Jenner; you called her. I just left her at her apartment; we were to meet tomorrow and now I find that I may not be able to. It's foolish but I forgot to get her telephone number, and I can't find it in the book. I wondered . . ."

"Mr. Spaulding." The girl interrupted him, her tone sharp, no longer blurred with sleep. "If this is a joke, I think it's in bad taste. I *do* remember your name. . . . I did *not* see you this afternoon and I wasn't exchanging . . . I wasn't in Rogers Peet. My husband was killed four months ago. In Sicily. . . . I haven't spoken to Leslie Jenner . . . Hawkwood, I think now . . . in over a year. She moved to California. Pasadena, I believe. . . . We haven't been in touch. Nor is it likely we would be."

David heard the abrupt click of the broken connection.

17

DECEMBER 31, 1943, NEW YORK CITY

It was the morning of New Year's Eve.

His first day of "employment" for Meridian Aircraft, Blueprint Division.

He had stayed most of the previous day in his hotel room, going out briefly for lunch and magazines, dinner through room service, and finally a pointless taxi to Greenwich Village, where he knew he would not find Leslie Jenner at ten o'clock.

He had remained confined for two reasons. The first was a confirmation of the Mitchell Field doctor's diagnosis: he was exhausted. The second reason was equally important. Fairfax was running checks on Leslie Jenner Hawkwood, Cindy Tottle Bonner, and a naval officer named Jack or John Webster, whose wife was conveniently in California. David wanted this data before progressing further, and Ed Pace had promised to be as thorough as forty-eight hours allowed.

Spaulding had been struck by Cindy Bonner's words concerning Leslie Jenner.

She moved to California. Pasadena, I believe. . . .

And a routine phone call to the Greenwich Village apartment's superintendent had confirmed that, indeed, the Websters *did* live there; the husband was in the navy, the wife was visiting him someplace in California. The superintendent was holding the mail.

Someplace in California.

She moved to California. . . .

Was there a connection? Or simple coincidence.

Spaulding looked at his watch. It was eight o'clock. The morning of New Year's Eve. Tomorrow would be 1944.

This morning, however, he was to report to one Walter Kendall and one Eugene Lyons at Meridian's temporary offices on Thirty-eighth Street.

Why would one of the largest aircraft companies in the United States have "temporary" offices?

The telephone rang. David reached for it.

"Spaulding?"

"Hello, Ed."

"I got what I could. It doesn't make a hell of a lot of sense. To begin with, there's no record of a divorce between the Hawkwoods. And he *is* in England. Eighth Air Force, but nothing classified. He's a pilot, Tenth Bomber Command down in Surrey."

"What about her living in California?"

"Eighteen months ago she left New York and moved in with an aunt in Pasadena. Very rich aunt, married to a man named Goldsmith; he's a banker—Social Register, polo set. From what we've learned—and it's sketchy—she just likes California."

"O.K. What about this Webster?"

"Checks out. He's a gunnery officer on the *Saratoga*. It pulled into San Diego for combat repairs. It's scheduled for sea duty in two weeks, and the date holds. Until then there are a lot of forty-eights, seventy-twos; no extended leaves, though. The wife Margaret joined her lieutenant a couple of days ago. She's at the Greenbrier Hotel."

"Anything on the Bonners?"

"Only what you know, except that he was a bona fide hero. Posthumous Silver Star, infantry. Killed on a scout patrol covering an ambush evacuation. Sicily invasion."

"And that's it?"

"That's it. Obviously they all know each other, but I can't find anything to relate to your DW assignment."

"But you're not the control, Ed. You said you didn't know what the assignment was."

"True. But from the fragments I *do* know about, I can't find anything."

"My room was searched. I'm not mistaken about that."

"Maybe theft. Rich soldier in a rich hotel, home from an extended tour. Could be someone figured you were carrying a lot of back pay, discharge money."

"I doubt that. It was too pro."

"A lot of pros work those hotels. They wait for guys to start off on an alcoholic evening and . . ."

Spaulding interrupted. "I want to follow up something."

"What?"

"The Bonner girl said it 'wasn't likely' she'd be in touch with Leslie Jenner, and she wasn't kidding. That's an odd thing to say, isn't it? I'd like to know why she said it."

"Go ahead. It was your hotel room, not mine. . . . You know what I think? And I've thought about it; I've had to."

"What?"

"That New York crowd plays a fast game of musical beds. Now, you didn't elaborate, but isn't it logical the lady was in New York for a few days, perhaps saw you herself, or knew someone who had, and figured, why not? I mean, what the hell, she's headed back to California; probably never see you again. . . ."

"No, it's not logical. She was too complicated; she didn't have to be. She was keeping me away from the hotel."

"Well, you were there. . . ."

"I certainly was. You know, it's funny. According to your major at Mitchell Field, you think the Azores thing was directed at me. . . ."

"I said *might* be," interjected Pace.

"And I don't. Yet here I am, convinced the other night was, and *you* don't. Maybe we're both getting tired."

"Maybe I'm also concerned for your source control. This Swanson, he's very nervous; this isn't his ball park. I don't think he can take many more complications."

"Then let's not give him any. Not now. I'll know if I should."

Spaulding watched the disheveled accountant as he outlined the Buenos Aires operation. He had never met anyone quite like Walter Kendall. The man was positively unclean. His body odor was only partially disguised by liberal doses of bay rum. His shirt collar was dirty, his suit unpressed, and David was fascinated to watch the man breathe simultaneously through his mouth and nostrils. The agent in Terceira had said Eugene Lyons was "odd"; if this Kendall was "normal," he couldn't wait to meet the scientist.

The Buenos Aires operation seemed simple enough, far

less complicated than most of the Lisbon work. So simple, in fact, that it angered him to think he had been removed from Lisbon for it. Had anyone bothered to fill him in a few weeks ago, he could have saved Washington a lot of planning, and probably money. He had been dealing with the German underground since that organization had consolidated its diverse factions and become an effective force. If this Erich Rhinemann was capable of buying the designs, removing them from the Peenemünde complex, he—the man in Lisbon—could have gotten them out of the country. Probably with more security than trying to slip them out of North Sea or Channel ports. Those ports were clamped tight, obsessively patrolled. Had they not been, much of his own work would have been unnecessary. The only really remarkable aspect of the operation was that Rhinemann *could* get blueprints—on *anything*—related to Peenemünde. That *was* extraordinary. Peenemünde was a concrete and steel vault buried in the earth. With the most complex system of safeguards and backups ever devised. It would be easier to get a man out—for any number of invented reasons—than to remove a single page of paper.

Further, Peenemünde kept its laboratories separate, vital stages coordinated by only a handful of elite scientific personnel under Gestapo check. In Buenos Aires terms, this meant that Erich Rhinemann was able to (1) reach and buy diverse laboratory heads in a systematic order; (2) circumvent or buy (impossible) the Gestapo; or (3) enlist the cooperation of those handful of scientists who crossed laboratory lines.

David's experience led him to disqualify the last two possibilities; there was too much room for betrayal. Rhinemann must have concentrated on the laboratory heads; that was dangerous enough but more feasible.

As Kendall talked, David decided to keep his conclusions to himself. He would ask several questions, one or two of which he really wanted answered, but he would not form a partnership with Walter Kendall at this time. It was an easy decision to make. Kendall was one of the least likable men he'd ever met.

"Is there any particular reason why the designs have to be delivered in stages?" Spaulding asked.

"They may not be. But Rhinemann's smuggling them out section by section. Everybody's got a schedule; he says it's safer that way. From his projections, we figure a period of a week."

"All right, that makes sense. . . . And this Lyons fellow can authenticate them?"

"There's no one better. I'll get to him in a few minutes; there are a couple of things you'll have to know. Once in Argentina, he's your property."

"That sounds ominous."

"You can handle him. You'll have help. . . . The point is, as soon as he's cleared those blueprints, you send the codes and Rhinemann gets paid. Not before."

"I don't understand. Why so complicated? If they check out, why not pay him off in Buenos Aires?"

"He doesn't want that money in an Argentine bank."

"It must be a bundle."

"It is."

"From what little I know of this Rhinemann, isn't it unusual for him to be working with the German underground?"

"He's a Jew."

"Don't tell any graduates of Auschwitz. They won't believe you."

"War makes necessary relationships. Look at us. We're working with the Reds. Same thing: common goals, forget the disagreements."

"In this case, that's a little cold-blooded."

"Their problem, not ours."

"I won't pursue it. . . . One obvious question. Since I'm on my way to Buenos Aires, the embassy, why this stop in New York? Wouldn't it have been easier to just rotate from Lisbon to Argentina?"

"A last-minute decision, I'm afraid. Awkward, huh?"

"Not too smooth. Am I on a transfer list?"

"A what?"

"Foreign Service transfer sheet. State Department. Military attaché."

"I don't know. Why?"

"I'd like to find out if it's common knowledge that I left Lisbon. Or could be common knowledge. I didn't think it was supposed to be."

"Then it wasn't. *Why?*"

"So I know how to behave, that's all."

"We thought you should spend a few days getting familiar with everything. Meet Lyons, me; go over the schedule. What we're after, that sort of thing."

"Very considerate." David saw the questioning look on Kendall's face. "No, I mean that. So often we get thrown field problems knowing too little background. I've done it to men myself. . . . Then this discharge, the combat in Italy, they're the cover for my Lisbon activities? For New York only."

"Yeah, I guess that's right." Kendall, who'd been sitting on the edge of his desk, got up and walked around to his chair.

"How far am I to carry it?"

"Carry what?" Kendall avoided looking at David, who was leaning forward on an office couch.

"The cover. The papers mention Fifth Army—that's Clark; Thirty-Fourth Division, One Hundred and Twelfth Battalion, et cetera. Should I bone up? I don't know much about the Italian Theater. Apparently I got hit beyond Salerno; are there circumstances?"

"That's army stuff. As far as I'm concerned you'll be here five, six days, then Swanson will see you and send you down to Buenos Aires."

"All right, I'll wait for General Swanson." David realized there was no point in pursuing G-2 rituals with Kendall. . . . Part professional, part amateur. The hesitation waltz.

"Until you leave you'll spend whatever time you think is necessary with Lyons. In his office."

"Fine. I'd like to meet him." David stood up.

"Sit down, he's not here today. Nobody's here today but the receptionist. Till one o'clock. It's New Year's Eve." Kendall slumped into his chair and took out a cigarette, which he squeezed. "I've got to tell you about Lyons."

"All right." David returned to the couch.

"He's a drunk. He spent four years in jail, in a penitentiary. He can hardly talk because his throat got burned out with raw alcohol. . . . He's also the smartest son of a bitch in aerophysics."

Spaulding stared at Kendall without replying for several moments. When he did speak, he made no attempt to conceal his shock. "That's kind of a contradictory recommendation, isn't it?"

"I said he's smart."

"So are half the lunatics in Bellevue. Can he *function?* Since he's going to be my 'property'—as you put it—I'd like to know what the hell you've given me. And *why*, not incidentally."

"He's the best."

"That doesn't answer my question. Questions."

"You're a soldier. You take orders."

"I give them, too. Don't start that way."

"All right. . . . O.K. You're entitled, I guess."

"I'd say so."

"Eugene Lyons wrote the book on physical aerodynamics; he was the youngest full professor at the Massachusetts Institute of Technology. Maybe he was too young; he went downhill fast. Bum marriage, a lot of drinking, a lot of debts; the debts did it, they usually do. That and too many brains no one wants to pay for."

"Did what?"

"He went out of his skull, a week's bender. When he woke up in a South Side Boston hotel room, the girl he was with was dead. He'd beaten her to death. . . . She was a whore so nobody cared too much; still, he did it. They called it unpremeditated murder and MIT got him a good lawyer. He served four years, got out and nobody would hire him, wouldn't touch him. . . . That was 1936. He gave up; joined the skid row bums. I mean he really joined them." Kendall paused and grinned.

David was disturbed by the accountant's smile; there was nothing funny in the story. "Obviously he didn't stay there." It was all he could think to say.

"Did for damn near three years. Got his throat burned out right down on Houston Street."

"That's very sad."

"Best thing that happened to him. In the hospital ward they took his history and a doctor got interested. He was shipped off to the goddamned CCC, was reasonably rehabilitated, and what with the war coming he got into defense work."

"Then he's all right now." Spaulding made the statement positively. Again, it was all he could think to say.

"You don't clean out a man like that overnight. Or in a couple of years. . . . He has lapses, falls into the booze barrel now and then. Since working on classified stuff he's cooped up with his own personal wardens. For instance, here in New York he's got a room at St. Luke's Hospital. He's taken back and forth just like your socialite drunks. . . . In California, Lockheed's got him in a garden apartment with male nurses round the clock, when he's away from the plant. Actually, he's got it pretty good."

"He must be valuable. That's a lot of trouble. . . ."

"I told you," interrupted Kendall. "He's *the best*. He's just got to be watched."

"What happens when he's on his own? I mean, I've known alcoholics; they can slip away, often ingeniously."

"That's no problem. He'll get liquor—when he wants it; he'll be ingenious about that. But he doesn't go outside by himself. He won't go where there are any people, if you know what I mean."

"I'm not sure I do."

"He doesn't talk. The best he can manage is a hoarse whisper; remember, his throat was boiled out. He stays away from people. . . . Which is fine. When he's not drinking—which is most of the time—he's reading and working. He'll spend days in a laboratory stone sober and never go outside. It's just fine."

"How does he communicate? In the lab? In a meeting?"

"Pad and pencil, a few whispers, his hands. Mostly a pad and pencil. It's just numbers, equations, diagrams. That's his language."

"His entire language?"

"That's right. . . . If you're thinking about holding a conversation with him, forget it. He hasn't had a conversation with anyone in ten years."

18

DECEMBER 31, 1943, NEW YORK CITY

Spaulding hurried down Madison Avenue to the northeast corner of B. Altman's. There was a light snow falling; taxis rushed past the few pedestrians signaling in the middle of the block. The better fares were at the department store's entrance, carrying last-minute purchases for New Year's Eve. People who shopped at Altman's on the afternoon of New Year's Eve were prime passengers. Why waste gas on less?

David found himself walking faster than he had reason to; he wasn't going anywhere, to any specific place that required his presence at a specific time; he was getting away from Walter Kendall as fast as he could.

Kendall had finished his briefing on Eugene Lyons with the statement that "two hulks" would accompany the scientist to Buenos Aires. There'd be no liquor for the hermit-mute with his throat burned out; the male nurses carried "horse pills" at all times. Eugene Lyons, with no drink available, would spend hours over the work problems. Why not? He didn't do anything *else*. No conversations, David mused.

David turned down Kendall's offer of lunch on the pretext of looking up family friends. After all, it had been over three years. . . . He'd be in the office on January 2.

The truth was that Spaulding just wanted to get away from the man. And there was another reason: Leslie Jenner Hawkwood.

He didn't know where he'd begin, but he had to begin quickly. He had roughly a week to learn the story behind that incredible evening two nights ago. The beginning would include a widow named Bonner, that much he knew.

Perhaps Aaron Mandel could help him.

He took a dollar bill from his pocket and approached the doorman in front of Altman's. A taxi was found in less than a minute.

The ride uptown was made to the accompanying loquaciousness of the driver, who seemed to have an opinion on most any subject. David found the man annoying; he wanted to think and it was difficult. Then suddenly he was grateful to him.

"I was gonna catch the New Year's Eve crowds, like up at the Plaza, you know what I mean? There's big tips over at those war relief things. But the wife said no. She said come home, drink a little wine, pray to God our boy gets through the year. Now, I gotta. I mean if anything happened, I'd figure it was the tips I made New Year's Eve. Superstitions! What the hell, the kid's a typist in Fort Dix."

David had forgotten the obvious. No, not forgotten; he just hadn't considered the possibilities because they did not relate to him. Or he to them. He was in New York. On New Year's Eve. And that meant parties, dances, charity balls and an infinite variety of war-created celebrations in a dozen ballrooms and scores of townhouses.

Mrs. Paul Bonner would be at one of those places, at one of those parties. It had been four months since her husband had been killed. It was sufficient mourning under the circumstances, for the times. Friends—other women like Leslie Jenner, but of course not Leslie Jenner—would make that clear to her. It was the way social Manhattan behaved. And quite reasonable, all things considered.

It shouldn't be too difficult to find out where she was going. And if he found her, he'd find others . . . it was a place to start.

He tipped the driver and walked rapidly into the Montgomery lobby.

"Oh, Mr. Spaulding!" The old desk clerk's voice echoed in the marble enclosure. "There's a message for you."

He crossed to the counter. "Thank you." He unfolded the paper; *Mr. Fairfax had telephoned. Would he return the call as soon as possible?*

Ed Pace wanted to reach him.

The thread was intact under the door lock. He entered his room and went directly to the telephone.

"We got something in on the Hawkwood girl," Pace said. "Thought you'd want to know."

"What is it?" Why, oh *why*, did Pace *always* start conversations like that? Did he expect him to say, no, I don't want to know anything, and hang up?

"It fits in, I'm afraid, with my opinion of the other night. Your antenna's been working overtime."

"For Christ's sake, Ed, I'll pin a medal on you whenever you like. What *is* it?"

"She plays around. She's got a wide sex life in the Los Angeles area. Discreet but busy. A high-class whore, if I don't offend you."

"You don't offend me. What's the source?"

"Several brother officers to begin with; navy and air force. Then some of the movie people, actors and a couple of studio executives. And the social-industrial crowd: Lockheed, Sperry Rand. She's not the most welcome guest at the Santa Monica Yacht Club."

"Is there a G-2 pattern?"

"First thing we looked for. Negative. No classified personnel in her bed. Just rank: military and civilian. And she *is* in New York. Careful inquiry says she went back to visit her parents for Christmas."

"There are no Jenners listed in the phone book who've ever heard of her."

"In Bernardsville, New Jersey?"

"No," said David wearily. "Manhattan. You *did* say New York."

"Try Bernardsville. If you want to find her. But don't hand in any expense vouchers; you're not on a courier run in the north country."

"No. Bernardsville is hunt country."

"What?"

"Very social territory. Stables and stirrup cups. . . . Thanks, Ed. You just saved me a lot of work."

"Think nothing of it. All you've had is the conduit center of Allied Intelligence solving the problems of your sex life. We try to please our employees."

"I promise to reenlist when it's all over. Thanks again."

"Dave?"

"Yes?"

"I'm not cleared for the Swanson job, so no specifics, but how does it strike you?"

"I'll be damned if I know why you're *not* cleared. It's a simple purchase being handled by some oddballs—at least one . . . no, two that I know about. The one I've met is a winner. It seems to me they've complicated the deal, but that's because they're new at it. . . . We could have done it better."

"Have you met Swanson?"

"Not yet. After the holidays, I'm told. What the hell, we wouldn't want to interfere with the brigadier's Christmas vacation. School doesn't start until the first week in January."

Pace laughed on the other end of the line. "Happy New Year, Dave."

"The same, Ed. And thanks."

Spaulding replaced the receiver. He looked at his watch; it was one fifteen. He could requisition an army vehicle somewhere, he supposed, or borrow a car from Aaron Mandel. Bernardsville was about an hour outside New York, west of the Oranges, if he remembered correctly. It might be best to take Leslie Jenner by surprise, giving her no chance to run. On the other hand, on the premise he had considered before Pace's call, Leslie was probably in New York, preparing for the New Year's Eve she'd promised him. Somewhere, someplace. In an apartment or a brownstone or a hotel room like his own.

Spaulding wondered for a moment whether Pace had a point. Was he trying to find Leslie for reasons quite apart from his suspicions? The lies, the search. . . . It was possible. Why not? But a two- to three-hour drive to west Jersey and back would bring him no closer to either objective, investigatory or Freudian. If she wasn't there.

He asked the Montgomery switchboard to get him the number of the Jenner residence in Bernardsville, New Jersey. Not to place the call, just get the telephone number. And the address. Then he called Aaron Mandel.

He had postponed it for as long as he could; Aaron would be filled with tears and questions and offers of anything under the Manhattan sun and moon. Ed Pace told him he had interviewed the old concert manager four years ago before approaching David for Lisbon; that would mean he could reasonably avoid any lengthy discussions about his work.

And Aaron might be able to help him, should he need the old man's particular kind of assistance. Mandel's New York contacts were damn near inexhaustible. David would know more after he reached Bernardsville; and it would be less awkward to have made his duty call to Aaron before asking favors.

At first Spaulding thought the old man would have a coronary over the telephone. Aaron's voice choked, conveying his shock, his concern . . . and his love. The questions came faster than David could answer them: his mother, his father, his own well-being.

Mandel did not ask him about his work, but neither would he be satisfied that David was as healthy as he claimed. Aaron insisted on a meeting, if not this evening then certainly tomorrow.

David agreed. In the morning, late morning. They would have a drink together, perhaps a light lunch; welcome the New Year together.

"God be praised. You are well. You'll come around tomorrow?"

"I promise," David said.

"And you've never broken a promise to me."

"I won't. Tomorrow. And Aaron . . ."

"Yes?"

"It's possible I may need to find someone tonight. I'm not sure where to look but probably among the Social Register crowd. How are your Park Avenue connections?"

The old man chuckled in the quiet, good-humored, slightly arrogant way David remembered so well. "I'm the only Jew with a Torah stand in St. John the Divine. Everybody wants an artist—for nothing, of course. Red Cross, green cross; debutantes for war bandages, dances for fancy-sounding French medal winners. You name it, Mandel's on the hook for it. I got three coloraturas, two pianists and five Broadway baritones making appearances for 'our boys' tonight. All on the Upper East Side."

"I may call you in a little while. Will you still be at the office?"

"Where else? For soldiers and concert managers, when are the holidays?"

"You haven't changed."

"The main thing is that you're well. . . ."

No sooner had David hung up the phone than it rang.

"I have the telephone number and the address of your party in Bernardsville, Mr. Spaulding."

"May I have them, please?"

The operator gave him the information and he wrote it down on the ever-present stationery next to the phone.

"Shall I put the call through, sir?"

David hesitated, then said, "Yes, please. I'll stay on the line. Ask for a Mrs. Hawkwood, please."

"Mrs. Hawkwood. Very well, sir. But I can call you back when I have the party."

"I'd rather stay on an open circuit. . . ." David caught himself, but not in time. The blunder was minor but confirmed by the operator. She replied in a knowing voice.

"Of course, Mr. Spaulding. I assume if someone other than Mrs. Hawkwood answers, you'll wish to terminate the call?"

"I'll let you know."

The operator, now part of some sexual conspiracy, acted her role with firm efficiency. She dialed the outside operator and in moments a phone could be heard ringing in Bernardsville, New Jersey. A woman answered; it was not Leslie.

"Mrs. Hawkwood, please."

"Mrs. . . ." The voice on the Bernardsville line seemed hesitant.

"Mrs. Hawkwood, please. Long distance calling," said the Montgomery operator, as if she were from the telephone company, expediting a person-to-person call.

"Mrs. Hawkwood isn't here, operator."

"Can you tell me what time she's expected, please?"

"What time? Good heavens, she's not expected. At least, I didn't think she was. . . ."

Not fazed, the Montgomery employee continued, interrupting politely. "Do you have a number where Mrs. Hawkwood can be reached, please?"

"Well . . ." The voice in Bernardsville was now bewildered. "I suppose in California. . . ."

David knew it was time to intercede. "I'll speak to the party on the line, operator."

"Very well, sir." There was a *ther-ump* sound indicating the switchboard's disengagement from the circuit.

"Mrs. Jenner?"

"Yes, this is Mrs. Jenner," answered Bernardsville, obviously relieved with the more familiar name.

"My name is David Spaulding, I'm a friend of Leslie's and . . ." *Jesus!* He'd forgotten the husband's first name. ". . . Captain Hawkwood's. I was given this number. . . ."

"Well, *David Spaulding!* How are you, dear? This is Madge Jenner, you silly boy! Good heavens, it must be eight, ten years ago. How's your father and mother? I hear they're living in London. So very brave!"

Christ! thought Spaulding, it never occurred to him that Leslie's mother would remember two East Hampton months almost a decade ago. "Oh, Mrs. Jenner. . . . They're fine. I'm sorry to disturb you. . . ."

"You could never disturb us, you dear boy. We're just a couple of old stablehands out here. James has doubled our colors; no one wants to keep horses anymore. . . . You thought Leslie was here?"

"Yes, that's what I was told."

"I'm sorry to say she's not. To be quite frank, we rarely hear from her. She moved to California, you know."

"Yes, with her aunt."

"Only half-aunt, dear. My stepsister; we've not gotten along too well, I'm afraid. She married a Jew. He calls himself Goldsmith—hardly a disguise for Goldberg or Goldstein, is it? We're convinced he's in the black market and all that profiteering, if you know what I mean."

"Oh? Yes, I see. . . . Then Leslie didn't come East to visit you for Christmas?"

"Good heavens, no! She barely managed to send us a card. . . ."

He was tempted to call Ed Pace in Fairfax; inform the Intelligence head that California G-2 had come up with a Bernardsville zero. But there was no point. Leslie Jenner Hawkwood was in New York.

He had to find out why.

He called Mandel back and gave him two names: Leslie's and Cindy Tottle Bonner, widow of Paul Bonner, hero. Without saying so, David indicated that his curiosity might well be more professional than personal. Mandel did not question; he went to work.

Spaulding realized that he could easily phone Cindy Bonner, apologize and ask to see her. But he couldn't risk her turning him down; which she probably would do in light of the crude telephone call he had placed two nights ago. There simply wasn't the time. He'd have to see her, trust the personal contact.

And even then she might not be able to tell him anything. Yet there were certain instincts one developed and came to recognize. Inverted, convoluted, irrational. . . . Atavistic.

Twenty minutes passed; it was quarter to three. His telephone rang.

"David? Aaron. This Hawkwood lady, there's absolutely nothing. Everyone says she moved to California and nobody's heard a word. . . . Mrs. Paul Bonner: there's a private party tonight, on Sixty-second Street, name of Warfield. Number 212."

"Thanks. I'll wait outside and crash it with my best manners."

"No need for that. You have an invitation. Personal from the lady of the house. Her name's Andrea and she's delighted to entertain the soldier son of the famous you-know-who. She also wants a soprano in February, but that's my problem."

19

DECEMBER 31, 1943, NEW YORK CITY

The dinner clientele from the Gallery could have moved intact to the Warfield brownstone on Sixty-second Street. David mixed easily. The little gold emblem in his lapel served its purpose; he was accepted more readily, he was also more available. The drinks and buffet were generous, the small Negro jazz combo better than good.

And he found Cindy Bonner in a corner, waiting for her escort—an army lieutenant—to come back from the bar. She was petite, with reddish hair and very light, almost pale skin. Her posture was Vogue, her body slender, supporting very expensive, very subdued clothes. There was a pensive look about her; not sad, however. Not the vision of a hero's widow, not heroic at all. A rich little girl.

"I have a sincere apology to make," he told her. "I hope you'll accept it."

"I can't imagine what for. I don't think we've met." She smiled but not completely, as if his presence triggered a memory she could not define. Spaulding saw the look and understood. It was his voice. The voice that once had made him a good deal of money.

"My name is Spaulding. David . . ."

"You telephoned the other night," interrupted the girl, her eyes angry. "The Christmas gifts for Paul. Leslie . . ."

"That's why I'm apologizing. It was all a terrible misunderstanding. Please forgive me. It's not the sort of joke I'd enter into willingly; I was as angry as you were." He spoke calmly, holding her eyes with his own. It was sufficient; she blinked, trying to understand, her anger fading. She looked briefly at the tiny brass eagle in his lapel, the small insignia that could mean just about anything.

"I think I believe you."

"You should. It was sick; I'm not sick."

The army lieutenant returned carrying two glasses. He was drunk and hostile. Cindy made a short introduction; the lieutenant barely acknowledged the civilian in front of him. He wanted to dance; Cindy did not. The situation—abruptly created—was about to deteriorate.

David spoke with a trace of melancholy. "I served with Mrs. Bonner's husband. I'd like to speak with her for just a few minutes. I'll have to leave shortly, my wife's waiting for me uptown."

The combination of facts—reassurances—bewildered the drunken lieutenant as well as mollified him. His gallantry was called; he bowed tipsily and walked back toward the bar.

"Nicely done," Cindy said. "If there *is* a Mrs. Spaulding uptown, it wouldn't surprise me. You said you were out with Leslie; that's par for her course."

David looked at the girl. *Trust the developed instincts*, he thought to himself. "There is no Mrs. Spaulding. But there was a Mrs. Hawkwood the other night. I gather you're not very fond of her."

"She and my husband were what is politely referred to as 'an item.' A long-standing one. There are some people who say I forced her to move to California."

"Then I'll ask the obvious question. Under the circumstances, I wonder why she used your name? And then disappeared. She'd know I'd try to reach you."

"I think you used the term *sick*. She's sick."

"Or else she was trying to tell me something."

David left the Warfields' shortly before the New Year arrived. He reached the corner of Lexington Avenue and turned south. There was nothing to do but walk, think, try to piece together what he had learned; find a pattern that made sense.

He couldn't. Cindy Bonner was a bitter widow; her husband's death on the battlefield robbed her of any chance to strike back at Leslie. She wanted, according to her, simply to forget. But the hurt had been major. Leslie and Paul Bonner had been more than an "item." They had reached—again, according to Cindy—the stage where the Bonners had mutually sued for divorce. A confrontation between the two women, however, did not confirm Paul Bonner's story; Leslie Jenner Hawkwood had no *intention* of divorcing *her* husband.

It was all a messy, disagreeable Social Register foul-up; Ed Pace's "musical beds."

Why, then, would Leslie use Cindy's name? It was not only provocative and tasteless, it was senseless.

Midnight arrived as he crossed Fifty-second Street. A few horns blared from passing automobiles. In the distance could be heard tower bells and whistles; from inside bars came the shrill bleats of noisemakers and a cacophony of shouting. Three sailors, their uniforms filthy, were singing loudly off key to the amusement of pedestrians.

He walked west toward the string of cafes between Madison and Fifth. He considered stopping in at Shor's or 21 . . . in ten minutes or so. Enough time for the celebrations to have somewhat subsided.

"Happy New Year, Colonel Spaulding."

The voice was sharp and came from a darkened doorway.

"What?" David stopped and looked into the shadows. A tall man in a light grey overcoat, his face obscured by the brim of his hat, stood immobile. "What did you say?"

"I wished you a Happy New Year," said the man. "Needless to say, I've been following you. I overtook you several minutes ago."

The voice was lined with an accent, but David couldn't place it. The English was British tutored, the origin somewhere in Middle Europe. Perhaps the Balkans.

"I find that a very unusual statement and . . . needless to say . . . quite disturbing." Spaulding held his place; he had no weapon and wondered if the man recessed in the doorway was, conversely, armed. He couldn't tell. "What do you want?"

"Welcome you home, to begin with. You've been away a long time."

"Thank you. . . . Now, if you don't mind . . ."

"I mind! Don't move, colonel! Just stand there as if you were talking with an old friend. Don't back away; I'm holding a .45 leveled at your chest."

Several passersby walked around David on the curb side. A couple came out of an apartment entrance ten yards to the right of the shadowed doorway; they were in a hurry and crossed rapidly between Spaulding and the tall man with the unseen gun. David was first tempted to use them, but two considerations prevented him. The first was the grave danger to the couple; the second, the fact that the man with the gun had something to say. If he'd wanted to kill him, he would have done so by now.

"I won't move. . . . What is it?"

"Take two steps forward. Just *two*. No more."

David did so. He could see the face better now, but not clearly. It was a thin face, gaunt and lined. The eyes were deepset with hollows underneath. Tired eyes. The dull finish of the pistol's barrel was the clearest object David could distinguish. The man kept shifting his eyes to his left, behind Spaulding. He was looking for someone. Waiting.

"All right. Two steps. Now no one can walk between us. . . . Are you expecting someone?"

"I'd heard that the main agent in Lisbon was very controlled. You bear that out. Yes, I'm waiting; I'll be picked up shortly."

"Am I to go with you?"

"It won't be necessary. I'm delivering a message, that is all. . . . The incident at Lajes. It is to be regretted, the work of zealots. Nevertheless, accept it as a warning. We can't always control deep angers; surely you must know that. Fairfax should know it. Fairfax *will* know it before this first day of the New Year is over. Perhaps by now. . . . There is my car. Move to my right, your *left*." David did so as the man edged toward the curb, hiding the pistol under the cloth of his coat. "Heed us, colonel. There are to be no negotiations with Franz Altmüller. They are finished!"

"Wait a minute! I don't know what you're talking about. I don't *know* any Altmüller!"

"*Finished!* Heed the lesson of Fairfax!"

A dark brown sedan with bright headlights pulled up to the curb. It stopped, the rear door was thrown open, and the tall man raced across the sidewalk between the pedestrians and climbed in. The car sped away.

David rushed to the curb. The least he could do was get the vehicle's license number.

There was none. The rear license plate was missing.

Instead, above the trunk in the oblong rear window, a face looked back at him. His shock caused him to lose his breath. For the briefest of moments he wondered if his eyes, his senses were playing tricks on him, transporting his imagination back to Lisbon.

He started after the car, running in the street, dodging automobiles and the goddamned New Year's Eve revelers.

The brown sedan turned north on Madison Avenue and sped off. He stood in the street, breathless.

The face in the rear window was a man he had worked with in the most classified operations out of Portugal and Spain.

Marshall. Lisbon's master cryptographer.

The taxi driver accepted David's challenge to get him to the Montgomery in five minutes or less. It took seven, but considering the traffic on Fifth Avenue, Spaulding gave him five dollars and raced into the lobby.

There were no messages.

He hadn't bothered to thread his door lock; a conscious oversight, he considered. In addition to the maid service, if he could have offered an open invitation to those who had searched his room two nights ago, he would have done so. A recurrence might cause carelessness, some clues to identities.

He threw off his coat and went to his dresser, where he kept a bottle of Scotch. Two clean glasses stood on a silver tray next to the liquor. He'd take the necessary seconds to pour himself a drink before calling Fairfax.

"A very Happy New Year," he said slowly as he lifted the glass to his lips.

He crossed to the bed, picked up the telephone and gave the Virginia number to the switchboard. The circuits to the Washington area were crowded; it would take several minutes to get through.

What in God's name did the man mean? *Heed the lesson of Fairfax.* What the hell was he talking about? Who was Altmüller? . . . What was the first name? . . . Franz. Franz Altmüller.

Who was he?

So the Lajes Field "incident" *was* aimed at him. For Christ's sake, what *for*?

And *Marshall.* It *was* Marshall in that rear window! He *hadn't* been mistaken!

"Field Division Headquarters" were the monotoned words from the State of Virginia, County of Fairfax.

"Colonel Edmund Pace, please."

There was a slight pause at the other end of the line. David's ears picked up a tiny rush of air he knew very well.

It was a telephone intercept, usually attached to a wire recorder.

"Who's calling Colonel Pace?"

It was David's turn to hesitate. He did so thinking that perhaps he'd missed the interceptor sound before. It was entirely possible, and Fairfax was, after all . . . well, Fairfax.

"Spaulding. Lieutenant Colonel David Spaulding."

"Can I give the colonel a message, sir? He's in conference."

"No, you may not. You may and can give me the colonel."

"I'm sorry, sir." Fairfax's hesitation was now awkward. "Let me have a telephone number. . . ."

"Look, soldier, my name is Spaulding. My clearance is four-zero and this is a four-zero priority call. If those numbers don't mean anything to you, ask the son of a bitch on your intercept. Now, it's an emergency. Put me through to Colonel Pace!"

There was a loud double click on the line. A deep, hard voice came over the wire.

"And this is Colonel Barden, Colonel Spaulding. I'm also four-zero and any four-zeros will be cleared with this son of a bitch. Now, I'm in no mood for any rank horseshit. What do you want?"

"I like your directness, colonel," said David, smiling in spite of his urgency. "Put me through to Ed. It's really priority. It concerns Fairfax."

"I can't put you through, colonel. We don't have any circuits, and I'm not trying to be funny. Ed Pace is dead. He was shot through the head an hour ago. Some goddamned son of a bitch killed him right here in the compound."

20

JANUARY 1, 1944, FAIRFAX, VIRGINIA

It was four thirty in the morning when the army car carrying Spaulding reached the Fairfax gate.

The guards had been alerted; Spaulding, in civilian clothes, possessing no papers of authorization, was matched against his file photograph and waved through. David had been tempted to ask to see the photograph; to the best of his knowledge, it was four years old. Once inside, the automobile swung left and headed to the south area of the huge compound. About a half mile down the gravel road, past rows of metal Quonset huts, the car pulled up in front of a barracks structure. It was the Fairfax Administration Building.

Two corporals flanked the door. The sergeant driver climbed out of the car and signaled the noncoms to let Spaulding through; he was already in front of them.

David was shown to an office on the second floor. Inside were two men: Colonel Ira Barden and a doctor named McCleod, a captain. Barden was a thick, short man with the build of a football tackle and close-cropped black hair. McCleod was stooped, slender, bespectacled—the essence of the thoughtful academician.

Barden wasted the minimum time with introductions. Completed, he went immediately to the questions at hand.

"We've doubled patrols everywhere, put men with K-9s all along the fences. I'd like to think no one could get out. What bothers us is whether someone got out beforehand."

"How did it happen?"

"Pace had a few people over for New Year's. Twelve, to be exact. Four were from his own Quonset, three from

Records, the rest from Administration. Very subdued . . . what the hell, this is Fairfax. As near as we can determine, he went out his back door at about twenty minutes past midnight. Carrying out garbage, we think; maybe just to get some air. He didn't come back. . . . A guard down the road came to the door, saying he'd heard a shot. No one else had. At least, not inside."

"That's unusual. These quarters are hardly soundproof."

"Someone had turned up the phonograph."

"I thought it was a subdued party."

Barden looked hard at Spaulding. His glare was not anger, it was his way of telegraphing his deep concern. "That record player was turned up for no more than thirty seconds. The rifle used—and ballistics confirms this—was a training weapon, .22 caliber."

"A sharp crack, no louder," said David.

"Exactly. The phonograph was a signal."

"Inside. At the party," added Spaulding.

"Yes. . . . McCleod here is the base psychiatrist. We've been going over everyone who was inside. . . ."

"Psychiatrist?" David was confused. It was a security problem, not medical.

"Ed was a hardnose, you know that as well as I do. He trained you. . . . I looked you up, Lisbon. It's one angle. We're covering the others."

"Look," interrupted the doctor, "you two want to talk, and I've got files to go over. I'll call you in the morning; later this morning, Ira. Nice to meet you, Spaulding. Wish it wasn't this way."

"Agreed," said Spaulding, shaking the man's hand.

The psychiatrist gathered up the twelve file folders on the colonel's desk and left.

The door closed. Barden indicated a chair to Spaulding. David sat down, rubbing his eyes. "One hell of a New Year's, isn't it?" said Barden.

"I've seen better," Spaulding replied.

"Do you want to go over what happened to you?"

"I don't think there's any point. I was stopped; I told you what was said. Ed Pace was obviously the 'Fairfax lesson.' It's tied to a brigadier named Swanson at DW."

"I'm afraid it isn't."

"It has to be."

"Negative. Pace wasn't involved with the DW thing. His only tie was recruiting you; a simple transfer."

David remembered Ed Pace's words: *I'm not cleared . . . how does it strike you? Have you met Swanson?* He looked at Barden. "Then someone thinks he was. Same motive. Related to the sabotage at Lajes. In the Azores."

"How?"

"The son of a bitch said so on Fifty-second Street! Five *hours* ago. . . . Look, Pace is dead; that gives you certain latitude under the circumstances. I want to check Ed's four-zero files. Everything connected to my transfer."

"I've already done that. After your call there was no point in waiting for an inspector general. Ed was about my closest friend. . . ."

"And?"

"There are no files. Nothing."

"There *has* to be! There's got to be a record for Lisbon. For *me*."

"There is. It states simple transfer to DW. No names. Just a word. A single word: 'Tortugas.' "

"What about the papers you prepared? The discharge, the medical record; Fifth Army, One Hundred and Twelfth Battalion? Italy? . . . Those papers aren't manufactured without a Fairfax file!"

"This is the first I've heard of them. There's nothing about them in Ed's vaults."

"A major—Winston, I think his name is—met me at Mitchell Field. I flew in from Newfoundland on a coastal patrol. He brought me the papers."

"He brought you a sealed envelope and gave you verbal instructions. That's all he knows."

"*Jesus!* What the hell happened to the so-called Fairfax efficiency?"

"You tell me. And while you're at it, who murdered Ed Pace?"

David looked over at Barden. The word *murder* hadn't occurred to him. One didn't commit *murder*; one killed, yes, that was part of it. But murder? Yet it *was* murder.

"I can't tell you that. But I can tell you where to start asking questions."

"Please do."

"Raise Lisbon. Find out what happened to a cryptographer named Marshall."

JANUARY 1, 1944, WASHINGTON, D.C.

The news of Pace's murder reached Alan Swanson indirectly; the effect was numbing.

He had been in Arlington, at a small New Year's Eve dinner party given by the ranking general of Ordnance when the telephone call came. It was an emergency communication for another guest, a lieutenant general on the staff of the Joint Chiefs. Swanson had been near the library door when the man emerged; the staffer had been white, his voice incredulous.

"My God!" he had said to no one in particular. "Someone shot Pace over at Fairfax. He's dead!"

Those few in that small gathering in Arlington comprised the highest echelons of the military; there was no need for concealing the news; they would all, sooner or later, be told.

Swanson's hysterical first thoughts were of Buenos Aires. Was there *any possible connection*?

He listened as the brigadiers and the two- and three-stars joined in controlled but excited speculations. He heard the words . . . *infiltrators, hired assassins, double agents.* He was stunned by the wild theories . . . advanced rationally . . . that one of Pace's undercover agents had to be behind the murder. Somewhere a defector had been paid to make his way back to Fairfax; somewhere there was a weak link in a chain of Intelligence that had been bought.

Pace was not just a crack Intelligence man, he was one of the best in Allied Central. So much so that he twice had requested that his brigadier star be officially recorded but not issued, thus protecting his low profile.

But the profile was not low enough. An extraordinary man like Pace would have an extraordinary price on his head. From Shanghai to Berne; with Fairfax's rigid security the killing had to have been planned for months. Conceived as a long-range project, to be executed internally. There was no other way it could have been accomplished. And there were currently over five hundred personnel in the compound, including a rotating force of espionage units-in-training—nationals from many countries. No security system could be that absolute under the circumstances. All that was needed was one man to slip through.

Planned for months . . . a defector who had made his way back to Fairfax . . . a double agent . . . a weak Intelligence link paid a fortune. Berne to Shanghai.

A long-range project!

These were the specific words and terms and judgments that Swanson heard clearly because he wanted to hear them.

They removed the motive from Buenos Aires. Pace's death had nothing to *do* with Buenos Aires because the time element prohibited it.

The Rhinemann exchange had been conceived barely three weeks ago; it was inconceivable that Pace's murder was related. For it to be so would mean that he, himself, had broken the silence.

No one else on earth knew of Pace's contribution. And even Pace had known precious little.

Only fragments.

And all the background papers concerning the man in Lisbon had been removed from Pace's vault. Only the War Department transfer remained.

A fragment.

Then Alan Swanson thought of something and he marveled at his own cold sense of the devious. In a way, it was chilling that it could escape the recesses of his mind. With Edmund Pace's death, not even Fairfax could piece together the events leading up to Buenos Aires. The government of the United States was removed one step further.

As if abstractly seeking support, he ventured aloud to the small group of his peers that he recently had been in communication with Fairfax, with Pace as a matter of fact, over a minor matter of clearance. It was insignificant really, but he hoped to Christ . . .

He found his support instantly. The lieutenant general from staff, two brigs and a three-star all volunteered that they, too, had used Pace.

Frequently. Obviously more than he did.

"You could save a lot of time dealing directly with Ed," said the staffer. "He cut tape and shot you off a clearance right away."

One step further removed.

Once back in his Washington apartment, Swanson experienced the doubts again. Doubts and opportunities alike. Pace's murder was potentially a problem because of the shock waves it would produce. There would be a major investigation, all avenues explored. On the other hand, the concentration would be on Fairfax. It would consume Allied Central Intelligence. At least for a while. He had to move now. Walter Kendall had to get to Buenos Aires and conclude the arrangements with Rhinemann.

The guidance designs from Peenemünde. Only the designs were important.

But first tonight, this morning. David Spaulding. It was time to give the former man in Lisbon his assignment.

Swanson picked up the telephone. His hand shook.

The guilt was becoming unbearable.

JANUARY 1, 1944, FAIRFAX, VIRGINIA

"Marshall was killed several miles from a place called Valdero's. In the Basque province. It was an ambush."

"That's horseshit! Marsh never went into the north country! He wasn't trained, he wouldn't know what to do!" David was out of the chair, confronting Barden.

"Rules change. You're not the man in Lisbon now. . . . He went, he was killed."

"Source?"

"The ambassador himself."

"*His* source?"

"Your normal channels, I assume. He said it was confirmed. Identification was brought back."

"Meaningless!"

"What do you want? A body?"

"This may surprise you, Barden, but a hand or a finger isn't out of the question. *That's* identification. . . . Any photographs? Close shots, wounds, the eyes? Even those can be doctored."

"He didn't indicate any. What the hell's eating you? This is *confirmed*."

"Really?" David stared at Barden.

"For Christ's sake, Spaulding! What the hell is . . . 'Tortugas'? If it killed Ed Pace, I want to know! And I'm going to goddamned well find out! I don't give a shit about Lisbon cryps!"

The telephone rang on Barden's desk; the colonel looked briefly at it, then pulled his eyes back to Spaulding.

"Answer it," said David. "One of those calls is going to be Casualty. Pace has a family. . . . Had."

"Don't complicate my life any more than you have." Barden crossed to his desk. "Ed was due for an escort leave this Friday. I'm putting off calling—till morning. . . . Yes?" The colonel listened to the phone for several seconds, then looked at Spaulding. "It's the trip-line operator in New York; the one we've got covering you. This General Swanson's been trying to reach you. He's got him holding now. Do you want him to put the old man through?"

David remembered Pace's appraisal of the nervous brigadier. "Do you have to tell him I'm here?"

"Hell, no."

"Then put him through."

Barden walked from behind the desk as Spaulding took the phone and repeated the phrase "Yes, sir" a number of times. Finally he replaced the instrument. "Swanson wants me in his office this morning."

"I want to know why the hell they ripped you out of Lisbon," Barden said.

David sat down in the chair without at first answering. When he spoke he tried not to sound military or officious. "I'm not sure it had anything to do with . . . anything. I don't want to duck; on the other hand, in a way I have to. But I want to keep a couple of options open. Call it instinct, I don't know. . . . There's a man named Altmüller. Franz Altmüller. . . . Who he is, where he is—I have no idea. German, Swiss, I don't know. . . . Find out what you can on a four-zero basis. Call me at the Hotel Montgomery in New York. I'll be there for at least the rest of the week. Then I go to Buenos Aires."

"I will if you flex the clearances . . . tell me what the hell is going on."

"You won't like it. Because if I do, and if it *is* connected, it'll mean Fairfax has open code lines in Berlin."

JANUARY 1, 1944, NEW YORK CITY

The commercial passenger plane began its descent toward La Guardia Airport. David looked at his watch. It was a little past noon. It had all happened in twelve hours: Cindy Bonner, the stranger on Fifty-second Street, Marshall, Pace's murder, Barden, the news from Valdero's . . . and finally the awkward conference with the amateur source control, Brigadier General Alan Swanson, DW.

Twelve hours.

He hadn't slept in nearly forty-eight. He needed sleep to find some kind of perspective, to piece together the elusive pattern. Not the one that was clear.

Erich Rhinemann was to be killed.

Of *course* he had to be killed. The only surprise for David was the bumbling manner in which the brigadier had given the order. It didn't require elaboration or apology. And it—at *last*—explained his transfer from Lisbon. It filled in the gaping hole of *why*. He was no gyroscope specialist; it hadn't made sense. But now it did. He was a good selection; Pace had made a thoroughly professional choice. It was a job for which he was suited—in addition to being a bilingual liaison between the mute gyroscopic scientist, Eugene Lyons, and Rhinemann's blueprint man.

That picture was clear; he was relieved to see it come into focus.

What bothered him was the unfocused picture.

The embassy's Marshall, the cryp who five days ago picked him up at a rain-soaked airfield outside of Lisbon. The man he *had* seen looking at him through the automobile window on Fifty-second Street; the man supposedly killed in an ambush in the north country, into which he never had ventured. Or would venture.

Leslie Jenner Hawkwood. The resourceful ex-lover who had lied and kept him away from his hotel room, who foolishly used the ploy of Cindy Bonner and the exchange of gifts for a dead husband she had stolen. Leslie was not an idiot. She *was* telling him something.

But what?

And Pace. Poor, humorless Ed Pace cut down within the most security-conscious enclosure in the United States.

The *lesson of Fairfax*, predicted with incredible accuracy—nearly to the moment—by a tall, sad-eyed man in shadows on Fifty-second Street.

That . . . *they* were the figures in the unfocused picture.

David had been harsh with the brigadier. He had demanded—professionally, of course—to know the exact date the decision had been reached to eliminate Erich Rhinemann. Who had arrived at it? How was the order transmitted? Did the general know a cryptographer named Marshall? Had Pace ever mentioned him? Had *anyone* ever mentioned him? And a man named Altmüller. Franz Altmüller. Did that name mean anything?

The answers were no help. And God knew Swanson wasn't lying. He wasn't pro enough to get away with it.

The names Marshall and Altmüller were unknown to him. The decision to execute Rhinemann was made within hours. There was absolutely no way Ed Pace could have known; he was not consulted, nor was anyone at Fairfax. It was a decision emanating from the cellars of the White House; no one at Fairfax or Lisbon could have been involved. For David that absence of involvement was the important factor. It meant simply that the whole unfocused picture had nothing to do with Erich Rhinemann. And thus, as far as could be determined, was unrelated to Buenos Aires. David made the quick decision not to confide in the nervous brigadier. Pace had been right: the man couldn't take any more complications. He'd use Fairfax, source control be damned.

The plane landed; Spaulding walked into the passenger terminal and looked for the signs that read Taxis. He went through the double doors to the platform and heard the porters shouting the various destinations of the unfilled cabs. It was funny, but the shared taxis were the only things that caused him to think La Guardia Airport knew there was a war going on somewhere.

Simultaneously he recognized the foolishness of his thoughts. And the pretentiousness of them.

A soldier with no legs was being helped into a cab. Porters and civilians were touched, helpful.

The soldier was drunk. What was left of him, unstable.

Spaulding shared a taxi with three other men, and they

talked of little but the latest reports out of Italy. David decided to forget his cover in case the inevitable questions came up. He wasn't about to discuss any mythical combat in Salerno. But the questions did not arise. And then he saw why.

The man next to him was blind; the man shifted his weight and the afternoon sun caused a reflection in his lapel. It was a tiny metal replica of a ribbon: South Pacific.

David considered again that he was terribly tired. He was about the most unobservant agent ever to have been given an operation, he thought.

He got out of the cab on Fifth Avenue, three blocks north of the Montgomery. He had overpaid his share; he hoped the other two men would apply it to the blind veteran whose clothes were one hell of a long way from Leslie Jenner's Rogers Peet.

Leslie Jenner . . . Hawkwood.

A cryptographer named Marshall.

The unfocused picture.

He had to put it all out of his mind. He had to sleep, forget; let everything settle before he thought again. Tomorrow morning he would meet Eugene Lyons and begin . . . again. He had to be ready for the man who'd burned his throat out with raw alcohol and had not had a conversation in ten years.

The elevator stopped at the sixth floor. His was the seventh. He was about to tell the elevator operator when he realized the doors were not opening.

Instead, the operator turned in place. In his hand he gripped a short-barreled Smith & Wesson revolver. He reached behind him to the lever control and pushed it to the left, the enclosed box jerked and edged itself up between floors.

"The lobby lights go out this way, Colonel Spaulding. We may hear buzzers, but there's a second elevator used in emergencies. We won't be disturbed."

The accent was the same, thought David. British overlay, Middle Europe. "I'm glad of that. I mean, Jesus, it's been so long."

"I don't find you amusing."

"Nor I, you . . . obviously."

"You've been to Fairfax, Virginia. Did you have a pleasant journey?"

"You've got an extraordinary pipeline." Spaulding wasn't only buying time with conversation. He and Ira Barden had taken the required precautions. Even if the Montgomery switchboard reported everything he said, there was no evidence that he had flown to Virginia. The arrangements were made from telephone booths, the flight from Mitchell to Andrews under an assumed name on a crew sheet. Even the Manhattan number he had left with the Montgomery desk had a New York address under constant surveillance. And *in* the Fairfax compound, only the security gate had his name; he had been seen by only four, perhaps five men.

"We have reliable sources of information. . . . Now you have learned firsthand the lesson of Fairfax, no?"

"I've learned that a good man was murdered. I imagine his wife and children have been told by now."

"There is no murder in war, colonel. A misapplication of the word. And don't speak to us. . . ."

A buzzer interrupted the man. It was short, a polite ring.

"Who is 'us'?" asked David.

"You'll know in time, if you cooperate. If you don't cooperate, it will make no difference; you'll be killed. . . . We don't make idle threats. Witness Fairfax."

The buzzer sounded again. This time prolonged, not quite polite.

"How am I supposed to cooperate? What about?"

"We must know the precise location of Tortugas."

Spaulding's mind raced back to five o'clock that morning. In Fairfax. Ira Barden had said that the name "Tortugas" was the single word opposite his transfer specification. No other data, nothing but the word "Tortugas." And it had been buried in Pace's "vaults." Cabinets kept behind steel doors, accessible only to the highest echelon Intelligence personnel.

"Tortugas is part of an island complex off the coast of Florida. It's usually referred to as the Dry Tortugas. It's on any map."

The buzzer again. Now repeated; in short, angry spurts.

"Don't be foolish, colonel."

"I'm not being anything. I don't know what you're talking about."

The man stared at Spaulding. David saw that he was unsure, controlling his anger. The elevator buzzer was incessant now; voices could be heard from above and below.

"I'd prefer not to have to kill you but I will. *Where is Tortugas?*"

Suddenly a loud male voice, no more than ten feet from the enclosure, on the sixth floor, shouted:

"*It's up here! It's stuck!* Are you all *right* up there?"

The man blinked, the shouting had unnerved him. It was the instant David was waiting for. He lashed his right hand out in a diagonal thrust and gripped the man's forearm, hammering it against the metal door. He slammed his body into the man's chest and brought his knee up in a single, crushing assault against the groin. The man screamed in agony; Spaulding grabbed the arched throat with his left hand and tore at the veins around the larynx. He hammered the man twice more in the groin, until the pain was so excruciating that no more screams could emerge, only low, wailing moans of anguish. The body went limp, the revolver fell to the floor, and the man slid downward against the wall.

Spaulding kicked the weapon away and gripped the man's neck with both hands, shaking the head back and forth to keep him conscious.

"Now, you tell *me*, you son of a bitch! What *is* 'Tortugas'?"

The shouting outside the elevator was now deafening. There was a cacophony of hysteria brought on by the screams of the battered operator. There were cries for the hotel management. For the police.

The man looked up at David, tears of terrible pain streaming from his eyes. "Why not kill me, pig," he said between agonizing chokes of breath. ". . . You've tried before."

David was bewildered. He'd never *seen* the man. The north country? Basque? Navarre?

There was no time to think.

"What is '*Tortugas*'?"

"Altmüller, pig. The pig Altmüller . . ." The man fell into unconsciousness.

There was the name again.

Altmüller.

Spaulding rose from the unconscious body and grabbed the control lever of the elevator. He swung it to the far left, accelerating the speed as fast as possible. There were ten floors in the Montgomery; the panel lights indicated that the first-, third-, and sixth-floor buttons had been activated. If he could reach the tenth before the hysterical voices followed him up the stairs, it was possible that he could get out of the elevator, race down the corridor to one of the corners, then double back into the crowd which surely would gather around the open elevator doors.

Around the unconscious man on the floor.

It *had* to be possible! This was no time for him to be involved with the New York police.

The man was carried away on a stretcher; the questions were brief.

No, he didn't know the elevator operator. The man had dropped him off at his floor ten or twelve minutes ago. He'd been in his room and came out when he'd heard all the shouting.

The same as everyone else.

What was New York coming to?

David reached his room on seven, closed the door and stared at the bed. Christ, he was exhausted! But his mind refused to stop racing.

He would postpone everything until he had rested, except for two items. He had to consider those now. They could not wait for sleep because a telephone might ring, or someone might come to his hotel room. And he had to make his decisions in advance. Be prepared.

The first item was that Fairfax no longer could be used as a source. It was riddled, infiltrated. He had to function without Fairfax, which, in a way, was akin to telling a cripple he had to walk without braces.

On the other hand, he was no cripple.

The second item was a man named Altmüller. He had to find a man named Franz Altmüller; find out who he was, what he meant to the unfocused picture.

David lay down on the bed; he didn't have the energy to remove his clothes, even his shoes. He brought his arm up to shade his eyes from the afternoon sun streaming in the hotel windows. The afternoon sun of the first day of the new year, 1944.

Suddenly, he opened his eyes in the black void of tweed cloth. There was a third item. Inextricably bound to the man named Altmüller.

What the hell did "Tortugas" mean?

21

JANUARY 2, 1944, NEW YORK CITY

Eugene Lyons sat at a drafting board in the bare office. He was in shirtsleeves. There were blueprints strewn about on tables. The bright morning sun bouncing off the white walls gave the room the antiseptic appearance of a large hospital cubicle.

And Eugene Lyons's face and body did nothing to discourage such thoughts.

David had followed Kendall through the door, apprehensive at the forthcoming introduction. He would have preferred not knowing anything about Lyons.

The scientist turned on the stool. He was among the thinnest men Spaulding had ever seen. The bones were surrounded by flesh, not protected by it. Light blue veins were in evidence throughout the hands, arms, neck and temples. The skin wasn't old, it was worn out. The eyes were deep-set but in no way dull or flat; they were alert and, in their own way, penetrating. His straight grey hair was thinned out before its time; he could have been any age within a twenty-year span.

There was, however, one quality about the man that seemed specific: disinterest. He acknowledged the intrusion, obviously knew who David was, but made no move to interrupt his concentration.

Kendall forced the break. "Eugene, this is Spaulding. You show him where to start."

And with those words Kendall turned on his heel and went out the door, closing it behind him.

David stood across the room from Lyons. He took the

necessary steps and extended his hand. He knew exactly what he was going to say.

"It's an honor to meet you, Dr. Lyons. I'm no expert in your field, but I've heard about your work at MIT. I'm lucky to have you spread the wealth, even if it's only for a short time."

There was a slight, momentary flicker of interest in the eyes. David had gambled on a simple greeting that told the emaciated scientist several things, among which was the fact that David was aware of Lyons's tragedy in Boston—thus, undoubtedly, the rest of his story—and was not inhibited by it.

Lyons's grip was limp; the disinterest quickly returned. Disinterest, not necessarily rudeness. On the borderline.

"I know we haven't much time and I'm a neophyte in gyroscopics," said Spaulding, releasing the hand, backing off to the side of the drafting board. "But I'm told I don't have to recognize much more than pretty basic stuff; be able to verbalize in German the terms and formulas you write out for me."

David emphasized—with the barest rise in his voice—the words *verbalize . . . you write out for me*. He watched Lyons to see if there was any reaction to his open acknowledgment of the scientist's vocal problem. He thought he detected a small hint of relief.

Lyons looked up at him. The thin lips flattened slightly against the teeth; there was a short extension at the corners of the mouth and the scientist nodded. There was even an infinitesimal glint of appreciation in the deep-set eyes. He got up from his stool and crossed to the nearest table where several books lay on blueprints. He picked up the top volume and handed it to Spaulding. The title on the cover was *Diagrammatics: Inertia and Precession.*

David knew it would be all right.

It was past six o'clock.

Kendall had gone; the receptionist had bolted at the stroke of five, asking David to close the doors if he was the last person to leave. If not, tell one of the others.

The "others" were Eugene Lyons and his two male nurses.

Spaulding met them—the male nurses—briefly in the reception room. Their names were Hal and Johnny. Both were large men; the talkative one was Hal, the leader was Johnny, an ex-marine.

"The old guy is on his real good behavior," said Hal. "Nothing to worry about."

"It's time to get him back to St. Luke's," said Johnny. "They get pissed off if he's too late for the night meal."

Together the men went into Lyons's office and brought him out. They were polite with the cadaverous physicist, but firm. Eugene Lyons looked indifferently at Spaulding, shrugged and walked silently out the door with his two keepers.

David waited until he heard the sound of the elevator in the hallway. Then he put down the *Diagrammatics* volume the physicist had given him on the receptionist's desk and crossed to Walter Kendall's office.

The door was locked, which struck him as strange. Kendall was on his way to Buenos Aires, he might not be back for several weeks. Spaulding withdrew a small object from his pocket and knelt down. At first glance, the instrument in David's hand appeared to be an expensive silver pocket knife, the sort so often found at the end of an expensive key chain, especially in very expensive men's clubs. It wasn't. It was a locksmith's pick designed to give that appearance. It had been made in London's Silver Vaults, a gift from an MI-5 counterpart in Lisbon.

David spun out a tiny cylinder with a flat tip and inserted it into the lock housing. In less than thirty seconds the appropriate clicks were heard and Spaulding opened the door. He walked in, leaving it ajar.

Kendall's office had no file cabinets, no closets, no bookshelves; no recesses whatsoever other than the desk drawers. David turned on the fluorescent reading lamp at the far edge of the blotter and opened the top center drawer.

He had to stifle a genuine laugh. Surrounded by an odd assortment of paper clips, toothpicks, loose Lifesavers, and note paper were two pornographic magazines. Although marked with dirty fingerprints, both were fairly new.

Merry Christmas, Walter Kendall, thought David a little sadly.

The side drawers were empty, at least there was nothing of interest. In the bottom drawer lay crumpled yellow pages of note paper, meaningless doodles drawn with a hard pencil, piercing the pages.

He was about to get up and leave when he decided to look once more at the incoherent patterns on the crumpled paper. There was nothing else; Kendall had locked his office door out of reflex, not necessity. And again by reflex, perhaps, he had put the yellow pages—not in a wastebasket, which had only the contents of emptied ashtrays—but in a drawer. Out of sight.

David knew he was reaching. There was no choice; he wasn't sure what he was looking for, if anything.

He spread two of the pages on top of the blotter, pressing the surfaces flat.

Nothing.

Well, something. Outlines of women's breasts and genitalia. Assorted circles and arrows, diagrams: a psychoanalyst's paradise.

He removed another single page and pressed it out. More circles, arrows, breasts. Then to one side, childlike outlines of clouds—billowy, shaded; diagonal marks that could be rain or multiple sheets of thin lightning.

Nothing.

Another page.

It caught David's eye. On the bottom of the soiled yellow page, barely distinguishable between criss-cross penciling, was the outline of a large swastika. He looked at it closely. The swastika had circles at the right-hand points of the insignia, circles that spun off as if the artist were duplicating the ovals of a Palmer writing exercise. And flowing out of these ovals were unmistakable initials. *JD.* Then *Joh D., J. Diet. . . .* The letters appeared at the end of each oval line. And beyond the final letters in each area were elaborately drawn *? ? ?*

? ? ?

David folded the paper carefully and put it in his jacket pocket.

There were two remaining pages, so he took them out simultaneously. The page to the left had only one large, indecipherable scribble—once more circular, now angry—and meaningless. But on the second paper, again toward the bottom of the page, was a series of scroll-like markings that could be interpreted as *J*s and *D*s. similar in flow to the letters after the swastika points on the other page.

And opposite the final *D* was a strange horizontal obelisk, its taper on the right. There were lines on the side as though they were edges. . . . A bullet, perhaps, with bore markings. Underneath, on the next line of the paper to the left, were the same oval motions that brought to mind the Palmer exercise. Only they were firmer here, pressed harder into the yellow paper.

Suddenly David realized what he was staring at.

Walter Kendall had subconsciously outlined an obscene caricature of an erect penis and testicles.

Happy New Year, Mr. Kendall, thought Spaulding.

He put the page carefully into his pocket with its partner, returned the others and shut the drawer. He switched off the lamp, walked to the open door, turning to see if he had left everything as it was, and crossed into the reception room. He pulled Kendall's door shut and considered briefly whether to lock the tumblers in place.

It would be pointless to waste the time. The lock was old, simple; janitorial personnel in just about any building in New York would have a key, and it was more difficult inserting tumblers than releasing them. To hell with it.

A half hour later it occurred to him—in an instant of reflection—that this decision probably saved his life. The sixty, or ninety, or one-hundred-odd seconds he eliminated from his departure placed him in the position of an observer, not a target.

He put on the Rogers Peet overcoat, turned off the lights, and walked into the corridor to the bank of elevators. It was nearly seven, the day after New Year's, and the building was practically deserted. A single elevator was working. It had passed his floor, ascending to the upper stories, where it seemed to linger. He was about to use the stairs—the offices were on the third floor, it might be quicker—when he heard rapid, multiple footsteps coming up the staircase. The sound was incongruous. Moments ago the elevator had been in the lobby; why would two—more than two?—people be racing up the stairs at seven at night? There could be a dozen reasonable explanations, but his instincts made him consider *un*reasonable ones.

Silently, he ran to the opposite end of the short floor, where an intersecting corridor led to additional offices on the south side of the building. He rounded the corner and pressed himself against the wall. Since the assault in the

Montgomery elevator, he carried a weapon—a small Beretta revolver—strapped to his chest, under his clothes. He flipped open his overcoat and undid the buttons of his jacket and shirt. Access to the pistol would be swift and efficient, should it be necessary.

It probably wouldn't be, he thought, as he heard the footsteps disappear.

Then he realized that they had not disappeared, they had faded, slowed down to a walk—a quiet, cautious walk. And then he heard the voices: whisper-like, indistinguishable. They came from around the edge of the wall, in the vicinity of the unmarked Meridian office, no more than thirty feet away.

He inched the flat of his face to the sharp, concrete corner and simultaneously reached his right hand under his shirt to the handle of the Berefta.

There were two men with their backs to him, facing the darkened glass of the unmarked office door. The shorter of the two put his face against the pane, hands to both temples to shut out the light from the corridor. He pulled back and looked at his partner, shaking his head negatively.

The taller man turned slightly, enough for Spaulding to recognize him.

It was the stranger in the recessed, darkened doorway on Fifty-second Street. The tall, sad-eyed man who spoke gently, in bastardized British-out-of-the-Balkans, and held him under the barrel of a thick, powerful weapon.

The man reached into his left overcoat pocket and gave a key to his friend. With his right hand he removed a pistol from his belt. It was a heavy-duty .45, army issue. At close range, David knew it would blow a person into the air and off the earth. The man nodded and spoke softly but clearly.

"He has to be. He didn't leave. I want him."

With these words the shorter man inserted the key and shoved at the door. It swung back slowly. Together, both men walked in.

At that precise moment the elevator grill could be heard opening, its metal frames ringing throughout the corridor. David could see the two men in the darkened reception room freeze, turn toward the open door and quickly shut it.

"*Chee-ryst Almighty!*" was the irate shout from the

angry elevator operator as the grill rang shut with a clamor.

David knew it was the instant to move. Within seconds one or both men inside the deserted Meridian offices would realize that the elevator had stopped on the third floor because someone had pushed the button. Someone not in evidence, someone they had not met on the stairs. Someone still on the floor.

He spun around the edge of the wall and raced down the corridor toward the staircase. He didn't look back; he didn't bother to muffle his steps—it would have reduced his speed. His only concern was to get down those steps and out of the building. He leaped down the right-angled staircase to the in-between landing and whipped around the corner.

And then he stopped.

Below him, leaning against the railing, was the third man. He *knew* he'd heard more than two sets of feet racing up the staircase minutes ago. The man was startled, his eyes widened in shocked recognition and his right hand jerked backwards toward his coat pocket. Spaulding didn't have to be told what he was reaching for.

David sprang off the landing straight down at the man, making contact in midair, his hands clawing for the man's throat and right arm. He gripped the skin on the neck below the left ear and tore at it, slamming the man's head into the concrete wall as he did so. David's heavier body crushed into the would-be sentry's chest; he twisted the right arm nearly out of its shoulder socket.

The man screamed and collapsed; the scalp was lacerated, blood flowing out of the section of his skull that had crashed into the wall.

David could hear the sounds of a door being thrown open and men running. Above him, of course; one floor above him.

He freed his entangled legs from the unconscious body and raced down the remaining flight of stairs to the lobby. The elevator had, moments ago, let out its cargo of passengers; the last few were going out the front entrance. If any had heard the prolonged scream from the battered man sixty feet away up the staircase, none acknowledged it.

David rushed into the stragglers, elbowing his way through the wide double doors and onto the sidewalk. He turned east and ran as fast as he could.

He had walked over forty city blocks—some two miles in Basque country, but here infinitely less pleasant.

He had come to several decisions. The problem was how to implement them.

He could not stay in New York; not without facing risks, palpably unacceptable. And he had to get to Buenos Aires at once, before any of those hunting him in New York knew he was gone.

For they were hunting him now; that much was clear.

It would be suicide to return to the Montgomery. Or for that matter, to the unmarked Meridian offices in the morning. He could handle both with telephone calls. He would tell the hotel that he had been suddenly transferred to Pennsylvania; could the Montgomery management pack and hold his things? He'd call later about his bill. . . .

Kendall was on his way to Argentina. It wouldn't make any difference what the Meridian office was told.

Suddenly, he thought of Eugene Lyons.

He was a little sad about Lyons. Not the man (of course the man, he reconsidered quickly, but not the man's affliction, in this instance), but the fact that he would have little chance to develop any sense of rapport before Buenos Aires. Lyons might take his sudden absence as one more rejection in a long series. And the scientist might really need his help in Buenos Aires, at least in the area of German translation. David decided that he had to have the books Lyons selected for him; he had to have as solid a grasp of Lyons's language as was possible.

And then David realized where his thoughts were leading him.

For the next few hours the safest places in New York were the Meridian offices and St. Luke's Hospital.

After his visits to both locations he'd get out to Mitchell Field and telephone Brigadier General Swanson.

The answer to the violent enigma of the past seven days —from the Azores to a staircase on Thirty-eighth Street and everything in between—was in Buenos Aires.

Swanson did not know it and could not help; Fairfax was infiltrated and could not be told. And *that* told *him* something.

He was on his own. A man had two choices in such a dilemma: take himself out of strategy, or dig for identities and blow the covers off.

The first choice would be denied him. The brigadier, Swanson, was paranoid on the subject of the gyroscopic designs. And Rhinemann. There'd be no out of strategy.

That left the second: the identity of those behind the enigma.

A feeling swept over him, one he had not experienced in several years: the fear of sudden inadequacy. He was confronted with an extraordinary problem for which there was no pat—or complicated—solution in the north country. No unraveling that came with moves or countermoves whose strategies he had mastered in Basque and Navarre.

He was suddenly in another war. One he was not familiar with; one that raised doubts about himself.

He saw an unoccupied taxi, its roof light dimly lit, as if embarrassed to announce its emptiness. He looked up at the street sign; he was on Sheridan Square—it accounted for the muted sounds of jazz that floated up from cellars and surged down crowded side streets. The Village was warming up for another evening.

He raised his hand for the taxi; the driver did not see him. He started running as the cab proceeded up the street to the corner traffic light. Suddenly he realized that someone else on the other side of the square was rushing toward the empty taxi; the man was closer to it than Spaulding, his right hand was gesturing.

It was now terribly important to David that he reach the car first. He gathered speed and ran into the street, dodging pedestrians, momentarily blocked by two automobiles that were bumper to bumper. He spread his hands from hood to trunk and jumped over into the middle of the street and continued racing toward his objective.

Objective.

He reached the taxi no more than half a second after the other man.

Goddamn it! It was the obstruction of the two automobiles!

Obstruction.

He slammed his hand on the door panel, preventing the other man from pulling it open. The man looked up at Spaulding's face, at Spaulding's eyes.

"Christ, fella. I'll wait for another one," the man said quickly.

David was embarrassed. What the hell was he *doing*?

The doubts? The goddamned doubts.

"No, really, I'm terribly sorry." He mumbled the words, smiling apologetically. "You take it. I'm in no hurry. . . . Sorry again."

He turned and walked rapidly across the street into the crowds of Sheridan Square.

He could have had the taxi. That was the important thing.

Jesus! The treadmill never let up.

PART 2

22

1944, BUENOS AIRES, ARGENTINA

The Pan American Clipper left Tampa at eight in the morning, with scheduled coastline stops at Caracas, São Luís, Salvador, and Rio de Janeiro before the final twelve hundred miles to Buenos Aires. David was listed on the passenger invoice as Mr. Donald Scanlan of Cincinnati, Ohio; occupation: mining surveyor. It was a temporary cover for the journey only. "Donald Scanlan" would disappear after the clipper landed at the Aeroparque in Buenos Aires. The initials were the same as his own for the simple reason that it was so easy to forget a monogrammed gift or the first letter of a hastily written signature. Especially if one was preoccupied or tired . . . or afraid.

Swanson had been close to panic when David reached him from the Mitchell Field Operations Room in New York. As a source control, Swanson was about as decisive as a bewildered bird dog. Any deviation from Kendall's schedule—Kendall's instructions, really—was abhorrent to him. And Kendall wasn't even *leaving* for Buenos Aires until the following morning.

David had not wasted complicated explanations on the general. As far as he was concerned, three attempts had been made on his life—at least, they could be so interpreted—and if the general wanted his "services" in Buenos Aires, he'd better get down there while he was still in one piece and functioning.

Were the attempts—the attacks—related to Buenos Aires? Swanson had asked the question as though he were afraid to name the Argentine city.

David was honest: there was no way to tell. The answer

was in Buenos Aires. It was reasonable to consider the possibility, but not to assume it.

"That's what Pace said," had been Swanson's reply. "Consider, don't assume."

"Ed was generally right about such things."

"He said when you operated in Lisbon, you were often involved in messy situations in the field."

"True. I doubt that Ed knew the particulars, though. But he was right in what he was trying to tell you. There are a lot of people in Portugal and Spain who'd rather see me dead than alive. Or at least they think they would. They could never be sure. Standard procedure, general."

There had been a prolonged pause on the Washington line. Finally, Swanson had said the words. "You realize, Spaulding, that we may have to replace you."

"Of course. You can do so right now, if you like." David had been sincere. He wanted very much to return to Lisbon. To go into the north country. To Valdero's. To find out about a cryp named Marshall.

"No. . . . No, everything's too far along. The designs. They're the important thing. Nothing else matters."

The remainder of the conversation concerned the details of transportation, American and Argentine currency, replenishing of a basic wardrobe, and luggage. Logistics which were not in the general's frame of reference and for which David took responsibility. The final command—request—was delivered, not by the general, but by Spaulding.

Fairfax was not to be informed of his whereabouts. Nor was anyone else for that matter, except the embassy in Buenos Aires; but make every effort to keep the information from Fairfax.

Why? Did Spaulding think . . .

"There's a leak in Fairfax, general. You might pass that on to the White House cellars."

"That's impossible!"

"Tell that to Ed Pace's widow."

David looked out the Clipper window. The pilot, moments ago, had informed the passengers that they were passing over the huge coastal lake of Mirim in Uruguay. Soon they'd be over Montevideo, forty minutes from Buenos Aires.

Buenos Aires. The unfocused picture, the blurred figures

of Leslie Jenner Hawkwood, the cryptographer Marshall, a man named Franz Altmüller; strange but committed men on Fifty-second and Thirty-eighth streets—in a darkened doorway, in a building after office hours, on a staircase. A man in an elevator who was so unafraid to die. An enemy who displayed enormous courage . . . or misguided zealousness. A maniac.

The answer to the enigma was in Buenos Aires, less than an hour away. The city was an hour away, the answer much longer. But no more than three weeks if his instincts were right. By the time the gyroscopic designs were delivered.

He would begin slowly, as he always did with a new field problem. Trying first to melt into the surroundings, absorb his cover; be comfortable, facile in his relationships. It shouldn't be difficult. His cover was merely an extension of Lisbon's: the wealthy trilingual attaché whose background, parents, and prewar associations in the fashionable centers of Europe made him a desirable social buffer for any ambassador's dinner table. He was an attractive addition to the delicate world of a neutral capital; and if there were those who thought someone, somewhere, had used money and influence to secure him such combat-exempt employment, so be it. It was denied emphatically, but not vehemently; there was a difference.

The "extension" for Buenos Aires was direct and afforded him top-secret classification. He was acting as a liaison between New York-London banking circles and the German expatriate Erich Rhinemann. Washington approved, of course; postwar financing in areas of reconstruction and industrial rebuilding were going to be international problems. Rhinemann could not be overlooked, not in the civilized marble halls of Berne and Geneva.

David's thoughts returned to the book on his lap. It was the second of six volumes Eugene Lyons had chosen for him.

"Donald Scanlan" went through the Aeroparque customs without difficulty. Even the embassy liaison, who checked in all Americans, seemed unaware of his identity.

His single suitcase in hand, David walked to the taxi station and stood on the cement platform looking at the drivers standing beside their vehicles. He wasn't prepared to assume the name of Spaulding or to be taken directly to the embassy just yet. He wanted to assure himself that "Donald Scanlan" was accepted for what he was—a mining surveyor, nothing more; that there was no unusual interest in such a man. For if there were, it would point to David Spaulding, Military Intelligence, Fairfax and Lisbon graduate.

He selected an obese, pleasant-looking driver in the fourth cab from the front of the line. There were protests from those in front, but David pretended not to understand. "Donald Scanlan" might know a smattering of Spanish, but certainly not the epithets employed by the disgruntled drivers cheated out of a fare.

Once inside he settled back and gave instructions to the unctuous driver. He told the man he had nearly an hour to waste before he was to be met—the meeting place not mentioned—and asked if the driver would give him a short tour of the city. The tour would serve two purposes: he could position himself so that he could constantly check for surveillance, and he would learn the main points of the city.

The driver, impressed by David's educated, grammatical Spanish, assumed the role of tour director and drove out of the airport's winding lanes to the exit of the huge Parque 3 de Febrero in which the field was centered.

Thirty minutes later David had filled a dozen pages with notes. The city was like a European insert on the southern continent. It was a strange mixture of Paris, Rome and middle Spain. The streets were not city streets, they were boulevards: wide, lined with color. Fountains and statuary everywhere. The Avenida 9 de Julio might have been a larger Via Veneto or Saint-Germain-des-Prés. The sidewalk cafes, profuse with brightly decorated awnings and greenery from hundreds of planter boxes, were doing a brisk summer afternoon business. The fact that it *was* summer in Argentina was emphasized for David by the perspiration on his neck and shirt front. The driver admitted that the day was inordinately warm, in the high seventies.

David asked to be driven—among other places—to a district called San Telmo. The cab owner nodded appreciatively, as if he had accurately assessed the rich American. Soon Spaulding understood. San Telmo was as Kendall had noted: elegant, secluded, beautifully kept old houses and apartment buildings with wrought-iron balustrades and brilliantly blossoming flowers lining the spotless streets.

Lyons would be comfortable.

From San Telmo the driver doubled back into the inner city and began the tour from the banks of the Río de la Plata.

The Plaza de Mayo, the Cabildo, the Casa Rosada, Calle Rivadavia. The names filled David's notebook; these were the streets, the squares, the locations he would absorb quickly.

La Boca. The waterfront, south of the city; this, the driver said, was no place for the tourist.

The Calle Florida. Here was the finest shopping area in all South America. The driver could take his American to several store owners personally known to him and extraordinary purchases could be made.

Sorry, there was no time. But David wrote in his notebook that traffic was banned at the borders of the Calle Florida.

The driver then sped out the Avenida Santa Fé toward the Palermo. No sight in Buenos Aires was as beautiful as the Palermo.

What interested David more than the beauty was the huge park—or series of individual parks; the quiet, immense, artificial lake. The acres of botanical gardens; the enormous zoo complex with rows of cages and buildings.

Beauty, yes. Secure areas of contact, more so. The Palermo might come in handy.

An hour had passed; there were no automobiles following the taxi. "Donald Scanlan" had not been under surveillance; David Spaulding could emerge.

Quietly.

He instructed the driver to leave him off at the cabstand outside the entrance to the Palermo zoo. He was to meet his party there. The driver looked crestfallen. Was there no hotel? No place of residence?

Spaulding did not reply, he simply asked the fare and quickly held out the amount. No more questions were in order.

David spent an additional fifteen minutes inside the zoo, actually enjoying it. He bought an ice from a vendor, wandered past the cages of marmosets and orangutans—finding extraordinary resemblances to friends and enemies

—and when he felt comfortable (as only a field man can feel comfortable), walked out to the cabstand.

He waited another five minutes while mothers and governesses and children entered the available taxis. It was his turn.

"The American embassy, *por favor*."

Ambassador Henderson Granville allowed the new attaché a half hour. There would be other days when they could sit and chat at length, but Sundays were hectic. The rest of Buenos Aires might be at church or at play; the diplomatic corps was at work. He had two garden parties still to attend—telephone calls would be made detailing the departures and arrivals of the German and the Japanese guests; *his* arrivals and departures would be timed accordingly. And after the second garden-bore there was dinner at the Brazilian embassy. Neither German nor Japanese interference was anticipated. Brazil was close to an open break.

"The Italians, you realize," said Granville, smiling at David, "don't count any longer. Never did really; not down here. They spend most of their time cornering us in restaurants, or calling from public phones, explaining how Mussolini ruined the country."

"Not too different from Lisbon."

"I'm afraid they're the only pleasant similarity. . . . I won't bore you with a tedious account of the upheavals we've experienced here, but a quick sketch—and emphasis —will help you adjust. You've read up, I assume."

"I haven't had much time. I left Lisbon only a week ago. I know that the Castillo government was overthrown."

"Last June. Inevitable. . . . Ramón Castillo was as inept a president as Argentina ever had, and it's had its share of buffoons. The economy was disastrous: agriculture and industry came virtually to a halt; his cabinet never made provisions to fill the beef market void created by the British struggle, even though the lot of them figured John Bull was finished. He deserved to be thrown out. . . . Unfortunately, what came in the front door—marched in phalanx up the Rivadavia, to be more precise—hardly makes our lives easier."

"That's the military council, isn't it? The junta?"

Granville gestured with his delicate hands; the chiseled

features of his aging, aristocratic face formed a sardonic grimace. "The Grupo de Oficiales Unidos! As unpleasant a band of goose-stepping opportunists as you will meet . . . I daresay, anywhere. You know, of course, the entire army was trained by the Wehrmacht officer corps. Add to that jovial premise the hot Latin temperament, economic chaos, a neutrality that's enforced but not believed in, and what have you got? A suspension of the political apparatus; no checks and balances. A police state rife with corruption."

"What maintains the neutrality?"

"The infighting, primarily. The GOU—that's what we call it—has more factions than the '29 Reichstag. They're all jockeying for the power spots. And naturally, the cold fear of an American fleet and air force right up the street, so to speak. . . . The GOU has been reappraising its judgments during the past five months. The colonels are beginning to wonder about their mentors' thousand-year crusade; extremely impressed by our supply and production lines."

"They should be. We've . . ."

"And there's another aspect," interrupted Granville thoughtfully. "There's a small, very wealthy community of Jews here. Your Erich Rhinemann, for example. The GOU isn't prepared to openly advocate the solutions of Julius Streicher. . . . It's already used Jewish money to keep alive lines of credit pretty well chewed up by Castillo. The colonels are afraid of financial manipulations, most military people are. But there's a great deal of money to be made in this war. The colonels intend to make it. . . . Do I sketch a recognizable picture?"

"A complicated one."

"I daresay. . . . We have a maxim here that serves quite well. Today's friend will probably be on the Axis payroll tomorrow; conversely, yesterday's Berlin courier might be for sale next week. Keep your options open and your opinions private. And publicly . . . allow for a touch more flexibility than might be approved of at another post. It's tolerated."

"And expected?" asked David.

"Both."

David lit a cigarette. He wanted to shift the conversation; old Granville was one of those ambassadors, professorial by nature, who would go on analyzing the subtleties of his station all day if someone listened. Such men were usually the best diplomats but not always the most desirable liaisons in times of active practicality. Henderson Granville was a good man, though; his concerns shone in his eyes, and they were fair concerns.

"I imagine Washington has outlined my purpose here."

"Yes. I wish I could say I approved. Not of you; you've got your instructions. And I suppose international finance will continue long after Herr Hitler has shrieked his last scream. . . . Perhaps I'm no better than the GOU. Money matters can be most distasteful."

"These in particular, I gather."

"Again, yes. Erich Rhinemann is a sworn companion of the wind. A powerful companion, make no mistake, but totally without conscience; a hurricane's morality. Unquestionably the least honorable man I've ever met. I think it's criminal that his resources make him acceptable to London and New York."

"Perhaps necessary is a more appropriate term."

"I'm sure that's the rationalization, at any rate."

"It's mine."

"Of course. Forgive an old man's obsolete limits of necessity. But we have no quarrel. You have an assignment. What can I do for you? I understand it's very little."

"Very little indeed, sir. Just have me listed on the embassy index; any kind of office space will do as long as it has a door and a telephone. And I'd like to meet your cryp. I'll have codes to send."

"My word, that sounds ominous," said Granville, smiling without humor.

"Routine, sir. Washington relay; simple Yes and Nos."

"Very well. Our head cryptographer is named Ballard. Nice fellow; speaks seven or eight languages and is an absolute whiz at parlor games. You'll meet him directly. What else?"

"I'd like an apartment. . . ."

"Yes, we know," interrupted Granville gently, snatching a brief look at the wall clock. "Mrs. Cameron has scouted one she thinks you'll approve. . . . Of course, Washington gave us no indication of your length of stay. So Mrs. Cameron took it for three months."

"That's far too long. I'll straighten it out. . . . I think

that's almost all, Mr. Ambassador. I know you're in a hurry."

"I'm afraid I am."

David got out of his chair, as did Granville. "Oh, one thing, sir. Would this Ballard have an embassy index? I'd like to learn the names here."

"There aren't that many," said Granville, leveling his gaze at David, a subtle note of disapproval in his voice. "Eight or ten would be those you'd normally come in contact with. And I can assure you we have our own security measures."

David accepted the rebuke. "That wasn't my point, sir. I really *do* like to familiarize myself with the names."

"Yes, of course." Granville came around the desk and walked Spaulding to the door. "Chat with my secretary for a few minutes. I'll get hold of Ballard; he'll show you around."

"Thank you, sir." Spaulding extended his hand to Granville, and as he did so he realized for the first time how tall the man was.

"You know," said the ambassador, releasing David's hand, "there was a question I wanted to ask you, but the answer will have to wait for another time. I'm late already."

"What was that?"

"I've been wondering why the boys on Wall Street and the Strand sent *you*. I can't imagine there being a dearth of experienced bankers in New York or London, can you?"

"There probably isn't. But then I'm only a liaison carrying messages; information best kept private, I gather. I *have* had experience in those areas . . . in a neutral country."

Granville smiled once more and once more there was no humor conveyed. "Yes, of course. I was sure there was a reason."

23

Ballard shared two traits common to most cryptographers, thought David. He was a casual cynic and a fount of information. Qualities, Spaulding believed, developed over years of deciphering other men's secrets only to find the great majority unimportant. He was also cursed with the first name of Robert, by itself acceptable but when followed by Ballard, invariably reduced to Bobby. Bobby Ballard. It had the ring of a 1920s socialite or the name in a cereal box cartoon.

He was neither. He was a linguist with a mathematical mind and a shock of red hair on top of a medium-sized, muscular body; a pleasant man.

"That's our home," Ballard was saying. "You've seen the working sections; big, rambling, baroque and goddamned hot this time of year. I hope you're smart and have your own apartment."

"Don't you? Do you live *here*?"

"It's easier. My dials are very inconsiderate, they hum at all hours. Better than scrambling down from Chacarita or Telmo. And it's not bad; we stay out of each other's way pretty much."

"Oh? A lot of you here?"

"No. They alternate. Six, usually. In the two wings, east and south. Granville has the north apartments. Besides him, Jean Cameron and I are the only permanents. You'll meet Jean tomorrow, unless we run into her on the way out with the old man. She generally goes with him to the diplobores."

"The what?"

"Diplo-bores. The old man's word . . . contraction. I'm surprised he didn't use it with you. He's proud of it.

Diplobore is an embassy duty bash." They were in a large, empty reception room; Ballard was opening a pair of French doors leading out onto a short balcony. In the distance could be seen the waters of the Río de la Plata and the estuary basin of the Puerto Nuevo, Buenos Aires' main port. "Nice view, isn't it?"

"Certainly is." David joined the cryptographer on the balcony. "Does this Jean Cameron and the ambassador . . . I mean, are they . . .?"

"Jean and the old *man*?" Ballard laughed loud and good-naturedly. "Christ, no! . . . Come to think of it, I don't know why it strikes me so funny. I suppose there're a lot of people who think that. And *that's* funny."

"Why?"

"Sad-funny, I guess I should say," continued Ballard without interruption. "The old man and the Cameron family go back to the original Maryland money. Eastern Shore yacht clubs, blazer jackets, tennis in the morning—you know: diplomat territory. Jean's family was part of it, too. She married this Cameron; knew him since they could play doctor together in their Abercrombie pup tents. A rich-people romance, childhood sweethearts. They got married, the war came; he chucked his law books for a TBF—aircraft carrier pilot. He was killed in the Leyte Gulf. That was last year. She went a little crazy; maybe more than a little."

"So the . . . Granville brought her down here?"

"That's right."

"Nice therapy, if you can afford it."

"She'd probably agree with that." Ballard walked back into the reception room; Spaulding followed. "But most people will tell you she pays her dues for the treatment. She works damned hard and knows what she's doing. Has rotten hours, too; what with the diplobores."

"Where's *Mrs.* Granville?"

"No idea. She divorced the old man ten, fifteen years ago."

"I still say it's nice work if you can get it." David was thinking, in an offhand way, of several hundred thousand other women whose husbands had been killed, living with reminders every day. He dismissed his thoughts; they weren't his concerns.

"Well, she's qualified."

"What?" David was looking at a rococo-styled corner pillar in the wall, not really listening.

"Jean spent four years—off and on—down here as a kid. Her father was in Foreign Service; probably would have been an ambassador by now if he'd stuck with it. . . . Come on, I'll show you the office Granville assigned you. Maintenance should have it tidied up by now," Ballard smiled.

"You've been employing a diversion," laughed David, following the cryp out the door into another hallway.

"I had to. You've got a room in the back. So far back it's been used for storage, I think."

"Obviously I made points with Granville."

"You sure did. He can't figure you out. . . . Me? I don't try." Ballard turned left into still another intersecting hallway. "This is the south wing. Offices on the first and second floors; not many, three on each. Apartments on the third and fourth. The roof is great for sunbathing, if you like that sort of thing."

"Depends on the company, I suppose."

The two men approached a wide staircase, preparing to veer to the left beyond it, when a feminine voice called down from the second landing.

"Bobby, is that you?"

"It's Jean," said Ballard. "Yes," he called out. "I'm with Spaulding. Come on down and meet the new recruit with enough influence to get his own apartment right off."

"Wait'll he sees the apartment!"

Jean Cameron came into sight from around the corner landing. She was a moderately tall woman, slender and dressed in a floor-length cocktail gown at once vivid with color yet simple in design. Her light brown hair was shoulder length, full and casual. Her face was a combination of striking features blended into a soft whole: wide, alive blue eyes; a thin, sharply etched nose; lips medium full and set as if in a half-smile. Her very clear skin was bronzed by the Argentine sun.

David saw that Ballard was watching him, anticipating his reaction to the girl's loveliness. Ballard's expression was humorously sardonic, and Spaulding read the message: Ballard had been to the font and found it empty—for those seeking other than a few drops of cool water. Ballard was now a friend to the lady; he knew better than to try being anything else.

Jean Cameron seemed embarrassed by her introduction on the staircase. She descended rapidly, her lips parted into one of the most genuine smiles David had seen in years. Genuine and totally devoid of innuendo.

"Welcome," she said, extending her hand. "Thank heavens I have a chance to apologize before you walk into that place. You may change your mind and move right back here."

"It's that bad?" David saw that Jean wasn't quite as young at close range as she seemed on the staircase. She was past thirty; comfortably past. And she seemed aware of his inspection, the approbation—or lack of it—unimportant to her.

"Oh, it's all right for a limited stay. You can't get anything else on that basis, not if you're American. But it's small."

Her handshake was firm, almost masculine, thought Spaulding. "I appreciate your taking the trouble. I'm sorry to have caused it."

"No one else here could have gotten you anything but a hotel," said Ballard, touching the girl's shoulder; was the contact protective? wondered David. "The *porteños* trust Mother Cameron. Not the rest of us."

"*Porteños*," said Jean in response to Spaulding's questioning expression, "are the people who live in BA. . . ."

"And BA—don't tell me—stands for Montevideo," replied David.

"Aw, they sent us a *bright* one," said Ballard.

"You'll get used to it," continued Jean. "Everyone in the American and English settlements calls it BA. Montevideo, of course," she added, smiling. "I think we see it so often on reports, we just do it automatically."

"Wrong," interjected Ballard. "The vowel juxtaposition in 'Buenos Aires' is uncomfortable for British speech."

"That's something else you'll learn during your stay, Mr. Spaulding," said Jean Cameron, looking affectionately at Ballard. "Be careful offering opinions around Bobby. He has a penchant for disagreeing."

"Never so," answered the cryp. "I simply care enough for my fellow prisoners to want to enlighten them. Prepare them for the outside when they get paroled."

"Well, I've got a temporary pass right now, and if I don't get over to the ambassador's office, he'll start on that damned address system. . . . Welcome again, Mr. Spaulding."

"Please. The name's David."

"Mine's Jean. Bye," said the girl, dashing down the hallway, calling back to Ballard. "Bobby? You've got the address and the key? For . . . David's place?"

"Yep. Go get irresponsibly drunk, I'll handle everything."

Jean Cameron disappeared through a door in the right wall.

"She's very attractive," said Spaulding, "and you two are good friends. I should apologize for . . ."

"No, you shouldn't," interrupted Ballard. "Nothing to apologize for. You formed a quick judgment on isolated facts. I'd've done the same, thought the same. Not that you've changed your mind; no reason to, really."

"She's right. You disagree . . . before you know what you're disagreeing to; and then you debate your disagreement. And if you go on, you'll probably challenge your last position."

"You know what? I can follow that. Isn't it frightening?"

"You guys are a separate breed," said David, chuckling, following Ballard beyond the stairs into a smaller corridor.

"Let's take a quick look at your Siberian cubicle and then head over to your other cell. It's on Córdoba; we're on Corrientes. It's about ten minutes from here."

David thanked Bobby Ballard once again and shut the apartment door. He had pleaded exhaustion from the trip, preceded by too much welcome home in New York—and God knew that was the truth—and would Ballard take a raincheck for dinner?

Alone now, he inspected the apartment; it wasn't intolerable at all. It was small: a bedroom, a sitting room-kitchen, and a bath. But there was a dividend Jean Cameron hadn't mentioned. The rooms were on the first floor, and at the rear was a tiny brick-leveled patio surrounded by a tall concrete wall, profuse with hanging vines and drooping flowers from immense pots on the ledge. In the center of the enclosure was a gnarled fruit-bearing tree he could not identify; around the trunk were three rope-webbed chairs that had seen better days but looked extremely comfortable. As far as he was concerned, the dividend made the dwelling.

Ballard had pointed out that his section of the Avenida Córdoba was just over the borderline from the commercial area, the "downtown" complex of Buenos Aires. Quasi residential, yet near enough to stores and restaurants to be easy for a newcomer.

David picked up the telephone; the dial tone was delayed but eventually there. He replaced it and walked across the small room to the refrigerator, an American Sears Roebuck. He opened it and smiled. The Cameron girl had provided—or had somebody provide—several basic items: milk, butter, bread, eggs, coffee. Then happily he spotted two bottles of wine: an Orfila *tinto* and a Colón *blanco*. He closed the refrigerator and went back into the bedroom.

He unpacked his single suitcase, unwrapping a bottle of Scotch, and remembered that he'd have to buy additional clothes in the morning. Ballard had offered to go with him to a men's shop in the Calle Florida—if his goddamned dials weren't "humming." He placed the books Eugene Lyons had given him on the bedside table. He had gone through two of them; he was beginning to gain confidence in the aerophysicists' language. He would need comparable studies in German to be really secure. He would cruise around the bookshops in the German settlement tomorrow; he wasn't looking for definitive texts, just enough to understand the terms. It was really a minor part of his assignment, he understood that.

Suddenly, David remembered Walter Kendall. Kendall was either in Buenos Aires by now or would be arriving within hours. The accountant had left the United States at approximately the same time he had, but Kendall's flight from New York was more direct, with far fewer stopovers.

He wondered whether it would be feasible to go out to the airport and trace Kendall. If he hadn't arrived, he could wait for him; if he had, it would be simple enough to check the hotels—according to Ballard there were only three or four good ones.

On the other hand, any additional time—more than absolutely essential—spent with the manipulating accountant was not a pleasant prospect. Kendall would be upset at finding him in Buenos Aires before he'd given the order to

Swanson. Kendall, no doubt, would demand explanations beyond those David wished to give; probably send angry cables to an already strung-out brigadier general.

There were no benefits in hunting down Walter Kendall until Kendall expected to find him. Only liabilities.

He had other things to do: the unfocused picture. He could begin that search far better alone.

David walked back into the living room-kitchen carrying the Scotch and took out a tray of ice from the refrigerator. He made himself a drink and looked over at the double doors leading to his miniature patio. He would spend a few quiet twilight moments in the January summertime breeze of Buenos Aires.

The sun was fighting its final descent beyond the city; the last orange rays were filtering through the thick foliage of the unidentified fruit tree. Underneath, David stretched his legs and leaned back in the rope-webbed chair. He realized that if he kept his eyes closed for any length of time, they would not reopen for a number of hours. He had to watch that; long experience in the field had taught him to eat something before sleeping.

Eating had long since lost its pleasure for him—it was merely a necessity directly related to his energy level. He wondered if the pleasure would ever come back; whether so much he had put aside would return. Lisbon had probably the best accommodations—food, shelter, comfort—of all the major cities, excepting New York, on both continents. And now he was on a third continent, in a city that boasted undiluted luxury.

But for him it was the field—as much as was the north country in Spain. As much as Basque and Navarre, and the freezing nights in the Galician hills or the sweat-prone silences in ravines, waiting for patrols—waiting to kill.

So much. So alien.

He brought his head forward, took a long drink from the glass and let his neck arch back into the frame of the chair. A small bird was chattering away in the midsection of the tree, annoyed at his intrusion. It reminded David of how he would listen for such birds in the north country. They telegraphed the approach of men unseen, often falling into different rhythms that he began to identify—or thought he identified—with the numbers of the unseen, approaching patrols.

Then David realized that the small chattering bird was not concerned with him. It hopped upward, still screeching its harsh little screech, only faster now, more strident.

There was someone else.

Through half-closed eyes, David focused above, beyond the foliage. He did so without moving any part of his body or head, as if the last moments were approaching before sleep took over.

The apartment house had four stories and a roof that appeared to have a gentle slope covered in a terra-cotta tile of sorts—brownish pink in color. The windows of the rooms above him were mostly open to the breezes off the Río de la Plata. He could hear snatches of subdued conversation, nothing threatening, no loud vibrations. It was the Buenos Aires siesta hour, according to Ballard; quite different from Rome's afternoon or the Paris lunch. Dinner in BA was very late, by the rest of the world's schedule. Ten, ten thirty, even midnight was not out of the question.

The screeching bird was not bothered by the inhabitants of the Córdoba apartment house; yet still he kept up his strident alarms.

And then David saw why.

On the roof, obscured but not hidden by the branches of the fruit tree, were the outlines of two men.

They were crouched, staring downward; staring, he was sure, at him.

Spaulding judged the position of the main intersecting tree limb and rolled his head slightly, as if the long-awaited sleep were upon him, his neck resting in exhaustion on his right shoulder, the drink barely held by a relaxed hand, millimeters from the brick pavement.

It helped; he could see better, not well. Enough, however, to make out the sharp, straight silhouette of a rifle barrel, the orange sun careening off its black steel. It was stationary, in an arrest position under the arm of the man on the right. No movement was made to raise it, to aim it; it remained immobile, cradled.

Somehow, it was more ominous that way, thought Spaulding. As though in the arms of a killer guard who was sure his prisoner could not possibly vault the stockade; there was plenty of time to shoulder and fire.

David carried through his charade. He raised his hand slightly and let his drink fall. The sound of the minor crash "awakened" him; he shook the pretended sleep from his head and rubbed his eyes with his fingers. As he did so, he maneuvered his face casually upward. The figures on the roof had stepped back on the terra-cotta tiles. There would be no shots. Not directed at him.

He picked up a few pieces of the glass, rose from the chair and walked into the apartment as a tired man does when annoyed with his own carelessness. Slowly, with barely controlled irritation.

Once he crossed the saddle of the door, beneath the sightline of the roof, he threw the glass fragments into a wastebasket and walked rapidly into the bedroom. He opened the top drawer of the bureau, separated some handkerchiefs and withdrew his revolver.

He clamped it inside his belt and picked up his jacket from the chair into which he'd thrown it earlier. He put it on, satisfied that it concealed the weapon.

He crossed out into the living room, to the apartment door, and opened it silently.

The staircase was against the left wall and David swore to himself, cursing the architect of this particular Avenida Córdoba building—or the profuseness of lumber in Argentina. The stairs were made of wood, the brightly polished wax not concealing the obvious fact that they were ancient and probably squeaked like hell.

He closed his apartment door and approached the staircase, putting his feet on the first step.

It creaked the solid creak of antique shops.

He had four flights to go; the first three were unimportant. He took the steps two at a time, discovering that if he hugged the wall, the noise of his ascent was minimized.

Sixty seconds later he faced a closed door marked with a sign—in goddamned curlicued Castilian lettering:

El Techo.

The roof.

The door, as the stairs, was old. Decades of seasonal heat and humidity had caused the wood to swell about the hinges; the borders were forced into the frame.

It, too, would scream his arrival if he opened it slowly.

There was no other way: he slipped the weapon out of his belt and took one step back on the tiny platform. He judged the frame—the concrete walls—surrounding the old wooden door and with an adequate intake of breath, he pulled at the handle, yanked the door open and jumped diagonally into the right wall, slamming his back against the concrete.

The two men whirled around, stunned. They were thirty feet from David at the edge of the sloping roof. The man with the rifle hesitated, then raised the weapon into waist-firing position. Spaulding had his pistol aimed directly into the man's chest. However, the man with the gun did not have the look of one about to fire at a target; the hesitation was deliberate, not the result of panic or indecision.

The second man shouted in Spanish; David recognized the accent as southern Spain, not Argentine. "*Por favor, señor!*"

Spaulding replied in English to establish their understanding, or lack of it. "Lower that rifle. *Now!*"

The first man did so, holding it by the stock. "You are in error," he said in halting English. "There have been . . . how do you say, *ladrones* . . . thieves in the neighborhood."

David walked over the metal transom onto the roof, holding his pistol on the two men. "You're not very convincing. *Se dan corte, amigos.* You're not from Buenos Aires."

"There are a great many people in this neighborhood who are as we: displaced, *señor*. This is a community of . . . not the native born," said the second man.

"You're telling me you weren't up here for my benefit? You weren't watching me?"

"It was coincidental, I assure you," said the man with the rifle.

"*Es la verdad,*" added the other. "Two *habitaciones* have been broken into during the past week. The police do not help; we are . . . *extranjeros,* foreigners to them. We protect ourselves."

Spaulding watched the men closely. There was no waver in either man's expression, no hint of lies. No essential fear.

"I'm with the American embassy," said David curtly. There was no reaction from either *extranjero*. "I must ask you for identification."

"*Qué cosa?*" The man with the gun.

"Papers. Your names. . . . *Certificados.*"

"*Por cierto, en seguida.*" The second man reached back

into his trousers pocket; Spaulding raised the pistol slightly, in warning.

The man hesitated, now showing his fear. "Only a *registro, señor*. We all must carry them. . . . Please. In my *cartera*."

David held out his left hand as the second man gave him a cheap leather wallet. He flipped it open with minor feelings of regret. There was a kind of helplessness about the two *extranjeros*; he'd seen the look thousands of times. Franco's Falangistas were experts at provoking it.

He looked quickly down at the cellophane window of the billfold; it was cracked with age.

Suddenly, the barrel of the rifle came crashing across his right wrist; the pain was excruciating. Then his hand was being twisted expertly inward and down; he had no choice but to release the weapon and try to kick it away on the sloping roof. To hold it would mean breaking his wrist.

He did so as his left arm was being hammerlocked—again expertly—up over his neck. He lashed his foot out at the unarmed *extranjero*, who had hold of his hand. He caught him in the stomach and as the man bent forward, David crossed his weight and kicked again, sending the man tumbling down on the tiled incline.

David fell in the thrust direction of the hammerlock—downward, to his rear—and as the first man countered the position, Spaulding brought his right elbow back up, crushing into the man's groin. The arm was released as the *extranjero* tried to regain his balance.

He wasn't quick enough; Spaulding whipped to his left and brought his knee up into the man's throat. The rifle clattered on the tiles and rolled downward on the slope. The man sank, blood dribbling from his mouth where his teeth had punctured the skin.

Spaulding heard the sound behind him and turned.

He was too late. The second *extranjero* was over him, and David could hear the whistling of his own pistol piercing the air above him, crashing down into his skull.

All was black. Void.

"They described the right attitude but the wrong section of town," said Ballard, sitting across the room from David, who held an ice pack to his head. "The *extranjeros* are concentrated in the west areas of the La Boca district.

They've got a hell of a crime rate over there; the *policía* prefer strolling the parks rather than those streets. And the Grupo—the GOU—has no love for *extranjeros*."

"You're no help," said Spaulding, shifting the ice pack around in circles on the back of his head.

"Well, they weren't out to kill you. They could have thrown you off or just left you on the edge; five to one you'd've rolled over and down four flights."

"I knew they weren't intent on killing me. . . ."

"How?"

"They could have done that easily before. I think they were waiting for me to go out. I'd unpacked; they'd have the apartment to themselves."

"What for?"

"To search my things. They *have* done that before."

"Who?"

"Damned if I know."

"Now who's no help?"

"Sorry. . . . Tell me, Bobby, who exactly knew I was flying in? How was it handled?"

"First question: three people. I did, of course; I'm on the dials. Granville, obviously. And Jean Cameron; the old man asked her to follow up on an apartment . . . but you know that. Question two: very confidentially. Remember, your orders came through at night. From Washington. Jean was playing chess with Granville in his quarters when I brought him the eggs. . . ."

"The what?" interrupted David.

"The scrambler; it's marked. Washington had your sheet radioed in on a scrambler code. That means only myself or my head man can handle it, deliver it to the ambassador."

"O.K. Then what?"

"Nothing. I mean nothing you don't know about."

"Tell me anyway."

Ballard exhaled a long, condescending breath. "Well, the three of us were alone; what the hell, I'd read the scramble and the instructions were clear about the apartment. So Granville figured—apparently—that Jean was the logical one to scout one up. He told her you were coming in; to do what she could on such short notice." Ballard looked about the room and over at the patio doors. "She didn't do badly, either."

"Then that's it; they've got a network fanned out over

the city; nothing unusual. They keep tabs on unoccupied places: apartments, rooming houses; hotels are the easiest."

"I'm not sure I follow you," said Ballard, trying to.

"We can all be smart as whips, Bobby, but we can't change a couple of basics: we have to have a place to sleep and take a bath."

"Oh, I follow *that*, but you can't apply it here. Starting tomorrow you're no secret; until then you are. D.C. said you were coming down on your own; we had no idea precisely when or how. . . . Jean didn't get this apartment for *you*. Not in *your name*."

"Oh?" David was far more concerned than his expression indicated. The two *extranjeros* had to have been on the roof before he arrived. Or, at least, within minutes after he did so. "How did she lease it then? Whose name did she use? I didn't want a cover; we didn't ask for one."

"Jesus, I thought *I* talked fast. Sunday is *Sunday*, Monday is *Monday*. Sunday we don't know you; Monday we do. That's what Washington spelled out. They wanted no advance notice of your arrival and, incidentally, if *you* decided to stay out of sight, we were to adhere to your wishes. I'm sure Granville will ask you what you want to do in the morning. . . . How did Jean lease the place? Knowing her, she probably implied the ambassador had a girl on the side, or something. The *porteños* are very *simpático* with that sort of thing; the Paris of South America and all that. . . . One thing I *do* know, she wouldn't have used your name. Or any obvious cover. She'd use her own first."

"Oh, boy," said Spaulding wearily, removing the ice pack and feeling the back of his head. He looked at his fingers. Smudges of blood were apparent.

"I hope you're not going to play hero with that gash. You should see a doctor."

"No hero." David smiled. "I've got to have some sutures removed, anyway. Might as well be tonight, if you can arrange it."

"I can arrange it. Where did you get the stitches?"

"I had an accident in the Azores."

"Christ, you travel, don't you?"

"So does something ahead of me."

24

"Mrs. Cameron is here at my request, Spaulding. Come in. I've talked with Ballard and the doctor. Stitches taken out and new ones put in; you must feel like a pincushion."

Granville was behind his baroque desk, reclining comfortably in his highbacked chair. Jean Cameron sat on the couch against the left wall; one of the chairs in front of the desk was obviously meant for David. He decided to wait until Granville said so before sitting down. He remained standing; he wasn't sure he liked the ambassador. The office assigned to him was, indeed, far back and used for storage.

"Nothing serious, sir. If it was, I'd say so." Spaulding nodded to Jean and saw her concern. Or, at least, that's what he thought he read in her eyes.

"You'd be foolish not to. The doctor says the blow to the head fortunately fell between concussion areas. Otherwise, you'd be in rather bad shape."

"It was delivered by an experienced man."

"Yes, I see. . . . Our doctor didn't think much of the sutures he removed."

"That seems to be a general medical opinion. They served their purpose; the shoulder's fine. He strapped it."

"Yes. . . . Sit down, sit down."

David sat down. "Thank you, sir."

"I gather the two men who attacked you last evening were *provincianos*. Not *porteños*."

Spaulding gave a short, defeated smile and turned to Jean Cameron. "I got to *porteños*; I guess *provincianos* means what it says. The country folk? Outside the cities."

"Yes," said the girl softly. "*The* city. BA."

"Two entirely different cultures," continued Granville.

"The *provincianos* are hostile and with much legitimacy. They're really quite exploited; the resentments are flaring up. The GOU has done nothing to ease matters, it only conscripts them in the lowest ranks."

"The *provincianos* are native to Argentina, though, aren't they?"

"Certainly. From their point of view, much more so than Buenos Airens, *porteños*. Less Italian and German blood, to say nothing of Portuguese, Balkan and Jewish. There were waves of immigrations, you see. . . ."

"Then, Mr. Ambassador," interrupted David, hoping to stem another post analysis by the pedagogical diplomat, "these were not *provincianos*. They called themselves *extranjeros*. Displaced persons, I gathered."

"*Extranjero* is a rather sarcastic term. Inverse morbidity. As though employed by a reservation Indian in our Washington. A foreigner in his own native land, you see what I mean?"

"These men were not from Argentina," said David quietly, dismissing Granville's question. "Their speech pattern was considerably alien."

"Oh? Are you an expert?"

"Yes, I am. In these matters."

"I see." Granville leaned forward. "Do you ascribe the attack to embassy concerns? Allied concerns?"

"I'm not sure. It's my opinion I was the target. I'd like to know how they knew I was here."

Jean Cameron spoke from the couch. "I've gone over everything I said, David." She stopped and paused briefly, aware that the ambassador had shot her a look at her use of Spaulding's first name. "Your place was the fourth apartment I checked into. I started at ten in the morning and got there around two o'clock. And leased it immediately. I'm sorry to say it was the patio that convinced me."

David smiled at her.

"Anyway, I went to a real estate office at Viamonte. Geraldo Baldez is the owner; we all know him. He's partisan; has no use for Germans. I made it clear that I wanted to rent the apartment for one of our people who was living here and who, frankly, found the embassy restrictions too limiting. He laughed and said he was sure it was Bobby. I didn't disagree."

"But it was a short lease," said David.

"I used it as an excuse in case you didn't like the apartment. It's a standard three-month clause."

"Why wouldn't Bobby—or anyone else—get his own place?"

"Any number of reasons. Also standard . . . here." Jean smiled, a touch embarrassed, thought David. "I know the city better than most; I lived here for several years. Also there's a little matter of expense allowance; I'm a pretty good bargainer. And men like Bobby have urgent work to do. My hours are more flexible; I have the time."

"Mrs. Cameron is too modest, Spaulding. She's an enormous asset to our small community."

"I'm sure she is, sir. . . . Then you don't think anyone had reason to suspect you were finding a place for an incoming attaché."

"Absolutely not. It was all done in such a . . . lighthearted way, if you know what I mean."

"What about the owner of the building?" David asked.

"I never saw him. Most apartments are owned by wealthy people who live in the Telmo or Palermo districts. Everything's done through rental agencies."

David turned to Granville. "Have there been any calls for me? Messages?"

"No. Not that I'm aware of, and I'm sure I would be. You would have been contacted, of course."

"A man named Kendall. . . ."

"Kendall?" interrupted the ambassador. "I know that name. . . . Kendall. Yes, Kendall." Granville riffled through some papers on his desk. "Here. A Walter Kendall came in last night. Ten thirty flight. He's staying at the Alvear; that's near the Palermo Park. Fine old hotel." Granville suddenly looked over at Spaulding. "He's listed on the sheet as an industrial economist. Now that's a rather all-inclusive description, isn't it? Would he be the banker I referred to yesterday?"

"He'll make certain arrangements relative to my instructions." David did not conceal his reluctance to go into the matter of Walter Kendall. On the other hand, he instinctively found himself offering a token clarification to Jean Cameron. "My primary job here is to act as liaison between financial people in New York and London and banking interests here in Buenos . . . BA." David smiled; he hoped as genuinely as Jean smiled. "I think it's a little silly. I don't know a debit from an asset. But Washington okayed me. The ambassador is worried that I'm too inexperienced."

Spaulding quickly shifted his gaze to Granville, reminding the old man that "banking interests" was the limit of identities. The name of Erich Rhinemann was out of bounds.

"Yes, I admit, I was. . . . But that's neither here nor there. What do you wish to do about last night? I think we should lodge a formal complaint with the police. Not that it will do a damn bit of good."

David fell silent for a few moments, trying to consider the pros and cons of Granville's suggestion. "Would we get press coverage?"

"Very little, I'd think," answered Jean.

"Embassy attachés usually have money," said Granville. "They've been robbed. It will be called an attempted robbery. Probably was."

"But the Grupo doesn't like that kind of news. It doesn't fit in with the colonels' view of things, and they control the press." Jean was thinking out loud, looking at David. "They'll play it down."

"And if we don't complain—assuming it was not robbery—we're admitting we think it was something else. Which I'm not prepared to do," said Spaulding.

"Then by all means, a formal complaint will be registered this morning. Will you dictate a report of the incident and sign it, please?" Obviously, Granville wished to terminate the meeting. "And to be frank with you, Spaulding, unless I'm considerably in the dark, I believe it *was* an attempt to rob a newly arrived rich American. I'm told the airport taxi drivers have formed a veritable thieves' carnival. *Extranjeros* would be perfectly logical participants."

David stood up; he was pleased to see that Jean did the same. "I'll accept that, Mr. Ambassador. The years in Lisbon have made me overly . . . concerned. I'll adjust."

"I daresay. Do write up the report."

"Yes, sir."

"I'll get him a stenographer," said Jean. "Bilingual."

"Not necessary. I'll dictate it in Spanish."

"I forgot." Jean smiled. "Bobby said they'd sent us a bright one."

David supposed it began with that first lunch. Later she told him it was before, but he didn't believe her. She claimed it was when he said that BA stood for Montevideo; that was silly, it didn't make sense.

What made sense—and they both recognized it without any attempt to verbalize it—was the total relaxation each felt in the other's company. It was as simple as that. It was a splendid comfort; the silences never awkward, the laughter easy and based in communicated humor, not forced response.

It was remarkable. Made more so, David believed, because neither expected it, neither sought it. Both had good and sufficient reasons to avoid any relationships other than surface or slightly below. He was an impermanent man, hoping only to survive and start somewhere again with a clear head and suppressed memories. That was important to him. And he knew she still mourned a man so deeply she couldn't possibly—without intolerable guilt—push that man's face and body and mind behind her.

She told him partially why herself. Her husband had not been the image of the dashing carrier pilot so often depicted by navy public relations. He'd had an extraordinary fear—not for himself—but of taking lives. Were it not for the abuse he knew would have been directed at his Maryland wife and Maryland family, Cameron would have sought conscientious objector status. Then, too, perhaps he hadn't the courage of his own convictions.

Why a pilot?

Cameron had been flying since he was in his teens. It seemed natural and he believed his civilian training might lead to a Stateside instructor's berth. He rejected military law; too many of his fellow attorneys had gone after it and found themselves in the infantry and on the decks of battleships. The military had enough lawyers; they wanted pilots.

David thought he understood why Jean told him so much about her dead husband. There were two reasons. The first was that by doing so openly, she was adjusting to what she felt was happening between them; atoning, perhaps. The second was less clear but in no way less important. Jean Cameron hated the war; hated what it had taken away from her. She wanted him to know that.

Because—David realized—her instincts told her he was

very much involved. And she would have no part of that involvement; she owed that much to Cameron's memory.

They'd gone to lunch at a restaurant overlooking the waters of the Riachúelo Basin near the piers of Dársena Sud. She had suggested it—the restaurant and the lunch. She saw that he was still exhausted; what sleep he'd managed had been interrupted constantly with pain. She insisted that he needed a long, relaxing lunch, then home to bed and a day's recuperation.

She hadn't meant to go with him.

He hadn't meant for her to.

"Ballard's a nice guy," said Spaulding, pouring a clear white Colón.

"Bobby's a dear," she agreed. "He's a kind person."

"He's very fond of you."

"And I of him. . . . What you're speculating on is perfectly natural, and I'm sorry to spoil the wilder melody. Is melody right? Granville told me who your parents were. I'm impressed."

"I've refused to read music since the age of eight. But 'melody's' fine. I just wondered."

"Bobby gave me a thoroughly professional try, with enormous charm and good humor. A better girl would have responded. He had every right to be angry. . . . I wanted his company but gave very little in return for it."

"He accepted your terms," said David affirmatively.

"I said he was kind."

"There must be ten other fellows here. . . ."

"Plus the marine guard," interjected Jean, feigning a lovely, unmilitary salute. "Don't forget them."

"A hundred and ten, then. You're Deanna Durbin."

"Hardly. The marines rotate off the FMF base south of La Boca; the staff—those without wives and kinder—are plagued with the embassy syndrome."

"What's that?"

"State Department-eye-tis. . . . The quivers. You seem to be singularly lacking in them."

"I don't know whether I am or not. I don't know what they are."

"Which tells me something about you, doesn't it?"

"What does it tell you?"

"You're not a State Department climber. The 'eye-tis'

syndrome is treading lightly and making damned sure everybody above you—especially the ambassador—is happy with your *sincerest efforts*." Jean grimaced like a boxer puppy, her delicate chin forward, her eyebrows down—mocking the words. Spaulding broke out laughing; the girl had captured the embassy look and voice with devastating accuracy.

"Christ, I'm going to put you on the radio." He laughed again. "You've described the syndrome. I see it, Lord! I see it!"

"But you're not infected by it." Jean stopped her mimicry and looked into his eyes. "I watched you with Granville; you were just barely polite. You weren't looking for a fitness report, were you?"

He returned her gaze. "No, I wasn't. . . . To answer the question that's rattling around that lovely head of yours so loud it vibrates—I'm not a Foreign Service career officer. I'm strictly wartime. I *do* work out of embassies on a variety of related assignments for a couple of related reasons. I speak four languages and because of those parents that impressed you so, I have what is euphemistically described as access to important people in government, commerce, those areas. Since I'm not a complete idiot, I often circulate confidential information among corporations in various countries. The market place doesn't stop humming for such inconveniences as war. . . . That's my contribution. I'm not very proud of it, but it's what they handed me."

She smiled her genuine smile and reached for his hand. "*I* think you do whatever you do very intelligently and well. There aren't many people who can say that. And God knows you can't choose."

" 'What did you do in the war, daddy?' . . . 'Well, son,' " David tried his own caricature. " 'I went from place to place telling friends of the Chase Bank to sell high and buy low and clear a decent profit margin.' " He kept her hand in his.

"And got attacked on Argentine rooftops and . . . and what were those stitches in your shoulder?"

"The cargo plane I was on in the Azores made a rotten landing. I think the pilot and his whole crew were plastered."

"There. See? You live as dangerously as any man at the front. . . . If I meet that boy you're talking to, I'll tell him that."

Their eyes were locked; Jean withdrew her hand, embarrassed. But for Spaulding the important thing was that she believed him. She accepted his cover extension without question. It occurred to him that he was at once greatly relieved and yet, in a way, quite sorry. He found no professional pride in lying to her successfully.

"So now you know how I've avoided the State Department syndrome. I'm still not sure why it's relevant. What the hell, with a hundred and ten men and marines. . . ."

"The marines don't count. They have sundry interests down here in La Boca."

"Then the staff—those without the 'Wives and kinder'—they can't all be quivering."

"But they do and I've been grateful. They'd like to get to the Court of St. James's someday."

"Now you're playing mental gymnastics. I'm not following you."

"No, I'm not. I wanted to see if Bobby had told you. He hasn't. I said he was kind. . . . He was giving me the chance to tell you myself."

"Tell me what?"

"My husband was Henderson Granville's stepson. They were very close."

They left the restaurant shortly past four and walked around the docks of the Dársena Sud waterfront, breathing in the salt air. It seemed to David that Jean was enjoying herself in a way she hadn't in too long a time. That it was part of the instant comfort between them, he realized, but it went further. As if some splendid relief had swept over her.

Her loveliness had been evident from those first moments on the staircase, but as he thought back on that brief introduction, he knew what the difference was. Jean Cameron had been outgoing, good-natured . . . welcoming charm itself. But there'd been something else: a detachment born of self-control. Total control. A patina of authority that had nothing to do with her status at the embassy or whatever other benefits derived from her marriage to the ambassador's stepson. It was related solely to her own decisions, her own outlook.

He had seen that detached authority throughout the morning—when she introduced him to various embassy employees; when she gave directions to her secretary; when she answered her telephone and rendered quick instructions.

Even in the byplay with Bobby Ballard she glided firmly, with the assurance of knowing her own pattern. Ballard could shout humorously that she could "get irresponsibly drunk" because by no stretch of the imagination would she allow herself to do that.

Jean kept a tight rein on herself.

The rein was loosening now.

Yesterday he had looked at her closely, finding the years; and she was completely unconcerned, without vanity. Now, walking along the docks, holding his arm, she was pleasantly aware of the looks she received from the scores of waterfront *Bocamos*. Spaulding knew she hoped he was aware of those looks.

"Look, David," she said excitedly. "Those boats are going to crash head on."

Several hundred yards out in the bay, two trawlers were on a collision course, both steam whistles filling the air with aggressive warnings, both crews shouting at each other from port and starboard railings.

"The one on the right will veer."

It did. At the last moment, amid dozens of guttural oaths and gestures.

"How did you know?" she said.

"Simple right of way; the owner would get clobbered with damages. There'll be a brawl on one of these piers pretty soon, though."

"Let's not wait for it. You've had enough of that."

They walked out of the dock area into the narrow La Boca streets, teeming with small fish markets, profuse with fat merchants in bloodied aprons and shouting customers. The afternoon catch was in, the day's labor on the water over. The rest was selling and drinking and retelling the misadventures of the past twelve hours.

They reached a miniature square called—for no apparent reason—Plaza Ocho Calle; there was no street number eight, no plaza to speak of. A taxi hesitantly came to a stop at the corner, let out its fare and started up again, blocked by pedestrians unconcerned with such vehicles. David looked at Jean and she nodded, smiling. He shouted at the driver.

Inside the taxi he gave his address. It didn't occur to him to do otherwise.

They rode in silence for several minutes, their shoulders touching, her hand underneath his arm.

"What are you thinking of?" David asked, seeing the distant but happy expression on her face.

"Oh, the way I pictured you when Henderson read the scramble the other night. . . . Yes, I call him Henderson; I always have."

"I can't imagine anyone, even the president, calling him Henderson."

"You don't know him. Underneath that Racquet Club jacket is lovable Henderson."

"How did you picture me?"

"Very differently."

"From what?"

"You. . . . I thought you'd be terribly short, to begin with. An attaché named David Spaulding who's some kind of financial whiz and is going to have conferences with the banks and the colonels about money things is short, at least fifty years old and has *very* little hair. He also wears spectacles—not glasses—and has a thin nose. Probably has an allergy as well—he sneezes a lot and blows his nose all the time. And he speaks in short, clipped sentences; very precise and quite disagreeable."

"He chases secretaries, too; don't leave that out."

"My David Spaulding doesn't chase secretaries. He reads dirty books."

David felt a twinge. Throw in an unkempt appearance, a soiled handkerchief and replace the spectacles with glasses —worn occasionally—and Jean was describing Walter Kendall.

"Your Spaulding's an unpleasant fellow."

"Not the new one," she said, tightening her grip on his arm.

The taxi drew up to the curb in front of the entrance on Córdoba. Jean Cameron hesitated, staring momentarily at the apartment house door. David spoke softly, without emphasis.

"Shall I take you to the embassy?"

She turned to him. "No."

He paid the driver and they went inside.

The field thread was invisibly protruding from the knob; he felt it.

He inserted the key in the lock and instinctively, gently shouldered her aside as he pushed the door open. The apartment was as he had left it that morning; he knew she felt his relief. He held the door for her. Jean entered and looked around.

"It really *isn't* so bad, is it?" she said.

"Humble but home." He left the door open and with a smile, a gesture—without words—he asked her to stay where she was. He walked rapidly into the bedroom, returned and went through the double doors onto his miniature, high-walled patio. He looked up, scanning the windows and the roof carefully. He smiled again at her from under the branches of the fruit tree. She understood, closed the door and came out to him.

"You did that very professionally, Mr. Spaulding."

"In the best traditions of extreme cowardice, Mrs. Cameron."

He realized his mistake the minute he'd made it. It was not the moment to use the married title. And yet, in some oblique way she seemed grateful that he had. She moved again and stood directly in front of him.

"Mrs. Cameron thanks you."

He reached out and held her by the waist. Her arms slowly, haltingly, went up to his shoulders; her hands cupped his face and she stared into his eyes.

He did not move. The decision, the first step, had to be hers; he understood that.

She brought her lips to his. The touch was soft and lovely and meant for earthbound angels. And then she trembled with an almost uncontrollable sense of urgency. Her lips parted and she pressed her body with extraordinary strength into his, her arms clutched about his neck.

She pulled her lips away from his and buried her face into his chest, holding him with fierce possession.

"Don't say anything," she whispered. "Don't say anything at all. . . . *Just take me.*"

He picked her up silently and carried her into the bedroom. She kept her face pressed into his chest, as if she were afraid to see light or even him. He lowered her gently onto the bed and closed the door.

In a few moments they were naked and he pulled the blankets over them. It was a moist and beautiful darkness. A splendid comfort.

"I want to say something," she said, tracing her finger over his lips, her face above his, her breasts innocently on his chest. And smiling her genuine smile.

"I know. You want the other Spaulding. The thin one with spectacles." He kissed her fingers.

"He disappeared in an explosion of sorts."

"You're positively descriptive, young lady."

"And not so young. . . . That's what I want to talk about."

"A pension. You're angling for Social Security. I'll see what I can do."

"Be serious, silly boy."

"And not so silly. . . ."

"There's no commitment, David," she said, interrupting him. "I want you to know that. . . . I don't know how else to say it. Everything happened so fast."

"Everything happened very naturally. Explanations aren't required."

"Well, I think some are. I didn't expect to be here."

"I didn't expect that you would be. I suppose I hoped, I'll admit that. . . . I didn't plan; neither of us did."

"I don't know; I think I did. I think I saw you yesterday and somewhere in the back of my mind I made a decision. Does that sound brazen of me?"

"If you did, the decision was long overdue."

"Yes, I imagine it was." She lay back, pulling the sheet over her. "I've been very selfish. Spoiled and selfish and behaving really quite badly."

"Because you haven't slept around?" It was his turn to roll over and touch her face. He kissed both her eyes, now open; the deep speckles of blue made bluer, deeper, by the late afternoon sun streaming through the blinds. She smiled; her perfect white teeth glistening with the moisture of her mouth, her lips curved in that genuine curve of humor.

"That's funny. I must be unpatriotic. I've withheld my charms only to deliver them to a noncombatant."

"The Visigoths wouldn't have approved. The warriors came first, I'm told."

"Let's not tell them." She reached up for his face. "Oh, David, David, *David*."

25

"I hope I didn't wake you. I wouldn't have troubled you but I thought you'd want me to."

Ambassador Granville's voice over the telephone was more solicitous than David expected it to be. He looked at his watch as he replied. It was three minutes of ten in the morning.

"Oh? . . . No, sir. I was just getting up. Sorry I overslept."

There was a note on the telephone table. It was from Jean.

"Your friend was in contact with us."

"Friend?" David unfolded the note. *My Darling—You fell into such a beautiful sleep it would have broken my heart to disturb you. Called a taxi. See you in the morning. At the Bastile. Your ex-regimented phoenix.* David smiled, remembering her smile.

". . . the details, I'm sure, aren't warranted." Granville had said something and he hadn't been listening.

"I'm sorry, Mr. Ambassador. This must be a poor connection; your voice fades in and out." All telephones beyond the Atlantic, north, middle and south, were temperamental instruments. An unassailable fact.

"Or something else, I'm afraid," said Granville with irritation, obviously referring to the possibility of a telephone tap. "When you get in, please come to see me."

"Yes, sir. I'll be there directly."

He picked up Jean's note and read it again.

She had said last night that he was complicating her life. But there were no commitments; she'd said that, too.

What the hell was a commitment? He didn't want to speculate. He didn't want to think about the awful discovery—the instant, splendid comfort they both recognized. It wasn't the time for it. . . .

Yet to deny it would be to reject an extraordinary reality. He was trained to deal with reality.

He didn't want to think about it.

His "friend" had been in contact with the embassy.

Walter Kendall.

That was another reality. It couldn't wait.

He crushed out his cigarette angrily, watching his fingers stab the butt into the metal ashtray.

Why was he angry?

He didn't care to speculate on that, either. He had a job to do. He hoped he had the commitment for it.

"Jean said you barely made it through dinner. You needed a good night's sleep; I must say you look better." The ambassador had come from around his desk to greet him as he entered the large, ornate office. David was a little bewildered. The old diplomat was actually being solicitous, displaying a concern that belied his unconcealed disapproval of two days ago. Or was it his use of the name Jean instead of the forbidding Mrs. Cameron.

"She was very kind. I couldn't have found a decent restaurant without her."

"I daresay. . . . I won't detain you, you'd better get cracking with this Kendall."

"You said he's been in contact. . . ."

"Starting last night; early this morning to be accurate. He's at the Alvear and apparently quite agitated, according to the switchboard. At two thirty this morning he was shouting, demanding to know where you were. Naturally, we don't give out that information."

"I'm grateful. As you said, I needed the sleep; Kendall would have prevented it. Do you have his telephone number? Or shall I get it from the book?"

"No, right here." Granville walked to his desk and picked up a sheet of notepaper. David followed and took it from the ambassador's outstretched hand.

"Thank you, sir. I'll get on it." He turned and started for the door, Granville's voice stopping him.

"Spaulding?"

"Yes, sir?"

"I'm sure Mrs. Cameron would like to see you. Assess

your recovery, I daresay. Her office is in the south wing. First door from the entrance, on the right. Do you know where that is?"

"I'll find it, sir."

"I'm sure you will. See you later in the day."

David went out the heavy baroque door, closing it behind him. Was it his imagination or was Granville reluctantly giving an approval to his and Jean's sudden . . . alliance? The words were approving, the tone of voice reluctant.

He walked down the connecting corridor toward the south wing and reached her door. Her name was stamped on a brass plate to the left of the doorframe. He had not noticed it yesterday.

Mrs. Andrew Cameron.

So his name had been Andrew. Spaulding hadn't asked his first name; she hadn't volunteered it.

As he looked at the brass plate he found himself experiencing a very strange reaction. He resented Andrew Cameron; resented his life, his death.

The door was open and he entered. Jean's secretary was obviously an Argentine. A *porteña.* The black Spanish hair was pulled back into a bun, her features Latin.

"Mrs. Cameron, please. David Spaulding."

"Please go in. She's expecting you." David approached the door and turned the knob.

She was taken by surprise, he thought. She was at the window looking out at the south lawn, a page of paper in her hand, glasses pushed above her forehead, resting on top of her light brown hair.

Startled, she removed her glasses from their perch and stood immobile. Slowly, as if studying him first, she smiled.

He found himself afraid. More than afraid, for a moment. And then she spoke and the sudden anguish left him, replaced by a deeply felt relief.

"I woke up this morning and reached for you. You weren't there and I thought I might cry."

He walked rapidly to her and they held each other. Neither spoke. The silence, the embrace, the splendid comfort returning.

"Granville acted like a procurer a little while ago," he said finally, holding her by the shoulders, looking at her blue speckled eyes that held such intelligent humor.

"I told you he was lovable. You wouldn't believe me."

"You didn't *tell* me we had dinner, though. Or that I could barely get through it."

"I was hoping you'd slip; give him more to think about."

"I don't understand him. Or you, maybe."

"Henderson has a problem. . . . Me. He's not sure how to handle it—me. He's overprotective because I've led him to believe I wanted that protection. I did; it was easier. But a man who's had three wives and at least twice that many mistresses over the years is no Victorian. . . . And he knows you're not going to be here long. As he would put it: do I sketch a reasonable picture?"

"I daresay," answered David in Granville's Anglicized manner.

"That's unkind." Jean laughed. "He probably doesn't approve of you, which makes his unspoken acceptance very difficult for him."

David released her. "I know damned well he doesn't approve. . . . Look, I have to make some calls; go out and meet someone. . . ."

"Just someone?"

"A ravishing beauty who'll introduce me to lots of other ravishing beauties. And between the two of us, I can't stand him. But I have to see him. . . . Will you have dinner with me?"

"Yes, I'll have dinner with you. I'd planned to. You didn't have a choice."

"You're right; you're brazen."

"I made that clear. You broke down the regimens; I'm flying up out of my own personal ash heap. . . . The air feels good."

"It was going to happen. . . . I was here." He wasn't sure why he said it but he had to.

Walter Kendall paced the hotel room as though it were a cage. Spaulding sat on the couch watching him, trying to decide which animal Kendall reminded him of; there were several that came to mind, none pets.

"You listen to *me*," Kendall said. "This is no military operation. You *take* orders, you don't give them."

"I'm sorry; I think you're misreading me." David was tempted to answer Kendall's anger in kind, but he decided not to.

"I misread, bullshit! You told Swanson you were in some trouble in New York. That's *your* problem, not *ours*."

"You can't be sure of that."

"Oh yes I can! You tried to sell that to Swanson and he bought it. You could have involved *us*!"

"Now just a minute." Spaulding felt he could object legitimately—within the boundaries he had mentally staked off for Kendall. "I told Swanson that in my opinion the 'trouble' in New York might have been related to Buenos Aires. I didn't say it *was*, I said it might have been."

"That's not possible!"

"How the hell can you be so sure?"

"Because I am." Kendall was not only agitated, thought David, he was impatient. "This is a business proposition. The deal's been made. There's no one trying to stop it. Stop *us*."

"Hostilities don't cease because a deal's been made. If the German command got wind of it they'd blow up Buenos Aires to stop it."

"Yeah . . . well, that's not possible."

"You *know* that?"

"We know it. . . . So don't go confusing that stupid bastard Swanson. I'll level with you. This is strictly a money-line negotiation. We could have completed it without any help from Washington, but they insisted—Swanson insisted—that they have a man here. O.K., you're him. You can be helpful; you can get the papers out and you speak the languages. But that's *all* you've got to do. Don't call attention to yourself. We don't want anyone upset."

Grudgingly, David began to understand the subtle clarity of Brigadier General Swanson's manipulation. Swanson had maneuvered him into a clean position. The killing of Erich Rhinemann—whether he did it himself or whether he bought the assassin—would be totally unexpected. Swanson wasn't by any means the "stupid bastard" Kendall thought he was. Or that David had considered.

Swanson was nervous. A neophyte. But he was pretty damned good.

"All right. My apologies," said Spaulding, indicating a sincerity he didn't feel. "Perhaps the New York thing was exaggerated. I made enemies in Portugal, I can't deny that. . . . I got out under cover, you know."

"What?"

"There's no way the people in New York could know I left the city."

"You're sure?"

"As sure as you are that no one's trying to stop your negotiations."

"Yeah. . . . O.K. Well, everything's set. I got a schedule."

"You've seen Rhinemann?"

"Yesterday. All day."

"What about Lyons?" asked David.

"Swanson's packing him off at the end of the week. With his nursemaids. Rhinemann figures the designs will be arriving Sunday or Monday."

"In steps or all together?"

"Probably two sets of prints. He's not sure. It doesn't make any difference; they'll be here in full by Tuesday. He guaranteed."

"Then we've moved up. You estimated three weeks." David felt a pain in his stomach. He knew it wasn't related to Walter Kendall or Eugene Lyons or designs for high-altitude gyroscopes. It was Jean Cameron and the simple fact that he'd have only one week with her.

It disturbed him greatly and he speculated—briefly—on the meaning of this disturbance.

And then he knew he could not allow himself the indulgence; the two entities had to remain separate, the worlds separate.

"Rhinemann's got good control," said Kendall, more than a hint of respect showing in his voice. "I'm impressed with his methods. Very precise."

"If you think that, you don't need me." David was buying a few seconds to steer their conversation to another area. His statement was rhetorical.

"We don't; that's what I said. But there's a lot of money involved and since the War Department—one way or another—is picking up a large share of the tab, Swanson wants his accounts covered. I don't sweat him on that. It's business."

Spaulding recognized his moment. "Then let's get to the

codes. I haven't wasted the three days down here. I've struck up a friendship of sorts with the embassy cryp."

"The what?"

"The head cryptographer. He'll send out the codes to Washington; the payment authorization."

"Oh. . . . Yeah, that." Kendall was squeezing a cigarette, prepared to insert it in his mouth. He was only half-concerned with codes and cryptographers, thought David. They were the wrap-up, the necessary details relegated to others. Or was it an act? wondered Spaulding.

He'd know in a moment or two.

"As you pointed out, it's a great deal of money. So we've decided to use a scrambler with code switches every twelve hours. We'll prepare the cryp schedule tonight and send it out by patrol courier to Washington tomorrow. The master plate will allow for fifteen letters. . . . Naturally, the prime word will be 'Tortugas.' "

Spaulding watched the disheveled accountant.

There was no reaction whatsoever.

"O.K. . . . Yeah, O.K." Kendall sat down in an easy chair. His mind seemed somewhere else.

"That meets with your approval, doesn't it?"

"Sure. Why not? Play any games you like. All I give a shit about is that Geneva radios the confirmation and you fly out of here."

"Yes, but I thought the reference had to include the . . . code factor."

"What the hell are you talking about?"

" 'Tortugas.' Hasn't it got to be 'Tortugas'?"

"Why? What's 'Tortugas'?"

The man wasn't acting. David was sure of that. "Perhaps I misunderstood. I thought 'Tortugas' was part of the authorization code."

"Christ! You and Swanson! All of you. Military geniuses! *Jesus!* If it doesn't sound like Dan Dunn, Secret Agent, it's not the real McCoy, huh? . . . Look. When Lyons tells you everything's in order, just say so. Then drive out to the airport . . . it's a small field called Mendarro . . . and Rhinemann's men will tell you when you can leave. O.K.? You got that?"

"Yes, I've got it," said Spaulding. But he wasn't sure.

Outside, David walked aimlessly down the Buenos Aires streets. He reached the huge park of the Plaza San Martín, with its fountains, its rows of white gravel paths, its calm disorder.

He sat down on a slatted bench and tried to define the elusive pieces of the increasingly complex puzzle.

Walter Kendall hadn't lied. "Tortugas" meant nothing to him.

Yet a man in an elevator in New York City had risked his life to learn about "Tortugas."

Ira Barden in Fairfax had told him there was only a single word opposite his name in the DW transfer in Ed Pace's vaults: "Tortugas."

There was an obvious answer, perhaps. Ed Pace's death prohibited any real knowledge, but the probability was genuine.

Berlin had gotten word of the Peenemünde negotiation—too late to prevent the theft of the designs—and was now committed to stopping the sale. Not only stopping it, but if possible tracing the involvement of everyone concerned. Trapping the entire Rhinemann network.

If this was the explanation—and what other plausible one existed?—Pace's code name, "Tortugas," had been leaked to Berlin by Fairfax infiltration. That there was a serious breach of security at Fairfax was clear; Pace's murder was proof.

His own role could be easily assessed by Berlin, thought David. The man in Lisbon suddenly transferred to Buenos Aires. The expert whose skill was proven in hundreds of espionage transactions, whose own network was the most ruthlessly efficient in southern Europe, did not walk out of his own creation unless his expertise was considered vital someplace else. He'd long ago accepted the fact that Berlin more than suspected him. In a way it was his protection; he'd by no means won every roll of the dice. If the enemy killed him, someone else would take his place. The enemy would have to start all over again. He was a known commodity . . . accept an existing devil.

Spaulding considered carefully, minutely, what he might do were he the enemy. What steps would he take at this specific juncture?

Barring panic or error, the enemy would not kill him.

Not now. Because he could *not* by himself inhibit the delivery of the designs. He could, however, lead his counterparts to the moment and place of delivery.

What is the location of Tortugas!?

The desperate . . . hysterical man in the Montgomery elevator had screamed the question, preferring to die rather than reveal those whose orders he followed. The Nazis reveled in such fanaticism. And so did others, for other reasons.

He—Spaulding—would therefore be placed under *äusserste Überwachung*—foolproof surveillance, three- to four-man teams, twenty-four hours a day. That would account for the recruitment of the extraterritorial personnel on the Berlin payroll. Agents who operated outside the borders of Germany, *had* operated—for profit—for years. The languages and dialects would vary; deep-cover operatives who could move with impunity in neutral capitals because they had no Gestapo or Gehlen or Nachrichtendienst histories.

The Balkans and the Middle East countries had such personnel for hire. They were expensive; they were among the best. Their only loyality was to the pound sterling and the American dollar.

Along with this round-the-clock surveillance, Berlin would take extraordinary measures to prevent him from developing his own network in Buenos Aires. That would mean infiltrating the American embassy. Berlin would not overlook that possibility. A great deal of money would be offered.

Who at the embassy could be bought?

To attempt corrupting an individual too highly placed could backfire; give him, Spaulding, dangerous information. . . . Someone not too far up on the roster; someone who could gain access to doors and locks and desk-drawer vaults. And codes. . . . A middle-level attaché. A man who'd probably never make it to the Court of St. James's anyway; who'd settle for another kind of security. Negotiable at a very high price.

Someone at the embassy would be Spaulding's enemy.

Finally, Berlin would order him killed. Along with numerous others, of course. Killed at the moment of delivery; killed after the *äusserste Überwachung* had extracted everything it could.

David got up from the slatted green bench and stretched, observing the beauty that was the Plaza San Martín park. He wandered beyond the path onto the grass, to the edge of a pond whose dark waters reflected the surrounding trees like a black mirror. Two white swans paddled by in alabaster obliviousness. A little girl was kneeling by a rock on the tiny embankment, separating the petals from a yellow flower.

He was satisfied that he had adequately analyzed the immediate options of his counterparts. Options and probable courses of action. His gut feeling was positive—not in the sense of being enthusiastic, merely not negative.

He now had to evolve his own counterstrategy. He had to bring into play the lessons he had learned over the years in Lisbon. But there was so little time allowed him. And because of this fact, he understood that a misstep could be fatal here.

Nonchalantly—but with no feelings of nonchalance—he looked around at the scores of strollers on the paths, on the grass; the rowers and the passengers in the small boats on the small dark lake. Which of them were the enemy?

Who were the ones watching him, trying to think what he was thinking?

He would have to find them—one or two of them anyway—before the next few days were over.

That was the genesis of his counterstrategy.

Isolate and break.

David lit a cigarette and walked over the miniature bridge. He was primed. The hunter and the hunted were now one. There was the slightest straining throughout his entire body; the hands, the arms, the legs: there was a muscular tension, an awareness. He recognized it. He was back in the north country.

And he was good in that jungle. He was the best there was. It was here that he built his architectural monuments, his massive structures of concrete and steel. In his mind.

It was all he had sometimes.

26

He looked at his watch. It was five thirty; Jean had said she'd be at his apartment around six. He had walked for nearly two hours and now found himself at the corner of Viamonte, several blocks from his apartment. He crossed the street and walked to a newsstand under a storefront awning, where he bought a paper.

He glanced at the front pages, amused to see that the war news—what there was of it—was relegated to the bottom, surrounded by accounts of the Grupo de Oficiales' latest benefits to Argentina. He noted that the name of a particular colonel, one Juan Perón, was mentioned in three separate subheadlines.

He folded the paper under his arm and, because he realized he had been absently musing, looked once again at his watch.

It was not a deliberate move on David's part. That is to say, he did not calculate the abruptness of his turn; he simply turned because the angle of the sun caused a reflection on his wristwatch and he unconsciously shifted his body to the right, his left hand extended, covered by his own shadow.

But his attention was instantly diverted from his watch. Out of the corner of his eye he could discern a sudden, sharp break in the sidewalk's human traffic. Thirty feet away across the street two men had swiftly turned around, colliding with oncoming pedestrians, apologizing, stepping into the flow on the curbside.

The man on the left had not been quick enough; or he was too careless—too inexperienced, perhaps—to angle his shoulders, or hunch them imperceptibly so as to melt into the crowd.

He stood out and David recognized him.

He was one of the men from the roof of the Córdoba apartment. His companion David couldn't be sure of, but he *was* sure of that man. There was even the hint of a limp in his gait; David remembered the battering he'd given him.

He was being followed, then, and that was good.

His point of departure wasn't as remote as he'd thought.

He walked another ten yards, into a fairly large group approaching the corner of Córdoba. He sidestepped his way between arms and legs and packages, and entered a small jewelry store whose wares were gaudy, inexpensive. Inside, several office girls were trying to select a gift for a departing secretary. Spaulding smiled at the annoyed proprietor, indicating that he could wait, he was in no hurry. The proprietor made a gesture of helplessness.

Spaulding stood by the front window, his body concealed from outside by the frame of the door.

Before a minute was up he saw the two men again. They were still across the street; David had to follow their progress through the intermittent gaps in the crowd. The two men were talking heatedly, the second man annoyed with his limping companion. Both were trying to glance above the heads of the surrounding bodies, raising themselves up on their toes, looking foolish, amateur.

David figured they would turn right at the corner and walk east on Córdoba, toward his apartment. They did so and, as the owner of the jewelry store protested, Spaulding walked swiftly out into the crowds and ran across the Avenida Callao, dodging cars and angry drivers. He had to reach the other side, staying out of the sightlines of the two men. He could not use the crosswalks or the curbs. It would be too easy, too logical, for the men to look backward as men did when trying to spot someone they had lost in surveillance.

David knew his objective now. He had to separate the men and take the one with a limp. Take him and force answers.

If they had any experience, he considered, they would reach his apartment and divide, one man cautiously going inside to listen through the door, ascertaining the subject's presence, the other remaining outside, far enough from the entrance to be unobserved. And common sense would dictate that the man unknown to David would be the one to enter the apartment.

Spaulding removed his jacket and held up the newspaper —not full but folded; not obviously but casually, as if he were uncertain of the meaning of some awkwardly phrased headline—and walked with the crowds to the north side of Córdoba. He turned right and maintained a steady, unbroken pace east, remaining as far left on the sidewalk as possible.

His apartment was less than a block and a half away now. He could see the two men; intermittently they *did* look back, but on their own side of the street.

Amateurs. If he taught surveillance, they'd fail his course.

The men drew nearer to the apartment, their concentration on the entrance. David knew it was his moment to move. The only moment of risk, really; the few split seconds when one or the other might turn and see him across the street, only yards away. But it was a necessary gamble. He had to get beyond the apartment entrance. That was the essence of his trap.

Several lengths ahead was a middle-aged *porteña* housewife carrying groceries, hurrying, obviously anxious to get home. Spaulding came alongside and without breaking stride, keeping in step with her, he started asking directions in his best, most elegant Castilian, starting among other points that he knew this was the right street and he was late. His head was tilted from the curb.

If anyone watched them, the housewife and the shirtsleeved man with a jacket under one arm and a newspaper under the other looked like two friends hastening to a mutual destination.

Twenty yards beyond the entrance on the other side, Spaulding left the smiling *porteña* and ducked into a canopied doorway. He pressed himself into the wall and looked back across the street. The two men stood by the curb and, as he expected, they separated. The unknown man went into his apartment house; the man with the limp looked up and down the sidewalk, checked oncoming vehicles, and started across Córdoba to the north side. David's side.

Spaulding knew it would be a matter of seconds before

the limping figure passed him. Logic, again; common sense. The man would continue east—he would not reverse direction—over traversed ground. He would station himself at a vantage point from which he could observe those approaching the apartment from the west. David's approach.

The man did not see him until David touched him, grabbed his left arm around the elbow, forced the arm into a horizontal position, and clamped the man's hand downward so that the slightest force on David's part caused an excruciating pain in the man's bent wrist.

"Just keep walking or I'll snap your hand off," said David in English, pushing the man to the right of the sidewalk to avoid the few pedestrians walking west on Córdoba.

The man's face grimaced in pain; David's accelerated walk caused him to partially stumble—his limp emphasized —and brought further agony to the wrist.

"You're breaking my arm. You're *breaking* it!" said the anguished man, hurrying his steps to relieve the pressure.

"Keep up with me or I will." David spoke calmly, even politely. They reached the corner of the Avenida Paraná and Spaulding swung left, propelling the man with him. There was a wide, recessed doorway of an old office building—the type that had few offices remaining within it. David spun the man around, keeping the arm locked, and slammed him into the wooden wall at the point farthest inside. He released the arm; the man grabbed for his strained wrist. Spaulding took the moment to flip open the man's jacket, forcing the arms downward, and removed a revolver strapped in a large holster above the man's left hip.

It was a Lüger. Issued less than a year ago.

David clamped it inside his belt and pushed a lateral forearm against the man's throat, crashing his head into the wood as he searched the pockets of the jacket. Inside he found a large rectangular European billfold. He slapped it open, removed his forearm from the man's throat, and shoved his left shoulder into the man's chest, pinning him unmercifully against the wall. With both hands, David removed identification papers.

A German driver's license; an Autobahn vehicle pass;

rationing cards countersigned by Oberführers, allowing the owner to utilize them throughout the Reich—a privilege granted to upper-level government personnel and above.

And then he found it.

An identity pass with a photograph affixed; for the ministries of Information, Armaments, Air and Supply.

Gestapo.

"You're about the most inept recruit Himmler's turned out," said David, meaning the judgment profoundly, putting the billfold in his back pocket. "You must have relatives. . . . *Was ist 'Tortugas'?*" Spaulding whispered harshly, suddenly. He removed his shoulder from the man's chest and thrust two extended knuckles into the Nazi's breastbone with such impact that the German coughed, the sharp blow nearly paralyzing him. "*Wer ist Altmüller? Was wissen Sie über Marshall?*" David repeatedly hammered the man's ribs with his knuckles, sending shock waves of pain throughout the Gestapo agent's rib cage. "*Sprechen Sie! Sofort!*"

"*Nein! Ich weiss nichts!*" the man answered between gasps. "*Nein!*"

Spaulding heard it again. The dialect. Nowhere near *Berliner*; not even a mountainized *Bavarian.* Something else.

What was it?

"*Noch 'mal!* Again! *Sprechen Sie!*"

And then the man did something quite out of the ordinary. In his pain, his fear, he stopped speaking German. He spoke in English. "I have not the information you want! I follow orders. . . . That is all!"

David shifted his stand to the left, covering the Nazi from the intermittent looks they both received from the passersby on the sidewalk. The doorway was deep, however, in shadows; no one stopped. The two men could have been acquaintances, one or both perhaps a little drunk.

Spaulding clenched his right fist, his left elbow against the wall, his left hand poised to clamp over the German's mouth. He leaned against the slatted wood and brought his fist crashing into the man's stomach with such force that the agent lurched forward, held only by David's hand, now gripping him by the hairline.

"I can keep this up until I rupture everything inside you. And when I'm finished I'll throw you in a taxi and drop you off at the German embassy with a note attached. You'll get it from both sides then, won't you? . . . Now, tell me what I want to know!" David brought his two bent knuckles up into the man's throat, jabbing twice.

"Stop. . . . *Mein Gott!* Stop!"

"Why don't you yell? You can scream your head off, you know. . . . Of course, then I'll have to put you to sleep and let your own people find you. Without your credentials, naturally. . . . Go on! Yell!" David knuckled the man once more in the throat. "Now, you start telling me. What's 'Tortugas'? Who's Altmüller? How did you get a cryp named Marshall?"

"I swear to God! I know nothing!"

David punched him again. The man collapsed; Spaulding pulled him up against the wall, leaning against him, hiding him, really. The Gestapo agent opened his lids, his eyes swimming uncontrollably.

"You've got five seconds. Then I'll rip your throat out."

"No! . . . Please! Altmüller. . . . Armaments. . . . Peenemünde. . . ."

"What about Peenemünde?"

"The tooling. . . . 'Tortugas.' "

"What does that *mean*!?" David showed the man his two bent fingers. The recollection of pain terrified the German. "What is 'Tortugas'?"

Suddenly the German's eyes flickered, trying to focus. Spaulding saw that the man was looking above his shoulder. It wasn't a ruse; the Nazi was too far gone for strategies.

And then David felt the presence behind him. It was an unmistakable feeling that had been developed over the recent years; it was never false.

He turned.

Coming into the dark shadows from the harsh Argentine sunlight was the second part of the surveillance team, the man who'd entered his apartment building. He was Spaulding's size, a large man and heavily muscular.

The light and the onrushing figure caused David to wince. He released the German, prepared to throw himself onto the opposite wall.

He couldn't!

The Gestapo agent—in a last surge of strength—held onto his arms!

Held his arms, threw his hands around David's chest and hung his full weight on him!

Spaulding lashed out with his foot at the man attacking, swung his elbows back, slamming the German back into the wood.

It was too late and David knew it.

He saw the huge hand—the long fingers spread—rushing into his face. It was as if a ghoulish film was being played before his eyes in slow motion. He felt the fingers clamp into his skin and realized that his head was being shoved with great strength into the wall.

The sensations of diving, crashing, spinning accompanied the shock of pain above his neck.

He shook his head; the first thing that struck him was the stench. It was all around him, sickening.

He was lying in the recessed doorway, curled up against the wall in a fetal position. He was wet, drenched around his face and shirt and in the crotch area of his trousers.

It was cheap whisky. Very cheap and very profuse.

His shirt had been ripped, collar to waist; one shoe was off, the sock removed. His belt was undone, his fly partially unzipped.

He was the perfect picture of a derelict.

He rose to a sitting position and remedied as best he could his appearance. He looked at his watch.

Or where his watch had been; it was gone.

His wallet, too. And money. And whatever else had been in his pockets.

He stood up. The sun was down, early night had begun; there were not so many people on the Avenida Paraná now.

He wondered what time it was. It couldn't be much more than an hour later, he supposed.

He wondered if Jean were still waiting for him.

She removed his clothes, pressed the back of his head with ice and insisted that he take a long, hot shower.

When he emerged from the bathroom, she fixed him a drink, then sat down next to him on the small couch.

"Henderson will insist on your moving into the embassy; you know that, don't you?"

"I can't."

"Well, you can't go on being beaten up every day. And don't tell me they were *thieves*. *You* wouldn't swallow that when Henderson and Bobby *both* tried to tell you that about the men on the roof!"

"This was different. For God's *sake*, Jean, I was robbed of everything on me!" David spoke sternly. It was important to him that she believe him now. And it was entirely possible that he'd find it necessary to avoid her from now on. That might be important, too. And terribly painful.

"People don't rob people and then douse them with whisky!"

"They do if they want to create sufficient time to get out of the area. It's not a new tactic. By the time a mark gets finished explaining to the police that he's a sober citizen, the hustlers are twenty miles away."

"I don't believe you. I don't even think you expect me to." She sat up and looked at him.

"I do expect you to because it's the truth. A man doesn't throw away his wallet, his money, his watch . . . in order to impress a girl with the validity of a lie. Come *on*, Jean! I'm very thirsty and my head still hurts."

She shrugged, obviously realizing it was futile to argue. "You're just about out of Scotch, I'm afraid. I'll go buy a bottle for you. There's a liquor store on the corner of Talcahuano. It's not far. . . ."

"No," he said, interrupting, recalling the man with huge hands who'd entered his building. "I will. Lend me some money."

"We'll both go," she responded.

"Please? . . . Would you mind waiting? I may get a phone call; I'd like the person to know I'll be right back."

"Who?"

"A man named Kendall."

Out on the street, he asked the first man he saw where the nearest pay phone could be found. It was several blocks away, on Rodríguez Peña, in a newspaper store.

David ran as fast as he could.

The hotel page found Kendall in the dining room. When he got on the phone he spoke while chewing. Spaulding pictured the man, the doodled obscenities, the animal-like breathing. He controlled himself. Walter Kendall was sick.

"Lyons is coming in in three days," Kendall told him. "With his nurses. I got him a place in this San Telmo district. A quiet apartment, quiet street. I wired Swanson the address. He'll give it to the keepers and they'll get him set up. They'll be touch with you."

"I thought *I* was to get him settled."

"I figured you'd complicate things," interrupted Kendall. "No piss lost. They'll call you. Or I will. I'll be here for a while."

"I'm glad. . . . Because so's the Gestapo."

"*What?*"

"I said so's the Gestapo. You figured a little inaccurately, Kendall. Someone *is* trying to stop you. It doesn't surprise me."

"You're out of your fucking mind!"

"I'm not."

"What happened?"

So David told him, and for the first time in his brief association with the accountant, he detected fear.

"There was a break in Rhinemann's network. It doesn't mean the designs won't get here. It does mean we have obstacles—if Rhinemann's as good as you say. As I read it, Berlin found out the designs were stolen. They know they're filtering down or across or however Rhinemann's routing them out of Europe. The High Command got wind of the transactions. The Reichsführers aren't going to broadcast, they're going to try and intercept. With as little noise as possible. But you can bet your ass there's been a slew of executions in Peenemünde."

"It's crazy. . . ." Kendall could hardly be heard. And then he mumbled something; David could not understand the words.

"What did you say?"

"The address in this Telmo. For Lyons. It's three rooms. Back entrance." Kendall still kept his voice low, almost indistinct.

The man was close to panic, thought Spaulding. "I can barely hear you, Kendall. . . . Now, calm down! I think it's time I introduced myself to Rhinemann, don't you?"

"The Telmo address. It's Fifteen Terraza Verde . . . it's quiet."

"Who's the contact for Rhinemann?"

"The what?"

"Rhinemann's contact."

"I don't know. . . ."

"For Christ's sake, Kendall, you held a five-hour conference with him!"

"I'll be in touch. . . ."

David heard the click. He was stunned. Kendall had hung up on him. He considered calling again but in Kendall's state of anxiety it might only make matters worse.

Goddamned amateurs! What the hell did they expect? Albert Speer himself to get in touch with Washington and lend the army air corps a few designs because he heard they had problems!?

Jesus!

David walked angrily out of the telephone booth and the store and into the street.

Where the goddamned hell was he? Oh, yes, the Scotch. The store was back at Talcahuano, Jean said. Four blocks west. He looked at his watch and, of course, there was no watch.

Goddamn.

"I'm sorry I took so long. I got confused. I walked the wrong way for a couple of blocks." David put the package of Scotch and soda water on the sink. Jean was sitting on the sofa; disturbed about something, he thought. "Did I get the call?"

"Not the one you expected," said Jean softly. "Someone else. He said he'd phone you tomorrow."

"Oh? Did he leave a name?"

"Yes, he did." When she answered, David heard the questioning fear in her voice. "It was Heinrich Stoltz."

"Stoltz? Don't know him."

"You should. He's an undersecretary at the German embassy. . . . David, what are you doing?"

27

"Sorry, *señor*. Mister Kendall checked out last night. At ten thirty, according to the card."

"Did he leave any other address or telephone number here in Buenos Aires?"

"No, *señor*. I believe he was going back to the United States. There was a Pan American flight at midnight."

"Thank you." David put down the telephone and reached for his cigarettes.

It was incredible! Kendall had shot out at the first moment of difficulty.

Why?

The telephone rang, startling David.

"Hello?"

"Herr Spaulding?"

"Yes."

"Heinrich Stoltz. I called last night but you were out."

"Yes, I know. . . . I understand you're with the German embassy. I hope I don't have to tell you that I find your contacting me unorthodox. And not a little distasteful."

"Oh, come, Herr Spaulding. The man from *Lisbon? He* finds unorthodoxy?" Stoltz laughed quietly but not insultingly.

"I am an embassy attaché specializing in economics. Nothing more. If you know anything about me, surely you know that. . . . Now, I'm late. . . ."

"Please," interrupted Stoltz. "I call from a public telephone. Surely *that* tells *you* something."

It did, of course.

"I don't talk on telephones."

"Yours is clean, I checked thoroughly."

"If you want to meet, give me a time and an address. . . .

Somewhere in the downtown area. With people around; no outside locations."

"There's a restaurant, Casa Langosta del Mar, several blocks north of the Parque Lezama. It's out of the way, not outside. There are back rooms. Curtains, no doors; no means of isolation. Only seclusion."

"Time?"

"Half past twelve."

"Do you smoke?" asked David sharply.

"Yes."

"Carry a pack of American cigarettes from the moment you get out of the car. In your left hand; the foil off one end of the top, two cigarettes removed."

"It's quite unnecessary. I know who you are. I'll recognize you."

"That's not my concern. I don't know you." David hung up the phone abruptly. As in all such rendezvous, he would arrive at the location early, through a delivery entrance if possible, and position himself as best he could to observe his contact's arrival. The cigarettes were nothing more than a psychological device: the contact was thrown off balance with the realization that he was an identified mark. A target. A marked contact was reluctant to bring trouble. And if trouble was his intent, he wouldn't show up.

Jean Cameron walked down the corridor toward the metal staircase that led to the cellars.

To the "Caves."

The "Caves"—a name given without affection by Foreign Service officers the world over—were those underground rooms housing file cabinets containing dossiers on just about everybody who had the slightest contact with an embassy, known and unknown, friend and adversary. They included exhaustive checks and counterchecks on all embassy personnel; service background, State Department evaluations, progress reports. Nothing was left out if it was obtainable.

Two signatures were required to gain entrance into the "Caves." The ambassador's and that of the senior attaché seeking information.

It was a regulation that was occasionally bypassed in the interests of haste and emergency. The marine officer of the guard generally could be convinced that an established attaché *had* to have immediate background material; the marine would list both the names of the embassy man and his subject on the check sheet, then stand in attendance while the file was removed. If there were repercussions, they were the attaché's responsibility.

There never were. Violations of this sort guaranteed a post in Uganda. The check sheet was sealed daily and sent only to the ambassador.

Jean rarely took advantage of her relationship to Henderson Granville in embassy matters. In truth, the occasion rarely arose, and when it did, the matter was always insignificant.

It was not insignificant now. And she intended to use fully her status as *family*, as well as a respected member of the staff. Granville had left for lunch; he would not return for several hours. She had made up her mind to tell the marine guard that her "father-in-law, the ambassador" had asked her to make a discreet inquiry regarding a new transfer.

Spaulding, David.

If Henderson wished to call her down for it, she would tell him the truth. She found herself very, *very* involved with the enigmatic Mr. Spaulding, and if Henderson did not realize it, he was a damn fool.

The marine officer of the guard was a young lieutenant from the FMF base south of La Boca. The personnel from FMF were sped in civilian clothes through the city to their posts at the embassy; the treaty that permitted the small, limited base did not condone uniformed men outside either territory. These restrictions tended to make the young officers sensitive to the functionary, faceless roles they were forced to play. So it was understandable that when the ambassador's daughter-in-law called him by name and spoke confidentially of a discreet matter, the marine complied without question.

Jean stared at David's file. It was frightening. It was not like any file she had ever seen. There was no dossier; no State Department records, no reports, no evaluations, no listing of post assignments.

There was only a single page.

It gave his description by sex, height, weight, coloring and visible markings.

Beneath this cursory data, separated by a three-line space, was the following:

> *War Dept. Transfer. Clandestine Operations. Finance. Tortugas.*

And nothing more.

"Finding what you need, Mrs. Cameron?" asked the marine lieutenant by the steel-grilled gate.

"Yes. . . . Thank you." Jean slipped David's thin folder back into place in the cabinet, smiled at the marine, and left.

She reached the staircase and walked slowly up the steps. She accepted the fact that David was involved with an undercover assignment—accepted it while hating it; loathing the secrecy, the obvious danger. But in a conscious way she had prepared herself, expecting the worst and finding it. She was not at all sure she could handle the knowledge, but she was willing to try. If she could not handle it she'd take what moments of selfish pleasure she could and kiss David Spaulding good-bye. She had made up her mind to that . . . unconsciously, really. She could not allow herself more pain.

And there was something else. It was only a dim shadow in a half-lit room but it kept falling across her eyes. It was the word.

"Tortugas."

She had seen it before. Recently. Only days ago.

It had caught her attention because she'd thought of the Dry Tortugas . . . and the few times she and Andrew had sailed there from the Keys.

Where was it? Yes. . . . Yes, she remembered.

It had been in a very mechanical paragraph within the context of an area surveillance report on Henderson Granville's desk. She had read it rather absently one morning . . . only a few days ago. But she hadn't read it closely. Area surveillance reports were composed of short, choppy informational sentences devoid of rhythm and color. Written by unimaginative men concerned only with what they could describe briefly, with data.

It had been down at La Boca.

Something about the captain of a trawler . . . and cargo.

Cargo that had a lading destination of Tortugas. A violation of coastal limits; said destination rescinded, called an obvious error by the trawler's captain.

Yet the lading papers had said Tortugas.

And David Spaulding's classified operation—*clandestine* operation—was coded "Tortugas."

And Heinrich Stoltz of the German embassy had called David.

And Jean Cameron was suddenly afraid.

Spaulding was convinced that Stoltz was alone. He signaled the German to follow him to the back of the restaurant, to the curtained cubicle David had arranged for with the waiter a half hour ago.

Stoltz entered carrying the pack of cigarettes in his left hand. Spaulding circled the round table and sat facing the curtain.

"Have a seat," said David, indicating the chair opposite him. Stoltz smiled, realizing that his back would be to the entrance.

"The man from Lisbon is a cautious man." The German pulled out the chair and sat down, placing the cigarettes on the table. "I can assure you I'm not armed."

"Good. I am."

"You are *too* cautious. The colonels look askance at belligerents carrying weapons in their neutral city. Your embassy should have told you."

"I understand they also arrest Americans quicker than they do you fellows."

Stoltz shrugged. "Why not? After all, we trained them. You only buy their beef."

"There'll be no lunch, incidentally. I paid the waiter for the table."

"I'm sorry. The langosta . . . the lobster here is excellent. Perhaps a drink?"

"No drinks. Just talk."

Stoltz spoke, his voice flat. "I bring a welcome to Buenos Aires. From Erich Rhinemann."

David stared at the man. "You?"

"Yes. I'm your contact."

"That's interesting."

"That's the way of Erich Rhinemann. He pays for allegiances."

"I'll want proof."

"By all means. From Rhinemann himself. . . . Acceptable?"

Spaulding nodded. "When? Where?"

"That's what I'm here to discuss. Rhinemann is as cautious as the man from Lisbon."

"I was attached to the diplomatic corps in Portugal. Don't try to make anything more of it than that."

"Unfortunately, I have to speak the truth. Herr Rhinemann is most upset that the men in Washington saw fit to send you as the liaison. Your presence in Buenos Aires could attract attention."

David reached for the cigarettes Stoltz had placed on the table. He lit one. . . . The German was right, of course; Rhinemann was right. The one liability in his having been chosen was the enemy's probable knowledge of his Lisbon operations. Ed Pace, he was sure, had considered that aspect, discarding it in favor of the overriding assets. Regardless, it was not a subject to discuss with Heinrich Stoltz. The German attaché was still an unproven factor.

"I have no idea what you're referring to. I'm in Buenos Aires to transmit preliminary recommendations from New York and London banking circles relative to postwar reconstruction negotiations. You see, we *do* believe we'll win. Rhinemann can't be overlooked in such projected discussions."

"The man from Lisbon is most professional."

"I wish you'd stop repeating that nonsense. . . ."

"And convincing," interrupted Stoltz. "The cover is one of your better ones. It has more stature than a cowardly American socialite. . . . Even Herr Kendall agrees with that."

David paused before replying. Stoltz was circling in, about to deliver his proof. "Describe Kendall," he said quietly.

"In short words?"

"It doesn't matter."

Stoltz laughed under his breath. "I'd prefer as few as possible. He's a most unattractive biped. He must be an extraordinary man with figures; there's no other earthly reason to stay in the same room with him."

"Have you stayed in the same room with him?"

"For hours, unfortunately. With Rhinemann. . . . Now. May we talk?"

"Go ahead."

"Your man Lyons will be here the day after tomorrow. We can accomplish everything very quickly. The designs will be delivered in one package, not two as Kendall believes."

"Does he believe that?"

"It's what he was told."

"Why?"

"Because until late last evening Herr Rhinemann thought it was so. I myself did not know of the change until this morning."

"Then why did you call me last night?"

"Instructions from Walter Kendall."

"Please explain that."

"Is it necessary? One has nothing to do with the other. Herr Kendall telephoned *me.* Apparently he had just spoken with you. He said he was called back to Washington suddenly; that I was to contact you immediately so there's no break in communications. He was most adamant."

"Did Kendall say why he was returning to the States?"

"No. And I saw no reason to inquire. His work here is finished. He's of no concern to us. You are the man with the codes, not him."

David crushed out his cigarette, staring at the tablecloth. "What's your rank at the embassy?"

Stoltz smiled. "Third . . . fourth in command would be a modest appraisal. My loyalty, however, is to the Rhinemann interests. Surely that's apparent."

"I'll know when I talk to Rhinemann, won't I?" David looked up at the German. "Why are the Gestapo here in Buenos Aires?"

"They're not. . . . Well, there's one man; no more than a clerk, really. As all Gestapo he thinks of himself as the personal spokesman for the Reich and overburdens the couriers—who, incidentally, cooperate with us. He is, as you *Amerikaner* say, a jackass. There is no one else."

"Are you sure?"

"Of course. I would be the first to know; before the ambassador, I assure you. This game is quite unnecessary, Herr Spaulding."

"You'd better set up that meeting with Rhinemann . . . *that's* necessary."

"Yes. Certainly. . . . Which brings us back to Herr Rhinemann's concerns. Why is the man from Lisbon in Buenos Aires?"

"I'm afraid he has to be. You said it. I'm cautious. I'm experienced. And I have the codes."

"But why *you*? To remove you from Lisbon is costly. I speak both as an enemy and as an objective neutral, allied with Rhinemann. Is there some side issue of which we're not aware?"

"If there is, I'm not aware of it, either," answered Spaulding, neutralizing Stoltz's inquisitorial look with one of his own. "Since we're talking plain, I want to get those designs okayed, send the codes for your goddamned money and get the hell out of here. Since a large share of that financing will come from the government, Washington obviously thinks I'm the best man to see we're not cheated."

Both men remained silent for several moments. Stoltz spoke.

"I believe you. You Americans always worry about being cheated, don't you?"

"Let's talk about Rhinemann. I want the meeting immediately. I won't be satisfied that Kendall's arrangements are solid until I hear it from him. And I won't organize a code schedule with Washington until I'm satisfied."

"There's no schedule?"

"There won't be any until I see Rhinemann."

Stoltz breathed deeply. "You are what they say, a thorough man. You'll see Rhinemann. . . . It will have to be after dark, two transfers of vehicles, his residence. He can't take the chance of anyone seeing you together. . . . Do these precautions disturb you?"

"Not a bit. Without the codes there's no money transferred in Switzerland. I think Herr Rhinemann will be most hospitable."

"Yes, I'm sure. . . . Very well. Our business is concluded. You'll be contacted this evening. Will you be at home?"

"If not, I'll leave word at the embassy switchboard."

"*Denn auf Wiedersehen, mein Herr.*" Stoltz got out of the chair and gave a diplomatic nod of his head. "*Heute Abend.*"

"*Heute Abend,*" replied Spaulding as the German parted the curtain and walked out of the cubicle. David saw that Stoltz had left his cigarettes on the table; a minor gift or a minor insult. He removed one and found himself squeezing the tip as he remembered Kendall doing—incessantly, with every cigarette the accountant prepared to smoke. David broke the paper around the tobacco and dropped it in the ashtray. Anything reminding him of Kendall was distasteful now. He couldn't think about Kendall and his sudden, fear-induced departure.

He had something else to think about.

Heinrich Stoltz, "third, fourth in command" at the German embassy, was not so highly placed as he believed. The Nazi had not been lying—he *did not* know the Gestapo was in Buenos Aires. And if he didn't know, that meant someone wasn't telling him.

It was ironic, thought David, that he and Erich Rhinemann would be working together after all. Before he killed Rhinemann, of course.

Heinrich Stoltz sat down at his desk and picked up the telephone. He spoke in his impeccable academic German.

"Get me Herr Rhinemann in Luján."

He replaced the phone, leaned back in his chair and smiled. Several moments later his buzzer hummed.

"Herr Rhinemann? . . . Heinrich Stoltz. . . . Yes, yes, everything went smoothly. Kendall spoke the truth. This Spaulding knows nothing about Koening or the diamonds; his only concerns are the designs. His only threat—that of withholding funds. He plays unimpressive games but we need the codes. The American fleet patrols could be ordered to seal off the harbor; the trawler will have to get out. . . . Can you imagine? All this Spaulding is interested in is not being cheated!"

28

At first he thought he was mistaken. . . . No, that wasn't quite right, he considered; that wasn't his first thought. He didn't have a first *thought*, he had only a *reaction*.

He was stunned.

Leslie Hawkwood!

He saw her from his taxi window talking with a man at the south end of the fountain in the Plaza de Mayo. The cab was slowly making its way through the traffic around the huge square; he ordered the driver to pull over and stop.

David paid the driver and got out. He was now directly opposite Leslie and the man; he could see the blurred figures through the spray of the fountain.

The man handed Leslie an envelope and bowed a European bow. He turned and went to the curb, his hand held up for a taxi. One stopped and the man got in; the cab entered the flow of traffic and Leslie went to the crosswalk, waiting for the pedestrian signal.

David made his way cautiously around the fountain and dashed to the curb just as the crosswalk light flashed.

He dodged the anxious vehicles, arousing horns and angry shouts, angling his path to the left in case she turned around at the commotion. She was at least fifty yards ahead of him; she couldn't spot him, he was sure of that.

On the boulevard, Leslie headed west toward Avenida 9 de Julio. David closed the gap between them but kept himself obscured by the crowds. She stopped briefly at several store windows, twice obviously trying to make up her mind whether to enter or not.

So like Leslie; she had always hated to give up the acquisition of something new.

She kept walking, however. Once she looked at her wristwatch; she turned north on Julio and checked the numbers of two storefront addresses, apparently to determine the directional sequence.

Leslie Hawkwood had never been to Buenos Aires.

She continued north at a leisurely pace, taking in the extraordinary color and size of the boulevard. She reached the corner of Corrientes, in the middle of the theater district, and wandered past the billboards, looking at the photographs of the performers.

Spaulding realized that the American embassy was less than two blocks away—between the Avenidas Supacha and Esmeralda. There was no point in wasting time.

She saw him before he spoke. Her eyes widened, her jaw fell, her whole body trembled visibly. The blood drained from her suntanned face.

"You have two alternatives, Leslie," said Spaulding as he came within a foot of her, looking down at her terrified face. "The embassy is right up there; it's United States territory. You'll be arrested as a citizen interfering with national security, if not espionage. Or you can come with me. . . . And answer questions. Which will it be?"

The taxi took them to the airport, where Spaulding rented a car with the papers identifying him as "Donald Scanlan, mining surveyor." They were the sort of identifications he carried when making contact with such men as Heinrich Stoltz.

He had held Leslie by the arm with sufficient pressure to warn her not to attempt running; she was his prisoner and he was deadly serious about the fact. She said nothing at all during the ride to the airport; she simply stared out the window, avoiding his eyes.

Her only words at the rental counter were, "Where are we going?"

His reply was succinct: "Out of Buenos Aires."

He followed the river road north toward the outskirts, into the hills above the city. A few miles into the Sante Fé province, the Río Luján curved westward, and he descended the steep inclines onto the highway paralleling the water's edge. It was the territory of the Argentine rich. Yachts were moored or cruising slowly; sailboats of all classes were lazily catching the upriver winds, tacking harmoniously among the tiny green islands which sprung out of the water like lush gardens. Private roads veered off the highway—now subtly curving west, away from the water. Enormous villas dotted the banks; nothing was without visual effect.

He saw a road to his left that was the start of a hill. He swung up into it, and after a mile there was a break in the area.

Vigía Tigre.

A lookout. A courtesy for tourists.

He drove the car to the front of the parking ground and pulled to a stop, next to the railing. It was a weekday; there were no other automobiles.

Leslie had said nothing throughout the hour's ride. She had smoked cigarettes, her hands trembling, her eyes refusing to make contact with his. And through experience, David knew the benefits of silence under such conditions. The girl was close to breaking.

"All right. Now come the questions." Spaulding turned in the seat and faced her. "And please believe me, I won't hesitate to run you into military arrest if you refuse."

She swung her head around and stared at him angrily—yet still in fear. "Why didn't you do that an hour ago?"

"Two reasons," he answered simply. "Once the embassy is involved, I'd be locked into a chain of command; the decisions wouldn't be mine. I'm too curious to lose that control. . . . And second, old friend, I think you're in way the hell over your head. What is it, Leslie? What *are* you into?"

She put the cigarette to her lips and inhaled as though her life depended on the smoke. She closed her eyes briefly and spoke barely above a whisper. "I can't tell you. Don't force me to."

He sighed. "I don't think you understand. I'm an Intelligence officer assigned to Clandestine Operations—I'm not telling you anything you don't know. You made it possible for my hotel room to be searched; you lied; you went into hiding; for all I know, you were responsible for several assaults which nearly cost me my life. Now, you turn up in Buenos Aires, four thousand miles away from that Park Avenue apartment. You followed me four thousand miles! . . . *Why?*"

"I can't *tell* you! I haven't been *told* what I can tell you!"

"You haven't been . . . *Christ!* With what I can piece

together—and testify to—you could spend twenty years in prison!"

"I'd like to get out of the car. May I?" she said softly, snuffing out her cigarette in the ashtray.

"Sure. Go ahead." David opened his door and rapidly came around the automobile. Leslie walked to the railing, the waters of the Río Luján far below in the distance.

"It's very beautiful here, isn't it?"

"Yes. . . . Did you try to have me killed?"

"Oh, *God!*" She whirled on him, spitting out the words. "I tried to save your *life!* I'm here because I don't *want* you killed!"

It took David a few moments to recover from the girl's statement. Her hair had fallen carelessly around her face, her eyes blinking back tears, her lips trembling.

"I think you'd better explain that," he said in a quiet monotone.

She turned away from him and looked down at the river, the villas, the boats. "It's like the Riviera, isn't it?"

"*Stop it*, Leslie!"

"Why? It's part of it." She put her hands on the railing. "It used to be all there was. Nothing else mattered. *Where* next; *who* next? *What* a lovely party! . . . You were part of it."

"Not really. You're wrong if you thought that. Just as you're wrong now. . . . I won't be put off."

"I'm not putting you off." She gripped the railing harder; it was a physical gesture telegraphing her indecision with her words. "I'm trying to tell you something."

"That you followed me because you wanted to save my *life?*" He asked the question with incredulity. "You were filled with dramatics in New York, too, if I recall. You waited, how long was it? Five, six, eight years to get me on the boathouse floor again. You're a bitch."

"And *you're insignificant!*" She flung the words at him in heat. And then she subsided, controlling herself. "I don't mean you . . . *you*. Just compared to everything else. We're all insignificant in that sense."

"So the lady has a cause."

Leslie stared at him and spoke softly. "One she believes in very deeply."

"Then you should have no reservations explaining it to me."

"I *will*, I promise you. But I can't *now*. . . . Trust me!"

"Certainly," said David casually. And then he suddenly whipped out his hand, grabbing her purse, which hung from her shoulder by a leather strap. She started to resist; he looked at her. She stopped and breathed deeply.

He opened the purse and took out the envelope she had been given at the fountain in the Plaza de Mayo. As he did so, his eyes caught sight of a bulge at the bottom of the bag, covered by a silk scarf. He held the envelope between his fingers and reached down. He separated the scarf from the object and pulled out a small Remington revolver. Without saying anything, he checked the chamber and the safety and put the weapon in his jacket pocket.

"I've learned to use it," said Leslie tentatively.

"Good for you," replied Spaulding, opening the envelope.

"At least you'll see how efficient we are," she said, turning, looking down at the river.

There was no letterhead, no origin of writer or organization. The heading on the top of the paper read:

> *Spaulding, David. Lt. Col. Military Intelligence, U.S. Army. Classification 4-0. Fairfax.*

Beneath were five complicated paragraphs detailing every move he had made since he was picked up on Saturday afternoon entering the embassy. David was pleased to see that "Donald Scanlan" was not mentioned; he'd gotten through the airport and customs undetected.

Everything else was listed: his apartment, his telephone, his office at the embassy, the incident on the Córdoba roof, the lunch with Jean Cameron at La Boca, the meeting with Kendall at the hotel, the assault on the Avenida Paraná, his telephone call in the store on Rodríguez Peña.

Everything.

Even the "lunch" with Heinrich Stoltz at the Langosta del Mar, on the border of Lezama. The meeting with Stoltz was estimated to last "a minimum of one hour."

It was the explanation for her leisurely pace on the Avenida de Mayo. But David had cut the meeting short; there'd been no lunch. He wondered if he had been picked up after he'd left the restaurant. He had not been concerned. His thoughts had been on Heinrich Stoltz and the presence of a Gestapo Stoltz knew nothing about.

"Your people are *very* thorough. Now, who are they?"

"Men . . . and women who have a calling. A purpose. A *great* calling."

"That's not what I asked you. . . ."

There was the sound of an automobile coming up the hill below the parking area. Spaulding reached inside his jacket for his pistol. The car came into view and proceeded upward, past them. The people in the car were laughing. David turned his attention back to Leslie.

"I asked you to trust me," said the girl. "I was on my way to an address on that street, the boulevard called Julio. I was to be there at one thirty. They'll wonder where I am."

"You're not going to answer me, are you?"

"I'll answer you in one way. I'm here to convince you to get out of Buenos Aires."

"Why?"

"Whatever it is you're doing—and I don't *know* what it is, they haven't told me—it can't happen. We can't let it happen. It's wrong."

"Since you don't know what it is, how can you say it's wrong?"

"Because I've been told. That's enough!"

"*Ein Volk, ein Reich, ein Führer*," said David quietly. "Get in the car!"

"No. You've got to listen to me! Get out of Buenos Aires! Tell your generals it can't be done!"

"Get in the car!"

There was the sound of another automobile, this time coming from the opposite direction, from above. David put his hand once more under his jacket, but then removed it casually. It was the same vehicle with the laughing tourists that had passed by moments ago. They were still laughing, still gesturing; probably drunk with luncheon wine.

"You can't take me to the embassy! You *can't!*"

"If you don't get in the car, you'll just wake up there! Go *on*."

There was the screeching of tires on the gravel. The descending automobile had turned abruptly—at the last second—and swung sharply into the parking area and come to a stop.

David looked up and swore to himself, his hand immobile inside his jacket.

Two high-powered rifles protruded from the open windows of the car. They were aimed at him.

The heads of the three men inside were covered with silk stockings, the faces flattened, grotesque beyond the translucent masks. The rifles were held by one man next to the driver in the front seat and by another in the back.

The man in the rear opened the door, his rifle held steady. He gave his command in a calm voice. In English.

"Get in the car, Mrs. Hawkwood. . . . And you, colonel. Remove your weapon by the handle—with two fingers."

David did so.

"Walk to the railing," continued the man in the back seat, "and drop it over the side, into the woods."

David complied. The man got out of the car to let Leslie climb in. He then returned to his seat and closed the door.

There was the gunning of the powerful engine and the sound once more of spinning tires over the loose gravel. The car lurched forward out of the parking area and sped off down the hill.

David stood by the railing. He would go over it and find his pistol. There was no point in trying to follow the automobile with Leslie Hawkwood and three men in stocking masks. His rented car was no match for a Duesenberg.

29

The restaurant had been selected by Jean. It was out of the way in the north section of the city, beyond Palermo Park, a place for assignation. Telephone jacks were in the wall by the booths; waiters could be seen bringing phones to and from the secluded tables.

He was mildly surprised that Jean would know such a restaurant. Or would choose it for them.

"Where did you go this afternoon?" she asked, seeing him looking out over the dim room from their booth.

"A couple of conferences. Very dull. Bankers have a penchant for prolonging any meeting way beyond its finish. The Strand or Wall Street, makes no difference." He smiled at her.

"Yes. . . . Well perhaps they're always looking for ways to extract every last dollar."

"No 'perhaps.' That's it. . . . This is quite a place, by the way. Reminds me of Lisbon."

"Rome," she said. "It's more like Rome. Way out. Via Appia. Did you know that the Italians comprise over thirty per cent of the population in Buenos Aires?"

"I knew it was considerable."

"The Italian hand. . . . That's supposed to mean evil."

"Or clever. Not necessarily evil. The 'fine Italian hand' is usually envied."

"Bobby brought me here one night. . . . I think he brings lots of girls here."

"It's . . . discreet."

"I think he was worried that Henderson might find out he had dishonorable designs. And so he brought me here."

"Which confirmed his designs."

"Yes. . . . It's for lovers. But we weren't."

"I'm glad you chose it for us. It gives me a nice feeling of security."

"Oh, no! Don't look for that. No one's in the market for that this year. No. . . . Security's out of the question. And commitments. Those, too. No commitments for sale." She took a cigarette from his open pack; he lit it for her. Over the flame he saw her eyes staring at him. Caught, she glanced downward, at nothing.

"What's the matter?"

"Nothing. . . . Nothing at all." She smiled, but only the outlines were there; not the ingenuousness, not the humor. "Did you talk to that man Stoltz?"

"Good Lord, is that what's bothering you? . . . I'm sorry, I suppose I should have said something. Stoltz was selling fleet information; I'm in no position to buy. I told him to get in touch with Naval Intelligence. I made a report to the base commander at FMF this morning. If they want to use him, they will."

"Strange he should call you."

"That's what I thought. Apparently German surveillance picked me up the other day and the financial data was on their sheet. That was enough for Stoltz."

"He's a defector?"

"Or selling bad stuff. It's FMF's problem, not mine."

"You're very glib." She drank her coffee unsteadily.

"What's that supposed to mean?"

"Nothing. . . . Just that you're quick. Quick and facile. You must be very good at your work."

"And you're in a godawful mood. Does an excess of gin bring it on?"

"Oh, you think I'm drunk?"

"You're not sober. Not that it matters." He grinned. "You're hardly an alcoholic."

"Thanks for the vote of confidence. But don't speculate. That implies some kind of permanence. We must avoid that, mustn't we?"

"Must we? It seems to be a point with you tonight. It wasn't a problem I was considering."

"You just brushed it aside, I assume. I'm sure you have other, more pressing matters." In replacing her cup, Jean spilled coffee on the tablecloth. She was obviously annoyed with herself. "I'm doing it badly," she said after a moment of silence.

"You're doing it badly," he agreed.

"I'm frightened."

"Of what?"

"You're not here in Buenos Aires to talk to bankers, are you? It's much more than that. You won't tell me, I know. And in a few weeks, you'll be gone . . . if you're alive."

"You're letting your imagination take over." He took her hand; she crushed out her cigarette and put her other hand over his. She gripped him tightly.

"All right. Let's say you're right." She spoke quietly now; he had to strain to hear her. "I'm making everything up. I'm crazy and I drank too much. Indulge me. Play the game for a minute."

"If you want me to . . . O.K."

"It's hypothetical. My David isn't a State Department syndromer, you see. He's an agent. We've had a few here; I've met them. The colonels call them *provocarios*. . . . So, my David is an agent and being an agent is called . . . high-risk something-or-other because the rules are different. That is, the rules don't have any meaning. . . . There aren't any rules for these people . . . like my hypothetical David. Do you follow?"

"I follow," he replied simply. "I'm not sure what the object is or how a person scores."

"We'll get to that." She drank the last of her coffee, holding the cup firmly—too firmly; her fingers shook. "The point is, such a man as my . . . mythical David could be killed or crippled or have his face shot off. That's a horrible thought, isn't it?"

"Yes. I imagine that possibility has occurred to several hundred thousand men by now. It's horrible."

"But they're different. They have armies and uniforms and certain rules. Even in airplanes . . . their chances are better. And I say this with a certain expertise."

He looked at her intently. "Stop."

"Oh, not yet. Now, I'm going to tell you how you can score a goal. Why does my hypothetical David do what he does? . . . No, don't answer yet." She stopped and smiled weakly. "But you weren't about to answer, were you? It doesn't matter; there's a second part of the question. You get extra points for considering it."

"What's the second part?" He thought that Jean was

recapitulating an argument she had memorized. Her next words proved it.

"You see, I've thought about it over and over again . . . for this make-believe game . . . this make-believe agent. He's in a very unique position: he works alone . . . or at least with very, *very* few people. He's in a strange country and he's alone. . . . Do you understand the second part now?"

David watched her. She had made some abstract connection in her mind without verbalizing it. "No, I don't."

"If David is working alone and in a strange country and has to send codes to Washington . . . Henderson told me that . . . that means the people he's working for have to believe what he tells them. He can tell them anything he wants to. . . . So now we come back to the question. Knowing all this, why does the mythical David do what he does? He can't really believe that he'll influence the outcome of the whole war. He's only one among millions and millions."

"And . . . if I'm following you . . . this make-believe man can send word to his superiors that he's having difficulties. . . ."

"He has to stay on in Buenos Aires. For a long time," she interrupted, holding his hand fiercely.

"And if they say no, he can always hide out in the pampas."

"Don't make fun of me!" she said intensely.

"I'm not. I won't pretend that I can give you logical answers, but I don't think the man you're talking about has such a clear field. Tight reins are kept on such men, I believe. Other men could be sent into the area . . . would be sent, I'm sure. Your strategy is only a short-term gain; the penalties are long and damned stiff."

She withdrew her hands slowly, looking away from him. "It's a gamble that might be worth it, though. I love you very much. I don't want you hurt and I know there are people trying to hurt you." She stopped and turned her eyes back to him. "They're trying to kill you, aren't they? . . . One among so many millions . . . and I keep saying to myself, 'Not him. Oh, God, not him.' Don't you see? . . . Do we need them? Are those people—whoever they are—so important? To us? Haven't you done enough?"

He returned her stare and found himself understanding the profundity of her question. It wasn't a pleasant realization. . . . He *had* done enough. His whole life had been turned around until the alien was an everyday occurrence.

For what?

The amateurs? Alan Swanson? Walter Kendall?

A dead Ed Pace. A corrupt Fairfax.

One among so many millions.

"Señor Spaulding?" The words shocked him momentarily because they were so completely unexpected. A tuxedoed maître d' was standing by the edge of the booth, his voice low.

"Yes?"

"There's a telephone call for you."

David looked at the discreet man. "Can't you bring the telephone to the table?"

"Our sincere apologies. The instrument plug at this booth is not functioning."

A lie, of course, Spaulding knew.

"Very well." David got out of the booth. He turned to Jean. "I'll be right back. Have some more coffee."

"Suppose I wanted a drink?"

"Order it." He started to walk away.

"David?" She called out enough to be heard; not loudly.

"Yes." He turned back; she was staring at him again.

" 'Tortugas' isn't worth it," she said quietly.

It was as if he'd been hit a furious blow in the stomach. Acid formed in his throat, his breath stopped, his eyes pained him as he looked down at her.

"I'll be right back."

"Heinrich Stoltz here," the voice said.

"I've been expecting your call. I assume the switchboard gave you the number."

"It was not necessary to telephone. The arrangements have been made. In twenty minutes a green Packard automobile will be outside the restaurant. A man will have his left arm out the window, holding an open pack of German cigarettes this time. I thought you would appreciate the symbolic repetition."

"I'm touched. But you may have to alter the time and the car."

"There can be no changes. Herr Rhinemann is adamant."

"So am I. Something's come up."

"Sorry. Twenty minutes. A green Packard automobile."

The connection was severed.

Well, that was Stoltz's problem, thought David. There was only one thought in mind. To get back to Jean.

He made his way out of the dimly lit corner and sidled awkwardly past the bar patrons whose stools were blocking the aisle. He was in a hurry; the human and inanimate obstructions were frustrating, annoying. He reached the arch into the dining area and walked rapidly through the tables to the rear booth.

Jean Cameron was gone. There was a note on the table.

It was on the back of a cocktail napkin, the words written in the heavy wax of an eyebrow pencil. Written hastily, almost illegibly:

> David. I'm sure you have things to do—
> places to go—and I'm a bore tonight

Nothing else. As if she just stopped.

He crumpled the napkin in his pocket and raced back across the dining room to the front entrance. The maître d' stood by the door.

"*Señor?* Is there a problem?"

"The lady at the booth. Where did she go?!"

"Mrs. Cameron?"

Christ! thought David, looking at the calm *porteño*. What was happening? The reservation was in *his* name. Jean had indicated that she'd been to the restaurant only once before.

"Yes! Mrs. Cameron! Goddamn you, where is she!?"

"She left a few minutes ago. She took the first taxi at the curb."

"You *listen* to me. . . ."

"*Señor*," interrupted the obsequious Argentine, "there is a gentleman waiting for you outside. He will take care of your bill. He has an account with us."

Spaulding looked out the large windowpanes in the heavy front door. Through the glass he could see a man standing on the sidewalk. He was dressed in a white Palm Beach suit.

David pushed the door open and approached him.

"You want to see me?"

"I'm merely waiting for you, Herr Spaulding. To escort you. The car should be here in fifteen minutes."

30

The green Packard sedan came to a stop across the street, directly in front of the restaurant. The driver's arm appeared through the open window, an indistinguishable pack of cigarettes in his hand. The man in the white Palm Beach suit gestured politely for Spaulding to accompany him.

As he drew nearer, David could see that the driver was a large man in a black knit, short-sleeved shirt that both revealed and accentuated his muscular arms. There was a stubble of beard, thick eyebrows; he looked like a mean-tempered longshoreman, the rough image intended, Spaulding was sure. The man walking beside him opened the car door and David climbed in.

No one spoke. The car headed south back toward the center of Buenos Aires; then northeast into the Aeroparque district. David was mildly surprised to realize that the driver had entered the wide highway paralleling the river. The same road he had taken that afternoon with Leslie Hawkwood. He wondered whether the route was chosen deliberately, if they expected him to make some remark about the coincidence.

He sat back, giving no indication that he recognized anything.

The Packard accelerated on the wide river road which now swung to the left, following the water into the hills of the northwest. The car did not, however, go up any of the offshoot roads as David had done hours ago. Instead the driver maintained a steady, high speed. A reflecting highway sign was caught momentarily in the glare of the headlights: *Tigre 12 kil.*

The traffic was mild; cars rushed past intermittently from the opposite direction; several were overtaken by the

Packard. The driver checked his rear- and side-view mirrors constantly.

In the middle of a long bend in the road, the Packard slowed down. The driver nodded his head to the man in the white Palm Beach suit beside David.

"We will exchange cars now, Herr Spaulding," said the man, reaching into his jacket, withdrawing a gun.

Ahead of them was a single building, an outskirts restaurant or an inn with a circular drive that curved in front of an entrance and veered off into a large parking area on the side. Spotlights lit the entrance and the lawn in front.

The driver swung in; the man beside Spaulding tapped him.

"Get out here, please. Go directly inside."

David opened the door. He was surprised to see a uniformed doorman remain by the entrance, making no move toward the Packard. Instead, he crossed rapidly in front of the entrance and started walking on the graveled drive in the direction of the side parking lot. Spaulding opened the front door and stepped into the carpeted foyer of the restaurant; the man in the white suit was at his heels, his gun now in his pocket.

Instead of proceeding toward the entrance of the dining area, the man held David by the arm—politely—and knocked on what appeared to be the door of a small office in the foyer. The door opened and the two of them walked inside.

It was a tiny office but that fact made no impression on Spaulding. What fascinated him were the two men inside. One was dressed in a white Palm Beach suit; the other—and David instantly, involuntarily, had to smile—was in the identical clothes he himself was wearing. A light blue, striped cord jacket and dark trousers. The second man was his own height, the same general build, the same general coloring.

David had no time to observe further. The light in the small office—a desk lamp—was snapped off by the newly appeared white suit. The German who had accompanied Spaulding walked to the single window that looked out on the circular drive. He spoke softly.

"Schnell. Beeilen Sie sich . . . Danke."

The two men quickly walked to the door and let themselves out. The German by the window was silhouetted in the filtered light of the front entrance. He beckoned David.

"*Kommen Sie her.*"

He went to the window and stood beside the man. Outside, their two counterparts were on the driveway, talking and gesturing as if in an argument—a mild disagreement, not violent. Both smoked cigarettes, their faces more often covered by their hands than not. Their backs were to the highway beyond.

Then an automobile came from the right, from the direction of the parking lot, and the two men got inside. The car moved slowly to the left, to the entrance of the highway. It paused for several seconds, waiting for an opportune moment in the thinned-out night traffic. Suddenly it lurched forward, crossed to the right of the highway and sped off south, toward the city.

David wasn't sure why the elaborate ploy was considered necessary; he was about to ask the man beside him. Before he spoke, however, he noticed the smile on the man's face, inches from his in the window. Spaulding looked out.

About fifty yards away, off the side of the river road, headlights were snapped on. A vehicle, facing north, made a fast U-turn on the wide highway and headed south in a sudden burst of speed.

The German grinned. "*Amerikanische . . . Kinder.*"

David stepped back. The man crossed to the desk and turned on the lamp.

"That was an interesting exercise," said Spaulding.

The man looked up. "Simply a—what are your words, *eine Vorsichtsmassnahme*—a . . ."

"A precaution," said David.

"*Ja.* That's right, you speak German. . . . Come. Herr Rhinemann must not be kept waiting longer than the . . . *precautions* require."

Even in daylight, Spaulding realized, the dirt road would be difficult to find. As it was, with no streetlamps and only the misty illumination of the moon, it seemed as though the Packard had swung off the hard pavement into a black wall of towering overgrowth. Instead, there was the unmistakable sound of dirt beneath the wheels as the car plunged forward, the driver secure in his knowledge of the numerous turns and straightaways. A half mile into the forest the dirt road suddenly widened and the surface became smooth and hard again.

There was an enormous parking area. Four stone gateposts—wide, medieval in appearance—were spaced equidistant from one another at the far end of the black-topped field. Above each stone post was a massive flood-lamp, the spills intersecting, throwing light over the entire area and into the woods beyond. Between the huge posts was a thick-grilled iron fence, in the center of which was a webbed steel gate, obviously operated electrically.

Men dressed in dark shirts and trousers—quasi-military in cut—stood around, several with dogs on leashes.

Dobermans. Massive, straining at their leather straps, barking viciously.

Commands could be heard from the handlers and the dogs subsided.

The man in the white Palm Beach suit opened the door and got out. He walked to the main gatepost, where a guard appeared at the fence from inside the compound. The two men talked briefly; David could see that beyond the guard stood a dark concrete or stucco enclosure, perhaps twenty feet in length, in which there were small windows with light showing through.

The guard returned to the miniature house; the man in the white suit came back to the Packard.

"We will wait a few minutes," he said, climbing into the rear seat.

"I thought we were in a hurry."

"To be here; to let Herr Rhinemann know we have arrived. Not necessarily to be admitted."

"Accommodating fellow," said David.

"Herr Rhinemann can be what he likes."

Ten minutes later the steel-webbed gate swung slowly open and the driver started the engine. The Packard cruised by the gatehouse and the guards; the Dobermans began their rapacious barking once again, only to be silenced by their masters. The road wound uphill, ending in another huge parking area in front of an enormous white mansion with wide marble steps leading to the largest pair of oak doors David had ever seen. Here, too, floodlights covered the whole area. Unlike the outside premises, there was a fountain in the middle of the courtyard, the reflection of the lights bouncing off the spray of the water.

It was as if some extravagant plantation house from the antebellum South had been dismantled stone by stone, board by board, marble block by marble block, and rebuilt deep within an Argentine forest.

An extraordinary sight, and not a little frightening in its massive architectural concept. The construction engineer in David was provoked and stunned at the same time. The materials-logistics must have been staggering; the methods of leveling and transport incredible.

The cost unbelievable.

The German got out of the car and walked around to David's door. He opened it.

"We'll leave you now. It's been a pleasant trip. Go to the door; you'll be admitted. *Auf Wiedersehen.*"

David got out and stood on the hard surface before the marble steps. The green Packard started off down the winding descent.

Spaulding stood alone for nearly a minute. If he was being watched—and the thought crossed his mind—the observer might think he was an astonished caller overwhelmed by the magnificence in front of him. That judgment would have been partially accurate; his remaining concentration, however, was on the mansion's more mundane specifics: the windows, the roof, the grounds on both visible sides.

Ingress and egress were matters to be considered constantly; the unexpected was never to be projected as too unlikely.

He walked up the steps and approached the immense, thick wooden doors. There was no knocker, no bell; he hadn't thought there would be.

He turned and looked down at the floodlit area. Not a person in sight; neither guards nor servants. No one.

Quiet. Even the sounds of the forest seemed subdued. Only the splash of the fountain interrupted the stillness.

Which meant, of course, that there were eyes unseen and whispers unheard, directing their attention on him.

The door opened. Heinrich Stoltz stood in the frame.

"Welcome to Habichtsnest, Herr Spaulding. The Hawk's Lair; appropriately—if theatrically—named, is it not?"

David stepped inside. The foyer, as might be expected, was enormous; a marble staircase rose beyond a chandelier of several thousand crystal cones. The walls were covered with gold cloth; Renaissance paintings were hung beneath silver portrait lamps.

"It's not like any bird's nest I've ever seen."

"True. However, Habichtsnest, I think, loses something in your translation. Come with me, please. Herr Rhinemann is outside on the river balcony. It's a pleasant evening."

They walked underneath the grotesque yet beautiful chandelier, past the marble staircase to an archway at the end of the great hall. It led out to an enormous terrace that stretched the length of the building. There were white wrought-iron tables topped with spotless glass, chairs of varying sizes with brightly colored cushions. A series of large double doors could be seen on both sides of the arch; they presumably led to diverse sections of the huge house.

Bordering the terrace was a stone balustrade, waist high, with statuary and plants on the railing. Beyond the balcony, in the distance, were the waters of the Río Luján. At the left end of the terrace was a small platform, blocked by a gate. Enormously thick wires could be seen above. It was a dock for a cable car, the wires evidently extending down to the river.

David absorbed the splendor, expecting his first view of Rhinemann. There was no one; he walked to the railing and saw that beneath the balcony was another terrace perhaps twenty feet below. A large swimming pool—complete with racing lines in the tile—was illuminated by floodlights under the blue green water. Additional metal tables with sun umbrellas and deck chairs were dotted about the pool and the terrace. And surrounding it all was a manicured lawn that in the various reflections of light looked like the thickest, fullest putting green David had ever seen. Somewhat incongruously, there were the silhouettes of poles and wickets; a croquet course had been imposed on the smooth surface.

"I hope you'll come out one day and enjoy our simple pleasures, Colonel Spaulding."

David was startled by the strange, quiet voice. He turned. The figure of a man stood in shadows alongside the arch of the great hall.

Erich Rhinemann had been watching him, of course.

Rhinemann emerged from the darkened area. He was a moderately tall man with greying straight hair combed rigidly back—partless. He was somewhat stocky for his size—"powerful" would be the descriptive word, but his stomach girth might deny the term. His hands were large, beefy, yet somehow delicate, dwarfing the wineglass held between his fingers.

He came into a sufficient spill of light for David to see his face clearly. Spaulding wasn't sure why, but the face startled him. It was a broad face; a wide forehead above a wide expanse of lip beneath a rather wide, flat nose. He was deeply tanned, his eyebrows nearly white from the sun. And then David realized why he was startled.

Erich Rhinemann was an aging man. The deeply tanned skin was a cover for the myriad lines the years had given him; his eyes were narrow, surrounded by swollen folds of age; the faultlessly tailored sports jacket and trousers were cut for a much, much younger man.

Rhinemann was fighting a battle his wealth could not win for him.

"*Habichtsnest ist prächtig. Unglaublich,*" said David politely but without commensurate enthusiasm.

"You are kind," replied Rhinemann, extending his hand. "And also courteous; but there is no reason not to speak English. . . . Come, sit down. May I offer you a drink?" The financier led the way to the nearest table.

"Thank you, no," said David, sitting across from Rhinemann. "I have urgent business in Buenos Aires. A fact I tried to make clear to Stoltz before he hung up."

Rhinemann looked over at an unperturbed Stoltz, who was leaning against the stone balustrade. "Was that necessary? Herr Spaulding is not to be so treated."

"I'm afraid it *was* necessary, *mein Herr*. For our American friend's own benefit. It was reported to us that he was followed; we were prepared for such an occurrence."

"If I was followed, you were doing the following."

"*After* the fact, colonel; I don't deny it. Before, we had no *reason*."

Rhinemann's narrow eyes pivoted to Spaulding. "This is disturbing. Who would have you followed?"

"May we talk privately?" David said, glancing at Heinrich Stoltz.

The financier smiled. "There's nothing in our arrangements that excludes the *Botschaftssekretär*. He is among my most valued associates in South America. Nothing should be withheld."

"I submit that you won't know unless we speak alone."

"Our American colonel is perhaps embarrassed," interrupted Stoltz, his voice laced with invective. "The man from Lisbon is not considered competent by his own government. He's placed under American surveillance."

David lit a cigarette; he did not reply to the German attaché. Rhinemann spoke, gesturing with his large, delicate hands.

"If this is so, there is no cause for exclusion. And obviously, there can be no other explanation."

"We're buying," said David with quiet emphasis. "You're selling. . . . Stolen property."

Stoltz was about to speak but Rhinemann held up his hand.

"What you are implying is not possible. Our arrangements were made in complete secrecy; they have been totally successful. And Herr Stoltz is a confidant of the High Command. More so than the ambassador."

"I don't like repeating myself." David spoke angrily. "Especially when I'm paying."

"Leave us, Heinrich," said Rhinemann, his eyes on Spaulding.

Stoltz bowed stiffly and walked rapidly, furiously, through the arch into the great hall.

"Thank you." David shifted his position in the chair and looked at up several small balconies on the second and third stories of the house. He wondered how many men were near the windows; watching, prepared to jump if he made a false move.

"We're alone as requested," said the German expatriate, hardly concealing his irritation. "What is it?"

"Stoltz is marked," said Spaulding. He paused to see what kind of reaction the financier would register at such news. As he might have expected, there was none. David continued, thinking perhaps that Rhinemann did not entirely understand. "He's not being given straight information at the embassy. He may do better at ours."

"Preposterous." Rhinemann remained immobile, his narrow eyelids half squinting, staring at David. "On what do you base such an opinion?"

"The Gestapo. Stoltz claims there's no active Gestapo in Buenos Aires. He's wrong. It's here. It's active. It's determined to stop you. Stop us."

Erich Rhinemann's composure cracked—if only infinitesimally. There was the slightest, tiny vibration within the rolls of flesh beneath his eyes, and his stare—if possible, thought David—was harder than before.

"Please clarify."

"I want questions answered first."

"*You want questions . . . ?*" Rhinemann's voice rose, his hand gripped the table; the veins were pronounced at his greying temples. He paused and continued as before. "Forgive me. I'm not used to conditions."

"I'm sure you're not. On the other hand, I'm not used to dealing with a contact like Stoltz who's blind to his own vulnerability. That kind of person annoys me . . . and worries me."

"These questions. What are they?"

"I assume the designs have been gotten out?"

"They have."

"En route?"

"They arrive tonight."

"You're early. Our man won't be here until the day after tomorrow."

"Now it is you who have been given erroneous information, Herr Colonel. The American scientist, Lyons, will be here tomorrow."

David was silent for several moments. He'd used such a ploy on too many others in the past to show surprise.

"He's expected in San Telmo the day *after* tomorrow," David said. "The change is insignificant but that's what Kendall told me."

"Before he boarded the Pan American Clipper. We spoke subsequently."

"Apparently he spoke to a lot of people. Is there a point to the change?"

"Schedules may be slowed or accelerated as the necessities dictate. . . ."

"Or altered to throw someone off balance," interrupted David.

"Such is not the case here. There would be no reason. As you phrased it—most succinctly—we're selling, you're buying."

"And, of course, there's no reason why the Gestapo's in Buenos Aires. . . ."

"May we *return* to that subject, please?" interjected Rhinemann.

"In a moment," answered Spaulding, aware that the German's temper was again stretched. "I need eighteen hours to get my codes to Washington. They have to go by courier, under chemical seal."

"Stoltz told me. You were foolish. The codes should have been sent."

"*Eine Vorsichtsmassnahme, mein Herr,*" said David. "Put plainly, I don't know who's been bought at our embassy but I'm damned sure someone has. Codes have ways of getting sold. The authentic ones will be radioed only when Lyons verifies the designs."

"Then you must move quickly. You fly out your codes in the morning; I will bring the first set of prints to San Telmo tomorrow night. . . . *Eine Vorsichtsmassnahme.* You get the remaining set when you have assured us Washington is prepared to make payment in Switzerland . . . as a result of receiving your established code. You won't leave Argentina until I have word from Berne. There is a small airfield called Mendarro. Near here. My men control it. Your plane will be there."

"Agreed." David crushed out his cigarette. "Tomorrow evening, the first set of prints. The remaining within twenty-four hours. . . . Now we have a schedule. That's all I was interested in."

"*Gut!* And now we will return to this Gestapo business." Rhinemann leaned forward in his chair, the veins in his temples once more causing blue rivulets in his sun-drenched skin. "You said you would clarify!"

Spaulding did.

When he was finished, Erich Rhinemann was breathing deeply, steadily. Within the rolls of flesh, his narrow eyes were furious but controlled.

"Thank you. I'm sure there is an explanation. We'll proceed on schedule. . . . Now, it has been a long and complicated evening. You will be driven back to Córdoba. Good night."

"*Altmüller!*" Rhinemann roared. "An *idiot!* A *fool!*"

"I don't understand," Stoltz said.

"Altmüller. . . ." Rhinemann's voice subsided but the violence remained. He turned to the balcony, addressing the vast darkness and the river below. "In his insane attempts to *disassociate* the High Command from Buenos Aires . . . to *absolve* his precious ministry, he's *caught* by his own *Gestapo!*"

"There is *no Gestapo* in Buenos Aires, Herr Rhinemann," said Stoltz firmly. "The man from Lisbon lies."

Rhinemann turned and looked at the diplomat. His speech was ice. "I know when a man is lying, Herr Stoltz. This Lisbon told the truth; he'd have no reason to do otherwise. . . . So if Altmüller was *not* caught, he's betrayed me. He's sent in the Gestapo; he has no intention of going through with the exchange. He'll take the diamonds and destroy the designs. The Jew-haters have led me into a trap."

"I, myself, am the sole coordinator with Franz Altmüller." Stoltz spoke in his most persuasive tones, nurtured for decades in the Foreign Corps. "You, Herr Rhinemann, arranged for that. You have no cause to question me. The men at the warehouse in Ocho Calle have nearly finished. The Koening diamonds will be authenticated within a day or two; the courier will deliver the designs before the night is over. Everything is as we planned. The exchange will be made."

Rhinemann turned away again. He put his thick yet delicate hands on the railing and looked into the distance. "There is one way to be sure," he said quietly. "Radio Berlin. I want Altmüller in Buenos Aires. There will be no exchange otherwise."

31

The German in the white Palm Beach suit had changed into the paramilitary dress worn by the Rhinemann guards. The driver was not the same one as before. He was Argentine.

The automobile was different, too. It was a Bentley six-seater complete with mahogany dashboard, grey felt upholstery, and window curtains. It was a vehicle suited to the upper-level British diplomatic service, but not so high as to be ambassadorial; just eminently respectable. Another Rhinemann touch, David assumed.

The driver swung the car out onto the dark river highway from the darker confines of the hidden dirt road. He pressed the accelerator to the floor and the Bentley surged. The German beside Spaulding offered him a cigarette; David declined with a shake of his head.

"You say you wish to be driven to the American embassy, *señor?*" said the driver, turning his head slightly, not taking his eyes off the onrushing road. "I'm afraid I cannot do so. Señor Rhinemann's orders were to bring you to the apartment house on Córdoba. Forgive me."

"We may not deviate from instructions," added the German.

"Hope you never do. We win the wars that way."

"The insult is misdirected. I'm completely indifferent."

"I forgot. Habichtsnest is neutral." David ended the conversation by shifting in the seat, crossing his legs and staring in silence out the window. His only thought was to get to the embassy and to Jean. She had used the word "Tortugas."

Again the elusive "Tortugas"!

How could she know? Was it conceivable she was part of it? Part of the unfocused picture?

No.

"Tortugas" isn't worth it. Jean had said those words. She had pleaded.

Leslie Hawkwood had pleaded, too. Leslie had traveled four thousand miles to plead in defiance. Fanatically so.

Get out of Buenos Aires, David!

Was there a connection?

Oh, Christ! he thought. *Was there really a connection?*

"Señores!"

The driver spoke harshly, jolting David's thoughts. The German instantly—instinctively—whipped around in his seat and looked out the rear window. His question was two words.

"How long?"

"Too long for doubt. Have you watched?"

"No."

"I passed three automobiles. Without pattern. Then I slowed down, into the far right lane. He's with us. Moving up."

"We're in the Hill Two district, yes?" asked the German.

"*Sí*. . . . He's coming up rapidly. It's a powerful car; he'll take us on the highway."

"Head up into the Colinas Rojas! Take the next road on the right! Any one!" commanded Rhinemann's lieutenant, taking his pistol from inside his jacket as he spoke.

The Bentley skidded into a sudden turn, swerving diagonally to the right, throwing David and the German into the left section of the back seat. The Argentine gunned the engine, starting up a hill, slamming the gears into first position, reaching maximum speed in seconds. There was a slight leveling off, a connecting, flatter surface before a second hill, and the driver used it to race the motor in a higher gear for speed. The car pitched forward in a burst of acceleration, as if it were a huge bullet.

The second hill was steeper but the initial speed helped. They raced upward; the driver knew his machine, thought David.

"There are the lights!" yelled the German. "They follow!"

"There are flat stretches . . . I think," said the driver, concentrating on the road. "Beyond this section of hills. There are many side roads; we'll try to hide in one. Perhaps they'll pass."

"No." The German was still peering out the rear window. He checked the magazine of his pistol by touch; satisfied, he locked it in place. He then turned from the window and reached under the seat. The Bentley was pitching and vibrating on the uphill, back country road, and the German swore as he worked his hand furiously behind his legs.

Spaulding could hear the snap of metal latches. The German slipped the pistol into his belt and reached down with his free hand. He pulled up a thick-barreled automatic rifle that David recognized as the newest, most powerful front-line weapon the Third Reich had developed. The curved magazine, rapidly inserted by the German, held over forty rounds of .30 caliber ammunition.

Rhinemann's lieutenant spoke. "Reach your flat stretches. Let them close in."

David bolted up; he held onto the leather strap across the rear of the front seat and braced his left hand against the window frame. He spoke to the German harshly.

"Don't use that! You don't know who they are."

The man with the gun glanced briefly at Spaulding, dismissing him with a look. "I know my responsibilities." He reached over to the right of the rear window where there was a small metal ring imbedded in the felt. He inserted his forefinger, pulled it up, and yanked it toward him, revealing an open-air slot about ten inches wide, perhaps four inches high.

David looked at the left of the window. There was another ring, another opening.

Rhinemann's car was prepared for emergencies. Clean shots could be fired at any automobile pursuing it; the sightlines were clear and there was a minimum of awkwardness at high speeds over difficult terrain.

"Suppose it's American surveillance covering *me?*" David shouted as the German knelt on the seat, about to insert the rifle into the opening.

"It's not."

"You don't *know* that!"

"*Señores!*" shouted the driver. "We go down the hill; it's very long, a wide bend. I remember it! Below there are high-grass fields. Flat. . . . Roads. Hold *on!*"

The Bentley suddenly dipped as if it had sped off the edge of a precipice. There was an immediate, sustained thrust of speed so abrupt that the German with the rifle was thrown back, his body suspended for a fraction of a second in midair. He crashed into the front seat support, his weapon held up to break the fall.

David did not—could not—hesitate. He grabbed the rifle, gripping his fingers around the trigger housing, twisting the stock inward and jerking it out of the German's hands. Rhinemann's lieutenant was stunned by Spaulding's action. He reached into his belt for his pistol.

The Bentley was now crashing down the steep incline at an extraordinary speed. The wide bend referred to by the Argentine was reached; the car entered a long, careening pattern that seemed to be sustaining an engineering improbability: propelled by the wheels of a single side, the other off the surface of the ground.

David and the German braced themselves with their backs against opposite sides, their legs taut, their feet dug into the felt carpet.

"Give me that *rifle!*" The German held his pistol on David's chest. David had the rifle stock under his arm, his finger on the trigger, the barrel of the monster weapon leveled at the German's stomach.

"You fire, I fire," he shouted back. "I might come out of it. You won't. You'll be all over the car!"

Spaulding saw that the driver had panicked. The action in the back seat, coupled with the problems of the hill, the speed and the curves created a crisis he was not capable of handling.

"*Señores! Madre de Jesús!* . . . You'll *kill* us!"

The Bentley briefly struck the rocky shoulder of the road; the jolt was staggering. The driver swung back toward the center line. The German spoke.

"You behave stupidly. Those men are after you, not us!"

"I can't be sure of that. I don't kill people on speculation."

"You'll kill us, then? For what purpose?"

"I don't want anyone killed. . . . Now, put down that gun! We both know the odds."

The German hesitated.

There was another jolt; the Bentley had struck a large rock or a fallen limb. It was enough to convince Rhinemann's lieutenant. He placed the pistol on the seat.

The two adversaries braced themselves; David's eyes on the German's hand, the German's on the rifle.

"*Madre de Dios!*" The Argentine's shout conveyed relief, not further panic. Gradually the Bentley was slowing down.

David glanced through the windshield. They were coming out of the hill's curve; in the distance were flat blankets of fields, miniature pampas reflecting the dull moonlight. He reached over and took the German's pistol from the seat. It was an unexpected move; Rhinemann's lieutenant was annoyed with himself.

"Get your breath," said Spaulding to the driver. "Have a cigarette. And get me back to town."

"Colonel!" barked the German. "You may hold the weapons, but there's a car back there! If you won't follow my advice, at least let us get off the road!"

"I haven't the time to waste. I didn't tell him to slow down, just to relax."

The driver entered a level stretch of road and reaccelerated the Bentley. While doing so he took David's advice and lit a cigarette. The car was steady again.

"Sit back," ordered Spaulding, placing himself diagonally in the right corner, one knee on the floor—the rifle held casually, not carelessly.

The Argentine spoke in a frightened monotone. "There are the headlights again. They approach faster than I can drive this car. . . . What would you have me do?"

David considered the options. "Give them a chance to respond. . . . Is there enough moon to see the road? With your lights off?"

"For a while. Not long. I can't remember. . . ."

"Flick them on and off! Twice. . . . Now!"

The driver did as he was instructed. The effect was strange: the sudden darkness, the abrupt illumination—while the Bentley whipped past the tall grass on both sides of the road.

David watched the pursuing vehicle's lights through the rear window. There was no response to the signals. He wondered whether they'd been clear, whether they conveyed his message of accommodation.

"Flick them again," he commanded the driver. "Hold a couple of beats. . . . seconds. Now!"

The clicks were heard from the dashboard; the lights

remained off for three, four seconds. The clicks again; the darkness again.

And then it happened.

There was a burst of gunfire from the automobile in pursuit. The glass of the rear window was shattered; flying, imbedding itself into skin and upholstery. David could feel blood trickling down his cheek; the German screamed in pain, grasping his bleeding left hand.

The Bentley swerved; the driver swung the steering wheel back and forth, zigzagging the car in the road's path.

"There is your *reply!*" roared Rhinemann's lieutenant, his hand bloodied, his eyes a mixture of fury and panic.

Quickly, David handed the rifle to the German. "Use it!"

The German slipped the barrel into the opening; Spaulding sprang up into the seat and reached for the metal ring on the left side of the window, pulled it back and brought the pistol up.

There was another burst from the car behind. It was the volley of a submachine gun, scattershot, heavy caliber; spraying the rear of the Bentley. Bulges appeared throughout the felt top and sides, several bullets shattered the front windshield.

The German began firing the automatic; David aimed as best he could—the swerving, twisting Bentley kept pushing the pursuing car out of sightlines. Still he pulled the trigger, hoping only to spray the oncoming tires.

The roars from the German's weapon were thunderous; repeated crescendos of deafening *booms*, the shock waves of each discharge filling the small, elegant enclosure.

David could see the explosion the instant it happened. The hood of the onrushing automobile was suddenly a mass of smoke and steam.

But still the machine-gun volleys came *out* of the enveloping vapor.

"*Eeaagh!*" the driver screamed. David looked and saw blood flowing out of the man's head; the neck was half shot off. The Argentine's hands sprang back from the wheel.

Spaulding leaped forward, trying to reach the wheel, but he couldn't. The Bentley careened off the road, sideslipping into the tall grass.

The German took his automatic weapon from the opening. He smashed the side window with the barrel of the rifle and slammed in a second magazine as the Bentley came to a sharp, jolting stop in the grass.

The pursuing car—a cloud of smoke and spits of fire—was parallel now on the road. It braked twice, lurched once and locked into position, immobile.

Shots poured from the silhouetted vehicle. The German kicked the Bentley's door open and jumped out into the tall grass. David crouched against the left door, fingers searching for the handle, pushing his weight into the panel so that upon touch, the door would fly open and he could thrust himself into cover.

Suddenly the air was filled with the overpowering thunder of the automatic rifle held steady in a full-firing discharge.

Screams pierced the night; David sprung the door open, and as he leaped out he could see Rhinemann's lieutenant rising in the grass. *Rising* and *walking* through the shots, his finger depressing the automatic's trigger, his whole body shaking, staggering under the impact of the bullets entering his flesh.

He fell.

As he did so a second explosion came from the car on the road.

The gas tank burst from under the trunk, sending fire and metal into the air.

David sprang around the tail of the Bentley, his pistol steady.

The firing stopped. The roar of the flames, the hissing of steam was all there was.

He looked past the Bentley's trunk to the carnage on the road.

Then he recognized the automobile. It was the Duesenberg that had come for Leslie Hawkwood that afternoon.

Two dead bodies could be seen in the rear, rapidly being enveloped by fire. The driver was arched over the seat, his arms limp, his neck immobile, his eyes wide in death.

There was a fourth man, splayed out on the ground by the open right door.

The hand moved! Then the head!

He was alive!

Spaulding raced to the flaming Duesenberg and pulled the half-conscious man away from the wreckage.

He had seen too many men die to mistake the rapid ebbing of life. There was no point in trying to stem death; only to use it.

David crouched by the man. "Who are you? Why did you want to kill me?"

The man's eyes—swimming in their sockets—focused on David. A single headlight flickered from the smoke of the exploded Duesenberg; it was dying, too.

"Who *are* you? Tell me who you are!"

The man would not—or could not—speak. Instead, his lips moved, but not to whisper.

Spaulding bent down further.

The man died trying to spit in David's face. The phlegm and blood intermingled down the man's chin as his head went limp.

In the light of the spreading flames, Spaulding pulled the man's jacket open.

No identification.

Nor in the trousers.

He ripped at the lining in the coat, tore the shirt to the waist.

Then he stopped. Stunned, curious.

There were marks on the dead man's stomach. Wounds but not from bullets. David had seen those marks before.

He could not help himself. He lifted the man by the neck and yanked the coat off the left shoulder, tearing the shirt at the seams to expose the arm.

They were there. Deep in the skin. Never to be erased.

The tattooed numbers of a death camp.

Ein Volk, ein Reich, ein Führer.

The dead man was a Jew.

32

It was nearly five o'clock when Spaulding reached his apartment on Córdoba. He had taken the time to remove what obvious identification he could from the dead Argentine driver and Rhinemann's lieutenant. He found tools in the trunk and unfastened the Bentley's license plates; moved the dials of the dashboard clock forward, then smashed it. If nothing else, these details might slow police procedures—at least a few hours—giving him valuable time before facing Rhinemann.

Rhinemann would demand that confrontation.

And there was too much to learn, to piece together.

He had walked for nearly an hour back over the two hills—the Colinas Rojas—to the river highway. He had removed the fragments of window glass from his face, grateful they were few, the cuts minor. He had carried the awesome automatic rifle far from the scene of death, removed the chamber loading clip and smashed the trigger housing until the weapon was inoperable. Then he threw it into the woods.

A milk truck from the Tigre district picked him up; he told the driver an outrageous story of alcohol and sex—he'd been expertly rolled and had no one to blame but himself.

The driver admired the foreigner's spirit, his acceptance of risk and loss. The ride was made in laughter.

He knew it was pointless, even frivolous, to attempt sleep. There was too much to do. Instead he showered and made a large pot of coffee.

It was time. Daylight came up from the Atlantic. His head was clear; it was time to call Jean.

He told the astonished marine night operator on the

embassy switchboard that Mrs. Cameron expected the call; actually he was late, he'd overslept. Mrs. Cameron had made plans for deep-sea fishing; they were due at La Boca at six.

"Hello? . . . Hello." Jean's voice was at first dazed, then surprised.

"It's David. I haven't time to apologize. I've got to see you right away."

"David? Oh, God! . . ."

"I'll meet you in your office in twenty minutes."

"*Please. . . .*"

"There's no *time!* Twenty minutes. Please, be there. . . . I need you, Jean. *I need you!*"

The OD lieutenant at the embassy gate was cooperative, if disagreeable. He consented to let the inside switchboard ring Mrs. Cameron's office; if she came out and personally vouched for him, the marine would let him pass.

Jean emerged on the front steps. She was vulnerable, lovely. She walked around the driveway path to the gatehouse and saw him. The instant she did so, she stifled a gasp.

He understood.

The styptic pencil could not eradicate the cuts from the half dozen splinters of glass he had removed from his cheeks and forehead. Partially conceal, perhaps; nothing much more than that.

They did not speak as they walked down the corridor. Instead, she held his arm with such force that he shifted to her other side. She had been tugging at the shoulder not yet healed from the Azores crash.

Inside her office she closed the door and rushed into his arms. She was trembling.

"David, I'm *sorry, sorry, sorry*. I was dreadful. I behaved so badly."

He took her shoulders, holding her back very gently. "You were coping with a problem."

"It seems to me I *can't* cope anymore. And I always thought I was so good at it. . . . What happened to your face?" She traced her fingers over his cheek. "It's swollen here."

" 'Tortugas.' " He looked into her eyes. " 'Tortugas' happened."

"Oh, God." She whispered the words and buried her head in his chest. "I'm too disjointed; I can't say what I want to say. Don't. Please, don't . . . let anything more happen."

"Then you'll have to help me."

She pulled back. "*Me?* How can I?"

"Answer my questions. . . . I'll know if you're lying."

"*Lying?* . . . Don't joke. *I* haven't lied to *you.*"

He believed her . . . which didn't make his purpose any easier. Or clearer. "Where did you learn the name 'Tortugas'?"

She removed her arms from around his neck; he released her. She took several steps away from him but she was not retreating.

"I'm not proud of what I did; I've never done it before." She turned and faced him.

"I went down to the 'Caves' . . . without authorization . . . and read your file. I'm sure it's the briefest dossier in the history of the diplomatic corps."

"What did it say?"

She told him.

"So you see, my mythical David of last evening had a distinct basis in reality."

Spaulding walked to the window overlooking the west lawn of the embassy. The early sun was up, the grass flickered with dew; it brought to mind the manicured lawn seen in the night floodlights below Rhinemann's terrace. And that memory reminded him of the codes. He turned. "I have to talk to Ballard."

"Is that all you're going to say?"

"The not-so-mythical David has work to do. That doesn't change."

"I can't change it, you mean."

He walked back to her. "No, you can't. . . . I wish to God you could; I wish *I* could. I can't convince myself—to paraphrase a certain girl—that what I'm doing will make that much difference . . . but I react out of habit, I guess. Maybe ego; maybe it's as simple as that."

"I said you were good, didn't I?"

"Yes. And I am. . . . Do you know *what* I am?"

"An intelligence officer. An agent. A man who works with other men; in whispers and at night and with a great deal of money and lies. That's the way I think, you see."

"Not that. That's new. . . . What I *really* am. . . . I'm a construction engineer. I build buildings and bridges and dams and highways. I once built an extension for a zoo in Mexico; the best open-air enclosure for primates you ever saw. Unfortunately, we spent so much money the Zoological Society couldn't afford monkeys, but the space is there."

She laughed softly. "You're funny."

"I liked working on the bridges best. To cross a natural obstacle without marring it, without destroying its own purpose. . . ."

"I never thought of engineers as romantics."

"*Construction* engineers are. At least, the best ones. . . . But that's all long ago. When this mess is over I'll go back, of course, but I'm not a fool. I know the disadvantages I'll be faced with. . . . It's not the same as a lawyer putting down his books only to pick them up again; the law doesn't change that much. Or a stockbroker; the market solutions *can't* change."

"I'm not sure what you're driving at. . . ."

"Technology. It's the only real, civilized benefit war produces. In construction it's been revolutionary. In three years whole new techniques have been developed. . . . I've been out of it. My postwar references won't be the best."

"Good Lord, you're sorry for yourself."

"Christ, *yes!* In one way. . . . More to the point, I'm angry. Nobody held a gun to my head: I walked into this . . . this job for all the wrong reasons and without any foresight. . . . That's why I have to be good at it."

"What about us? Are we an 'us'?"

"I love you," he said simply. "I know that."

"After only a week? That's what I keep asking myself. We're not children."

"We're not children," he replied. "Children don't have access to State Department dossiers." He smiled, then grew serious. "I need your help."

She glanced at him sharply. "What is it?"

"What do you know about Erich Rhinemann?"

"He's a despicable man."

"He's a Jew."

"Then he's a despicable Jew. Race and religion notwithstanding, immaterial."

"Why is he despicable?"

"Because he uses people. Indiscriminately. Maliciously. He uses his money to corrupt whatever and whomever he can. He buys influence from the junta; that gets him land, government concessions, shipping rights. He forced a number of mining companies out of the Patagonia Basin; he took over a dozen or so oil fields at Comodoro Rivadavia. . . ."

"What are his politics?"

Jean thought for a second; she leaned back in the chair, looking for an instant at the window, then over to Spaulding. "Himself," she answered.

"I've heard he's openly pro-Axis."

"Only because he believed England would fall and terms would be made. He still owns a power base in Germany, I'm told."

"But he's a Jew."

"Temporary handicap. I don't think he's an elder at the synagogue. The Jewish community in Buenos Aires has no use for him."

David stood up. "Maybe that's it."

"What?"

"Rhinemann turned his back on the tribe, openly supports the creators of Auschwitz. Maybe they want him killed. Take out his guards first, then go after him."

"If by 'they' you mean the Jews here, I'd have to say no. The Argentine *judĭos* tread lightly. The colonels' legions are awfully close to a goose step; Rhinemann has influence. Of course, nothing stops a fanatic or two. . . ."

"No. . . . They may be fanatics, but not one or two. They're organized; they've got backing—considerable amounts, I think."

"And they're after Rhinemann? The Jewish community would panic. Frankly, we'd be the first they'd come to."

David stopped his pacing. The words came back to him again: *there'll be no negotiations with Altmüller*. A darkened doorway on New York's Fifty-second Street.

"Have you ever heard the name Altmüller?"

"No. There's a plain Müller at the German embassy, I think, but that's like Smith or Jones. No Altmüller."

"What about Hawkwood? A woman named Leslie Jenner Hawkwood?"

"No again. But if these people are intelligence oriented, there'd be no reason for me to."

"They're Intelligence but I didn't think they were undercover. At least not this Altmüller."

"What does that mean?"

"His name has been used in a context that assumes recognition. But I can't find him."

"Do you want to check the 'Caves'?" she asked.

"Yes. I'll do it directly with Granville. When do they open?"

"Eight thirty. Henderson's in his office by quarter to nine." She saw David hold up his wrist, forgetting he had no watch. She looked at her office clock. "A little over two hours. Remind me to buy you a watch."

"Thanks. . . . Ballard. I have to see him. How is he in the early morning? At this hour?"

"I trust that question's rhetorical. . . . He's used to being roused up for code problems. Shall I call him?"

"Please. Can you make coffee here?"

"There's a hotplate out there." Jean indicated the door to the anteroom. "Behind my secretary's chair. Sink's in the closet. . . . Never mind, I'll do it. Let me get Bobby first."

"I make a fine pot of coffee. You call, I'll cook. You look like such an executive, I'd hate to interfere."

He was emptying the grounds into the pot when he heard it. It was a footstep. A single footstep outside in the corridor. A footstep that should have been muffled but wasn't. A second step would ordinarily follow but didn't.

Spaulding put the pot on the desk, reached down and removed both his shoes without a sound. He crossed to the closed door and stood by the frame.

There it was again. Steps. Quiet; unnatural.

David opened his jacket, checking his weapon, and put his left hand on the knob. He turned it silently, then quickly opened the door and stepped out.

Fifteen feet away a man walking down the corridor spun around at the noise. The look on his face was one Spaulding had seen many times.

Fright.

"Oh, hello there, you must be the new man. We haven't met. . . . The name's Ellis. Bill Ellis. . . . I have a beastly conference at seven." The attaché was not convincing.

"Several of us were going fishing but the weather reports are uncertain. Care to come with us?"

"I'd love to except I have this damned ungodly hour meeting."

"Yes. That's what you said. How about coffee?"

"Thanks, old man. I really should bone up on some paperwork."

"O.K. Sorry."

"Yes, so am I. . . . Well, see you later." The man named Ellis smiled awkwardly, gestured a wave more awkwardly —which David returned—and continued on his way.

Spaulding went back into Jean's office and closed the door. She was standing by the secretary's desk.

"Who in heaven's name were you talking to at this hour?"

"He said his name was Ellis. He said he had a meeting with someone at seven o'clock. . . . He doesn't."

"What?"

"He was lying. What's Ellis's department?"

"Import-export clearances."

"That's handy. . . . What about Ballard?"

"He's on his way. He says you're a mean man. . . . What's 'handy' about Ellis?"

Spaulding went to the coffee pot on the desk, picked it up and started for the closet. Jean interrupted his movement, taking the pot from him. "What's Ellis's rating?" he asked.

"Excellent. Strictly the syndrome; he wants the Court of St. James's. You haven't answered me. What's 'handy'?"

"He's been bought. He's a funnel. It could be serious or just penny-ante waterfront stuff."

"Oh?" Jean, perplexed, opened the closet door where there was a washbasin. Suddenly, she stopped. She turned to Spaulding. "David. What does 'Tortugas' mean?"

"Oh, Christ, stop kidding."

"Which means you can't tell me."

"Which means I don't *know*. I wish to heaven I *did*."

"It's a code word, isn't it? That's what it says in your file."

"It's a code I've never been told about and I'm the one responsible!"

"Here, fill this; rinse it out first." Jean handed him the coffee pot and walked rapidly into her office, to the desk. David followed and stood in the doorway.

"What are you doing?"

"Attachés, even undersecretaries, if they have very early appointments, list them with the gate."

"Ellis?"

Jean nodded and spoke into the telephone; her conversation was brief. She replaced the instrument and looked over at Spaulding. "The first gate pass is listed for nine. Ellis has no meeting at seven thirty."

"I'm not surprised. Why are you?"

"I wanted to make sure. . . . You said you didn't know what 'Tortugas' meant. I might be able to tell you."

David, stunned, took several steps into the office. "*What?*"

"There was a surveillance report from La Boca—that's Ellis's district. His department must have cleared it up, given it a clean bill. It was dropped."

"What was dropped? What are you talking about?"

"A trawler in La Boca. It had cargo with a destination lading that violated coastal patrols . . . they called it an error. The destination was Tortugas."

The outer office door suddenly opened and Bobby Ballard walked in.

"*Jesus!*" he said. "The Munchkins go to work early in this wonderful world of Oz!"

33

The code schedules with Ballard took less than a half hour. David was amazed at the cryptographer's facile imagination. He developed—on the spot—a geometrical progress of numbers and corresponding letters that would take the best cryps Spaulding knew a week to break.

At maximum, all David needed was ninety-six hours.

Bobby placed Washington's copy in an official courier's envelope, sealed it chemically, placed it in a triple-locked pouch and called the FMF base for an officer—captain's rank or above—to get to the embassy within the hour. The codes would be on a coastal pursuit aircraft by nine; at Andrews Field by late afternoon; delivered to General Alan Swanson's office in the War Department by armored courier van shortly thereafter.

The confirmation message was simple; Spaulding had given Ballard two words: *Cable Tortugas.*

When the code was received in Washington, Swanson woud know that Eugene Lyons had authenticated the guidance designs. He could then radio the bank in Switzerland and payment would be made to Rhinemann's accounts. By using the name "Tortugas," David hoped that someone, somewhere, would understand his state of mind. His anger at being left with the full responsibility without all of the facts.

Spaulding was beginning to think that Erich Rhinemann was demanding more than he was entitled to. A possibility that would do him little good.

Rhinemann was to be killed.

And the outlines of a plan were coming into focus that would bring about that necessary death. The act itself might be the simplest part of his assignment.

There was no point in *not* telling Jean and Bobby Ballard about the guidance designs. Kendall had flown out of Buenos Aires—without explanation; David knew he might need assistance at a moment when there was no time to brief those helping him. His cover was superfluous now. He described minutely Rhinemann's schedule, the function of Eugene Lyons and Heinrich Stoltz's surfacing as a contact.

Ballard was astonished at Stoltz's inclusion. "*Stoltz!* That's a little bit of lightning. . . . I mean, he's a *believer.* Not the Hitler fire 'n' brimstone—he dismisses that, I'm told. But *Germany.* The Versailles motive, the reparations —bled giant, export or die—the whole thing. I figured him for the real Junker item. . . ."

David did not pay much attention.

The logistics of the morning were clear in Spaulding's mind and at eight forty-five he began.

His meeting with Henderson Granville was short and cordial. The ambassador was content not to know David's true purpose in Buenos Aires, as long as there was no diplomatic conflict. Spaulding assured him that to the best of his knowledge there was none; certainly less of a possibility if the ambassador remained outside the hard core of the assignment. Granville agreed. On the basis of David's direct request, he had the "Caves" checked for files on Franz Altmüller and Leslie Jenner Hawkwood.

Nothing.

Spaulding went from Granville's office back to Jean's. She had received the incoming passengers manifest from Aeroparque. Eugene Lyons was listed on clipper flight 101, arriving at two in the afternoon. His profession was given as "physicist"; the reason for entry, "industrial conferences."

David was annoyed with Walter Kendall. Or, he thought, should his annoyance be with the bewildered amateur, Brigadier General Alan Swanson? The least they could have done was term Lyons a "scientist"; "physicist" was stupid. A physicist in Buenos Aires was an open invitation to surveillance—even *Allied* surveillance.

He walked back to his own isolated, tiny office. To think.

He decided to meet Lyons himself. Walter Kendall had told him that Lyons's male nurses would settle the mute, sad man in San Telmo. Recalling the two men in question, David had premonitions of disaster. It wasn't beyond Johnny and Hal—those were the names, weren't they?—to deliver Lyons to the steps of the German embassy, thinking it was another hospital.

He would meet Pan Am Clipper 101. And proceed to take the three men on a complicated route to San Telmo.

Once he'd settled Lyons, David estimated that he would have about two, possibly three, hours before Rhinemann—or Stoltz—would make contact. Unless Rhinemann was hunting him now, in panic over the killings in the Colinas Rojas. If so, Spaulding had "built his shelter." His irrefutable alibi. . . . He hadn't been there. He'd been dropped off at Córdoba by two in the morning.

Who could dispute him?

So, he would have two or three hours in midafternoon.

La Boca.

Discreetly, Jean had checked naval surveillance at FMF. The discretion came with her utterly routine, bored telephone call to the chief of operations. She had a "loose end" to tie up for a "dead file"; there was no significance, only a bureaucratic matter—someone was always looking for a good rating on the basis of closing out. Would the lieutenant mind filling in? . . . The trawler erroneously listed for Tortugas was moored by a warehouse complex in Ocho Calle. The error was checked and confirmed by the embassy attaché, Mr. William Ellis, Import-Export Clearance Division.

Ocho Calle.

David would spend an hour or so looking around. It could be a waste of time. What connection would a fishing trawler have with his assignment? There was none that he could see. But there *was* the name "Tortugas"; there *was* an attaché named Ellis who crept silently outside closed doors and lied about nonexistent conferences in the early morning.

Ocho Calle was worth looking into.

Afterward, he would stay by his telephone at Córdoba.

"Are you going to take me to lunch?" asked Jean, walking into his office. "Don't look at your watch; you haven't got one."

Spaulding's hand was in midair, his wrist turned. "I didn't realize it was so late."

"It's not. It's only eleven, but you haven't eaten—probably didn't sleep, either—and you said you were going to the airport shortly after one."

"I was right; you're a corporate executive. Your sense of organization is frightening."

"Nowhere near yours. We'll stop at a jewelry store first. I've already called. You have a present."

"I like presents. Let's go." Spaulding got out of his chair as the telephone rang. He looked down at it. "Do you know that's the first time that thing has made a sound?"

"It's probably for me. I told my secretary I was here. . . . I don't think I really *had* to tell her."

"Hello?" said David into the phone.

"Spaulding?"

David recognized the polished German of Heinrich Stoltz. His tension carried over the wire. "Isn't it a little foolish to call me here?"

"I have no choice. Our mutual friend is in a state of extreme anxiety. Everything is jeopardized."

"What are you talking about?"

"This is no time for foolishness! The situation is grave."

"It's no time for games, either. What the hell are you talking about?"

"Last night! This morning. What happened?"

"What happened where?"

"*Stop it!* You were *there!*"

"Where?"

Stoltz paused; David could hear his breath. The German was in panic, desperately trying to control himself. "The men were killed. We must know what happened!"

"Killed? . . . You're *crazy*. How?"

"I *warn you. . . .*"

"Now *you* cut it out! I'm *buying,* and don't you forget it. . . . I don't want to be mixed up in any organization problems. Those men dropped me off around one thirty. Incidentally, they met your other boys, the ones covering my apartment. And also incidentally, I don't like this round-the-clock surveillance!"

Stoltz was blanked—as David expected he would be. "The others? . . . What others?"

"Get off it! You know perfectly well." Spaulding let the inference hang.

"This is all most disturbing. . . ." Stoltz tried to compose himself.

"I'm sorry," said David noncommittally.

Exasperated, Stoltz interrupted. "I'll call you back."

"Not here. I'll be out most of the afternoon. . . . As a matter of fact," added Spaulding quickly, pleasantly, "I'll be in one of those sailboats our mutual friend looks down upon so majestically. I'm joining some diplomatic friends almost as rich as he is. Call me after five at Córdoba."

David hung up instantly, hearing the beginning of Stoltz's protest. Jean was watching him, fascinated.

"You did that very well," she said.

"I've had more practice than him."

"Stoltz?"

"Yes. Let's go into your office."

"I thought we were going to lunch."

"We are. Couple of things first. . . . There's a rear exit, isn't there?"

"Several. Back gate."

"I want to use an embassy vehicle. Any trouble?"

"No, of course not."

"Your secretary. Could you spare her for a long lunch?"

"You're sweet. I had the insane idea you were taking *me*."

"I am. Could she put her hair up and wear a floppy hat?"

"Any woman can."

"Good. Get that yellow coat you wore last night. And point out any man around here relatively my size. One that your secretary might enjoy that long lunch with. Preferably wearing dark trousers. He'll have my jacket."

"What *are* you *doing?*"

"Our friends are good at playing jokes on other people. Let's see how they take it when one's played on them."

Spaulding watched from the third-floor window, concealed by the full-length drapes. He held the binoculars to his eyes. Below, on the front steps, Jean's secretary—in a wide-brimmed hat and Jean's yellow coat—walked rapidly down to the curb of the driveway. Following her was one of Ballard's assistants, a tall man in dark trousers and David's jacket. Both wore sunglasses. Ballard's man paused momentarily on the top step, looking at an unfolded road map. His face was covered by the awkward mass of paper. He descended the stairs and together he and the girl climbed into the embassy limousine—an upper-level vehicle with curtains.

Spaulding scanned the Avenida Corrientes in front of the gates. As the limousine was passed through, a Mercedes coupe parked on the south side of the street pulled away from the curb and followed it. And then a second automobile on the north side made a cautious U-turn and took up its position several vehicles behind the Mercedes.

Satisfied, David put down the binoculars and went out of the room. In the corridor he turned left and walked swiftly past doors and around staircases toward the rear of the building, until he came to a room that corresponded to his observation post in front. Bobby Ballard sat in an armchair by the window; he turned around at the sound of David's footsteps, binoculars in his hands.

"Anything?" Spaulding asked.

"Two," answered the cryp. "Parked facing opposite directions. They just drove away."

"Same up front. They're in radio contact."

"Thorough, aren't they?"

"Not as much as they think," Spaulding said.

Ballard's sports coat was loose around the midsection and short in the sleeves, but it showed off David's new wristwatch. Jean was pleased about that. It was a very fine chronometer.

The restaurant was small, a virtual hole-in-the-wall on a side street near San Martín. The front was open; a short awning protected the few outside tables from the sun. Their table, however, was inside. Spaulding sat facing the entrance, able to see clearly the passersby on the sidewalk.

But he was not watching them now. He was looking at Jean. And what he saw in her face caused him to say the words without thinking.

"It's going to be over soon. I'm getting out."

She took his hand, searching his eyes. She did not reply for several moments. It was as if she wanted his words suspended, isolated, thought about. "That's a remarkable thing to say. I'm not sure what it means."

"It means I want to spend years and years with you. The

rest of my life. . . . I don't know any other way to put it."

Jean closed her eyes briefly, for the duration of a single breath of silence. "I think you've put it . . . very beautifully."

How could he tell her? How could he explain? He had to try. It was so damned important. "Less than a month ago," he began softly, "something happened in a field. At night, in Spain. By a campfire. . . . *To me.* The circumstances aren't important, but what happened to me was . . . the most frightening thing I could imagine. And it had nothing to do with the calculated risks in my work; nothing to do with being afraid—and I was always afraid, you can bet your life on that. . . . But I suddenly found I had no *feeling.* No feeling at all. I was given a report that should have shaken me up—made me weep, or made me angry, *goddamned angry.* But I didn't feel anything. I was numb. I accepted the news and criticized the man for withholding it. I told him not to make conditions. . . . You see, he *rightfully* thought that I would." David stopped and put his hand over Jean's. "What I'm trying to tell you is that you've given me back something I thought I'd lost. I don't ever want to take the chance of losing it again."

"You'll make me cry," she said quietly, her eyes moist, her lips trembling to a smile. "Don't you know girls cry when things like that are said to them? . . . I'll have to teach you so much. . . . Oh, Lord," she whispered. "Please, *please* . . . years."

David leaned over the small table; their lips touched and as they held lightly together, he removed his hand from hers and gently ran his fingers over the side of her face.

The tears were there.

He felt them, too. They would not come for him, but he *felt* them.

"I'm going back with you, of course," she said.

Her words brought back the reality . . . the other reality, the lesser one. "Not *with* me. But soon. I'm going to need a couple of weeks to settle things. . . . And you'll have to transfer your work down here."

She looked at him questioningly but did not ask a question. "There are . . . special arrangements for you to take back the blueprints or designs or whatever they are."

"Yes."

"When?"

"If everything goes as we expect, in a day or two. At the most, three."

"Then why do you need a couple of weeks?"

He hesitated before answering. And then he realized he wanted to tell her the truth. It was part of the beginning for him. The truth. "There's a breach of security in a place called Fairfax. . . ."

"Fairfax," she interrupted. "That was in your file."

"It's an intelligence center in Virginia. Very classified. A man was killed there. He was a friend of mine. I purposely withheld information that might stop the leaks and, more important, find out who killed him."

"For heaven's sake, why?"

"In a way, I was forced to. The men in Fairfax weren't cleared for the information I had; the one man who was, is ineffectual . . . especially in something like this. He's not Intelligence oriented; he's a requisition general. He buys things."

"Like gyroscopic designs?"

"Yes. When I get back I'll force him to clear the data." David paused and then spoke as much to himself as to Jean. "Actually, I don't give a damn whether he does or not. I've got a long accumulated leave coming to me. I'll use a week or two of it in Fairfax. There's a German agent walking around in that compound with a four-zero rating. He killed a very good man."

"That frightens me."

"It shouldn't." David smiled, answering her with the truth. "I have no intention of risking those years we talked about. If I have to, I'll operate from a maximum security cell. . . . Don't worry."

She nodded. "I won't. I believe you. . . . I'll join you in, say, three weeks. I owe that to Henderson; there *will* be a lot of adjustments for him. Also, I'll have something done about Ellis."

"Don't touch him. We don't *know* anything yet. If we find out he's on an outside payroll he can be valuable right where he is. Reverse conduits are jewels. When we uncover one we make sure he's the healthiest man—or woman—around."

"What kind of a world do you live in?" Jean asked the question with concern, not humor.

"One that you'll help me leave. . . . After Fairfax, I'm finished."

Eugene Lyons edged into the back seat of the taxi between Spaulding and the male nurse named Hal. The other attendant, Johnny, sat in front with the driver. David gave his instructions in Spanish; the driver started out the long, smooth roadway of the Aeroparque.

David looked at Lyons; it wasn't easy to do so. The proximity of the sad, emaciated face emphasized the realization that what he saw was self-inflicted. Lyons's eyes were not responding; he was exhausted from the flight, suspicious of the new surroundings, annoyed by David's aggressive efficiency at hurrying them all out of the terminal.

"It's good to see you again," David told him.

Lyons blinked; Spaulding wasn't sure whether it was a greeting or not.

"We didn't expect you," said Johnny from the front seat. "We expected to get the professor set ourselves."

"We've got it all written down," added Hal, leaning forward on Lyons's right, taking a number of index cards out of his pocket. "Look. The address. Your telephone number. And the embassy's. And a wallet full of Argentine money."

Hal pronounced Argentine, "Argentyne." David wondered how he could be given a course in hypodermic injection; who would read the labels? On the other hand his partner Johnny—less talkative, more knowing somehow—was obviously the leader of the two.

"Well, these things are usually fouled up. Communications break down all the time. . . . Did you have a good flight down, doctor?"

"It wasn't bad," answered Hal. "But bumpy as a son of a bitch over Cuba."

"Those were probably heavy air masses coming up from the island," said David, watching Lyons out of the corner of his eye. The physicist responded now; a slight glance at Spaulding. And there was humor in the look.

"Yeah," replied Hal knowingly, "that's what the stewardess said."

Lyons smiled a thin smile.

David was about to capitalize on the small breakthrough

when he saw a disturbing sight in the driver's rear-view mirror—instinctively he'd been glancing at the glass.

It was the narrow grill of an automobile he'd previously spotted, though with no alarm. He had seen it twice: on the long curb in the taxi lineup and again on the turnout of the front park. Now it was there again, and David slowly shifted his position and looked out the taxi's rear window. Lyons seemed to sense that Spaulding was concerned; he moved to accommodate him.

The car was a 1937 La Salle, black, with rusted chrome on the grillwork and around the headlights. It remained fifty to sixty yards behind, but the driver—a blond-haired man—refused to let other vehicles come between them. He would accelerate each time his position was threatened. The blond-haired man, it appeared, was either inexperienced or careless. If he *was* following them.

David spoke to the taxi driver in urgent but quiet Spanish. He offered the man five dollars over the meter if he would reverse his direction and head away from San Telmo for the next several minutes. The *porteño* was less of an amateur than the driver of the La Salle; he understood immediately, with one look in his mirror. He nodded silently to Spaulding, made a sudden, awkwardly dangerous U-turn, and sped west. He kept the taxi on a fast zigzag course, weaving in and around the traffic, then turned abruptly to his right and accelerated the car south along the ocean drive. The sight of the water reminded David of Ocho Calle.

He wanted very much to deposit Eugene Lyons in San Telmo and get back to Ocho Calle.

The La Salle was no longer a problem.

"Christ!" said Hal. "What the hell was that?" And then he answered his own question. "We were being followed, right?"

"We weren't sure," said David.

Lyons was watching him, his look inexpressive. Johnny spoke from the front seat.

"Does that mean we can expect problems? You had this guy tooling pretty hard. Mr. Kendall didn't mention anything about trouble. . . . Just our job." Johnny did not turn around as he spoke.

"Would it bother you if there were?"

Johnny turned to face Spaulding; he was a very serious

fellow, thought David. "It depends," said the male nurse. "Our job is to watch out for the professor. Take care of him. If any trouble interfered with that, I don't think I'd like it."

"I see. What would you do?"

"Get him the hell out of here," answered Johnny simply.

"Dr. Lyons has a job to do in Buenos Aires. Kendall must have told you that."

Johnny's eyes leveled with Spaulding's. "I'll tell you straight, mister. That dirty pig can go screw. I never took so much shit from anyone in my life."

"Why don't you quit?"

"We don't work for Kendall," said Johnny, as if the thought was repulsive. "We're paid by the Research Center of Meridian Aircraft. That son of a bitch isn't even from Meridian. He's a lousy bookkeeper."

"You understand, Mr. Spaulding," said Hal, retreating from his partner's aggressiveness. "We have to do what's best for the professor. That's what the Research Center hires us for."

"I understand. I'm in constant touch with Meridian Research. The last thing anyone would wish is to harm Dr. Lyons. I can assure you of that." David lied convincingly. He couldn't give assurance because he himself was far from sure. His only course with Johnny and Hal was to turn this newfound liability into an asset. The key would be Meridian's Research Center and his fictional relationship to it; and a common repugnance for Kendall.

The taxi slowed down, turning a corner into a quiet San Telmo street. The driver pulled up to a narrow, three-storied, white stucco house with a sloping, rust-tiled roof. It was 15 Terraza Verde. The first floor was leased to Eugene Lyons and his "assistants."

"Here we are," said Spaulding, opening the door.

Lyons climbed out after David. He stood on the sidewalk and looked up at the quaint, colorful little house on the peaceful street. The trees by the curb were sculptured. Everything had a scrubbed look; there was an Old World serenity about the area. David had the feeling that Lyons had suddenly found something he'd been looking for.

And then he thought he saw what it was. Eugene Lyons was looking up at a lovely resting place. A final resting place. A grave.

34

There wasn't the time David thought there would be. He had told Stoltz to call him after five at Córdoba; it was nearly four now.

The first boats were coming into the piers, whistles blowing, men throwing and catching heavy ropes, nets everywhere, hanging out for the late drying rays of the sun.

Ocho Calle was in the Dársena Norte, east of the Retiro freight yards in a relatively secluded section of La Boca. Railroad tracks, long out of use, were implanted in the streets along the row of warehouses. Ocho Calle was not a prime storage or loading area. Its access to the sea channels wasn't as cumbersome as the inner units of the La Plata, but the facilities were outmoded. It was as if the management couldn't decide whether to sell its fair waterfront real estate or put it into good operating order. The indecision resulted in virtual abandonment.

Spaulding was in shirtsleeves; he had left Ballard's tan jacket at Terraza Verde. Over his shoulder was a large used net he had bought at an outdoor stall. The damn thing was rancid from rotting hemp and dead fish but it served its purpose. He could cover his face at will and move easily, comfortably among his surroundings—at one with them. David thought that should he ever—God forbid!—instruct recruits at Fairfax, he'd stress the factor of comfort. Psychological comfort. One could feel it immediately; just as swiftly as one felt the discomfort of artificiality.

He followed the sidewalk until it was no more. The final block of Ocho Calle was lined on the far side by a few old buildings and fenced-off abandoned lots once used for outside storage, now overgrown with tall weeds. On the water side were two huge warehouses connected to each other by a framed open area. The midships of a trawler could be seen moored between the two buildings. The next pier was across a stretch of water at least a quarter of a mile away. The Ocho Calle warehouses were secluded indeed.

David stopped. The block was like a miniature peninsula; there were few people on it. No side streets, no buildings beyond the row of houses on his left, only what appeared to be other lots behind the houses and further pilings that were sunk into the earth, holding back the water of a small channel.

The last stretch of Ocho Calle *was* a peninsula. The warehouses were not only secluded, they were isolated.

David swung the net off his right shoulder and hoisted it over his left. Two seamen walked out of a building; on the second floor a woman opened a window and shouted down, berating her husband about the projected hour of his return. An old man with dark Indian features sat in a wooden chair on a small, dilapidated stoop in front of a filthy bait store. Inside, through the glass stained with salt and dirt, other old men could be seen drinking from wine bottles. In the last house, a lone whore leaned out a first-floor window, saw David and opened her blouse, displaying a large, sagging breast. She squeezed it several times and pointed the nipple at Spaulding.

Ocho Calle was the end of a particular section of the earth.

He walked up to the old Indian, greeted him casually, and went into the bait store. The stench was overpowering, a combination of urine and rot. There were three men inside, more drunk than sober, nearer seventy than sixty.

The man behind the planked boards which served as a counter seemed startled to see a customer, not really sure what to do. Spaulding took a bill from his pocket—to the astonishment of all three surrounding him—and spoke in Spanish.

"Do you have squid?"

"No. . . . No, no squid. Very little supplies today," answered the owner, his eyes on the bill.

"What have you got?"

"Worms. Dog meat, some cat. Cat is very good."

"Give me a small container."

The man stumbled backward, picked up pieces of intestine and wrapped them in a dirty newspaper. He put it on the plank next to the money. "I have no change, señor. . . ."

"That's all right," replied Spaulding. "This money's for you. And keep the bait."

The man grinned, bewildered. "*Señor?* . . ."

"You keep the money. Understand? . . . Tell me. Who works over there?" David pointed at the barely translucent front window. "In those big dock houses?"

"Hardly anybody. . . . A few men come and go . . . now and then. A fishing boat . . . now and then."

"Have you been inside?"

"Oh yes. Three, four years ago, I work inside. Big business, three, four . . . five years ago. We all work." The other two old men nodded, chattering old men's chatter.

"Not now?"

"No, no. . . . All closed down. Finished. Nobody goes inside now. The owner is a very bad man. Watchmen break heads."

"Watchmen?"

"Oh, yes. With guns. Many guns. Very bad."

"Do automobiles come here?"

"Oh, yes. Now and then. . . . One or two. . . . They don't give us work."

"Thank you. You keep the money. Thank you, again." David crossed to the filthy storefront window, rubbed a small section of the glass and looked out at the block-long stretch of warehouse. It appeared deserted except for the men on the pier. And then he looked closer at those men.

At first he wasn't sure; the glass—though rubbed—still had layers of film on the outside pane; it wasn't clear and the men were moving about, in and out of the small transparent area.

Then he was sure. And suddenly very angry.

The men in the distance on the pier were wearing the same paramilitary clothes the guards at Rhinemann's gate had worn.

They were Rhinemann's men.

The telephone rang at precisely five thirty. The caller was not Stoltz, and because it wasn't, David refused to accept the instructions given him. He hung up and waited less than two minutes for the phone to ring again.

"You are most obstinate," said Erich Rhinemann. "It is we who should be cautious, not you."

"That's a pointless statement. I have no intention of following the directions of someone I don't know. I don't expect airtight controls but that's too loose."

Rhinemann paused. Then he spoke harshly. "What happened last night?"

"I told Stoltz exactly what happened to *me*. I don't know anything else."

"I don't believe you." Rhinemann's voice was tense, sharp, his anger very close to the surface.

"I'm sorry," said David. "But that doesn't really concern me."

"Neither of those men would have left Córdoba! Impossible!"

"They left; take my word for it. . . . Look, I told Stoltz I don't want to get mixed up in your problems. . . ."

"How do you know you're not . . . mixed up?"

It was, of course, the logical question and Spaulding realized that. "Because I'm here in my apartment, talking to you. According to Stoltz, the others are dead; that's a condition I intend to avoid. I'm merely purchasing some papers from you. Let's concentrate on that."

"We'll talk further on this subject," said Rhinemann.

"Not now. We have business to transact."

Again the German Jew paused. "Do as the man told you. Go to the Casa Rosada on the Plaza de Mayo. South gate. If you take a taxi, get off at the Julio and walk."

"Your men will pick me up when I leave the apartment, I assume."

"Discreetly. To see if you're followed."

"Then I'll walk from here. It'll be easier."

"Very intelligent. A car will be waiting for you at the Rosada. The same automobile that brought you here last evening."

"Will you be there?" asked David.

"Of course not. But we'll meet shortly."

"I take the designs straight to Telmo?"

"If everything is clear, you may."

"I'll leave in five minutes. Will your men be ready?"

"They are ready now," answered Rhinemann. He hung up.

David strapped the Beretta to his chest and put on his jacket. He went into the bathroom, grabbed a towel from the rack and rubbed his shoes, removing the Aeroparque and La Boca dirt from the leather. He combed his hair and patted talcum powder over the scratches on his face.

He couldn't help but notice the dark crescents under his eyes. He needed sleep badly, but there was no time. For his own sake—survival, really—he knew he had to take the time.

He wondered when it would be.

He returned to the telephone. He had two calls to make before he left.

The first was to Jean. To ask her to stay in the embassy; he might have reason to call her. At any rate, he would talk to her when he returned. He said he would be with Eugene Lyons at Terraza Verde. And that he loved her.

The second call was to Henderson Granville.

"I told you I wouldn't involve the embassy or yourself in my work here, sir. If that's changed it's only because a man on your staff closed a naval surveillance file improperly. I'm afraid it directly affects me."

"How do you mean 'improperly'? That's a serious implication. If not a chargeable offense."

"Yes, sir. And for that reason it's imperative we raise no alarm, keep everything very quiet. It's an Intelligence matter."

"Who is this man?" asked Granville icily.

"An attaché named Ellis. William Ellis—please don't take *any* action, sir." Spaulding spoke rapidly, emphatically. "He may have been duped; he may *not* have been. Either way we can't have him alerted."

"Very well. I follow you. . . . Then why have you told me . . . if you want no action taken?"

"Not against Ellis, sir. We *do* need a clarification on the surveillance." David described the warehouses on Ocho Calle and the trawler moored between the two buildings.

Granville interrupted quietly. "I remember the report. Naval surveillance. It was a lading destination . . . let me think."

"Tortugas," supplied Spaulding.

"Yes, that was it. Coastal violations. An error, of course. No fishing boat would attempt such a trip. The actual destination was *Torugos*, a small port in northern Uruguay, I think."

David thought for a second. Jean hadn't mentioned the switch—or similarity—of names. "That may be, sir, but it would be advantageous to know the cargo."

"It was listed. Farm machinery, I believe."

"We don't think so," said Spaulding.

"Well, we have no right to inspect cargo. . . ."

"Mr. Ambassador?" David cut off the old gentleman. "Is there anyone in the junta we can trust, *completely* trust?"

Granville's reply was hesitant, cautious; Spaulding understood. "One. Two, perhaps."

"I won't ask you their names, sir. I *will* ask you to request their help. With priority security measures. Those warehouses are guarded . . . by Erich Rhinemann's men."

"*Rhinemann?*" The ambassador's distaste carried over the telephone. That was an asset, thought David.

"We have reason to believe he's aborting a negotiation or tying contraband into it. Smuggling, sir. We have to know what that cargo is." It was all David could think to say. A generalization without actual foundation. But if men were willing to kill and be killed for "Tortugas," perhaps that was foundation enough. If Fairfax could list the name on his transfer orders without telling him—that was *more* than enough.

"I'll do what I can, Spaulding. I can't promise anything, of course."

"Yes, sir. I realize. And thank you."

The Avenida de Mayo was jammed with traffic, the Plaza worse. At the end of the square the pinkish stone of Casa Rosada reflected the orange flood of the setting sun. Befitting a capital controlled by soldiers, thought David.

He crossed the Plaza, stopping at the fountain, recalling yesterday and Leslie Jenner Hawkwood. Where was she now? In Buenos Aires; but where? And more important, why?

The answer might lie in the name "Tortugas" and a trawler in Ocho Calle.

He circled the fountain twice, then reversed his steps once, testing himself, testing Erich Rhinemann. Where were the men watching him? Or were they women?

Were they in cars or taxis or small trucks? Circling as he was circling?

He spotted one. It wasn't hard to do. The man had seated himself on the edge of the fountain's pool, the tail of his jacket in the water. He'd sat down too quickly, trying to be inconspicuous.

David started across the pedestrian walk—the same pedestrian walk he'd used following Leslie Hawkwood—and at the first traffic island waited for a change of light. Instead of crossing, however, he walked back to the fountain. He stepped up his pace and sat down at the pool's edge and watched the crosswalk.

The man with the wet jacket emerged with the next contingent of pedestrians and looked anxiously around. Finally he saw Spaulding.

David waved.

The man turned and raced back across the street.

Spaulding ran after him, just making the light. The man did not look back; he seemed hell-bent to reach a contact, thought David; to have someone take over, perhaps. The man turned left at the Casa Rosada and Spaulding followed, keeping himself out of sight.

The man reached a corner and to David's surprise he slowed down, then stopped and entered a telephone booth.

It was a curiously amateurish thing to do, mused Spaulding. And it told him something about Erich Rhinemann's personnel: they weren't as good as they thought they were.

There was a long blasting of a horn that seemed louder than the normally jarring sounds of the Mayo's traffic. The single horn triggered other horns and in a few seconds a cacophony of strident honking filled the streets. David looked over. It was nothing; an irritated motorist had momentarily reached the end of his patience. Everything returned to normal chaos with the starting up of the automobiles at the crosswalk.

And then there was a scream. A woman's scream. And another; and still another.

A crowd gathered around the telephone booth.

David pushed his way through, yanking arms, pulling shoulders, shoving. He reached the edge of the booth and looked inside.

The man with the wet jacket was slumped awkwardly to the floor of the tiny glass enclosure, his legs buckled under him, his arms stretched above, one hand still gripping the telephone receiver so that the wire was taut. His head was sprung back from his neck. Blood was streaming down the back of his skull. Spaulding looked up at the walls of the booth. On the street side were three distinct holes surrounded by cracked glass.

He heard the piercing sounds of police whistles and pushed his way back through the crowd. He reached the iron fence that surrounded the Casa Rosada, turned right and started rapidly around the building to the south side.

To the south gate.

The Packard was parked in front of the entrance, its motor running. A man about his size approached him as David started for the automobile.

"Colonel Spaulding?"

"Yes?"

"If you'll hurry, please?" The man opened the back door and David climbed in quickly.

Heinrich Stoltz greeted him. "You've had a long walk. Sit. The ride will be relaxing."

"Not now." David pointed to the panels below the front dashboard. "Can you reach Rhinemann on that thing? Right away?"

"We're in constant contact. Why?"

"Get him. Your man was just killed."

"Our man?"

"The one following me. He was shot in a telephone booth."

"He wasn't our man, colonel. And *we* shot him," said Stoltz calmly.

"*What?*"

"The man was known to us. He was a hired killer out of Rio de Janeiro. You were his target."

Stoltz's explanation was succinct. They'd picked up the killer within moments after David left his apartment house. He was a Corsican, deported out of Marseilles before the war; a gun for the Unio Corso who had murdered one prefect too many under orders from the *contrabandistes* of southern France.

"We couldn't take a chance with the American who possesses the codes. A silencer in heavy traffic you'll agree is adequate."

"I don't think he was trying to kill me," said Spaulding. "I think you moved too soon."

"Then he was waiting for you to meet with *us*. Forgive me, but we couldn't permit that. You agree?"

"No. I could have taken him." David sat back and brought his hand to his forehead, tired and annoyed. "I was *going* to take him. Now we both lose."

Stoltz looked at David. He spoke cautiously; a question. "The same? You wonder also."

"Don't you? . . . You still think the Gestapo's not in Buenos Aires?"

"*Impossible!*" Stoltz whispered the word intensely through his teeth.

"That's what our mutual friend said about your men last night. . . . I don't know a goddamned thing about that, but I understand they're dead. So what's impossible?"

"The Gestapo *can't* be involved. We've learned that at the highest levels."

"Rhinemann's Jewish, isn't he?" David watched Stoltz as he asked the unexpected question.

The German turned and looked at Spaulding. There was a hint of embarrassment in his expression. "He practices no religion; his mother was Jewish. . . . Frankly, it's not pertinent. The racial theories of Rosenberg and Hitler are not shared unequivocally; far too much emphasis has been placed upon them. . . . It is—was—primarily an economic question. Distribution of banking controls, decentralization of financial hierarchies. . . . An unpleasant topic."

David was about to reply to the diplomat's evasions when he stopped himself. . . . Why did Stoltz find it necessary even to attempt a rationalization? To offer a weak explanation he himself knew was devoid of logic?

Heinrich Stoltz's loyalty was supposedly to Rhinemann, not the Third Reich.

Spaulding looked away and said nothing. He was, frankly, confused, but it was no time to betray that confusion. Stoltz continued.

"It's a curious question. Why did you bring it up?"

"A rumor. . . . I heard it at the embassy." And that was the truth, thought David. "I gathered that the Jewish community in Buenos Aires was hostile to Rhinemann."

"Mere speculation. The Jews here are like Jews elsewhere. They keep to themselves, have little to do with those outside. Perhaps the ghetto is less definable, but it's there. They have no argument with Rhinemann; there's no contact, really."

"Cross off one speculation," said Spaulding.

"There's another," said Stoltz. "Your own countrymen."

David turned slowly back to the German. "This is a good game. How did you arrive at that?"

"The purchase of the designs is being made by one aircraft corporation. There are five, six major companies in competition for your unending government contracts. Whoever possesses the gyroscope designs will have a powerful—I might even say irresistible—lever. All other guidance systems will be obsolete."

"Are you serious?"

"Most assuredly. We have discussed the situation at length . . . in depth. We are nearly convinced that this is the logical answer." Stoltz looked away from David and stared to the front. "There's no other. Those trying to stop us are American."

35

The green Packard made crisscross patterns over the Buenos Aires streets. The route was programmed aimlessness, and Spaulding recognized it for what it was: an extremely thorough surveillance check. Intermittently, the driver would pick up the microphone from beneath the dashboard and recite a prearranged series of numbers. The crackling response over the single speaker would repeat the numbers and the Packard would make yet another—seemingly aimless—turn.

Several times David spotted the corresponding vehicles making the visual checks. Rhinemann had a minimum of five automobiles involved. After three-quarters of an hour, it was certain beyond doubt that the trip to San Telmo was clean.

The driver spoke to Stoltz.

"We are clear. The others will take up their positions."

"Proceed," said Stoltz.

They swung northwest; the Packard accelerated toward San Telmo. David knew that at least three other cars were behind them; perhaps two in front. Rhinemann had set up his own transport column, and that meant the gyroscopic designs were in one of the automobiles.

"Have you got the merchandise?" he asked Stoltz.

"Part of it," replied the attaché, leaning forward, pressing a section of the felt backing in front of him. A latch sprung; Stoltz reached down and pulled out a tray from beneath the seat. Inside the concealed drawer was a thin metal box not unlike the containers used in libraries to protect rare manuscripts from possible loss by fire. The German picked it up, held it in his lap and pushed the drawer back with his foot. "We'll be there in a few minutes," he said.

The Packard pulled up to the curb in front of the white stucco house in San Telmo. Spaulding reached for the door handle but Stoltz touched his arm and shook his head. David withdrew his hand; he understood.

About fifty yards ahead, one of the checkpoint automobiles had parked and two men got out. One carried a thin metal container, the other an oblong leather case—a radio. They walked back toward the Packard.

David didn't have to look out the rear window to know what was happening behind him, but to confirm his thoughts he did so. Another automobile had parked. Two additional men were coming up the sidewalk; one, of course, carrying a container, the second, a leather-encased radio.

The four men met by the door of the Packard. Stoltz nodded to Spaulding; he got out of the car and walked around the vehicle, joining Rhinemann's contingent. He was about to start up the short path to the front entrance when Stoltz spoke through the automobile window.

"Please wait. Our men are not yet in position. They'll tell us."

Static could be heard over the radio beneath the Packard's dashboard. There followed a recitation of numbers; the driver picked up his microphone and repeated them.

Heinrich Stoltz nodded and got out of the car. David started toward the door.

Inside, two of Rhinemann's men remained in the hallway; two walked through the apartment to the kitchen and a rear door that opened onto a small, terraced back yard. Stoltz accompanied David into the living room where Eugene Lyons was seated at a large dining table. The table was cleared except for two note pads with a half dozen pencils.

The male nurses, Johnny and Hal, accepted Spaulding's terse commands. They stood at opposite ends of the room in front of a couch, in shirtsleeves, their pistols strapped in shoulder holsters emphasized by the white cloth of their shirts.

Stoltz had relieved one man of his metal case and told David to take the other. Together, Stoltz and Spaulding placed the three containers on the large table, and Stoltz unlocked them. Lyons made no effort to greet his visitors—his intruders—and only the most perfunctory salutation came from Stoltz. It was apparent that Kendall had described the scientist's afflictions; the German diplomat conducted himself accordingly.

Stoltz spoke from across the table to the seated Lyons. "From your left, the designs are in order of sequence. We have prepared bilingual keys attached to each of the schematics, and wherever processes are described, they have been translated verbatim, utilizing English counterpart formulae or internationally recognized symbols, and often both. . . . Not far from here, and easily contacted by our automobile radio, is an aeronautical physicist from Peenemünde. He is available for consultation at your request. . . . Finally, you understand that no photographs may be taken."

Eugene Lyons picked up a pencil and wrote on a pad. He tore off the page and handed it to Spaulding. It read:

How long do I have? Are these complete?

David handed the note to Stoltz, who replied.

"As long as you need, *Herr Doktor*. . . . There is one last container. It will be brought to you later."

"Within twenty-four hours," interrupted Spaulding. "I insist on that."

"When we receive confirmation that the codes have arrived in Washington."

"That message is undoubtedly at the embassy now." David looked at his watch. "I'm sure it is."

"If you say it, I believe it," said Stoltz. "It would be pointless to lie. You won't leave Argentina until *we* have received word from . . . Switzerland."

Spaulding couldn't define why but there was something questioning about the German's statement; a questioning that didn't belong with such a pronouncement. David began to think that Stoltz was far more nervous than he wanted anyone to realize. "I'll confirm the codes when we leave. . . . By the way, I also insist the designs remain here. Just as Doctor Lyons has checked them."

"We anticipated your . . . request. You Americans are so mistrustful. Two of our men will also remain. Others will be outside."

"That's a waste of manpower. What good is three-fourths of the merchandise?"

"Three-fourths better than you have," answered the German.

The next two and a half hours were marked by the scratches of Lyons's pencil; the incessant static of the radios from the hallway and the kitchen, over which came the incessant, irritating recitation of numbers; the pacing of Heinrich Stoltz—his eyes constantly riveting on the pages of notes taken by an exhausted Lyons, making sure the scientist did not try to pocket or hide them; the yawns of the male nurse, Hal; the silent, hostile stares of his partner, Johnny.

At ten thirty-five, Lyons rose from the chair. He placed the pile of notes to his left and wrote on a pad, tearing off the page and handing it to Spaulding.

So far—authentic. I have no questions.

David handed the note to an anxious Stoltz.

"Good," said the German. "Now, colonel, please explain to the doctor's companions that it will be necessary for us to relieve them of their weapons. They will be returned, of course."

David spoke to Johnny. "It's all right. Put them on the table."

"It's all right by who-says?" said Johnny, leaning against the wall, making no move to comply.

"I do," answered Spaulding. "Nothing will happen."

"These fuckers are Nazis! You want to put us in blindfolds, too?"

"They're German. Not Nazis."

"Horseshit!" Johnny pushed himself off the wall and stood erect. "I don't like the way they talk."

"Listen to me." David approached him. "A great many people have risked their lives to bring this thing off. For different reasons. You may not like them any more than I do, but we can't louse it up now. Please, do as I ask you."

Johnny stared angrily at Spaulding. "I hope to Christ you know what you're doing. . . ." He and his partner put down their guns.

"Thank you, gentlemen," said Stoltz, walking into the hallway. He spoke quietly in German to the two guards. The man with the radio walked rapidly through the sitting room into the kitchen; the other picked up the two weapons, placing one in his belt, the second in his jacket pocket. He then returned to the hallway without speaking.

Spaulding went to the table, joined by Stoltz. Lyons had replaced the designs in the manila envelopes; there were three. "I'd hate to think of the money our mutual friend is getting for these," said David.

"You wouldn't pay it if they weren't worth it."

"I suppose not. . . . No reason not to put them in one case. Along with the notes." Spaulding looked over at Lyons, who stood immobile at the end of the table. "Is that all right, doctor?"

Lyons nodded, his sad eyes half closed, his pallor accentuated.

"As you wish," said Stoltz. Picking up the envelopes and the notes, he put them in the first container, locked it, closed the other two and placed them on top of the first, as if he were performing a religious exercise in front of an altar.

Spaulding took several steps toward the two men by the window. "You've had a rough day. Doctor Lyons, too. Turn in and let your guests walk guard duty; I think they're on overtime."

Hal grinned. Johnny did not.

"Good evening, doctor. It's been a privilege meeting such a distinguished man of science." Across the room, Stoltz spoke in diplomatic tones, bowing a slight diplomatic bow.

The guard with the radio emerged from the kitchen and nodded to the German attaché. They left the room together. Spaulding smiled at Lyons; the scientist turned without acknowledging and walked into his bedroom to the right of the kitchen door.

Outside on the sidewalk, Stoltz held the car door for David. "A very strange man, your Doctor Lyons," he said as Spaulding got into the Packard.

"He may be, but he's one of the best in his field. . . . Ask your driver to stop at a pay phone. I'll check the embassy's radio room. You'll get your confirmation."

"Excellent idea. . . . Then, perhaps, you'll join me for dinner?"

David looked at the attaché who sat so confidently, so half-mockingly, beside him. Stoltz's nervousness had disappeared. "No, Herr Botschaftssekretär. I have another engagement."

"With the lovely Mrs. Cameron, no doubt. I defer."

Spaulding did not reply. Instead, he looked out the window in silence.

The Terraza Verde was peaceful. The streetlamps cast a soft glow on the quiet, darkened sidewalks; the sculptured trees in front of the picturesque Mediterranean houses were silhouetted against pastel-colored brick and stone. In windows beyond flower boxes, the yellow lamps of living rooms and bedrooms shone invitingly. A man in a business suit, a newspaper under his arm, walked up the steps to a door, taking a key from his pocket; a young couple were laughing quietly, leaning against a low wrought-iron fence. A little girl with a light brown cocker spaniel on a leash was skipping along the sidewalk, the dog jumping happily out of step.

Terraza Verde was a lovely place to live.

And David thought briefly of another block he'd seen that day. With old men who smelled of rot and urine; with a toothless whore who leaned on a filthy sill. With cat intestines and dirt-filmed windows. And with two huge warehouses that provided no work, and a trawler at anchor, recently destined for Tortugas.

The Packard turned the corner into another street. There were a few more lights, less sculptured trees, but the street was very much like Terraza Verde. It reminded David of those offshoot streets in Lisbon that approached the rich *caminos;* dotted with expensive shops, convenient for wealthy inhabitants a few hundred yards away.

There were shops here, too; with windows subtly lit, wares tastefully displayed.

Another block; the Packard slowed down at the intersecting street and then started across. More shops, less trees, more dogs—these often walked by maids. A group of teenagers were crowded around an Italian sportscar.

And then David saw the overcoat. It was just an overcoat at first; a light grey overcoat in a doorway.

A grey overcoat. A recessed doorway.

The man was tall and thin. A tall, thin man in a light grey overcoat. In a doorway!

My God! thought David. *The man on Fifty-second Street!*

The man was turned sideways, looking down into a dimly lit store window. Spaulding could not see them but he could picture the dark, hollow eyes; could hear the bastardized English out of somewhere in the Balkans; sense the desperation in the man's eyes:

There are to be no negotiations with Franz Altmüller. . . . Heed the lesson of Fairfax!

He had to get out of the Packard. Quickly!

He had to go back to Terraza Verde. Without Stoltz. He *had* to!

"There's a café in the next block," said Spaulding, pointing to an orange canopy with lights underneath, stretching across the sidewalk. "Stop there. I'll call the embassy."

"You seem anxious, colonel. It can wait. I believe you."

Spaulding turned to the German. "You want me to spell it out? O.K., I'll do that. . . . I don't like you, Stoltz. And I don't like Rhinemann; I don't like men who yell and bark orders and have me followed. . . . I'm buying from you, but I don't have to associate with you. I don't have to have dinner or ride in your automobile once our business for the day is over. Do I make myself clear?"

"You're clear. Though somewhat uncivilized. And ungrateful, if you don't mind my saying so. We saved your life earlier this evening."

"That's your opinion. Not mine. Just let me off, I'll telephone and come out with your confirmation. . . . As you said, there's no point in my lying. You go on your way, I'll grab a taxi."

Stoltz instructed the driver to pull up at the orange canopy. "Do as you please. And should your plans include Doctor Lyons, be advised we have men stationed about the area. Their orders are harsh. Those designs will stay where they are."

"I'm not paying for three-quarters of the merchandise regardless of what there is back home. And I have no intention of walking into that phalanx of robots."

The Packard drew up to the canopy. Spaulding opened the door quickly, slamming it angrily behind him. He walked swiftly into the lighted entrance and asked for the telephone.

"The ambassador has been trying to reach you for the past half-hour or so," said the night operator. "He says it's urgent. I'm to give you a telephone number." The operator drawled out the digits.

"Thank you," David said. "Now connect me with Mr. Ballard in Communications, please."

"O'Leary's Saloon," came the uninterested voice of Bobby Ballard over the wire.

"You're a funny man. I'll laugh next Tuesday."

"The 'switch' said it was you. You know Granville's trying to find you."

"I heard. Where's Jean?"

"In her room; pining away just like you ordered."

"Did you get word from D.C.?"

"All wrapped. Came in a couple of hours ago; your codes are cleared. How's the erector set?"

"The instructions—three-quarters of them—are in the box. But there are too many playmates."

"Terraza Verde?"

"Around there."

"Shall I send out a few FMF playground attendants?"

"I think I'd feel better," said Spaulding. "Tell them to cruise. Nothing else. I'll spot them and yell if I need them."

"It'll take a half-hour from the base."

"Thanks. No parades, please, Bobby."

"They'll be so quiet no one'll know but us Munchkins. Take care of yourself."

Spaulding held down the receiver with his finger, tempted to lift it, insert another coin and call Granville. . . . There wasn't time. He left the booth and walked out the restaurant door to the Packard. Stoltz was at the window; David saw that a trace of his previous nervousness had returned.

"You've got your confirmation. Deliver the rest of the goods and enjoy your money. . . . I don't know where you come from, Stoltz, but I'll find out and have it bombed off the map. I'll tell the Eighth Air Force to name the raid after you."

Stoltz seemed relieved at David's surliness—as David thought he might be. "The man from Lisbon is complicated. I suppose that's proper for a complicated assignment. . . . We'll call you by noon." Stoltz turned to the driver. "*Los, abfahren, machen Sie schnell!*"

The green Packard roared off down the street. Spaulding

waited under the canopy to see if it made any turns; should it do so, he would return to the cafe and wait.

It did not; it maintained a straight course. David watched until the taillights were infinitesimal red dots. Then he turned and walked as fast as he could without calling attention to himself toward Terraza Verde.

He reached the short block in which he'd seen the man in the light grey overcoat and stopped. His concerns made him want to rush on; his instincts forced him to wait, to look, to move cautiously.

The man was not on the block now; he was nowhere to be seen. David reversed his direction and walked to the end of the sidewalk. He turned left and raced down the street to the next corner, turning left again, now slowing down, walking casually. He wished to God he knew the area better, knew the buildings behind Lyons's white stucco house. Others did; others were positioned in dark recesses he knew nothing about.

Rhinemann's guards. The man in the light grey overcoat; how many more were with *him?*

He approached the intersection of Terraza Verde and crossed the road diagonally, away from the white stucco house. He stayed out of the spill of the lamps as best he could and continued down the pavement to the street behind the row of houses on Terraza Verde. It was, of course, a block lined with other houses; quaint, picturesque, quiet. Spaulding looked up at the vertical sign: *Terraza Amarilla.*

San Telmo fed upon itself.

He remained at the far end of the corner under a sculptured tree and looked toward the section of the adjacent street where he judged the rear of Lyons's house to be. He could barely make out the sloping tiled roof, but enough to pinpoint the building behind it—about 150 yards away.

He also saw Rhinemann's automobile, one of those he'd spotted during the long, security-conscious drive from the Casa Rosada. It was parked opposite a light-bricked Italian townhouse with large gates on both sides. David assumed those gates opened to stone paths leading to a wall or a fence separating Lyons's back terrace from the rear entrance of the townhouse. It had to be something like that; Rhinemann's guards were posted so that anyone emerging from those gates was equally in their sightlines.

And then Spaulding remembered the crackling static of the radios from the hallway and the kitchen and the incessant repetition of the German numbers. Those who carried the radios had weapons. He reached beneath his jacket to his holster and took out the Beretta. He knew the clip was filled; he unlatched the safety, shoved the weapon into his belt and started across the street toward the automobile.

Before he reached the opposite corner, he heard a car drive up behind him. He had no time to run, no moment to make a decision—good or bad. His hand went to his belt; he tried to assume a posture of indifference.

He heard the voice and was stunned.

"Get in, you goddamned *fool!*"

Leslie Hawkwood was behind the wheel of a small Renault coupe. She had reached over and unlatched the door. David caught it, his attention split between his shock and his concern that Rhinemann's guard—or guards—a hundred yards away might hear the noise. There were fewer than a dozen pedestrians within the two-block area. Rhinemann's men *had* to have been alerted.

He jumped into the Renault and with his left hand he grabbed Leslie's right leg above the knee, his grip a restraining vise, pressing on the nerve lines. He spoke softly but with unmistakable intensity.

"You back this car up as quietly as you can, and turn left down that street."

"Let *go!* Let . . ."

"Do as I say or I'll break your kneecap off!"

The Renault was short; there was no need to use the reverse gear. Leslie spun the wheel and the car veered into a sharp turn.

"Slowly!" commanded Spaulding, his eyes on Rhinemann's car. He could see a head turn—two heads. And then they were out of sight.

David took his hand off the girl's leg; she pulled it up and doubled her shoulders down in agony. Spaulding grabbed the wheel and forced the gears into neutral. The car came to a stop halfway down the block, at the curb.

"You bastard! You broke my leg!" Leslie's eyes were filled with tears of pain, not sorrow. She was close to fury but she did not shout. And that told David something about Leslie he had not known before.

"I'll break more than a leg if you don't start telling me

what you're doing here! How many others are there? I saw one; how many more?"

She snapped her head up, her long hair whipping back, her eyes defiant. "Did you think we couldn't find him?"

"Who?"

"Your *scientist*. This Lyons! We found him!"

"Leslie, for Christ's sake, what are you *doing?*"

"Stopping you!"

"*Me?*"

"You. Altmüller, Rhinemann. Koening! Those pigs in Washington. . . . Peenemünde! It's all over. They won't trust you anymore. 'Tortugas' is finished!"

The faceless name—Altmüller again. Tortugas. . . . Koening? Words, names . . . meaning and no meaning. The tunnels had no light.

There was no *time!*

Spaulding reached over and pulled the girl toward him. He clutched the hair above her forehead, yanking it taut, and with his other hand he circled his fingers high up under her throat, just below the jawbone. He applied pressure in swift, harsh spurts, each worse than the last.

So much, so alien.

"You want to play this game, you play it out! Now tell me! What's *happening? Now?*"

She tried to squirm, lashing out her arms, kicking at him; but each time she moved he ripped his fingers into her throat. Her eyes widened until the sockets were round. He spoke again.

"Say it, Leslie! I'll have to kill you if you don't. I don't have a choice! Not now. . . . For Christ's sake, don't *force* me!"

She slumped; her body went limp but not unconscious. Her head moved up and down; she sobbed deep-throated moans. He released her and gently held her face. She opened her eyes.

"Don't touch me! Oh, *God*, don't touch me!" She could barely whisper, much less scream. "Inside. . . . We're going inside. Kill the scientist; kill Rhinemann's men. . . ."

Before she finished, Spaulding clenched his fist and hammered a short, hard blow into the side of her chin. She slumped, unconscious.

He'd heard enough. There *was* no time.

He stretched her out in the small front seat, removing

the ignition keys as he did so. He looked for her purse; she had none. He opened the door, closed it firmly and looked up and down the street. There were two couples halfway down the block; a car was parking at the corner; a window was opened on the second floor of a building across the way, music coming from within.

Except for these—nothing. San Telmo was at peace.

Spaulding ran to within yards of Terraza Amarilla. He stopped and edged his way along an iron fence that bordered the corner, swearing at the spill of the streetlamp. He looked through the black grillwork at Rhinemann's car less than a hundred yards away. He tried to focus on the front seat, on the two heads he'd seen moving minutes ago. There was no movement now, no glow of cigarettes, no shifting of shoulders.

Nothing.

Yet there was a break in the silhouette of the left window frame; an obstruction that filled the lower section of the glass.

David rounded the sharp angle of the iron fence and walked slowly toward the automobile, his hand clamped on the Beretta, his finger steady over the trigger. *Seventy yards, sixty, forty-five.*

The obstruction did not move.

Thirty-five, thirty . . . he pulled the pistol from his belt, prepared to fire.

Nothing.

He saw it clearly now. The obstruction was a head, sprung back into the glass—not resting, but wrenched, twisted from the neck; immobile.

Dead.

He raced across the street to the rear of the car and crouched, his Beretta level with his shoulders. There was no noise, no rustling from within.

The block was deserted now. The only sounds were the muffled, blurred hums from a hundred lighted windows. A latch could be heard far down the street; a small dog barked; the wail of an infant was discernible in the distance.

David rose and looked through the automobile's rear window.

He saw the figure of a second man sprawled over the felt top of the front seat. The light of the streetlamps illuminated the upper part of the man's back and shoulders. The whole area was a mass of blood and slashed cloth.

Spaulding slipped around the side of the car to the front right door. The window was open, the sight within sickening. The man behind the wheel had been shot through the side of his head, his companion knifed repeatedly.

The oblong, leather-cased radio was smashed, lying on the floor beneath the dashboard.

It had to have happened within the past five or six minutes, thought David. Leslie Hawkwood had rushed down the street in the Renault to intercept him—at the precise moment men with silenced pistols and long-bladed knives were heading for Rhinemann's guards.

The killings complete, the men with knives and pistols must have raced across the street into the gates toward Lyons's house. Raced without thought of cover or camouflage, knowing the radios were in constant contact with those inside 15 Terraza Verde.

Spaulding opened the car door, rolled up the window, and pulled the lifeless form off the top of the seat. He closed the door; the bodies were visible, but less so than before. It was no moment for alarms in the street if it could be avoided.

He looked over at the gates across the way on each side of the townhouse. The left one was slightly ajar.

He ran over to it and eased himself through the opening, touching nothing, his gun thrust laterally at his side, aiming forward. Beyond the gate was a cement passageway that stretched the length of the building to some sort of miniature patio bordered by a high brick wall.

He walked silently, rapidly to the end of the open alley; the patio was a combination of slate paths, plots of grass and small flower gardens. Alabaster statuary shone in the moonlight; vines crawled up the brick wall.

He judged the height of the wall: seven feet, perhaps seven and a half. Thickness: eight, ten inches—standard. Construction: new, within several years, strong. It was the construction with which he was most concerned. In 1942 he took a nine-foot wall in San Sebastián that collapsed under him. A month later it was amusing; at the time it nearly killed him.

He replaced the Beretta in his shoulder holster, locking the safety, shoving in the weapon securely. He bent down and rubbed his hands in the dry dirt at the edge of the cement, absorbing whatever sweat was on them. He stood up and raced toward the brick wall.

Spaulding leaped. Once on top of the wall, he held—silent, prone; his hands gripping the sides, his body motionless—a part of the stone. He remained immobile, his face toward Lyons's terrace, and waited several seconds. The back door to Lyons's flat was closed—no lights were on in the kitchen; the shades were drawn over the windows throughout the floor. No sounds from within.

He slid down from the wall, removed his gun and ran to the side of the kitchen door, pressing his back against the white stucco. To his astonishment he saw that the door was *not* closed; and then he saw why. At the base, barely visible in the darkness of the room beyond, was a section of a hand. It had gripped the bottom of the doorframe and been smashed into the saddle; the fingers were the fingers of a dead man.

Spaulding reached over and pressed the door. An inch. Two inches. Wood against dead weight; his elbow ached from the pressure.

Three, four, five inches. A foot.

Indistinguishable voices could be heard now; faint, male, excited.

He stepped swiftly in front of the door and pushed violently—as quietly as possible—against the fallen body that acted as a huge, soft, dead weight against the frame. He stepped over the corpse of Rhinemann's guard, noting that the oblong radio had been torn from its leather case, smashed on the floor. He closed the door silently.

The voices came from the sitting room. He edged his way against the wall, the Beretta poised, unlatched, ready to fire.

An open pantry against the opposite side of the room caught his eye. The single window, made of mass-produced stained glass, was high in the west wall, creating eerie shafts of colored light from the moon. Below, on the floor, was Rhinemann's second guard. The method of death he could not tell; the body was arched backward—probably a bullet from a small-caliber pistol had killed him. A pistol with a silencer attached. It would be very quiet. David felt the perspiration rolling down his forehead and over his neck.

How many were there? They'd immobilized a garrison. He had no commitment matching those odds.

Yet he had a strange commitment to Lyons. He had commitment enough for him at the moment. He dared not think beyond that instant.

And he was good; he could—should—never forget that. He was the best there was.

If it was important to anyone.

So much, so alien.

He pressed his cheek against the molding of the arch and what he saw sickened him. The revulsion, perhaps, was increased by the surroundings: a well-appointed flat with chairs and couches and tables meant for civilized people involved with civilized pursuits.

Not death.

The two male nurses—the hostile Johnny, the affable, dense Hal—were sprawled across the floor, their arms linked, their heads inches from each other. Their combined blood had formed a pool on the parquet surface. Johnny's eyes were wide, angry—dead; Hal's face composed, questioning, at rest.

Behind them were Rhinemann's two other guards, their bodies on the couch like slaughtered cattle.

I hope you know what you're doing!

Johnny's words vibrated painfully—in screams—in David's brain.

There were three other men in the room—standing, alive, in the same grotesque stocking masks that had been worn by those in the Duesenberg who had cut short the few moments he'd had alone with Leslie Hawkwood high in the hills of Luján.

The Duesenberg that had exploded in fire in the hills of Colinas Rojas.

The men were standing—none held weapons—over the spent figure of Eugene Lyons—seated gracefully, without fear, at the table. The look in the scientist's eyes told the truth, as Spaulding saw it: he welcomed death.

"You see what's around you!" The man in the light grey overcoat spoke to him. "We will not hesitate further! You're dead! . . . Give us the designs!"

Jesus Christ! thought David. Lyons had hidden the plans!

"There's no point in carrying on, please believe me," continued the man in the overcoat, the man with the hollow crescents under his eyes Spaulding remembered so well. "You may be spared, but only if you tell us! *Now!*"

Lyons did not move; he looked up at the man in the overcoat without shifting his head, his eyes calm. They touched David's.

"Write it!" said the man in the light grey overcoat.

It was the moment to move.

David spun around the molding, his pistol leveled.

"Don't reach for guns! *You!*" he yelled at the man nearest him. "Turn around!"

In shock, without thinking, the man obeyed. Spaulding took two steps forward and brought the barrel of the Beretta crashing down into the man's skull. He collapsed instantly.

David shouted at the man next to the interrogator in the grey overcoat. "Pick up that chair! *Now!*" He gestured with his pistol to a straight-backed chair several feet from the table. "*Now*, I said!"

The man reached over and did as he was told; he was immobilized. Spaulding continued. "You drop it and I'll kill you. . . . Doctor Lyons. Take their weapons. You'll find pistols and knives. Quickly, please."

It all happened so fast. David knew his only hope of avoiding gunfire was in the swiftness of the action, the rapid immobilization of one or two men, an instant reversal of the odds.

Lyons got out of the chair and went first to the man in the light grey overcoat. It was apparent that the scientist had observed where the man had put his pistol. He took it out of the overcoat pocket. He went to the man holding the chair and removed an identical gun, then searched the man and took a large knife from his jacket and a second, short revolver from a shoulder holster. He placed the weapons on the far side of the table and walked to the unconscious third man. He rolled him over and removed two guns and a switchblade knife.

"Take off your coats. *Now!*" Spaulding commanded both men. He took the chair from the one next to him and pushed him toward his companion. The men began removing their coats when Spaulding suddenly spoke, before either had completed their actions. "Stop right there! Hold it! . . . Doctor, please bring over two chairs and place them behind them."

Lyons did so.

"Sit down," said Spaulding to his captives.

They sat, coats half off their shoulders. David approached them and yanked the garments further—down to the elbows.

The two men in the grotesque stocking masks were seated now, their arms locked by their own clothes.

Standing in front of them, Spaulding reached down and ripped the silk masks off their faces. He moved back and leaned against the dining table, his pistol in his hand.

"All right," he said. "I estimate we've got about fifteen minutes before all hell breaks loose around here. . . . I have a few questions. You're going to give me the answers."

36

Spaulding listened in disbelief. The enormity of the charge was so far-reaching it was—in a very real sense—beyond his comprehension.

The man with the hollow eyes was Asher Feld, commander of the Provisional Wing of the Haganah operating within the United States. He did the talking.

"The operation . . . the exchange of the guidance designs for the industrial diamonds . . . was first given the name 'Tortugas' by the Americans—one American, to be exact. He had decided that the transfer should be made in the Dry Tortugas, but it was patently rejected by Berlin. It was, however, kept as a code name by this man. The misleading association dovetailed with his own panic at being involved. It came—for him and for Fairfax—to mean the activities of the man from Lisbon.

"When the War Department clearances were issued to the Koening company's New York offices—an Allied requisite—this man coded the clearance as 'Tortugas.' If anyone checked, 'Tortugas' was a Fairfax operation. It would not be questioned.

"The concept of the negotiation was first created by the Nachrichtendienst. I'm sure you've heard of the Nachrichtendienst, colonel. . . ."

David did not reply. He could not speak. Feld continued.

"We of the Haganah learned of it in Geneva. We had word of an unusual meeting between an American named Kendall—a financial analyst for a major aircraft company—and a very despised German businessman, a homosexual, who was sent to Switzerland by a leading administrator in the Ministry of Armaments, Unterstaatssekretär

Franz Altmüller. . . . The Haganah is everywhere, colonel, including the outer offices of the ministry and in the Luftwaffe. . . ."

David continued to stare at the Jew, so matter of fact in his extraordinary . . . unbelievable . . . narrative.

"I think you'll agree that such a meeting was unusual. It was not difficult to maneuver these two messengers into a situation that gave us a wire recording. It was in an out-of-the-way restaurant and they were amateurs.

"We then knew the basics. The materials and the general location. But not the specific point of transfer. And that was the all-important factor. Buenos Aires is enormous, its harbor more so—stretching for miles. Where in this vast area of land and mountains and water was the transfer to take place?

"Then, of course, came word from Fairfax. The man in Lisbon was being recalled. A most unusual action. But then how well thought out. The finest network specialist in Europe, fluent German and Spanish, an expert in blueprint designs. How logical. Don't you agree?"

David started to speak, but stopped. Things were being said that triggered flashes of lightning in his mind. And unbelievable cracks of thunder . . . as unbelievable as the words he was hearing. He could only nod his head. Numbly.

Feld watched him closely. Then spoke.

"In New York I explained to you, albeit briefly, the sabotage at the airfield in Terceira. Zealots. The fact that the man in Lisbon could turn and be a part of the exchange was too much for the hot-tempered Spanish Jews. No one was more relieved than we of the Provisional Wing when you escaped. We assumed your stopover in New York was for the purposes of refining the logistics in Buenos Aires. We proceeded on that assumption.

"Then quite abruptly there was no more time. Reports out of Johannesburg—unforgivably delayed—said that the diamonds had arrived in Buenos Aires. We took the necessary violent measures, including an attempt to kill you. Prevented, I presume, by Rhinemann's men." Asher Feld stopped. Then added wearily, "The rest you know."

No! The rest he did not know! Nor any other part!

Insanity!

Madness!

Everything was nothing! Nothing was everything!

The years! The lives! . . . The terrible nightmares of fear . . . the killing! Oh, my God, the killing!

For what?! . . . Oh, my God! For what?!

"You're *lying!*" David crashed his hand down on the table. The steel of the pistol cracked against the wood with such force the vibration filled the room. "You're *lying!*" he cried; he did not shout. "I'm in Buenos Aires to buy gyroscopic designs! To have them authenticated! Confirmed by code so that son of a bitch gets paid in Switzerland! That's *all. Nothing else! Nothing else at all! Not this!*"

"Yes. . . ." Asher Feld spoke softly. "It is this."

David whirled around at nothing. He stretched his neck; the crashing thunder in his head would not stop, the blinding flashes of light in front of his eyes were causing a terrible pain. He saw the bodies on the floor, the blood . . . the corpses on the sofa, the blood.

Tableau of death.

Death.

His whole shadow world had been ripped out of orbit. A thousand gambles . . . pains, manipulations, death. And more death . . . all faded into a meaningless void. The betrayal—if it was a betrayal—was so immense . . . hundreds of thousands had been sacrificed for absolutely nothing.

He had to stop. He had to think. To concentrate.

He looked at the painfully gaunt Eugene Lyons, his face a sheet of white.

The man's dying, thought Spaulding.

Death.

He had to concentrate.

Oh, Christ! He had to *think.* Start *somewhere. Think.*

Concentrate.

Or he would go out of his mind.

He turned to Feld. The Jew's eyes were compassionate. They might have been something else, but they were not. They were compassionate.

And yet, they were the eyes of a man who killed in calm deliberation.

As he, the man in Lisbon, had killed.

Execution.

For what?

There were questions. *Concentrate on the questions.*

Listen. Find error. *Find error*—if ever error was needed in this world it was *now!*

"I don't believe you," said David, trying as he had never tried in his life to be convincing.

"I think you do," replied Feld quietly. "The girl, Leslie Hawkwood, told us you didn't know. A judgment we found difficult to accept. . . . I accept it now."

David had to think for a moment. He did not, at first, recognize the name. *Leslie Hawkwood.* And then, of course, he did instantly. Painfully. "How is she involved with you?" he asked numbly.

"Herold Goldsmith is her uncle. By marriage, of course; she's not Jewish."

"Goldsmith? The name . . . doesn't mean anything to me." . . . *Concentrate!* He had to concentrate and speak rationally.

"It does to thousands of Jews. He's the man behind the Baruch and Lehman negotiations. He's done more to get our people out of the camps than any man in America. . . . He refused to have anything to do with us until the civilized, compassionate men in Washington, London and the Vatican turned their backs on him. Then he came to us . . . in fury. He created a hurricane; his niece was swept up in it. She's overly dramatic, perhaps, but committed, effective. She moves in circles barred to the Jew."

"*Why?*" . . . *Listen!* For God's sake, *listen.* Be *rational. Concentrate!*

Asher Feld paused for a moment, his dark, hollow eyes clouded with quiet hatred. "She met dozens . . . hundreds, perhaps, of those Herold Goldsmith got out. She saw the photographs, heard the stories. It was enough. She was ready."

The calm was beginning to return to David. Leslie was the springboard he needed to come back from the madness. There were questions. . . .

"I can't reject the premise that Rhinemann bought the designs. . . ."

"Oh, come!" interrupted Feld. "You were the man in Lisbon. How often did your own agents—your best men—find Peenemünde invulnerable. Has not the German underground itself given up penetration?"

"No one ever gives up. On either side. The German

underground is *part* of this!" *That was the error,* thought David.

"If that were so," said Feld, gesturing his head toward the dead Germans on the couch, "then those men were members of the underground. You know the Haganah, Lisbon. We don't kill such men."

Spaulding stared at the quiet-spoken Jew and knew he told the truth.

"The other evening," said Spaulding quickly, "on Paraná. I was followed, beaten up . . . but I saw the IDs. They were Gestapo!"

"They were Haganah," replied Feld. "The Gestapo is our best cover. If they had been Gestapo that would presume knowledge of your function. . . . Would they have let you live?"

Spaulding started to object. The Gestapo would not risk killing in a neutral country; not with identification on their persons. Then he realized the absurdity of his logic. Buenos Aires was not Lisbon. Of course, they would kill him. And then he recalled the words of Heinrich Stoltz.

We've checked at the highest levels . . . not the Gestapo . . . impossible. . . .

And the strangely inappropriate apologia: *the racial theories of Rosenberg and Hitler are not shared . . . primarily an economic . . .*

A defense of the indefensible offered by a man whose loyalty was purportedly *not* to the Third Reich but to *Erich Rhinemann.* A Jew.

Finally, Bobby Ballard:

. . . he's a believer . . . the real Junker item. . . .

"Oh, my God," said David under his breath.

"You have the advantage, colonel. What is your choice? We're prepared to die; I say this in no sense heroically, merely as a fact."

Spaulding stood motionless. He spoke softly, incredulously. "Do you understand the implications? . . ."

"We've understood them," interrupted Feld, "since that day in Geneva your Walter Kendall met with Johann Dietricht."

David reacted as though slapped. "Johann . . . *Dietricht?*"

"The expendable heir of Dietricht Fabriken."

"J.D.," whispered Spaulding, remembering the crumpled yellow pages in Walter Kendall's New York office. The breasts, the testicles, the swastikas . . . the obscene, nervous scribblings of an obscene, nervous man. "Johann Dietricht . . . *J.D.*"

"Altmüller had him killed. In a way that precluded any . . ."

"*Why?*" asked David.

"To remove any connection with the Ministry of Armaments, is our thought; any association with the High Command. Dietricht initiated the negotiations to the point where they could be shifted to Buenos Aires. To Rhinemann. With Dietricht's death the High Command was one more step removed."

The items raced through David's mind: Kendall had fled Buenos Aires in panic; something had gone wrong. The accountant would not allow himself to be trapped, to be killed. And he, David, was to kill—or have killed—Erich Rhinemann. Second to the designs, Rhinemann's death was termed paramount. And with his death, Washington, too, was "one more step removed" from the exchange.

Yet there was Edmund Pace.

Edmund *Pace.*

Never.

"A man was killed," said David. "A Colonel Pace. . . ."

"In Fairfax," completed Asher Feld. "A necessary death. He was being used as you are being used. We deal in pragmatics. . . . Without knowing the consequences—or refusing to admit them to himself—Colonel Pace was engineering 'Tortugas.' "

"You could have *told* him. Not kill him! You could have stopped it! You *bastards!*"

Asher Feld sighed. "I'm afraid you don't understand the hysteria among your industrialists. Or those of the Reich. He would have been eliminated. . . . By removing him ourselves, we neutralized Fairfax. And all its considerable facilities."

There was no point in dwelling on the *necessity* of Pace's death, thought David. Feld, the pragmatist, was right: Fairfax had been removed from "Tortugas."

"Then Fairfax doesn't know."

"Our man does. But not enough."

"Who is he? Who's your man in Fairfax?"

Feld gestured to his silent companion. "He doesn't know and I won't tell you. You may kill me but I won't tell you."

Spaulding knew the dark-eyed Jew spoke the truth. "If Pace was used . . . and me. Who's using us?"

"I can't answer that."

"You know this much. You must have . . . thoughts. Tell me."

"Whoever gives you orders, I imagine."

"One man. . . ."

"We know. He's not very good, is he? There are others."

"*Who? Where does it stop?* State? The War Department? *The White House? Where,* for Christ's sake!?"

"Such territories have no meaning in these transactions. They vanish."

"*Men don't!* Men don't vanish!"

"Then look for those who dealt with Koening. In South Africa. Kendall's men. They created 'Tortugas.'" Asher Feld's voice grew stronger. "That's your affair, Colonel Spaulding. We only wish to stop it. We'll gladly *die* to stop it."

David looked at the thin-faced, sad-faced man. "It means that much? With what you know, what you believe? Is either side worth it?"

"One must have priorities. Even in lessening descent. If Peenemünde is saved . . . put back on schedule . . . the Reich has a bargaining power that is unacceptable to us. Look to Dachau; look to Auschwitz, to Belsen. Unacceptable."

David walked around the table and stood in front of the Jews. He put his Beretta in his shoulder holster and looked at Asher Feld.

"If you've lied to me, I'll kill you. And then I'll go back to Lisbon, into the north country, and wipe out every Haganah fanatic in the hills. Those I don't kill, I'll expose. . . . Put on your coats and get out of here. Take a room at the Alvear under the name of . . . Pace. *E. Pace.* I'll be in touch."

"Our weapons?" asked Feld, pulling his light grey overcoat over his shoulders.

"I'll keep them. I'm sure you can afford others. . . . And don't wait for us outside. There's an FMF vehicle cruising for me."

"What about 'Tortugas'?" Asher Feld was pleading.

"I said I'll be in touch!" shouted Spaulding. "Now, get out of here! . . . Pick up the Hawkwood girl; she's around the corner in the Renault. Here are the keys." David reached in his pocket and threw the keys to Asher Feld's companion, who caught them effortlessly. "Send her back to California. Tonight, if you can. No later than tomorrow morning. Is that clear?"

"Yes. . . . You *will* be in touch?"

"Get out of here," said Spaulding in exhaustion.

The two Haganah agents rose from their chairs, the younger going to the unconscious third man and lifting him off the floor, onto his shoulders. Asher Feld stood in the front hallway and turned, his gaze resting momentarily on the dead bodies, then over to Spaulding.

"You and I. We must deal in priorities. . . . The man from Lisbon is an extraordinary man." He turned to the door and held it open as his companion carried out the third man. He went outside, closing the door behind him.

David turned to Lyons. "Get the designs."

37

When the assault on 15 Terraza Verde had begun, Eugene Lyons had done a remarkable thing. It was so simple it had a certain cleanliness to it, thought Spaulding. He had taken the metal container with the designs, opened his bedroom window and dropped the case five feet below into the row of tiger lilies that grew along the side of the house. The window shut, he had then run into his bathroom and locked the door.

All things considered—the shock, the panic, his own acknowledged incapacities—he had taken the least expected action: he had kept his head. He had removed the container, not tried to conceal it; he had transferred it to an *accessible* place, and that was not to be anticipated by the fanatic men who dealt in complicated tactics and convoluted deceits.

David followed Lyons out of the house through the kitchen door and around to the side. He took the container from the physicist's trembling hands and helped the near-helpless man over the small fence separating the adjacent property. Together they ran behind the next two houses and cautiously edged their way toward the street. Spaulding kept his left hand extended, gripping Lyon's shoulder, holding him against the wall, prepared to throw him to the ground at the first hint of hostilities.

Yet David was not really expecting hostilities; he was convinced the Haganah had eliminated whatever Rhinemann guards were posted in front, for the obvious reason that Asher Feld had left by the front door. What he did think was possible was a last-extremity attempt by Asher Feld to get the designs. Or the sudden emergence of a Rhinemann vehicle from some near location—a vehicle whose occupants were unable to raise a radio signal from 15 Terraza Verde.

Each possible; neither really expected.

It was too late and too soon.

What David profoundly hoped he would find, however, was a blue green sedan cruising slowly around the streets. A car with small orange insignias on the bumpers that designated the vehicle as U.S. property. Ballard's "playground attendants"; the men from the FMF base.

It wasn't cruising. It was stationary, on the far side of the street, its parking lights on. Three men inside were smoking cigarettes, the glows illuminating the interior. He turned to Lyons.

"Let's go. Walk slowly, casually. The car's over there."

The driver and the man next to him got out of the automobile the moment Spaulding and Lyons reached the curb. They stood awkwardly by the hood, dressed in civilian clothes. David crossed the street, addressing them.

"Get in that goddamned car and get us out of here! And while you're at it, why don't you paint bull's-eyes all over the vehicle? You wouldn't be any more of a target than you are now!"

"Take it easy, buddy," replied the driver. "We just got here." He opened the rear door as Spaulding helped Lyons inside.

"You were supposed to be cruising, not parked like watchdogs!" David climbed in beside Lyons; the man at the far window squeezed over. The driver got behind the wheel, closed his door and started the engine. The third man remained outside. "Get him in here!" barked Spaulding.

"He'll remain where he is, colonel," said the man in the back seat next to Lyons. "He stays here."

"Who the hell are you?"

"Colonel Daniel Meehan, Fleet Marine Force, Naval Intelligence. And we want to know what the fuck's going on."

The car started up.

"You have no control over this exercise," said David slowly, deliberately. "And I don't have time for bruised egos. Get us to the embassy, please."

"Screw egos! We'd like a little simple clarification! You know what the hell is going on down in our section of town? This side trip to Telmo's just a minor inconvenience! I wouldn't be here except your goddamned name was mentioned by that smart-ass cryp! . . . *Jesus!*"

Spaulding leaned forward on the seat, staring at Meehan. "You'd better tell me what's going on in your section of town. And why my name gets you to Telmo."

The marine returned the look, glancing once—with obvious distaste—at the ashen Lyons. "Why not? Your friend cleared?"

"He is now. No one more so."

"We have three cruisers patrolling the Buenos Aires coastal zone plus a destroyer and a carrier somewhere out there. . . . Five hours ago we get a blue alert: prepare for a radio-radar blackout, all sea and aircraft to hold to, no movement. Forty-five minutes later there's a scrambler from Fairfax, source four-zero. Intercept one Colonel David Spaulding, also four-zero. He's to make contact pronto."

"With Fairfax?"

"*Only* with Fairfax. . . . So we send a man to your address on Córdoba. He doesn't find you but he *does* find a weird son of a bitch tearing up your place. He tries to take him and gets laid out. . . . He gets back to us a couple of hours later with creases in his head and guess who calls? Right on an open-line telephone!"

"Ballard," answered David quietly. "The embassy cryp."

"The smart-ass! He makes jokes and tells us to play games out at Telmo! Wait for you to decide to show." The marine colonel shook his head in disgust.

"You said the blue alert was preparation for radar silence . . . and radio."

"And all ships and planes immobilized," interrupted Meehan. "What the hell's coming *in* here? The whole goddamned General *Staff? Roosevelt? Churchill? Rin-tin-tin?* And what are *we?* The *enemy!*"

"It's not what's coming in, colonel," said David softly. "It's what's going out. . . . What's the time of activation?"

"It's damn loose. Anytime during the next forty-eight hours. How's that for a tight schedule?"

"Who's my contact in Virginia?"

"Oh. . . . Here." Meehan shifted in his seat, proffering a sealed yellow envelope that was the mark of a scrambled message. David reached across Lyons and took it.

There was the crackling static of a radio from the front seat followed by the single word "Redbird!" out of the speaker. The driver quickly picked up the dashboard microphone.

"Redbird acknowledge," said the marine.

The static continued but the words were clear. "The Spaulding intercept. Pick him up and bring him in. Four-zero orders from Fairfax. No contact with the embassy."

"You heard the man," laughed Meehan. "No embassy tonight, colonel."

David was stunned. He started to object—angrily, furiously; then he stopped. . . . Fairfax. No Nazi, but Haganah. Asher Feld had said it. The Provisional Wing dealt in practicalities. And the most practical objective during the next forty-eight hours was to immobilize the man with the codes. Washington would not activate a radio-radar blackout without them; and an enemy submarine surfacing to rendezvous with a trawler would be picked up on the screens and blown out of the water. The Koening diamonds—the Peenemünde tools—would be sent to the bottom of the South Atlantic.

Christ! The *irony*, thought David. Fairfax—*someone* at Fairfax—was doing precisely what *should* be done, motivated by concerns Washington—and the aircraft companies—refused to acknowledge! It—they—had other concerns: three-quarters of them were at Spaulding's feet. High-altitude gyroscopic designs.

David pressed his arm into Lyons's shoulder. The emaciated scientist continued to stare straight ahead but responded to Spaulding's touch with a hesitant nudge of his left elbow.

David shook his head and sighed audibly. He held up the yellow envelope and shrugged, placing it into his jacket pocket.

When his hand emerged it held a gun.

"I'm afraid I can't accept those orders, Colonel Meehan." Spaulding pointed the automatic at the marine's head; Lyons leaned back into the seat.

"What the hell are you doing!?" Meehan jerked forward; David clicked the firing pin of the weapon into hair-release.

"Tell your man to drive where I say. I don't want to kill you, colonel, but I will. It's a matter of priorities."

"You're a goddamned double agent! That's what Fairfax was onto!"

David sighed. "I wish it were that simple."

Lyons's hands trembled as he tightened the knots around Meehan's wrists. The driver was a mile down the dirt road, bound securely, lying in the border of the tall grass. The area was rarely traveled at night. They were in the hills of Colinas Rojas.

Lyons stepped back and nodded to Spaulding.

"Get in the car."

Lyons nodded again and started toward the automobile. Meehan rolled over and looked up at David.

"You're dead, Spaulding. You got a firing squad on your duty sheet. You're stupid, too. Your Nazi friends are going to lose this war!"

"They'd better," answered David. "As to executions, there may be a number of them. Right in Washington. That's what this is all about, colonel. . . . Someone'll find you both tomorrow. If you like, you can start inching your way west. Your driver's a mile or so down the road. . . . I'm sorry."

Spaulding gave Meehan a half-felt shrug of apology and ran to the FMF automobile. Lyons sat in the front seat and when the door light spilled over his face, David saw his eyes. Was it possible that in that look there was an attempt to communicate a sense of gratitude? Or approval? There wasn't time to speculate, so David smiled gently and spoke quietly.

"This has been terrible for you, I know. . . . But I can't think what else to do. I don't know. If you like, I'll get you back to the embassy. You'll be safe there."

David started the car and drove up a steep incline—one of many—in the Colinas Rojas. He would double back on a parallel road and reach the highway within ten or fifteen minutes; he would take Lyons to an outskirts taxi and give the driver instructions to deliver the physicist to the American embassy. It wasn't really what he wanted to do; but what else was there?

Then the words came from beside him. *Words!* Whispered, muffled, barely audible but clear! From the recesses of a tortured throat.

"I . . . stay with . . . you. Together. . . ."

Spaulding had to grip the wheel harshly for fear of losing control. The shock of the pained speech—and it *was* a speech for Eugene Lyons—had nearly caused him to drop his hands. He turned and looked at the scientist. In the flashing shadows he saw Lyons return his stare; the lips were set firmly, the eyes steady. Lyons knew exactly what he was doing; what they both were doing—*had* to do.

"All right," said David, trying to remain calm and precise. "I read you clearly. God knows I need all the help I can get. We both do. It strikes me we've got two powerful enemies. Berlin *and* Washington."

"I don't want any interruptions, Stoltz!" David yelled into the mouthpiece of the telephone in the small booth near Ocho Calle. Lyons was now behind the wheel of the FMF car ten yards away on the street. The motor was running. The scientist hadn't driven in twelve years but with half-words and gestures he convinced Spaulding he would be capable in an emergency.

"You can't behave this way!" was the panicked reply.

"I'm Pavlov, you're the dog! Now shut up and listen! There's a mess in Terraza Verde, if you don't know it by now. Your men are dead; so are mine. I've got the designs *and* Lyons. . . . Your nonexistent Gestapo are carrying out a number of executions!"

"*Impossible!*" screamed Stoltz.

"Tell that to the corpses, you incompetent son of a bitch! While you clean up that mess! . . . I want the rest of those designs, Stoltz. Wait for my call!" David slammed down the receiver and bolted out of the booth to the car. It was time for the radio. After that the envelope from Fairfax. Then Ballard at the embassy. One step at a time.

Spaulding opened the door and slid into the seat beside Lyons. The physicist pointed to the dashboard.

"Again . . ." was the single, painful word.

"Good," said Spaulding. "They're anxious. They'll listen hard." David snapped the panel switch and lifted the microphone out of its cradle. He pressed his fingers against the tiny wire speaker with such pressure that the mesh was bent; he covered the instrument with his hand and held it against his jacket as he spoke, moving it in circles so as to further distort the sound.

"Redbird to base . . . Redbird to base."

The static began, the voice angry. "Christ, Redbird! We've been trying to raise you for damn near two hours! That Ballard keeps calling! Where the hell are you!?"

"Redbird. . . . Didn't you get our last transmission?"

"*Transmission?* Shit, man! I can hardly hear this one. Hold on; let me get the CO."

"Forget it! No sweat. You're fading here again. We're on Spaulding. We're following him; he's in a vehicle . . . twenty-seven, *twenty-eight miles north.* . . ." David abruptly stopped talking.

"Redbird! Redbird! . . . Christ, this frequency's puke! . . . Twenty-eight miles north *where?* . . . I'm not reading you, Redbird! Redbird, acknowledge!"

". . . bird, acknowledge," said David directly into the microphone. "This radio needs maintenance, pal. Repeat. No problems. Will *return to base in approximately.* . . ."

Spaulding reached down and snapped the switch into the off position.

He got out of the car and went back to the telephone booth.

One step at a time. No blurring, no overlapping—each action defined, handled with precision.

Now it was the scramble from Fairfax. The deciphered code that would tell him the name of the man who was having him intercepted; the source four-zero, whose priority rating allowed him to send such commands from the transmission core of the intelligence compound.

The agent who walked with impunity in the highest classified alleyways and killed a man named Ed Pace on New Year's Eve.

The Haganah infiltration.

He had been tempted to rip open the yellow envelope the moment the FMF officer had given it to him in San Telmo, but he had resisted the almost irresistible temptation. He knew that he would be stunned no matter who it was—whether known to him or not; and no *matter* who it was he would have a name to fit the revenge he planned for the killer of his friend.

Such thoughts were obstructions. Nothing could hinder their swift but cautious ride to Ocho Calle; nothing could interfere with his thought-out contact with Heinrich Stoltz.

He withdrew the yellow envelope and slid his finger across the flap.

At first, the name meant nothing.

Lieutenant Colonel Ira Barden.

Nothing.

Then he remembered.

New Year's Eve!

Oh, *Christ*, did he remember! The tough-talking hard-nose who was second in command at Fairfax. Ed Pace's "best friend" who had mourned his "best friend's" death with army anger; who secretly had arranged for David to be flown to the Virginia base and participate in the wake-investigation; who had used the tragic killing to enter his "best friend's" dossier vaults . . . only to find nothing.

The man who insisted a Lisbon cryptographer named Marshall had been killed in the Basque country; who said he would run a check on Franz Altmüller.

Which, of course, he never did.

The man who tried to convince David that it would be in everyone's interest if Spaulding would flex the clearance regulations and explain his War Department assignment.

Which David nearly did. And now wished he had.

Oh, God! Why hadn't Barden *trusted* him? On the other hand, he could not. For to do so would have raised specific, unwanted speculations on Pace's murder.

Ira Barden was no fool. A fanatic, perhaps, but not foolish. He knew the man from Lisbon would kill him if Pace's death was laid at his feet.

Heed the lesson of Fairfax. . . .

Jesus! thought David. We fight each other, kill each other . . . we don't know our enemies any longer.

For *what?*

There was now a second reason to call Ballard. A name was not enough; he needed more than just a name. He would confront Asher Feld.

He picked up the telephone's receiver off the hook, held his coin and dialed.

Ballard got on the line, no humor in evidence.

"*Look*, David." Ballard had not used his first name in conversation before. Ballard was suppressing a lot of anger. "I won't pretend to understand how you people turn your dials, but if you're going to use *my* set, keep me informed!"

"A number of people were killed; I wasn't one of them.

That was fortunate but the circumstances prohibited my contacting you. Does that answer your complaint?"

Ballard was silent for several seconds. The silence was not just his reaction to the news, thought David. There was someone with Bobby. When the cryp spoke, he was no longer angry; he was hesitant, afraid.

"You're all right?"

"Yes. Lyons is with me."

"The FMF were too late. . . ." Ballard seemed to regret his statement. "I keep phoning, they keep avoiding. I think their car's lost."

"Not really. I've got it. . . ."

"Oh, Christ!"

"They left one man at Telmo—for observation. There were two others. They're not hurt; they've disqualified."

"What the hell does *that* mean?"

"I haven't got time to explain. . . . There's an intercept order out for me. From Fairfax. The embassy's not supposed to know. It's a setup; I can't let them take me. Not for a while. . . ."

"Hey, we don't mess with Fairfax," said Ballard firmly.

"You can this time. I told Jean. There's a security breach in Fairfax. I'm not it, believe that. . . . I've *got* to have time. Maybe as much as forty-eight hours. I need questions answered. Lyons can help. For God's sake, trust me!"

"I can trust you but I'm no big deal here. . . . Wait a minute. Jean's with me. . . ."

"I thought so," interrupted Spaulding. It had been David's intention to ask Ballard for the help he needed. He suddenly realized that Jean could be far more helpful.

"Talk to her before she scratches the skin off my hand."

"Before you get off, Bobby. . . . Could you run a priority check on someone in Washington? In Fairfax, to be exact?"

"I'd have to have a reason. The subject—an Intelligence subject, *especially* Fairfax—would probably find out."

"I don't give a damn if he does. Say I demanded it. My rating's four-zero; G-2 has that in the records. I'll take the responsibility."

"Who is it?"

"A lieutenant colonel named Ira Barden. Got it?"

"Yes. Ira Barden. Fairfax."

"Right. Now let me talk to . . ."

Jean's words spilled over one another, a mixture of fury and love, desperation and relief.

"Jean," he said when she had finished a half-dozen questions he couldn't possibly answer, "the other night you made a suggestion I refused to take seriously. I'm taking it seriously now. That mythical David of yours needs a place to hide out. It can't be the pampas, but any place nearer will do. . . . Can you help me? Help us? For *God's sake!*"

38

He would call Jean later, before daybreak. He and Lyons had to move in darkness, wherever they were going. Wherever Jean could find them sanctuary.

There would be no codes sent to Washington, no clearance given for the obscene exchange, no radio or radar blackouts that would immobilize the fleet. David understood that; it was the simplest, surest way to abort "Tortugas."

But it was not enough.

There were the men behind "Tortugas." They had to be yanked up from the dark recesses of their filth and exposed to the sunlight. If there was any meaning left, if the years of pain and fear and death made any sense at all, they had to be given to the world in all their obscenity.

The world deserved that. Hundreds of thousands—on both sides—who would carry the scars of war throughout their lives, deserved it.

They had to understand the meaning of *For what*.

David accepted his role; he would face the men of "Tortugas." But he could not face them with the testimony of a fanatical Jew. The words of Asher Feld, leader of the Haganah's Provisional Wing, were no testimony at all. Fanatics were madmen; the world had seen enough of both, for both were one. And they were dismissed. Or killed. Or both.

David knew he had no choice.

When he faced the men of "Tortugas," it would not be with the words of Asher Feld. Or with deceptive codes and manipulations that were subject to a hundred interpretations.

Deceits. Cover-ups. Removals.

He would face them with what he saw. What he knew, because he had borne witness. He would present them with the irrefutable. And then he would destroy them.

To do this—all this—he had to get aboard the trawler in Ocho Calle. The trawler that would be blown out of the water should it attempt to run the harbor and rendezvous with a German submarine.

That it ultimately would attempt such a run was inevitable. The fanatic mind would demand it. Then there would be no evidence of things seen. Sworn to.

He had to get aboard that trawler now.

He gave his final instructions to Lyons and slid into the warm, oily waters of the Río de la Plata. Lyons would remain in the car—drive it, if necessary—and, if David did not return, allow ninety minutes to elapse before going to the FMF base and telling the commanding officer that David was being held prisoner aboard the trawler. An American agent held prisoner.

There was logic in the strategy. FMF had priority orders to bring in David; orders from Fairfax. It would be three thirty in the morning. Fairfax called for swift, bold action. Especially at three thirty in the morning in a neutral harbor.

It was the bridge David tried always to create for himself in times of high-risk infiltration. It was the trade-off; his life for a lesser loss. The lessons of the north country.

He did not want it to happen that way. There were too many ways to immobilize him; too many panicked men in Washington and Berlin to let him survive, perhaps. At best there would be compromise. At worst. . . . The collapse of "Tortugas" was not enough, the indictment was everything.

His pistol was tight against his head, tied with a strip of his shirt, the cloth running through his teeth. He breaststroked toward the hull of the ship, keeping his head out of the water, the firing pin mechanism of his weapon as dry as possible. The price was mouthfuls of filthy, gasoline-polluted water, made further sickening by the touch of a large conger eel attracted, then repelled, by the moving white flesh.

He reached the hull. Waves slapped gently, unceasingly, against the hard expanse of darkness. He made his way to the stern of the ship, straining his eyes and his ears for evidence of life.

Nothing but the incessant lapping of water.

There was light from the deck but no movement, no shadows, no voices. Just the flat, colorless spill of naked bulbs strung on black wires, swaying in slow motion to the sluggish rhythm of the hull. On the port side of the ship—the dockside—were two lines looped over the aft and midships pilings. Rat disks were placed every ten feet or so; the thick manila hemps were black with grease and oil slick. As he approached, David could see a single guard sitting in a chair by the huge loading doors, which were shut. The chair was tilted back against the warehouse wall; two wire-mesh lamps covered by metal shades were on both sides of the wide doorframe. Spaulding treaded backward to get a clearer view. The guard was dressed in the paramilitary clothes of Habichtsnest. He was reading a book; for some reason that fact struck David as odd.

Suddenly, there were footsteps at the west section of the warehouse dock. They were slow, steady; there was no attempt to muffle the noise.

The guard looked up from his book. Between the pilings David could see a second figure come into view. It was another guard wearing the Rhinemann uniform. He was carrying a leather case, the same radio case carried by the men—dead men—at 15 Terraza Verde.

The guard in the chair smiled and spoke to the standing sentry. The language was German.

"I'll trade places, if you wish," said the man in the chair. "Get off your feet for a while."

"No, thanks," replied the man with the radio. "I'd rather walk. Passes the time quicker."

"Anything new from Luján?"

"No change. Still a great deal of excitement. I can hear snatches of yelling now and then. Everybody's giving orders."

"I wonder what happened in Telmo."

"Bad trouble is all I know. They've blocked us off; they've sent men to the foot of Ocho Calle."

"You heard that?"

"No. I spoke with Geraldo. He and Luis are here. In front of the warehouse; in the street."

"I hope they don't wake up the whores."

The man with the radio laughed. "Even Geraldo can do better than those dogs."

"Don't bet good money on that," replied the guard in the chair.

The guard on foot laughed again and proceeded east on his solitary patrol around the building. The man in the chair returned to his book.

David sidestroked his way back toward the hull of the trawler.

His arms were getting tired; the foul-smelling waters of the harbor assaulted his nostrils. And now he had something else to consider: Eugene Lyons.

Lyons was a quarter of a mile away, diagonally across the water, four curving blocks from the foot of Ocho Calle. If Rhinemann's patrols began cruising the area, they would find the FMF vehicle with Lyons in it. It was a bridge he hadn't considered. He should have considered it.

But he couldn't think about that now.

He reached the starboard midships and held onto the waterline ledge, giving the muscles of his arms and shoulders a chance to throb in relief. The trawler was in the medium-craft classification, no more than seventy or eighty feet in length, perhaps a thirty-foot midship beam. By normal standards, and from what David could see as he approached the boat in darkness, the mid and aft cabins below the wheel shack were about fifteen and twenty feet long, respectively, with entrances at both ends and two portholes per cabin on the port and starboard sides. If the Koening diamonds *were* on board, it seemed logical that they'd be in the aft cabin, farthest away from the crew's normal activity. Too, aft cabins had more room and fewer distractions. And if Asher Feld was right, if two or three Peenemünde scientists were microscopically examining the Koening products, they would be under a pressured schedule and require isolation.

David found his breath coming easier. He'd know soon enough whether and where the diamonds were or were not. In moments.

He untied the cloth around his head, treading water as he did so, holding the pistol firmly. The shirt piece drifted away; he held onto the line ledge and looked above. The gunwale was six to seven feet out of the water; he would need both his hands to claw his way up the tiny ridges of the hull.

He spat out what harbor residue was in his mouth and clamped the barrel of the gun between his teeth. The only clothing he wore was his trousers; he plunged his hands beneath the water, rubbing them against the cloth in an effort to remove what estuary slick he could.

He gripped the line ledge once again and with his right hand extended, kicked his body out of the water and reached for the next tiny ridge along the hull. His fingers grasped the half-inch sprit; he pulled himself up, slapping his left hand next to his right, pushing his chest into the rough wood for leverage. His bare feet were near the water's surface, the gunwale no more than three feet above him now.

Slowly he raised his knees until the toes of both feet rested on the waterline ledge. He paused for breath, knowing that his fingers would not last long on the tiny ridge. He tensed the muscles of his stomach and pressed his aching toes against the ledge, pushing himself up as high as possible, whipping out his hands; knowing, again, that if he missed the gunwale he would plunge back into the water. The splash would raise alarms.

The left hand caught; the right slipped off. But it was enough.

He raised himself to the railing, his chest scraping against the rough, weathered hull until spots of blood emerged on his skin. He looped his left arm over the side and removed the pistol from his mouth. He was—as he hoped he would be—at the midpoint between the fore and aft cabins, the expanse of wall concealing him from the guards on the loading dock.

He silently rolled over the gunwale onto the narrow deck and took the necessary crouching steps to the cabin wall. He pressed his back into the wooden slats and slowly stood up. He inched his way toward the first aft porthole; the light from within was partially blocked by a primitive curtain of sorts, pulled back as if parted for the night air. The second porthole farther down had no such obstruction, but it was only feet from the edge of the wall; there was the possibility that a sentry—unseen from the water—might be stern watch there. He would see whatever there was to see in the first window.

His wet cheek against the rotted rubber surrounding the porthole, he looked inside. The "curtain" was a heavy sheet of black tarpaulin folded back at an angle. Beyond, the light was as he had pictured it: a single bulb suspended from the ceiling by a thick wire—a wire that ran out a port window to a pier outlet. Ship generators were not abused while at dock. There was an odd-shaped, flat piece of metal hanging on the side of the bulb, and at first David was not sure why it was there. And then he understood: the sheet of metal deflected the light of the bulb from the rear of the cabin, where he could make out—beyond the fold of the tarp—two bunk beds. Men were sleeping; the light remained on but they were in relative shadow.

On the far side of the cabin, butted against the wall, was a long table that had the incongruous appearance of a hospital laboratory workbench. It was covered by a taut, white, spotless oilcloth and on the cloth, equidistant from one another, were four powerful microscopes. Beside each instrument was a high-intensity lamp—all the wires leading to a twelve-volt utility battery under the table. On the floor in front of the microscopes were four high-backed stools—four white, spotless stools standing at clinical attention.

That was the effect, thought David. Clinical. This isolated section of the trawler was in counterpoint to the rest of the filthy ship: it was a small, clinical island surrounded by rotted sea waste and rat disks.

And then he saw them. In the corner.

Five steel crates, each with metal strips joined at the top edges and held in place with heavy vault locks. On the front of each crate was the clearly stenciled name: KOENING MINES, LTD.

He'd seen it now. The undeniable, the irrefutable.

Tortugas.

The obscene exchange funneled through Erich Rhinemann.

And he was so close, so near possession. The final indictment.

Within his fear—and he *was* afraid—furious anger and deep temptation converged. They were sufficient to suspend his anxiety, to force him to concentrate only on the objective. To believe—knowing the belief was false—in some mystical invulnerability, granted for only a few precious minutes.

That was enough.

He ducked under the first porthole and approached the second. He stood up and looked in; the door of the cabin was in his direct line of sight. It was a new door, not part of the trawler. It was steel and in the center was a bolt at least an inch thick, jammed into a bracket in the frame.

The Peenemünde scientists were not only clinically isolated, they were in a self-imposed prison.

That bolt, David realized, was his personal Alpine pass—to be crossed without rig.

He crouched and passed under the porthole to the edge of the cabin wall. He remained on his knees and, millimeter by millimeter, the side of his face against the wood, looked around the corner.

The guard was there, of course, standing his harbor watch in the tradition of such sentry duty: on deck, the inner line of defense; bored, irritated with his boredom, relaxed in his inactivity yet annoyed by its pointlessness.

But he was not in the paramilitary clothes of Habichtsnest. He was in a loose-fitting suit that did little to conceal a powerful—military—body. His hair was cut short, Wehrmacht style.

He was leaning against a large fishing net winch, smoking a thin cigar, blowing the smoke aimlessly into the night air. At his side was an automatic rifle, .30 caliber, the shoulder strap unbuckled, curled on the deck. The rifle had not been touched for quite some time; the strap had a film of moisture on the surface of the leather.

The strap. . . . David took the belt from his trousers. He stood up, inched back toward the porthole, reached underneath the railing and removed one of two gunwale spikes which were clamped against the inner hull for the fish nets. He tapped the railing softly twice; then twice again. He heard the shuffling of the guard's feet. No forward movement, just a change of position.

He tapped again. Twice. Then twice more. The quietly precise tapping—intentional, spaced evenly—was enough to arouse curiosity; insufficient to cause alarm.

He heard the guard's footsteps now. Still relaxed, the forward motion easy, not concerned with danger, only curious. A piece of harbor driftwood, perhaps, slapping against the hull, caught in the push-pull of the current.

The guard rounded the corner; Spaulding's belt whipped around his neck, instantly lashed taut, choking off the cry.

David twisted the leather as the guard sank to his knees, the face darkening perceptibly in the dim spill of light from the porthole, the lips pursed in strangled anguish.

David did not allow his victim to lose consciousness; he had the Alpine pass to cross. Instead, he wedged his pistol into his trousers, reached down to the scabbard on the guard's waist, and took out the carbine bayonet—a favorite knife of combat men, rarely used on the front of any rifle. He held the blade under the guard's eyes and whispered.

"*Español* or *Deutsch?*"

The man stared up in terror. Spaulding twisted the leather tighter; the guard choked a cough and struggled to raise two fingers. David whispered again, the blade pushing against the skin under the right eyeball.

"*Deutsch?*"

The man nodded.

Of course he was German, thought Spaulding. And Nazi. The clothes, the hair. Peenemünde *was* the Third Reich. Its scientists would be guarded by their own. He twisted the blade of the carbine bayonet so that a tiny laceration appeared under the eye. The guard's mouth opened in fright.

"You do exactly what I tell you," whispered David in German into the guard's ear, "or I'll carve out your sight. Understand?"

The man, nearly limp, nodded.

"Get up and call through the porthole. You have an urgent message from . . . Altmüller, Franz Altmüller! They must open the door and sign for it. . . . Do it! Now! And remember, this knife is inches from your eyes."

The guard, in shock, got up. Spaulding pushed the man's face to the open porthole, loosened the belt only slightly, and shifted his position to the side of the man and the window, his left hand holding the leather, his right the knife.

"*Now!*" whispered David, flicking the blade in half circles.

At first the guard's voice was strained, artificial. Spaulding moved in closer; the guard knew he had only seconds to live if he did not perform.

He performed.

There was stirring in the bunk beds within the cabin. Grumbling complaints to begin with, ceasing abruptly at the mention of Altmüller's name.

A small, middle-aged man got out of the left lower bunk and walked sleepily to the steel door. He was in undershorts, nothing else. David propelled the guard around the corner of the wall and reached the door at the sound of the sliding bolt.

He slammed the guard against the steel panel with the twisted belt; the door flung open, David grabbed the knob, preventing it from crashing into the bulkhead. He dropped the knife, yanked out his pistol, and crashed the barrel into the skull of the small scientist.

"*Schweigen!*" he whispered hoarsely. "*Wenn Ihnen Ihr Leben lieb ist!*"

The three men in the bunks—older men, one old man—stumbled out of their beds, trembling and speechless. The guard, choking still, began to focus around him and started to rise. Spaulding took two steps and slashed the pistol diagonally across the man's temple, splaying him out on the deck.

The old man, less afraid than his two companions, stared at David. For reasons Spaulding could not explain to himself, he felt ashamed. Violence was out of place in this antiseptic cabin.

"I have no quarrel with you," he whispered harshly in German. "You follow orders. But don't mistake me, I'll kill you if you make a sound!" He pointed to some papers next to a microscope; they were filled with numbers and columns. "You!" He gestured his pistol at the old man. "Give me those! Quickly!"

The old man trudged haltingly across the cabin to the clinical work area. He lifted the papers off the table and handed them to Spaulding, who stuffed them into his wet trousers pocket.

"Thanks. . . . Now!" He pointed his weapon at the other two. "Open one of those crates! Do it now!"

"No! . . . No! For God's sake!" said the taller of the middle-aged scientists, his voice low, filled with fear.

David grabbed the old man standing next to him. He clamped his arm around the loose flesh of the old neck and brought his pistol up to the head. He thumbed back the firing pin and spoke calmly. "You will open a crate or I will kill this man. When he's dead, I'll turn my pistol on you. Believe me, I have no alternative."

The shorter man whipped his head around, pleading silently with the taller one. The old man in David's grasp was the leader; Spaulding knew that. An old . . . *alter-Anführer*; always take the German leader.

The taller Peenemünde scientist walked—every step in fear—to the far corner of the clinical workbench, where there was a neat row of keys on the wall. He removed one and hesitantly went to the first steel crate. He bent down and inserted the key in the vault lock holding the metal strip around the edge; the strip snapped apart in the center.

"Open the lid!" commanded Spaulding, his anxiety causing his whisper to become louder; too loud, he realized.

The cover of the steel crate was heavy; the German had to lift it with both hands, the wrinkles around his eyes and mouth betraying the effort required. Once at a ninety-degree angle, chains on both sides became taut; there was a click of a latch and the cover was locked in place.

Inside were dozens of identically matched compartments in what appeared to be sliding trays—something akin to a large, complicated fishing tackle box. Then David understood: the front of the steel case was on hinges; it too could be opened—or lowered, to be exact—allowing the trays to slide out.

In each compartment were two small, heavy, paper envelopes, apparently lined with layers of soft tissue. There were dozens of envelopes on the top tray alone.

David released the old man, propelling him back toward the bunk beds. He waved his pistol at the tall German who had opened the crate, ordering him to join the other two. He reached down into the steel crate, picked out a small envelope and brought it to his mouth, tearing the edge with his teeth. He shook it toward the ground; tiny translucent nuggets spattered over the cabin deck.

The Koening diamonds.

He watched the German scientists as he crumpled the envelope. They were staring at the stones on the floor.

Why not? thought David. In that cabin was the solution for Peenemünde. In those crates were the tools to rain death on untold thousands . . . as the gyroscopic designs for which they were traded would make possible further death, further massacre.

He was about to throw away the envelope in disgust and fill his pockets with others when his eyes caught sight of some lettering. He unwrinkled the envelope, his pistol steady on the Germans, and looked down. The single word:

echt

True. Genuine. This envelope, this tray, this steel case had passed inspection.

He reached down and grabbed as many envelopes as his left hand could hold and stuffed them into his trousers pocket.

It was all he needed for the indictment.

It was everything. It was the meaning.

There was one thing more he could do. Of a more immediately practical nature. He crossed to the workbench and went down the line of four microscopes, crashing the barrel of his pistol up into each lens and down into the eyepieces. He looked for a laboratory case, the type which carried optical equipment. There had to be one!

It was on the floor beneath the long table. He kicked it out with his bare foot and reached down to open the hasp.

More slots and trays, only these filled with lenses and small black tubes in which to place them.

He bent down and overturned the case; dozens of circular lenses fell out onto the deck. As fast as he could he grabbed the nearest white stool and brought it down sideways into the piles of glass.

The destruction wasn't total, but the damage was enough, perhaps, for forty-eight hours.

He started to get up, his weapon still on the scientists, his ears and eyes alert.

He heard it! He sensed it! And simultaneously he understood that if he did not spin out of the way he would be dead!

He threw himself on the floor to the right; the hand above and behind him came down, the carbine bayonet slicing the air, aimed for the spot where his neck had been less than a second ago.

He had left the goddamned bayonet on the floor! He

had discarded the goddamned *bayonet!* The guard had revived and *taken* the goddamned *bayonet!*

The Nazi's single cry emerged before Spaulding leaped on his kneeling form, smashing his skull into the wood floor with such force that blood spewed out in tiny bursts throughout the head.

But the lone cry was enough.

"Is something wrong?" came a voice from outside, twenty yards away on the loading dock. "Heinrich! Did you call?"

There was no second, no instant, to throw away on hesitation.

David ran to the steel door, pulled it open and raced around the corner of the wall to the concealed section of the gunwale. As he did so, a guard—the sentry on the bow of the trawler—came into view. His rifle was waist high and he fired.

Spaulding fired back. But not before he realized he was hit. The Nazi's bullet had creased the side of his waist; he could feel the blood oozing down into his trousers.

He threw himself over the railing into the water; screams and shouts started from inside the cabin and farther away on the pier.

He thrashed against the dirty Río slime and tried to keep his head. Where was he? What direction! Where? For Christ's sake, *where!*

The shouts were louder now; searchlights were turned on all over the trawler, crisscrossing the harbor waters. He could hear men screaming into radios as only panicked men can scream. Accusing, helpless.

Suddenly, David realized there were no boats! No boats were coming out of the pier with the searchlights and high-powered rifles that would be his undoing!

No boats!

And he nearly laughed. The operation at Ocho Calle was so totally secretive they had allowed no small craft to put into the deserted area!

He held his side, going under water as often as he could, as fast as he could.

The trawler and the screaming Rhinemann-Altmüller guards were receding in the harbor mist. Spaulding kept bobbing his head up, hoping to God he was going in the right direction.

He was getting terribly tired, but he would not allow himself to grow weak. He *could not* allow that! Not now!

He had the "Tortugas" indictment!

He saw the pilings not far away. Perhaps two, three hundred yards. They *were* the right pilings, the right piers! They . . . it, *had* to be!

He felt the waters around him stir and then he saw the snakelike forms of the conger eels as they lashed blindly against his body. The blood from his wound was attracting them! A horrible mass of slashing giant worms were converging!

He thrashed and kicked and fought down a scream. He pulled at the waters in front of him, his hands in constant contact with the oily snakes of the harbor. His eyes were filled with flashing dots and streaks of yellow and white; his throat was dry in the water, his forehead pounded.

When it seemed at last the scream would come, *had* to come, he felt the hand in his hand. He felt his shoulders being lifted, heard the guttural cries of his own terrified voice—deep, frightened beyond his own endurance. He could look down and see, as his feet kept slipping off the ladder, the circles of swarming eels below.

Eugene Lyons carried him—*carried* him!—to the FMF automobile. He was aware—yet not aware—of the fact that Lyons pushed him gently into the back seat.

And then Lyons climbed in after him, and David understood—yet did not understand—that Lyons was slapping him. Hard. Harder.

Deliberately. Without rhythm but with a great deal of strength.

The slapping would not stop! He couldn't make it stop! He couldn't stop the half-destroyed, throatless Lyons from slapping him.

He could only cry. Weep as a child might weep.

And then suddenly he *could* make him stop. He took his hands from his face and grabbed Lyons's wrists, prepared, if need be, to break them.

He blinked and stared at the physicist.

Lyons smiled in the shadows. He spoke in his tortured whisper.

"I'm sorry. . . . You were . . . in temporary . . . shock. My friend."

39

An elaborate naval first aid kit was stored in the trunk of the FMF vehicle. Lyons filled David's wound with sulfa powder, laid on folded strips of gauze and pinched the skin together with three-inch adhesive. Since the wound was a gash, not a puncture, the bleeding stopped; it would hold until they reached a doctor. Even should the wait be a day or a day and a half, there would be no serious damage.

Lyons drove.

David watched the emaciated man behind the wheel. He was unsure but willing; that was the only way to describe him. Every now and then his foot pressed too hard on the accelerator, and the short bursts of speed frightened him—then annoyed him. Still, after a few minutes, he seemed to take a careful delight in manipulating the car around corners.

David knew he had to accomplish three things: reach Henderson Granville, talk to Jean and drive to that sanctuary he hoped to Christ Jean had found for them. If a doctor could be brought to him, fine. If not, he would sleep; he was beyond the point of functioning clearly without rest.

How often in the north country had he sought out isolated caves in the hills? How many times had he piled branches and limbs in front of small openings so his body and mind could restore the balance of objectivity that might save his life? He had to find such a resting place now.

And tomorrow he would make the final arrangements with Erich Rhinemann.

The final pages of the indictment.

"We have to find a telephone," said David. Lyons nodded as he drove.

David directed the physicist back into the center of Buenos Aires. By his guess they still had time before the FMF base sent out a search. The orange insignias on the bumpers would tend to dissuade the BA police from becoming too curious; the Americans were children of the night.

He remembered the telephone booth on the north side of the Casa Rosada. The telephone booth in which a hired gun from the Unio Corso—sent down from Rio de Janeiro—had taken his last breath.

They reached the Plaza de Mayo in fifteen minutes, taking a circular route, making sure they were not followed. The Plaza was not deserted. It was, as the prewar travel posters proclaimed, a Western Hemisphere Paris. Like Paris, there were dozens of early stragglers, dressed mainly in expensive clothes. Taxis stopped and started; prostitutes made their last attempts to find profitable beds; the streetlights illuminated the huge fountains; lovers dabbled their hands in the pools.

The Plaza de Mayo at three thirty in the morning was not a barren, dead place to be. And David was grateful for that.

Lyons pulled the car up to the telephone booth and Spaulding got out.

"Whatever it is, you've hit the rawest nerve in Buenos Aires." Granville's voice was hard and precise. "I must demand that you return to the embassy. For your own protection as well as the good of our diplomatic relations."

"You'll have to be clearer than that, I'm afraid," replied David.

Granville was.

The "one or two" contacts the ambassador felt he could reach in the Grupo were reduced, of course, to one. That man made inquiries as to the trawler in Ocho Calle and subsequently was taken from his home under guard. That was the information Granville gathered from a hysterical wife.

An hour later the ambassador received word from a GOU liaison that his "friend" had been killed in an automobile accident. The GOU wanted him to have the news. It was most unfortunate.

When Granville tried reaching the wife, an operator cut in, explaining that the telephone was disconnected.

"You've involved us, Spaulding! We can't function with Intelligence dead weight around our necks. The situation in Buenos Aires is extremely delicate."

"You *are* involved, sir. A couple of thousand miles away people are shooting at each other."

"Shit!" It was just about the most unexpected expletive David thought he could hear from Granville. "Learn your lines of demarcation! We all have jobs to do within the . . . artificial, if you like, parameters that are set for us! I repeat, sir. Return to the embassy and I'll expedite your immediate return to the United States. Or if you refuse, take yourself to FMF. *That's* beyond my jurisdiction; you will be no part of the embassy!"

My God! thought David. *Artificial parameters. Jurisdictions. Diplomatic niceties.* When men were dying, armies destroyed, cities obliterated! And men in high-ceilinged rooms played games with words and attitudes!

"I can't go to FMF. But I can give you something to think about. Within forty-eight hours all American ships and aircraft in the coastal zones are entering a radio and radar blackout! Everything grounded, immobilized. That's straight military holy writ. And I think you'd better find out why! Because I think I know, and if I'm right, your *diplomatic wreck* is filthier than anything you can imagine! Try a man named Swanson at the War Department. Brigadier Alan Swanson! And tell him I've found 'Tortugas'!"

David slammed down the receiver with such force that chips of Bakelite fell off the side of the telephone. He wanted to run. Open the door of the suffocating booth and race away.

But where to? There was nowhere.

He took several deep breaths and once more dialed the embassy.

Jean's voice was soft, filled with anxiety. But she had found a place!

He and Lyons were to drive due west on Rivadavia to the farthest outskirts of Buenos Aires. At the end of Rivadavia was a road bearing right—it could be spotted by a large statue of the Madonna at its beginning. The road led to the flat grass country, *provinciales* country. Thirty-six miles beyond the Madonna was another road—on the left—this marked by telephone junction wires converging into a transformer box on top of a double-strapped telephone pole. The road led to a ranch belonging to one Alfonso Quesarro. Señor Quesarro would not be there . . . under the circumstances. Neither would his wife. But a skeleton staff would be on; the remaining staff quarters would be available for Mrs. Cameron's unknown friends.

Jean would obey his orders: she would not leave the embassy.

And she loved him. Terribly.

Dawn came up over the grass country. The breezes were warm; David had to remind himself that it was January. The Argentine summer. A member of the skeleton staff of Estancia Quesarro met them several miles down the road past the telephone junction wires, on the property border, and escorted them to the *ranchería*—a cluster of small one-story cottages—near but not adjacent to the main buildings. They were led to an adobe farthest from the other houses; it was on the edge of a fenced grazing area, fields extending as far as the eye could see. The house was the residence of the *caporal*—the ranch foreman.

David understood as he looked up at the roof, at the single telephone line. Ranch foremen had to be able to use a telephone.

Their escort opened the door and stood in the frame, anxious to leave. He touched David's arm and spoke in a Spanish tempered with pampas Indian.

"The telephones out here are with operators. The service is poor; not like the city. I am to tell you this, *señor*."

But that information was not what the gaucho was telling him. He was telling him to be careful.

"I'll remember," said Spaulding. "Thank you."

The man left quickly and David closed the door. Lyons was standing across the room, in the center of a small monastery arch that led to some sort of sunlit enclosure. The metal case containing the gyroscopic designs was in his right hand; with his left he beckoned David.

Beyond the arch was a cubicle; in the center, underneath an oblong window overlooking the fields, there was a bed.

Spaulding undid the top of his trousers and peeled them off.

He fell with his full weight into the hard mattress and slept.

40

It seemed only seconds ago that he had walked through the small arch into the sunlit cubicle.

He felt the prodding fingers around his wound; he winced as a cold-hot liquid was applied about his waist and the adhesive ripped off.

He opened his eyes fiercely and saw the figure of a man bent over the bed. Lyons was standing beside him. At the edge of the hard mattress was the universal shape of a medical bag. The man bending over him was a doctor. He spoke in unusually clear English.

"You've slept nearly eight hours. That is the best prescription one could give you. . . . I'm going to suture this in three places; that should do it. There will be a degree of discomfort, but with the tape you'll be quite mobile."

"What time is it?" asked David.

Lyons looked at his watch. He whispered, and the words were clear. "Two . . . o'clock."

"Thank you for coming out here," said Spaulding, shifting his weight for the doctor's instruments.

"Wait until I'm back at my office in Palermo." The doctor laughed softly, sardonically. "I'm sure I'm on one of their lists." He inserted a suture, reassuring David with a tight smile. "I left word I was on a maternity call at an outback ranch. . . . There." He tied off the stitch and patted Spaulding's bare skin. "Two more and we're finished."

"Do you think you'll be questioned?"

"No. Not actually. The junta closes its eyes quite often. There's not an abundance of doctors here. . . . And amusingly enough, interrogators invariably seek free medical advice. I think it goes with their mentalities."

"And I think you're covering. I think it *was* dangerous."

The doctor held his hands in place as he looked at David. "Jean Cameron is a very special person. If the history of wartime Buenos Aires is written, she'll be prominently mentioned." He returned to the sutures without elaboration. David had the feeling that the doctor did not wish to talk further. He was in a hurry.

Twenty minutes later Spaulding was on his feet, the doctor at the door of the adobe hut. David shook the medical man's hand. "I'm afraid I can't pay you," he said.

"You already have, colonel. I'm a Jew."

Spaulding did not release the doctor's hand. Instead, he held it firmly—not in salutation. "Please explain."

"There's nothing to explain. The Jewish community is filled with rumors of an American officer who pits himself against the pig. . . . Rhinemann the pig."

"That's all?"

"It's enough." The doctor removed his hand from Spaulding's and walked out. David closed the door.

Rhinemann the pig. It was time for Rhinemann.

The teutonic, guttural voice screamed into the telephone. David could picture the blue-black veins protruding on the surface of the bloated, suntanned skin. He could see the narrow eyes bulging with fury.

"*It was you! It was you!*" The accusation was repeated over and over again, as if the repetition might provoke a denial.

"It was me," said David without emphasis.

"You are *dead!* You are a *dead man!*"

David spoke quietly, slowly. With precision. "If I'm dead, no codes are sent to Washington; no radar or radio blackout. The screens will pick up that trawler and the instant a submarine surfaces anywhere near it, it'll be blown out of the water."

Rhinemann was silent. Spaulding heard the German Jew's rhythmic breathing but said nothing. He let Rhinemann's thoughts dwell upon the implication. Finally Rhinemann spoke. With equal precision.

"Then you have something to say to me. Or you would not have telephoned."

"That's right," agreed David. "I have something to say. I

assume you're taking a broker's fee. I can't believe you arranged this exchange for nothing."

Rhinemann paused again. He replied cautiously, his breathing heavy, carried over the wire. "No. . . . It is a transaction. Accommodations must be paid for."

"But that payment comes later, doesn't it?" David kept his words calm, dispassionate. "You're in no hurry; you've got everyone where you want them. . . . There won't be any messages radioed out of Switzerland that accounts have been settled. The only message you'll get—or *won't* get—is from a submarine telling you the Koening diamonds have been transferred from the trawler. That's when I fly out of here with the designs. That's the signal." Spaulding laughed a brief, cold, quiet laugh. "It's very pro, Rhinemann. I congratulate you."

The financier's voice was suddenly low, circumspect. "What's your point?"

"It's also very pro . . . I'm the only one who can bring about that message from the U-boat. No one else. I have the codes that turn the lights off; that make the radar screens go dark. . . . But I expect to get paid for it."

"I see. . . ." Rhinemann hesitated, his breathing still audible. "It is a presumptuous demand. Your superiors expect the gyroscopic designs. Should you impede their delivery, your punishment, no doubt, will be execution. Not formally arrived at, of course, but the result will be the same. Surely you know that."

David laughed again, and again the laugh was brief—but now good-natured. "You're way off. *Way* off. There may be executions, but not mine. Until last night I only knew half the story. Now I know it *all*. . . . No, not *my* execution. On the other hand, you *do* have a problem. I know *that;* four years in Lisbon teaches a man some things."

"What is my problem?"

"If the Koening merchandise in Ocho Calle is not delivered, Altmüller will send an undercover battalion into Buenos Aires. You won't survive it."

The silence again. And in that silence was Rhinemann's acknowledgment that David was right.

"Then we are allies," said Rhinemann. "In one night you've gone far. You took a dangerous risk and leaped many plateaus. I admire such aggressive ambitions. I'm sure arrangements can be made."

"I was sure you'd be sure."

"Shall we discuss figures?"

Again David laughed softly. "Payment from you is like . . . before last night. Only half the story. Make your half generous. In Switzerland. The second half will be paid in the States. A lifetime of *very* generous retainers." David suddenly spoke tersely. "I want names."

"I don't understand. . . ."

"*Think* about it. The men *behind* this operation. The Americans. Those are the names I want. Not an accountant, not a confused brigadier. The others. . . . Without those names there's no deal. No codes."

"The man from Lisbon is remarkably without conscience," said Rhinemann with a touch of respect. "You are . . . as you Americans say . . . quite a rotten fellow."

"I've watched the masters in action. I thought about it. . . . Why not?"

Rhinemann obviously had not listened to David's reply. His tone was abruptly suspicious. "If this . . . gain of personal wealth is the conclusion you arrived at, why did you do what you did last night? I must tell you that the damage is not irreparable, but why *did* you?"

"For the simplest of reasons. I hadn't thought about it last night. I hadn't arrived at this conclusion . . . last night." God knew, that was the truth, thought David.

"Yes. I think I understand," said the financier. "A very human reaction. . . ."

"I want the rest of these designs," broke in Spaulding. "And you want the codes sent out. To stay on schedule, we have thirty-six hours, give or take two or three. I'll call you at six o'clock. Be ready to move."

David hung up. He took a deep breath and realized he was perspiring . . . and the small concrete house was cool. The breezes from the fields were coming through the windows, billowing the curtains. He looked at Lyons, who sat watching him in a straight-backed wicker chair.

"How'd I do?" he asked.

The physicist swallowed and spoke, and it occurred to Spaulding that either he was getting used to Lyons's strained voice or Lyons's speech was improving.

"Very . . . convincing. Except for the . . . sweat on your face and the expression . . . in your eyes." Lyons smiled; then followed it instantly with a question he took seriously. "Is there a chance . . . for the remaining blueprints?"

David held a match to a cigarette. He inhaled the smoke, looked up at the gently swaying curtains of an open window, then turned to the physicist. "I think we'd better understand one another, doctor. I don't give a goddamn about those designs. Perhaps I should, but I don't. And if the way to get our hands on them is to risk that trawler reaching a U-boat, it's out of the question. As far as I'm concerned we're bringing out three-quarters more than what we've got. And that's too goddamn much. . . . There's only one thing I want: the names. . . . I've got the evidence; now I want the names."

"You want revenge," said Lyons softly.

"*Yes! . . . Jesus! Yes, I do!*" David crushed out his barely touched cigarette, crossed to the open window and looked out at the fields. "I'm sorry, I don't mean to yell at you. Or maybe I should. You heard Feld; you saw what I brought back from Ocho Calle. You know the whole putrid . . . obscene thing."

"I know . . . the men who fly those planes . . . are not responsible. . . . I know I believe that . . . Germany must lose this war."

"For Christ's *sake!*" roared David, whirling from the window. "You've *seen!* You've *got* to *understand!*"

"Are you saying . . . there's no difference? I don't believe that. . . . I don't think you believe it."

"I don't know *what* I believe! . . . No. I *do* know. I know what I object to; because it leaves no *room* for belief. . . . And I know I want those names."

"You should have them. . . . Your questions are great . . . moral ones. I think they will pain you . . . for years." Lyons was finding it difficult to sustain his words now. "I submit only . . . no matter what has happened . . . that Asher Feld was right. This war must *not* be settled . . . it must be won."

Lyons stopped talking and rubbed his throat. David walked to a table where Lyons kept a pitcher of water and poured a glass. He carried it over to the spent physicist and handed it to him. It occurred to David, as he acknowledged the gesture of thanks, that it was strange. . . . Of all men, the emaciated recluse in front of him would profit least from the outcome of the war. Or the shortening of it. Yet Eugene Lyons had been touched by the commitment of Asher Feld. Perhaps, in his pain, Lyons understood the simpler issues that his own anger had distorted.

Asher Feld. The Alvear Hotel.

"Listen to me," said Spaulding. "If there's a chance . . . and there may be, we'll try for the blueprints. There's a trade-off possible; a dangerous one . . . not for us, but for your friend, Asher Feld. We'll see. No promises. The names come first. . . . It's a parallel route; until I get the names, Rhinemann has to believe I want the designs as much as he wants the diamonds. . . . We'll see."

The weak, erratic bell of the country telephone spun out its feeble ring. Spaulding picked it up.

"It's Ballard," said the voice anxiously.

"Yes, Bobby?"

"I hope to Christ you're clean, because there's a lot of flak to the contrary. I'm going on the assumption that a reasonable guy doesn't court-martial himself into a long prison term for a few dollars."

"A reasonable assumption. What is it? Did you get the information?"

"First things first. And the first thing is that the Fleet Marine Force wants you dead or alive; the condition is immaterial, and I think they'd prefer you dead."

"They found Meehan and the driver. . . ."

"You bet your ass they did! After they got rolled and stripped to their skivvies by some wandering *vagos*. They're mad as hell! They threw out the bullshit about not alerting the embassy that Fairfax wants you picked up. Fairfax's incidental; *they* want you. Assault, theft, et cetera."

"All right. That's to be expected."

"Expected? Oh, you're a pistol! I don't suppose I have to tell you about Granville. You got him burning up my dials! Washington's preparing a top-level scramble, so I'm chained to my desk till it comes in."

"Then he doesn't know. They're covering," said Spaulding, annoyed.

"The hell he doesn't! The hell they *are!* This radio silence; you walked into a High Command *defection!* An Allied Central project straight from the War Department."

"I'll bet it's from the War Department. I can tell you which office."

"It's true. . . . There's a U-boat bringing in a couple of very important Berliners. You're out of order; it's not your action. Granville will tell you that."

"Horseshit!" yelled David. "Pure horseshit! *Transparent* horseshit! Ask any network agent in Europe. You couldn't get a *Briefmarke* out of *any* German port! No one knows that better than me!"

"Interesting, ontologically speaking. Transparency isn't a quality one associates . . ."

"No jokes! My humor's strained!" And then suddenly David realized he had no cause to yell at the cryp. Ballard's frame of reference was essentially the same as it had been eighteen hours ago—with complications, perhaps, but not of death and survival. Ballard did not know about the carnage at San Telmo or the tools for Peenemünde in Ocho Calle; and a Haganah that reached into the most secret recesses of Military Intelligence. Nor would he be told just now. "I'm sorry. I've got a lot on my mind."

"Sure, sure." Ballard replied as if he were used to other people's tempers. Another trait common to most cryptographers, David reflected. "Jean said you were hurt; fell and cut yourself pretty badly. Did somebody push?"

"It's all right. The doctor was here. . . . Did you get the information? On Ira Barden."

"Yeah. . . . I used straight G-2 in Washington. A dossier Teletype request over your name. This Barden's going to know about it."

"That's O.K. What's it say?"

"The whole damn *thing?*"

"Whatever seems . . . unusual. Fairfax qualifications, probably."

"They don't use the name Fairfax. Just high-priority classification. . . . He's in the Reserves, not regular army. Family company's in importing. Spent a number of years in Europe and the Middle East; speaks five languages. . . ."

"And one of them's Hebrew," interrupted David quietly.

"That's right. How did . . . ? Never mind. He spent two years at the American University in Beirut while his father represented the firm in the Mediterranean area. The company was very big in Middle East textiles. Barden transferred to Harvard, then transferred again to a small college in New York State. . . . I don't know it. He majored in Near East studies, it says here. When he graduated he went into the family business until the war. . . . I guess it was the languages."

"Thanks," said David. "Burn the Teletype, Bobby."

"With pleasure. . . . When are you coming in? You better get here before the FMF finds you. Jean can probably convince old Henderson to cool things off."

"Pretty soon. How's Jean?"

"Huh? Fine. . . . Scared; nervous, I guess. You'll see. She's a strong girl, though."

"Tell her not to worry."

"Tell her yourself."

"She's there with you?"

"No. . . ." Ballard drew out the word, telegraphing a note of concern that had been absent. "No, she's not with me. She's on her way to see you. . . ."

"What?"

"The nurse. The doctor's nurse. She called about an hour ago. She said you wanted to see Jean." Ballard's voice suddenly became hard and loud. "*What the hell's going on, Spaulding?*"

41

"Surely the man from Lisbon expected countermeasures. I'm amazed he was so derelict." Heinrich Stoltz conveyed his arrogance over the telephone. "Mrs. Cameron was a flank you took for granted, yes? A summons from a loved one is difficult to resist, is it not?"

"Where is she?"

"She is on her way to Luján. She will be a guest at Habichtsnest. An honored guest, I can assure you. Herr Rhinemann will be immensely pleased; I was about to telephone him. I wanted to wait until the interception was made."

"You're out of line!" David said, trying to keep his voice calm. "You're asking for reprisals in every neutral area. Diplomatic hostages in a neutral . . ."

"A guest," interrupted the German with relish. "Hardly a prize; a *step*daughter-in-law; the husband *deceased*. With no official status. So complicated, these American social rituals."

"You know what I mean! You don't need diagrams!"

"I said she was a *guest!* Of an eminent financier you yourself were sent to contact . . . concerning international economic matters, I believe. A Jew expelled from his own country, that country your enemy. I see no cause for immediate alarm. . . . Although, perhaps, you should."

There was no reason to procrastinate. Jean was no part of the bargain, no part of the indictment. To hell with the indictment! To hell with a meaningless commitment! There *was* no meaning!

Only Jean.

"Call the moves," said David.

"I was sure you'd cooperate. What difference does it

make to you? Or to me, really. . . . You and I, we take orders. Leave the philosophy to men of great affairs. We survive."

"That doesn't sound like a true believer. I was told you were a believer." David spoke aimlessly; he needed time, only seconds. To think.

"Strangely enough, I am. In a world that passed, I'm afraid. Only partially in the one that's coming. . . . The remaining designs are at Habichtsnest. You and your aerophysicist will go there at once. I wish to conclude our negotiations this evening."

"Wait a minute!" David's mind raced over conjectures—his counterpart's options. "That's not the cleanest nest I've been in; the inhabitants leave something to be desired."

"So do the guests. . . ."

"Two conditions. One: I see Mrs. Cameron the minute I get there. Two: I don't send the codes—if they're to be sent—until she's back at the embassy. With Lyons."

"We'll discuss these points later. There is one prior condition, however." Stoltz paused. "Should you not be at Habichtsnest this afternoon, you will *never* see Mrs. Cameron. As you last saw her. . . . Habichtsnest has so many diversions; the guests enjoy them so. Unfortunately, there have been some frightful accidents in the past. On the river, in the pool . . . on horseback. . . ."

The foreman gave them a road map and filled the FMF automobile's gas tank with fuel from the ranch pump. Spaulding removed the orange medallions from the bumpers and blurred the numbers of the license plates by chipping away at the paint until the 7s looked like 1s, and 8s like 3s. Then he smashed the ornament off the tip of the hood, slapped black paint over the grill and removed all four hubcaps. Finally, he took a sledgehammer and, to the amazement of the silent gaucho, he crashed it into the side door panels, trunk and roof of the car.

When he had finished, the automobile from Fleet Marine Force looked like any number of back country wrecks.

They drove out the road to the primitive highway by the telephone junction box and turned east toward Buenos Aires. Spaulding pressed the accelerator; the vibrations caused the loose metal to rattle throughout the car. Lyons held the unfolded map on his knees; if it was correct, they could reach the Luján district without traveling the major highways, reducing the chances of discovery by the FMF patrols that were surely out by now.

The goddamned irony of it! thought David. Safety . . . safety for Jean, for him, too, really . . . lay in contact with the same enemy he had fought so viciously for over three years. An enemy made an ally by incredible events . . . treasons taking place in Washington and Berlin.

What had Stoltz said? *Leave the philosophy to men of great affairs.*

Meaning and no meaning at all.

David nearly missed the half-concealed entrance to Habichtsnest. He was approaching it from the opposite direction on the lonely stretch of road he had traveled only once, and at night. What caused him to slow down and look to his left, spotting the break in the woods, were sets of black tire marks on the light surface of the entrance. They had not been there long enough to be erased by the hot sun or succeeding traffic. And Spaulding recalled the words of the guard on the pier in Ocho Calle.

. . . There is a lot of shouting.

David could visualize Rhinemann screaming his orders, causing a column of racing Bentleys and Packards to come screeching out of the hidden road from Habichtsnest on its way to a quiet street in San Telmo.

And no doubt later—in the predawn hours—other automobiles, more sweating, frightened henchmen—racing to the small isolated peninsula that was Ocho Calle.

With a certain professional pride, Spaulding reflected that he had interdicted well.

Both enemies. All enemies.

A vague plan was coming into focus, but only the outlines. So much depended on what faced them at Habichtsnest.

And the soft-spoken words of hatred uttered by Asher Feld.

The guards in their paramilitary uniforms leveled their rifles at the approaching automobile. Others held dogs that were straining at leashes, teeth bared, barking viciously. The man behind the electric gate shouted orders to those in front; four guards ran to the car and yanked the smashed panels open. Spaulding and Lyons got out; they were pushed against the FMF vehicle and searched.

David kept turning his head, looking at the extended fence beyond both sides of the gate. He estimated the height and the tensile strength of the links, the points of electrical contact between the thick-poled sections. The angles of direction.

It was part of his plan.

Jean ran to him from across the terraced balcony. He held her, silently, for several moments. It was a brief span of sanity and he was grateful for it.

Rhinemann stood at the railing twenty feet away, Stoltz at his side. Rhinemann's narrow eyes stared at David from out of the folds of suntanned flesh. The look was one of despised respect, and David knew it.

There was a third man. A tall, blond-haired man in a white Palm Beach suit seated at a glass-topped table. Spaulding did not know him.

"David, *David*. What have I *done?*" Jean would not let him go; he stroked her soft brown hair, replying quietly.

"Saved my life among other things. . . ."

"The Third Reich has extraordinarily thorough surveillance, Mrs. Cameron," interrupted Stoltz, smiling. "We keep watch on all Jews. Especially professional men. We knew you were friendly with the doctor in Palermo; and that the colonel was wounded. It was all quite simple."

"Does your surveillance of Jews include the man beside you?" asked Spaulding in a monotone.

Stoltz paled slightly, his glance shifting unobtrusively from Rhinemann to the blond-haired man in the chair. "Herr Rhinemann understands my meaning. I speak pragmatically; of the necessary observation of hostile elements."

"Yes, I remember," said David, releasing Jean, putting his arm around her shoulders. "You were very clear yesterday about the regrettable necessity of certain practicalities. I'm sorry you missed the lecture, Rhinemann. It concerned the concentration of Jewish money. . . . We're here. Let's get on with it."

Rhinemann stepped away from the railing. "We shall. But first, so the . . . circle is complete, I wish to present to you an acquaintance who has flown in from Berlin. By way of neutral passage, of course. I want you to have the opportunity of knowing you deal *directly* with *him*. The exchange is more *genuine* this way."

Spaulding looked over at the blond-haired man in the white Palm Beach suit. Their eyes locked.

"Franz Altmüller, Ministry of Armaments. Berlin," said David.

"Colonel David Spaulding. Fairfax. Late of Portugal. The man in Lisbon," said Altmüller.

"You are jackals," added Rhinemann, "who fight as traitors fight and dishonor your houses. I say this to you both. For both to hear. . . . Now, as you say, colonel, we shall get on with it."

Stoltz took Lyons below to the manicured lawn by the pool. There, at a large, round table, a Rhinemann guard stood with a metal attaché case in his hand. Lyons sat down, his back to the balcony; the guard lifted the case onto the table.

"Open it," commanded Erich Rhinemann from above.

The guard did so; Lyons took out the plans and spread them on the table.

Altmüller spoke. "Remain with him, Stoltz."

Stoltz looked up, bewildered. However, he did not speak. He walked to the edge of the pool and sat in a deck chair, his eyes fixed on Lyons.

Altmüller turned to Jean. "May I have a word with the colonel, please?"

Jean looked at Spaulding. She took her hand from his and walked to the far end of the balcony. Rhinemann remained in the center, staring down at Lyons.

"For both our sakes," said Altmüller, "I think you should tell me what happened in San Telmo."

David watched the German closely. Altmüller was not lying; he was not trying to trap him. *He did not know about the Haganah. About Asher Feld*. It was Spaulding's only chance.

"Gestapo," said David, giving the lie the simplicity of conviction.

"*Impossible!*" Altmüller spat out the word. "You *know* that's impossible! *I* am here!"

"I've dealt with the Gestapo—in various forms—for

nearly four years. I know the enemy. . . . Grant me that much credit."

"You're wrong! There's *no possible way!*"

"You've spent too much time in the ministry, not enough in the field. Do you want a professional analysis?"

"What is it?"

David leaned against the railing. "You've been had."

"*What?*"

"Just as I've been had. By those who employ our considerable talents. In Berlin and Washington. There's a remarkable coincidence, too. . . . They both have the same initials. . . . A.S."

Altmüller stared at Spaulding, his blue eyes penetrating, his mouth parted slightly—in disbelief. He spoke the name under his breath.

"*Albert Speer. . . .*"

"*Alan Swanson,*" countered David softly.

"It can't *be,*" said Altmüller with less conviction than he wished to muster. "He doesn't know. . . ."

"Don't go into the field without some advanced training. You won't last. . . . Why do you think I offered to make a deal with Rhinemann?"

Altmüller was listening but not listening. He took his eyes from Spaulding, seemingly consumed with the pieces of an incredible puzzle. "If what you say is true—and by no means do I agree—the codes would not be sent, the transfer aborted. There would be no radio silence; your fleet cruising, radar and aircraft in operation. Everything lost!"

David folded his arms in front of him. It was the moment when the lie would either be bought or rejected out of hand. He knew it; he felt as he had felt scores of times in the north country when *the lie* was the keystone. "Your side plays rougher than mine. It goes with the New Order. My people won't kill me; they just want to make sure I don't know anything. All they care about are those designs. . . . With you it's different. Your people keep their options open."

David stopped and smiled at Rhinemann, who had turned from his sentry position by the balcony and was looking at them. Altmüller kept his eyes on Spaulding . . . the inexperienced "runner" being taught, thought David.

"And in your judgment, what are these options?"

"A couple I can think of," replied Spaulding. "Immobilize me, force in another code man at the last minute, substitute faulty blueprints; or get the diamonds out from Ocho Calle some other way than by water—difficult with those crates, but not impossible."

"Then why should I not let these options be exercised? You tempt me."

Spaulding had been glancing up, at nothing. Suddenly he turned and looked at Altmüller. "Don't *ever* go into the field; you won't last a day. Stay at your ministry."

"What does that mean?"

"Any alternate strategy used, you're dead. You're a liability now. You 'dealt' with the enemy. Speer knows it, the Gestapo knows it. Your only chance is to *use* what you know. Just like me. You for your life; me for a great deal of money. Christ knows, the aircraft companies will make a pile; I deserve some of it."

Altmüller took two steps to the railing and stood alongside David, looking down at the distant river below. "It's all so pointless."

"Not when you think about it," said Spaulding. "Something for nothing never is in this business."

David, staring straight ahead, could feel Altmüller's eyes abruptly on him. He could sense the new thought coming into focus in Altmüller's mind.

"Your generosity may be your undoing, colonel. . . . We can still have something for nothing. And I, a hero's medal from the Reich. We have you. Mrs. Cameron. The physicist's expendable, I'm sure. . . . You *will* send the codes. You were willing to negotiate for money. Surely you'll negotiate for your lives."

Like Altmüller, David stared straight ahead when he replied. His arms still folded, he was irritatingly relaxed, as he knew he had to be. "Those negotiations have been concluded. If Lyons approves the blueprints, I'll send the codes when he and Mrs. Cameron are back at the embassy. Not before."

"You'll send them when I *order* you to." Altmüller was finding it difficult to keep his voice low. Rhinemann looked over again but made no move to interfere. Spaulding understood. Rhinemann was toying with his jackals.

"Sorry to disappoint you," said David.

"Then extremely unpleasant things will happen. To Mrs. Cameron first."

"Give it up." David sighed. "Play by the original rules. You haven't a chance."

"You talk confidently for a man alone."

Spaulding pushed himself off the railing and turned, facing the German. He spoke barely above a whisper. "You really are a goddamned fool. You wouldn't last an hour in Lisbon. . . . Do you think I drove in here without any backups? Do you think Rhinemann *expected* me to? . . . We men in the field are very cautious, very cowardly; we're not heroic at all. We don't blow up buildings if there's a chance we'll still be inside. We won't destroy an enemy bridge unless there's another way back to our side."

"You *are* alone. There are no bridges left for you!"

David looked at Altmüller as if appraising a bad cut of meat, then glanced at his watch. "Your Stoltz was a fool. If I don't make a call within fifteen minutes, there'll be a lot of busy telephones resulting in God knows how many very official automobiles driving out to Luján. I'm a military attaché stationed at the American embassy. I accompanied the ambassador's daughter to Luján. That's enough."

"That's preposterous! This is a neutral city. Rhinemann would . . ."

"*Rhinemann* would open the gates and throw the jackals out," interrupted Spaulding quietly and very calmly. "We're liabilities, both of us. 'Tortugas' could blow up in his postwar face. He's not going to allow that. Whatever he thinks of the systems, yours *or* mine, it doesn't matter. Only one thing matters to him: the cause of Erich Rhinemann. . . . I thought you knew that. You picked him."

Altmüller was breathing steadily, a bit too deeply, thought David. He was imposing a control on himself and he was only barely succeeding.

"You . . . have made arrangements to send the codes? From here?"

The lie was bought. The keystone was now in place.

"The rules are back in force. Radio and radar silence. No air strikes on surfacing submarines, no interceptions of trawlers . . . under Paraguayan flags entering the coastal zones. We both win. . . . Which do you want, jackal?"

Altmüller turned back to the railing and placed his hands on the marble top. His fingers were rigid against the stone. The tailored folds of his white Palm Beach suit were starchly immobile. He looked down at the river and spoke.

"The rules of 'Tortugas' are reinstated."

"I have a telephone call to make," said David.

"I expected you would," replied Rhinemann, looking contemptuously at Franz Altmüller. "I have no stomach for an embassy kidnapping. It serves no one."

"Don't be too harsh," said Spaulding agreeably. "It got me here in record time."

"Make your call." Rhinemann pointed to a telephone on a table next to the archway. "Your conversation will be amplified, of course."

"Of course," answered David, walking to the phone.

"Radio room . . . ," came the words from the unseen speakers.

"This is Lieutenant Colonel Spaulding, military attaché," said David, interrupting Ballard's words.

There was the slightest pause before Ballard replied.

"Yes, sir, Colonel Spaulding?"

"I issued a directive of inquiry prior to my conference this afternoon. You may void it now."

"Yes, sir. . . . Very good, sir."

"May I speak with the head cryptographer, please? A Mr. Ballard, I believe."

"I'm . . . Ballard, sir."

"Sorry," said David curtly, "I didn't recognize you, Ballard. Be ready to send out the sealed code schedules I prepared for you. The green envelope; open it and familiarize yourself with the progressions. When I give you the word, I want it transmitted immediately. On a black-drape priority."

"What . . . sir?"

"My authorization is black drape, Ballard. It's in the lex, so clear all scrambler channels. You'll get no flak with that priority. I'll call you back."

"Yes, sir. . . ."

David hung up, hoping to Christ that Ballard was as good at his job as David thought he was. Or as good at parlor games as Henderson Granville thought he was.

"You're very efficient," said Rhinemann.

"I try to be," said David.

Ballard stared at the telephone. What was Spaulding trying to tell him? Obviously that Jean was all right; that he and Lyons were all right, too. At least for the time being.

Be ready to send out the sealed code schedules I prepared. . . .

David had not prepared any codes. *He* had. Spaulding had memorized the progressions, that was true, but only as a contingency.

What goddamned *green envelope?*

There was no envelope, red, blue or green!

What the hell was that nonsense . . . *black-drape priority?*

What was a black drape? It didn't make sense!

But it *was* a key.

It's in the lex. . . .

Lex. . . . Lexicon. The Lexicon of Cryptography!

Black drape. . . . He recalled something . . . something very obscure, way in the past. *Black drape* was a very old term, long obsolete. But it *meant* something.

Ballard got out of his swivel chair and went to the bookshelf on the other side of the small radio room. He had not looked at *The Lexicon of Cryptography* in years. It was a useless, academic tome. . . . Obsolete.

It was on the top shelf with the other useless references and, like the others, had gathered dust.

He found the term on page 71. It was a single paragraph sandwiched between equally meaningless paragraphs. But it had meaning now.

"The Black Drape, otherwise known as *Schwarztuchchiffre,* for it was first employed by the German Imperial Army in 1916, is an entrapment device. It is hazardous for it cannot be repeated in a sector twice. It is a signal to proceed with a code, activating a given set of arrangements with intent to terminate, canceling said arrangements. The termination factor is expressed in minutes, specifically numbered. As a practice, it was abandoned in 1917 for it nullified . . ."

Proceed . . . with intent to terminate.

Ballard closed the book and returned to his chair in front of the dials.

Lyons kept turning the pages of the designs back and forth as if double-checking his calculations. Rhinemann called down twice from the balcony, inquiring if there were problems. Twice Lyons turned in his chair and shook his head. Stoltz remained in the deck chair by the pool, smoking cigarettes. Altmüller talked briefly with Rhinemann, the conversation obviously unsatisfactory to both. Altmüller returned to the chair by the glass-topped table and leafed through a Buenos Aires newspaper.

David and Jean remained at the far end of the terrace, talking quietly. Every once in a while Spaulding let his voice carry across; if Altmüller listened, he heard references to New York, to architectural firms, to vague postwar plans. Lovers' plans.

But these references were non sequiturs.

"At the Alvear Hotel," said David softly, holding Jean's hand, "there's a man registered under the name of E. Pace. *E. Pace*. His real name is Asher Feld. Identify yourself as the contact from me . . . and a Fairfax agent named Barden. Ira Barden. Nothing else. Tell him I'm calling his . . . priorities. In precisely two hours from . . . the minute you telephone from the embassy. . . . I *mean* the minute, Jean, he'll understand. . . ."

Only once did Jean Cameron gasp, an intake of breath that caused David to glare at her and press her hand. She covered her shock with artificial laughter.

Altmüller looked up from the newspaper. Contempt was in his eyes; beyond the contempt, and also obvious, was his anger.

Lyons got up from the chair and stretched his emaciated frame. He had spent three hours and ten minutes at the table; he turned and looked up at the balcony. At Spaulding.

He nodded.

"Good," said Rhinemann, crossing to Franz Altmüller. "We'll proceed. It will be dark soon; we'll conclude everything by early morning. No more delay! Stoltz! *Kommen Sie her! Bringen Sie die Aktenmappe!*"

Stoltz went to the table and began replacing the pages in the briefcase.

David took Jean's arm and guided her toward Rhinemann and Altmüller. The Nazi spoke.

"The plans comprise four hundred and sixty-odd pages of causal data and progressive equations. No man can retain such information; the absence of any part renders the designs useless. As soon as you contact the cryptographer and relay the codes, Mrs. Cameron and the physicist are free to leave."

"I'm sorry," said Spaulding. "My agreement was to send the codes when they were back at the embassy. That's the way it has to be."

"*Surely,*" interjected Rhinemann angrily, "you don't think I would permit . . ."

"No, I don't," broke in David. "But I'm not sure what you can control outside the gates of Habichtsnest. This way, I know you'll try harder."

42

It was an hour and thirty-one minutes before the telephone rang. Nine fifteen exactly. The sun had descended behind the Luján hills; the light along the distant riverbank flickered in the enveloping darkness.

Rhinemann picked up the receiver, listened and nodded to David.

Spaulding got out of his chair and crossed to the financier, taking the receiver. Rhinemann flicked a switch on the wall. The speakers were activated.

"We're here, David." Jean's words were amplified on the terrace.

"Fine," answered Spaulding. "No problems then?"

"Not really. After five miles or so I thought Doctor Lyons was going to be sick. They drove so fast. . . ."

After . . . five. . . .

*A*sher . . . *F*eld. . . .

Jean had done it!

"But he's all right now?"

"He's resting. It'll take some time before he feels himself. . . ."

Time.

Jean had given Asher Feld the precise *time.*

"All right. . . ."

"*Genug! Genug!*" said Altmüller, standing by the balcony. "That's enough. You have your proof; they are there. The codes!"

David looked over at the Nazi. It was an unhurried look, not at all accommodating.

"Jean?"

"Yes?"

"You're in the radio room?"

"Yes."

"Let me speak to that Ballard fellow."

"Here he is."

Ballard's voice was impersonal, efficient. "Colonel Spaulding?"

"Ballard, have you cleared all scrambler channels?"

"Yes, sir. Along with your priority. The drape's confirmed, sir."

"Very good. Stand by for my call. It shouldn't be more than a few minutes." David quickly hung up the phone.

"What are you doing?!" yelled Altmüller furiously. "The *codes! Send them!*"

"He's *betraying* us!" screamed Stoltz, jumping up from his chair.

"I think you should explain yourself." Rhinemann spoke softly, his voice conveying the punishment he intended to inflict.

"Just last-minute details," said Spaulding, lighting a cigarette. "Only a few minutes. . . . Shall we talk alone, Rhinemann?"

"That is unnecessary. What is it?" asked the financier. "Your method of departure? It's arranged. You'll be driven to the Mendarro field with the designs. It's less than ten minutes from here. You won't be airborne, however, until we have confirmation of the Koening transfer."

"How long will that be?"

"What difference does it make?"

"Once the blackout starts I have no protection, *that's* the difference."

"*Ach!*" Rhinemann was impatient. "For four hours you'll have the best protection in the world. I have no stomach for offending the men in Washington!"

"You see?" said David to Franz Altmüller. "I told you we were liabilities." He turned back to Rhinemann. "All right. I accept that. You've got too much to lose. Detail number one, crossed off. Now detail number two. My payment from you."

Rhinemann squinted his eyes. "You *are* a man of details. . . . The sum of five hundred thousand American dollars will be transferred to the Banque Louis Quatorze in Zürich. It's a nonnegotiable figure and a generous one."

"Extremely. More than I would have asked for. . . . What's my guarantee?"

"Come, colonel. We're not *salesmen.* You know where I live; your abilities are proven. I don't wish the specter of the man from Lisbon on my personal horizon."

"You flatter me."

"The money will be deposited, the proper papers held in Zürich for you. At the bank; normal procedures."

David crushed out his cigarette. "All right. Zürich. . . . Now the last detail. Those generous payments I'm going to receive right at home. . . . The names, please. Write them on a piece of paper."

"Are you so sure I possess these names?"

"It's the only thing I'm really sure of. It's the one opportunity you wouldn't miss."

Rhinemann took a small black leather notebook from his jacket pocket and wrote hastily on a page. He tore it out and handed it to Spaulding.

David read the names:

Kendall, Walter
Swanson, A. U.S. Army
Oliver, H. Meridian Aircraft
Craft, J. Packard

"Thank you," said Spaulding. He put the page in his pocket and reached for the telephone. "Get me the American embassy, please."

Ballard read the sequence of the code progressions David had recited to him. They were not perfect but they were not far off, either; Spaulding had confused a vowel equation, but the message was clear.

And David's emphasis on the "frequency megacycle of 120 for all subsequent scrambles" was meaningless gibberish. But it, too, was very clear.

120 minutes.

Black Drape.

The original code allowed for thirteen characters:

CABLE TORTUGAS

The code Spaulding had recited, however, had fifteen characters.

Ballard stared at the words.

DESTROY TORTUGAS

In two hours.

David had a final "detail" which none could fault professionally, but all found objectionable. Since there were four hours—more or less—before he'd be driven to the Mendarro airfield, and there were any number of reasons during this period why he might be out of sight of the designs—or Rhinemann might be out of sight of the designs—he insisted that they be placed in a single locked metal case and chained to any permanent structure, the chain held by a new padlock, the keys given to him. Further, he would also hold the keys to the case and thread the hasps. If the designs were tampered with, he'd know it.

"Your precautions are now obsessive," said Rhinemann disagreeably. "I should ignore you. The codes have been sent."

"Then humor me. I'm a Fairfax four-zero. We might work again."

Rhinemann smiled. "That is always the way, is it not? So be it."

Rhinemann sent for a chain and a padlock, which he took a minor delight in showing to David in its original box. The ritual was over in several minutes, the metal case chained to the banister of the stairway in the great hall. The four men settled in the huge living room, to the right of the hall, an enormous archway affording a view of the staircase . . . and the metal briefcase.

The financier became genial host. He offered brandies; only Spaulding accepted at first, then Heinrich Stoltz followed. Altmüller would not drink.

A guard, his paramilitary uniform pressed into starched creases, came through the archway.

"Our operators confirm radio silence, sir. Throughout the entire coastal zone."

"Thank you," said Rhinemann. "Stand by on all frequencies."

The guard nodded. He turned and left the room as quickly as he had entered.

"Your men are efficient," observed David.

"They're paid to be," answered Rhinemann, looking at his watch. "Now, we wait. Everything progresses and we have merely to wait. I'll order a buffet. Canapes are hardly filling . . . and we have the time."

"You're hospitable," said Spaulding, carrying his brandy to a chair next to Altmüller.

"And generous. Don't forget that."

"It would be hard to. . . . I was wondering, however, if I might impose further?" David placed his brandy glass on the side table and gestured at his rumpled, ill-fitting clothes. "These were borrowed from a ranch hand. God knows when they were last washed. Or me. . . . I'd appreciate a shower, a shave; perhaps a pair of trousers and a shirt, or a sweater. . . ."

"I'm sure your army personnel can accommodate you," said Altmüller, watching David suspiciously.

"For Christ's sake, Altmüller, I'm not *going* anywhere! Except to a shower. The designs are over there!" Spaulding pointed angrily through the archway to the metal case chained to the banister of the stairway. "If you think I'm leaving without *that*, you're retarded."

The insult infuriated the Nazi; he gripped the arms of his chair, controlling himself. Rhinemann laughed and spoke to Altmüller.

"The colonel has had a tiresome few days. His request is minor; and I can assure you he is going nowhere but to the Mendarro airfield. . . . I wish he were. He'd save me a half million dollars."

David responded to Rhinemann's laugh with one of his own. "A man with that kind of money in Zürich should at least *feel* clean." He rose from the chair. "And you're right about the last few days. I'm bushed. And sore all over. If the bed is soft I'll grab a nap." He looked over at Altmüller. "With a battalion of armed guards at the door if it'll ease the little boy's concerns."

Altmüller shot up, his voice harsh and loud. "*Enough!*"

"Oh sit down," said David. "You look foolish."

Rhinemann's guard brought him a pair of trousers, a lightweight turtleneck sweater and a tan suede jacket. David saw that each was expensive and he knew each would fit. Shaving equipment was in the bathroom; if there was anything else he needed, all he had to do was open the door and ask. The man would be outside in the hall. Actually, there would be two men.

David understood.

He told the guard—a *porteño*—that he would sleep for an hour, then shower and shave for his journey. Would the guard be so considerate as to make sure he was awake by eleven o'clock?

The guard would do so.

It was five minutes past ten on David's watch. Jean had phoned at precisely nine fifteen. Asher Feld had exactly two hours from nine fifteen.

David had one hour and six minutes.

Eleven fifteen.

If Asher Feld really believed in his priorities.

The room was large, had a high ceiling and two double-casement windows three stories above the ground, and was in the east wing of the house. That was all Spaulding could tell—or wanted to study—while the lights were on.

He turned them off and went back to the windows. He opened the left casement quietly, peering out from behind the drapes.

The roof was slate; that wasn't good. It had a wide gutter; that was better. The gutter led to a drainpipe about twenty feet away. That was satisfactory.

Directly beneath, on the second floor, were four small balconies that probably led to four bedrooms. The farthest balcony was no more than five feet from the drainpipe. Possibly relevant; probably not.

Below, the lawn like all the grounds at Habichtsnest: manicured, greenish black in the moonlight, full; with white wrought-iron outdoor furniture dotted about, and flagstone walks bordered by rows of flowers. Curving away from the area beneath his windows was a wide, raked path that disappeared into the darkness and the trees. He remembered seeing that path from the far right end of the terrace overlooking the pool; he remembered the intermittent, unraked hoofprints. The path was for horses; it had to lead to stables somewhere beyond the trees.

That *was* relevant; relevancy, at this point, being relative.

And then Spaulding saw the cupped glow of a cigarette behind a latticed arbor thirty-odd feet from the perimeter of the wrought-iron furniture. Rhinemann may have expressed confidence that he, David, would be on his way to

Mendarro in a couple of hours, but that confidence was backed up by men on watch.

No surprise; the surprise would have been the absence of such patrols. It was one of the reasons he counted on Asher Feld's priorities.

He let the drapes fall back into place, stepped away from the window and went to the canopied bed. He pulled down the blankets and stripped to his shorts—coarse underdrawers he had found in the adobe hut to replace his own bloodstained ones. He lay down and closed his eyes with no intention of sleeping. Instead, he pictured the high, electrified fence down at the gate of Habichtsnest. As he had seen it while Rhinemann's guards searched him against the battered FMF automobile.

To the right of the huge gate. To the east.

The floodlights had thrown sufficient illumination for him to see the slightly angling curvature of the fence line as it receded into the woods. Not much but definite.

North by northeast.

He visualized once again the balcony above the pool. Beyond the railing at the far right end of the terrace where he had talked quietly with Jean. He concentrated on the area below—in front, to the right.

North by northeast.

He saw it clearly. The grounds to the right of the croquet course and the tables sloped gently downhill until they were met by the tall trees of the surrounding woods. It was into these woods that the bridle path below him now entered. And as the ground descended—ultimately a mile down to the river banks—he remembered the breaks in the patterns of the far off treetops. Again to the right.

Fields.

If there were horses—and there *were* horses—and stables—and there *had* to be stables—then there were fields. For the animals to graze and race off the frustrations of the wooded, confining bridle paths.

The spaces between the descending trees were carved-out pasture lands, there was no other explanation.

North by northeast.

He shifted his thoughts to the highway two miles south of the marble steps of Habichtsnest, the highway that cut through the outskirts of Luján toward Buenos Aires. He remembered: the road, although high above the river at the

Habichtsnest intersection, curved to the *left* and went *downhill* into the Tigre district. He tried to recall precisely the first minutes of the nightmare ride in the Bentley that ended in smoke and fire and death in the Colinas Rojas. The car had swung out of the hidden entrance and for several miles sped east *and* down *and* slightly north. It finally paralleled the shoreline of the river.

North by northeast.

And then he pictured the river below the terraced balcony, dotted with white sails and cabin cruisers. It flowed diagonally away . . . to the right.

North by northeast.

That was his escape.

Down the bridle path into the protective cover of the dark woods and northeast toward the breaks in the trees—the fields. Across the fields, always heading to the right—east, and downhill, north. Back into the sloping forest, following the line of the river, until he found the electrified fence bordering the enormous compound that was Habichtsnest.

Beyond that fence was the highway to Buenos Aires. And the embassy.

And Jean.

David let his body go limp, let the ache of his wound run around in circles on his torn skin. He breathed steadily, deeply. He had to remain calm; that was the hardest part.

He looked at his watch—his gift from Jean. It was nearly eleven o'clock. He got out of the bed and put on the trousers and the sweater. He slipped into his shoes and pulled the laces as tight as he could, until the leather pinched his feet, then reached for the pillow and wrapped the soiled shirt from the outback ranch around it. He replaced the pillow at the top of the bed and pulled the blanket partially over it. He lifted the sheets, bunched them, inserted the ranch hand's trousers and let the blankets fall back in place.

He stood up. In the darkness, and with what light would come from the hallway, the bed looked sufficiently full at least for his immediate purpose.

He crossed to the door and pressed his back into the wall beside it.

His watch read one minute to eleven.

The tapping was loud; the guard was not subtle.

The door opened.

"*Señor? . . . Señor?*"

The door opened further.

"*Señor*, it's time. It's eleven o'clock."

The guard stood in the frame, looking at the bed. "*Él duerme*," he said casually over his shoulder.

"*Señor Spaulding!*" The guard walked into the darkened room.

The instant the man cleared the door panel, David took a single step and with both hands clasped the guard's neck from behind. He crushed his fingers into the throat and yanked the man diagonally into him.

No cry emerged; the guard's windpipe was choked of all air supply. He went down, limp.

Spaulding closed the door slowly and snapped on the wall switch.

"*Thanks very much*," he said loudly. "Give me a hand, will you please? My stomach hurts like *hell. . . .*"

It was no secret at Habichtsnest that the American had been wounded.

David bent over the collapsed guard. He massaged his throat, pinched his nostrils, put his lips to the man's mouth and blew air into the damaged windpipe.

The guard responded; conscious but not conscious. In semishock.

Spaulding removed the man's Lüger from his belt holster and a large hunting knife from a scabbard beside it. He put the blade underneath the man's jaw and drew blood with the sharp point. He whispered. In Spanish.

"Understand me! I want you to laugh! You start laughing *now!* If you don't, this goes home. Right up through your neck! . . . Now. *Laugh!*"

The guard's crazed eyes carried his total lack of comprehension. He seemed to know only that he was dealing with a maniac. A madman who would kill him.

Feebly at first, then with growing volume and panic, the man laughed.

Spaulding laughed with him.

The laughter grew; David kept staring at the guard, gesturing for louder, more enthusiastic merriment. The man—perplexed beyond reason and totally frightened—roared hysterically.

Spaulding heard the click of the doorknob two feet from his ear. He crashed the barrel of the Lüger into the guard's head and stood up as the second man entered.

"*Qué pasa, Antonio? Tu re*——"

The Lüger's handle smashed into the Argentine's skull with such force that the guard's expulsion of breath was as loud as his voice as he fell.

David looked at his watch. It was eight minutes past eleven. Seven minutes to go.

If the man named Asher Feld believed the words he spoke with such commitment.

Spaulding removed the second guard's weapons, putting the additional Lüger into his belt. He searched both men's pockets, removing whatever paper currency he could find. And a few coins.

He had no money whatsoever. He might well need money.

He ran into the bathroom and turned on the shower to the hottest position on the dial. He returned to the hallway door and locked it. Then he turned off all lights and went to the left casement window, closing his eyes to adjust to the darkness outside. He opened them and blinked several times, trying to blur out the white spots of anxiety.

It was nine minutes past eleven.

He rubbed his perspiring hands over the expensive turtleneck sweater; he took deep breaths and waited.

The waiting was nearly unendurable.

Because he could not know.

And then he heard it! And he knew.

Two thunderous explosions! So loud, so stunning, so totally without warning that he found himself trembling, his breathing stopped.

There followed bursts of machine-gun fire that ripped through the silent night.

Below him on the ground, men were screaming at one another, racing toward the sounds that were filling the perimeter of the compound with growing ferocity.

David watched the hysteria below. There were five guards beneath his windows, all running now out of their concealed stations. He could see the spill of additional floodlights being turned on to his right, in the elegant front courtyard of Habichtsnest. He could hear the roar of powerful automobile engines and the increasing frequency of panicked commands.

He eased himself out of the casement window, holding onto the sill until his feet touched the gutter.

Both Lügers were in his belt, the knife between his teeth. He could not chance a blade next to his body; he could always spit it out if necessary. He sidestepped his way along the slate roof. The drainpipe was only feet away.

The explosions and the gunfire from the gate increased. David marveled—not only at Asher Feld's commitment, but at his logistics. The Haganah leader must have brought a small, well-supplied army into Habichtsnest.

He lowered his body cautiously against the slate roof; he reached out, gripped the gutter on the far side of the drainpipe with his right hand and slowly, carefully crouched sideways, inching his feet into a support position. He pushed against the outside rim of the gutter, testing its strength, and in a quick-springing short jump, he leaped over the side, holding the rim with both hands, his feet against the wall, straddling the drainpipe.

He began his descent, hand-below-hand on the pipe.

Amid the sounds of the gunfire, he suddenly heard loud crashing above him. There were shouts in both German and Spanish and the unmistakable smashing of wood.

The room he had just left had been broken into.

The extreme north second-floor balcony was parallel with him now. He reached out with his left hand, gripped the edge, whipped his right hand across for support and swung underneath, his body dangling thirty feet above the ground but out of sight.

Men were at the casement windows above. They forced the lead frames open without regard to the handles; the glass smashed; metal screeched against metal.

There was another thunderous explosion from the battleground a quarter of a mile away in the black-topped field cut out of the forest. A far-off weapon caused a detonation in the front courtyard; the spill of floodlight suddenly disappeared. Asher Feld was moving up. The crossfire would be murderous. Suicidal.

The shouts above Spaulding receded from the window, and he kicked his feet out twice to get sufficient swing to lash his hands once more across and around the drainpipe.

He did so, the blade between his teeth making his jaws ache.

He slid to the ground, scraping his hands against the weathered metal, insensitive to the cuts on his palms and fingers.

He removed the knife from his mouth, a Lüger from his belt and raced along the edge of the raked bridle path toward the darkness of the trees. He ran into the pitch-black, tree-lined corridor, skirting the trunks, prepared to plunge between them at the first sound of nearby shots.

They came; four in succession, the bullets thumping with terrible finality into the surrounding tall shafts of wood.

He whipped around a thick trunk and looked toward the house. The man firing was alone, standing by the drain-pipe. Then a second guard joined him, racing from the area of the croquet course, a giant Doberman straining at its leash in his hand. The men shouted at one another, each trying to assert command, the dog barking savagely.

As they stood yelling, two bursts of machine-gun fire came from within the front courtyard; two more flood-lights exploded.

David saw the men freeze, their concentration shifted to the front. The guard with the dog yanked at the straps, forcing the animal back into the side of the house. The second man crouched, then rose and started sidestepping his way rapidly along the building toward the courtyard, ordering his associate to follow.

And then David saw him. Above. To the right. Through foliage. On the terrace overlooking the lawn and the pool.

Erich Rhinemann had burst through the doors, screaming commands in fury, but not in panic. He was marshaling his forces, implementing his defenses . . . somehow in the pitch of the assault, he was the messianic Caesar ordering his battalions to attack, attack, *attack*. Three men came into view behind him; he roared at them and two of the three raced back into Habichtsnest. The third man argued; Rhinemann shot him without the slightest hesitation. The body collapsed out of David's sight. Then Rhinemann ran to the wall, partially obscured by the railing, but not entirely. He seemed to be yelling into the wall.

Screeching *into the wall.*

Through the bursts of gunfire, David heard the muted, steady whirring and he realized what Rhinemann was doing.

The cable car from the riverbank was being sent up for him.

While the battle was engaged, this Caesar would escape the fire.

Rhinemann the pig. The ultimate manipulator. Corruptor of all things, honoring nothing.

We may work again. . . .

That is always the way, is it not?

David sprang out of his recessed sanctuary and ran back on the path to the point where the gardens and woods joined the lawn below the balcony. He raced to a white metal table with the wrought-iron legs—the same table at which Lyons had sat, his frail body bent over the blueprints. Rhinemann was nowhere in sight.

He had to be there!

It was suddenly . . . inordinately clear to Spaulding that the one meaningful aspect of his having been ripped out of Lisbon and transported half a world away—through the fire and the pain—was the man above him now, concealed on the balcony.

"Rhinemann! . . . Rhinemann! I'm here!"

The immense figure of the financier came rushing to the railing. In his hand was a Sternlicht automatic. Powerful, murderous.

"*You. You are a dead man!*" He began firing; David threw himself to the ground behind the table, overturning it, erecting a shield. Bullets thumped into the earth and ricocheted off the metal. Rhinemann continued screaming. "Your tricks are *suicide*, Lisbon! My men come from everywhere! *Hundreds!* In minutes! . . . Come, Lisbon! Show yourself. You merely move up your death! You think I would have let *you live? Never!* Show yourself! You're *dead!*"

David understood. The manipulator would not offend the men in Washington, but neither would he allow the man from Lisbon to remain on his *personal horizon*. The designs would have gone to Mendarro. Not the man from Lisbon.

He would have been killed on his way to Mendarro.

It was *so* clear.

David raised his Lüger; he would have only an instant. A diversion, then an instant.

It would be enough. . . .

The lessons of the north country.

He reached down and clawed at the ground, gathering chunks of earth and lawn with his left hand. When he had a large fistful, he lobbed it into the air, to the *left* of the rim of metal. Black dirt and blades of grass floated up, magnified in the dim spills of light and the furious activity growing nearer.

There was a steady burst of fire from the Sternlicht. Spaulding sprang to the *right* of the table and squeezed the trigger of the Lüger five times in rapid succession.

Erich Rhinemann's face exploded in blood. The Sternlicht fell as his hands sprang up in the spasm of death. The immense body snapped backward, then forward; then lurched over the railing.

Rhinemann plummeted down from the balcony.

David heard the screams of the guards above and raced back to the darkness of the bridle path. He ran with all his strength down the twisting black corridor, his shoes sinking intermittently into the soft, raked edges.

The path abruptly curved. To the *left.*

Goddamn it!

And then he heard the whinnies of frightened horses. His nostrils picked up their smells and to his right he saw the one-story structure that housed the series of stalls that was the stables. He could hear the bewildered shouts of a groom somewhere within trying to calm his charges.

For a split second, David toyed with an idea, then rejected it. A horse would be swift, but possibly unmanageable.

He ran to the far end of the stables, turned the corner and stopped for breath, for a moment of orientation. He thought he knew where he was; he tried to picture an aerial view of the compound.

The fields! The fields had to be nearby.

He ran to the opposite end of the one-story structure and saw the pastures beyond. As he had visualized, the ground sloped gently downward—north—but not so much as to make grazing or running difficult. In the distance past the fields, he could see the wooded hills rise in the moonlight. To the right—east.

Between the slope of the fields and the rise of the hills was the line he had to follow. It was the most direct, concealed route to the electrified fence.

North by northeast.

He sped to the high post-and-rail fence that bordered the pasture, slipped through and began racing across the field. The volleys and salvos of gunfire continued behind him—in the distance now, but seemingly no less brutal. He reached a ridge in the field that gave him a line of sight to the river a half mile below. It, too, was bordered by a high post-and-rail, used to protect the animals from plummeting down the steeper inclines. He could see lights being turned on along the river; the incessant crescendos of death were being carried by the summer winds to the elegant communities below.

He spun in shock. A bullet whined above him. It had been *aimed* at him! He had been spotted!

He threw himself into the pasture grass and scrambled away. There was a slight incline and he let himself roll down it, over and over again, until his body hit the hard wood of a post. He had reached the opposite border of the field; beyond, the woods continued.

He heard the fierce howling of the dogs, and knew it was directed at him.

On his knees, he could see the outlines of a huge animal streaking toward him across the grass. His Lüger was poised, level, but he understood that by firing it, he would betray his position. He shifted the weapon to his left hand and pulled the hunting knife out of his belt.

The black monstrosity leaped through the air, honed by the scent into his target of human flesh. Spaulding lashed out his left hand with the Lüger, feeling the impact of the hard, muscular fur of the Doberman on his upper body, watching the ugly head whip sideways, the bared teeth tearing at the loose sweater and into his arm.

He swung his right hand upward, the knife gripped with all the strength he had, into the soft stomach of the animal. Warm blood erupted from the dog's lacerated belly; the swallowed sound of a savage roar burst from the animal's throat as it died.

David grabbed his arm. The Doberman's teeth had ripped into his skin below the shoulder. And the wrenching, rolling, twisting movements of his body had broken at least one of the stitches in his stomach wound.

He held onto the rail of the pasture fence and crawled east.

North by northeast! *Not east*, goddamn it!

In his momentary shock, he suddenly realized there was a perceptible reduction of the distant gunfire. How many minutes had it *not* been there? The explosions seemed to continue but the small-arms fire was subsiding.

Considerably.

There were shouts now; from across the field by the stables. He looked between and over the grass. Men were running with flashlights, the beams darting about in shifting diagonals. David could hear shouted commands.

What he saw made him stop all movement and stare incredulously. The flashlights of the men across the wide pasture were focused on a figure coming out of the stable —on horseback! The spill of a dozen beams picked up the glaring reflection of a white Palm Beach suit.

Franz Altmüller!

Altmüller had chosen the madness he, David, had rejected.

But, of course, their roles were different.

Spaulding knew he was the quarry now. Altmüller, the hunter.

There would be others following, but Altmüller would not, *could* not wait. He kicked at the animal's flanks and burst through the opened gate.

Spaulding understood again. Franz Altmüller was a dead man if David lived. His only means of survival in Berlin was to produce the corpse of the man from Lisbon. The Fairfax agent who had crippled "Tortugas"; the body of the man the patrols and the scientists in Ocho Calle could identify. The man the "Gestapo" had unearthed and provoked.

So much, so alien.

Horse and rider came racing across the field. David stayed prone and felt the hard earth to the east. He could not stand; Altmüller held a powerful, wide-beamed flashlight. If he rolled under the railing, the tall weeds and taller grass beyond might conceal him but just as easily might bend, breaking the pattern.

If . . . might.

He knew he was rationalizing. The tall grass would be best; out of sight. But also out of strategy. And he knew why that bothered him.

He wanted to be the hunter. Not the quarry.

He wanted Altmüller dead.

Franz Altmüller was not an enemy one left alive. Altmüller was every bit as lethal in a tranquil monastery during a time of peace as he was on a battlefield in war. He was the absolute enemy; it was in his eyes. Not related to the cause of Germany, but from deep within the man's arrogance: Altmüller had watched his masterful creation collapse, had seen "Tortugas" destroyed. By another man who had told him he was inferior.

That, Altmüller could not tolerate.

He would be scorned in the aftermath.

Unacceptable!

Altmüller would lie in wait. In Buenos Aires, in New York, in London; no matter where. And his first target would be Jean. In a rifle sight, or a knife in a crowd, or a concealed pistol at night. Altmüller would make him pay. It was in his eyes.

Spaulding hugged the earth as the galloping horse reached the midpoint of the field, plunging forward, directed by the searchlight beam from the patrols back at the stables a quarter of a mile away. They were directed at the area where the Doberman was last seen.

Altmüller reined in the animal, slowing it, not stopping it. He scanned the ground in front with his beam, approaching cautiously, a gun in his hand, holding the straps but prepared to fire.

Without warning, there was a sudden, deafening explosion from the stables. The beams of light that had come from the opposite side of the field were no more; men who had started out across the pasture after Altmüller stopped and turned back to the panic that was growing furiously at the bordering fence. Fires had broken out.

Altmüller continued; if he was aware of the alarms behind him he did not show it. He kicked his horse and urged it forward.

The horse halted, snorted; it pranced its front legs awkwardly and backstepped in spite of Altmüller's commands. The Nazi was in a frenzy; he screamed at the animal, but the shouts were in vain. The horse had come upon the dead Doberman; the scent of the fresh blood repelled it.

Altmüller saw the dog in the grass. He swung the light first to the left, then to the right, the beam piercing the space above David's head. Altmüller made his decision instinctively—or so it seemed to Spaulding. He whipped the reins of the horse to his right, toward David. He walked the horse; he did not run it.

Then David saw why. Altmüller was following the stains of the Doberman's blood in the grass.

David crawled as fast as he could in front of the spill of Altmüller's slow-moving beam. Once in relative darkness, he turned abruptly to his right and ran close to the ground back toward the *center* of the field. He waited until horse and rider were between him and the bordering post-and-rail, then inched his way toward the Nazi. He was tempted to take a clean shot with the Lüger, but he knew that had to be the last extremity. He had several miles to go over unfamiliar terrain, with a dark forest that others knew better. The loud report of a heavy-caliber pistol shot would force men out of the pandemonium a quarter of a mile away.

Nevertheless, it might be necessary.

He was within ten feet now, the Lüger in his left hand, his right free. . . . A little closer, just a bit closer. Altmüller's flashlight slowed to a near stop. He had approached the point where he, David, had lain in the grass immobile.

Then Spaulding felt the slight breeze from behind and knew—in a terrible instant of recognition—that it was the moment to move.

The horse's head yanked up, the wide eyes bulged. The scent of David's blood-drenched clothing had reached its nostrils.

Spaulding sprang out of the grass, his right hand aimed at Altmüller's wrist. He clasped his fingers over the barrel of the gun—it was a Colt! a U.S. Army issue Colt .45!—and forced his thumb into the trigger housing. Altmüller whipped around in shock, stunned by the totally unexpected attack. He pulled his arms back and lashed out with his feet. The horse reared high on its hind legs; Spaulding held on, forcing Altmüller's hand down, *down.* He yanked with every ounce of strength he had and literally ripped Altmüller off of the horse into the grass. He slammed the

Nazi's wrist into the ground again and again, until flesh hit rock and the Colt sprang loose. As it did so, he crashed his Lüger into Altmüller's face.

The German fought back. He clawed at Spaulding's eyes with his free left hand, kicked furiously with his knees and feet at David's testicles and legs and rocked violently, his shoulders and head pinned by Spaulding's body. He screamed.

"*You!* You and . . . *Rhinemann! Betrayal!*"

The Nazi saw the blood beneath David's shoulder and tore at the wound, ripping the already torn flesh until Spaulding thought he could not endure the pain.

Altmüller heaved his shoulder up into David's stomach, and yanked at David's bleeding arm, sending him sprawling off to the side. The Nazi leaped up on his feet, then threw himself back down on the grass where the Colt .45 had been pried loose. He worked his hands furiously over the ground.

He found the weapon.

Spaulding pulled the hunting knife from the back of his belt and sprang across the short distance that separated him from Altmüller. The Colt's barrel was coming into level position, the small black opening in front of his eyes.

As the blade entered the flesh, the ear-shattering fire of the heavy revolver exploded at the side of David's face, burning his skin, but missing its mark.

Spaulding tore the knife downward into Altmüller's chest and left it there.

The absolute enemy was dead.

David knew there was no instant to lose, or he was lost. There would be other men, other horses . . . many dogs.

He raced to the bordering pasture fence, over it and into the darkness of the woods. He ran blindly, trying desperately to swing partially to his left. North.

North by northeast.

Escape!

He fell over rocks and fallen branches, then at last penetrated deepening foliage, lashing his arms for a path, any kind of a path. His left shoulder was numb, both a danger and a blessing.

There was no gunfire in the distance now; only darkness and the hum of the night forest and the wild, rhythmic pounding of his chest. The fighting by the stables had stopped. Rhinemann's men were free to come after him now.

He had lost blood; how much and how severely he could not tell. Except that his eyes were growing tired, as his body was tired. The branches became heavy, coarse tentacles; the inclines, steep mountains. The slopes were enormous ravines that had to be crossed without ropes. His legs buckled and he had to force them taut again.

The fence! There was the fence!

At the bottom of a small hill, between the trees.

He began running, stumbling, clawing at the ground, pushing forward to the base of the hill.

He was there. *It* was there.

The fence.

Yet he could not touch it. But, perhaps. . . .

He picked up a dry stick from the ground and lobbed it into the wire.

Sparks and crackling static. To touch the fence meant death.

He looked up at the trees. The sweat from his scalp and forehead stung his eyes, blurring his already blurred vision. There had to be a tree.

A tree. The *right* tree.

He couldn't be sure. The darkness played tricks on the leaves, the limbs. There were shadows in the moonlight where substance should be.

There were no limbs! No limbs hanging over the fence whose touch meant oblivion. Rhinemann had severed—on both sides—whatever growths approached the high, linked steel wires!

He ran as best he could to his left—north. The river was perhaps a mile away. Perhaps.

Perhaps the water.

But the river, if he could reach it down the steep inclines barred to horses, would slow him up, would rob him of the time he needed desperately. And Rhinemann would have patrols on the river banks.

Then he saw it.

Perhaps.

A sheared limb several feet above the taut wires, coming to within a few feet of the fence! It was thick, widening into suddenly greater thickness as it joined the trunk. A laborer had taken the means of least resistance and had angled his chain saw just before the final thickness. He would not be criticized; the limb was too high, too far away, for all practical purposes.

But Spaulding knew it was his last chance. The only one left. And that fact was made indelibly clear to him with the distant sounds of men and dogs. They were coming after him now.

He removed one of the Lügers from his belt and threw it over the fence. One bulging impediment in his belt was enough.

He jumped twice before gripping a gnarled stub; his left arm aching, no longer numb, no longer a blessing. He scraped his legs up the wide trunk until his right hand grasped a higher branch. He struggled against the sharp bolts of pain in his shoulder and stomach and pulled himself up.

The sawed-off limb was just above.

He dug the sides of his shoes into the bark, jabbing them repeatedly to make tiny ridges. He strained his neck, pushing his chin into the calloused wood, and whipped both arms over his head, forcing his left elbow over the limb, pulling maniacally with his right hand. He hugged the amputated limb, pedaling his feet against the tree until the momentum allowed him the force to throw his right leg over it. He pressed his arms downward and thrust himself into a sitting position, his back against the trunk.

He had managed it. Part of it.

He took several deep breaths and tried to focus his sweat-filled, stinging eyes. He looked down at the electrified barbed wire on top of the fence. It was less than four feet below him but nearly three feet in front. From the crest of the ground, about eight. If he was going to clear the wire, he had to twist and jack his body into a lateral vault. And should he be able to do that, he was not at all sure his body could take the punishment of the fall.

But he could hear the dogs and the men clearly now. They had entered the woods beyond the fields. He turned his head and saw dim shafts of light piercing the dense foliage.

The other punishment was death.

There was no point in thinking further. Thoughts were out of place now. Only motion counted.

He reached above with both hands, refusing to acknowledge the silent screams from his shoulder, grabbed at the thin branches, pulled up his legs until his feet touched the top of the thick limb, and lunged, hurling himself straight out above the taut wires until he could see their blurred image. At that split-instant, he twisted his body violently to the right and down, jackknifing his legs under him.

It was a strange, fleeting sensation: disparate feelings of final desperation and, in a very real sense, clinical objectivity. He had done all he could do. There wasn't any more.

He hit the earth, absorbing the shock with his right shoulder, rolling forward, his knees tucked under him—rolling, rolling, not permitting the roll to stop; distributing the impact throughout his body.

He was propelled over a tangle of sharp roots and collided with the base of a tree. He grabbed his stomach; the surge of pain told him the wound was open now. He would have to hold it, clutch it . . . blot it. The cloth of the turtleneck sweater was drenched with sweat and blood—his own and the Doberman's—and torn in shreds from the scores of falls and stumbles.

But he had made it.

Or nearly.

He was out of the compound. He was free from Habichtsnest.

He looked around and saw the second Lüger on the ground in the moonlight. . . . The one in his belt would be enough. If it wasn't, a second wouldn't help him; he let it stay there.

The highway was no more than half a mile away now. He crawled into the underbrush to catch his spent breath, to temporarily restore what little strength he had left. He would need it for the remainder of his journey.

The dogs were louder now; the shouts of the patrols could be heard no more than several hundred yards away. And suddenly the panic returned. What in God's name had he been *thinking* of!? What was he *doing!?*

What *was* he doing?

He was lying in the underbrush assuming—*assuming* he was *free!*

But *was* he?

There were men with guns and savage—viciously savage—animals within the sound of his voice and the sight of his running body.

Then suddenly he heard the words, the commands, shouted—screamed in anticipation. In rage.

"Freilassen! Die Hunde freilassen!"

The dogs were being released! The handlers thought their quarry was cornered! The dogs were unleashed to tear the quarry apart!

He saw the beams of light come over the small hill before he saw the animals. Then the dogs were silhouetted as they streaked over the ridge and down the incline. Five, eight, a dozen racing, monstrous forms stampeding toward the hated object of their nostrils; growing nearer, panicked into wanting, needing the wild conclusion of teeth into flesh.

David was mesmerized—and sickened—by the terrible sight that followed.

The whole area lit up like a flashing diadem; crackling, hissing sounds of electricity filled the air. Dog after dog crashed into the high wire fence. Short fur caught fire; horrible, prolonged, screeching yelps of animal death shattered the night.

In alarm or terror or both, shots were fired from the ridge. Men ran in all directions—some to the dogs and the fence, some to the flanks, most away in retreat.

David crawled out of the brush and started running into the forest.

He *was* free!

The prison that was Habichtsnest confined his pursuers.

. . . but *he* was free!

He held his stomach and ran into the darkness.

The highway was bordered by sand and loose gravel. He stumbled out of the woods and fell on the sharp, tiny stones. His vision blurred; nothing stayed level; his throat was dry, his mouth rancid with the vomit of fear. He realized that he could not get up. He could not stand.

He saw an automobile far in the distance, to his right. West. It was traveling at high speed; the headlights kept flashing. Off . . . on, off . . . on. On, on, on . . . off, off, off, interspersed.

It was a signal!

But he could not stand! He could not rise!

And then he heard his name. Shouted in unison through

open windows, by several voices. In unison! As a chant might be sung!

"... Spaulding, Spaulding, Spaulding. ..."

The car was about to pass him! He could not get up!

He reached into his belt and yanked out the Lüger.

He fired it twice, barely possessing the strength to pull the trigger.

With the second shot ... all was blackness.

He felt the gentle fingers around his wound, felt the vibrations of the moving automobile.

He opened his eyes.

Asher Feld was looking down at him; his head was in Feld's lap. The Jew smiled.

"Everything will be answered. Let the doctor sew you up. We must patch you together quickly."

David raised his head as Feld held his neck. A second man, a young man, was also in the back seat, bending over his stomach; Spaulding's legs were stretched over the young man's knees. The man held gauze and pincers in his hands.

"There will be only minor pain," he said in that same bastardized British accent David had heard so often. "I think you've had enough of that. You're localized."

"I'm what?"

"Simple Novocain," replied the doctor. "I'll retie the stitches here; your arm is filled with an antibiotic—refined in a Jerusalem laboratory, incidentally." The young man smiled.

"What? Where ..."

"There isn't time," interrupted Feld quietly, urgently. "We're on our way to Mendarro. The plane is waiting. There'll be no interference."

"You got the designs?"

"Chained to the staircase, Lisbon. We did not expect such accommodation. We thought probably the balcony, perhaps an upper floor. Our invasion was swift, thanks be to God. Rhinemann's troops came swiftly. Not swiftly enough. . . . Good work, that staircase. How did you manage it?"

David smiled through the "minor pain." It was difficult to talk. "Because . . . no one wanted the blueprints out of his sight. Isn't that funny?"

"I'm glad you think so. You'll need that quality."

"*What? . . . Jean?*" Spaulding started to rise from the awkward position. Feld restrained his shoulders, the doctor his midsection.

"No, colonel. There are no concerns for Mrs. Cameron or the physicist. They will, no doubt, be flown out of Buenos Aires in the morning. . . . And the coastal blackout will be terminated within minutes. The radar screens will pick up the trawler. . . ."

David held up his hand, stopping the Jew. He took several breaths in order to speak. "Reach FMF. Tell them the rendezvous is scheduled for approximately . . . four hours . . . from the time the trawler left Ocho Calle. Estimate the maximum speed of the trawler . . . semicircle the diameter . . . follow that line."

"Well done," said Asher Feld. "We'll get word to them."

The young doctor had finished. He leaned over and spoke pleasantly.

"All things considered, these patches are as good as you'd get at Bethesda. Better than the job someone did on your right shoulder; that was awful. You can sit up. Easy, now."

David had forgotten. The British medic in the Azores—centuries ago—had taken a lot of criticism from his professional brothers. Misdirected; his orders had been to get the American officer out of Lajes Field within the hour.

Spaulding inched his way stiffly into a sitting position, aided gently by the two Haganah men.

"Rhinemann is dead," he said simply. "Rhinemann the pig is gone. There'll be no more negotiations. Tell your people."

"Thank you," said Asher Feld.

They drove in silence for several minutes. The searchlights of the small airfield could be seen now; they were shafting their beams into the night sky.

Feld spoke. "The designs are in the aircraft. Our men are standing guard. . . . I'm sorry you have to fly out tonight. It would be simpler if the pilot were alone. But that's not possible."

"It's what I was sent down here for."

"It's a bit more complicated, I'm afraid. You've been through a great deal, you've been wounded severely. By all rights, you should be hospitalized. . . . But that will have to wait."

"Oh?" David understood that Feld had something to say that even this pragmatic Jew found difficult to put into words. "You'd better tell me. . . ."

"You'll have to deal with this in your *own* way, colonel," interrupted Feld. "You see . . . the men in Washington do not expect you on that plane. They've ordered your execution."

43

Brigadier General Alan Swanson, lately of the War Department, had committed suicide. Those who knew him said the pressures of his job, the immense logistics he was called upon to expedite daily, had become too much for this dedicated, patriotic officer. They also served who, far behind the lines, primed the machinery of war with all the selfless energy they possessed.

In Fairfax, Virginia, at the huge, security-conscious compound that held the secrets of Allied Central Intelligence, a lieutenant colonel named Ira Barden disappeared. Simply disappeared; substance one day, vapor the next. With him went a number of highly classified files from the vaults. What bewildered those who knew about them was the information these files contained. In the main they were personal dossiers of ranking Nazis involved with the concentration camps. Not the sort of intelligence data a defector would steal. Ira Barden's own dossier was pulled and placed in the archives. Regrets were sent to his family; Lieutenant Colonel Barden was MOA. Missing while on assignment. Strange, but the family never insisted upon an investigation. Which was their right, after all. . . . Strange.

A cryptographer in Lisbon, a man named Marshall, was found in the hills of the Basque country. He had been wounded in a border skirmish and nursed back to health by partisans. The reports of his death had been greatly exaggerated as intended. German Intelligence was onto him. For the time being, however, he was confined to the embassy and returned to duty. He had sent a personal message to an old friend he thought might be concerned; to Colonel David Spaulding. The message was amusing, in an oddly phrased way. He wanted Spaulding to know there were no hard feelings about the colonel's vacation in South America. The cryp had taken a vacation, too. There were codes that had to be broken—if they could be found. They both should plan better in the future; they should get together on vacations. Good friends should always do that.

There was another cryptographer. In Buenos Aires. One Robert Ballard. The State Department was very high on Ballard these days. The Buenos Aires cryptographer had spotted an enormous error in a scrambler and had taken the personal initiative to not only question it, but to refuse to *authenticate* it. Through a series of grave misunderstandings and faulty intelligence, an order for the on-sight execution of Colonel Spaulding had been issued by the War Department. Code: treason. Defection to the enemy while on assignment. It took a great deal of courage on Ballard's part to refuse to acknowledge so high priority a command. And State was never averse to embarrassing the Department of War.

The aerophysicist, Eugene Lyons, Ph.D., was flown back to Pasadena. Things . . . things had happened to Doctor Lyons. He was offered and accepted a lucrative, meaningful contract with Sperry Rand's Pacific laboratories, the finest in the country. He had entered a Los Angeles hospital for throat surgery—prognosis: sixty-forty in his favor, if the will was there. . . . It was. And there was something else about Lyons. On the strength of his contract he had secured a bank loan and was building an oddly shaped, Mediterranean-style house in a peaceful section of the San Fernando Valley.

Mrs. Jean Cameron returned to the Eastern Shore of Maryland—for two days. The State Department, at the personal behest of Ambassador Henderson Granville in Buenos Aires, issued a letter of commendation to Mrs. Cameron. Although her status was not official, her presence at the embassy had been most valuable. She had kept open lines of communication with diverse factions within the neutral city; lines of communication often jeopardized by diplomatic necessities. Officials at State decided to present Mrs. Cameron with the letter in a small ceremony, presided over by a prominent undersecretary. State was somewhat surprised to learn that Mrs. Cameron could not be reached at her family home on Maryland's Eastern Shore. She was in Washington. At the Shoreham Hotel.

The Shoreham was where Colonel David Spaulding was registered. . . . More than a coincidence, perhaps, but in no way would it interfere with the letter of commendation. Not these days. Not in Washington.

Colonel David Spaulding looked up at the light brown stone and square pillars of the War Department. He pulled at his army overcoat, adjusting the heavy cloth over the sling on his arm underneath. It was the last time he would wear a uniform or enter this building. He started up the steps.

It was curious, he mused. He had been back for nearly three weeks, and every day, every night he had thought about the words he was going to say this afternoon. The fury, the revulsion . . . the waste. Resentments for a lifetime. But life would go on and in some curious way the violent emotions had crested. He felt only a weariness now, an exhaustion that demanded that he get it over with and return to somcthing of value. Somewhere.

With Jean.

He knew the men of "Tortugas" could not be reached with words. Words of conscience had lost meaning for such men. As they had so often lost meaning for him. That, too, was one of their crimes: they had stolen . . . decency. From so many. For so little.

Spaulding left his overcoat in the outer office and walked into the small conference room. They were there, the men of "Tortugas."

Walter Kendall.

Howard Oliver.

Jonathan Craft.

None got up from the table. All were silent. Each stared at him. The looks were mixtures of hate and fear—so often inseparable.

They were prepared to fight, to protest . . . to salvage. They had held their *discussions*, they had arrived at *strategies*.

They were so obvious, thought David.

He stood at the end of the table, reached into his pocket and took out a handful of carbonado diamonds. He threw them on the hard surface of the table; the tiny nuggets clattered and rolled.

The men of "Tortugas" remained silent. They shifted their eyes to the stones, then back to Spaulding.

"The Koening transfer," said David. "The tools for Peenemünde. I wanted you to see them."

Howard Oliver exhaled a loud, impatient breath and spoke in practiced condescension. "We have no idea what . . ."

"I know," interrupted Spaulding firmly. "You're busy men. So let's dispense with unnecessary conversation; as a matter of fact, there's no reason for you to talk at all. Just listen. I'll be quick. And you'll always know where to reach me."

David put his left hand into his arm sling and pulled out an envelope. It was an ordinary business envelope; sealed, thick. He placed it carefully on the table and continued.

"This is the history of 'Tortugas.' From Geneva to Buenos Aires. From Peenemünde to a place called Ocho Calle. From Pasadena to a street . . . Terraza Verde. It's an ugly story. It raises questions I'm not sure should be raised right now. Perhaps ever. For the sake of so much sanity . . . everywhere.

"But that's up to you here at this table. . . . There are several copies of this . . . this indictment. I won't tell you where and you'll never be able to find out. But they exist. And they'll be released in a way that will result in simultaneous headlines in New York and London and Berlin. Unless you do exactly as I say. . . .

"Don't protest, Mr. Kendall. It's useless. . . . This war is won. The killing will go on for a while but we've won it. Peenemünde hasn't been idle; they've scoured the earth. A few thousand rockets will be built, a few thousand killed. Nowhere near what they conceived of. Or needed. And our aircraft will blow up half of Germany; we'll be the victors now. And that's how it should be. What must come after the killing is the healing. And you gentlemen will dedicate the rest of your natural lives to it. You will sever all connections with your companies; you will sell all your holdings above a bare subsistence level—as defined by the national economic guidelines—donating the proceeds to charities—anonymously but with substantiation. And you will offer your considerable talents to a grateful government—in exchange for government salaries.

"For the rest of your lives you will be skilled government clerks. And that is all you'll be.

"You have sixty days to comply with these demands. Incidentally, since you ordered my execution once, you should know that part of our contract is my well-being. And the well-being of those close to me, of course.

"Lastly, because it occurred to me that you might wish to recruit others under this contract, the indictment makes it clear that you could not have created 'Tortugas' alone. . . . Name who you will. The world is in a sorry state, gentlemen. It needs all the help it can get."

Spaulding reached down for the envelope, picked it up and dropped it on the table. The slap of paper against wood drew all eyes to the spot.

"Consider *everything*," said David.

The men of "Tortugas" stared in silence at the envelope. David turned, walked to the door and let himself out.

March in Washington. The air was chilly, the winds were of winter but the snows would not come.

Lieutenant Colonel David Spaulding dodged the cars as he crossed Wisconsin Avenue to the Shoreham Hotel. He was unaware that his overcoat was open; he was oblivious to the cold.

It was over! He was finished! There would be scars—deep scars—but with time. . . .

With Jean. . . .